S0-AGU-340

Evergence

The Prodigal Sun
The Dying Light
A Dark Imbalance

SEAN WILLIAMS
SHANE DIX

Publishing History: Ace paperback, November 1999

Publishing History: Ace paperback, July 2000

Publishing History: Ace Paperback, March 2001

First SFBC Science Fiction Printing: May 2001

Published by arrangement with:
The Berkley Publishing Group
a division of Penguin Putnam Inc.
375 Hudson Street
New York, NY 10014

Visit our website at *www.sfbc.com*

ISBN 0-7394-1746-0

PRINTED IN THE UNITED STATES OF AMERICA

Contents

The Prodigal Sun

For Peter McNamara, Patrick McNamara, Andrew Stunnell, Peter Stunnell and everyone involved in the Cogal project, without whom this book would not have been possible.

"Violence can only be concealed by a lie, and the lie can only be maintained by violence. Any man who has once proclaimed violence as his method is inevitably forced to take the lie as his principle."

Alexander Solzhenitsyn

"Darkness is looking back and saying: 'I have been deluded from the start; it has all been a mistake.'"

Hubert van Zeller

PROLOGUE

The pillow-shaped capsule tumbled end over end through the gulf between stars. Every point of its four-meter length showed evidence of age: its matte-grey surface was pitted from microimpacts; the molecules of its ablative shield were scarred by radiation; gravity waves from distant black holes spiraling inevitably to collision had warped it from true. Had it been noticed by any passing ship, it would have been ignored as flotsam, for after millennia of exploration and trade such drifting junk was common in the galaxy. It wouldn't even have been worth the effort required to destroy it.

Had it been noticed . . .

Junk it may have appeared to be, but it was far from that. A detailed analysis of the skin of the capsule would have revealed that nothing—not even radiation—penetrated deeper than five centimeters. It had retained its structural integrity despite the forces tugging at it. And, had its density been measured, the fact that it was hollow would have become immediately obvious.

As it tumbled through the void, sensors within monitored the frequency and intensity of incident radiation. It emitted nothing, yet analyzed in minute detail everything that fell upon it. Data was collated and processed. Three-dimensional maps were drawn, on which the course of the capsule—past and future—was plotted. Options were considered.

The capsule had passed through numerous governments and territories during its long journey: from the Giel, remote and aloof in the Perseus Arm, to the Bright Suzerains tucked hot and hardy close to the galactic core. There was hardly a solar system in the Milky Way that had not been colonized or explored at least once by the Human race in all its forms. The descendants of the apes who had once reached in wonder for the night sky now owned the stars. They were the sole heirs of a galaxy ripe for the taking.

Decisions were made.

Patient exploitation of the local magnetic field brought the capsule to the boundary between two nations: one an unwieldy alliance that had outlived its usefulness and was already dissolving under the weight of administration and ennui; the other a small but heated theocracy bursting like a boil from its parent's side. Stray emissions—some almost certainly decades out of date—carried reports of occasional conflict, harried officials, rising tension. . . . The capsule didn't care much for the details, just as long as there was friction, an ambient heat it could exploit. Who fought whom was irrelevant. There was only one Right and Wrong it cared to recall, for it was this duality the capsule existed to serve.

It was a seed looking for soil in which to germinate. A seed that had come a long way and waited a long, long time to bear fruit. A seed whose interior became increasingly active the more certain it was that the end of its journey was near. . . .

PART ONE:

MIDNIGHT

1

COEA *Midnight*
'954.10.30 EN
0235

Morgan Roche was trapped, and she knew it. Trapped by orders, by circumstance, by the bracelet around her left wrist, and by the stare of the wide-shouldered, middle-aged man standing in front of the main viewscreen of the frigate *Midnight.*

"We have discussed this before," he said, frowning down at her from his elevated position. The captain's podium normally remained flush to the floor except during battle, but Proctor Klose preferred it at its full one-meter extension. Surrounded by the half-light of the bridge, with its flashing displays and blank-faced officers, he reminded Roche of a half-finished statue—so full of self-importance that, had she not been so frustrated, she would have found him laughable. "Has anything changed since then, Commander?"

"No, sir," she replied. "All I ask is that you reconsider your decision."

Klose shook his head. "Call me inflexible, if you like, but I see no reason to entertain the whims of my passengers."

"It's more than a *whim*, Captain," she snapped.

"No, Commander," said Klose, the ghost of a grin hovering at the corners of his mouth. "It is not. What you request is clearly outside your jurisdiction."

"Not necessarily." Her free hand betrayed the half-lie by adjusting the tight-fitting neck of her uniform, making her look nervous. When she realized what she was doing, she returned the hand to her side. The cord connecting the bracelet to the valise brushed against her leg as she straightened her posture, but she had learned long ago to ignore it.

"Without access to the relevant information," she said, "I am unable to determine where my jurisdiction lies in this matter. Perhaps if you would explain your reason for denying me access to the capsule, then I might understand."

Klose's frown deepened. "I am not required to explain anything to you, Commander. Need I remind you who is the commanding officer of this vessel?"

"No, sir." Roche gritted her teeth on an angry retort.

"Then I think that concludes our discussion." He turned to face the viewscreen.

Roche remained where she was, unwilling to let the matter rest—although she knew that technically he was in the right. But there was more than the life capsule and its contents at stake. There was a *principle.*

"Captain . . ."

Klose sighed. "Yes, Commander?"

"Forgive me for saying this, but your manner seems to indicate a resentment of my presence aboard this ship. I hope you have not allowed your feelings to cloud your judgment."

Klose faced her once again, his narrowed eyes displaying an indignation that told Roche her remark had hit home.

The captain of the *Midnight* outranked Roche, but *her* superior officer—and, therefore, her mission—outranked *his*. In the course of their voyage, the unassuming valise she carried had become a focus for every slight, real or imagined. That she carried it because of the cord and bracelet ensuring its permanent attachment to her person, rather than out of any real choice, he seemed to have forgotten. Orders were orders, and she had less choice than he did, if only in the short term. But the basic fact, the one the captain detested, remained: Klose was just a donkey for the courier on his back.

The situation might never have become a problem had it not been for the length of time available for circumstance to rub shoulders with resentment. In six weeks, the gentle but constant friction had generated enough heat to spark flame. The matter of the capsule and its mysterious occupant, although trivial in itself, was the catalyst of a much more significant reaction.

"On the contrary," replied the captain, responding to her comment with frosty politeness. "It is not I who has allowed emotions to interfere. Frankly, Commander, I would say that your curiosity has gotten the better of you."

"I'm an active field agent for COE Intelligence," she retorted. "It comes with the job."

"Nevertheless." Klose folded his arms. "The most intelligent thing for you to do right now is let the matter rest."

"With respect, sir—"

"Commander, the simple fact of the matter is that I am not permitted to allow you to place yourself in a situation that is potentially dangerous."

"I'm quite capable of looking after myself."

"I don't doubt that, Commander. But I think you underestimate the risk—"

"How can I underestimate him if I know nothing *about* him?"

"'Him'? You seem to have learned too much as it is."

She ignored this. "If you would simply let me view the science officer's report—"

"Which is classified."

"My security rating is as high as yours, Captain." It was higher, in fact, but she didn't press the fact. "At least give me the opportunity to use my position as I have been trained to do."

Klose sighed in resignation. "Very well, then. I will consider letting you view the report, but only after we have arrived at Sciacca's World and off-loaded our cargo. In the meantime, your mission—and mine—is best served by you returning to your quarters and remaining there."

"But—"

"Shields detecting microimpacts." The voice came from somewhere behind Roche, but Klose didn't take his eyes from hers to acknowledge it. "Captain, we are brushing the halo."

"Please, Commander," he said evenly, gesturing at the exit from the bridge. "Or will I have to have you removed?"

Roche fumed silently to herself. Klose's promises to "consider" or "review" the situation had proven worthless before, and she doubted that this time would be any different. But she had to admit that he did have a point. The *Midnight* was about to insert itself into orbit around one of the most hazardous destinations in the Commonwealth of Empires; he and his crew needed to concentrate on their work without distraction.

Refusing to concede defeat by speaking, she turned away from Klose and moved toward the exit. The door slid aside with a grind of metal on metal, but instead of stepping through, Roche stopped on the threshold and turned to watch the goings-on of the bridge. It was both a show of strength and a demonstration of her independence.

The main screen displayed an image of Sciacca's World. The grey-brown orb floated in the center of the screen, with the ring of densely packed moonlets that girdled the planet's equator glistening in the light from the system's primary. The occasional explosion flaring from some of the larger rocks made the miniature asteroid belt look deceptively attractive from the *Midnight*'s distance. Roche knew how dangerous it could be. Some of the moonlets were over ten kilometers in diameter; one slip near something that size would rip the *Midnight* in two.

Apart from the belt, what really struck her about the view was something that might have been lost on the average deep-space tourist. Few people outside military service would have noted the absence of orbital towers girding the planet; if they had, it was doubtful they would have understood the significance of the fact. To Roche, the planet appeared uninhabited, with nothing but a handful of navigation stations in orbit and the pocket asteroid belt to keep it company—like a reef holding all but the most determined at bay; a shoal around a desert island.

<They call it the Soul—not the *shoal*,> said a voice deep in her skull, intruding upon her subvocal thoughts. <The origins of the name are clouded, but one recurring folk myth from the planet's inhabitants asserts that the band of light—as the asteroid belt appears to those living on the planet—is composed of the souls of people who have died in captivity. The myth of transubstantiation from the mortal to the sublime is common to many repressed societies—but the image is still evocative, don't you think, Morgan?>

The voice fell silent. No one else on the bridge had heard it speak.

"You can go to hell too," Roche whispered, and walked out.

The Retriever Class Frigate *Midnight*, one of the few ships to survive the Ataman and Secession Wars, had been built around the 43rd-generation anchor drive common in the years '212 to '286 EN. Shaped like a fat sausage, with a shaft containing the drive mechanism running along its axis, she had five levels of concentric decking to house a 450-odd crew, two freight-locks and enough storage space to hold five independent fighters. Artificial gravity, produced as an aftereffect of the drive, had resulted in a sense of down being inward rather than outward as was the case on centrifugal ships. This feature also gave her a degree of maneuverability far superior than that of other ships of her day—which was one reason she endured both Ataman Wars relatively unscathed.

The centuries since, however, had left her behind, despite numerous remods and even complete refits in dry dock. Her drive systems had been replaced in '755 EN, upgrading her to 46th generation and full battle status. Her most recent overhaul had been after service as a supply vessel during the Secession War. In '837 EN, only weeks after the Terms of Revocation had been agreed between the Commonwealth of Empires and the newly independent Dato Bloc, she had received new viewscreens and E-shields but little in the way of either fundamental or cosmetic changes.

To Roche's eyes, as she left the bridge and headed through the cramped and dimly lit corridors to her quarters, the *Midnight* looked more like a museum piece than an active frigate. Doors clicked and hissed, elevators shuddered, manual systems still operated where in recent ships crude but efficient AIs had taken over. Current hyperspace technology in the COE—kept homogeneous by the nearby Eckandar Trade Axis and its links with the Commerce Artel—stood at 49th generation, three orders of magnitude more efficient and responsive than that propelling the ancient frigate. The discrepancy between the *Midnight* and other Armada vessels didn't surprise her, however; prison ships were renowned for being poorly outfitted, outdated relics fit for little more than so-called "cattle runs" and other routine jobs.

The uppermost level housed officers and command stations; levels two and three were the crew quarters. The lowest levels contained cells for the transportees heading to the penal colony on Sciacca's World. Roche's room—her own cell, as she thought of it—was the last on the first floor, sandwiched between the drive shielding and a water reclamation plant. Straining engines kept her awake during maneuvers, with bubbling pipes a constant counterpoint. She doubted that the room was used often, being too uncomfortable for either a regular officer or an important guest. As she was neither, it was her dubious honor to be its occupant.

The bulkhead leading to her section slid aside with a noise like tearing metal, jamming as it always did when it was only three-quarters opened. Set into the wall opposite the door was a security station inhabited by a single crewman. He saluted as she approached, recognizing her on sight, and she returned the gesture automatically. Behind him, a battered flatscreen followed the progress of the *Midnight.*

The view of Sciacca's World hadn't changed much. The *Midnight*'s contingent of fighters, standard escort for a prison ship, had adopted a defensive configuration for planetary approach.

Catching the direction of her glance, the crewman nodded. "Almost there," he said. "Not that we'll see much of it."

Roche felt compelled to respond, although her anger at Klose still burned. "We're not landing?"

"No, sir. We'll simply dock at Kanaga Station to off-load the cattle and to refuel." He shrugged. "No one goes down; no one comes up. That's the rules. No one escapes from this place."

"What about staffing changes?"

"Oh, DAOC sends a shuttle every year or so, independent of us. This is the fifth time I've been this way, and it's always the same. Occasionally we bring supplies to trade for service credit, but not this time. I wouldn't let it worry you though, sir," he added quickly, mistaking her dark expression for concern. "It's all very routine."

Roche nodded distantly—the last thing she needed at the moment was *more* routine—and continued on her way. The entrance to her room lay at the end of the corridor. Halfway there, the voice inside her head spoke again. She ignored it. It wouldn't do for the crewman to hear her talking to empty air. Rumors had spread as it was.

With a sigh of relief, she keyed the palmlock and opened the door to her room. Stale air gusted past her face as pressures equalized, indicating a faulty valve somewhere in the life-support system. Nothing serious; just an irritation. No doubt it was on a maintenance list somewhere, awaiting repair.

When the door slid shut behind her, she ran a hand across her close-cropped scalp and vented her frustration on the empty room.

"*Damn* him."

<Who?>

"Klose. Weren't you listening?"

The voice in her head chided her gently. <You know that I am unable to study information to which I have no direct access. Besides, it would be immoral to eavesdrop without your permission.>

Roche doubted both statements but kept her thoughts to herself, not wishing to encourage conversation. A short corridor led from the doorway to a small work space; the far end of her quarters housed a toilet, bathroom, and sleeping chamber. In cross section, the space was shaped like a narrow triangle with the door at its apex, its size dictated by the space available rather than by comfort or aesthetics. Nowhere within it was there room for someone of her height to lie fully outstretched, let alone swing a cat.

The voice remained silent, perhaps considerate of her mood for a change. Before it could begin again, she walked to the work space and put the valise on the desk. The cuff was made of monofilament cord wrapped in black leather and ended in the bracelet that fitted around her left wrist tightly enough to prevent it slipping loose—or being removed by force—but not so tight that it caused her discomfort. Tiny contacts on its inner surface matched nodes on her skin, which in turn patched into a modified ulnar nerve leading up her forearm and into her spinal column, thus enabling data to flow in either direction. The voice in her head—intrusive, often unwelcome even though it was her only company—was not so much heard as insinuated directly in the aural centers of her brain.

Flipping open the valise's grey lid, she studied its interior with an emotion bordering on hatred.

"Oh, for an axe," she whispered out loud, although she had no need to.

<It wouldn't do any good, Morgan,> said the voice. <I am graded to withstand—>

"—a nuclear strike from one hundred meters." She nodded wearily. "I know, I know, but if it wasn't for you I wouldn't be in this mess. Can you understand how frustrating it is to be cooped up in here with nothing to do?"

<As a matter of fact, Morgan, I can.>

Roche bit her lip. Of course it understood. The AI's previous environment had been the massive information workshops of Trinity, the planet of its birth. There, protected by the system's neutral status, secretive craftspersons in the service of High Humanity produced the AIs of the COE—rare and precious mind-machines lovingly crafted by carefully guarded techniques. Few people were allowed onto the planet itself, and she had been no exception. As she'd waited in orbit for the envoy from the manufacturers to arrive, then for the *Midnight* to collect her on its way past the system, she had had almost a week to watch the world below, but had learned little. Only a handful of what might have been cities were visible above the smoky-orange surface of the planet; apart from a ring of five skyhooks circling the equator, there was little sign of advanced life. And yet . . .

Somehow she had been rendered unconscious prior to their arrival. She had no memory of the High Caste manufacturers—who they were, what they looked like, or how they behaved. There was just a blankness, after which she had woken in her singleship with the valise already strapped to her. The experience had been dreamlike, surreal—and frustrating. Such levels of secrecy were paranoid to an extreme—all for the sake of technology no mundane Human could understand anyway.

The valise's imitation cover fitted over an ebony rectangular box with a small keypad of touch points and recessed nodes along its top. The heart of the valise was a densely packed mass of complex microtechnology, crammed neatly into the small space available, both shielded and camouflaged by the shell of the briefcase itself. Molded in superhard composite along the inside of the lid was the AI's identification tag: JW111101000, one digit longer than usual. Without a name in the usual sense of the word to fall back on, Roche resorted as billions of people had before her to popular slang. In this case, the term "Black Box" was even more appropriate, given the shape of the AI's container.

"The sooner we're back in HQ, Box, the better."

<I agree, Morgan, although I feel no distress at our union; I am a burden upon you, not the other way around. If it makes you feel any better, it should take only another six weeks to reach Intelligence HQ.>

"*Only* six weeks . . ." She forced a short-lived smile. "If it wasn't for Klose being so pedantic, I'd probably enjoy the break from normal duties."

<I sense—>

"I don't want to talk about it." Swiveling the room's only chair to face the workstation and placing her left palm on the contact pad, she activated the console and called up the ship's outlet of the Information Dissemination Network. IDnet granted her access to all nonrestricted data, from the volume of processed foodstuff in the *Midnight*'s holds to current affairs on any of the worlds in the COE. Raw data coursed up her arm into the small processor at the base of her skull, where it was interpreted as visual and audio signals and routed to the implanted systems in her left eye and ear. Her implants were by no means the most sophisticated available—lacking three-dimensional clarity and line-of-sight commands—but set her above ninety percent of Armada employees. Such subtle means of communication were sometimes required of Intelligence operatives, so these basic implants were standard to all of her rank.

A virtual screen appeared over her field of vision, seeming to hang two meters from her, impossibly deep in the bulkhead. Skimming at random through the channels, she found a station devoted to general COE news and settled back to discover what the rest of the universe was up to. Try as she might, however, her mind kept returning to Klose and his reasons for denying her what she wanted, while the patient, steady voice of IDnet murmured into her ear, an incessant counterpoint to her thoughts.

// in the wake of crippling solar flares, which destroyed asteroid mining facilities and a hydrogen purification plant in orbit around the system's innermost gas giant. Ede Prime's Presiding Minister today released a statement exonerating two members of her advisory staff who yesterday committed ritual suicide, after it was revealed that the Eckandar Trade Axis has been conclusively linked to corruption within a local chapter of the Commerce Artel //

Ship and captain: for better or for worse, their destinies and characters were intertwined. The post of ship command, contrary to popular opinion, offered not liberation but a lifetime of snaillike confinement. With a prison strapped to his or her back, unable to shrug free even for a moment, every captain had the power to travel vast distances but in reality no more freedom than any of the convicts on Sciacca's World.

Few deep-space commands led to promotion, at least in the COE Armada; captains quickly learned that the chance of achieving advancement via success in battle was slim, as battles themselves were rare and usually fatal to those involved, and most missions were more concerned with distribution of resources across that region of the galaxy than the expansion of the COE—the Commonwealth of Empires, which had ceased expanding entirely some centuries ago and indeed had, upon the secession of the Dato Bloc, begun to shrink. If they failed to die in space, captains inevitably retired to one of the bleak Space Command planets (whose very architecture mirrored deep-space engineering) and spent their remaining days reminiscing about imagined glories. Meanwhile their ships, unfaithful lovers at best, flew on, piloted by younger versions of themselves who were no less doomed than their predecessors. Doomed to a life of confinement, first in their ships and later in retirement or death.

In a very real sense, then, Proctor Klose *was* the *Midnight*, but only for a little while. Jealous of his small command, he would resist any attempt to undermine it. And therein lay the problem.

Roche didn't want to take over. She just wanted something to do. Armada training had prepared her for a wide range of combat scenarios, not months of being cooped up on a worn-out frigate acting as nursemaid for an artificial mind. She knew she should be patient, and perhaps even grateful for the undemanding task, but it wasn't in her nature to sit still for long. She wanted to move, to act, to investigate.

// shock discovery of remains in the Greater Vexisen Republic dating the emergence of Pristine Humanity into the wider galaxy fifty thousand years earlier than the previous best estimate. Renowned xenoarchaeologist Linegar Rufo, nominal overseer of the excavation, was not available for comment, but acting overseer Dev Bogasi commented that "This find represents the most exciting development in the field for over five hundred years. I'm not saying we've found the ultimate source of the Human race, but we're well on the way. The further back we push the envelope—and we're up to half a million years, now—the closer we're coming to a pure genetic strain. Give us another discovery of this magnitude and I predict we'll be able to narrow our field of search to a handful of //

Feeling the tension knotting her muscles, Roche shifted in her seat and unbuttoned the tight collar of her uniform. Brooding on it wasn't going to do her any good, and talking was better than doing nothing. The Box wasn't the confidant she would have chosen, but she had no choice. It was either that or go stir crazy.

"To be fair, Box," she said, picking up the conversation where she had ended it earlier, "it's partly my fault. You remember that derelict we picked up seven days ago?"

<I do recall it in the daysheets.>

"Well, I've been hearing rumors among the crew—"

An all-stations announcement interrupted her, warning the crew and transportees alike of imminent deceleration. The *Midnight* had come out of the anchor point at the edge of the system seven days earlier; this final maneuver would bring the frigate into an inclined polar orbit around the planet, dipping through the belt of moonlets once every two hours. Within moments of the announcement, the engines groaned through the bulkheads of Roche's room, and a wave of rattles and clatters shivered through the ship.

<You were saying, Morgan?>

"Hang on." She adjusted the workstation to bring up a view of the planet, overlaying IDnet. "It's nothing, really. The derelict was a life-support capsule with one man inside."

<Alive?>

"Apparently. No one knows where he's from, though, which makes me curious. The other eight capsules we picked up coming here all contained survivors ejected from the wreckage of the *Courtesan*, the passenger cruiser that broke up near Furioso. But this one . . . They don't recognize him. I asked Klose if I could interview the man, but he told me to mind my own business." She shrugged. "That's it, I guess."

She didn't mention the other snippets of gossip she'd heard: that the capsule had been drifting through space far longer than usual before being detected by the *Midnight*, and that its design was anything but orthodox.

<Your curiosity is understandable, Morgan,> said the Box. <And commendable.>

The AI's overt praise surprised her. "It is?"

<Of course. The man in the capsule might be anyone. He might even be a threat to your mission, a saboteur posing as a castaway to cover his true intentions.>

"That doesn't seem likely."

<Nevertheless, it is a possibility. The capsule might contain a bomb, or some sort of communication device. Or a virus. I am, after all, an information-retrieval device—albeit one of spectacular sophistication.>

"Not forgetting modesty," Roche cut in.

The Box ignored her. <The point is, Morgan, that the plan may not be to destroy me, but to corrupt my function.>

Roche rubbed her chin thoughtfully. She hadn't considered this possibility before. The *Midnight* had been chosen as the vehicle to carry the Box because its route to Intelligence HQ was circuitous, not the direct route one might expect for such an important cargo. If the man in the capsule was a spy, all he had to do was ascertain that the Box was definitely aboard *this* ship, instead of one of the many decoy ships, and notify his superiors.

It was barely plausible, certainly not likely.

And it didn't make sense, not if the capsule was older than the plans to ferry the Box to Intelligence HQ. Still, it would be an interesting point to raise when she and Klose were next at loggerheads.

// until the vector has been isolated and the outbreak contained, all scheduled traffic in- and out-system—including that for the purpose of trade and Armada activity—is either severely restricted or canceled indefinitely. Anyone attempting to break the blockade will be in violation of the Commonwealth of Empires Security Act and liable to face the severest penalty, by order of Chief Liaison Officer for the COE

Armada, Burne Absenger. Repeat: Palasian System has been declared a no-go zone as a result of a Class Three Medical Emergency //

The *Midnight*'s engines roared again, swinging its ponderous bulk around to the correct attitude for polar insertion.

"So this is the way you spend your time, Box. Is there anything that could go wrong that you *haven't* thought about?"

<Of course there isn't. The datapool of this ship is too small to provide stimulating conversation, and I am hesitant to intrude upon you any more than I already do. I am therefore left with one means of amusement: to explore possible situations and prepare contingency plans.>

"Such as?"

Before it could answer, a red light flashed in the virtual screen, indicating a deviation from the mission plan. She returned her attention to the view of the planet and its attendant asteroid belt—"the Soul," she reminded herself. The halo of moonlets had grown in size dramatically; individual motes of light now stood out against the indistinct glow of dust and pebbles. Nothing seemed immediately out of the ordinary, so she superimposed a navigation overlay across the view. Multicolored lines defined the vectors and mass of the largest rocks, while bold green angles indicated the *Midnight*'s orbital approach. The latter should have been clear of all obstacles larger than the frigate's shields could handle, but it wasn't.

Four red circles—ships, judging by their mass and velocity—occupied the exact center of the *Midnight*'s path.

"That's strange," Roche mused, more to herself than to her artificial companion. "The corridor should be clear by now."

<I agree,> replied the Box. <I am monitoring this development through the bridge log. The ships moved into this orbit fifteen minutes ago and have not made any attempt to alter their course since then.>

"Any ident?"

<Surface scan indicates ore freighters from the Eckandar Trade Axis, although their size suggests otherwise.> The Box hesitated for the briefest of moments, as though scanning data. <Captain Klose has received a communication from the commanding officer of the largest ship. It is this woman's opinion that she has right of way in this corridor, and that the *Midnight* should adjust its course to compensate. We will overtake the nearest vessel in approximately fifteen minutes. A course correction is required shortly. Captain Klose has denied her request.>

"Typical." Roche could well imagine the *Midnight*'s captain fuming at the woman's impudence. All maneuvers by the Armada were booked well in advance; there was no question that Klose was in the right. That didn't mean, of course, that he couldn't do the courteous thing and oblige her, but it wasn't in his nature to deviate from the regulations one iota. Not for COE Intelligence, as Roche knew well, and especially not for a civilian.

<A compromise has been reached,> announced the Box shortly. <The captain of the freighter will instruct her ships to spread their formation. The *Midnight* will pass between the three smaller vessels without need for course correction in—fourteen minutes and seventeen seconds.>

"*Between* the freighters?" Roche frowned, concerned.

<Although unorthodox, the maneuver has been authorized by Kanaga Station traffic control.>

"That's not what worries me. What if they're freebooters? We'll be at a disadvantage should one of them take a shot at us. It goes against everything I learned in Tactics."

<It would seem that Captain Klose does not share your concern.> Something in the Box's tone suggested that it was playing devil's advocate, rather than honestly defending the captain.

"Captain Klose is—" *A fool*, she had been about to say, but thought better of it. He had traveled this route many times, after all, and knew its dangers better than she. A course correction would cost them energy and delay their docking at Kanaga Station. Why *should* he give way, when he was so obviously in the right? Besides, fears of freebooting and other forms of treachery seemed naive even to her.

"—just doing his job, I guess," she concluded with a sigh, and settled back into the chair to watch the approach. The red circles on the navigation display drifted apart, widening like a mouth to swallow the *Midnight*. Although she was no longer protesting, she was unable to quell the flutter in her stomach.

// continuing hostilities forced intervention on the behalf of the Commerce Artel. The long-running dispute between the Hierocratic Kingdom of Shurdu and the Pan-Rationalist Alliance of neighboring Zanshin flared into open warfare two months ago, following racist comments made by Hierocrat Kaatje Lene in response to a plea for peace from his opposite number, Provost Hemi Felucca. The exacerbation of inter-Caste tensions as a result of these comments has been cited by concerned observers as a major contributing factor to the current situation. Some have even suggested that the comments were made deliberately, in order to incite war. Exactly why the Hierocrat would do such a thing remains a mystery at this time, although some delegates have not ruled out interference from an unknown third party keen to see war between the two nations.

Meanwhile, on a more cheerful note, an explanation has come from High Human Interventionist, the Crescend, regarding a garbled transmission received from the homeworld of the Jaaf Caste—which, it turns out, has successfully Transcended to the status of High Human, not been annihilated by the nova of their primary star as was first thought. Concerned friends and business associates can contact //

A brisk rap at her door startled her from both the view and IDnet's incessant patter. She stood automatically and straightened her uniform. The moment her hand left the contact pad without canceling her link to IDnet, an inactive screen mounted in the wall above the workstation flickered to life, continuing the display of the *Midnight*'s approach.

"Who is it?" she called into the intercom.

"To be honest, I was hoping you might be able to help me answer that question."

Her hand hovered over the switch that would open the door. The voice had been male, deep and articulate, but the statement itself suggested anything but conviction. "If this is some sort of joke—?"

"I assure you it's not." There was a moment's pause before the man on the other side of the door spoke again. "Look, my name is Adoni Cane, but that's about all I can tell you. Everything else is just—" Another pause. "Please, I need to speak to you."

Roche removed her hand from the switch and checked the name in the ship's datapool; it didn't register. Although she was no rigid stickler for standard military procedure, as Klose was, there were some broad guidelines she simply wouldn't break. Admitting a mysterious visitor at her door in the middle of a potentially dangerous maneuver while on a priority mission was one of them.

"I'm sorry," she said. "I'm going to need a positive ident before I let you in. Come back later, when we've docked, and maybe we can discuss it."

Symbolically turning her back on the door, she switched off the intercom.

With a hiss, the door slid open behind her. Roche's left hand was instantly on the cover of the valise, slamming it closed, while her right reached across the narrow work space for her service pistol. The grip slid smoothly into place as she snap-turned to face the intruder.

Her breath caught in her throat.

His skin was very dark, almost chocolate-brown, and he was tall, a full half-head taller even than herself, with strong shoulders, a wide chest, and powerful hips and upper legs. He was dressed in a simple grey shipsuit, and its narrow fit accentuated the impression of power. He reminded Roche of an oversized Surin war-dancer—exuding a rare physical presence that went beyond simple strength—except that he appeared to be completely hairless. And looked like a Pristine Human, not an Exotic.

The smooth dome of his skull was lit by the overhead door-light as he took a step forward into the room. The flow of muscle beneath his shipsuit was powerful, oddly graceful, and potentially very dangerous.

Roche reacted with alarm. "Hold it right there," she barked, gesturing with the pistol.

"I don't understand," he said, raising his hands placatingly. "Why did you let me in if—"

"*Me* let you in? I told you to go away. The door was locked."

Despite the pistol trained on him, his eyes betrayed not the slightest hint of fear.

"I didn't open it." He glanced over his shoulder at the door, which remained open, then back to her. "If you want me to leave—"

"No, wait." She grasped the handle of the valise and lifted it off the desk. "I want to know what you're doing here."

He lowered his hands slightly and took another step inside. The door slid shut behind him. "I was told to see you."

"See *me*? Who told you this?"

He shrugged. "Somebody spoke to me through the security intercom in my cell. He told me that when the doors opened I was to come here to you, to these quarters. He gave me directions, but no name." His face, when the light caught it, displayed a genuine puzzlement. "I'm sorry I can't be any more specific than that."

"You said you were in a cell," said Roche, keeping the pistol trained upon him. "What happened to the guards? Didn't they try to stop you?"

"I suppose they should have. But when the door opened, there was no one there."

Suspicion made Roche apply slightly more pressure upon the trigger. "Conveniently allowing your escape."

His eyes dropped to the muzzle of the pistol; when they met her own a second later, he was smiling. "If 'escape' is the appropriate word. After all, no one ever told me why I was locked up in the first place."

"You're not a transportee?" she asked, although something about his manner had already convinced her of that. He didn't seem like a petty criminal: too self-possessed, perhaps, or too confident. And despite the absurdity of his tale, he didn't seem to be lying. Roche's curiosity began to outweigh her sense of caution.

"I don't know what I am," he said. "All I know is that I awoke a week ago and have been confined to a cell ever since. I have no memories of a time before that. All I have is my name." He shrugged. "I was told that you would be able to help me."

"*Help* you? In what way?"

He offered his hands, palms up, to demonstrate that he had no answer to that question either. If she wanted answers, she would have to deduce them herself from what scant information he had to offer.

Roche swallowed her frustration with difficulty, kicked the chair to him, and indicated for him to sit. Keeping the pistol trained carefully on his chest, she retreated to the far corner of the room to think.

Adoni Cane. If he wasn't a transportee, then he could have been a passenger, but then why didn't his name register in the datapool? He *had* to be lying. But why? She could ask the Box to investigate the mysterious message that had led Cane to her; it would have been recorded by security monitors, if it existed at all. And if it didn't—

Her hand instinctively tightened on the valise as she realized the stranger's intentions. Before she could express her concerns to the Box, the AI's voice cut across her train of thought:

<Morgan, that freighter has just—>

She blinked and subvocalized: <Not now. Listen—>

<I strongly suggest that you check the monitor, Morgan.>

Roche swung her gaze to the screen. It showed an overhead view of the *Midnight*'s bridge, from cameras mounted above the access locks at the rear of the chamber, and took in most if not all of the hemispherical sweep of workstations.

Klose was standing on the podium, his first officer, Terrison, with him; both were studying the forward displays. There was a superficial impression of calm about the scene that belied the tension in their stances. Roche could tell at a glance that they and the other personnel on the bridge were operating under unusual pressure. Something had gone wrong.

As she watched, Janek, the tactician, turned from her station to face Klose and Terrison.

"Ident confirmed," the tactician said. "Dato warships. Four of them."

Roche slipped her hand onto the contact pad to overlay the navigation display in one corner of the screen, hardly believing what she was hearing. *Dato* ships? From where? The Dato Bloc had no business this side of the border.

A moment's glance showed her what had happened: the three Eckandi "freighters" had deactivated their sophisticated camouflage systems, revealing the truth beneath. A dreadnought and three raiders, plus at least a dozen tiny fighters, swooping free of the dreadnought even as she watched.

// disturbance within the sector under Olmahoi control has both puzzled and concerned COE observers. Reaves in neighboring systems have reported surges in epsense //

Roche irritably killed IDnet and swore softly to herself. Cane leaned closer; out of the corner of her eye she saw him echo her frown.

"Trouble?" he asked.

"You might say that." Mindful that her pistol no longer covered him, she waved him back. "We've just cruised straight into an ambush."

"Is there conflict between your people and the owners of these ships?"

"Are you serious?" She saw no indication of irony in his composed features. She had never met anyone who wasn't at least vaguely aware of the political realities of the region. "How long have you been imprisoned here?"

"Seven days, as I said."

"This really isn't turning into a very good day for me," she said, shaking her head. Then, returning to the screen before her, she added, "Officially the Commonwealth of Empires and the Dato Bloc are at peace." She focused her attention on the ships on the screen. "But I get the impression that this isn't official business."

"Could it be a mistake?"

She glanced down at the valise. "Unlikely."

The Dato ships had assumed a tight arrowhead formation and were powering up their drives to meet the incoming frigate. Alert strips above the door to her room flashed to amber simultaneously with the light in the tank. A sterile voice announced an order for provisional battle stations.

"Four against one," mused Cane, studying the formation intently. "Not insuperable odds. Why hasn't the captain—" He stopped in mid-sentence and glanced at Roche quizzically, as though suddenly remembering her presence. "You're an officer. Why aren't *you* on the bridge?"

"I'm just a guest, noncombat." She turned to study him in return. If the impending battle concerned him, he didn't show it. Even his voice echoed the easy strength and confidence of his physique. "What were you about to say? Do you know something about this?"

"Nothing." Klose's voice had taken Cane's attention back to the screen, and Roche followed it at once.

"Any communication?" the captain had asked.

"None, sir." The officer glanced up from his console. "They are not responding to our signals."

"Janek: ETA?"

"Three minutes, sir," replied the tactician without looking up. Then she leaned in close to her console. "Sir, that dreadnought—"

"What about it?"

"It's not a dreadnought. Configuration reads way off." She leaned in close again. "It could be the ship we've heard rumors about—the new Marauder."

Roche studied the image forming on the screen. The ship *did* look different: a large dolioform drive facility connected to seven pointed nacelles by a complicated web of what looked like threads but were probably access tubes and girders made small by distance. Streamlined mouths at either end of the drive flashed red as the ship maneuvered; smaller spiracles on five of the nacelles were inactive but open, obviously weapon bays or fighter launchers ready for action. The ship looked like nothing Roche had seen before, but she could tell just by its appearance—an ominous cross between a spider and shark—that it was designed for speed and resilience in battle.

"Broadcast full battle alert," announced Klose, his voice booming. "Seal the bridge and all compartments! Prepare for defensive maneuvers!"

"Too late," mumbled Cane. "Much too late."

"What is?"

"The captain should have attacked the moment he saw them."

"Not Klose." She grimaced bitterly. "He'd never risk a diplomatic incident on the off chance there'd been some sort of misunderstanding."

"What do you think?" The approaching Dato ships glinted in Cane's eyes. "Does this look like a misunderstanding to you?"

"They haven't attacked us—"

"But they will," Cane interjected calmly. "And if the captain waits any longer—"

A groan from the bulkheads interrupted him. The view in the telemetry display shifted suddenly as the *Midnight*'s engines kicked into life, thrusting the ship along a different course. Life support dampened the violent shift in momentum, leaving a lingering sense of disorientation in its wake.

Roche blinked and shook her head. Cane seemed entirely unaffected, although she realized with alarm that he was standing much closer than he had been before. If he had wanted to overpower her, he could have done so easily during the maneuver. The fact that he hadn't did not reassure her. That she had let him get that close in the first place—

Another disturbance rolled through the ship, more violent than the previous one. Cane's hand came down on her shoulder. She brushed it aside with the hand holding the pistol before realizing that he was only steadying her.

He raised an eyebrow at her confusion, then turned back to the screen.

Klose had sent the *Midnight* angling along a path heading below the approaching triangle of Dato ships, demonstrating an initial reluctance to engage but without placing the ship in too vulnerable a position. The frigate's contingent of five fighters peeled away to draw fire. Instantly, the arrowhead formation dissolved, with the Marauder swooping to intercept the *Midnight* and the three raiders at the rear peeling to either side and below to pen the COE frigate in a potential cross fire.

The *Midnight* turned again, to port, disturbing the deadly symmetry of the pattern. The Marauder followed while the raiders jockeyed for new positions.

Klose ordered the raising of hyperspace disrupters and E-shields. The *Midnight*'s armory targeted and tracked the Dato ships, awaiting the order to fire.

Roche's hands gripped the valise tightly. Cane's observations had been acute: she did want to be on the bridge, instead of watching the action impotently from her room; and Klose had indeed waited too long to act. Her heart beat faster; she was reluctant to take her eyes off the screen for fear she would miss the crucial moment.

When it came, however, it surprised her. The Dato raider to starboard of *Midnight* was the first to fire—not the Marauder. A salvo of flicker-bombs, dropping in and out of hyperspace with intermittent flashes of light, lashed toward the green dot at the center of the telemetry screen. Fast in its wake came a wave of A-P fire.

The first of the missiles struck the aft disrupters, making the ship shudder. Roche flinched automatically.

"Lucky," said Cane, as Klose finally ordered the firing of the *Midnight*'s laser and A-P cannon. The power in Roche's room flickered at the same time as spears of light darted across the telemetry screen in the direction of the dots representing the Dato ships. "If the trailing ship had fired first, a missile could have passed through the afterwash shields and blown the engines."

"So why didn't it?"

"I would have thought that was obvious," he said. "They don't intend to destroy us." He glanced at her and the valise in turn. "There's something aboard the *Midnight* they want."

She ignored the unspoken implication. On the screen, the battle was proceeding rapidly. The lights flickered again, followed by wave after wave of subtle nausea as the *Midnight* weaved for position. Two of the fighters vanished as they engaged the Dato; outnumbered by ten to one, the *Midnight*'s contingent would not last long.

The Marauder, however, had not fired once. Under combined fire from the three raiders—two were easily a match for the aged frigate—the tiny singleship fighters were little more than target practice. A steady stream of missiles battered the *Midnight*'s disrupters and E-shields, gradually weakening them. It was only a matter of time before the shields failed entirely, leaving the frigate open to direct assault—or a boarding party.

Klose was no master tactician, but Roche doubted she could do any better herself. Besides, she had other priorities to consider.

The lights went out entirely for a split-second, then returned in emergency red. A tang of smoke filtered into the room, and the pit of her stomach rolled disturbingly. The last COE fighter fell with a flare of light. On the screen, the Dato raiders swooped nearer, harrowing the beleaguered frigate.

Roche came to a decision.

"Okay," she said, swinging the valise into a more accessible position. Cane watched curiously from his position nearby, and she reverted to subvocals. <Box, we're in trouble, aren't we?>

<It would seem so. The *Midnight* is experiencing gravity fluctuations, which means the disrupters are failing. Quite soon now the shields will collapse entirely and we will be boarded—unless Captain Klose orders a self-destruct.>

<Klose won't do that,> she said. <He'd rather be killed than commit suicide.>

<Be that as it may. We probably only have a short time in which to act. Should Klose either surrender or otherwise allow the ship to be boarded, that would be tantamount to handing me over to the Dato Bloc, in direct contradiction of his orders—which are, of course, to prevent my capture at any cost. He should therefore allow the ship to be destroyed in the hope that the wreckage of the *Midnight* will conceal my remains. Fortunately, due to my structural resilience, I will not be harmed.>

<Great,> said Roche dryly. <But what about *me*?>

<Patience, Morgan. Remember your own orders.>

<I *know* my orders, Box,> she snapped impatiently. Then, more calmly, she added, <Look, is there any way out of this?>

<Would I waste time like this if there wasn't?>

<I don't know. *Would* you?>

<Perhaps, if things were totally hopeless.> The Box seemed almost to be enjoying her discomfort. <I suppose I might attempt to take your mind off the situation. However, it is not. The solution, clearly, is to evacuate the ship.>

On the screen, one of the Dato raiders loomed, partially occluding the image of Sciacca's World.

<A great plan, Box. Any ideas *how*?>

<In one of *Midnight*'s landers would seem our best option.>

<But the launch controls are locked from the bridge.>

<With your approval I can override the locks.>

<Do it.> She glanced at the screen as more missiles barraged the Frigate's struggling defenses. <Just do whatever it takes to get us out of here.>

<Very well.> The Box fell silent, then returned a moment later, sounding faintly surprised. <It would seem that somebody else has thought along the same lines. The doors to Lander Bay Three are already open, and all approaches to it have been sealed off—except from the lower levels. The bay is two sectors away. I have opened the corridors between here and there.> After a further pause of a few seconds, the voice spoke again inside Roche's head: <Haste at this juncture would be prudent, Morgan.>

"Right." She stood to leave, the valise gripped tightly in her hand. Cane, forgotten during her exchange with the Box, startled her as she turned to face the door.

"You're leaving?"

She hesitated briefly. "I'm sorry," she said. "I have no choice."

<Take him with you, Morgan.> The Box's words broke across her thoughts like the voice of a guilty conscience.

"What? *Why*?" Startled by the Box's request, she spoke aloud. Cane frowned, but didn't speak.

<Remember your dispute with Captain Klose?>

"What about it?"

<The man standing before you is the subject of that dispute.>

"He is? How do you know that?"

<His name does not appear in the ship's log. Ergo, he was not on board when we left Ivy Green Station. Ergo, he must have been in the last life capsule we salvaged.>

"I—" She stopped. It made sense—but explained nothing. If that was so, why was he *here*?

Confusion wrinkled Cane's brow. Roche belatedly realized that she'd been talking to the Box out loud, rather than by subvocalizing. What he made of her side of the conversation, she couldn't even guess.

Torn between her mission, curiosity, and basic Human compassion, she tried to decide what to do with him. If she left him behind, he would surely be captured by the Dato Bloc—at best—and she would never learn who he was, nor why Klose had not wanted her to see him. On the other hand, she knew too little about him to risk him coming along; having a total stranger in tow at a time such as this could prove a threat to her mission.

<I remind you, Morgan, that time is not what you might call an ally at this point.>

"Okay, okay." Cane's stare hadn't faded, and she returned it with one of equal intensity. "My name is Commander Roche of COE Intelligence," she said quickly, collecting as she did a handful of magazine charges for her pistol and slipping them into her belt. "I'm going to try to escape in one of the landers. You can tag along, but only on the understanding that I give the orders. Clear?"

"I understand." His smile was slight but genuine. "And I agree."

"Good. Because should you so much as cross me once, I swear I'll shoot you."

"That won't be necessary."

She wrapped the belt loosely about her waist and keyed the door with her palm. "Okay, then let's move it."

The ship lurched as they stepped out into the corridor. Roche swayed, steadying herself with the walls. Ahead of her, Cane hardly missed a step. For the second time she shrugged away his helping hand.

"That way," she said, gesturing with the pistol.

Nodding, he obeyed, and Roche followed a pace behind. His steady pace displayed no concern at the gun at his back, and neither did he stop to question her plans. That sudden—and unreciprocated—trust bothered her more than anything else about him. Whoever he was, he seemed quite content to place his fate in her hands. Perhaps, she thought, the only alternative open to him was worse than mere imprisonment by the Dato.

<You had better be right about this, Box.>

The Box might have chuckled softly at that, but she couldn't be certain.

<Aren't I always?>

2

COEA *Midnight*
'954.10.30 EN
0710

Lander Bay Three was one of two on the officers' deck, situated at the fore of the *Midnight*. Due to the frigate's unusual configuration, the ceiling of the uppermost decks comprised the outer shell of the hull; Roche's quarters, being the last on the officers' deck, were near the midway point. To reach the lander bay, she and Cane had to follow one of the main access corridors along half the length of the ship—but at least they were not required to change levels.

The security station at the end of her corridor was empty, the crewman who had occupied it earlier obviously performing battle duties elsewhere. The main access corridor was likewise unoccupied. The occasional rolling boom echoed along its length as Dato weapons exploded near the hull of the frigate. Perhaps it was Roche's imagination, but the explosions seemed to grow louder, and more frequent, as the minutes passed. If so, the disruption shields were failing, allowing the blink-bombs to jump out of hyperspace and explode a little closer to the frigate every time. It was only a matter of time before one snuck through entirely and detonated deep in the heart of the ship. Although small enough to defeat the constraints that normally prevented matter from slow-jumping in a gravity well, just one contained sufficient explosive to cripple a vessel.

Gravity fluctuations kept their pace to a steady jog; any faster risked a fall, especially with the weight of the valise to upset her balance. Cane matched her stride easily, moving with the powerful grace of a trained athlete. The occasional lurch of the floor didn't even break his stride, and it was he who occasionally lent her a hand, never the other way around. Not bad, she thought, for someone who had just emerged from a life-support coma.

By the time they reached the end of the corridor, smoke had begun to filter in—a slowly thickening blue haze coming from somewhere beyond the abandoned security point. She watched it carefully as they neared it, assessing the inflow. Her first impressions were correct: the buildup was gradual, probably isolated to the local ventilation system, and not a serious problem—yet.

Roche turned left at the end of the corridor, away from the source of the smoke. A series of doglegs led to EVA control, a large self-contained chamber onto which the two lander bays opened.

<Lander Three has been breached,> the Box said as they took the first corner. <Whoever we are following has beaten us to it.>

<How many can the landers hold?>

<Full complement is five, although four is optimal.>

<What about Lander Two?>

There was a momentary hesitation as the AI assessed the available data. <The smoke you saw earlier is coming from burning insulation, caused by an overheating E-shield generator. The source of the fire is dangerously close to Lander Two, suggesting that the vessel may be damaged, or soon will be.>

<How long do we have?>

<That depends on Captain Klose. The disrupters are close to failing.>

<Not long, then. Certainly not enough time to try another bay. We'll have to make do with what we've got.> Turning to Cane, she explained the situation. "We need that lander. If whoever's got there ahead of us amounts to more than three people, we may have to fight for it."

Cane nodded calmly. The idea of combat didn't appear to faze him in any way. "Understood, Commander. You'll have my full support."

"Good." Although she halfheartedly listened for accent or anomalies of syntax, there were none. He spoke with the sort of generalized Standard that one heard all over the galaxy. "Not far now."

They rounded the last corner slowly. Roche was up front, her pistol at the ready. The all-purpose magazine clipped in the long barrel allowed her a number of diverse selections; before turning the corner, she set it for scatter.

EVA control was empty. The outer airlock to Lander Three stood open. Beyond the airlock was the lander bay—a round antechamber roughly three times the size of her room—then a steep ramp that curved upward to the lander, doubling back on itself once along the way. The manual controls for the outer airlock were next to the entrance to the ramp. Roche inched forward through the airlock, into the bay. It too was empty, so she kept moving.

Cane's hand gripped her forearm, bringing her to a sudden halt only meters from the ramp. Instinctively she tried to pull the arm free, but found she could not.

"What?" she hissed, uneasy in his firm grip.

His gaze was fixed on the open doorway, and for the first time she noticed that his head was cocked slightly. He was listening to sounds coming from within the lander.

"Someone's coming," he said. "Down the ramp."

"Are you sure?" She could hear nothing.

Instead of answering, he pulled her away from the entrance to the lander, back into EVA control. Moments later, the sound of soft footsteps padded toward them.

Cane let go of her arm and put his mouth close to her ear. "Only one. I'll draw that one's fire while you shoot from here. Can you do that?"

"Of course I can," she said with some annoyance, although whether that annoyance came from his questioning her ability or from his suddenly taking charge of the situation, she wasn't sure. "But you're putting rather a lot of faith in your speed, aren't you?"

"No," he said, the faint trace of a grin splitting his dark features. "I'm putting it in your ability to hit them before they hit me."

She opened her mouth to voice her doubts, but got no further. An explosion shook the ship, the shock wave slamming through the bulkheads and snapping her head back into the wall. Cane maintained his balance and caught her with astonishing ease, held her until she regained her footing.

The tang of smoke in the air thickened almost immediately, and the lights dimmed.

<That was primary life-support,> said the Box. <The disrupters are failing. E-shields are down to five percent.>

As though he had heard the Box's words, Cane let her go and inched sideways to the entrance of the bay. "We haven't got time to play it safe, Commander," he whispered back to her. "We have to go in now, while they're still reeling from that explosion."

Raising the pistol to her chest, she nodded once. Cane immediately leapt through the door with a speed and agility she would not have believed possible—so fast that her own movements seemed belated and slow in comparison.

Following the small of his back with her eyes and swiveling her entire body to face the airlock, she covered the interior of the bay with one sweep, gun held at shoulder height in her right hand.

The first thing she saw was the light: the flash of blue laser fire from somewhere to her left, slicing through the air toward Cane's back. Only his speed saved him, kept him ahead of the beam.

Then she was through the door herself, the Box tucked up against her rib cage, cushioned from the Armada-trained roll that she executed with a sureness her instructors would have been proud of. All the time her eyes were focused left, her free hand and the pistol clear of the floor, tilted toward the expected target—

—a thin figure in a grey transportee uniform, definitely an Exotic Caste, Eckandi perhaps, with white hair, a gaunt face, and an industrial laser held in a double-handed grip, arms swinging to follow Cane's progress across the open bay floor, the trigger held tightly down, blue light arcing lethally toward Cane's retreating back—

Roche's scatter-fire took the transportee full in the chest. The man crumpled where he stood, then fell forward onto his face. The blue beam flickered out, but not before scoring an ugly black line across the floor of the bay, terminating in a rough interrogative just short of Roche's toes.

Cane's momentum carried him up the ramp and out of sight into the lander, his feet soundless on the metal deck. Roche lingered for a moment to ensure that the transportee had not been unduly harmed. An Eckandi prisoner on a COE ship was rare enough to be treated delicately under any circumstance. The elderly man—perhaps over a century in age, middle-aged, but not infirm—had fallen awkwardly onto his side. His respiration was even, if a little slow, and his staccato pulse regular. Although no expert in Exotic physiognomy, she suspected he would recover before long.

With a grunt, she rose to her feet and went to run up the ramp to see what Cane was up to. Barely had she taken a step when something dark and cold thrust itself into her mind.

She stopped in her tracks, reeling with panic and confusion as the force squeezed her entire brain in an invisible psychic fist, sending a retching wave of sickness and self-hatred deep into her gut, where it blossomed into a bitter flower of bile.

The muscles in her hand relaxed involuntarily, and the gun clattered to the floor.

A reave.

She wasn't sure if she spoke the words or thought them. The mental intrusion had caught Roche unaware, not allowing her to employ the epsense resistance techniques she had been taught at Military College. She slipped to her knees, clutching first at her stomach, then her head, wanting desperately for the intrusion to cease. This was different from anything she had ever experienced before—much more intense.

Her vision greyed, became cluttered with images that confused her: the inside of the lander, and huddled within its shadows the reave—a Surin, not more than fifteen years old by the sheen of her fur. She was small of stature and, cowering, looked deceptively vulnerable. And frightened, Roche noted through her own suffocating anxiety. The girl was terribly frightened. Which perhaps explained the intensity of the intrusion.

And her face—

A narrow, stained bandage wrapped about the girl's head hid her eyes from view. Fully developed reaves "borrowed" the eyes and ears of the people around them rather than using their own senses, and communicated purely by thought. Roche sucked air sharply in sudden revulsion as she recalled that some fundamentalist factions of the Surin Agora actually *forced* their latent psychics to do so by a mutilation ceremony that accompanied the completion of their training. It was either that or go mad from sensory deprivation. This Surin girl, Roche guessed, was eyeless behind the bandage—probably declawed and a deaf-mute as well.

Despite her own discomfort, Roche couldn't help but feel pity for the girl. The ritual mutilation usually occurred in the very last stages of the transition from latent talent to full-fledged epsense adept—a process that often took decades. Yet the Surin in the lander was less than half Roche's age. Power at such a price had to be a dubious gift.

"You're reading my mind," said a familiar voice, disconcertingly nearby. It belonged to the reave's primary subject.

Cane, Roche realized. The voice belonged to Cane!

<Stay back.> The reave's words reached Roche's mind as thoughts rather than sound. She could feel the creeping tendrils of the Surin girl deep within herself, holding her at bay, their very presence aching dully. Yet the will that had so incapacitated her hardly seemed to be affecting Cane.

"Why?" he said, taking a step closer, his eyes—and thus Roche's—fixed upon the girl. "You have no reason to be afraid of me. I have no wish to harm you."

<What about Veden? You killed Veden!>

Roche winced as the Surin's grief twisted at her mind.

"Your friend fired upon us first. My companion was merely defending herself." Roche felt the reave's tentacles tighten a little at that, searching for the truth, as Cane took another step forward. "Listen to me; we haven't much time. We need this ship to escape. If we can just work—"

<No! Stay back or I'll—> The Surin hesitated, and Roche realized that, despite the clarity of mind generally required to enable epsense transfer, the reave was close to panic. <If you come any closer, I'll kill your friend!>

Roche hissed through her teeth as the pain increased. She swore she wouldn't scream, no matter how bad the pain. Half-formed words blossomed in her throat, but were stifled by the reave.

She's bluffing! she wanted to scream. Reaves rarely killed someone they were riding. The personal consequences were too great.

Cane either suspected this or simply didn't care what happened to Roche. Taking another step forward, he came within arm's reach of the Surin, who turned her face away.

<I can't read you.> Roche sensed fear and timidity in the girl's words.

The view of the cockpit vanished as the reave switched from Cane's point of view to Roche's. The lander bay was filled with dense smoke, billowing through the airlock leading to EVA control. The fire had either worsened dramatically or spread to the corridor outside. Through the pain in her head, she could hear klaxons wailing.

The reave's voice superimposed itself over everything—pervasive and irresistible: <Can you pilot the lander?>

Cane's response was prompt and without concern: "No."

Roche felt the pain in her head increase once more, slicing through her thoughts as though it were a red-hot scalpel.

<Morgan Roche.> The tone was cut with panic and confusion. <That case you carry—why do you believe that it can fly the lander?>

Roche clenched her mouth shut, using every iota of Armada training to resist replying.

Even as she struggled, a series of small explosions, quite near, rumbled through the hull. Then, with a sudden high-pitched screaming noise, the smoke began to fly away from her back down the corridor.

The pressure from the reave suddenly vanished, and full control of her body returned. Gasping, she fell forward onto the deck, scrabbling for the pistol. Her muscles felt spastic, jerky, as she struggled to her feet and staggered for the airlock controls. She thumped the SEAL prompts in quick succession, hoping that her training would overcome the fogginess in her head.

The outer door slammed shut. The sound of klaxons diminished.

<Morgan,> said the Box, <we have very little time. Klose has surrendered to the Dato Bloc.>

Fighting the haze, she tried to concentrate. "He's *what*?"

<He has given permission for one of the raiders to dock. It may be a ruse, of course. Either way—>

"I understand." Blinking to clear her vision, she stumbled for the ramp and the lander. Cane met her halfway, raised his arms in mock surrender as her pistol swung at him. Then he smiled. The calm with which he did that, his ability to instantly relax once a moment of tension passed, disturbed her. It was more than control. It was almost inhuman.

His resistance to epsense was no less remarkable. Armada cadets received a basic training in mental defense, but no one she knew of, least of all herself, had the degree of control necessary to resist a reave as he had—and she hadn't—without actually being an epsense adept as well.

"Hull's punctured," she said with a calmness she didn't feel. "Not far away. The airlock is sealed. We're here to stay."

"Understood." He steadied her with a hand on her arm, then continued down the ramp. Moments later he returned with the semiconscious Eckandi draped over his shoulder. "The mind-rider will need him when she regains consciousness," he explained in response to her sharp look.

"Mind—? Oh, the reave." The outdated term threw her for a moment. He was making sense, though; the Surin would need someone to give her sensory input, preferably neither her nor Cane. "What did you do to her?"

"Nothing serious. She will awaken shortly."

Roche wasn't sure how she felt about that, and couldn't fight the sensation that she was being backed into a corner: first Cane, and now two others. Her mission was in enough jeopardy without complicating things further. But without saying anything, she hurried the short distance to the lander itself. When Cane had ducked through the inner airlock, she keyed it closed and made sure the seals were tight.

A short companionway led to the cockpit and its standard, if slightly out of date, hemispherical layout: five acceleration couches, centrally placed in rows of two and three; main controls located ahead of the front row; pilot's position right and backup to the left, auxiliary systems away to either side and rear. There were no viewports this far forward; heat shields covered the nose completely.

Roche dropped into the pilot's couch, made the fundamental adjustments to suit her physique, and placed the valise on her knees. "Out of curiosity, Box, *can* you fly this thing?"

<Of course, Morgan. Its interface is simple and will respond to my commands.>

"Good." She turned in her seat to see what Cane was up to. He had strapped the Eckandi into the chair in the center of the rear row and lifted the Surin from where she lay on the floor. The girl, limp and even smaller than Roche had guessed, went into the seat on the far side of the cockpit from Roche. "We have a reave on board, Box."

<I know—>

"If she wakes up and takes me over, you have my permission to fly the ship on your own. I don't want us stuck in limbo again waiting for her to decide whether or not she should trust us."

<A sensible precaution, Morgan.>

Cane strapped himself into the copilot's seat next to her, and Roche belatedly realized that she had been talking aloud.

"The briefcase," he said. "It's some sort of computer, isn't it?"

"Yes." She cursed the slip. "It's going to fly us out of here in—how long, Box?"

<Shortly.> The Box paused. <The *Midnight*'s fuel reserve will self-destruct at any moment.>

"What? Klose gave the order to scuttle the ship?"

Before the Box could reply, Roche had to grasp at the armrests as the frigate's gravity stabilizers failed completely.

"Shouldn't we be launching, then?" If the stabilizers had gone, the main energy pile wouldn't be far behind. And if the Box was right about Klose's order to free the antimatter reserve—

She was suddenly aware of perspiration beading her forehead.

<A little decorum, Morgan,> the voice lilted in her ear. <We have almost a full minute left to us.>

Roche forced herself to stay calm. "To hell with decorum, Box. Would you just get us out of here?"

<Morgan, must I explain the obvious? If we launch immediately, we will be picked up at once by Dato fighters—an easy target for their gunnery. There is a high probability they will take us for unimportant crew attempting to abandon ship, not the valued personnel we most certainly are, and destroy the lander. Do you agree?>

"Yes. So?"

<The magnetic bottle containing the antimatter reserve will fail in twenty seconds.>

"Box!" It was an exclamation of disbelief, nothing more. She had passed beyond panic.

<Outer door sequence employed. Stay calm, Morgan. Put colloquially: by the time they react to the opening of the outer doors, the ship will be history.>

"Just don't cut it too fine—"

<Ignition sequence commenced, Morgan. Take position.>

"Brace yourself!" Roche shouted to Cane, remembering that she alone could hear the voice in her ear. "We're launching!"

<Three seconds,> intoned the Box. <Launch.>

Riding a wave of energy as mighty as that on the surface of a small sun, the lander ejected itself into space. Roche closed her eyes against the sudden pressure, and put her fate into the Box's hands.

3

DBMP *Ana Vereine*
'954.10.30 EN
0765

From his coffin in life support, Captain Uri Kajic viewed the assault on the *Midnight* via his ship's various external sensors with interest.

The battlefield was complex. At its heart, the angry speck that represented the COE frigate spun like a primitive atom in primordial soup. A ring of Dato fighters harried this defensive position, swooping closer with every pass, supported by the greater might of the three raiders and, further back still, the Marauder itself: the *Ana Vereine*.

Occasional stray bolts spun free from the intense web of destruction woven by the raiders about the blazing frigate. Some were deflected from the *Midnight*'s remaining shields; others might have originated from the frigate itself. Although most dissipated harmlessly, the potential remained for an unlucky mishap. The narrow channel through Sciacca's World's asteroid field had been mapped in advance and was updated every millisecond by the Marauder's battle computers—but every new, unplanned explosion altered the orbits of nearby asteroids and increased the risk of collision.

When the *Midnight*'s antimatter reserve suddenly spilled free of its containment and annihilated the ordinary matter surrounding it, that risk increased tenfold.

"Pull the fighters back!" Kajic ordered, sending the command hurtling down electromagnetic paths to the bridge in the Marauder's primary nacelle, where his holographic image appeared a moment later. "Prepare for impact!"

His second in command, Atalia Makaev, turned away to relay the order. The expanding bubble of energy reached the *Ana Vereine*, making it shudder. Kajic's image flickered slightly with the energy surge, but otherwise remained steadfast. The officers on the bridge gripped their stations as the disturbance washed over them, steadying themselves against the lurching motion. When it eased, and the ship's g-field restabilized, the normal bustle resumed.

"Report!" Kajic was unable to suppress his impatience. If the ship had been holed, he would have known immediately, but there were thousands of smaller ailments that might slip by unnoticed. The inevitable lag between his orders and their enactment was never as irritating as it was in battle.

"Telemetry reports—" The ship shuddered again as the shields sustained another impact, draining power. Makaev waited for her superior's image to reconfigure itself properly before continuing. Not that it was necessary—Kajic could receive the information with or without the presence of his hologram—but it was considered polite. "Telemetry reports that the *Midnight* has broken into seven substantial fragments." She paused again, adjusting the communication bud in her left ear. "Their trajectories have been noted and extrapolated."

"Damage to the raiders?" Although Kajic's primary concern was the *Ana Vereine*, the information available to him showed an alarming void where moments earlier a dozen fighters had been.

"*Paladin* has sustained minor damage. *Lansquenet* reports no incident. Awaiting word from Captain Hage regarding *Galloglass*."

Kajic sighed, folding his simulated hands behind his back—using body language consciously, as just another means of communication of the many in his repertoire—and did his best to radiate calm. On the bridge's main screen, the brilliant fireball that had once been the COEA *Midnight* boiled away into space, leaving a shower of particles and radioactive dust in its wake. The larger fragments that telemetry had noted were ringed in warning red to aid navigation: bull's-eyes where perhaps gravestones should have been.

Kajic knew from intelligence reports that every COE frigate carried a crew of two hundred and fifty, each with families scattered throughout the Commonwealth of Empires; some of these people might conceivably have had ties with the Dato Bloc, no matter how distant. The *Midnight* had also been carrying a score of transportees. . . .

Gone, all of them, in a single blinding explosion as the *Midnight*'s pile went critical.

Gone also—and more important—was his hope of executing his mission smoothly and without error.

"Captain?"

Atalia Makaev regarded him with a steely expression. It always felt to Kajic as though she were looking into his soul, seeing all of his personal doubts, searching out his weaknesses.

"Yes, Atalia?" he said.

"We have regained contact with Captain Hage. Communications are currently restricted to coherent transmissions. *Galloglass*'s main communications nexus was overloaded by neutrino flux at the peak of the explosion."

He nodded. "As would be expected, given the *Galloglass*'s close proximity to the *Midnight*. It was ready to dock the moment the frigate's shields fell."

"With all due respect, sir," said Makaev. "The self-destruction of the *Midnight* should have been anticipated."

Kajic noted her thin, almost imperceptible smile with some irritation. "It was not a consideration," he said. "There was nothing within Captain Klose's professional or personal profiles to suggest that he would take such drastic action."

"Nevertheless, Captain," said Makaev, "he did self-destruct."

Kajic hesitated, fixing his stare squarely upon her for almost a full minute. He had his doubts about her true role aboard the ship, and how that role related to his own, but this wasn't the time to let suspicion interfere with duty.

"Bring us back to yellow alert," he said eventually. "Stabilize our orbits and commence repairs. I want all fighters returned to the *Ana Vereine*. We must be ready to leave at a moment's notice."

"Yes, sir."

"What of the target? Has a sighting been confirmed?"

"Debris scanning is under way."

He returned his attention to the data flowing from the sensors. "Replay the destruct sequence. Bring reserve computers on-line to plot the dispersal pattern and extend scan accordingly. It has to be out there somewhere," he said. "I want it found."

"Sir." Makaev's left arm snapped a salute; then she turned away.

On the main screen the fiery death of the *Midnight* returned to haunt him. He could have accessed the data directly, but for the moment he preferred the luxury of viewing the information from a distance, allowing him a more . . . *Human* perspective.

The outcome of the battle had indeed taken him by surprise. A protracted engagement had always been a possibility; on that point the tacticians agreed, and Kajic had prepared himself for Dato Bloc losses—but not for this. Not for the complete annihilation of the frigate and all its contents.

detain or disable COEA Midnight

His orders, hardwired into his circuitry, sprang into his thoughts unbidden. With his mission suffering such a spectacular setback, he was not surprised that they had. They were intended as a prompt, to surface with any doubt or uncertainty over the success of his mission.

capture and return Commander Roche and AI JW111101000

They continued—and would keep doing so until his thoughts were once again focused upon his mission, and all reservations concerning its success were dispelled.

priority gold-one

He shrugged aside the mental prompts and concentrated upon the recent battle:

Operationally, the strategy had been a simple one, and had been well executed. With the DBMP *Lansquenet*, *Galloglass*, and *Paladin* in support, the *Ana Vereine* had translated with extreme precision to the coordinates provided. The *Midnight* had been exactly where the Espionage Corps had reckoned it would be—too far in-system to make a run for the nearest anchor point, and foolishly vulnerable in Sciacca's World's orbital ring. Decelerating, outflanked, and outgunned, the *Midnight* had, ultimately, no choice other than surrender—or so reason would have had it.

The destruction of an Armada frigate in COE space, by its own hand or not, unplanned or not, had all the makings of a major diplomatic incident. A high cost, even if the mission ultimately proved to be successful—which was still by no means certain.

While the bridge bustled around him, Kajic accessed Klose's files and restudied the captain's profile. Klose's service record, stolen by Espionage Corps spies from COE Armada databanks, was long and unremarkable. CEO of an old frigate, normally given unimportant duties, Klose had been marked as a conservative living off remembered glories, full of hubris, disrespectful of the "new breed" of well-educated military administrators, stubborn and authoritarian—much like the Commonwealth he served. The possibility that Klose had also been unstable was something Kajic had not considered—had no *reason* to consider. There was nothing in the man's records to warrant it.

Klose had taken his own orders—to prevent the Dato Bloc from capturing the AI—to the absolute extreme. He had done so knowingly, choosing death before surrender, and had taken his crew with him, regardless of what their individual choices might have been.

Unexpected, yes. But if Kajic had not counted on Proctor Klose's reaction, then the opposite was also true: Klose could not have anticipated Kajic's own response to the situation. He had no intention of letting the destruction of the *Midnight* prevent him from fulfilling his mission. Nor would he permit any interference from the prison planet itself to stop him. Nothing was going to get in the way. Not even his often debilitating fear of failure.

priority gold-one

He forced the fear down, away from the surface. If there was one thing Kajic was, it was focused on the mission.

His orders had been explicit, and ranked in order of priority. These three priorities had been stamped into the fine mesh of bio-implants infiltrating the tissues of his living brain to ensure that there could be no possibility of misunderstanding their significance. No matter how omnipotent he felt at times—with his mind roving the labyrinthine networks of the *Ana Vereine*—priorities A to C were a constant reminder of his limitations, of just how much he owed the machines in his coffin.

Life. Senses. Command. Duty:

(A) capture the AI;

(B) capture Roche;

(C) perform (A) and (B) with as much stealth and speed as possible.

Focused.

"Atalia?"

His second returned instantly to his side, as though proximity to his image actually meant something. Microphones and cameras scattered throughout the Marauder provided him with the ability to communicate with anyone, anywhere, at any time he wished. She, of all the people on board, should have known that. Had she forgotten this, he wondered, or was it a deliberate action?

But then, he reminded himself, this was one of the many things the experiment was designed to test. Was effective command dependent on genuine physical presence, or could it be simulated? Could a simulation breed resentment, even fear, among those it was supposed to deal with most effectively?

"Sir?" Makaev's voice was as controlled as it always was.

"Dispatch shuttles to examine the larger pieces in situ."

She frowned. "If we do that, sir, we will be unable to leave until the shuttles have returned."

He manufactured a glower and turned its full force on her. "Are you questioning my orders?"

"Of course not, sir, but—"

"Then see that they are carried out immediately."

Makaev turned away and relayed the order to a subordinate while Kajic watched the *Midnight* explode an uncounted time and let the anger percolate through him.

He would not allow this temporary setback to get on top of him. He would not allow himself to doubt that he was capable of fulfilling the expectations of those who had designed him. He would not, *could* not, afford to fail.

It was just a matter of time.

4

COEA Lander *M-3*
'954.10.30 EN
0775

Roche slammed back into the couch, the valise crushing her rib cage and forcing the air from her lungs. The roar of the thrusters threatened to split her eardrums. She wanted to turn her head to check on the others, but the acceleration would not allow her.

Thrust increased twofold for an instant, accompanied by a thunderous rattling on the hull. The lander slewed violently, as though flying through atmospheric turbulence.

<What's happening, Box?> Her mental voice was faint beneath the noise.

<We're riding the *Midnight*'s shock wave, Morgan. I apologize for the bumpy ride, but it cannot be avoided.>

She forced herself to relax as much as she could, letting her abnormally heavy body roll with the vibrations and trying not to worry about damage to the lander's hull. It was out of her hands entirely now. All she could do was hope that the Box knew what it was doing.

<Applying lateral thrust to alter our course.> The voice of the AI was no different from normal, as though riding the envelope of a thermonuclear explosion was all in a day's work. <The Dato do not seem to have noticed our launch, obviously confused by the general debris around us. However, to avoid the increasing likelihood of thruster detection, I am cutting the main burn—now.>

Roche felt herself lift from the couch, her body pressing momentarily against the sudden tautness of the restraints. The rattling on the hull continued for a while before fading into silence. The occasional *tap-tap* of smaller thrusters came through the hull, changing the attitude of the lander slightly and making her stomach roll. A few minutes later she was weightless.

Her mind was heavy, however, with the knowledge of the carnage they had left behind.

<I have set a course for Sciacca's World,> said the Box. <Our orbit is highly elliptical, first taking us away from the planet and then back to perihelion at the edge of the atmosphere. We will exit the Soul in approximately ten minutes. Reentry will be in approximately nine hours.>

Roche forced herself to think about the future. <How long to perihelion?>

<Six hours. A slow trip, I know, Morgan, but this way we continue the pretense of debris.>

She nodded. It was a sensible strategy, given the situation: with no anchor or slow-jump drive and only a small amount of fuel, their possible destinations were limited to Kanaga Station in orbit or Port Parvati on the surface. Their decision would depend on the Dato and the movements of the Marauder. <Could be worse, I suppose.>

<Indeed. The pretense might have been reality.>

Roche loosened her restraint harness and massaged her aching muscles. The Box was right: had the *Midnight* exploded a minute sooner, they wouldn't have made it. <So what now?>

<Nothing. Rest, perhaps, if you feel the need to. I can handle the lander. Apart from monitoring the Dato, there is little to do.>

"Except find a few answers, perhaps," she muttered as she swung herself free of the chair, hooking the fingers of one hand around a grip to stabilize herself in the zero-g.

Cane watched unblinkingly from his seat at the copilot's station as she swiveled in midair to face him.

"We survived," he said. His natural smile reflected his calm disposition. Their abrupt departure didn't appear to have affected him in any way. "Whoever it was that spoke to me in my cell was right: you have been able to help me."

"So it would seem." She sensed no dissembling in his face and posture—and his gratitude seemed genuine—but she still couldn't afford to trust him. She knew too little to turn her back on him just yet.

She moved over to check on the Eckandi and the Surin, her movements within the cramped lander awkward and clumsy. A quick look confirmed her suspicions.

"Good. They won't wake for a while." She returned to her own couch and looked across at Cane. "I think it's time we talked."

"Whatever you want, Commander."

"How much do you actually remember?"

"I told you: I woke up a few days ago on the ship with no memory beyond my name. Since then, apart from a few visits from the ship's science officer, I've been left alone."

"Do you know that you were picked up in a life-support capsule?"

"I was told that much, but little else."

"They didn't tell you how long you'd been drifting?"

"I did overhear something to the effect that it might have been a while," he said. "But nothing was officially mentioned."

"I don't suppose you happened to 'overhear' anything else, did you?"

"Little. Why?"

"Because the science officer's report was destroyed with the *Midnight*." Along with any records of the conversation that had led him to her, she added to herself, rubbing a hand across tired eyes. The rush of adrenaline she had experienced over the last few hours had left her feeling more than a little exhausted. "Your recollections are all we have left to go on, I'm afraid."

Cane raised an eyebrow. "Well, I know I was picked up near an anchor point leading here. Not by chance, either: the *Midnight* apparently detected a distress signal. Where the signal came from, however, is a mystery; the capsule had no transmitter, and the signal vanished once they picked up the capsule on scan." He shrugged. "I can't explain it, and neither could the science officer."

Roche nodded, absorbing the information. "What else?"

"Not much. He wanted to know more about the way the capsule worked. I gather it contained a lot of equipment not normally required for any sort of emergency coma."

"Such as?"

"Biofeedback systems, I believe, but I really don't know." He shook his head. "I have no memory at all of any time before the capsule. If there was any."

Roche frowned. "What do you mean by that?"

"Nothing." A smile touched his lips but was gone a moment later. "It sometimes feels as though I was born inside the capsule."

"If you were, then you've grown up quick; you can talk, think, and move like an adult." And a very adept one at that, she thought to herself. She could see his potential in the way he held himself: constantly primed, ready to act, and yet, paradoxically, always at ease with his situation. The way he had carried himself in the lander bay had been more than impressive. An army of soldiers like Cane would be hard to stop. "Perhaps you were a combat soldier?"

"Maybe," he said, but without conviction.

A groan from behind them made them both turn. Roche instinctively reached for her pistol, then saw it was the old Eckandi, struggling in his chair. He was little more than semiconscious, and she noted with approval that Cane had locked the harness tight—something she should have done herself. Still, she kept the pistol ready. If the Surin had been a reave, who knew what the Eckandi—the Surin had called him "Veden," she recalled—would be.

Veden shook his head, opened his eyes. Taking in the interior of the lander with one quick glance, he turned to face Roche and Cane.

"Where—?" His voice was thin and accented faintly, but clear. His wide-pupiled eyes were startled, flitting between Roche and Cane, their movement beneath the fine milky film that was peculiar to the Eckandar Caste causing Roche some discomfort. "Where am I?"

"On the lander," Roche replied. "Heading for Sciacca's World."

"The *Midnight*?" Without waiting for a reply he turned to the unconscious Surin strapped into the seat beside him. "Maii?" He made to move, then realized that he too was restrained. "What have you done to her?"

Roche watched with interest the concern on the Eckandi's face. "She'll be okay."

"You know she's a reave?" Roche nodded; Veden shook his head. "I can't even begin to imagine how you managed to get past her."

Nor can I, Roche admitted to herself, but said: "We surprised you in the lander bay. Do you remember that?"

"I remember you shot me." Thin but distinct muscles tightened around the Eckandi's eyes. "I remember that much."

"You fired upon us first," said Cane.

"What else was I supposed to do? We had to get out of there. The ship was about to blow."

"How could you have known that?" Using a hand-grip, Roche pulled herself forward slightly. "And how did you escape from your cell?"

"Maii—" He hesitated, glancing again at the Surin. "She was monitoring the guards when the Dato hit. She got one of them to open the cell and let us go. It's considerably easier to manipulate people when they are panicked or confused, you see, so the attack on the *Midnight* was fortuitous in a way." He shifted beneath his restraints. "After that it was a simple matter of getting to the lander bay. I've flown landers like this all my life; launching wouldn't have been a problem." He seemed about to say something further, but decided against it and fell silent.

"Sounds a bit too easy," said Roche doubtfully. "If it was that simple to escape, then why didn't you do it sooner? I mean, surely there would have been other times in other systems when the guards were vulnerable. Why wait until we're at Sciacca's World?"

"That's none of your business." His milky glare fixed on Roche for a few seconds before he turned away and faced Cane. "Who's *he*, anyway?"

Cane met Veden's unexpected hostility with a broad grin, the lights from the lander's displays flashing in his steady eyes. "That would appear to be none of *your* business," he said.

Veden's gaze returned to Roche. "He's working undercover for the Armada—for COE Intelligence—is that it? I don't remember seeing him in the brig." Roche ignored the question. "Whoever he is, he moves like one of those damned jarapines from Proebis-12."

<Morgan.> The Box's voice sounded in her mind.

<Yes, Box?> She was careful to subvocalize in front of the Eckandi.

<There is an Eckandi named Makil Veden listed on the *Midnight*'s freight transcript.>

<What was his charge?>

<Code violation and gross misconduct. Apparently he trod quite heavily on someone's toes—someone in the Commerce Artel, I would guess, given that he used to work for them. Death sentence commuted to transportation.>

<Any mention of the Surin?>

<Conspirator. Same charges.>

<Thanks, Box.> She returned her attention to Veden, regarding the Eckandi silently for a few moments before speaking. "So," she said, "was it fraud, or outright robbery?"

His eyes widened. "I don't know what you mean."

"The code violation. You must be more stupid than you look to mess with the Commerce Artel."

"If you say so, Commander." He dismissed her accusation with a flick of his head. If he was surprised by her knowledge of his history, he showed no sign of it. There was more than just a hint of contempt in his crooked smile. "Who am I to question an Armada officer?"

Their eyes locked for thirty seconds or so before he finally looked away, his smile fading beneath a sigh. "At least we're alive," he said, closing his eyes and lying back into the chair. "That's all that matters right now."

"For you, maybe," Roche muttered. "What matters to me is that I'm stuck with you for at least another five hours." She watched the Eckandi closely for a reaction, but there was none. With the typical arrogance of his Caste, he had decided to terminate the conversation. For all intents and purposes, he had totally closed himself off, and Roche knew that further questioning would be useless for the time being. Maybe, she hoped, things would change when the Surin awoke.

To Cane she said: "I'm going to check out the lander, see what we've got in the way of supplies. Can I rely on you to keep an eye on him?"

Cane nodded. “Of course.”

“If the reave tries anything when she wakes, knock her out again.” The words elicited no response from the supine Eckandi. “We’re some way from safety, and I don’t want anything else to go wrong.”

“Understood.” He folded his arms as she left the cockpit. When she returned five minutes later to check on him, he hadn’t moved a muscle. *A perfect sentry*, she thought. Almost too good, in fact.

<Box?>

<Yes, Morgan.>

<Watch him via the cabin monitors. If he makes the slightest move, let me know.>

<You’re a trusting soul, aren’t you?>

She didn’t smile as she returned to the storeroom. “That’s a luxury I can’t afford at the moment,” she said, more to herself than to the Box.

Four hours later, a voice roused her from a deep slumber she couldn’t remember entering:

<Wakey-wakey, Morgan.>

Her head jerked up, and the sudden movement sent her drifting across the room. More by chance than anything else, she managed to catch hold of a stanchion and bring herself to a halt. A rush of panic subsided when her eyes adjusted to the dim light of her surroundings and she realized where she was: the lander’s storeroom. She had come in to check on what equipment was available to them, but the low lights coupled with her exhaustion had seduced her into sleep. Not, however, before she had ascertained how little in the way of supplies they actually had: two medical kits, three basic communicators, six survival suits, and enough food to last them two days—five if rationed severely. The only weapons on board were Veden’s laser and her own pistol.

<Morgan.> The voice was sterner this time, cutting through her tired thoughts.

Roche rubbed her eyes, shook her head. “Yes, Box,” she said. “I’m awake. How long have I been out?”

<Too long. I would have let you sleep longer, but there has been a development.>

“Oh? What?”

<The Surin has regained consciousness.>

She shook her head one last time to clear it of the residue of sleep, then pushed herself toward the door. It slid aside with a hiss, and she slipped out into the narrow accessway. The only other room in the lander, a privacy and waste cubicle opposite the storeroom, was sealed, occupied. Sparing it but a glance, she brushed past it and into the cockpit.

Cane had moved to a position by the main entrance. The Surin lay with her back to Roche, still strapped into the central couch. The only movement as she entered the room came from Cane’s eyes, which glanced at her before returning to the reave.

<I can detect peripheral vision also.> The reave’s voice echoed deep in Roche’s head, although the statement was intended for Cane. It was a strange and intimate kind of intrusion—almost a rape—and felt as though someone was using her brain to think their own thoughts. It was very different from the Box’s clear input, and Roche detested it. <I admire your perseverance,> continued the Surin. <But I knew Roche

was awake the moment she did. I could have taken her then, if I'd wanted to. Doesn't that mean anything to you? That I didn't?>

Roche watched from the other side of the cockpit as Cane kept his eyes still. Nothing was spoken aloud, but a conversation took place nonetheless.

<I'm trying to tell you that you can trust me!> The Surin's tone was desperate. She was clearly uncomfortable in her restraints. <I know I can't hurt *you*. But, Roche—Yes, I am aware of what would happen if I tried. I'm just saying that I *could*. Why don't you *believe* me?>

Roche cleared her throat pointedly. "Where's Veden?" The couch next to the Surin was empty.

<He's in the privacy cabin,> replied the reave. <And stop thinking of me as just a Surin. My name is Maii.>

Roche forced herself to reply civilly. "Thank you," she said, "Maii."

<You don't trust me, do you?>

"Should I?"

<You tell her, Cane.>

"She's telling the truth." Cane finally wrenched his eyes away from the Surin's. "He's locked in the cubicle. The couch was too uncomfortable for an old man to be confined to for such a long period of time."

Roche nodded. It seemed reasonable, she supposed. "What about you two?"

Cane shrugged noncommittally.

<He's trying to resist me,> explained the Surin. <He doesn't like me using his eyes, and keeps them focused on my face to stop me seeing anything. But it isn't working.> Roche sensed amusement as the girl added: <It's okay now, Cane. You can relax. I'm not using them anymore.>

Roche suppressed a shudder, and barely caught herself from using her training to keep the girl out of her head, if she could at all. There was no point. If the reave noticed her revulsion, she didn't mention it.

"Maii, I want you to tell me about Veden. Who is he, and what were you doing with him?"

<Cane can answer that,> said the girl. <I've already told him.>

Roche turned to Cane, who shrugged. "She says they're not really transportees—or rather, they are, but not criminals."

"That doesn't make sense."

<I know, but that's all I can say.> The Surin's narrow tongue licked at the fine hair around her black lips. <You'll have to ask Veden.>

"I did," said Cane.

Roche's eyes flicked from Maii to Cane. "And what did he say?"

"Nothing."

"I didn't think he would." Roche moved around the cockpit and came up beside the girl's couch. "Is he using you against your will?"

Something rippled gently through Roche's mind—Maii was chuckling. <I'm not a *slave*, if that's what you're suggesting. Veden wouldn't dream of doing anything like that.>

"No, I meant . . ." She shook her head. "You know what I meant."

The girl looked annoyed for an instant, the flash of emotion the first true vitality Roche had seen in the Surin's face. <I don't know *everything* about you. Just the surface thoughts; the obvious details. I could read deeper, of course, if you'd let me.>

"That didn't stop you before," said Roche. "Back in the lander bay." The experience was still vivid in her mind.

<You caught me by surprise. One moment Veden was going to seal the airlock, and the next he'd been knocked out. I panicked.> The girl looked genuinely sad for a moment. <Contrary to popular belief, Commander, we epsense adepts do have some moral standards.>

Roche snorted. "Yeah, they just aren't very high."

<That isn't fair,> said the Surin. <You make it sound as though what happened back on the *Midnight* is something I enjoy doing. But I don't. It happens to be very draining.>

"Not to mention immoral."

<And a pistol isn't?>

Roche mentally conceded the point, and wondered if she was being more than a little paranoid. She was imagining dark motives behind everything the reave said and did—sophisticated deceits that only an adult would be capable of. The ritually blinded Surin, for all her psychic talents, was still little more than a child. Petulant sometimes, perhaps even vicious, but a child nonetheless.

What the Surin had been doing in the company of Makil Veden remained a concern, however. To Roche, the long-faced and grey-skinned Eckandi made an odd figure beside the tawny Surin, with her wide jaws and lightly fuzzed complexion. Obviously their relationship went back a lot farther than the *Midnight*, perhaps even as far as the Surin's birth. Certainly Maii seemed to regard Veden in a respectful light; maybe the Eckandi had adopted her as his surrogate daughter.

"You're very young," said Roche. "Far younger than any other reave I've met."

Maii's face closed instantly. <I developed young. Let's leave it at that, okay?>

"Hey, I was just—"

<I'm sorry to interrupt, Morgan.>

Roche turned away from the Surin. <What is it, Box?>

<Good and bad news, I'm afraid.>

She groaned inwardly. <Let's have it.>

<First: despite my precautions, we have been located. The undamaged raider has changed course to pursue us. They clearly intend a leapfrog maneuver—overtaking us and launching interceptors before we reach perihelion—which seems sensible under the circumstances.>

<Okay.> She braced herself against the nearest couch. <The good news?>

<That was it.>

<Come on, Box. This is no time for—>

<I am being completely serious, Morgan. Relatively speaking, that *was* the good news: they haven't decided to destroy us outright. The bad news is that the local authority in orbit around Sciacca's World has made no move to avenge the destruction of the *Midnight*. Furthermore, I have detected coded transmissions between the Dato Marauder and Kanaga Station.>

Roche frowned, trying to comprehend what the Box was implying. <The Dato wouldn't take over a COE Communications Base, would they? That'd be tantamount to a declaration of war.>

<You misunderstand me, Morgan. Ask yourself why these transmissions are coded in the first place.>

Even as the Box posed the question, the answer had formed in her own mind.

<Because neither party wants what they have to say to go public. A strictly private exchange.>

<Precisely. Now consider: four ships from the Dato Bloc attacked and destroyed an Armada frigate within a planetary system under the nominal control—or at least the scrutiny—of the Commonwealth. How could they hope to execute such an attack and get away with it, camouflaged or not? The repercussions would be severe.>

<I don't like the sound of this, Box.>

<It is decidedly unpleasant. I have recorded the times each transmission took place; you may need the detail later. For now, it is sufficient that you know that the command on Kanaga Station is, to some degree at least, corrupt.>

<Dato sympathizers?>

<It is unlikely to be anything so moral. Just corrupt. The attack on the *Midnight* was no incident of opportunity; it was carefully planned in advance, using information gathered even higher—from the very top of the COE Armada. A high-priced deal was struck with those in power here around Sciacca's World in order to facilitate it. It is also likely that an even more generous deal is being negotiated to ensure our recapture.>

<So it *is* you they're after?>

<Both of us, it seems, or else they would have destroyed the lander immediately upon sighting it. Negotiations will currently be determining the true extent of our value to your opposite numbers in the Dato Bloc Espionage Corps. I would guess the ultimate figure will be exceedingly high.>

<That's something, I guess.> Roche tugged herself forward to the lander's array of instrumentation and the pilot's couch. The feel of cushions against her back was somehow reassuring. <So, let me guess what happens next. Either we dock at Kanaga Station and are handed over to the Dato—for a tidy sum and no questions asked—or we go into the atmosphere and take our chances on the ground. We have no way of knowing how Port Parvati figures in this, but we know that it'll cost the Dato considerably more to land a search party, or pay for one to be sent after us. Either way, going to ground is our best option.>

<An essentially accurate summary.>

<Then do it. Take us down. Try to put us down at Port Parvati's landing field, or nearby. They'll have communicators there. At the very least we'll be able to let HQ know what happened.>

<As you wish.> The Box paused for a moment, then added, almost as an afterthought: <I suggest you get everybody into the acceleration couches. In order to take the Dato raider by surprise, I will have to use maximum thrust.>

<Right.>

Roche sat up and looked around. Cane was studying her closely.

"From the look on your face," he said quietly, "I take it we're in trouble."

"We are. Get yourself strapped in. No, wait—we need to wake Veden."

Cane stepped from the room to get the Eckandi. At least with him nearby, Roche thought, the Surin would no longer need her senses, or those of Cane.

A couple of minutes later, when Cane had returned with Veden, Roche turned and addressed everyone. "The Dato are on to us, but there's a chance we can outrun them. We'll be thrusting at max, so make sure your harnesses are firm. Let me know when you're set."

Cane dropped into his couch and fastened the harness with all the speed and surety of a veteran. He smiled reassuringly at Roche but said nothing. She didn't respond. Veden swung himself into the couch next to Maii and sealed himself in.

<We're fine,> said Maii a moment later.

"Okay here," Cane added.

Roche locked the clasps around her own chest and midriff and let the couch enfold her.

<When you're ready, Box.>

Immediately the thrusters crushed them back into the couches. Roche felt the air empty from her lungs, and struggled against the acceleration to refill them. Purple spots floated in her eyes as blood drained from her retinae. She wondered briefly how Veden was managing; he was an aging man, surely not up to such strain. If the burn continued for too long, he might exhaust himself, be in danger of asphyxiating—

Her thoughts were interrupted when she felt the Surin's mind-touch come and go. She glanced up to the monitors above her and had the Box display a view of the others. Maii's face was turned up, her breathing strong and even. She at least was having no difficulties. Veden also seemed to be breathing steadily, which surprised Roche. His eyes were closed, almost as if he were asleep. He was handling the burn with considerable ease.

Then Roche realized why: Maii had taken over his autonomous systems. The girl was regulating his breathing and heart rate in sympathy with her own. Veden was in a state far deeper than sleep; he had given himself over completely to the reave.

The degree of the invasion was abominable, but Roche knew that the acceleration would be life-threatening for Veden if Maii had not been controlling him. And she had checked on Roche in passing—to make sure that she hadn't required similar assistance.

Roche shuddered. It made her skin crawl just thinking about it.

She withdrew into herself, concentrated on riding out the burn. She thought about asking the Box how long it planned to stay at max, but decided it was better not to know. She cleared her mind and focused inward upon her body, riding the stress rather than fighting it.

Even so, the burn seemed to last forever. When the pressure suddenly lapsed, there came in its place a sensation of relative weightlessness, but Roche knew from experience how false the feeling was. The Box was still holding the lander at somewhere between two and three gees. Although the lander's instruments had come to life—now that the pretense of dereliction was over—her eyes wouldn't focus properly.

<What's the situation, Box?>

The Box's voice was annoyingly free of strain. <It would appear that the opposition lacks a decisive strategist. The raider moved to overlap us, but declined to drop its interceptor craft. They seem reluctant to maneuver so deep within the Soul—probably because of the threat of damage to hull integrity posed by the ever-present dust—and so have opted to allow us to land. The safer but more expensive option.>

<So why are we still accelerating?>

<To put it colloquially, Morgan: I do not wish to tip our hand too soon. We have an advantage in that the opposition does not know that I know about their communications with Kanaga Station, and I intend to keep that advantage as long as possible. My strategy is to continue to give the appearance of a pursued vessel. This means a hot descent to Port Parvati—which will, unfortunately, be uncomfortable.> The Box

hesitated before continuing: <I believe the time has come, Morgan, to abandon our heretofore one-on-one communication status.>

Roche didn't answer immediately. One-on-one was a basic security precaution prescribed by her superiors in COE Intelligence. Technically, she could not countermand it.

<Why?> she asked, instinctively suspicious.

<I am simply suggesting that we open an internal com channel so that I will be able to communicate directly with everybody in the lander. If I am to make decisions based on constantly changing random factors, then critical information will have to be available to everybody. A successful outcome may depend on the swiftness of our response to an unforeseen emergency.>

Roche felt weary. The move made good sense, and the Box could open the channel itself if it really wanted to. But to go against a direct order . . .

With difficulty, she reached for the pilot's console, selected an internal com channel, and flicked it open. "Okay, Box. You've got what you want. The stage is yours."

<Thank you,> the Box lilted. <Internal com will not come through your implant.> Even as Roche heard the voice in her ear, it delivered a separate message over the newly opened channel.

"The thrusters are about to be cut," it said loudly, employing more than enough volume to gain attention over the background noise of the burn.

Roche glanced at Cane, then at the others. Cane's eyebrows had risen sharply when the voice of the Box broke the relative silence of the cabin, but he quickly regained his composure. Veden looked completely relaxed, his eyes focused somewhere ahead of him. He gave no indication that he was even listening.

"We will be entering the atmosphere of Sciacca's World within minutes," the Box went on, sounding more like a tour guide than the present arbiter of their destinies. "It will be a hot and bumpy descent. Further maneuvers will be necessary once we're able to deploy our glide foils, so please remain in your harnesses. I will inform you when it is safe to release them."

<I hope your little black box knows what it's doing.> Maii's tone was sharp. AIs, Roche remembered, were regularly used to counteract reaves, unable as the latter were to read electronic thoughts.

"It knows," Roche said aloud, but with an uncertainty that mirrored the Surin's own feelings. Then the burn died, and suddenly they were weightless again.

She looked toward Cane, found him watching her impassively. "That was the Box?" he asked.

"Yes."

"Interesting," he said thoughtfully. "It sounds very . . . Human."

Something struck the hull of the lander with a short but decisive bang, and Roche jumped in her seat. "Box?"

<Particulate debris,> replied the AI, in her ears only. <Nothing to be greatly concerned about. At our velocity, small impacts are inevitable.>

<The hull will hold?>

<It is being damaged but, yes, it will hold.>

<How long until we hit atmosphere?>

<Not long. The burn changed our orbit significantly. Using the velocity we already possessed as a result of the downward leg of our ellipse, I have directed the

lander into a near-vertical descent. Our trajectory will change in approximately five minutes to soften the impact with the upper atmosphere.>

Roche closed her eyes and tried to relax, hard though it was with the lander hurtling straight down into an unknown situation. Two minutes passed, then three, and no one in the cockpit made a sound. Then:

<Slight change of plans, Morgan.>

<What's happened?>

<Port Parvati has launched a squadron of fighters to intercept us before we land.>

She groaned. <So they're involved as well.>

<It would seem so. We can't rely on them for assistance, in any case. That forces us to reassess our intentions. I suggest we continue along our current course, to present the illusion of surrender, then peel away from the landing field at the last possible moment.>

<Peel away to where?>

<That, Morgan, is something I do not yet know.>

Roche blinked. She had never heard the Box admit anything but omniscience before. <But you will, right? When the time comes?>

<Let us say that I will go with what seems the best option at the time.>

Roche could hardly believe what she was hearing. She knew that independent Boxes could be unpredictable—unlike their rigidly controlled, and therefore less flexible, counterparts in the COE Armada—but they simply didn't *say* things like that.

<At the risk of sounding critical,> she said, with a growing disquiet, <your strategy seems to be constructed of and entirely dependent on random factors.>

<Yes, Morgan. Exciting, is it not?>

The thrusters burned again, bringing the lander into a less steep descent.

"Not the word I would have used," she said quietly. Then, shouting over the noise to the others in the cockpit: "We can't afford to trust anyone on the ground. The government here is corrupt. If we fall into their hands, they'll turn us over to the Dato Bloc. The Box's strategy is to let them think we're coming straight in—that we know none of this. We'll change course as late as possible and look for other hands to fall into. Everyone happy with that?"

On the monitors she saw Cane cock an eyebrow and give the faintest of shrugs. At the same time she heard Maii mind-whisper: <Too bad if we're not.> Roche saw Veden grin at this.

Roche could appreciate the irony of his situation. The Dato were after Roche and the Box, not the transportees. Perhaps Veden had expected to be turned over to the authorities in Port Parvati as soon as the lander made planetfall. Had that indeed been Roche's intention—and she'd had very little time to consider her plans for him and the Surin—then the discovery of treachery on the planet rendered it unlikely. From Veden's point of view, as long as he pleaded ignorance, the betrayal of Port Parvati's wardens was good news, not bad.

Accordingly, it was Veden who spoke next:

"Your Box should know that outlaw forces are currently operating on Sciacca's World."

"I hear you, Veden," the Box said through the com. "Elaborate, please."

"There's a group operating in the mountainous area to the north of Port Parvati. They may be able to assist us."

"I have relief maps on file. Can you provide coordinates?"

"They're a mobile group. That's how they survive."

"Then your information has little value." A viewtank winked into life on the pilot's display, showing an expanded view of Sciacca's World. The main continental mass zoomed close; Port Parvati was in the center of a large but relatively featureless desert with a forbidding range of mountains to the immediate north. A cursor traced a wide arc along the southernmost peaks. "We must assume that our hypothetical allies exist somewhere in this region. The range known as Behzad's Wall offers sufficient cover not too far from the port for any number of resistance operations."

"Take us along the spine of the range, then," said Veden. "There's a plateau containing an old strip mine and an abandoned town. Land us as close us possible to that location. They'll find us, if they want to."

"Understood."

Both the Box and Veden fell silent. Roche turned to look at the old man. "Just who are these people?"

"Commander, you belong to COE Intelligence. As such, you're the last person I should discuss this information with."

Roche felt mounting exasperation. "But if the Port Parvati authorities are corrupt, then COE Intelligence needs to be informed. If your friends have formed some sort of resistance, then they should be making every attempt to communicate with us. We can help them."

Veden frowned. "COE Intelligence is an arm of the Commonwealth, just as the Enforcers in Port Parvati are. Why should one arm act against another?"

Roche stared at him, unable to believe that her government could be so distrusted. But Veden went on before she could protest.

"Anyway, they are not my friends. They are merely clients. I was coming here to do a job. Why they have done or not done certain things is not my concern."

"But you're a transportee," Roche said. "How could you—?" She stopped in mid-sentence. There could be only one answer, the one Maii had provided earlier.

Veden confirmed it. "As a transportee, I could be moved here without arousing suspicion. All I needed was a conviction and a life sentence."

Easy, Roche thought, although not without skepticism. "You're being well paid for this, I take it?"

"Perhaps."

"To do what, exactly?"

"That, Commander, is a matter safeguarded by professional confidentiality. I'm in business, after all, not an agent of COE Intelligence."

"I—uh!" The lander suddenly shifted, jolting Roche violently against her harness. She saw Veden's face twist in pain, felt Maii's desperation as she quickly tried to regain control over the old man's autonomous systems. "Box! What the hell is going on?"

"We are about to strike the ionosphere." The Box's voice came loudly over the com. "Most of our reentry velocity will be shed by aerobraking, during which time I will maintain a standard approach to Port Parvati. At the last moment, however, we will overfly the landing area and proceed north at roughly treetop level. Somewhere in the mountains I shall attempt to simulate a crash."

"'Attempt' . . . ?" Roche gaped. Landing in a gravity well was the most difficult maneuver a pilot could be asked to perform; she knew it would be all too easy to *genuinely* crash, no matter what the Box's intentions were.

But the Box had obviously anticipated her misgivings. In her ear only, it said: <This is the best strategy, Morgan. If we appear to perish, they might lose interest in us. Trust me on this, please. It is the only option open to us at this time.>

Over the com, the Box continued its spiel. "I will attempt to land as close to Veden's target as possible. Once down, there will be very little time to get clear before the engines overload."

"How long exactly?" said Roche.

"That I cannot predict. It depends on the severity of damage sustained as a result of the impact. Regardless, a hasty departure will certainly be in order."

"Will we have time to gather supplies?"

"Perhaps. We will have to see what happens."

The retros ceased their noisy burn. A few seconds of weightless glide followed; then the atmosphere touched the hull, feather-light at first but with a steadily increasing force. The lander began to bump and slew, the series of jolts gradually building in violence. As friction tore at the pockmarked nose of the vessel, the temperature inside the cockpit began to rise, and Roche began to feel decidedly uncomfortable.

In her ear, the Box's emotionless voice whispered: <The fighters from Port Parvati are tracking us. They are also attempting to communicate. I am ignoring them, of course. Thus far, they have made no overtly hostile moves. It could be that they are present simply to ensure that we head for the landing field.>

The lurching descent continued, and the temperature continued to rise. Roche heard a mental curse from Maii, but the girl sounded in control—which meant that Veden was all right also. And she knew that Cane would be coping as easily as he seemed to cope with everything else.

She tried to push the mounting heat aside, but her mind refused to settle. There were too many unknowns swirling about her: Veden with his connections to whatever waited on the surface, Maii's connection with him and her ability to know anything and everything Roche herself knew, and a Box that was trying its best to cook them all.

Not quite. Just when she felt she could stand it no longer, the temperature began to fall again. The wild ride was finally easing.

"Box?"

"Extending glide foils in thirty seconds. Lining up on the landing area."

The cabin jolted again as the airfoils extended and the lander began to maneuver in clear air. Moments later, the ride became relatively smooth.

"Accelerating again in twelve seconds," the Box announced. "Brace yourselves."

Roche counted down the seconds, clutched the arms of the couch tightly to steady herself, but was slapped back into the cushions anyway. The lander slewed violently to the left, and the wild ride began afresh.

In her ear: <I'm making it look as if we've lost control. We'll put down near this end of the range, just as soon as I get us into radio shadow.>

Over the com: "Hard landing in approximately one minute. The cargo doors will be open. Be ready to disembark. Try to put as much distance as possible between yourselves and the lander. That or some large objects."

And again in her ear: <It's going to be rough, so don't worry about supplies. Just up and run.>

<You're one hell of a strategist, Box.>

<Don't knock it, Morgan. We're still in the game.>

"Twenty seconds to impact," it said over the com.

Roche braced herself yet again. The lander swayed extravagantly, but she noticed that the vertical component of the glide remained smooth. The Box had full control. Still, she was glad there was no viewing portal. Better not to see what was happening outside.

Then came a frightening few seconds of silence—no slewing, no whining of the airfoils, just waiting for impact. She didn't know what was worse.

<Hold onto me, Morgan,> the Box said to her.

Then they hit.

Roche was thrown against her harness with such force that it felt as if the couch would tear loose from its mountings. A long, terrible scream of ripping metal shrieked through the cabin; smoke suddenly filled the air. Anything not secured ricocheted around the cockpit.

Something clipped the side of Roche's skull, making her head ring. She closed her eyes and tried not to scream.

Cane called out something, but his words were lost in the noise.

The lander bounced once, twice, then careened violently to the right. Another lurch—this time upward, giving the impression that the craft was about to tip end over end. Sparks and blue flame erupted about them as the control panels and monitors exploded simultaneously. A series of small slews and lurches, a long dull grinding noise—

Then nothing but smoke.

"Evacuate immediately," the Box said into the ringing silence. Roche wasn't sure whether it was in her ear or over the com, but she needed no further prompting.

"Okay," she gasped, slipping the clasps on her harness. "Let's get out of here."

Cane reached across her and freed her rear clasps. Before she could move, he was doing the same for a badly dazed Veden. Roche couldn't help but marvel at him. He had been out of his harness almost instantly; with no sense of undue rush, he was moving faster than she could manage with all her Armada training.

"Help him out of here," she ordered as Veden stumbled, disoriented. Cane put an arm around the Eckandi's shoulders and guided him to the airlock.

Roche tucked the Box under her left arm, slid off the couch, and helped Maii to her feet. The Surin shrugged her hand away; the smoke in the air made her cough, but otherwise she was unharmed.

<I can walk,> Maii whispered in her mind. <Just point me in the right direction.>

Roche smiled to herself. "That way," she said, and started the girl forward. "Just keep moving. I won't be far behind."

Cane and Veden had already vanished. It was hard to tell through the thickening smoke exactly where she was. Something exploded with a *crump* beyond a bulkhead, showering her with sparks and temporarily blinding her. She had to rely on her hands to guide her along. At the storeroom, she stopped and tried the door.

"How long, Box?"

<Sixty seconds. I told you—>

"I know, I know. But we *need* those supplies."

The door to the storeroom had jammed shut, the frame warped by the impact. She kicked it open and stumbled through. The smoke was thicker in the tiny room, and the heat more oppressive. More sparks showered in a stream from one corner, burning her exposed skin. She clutched randomly at containers and, gagging upon the suffocating fumes, quickly thrust them into a plastic sack.

<Thirty seconds.>

"Okay," she said, coughing. "I hear you." Shrugging the half-empty sack over a shoulder, she hastened out of the room and through the cockpit. Halfway to the airlock, her foot tangled in a strip of burning insulation, making her stumble. Barely had she regained her feet when she felt strong hands clutch at her shoulders.

"Roche!" Cane's voice bellowed in her ear, straining to be heard over the rising rumble from the depleted fuel tanks. "Come on!"

Unable to reply, Roche let herself be hauled through the lander. As they crossed the lip of the airlock, her legs gave out entirely, sending her tumbling forward. As one, she and Cane fell down the steep egress ramp and onto rocky ground.

Maii was at their side immediately, pulling Cane to his feet. Roche had landed heavily beneath him, with the Box crushed up against her ribs. She had a bad feeling that one or more of them was broken. She reached for Maii's hand and heard Cane shout from somewhere above them: "I'll carry her! You get clear!"

Roche's head was swimming now. She was aware of Cane standing over her, and of his powerful arms dragging her upright. Pain shot across her chest as he lifted her onto his shoulders.

"*The sack*," she tried to say. If he replied, she didn't hear.

The pain increased when he started to run, but she fought against unconsciousness as long as she could. A loud explosion slapped the world behind her, and a flash of heat seared one side of her face—and then, finally, she blacked out.

PART TWO:

HOUGHTON'S CROSS

5

DBMP *Ana Vereine*
'954.10.30 EN
1225

Down through the complex matrix of information that represented the Dato Marauder, *Ana Vereine*, the soul of Captain Uri Kajic flew like an electric bird of prey—

feeling

—the hull humming with energy, singing like vibrating glass—

seeing

—sensors alive with light and radiation, feeding a constant stream of tactical and telemetry data directly to his nervous system—

tasting

—the drive mix: potent and powerful, exactly the right texture of elements at exactly the right temperature—

hearing

—the babble of voices chanting an epiphany to the process that was war and the great metal beasts that served its purpose—

dreaming

—of a faceless woman whose very presence threatened his existence in some vague, unstated manner.

While the remains of his body lay in its fluid-filled coffin, attended by patient machines, the various networks and subroutines implanted in the tissues of his brain ticked over without rest. From spinal column to cerebrum, every ganglion of his nervous system had been rewired to interface with some aspect of the ship. As a result, only part of his mind slept while the remainder continued its perpetual chores of monitoring the ship's activities.

His previous life—before the slow-jump accident and the operation—had been completely forgotten. Erased by surgery. The wire net lacing his plastic skull caught any ghosts long before they could disturb his thoughts, waking or unconscious. On every level of his being, he was the captain of the *Ana Vereine*—capable, efficient, and, above all, loyal. His dreams were always of the ship, his new body, and his mission; the never-ending flow of information from the *Ana Vereine* rarely allowed him anything else. Most filtered through his subconscious without ever requiring further attention, although occasionally certain elements of a dream would catch his interest and linger longer than normal.

Such as this threatening, faceless woman. . . .

He had no doubts that the dream was a warning, and that the woman was his second in command, Atalia Makaev. Since the beginning of the mission she had been undermining his leadership at every opportunity. Not overtly—that would constitute treason—but certainly subtly. It was in the things she said, the *way* she said them, and the manner in which she looked at him. Everything was a threat to his authority.

He had been designed and rebuilt to *lead*. Any challenge to that was a challenge to the very core of his being.

A soft but insistent alarm purred through his coffin, distracting him from his reverie. The image of the woman faded almost immediately, although he was unable to free himself of the apprehension that the dream had brought.

Focusing his thoughts on the specific rather than the general, Kajic glanced at the message. Makaev, with an uncanny sense of timing, had summoned him.

His sensory input jumped from sensors scattered across the ship to the two task-specific cameras mounted on the bridge command dais. They swung to focus on the position Makaev usually occupied, but found it empty. Belatedly studying the summons in detail, he discovered her in the command module, a small niche used for privacy at the rear of the bridge.

Changing his position took less will than the blink of an eyelid. His hologram faded from the bridge and reappeared in the module, where Makaev stood watching him with her hands folded behind her back, her lips parted in a slight and narrow smile.

"News, sir." Her voice was brisk and businesslike, a sharp contrast to the way his brain presently felt. The hormone delivery systems of his life support needed tuning again, he guessed. He nodded, gesturing for her to continue.

"Our mole in DAOC flight control reports that the shuttle has crash-landed in a region to the north of Port Parvati, under cover of mountains."

He stared at her, momentarily disoriented.

priority gold-one

"*What* shuttle?" He quickly accessed the relevant data that had collected in his "memory" banks during his artificial slumber, waiting for him to find the opportunity to review it. There was nothing Makaev could tell him that wasn't already there, but a lesson in respect and humility wouldn't hurt the woman.

She inclined her head with an expression that approximated genuine bafflement. "I'm sorry, sir. I assumed you were observing—"

"You don't *assume* anything, Commander," he snapped, scowling. "I have been resting for the last three hours, and therefore disconnected from virtually all data input."

"I had no idea—"

He interrupted her again. "Don't play the fool with me, Commander."

"Sir, I swear . . ." She faltered. Then, more surely: "All information regarding your bodily needs and/or states of mind is restricted, and no inferior officer may access your network without reasonable cause. Given the nature of this mission, the only acceptable cause would be that your actions had somehow threatened its success. Anything else would be regarded as mutiny." She added, "Sir."

Kajic studied her carefully. The expression on her face was one of concern, but he was suspicious of what lay underneath—of what intentions her thoughts kept hidden.

"I'm aware of the regulations, Commander," he said distractedly. "Nevertheless, there is a back door in my life-support program. I found it in the mainframe two days ago." He hesitated before voicing his suspicions. "*Someone* has been monitoring me."

The crease in her brow was slight and forced. "A back door? But who—? I mean, *why* would there be such a thing?"

"To spy on me, of course. To make sure I behave." His image leaned closer to Makaev. "And please, Commander, if you must play the fool, then do it with more conviction."

Makaev's back straightened, and she met the stare of the hologram evenly and without flinching. "I have no knowledge of what you speak, sir," she said. "Clearly the leak must have been placed there before we left Jralevsky Minor."

Kajic allowed himself a wry grin. "Clearly."

"Whoever is behind it must be somehow involved in the design of your program itself."

"Or somebody opposed to it." He shrugged. "One of the conservatives, perhaps."

Kajic, although he had been deep in the surgical process at the time, was aware of the controversy the Andermahr Experiment had caused. While extremes of genetic modification remained illegal, the Ethnarch's Military Presidium still had a keen interest in bettering its troops. The long-dead Ataman Ana Vereine—after whom the Marauder was named, and who had begun the research centuries ago—had desired captains who were as much a part of their ships as was the anchor drive, an integral, reliable system rather than a merely flesh-and-blood addition to it.

Kajic was the first prototype of a radical new technique, one that had the potential to transform the Ethnarch's Military Presidium into an unopposable force across the region. Naturally, there would be resistance to the idea. Those sympathetic to the cause of coexistence, and those who believed the process itself to be an immoral perversion of the "natural" Pristine state, would be eager to see the project fail.

"I'm still being tested," he said, almost to himself. Despite all the implants, and his three unalterable priorities—which, even now, throbbed in his mind like guilt—he still wasn't completely trusted.

And if he failed to complete the mission—and thereby failed the test—what would happen to him? Would he be excised from the ship and thrown out with the scraps? Of what possible use would a man such as he be—one flayed and twisted, unable even to live without the aid of expensive machines?

capture AI and Roche with as much stealth as possible

Priority C stabbed at his thoughts like a physical pain, an ache in his left temple. In this, at least, he had failed—and whoever was watching him knew it too.

But the mission wasn't lost yet. Priorities A and B remained to be fulfilled. If he could only do so quickly enough, he could salvage his honor.

Focus, he told himself, dispensing with his doubts. *Focus.*

Makaev hadn't moved during the split second it took him to think the situation through. She denied knowing about the back door. Perhaps it was true, although he doubted it. She may not have been directly involved, but she must surely have been aware of the monitoring taking place.

He sighed. "We can discuss this later. For now, though, tell me about this shuttle."

"It seems that it escaped the destruction of the COE frigate under cover of the debris," she explained, her face carefully deadpan. "The *Paladin* moved to intercept, but it managed to evade them."

"You said it crashed," said Kajic. "Were there any survivors?"

"Unknown at this stage, but unlikely. The explosion was detectable from orbit."

Kajic mulled this over. "Any progress yet in the wreckage of the frigate?"

Makaev shook her head. "The dispersal pattern of the fragments has been thoroughly mapped and studied—twice—but our scanners and probes have failed to locate the AI."

"So it must have been in the shuttle."

"That conclusion seems obvious, sir."

Kajic glanced sharply at his second in command, but her face was still stonily blank.

"Has the wreckage of the shuttle been investigated?" he asked.

"Not yet. A search party is on its way as we speak. The authorities at Port Parvati assure me that no detail will escape their attention."

"Have you told them what we're looking for?"

"Of course not, sir. They are simply to study the wreckage and convey the data to us."

"At considerable expense, no doubt." The Port Parvati wardens were voracious—and if there was one thing Kajic hated, it was fighting a war with money—but there was no other option. His future, if not his life, might well depend on their help.

Kajic's instincts continued to nag at him. He felt that he was in danger of letting success slip through his fingers unless he acted decisively.

at all costs

If the AI wasn't in the wreckage of the *Midnight*, then it must have escaped in the shuttle. The Espionage Corps had, however, reported that in its present form the AI wasn't able to move itself. Its escape must therefore have been facilitated by someone else. And as it was also known to be secure-cuffed to the wrist of a COE Intelligence agent . . .

"Instruct them to expand the search," he said. "Tell them we are looking for survivors."

"Sir?"

"We have underestimated our opponent, Atalia."

"Opponent?" Atalia Makaev could not conceal her bemusement. "Sir, we *have* no opponent. The *Midnight* and the shuttle which escaped from it were totally destroyed. It is just a matter of searching through the wreckage and retrieving the AI."

"I'll wager that the AI will not be found."

Makaev frowned. "Sir, may I ask what you are basing this assumption on? Have you access to information I have not been privy to?" There was a hint of mockery in her voice.

"Call it a gut feeling," said Kajic. Then, seeing his second in command's expression of disbelief, he added, "Inform the search party that we are looking for a Commander Morgan Roche, and have her image relayed down to them."

"The AI's courier?"

"We have unwittingly locked horns with a formidable enemy, Atalia." He nodded thoughtfully as something else occurred to him. "And I think we have found the cause of the *Midnight*'s destruction."

"But, sir," said Makaev, annoyance flaring in her eyes, her voice. "Proctor Klose was the only one who could have—"

"That is what we are meant to believe, Commander. In the same way we were meant to believe that nothing could have survived the destruction of the frigate; and in the same way we are now meant to believe that there are no survivors from the shuttle. But all the while we search that wreckage, the further away she gets." He set his gaze firmly upon her. "Commander, I want the search for survivors extended immediately. Roche must not elude us!"

"Sir." Makaev straightened her posture and snapped a salute. Nevertheless, Kajic detected cynicism in her tone. "I will convey your request to Warden Delcasalle. If there are any survivors, they will be found."

"Indeed they will, Commander. And this time you *will* keep me informed."

"Yes, sir." Makaev turned away as Kajic's image faded. While the bridge staff attended to their duties, he retired to his usual pattern of overall monitoring, letting his thoughts surf the vast sea of data crashing mercilessly on the sands of his mind.

Roche was the key. He had been a fool not to have seen it earlier. He hadn't misjudged Klose at all; his assessment of the man had been sound. It was Roche he had underestimated; her personal files had deceived him. Yet his subconscious mind had suspected, and had tried to warn him with the image of the faceless enemy. Had he analyzed the hunch in more detail, he might have been prepared.

At least now the problem was isolated, and all he had to do was focus his attention upon it. The Intelligence officer would not outwit him again. Not now . . .

Leaving the running of the ship in the hands of his junior officers, he opened the mission portfolio and began to study his adversary in more detail. And as the information filtered through his mainframe, he found something akin to admiration for the woman who momentarily distracted him.

priority gold-one

The prompt was sharp and burning. He cast aside the unwanted emotion and continued with his research.

6

Sciacca's World
Behzad's Wall
'954.10.30 EN
1650

All her life, Morgan Roche had enjoyed working with machines. Left without parents at an early age, she had been raised in an orphanage on Ascensio run by the planet's social welfare AIs. The orphanage's environment was one in which her social skills lagged (although contact with other children and adults was not rare—the orphanage understood the need for the Human interaction that a biochip could not provide, and so stays with a host family were frequent), but her proficiency with AIs soared.

By the age of eight she was entertaining herself by devising ways to circumvent the programming of her tutors; by the age of ten she had been so successful in this venture that she knew the inner logic of the AIs better than the programmers themselves. Every foible, inconsistency, and subtle glitch was committed to memory along with her basic education, which she absorbed by default.

At seventeen she left the orphanage to seek employment, although with Ascensio in the shadow of a local recession there were few jobs to offer someone whose expertise lay in artificial intelligence. By circumstance rather than choice, she was drawn toward the Armada (the preferable alternative to poverty or prostitution). Within a year of being out on her own she had applied for and taken the entrance exam; a further three years saw her inducted into the COE Intelligence training course.

The course itself was held on the second moon of Bodh Gaya, and it was here that she received her first neural implants and was thus exposed to the glowing web data that surrounded each and every being in the Commonwealth of Empires. To access this epiphany of information, all she had to do was touch a contact with the fake skin of her palm, and her mind would receive unimaginable tracts of data, fed directly into her cortex by the most sophisticated technology available in the Commonwealth of Empires.

Lessons were conducted from her quarters in the Intelligence dormitories, plugged directly into the vast virtual reality that comprised the college's mind-pool. She had no way of knowing if the minds she conversed with—her teachers and fellow students—were Human or artificial. Even those she suspected to possess manufactured origins were of a sort far superior to the lowly educators she had sabotaged in her childhood. Yet still she attempted to fathom them: probing their weaknesses, assaying their strengths, all the while allowing them to guide her in the ways of COE Intelligence.

Along the way she learned something of the history of the Commonwealth itself, and of the wider galaxy surrounding it: of the way Humanity had speciated following its colonization of the stars, from the High Humans, who had transcended their biological origins and existed in isolation from the mundane Castes (themselves divided into Exotic and Pristine categories), to the Low, who eked out primitive, animal-like lives on unnoticed worlds; of the immense number of empires that had risen and fallen down the millennia, waxing and waning like tides, many of them forgotten; of the lesser—although still extensive—number of such empires currently in existence, in varying degrees of torpidity. There was so much about Humanity to learn, both past and present, and the first thing she had learned was that one could *never* know it all. Perhaps only the High Humans could even hope to come close, but few mundanes ever had the chance to ask them.

On completion of the Intelligence course, Roche was assigned to the Quyrend System to work as a passive agent with a team of scientists repairing a major COE information network. It was there that she learned the basic rule of AI science: that no truly intelligent mind had yet been created to equal in every way that of a mundane Human. Minds equivalent to animals had been built, and it was these that fueled all of the AIs currently in service. Empowered by vast resources of information, they might have seemed equal or even superior to a Pristine Human, but they lacked the sophistication of thought, the degree of creativity, that every individual possessed. The quest for true artificial intelligence, she learned, had floundered centuries earlier, confounded by some unfathomable failure of design and theory that no amount of thought could remedy.

It came as no surprise to learn, five years later, after ten missions in as many solar systems, that the quest for true AI had been all but abandoned. The adept minds of COE Intelligence adequately filled the gaps machines could not. Yet rumors persisted: somewhere in the galaxy, perhaps even in the COE itself, work was continuing apace on a new theory, one that would render every early model of Box instantly obsolete. The ramifications of such a rumor, if it was true, were enormous, but it was dismissed by all in authority, including—and especially—the invisible rulers of Trinity, where all Boxes were made. Only the High Humans could build such a thing, and if they did it was doubtful that they would ever allow it to be released into the hands of a mundane government.

On the anniversary of her twelfth year of service in Intelligence, Roche received word of a new mission. The head of COE Intelligence, Auberon Chase, had requested her specifically. She was to travel alone to Trinity to collect a Box commissioned by the Armada and return it to COE Intelligence HQ. The AI had been designed to meet certain demanding specifications, and was thus highly expensive, yet it would receive no special escort. It would instead travel with her along a route remarkable only for its apparent randomness. Twelve other ships would leave Trinity at the same time, however, each carrying an Intelligence field agent, thus confusing any attempt to follow her and her ward. Such extreme measures to ensure secrecy made her curious, of course, but she knew better than to pry. She knew her place. Morgan Roche's service had been diligent and faithful, though not particularly distinguished. If she could complete this mission successfully, then she imagined she would earn another promotion; if she were to rock the boat, on the other hand, she might find herself off the mission entirely, or relegated to one of the dummy ships, headed nowhere. Whether the Box was the first of a new generation of super-Boxes or nothing more than a device to decode the transmissions of the Dato Bloc, she would be better off not knowing. At the very least, she would have plenty of time to converse with this Box. Who knew what she might learn in the process?

Two months on the *Midnight*, however, with little more than this Box for company, had been nearly enough to make her doubt even the most basic tenet of her short life. One machine at least, it seemed, she simply couldn't fathom—no matter how she tried. And neither, as a result, could she bring herself to like it. . . .

<Morgan.>

The voice was gentle but insistent, drifting through her thoughts, her dream. There had been shouting and panic and running—but she hadn't been able to move properly, hadn't been able to get clear of the explosion.

And pain. There had been a lot of pain.

<Wake up, Morgan.>

The voice continued to whisper through her half-sleep, compelling her to leave the dream behind.

With some effort, her eyelids flickered open. She squinted as the light from the yellow-hued sky stabbed at her eyes, dispelling some of her confusion, and what she had mistaken for a dream quickly adjusted itself and became a memory. Only the pain remained; in her shoulder, across her back, down one side of her face.

<Wake up now, Morgan,> the Box said, persisting.

Then another sound, this time the snarl of engines, ripped the quiet around her. Above, through a tangle of dead, petrified branches, she saw a flyer bank sharply, turning a tight figure eight before continuing back the way it had come.

As the whine of its engines faded into the distance, two voices sounded simultaneously in her head:

<Welcome back on-line, Morgan.>

And: <Do you think they saw us?>

The figure of Maii unfolded from the narrow crack in the rock face. Cane was beside her, staring in the direction in which the flyer had disappeared.

"Without a doubt." Roche recognized Veden's voice. "And even if they didn't, it's only a matter of time."

"Perhaps," said Cane. His head was cocked, as if listening to the fading engines.

"What's going on?" The words felt awkward in Roche's dry mouth. She tried to stand but found herself unable to move her left arm.

Cane glanced down at her, the thin suggestion of a smile creasing his otherwise composed features. He reached out and helped her to her feet. Waves of agony shot from her shoulder along her arm, making her dizzy for a moment. Cane's strong hands held her firm until he was sure she had her balance.

"You okay?" he asked.

Roche noted that her arm had been strapped firmly to her side using strips of cloth from Cane's uniform. "Dislocated?" she asked.

Cane nodded. "You'll be all right."

Roche quickly checked around her and saw they had taken refuge in a long and shallow ravine. Maii was slumped against a boulder, the slight movements of her head synchronized with Veden crouching a meter away. He was scowling at Roche and Cane.

"We should be going before they come back," he said.

Roche turned to Cane. "I take it our plan didn't work?"

Cane shook his head grimly. "A couple of flyers appeared on the scene not long after we bandaged you up. They've been scouting the area ever since, so our progress has been a little slow."

"Do you know where they're from?" said Roche.

"No idea," replied Cane. "But whoever they are, they seem to be heading back toward the wreck of the lander."

"So you say," Veden hissed, rising to his feet.

Roche ignored him. "Let's have a proper look," she said, gesturing upward. "We can't see a thing from down here."

"Good idea," said Cane.

Veden turned away. "We're wasting *time*," he muttered, just loud enough to be heard.

Cane clambered up a relatively shallow section of the wall, then leaned back to give Roche a hand. With difficulty she followed him, the valise scraping against the rock face as she went. The biofilaments lacing the skin of Roche's suit were fueled by sunlight, and chilled perceptibly at the sudden exertion, but the air on her face and right hand seemed only hotter in comparison, and as dry as a furnace. The earth beneath her fingertips, completely devoid of life, crumbled into dust. It smelled of ancient spices mixed with gunpowder.

When they reached the surface of the stony plain, they crouched behind a rock outcrop to peer at their surroundings. With no suggestion of Maii's presence in her mind, Roche realized that the girl must be using Cane's senses to view the scene.

The ravine in which they had taken refuge snaked across the orange lava plain, a jagged crack three meters wide and ten deep leading upward into the foothills; not a dry riverbed, but a fracture resulting from gentle seismic expansion, the only such fracture—and therefore the only true cover—for many kilometers. Farther ahead, shadowing the horizon like bulky storm clouds, lay a range of mountains. Behind them, back the way they had come, a tower of smoke rose against the backdrop of a pink-brown sky: the wreckage of the lander, still burning. A glint of light at the base of the tower of smoke might have been the flyer, although at this distance Roche could only guess.

With pursuit so close at hand, she could understand Veden's sense of urgency, but she was grateful at the same time for the opportunity to get her bearings. Unlike the others, she'd had no opportunity to view the world upon which they had crash-landed.

The sky directly above was a uniform sand-yellow, deepening to pink toward the horizon. Running the length of the sky was a faint, white streak that Roche had first assumed to be a cloud, but was, she now realized, the planet's belt of moonlets—the Soul. The rising sun hung low in the horizon, at the base of the Soul, its light a dull orange tinged with green. Away to her left, a large cloud mass was gathering.

The axial tilt of Sciacca's World was large enough for pronounced seasons, she knew. During winter or summer, the sun appeared at either side of the Soul—above or below, depending on the observer's latitude. At other times it would be partially occluded by the orbital debris. The Soul, therefore, indicated the direction of the planet's rotation, and the displacement of the sun to either above or below geographical north or south.

With this as a rough guide, but without knowing the season, she guessed that the ravine headed roughly northeast.

Roche turned to Cane. "That flyer," she said. "Did you get a look at its insignia?"

He nodded. "A circle, with a green cross on a white background."

"Not Armada or Dato Bloc, then." Roche frowned. "Still, whoever they are, they seem pretty eager to find us." Looking back to the wreckage of the lander, she added, "Box?"

<Yes, Morgan?>

"Anything you can tell me about this place that might give us an idea of who we're dealing with?"

<As you may know,> it said in a patient, lecturing tone, <it possesses a turbulent history—owing mainly to the fact that Sciacca's World lies close to Dato Bloc territory. In '112 EN, before the Commonwealth reached this far, the original Dominion colony was razed by Olmahoi retribution units under the orders of the Dato Bloc, then known as the Ataman Theocracy. This incident triggered the Ghost War, even though the Theocracy never laid claim to the system. Not until '293 EN, during the First Ataman War, was the Hutton-Luu System captured by the Ataman Theocracy and Sciacca's World annexed. In '442 EN, during the Second Ataman War, when the Theocracy finally submitted to the Commonwealth, the COE took control and the planet changed hands again. Despite, or perhaps because of, its strategic location, the COE leaders of the time chose not to house an Intelligence base upon it, opting instead for a small penal colony overseen by the Armada; it is possible that they might have intended it as a beachhead for covert operations into the Dato Bloc, although whether they did or not is unrecorded. In '474 EN, when the extensive mineral deposits of the Soul were discovered, a private contractor—OPUS—applied for mining rights to the system. The rights were granted, clearing the way for OPUS to begin surveying.>

"If there is a point to all of this," said Roche, "then I wish you'd get to it."

<Morgan, the presence of the penal colony on the planet could not be ignored by OPUS. They recognized cheap labor when they saw it. By the time OPUS folded and Dirt & Other Commodities Inc.—DAOC—assumed control of the operation, the previous Armada command had been replaced by a system of private overseers and hired security. Today, only a token Enforcement and Armada contingent remains, divided between orbit and Port Parvati. DAOC is the main socioeconomic force on the planet which—"

Roche interrupted. "So you're saying that the flyer was a DAOC Enforcement vessel?"

<Yes, Morgan.>

"You're sure?"

<The ship did bear the DAOC insignia.>

Roche's tired sigh was lost to a flurry of scalding wind that skittered off across the plain, raising a cloud of orange dust in its wake. "And you couldn't have just *told* me that?"

<Morgan, survival in any culture depends principally upon having an understanding *of* that culture.>

Roche shook her head. “Is there anything else you can tell me that might be relevant to us here and now?”

<Little, I’m afraid. I have been cut off from my usual sources of information. Before the lander crashed, however, I did record an aerial view of the region. If we are to head for the village Veden indicated, then I recommend a course due north, into the foothills. I estimate our distance to be roughly thirty-five kilometers—>

“They definitely landed at the wreck.” Cane’s words distracted Roche from the voice in her head. She faced him again, saw him squinting into the distance. “I can make out their downdraft swirling the smoke.”

“You can *see* that?” Once again Roche was amazed at his abilities. She was beginning to wonder if there was anything he couldn’t do better than she. “I don’t suppose you can make out how many there are of them, can you?” she added wryly.

The humor seemed lost on Cane. “No. I’d need some binoculars to discern anything more at this distance.”

She leapt on the word instantly: “Binoculars? You remember using them before the capsule?”

His eyes met hers evenly. “No. But I know what they are.”

“Just like you knew how to splint my arm?”

“That was Veden’s doing.” Cane shrugged. “I merely assisted him.”

Roche sighed. If he was lying about how much he remembered, then she could trap him—unless, of course, he was better at lying, too. In the hours she had known him, he had demonstrated nothing but trustworthiness in her presence—and had, in fact, saved her life once already. She wasn’t sure whether that bothered her more or less than if he hadn’t.

<Veden is growing impatient,> said Maii. <He says he’ll leave without you if you delay much longer.>

“Tell him we’re on our way.” Roche mentally prepared herself for the descent into the ravine. Her shoulder ached right down to the bone, the pain reaching from her neck to the tips of her fingers. The secure-cuffing around her wrist had left yellow-black bruises where she had hit the ground after the explosion of the lander, but the Box looked little the worse for wear. Its outer casing had been scarred quite badly from the explosion, but was otherwise intact. The handle still slotted into her hand perfectly, even though she was unable to bear its weight with her left arm.

As she clambered back down the slope into the ravine, she took one last look around at the surface of Sciacca’s World. An arid moonscape, plus an atmosphere. Not a pleasant place to live by any means. But for its mineral content, it would probably never have been settled in the first place.

She failed to see why anyone would *want* to come here. . . .

Veden and Maii were waiting for them at the bottom of the ravine. Barely had they regained their wind before the Eckandi headed off up the ragged slope, toward the foothills.

Roche took a deep breath and followed. Cane stayed with her, considerate of her weakness rather than of his own strength. She had no doubt that he could outperform the Eckandi easily, in both speed and endurance.

“Has he said anything?” she asked him, not loud enough for the other two to hear.

“About what?”

"About why he's here."

Cane shook his head. "No, but he is impatient to get to wherever it is he wants to go. That much is obvious."

"Patently." She spat a mixture of saliva and dust into the rocks. The spittle was stained red. "But why? What does he expect to find here?"

Cane shrugged. "Exercise?"

<Hope.> Maii's silent voice was barely audible above Roche's own thoughts.

Roche glanced ahead. The set of the Surin's narrow shoulders told her that the message had been intended for her alone.

"On a prison planet?" Roche mumbled to herself.

Cane turned to her. "What did you say?"

"Nothing," she said, and kept on walking.

The day darkened, paradoxically, as the sun rode higher into the sky. Once, the flyer passed overhead again, but this time didn't turn immediately back. Her mind was fogged by exhaustion, and she could only vaguely guess that their intentions were to intensify their search by looking farther from the wreckage. Not that it mattered. With the wind lifting the dust the way it was, in another hour or so the people in the flyer were going to have a visibility factor of about zero.

To while away the time, and to distract herself from the constant pain, she tried to talk to the Box. Something more substantial—even access to a basic medical database, accessible by the contact pad in her quarters—would have been preferable, but the Box was all she had. It could add little to what she had already learned from Cane: that the lander had exploded shortly after landing, as planned; that Maii and Veden had made it to shelter in time, but that she and Cane had taken a touch of heat-flash, in addition to Roche's dislocated shoulder and bruised ribs; that she had been carried on Cane's back away from the burning wreckage like a sack of potatoes; that Cane hadn't wanted to move her at all until she had regained consciousness and had agreed to do so only after Veden had threatened to leave them behind.

Among the supplies Roche had managed to rescue from the lander were a sack containing five survival suits and two basic ration packs. There was no medical kit, no painkillers to numb the aching, and as their trek continued her discomfort worsened. Despite her Armada biofeedback training, it was all she could do to keep her eyes focused on the ground ahead. Only when the Box finally complained that she had asked the same question three times in five minutes did she stop talking altogether and concentrate solely on walking.

Then, as the sun reached a position corresponding to late afternoon, she could take it no longer.

"Stop," she gasped, clutching at Cane for support as she staggered to halt. Pain from her shoulder and ribs made her head spin. Only with difficulty did she fight nausea back down. "I have to rest."

"No," Veden spat, his tone a whiplash of irritation. "We must keep moving until nightfall."

"I can't. Please. Just five minutes. That's all I ask."

"No." Without looking back, Veden kept walking.

Roche was unable to prevent the collapse of her thigh muscles. Cane made sure she was stable and went to follow the Eckandi.

"Let him go, Cane." That she had to raise her voice to be heard made her realize just how much the wind had risen in the last hour.

"We should stick together," asserted Cane. "Separated, we will be more vulnerable."

"If he wants to risk an ambush, let him." Roche felt only contempt for the old Eckandi, but the overriding emotion was one of despair at her own fading strength. It would come as something of a relief, she noted with alarm, to be captured. At least the wait, and the walk, would be over.

She shook her head firmly, denying the thoughts. Yes, the *Midnight* had been destroyed with all hands; yes, she was trapped on an unfamiliar planet, being pursued by a hostile security force; and yes, she was in a great deal of pain—but that was no reason to give in. Her passage into COE Intelligence had taught her that hard work and sheer determination could take a great deal of the edge off fate's sometimes cruel sting.

But the feeling wouldn't dissipate, no matter how she tried.

Biting down on the sense of hopelessness, she forced herself to smile up at Cane. "We'll catch up. You'll see. They'll stop when night falls, and—"

"Wait." Cane's head cocked; his eyes darted along the edges of the ravine.

Roche glanced upward, startled. The sky had grown dark without warning. As she watched, it darkened even further to a deep ochre mottled with grey. Small sprays of dirt leapt from one wall of the ravine to the other, occasionally showering down on them.

Then she heard it: a rumble, distant at first but growing louder with every second. The low-frequency sound reminded her of a heavy-armor tank, or an unusually large ground-effect vehicle.

"What is it?"

Cane shook his head. "I don't know, but I don't like it."

Roche's despair abruptly deepened, and she found herself fighting an overwhelming urge to cry. She cursed herself. She had never experienced anything quite like this before. Why was she feeling it now? Her entire body trembled with the intensity of the emotion.

She reached out to steady herself on the nearest wall, but withdrew the hand as a tiny spark arced from her fingertips to the stone.

"What—?"

Suddenly, Cane took her by her good arm and flattened her against the wall of the ravine. "Cover your face!" he hissed, his voice nearly drowned under the now-deafening sound.

She stared at him, too surprised to move. When she failed to obey him immediately, he reached behind her head for the hood of her survival suit. Tugging it over her face, he did the same with his own, holding the edges closed with one hand. Only his eyes stared at her, unblinking and frighteningly rational.

"What the—?"

"Close your eyes," he shouted. "Now!"

Roche blinked, delayed a second longer than he. At that moment, something roared across the top of the ravine—a dark, swirling mass of dust traveling at an awesome speed. The air in the ravine, sucked by the low pressure of the front, exploded upward. The turbulence created a partial vacuum, which in turn rolled a layer of dense air at the bottom of the front down into the ravine, instantly filling it with swirling clouds of choking dust.

Roche gasped, then coughed, doubling up into Cane's wind-shadow. Her one good hand flew to her face in a belated attempt to seal her nose. Her ears rang with the sound of tortured, screaming air. Only Cane's hand on her back prevented her from toppling forward. Even as she struggled to breathe, she finally understood what was happening:

A dust storm had struck them, one more violent than any she had previously encountered. That explained her sudden mood swing and the spark of static electricity: the charge in the air, rolling ahead of the storm, pervading everything.

After half a minute of the onslaught, Cane knelt beside her to bring his mouth close to her head.

"The front will be the most turbulent!" he shouted. "If we can hold on for a moment longer, it should ease slightly!"

She wanted to yell back—*How do you know*?—but her throat only rasped, irritated by dust and dry air. She concentrated on holding herself still, waiting for the tumult to release her.

Then, over the howling wind, came the reave's voice:

<Roche! Cane!>

Roche opened her eyes, and was instantly stung by a thousand particles of dust. There was no denying the urgency in the voice. But—how did one reply to a reave?

"What's wrong?" she shouted back.

She was unsure whether the Surin had heard her call, but a reply came nonetheless: <They're here! I—we—need help!>

"*Who* are here?"

"Listen!" Cane had his head cocked again. "Gunshots."

This time even Roche could hear the discharge of weapons over the storm. "We have to help them," she said, trying in vain to climb to her feet.

"No." He pressed her back. "I'll go." He opened his suit and slipped her pistol and Veden's makeshift laser from the pockets of his transportee uniform. Handing her the pistol, he glanced around him, eyes narrowed to slits. In the darkness of the storm, little could be seen but swirling, dust-filled air. The mouth of the ravine showed as a faint lightening in the air above them. Apart from that, Roche was blind.

"Could be Veden's friends," Cane said. "But then again—"

"Better safe than sorry."

"Exactly. Stay here." With one smooth movement he ducked away from her and was swallowed by the storm. Roche leaned back against the wall of the ravine, clutching the pistol to her chest while protecting her eyes as best she could.

Moments later, a sharp rattle of projectile weapons issued from farther up the ravine. Voices followed, shouting in confusion. With the sounds came the realization that she was hearing more clearly; the fury of the storm front had indeed abated slightly.

Maii said nothing more, however, and Roche couldn't stand aside when help might be needed. The wind allowed her to reach a standing position; from there, with the hand holding the pistol on the ravine wall, keeping her upright, she made her way cautiously across the ragged rock face.

Another round of shouting and gunshots broke the silence, followed by the sharp hiss of an energy weapon discharging through the atmosphere. Then the muffled thump of impact. She flinched instinctively but continued forward.

The voices ceased in the wake of the explosion, but the exchange of gunfire continued in ragged bursts. Roche pressed on as fast as she could, but the ravine seemed endless. Her breath burned in her chest as though her rib cage was on fire.

Then, almost before she realized it, she stumbled into a shallow section of the ravine. The rock walls stood barely chest-high, with open ground to either side. The wind was stronger here, and the dust more dense. A projectile whined past her, sent rock fragments flying a meter from her shoulder. She dropped instantly to a crouch and leveled the pistol in the direction from which she felt the weapon had been discharged.

Even as she did so, a man in a green uniform dropped into the ravine barely two meters farther on. He obviously hadn't seen her from above, hidden as she was by the swirling dust. The moment his feet touched rock, however, his pistol swung to target her. Roche fired instinctively, taking him squarely in the chest. He looked momentarily surprised; then his eyes rolled back and he toppled sideways to the ground.

Roche didn't move, frozen to the spot. In the wake of her surprise and the sudden movement, her ribs sang like a saw dragged across a wire, sending pain in waves through her chest. Her breath came in short gasps.

A pebble dropped on her head, and she rolled forward, twisted, and fired behind her. A second man, also in the green uniform, tumbled into the ravine, the back of his head black and smoking. Her own shot had missed. Someone else, outside the ravine, had been more accurate.

<You all right, Roche?> Maii's soundless voice filled her head.

The body of the second officer twitched once where it had fallen, then lay still. Roche formed the word <Okay> in her mind and tried her best to hold it steady for the reave to find.

<I sense no one else near you at the moment,> continued the Surin. <But stay down just in case.>

"What happened?"

<They took us by surprise.>

"Enforcers?"

<Yes, from Port Parvati. They were in the ravine, heading down from the foothills. Veden and I were arguing when the sandstorm hit. There was a cave, and we all headed there for shelter at the same time. I think we surprised them as much as they surprised us, but they had weapons and we didn't. If Cane hadn't come when he did—> Roche sensed something akin to a shrug touch her mind. <We're armed now, if that means anything.>

Roche stayed put as the Surin drifted off into silence. She doubted whether she'd be able to move anyway, even if she wanted to. In dust this dense, sight gave little advantage. She wondered how it would feel to be Maii, a hunter aiming for the very eyes that helped her see. . . .

If Maii caught the thought, she made no comment.

Roche heard a couple more shots, another thump of energy discharge, and a single strangled cry. Then the wind picked up again, reducing her world to a meter-wide circle with her in the center. Even with her eyelids half-closed, the dust forced her to blink. Effectively blinded and deaf, she huddled close to the wall of the ravine and waited. Small bolts of lightning, triggered by the charge in the air, crackled into the soil around the ravine, stabbing the darkness with an eerie light.

A hand reached out of the maelstrom to take her by the arm, and she raised the gun to strike it away. Someone shouted her name over the wind, but whatever other words followed were instantly swept away. The hand was large and strong, and she couldn't fight it off. With immense relief, she recognized the plastic of a survival suit above the wrist and guessed it to be Cane, although the rest of him was erased by the storm.

He dragged her to her feet and farther along the ravine. A flash of energy briefly lit the gloom, arcing over her shoulder and exploding harmlessly into rock.

Maii's voice rose out of the racket.

<We have to move. They know this weather better than we do. There's no way for us to tell how long the storm will last.>

Silence, then: <Agreed. We don't have any choice. The other two Enforcers only have to wait us out. Follow the ravine as before, try to put some distance between us and them before the storm breaks. We'll see—>

The reave's voice broke off suddenly. Roche glanced at Cane in alarm, but his face remained hidden. As though he too was alarmed, he urged her to move faster. The best she could manage was a quick shuffle, through the sand gathering at the bottom of the ravine, with her lack of sight and the constant buffeting of the wind constantly upsetting her balance, but she hurried as well as she could.

Again the energy weapon flashed, this time from farther away. Barely had she thought that they might be able to escape when something brushed against her, and a shadowy shape reached for her out of the dust. She flinched away, but not quickly enough to escape a pair of enormous, grasping hands. One seized her wrist; the other took her about the face, stifling her shout of alarm. She tried to raise the pistol, but the hand on her wrist twisted it savagely, sending agony burning through her shoulders.

When the hands tried to drag her away, however, they met the resistance of Cane's strength. She endured a brief, painful, tug-of-war between the two; then the unknown pair of hands fell away. The shape moved around her to confront Cane, and she thought she could hear voices shouting over the wind. Then, clearly silhouetted against a brief bolt of lightning, she saw a gun raised and pointed at Cane's head, aimed by a shambling bipedal figure at least as tall as Cane himself, and far broader.

Cane glanced at Roche, then nodded. Feeling his hand loosen, she clutched at him, trying to keep him close, but a cloud of dust erupted around them, and Roche suddenly lost sight of him. She called out in panic and tried to go back, but the large hands of her captor held her firm, dragging her away into the fury of the storm.

7

Sciacca's World
Behzad's Wall
'954.10.31 EN
0050

Darkness and silence wrapped themselves around Roche as the wind abruptly fell away. Startled by the sudden absence of noise, she stumbled. The strong hands of her captor roughly righted her.

"This way," he said, guiding her forward. His voice was coarse, almost guttural, and clearly Exotic. His Caste eluded her for a moment, until she caught a whiff of him. Mbatan, definitely. No other Caste possessed that distinctive bitter smell. A soft flare illuminated their surroundings a moment later and confirmed her suspicions. He was as solid as a bear beneath a brown, stained coverall, with a shaggy mane of hair and limbs like tree trunks.

In the Mbata common tongue, Roche asked the huge figure where he was taking her. He laughed, turning to face her in the dim light. The sound was a throaty bark, testimony to non-Pristine physiognomy.

"I don't speak Bantu." His voice was thickly accented, although intelligible nonetheless. "Not anymore." The blue-green light from the chemical flare flickered over the Mbatan's heavily bearded and tanned face, catching now and then in the weathered lines that covered his features. "My name is Emmerik," he said.

"You're a convict?" Cane's voice, coming from near Roche's shoulder, made her jump.

If Emmerik took offense at the question, he didn't show it. Instead, he grinned widely, revealing a complete, if slightly yellow, set of teeth. "Time for talk later. This way."

Again he guided Roche forward. The light revealed that they were traveling through a rough tunnel carved from ancient lava, barely high enough for Roche but broad enough to allow her and the Mbatan to walk side by side. The stone was a uniform, dirty orange, except for the occasional vein of dark grey. As the tunnel wound its jagged way underground, she noticed scars in the rock, suggesting that it had been carved by shaped explosives and with the bare minimum of finesse. A rush job.

"You were following us?" She began it as an accusation but ended it as a question.

"We expected the Eckandi and Surin in the next shipment. When the shuttle crashed, Haid sent me to investigate. I recognized Veden from the file we had on him—but you I wasn't so sure about." He shrugged mightily, all the muscles in his back and shoulders rippling. "No offense. It wasn't until the Enforcers moved in on you that I was fairly certain you were working with the Eckandi and not against him."

"So why take so long to help us?" Cane's voice was smooth in the cool quiet of the cave, but Roche thought she detected a hint of annoyance underlying his words. "We were struggling out there, in case you didn't notice."

"I felt it would be best to wait for the cover of the storm before acting. They come in waves on Sciacca. The one that just hit us was the second of a tri-rage. I knew it had to hit soon—as did the Enforcement—so I just kept my distance until it did."

"And this?" said Roche, indicating the tunnel they were walking along. "This is the base of the resistance?"

Roche had suspected they had been captured by the covert movement Veden had mentioned, and when Emmerik failed to deny it, she knew she was right.

"No. We just use these tunnels and the ravine for recon, mainly. If we need to get to the port unseen, and so on."

"Is that where we're going? Port Parvati?"

"Not yet." The Mbatan gestured for her to continue walking, but said nothing more.

The tunnel continued for five hundred meters or so farther, dipping downward at one point, until it opened onto a slightly larger chamber.

Veden looked up as they entered, his cold eyes glittering in the unnatural light. "What did you do to her?" he asked Emmerik, his tone harshly accusing. The Surin lay in a fetal position on the rough stone floor at his feet.

"Xarodine." The burly Mbatan ushered Roche and Cane into the chamber ahead of him. "If she'd squawked at the wrong moment, the Enforcers would have known where to find her."

"She has more control than that!" Veden barely kept his rage in check. "She's not some fledgling talent you'd buy for a copek at a local—"

"I couldn't take that chance," said Emmerik calmly over Veden's outrage. He slipped a filthy hand into his coverall and removed the dart gun that had administered the dose. "Besides, it'll wear off in a few hours—then we'll get to see exactly what she can and cannot do."

Roche, studying the curled form of the Surin, felt suddenly sorry for her. Xarodine inhibited the epsense ability. The girl was, as a result, cut off from her senses, trapped in her own skull like any other blind deaf-mute.

"You." Emmerik handed Roche a tablet with a flask of water. "Take this."

"Why?" She eyed it suspiciously. "What is it?"

"Painkiller. We need you fit if we're going to make the hills by nightfall."

Veden's glare doubled in intensity. "She's not with us. Nor is he."

Emmerik glanced from the Eckandi to Cane, but there was no suspicion in his expression. "If I'm not mistaken, he saved your life back there."

"She's with COE Intelligence," he said. "And he's with her."

"Regardless. The Enforcers fired at her too."

"I don't care," said Veden. "They're not *with* us."

"I'll keep that in mind next time you need help," said Roche.

Veden stared, the half-light highlighting the anger on his face. "I don't need the help of the Armada!"

"We could have left you on the *Midnight* to fry, and you know it."

"Hey!" Emmerik cut Veden's response off before the Eckandi had a chance to speak. "I don't give a damn *who* she's with. What happens to her is up to Haid, okay?" When he was certain that neither Roche nor Veden would continue the argument, Emmerik turned away and shrugged into an old, well-used backpack. "I leave in five minutes. Whoever wants to come with me can. Whoever doesn't can stay." The Mbatan's eyes settled on Roche again. "And if you don't want that tablet, give it back. Medical supplies aren't easily come by on Sciacca."

Roche placed the tablet in her mouth, wincing at the bitter taste. She quickly washed it down with water from the flask, which tasted of dirt and left an oily residue on her tongue.

"I'm with you," she said, handing back the flask. "Not that I have much choice."

"Too right, lady." The Mbatan came close to a smile. "You wouldn't last a day out there in your condition—even with your friend."

"What about Maii?" Veden interrupted brusquely.

"You can lead her." The Mbatan smiled, teeth glinting in the eerie chemical light. "Think she'll trust you?"

Veden turned to help the girl to her feet. Maii's hands fluttered for a moment over the Eckandi's face and hair, then became still. She allowed herself to be led across the room with her hand clutched tightly in his. Roche noted, however, that there was more desperation in the clasp than affection.

"Good." Emmerik nodded. "We'll move in a line with me in the middle. You," he said to Cane, "go first, then you." Roche nodded. "Then the others. And I'll have your weapons before we go, thanks."

Cane hesitated for a moment, then handed over the laser. Roche did likewise with the pistol. Veden produced a stolen Enforcement rifle from under his robes. All three vanished into the voluminous folds of the Mbatan's pack.

"Good." Emmerik swept the chamber with the flare to ensure that nothing had been overlooked, then gestured down the corridor. "Let's go."

<What do you think, Box?> Roche subvocalized as she walked along the dark and dank tunnels.

<It would be optimistic to believe we have been saved, Morgan,> replied the AI, <but pessimistic to succumb to despair.>

Roche nodded to herself, remembering the wave of gloom that had almost overwhelmed her earlier. The emotion had been accentuated by the ions presaging the dust storm, she knew, but that knowledge did little to console her. <Do you have anything in your datapool about the rebel movement on Sciacca's World?>

<No, but given the violent history of the planet, I'm not surprised it exists.>

<Nothing on what their aims might be?>

<One can only wonder. Given that the planet is a prison, liberation seems unlikely. The same with vengeance: even if the complete resources of the local Enforcement arm were turned over to them, they would possess little more than they already do. The only ships here are intrasystem vessels, with no ftl capability.>

<Apart from the Dato.>

<Yes, but surely that is a possibility too remote even to consider?>

Roche shrugged and sighed. They had been walking rapidly for almost half an hour without once leaving the underground tunnel. The painkiller Emmerik had given her had dulled her shoulder to a mere ache without numbing her mind as well. And, with little to distract her, she found herself slightly bored—despite her uncertain circumstances.

Cane's voice suddenly broke the quiet, his words resounding along the tunnel down which they walked. "Those people who attacked us," he said over his shoulder. Roche could tell he was talking past her to the Mbatan. "There were six of them, right?"

"That's right," said Emmerik. "Standard recon team."

"And we took out four."

"The Surin one, your friend one, and you two," the Mbatan confirmed. "You fight well in the dust, for an off-worlder. For anyone, to be honest. Where were you trained?"

"That leaves two," said Cane, ignoring the question.

Emmerik grunted a laugh. "Yes," he said. "That leaves two. If we're lucky, they'll believe you staggered off into the storm and died."

"And if we're not?" put in Roche.

"They'll have this area swarming with Enforcers."

"Will they find the tunnel?"

"Probably." Emmerik scratched his beard, the rustle of fingertips on hair clearly audible over the dull echoes of their footsteps. "But I don't believe that will happen. Most likely they'll just send another recon team to quarter the area."

"And then?"

"That depends on how badly they want you, doesn't it?" he said. "And why. What did you do? Blow up the ship?"

"No. We were ambushed by the Dato Bloc."

"Dato? Here?" Emmerik couldn't keep the surprise from his voice. "Well, well. That *is* interesting."

Silence fell for a moment. Roche could almost hear the Mbatan's mind turning, until Veden spoke up.

"She's carrying something they want. An AI. It's strapped to her back."

"They must want it badly to raid the Commonwealth."

"Obviously," said Veden.

"Maybe they'll even be prepared to pay for it," ventured Emmerik.

"A great deal, I'd imagine," said the Eckandi.

"Yes." The Mbatan's voice changed to mimic the Eckandi's suggestive tone. "And all we'd have to do is sell her out, right? Hand her over like some low-grade ore in exchange for a few credits?"

Veden fell silent.

"I don't like you much, Makil Veden," said Emmerik, "no matter what Haid says you can do for us. Remember that. I don't care what she is or what she's carrying; it's what she *did* that counts. On Sciacca's World, a life saved is worth something."

"My name is Roche, Emmerik. Morgan Roche. Not 'she.' "

Emmerik ignored her. "Do you hear me, Veden?"

"I hear." The Eckandi's voice was low and dangerous. "But I will raise the matter with Haid when we arrive. The reality of your situation makes sentiment meaningless. Perhaps he will see things differently."

"You obviously don't know him very well." The Mbatan's heavy palm descended onto Roche's shoulder. She couldn't tell whether the gesture was meant to reassure her, but she knew it wasn't threatening. "If the AI Roche carries is so valuable, then we may be able to use it to our advantage."

She said nothing, let the moment bury his words. Pledging herself and the Box to Emmerik's cause seemed premature, no matter how much she owed him.

"I will freely offer any assistance I can give," said Cane.

Roche frowned in the dark, surprised by Cane's words.

The Mbatan laughed. "That I expected. You are clearly a man of action: a trained soldier for certain, someone who recognizes debts of honor." He paused for a few steps. "I suspect that I can trust you, wherever you are from."

"My origins are unknown," said Cane. "Even to me."

"An unknown soldier, eh?" Emmerik shrugged, the fabric of his coverall shifting noisily over his large frame. "Then it must be a natural ability." His hand fell away from Roche's shoulder as he added, "Quiet now. The exit is nearby."

A few meters farther, and Emmerik called the party to a halt. He lit another chemical flare, and the weird light revealed that they had stopped in a chamber similar to the one they had left earlier. This time the tunnel did not continue on the other side. Instead, a rope ladder dangled from a gnarled cavity in the ceiling.

"I'll go first," said Emmerik, "to open the hatch and make sure the area is secure. Wait here."

The Mbatan swung his bulky form up the ladder with surprising speed. The mica in the rock wall flickered under the light from his flare as he ascended into the shadows. Moments later, a shaft of muddy light spilled through the hole, followed by the sound of wind and a shower of fine dust. Roche waited patiently, idly flexing the muscles of her right arm and wondering how she was going to climb the ladder one-handed.

Emmerik returned, his pack gone and his dirty teeth cutting a wide grin through his beard. "All's clear," he said. "You, soldier, go first." Cane nodded. "I'll bring the reave. Veden will follow me. Then I'll come back for you, Commander."

The rope ladder danced as Cane began his graceful ascent, his movements as nimble and surefooted as any Surin child Roche had seen. Emmerik reached out for Maii, who immediately retreated from his alien scent.

"Don't be afraid, little one." Emmerik's voice was gentle and soothing as he tried to ease his arms about the Surin's shoulders.

The girl shied away even farther.

"She can't hear you," said Roche. She reached out to touch the Surin's arm, to offer reassurance. Much to her surprise, the girl clutched at her hand with both of hers and held it tight.

"At least *she* trusts you," observed the Mbatan. "But that doesn't help us. You can't carry her."

"I know. Just give me a moment." Roche soothed the girl, stroking the fine hair of her cheeks and ears, feeling the grainy texture of the skin beneath it. Slowly Maii quietened, nestling into Roche as a small child might to its mother. When the girl was completely relaxed, Roche let Emmerik come closer and place his enormous arms in a clumsy embrace around her own. Then she slowly slipped aside.

The Surin stiffened for a moment, then seemed to accept the situation. With barely a grunt of effort, Emmerik slung her across his back. She clutched him tightly, looking like a rag doll tossed over the shoulder of a giant child.

"I won't be long," said the Mbatan. Tossing the chemical flare to her, he began the steady, careful climb up the ladder. The rope, although it stretched slightly, didn't break under their combined weight.

Shortly afterward, Emmerik called back down for Veden to follow. He did so, facing Roche briefly in the fading light of the flare. For a second she felt he was about to say something, but in the end he simply fixed her with a cold glare and scurried up the ladder.

Watching after him, she suddenly found herself smiling at the Eckandi's enmity toward her. His reluctance to have her and Cane along was understandable: after all, Enforcement was after *her,* not him. DAOC might not even be aware that he had escaped the *Midnight.* If he could get rid of her, he would be free to do whatever he had come to Sciacca's World to do. If, however, he stayed with her, the chances increased that he would be captured.

She could follow Veden's logic, but she didn't like it. Emmerik's uncomplicated way of thinking mirrored her own. She and Cane had saved the Eckandi's life twice now; that should have counted for something. But the Eckandar Trade Axis was renowned for its pragmatism in both business and life. The borders of its trading empire were far-flung, and its influence, in concert with the Commerce Artel, all-pervasive. Sharklike, the members of the Eckandar Caste had little room for sentiment or other emotions that she took for granted. In order to win his support, she would have to demonstrate her material worth to him: she had to prove that she offered more than her presence risked.

The answer to that, she suspected, lay in Veden's mission. Whatever that was.

A quiet murmur of voices broke the silence and her train of thought. She listened to them for a few minutes, following the rise and fall of inflection rather than the words themselves, which were mostly inaudible. They seemed to be arguing about something. Maybe Veden was trying to convince Emmerik to leave her behind again.

No. The voices were coming from behind her, from the tunnel, not from above.

She immediately smothered the chemical flare and moved away from the dull cone of radiance into the security of the shadows. The light from above was relatively dim, not bright enough to travel too far along the tunnel, but still a concern.

She fought the urge to warn Emmerik and the others, knowing that her voice would carry to whoever approached as surely as theirs had carried to her.

The voices grew louder: a woman talking into a radio, the static-dampened responses not reaching Roche clearly. There was no way of telling exactly how many approached, or how close they were. The echoes of voice and, faintly, footsteps might have traveled hundreds of meters through the stone tunnel or not very far at all.

As she watched, a faint glimmer of light appeared in the depths of the tunnel: an electric torch tracing their path in the dirt.

The movement of the ladder in the dim light startled her momentarily; she glanced up and saw Emmerik descending from the hole. When his night-sensitive eyes saw her in the shadows, he opened his mouth to say something, but Roche was quick to raise a hand and gesture him to silence. When she had his attention, she pointed along the tunnel.

He instantly realized what she meant. "Quick," he said softly, reaching out with his arm. "No time for a harness. Put your arm about my neck."

She did so, and Emmerik grunted with effort as he straightened, lifting her off the ground. Closing her eyes, she concentrated on holding onto his coverall as he slowly climbed upward. The ladder strained under their weight but held nonetheless.

Awkwardly, they moved up and out of the cavern, swaying slowly from side to side as Emmerik constantly shifted his balance.

"How many?" Emmerik whispered as they slipped through the narrow opening and into the confined space that led to the surface.

"Too far away to tell," said Roche. The calm of his voice surprised her. "But I think at least two—maybe the two from the ambush. They were talking to someone on a radio."

"Great," Emmerik muttered.

The footsteps from below grew steadily louder; the opening above them seemed impossibly distant.

The Mbatan fumbled a handhold and grunted under his breath. Roche gasped as they swung for a second from his other hand, until he regained his grip and took another step upward.

"Almost there . . ." His tone reflected her own doubts.

The voices from the tunnel took on an urgent note as the Enforcers came near enough to make out the dancing base of the ladder. The sturdy Mbatan began to move faster, muscles bunching in his back as he moved his hands from rung to rung. His lungs wheezed with the effort.

Then the ladder shook violently as one of the Enforcers grabbed the lowest rung and began to pull, shouting for them to halt. The extra load proved too much for the already straining material. With a stomach-wrenching lurch, one of the ropes snapped, sending Emmerik and Roche swinging into the stone wall of the chimney. Her hand bit into the Mbatan's neck as she fought to hold on. Dizziness swept her senses; pain flared through her injured shoulder. Flashing lights and shouting voices broke her concentration.

Her hand slipped at the same moment Cane reached down from above and grabbed the Mbatan's right hand. Emmerik grabbed her with his left and held as she scrambled to regain her grip.

Above her, the glare from another flare.

"Veden!" she called out as he threw it into the shaft, then felt it deflect off the valise strapped to her back. She glanced down to see it drop, its light illuminating the shaft as it fell. Below she could make out two figures scattering for cover.

Cane hauled on Emmerik's arm, pulling them upward, while the Mbatan's feet dug into the walls of the chimney. Clear of the opening, Cane dropped the Mbatan and Roche onto the dry, hard ground. In a single, smooth motion he moved back over the hole, reached in, and snapped the remaining strands of rope.

Three bursts of energy fire sounded from below; Roche watched in awe as Cane easily avoided the bolts that hissed from the opening, arcing harmlessly toward the sky. Then, with no sense of urgency, he was at her side, helping her to her feet and guiding her up a slope of tumbled rocks where Veden and Maii waited.

Raised voices issued from the shaft, and a quick patter of gunfire. Roche looked back to see Emmerik raise a device no larger than his fist and hurl it into the mouth of the shaft.

The gunfire ceased abruptly. A moment later, a muffled *crump* lifted the earth beneath them and sent a cloud of dust shooting out of the hole in the ground.

"And then there were none," said Emmerik without smiling. He grasped Roche's arm, indicating for her to move.

"If others heard the explosion . . ." Veden began.

"I know," Emmerik said. "We must hurry."

The Mbatan led them up a rough slope into a narrow valley between two low foothills. The ground was littered with grey stones, a rough shale that had flaked from the hills over thousands of seasons. The sandstorm had dissipated, but still the air was murky with dust; an erratic wind tugged and squeezed it into a series of small twisters that slid across the landscape before dissolving again into the larger mass.

Ahead, looming over them like the end of the world, were the mountains. The sun had almost set behind them, and the sky had deepened to the color of blood, darkened by the last tatters of the storm. The yellow-silver arc of the Soul bisected the sky like an enormous bow, taut with strain, its bright glow visible through the clouds.

They ran until the sun set, with Emmerik constantly casting glances behind them and at the sky, expecting pursuit to appear at any moment. When, as darkness fell, the distinctive buzz saw of a flyer broke the twilight, he tugged them under an overhanging shelf of rock, where they hid from view.

Roche took the opportunity to catch her breath, nursing her bruised ribs. The painkiller had worn off, and every mouthful of air burned through her throat and chest. Fighting her pride, she asked Emmerik for another painkiller, which he freely gave.

"We'll have to stay here for the night," said the Mbatan gloomily. His breathing was labored, as though he had found the run more wearying than he was prepared to admit. After quaffing from the flask, he passed it around for the others. "They'll be sweeping the area with infrared from now on, so it would be best if we just stayed put."

Roche dealt with the pain as best she could and forced herself to talk. "The survival suit," she wheezed to Cane, who stood nearby. He seemed none the worse for the exertion, perhaps even healthier than he had been before—more *alive*. ". . . I brought five . . . out of the lander?"

"That's right. Maii has the other, in one of the pockets of her own."

"Good." She turned to Emmerik.

"I'm too big," he said, understanding what she was about to suggest.

"Doesn't matter," said Cane. "It'll block IR. Any cover will help, just as long as we can keep on moving."

"That's right," added Roche. "As much as I'd like to rest . . . I don't think we can afford to."

He nodded. Veden calmed Maii while Cane rummaged through the Surin's pockets for the suit. The one-piece garment unfolded from a parcel scarcely larger than her hand. Roche showed the Mbatan how to activate the chameleon circuits and moisture reclaimer. The processor in the belt would do the rest. IR opacity was standard in all Armada survival suits; the heat would be absorbed to hold the desert chill at bay through the night.

Emmerik managed to get his arms into the elastic fabric, but had no luck with his legs. The rest of the suit, where it couldn't be tied into place, flapped from his body like an overcoat.

"Better than nothing," he said, the gruffness of his voice offset by the look of gratitude he directed at Roche. Leaning out from the overhang, he listened for a moment. "They've moved on, and so should we. The others will be waiting for us at the Cross."

"The Cross?" asked Cane.

"Houghton's Cross is the town we're heading for," said Emmerik. "And if we can get there by dawn, then we'll be able to rest."

"How far?" asked Cane.

"Four hours' walk, at a steady pace."

"Night here is how long?"

"This time of year, about eleven hours."

"Okay," said Cane. "Morgan? Are you sure you're up to it?"

Roche glanced at Cane. This was the first time he had used her first name; she supposed he had earned the right. "I'll manage," she said, "once this painkiller takes effect."

Cane smiled. "And maybe we can rustle up something to eat on the way. Anything edible in these hills, Emmerik?"

The Mbatan smiled. "Depends what you regard as edible," he said. "We should be able to find some vintu buds, and choss roots are closer to the surface at night. If you're really lucky we may be able to find some rapeworm-infected animal. It's a parasite indigenous to Sciacca. It paralyzes the host and injects the eggs into the animal's gut. Two weeks later, the young emerge. If you get the larvae on about the eight or ninth day, the meat can be quite delicious. . . ."

Roche listened with only half an ear as she performed brief stretching exercises to ease her aching muscles. Feeling confined under the shelf of rock, she stepped out to look at the stars. Despite a fine haze of lingering dust, it was a beautiful sight.

The sun, although it had set, was still shining on the Soul. At the eastern horizon, the band of moonlets twinkled a dull silver; above her, it brightened considerably, colored by the coppery light that filtered through the thin lens of the planet's atmosphere; to the west, it was brighter still, catching the full, unrefracted light of the sun. Occasionally, one of the larger moonlets would reflect the light, making it twinkle. Otherwise the belt was a solid band—a long, glowing cloud on fire with the colors of sunset.

She didn't hear the conversation behind her cease, or the Mbatan move to her shoulder, until his voice boomed in her ear. "Heartwarming, isn't it?"

She started slightly, then nodded. "Yes, very." When she turned to look at him, his face was beaming with an emotion almost like pride: pleased both by the sight and by her appreciation of it. "Small compensation, though, for being condemned here forever."

"Perhaps." The Mbatan returned her gaze steadily, and she wondered what crime he had committed to warrant transportation. Murder, perhaps; he'd certainly disposed of the two Enforcers in the tunnel easily enough. Yet he seemed so trustworthy, so at peace with himself, that she found it hard to imagine him committing a crime of passion. Maybe he had learned temperance, not achieved it naturally.

As though reading her mind, he said, "I was born here, you know."

Roche stared at him. "But you—I assumed—"

"My parents were transportees. I was conceived illegally, and should have been shipped back to Vasos when I came of age. Of course, I was an outcast by birth, and couldn't return, even if I wanted to." He shrugged his huge shoulders. "Regardless, I wouldn't have let them take me. *This* is my home." He paused again before saying, "I suppose it's hard for you to understand that anyone could feel genuine affection for a prison planet."

"Well, yes," she said slowly. She did find it difficult to believe, even though the proof was standing before her. "Are there many like you?"

"A few. We tend to stick together, away from the port, although we have our differences. You'll meet them soon enough."

"I'll look forward to it."

"Will you? I hope so. We need allies desperately."

She shivered then, catching herself by surprise. Night had fallen rapidly, and the temperature with it. Her survival suit's heating system had not yet responded to the change.

Emmerik noticed the small movement and nodded. "We should be going." He turned back to the others. "Veden, are you and Maii ready to move?"

"Almost," replied the Eckandi, opening his eyes as though stirring from a deep sleep. Rising to his feet, he stretched his legs experimentally and rubbed his hands. "Give me a moment."

<I am ready too.> The reave's words whispered through Roche's thoughts. Her voice might have belonged to the wind, it was so faint, but it was definitely there.

"How long have you been . . . ?" Roche stopped, unsure how to phrase the question.

<Long enough to take a look around.> The Surin smiled and turned to the Mbatan. <You have loving eyes, Emmerik.>

The burly man nodded awkwardly. "Thank you. I hope you will forgive me for the way I mistreated you."

<If I hadn't, you would already be dead.>

The Mbatan grinned, although the tone underlying her words was ominous. "I can believe it. Veden has warned me that you're not to be underestimated."

<I can do everything I am here to do, and more besides. You'll find me a worthy ally—and a formidable enemy.>

"Then here's to the former." Emmerik slapped his hands together. "And to our journey. We still have far to travel before we can resolve our differences. I think we should get moving."

<Agreed,> the Surin purred, then fell silent with her hands clasped behind her back, waiting.

"So let's go," Cane said. "Do you want me to lead the way again, Emmerik?"

The Mbatan shook his head. "No, I'll lead. You can take the rear, or wherever you feel most useful. I'll leave it up to you. Just keep your eyes and ears peeled. They won't be far away." He glanced at the ring of faces surrounding him. "That goes for all of you."

"Understood. Whether we like this or not," Roche said, deliberately catching Veden's steely eye, "we're in it together."

The night deepened with unnerving speed. The only light came from the Soul and its constantly changing colors. The last dregs of the dust storm gusted through the valleys and ravines of the foothills like short-lived ghosts, robbing warmth and occasionally blinding them. Roche quickly learned to anticipate their arrival, as Emmerik did, by the distinctive whistle each gust made, and bunched closer to the others to prevent losing them.

Conversation was hesitant, confined mainly to Emmerik's infrequent lectures on the vagaries of the weather. Dust storms had been known to last for days at this time of the year. Although the foothills were catchments, with a rudimentary vegetation and a small amount of insect life, the moisture-stealing wind made life difficult even for the hardiest of species.

Roche listened to him with half an ear, expending the remainder of her concentration on her surroundings. Occasionally flyers buzzed overhead, scanning the area, and a couple of times she even noticed the distant flicker of lights lower in the hills. Enforcers, Emmerik had told them, searching for evidence of their passage. Pursuit was never far behind, it seemed, and constantly at the forefront of her mind. She swore to herself, and to her distant superiors, that she would not let herself be captured.

That she was trapped on a prison planet many light-years from her destination with, as yet, no concrete plan to reach a communicator didn't deter her. There had to be some way left to complete her mission. The Box was too important to be allowed to fall into Dato hands.

The others, with the possible exception of Cane, seemed to share her tight-lipped determination. Veden kept to himself, his expression stony and unapproachable. Maii walked with a stubborn independence, as though the time spent severed from her secondhand senses had humiliated her and left her needing to prove her abilities. Emmerik plodded steadily onward with the sure footing of someone who knew his way well.

Cane just walked, silent and pensive, taking in everything around him.

After an hour or so, the foothills steepened into a mountainside with paths that doglegged through crevasses and gullies. Roche's side and shoulder began to ache again, but she didn't allow herself the luxury of complaint. She simply bit down on the pain and kept walking.

Then, after three hours, a warning from Maii:

<I can sense them.> The reave's words were cut with urgency. <Nearby.>

"How near?" asked Emmerik, keeping his voice low.

<Near enough to sense,> Maii replied. <Maybe five hundred meters. In this terrain, I cannot be more accurate.>

"Very well." The Mbatan scanned their surroundings. "Over there—in that small niche. We'll rest there."

They did so, squeezing awkwardly into the narrow split in the rock. Something crawled across Roche's hand, but had disappeared by the time she reached down to brush it away.

"Wait here," Emmerik said when they were settled. "I'll go look around." Cane followed him out of the niche, moving, Roche noted, with all the soundless grace of the silver dust-moths she had chased as a child on Ascensio.

Roche leaned into the rock and breathed deeply, cautiously, feeling the pain in her ribs but thinking through it, trying to negate it by willpower alone. Years of advanced medicine had undermined her basic survival training, however; the twinge in her bones refused to fade. At home, or on almost any other civilized planet in the galaxy, relief would have been moments away under the care of an automated medkit. She was slowly learning that, on Sciacca's World, access to such fundamental medical treatment would have been a luxury.

She wondered how Emmerik could stand it.

<He knows nothing else,> said the Surin suddenly. <This is the life he leads, and has led all his life. His fight is not simply against authority.>

Roche glanced at the Surin's blindfolded, unreadable face. She found it ironic that one who could appear so closed, so isolated from the viewpoint of others, could have such intimate access to her thoughts.

<Would you like to see me?> asked the reave unexpectedly. <As I truly am?>

"No, I—"

<Why not? Do you hate me that much?>

Roche gritted her teeth. She knew it was nothing more than her personal aversion to epsense that had made her react badly to the Surin, nothing to do with the girl herself.

<You know nothing about me,> said Maii. <But you knew as little when you helped me before, when Emmerik tried to carry me. How can you damn me now for something over which I have no control?>

"Because you *do* have control. It's not like any other sense. And I—I guess I find the power unnerving."

<No.> The Surin moved closer in the confined space. <You're afraid I'll expose you—reveal your weaknesses and Pristine frailties. Everything that your uniform hides.>

"You're wrong—"

<About what? Your fear or your self?>

Before she could answer, Maii had entered her mind and filled it with images:

A Surin woman with pendulous breasts bent over her, touching her, pleasing her, in a town called Erojen on an outpost far from the heart of the Surin domain, where outriders and social outcasts came for shelter, where those on the edge of society sought succor, where the normal could find what the rest of the Caste rejected—where anything that had a price could be bought. Yet somehow, in the squalor and perjury, was a strange dignity, a perverse pride, and dreams too, of betterment, profit, and sometimes, revenge . . .

. . . a place of passion, of vivid memories . . .

. . . a Surin adult taking her hand and leading her from her mother, her tears staining the front of her white smock, the world seeming so large and awful everywhere she looked, through ten kilometers in a jeep to the sanctuary, then the soft snick of the lock to her room sealing her in . . .

. . . in the hospital . . .

. . . learning to use the implants, with their gentle, cajoling voices, learning to avoid the discipline if she somehow got it wrong, learning to know what the doctor wanted in advance and what the treatment involved (if not what it meant), learning not to be afraid (or at least bottling it up where no one else would see it, where not even she could feel it, unless she wanted to), learning to forget what she had been, to concentrate on the now . . .

. . . feeling the sharp sting of the needle, feeling the voice of the doctor vibrating in the electric tingle of the implant (rather than hearing it pounding on her now-sensitive ears), feeling darkness creep over her from her toes up, feeling nothing in the end but an echo of the fear, and then feeling nothing at all for a very, very long (and yet somehow timeless) single moment . . .

. . . then . . . awakening to nothing.

Her higher senses—visual and aural, not the primal, animal senses of touch, taste, and smell—were gone, as was her ability to talk. The implant could still communicate with her, but it did so reluctantly, to quell her overwhelming panic, and then only via the bones in her skull, tapping out words of instruction and guidance into the outer layers of her brain itself. It monitored her every neuron, testing, probing, rearranging, rebuilding, using the tissues that had once belonged to her severed senses to rebuild a new sense, a new ability, one that (it said) would make her more valuable than anyone else on the planet.

She was the first successful outcome of a new procedure, one that could replicate in months what years of training could only hope to achieve. A procedure that was both illegal and immoral—in that it could only succeed when applied to children in their prepubescent years—but one that had the potential to increase her worth by millions after one simple operation.

All this, and more, she learned from the doctor in the spectacular moment her mind first opened—when, effortlessly, she reached into him with an invisible hand, searching, feeling, sensing, and leaving nothing but a burned-out ruin in her wake.

She was a reave. And she had been *made* that way.

It took time—and practice—to come to terms with this wondrous new ability of hers. And in a way it was perhaps fortunate for her that of every ten subjects she practiced upon, nine of them died. Had the doctor lived, and the process been completely successful, who knew what might have happened to her, to whom she might have been sold?

Even as her control improved—and she came to realize that the years of training endured by naturally occurring psychics were not necessary so much to develop the power, but to control it when it finally appeared—she understood that they would never use the process again. Not only had much of the theory gone with the doctor, but the risks were too great—the risk of creating a monster, of creating a failure, of being caught. Of creating another *her*, whom they would have to get rid of somehow, without her realizing it.

So she escaped. And entered the real world. And came to realize that what she had was even less of a gift than she had thought.

It wasn't sight—not sight as she had once known it, but an impression of sight, sight with all the baggage. Someone saw a knife and thought of a lost lover; buildings evoked memories of people long dead, of past events that had no relevance to her, the observer. Sounds were even worse, bringing unwanted impressions of voices, songs, screams, and sighs. Her world was secondhand, passing through the filters of other peoples' minds and emerging tainted rather than purified. She began to lose her own voice in the relentless ambience of echoes, overwhelmed by a world full of other peoples' thoughts.

But she maintained, grew bolder, traveled . . .

. . . received guidance from a bonded reave on Fal-Soma, many light-years from home . . .

. . . worked . . .

. . . and . . .

. . . returned with no thoughts left for herself. Not for a long while. All she saw—through her own eyes, her own sense of touch—was the orange-grey shelf of rock before her and the grit of dust on her fingertips.

Roche. Not Maii, the child sold, the experimental subject, the wanderer—the young Surin woman sitting opposite her, her mind elsewhere, far away and unreadable—whom she *had been* for an instant. Not Maii, not anymore.

All Roche felt was herself.

* * *

When Emmerik returned, he was pale-faced behind his beard. Cane followed, as soft and as silent as the Mbatan's shadow, yet full of the same vitality Roche had glimpsed earlier.

"Did you find them?" asked Veden.

Emmerik glanced at Cane and did not reply immediately.

"We found them," said Emmerik softly.

"And?" Veden prompted.

<I can no longer sense them,> Maii said. <At all.>

"We should keep moving," said the Mbatan, shifting his pack awkwardly, impatiently. "More could be following, and the Cross isn't far away now."

"Good." Veden was on his feet before Emmerik had finished speaking. "We've wasted enough time for one night."

In a wordless silence broken only by the crunch of their footfalls, they filed out of the niche and headed up the path.

8

Sciacca's World
Behzad's Wall
'954.10.31 EN
0325

The wind picked up as they crested the ridge of the mountains and rose above the dense layers of the storm. From the ridge, illuminated by the Soul, a wide plateau stretched below them: a deep bowl ringed by cliffs, perhaps an ancient, collapsed volcanic crater, with a small town in its center, too far away and too low in the dust to be seen clearly. The uppermost levels of two thin towers connected to each other by walkways were the only obvious detail.

"Houghton's Cross," said Emmerik, speaking for the first time in almost an hour.

"*That's* where we're headed?" Although he hadn't said so, Roche could tell that the town was dead, and had been for many years.

"Yes. The others are waiting for us there."

"'Haid'?" The name had been mentioned a couple of times earlier, in a context suggesting leadership or at least some sort of coordinating role. If Roche was ever going to find help getting off the planet, she guessed that he was the person she needed to talk to.

"Maybe. Depends what's happening in the port." The burly Mbatan shifted his pack into a more comfortable position. "We'll talk when we arrive. Let's keep moving."

They descended along a thin path barely wide enough for one person. An avalanche of dust falling through a dip in the ridge enveloped them, reducing their line of sight to the back of the person in front, but at the same time effectively hiding them from the eyes of anyone in the area. If the air within the crater was as gloomy as it appeared to be, they would be invisible to Enforcers standing on the ridge.

Roche walked grimly onward, the pain somehow keeping her focused on who she was and what she was doing. The straps holding the Box to her back were like whips in slow motion, digging into her bruised and battered shoulders with each step she took. The valise itself had been attached to her for so long that it was starting to feel like an extra limb—and a useless, hindering limb at that, dragging as it did behind her. In a way it seemed more of an inconvenience than her strapped left arm, yet without it she doubted she would ever feel complete again.

That thought depressed her more than any merely physical pain. That, and the still-ringing echoes of Maii's life.

The floor of the crater was relatively flat and composed of a loose, grey dirt.

Although the soil here seemed as parched as that of the neighboring foothills, hardy weeds grew from it, clinging to the ground in a desperate embrace against the severe winds. They crossed an unused road at one point, then a wide, flat area that might once have been a landing strip. An abandoned machine—an ore carrier—loomed out of the gloom, rusted and hulking, left to the elements centuries ago and now barely recognizable. Dust had sanded its paint and windshield back to bare metal, which itself was scored and pitted. A ragged hole in one side offered a mute explanation for the neglect, although Roche was unable to tell if the hole had been caused by an internal malfunction or external interference.

Closer to the town, the crater floor undulated in a series of low dunes, possibly a forestalled attempt at irrigation. Something glinting in the dirt at the bottom of one of the trenches caught Roche's eye, and she stopped to pick it up. It was a silver coin, heavy in her palm, with a bold "U" on one side. She didn't recognize the denomination.

<Underground currency,> said the Box. <Early Ataman Theocracy.>

<Here?>

<No need to be concerned, Morgan. Such coins have been out of circulation for over seven hundred years; this one was no doubt left by an early colonist. Furthermore, being a penal colony, Sciacca's World has no official economy, and therefore no use for money.>

"Except to deal with outsiders," she muttered.

<Who are unable to come here anyway.>

Roche glanced at Veden, whose back was receding up the slope of the trench. <No money at all?>

<DAOC trades for credit with the Pan-Human Finance Trust. The transportees work to gain what comforts they can, with benefits such as health care and rations accrued by points. Officially, there is no commerce between parties on the surface, with no economic medium to enable it.>

<And unofficially?>

<We have no way of knowing that until we see it at work—although the existence of this coin, here, could be taken as suggestive.>

<That's what I think.> Roche dropped the coin into the dirt and hurried to catch up with the others, suspicious yet again of the Eckandi's motives. If the rebels on Sciacca's World had no current means of paying Veden for his services, what did he hope to gain from coming here?

Emmerik glanced back at her as she approached. "Don't wander," he said. "We're almost there."

Made curious by the forbidding tone in his voice, Roche obeyed but kept her eyes peeled. Another road crossed their path, and Emmerik turned to follow it. The brown, stony surface was cracked and split in places, and puddles of sand had collected in the cracks, making footing treacherous. The ever-present dust allowed them to see no more than six meters in any direction; even via infrared, the world was dim and featureless. Roche wondered how Emmerik could tell their position relative to the town.

Then, rising out of the haze, shapes appeared lining the road and spreading off into the distance: a field of posts, perhaps, barely a meter high, or the trunks of long-dead shrubs, stripped of their branches. Roche couldn't tell exactly what they were, except that there were a lot of them. The wind moaned eerily through them, making the hair on the back of her neck rise.

She approached the edge of the road to look closer at one of the objects. Through the haze of dirt, she recognized the dull sheen of blackened metal and the sweep of a stock, sight, and barrel. It was a weapon, buried barrel-first in the dirt.

<Mbatan high-frequency microwave combat rifle,> said Box. <A very old model.>

She crouched down to study it more closely. She hadn't seen a HFM peace gun outside the Armada Museum, but the distinctive line of the trigger guard, designed for digits larger than her own, confirmed that the Box was right at least about the Caste that had built it. <There must be hundreds of them.> She reached out a hand to touch it.

"Roche!" Emmerik's warning snapped at her.

She glanced guiltily upward. An indistinct figure was moving toward her through the gloom from deeper in the field, a vaguely Human shape wrapped in rags, hissing menacingly. She jerked upright, reaching automatically for her empty holster.

The figure stopped in its tracks and stared at her. Two more approached out of the dust, and stood on either side of the first. She stared back, mystified, waiting for them to make a move. It was only when Emmerik's gently restraining hand came down on her shoulder that she realized they would approach no closer while she stayed away from the rifle.

"Leave them alone," Emmerik said from behind her. "We have no right to interfere with them, and what belongs to them."

"Who are they?"

"Caretakers." Emmerik's hand, now on her good arm, led her away from the edge of the road. "They preserve the killing fields."

"The guns?" she said.

"No," said Emmerik firmly. "This is neither the time nor the place to discuss what happened here, Roche."

Roche opened her mouth to speak, but Emmerik was already moving off down the road, into the dust. She followed slowly after him, her attention caught by the three ghostly figures disappearing once again into the gloom. The movements of one of them disturbed her a little. With each step it took, its garments moved in such a way as to suggest that it had more than one right arm.

When the three figures completely vanished into the haze, Roche hurried her pace to catch up with Emmerik.

"How many?" she asked, coming to his side. "The guns, I mean."

Emmerik kept his attention on the road ahead. "Not now, I said."

"*When*, then?" she snapped. "I'm sick of not knowing anything."

"When we meet the others."

"You keep saying that." Roche fought to control her anger, but she could still hear the snap in her voice.

"Not far now," he said, adjusting his dust-specs. "The town's just a little further on."

The field of rifles petered out after a hundred meters. Moments later, a large shape appeared through the dust, glowing with the remnants of the day's heat: a wall, natural for the first five meters, then artificial above. Exactly how high it rose above the floor of the crater, Roche couldn't tell, but it showed no sign of ending at the limits of her infrared vision. She supposed that the builders had situated the wall, and the city within, on the central peak of the ancient impact crater to thereby gain the strategic advantage that would give the town. Higher than the crater floor, it was well placed to repel ground attacks—the unbroken expanse of the floor itself gave little cover for an attacking army—and the ring of mountains was far enough away to reduce the accuracy of sniping.

The road came to a halt at the base of a gentle ramp, which led to a wide pair of sliding doors set into the natural base of the wall. The doors were firmly shut, and looked as though they weighed tons. A sign on the door proclaimed a brief message in letters almost too faint to read, in a script Roche recognized but could not decipher.

<'Ul-æmato,'> read the Box. <Dominion alphabet, circa twenty-fifth century EN.>

<What does it mean?>

<'Founder's Rock.'>

<Could be the name of the town, before the Ataman Theocracy took over.>

<One would assume so.>

<Does it appear in your datapool?>

<Briefly.> The Box paused, as though scanning its extensive memory. <The Hutton-Luu System was the first of many fought over by the Ataman Theocracy and the Dominion during the Ghost War, as I said earlier. The city of Ul-æmato was a target during this period. Beyond that, I can tell you little.>

Roche absorbed this information while Emmerik approached the massive doors. <Olmahoi greyboots, Mbatan peace guns, Theocracy coins, Dominion ruins . . .>

<And a Commonwealth of Empires penal colony,> chimed the Box.

Roche nodded. <This place has seen a lot in its time.>

<It is steeped in death.> Maii's words intruded, suddenly, upon their silent conversation.

Roche glanced at the Surin, who had spoken even less than Emmerik since their brief break in the mountains. The girl shivered deep in her survival suit—which had turned a deep, gloomy grey, mirroring both the night and Maii's mood.

<What do you mean by that?> asked Roche.

<I can sense echoes of the people who live nearby,> said the reave. <They do not enter the city itself. They remember suffering and terrible pain—and they believe it to be inhabited by the shelaigh.> Maii read Roche's confusion and answered the question that had arisen in her thoughts: <Spirits, ghosts, *qacina*, jezu . . . >The explanation ceased the moment Roche's confusion cleared.

<Can you read anything more about them?>

<No. Their minds are confused, vague. Sickened.>

Roche felt a slight chill at the reave's words. Not sick, but *sickened*. By something.

A deep, bone-jarring rumble distracted her. She looked up in time to see the mighty doors slide open a meter, then crash to a halt. Emmerik slid his bulk through the crack and gestured that they should follow. Cane did so first, sniffing at the air before entering the darkness. Veden and Maii went next, leaving Roche alone in the chill night air. If it was a trap, she reasoned, better to face it with the others than alone.

Darkness overwhelmed her as she slipped through the narrow space—a deep black broken only by the faint heat profiles of those ahead of her. Echoes told her that the passage was slightly wider than the doors, and barely as high. She was reminded of their earlier journey through the tunnel leading from the ravine. This passage seemed more oppressive despite its greater width—perhaps because it was designed to be lit, and was not.

Several minutes passed before anything changed. Veden grunted with surprise, and Roche tensed. Then she realized that his heat image was rising, as were those of Emmerik, Maii, and Cane. A second later, she too hit the ramp and began to climb. The passage had been designed to accommodate wheeled vehicles, not pedestrians, for the slope was steep and the walls lacked handholds. She maintained her balance carefully, conscious that if she slipped she might not be able to arrest a slide back to the bottom with only one arm to stop her.

The ramp leveled out after twenty paces, and reached another set of doors. Emmerik again approached them, and manipulated the controls of what could only be a magnetic lock, although one of ancient design. Roche felt the tingle in her implants as powerful fields shifted to a new configuration and the heavy barrier slid aside.

They stepped out of the tunnel into a square on the edge of the town.

The pearly sheen of the Soul, diffused though it was by the dust-laden air, seemed bright in comparison to the interior of the tunnel. Roche glanced behind her, and realized that their journey had taken them only as far as the inner edge of the wall, the base of which must therefore have been nearly thirty meters thick. Its top was studded with ramps and walkways, and sturdier emplacements where weapons might once have peered over the wall at the crater below. Every fixture seemed perfectly designed, intended to last centuries—as it seemed they already had. Roche could only admire the builders of the wall, and the military function it performed so well.

The square split traffic from the tunnel into five wide roadways that diverged as they led deeper into the town. The buildings were uniformly squat and solid, with rounded corners and domed roofs—an architecture common to Dominion military emplacements. Apart from the efforts of wind and time, not one of the buildings appeared damaged in any way. Every door was open, and the few windows were utterly black. In the absence of wind, the square seemed unnaturally still.

Raising her eyes from the buildings before her, she saw the two large towers at the heart of the city: the only buildings higher than two stories. From this close—less than two kilometers—they were far more impressive. The shorter stood at least one hundred meters high; its taller twin might have reached one hundred and twenty, although dust hazed its upper limits. They stood roughly ten meters apart with a tracery of scaffolding connecting the two, as though they had been undergoing repair when the town had been abandoned.

No, Roche reminded herself, not abandoned. Emmerik intended to meet someone here.

"Which way?" prompted Cane, gesturing at the five roads.

"Second from the left." The Mbatan's voice was muted, muffled by an emotion Roche could not read. "Please stick to the road and don't disturb anything. I'll follow in a moment."

"Are we in danger?" Cane studied the darkened doorways with suspicion.

"No." Emmerik shook his head. "It's not that."

Roche suddenly guessed what was bothering the Mbatan. Studying the silent streets more closely, she could see the way sand had gathered in every crevice, untouched for decades, perhaps centuries; the very air tasted pure, despite the tang of dust, untainted by the outside world. It was as though the whole town had been sealed in memoriam to whatever in its past had killed it. The town was a shrine, and they were violating it simply with their presence.

Again she swallowed her curiosity and forced herself to walk, eager to reach the end of their long journey. The others followed her lead, heading slowly along the road with their footsteps echoing off the stubborn buildings. Cane took the rear, his keen gaze studying the shadows for movement. Roche looked also, but from training rather than suspicion; in those deserted streets she didn't expect to find life of *any* kind. Still, the absence of Emmerik's steady steps among theirs made the procession seem somewhat unnatural, even tense. And the fact that he had their weapons only made her feel more uneasy.

Roche trod onward, refusing to look behind her. There were other ways to find out what was going on.

"What's he doing, Maii?" she asked, once they were out of earshot.

<I don't know.> There was a hint of resignation in the reave's tone. <He has a very effective epsense shield.>

"Can you sense anybody else? The people he's supposed to be meeting, for example?"

<Faintly. They are not far away.> She hesitated for a few moments. <They seem to be waiting. Perhaps they noticed the doors opening.>

Roche sighed. <Box? Do you have a map of this place?>

<Only an aerial reconnaissance photo.> The display in Roche's left eye flickered and superimposed a grainy picture over the dimly lit street: a high-altitude, low-res scan of the city. A bright dot of light moved across the image. <This is the street we are following. Note that it doglegs shortly before we reach the central square.>

Roche looked ahead, trying to locate the corner but failing. <How far?>

<Perhaps a kilometer, maybe more.> The image zoomed closer, became even grainier. <Note also that the scaffolding around the towers appears to be missing.>

<You can see that? I can't see any such thing.>

<Well, it's missing, although I am unable to explain why.>

<So the picture was obviously taken before it went up.>

<I had realized that, Morgan.> Did she detect indignation in the AI's tone? <The question is: what purpose does it serve now that did not require servicing earlier?>

<I don't know.>

<Quite.> The Box fell silent for a moment, and the image in her eye disappeared. <Speculation is useless in the absence of data.>

<Not really. We could at least form a hypothesis to test later, when we do have the data.>

<Better to have no hypothesis at all, than an incorrect one.>

<Perhaps.> Roche withdrew into herself, rubbing her aching shoulder through the survival suit and makeshift bandages. The road seemed endless, and the night deeper and colder than ever. Her survival suit, and those of her companions, had turned a deep charcoal black. But for the faint heat signatures, they would have been totally invisible. "Damn him," she muttered. "He could have at least left us some water."

They reached the dogleg fifteen minutes later. Roche studied it cautiously before sending Cane ahead. The blind corner would be the perfect place for an ambush, and she wasn't prepared to risk anything in this place. The lanky figure of her only Pristine companion strode confidently across the open space until he disappeared from sight. Roche found herself holding her breath until he appeared again, waving an "all clear." Tenuous though her connection to him was, right now, in this town, she felt she would be lost without his presence. It wasn't an emotional issue, but one that any realist would admit to. In her weakened state, she needed someone strong to rely on. And if she was wrong to place her trust in him, then . . .

Not that she had any choice. She was vulnerable, cut off from the support structures that usually surrounded her. She had to take what she could get, and learn to live without the rest.

As they approached the heart of the abandoned town, the towers loomed higher than ever. The scaffolding became clearer, although its purpose remained a mystery. Wires and thin poles tangled like an abstract sculpture across the gap between the towers; the faint light from the Soul touching various sections gave it the appearance of a giant spider's web. Roche strained her eyes to see more clearly: could she see something, a tiny speck, in the center of the web, or was that just her imagination?

The road turned once more before reaching the central square, which occupied the space between the towers. The curve was gentle, hardly threatening, but Roche's nervousness increased with every step along it.

"I don't like this," she said. "I feel like we're walking into a trap."

"Don't be stupid," said Veden, his grey eyes glinting in the darkness. "They know who I am."

"Still . . ."

<It has become very quiet.> Maii's words cut across Roche's unfinished sentence. <I don't like it either.>

"There are two people ahead," said Cane.

Roche stopped in mid-stride. "Where?"

"In the square."

She squinted into the gloom. "I can't see them."

"I can just make out the shapes of their arms and legs," said Cane, his eyes narrowed. "Only just, but they are definitely there."

<Ask him what color, Morgan,> said the Box.

"What color, Cane?"

"A very deep purple, around the edges. Like silhouettes."

<They are shielded, then. He is detecting high-frequency interference where the fields are narrowest.>

<Are you saying he can see in ultraviolet?> Roche couldn't contain her disbelief.

<It is the only possibility. You yourself can see nothing in either visible or infrared, so therefore—>

<Okay, okay.> Roche fought to concentrate. Should they separate, or move in en masse and risk being cornered?

<I detect no ill intent,> said the reave.

"You can read them?"

<Now, yes. They were closed before. Their camouflage shields are simply precautionary, to prevent them being seen from the city walls or from the air. They await Veden.>

"Should we keep going?"

<We are in no danger,> said Maii, <from them.>

Roche noted the qualifying phrase, and nodded. “Okay. But keep an eye out. Or whatever.” She wished Emmerik were back with them; at least then they would have somebody to speak on their behalf. It was unlikely that Veden would.

They continued onward, closer to the square. As they approached, the shields fell away from the pair, revealing a short man and a tall woman, both dressed in black. Beyond the dropping of the shields, neither made any move.

Roche walked until she was within ten meters of the pair, then stopped. Cane did likewise, as did Maii. Veden hesitated, then continued walking.

“Makil Veden?” said the man, his voice booming into the silence.

“Yes,” replied the Eckandi. “I am he.”

The man and the woman moved simultaneously, drawing heavy weapons from beneath their tunics and directing them at the Eckandi. “Come no closer.”

Veden stopped immediately, with his hands half-raised in an automatic gesture of surrender. “What—?”

“Take another step and we will execute you for the crimes your Caste has committed against us.”

<They don’t mean it,> gasped the reave, her voice urgent. <It’s a distraction. They’re trying to—>

Cane moved. From a standing start to a rapid sprint, he ran for the shadows cloaking the square. Roche gaped, startled by the swiftness of his response; his legs almost seemed to blur in the darkness. The woman spun to follow him. Chattering gunfire chased his heels, too late to catch him. He disappeared into an open doorway, reappeared an instant later through an alleyway, then disappeared again.

Roche automatically extrapolated his path. He was circling the square, not running away. Stunned by his sheer speed, she could only watch, frozen.

The man and woman turned to face her and Maii.

“Put your hands on your head,” said a voice from behind them. “Lie facedown on the ground and do not try to resist.”

Roche spun to face the familiar voice. Six more people had appeared from the shadows with rifles in their hands. One of them was Emmerik.

“Do it,” he spat, gesturing with the rifle. “Now!”

Roche obeyed, clumsily lowering herself to her knees, then lying flat on the road with the cold stone against her cheek.

“We’ll kill her!” Emmerik shouted, his voice echoing through the empty square. The words chilled her less than the tone of his voice. The Mbatan’s eyes searched the shadows, desperate for any sign of the fugitive.

Something moved on the far side of the square, and the woman’s rifle turned to face it.

“I mean it,” Emmerik said, less loudly than before. The rifle clicked at her back: a projectile weapon, she absently noted; lethal at such close range. “I swear.”

<They want *you*, Cane,> said Maii, her mental voice stabbing the night. <Just you. They won’t hurt Roche if you come out. They *will* hurt her if you don’t.>

Emmerik nodded. “She’s telling the truth. Too many people have died here for another to make a difference.”

Silence answered him, heavy with potential violence.

Then a shadow moved, and Cane stepped into view. His hands hung clenched at his sides. His expression was one of anger, tightly reined.

“Down.” Emmerik gestured with the rifle.

With his eyes focused on the Mbatan, Cane obeyed. A rifle butt, held by the woman, jammed into the back of his neck as her companion fixed his hands and feet in carbon-steel cuffs. Cane made no sound at all as he was bound, although Roche could see the rage boiling inside him, waiting for a chance to escape. But with the gun at his neck, he had no opportunity to break free.

When he was securely bound, rough hands lifted Roche upright. She gasped, staring in confusion at the Mbatan.

"What the hell—?"

"We had to do it," he said, his eyes pleading for her to believe him.

"But he swore to help you," she hissed. "He deserves better than this."

"He's too dangerous, too unpredictable," the Mbatan said. "You saw how fast he moved. Until he tells us who or what he is, he stays like this. I'm sorry."

Roche glanced at Cane, prostrate on the ground, then at Maii and Veden. The Eckandi was looking smugly superior now that the object of the trap had been revealed: not Veden himself, or even Roche and the Box, but Cane alone.

Roche turned away, feeling frustration bubbling within her like a ball of superheated water. She couldn't bear to look at him, potentially the most powerful fighter she had ever met betrayed by a handful of low-life rebels.

"What about honesty?" she snapped back. "Integrity? Trust?"

"Look up," said one woman standing close behind her.

"What?" said Roche.

"Look up," the woman repeated. "Between the towers."

Roche did so, and was gratified to hear Veden echo her own involuntary gasp of revulsion.

Suspended by the scaffolding between the two towers, crucified horizontally by wires and impaled upon iron spars, hung the mummified body of a naked Eckandi male.

"Blind trust on Sciacca can often prove expensive," said Emmerik, and gestured with the rifle that she should walk ahead of him to join the others.

9

Sciacca's World
Behzad's Wall
'954.10.31 EN
0750

"Newcomers to our planet usually mean trouble." The woman brushed strands of black hair from her narrow face. Roche had heard Emmerik address her as "Neva," although she hadn't been formally introduced. "It's an unfortunate fact of life," she added.

Roche glanced inquiringly at Neva from where she sat, but the woman averted her face and busied herself at one of the tables. Emmerik crouched nearby with a gun in his lap, his attention fixed on Cane sitting against the wall opposite Roche. Through the only doorway leading into the room, Roche could make out Veden and Maii discussing business with a half dozen other rebels, their conversation kept carefully out of earshot.

If the woman's remark had been an overture to an explanation, it seemed Roche would have to wait a little longer for the rest.

They had been brought to the shorter of the two towers, which obviously served as an impromptu base for the rebels in the town. The room they were in was slightly run-down and thick with dust; around them were scattered ten camp beds, a number of the crude projectile weapons she had seen earlier, a small cache of food and water, and a dozen or so unmarked containers. The only light in the room came from a battered fuel-cell heater in the corner; the only window was currently shielded by a carbon-mat, presumably to prevent their heat from being detected at night.

Neva came to Roche's side to tend her injuries, gently peeling back the survival suit to take a closer look. Roche winced as her bruised muscles submitted to the woman's examination.

"I think you're being a little harsh on us," said Roche. "I never wanted to be here in the first place—and if the only way to leave is by helping you, then that's what I'll do."

Neva grinned wryly. "Whether you want to or not." She slipped a ration-stick into Roche's mouth. The stick burst upon chewing and became a thick, sweet gel. "The transportees don't want to be here either, remember."

Roche nodded in appreciation for the food, but couldn't bring herself to offer her gratitude. The rebels may have helped her so far, but she was still decidedly wary of their motives.

"Well," she said, "this *is* a penal planet—"

"That's not the half of it." Neva roughly unstrapped the Box from her back. "If you think *we're* being harsh, then you don't know the meaning of the word."

"Not now," Emmerik interrupted. "She needs rest, not a lecture."

"Be quiet, Emmerik," said the woman evenly. It was clear to Roche from Neva's tone that her rank in the rebels was higher than that of the Mbatan. "She wants to know who we are. She *needs* to if she expects us to help her."

"And if you expect us to help you." Roche smiled, but the light from the heater reflected in the woman's eyes was cold. That she wanted to talk, though, was obvious. "Why don't you tell me what happened?"

"What happened was the Ghost War," Neva said, settling back onto her haunches and continuing to work on Roche's injured shoulder. "Prior to then, this was a comfortable planet, with forests and lakes and fields of grain. And rivers."

"It's hard to imagine."

Neva's fingers dug deep into Roche's shoulder, making her wince with pain. *Be quiet* was the obvious message.

"A strike on a Dominion installation in the Soul changed—*ruined*—everything," the woman went on. "There was massive destruction. Three large moonlets fell from orbit. Killed millions, smashed the ecosphere. A few small cities survived, such as this one, but the moonlets—along with the quakes and volcanic activity that followed—left virtually nothing else standing. The Ataman Theocracy didn't even bother to hang around to mop up the survivors. Bigger wars to attend to, perhaps. I don't know. History doesn't supply an explanation. And it doesn't matter. The old world was gone."

Neva's fingers stopped working, and for a few moments she remained very still, staring off over Roche's injured shoulder. Roche made no attempt to prompt her, but glanced over to where Cane sat huddled beneath a cowl of shadows, attentive as always. His eyes were fixed upon her, but she suspected he would be listening to every word that Neva or Emmerik said.

Then Neva's fingers began to move again, and with them her labored account of Ul-æmato's history. "For the survivors, life went on. They adapted to the new environment: the deserts, the sandstorms, the predators. Sciacca's World was still home to a couple of million people, and I guess they believed they could tame it again. They became a harder breed, tougher than their ancestors. A more resilient type of Pristine altogether, although not a new Caste.

"The First Ataman War came and went. Officially, from then on, we were part of the Theocracy, but they had no substantial presence, so it didn't mean much to people here. Only during the Second Ataman War did things change. The Commonwealth of Empires took the system, and they invaded in force. But we were stronger on the ground, and we held a number of small territories in the hills and mountains free from the invading forces."

"Such as Houghton's Cross?" Roche said, noting Neva's unconscious switch from "they" to "we."

"It wasn't called Houghton's Cross back then," said Neva. "It was called Ul-æmato, and it became the capital of this region." She shrugged. "And although the Commonwealth occasionally conducted raids in the hope of destabilizing the Dominion population, the two nations coexisted in relative peace for quite a while."

"It was around then that the penal colony was founded," put in Emmerik. "To mine the Soul, and the places on the shattered crust where minerals had come to the surface."

Neva nodded once more. "The Theocracy, when it destroyed the planet, ignored that resource, just as its soldiers ignored the Human suffering they left behind."

She paused, concentrating for a moment on Roche's shoulder. Then: "Port Parvati was rebuilt—along with the installations in the Soul—and the entire project was turned over to OPUS, a mining consortium. The planet became a business venture, and the board of directors wouldn't tolerate competition or interference from unruly neighbors. Ul-æmato became *competition*."

Neva began to rub salve into Roche's shoulder. It burned and stung, but she didn't interrupt the woman's narrative with complaint.

"Then DAOC, another mining company, took over the administration of the planet. Its prospectors exhausted low-lying deposits and decided they wanted the hills. They mounted a full-scale military campaign against Sciacca's people. There are ruins all through these mountains where DAOC troops—mercenaries, most of them—razed entire communities to the ground, leaving nothing but rubble and ashes in their wake. Yet, despite being outgunned in almost every way, the defenses of Ul-æmato held while other towns fell around it. The fight went on for weeks, until Ul-æmato was teeming with injured and frightened refugees.

"Food and water were scarce. DAOC had destroyed irrigation and mist-collection plants. The siege of the city was in its seventh week when a lucky strike crippled one of only two fusion generators in the area. It all seemed hopeless until a gunrunner approached the defenders from out-system with a large supply of weapons."

Neva paused to tie a bandage in place. "Word must have spread, and I guess it was only a matter of time before somebody tried to profit from the situation. But any chance of improving the odds had to be considered seriously. DAOC was well armed, whereas Ul-æmato was relying on technology centuries out of date. The Mbatan rifles, nearly five thousand in all, were high-frequency microwave weapons—designed to disable electronic equipment rather than to kill. They would be effective against the battle armor of the attacking troops. They were cheap, efficient, and honorable, and the gunrunner agreed to sell the weapons on credit."

"Credit?" said Roche. "What sort of illegal—?"

Neva raised a hand to silence her. "He agreed to supply the weapons in exchange for a substantial down payment in underground currency. The deal was signed. With the weapons, the troops of Ul-æmato went into battle.

"And they did well, taking first one and then another DAOC squadron by surprise and forcing them back. As the squadrons retreated, Ul-æmato's territory expanded to something like its original size. Anything with powered systems could not enter this area, or the peace guns would disable them, and the Ul-æmato fighters were so well trained at more primitive methods of combat—having practiced them for generations—that DAOC was reluctant to send troops in unarmored. Orbital bombardment was ruled out, because that method of fighting would be frowned upon by the interstellar community. For the first time in several months, it seemed that DAOC would have to capitulate and allow the original owners of the planet their small territory."

Having finished ministering to Roche's shoulder—as well as changing her makeshift bandages—Neva strapped the injured arm into a more comfortable position, leaving the valise free. She sat back upon the gritty floor, facing Roche.

"Then, for no obvious reason, Ul-æmato's troops began to weaken. A tiredness afflicted them: a terrible malaise that sapped both strength and will. It caused bleeding, skin damage, and occasional loss of hair; in the long term, it led to death. No physical cause could be found. The popular theory was that a biological agent had been unleashed by DAOC to quash the town's resistance.

"The strange thing about it, though, was that the disease only affected those who fought in battle, never noncombatants. And as the battle continued, the weakened fighters were replaced by others, who in turn fell to the mysterious illness. Lacking an advanced medical center, the colonists had no means of determining the illness's cause until it was far too late. And even then, it was only by chance. By that time, nearly three quarters of the town had fallen prey to the disease."

"The rifles," said Cane softly.

Neva nodded. "One of the town's elders, a woman named Madra Hazeal, returned from the front with one of the Mbatan peace guns. Its batteries were dead, and she intended to recharge them the following day. Legend has it that, feeling tired and sick with the disease, she retired to bed and absently left the weapon near a tub of water. Somehow the weapon slipped and fell into the water and remained immersed for a number of hours. When she retrieved it the following morning, she discovered something very peculiar: despite the chill of the desert night, the water in the tub was distinctly warm."

"Beta decay," said Roche, echoing the voice of the Box in her skull.

Neva nodded again. "The rifles were radioactive—so contaminated that only a few doses resulted in debilitating sickness. The gunrunner had deliberately sold them, knowing the harm they would do. This left the people of Ul-æmato in a bind: continuing the defense of the town with the weapons meant slow death by radiation sickness, while surrender meant that they would be invaded." She lowered her eyes to the floor. "So the town fell to DAOC without a fight, killed by the rifles that had almost liberated it."

Roche waited for her to continue, but Emmerik picked up the tale.

"Shortly after taking the town," he said, "the DAOC troops learned what had happened. Naturally, they were appalled. Along with orbital bombardment, the use of radiation weapons was forbidden. Breaking the Warfare Protocol carried a heavy penalty. If conciliatory measures were not taken immediately to demonstrate their innocence, word would spread that the DAOC troops had planted the weapons themselves."

"So," Cane guessed, "as a gesture of goodwill, DAOC allowed the few remaining survivors to keep the town?"

Neva glanced back to him in the shadows. "Yes," she said. "Although they took the mountains around it, the security forces vowed to leave the town and its inhabitants alone." Again she faced Roche. "In the weeks remaining to them, the dying townsfolk buried the dead in a ring around the town, using the poisoned rifles as gravestones."

Roche remembered the endless field of rifles pointing at the sky, and shivered. "And the gunrunner?" she asked.

Emmerik snorted. "You've seen what happened to him," he said.

Roche nodded slowly. "The Eckandi."

"Lazaro Houghton," said Neva, her voice cold, "was eventually captured by the Dominion with the help of the COE—in a further gesture of goodwill. After his trial, he was sent to Sciacca's World as a convict. He only lasted a year before the inhabitants hunted him down and meted out their own justice."

"Thus 'Houghton's Cross,'" muttered Cane.

"That's right." Emmerik stared at him in the half-light, the glow from the heater catching his intense expression. "Only a handful of children survived the radiation sickness, but DAOC's promise still holds. They won't attack us here. The Cross, the old city, has become a symbol of everything we strive for: justice for past wrongs, freedom to live as we wish—"

"And it's safe," said Cane, cutting through the Mbatan's rhetoric with hard-edged pragmatism.

"That too." Emmerik glanced at Neva, and Roche noted the look that passed between them. "We do not seek a bloodbath, and we are not interested in leaving the planet. Our cause does not belong with the convicts, or the wardens. We were born here, all of us. This is where we want to live, in peace, for the rest of our lives. In order to do so, we will attempt diplomacy, but not open rebellion."

"Except as a last resort," added Neva. "Our reluctance to trust off-worlders is ingrained, you see. Sciacca's World has been betrayed at various times by the Ataman Theocracy, the Dato Bloc, the Commonwealth of Empires, and even by the Dominion, who abandoned it to its fate eight hundred years ago. Any treaty would be regarded as suspect until proved by time."

"Patience is what we should be embracing, Neva," said the Mbatan wearily, as though they had had this disagreement many times. "There has been enough death here."

"But not enough, it seems, to convince the wardens to agree to our terms." Neva returned her attention to Roche. "Haid seeks a hearing with the High Equity Court of the COE to discuss our claim of sovereignty. To do this we need a hyperspace communicator. But our requests to use the MiCom facilities at the landing field have been denied, and Warden Delcasalle refuses to negotiate."

"So you fight," said Roche, finally feeling that she understood the nature of the rebels. The why of their actions, if not the how.

"No, we *resist*." Emmerik leaned forward to accentuate the word. "We will never give up hope of finding a peaceful solution."

"Even if it means using a stranded Armada officer as a bargaining point?"

"Perhaps," said Neva. "It might come to that."

"But it won't." Emmerik gave the woman a warning look. "We have other plans, plans that don't involve betrayal."

"But do they involve Veden?" said Roche.

Neva glanced at Emmerik, and the Mbatan looked away. "It's important that you understand us," said the woman, "to enable you to decide where you stand. But until you make that decision, we will tell you nothing more."

Roche took the hint, although she was more curious than ever about how Veden intended to help. She looked into the adjacent room to see what Veden was doing, but the Eckandi and Maii, along with the other rebels, had gone.

Until you make that decision . . . Neva's sentiment bothered her. Although she could sympathize with the rebels' plight, she wasn't sure she should take a stand at all. It wasn't her job to get involved—unless that was the only way she could get off-world.

Roche lay back on the bed that Neva had prepared for her and closed her eyes. <What do you think, Box?>

<Intriguing,> said the familiar voice deep inside her head.

<But are they telling us the whole story?>

<Possibly not. Certainly there are a number of aspects that the official records do not corroborate, although that could be because the records I have were compiled by the Commonwealth of Empires and would certainly be biased, if what Neva says is true. We have no reason to disbelieve her. Her explanation does match the evidence we have gathered so far: the coin, the weapons, the town itself.>

<But where does Veden fit into it all?>

<Obviously they hope he will enable them to reach their goal. Perhaps he can talk reason to Warden Delcasalle; the Eckandi are renowned negotiators, after all. Or perhaps they intend to use Maii's epsense ability to force the warden into making the decision the rebels desire. There are a number of possibilities, none of which seems any more likely than the others at this time.> The Box paused for a moment, as though considering the situation. <When I said 'intriguing,' Morgan, I was actually referring to the curious way in which our needs almost exactly match theirs. We need access to communications, and so do they. The only difference is that we want to leave the planet, whereas they intend to stay.>

Roche tried to find a comfortable position. <And they're welcome to it.>

<I know you are tired, Morgan, but try to concentrate for just a few more minutes: the rebels have been attempting to get what they want for many years, and have failed thus far. Without Veden, we all lose. And that makes us—meaning you and me and Adoni Cane—dangerously vulnerable.>

Roche absorbed this disquieting thought in silence. Her fate rested in the Eckandi's hands: if he chose not to help the rebels because of her involvement, then she could hardly blame them for turning her in. What did she have to offer them in return for their help? All she had done so far was bring the Dato with her into the system, and increased Enforcement's presence in the mountain range—neither of which was likely to sit well with the rebels.

<At least all is not yet lost,> said the Box.

<Why's that?> she asked, beginning to feel the tug of sleep.

<You still have me.>

In defiance of sheer physical exhaustion, her mind wouldn't let her rest. She lay for two hours on the camp mattress—staring at the orange, unflickering glow the heater cast across the ceiling, and thinking about everything Neva had said—before finally giving in to restlessness.

The atmosphere of the room was thick and heavy with sleep. The floor was carpeted with a dense, aging fabric that might once have been a vibrant red, although the years had faded it to a musty brown. Roche tried to imagine the room filled with people—dignitaries, diplomats, soldiers, partisans—but failed. The town's oppressive stillness had penetrated every building, every room, robbing it of even ghosts of memory.

No one stirred as she climbed out of the bunk and donned her survival suit.

Cane's eyes were open, but he neither moved nor made a sound to disturb the others. Grasping the valise by its handle, she eased out of the room and into the hallway, where she waited a moment, listening. Still no sounds of alarm. When she felt certain she would not be followed, she swiftly and silently retraced the steps that had led to the room from the street below.

The wind had picked up in the hours she had been sheltered. It blustered around the base of the tower, snatching at her cropped scalp and stealing her warmth. Not yet certain where she was headed, she put down the valise for a moment to tug the hood of her suit over her head. As she did so, she happened to glance upward and glimpsed the Eckandi gunrunner, Lazaro Houghton, his twisted body silhouetted against the Soul.

She shivered, picked up the valise, and walked away, heading into the darkness of the city.

How long it took her to reach the town's outer wall she had no way of knowing, but when she arrived, the eastern span of the Soul had grown perceptibly brighter. Dawn was approaching. Randomly choosing a walkway, she climbed the network of ladders and platforms up the inside of the wall until she stood on its lip, thereby gaining an unobstructed view of both the town behind her and the crater around it. The wind moaned incessantly, seeking to tug her from her ancient perch. She gripped a brass rail with her one good hand and watched patiently, her mind empty of all thought, as the orange sun rose over the horizon.

Below her, still in shadow but growing more distinct with every second, was the field of graves encircling the town—rifle after rifle in an endless procession. So many graves, she thought. So much—

"You are restless," said a voice from behind her.

She turned, startled. It was Emmerik. She let herself relax. "Yes."

"Everyone has a still point, a focus, a place where one can find peace." Emmerik tipped his head to the sunrise, at the stain of blood spreading over the crater lip. "Mine is here. Houghton's Cross at dawn."

"You didn't follow me here, then?"

"Oh, I followed you. I was watching the tower from across the street. When you left, I chose not to stop you, thinking you might be headed here. Hoping." The burly Mbatan sighed deeply, the deep crinkles in the thick skin of his face smoothing slightly. "A moment of stillness is all I desire of every day. It's a shame you can't partake fully of it."

Roche turned back to the sunrise. "I have such a place also, but it's far away from here."

"Further than I can imagine, most likely. I have never traveled through space, even to a place so near as the Soul. Leaving my planet seems impossible, sometimes, although I hope to one day."

"How?"

"That will be up to Haid to tell you. It is not my place to discuss such matters."

"But Veden is essential to your plan?" Roche asked, and noted the contempt in her tone.

Emmerik heard it also, and smiled. "Don't let him worry you so."

"*Worry* me . . . ?" She stopped and sighed. "I guess he does a little. I can't help thinking that he will betray us to Enforcement the first opportunity he gets."

"He is simply afraid," said Emmerik.

"Afraid of what?"

"Of what you represent."

Roche studied the Mbatan's bearded face closely. "What about you? Are you afraid? Do I frighten you?"

Emmerik laughed, the thick sound rolling out across a sudden gust of wind. "No," he said. "You don't frighten me." He paused. "Your companion, however—Cane—he chills me to the bone."

"Why?"

Emmerik shook his head and folded his beefy arms against the wind. "When we halted in the mountain pass last night, while you and Maii and Veden waited in the rocks, Cane and I found a recon team up on the far side of the rift. They were waiting for us to come up. We'd doubled back another way and come on them from behind. They were scanning the path with infrared, waiting for us to appear."

"An ambush."

He nodded. "They were armed. We couldn't wait for them to lose interest and move elsewhere. We needed to get past them, and they had to be dealt with swiftly, but there were six of them and only two of us. I could see no easy way to approach them, or to overpower them without raising an alarm. I turned to Cane to suggest we return to your hiding place, but he wasn't there." Emmerik winced as the memory returned to him. "They didn't see him coming, or hear him. It was . . . unbelievable. I've never seen anyone move so fast. He killed them with his bare hands, soundlessly and efficiently. One of them, the last, had time to gasp for mercy, but Cane simply reached out and snapped his neck." Emmerik gestured with his right hand, imitating Cane's killing blow.

His eyes stayed on Roche. "What *is* he, Commander?"

"I don't know," she said, and recognized the doubt in his expression. "It's the truth. I wish I *did* know something more about him, but—" She looked out across the expanse of impromptu headstones. "You can always ask Maii if you don't believe me."

"I have. She says only that he is good at what he does, as are all of you, in your own ways."

"And that's all we can ever hope to be," she replied. "To fight ourselves is pointless. We must use what we have to the best of our ability and do as we see fit."

"And that includes killing in cold blood?"

"No!" She faced him angrily. He was twisting her words. "That's not what I mean. You can't blame Cane for what he did. They were the enemy. Given the chance, they would have done the same to us."

Emmerik didn't speak for several seconds. "I don't blame him," he said at last. "But if he ever turned against us—"

"He won't," Roche cut in quickly, although even as she spoke she could feel her own reservations. They were slight, but they were there. "He promised to support us," she said with more resolve. "And he will. I'm sure of it. I don't know much about him but I do know he is honorable. You yourself said that much."

Emmerik gestured to the makeshift graves below. "Needless killing is never honorable, Commander."

"That at least I can agree with," Roche said. "Perhaps we only disagree on our definition of 'need.' . . ."

Together they fell into silence, watching the dawn tighten its grip on the world.

The sky lightened to its familiar yellow-red, and the radiance of the Soul dimmed in comparison. The only blemish was a dark shadow looming over the crater's northern wall. Moving perceptibly, it seemed to creep over the lip, spilling into the bowl of stone to flood the town. Its speed surprised her. Although she had experienced once before the terrible power of a dust storm, she still had trouble comprehending the sheer ferocity of the front. The turbulent shock wave riding at the fore of an atmospheric war.

"Fodder for the Soul," said Emmerik, following her gaze. He caught the look of confusion on Roche's face and smiled. "It's something we say when a particularly bad storm is about to hit. Sort of a presage of doom. You see, some people believe that the Soul is made up—"

"—of the spirits of those that have died here," finished Roche.

Admiration flashed briefly in his eyes. "Exactly," he said. "Anyway, one myth has it that these storms are the hands of a god collecting spirits to illuminate the Soul." He glanced up at the sky. "Somebody invariably dies whenever one hits, so maybe there's some truth in it."

Roche stiffened. "If it is a god, then it's working with DAOC." She pointed in the direction of what else she had seen, hovering at the edge of the cloud. "Look!"

A tiny speck of light flickered as clouds of dust rolled around it. An instant later, it disappeared entirely, tossed by the unpredictable currents that had briefly brought it into view.

There was only one thing it could be: a flyer attempting to use the front as cover for an approach to the town.

"Quickly!" Emmerik gripped her good arm and dragged her away from the wall. "We have to warn the others!"

They climbed down from the top of the wall and started running through the empty streets of the city. The moaning of the storm was distant at first, but growing rapidly louder. Beneath it, Roche imagined she could hear the nasal buzzing of the flyer, swooping toward the city to catch them unaware.

"Do you think they saw us?"

"Undoubtedly," replied the Mbatan without breaking stride. His heavy legs pounded the pavement relentlessly, and it was all she could do to keep up. "But they knew we were here anyway, otherwise they wouldn't have come."

"It couldn't be a routine patrol?"

"No." Emmerik slowed his pace as they rounded the final corner. The looming shadow of the storm spread across the sky ahead of them, beyond the two towers and their grisly mascot. The day—not even half an hour old—began to darken. Again Roche felt the numbing despair that had crippled her the previous day, but this time she was ready for it and therefore able to resist it. Lightning flashed in the brown cloud with increasing frequency, as though the elements understood their predicament and actively encouraged a sense of emergency. "Flying a storm front is dangerous," Emmerik gasped. "Not to be undertaken lightly. Only a lunatic or a soldier would attempt to approach the town this way."

"I thought you said they wouldn't attack."

"They never have before. Perhaps that's why they're using this method of approach: to hide from eyes other than ours."

Even as he said this, a siren like the bellow of a dying animal sounded in the distance, seeming to come from all directions at once. Emmerik stumbled to a halt, listening, as the ululating cry resounded eerily across the town.

"They must have noticed it too," he said. "Good. Perhaps now we have a chance."

"Who—?" Roche used the pause to catch her breath. It seemed that she had been gasping ever since setting foot on the planet, and she wondered if the thin atmosphere was entirely to blame. "Who's making that noise?"

"The keepers of the city," Emmerik replied.

Roche remembered the strangely robed figures who had confronted her the previous night, when she had reached out to touch one of the cemetery-rifles. "The keepers? You mean the descendants of the Dominion colonists?"

"They have guarded the city for over five hundred years," he said. Then, with a wry smile, added: "They are also responsible for the rumors of it being haunted. If it is attacked, they will defend it."

"But they won't enter the city, you said."

"Not normally, and perhaps not on this occasion either. At the very least, they will repel a ground assault, should one be attempted." The Mbatan grabbed her arm again and dragged her forward. The first of the rebels had appeared in the foyer of the tower, summoned by the wail of the siren. "Come on."

Neva, still slightly sleep-fogged, led the evacuation from the tower, followed by Veden and Maii. Two rebels escorted Cane with pistols at the ready. Catching sight of Emmerik, Neva hailed him loudly, with words that belied her obvious relief at seeing him.

"I leave you on duty, and look what happens. You unlucky bastard."

Emmerik gestured helplessly at the storm. The massive clouds had almost reached the northern wall of the city. The wind had picked up to the point where its noise made speech difficult. Briefly, he explained the situation to Neva while Roche went to check on Cane.

"The underground, then," Neva said when Emmerik had finished. "That's our only hope."

"Let's pray there's enough time."

"But not too much."

"Aye." Emmerik grinned slightly. "It's cramped enough down there without Enforcement teams getting in the way."

Cane's ankle shackles had been removed, but his hands remained firmly pinned behind his back. The muscles of his shoulders flexed restlessly, as though he could sense the coming battle and yearned to be free. His face, however, betrayed none of this tension; his smile was casual, relaxed, when Roche approached.

"You're okay?"

A thin smile broke his easy expression. "Fine."

"Did you sleep?"

"No. I didn't need to."

She studied his face. He showed no sign of fatigue, despite everything they had done in the previous day. She reached out a hand to touch his shoulder, and a bright spark of static electricity snapped between them.

"We don't have long," Neva said.

Roche raised her head. The storm was on the far side of the tower, but she could feel its rumble in the air and through the soles of her feet. The sky had darkened to the color of dried blood.

As she stared, a flyer swooped around the towers, flying low over the buildings, scanning the area. The high-pitched scream of its motors was barely audible over the noise of the storm. It dipped its nose suddenly, swooped even lower, and dropped a handful of objects into the town: armored Enforcers, drifting on jets of gas onto the streets.

Neva gestured for them to move. As one, they began to run.

At that moment, the storm front hit. A solid wall of dust struck the tower and was bisected, each half curving around the circular wall to strike Roche and the rebels from opposite sides. All was instantly confusion, with opposing gusts of wind meeting and forming a giddying vortex around them.

Someone grabbed Roche's arm and tugged her along. She let herself be led, confident that the rebels knew where they were going and that the dust would hinder DAOC as much as it would them.

The imposing shadow of the Mbatan drifted closer, and he pressed something into her stomach. Shifting the valise to her injured arm, she grabbed at the object and felt the grip of a pistol enter her hand. The stocky projectile weapon was primitive, but she was grateful to have it nonetheless. At least she wouldn't be totally defenseless.

Neva led them along one of the arterial routes away from the towers, heading roughly east. After half a kilometer their route switched to narrower streets and alleyways, winding circuitously between empty buildings. Skull-like, empty doorways and windows gaped fleetingly at them as they passed, glimpsed and then gone in an instant, swallowed by the thick, choking dust.

Roche stumbled in a clogged gutter and lost her grip on the valise. The thin cord tangled, causing her to trip and wrench her shoulder. The pain was blinding, and she hardly felt Emmerik's hands lifting her to her feet, pressing the valise to her chest, and helping her along once again. The fall cost them seconds, during which time the others had disappeared from sight.

"It's okay!" Emmerik bellowed into her ear, his mouth only centimeters away. "I know the way!"

With her eyes protected by the dust-specs that Emmerik had pressed upon her, Roche peered into the thick dust and frowned. She could barely make out Emmerik, and he was standing right there beside her. "How . . . ?"

He couldn't have heard her half-muttered word, but he must have read her expression of bewilderment. "Trust me!" he shouted, and quickly moved on.

Roche stumbled along with him, grateful for the Mbatan's guiding hand on her shoulder. Together they rounded another corner, then another, and finally caught sight of a figure struggling through the wind.

Roche sighed with relief, despite Emmerik's assurance that he knew where he was going—until she realized that the figure approaching out of the gloom was wearing full ceramic battle armor and carried a cocked percussion rifle in both hands.

She instinctively ducked to one side and dragged the startled Mbatan with her behind a nearby pillar. The domed helmet of the Enforcer, its visor a deep nonreflective black, turned to scan the area around it. She tensed as the impassive gaze swept over their hiding place, then relaxed as it drifted past.

The suit's gloves tightened on the rifle's handgrip, and the Enforcer continued onward, heading away from them.

"Too close!" she shouted to Emmerik.

"Worse than that!" The Mbatan pointed in the direction the guard had headed. "We have to go that way!"

"The others—?"

"I'm afraid so!" Emmerik turned. "We'll have to get around the Enforcer somehow, to warn them!"

He lumbered off with Roche firmly in tow, heading down another route. The path they followed was even more elaborate, avoiding as it did any connection whatsoever with the road along which the Enforcer and the rebels had traveled. Roche kept her eyes peeled for other Enforcers searching the town, looking for them.

So intent was she on this task that she automatically ducked when a voice spoke into her ear:

<The Siegl-K powered combat armor was discontinued in '895 EN. Surprising to see a working model.>

Her internal voice wanted to shout, as her actual vocal cords needed to, but she resisted the impulse. <This is hardly the time—>

<The Armada must have sold them to DAOC on the cheap, decades ago,> returned the Box, <instead of mothballing them. Half of their systems will therefore be inactive, or removed.>

<Just armor?>

<Basic body-maintenance and power-assist, no sophisticated weapons or—>

An explosion ahead cut the Box off in mid-sentence, followed by the high-pitched scream of a low-flying vehicle arcing over their heads and away. The muted thud of percussion rifles pierced the aural veil of the storm and made the Mbatan's hand grip her arm even more tightly.

Abandoning stealth, he led her along a wide thoroughfare to the source of the noises. Shadowy figures crossed their path—more bulky armor, crunching heavily across the road—but quickly disappeared. Swerving to his right, Emmerik ducked through a narrow alleyway with Roche in tow. At its end, a small courtyard exploded into light as an energy weapon discharged into a wall, splintering the dust-laden air with a short-lived corona of sparks.

They stumbled to a halt and began to retreat. Out of the gloom, before either of them could dodge, an Enforcer appeared. The suit had lost its balance, and seemed more to fall into them than attack, knocking Roche to the ground. Emmerik kicked its left leg out from beneath it, dodged a flailing arm and fired two shots through the matte glass of the visor.

The Enforcer twitched, and the powered armor magnified the motion into a body-racking spasm. One heavy boot caught the Mbatan on the hip and sent him sprawling. Roche fired wildly at the thrashing figure, not caring where she hit. Sparks and spatters of blood issued from the smashed visor until finally the massive body fell still.

Roche clambered to her feet and helped the Mbatan do the same. As he rose, Emmerik grabbed the fallen Enforcer's percussion weapon. Shadows moved at the edge of the square, and this time she dodged quickly enough to avoid another armored figure as it staggered by, firing its percussion rifle in random, furious bursts.

A second figure danced out of the gloom, catching the armor square in the chest with one firmly planted foot, employing both balance and strength to tip it over its center of gravity. Roche and Emmerik fired as it fell. Black explosions flared on the armor's ceramic exoskeleton, stitching a ragged path from groin to throat, until something shorted in the power-assist mechanisms and the armor became still, locking its inhabitant in a coffinlike embrace.

Cane, who had delivered the overbalancing blow, nodded appreciatively at the Mbatan, then turned to go.

"Wait!" Roche called him back, then turned to Emmerik. "Free his hands!"

The Mbatan hesitated for an instant, obviously weighing the ease with which Cane, even with his hands shackled, had overpowered two Enforcers in full combat armor.

"Emmerik!" Roche shouted. "We *need* him!"

With a faint and uncertain shrug, Emmerik placed the muzzle of the rifle against Cane's outstretched wrists and severed the mesh chain with a single shot.

Cane smiled his gratitude at both of them. Then, leaving the second percussion rifle for Roche, he dashed off into the gloom with Roche and Emmerik vainly trying to keep up.

The sharp whiplash of projectile fire became increasingly loud as they ran, interspersed with shouts for help and cries of anger. Then, more ominous still, another sound rose above that of the wind: a deep, bone-tingling rumble that seemed to come from no particular direction. As it grew in volume, the smoke and dust around them began to agitate from side to side—not swirling as it normally did through the streets and openings in the buildings, but vibrating in confined circles. The sharp smell of ozone was almost overpowering.

A pair of Enforcers darted through the oscillating clouds, boots crunching as they came. Emmerik and Roche separated as the Enforcers' percussion rifles swiveled and spat at them. Returning fire, they ducked and weaved around the pair, using their small advantage of mobility over the suits' inertia. The Enforcers followed swiftly, however—the whine and clank of power-assist an atonal accompaniment to their every movement. The short hairs on Roche's scalp stiffened as a bolt narrowly missed her. She rolled to one side with the valise clutched to her chest, wishing she'd had time to strap it to her back, out of the way. Firing over her shoulder, she weaved across the courtyard as though heading for an inviting doorway, then ducked into an alley at the last moment. Running furiously, not knowing or caring where she was headed, she concentrated solely on putting distance between herself and the Enforcer, hoping to lose herself in the dust.

Pursued by the whirring armor, she burst out the far end of the alleyway and ran headlong into another person. Limbs tangled as she fell skidding to the ground. She scrambled to her hands and knees, feeling in the dust for the fallen rifle, while the person she had collided with fought for breath nearby.

The crunch of heavy boot treads arrived at the end of the alley at exactly the same moment that the bone-tingling rumble reached a peak. With a strange sensation—as though every item of clothing on her body had suddenly inflated—the dust around her vanished.

Blinking in the suddenly clear air, she looked up.

Hovering not twenty meters directly above her, all black carbon fiber and armored struts, was a troop carrier—slightly smaller than a salvage craft and shaped like a flat-bottomed bullet. The concave panels of the field-effect generators that striped its underside looked like ribs on the belly of some deep-sea beast.

The troop carrier was using its field-effect to clear the dust.

"Roche?" Emmerik's distant shout distracted her from the sight hanging above her. Blinking, she turned away, and belatedly realized that the footsteps of the Enforcer following her had ceased.

The armored figure stood at the entrance to the alley, not five meters from her, its rifle already rising. Her own rifle lay just out of arm's reach, too far away for a desperate lunge, and the nearest cover was farther away still. The Enforcer would shoot before she reached either. Yet she didn't feel any fear, just a vague anger for the undignified manner in which she was about to die: on her knees in a dusty square of some forgotten town on a backwater planet.

The black eye of the Enforcer's rifle stared at her for what seemed an excruciatingly long time before the Surin's words whispered in her thoughts:

<Hurry! I can't hold him forever.>

Roche gaped first at the motionless Enforcer, and then at the girl sprawled out on the ground next to her, into whom she had just stumbled.

She reached for her rifle and trained it on the Enforcer. "I owe you one, Maii," she said, preparing to fire.

<Morgan, wait!> protested the Box, before she could fire. <Don't shoot!>

Her finger froze on the trigger. <Why the hell not?>

<We can use the suit.>

The eye of the Enforcer's rifle began to waver. <If you think I'm getting into that thing—>

<We need a glove,> insisted the Box. <Along with its command nexus.>

<Roche?>

<Hang on, Maii.> She looked around. They were too exposed in the courtyard. Under heavy fire from below, the troop carrier had drifted, and the turbulent edge of the clear space was drawing closer—but the heavy tread of other Enforcers was too close for comfort, and the threat of fire from above was still very real. As she watched, two gun emplacements on the underside of the carrier began to swivel, targeting the source of attack below. <Can you walk him?>

The Surin nodded. <Yes, but not far. It's difficult.>

<Okay. Let's just get under cover.> She glanced around. <That building, over there. Is that too far away?>

The Surin shook her head, and the petrified Enforcer took one hesitant step forward, then another. The three of them reached the building's vacant doorway just as the storm reclaimed the area. As the howling wind descended, Roche thought she heard the Mbatan calling for her again.

<Tell Emmerik where we are,> she said to Maii. <We'll wait for him here.>

The Surin thought for a moment, then said: <He has met Veden and the others. They are trying to disable the troop carrier. He will be here as soon as he can.>

<Good.> Roche faced the Enforcer. "Now, Box, what did you have in mind?"

<Unseal the helmet. The clasps are hidden at the seal in the small of the back.>

Roche felt for the concealed tabs, found them, and pulled until they clicked. With a hiss, the helmet unsealed and fell forward, revealing the shaved head of a female Enforcer, her eyes staring vacantly. Roche raised the butt of her rifle and brought it down on the back of the Enforcer's skull, knocking her unconscious.

The suit shuddered but stayed upright, held immobile by emergency overrides.

<Now what?>

<Reach into the neck ring. There's a stud about five centimeters down, in the center. Push it.>

Roche did so, and the ceramic armor parted along invisible lines like a three-dimensional jigsaw puzzle. The slabs of armor lifted outward a centimeter, then remained in that position, awaiting her next move. The air inside stank of sweat and fear, and aging rubber seals.

With Maii's help, Roche managed to wrestle the limp Enforcer out of the suit's intimate embrace through a sliding panel in the back. The interior was black and uninviting, a nest of glistening cables and contacts with holes for limbs to pass through.

<Each glove will have a palm-link,> said the Box. <We need to get your left hand down the sleeve.>

Roche eyed the interior with distaste, but she had little choice. Slipping her left arm out of the bandages, wincing every time she moved her shoulder, she stepped into the suit. Maii slung the briefcase across her back, out of the way, and stepped back.

The moment her left hand made contact with the palm-link, the armor came to life.

<Wait!> She struggled to control the suit as it sealed around her. <I can't walk out of here like this. I'll be shot by the rebels!>

<Relax, Morgan,> said the Box. <Simply remove the helmet.>

<But the controls—>

<I can handle them, and display them via your implant.>

Roche shrugged herself into a more comfortable position and felt the armor imitate the motion. Reaching up with her gloved right hand, she ripped the helmet from its hinge on the chest-plate and threw it aside.

Taking an experimental step forward, she felt the seductive strength of the power-assist echo through her limbs. She hadn't used combat armor more than a couple of times in her career, but the old moves came back to her with ease. Although mindful not to shift her left arm more than was absolutely necessary, she began to feel confident for the first time in days.

<Okay, Box. We're in business. Where do we go?>

<Nowhere, unless you feel the need. Emmerik and the others have identified the problem succinctly: apart from the thirty to forty Enforcers on the ground, the main threat is from above. We could evade the Enforcers without the carrier clearing the air. I will attempt to neutralize that threat via the suit's command nexus.>

<Okay, you do that. In the meantime, Maii and I are going to help the others.> She swiveled to face the Surin. <Lead the way.>

Together they left the building and headed out into the storm. The Surin called out directions, using mental images of the town to find her way and her epsense abilities to target Enforcers through the dust. Four armored suits fell to Roche's percussion rifle before word of the rogue spread through the Enforcement communication network. Then the uneven rumble of the troop carrier began to grow louder again, and the dust agitated more violently than ever, stirred by the field-effects of the craft above. Maii led her away from danger, deeper into the cloud.

<We make a good team,> said the Surin at one point, and Roche, too caught up in combat to really think about what she was saying, could only agree.

They passed Cane moments later. His nimble form appeared out of the gloom, poised to strike her, but he realized who she was in time. He relaxed, made a gesture that might have been a salute but one Roche didn't recognize, and stepped back. He had acquired both a percussion rifle and a bloody gash across his forehead. His manner, although outwardly relaxed, was urgent.

"There are too many of them!" He had to shout to be heard over the sound of the troop carrier. "The others are holed up not far from here, and the big ship is on its way."

"What weapons do they have?"

"A handful of rifles. I've tried to pass on the ones I've come across, but . . ." He shrugged. "It hasn't been easy, and the charges on the ones they have won't last forever."

Roche imagined Cane flitting through the dust like a demon, reaching out of the gloom to snatch rifles from the hands of the Enforcers, then vanishing again. His major problem, as had been Roche's, was locating the others. It was all very well to have found weapons, but no use at all if he couldn't distribute them.

"Okay," she said, intending to ask him to lead the way, but getting no farther than that.

The vision through her left eye suddenly shifted, becoming clear. She blinked furiously, then realized that the Box was feeding her an external image taken from above the storm, or from a clear space within it. It showed the city not far below, moving slowly past. Armored Enforcers darted from building to building through the streets, converging on an area just inside the clear space.

With a jolt of surprise, she realized that the view was taken from one of the turret guns on the troop carrier itself.

An auxiliary view showed the airspace above the city. To her shock she saw not one flyer but five, circling the area like birds of prey, waiting for an opportunity to move in.

Furious sparks of light reached upward out of the clouds toward the troop carrier from a low building at the edge of a small courtyard. This, she assumed, was the work of the rebels. As she watched, her aerial view swiveled to focus on the building, and zoomed in to aim.

"The others are in trouble," she said, blinking the view aside for a moment to focus on the world around her. "The troop carrier's arrived. We have to hurry."

Cane nodded and moved off. "Follow me."

Roche lumbered after him, grateful for the power-assist enabling her to keep up. Maii sprinted behind, barely maintaining the pace.

<Veden's still with them,> mind-whispered the Surin. <If he is harmed, I'll never forgive them—or myself.>

<Don't worry,> said Roche, although she had little reassurance to offer in the face of such superior firepower. <We'll make it in time.>

The dust swirled around them, and the omnipresent rumble of the troop carrier reached a mind-numbing peak. Suddenly, and without warning, the three of them burst into clear air. Two Enforcers stood between them and the building, firing burst after burst at the roof where the others were hidden. Roche tackled one from behind while Cane tipped the other off balance. A third appeared from around the corner of a building, but Maii was quick to act and kept the Enforcer frozen until Cane could bring his weapon to bear.

Gasping, Roche looked around and up. The troop carrier had descended to a point not ten meters above the building. Turrets pumped powerful bolts of energy into the stone walls, sending short-lived blossoms of rock into the air. Sporadic fire lashed up at it from windows and smashed walls, as the rebels tried to fight back—but the superior weaponry of the troop carrier forced the defenders back under cover an instant later.

Behind her, two flyers swooped low over the city to lend the troop carrier support. They too concentrated their fire on the building.

Roche took one step forward, not certain what she was going to do but knowing she had to try something. Before she could fire a single shot, the Box suddenly whispered in triumph:

<Success, Morgan.>

Seconds later the troop carrier stopped firing and banked to the left, turning away from the building. Its turrets swiveled wildly, searching the earth below and the sky above. Lances of energy speared the air, striking a handful of locations in the city. Two higher bolts connected with the nearest of the two flyers, sending it spinning out of control. The high-tech arrowhead dipped low, bucked for control, then clipped an ancient building. With a shriek of engines, it crashed out of sight and exploded in a crimson and yellow fireball.

Roche watched, stunned. <Box? Are you doing this?>

<I have infiltrated the AI controlling the vessel via the command nexus of this suit, and have overridden the commands of the pilot. The troop carrier is now under my control.>

The battle below halted for a moment at the sudden reversal. Soon, though, the rebels took advantage of what must have been to them a mysterious turn of events. Firing at the Enforcers below, they began to clear the area for their escape. Likewise the underbelly turrets of the troop carrier picked out individual Enforcers, striking them from above.

Within moments, the Enforcers retaliated. The four remaining flyers swooped low to blast the treacherous troop carrier, while individual Enforcers fired from shelter underneath. The carrier was too bulky to successfully dodge the concentrated fire; only its heavy armor prevented it from being destroyed immediately. First one and then another of its underbelly turrets exploded, but not before a second flyer had been downed and perhaps ten more Enforcers shot from above.

With a bone-wrenching lurch, it ducked away, and the storm rushed into the area once more.

<They're leaving the building!> Maii cried. <I've told them what's going on—they say to meet us by the south gate.>

Roche looked around. <Do they say which way to go?>

<No need. I've constructed a map from their minds. I'll show you the way.> The lithe Surin danced off through the dust. Cane and Roche followed, the latter observing the continuing battle for control of the sky through the implant in her left eye.

Under heavy fire from the remaining flyers, the troop carrier spun in a lazy arc above the town. Its starboard flank was ablaze, and deep craters pitted its armored surface. Two of its gun turrets still functioned, however, and with these it managed to down another flyer. The heavy crunch of impact and subsequent explosion were nearly enough to make Roche stumble. The two remaining flyers darted away, then returned a moment later. Furious bolts lashed at the troop carrier's damaged flank, making it shudder. The steady rumble of its engines began to waver.

"It's going to blow!" Roche watched breathlessly as the troop carrier banked sharply to starboard, its injured side seeming to drag it down from the sky. Its remaining firepower surged at the most distant flyer, damaging it. The last one darted closer, preying on the hulk's damaged state. The rumble of the field-effect became a whine, and the troop carrier began to slow. Drifting in a sluggish circle, it passed over the area where the rebels were fleeing. The distinct dots of the dozen remaining Enforcers appeared out of the dust, doggedly pursuing the rebels. At that moment, Roche guessed what the Box was going to do and dragged the others to cover.

<Warn Veden!> Her message to the Surin was steeped in urgency. <Tell him to keep them moving as fast as they can!>

The last flyer dipped dangerously close to the troop carrier, strafing its bulk with concentrated fire. Suddenly the carrier banked again, this time swinging sharply around its center of gravity to bring its nose in line with the flyer's trajectory. With a flash of flame, the two collided, and the rumble of engines ceased altogether. Roche's view through the carrier began to fade, but not before she glimpsed the milling Enforcers rising up at her, slowly at first, but with increasing speed.

"Down!" She leapt for an open doorway, dragging Maii after her. Cane was a step ahead of them, rolling for safety within the stone walls.

With an earthshaking bellow of tortured metal, the crippled troop carrier crashed nose-first into the town. Its stricken power plant instantly exploded, enveloping everything around it in a ball of fiery heat. The shock wave flattened buildings, killed the Enforcers nearby despite their combat armor, and expanded at the speed of sound through the streets toward the building where Roche and the others had taken shelter.

The wall collapsed, and would have crushed Roche's legs but for her stolen suit. Fragments of molten metal and glowing stone rained down on the rubble. For an instant, everything was white, even through her closed eyelids. Then something else, an uncomfortable mix of panic and grief, washed through her, causing her to shudder.

<Veden? Veden!>

Roche wanted to bury her head in her hands as the cries intensified, but her position in the armor didn't allow her any movement. All she could do was lie there, pinned to the ground, screaming as Maii's hysterical anger burned ferociously, relentlessly, in her mind.

<No!>

PART THREE:

PORT PARVATI

10

DBMP *Ana Vereine*
’954.10.31 EN
1810

In the wake of the transmission from Port Parvati, a deathly silence fell.

On the main screen, a satellite view of the mountain range known as Behzad’s Wall replayed the explosion of the troop carrier in slow motion. The brilliant flash of light was followed by a billowing bubble of dust and superheated air, rising upward and obscuring the town. When it had passed, the storm once again enfolded the region. Like a blanket cast from the sky, the dust smothered the fires and enveloped the damage as though nothing had ever changed the eternal stillness of the doomed city.

“Summarize the report,” Kajic said to Atalia Makaev, when the video had finished. His hologram did not turn to face her.

“It would appear that—”

“In as few words as possible, if you please.” He kept his tone carefully controlled and even.

Makaev swallowed. “They have escaped, sir.”

“Succinctly put, Atalia.” Kajic killed the main screen and faced his second in command. “I can only be grateful that your analysis of the situation is not correct.”

Makaev frowned. “Sir, the warden’s report is quite clear.” She paused, obviously conscious that her remarks bordered on the insubordinate. “Evidence recovered from the wreckage of the lander has established that there were at least four people on board—two Pristines, an Eckandi, and possibly one Surin—yet the search team has found no traces of their bodies. The battle we have just witnessed, along with the disappearance of the recon team, strongly suggests that surface intransigents—”

“Nevertheless”—Kajic’s smooth voice washed smoothly over hers—“the fugitives have *not* escaped.”

“Sir?”

“They remain on Sciacca’s World, do they not?” The question did not require a response, nor did Kajic wait for one. “Commander Roche is obviously aware that the wardens are unsympathetic to her cause, or else she would have surrendered herself to the port upon planetfall. She must therefore know that she is unable to leave the planet by official means, and has thus allied herself with the local underground in order to escape.” Kajic smiled. “All we have to do is ensure that she cannot.”

“Naturally, but—”

“To that end,” he continued, “you will place the *Ana Vereine* in a geosynchronous orbit directly above Port Parvati. Any craft attempting to reach orbit from the landing field will be boarded and searched." He hesitated before adding, "Or destroyed in transit."

"But sir, this directly contravenes the—"

"Regardless." Kajic's image wavered slightly.

priority gold-one

"Nothing will leave Sciacca's World without our permission until the AI and the commander are in our hands. Is this clear, Atalia?" Again there was no expectation of a response, and again Makaev did not offer one. The straightening of her posture alone conveyed her understanding. "You will arrange this with Warden Delcasalle," Kajic said, "within the hour."

"The cost will be enormous," she protested.

Kajic's smile widened. "Cost is meaningless when the stakes are this high," he said. "Make sure the warden is aware of this. Let him know that I am prepared to raze the surface of Sciacca's World to slag and sift through the ruins to find that AI." He shrugged. "It is practically indestructible, after all. And this method would certainly save us a good deal of time and effort—not to mention money." Kajic's image froze momentarily, the only movement being the flicker of its light. Then: "When you have convinced him, dispatch one of our own teams to assist his incompetents in their search."

"Yes, sir. I shall lead it myself."

"No. Send Major Gyori. I prefer you here, where I can keep an eye on you."

Makaev winced slightly—which gave him some gratification—but she kept her eyes fixed upon Kajic. "As you wish, sir."

"Good. See to it immediately, then join me in the command module. I wish to speak with you privately."

Kajic let his hologram dissipate and his mind retreat from the bridge with a feeling of immense relief. The energy required to maintain a semblance of confident control had been enormous. His thoughts were in turmoil, his confidence was only an act—and these were facts he wished to keep carefully to himself, not parade in front of the bridge crew. But anyone with access to the back door in his mainframe could browse through his most intimate details at will.

With half a mind he followed the activities of his senior officers as they prepared the ship for reorientation and thrust. His virtual senses reported the firing of attitude jets and the priming of the reaction drive. The slowly changing orientation of the stars kept him occupied for several seconds. The sight was peaceful, and reminded him of his true purpose.

Where had he failed? His ship ran well; not one major system had been compromised on this, the *Ana Vereine*'s maiden voyage. And with the superior ability he possessed to study crew as well as ship, he had suffered none of the minor dissensions many new captains endured on their first command. Ship, crew, and captain were all in perfect working order, a unified system operating under his command.

Yet, to his dismay, there *was* evidence that he had failed, and it was mounting steadily. . . .

Priority C (stealth) had already been broken, and now, after the day's events, priority B had followed. Despite his denial, Roche *had* escaped from the ambush and was roaming free somewhere on the planet. She was the only person within easy reach who might be able to explain the operation and purpose of the AI, but the chances of her being captured alive were diminishing by the second, and his desperation to meet the last priority increased proportionately. If he failed at this mission, regardless how he had performed every other aspect of his mission, his command, and therefore his life, *would* be terminated. He had no doubts about that. To the Ethnarch's Military Presidium, there was only success or failure; there was nothing in between.

Priority A was all he had left to hope for now.

capture the AI

Destroying the planet to find it wasn't really an option, as far as he was concerned. Even his mission wasn't worth risking all-out war with the COE Armada, which would retaliate regardless of Port Parvati's inherent corruption. But he had no choice: whatever he did, it would *work*. He would achieve his goal and satisfy the orders written into his mind, branded onto his thoughts. What other choice did he have?

His priorities were like steel bars enclosing his free will: contemplating even the slightest deviation caused him severe mental pain. He could not disobey his superiors in the Military Presidium even to save his own life. And, to make matters worse, he would not want to. No matter how he might rationalize the alternatives, he would sacrifice his own life to meet his orders, if the situation demanded it. Where might once have been written "Do what thou wilt," now it read "*Obey* . . ."

Some minutes passed before Makaev came to meet him. When she did, he projected his image into an armchair and assumed a relaxed disposition.

"I received your message," he said without preamble. The memo had arrived just moments before the data from the warden of Port Parvati, leaving him little time to ponder it. The timing had seemed a little too unlucky, which only made him all the more anxious. "A full report, please."

"Yes, sir." Makaev remained at attention, standing with her arms at her sides in the center of the room. If what he suspected was true, she hid it well. "During your last rest period, as you instructed, I ordered a technician to examine your life support."

"And?"

She leaned over the desk to key a wall-screen. Complex schematics appeared, an endless series of lines and junctures scrolling from top to bottom. "The system matches the diagnostics in the *Ana Vereine*'s mainframe exactly, with only one exception. At the base of your brain-stem interface, there is this." The display zoomed in on one particular point, where a knot of biocircuits converged; highlighted in bold red was a denser clump, not unlike the network of fibers surrounding a dreibon root.

"The back door?" Kajic prompted.

"No, sir," said Makaev. "At least the technician doesn't believe so. The device is quite ingenious. It will lie dormant and not interfere with the overall system until it receives a coded command from an outside source." Makaev paused, her eyes suddenly restless. "Upon receiving that command, it will immediately sever all communication between your brain stem and the ship's mainframe."

"A kill-switch?" said Kajic.

"That appears to be its purpose," said Makaev. "Yes, sir."

"But who would dare sabotage a warship in such a way?" His ship—his very being—had been compromised!

"With respect, sir," Makaev said, "it is not sabotage. Although the device does not appear on the circuit diagrams we have access to, it is not an afterthought." Again she paused. "It's an integral aspect of the life support's design."

"Integral? What are you saying? That it cannot be removed without damaging the system?"

"No, sir. I'm saying that it's *supposed* to be there."

Kajic used every sense at his disposal to assure himself that she was being honest. All the data concurred: she was telling the truth. A truth that he feared, that brought his mind to a halt.

"Why?" he finally managed.

"I can hazard a guess, sir," said his second in command, then waited for him to indicate that she should continue. He did so irritably. "It makes sense, sir, if you examine the 'how' of it first. The plans for your life support were approved by the Presidium itself. If such a device was deliberately included, then the decision to do so could have come from nowhere else. As to the 'why,' well, we must remember that you are a prototype, one that has never been field-tested in genuine combat before. Who could anticipate what might happen, or how you would respond to the pressures of battle? The kill-switch must be a safeguard against command instability. Were you to become unstable at a critical moment—and I am not suggesting that you have, or will—your actions could cripple the ship. The kill-switch could then come into play, freeing the command systems for another officer to employ."

Kajic mulled it over. Yes, it made sense, and it mirrored almost exactly his first thoughts on the matter. Makaev put the case well. Too well for Kajic's liking. If she was lying, then her only fault was that she was too convincing.

"So where does the command signal come from?" he asked, following the argument to its conclusion. "And who decides whether to send the command or not?"

"One would assume, sir, that a high-ranking officer would enact that decision. Perhaps not the person who would actually assume control of the ship," she added quickly, "but someone at least who knows the truth and is in the correct position to act upon it."

"Which could be anyone from the bridge crew," he said. "Or even life support. Anyone, in fact, with access to the back door. He—or she—need not necessarily be high-ranking, either."

She nodded. "That is true."

"Nevertheless," said Kajic, "regardless who actually *gave* the order, it would be you who would assume command of the *Ana Vereine*." *Of my ship*. His unblinking image locked eyes with her, daring her to look away. *Of me*.

She nodded. "Yes, sir. It would seem that I am the most likely candidate."

"So tell me, Atalia," he said coldly, "*are* you the betrayer? Are you the one waiting for the first opportunity to strike me down?"

"If I said I wasn't, would you believe me?"

Kajic smiled, finding some pleasure in the confrontation. "I might," he said. "But I still wouldn't entirely *trust* you." He broke the locked gaze, letting his smile dissipate as he glanced again at the circuit diagram. "Perhaps I shouldn't even ask."

"Perhaps." She squared her shoulders and took a deep breath. "The only way to be sure is to watch every member of the senior crew as they go about their duties. Try to find the one who is acting suspiciously."

"That might work," he said. "But I am just like any other Pristine: I can only think one thing at a time; I am limited to one single point of view. And—"

priority gold-one

"And I have more important things to contemplate at the moment than my own personal survival."

She absorbed this in silence—perhaps with relief—and he watched her closely while she did so. How true his words were: the data he required might have been at his fingertips, but he had neither the ability nor the freedom to study it. He could feel the priorities bending his thoughts subtly back to his mission. Even now, at such a moment, he was unable to take concrete steps to save his own life. To remove or to interfere with the deadly mechanism would be to disobey the Ethnarch's Military Presidium itself.

"Atalia," he said after a moment. "This conversation will be kept between ourselves. We will continue our mission as though nothing has changed." What else *can* I do? he asked himself. The fact that the Presidium didn't fully trust him—had never trusted him—could not be allowed to interfere with his duty. Otherwise it would become a self-fulfilling prophecy—which was, perhaps, exactly what Makaev intended by telling him about the kill-switch, if she truly was the betrayer at his side. She could just as easily have lied about it to protect herself. Instead, she had thrown him off balance by sowing the seeds of distrust in his mind. . . .

"I agree, sir," she said, killing the display before them. "When we have recovered the AI and completed our mission, perhaps then we can discuss the matter in more detail."

Yes, he thought to himself, and in the meantime I have my neck on the line. The slightest mistake and—

"Atalia?"

"Sir?"

"Please reinforce with Major Gyori that our orders are to capture both the AI and its courier. I want those orders obeyed to the letter. I want Commander Roche taken *alive*." That way, he hoped, he might be able to improve his position with his superiors when the *Ana Vereine* returned from the mission.

"Yes, sir." Makaev snapped a salute and turned to leave.

"And one more thing," he said. She stopped and faced his shimmering image once again. "The investigation was to be conducted discreetly. The technician that you used—?"

"Has already been . . . transferred, sir," she said. "No one will ever know the truth."

Again Kajic studied her minutely, searching for the slightest sign of deception—and this time he thought he detected something. A tiny smile played across her lips, seeming to add silently but more evocatively than speech one single word:

Unless . . .

Kajic ignored it; better for her to think him a fool than to allow his fear to weaken his position further. "Good. You may return to your duties."

"Thank you, sir." She turned away for the final time and left the command module.

11

Sciacca's World
Port Parvati
'954.10.32 EN
0900

The orange sun rose above the horizon, casting brownish dawn-light over Port Parvati. Dull shafts crawled over the already bustling cityscape, here touching food-sellers arranging their produce in preparation for the day's business, there catching artisans dusting their wares. The light crept with casual sureness into dusty streets and garbage-strewn alleys, melting pockets of shadow that had gathered in the night and waking the few remaining curb-sleepers that had yet to join the growing throng.

Even at this early hour, business was brisk. The sound of complaining machinery was nearly drowned by a rising hubbub of bargaining and arguments. And over that, the constant arrhythmic chug of the truck that carried Roche and her party through the streets.

At first, Roche watched the proceedings going on around her with indifference. Then, as they moved through the streets and various marketplaces, she found herself succumbing to a profound melancholy—one she saw reflected in the faces of the people bustling around their truck.

If Port Parvati had been a city on any other planet, Roche thought, it would have been demolished years ago: flattened, pulped, and turned into artificial topsoil fit for treading on and little more.

There was also an unpleasant smell about the place—something other than the stench of sewage occasionally spilling from the inadequate drain system, or that of rotting food rising from the dirty market stalls. The air was thick with it, lingering through all the streets they passed along, strong enough even to penetrate the fumes issuing from the methane-fueled engine of their vehicle. It was with some revulsion that Roche suddenly realized what that smell was: disease.

"Destroyed," Roche muttered to herself, "*and* burned."

Emmerik leaned forward from his place on the flatbed to speak. "What was that?" He raised his voice to be heard above the noise of the truck.

Roche shook her head. "How much further?"

"About five minutes." The Mbatan raised a hand to shield his eyes from the sun and turned to bang on the cab of the truck. The truck suddenly veered down a narrow alleyway. Emmerik cursed aloud, steadying Roche. The abrupt turn unbalanced her before the armor's built-in overrides could react. The truck's suspension had needed an overhaul about twenty years ago, Roche thought; now, suspension was the least of its worries.

When their trajectory steadied, Roche turned her attention once more to the goings-on beyond the truck. This particular section of the city they were passing through appeared dirtier and more cluttered than other parts. The streets were certainly narrower and grimier, the dwellings often low and shabby. Wide and jutting verandahs shaded dark interiors from which dirty faces glanced briefly as they passed. Others paused upon the flimsy walkways that now and then arced between buildings, their solemn expressions enhancing the already growing melancholy that Roche was feeling.

Most of the people, she noted, were Pristine—but not all. The penal colony held all manner of nonviolent criminals, from habitual thieves to industrial conspirators, from Olmahoi to Hurn. Yet all looked the same beneath the universal garments of cheap robes and wide-brimmed hats, as dictated by environment and limited resources rather than fashion. Roche herself had donned similar garb to cover the combat armor. From a distance, she hoped, she would pass as a skinny Mbatan.

She ran her hands over the coarse and threadbare garment and frowned. "How the hell can people live like this?"

Despite the noise, Emmerik seemed to have heard her. "Ninety percent of the population lives here, Commander," he said. "But it's not as if we have any choice. There just isn't anywhere else."

<This is true, Morgan.> The Box's voice was clear beneath all the noise from the street. <With the planet's population of convicts and Enforcement staff, Port Parvati remains the capital and sole large settlement. Apart from the ruins of places like Houghton's Cross, there is nowhere else for them to go.>

<Couldn't they build—?>

<Yes, although the question of whether the inhabitants *want* to better their planet or not becomes an issue. The fact is, the authorities prefer it this way. It is easier to maintain order. The greater the number of towns, the more difficult security becomes.>

Roche nodded to herself, leaning away from Emmerik. Indeed, as she watched the crowd milling through the dusty streets, she realized that security was lighter than she had expected—and feared. Only infrequently did an Enforcement patrol serve to remind her that this was a supervised penal base, not one of the poorer COE planets.

Waving a hand to ward off the stench of a herd of vat-bred cattle, she looked back to Emmerik. Even his eyes seemed slightly more moist than usual in the high air of the city.

"Is all of Port Parvati like this?" she said.

He shook his head. "These are just the outskirts. Like any other city, we have varying standards."

The truck lurched again as it took another sharp corner. This time Roche was prepared, and the suit kept her balanced. When their motion had steadied somewhat, she glanced under the makeshift canopy tied over the truck's flatbed. The stretcher hadn't been disturbed by the sudden turn, and the Eckandi's face expressed no more distress than it had at any stage of their journey so far. Strapped to the Mbatan's back through the old mines honeycombing the mountains beneath Houghton's Cross, by petroleum-powered, propeller-driven airplane to one of Port Parvati's many makeshift airfields, passing through a casual security check (with the aid of several small bribes in a currency unfamiliar to Roche), then onto the truck for the penultimate leg of their journey—he had remained unconscious throughout it all, oblivious to the rough plaster encasing his head and the distressed Surin constantly at his side.

"How's he doing, Maii?" Roche asked, concerned as much for the reave as she was for her friend.

The girl didn't respond at first. Her posture hardly shifted. But Roche could tell that she had heard—by the subtle change of the girl's sullen expression, the way her head tilted ever so slightly to face Roche.

After a moment, the Surin's quiet voice filtered through the noise of traffic and animals into Roche's mind: <I can still feel him. He's deep—very deep. He has retreated to somewhere I can't reach him. Somewhere he can heal.>

Or die, Roche added to herself, forgetting that the reave could read the thought if she wanted. The shrapnel from the downed troop carrier that had struck Veden on the back of the head required delicate nanosurgery, not stubborn, blind denial. If she heard, however, Maii didn't contradict her.

Turning back to Emmerik, Roche picked up the conversation where it had left off. "You work underground here, too?"

The Mbatan spoke without taking his eyes from the road. "The city is built on the ruins of the original port. When the Commonwealth moved in, they decided it was cheaper to build over than rebuild. So that's what they did," he said. "And continue to do. The original city is buried under layer after layer of later settlements, but it's still intact in places." He grinned wryly. "The Dominion built well."

Roche nodded. Houghton's Cross was testament to that. "So you moved in?"

"The founders of our movement did. Some of the survivors of Ul-æmato had maps of the original city, and it was a simple matter to work out what had been what under the new surface." Emmerik faced Roche now, wiping at the dust around his eyes. "All it took was some digging equipment, a little patience, and a lot of care to keep the work hidden from the wardens. Whole sections of the original maglev subway were intact, although the tunnels had cracked open in a few places. The rubbish that had filtered down was cleared out, and there we had it—a means of crossing the city without being seen by the wardens. There are buildings dotted all over the city that act as entrances to the tunnels: little more than empty facades hiding their true purpose. Gain access to one of these and you can go almost anywhere."

"That's a major achievement," she said, studying him closely. When he went to look away again, she quickly added, "But why are you telling me about this now? Why the sudden trust?"

"I've always trusted you," he said soberly. "But your involvement with Cane made me a little apprehensive." The Mbatan shrugged wearily. "The difference now is that we need your help as much as you need ours. And the only way to begin helping each other is by talking—as equals."

"Trade secrets, you mean?" she said, glancing over her shoulder to where Cane was riding on the tail of the flatbed, his eyes constantly scanning the crowd.

"I was thinking more of your AI," put in the Mbatan. "I had no idea it was so powerful."

Roche turned back to him and offered a fleeting smile. "Neither did I, to be honest."

Emmerik grunted deep in his throat. The exhalation might have been a laugh, although his face displayed no amusement. "It's running the suit, isn't it?" he said.

Roche nodded. "Through the data glove."

"For that function alone it is valuable. Any advanced weaponry is priceless here."

Roche immediately understood what he was hinting at: the Dato wouldn't be the only ones interested in getting their hands on the AI. But what Emmerik almost certainly failed to realize was that without her—without her palm-link, her implants—the Box's value was reduced to zero. Without her in the driver's seat, the armor was little more than dead metal, and the Box a useless valise.

When she explained this to the Mbatan, he only smiled and said:

"*I* understand this, but there are others who won't. Take care to emphasize your own worth as much as the assets you bring with you. I am not typical of the bulk of our group, Commander."

She nodded, taking his warning to heart. Whether he was referring to Haid himself or just those surrounding him, it didn't matter. That the threat was real was enough for now. She would keep her guard up.

Moments later the truck swung into a sheltered garage and shuddered to a noisy halt. The rebels clambered out of the cab and off the flatbed and began to unload the truck. Emmerik joined them, leaving Roche to make her own way down. The bulky armor took the short drop with ease, thudding to the concrete floor like a lump of lead. Cushioned within, her injured shoulder was barely disturbed by the jar of impact.

She brushed some of the ubiquitous dust from her cloak and turned to help Cane with Veden's stretcher. One on each end, they swung it down and placed it against the far wall. Barely had they put it down when two unfamiliar rebels appeared through a door leading deeper into the building and spirited him away.

Maii, when she tried to follow, was politely but firmly rebuffed. Roche moved to comfort her, but the girl shrugged her away.

"You have medical facilities here, Emmerik?" said Roche.

The Mbatan paused in the middle of unloading the truck to look at her. "Some."

"How sophisticated?"

"I don't know," he said. "It's not my field."

"He'll need X-rays, CAT and QIP scans, nanosurgery if you have it—"

"We'll do what we can, Roche," he cut in sharply, more calmly adding, "*When* we can. Okay?" He returned to his work without another word.

Feeling impotent, Roche tried to find something to do. Two of the rebels were struggling with a large crate of projectile weapons retrieved from the ruins of their headquarters in Houghton's Cross. With the power-assists of the armor, she took the crate from them and placed it with others along one wall, then turned to do the same with the rest of the crates on the truck. The warning from Emmerik still rung in her mind; the more she could do to gratify herself to the locals, the better.

<I too have the original plans of the old port,> put in the Box unexpectedly, harking back to her conversation with the Mbatan. <We are approximately five kilometers from the current landing field, on the site of what was once a large university. The maglev network divides into three major routes not far from here. A good location for headquarters.>

Roche grunted, only half listening. <Do your files say anything about current security arrangements?>

<No, but I am still patched into the DAOC combat network through the suit.>

Roche put down the crate she was carrying. This was interesting. <Really? I thought they would've scrambled transmissions after you—>

<I took the precaution of erasing any record of my intrusion from all databases connected with the assault on Houghton's Cross. The only people aware of my intrusion were onboard the troop carrier; I was careful to prevent information being transmitted by radio at the time and, naturally, the people themselves are now dead. Therefore, DAOC is ignorant of my intrusion in its systems.>

<And?> Roche prompted when the Box fell silent. <What have you learned?>

<Surprisingly little of any importance. I can only access information and routines stored in a buffer accessible by combat computers and decentralized planning systems. Unfortunately the main work is done by the MiCom processing center in the landing field, which is quite separate. The combat network is updated hourly from this processor.>

<What does it say about us?>

<That there is a price on your head, Morgan. A high price, too. To be taken alive, if possible.>

<Only me? What about Cane and Veden and Maii? Hell, what about *you*?>

<The only person described in the bulletin is 'Morgan Roche,' no rank. You are said to be armed and in league with indigenous forces. Which, I suppose, means that you were seen with other people, and that, for some reason, it was determined that these others met you here rather than came with you from the *Midnight*.>

<How do they explain the troop carrier, then?>

<They do not. It would seem that Warden Delcasalle has no knowledge of either my existence or my capabilities.>

<That makes two of us,> she said, thinking of the way the Box had saved them at Houghton's Cross.

"Roche?"

Startled by the sudden intrusion on the conservation, Roche realized that she was standing stock-still in the middle of the garage, staring off into space. Feeling foolish, she turned to face the woman who had spoken. Cropped blonde hair, a sour face, and grey eyes stared back at her.

"You Roche?"

"I am." She automatically glanced around for the others and found Cane and Maii on the far side of the garage. Cane's eyes scanned the proceedings with his usual attention to detail; the Surin was motionless.

"Haid wants you out of that armor before he'll let you down. There's a cubicle and a change of clothes out back."

Roche flexed her fingers in the power-gloves. Although the armor had increased her sense of well-being for a while, she would be glad to be rid of it, if only temporarily. Sweat had pooled in the suit's crevices, making her entire body feel oily. "Any chance of a shower?"

The woman nodded reluctantly. "If you have to," she said. "But don't waste the water."

The woman walked through the door at the rear of the garage, and Roche followed, careful not to bump anything with the armor's wide shoulders. The corridor was narrow and cluttered with boxes. Some of them contained weapons similar to the ones they had brought back from Houghton's Cross; most seemed to contain provisions of a more harmless sort: food, clothes, medicinal supplies, and the like.

Although the Enforcement government allowed the inhabitants of the penal colony free rein over their internal affairs, they obviously kept a heavy hand on potentially dangerous matters, such as technology and communications. Thus far, the most sophisticated weapon Roche had seen in the hands of the rebels was a projectile rifle, and the most powerful engine one powered by petroleum. By thus keeping the population at a level barely approximating civilized, DAOC ensured that its relatively small but well-equipped force was more than capable of keeping the peace. Armed with nothing but pellet guns and cow-shit trucks, the rebels wouldn't last a moment against the landing field's defenses.

Yet somehow they had fashioned an extensive underground network capable of some small resistance. Utilizing the only assets available to them—ruins, untamed wilderness, and people—they had at least given themselves a chance. All they needed, she thought, was one even break, and they'd become dangerous. And, like all dangerous resistance movements, they'd probably be wiped out at the first opportunity.

Roche tried to rid herself of the thought, concentrating instead on her own problems.

The cubicle at the end of the corridor was half as large as the compartment Roche had occupied on the *Midnight*. A small toilet facility, including a shower, had been curtained off in one corner. There seemed to be no surveillance equipment or hidden entrances, just the door through which she had entered.

"Thanks," Roche said. "I owe you one already."

"I'll send the Surin girl through when you're finished."

"No, wait." Roche stopped the woman before she could leave. "I'd like to see her now, if possible. Don't worry," she added when the woman frowned, suspicious. "We're not going anywhere."

The woman shrugged and left the room. Roche waited a moment, then returned her attention to the Box.

<You heard what she said. We have to leave the suit behind. I don't think they plan to steal it.>

<Not that they could use it anyway,> said the Box. <Besides, it isn't important right now. I believe I have gathered enough information from DAOC for the time being.>

<Good. So unseal this thing and get me out of here.>

The armor hissed, split along its seams, and allowed her to wriggle free. The pain in her shoulder was muted, manageable, as her arm slipped out of the padded sleeve. The touch of fresh air on her exposed skin made her groan with relief.

The blonde woman arrived with Maii as Roche began the difficult process of extricating herself from the sweat-stained and torn remains of her Armada uniform.

The woman pointed at a small pile by the door. "Change of clothes. You're about my size, so they should fit. You'll find a towel in the shower." With that, she left Roche and the reave alone.

"Do you want a shower?"

Maii shrugged.

Roche took the hint and began to peel off her uniform, not bothering to hide herself from the blind Surin. Her skin was red where the suit had rubbed, and crusted with dirt where it hadn't. She doubted that even an hour in a gehan mineral spa followed by a complete body scrub could make her feel clean, but a brief rinse certainly wouldn't hurt.

The curtained-off area contained a small handheld nozzle and a recessed basin. Standing in the basin, with the valise resting just outside, she switched on the nozzle and gasped as a fan of cold water sprayed her thigh. Directing the jet across the entirety of her body, she did her best to clean herself, relishing the feel of the cool water.

She examined her skin as she washed, noting a variety of multicolored bruises she hadn't previously been aware of. The purple-yellow blotch enveloping her left shoulder was beginning to fade, but still spread down to her breast and as far back as she could see. The joint itself was tender to the touch, and, she noted, swapping the nozzle over to her left hand, stiff. Her right side was relatively intact, apart from a couple of grazes. The water washed across the smooth line of her muscles, down her hips and thighs, curling between her toes, its caress gentle and soothing. She could have stayed within the intimate embrace of the water indefinitely, but she kept in mind the woman's warning and, after one last scrub at her stubbled scalp, clicked off the nozzle and reached for the towel. Water was scarce on the planet, and doubly so in the port itself.

While drying herself off, she stepped from behind the curtain to find Maii standing in exactly the same position she had been minutes earlier.

"You look lost," she said, with feeling. The girl seemed so small and helpless that, despite years of programming to loathe reaves, she wanted to reach out and hug the child.

<Without Veden, I am nothing.> She shuddered gently. <He is my eyes, my ears. . . . > Roche could feel something else there also, but Maii managed to suppress the thought; her words in Roche's mind trailed into an uncomfortable silence.

"By yourself, you must feel terrible." Roche wondered at the depth of the girl's attachment to her ward. It seemed more than just the bond of friendship, and yet less than a physical attachment. Could the Surin and Eckandi Castes mate? It was not something she had ever heard of before.

<It is not a common practice.> There was annoyance in the reave's tone. <The Agora has forbidden it.>

"Then . . ." Roche wasn't quite sure what to say. From what she remembered of Maii's memories, the reave held the main governing body of the Surin Caste in no high regard. "Listen, if you and Veden are lovers or whatever . . ."

<We're not,> she cut in with indignation.

"Okay." Roche finished toweling herself dry, then turned to the pile of clothes. The loose outfit of brown cotton pants and shirt the woman had provided was slightly baggy, but comfortable enough. She tucked her left arm under the shirt, keeping it pressed against her stomach. The valise's cable dangled around her waist like a belt.

Turning back to Maii, she said: "We're in no hurry, it seems. Why not have a shower? It'll take your mind off things for a moment."

<I can't.>

"Why not?"

<Because I can't see.>

"You—" Roche did a mental double take. "What's wrong with my eyes?"

<You don't like me to use them,> said Maii. <And I respect that.>

Roche frowned. "But—"

<You regard it as theft. I haven't touched your mind for information since Houghton's Cross. You tried to help me there, and for that I am in your debt. At the moment, respecting your feelings is the only way I have to honor that debt.>

"So whose eyes have you been using?"

<Cane's, when he lets me. But his will is stronger than yours, and I am unable to read him without his noticing. Sometimes I use the rebels. Most often, I just wait.>

"For Veden."

Maii was silent. Grief radiated from her small form and into Roche's mind.

She sighed. "Look, Maii. You're exhausted, you need rest, and I don't know how long it's been since you slept. You *need* that shower. It'll make you feel better, if only for a while." Roche hesitated, then forged on. "You can use my eyes, if you want."

<Do you mean that?>

"You can check, if you like."

The reave didn't say anything for a moment, then sighed. <Thank you, Morgan. I know how much this disturbs you.>

"Yes, well, this time it won't be theft, but a gift." She paused. "Besides, we kind of need each other right now."

<You see yourself as alone also, don't you?>

Roche shrugged, knowing that, having let the reave into her head, she could no longer hide her feelings from the girl. "Just have a shower. We'll talk about it later."

Maii nodded and slipped out of her tunic and blindfold. Leaving the curtain open, she climbed into the basin and used the nozzle to clean her skinny body. Roche tried not to feel squeamish, and forced herself to keep her eyes on the girl as she washed.

Not "girl," she reminded herself. Not as she knew one to be. Naked, there was no mistaking the peculiar physiology before her for that of a Pristine: the graceful skeleton, with its high rib cage; the dark, protruding nipples; the stump of a vestigial tail protruding from the cleft between narrow, corded buttocks; the fine, ginger hair—not fur—that uniformly covered the Surin's body except at groin and armpits, exactly the reverse of Pristine hair. Girlish in form, but Exotic in detail.

As her eyes became accustomed to the sight, Roche noticed the fine network of scars across Maii's scalp. Whoever had operated on her—the rogue doctor unnamed in Maii's memories—had performed an intricate operation to convert the child into a fully functioning epsense adept. Exactly how it had been achieved, Maii did not remember, and Roche had never heard of the practice before. The moral question it raised may have forced the Surin Agora to ban the process while it was still in development, and thereby driven the doctor underground, where he had procured experimental subjects from the poor or the unscrupulous.

Children, all of them, too young to choose.

When Maii finished her brief shower, she climbed out of the basin and used the towel Roche had discarded to dry. Then she clambered back into her old shipsuit and smoothed the hair on her hands and scalp.

<Thank you,> she said. <You were right: I did need it.>

"That's okay." Roche glanced at the door. "Maybe you should call the woman—"

<Her name is Sabra, and she is Haid's assistant.>

"—Sabra, then, to let her know we're ready."

Maii nodded. Roche took a seat on a box in one corner of the room to rest while she waited. The enormous bulk of the armor dominated the center of the tiny room, like a statue of a dirty, beheaded giant. Old but still reliable, it had served her and the Box well during her brief occupation, and she regretted leaving it behind. If discussions went well with Haid, she promised herself, she would retrieve it later.

<It needs a name,> said Maii, eavesdropping on Roche's surface thought.

Roche nodded. "Any suggestions?"

<Only the one you're thinking of.>

Roche smiled to herself. Yes, it was appropriate.

"Okay. 'Proctor' it is. Here's hoping it gives us better luck than its previous owner."

<Which? The armor or the name?>

Roche laughed aloud at this. "Both."

A security card gained them entry to an unfurnished office at the back of the building, stained from years of neglect. Sabra stepped up to a sliding door set in one corner of the room and punched a code into a keypad. The metal door shuddered for a moment but failed to open. Without complaint, Sabra repeated the sequence. On the third attempt, the door finally opened with a slight hiss. Beyond was an elevator. The woman ushered Roche, Maii, and Cane inside. With a rattle and grind of machinery, the carriage and its four passengers dropped downward.

"Where are you taking us?" asked Cane.

"Downstairs," said Sabra. Her reticence could have been natural or cultivated; either way, it showed no signs of abating.

"The port is riddled with old tunnels and chambers," said Roche, "left over from the early colonial days, before the Ataman Theocracy and COE invasions. Everyone knows they're here, but no one apart from the resistance uses them; they're supposed to be unsafe. According to the Box, this section used to be a university. The resistance rebuilt it, and now uses it as a headquarters." She smiled sweetly at Sabra, who returned her gaze with obvious dislike. "And that's where we're going. To meet Haid, right?"

The woman shrugged. "Right enough."

Their journey ended with a stomach-wrenching jerk. When the door slid open, it revealed a narrow, ill-lit passageway. Sabra nudged them forward, then sealed the lift behind them. Poorly maintained gears groaned as the carriage slowly returned to the surface.

"This way," said Sabra, and headed down the corridor.

They passed through a security scanner and a corridor lined with a dozen locked doors, then entered a dimly lit chamber containing nothing but a wide wooden desk and five chairs. Behind the desk and its compulsory computer facility sat the most profoundly black man Roche had ever seen. His skin was as dark as that of an Olmahoi, with a similar bluish sheen. He was hairless, which only accentuated the color of his skin. One eye stared at them from behind an ocular lens—held permanently in place millimeters above the eye by microfilaments embedded in bone. The other was nothing but glass. His left arm, resting on the desk, lifted as they entered the room to gesture at the chairs.

"My name is Ameidio Haid," said the man. His voice was warm, patient, and solid. "I'm sorry to have kept you waiting."

Roche nodded, accepting the apology for what it was: a formality. She settled gratefully into an armchair, the upholstery of which was ripped in various places. Cane sat to her immediate left, Maii to her right. Sabra stood to one side of the desk, unobtrusive but undeniably present. Under the dim light above the desk, Roche could see deep scars etched in Haid's cheeks and temples. Not injuries, she noted, but surgery. Given the hollow look of his face, she suspected that items had been removed, not implanted.

Or perhaps, she thought, remembering DAOC's stern restrictions on technology, *confiscated.*

"I was beginning to wonder if you even existed," said Roche. When he smiled at this, she said, "It's good to finally talk to you face to face."

Haid's laugh was mellow, natural. He would have been an attractive man if not for his injuries. "I'm pleased to be able to say the same about you, Commander Roche. Only two days on the planet, and you're already something of a legend."

"Unintentionally, I assure you."

"If you say so. Although it is difficult to imagine how one could wipe out an entire squadron of DAOC personnel by accident."

Roche smiled now. "What I meant was, it wasn't my intention to become involved."

"No?" asked Haid. "Then what exactly was your intention?"

"To stay alive," she said. "And to complete my mission, of course."

"Ah, yes. Your mission." Haid leaned back in his seat, all business. "You have mentioned this to a number of my people but have neglected to *define* it even once." Haid raised an eyebrow. "I find this oversight slightly unnerving."

Roche said nothing, conflicting desires warring within her. She needed to tell him to gain his trust, but needed to trust him before she could tell him. There was no easy way out of the dilemma.

As though reading her thoughts, Haid said, "I understand your reluctance, Commander Roche. I am in a similar bind. As director of this small covert operation, I am honor-bound to follow its interests before my own. You could be a great boon to us, but you might also be a great threat. Perhaps only time will tell which you are."

He folded his hand into his lap. "I therefore suggest that we ignore the matter of your mission for the time being, and concentrate on other issues. DAOC security, for one. You are fleeing from them. Why?"

"Because they are corrupt. I was a passenger on the Armada ship destroyed two nights ago—"

"Yes, we saw the explosion. Local news reported it as a mining accident."

"It wasn't. The *Midnight* was ambushed by Dato ships during its approach through the Soul. We barely escaped with our lives by pretending to be debris flung from the wreckage. When we crashed on the planet, Enforcement attempted to capture us. The obvious conclusion is that the wardens are collaborating with the Dato Bloc."

"Treason?"

"Yes," said Roche. "In exchange for money."

"This planet encourages a mercenary attitude. It has, after all, little else to offer."

Haid seemed amused by the squabbles that had impinged upon his immediate life. "So close to the Dato border, such a security compromise would seem inevitable—or at least possible. That begs the question: what were you doing here in the first place? If you or what you're carrying is so valuable, why place it in such an unnecessarily risky position?"

Roche considered the alternatives for a long moment before eventually replying: "Cover."

Haid nodded, then smiled. "Cover you still seek to maintain. Understood. But tell me, why is it that when you speak of your escape from the ship you refer to 'we,' not 'I'?"

Roche glanced at Cane, who kept his stare fixed upon Haid. "I'm carrying an AI," she said. "That was my only companion before my escape. The others came with me by chance."

"Really? Veden and Maii I was expecting. The other, however, is a complete unknown." Turning to Cane, he tapped his teeth with his fingertips. They made a soft clinking noise, as though his fingers were made of plastic, not flesh.

Cane returned his steady gaze without blinking.

"You look like a soldier," said Haid. "Are you an Armada officer?"

"I have no allegiance to the Commonwealth of Empires."

"A bounty hunter, then? Or a mercenary?"

"No."

"A spy?"

"No."

"Then what are you? You're not a transportee, I can tell that much."

"I don't know what I am. A refugee, perhaps."

"I find it difficult to imagine what you would be seeking refuge *from*." Haid smiled. "Emmerik describes your strength with some awe. Yet you expect me to believe that it is simply a natural ability?"

"He was pulled from a survival capsule before we jumped to the Hutton-Luu System," Roche said. "He has no memory of the time before then. Just his name. If you don't believe me, ask Maii."

"Oh, I will." Haid's eyes didn't shift from his examination of Cane. The reave herself made no sound. "Interesting," Haid continued, still talking to Cane. "If you aren't with the Armada, why are you on Roche's side?"

Cane shrugged. "Expediency. It seemed appropriate when I first met her, and still does."

"A natural soldier with no orders, no past, latching onto the first officer he comes across? Is that the whole truth?"

"Yes." Cane's voice was even and unfazed.

Haid rolled his eyes. "I'm sorry. I'll need more than that. The stories are too wild for me to believe without evidence. Will you submit to a physical examination?"

Cane glanced at Roche, who nodded. This coincided with her own desire to find out more about Cane—and his origins.

"Good. Now we're getting somewhere." Haid leaned forward to run his hand along the edge of his desk. "I must admit, though, you make me nervous. You arrive on this planet, possibly the most potent task force I've ever seen, and refuse to answer my questions. I'm sure you can appreciate my frustration."

Roche frowned. "Are you suggesting—?"

"Cane with his natural strength and combat abilities, Maii with her mind power, your AI's apparent ability to manipulate the systems of hostile parties, and you, perhaps the leader and coordinator—how could I not be nervous with you sitting on the other side of my desk?"

"If we wanted to overthrow you, or infiltrate you, we could have made a move by now, and you know it. Besides, you *invited* Maii and Veden here."

"True." He said this thoughtfully. "Did they tell you why?"

"No."

"Can you guess?"

"Something to do with Maii's talents and Veden's negotiating skills, I imagine. I'm assuming you're not planning to control Warden Delcasalle directly." She shrugged lightly. "That's all I've managed to work out so far."

Haid smiled. "Emmerik trusts you. He told you about the need for a High Equity Court hearing to discuss our ownership of this planet. If Maii still won't tell you after this meeting, then that's the only clue I'll give you."

Roche sighed. She could understand his position, but that didn't mean she liked it. She was sick of fighting for every step and meeting obstacles everywhere she turned. Most of all, she lacked Cane's apparently indefatigable patience.

"Okay," said Haid, obviously tiring of letting the conversation wander, "here's the way it stands. You have to convince me, A, that I can help you without putting myself at risk, and B, that I *should* help you in the first place. You have to tell me what you want, then we'll negotiate."

"Fair enough." She paused for a moment to gather her thoughts. "I need to send a message to my superiors in Intelligence HQ informing them of the situation in Port Parvati."

"How do you propose to do that?"

"By gaining access to a high-power hyperspace transmitter, preferably one with encryption facilities."

"Relatively simple, it seems." Haid's fingers tapped a tune out upon the table. "Problem number one: there is only one such transmitter on Sciacca's World, and that belongs to the wardens. Problem number two: the only access to it is from within the landing field itself, well out of harm's way inside the MiCom installation. Three: even if you could get in, how do you expect to override the security systems designed to prevent such unauthorized transmissions? Four: you'll need my help to get at it, and I'm not yet convinced you deserve it."

"One and two we can deal with later," Roche responded, "when you give us more information. Four is up to you to decide. Three is this."

Rising to her feet in one smooth motion, she raised the battered valise and slammed it onto the desk. Haid jumped back involuntarily, and Sabra reached into her tunic and quickly withdrew a pistol. Before she had a chance to react, however, Cane had also risen from his chair and kicked the weapon from the woman's hand.

Haid's sudden shock evaporated just as quickly when his eyes settled upon the valise Roche had placed before him. "The AI, I presume," he said.

Sabra, nursing her hand, collected her pistol and, at Haid's instruction, slid it beneath her tunic. Only then did Cane return to his own seat.

Roche reached across the desk for the computer terminal and placed her hand on the palm-link.

"Box? Go to work."

A moment later, an artificial voice spoke from the terminal itself.

"Communications established. Nice work, Morgan. You have placed us right into the heart of the resistance. Very well done indeed."

Another look of concern briefly crossed Haid's black face, but it quickly yielded to curiosity. "This is the device you used to take control of the Enforcement vessel over Houghton's Cross?"

"With it," said Roche, "we can do whatever we like to the wardens, once we get in."

"Which explains why they want you." Haid nodded. "Did you steal it?"

"Nothing so dramatic. I was carrying it back to Intelligence HQ when the Dato ambushed us here."

"But how did the Dato know you were coming?" he asked. "Or expect to get away with it?"

"Courtesy of the wardens, as I said. They're as corrupt as hell. I can't hand it over to them—they'll just sell it to the Dato Bloc—so I've got to call for help. Which means getting into the landing field. And that's where *you* come in."

"Perhaps." Haid knitted his fingers together and leaned back in the chair. "Go on."

"If we can signal the Armada, they can send reinforcements."

"Perhaps you can even get off-planet first, and *then* signal for help."

"Impossible," interrupted the Box.

"Oh?" Haid leaned forward. "It would seem to be the safest option. It would avoid having to hold the landing field until reinforcements arrive."

"Not under the circumstances," the Box continued. "The Dato have imposed a blockade on Sciacca's World. Any unauthorized and uninspected departures will be shot down before reaching orbit."

"How do you know that?" Haid regarded the valise with suspicion.

"Your information network has failed to penetrate the wardens' higher security, but it does have access to the landing field's flight schedule. All flights have been canceled or severely delayed pending Morgan's capture."

Haid's smile tightened. "Drastic steps," he said. "This changes everything. Perhaps you're more trouble than you're worth."

"Your options are limited," said Roche. "You could kill us, or try to. You saw how we dealt with the Enforcement squadron; could you do any better? Or you could let us go and risk us being captured."

"I have copied your security files," added the Box. "My capture would mean the complete and utter destruction of everything you have built."

Haid paled at this. "Or I agree to help you."

"Precisely," cooed the Box.

Haid rubbed his hand across his chin. "But what's in it for me? How do I benefit? Apart from not being destroyed, I mean."

"I can help you attack the wardens," said Roche. "They are corrupt, the enemies of both of us. They deserve to be brought to justice."

"So you'll get a medal, and I'll get—what?"

"Revenge, at least," said Roche. "I'm hardly in a position to promise a reduction in your sentence."

"That's not what I want." Haid's sigh was deep and thoughtful, but his good humor was returning. "I never thought I'd hear an Armada officer swearing revenge on her fellows."

"I never thought I'd be doing it myself." Roche nodded and stepped away from the desk, severing contact with the palm-link. "But they're not my fellows, and I'd appreciate it if you wouldn't associate me with them."

"I'll try to remember." Haid glanced at Sabra, who was still rubbing at her hand where Cane had kicked it. His one good eye crinkled with amusement. "Well, you have me fascinated, Commander Roche. I was just about ready to turn you in when you arrived, but you've convinced me to reconsider.

"I suggest we all need time to think about our positions. Not long, though. If the Dato become impatient, who knows what they'll do?" Haid stood. "We'll meet again in six hours. Sabra, please show our guests to somewhere they can rest. Instruct Sylvester Teh to conduct an examination of Cane as soon as possible. And there may be other minor injuries requiring attention."

The sour-faced woman nodded briskly but said nothing.

"Wait," said Roche. "What about Veden? What's happening to him?"

"He's undergoing surgery. Our physician has been discussing his case with Maii while we talked. She can keep you updated in her own time." Haid held out his hand to her. "But thanks for asking. I'm relieved to see your concern for your companions, even for those that wish you harm."

Roche took the resistance leader's hand. The feel of his fingers convinced her of what she had suspected: the limb was artificial. Now that she saw him standing, she also realized that his other arm was missing entirely.

Haid noted the direction of her gaze. "Perhaps, when we meet again, we can exchange stories."

Roche held his monocled stare. "Perhaps."

With a slow-lidded wink, Haid bowed and left the room.

12

Sciacca's World
Port Parvati
'954.10.32 EN
1795

The hill was bald, stony, and round. A fringe of grey, long-stemmed grass ringed its base, lending it a striking resemblance to an Eckandi's skull. The view was extensive, even though the summit wasn't particularly high, with uniformly flat plains leading to a knife-edge horizon in every direction. The cold blue of the sky was dotted with small islands of cloud, and between them glimmered a handful of nearby stars that defied the light of the weak, white sun.

As she stood there watching through another's eyes, the largest of these stars, Kabos, winked once, twice, and then went out.

She buried her hands into the deep pockets of her thick overcoat and sighed.

"Child, we have been working together for . . . how long?"

She turned out of politeness to face the owner of the voice, and saw herself echo the movement through his eyes. <Five years,> she said.

"And in all that time, have I ever betrayed you?"

She hesitated, even though there was no doubt in her mind. <Never.>

The Eckandi nodded. "Not once."

<No.> Not for the first time, she cursed the fact that she couldn't see his face when they were alone. <Why won't you tell me what has happened?>

"Because nothing *has* happened—yet. I—" He stopped. For a moment the only sound was that of the wind whipping across the skull of the hill. "I've been struck from the Commerce Artel," he said at last, the words a long, slow exhalation of shame.

She gasped, despite herself. <But—>

"No, let me finish. It gets worse." She waited, wondering how it *could* get worse. "Remember that offer we had from the Hutton-Luu System? The job we refused?"

<Petty criminals on a petty penal colony, you said. Too hard to get in, impossible to get out. You said I was too valuable to risk on such a small-time deal.>

"Well, the Axis felt otherwise." She could sense the discomfort swell beneath his words. "They advised me to take it. What with this" —he waved vaguely at the now-invisible star—"they said I need to prove myself again; that I had to *demonstrate* to them that I still have what it takes."

<But you can't be blamed for *this*,> she protested. <The generator was faulty. It could have happened to any—>

"But it didn't," he cut in. "It happened to *me*." He paused before continuing, his breath catching in the sudden breeze. "Anyway, when I refused to comply to their 'recommendation,' they stripped me of my rank, ordered criminal proceedings to begin, and charged me with first-degree fraud."

She shuddered at this: fraud was the most serious crime a delegate of the Commerce Artel could be accused of. In their books, not even murder rated above *bad business*.

<So what happens now?>

"The COE transport arrives in a week." He laughed his wheezing, exotic laugh while she struggled to take in what he was saying. "That's right. I'm to be transported to the penal colony as a convict. A free ticket to exactly where they want me—and the only way I can escape is by doing what they want me to." Although she couldn't see it, she felt him shake his head. "I've been set up, Maii. And I didn't even see it coming."

She waited in silence as he breathed his bitterness into the wind. The plan he had devised was in his mind—only half finalized, but she could read it clearly. When she sensed that he was about to ask the question foremost on his mind, she preempted him easily:

<I'll come too.>

She sensed the relief this aroused in him. "There are no guarantees—"

<Please. I want to,> she said. <When T'Bul threatened to have me lobotomized back on Gorgone-8, you stepped in and helped me. This is my chance to do something in return.>

He squeezed her shoulder. "You know you don't owe me anything, child," he said. "But I'm glad you feel that way. The truth is, there's no way I can make it through this without you."

<I know.> She reached out to take his hand. <Show me the sky again.>

He turned his eyes again heavenward. The star called Kabos had reappeared, although now it burned a deep, angry red. It brightened visibly as they watched, until it flared and became too bright to stare at directly.

"Come on," he said, glancing down the hill. For the first time she noticed the trio of Olmahoi greyboots waiting for him at the hive's massive entrance. "We need to get below ground. The shock wave won't be far away."

She nodded, allowing him to lead her down the hill, and . . .

Roche woke with a gasp.

Sitting upright on the narrow bunk, she put a hand to her forehead, trying to massage away the intrusive thoughts, to free herself of the last threads of the dream. Except it wasn't a dream. She was sure of that. It was something else entirely, a memory that belonged to someone else. . . .

A supernova in colonized space—a population huddling underground because a shield supplied by the Eckandar Trade Axis had failed—the Commerce Artel delegate responsible tried and found guilty of fraud—

It was all so familiar; something she had come across recently while on the *Midnight*. She was certain the IDnet news reports had mentioned it on a number of occasions: Ede System, one of the Olmahoi provinces near the Commonwealth of Empires border, had been an insignificant backwater until it became the victim of a stellar disturbance and was nearly destroyed by the failure of a planetary shield.

And the name of the Artel delegate responsible for the sale of that shield had been—*Makil Veden*.

How could she not have connected the name sooner?

Completely awake, she looked around. Struggling from the thin, dirty mattress, she saw Maii sitting cross-legged on the upper bunk, features completely still. Whether she was asleep or meditating, Roche couldn't tell. Either way, she didn't acknowledge Roche's anger.

Roche was tempted to reach up and rouse the Surin but, sighing, decided against it. For the first time in what seemed like weeks, Roche felt alone—despite the young girl's presence in the room—and she found herself welcoming the solitude.

The room was small and practical, containing only a narrow double bunk and primitive toilet facilities. Minutes after Sabra had brought her to it, Roche had fallen into a deep sleep, blaming fatigue for her sudden and overwhelming tiredness. Now she wasn't so sure. . . .

"You awake, Commander?"

The voice, from the door, broke the quiet Roche had been enjoying. She crossed the short distance to see who it was.

"Sorry to disturb you," said Haid, his scarred, black face smiling at her. He was dressed in loose-fitting, black casuals that might once have been a shipsuit. "I was hoping to talk to you."

Roche shrugged aside her irritation. "Likewise. But give me a moment."

"Of course." He averted his eyes while she dressed and changed the sling on her left arm. Maii didn't move once, and Roche decided not to disturb her. If the girl really was asleep, then she obviously needed it. Accusations of mental tampering could wait until later—until she had decided which she was most angry about: the way the Surin's memories had been thrust into her thoughts, or the abrupt way in which her own had been suppressed.

When she was ready, the rebel leader took her through a series of dimly lit tunnels and chambers. The subterranean headquarters was busier than she had assumed it would be—containing the homes of hundreds of people, as well as rudimentary markets, hospitals, industries, and entertainment facilities; as though a miniature city had grown around the rebel installation. In one large room they passed, at least fifty people had gathered to dine together; the smell of roasted meat caused Roche to hesitate at the entrance.

Haid took her arm to encourage her on. "We'll eat soon," he said, smiling. "I promise."

"As long as it *is* soon," she said. Haid led her down a flight of curving, narrow stairs. The deeper they went, the damper the walls became, as though they were approaching some sort of water table. Yet, when she stopped to test the moisture with a fingertip, she realized that the source of the water was industrial rather than natural. It had a bitter, pungent smell.

"There's a leaky sewage outlet not far from here," explained Haid. Roche grimaced and wiped the hand on her clothes.

"And you live down here?" It wasn't disgust that stained her words, but rather amazement.

"I like to be near the others," he said. "Helps remind me that I'm one of them."

"More leaders should follow your example," Roche commented, thinking of Proctor Klose and his private suite on the executive floor of the *Midnight*. As far as she was concerned, being in command meant more than simply giving orders. And it meant more than just wearing a fancy uniform and having access to luxuries, too. When it came down to it, that extra star on Klose's uniform hadn't helped him when his ship had exploded. Part of her couldn't help wondering if the extra privilege may even have caused it, albeit indirectly. Had he been a better leader, more in tune with his crew and his ship, the *Midnight* might now be more than several thousand cubic kilometers of glowing, radioactive dust.

"This way." Haid took her arm and guided her to the next exit from the stairwell. On the other side was a floor much like the one they had left, although more extensively populated than the other.

They moved along the dank, slightly odorous passages for a while longer, until Haid arrived at a locked door. He keyed the lock by some unseen mechanism, and the panel slid aside. Entering first, he switched on lights and gestured at a chair.

Roche followed him cautiously, eyes scanning the room out of habit before actually stepping inside. It was furnished comfortably, but not ostentatiously so. One wall was dominated by an enormous desk, on which rested a complicated array of out-of-date computers. Two small, cushioned armchairs occupied the center of the room. A cloth hammock hung across one corner, near a narrow cupboard. Hanging from the wall opposite the desk was a multicolored mural. At least three meters wide and two high, it looked like a window to another world—and a familiar one at that.

Ignoring the chair, Roche approached the mural to take a better look. Grey sky rippled above a bleak and barren landscape, with jagged fingers of black rock clawing hopelessly for purchase on the clouds so far above. The scene was totally desolate, yet somehow managed to impart a sense of life—almost as though the rocks themselves were sentient.

"It's Montaban, isn't it?"

"That's right." Roche thought she detected admiration in the rebel leader's voice. "You've been there?"

"Read about it." COE Armada training covered several hundred of the more notable nearby worlds, including this one. "What made you paint it?"

"I was born there."

Roche turned to face him. "*Born* there?"

"All the others—Emmerik, Sabra, Neva—they're all natives of Sciacca, but not me." He moved to the cupboard and opened it, unhampered by his single arm. "Drink?"

"Thanks." She stepped over to the chair he had indicated and sat down. When he handed her a tall, thin glass filled with a clear liquid, she said: "So what's your story, Haid?"

He smiled, his monocular sight gleaming in the faint light of the room, and raised his glass in a wordless toast, which Roche imitated. She took a mouthful of the liquid and was momentarily puzzled by the lack of taste. Then she realized: the glass contained nothing but water. A moment later, a second realization: a full glass of clean drinking water on Sciacca's World would have been regarded as something of a treat to the rebels. Understanding this, Roche decided that sipping the drink would probably be the best means of acknowledging Haid's generosity.

"I was a mercenary before coming here," Haid began. "Tried and convicted after forty-seven successful juntas. Not that I'm boasting or anything. It's just a fact, the way my life panned out." He shrugged. "My parents were killed when I was fifteen, and they left me enough money to pay for anything I wanted. But theirs was a political killing, an underground thing, and I wasn't safe. So I skipped town, bought myself as many implants as I could afford, and set out to find my own niche.

"My parents' money," he went on, "certainly made up for any lack of talent in those early years. If I found it hard to keep up, I just bought a new implant. Easy. I started off as a vigilante for hire until I got a taste for killing."

Roche was somewhat surprised by the man's frankness. He seemed completely at ease with his admissions, speaking with a total absence of guilt. It must have shown on her face, too, because he carried on with a few words of explanation.

"You must understand, Commander, that it paid extremely well. And you'd be amazed how easy it can become after the first couple of times."

"How many?" said Roche. "How many people have you killed?"

"Hard to say." He shook his head. "What with assassinations, fighting in the M'taio System's Caste wars, the i-Hurn Uprising—hell, even with the implants I lost count."

"So what happened?"

He sighed. "I had a rival, a young blood by the name of Decima Frey. She sold me to COE Enforcers in exchange for clemency when they caught her. I was hauled in and tried—so far gone, I didn't really know what was going on. My implants were on a feedback kick, you see, with so many subroutines it was hard to tell where they stopped and I began." He wiggled his fingers by his right ear. "Anyway, I was initially sentenced to be executed, but appealed and had it reduced to this." He indicated his surroundings with a wave of his hand. "At a cost. I had to undergo rehabilitation first. And that didn't seem such a big deal at the time—I mean, I figured rehab would be easy to fake and was confident I'd be able to escape soon enough. I was a killing machine, after all. No backwater penal colony was going to be able to hold me for very long." The grin that touched his lips was wry and without humor. "At least that was what I thought, until I realized what the judge had meant by 'rehabilitation.'"

Roche had learned about the process during her early years of training in Military College. "They stripped you of your implants," she said.

The whirr of his monocle focusing upon her seemed loud in the sudden quiet.

"They dewired me from the inside out," he said. "Everything went. There wasn't a bone or a nerve untouched. My body weight must have dropped by about seventy-five percent. My neuronal mass went down by half. I tell you, I was jelly by the end of it—physically and mentally."

"But how could they have taken care of you in that condition?" said Roche. "I mean, Sciacca's World doesn't have the facilities—"

Haid's laugh startled her. "Take *care* of me?" He laughed again. "Boras—Delcasalle's predecessor—she washed her hands of me very quickly. I was sent into the streets to fend for myself." Light caught Haid's monocle as he leaned forward. "And I was a cripple at that stage. It wasn't until later that I salvaged this"—he tapped his arm on one leg—"and the eye from someone who was no longer . . . in need of it."

Roche's face creased in puzzlement. "You couldn't have managed to do that by yourself, surely?"

"One of my old shipmates rescued me from the gutter. Got to me before the rats could finish the job the authorities had started." He smiled self-deprecatingly. "I'm a far cry from the man I once was, but at least I'm alive, right?"

Roche nodded slowly. "For many here, that might not be something to be grateful for."

"That's why I'm with these people," he said. "They've had it rough, but they're not afraid to keep trying. They're determined to get what they want in the end. The only thing they needed was a good leader—someone with experience at fighting in a modern way." He tipped his head in an exaggerated manner. "And here I am. Gun for hire turned revolutionary."

Roche smiled back. "And doing well, it would seem. This installation is well organized."

"If a little underequipped and leaky at times. Yes. I try my best. It may be nothing compared to my old exploits, but it keeps me going. And I enjoy it, too. I guess having a personal stake in the outcome really makes the difference." His glass eye winked at her. "Which brings us to you, Commander." His expression became hard, grim. "You're a serious threat to everything I've built—in more ways than one. So let's hear your own story. Tell me about this mess you've brought to Sciacca."

Roche put the drink on the floor by her chair and began to talk. Midway through Haid's confession she'd realized that she had little to fear from the man, at least as far as secrecy was concerned. Her mission was of little relevance on the planet—except to her and the Dato Bloc—and any information she divulged would be unlikely to spread. Even in the improbable event that Haid decided to tell Warden Delcasalle, his word was sure to be doubted. Besides, she needed his help—there was no escaping this simple fact. And if the only way to gain that help was to tell the truth, then so be it.

He listened closely as she described how she had "collected" the Box from the AI factories on Trinity, and how she really had very little idea of either its potential or its purpose. He accepted her role as uninformed military courier as easily as she did: she wasn't required to know; therefore she didn't. When she described the ambush in the Soul and the means by which she and the others had slipped past the Dato ships and to the planet in the lander, he nodded appreciatively and commented that their tactics had been sound.

Cane's unexplained appearance on the scene, however, bothered him.

"You say that Cane was instructed by someone to come to your room prior to the *Midnight*'s destruction. Presumably the same someone who let him out of his cell." He frowned. "Any idea who that might have been?"

"No. The security records went up with the ship, and I've been too busy trying to stay alive since then to worry about anything else."

"Understandable." Haid sucked the tips of his plastic fingers. "Go on."

There was little more to add: the crash of the lander; their rescue by Emmerik and the battle in Houghton's Cross; their arrival in Port Parvati.

When she had finished, she refreshed her throat with a sip of water and leaned back into the chair. "What do you think?" she asked. "It's not as good a story as yours—"

"Don't be too quick to dismiss it," Haid said, frowning.

"Do you think you can trust me?"

"Perhaps," he said. "Half of what you've told me doesn't make sense, and what *does* bothers me."

Now Roche frowned. "So you *don't* believe me?"

He waved his hand dismissively. "That's not what I'm saying at all. I *do* believe you—totally. But you're not giving me the full picture, albeit unintentionally."

"I don't understand."

"Well, take your mission for instance. Granted, the *Midnight* was a form of cover—but why here? If the Box is so important, for whatever reason, why send it to such a high-risk region when thousands of other routes were available? The Hutton-Luu System is so close to the Dato border that it's almost begging to be annexed. All it would've taken was a small skirmish to put your mission in jeopardy. No. It doesn't make sense at all." Haid shook his head. "And then there's Cane."

Roche sighed. "I know. I've been trying to figure him out ever since I met him."

"That's not what I mean," said Haid. "Ignore what he is for a moment, and focus on how he came to be here. You said his life support capsule was plucked out of deep space near an interim anchor point. I can understand his lack of memory, perhaps—but not his escape from the cell. Who helped him? Why did they send him to you? And the timing of his release is suspicious, too. Did his ally know about the ambush? And if they did, how could they possibly have known that you, of all the people onboard the *Midnight*, were going to escape?"

Roche considered for a long moment. "They couldn't have. No one knew the ship was going to blow until it happened. Except maybe Klose—"

"But you said he did his best to keep you *away* from Cane."

"I know." Roche shook her head. As unlikely as coincidence was, it seemed the less ridiculous option. "You really think there's a conspiracy?"

"I don't know. But I'm not dismissing the possibility." Haid's monocle didn't waver, so tightly was his attention focused on her. "Everything Emmerik's told me warns me to be careful where Cane is concerned."

"Fair enough." She couldn't blame him for being wary. Someone with Cane's natural combat abilities deserved that, at the very least.

"And then there's Veden," Haid continued. "He's supposed to be on my side, but I have to tell you that the way you turn up together makes me a little . . . uneasy."

"Well, you can rule out the possibility of the two of us working in tandem against you. He's been wanting to cut loose from me ever since we met."

"So I understand." Haid smiled to himself and studied the last mouthful of water in his glass. "Maybe he knows something I don't."

"All he'd know would come through Maii. If she's told you nothing, then that leaves me in the clear. Right?"

"My thoughts exactly," he said. "Except that you and she have been fairly close since your arrival. Maybe the two of you have taken sides against Veden and me, for whatever reason. It's a possibility I have to consider." He downed the last of his water in a single gulp. "Yet you maintain that you don't know why she's here."

"That's not quite true anymore." Roche shuddered slightly, remembering the dream the Surin had given her. "I do know a little more now than I did."

"How much?"

"I'm not sure." The slab of Maii's memories had been dumped unceremoniously into Roche's head in the form of a dream, raw and requiring processing. Now that she had the chance, she belatedly tried to assimilate what she had learned with what she knew about Sciacca's World.

"Something about the DAOC hyperspace transmitter being off-planet?" she said.

Haid nodded. "The MiCom installation in the landing field controls all transmissions, but the hardware itself is in a remote polar orbit, well outside the Soul. The small station is unstaffed apart from a skeleton crew to oversee the equipment and to perform minor repairs. The crew is rotated once every fifty days with fresh personnel from Kanaga Station."

"So it's theoretically impossible for anyone on the ground to take over the transmitter."

"That's right."

"Unless you somehow infiltrate the crew of the station."

"Possible, but unlikely. This is a high-security installation; the transmitter will have command codes known only to the CEO."

"Warden Delcasalle," said Roche.

"Exactly. Without the codes, the only way to 'interfere' with any broadcast is to damage the transmitter itself."

Roche nodded to herself, the plan suddenly falling into place. First, Maii had to work her way into the warden's mind—not to take him over, for there were sure to be safeguards against that, but to steal the transmitter codes. Second, she had to reach out for the orbital station and select one of the crew. Someone who knew how to operate the transmitter, someone tired and easily influenced—perhaps at the end of a tour of duty, eager for recall to the main base. Someone who could be controlled by epsense to send a message from Sciacca's World—a message, more specifically, to the COE High Equity Court requesting a formal hearing on behalf of the rebels.

And that was where Veden came in. Such a request, from an undercover delegate of the Commerce Artel, would hardly go unnoticed.

Except that now Veden was in a coma.

When she outlined this to the leader of the rebels, he smiled widely.

"That's the gist of it," he said. "A long shot, but at least it doesn't involve the use of force. The Eckandar Trade Axis has been sympathetic ever since their outcast—Lazaro Houghton—betrayed the original settlers. The cost in bribes to get the message out to them nearly ruined us, but it'll be worth it." He shrugged. "At least we hope it will be. Veden's still under anesthetic; we won't know how he's doing until tomorrow morning. If he doesn't wake from the coma, then we'll have to rethink the situation."

Roche nodded. "The only other option, as far as I can see, is to raid the landing field and use the codes there. But given your current position—underarmed, that is—I wouldn't recommend it."

"Perhaps not. But maybe we should plan something anyway, just in case."

"It couldn't hurt."

Haid grinned suddenly. "You know, Commander, I think we're actually getting somewhere."

"That depends on how you look at it. I've decided to trust you—but, then, I have little choice."

"True. And I've decided not to turn you in to Enforcement for the bounty, although I won't deny we could use the cash. Apart from the fact that you might be able to help us, I've got little to lose if I support you. Should Veden's plan work, the High Equity Court can be told about you then. Or you can transmit a message to your superiors at the same time."

"My thoughts exactly."

"At least we agree on something." Haid leaned back into his chair. "We can discuss Plan B later, if you like. All I want is an assurance that if Veden's plan fails and yours works, you'll take him off the planet when you leave. I owe him that much, for coming here."

Roche thought about it. "I'm not really in a position to guarantee anything—"

"Nor I, Commander," Haid cut in.

Roche studied the man's intent expression for a moment. "But I can try, I guess."

"Good. That's as much as I can expect from anyone." Haid leaned back into his chair. "All that remains is for me to ask a small favor."

"Which is?"

Haid stood and crossed to the cupboard, rummaged around inside it for a time, then returned with a small box. Seating himself again, he keyed open the lid and showed her the contents.

Inside the box was a slim data glove with an infrared remote link.

"I want you to put this on," said Haid.

"Why?"

"So I can communicate with the Box, of course. If we're going to attempt anything together, we need to understand the tools at our disposal. And, given my past, I think you'll agree that I'm the closest thing we have to an expert on cybernetic systems."

Roche hesitantly reached into the box and picked up the glove. Did she have the right to allow a convicted criminal access to the Box? Regardless of her situation, and no matter how much she needed Haid's help, it went against all her training.

"I suppose it won't hurt," Roche agreed warily. "Although I doubt you'll learn much. I certainly haven't."

"Well, we'll see about that, won't we? I've never met an AI before with more intelligence than a retarded rodent, regardless how well appointed they may seem up front. Give me a day or two and I should have it figured out."

Still she vacillated. Yet she had to admit that she too was curious. If Haid could learn anything more than she had in the last few weeks, it might be worth the risk.

<Put on the glove, Morgan.> The Box spoke through her thoughts. <He will learn only what I want him to. And, besides, this will enable me to infiltrate their installation further. We have nothing to lose and much to gain.>

It made sense, she thought, slipping on the glove and snapping its wrist closed. She flexed her fingers. The mesh fabric was tight around her knuckles, but left her fingers otherwise unimpeded. Almost immediately she felt the tingle down her forearm that followed a transfer of data.

Haid smiled. "Good. I'll get started soon. For now, though, I suggest we find you some food."

Relieved by the offer, Roche stood and followed Haid from the room.

"It's not a matter of numbers," Roche insisted, "or of firepower. What I'm proposing is a quick surgical strike. If we do it properly, we'll be in before they can mount countermeasures. And once we're in, we can take effective control."

The unofficial tactical meeting had convened in an empty office in one of the deeper sections of the underground resistance complex. A large viewtank, oriented horizontally to the floor, served as a combined desk and map. Roche and Neva leaned on opposite sides of its glowing surface, secondhand diagrams painting patterns on their faces. Emmerik stood to one side, watching the interaction between the two women with interest.

Haid had given Roche over to the two of them not long after a hasty meal in the rebel refectory. She and Neva, it seemed, had been arguing ever since.

"Control?" The furrows on Neva's brow grew deeper. "There are more than two thousand Armada personnel in Port Parvati, in twenty-seven separate facilities. We have less than a thousand. At the very best, we can take control of *one* facility, and that doesn't give us effective control of anything. It just makes us effective targets. Ameidio won't risk our people for such a futile gesture."

"There'll be no risk to your overall organization," said Roche. "We can use a handful of volunteers, if necessary. And anyway, we'll control the communications nexus—MiCom."

"But MiCom is only the *instrument* of command," Neva quickly countered. "Delcasalle and his cronies could run their operation without it; they'd use carrier bats if they had to. You don't know these people like we do."

Roche shook her head. "One: MiCom is linked to the hyperspace transmitter in orbit—so once we have it, we can blow the whistle on them, right down the line to the Armada. And two: corrupt officials are the same anywhere. They—"

"I don't think Commander Roche plans to leave them on the loose," the Box interrupted, speaking through a terminal near the viewtank. Roche regarded the valise in surprise, unaware that it had been listening.

"Warden Delcasalle may well be in absolute control here," it continued, "but he is dependent on those immediately below him, and they in turn on the level below them. All levels below Delcasalle operate through the Administration Center; the key personnel may not be present, but the mechanism for decision-making and control always is. Cut out the Administration Center, and you effectively cut off Delcasalle's hands."

"*Administration?*" Neva waved her hand at the glowing map. "So now we're taking out more than one of the facilities?"

"No," the Box said firmly. "Merely extending our strike at the MiCom installation to include the Administration Center as well. Look at the map."

Neva looked down, and Roche, impressed by the Box's line of thought, did likewise. She saw at once where it was leading.

"MiCom and Administration," it said, "are features of the central port complex, isolated within the scorched-earth perimeter. Administration is adjacent to—and can be entered by way of—the main terminal building, which houses MiCom. So this can be a single operation. No untidy splitting of the strike force, no civilians, and no collateral damage."

Roche swung the Box onto the viewtank's edge. There was just enough free chain to allow her to reach across the main map.

"Both MiCom and Administration are secure modules," she said, following the Box's lead. "Probably prefab components shipped from an old orbital facility. But the main entrance to Administration is only about ten meters from the emergency stairs to MiCom. See, here." She tapped the point on the plan showing the map of the main terminal building. "We can go to that point as one group, split into separate strike forces, and be in a position to move simultaneously against the two targets."

"Seems almost made to order," Neva said dryly.

Roche glanced up at her, trying to read her face rather than her words. But the woman was impassive.

Roche returned to the plans. "Forget the lower floor and the navigation module; that's of no interest to us. The MiCom module occupies the three levels above that, right through to the roof installations; it's totally isolated from the ground floor, totally shielded and insulated, totally selfcontained. It even has its own emergency life-support system, controlled from the first floor. The only points of entry or exit are the elevator system—which can be disabled—and the equipment access stairwell from the ground—here. All we have to target is the first floor, and they'll be cut off from the outside."

Neva leaned over the map, her face finally revealing a hint of interest in Roche's plan.

"It's a simple operation," Roche said. "A single shot and the elevator will be inoperable. We go up the stairs, blow out the door, and enter fast under cover of the explosion. Three or four people could secure the floor in, say, thirty seconds. One heavy weapon to cover the stairwell—perhaps a portable shield to prevent them lobbing their own explosives in on us—gas via the emergency life support, or Maii, to knock out those above us—and we're secure. It'll only take a few seconds to interface the Box. Once we've done that, we'll control all command communication on Sciacca's World plus all intersystem channels, including the Armada's."

"What about Admin?" said Emmerik.

"Cane can take a small force in there," Roche said. "It's one level; he'll simply sweep through it. No need to be tidy."

Neva looked across at Emmerik. A frown creased her face.

The Mbatan nodded. "He's quite capable of doing it," he said.

"That's not what I was thinking."

"I know," said Emmerik, his eyes moving to meet Roche's.

Neva's gaze narrowed. Lowering her eyes to the map, she deliberated a moment, then said: "Okay, Commander. It seems sound enough, although it does rely heavily on the talents of a small number of individuals—namely the members of your own party. Should either you, Cane, or Maii fall early in the battle, success will be unlikely." She folded her arms and nodded to herself. "But supposing we grant you the possibility that your plan *might* work, there still remains the little matter of getting to the strike point you've identified. The terminal complex is well inside the landing field's electrified perimeter, some hundred meters back from the only gates. Not only is the gatehouse well served by Enforcement personnel, but so is the main guard block. Both lie between the gates and the front doors of the main complex. Needless to say, these people aren't technicians and administrators and will be highly sensitive to intruders. How do you plan to get us past them?" She brushed the back of a hand across the map as though wiping off crumbs. "Just send Cane in first?"

Roche smiled. "That's the least of our problems. What you have to decide is whether you want to continue to play good citizen, perhaps infiltrate the system and gain a few minor advantages—or whether you want to go with us and clean this bunch out once and for all."

Neva's expression tightened as she spoke. Obviously she had struck a nerve. "I shouldn't need to remind you, Commander," she said, "that we've built up a strong and efficient resistance here over a number of years. If we implement your plan and it fails, we stand to lose everything."

"Not necessarily. You risk maybe a dozen people. Surely you've set up field-operative cells with one person control?"

"Of course. That's how we work outside the city."

"Then use one of those cells."

Neva said nothing. She looked at Roche and the Box's valise in turn, then back to the map. Her frown intensified.

"Believe me," Roche pressed, "if we wait much longer, a Dato ground team will be next on the scene, and your little operation won't last a week. They're a distinct step up from the locals you've been dealing with."

Again Emmerik and Neva exchanged a glance. "We know," said the woman.

"There's just one thing I'd like to ask," said the Mbatan. "You seem quite confident about getting in, but what happens *afterward*?"

Roche hesitated. She hadn't dwelled on the aftermath as much as she had on the events leading up to it. "The message to the Armada will be sent on a broadband emergency frequency. The Dato will know instantly it's been sent, and might even back off without any further trouble, depending on how far they're willing to be involved. Even if they don't, we can use the Box to control the landing field's defense screen to keep them—and the Enforcers—at bay for a while. Long enough for a reply to arrive, at least. Reinforcements won't be far behind." She shrugged. "That should be enough to make Delcasalle think twice about attacking us."

"Perhaps." Neva still looked undecided. "But it still seems a little risky. We'll be sitting ducks in the MiCom building."

"I agree," put in the Box, surprising Roche. "I don't doubt that I can send the emergency message and simultaneously organize a ground defense while you keep MiCom secure. In a predictable world, this would be no mean feat. But in the real world I will have little control over the response time of the Armada or the actions of the Dato Bloc. Should the former be sluggish and the latter retaliatory rather than conciliatory, there will be little even I can do to delay the inevitable."

Emmerik nodded. "The longer we're under siege, the more time we give DAOC or the Dato to find a way in."

"The Armada could take days," Neva added.

"And that's not the worst of it," continued the Box. "A conflict of interests exists within the group itself. Assuming all goes well, we will be lifted from a combat zone by Armada dropships—hardly an inconspicuous way to leave the planet. Especially when more circumspect pathways are available. While it suits our needs admirably to choose this method of escape, others might not find it appropriate."

"What other way is there?" Roche asked.

"By betraying us to the Enforcers, a traitor might gain illegal exit from Sciacca's World from the Dato—thereby circumventing the judiciary system."

"It's a possibility," Emmerik said to Roche, his eyes dark.

"A very real one, I'm afraid," the Box continued. "In combat, as I am sure you are aware, there are crucial moments where one simple action, or failure to take action, can decide the ultimate outcome. It would be relatively easy for one person to shift the scales, should he or she so wish."

"That's a risk everyone takes in combat," Roche protested. "And besides, they won't have time to plan anything. The response from the Armada won't be slow. The *Midnight* was destroyed two days ago, and therefore hasn't reported to HQ. Someone might already be on their way to see what happened." Leaning over the map, she did her best to argue with a voice that had no face. "And besides, what other alternatives do we have?"

"At least one," said the Box. "We can commandeer a ground-to-orbit vessel and physically occupy the transmitter station."

"What?" Stunned by the audacity of the suggestion, Roche openly gaped. "Are you crazy?"

"Not at all," the Box purred. "The station is well defended—more so than the landing field and the MiCom installation, but not overwhelmingly so. I can get us past the Dato blockade and into a position to dock. The warden will not sanction a direct assault upon it, for fear of destroying it. This will place them in direct conflict with the Dato Bloc. A very real possibility exists that our enemies will go to war over the best way to capture us, while we sit back and await rescue."

"You really are crazy," said Neva, shaking her head. "I like Roche's plan much better. At least with her we stay on solid ground."

"Which is less defensible than—"

"Forget it, Box," Roche said. "The most we can hope for is control of MiCom. Push it any further and we risk losing everything."

"I agree," said Emmerik, nodding.

"But, Morgan—"

"I said, *forget it*." Roche glared at the valise, mentally daring it to argue further.

Before it could do so, the room's intercom beeped urgently for attention.

Neva stepped aside to take the call. While she waited, Roche ran over her plan in her mind. Yes, it seemed sound; there were only a handful of details left to be straightened out, and they would fall into place as the others applied their superior knowledge of the rebel forces and the city to the problem. Roche doubted COE Intelligence's head of Strategy, Page De Bruyn, could have done any better, given what she had to work with.

"Your AI is either far more clever than I gave it credit for," said Emmerik into the silence, "or dangerously abstracted from reality."

"What do you mean?" Roche responded.

"Well, its suggestion appears to have forced you and Neva to a consensus. Perhaps that was all it was intended to do, in which case the move was inspired." Emmerik shrugged. "If it meant it seriously, on the other hand . . ."

The Mbatan let the sentence trail off, and Roche didn't complete the thought out loud. Much as she disliked the idea of the Box being such a skilled debater, especially on her behalf, she found that less disturbing than the Box's plan itself.

Although, now that she thought about it, the Box's plan did make a certain kind of sense. It *was* feasible, in a crazy kind of way. Almost Human in its boldness; hardly what she would have expected from a mere machine.

When Neva returned, her face was grim. "That was Ameidio," she said. "He's received the results of Cane's tests."

"Excellent." Emmerik lifted his bulk off the table he had been leaning on. "Now we might get some answers."

"We already have, I'm afraid." Neva turned to look Roche squarely in the eye. "Ameidio's called a conference. It starts in fifteen minutes. He wants you to wait here until he calls a guard to show you down. We'll meet you there." Neva turned back to Emmerik. "Let's go. I'll fill you in on the way." Together they headed for the door.

"Wait!" Roche came around the viewtank. "At least give me a hint of what they've found."

Neva stopped on the threshold, glancing at Emmerik. After a moment, he nodded assent. "You won't like it," she said to Roche.

"Is he sick? Dying? What?"

"Worse than that, I'm afraid." Neva met Roche's stare and sighed. "Whatever Cane is, he *isn't* what he seems. . . ."

13

Sciacca's World
Port Parvati
'954.10.33 EN
1025

Nine people filed into the oval-shaped conference room and gathered about its long, polished, grey stone table. As they did, a warm and gentle light began to emanate from the rafters high above, replacing the shadows of the large room with a pervasive yellow glow.

Present at the table were Haid, at its head, with Emmerik and Neva on one side and Sabra on the other. Next to Sabra—and directly opposite Roche—was Sylvester Teh, the representative of the medical team that had examined Cane. He was a short and balding man in his middle years who spoke in a manner both soft and lacking in self-confidence. Roche got the impression that he was more comfortable talking to machines than to people.

To Roche's right were two guards, between which sat Cane himself. If he was aware that he was, to all intents and purposes, on trial, his face betrayed no apprehension. Not that she expected it to. She doubted whether there was anything the rebels could do to Cane to hurt him. Roche and Emmerik had seen Cane in action; they both knew that he could have overpowered his escort on any number of occasions on the way down to this meeting. The guards' presence was more for show than anything else.

Maii had declined to attend, saying she needed to concentrate in order to prepare for her part in Veden's plan. It felt unusual for Roche not to have someone whispering in her mind. Indeed, even the Box was silent—the tingle of data flowing through the glove still for the moment. She suspected it would be paying close attention to the proceedings just the same.

When all were seated, Haid called for order. "I'm sorry to drag you in at such short notice," he began, "but as you are probably aware, something has come up regarding our friend here." He nodded in Cane's direction. "You'll have to excuse the choice of venue, I'm afraid; unfortunately it's the only room guaranteed to be secure."

Roche glanced around the large and empty room. It was situated on one of the university's lower levels, and, from the disheveled appearance of the corridors leading to it, she suspected it wasn't used too often.

"Sylvester," continued Haid. "You want to tell us what we have here?"

Teh adjusted the neck of his tunic as he stood to address the small group. "Early this morning," he said, "we completed an in-depth physical examination of the subject known as Adoni Cane, our intention being to determine the cause of his amnesia. We also wanted to see if he had suffered any physical side-effects of what I am given to understand was an extended time spent in a life support capsule. Indeed, we thought the two facts might have been connected." Teh glanced down to the copious notes laid out before him.

"However, before we move on to the full findings of our investigation, I would like to begin by saying that, as far as we can tell, Adoni Cane's loss of memory is *not* the result of physical trauma. He has no memory of a time earlier than thirteen days ago because, quite simply, the memories never existed in the first place." Teh looked around the table to ensure that this conclusion was clearly understood. Noting Roche's obvious confusion, he said, "To put it another way, until a little more than a week ago, the Adoni Cane sitting before you did not exist."

"That's impossible," said Roche. "The recovery team on the *Midnight* physically pulled him out of the capsule."

Teh raised a hand. "Let me clarify that," he said. "Perhaps I should have said he did not exist as an *individual*."

Emmerik lifted his thick eyebrows. "He was someone else?"

"Or no one at all." Teh's nervous eyes dropped again to his notes. "Real-time analysis of the blood flow in his brain reveals an absence of lesions and clots—no physical damage, in other words, that would suggest the erasure of a previous personality. What we see before us is a man whose brain is functioning perfectly—albeit that it has only been *conscious* for a matter of days."

Neva leaned forward. "So how is it that he can talk? If he's only thirteen days old, surely he should be as helpless as a newborn baby. *And* as mindless."

"I don't know," said Teh. "One possibility is that the capsule in which he was found contained more than the usual life-suspend/support outfit. During his time adrift, it may have been educating him, training him." He shrugged. "We have no way of knowing."

"Training him for what?" Sabra asked.

"Why don't you ask the man himself?" put in Roche, gesturing at Cane.

"I have no memories at all prior to the *Midnight*," he said, preempting the question. "If I was educated subliminally, then I'm afraid I can offer no answers which might explain what my training was intended *for*."

"But why would anyone do such a thing?" asked Neva. "It's crazy."

Haid brought the matter to an end by standing and saying, "We'll come back to that later. First we should hear the other results of the examination."

Teh nodded. "We conducted the standard tests: X-rays, tissue typing, genetic analysis, and so on. Without exception, the results of these tests were anomalous."

"In what way?" Roche asked.

"See for yourself." The medic displayed a handheld computer down which scrolled test results. Roche caught perhaps one line in five and rapidly became lost among the endless procession of data.

"What you're seeing is Cane's genetic transcript, coding exons and introns both," Teh explained. "When you compare it to his overall physiognomy, the results are weird—to say the least. He may look normal on the surface, but *underneath* . . ." His voice trailed off as he scanned through a variety of holographic images, then returned: "Just look at his cell structure, his central nervous system, his gut, his lungs—and his brain. Have you ever seen anything like that before? Anywhere?"

"No," said Roche. "But that doesn't necessarily mean—"

"I understand your reluctance to accept the results of the test," Teh said. "But I'm afraid there can be no doubt. Our diagnostic database is customized to the Pristine form, and precisely because it's not equipped to deal with data outside certain guidelines, it is ideally suited to provide a direct comparison with what we would regard as usual. For instance, Adoni Cane's cellular structure is more compact than normal, resulting in tissue that is more elastic, yet stronger; likewise his skeleton is denser, his intestinal tract longer, his lungs of superior capacity, his heart more powerful, and his immune system more efficient than what would be regarded as typical of a Pristine Human. He possesses several glands that do not correspond with any I am aware of, yet lacks certain vestigial organs we all take for granted. His brain displays a quite remarkable number of structural anomalies, and his chromosomal map matches no known genotype.

"In short," Teh concluded, "Adoni Cane is *not* Pristine—although what he is, exactly, has yet to be determined."

"Any guesses?" asked Neva.

"Well, I'm not qualified enough to even guess," Teh said. Then, for Roche's benefit, he added, "You must understand, Commander, that we have no schools here. What training we indigenes receive comes from the convicts. My own was courtesy of a woman sent to Sciacca's World for malpractice." He smiled at a private memory. "She assured me she knew what she was talking about, even though her knowledge was not—"

"Don't feel the need to justify yourself, Sylvester," intruded Haid. "No one is doubting your ability."

Roche wasn't so confident, but she said nothing.

Embarrassed, Teh turned again to his notes. "Well," he said, "it seems to me that the differences between Cane and the Pristine Human are not random. That is, in each and every case they serve to make him superior to the norm. His kidneys absorb more toxins; he can see and hear things we cannot without artificial amplification; his tissue repairs faster than ours."

Not for the first time that day, Roche looked with some amazement at the thin scar that was all that remained of the gash Cane had suffered at Houghton's Cross.

"In fact," Teh continued, "the only area in which he is inferior to anyone sitting at this table is reproduction."

"He's sterile?" Sabra asked the question without taking her eyes from Cane's impassive face, her lips pursed in a mixture of repugnance and admiration. "A superhuman drone?"

"That would be one interpretation of the data, yes," said Teh.

"But he looks so *normal*."

"His appearance does belie the uniqueness of the rest of his physique," said Teh. "And I dare say that this has been deliberately programmed—"

"Programmed?" interrupted Emmerik.

"Isn't it obvious?" said Teh. "He can't be an Exotic we've never encountered before. Someone knew what they were doing when they built him. Someone who knows more about genetics and the Human form than I ever will."

Haid allowed the others a moment to absorb this before asking the obvious question:

"But why?"

Roche watched the faces of everyone in the room as they thought it through. Haid had had time to reach the obvious conclusion, as had Sylvester Teh. Neva shook her head in irritation; Sabra's lips pursed even tighter; Emmerik scowled deeply; the two security guards stiffened. Roche kept her expression carefully neutral, although the answer to the question seemed obvious enough, and indeed disturbing.

Surprisingly, Cane was the first to speak.

"To allow me to infiltrate Pristine society, I imagine." His voice was even and uncolored by emotion. He might have been talking about someone else. "Given the abilities I possess, I can only be either a spy or a weapon."

"Exactly." Haid leaned forward, his one arm splayed flat on the stone tabletop. "Emmerik warned me about your ability to kill without apparent remorse, when you need to. He and Neva also witnessed your extraordinary skill in combat; anyone able to disarm powered armor with hands cuffed deserves respect in my book—or suspicion. And there can be no questioning your intelligence, either. I have no doubt that, given time, you could do almost anything you wanted. But that brings us no closer to the answer: what *do* you want to do?" Haid shrugged helplessly. "I doubt that even you know the answer to that, do you?"

Cane shook his head.

"So it seems more appropriate to tackle the problem not from the *why* angle, but rather the *who*."

Cane shrugged. "Someone who doesn't like Pristine Humans?"

"That could be any one of a number of Castes," said Emmerik wryly.

"True." Roche knew that although none of the seven local Castes hated Pristine Humans specifically, at least one Caste's members despised everyone but themselves. And there were a number of splinter groups who would gladly accept responsibility. "But that leaves us with plenty of suspects."

"The Eckandar Trade Axis is the most advanced in this area," said Teh, "and it guards its knowledge jealously. Or so I've heard."

"It's true," Roche agreed. "The Eckandi will sell just about anything other than genetic technology."

"I don't understand." Sabra frowned. "What use would Eckandi genetics be to Pristines?"

"We all spring from a common, carbon-based organism," explained Teh. "Our genetic codes may speak a different language now, but it's still all written on the same paper. Genome maps and so on are frequently interchangeable."

"So they're the obvious suspects. Aren't they?" Sabra turned to face Roche when she hesitated to agree.

"Not necessarily," said Roche. "The Dato have been interested, too. One of their pre-Commonwealth leaders—Ataman Vereine, I believe—almost went to war with the Eckandar Trade Axis when they refused to sell what they knew. She may have got what she wanted, or developed it herself."

"I thought they'd moved into cyber-assist programs instead," said Haid.

"Maybe," said Roche, although she had heard nothing of the sort. "That could be a cover, though."

"True. Cane might be a Dato spy, which would explain why he was planted on an Armada vessel." Haid counted on his fingers. "That makes two. Who else?"

"The Kesh hate everyone," Emmerik mused, echoing Roche's earlier thought, "but they've never shown interest in this sort of warfare."

"And the Surin Agora is too busy squabbling within itself to attack anyone else," said Roche. "The same applies to most of the other major governments. Why spend so much time and money fighting Pristines when there are already enough problems at home?"

"If Veden was awake, we could ask him," said Neva. "About the Eckandi, I mean."

"He is awake," said Haid. "But he was not well enough to attend, I'm afraid. The nanomachines we had were an old paramilitary design, barely sufficient. Still, I doubt whether he would tell us even if he did know. Neither the Eckandar Trade Axis nor the Commerce Artel would ever risk spreading publicity like that."

"Maybe we're looking in the wrong place." Teh's voice intruded softly, uneasily, into the debate. "We're looking all around us for suspects, when maybe we should be looking in another direction entirely."

"Like where?" asked Roche. "Within? If you're suggesting that COE Intelligence—"

"No, no," cut in Teh quickly. "I mean into the *past*." He leaned back into his chair, away from the frowns and puzzled expressions around the table. "There was another group apart from the Eckandar Trade Axis which possessed more than the average working knowledge of genetics. In fact, if I'm not mistaken, they were the original source of the Eckandi's current know-how."

"Who?" said Sabra.

"A splinter group from the older Pristine governments. Pre-Commonwealth—even pre-Dominion, I think—but definitely local. Obsessed with Transcendence by means of biomodification. The Eckandi helped them build a base, if I remember correctly, and they traded knowledge for services. I don't recall what happened to them—except that there was some sort of backlash—but if what they gave the Eckandar Trade Axis was only a small amount of their complete knowledge, then they might have been just the right people to design something like Cane."

"I've never heard of anyone like that," said Haid.

"I have," said Emmerik. "My mother used to tell me stories about them when I was a child, along with all the other Transcendence stories about the Crescend."

Haid faced Emmerik. "What were they called?"

Emmerik shrugged, but it was Teh that spoke.

"I can't remember," said the physician. "And I'll admit it seems far-fetched—"

"More than that. It sounds crazy." Sabra didn't bother to hide her scepticism. "How long must Cane have been drifting out there for him to be one of them?"

"A *long* time." Teh shook his head. "Hundreds, maybe thousands, of years."

"And *was* he?" the woman asked Roche.

"I don't know," she said. "The science team on the *Midnight* might have analyzed the corrosion on the hull of the capsule, but their data was lost with the ship."

"It's pointless asking anyway." Sabra looked away. "No one could survive more than a month or two in a life-support capsule."

"That's the usual assumption," said Haid. "Which was why Sylvester suspected that such a stretch might have caused Cane's amnesia." He sighed. "And it seems we've come full circle. Does anybody have anything they'd like to say that hasn't already been covered?"

Sabra raised her hand. When Haid looked to her, she said, "He's obviously dangerous. We should get rid of him now. Turn him in to the wardens before he has a chance to destroy us. He only *says* he doesn't remember anything, after all. We would be gambling an awful lot simply on the strength of his word."

Haid grimaced. "How about you, Emmerik? What are your feelings on this?"

The Mbatan looked uncertainly at Cane, then back to Haid. "Having seen him fight, I'm still wary." After a few seconds of staring into Cane's unblinking eyes, he said, "But I've decided to trust him. He fought for *us*, after all."

"Whatever he was, and is," put in Neva, "he's on Roche's side. So as long as she remains with us, I don't think we're in any danger."

"Roche?" Haid indicated that it was her turn to speak.

"I can understand your suspicion," she said, "and your reluctance to put faith in someone you hardly know. But I'm in the same position. For the most part you've treated me fairly, and I respect that. As long as our goals remain the same, you can count on me for support. And I too believe you can count on Cane as well."

Haid nodded. "What about you, Cane? What do *you* think we should do with you? Dispose of you, or use you as a weapon?"

"The answer seems obvious." Cane smiled slightly, the only expression he had worn throughout the meeting. "If I am a biological weapon—one that has been programmed by others, what's more—then I am inherently unreliable. My instinct tells me to follow Roche, but that may change at any moment. Who knows when my programming will take over? Or what I might do? If I was in your position, faced with such a choice, I would rely on my own abilities and not take a chance on something so unpredictable."

Haid's expression was one of bafflement. "You're suggesting that we get rid of you?"

"No. I'm simply saying that that is what *I* would do in your position." His smile widened. "Or try to, anyway."

Haid called the meeting to an end moments later, saying he needed to think prior to reaching a decision. Before he could leave, Roche asked if she could go to the medical center.

"I don't know." Haid didn't hide his reservations. "Veden only regained consciousness an hour ago, and I don't think you're particularly high on his visiting list."

"I won't stay long," she said, not sure whether she was telling the truth. Teh's point about the Eckandi had been an interesting one. If Veden knew something, she might be able to persuade Maii to lever it out of him. "I just want to get my shoulder checked. While I'm there, I can make sure he's okay so I can put Maii at ease."

Haid hesitated. "All right. But leave when Sylvester tells you to."

"Don't worry. I only want a couple of minutes."

Haid nodded reluctantly. "You know the way?"

"That's okay," Sabra said, stepping forward. "I'll take her there."

"Thanks." Surprised by the friendly gesture, Roche almost missed the look that passed between the rebel leader and his assistant: a look of warning from Haid, and resentment from Sabra.

"Don't worry," said the woman. "I'll take good care of her."

"You do that." Haid turned back to Roche. "I'll see you later."

The two guards escorted Cane out of the conference room at the same time Roche and Sabra left, causing a moment's confusion in the narrow doorway. The corridor outside took them to an elevator that was, again, barely large enough for the five of them.

"We'll wait for the next one," said Sabra.

"No, it's all right." Roche slid into the carriage between one of the guards and the wall. "We'll fit."

The doors closed with a sullen hiss. As the elevator jerked upward, the butt of one guard's pistol jabbed Roche in the hip. She twisted away from him in the confined space.

"If you think this is bad," he said, smiling, "be thankful you're not topside. Delcasalle's got patrols in every quarter looking for you."

"He has?" Roche's brow creased. "I wasn't told that."

"Ameidio doesn't tell you everything," Sabra said, her eyes flashing. The good humor that had prompted her to take Roche to the sick bay appeared to be waning fast.

"I don't expect him to," said Roche.

"Really?" The elevator paused as they passed a floor, causing the carriage to sway. "It doesn't look like that to me."

Roche fixed her with a calm and unflinching stare. "No? What *does* it look like to you, Sabra?"

Sabra scowled silently to herself and faced the dented and scrawled doors of the elevator. Roche glimpsed one of the guards in the corner grimacing.

"There's a rumor in the ranks," said Cane. "I overhead it before the meeting. It's said that you're a spy for the wardens."

Roche groaned. "You're kidding."

"Unfortunately not," said Cane.

"But what about the *Midnight*? Houghton's Cross?"

"The full truth of your identity is being kept secret to prevent word leaking to Enforcement plants on the surface," said Cane. "In the absence of information, speculation spreads."

"But . . ." Roche fought to contain her sense of outrage in words. "If that's the case, then why would Haid be telling me anything at all?"

"It's not hard to seduce a cripple," said Sabra coldly.

"What?" Roche snapped.

"Why not?" Sabra's face flushed an angry red. "He was a proud man once, before coming here. And, as they say, a beautiful woman is a powerful poison."

"Your anger betrays your jealousy, Sabra," said Roche, fighting to keep her own temper in check. Then: "Is that what you really think of me?"

Sabra glared at her through the flickering light of the elevator. "I don't know what to think of you, Roche. But I'll tell you this much: I don't trust you *or* your friend here." She glanced pointedly at Cane. "And jealousy has nothing to do with it. I just don't like the idea of Haid's judgment being affected at this stage by some misplaced trust. It's too dangerous to our operations."

"Did he give you any reason to question his judgment at the meeting?"

The elevator shuddered to a halt. "We get out here," Sabra said, ignoring the question. "You coming or not?"

Roche squeezed her way past the guard and out of the elevator, her pulse racing with suppressed anger. What was wrong with the woman? If she wanted to make a scene, why do it now? Why didn't she do it back at the meeting?

"This way." Sabra headed off along the corridor without looking back. Roche gritted her teeth and followed.

"Listen," she said, her shoes slapping on the damp floor of the passage. "You can't be that worried about Cane and me, surely. Whatever your problem is, I'd rather you tell me now."

"I think we've already said enough, don't you?" Sabra's back remained rigid.

"No, I don't think we've even started—"

"Then let's not." Sabra stopped in mid-stride and turned to face her. Even in the poor light from the few working lamps, Roche could see hatred behind red-rimmed eyes. "Or I might be tempted to leave you down here."

Roche noted for the first time the grimy stains covering the walls and floor of the corridor, and realized with some alarm that they were in a part of the underground complex she had never seen before.

"Where the hell is this place?" she said uneasily. "What are you playing at?"

"Nothing." Sabra turned away and resumed her walk into the shadows. Over her shoulder she said, "I told Haid I'd take care of you, and that's exactly what I'll do."

Roche followed a half-step behind, matching the other woman's swift pace with stubborn determination. Whatever Sabra was up to—a test, perhaps, of the newcomer—she resolved to meet it without flinching.

<They named themselves after the system they colonized.> The Box's words intruded upon Roche's discomfort, and she fought back a curse. The last thing she needed at this moment was an interruption.

<*What?*>

<The splinter group Sylvester Teh mentioned,> said the Box. <They took the name of the system the Eckandar Trade Axis helped them take over.>

<So?>

<It may be relevant, Morgan. If you ever hope to understand Cane, you must consider all the available data. Otherwise—>

<Okay, okay. Just tell me what you have on them.>

<They reached their peak and were destroyed in the 37th Millennium, long before the Commonwealth reached this segment of the galaxy. They were a source of unrest for decades, until an alliance formed among their neighbors dedicated to putting a stop to them. In '577, at the climax of the Scion War, a flotilla of allied forces encircled their base, which they destroyed in order to prevent it being captured. The resulting explosion annihilated them as well, of course, but also decimated the flotilla. Of the four stations involved in the battle, only one survived, and that was severely damaged. So embarrassed was the alliance that the leaders of the day ordered the event stricken from history. They even closed the anchor point leading to the system to stop anyone finding out.> The Box paused—for effect, it seemed to Roche—then added: <Nothing survived of the base, and the rest of the system is an unsalvageable ruin.>

<No relics?>

<None known. No survivors, either, if that is your next question. The Sol Apotheosis Movement was, among other things, extremely thorough.>

<The who?>

<The Sol Apotheosis Movement. That was the name they chose—after the name of the system, as I said.>

Morgan absorbed this in silence for a moment. The name didn't ring a bell, and didn't seem particularly relevant. <And they tried to Transcend by altering their genetic code? I didn't think it could be done that way.> Most Transcendences took place when AI technology and consciousness research overlapped, resulting in Human-based artificial minds far larger and more complex than anything that could be housed in a biological frame.

<Conventional wisdom is in accord with that statement, yes,> the Box said. <My records indicate that their experiment, like others before it, was a failure. However—>

<Wait.> Sabra had stopped at one of the primitive wall phones that were scattered here and there throughout the rebel headquarters. Indicating for Roche to wait out of earshot, she made a quick call.

While she was doing so, Roche wandered back along the corridor, peering through doors at random. None of the rooms was occupied, and they hadn't been for some time. The floors were covered with a thin slime created from years of dust mixed with the moisture seeping down from the ceiling, and the walls had cracked and peeled with age. The farther they moved into this area of the rebels' headquarters, the more decrepit it became.

Stepping out of one room back into the hallway, Roche froze, her attention focusing upon a distant noise.

<Don't say anything, Box.>

<I wasn't going to, Morgan.>

<Quiet!>

She heard it again. A faint sound from the direction they had just come, right at the edge of hearing.

"When you're ready, Commander." Sabra's voice echoed down the corridor from behind her. Roche turned to face the woman—

And raised her hands.

"I'm not going to pretend I like you, Commander." Sabra kept the pistol aimed squarely at her stomach. "But I don't want to shoot you, either. So just walk along the wall, slowly, and keep doing so until I tell you to stop. Okay?"

Roche nodded, noting the tremor in Sabra's hands and the desperate look in her eyes. "Okay."

"Then let's move."

One step at a time, without breaking eye contact, Morgan began to move along the wall. Sabra swiveled to follow her, keeping well out of arm's reach. When Roche had passed her, she waved the pistol. "No, don't lower your hands."

Roche ignored the pain in her injured shoulder as best she could and walked along the passageway. Twenty meters ahead, the corridor branched into a T junction, with both arms of the T dark. It was clear to Roche that they had almost reached the edge of the inhabited areas and were about to enter the unrestored sections of the old university.

Whatever was about to happen to her, she supposed, would happen to her there. If she was going to do something, it had to be before then.

"I don't suppose you'd like to explain—"

"No." Sabra's voice was curt. "I know what I'm doing."

"Whatever it is, I guess it involves whoever's following us, right?"

"Please, Commander. Don't be so stupid. No one's been this way for years."

"Sabra, I'm serious. There *is* someone back there, and if they're not with you . . ."

The sound of Sabra's footsteps slowed, then stopped altogether. "Wait," she said.

Roche glanced around quickly and, seeing Sabra's back turned, made a dash for the intersection. The pistol cracked loudly, and something snatched at her side. Without breaking stride, Roche took the corner at a sprint, catching herself roughly on the wall as she did. Meters behind, the wet slap of Sabra's shoes followed.

The right-hand arm of the T was lit only by infrequent maintenance lights. Little could be seen through the gloom. The corridor angled to the left, and Roche made it around the bend just as Sabra fired a second time. The shot went well clear, ricocheting brightly in the near darkness. Roche's feet slipped in the slime as she took another corner. Quickly regaining her footing, she plunged ahead through the dimly lit corridors, dodging the occasional pile of rubble littering the floor. Row after row of inviting doorways passed her, but she ignored them. Her only hope was to lose Sabra, or somehow to double back to the T intersection.

Roche's long stride and years of exercise gradually widened her lead, although the sound of Sabra's footfalls was still too close for comfort. She took another left-hand turn, stumbled over a pile of broken furniture, then a right. Her shoulder began to ache. If she could only find a *weapon*—something solid enough that wouldn't disintegrate at the slightest touch—

Another corner brought her to a door. Through the light of a faded lamp above it, she saw the letters of a damaged sign: *F re E t.*

The door was locked.

Out of options, Roche spun to face the way she had come. She launched herself forward at the exact moment Sabra rounded the corner.

Taken by surprise, Sabra barely had time to raise the gun before Roche pushed it aside. Letting her weight carry her forward, she met Sabra's stomach with her shoulder, forcing them both to the ground. A third shot sparked crazily in the confined space, making Roche's ears ring.

Sabra punched wildly in the darkness and connected once above Roche's right ear. Roche kicked back and was gratified to feel her foot meet flesh. She grasped for purchase on her struggling adversary, wanting to use her Armada training but failing to obtain a grip; the data glove made her left hand stiff and unwieldy. The butt of the gun swung back to strike her injured shoulder, and she gasped involuntarily. Sabra rolled, brought her knee upward into her stomach. Roche fought the impulse to curl into a ball, then swung the Box's valise into exposed ribs and heard bone crack.

Sabra hissed and wrenched the pistol free. Roche tried to regain her footing and slipped in the moisture. Her flailing arm knocked the gun aside for a moment, but it returned a split-second later. Sabra's face behind it grimaced in triumph. She fired at exactly the moment Roche brought the valise up to protect her face.

The impact of the bullet knocked the valise from her hands. She kicked both legs into Sabra's chest with all her strength. The woman lifted into the air with relative ease, striking the wall on the far side of the cul-de-sac. Roche watched in total bewilderment. The kick hadn't been that hard. . . .

Then she glimpsed a shadowy figure rush past her through the gloom, its right arm still outstretched from the blow that had struck her assailant.

Sabra disappeared behind a flurry of limbs, screamed once, then reappeared a moment later, pinned by a hand at her throat against the wall under the broken sign.

Her face twisted into a rictus of pain and surprise. Roche sympathized. It had all happened so fast that not even she could quite believe it.

The arm that held the woman to the wall was attached by muscular shoulders to a profile Roche recognized instantly.

"She's dead," said Cane, his voice hushed and breathless, almost in awe. His eyes were fixed on the dying woman's face. "She just hasn't realized it yet."

Roche watched in horror as Sabra struggled once against the grip around her throat, then went still. Slowly, the pain went out of her eyes—although the fear remained.

"You can let her go, Cane." Roche clambered slowly upright, wincing. "*Cane!*"

"You die so easily," he mused, almost to himself, and let the woman's body slide to the floor. He followed it with his eyes, then turned to look over his shoulder at Roche. Seeing her shock, he said, "I don't enjoy it, you know."

"No—" She took a deep breath, and amazed herself by believing him. "I believe you."

"But I should," he said softly. "I feel it inside. I was made to kill, wasn't I?"

Roche gathered the courage to touch his arm. His skin was hot and dry and seemed to quiver under her fingertips. "I'm not going to damn you for that," she said. "You probably just saved my life—again."

He shook his head. She sensed that he was clearing his mind rather than disagreeing with her comment. She removed her hand.

When she gingerly touched behind her ear, where Sabra had punched her, her fingers came away slippery with blood: another injury to add to her collection. As she felt her side where Sabra's first shot had nicked her uniform, the tug of the chain on her wrist reminded her of the valise. There was a slight dent where the bullet had struck, but otherwise it was undamaged.

<I'm still here, Morgan.>

<I didn't doubt it, Box,> she said. <Not for a moment.>

Glancing down to Sabra's body, Roche sighed and said, "We'd better head back. If you remember the way, that is."

Cane nodded numbly in the near darkness. "Should we bring her with us?"

"No," she said, already dreading the reception they would receive. "I think she can wait here a little longer. We're going to have enough problems as it is."

14

Sciacca's World
Port Parvati
'954.10.33 EN
1500

Halfway along the corridor leading back to the elevator shaft, Roche's left arm began to tingle as data flowed through it.

<Box? What's going on?>

<I am in communication with Ameidio Haid,> replied the AI. <He desires to know your whereabouts.>

<Have you told him?>

<No.>

<Then don't. And don't tell him what happened, either.>

<He is very insistent, Morgan.> The Box paused, as though listening to another conversation, then added, <The two guards have been found.>

Roche groaned aloud. Turning to Cane, she said, "You didn't kill your guards as well, did you?"

"No. I knocked them out on the floor above where you got out." He shrugged. "I had no choice. If I was going to help you, I needed to act immediately."

Roche nodded, grateful for small mercies: at least they only had one body to explain, not three.

"But how did you *know*?" she said after a few more steps along the wet and litter-strewn floor. "About Sabra, I mean."

"She said she was taking you to the medical center," Cane replied. "But she got out of the elevator on the twenty-third floor. The medical center is on the fourteenth floor."

He made it seem simple. Almost too simple. She knew how it would sound to the rebels: easier to believe that Cane had deliberately set out to follow Roche and Sabra with the intention of killing the woman who had spoken out against him in the meeting. Even Roche found his story slightly incredible.

Yet Cane himself had urged caution at the meeting, agreeing with Sabra on almost every point. That alone was enough to convince Roche he was not lying—that and the fact that he had saved her life. But would it be enough for the rebels?

<Okay, Box. Tell Haid I'm on my way back with Cane. And tell him I need to talk to him. But don't tell him why, or what happened to Sabra. We need to handle this carefully.>

<Understood.> The Box fell silent, leaving Roche to consider how best to break the news.

Cane walked solidly beside her, as untroubled and indefatigable as ever—and with an expression that was, as always, impossible to read. His pace matched hers perfectly—slow but steady, in sympathy with her conflicting need both to hurry and to nurse new injuries. The fleeting moment of vulnerability she thought she had detected in him earlier had long since passed. She wondered if anyone could truly reach the innermost depths of him; indeed, so perfect was his control that sometimes it seemed as though he had no depth at all. Just another soldier doing his duty, without remorse or doubt—a robot in Pristine Human form, programmed to kill.

Yet Sabra *had* touched him; she was sure of that. Somehow. On a level Roche could never hope to reach, although she was—for the moment at least—his putative ally.

The remainder of the walk to the elevator passed in silence. As they rounded the final bend and the doors came into view, Roche realized that she had hardly begun to decide how she would break the news to Haid. Every time she went over it in her head, it sounded clumsy and clichéd:

Sabra started it—

Cane acted in self-defense—

I had no choice—

If there was any other way . . .

The elevator approached all too quickly. Had Haid followed Roche's request, he would already be waiting for her on one of the upper floors. She had only minutes left in which to decide how she was going to handle the explanation.

When they came to a halt by the doors, Roche eyed Cane uncertainly. "Maybe you should stay down here for a while," she said. "Until things quiet down."

"No," he said. "Better to get it over with."

He reached out for the elevator button. Before he could touch it, however, the doors pulled back with a hiss.

Facing them, in the elevator, were Haid and three rebel guards. Roche automatically backed away; Cane stood his ground without apparent concern for the projectile rifles raised and pointing at them.

Haid waved at the guards to lower their weapons and stepped out to greet the two of them. "Sorry to startle you," he said. "I thought it best to meet you halfway."

"How did you . . . ?" Roche fumbled for the words.

"Find you?" Haid smiled. "Simple, really. We triangulated the data glove's short-wave transmission, tracing the signal back through the receiving stations throughout the building. What the Box told me only confirmed what we had already learned for ourselves."

Annoyance and discomfort suddenly tangled inside her. "You didn't trust us?"

"One of the most important rules in covert operations is never to design a safe house without a back door. This way leads to one of ours, and given what you've learned since you arrived, it seemed sensible to—"

He stopped suddenly, peering along the dim corridor.

"Where's Sabra?" he asked. Catching the dark expression on Roche's face, he added: "What's happened to her?"

Roche opened her mouth to reply, but Cane spoke before the half-planned words had even formed in her mind.

"She's dead," he said simply and without emotion.

Haid's face hardened, and he stepped back as though Cane had physically struck him. The rifles came up again, and this time the rebel leader did not order them down.

"You're not joking, are you?" His artificial eye narrowed, fixing itself upon Cane.

"No," said Cane, returning Haid's monocular challenge evenly. "I killed her."

"I can explain." Roche stepped in quickly. "Please, Haid, just give me a chance. It's not what it seems."

"I hope so," said Haid, keeping his glare on Cane. "I honestly hope so."

"Okay." The scarred woman made no effort to conceal her hostility. "Tell me again, and this time don't leave anything out."

Roche floundered for a moment. Leave anything out? She had told her story as completely the last time as the time before, and the time before that, when Haid had interviewed her. What could she possibly have forgotten?

Then she realized: this was an oft-used trick of interrogation. By making the suspect feel that she had omitted something from a fabricated tale, new and crucial information might sometimes be forthcoming. Confession by overcompensation.

Roche sighed, and patiently began the recital from the beginning. She had left the meeting with Sabra, and had exited the elevator on the twenty-third floor. . . .

The woman rerecorded Roche's story, along with each and every nuance of her face. A thick scar warped the woman's own upper lip into a permanent sneer, and Roche wondered if a psychological trauma had similarly twisted her personality. This, the fourth time Roche had described the events of the last few hours, elicited no response other than wordless, yet obvious, contempt.

Apart from the woman, Roche was alone in the holding bay. Two armed rebels guarded the other side of the door. Cane had been removed to another cell after their initial interrogation by Haid, and Roche hadn't seen him since. If he was alive or dead, she had no way of knowing—although she suspected the former was more likely to be true, knowing the man's amazing constitution.

Halfway through her "confession," the intercom buzzed. The woman put aside her work slate to take the call, casting a warning look at Roche as she did.

Haid's voice over the intercom was terse. "That's enough for now, Rasia. Have the commander escorted back to her room and make sure she stays there. Tell the escort to talk to no one on the way. I don't want word leaking out before I'm ready."

Roche pushed forward to the intercom. "Ameidio, this is Roche. What the hell's going on?"

"I'll call you when I've decided." With a click, he severed the line.

Roche backed away from the intercom as the guards entered the room. "Okay, okay." She let herself be led from the holding bay, with the scarred woman bringing up the rear. She had no choice. Until she spoke to Haid, her options were severely limited.

On the way to her room, she passed a couple of faces she recognized from the refectory the previous day. One nodded at her, showing no awareness of the events that had transpired since they had last met. Roche nodded back, unable to prevent the blush that spread up her neck and into her hairline. She cursed herself for *feeling* like a traitor.

When they reached her room, the guards keyed it open and motioned for her to enter. She did so, noting first of all that Maii had left during her absence, and second that the lock on the inside of the door had been disabled. She turned to protest, but was met with the stony sneer of the scarred woman.

"Don't expect mercy," said the woman. "We look after our own down here."

With that, the woman slammed the door shut and locked it. When the sound of footsteps outside had faded into silence, she let go the breath she had been holding.

Mercy? Roche wasn't expecting mercy. She would settle for justice, any day.

Still, she supposed she shouldn't be too hasty. In their situation, she might have behaved the same.

<I have been denied access to the rebels' security system,> announced the Box into the silence.

She shrugged and sat down on the edge of the bed. "I guess that's to be expected," she said.

<If not a little frustrating.> The Box sounded annoyed, though Roche knew that this was impossible. <From the moment Haid learned what happened, all official channels have been closed.>

"How about unofficial?"

<We are too deep below ground to access anything useful. The most I can manage is an edited feed of the local IDnet outlet.>

"Okay," she said, lying back on the bunk. "Show me."

Her left eye greyed for a moment, then cleared. The familiar stream of news, from places near and distant, flowed past her: wars, accidents, negotiations, science, deaths. Even after so few days trapped on Sciacca's World, much of it made reference to current events that were unfamiliar to her, making her feel isolated from the rest of the COE and the galaxy beyond. At least three major conflicts near the Commonwealth were completely unfamiliar to her, and there were many more beyond—more than she was sure was normal. She wondered if the background level of violence in the galaxy had indeed risen without her being aware of it, or if that impression was merely a result of her recent isolation.

One name, however, stood out: Palasian System.

She recalled hearing about it being quarantined just prior to her leaving the *Midnight*. Now it had been declared the site of a "major catastrophe" and sealed off to all traffic. Not even aid or rescue ships could breach the blockade. No explanation was offered as to the cause of the catastrophe, however, before the data stream moved on to another war that had broken out in a distant part of the galaxy. Whatever had happened to Palasian System, it must have been serious to warrant such utter isolation.

Suddenly struck by a thought, she turned her attention back to the Box. "Have you been monitoring this?" she asked.

<As a matter of course. Why do you ask?>

"Has there been any mention of the *Midnight*?"

<None, I'm afraid. Either word has not reached the Armada, or the information is being suppressed. Both possibilities are disturbing. Perhaps help is not on the way, as we had hoped.>

Roche nodded. "Or they want to take the Dato by surprise."

<Unlikely. Any Armada ships entering the system will be visible well before any confrontation would be possible.>

"True." Roche frowned as another thought occurred to her. "But why would—?"

The sound of the door opening interrupted her in mid-sentence, although the question remained sharp in her thoughts: *Why would the COE Armada suppress the information*?

Making a mental note to follow this up later, she rose to greet her visitor.

"Roche," said Haid. The rebel leader looked haggard and drawn, as though he hadn't slept for a week. He was alone.

"I would invite you in," Roche said, unable to keep the bitterness from her voice. "But that seems inappropriate given the circumstances."

Haid closed the door behind him and turned to face her. "You have no reason to resent me," he said. "I'm not here officially."

"Does that mean you've reached a decision?"

"Well, your story checks out," he said. "As I said earlier, there's a shaft leading from the old sector to the surface—our back door. At the exit from the shaft, we found Edan Malogorski. Sabra had arranged to meet him there to take you to the landing field. It looks like she was going to sell you to the wardens for the bounty."

Roche sat up on the bunk. "That seems obvious."

"Maybe." The rebel leader sighed. "I have my doubts, though."

"I thought you just said that my story checked out."

"I have no doubts about what she intended to do; the facts are irrefutable. The why, though, is a different matter. In the elevator, according to your statement, Sabra said that she thought Cane was under your control. It's my guess she believed that by getting rid of you, she'd be rid of Cane as well. Maybe she was more concerned with my safety than the money."

"And maybe you're being overcharitable regarding her motives." Roche remembered the implied jealousy in the woman's words, the fierce resentment she had harbored toward the new woman in town. "She certainly made it clear, from the day I arrived, that she'd rather Cane and I weren't around. Regardless of Cane's past, or my dealings with you—"

"She was simply wary of you," Haid interrupted. "As we all are with strangers." Haid paced the length of the room once, then returned to face her. "If I *am* being overcharitable, as you say, then it's because I knew her better than you did. I served with her when she was a lieutenant on the *Transpicuous* before I went out on my own. When I was sentenced here . . ." He filled the pause with a sigh. "It was she who took me from the gutter. Everything I've done here, it was with her aid. If she had an ulterior motive in turning you in, then it was to help me, not for the money."

Haid stopped talking, his one empty eye socket red. Roche could sense his pain as palpably as the dust on his clothes, in the tone of voice and the lines of his face. He needed to believe what he was saying, needed to believe that his old friend hadn't betrayed his trust. And Roche could sympathize. She herself had been betrayed often enough in her youth, to the point where she had avoided close friendships ever since. Who was she to call into question the strength of a relationship she had had no part of? Furthermore, she conceded, he might even have been right.

"Unfortunately," Haid continued after a moment, "the facts have leaked. And they are damning, whichever way they are interpreted."

Roche took a deep breath. She could sense that they were approaching the real reason for his visit. "Go on."

"Well, on the one hand, I'm being pressured to turn you in myself, by those who think Sabra had the right idea. They're supported by another camp, who believe that you and Cane led Sabra into the old quarter to murder her. Taken together, these two factions comprise a majority of us down here."

"But you don't agree?"

"No," he said. "And therein lies the problem. If I decide not to turn you in, I'll be disobeying the wishes of the very people I'm supposed to serve." Haid ran his artificial fingers across his ebony scalp. "At the heart of the matter is the fact that I'm an outsider myself; some of the indigenes have always resented me taking over, and they will use that lever to call for a no-confidence vote. Given their clear majority in this matter, I'm bound to lose. And the new leader will no doubt turn you in anyway."

Roche kept her emotions carefully hidden. "So what happens now?"

"After all the resentment and anger you've stirred up, I don't really have much choice." Haid's mouth tightened. "We need an outlet, or the problem will just get worse. The last thing we need right now is a leadership crisis."

"But you *can't* blame us," Roche said urgently, sensing her last chance slipping through her fingers. "Make Cane and me scapegoats—kill us, or whatever—and the High Equity Court will never listen to you."

"I know that." Haid shook his head. "And Veden agrees with you. But there are two hundred Enforcers searching the city for you as we speak. Five of our safe houses have been breached. Twenty people have been taken for interrogation. Five have been killed for 'obstructing investigations.'

"And then there are the Dato. A landing party touched down yesterday and entered the city six hours ago. Reports are coming in of fires in the old subway, lit by the squad. It looks like they've found an entrance to our underground network. If that's the case, then it's only a matter of time before they find us here." Haid glanced briefly around at the walls of the cell before his gaze fell back upon Roche. "Twenty Enforcers we could bribe. Fifty we could fight in self-defense. But two hundred and a well-armed Dato squad . . ." He shrugged helplessly.

"But we need to do *something*," he went on. "Which is why I've decided to take you with us."

Roche studied him quizzically for a moment. "Take us where?"

"To the landing field, of course. We have to attack while they're busy in the city, and hope your plan works."

"*My* plan?"

"I spoke to Neva and Emmerik. They believe it's sound, and I'm prepared to go with their judgment. They'll be in the attacking party, along with you and me and five others."

"But what about the command codes? There's no point attacking until—"

"We have the codes. Maii learned them an hour ago."

"And weapons? We're hopelessly outgunned for a frontal assault—"

"Don't worry about that. I'll fix it."

Roche took a deep breath, resigning herself to the fact that the decision had been made, and nothing she said could change it. "We need time to prepare, then."

"We have two hours." Haid's artificial eye regarded her implacably. "You'll suit up and meet the others as we leave. Until then, you stay here." He reached into his jacket and removed a work slate—a small processor with a flatscreen and compressed keyboard—which he handed to her. "Whatever happens, we can't just sit back idly here, waiting for the Dato Bloc to arrive. You can still be useful, if you want." He nodded at the slate in Roche's hands. "The others will be busy getting equipment ready. Study this for us; make *sure* the plan will work. I'll send someone down with Cane as soon as we're ready.

"But remember: this isn't an official action. As far as the indigenes are concerned, I'm still considering your fate. When we leave, it'll supposedly be to turn you in. So do your best to look cowed, and don't breathe a word of this to anyone else."

With that, he keyed the door open and left.

Roche activated the slate and sat back down on the bed to study the image that appeared on the small screen and the heading above it:

PORT PARVATI SECURITY: CONFIDENTIAL

She stared at it for a moment, unable to absorb the sudden reversal. Haid was right, of course: if the Dato were actively hunting her, it would be only a matter of time before they found her here. They needed to move somewhere else, somewhere safe. But there was nowhere safe on the entire planet, nowhere to hide. And if the Enforcers truly were distracted by their own searches, then it made sense to attack the landing field while their defenses were down—to hunt instead of being hunted.

Yet, somehow, it was too much too soon. Her ribs still ached, and her newly injured side throbbed. She needed rest, time to gather her resources. Her allegiances—with Haid, with Cane, with the Box—were still too fragile to test during an all-out attack on the Enforcement stronghold. If any one of them failed, she would be worse off than when she had started.

And hadn't there already been enough death?

Even as her doubts assailed her, however, her conviction to the plan remained strong. She had a mission—to deliver the Box to COE Intelligence HQ—and this was the best way to achieve it. If she was to leave the planet—which she had to do, in order to succeed—then this was the only way.

She had no options anymore. Circumstances dictated that she should fight, so she would do so to the best of her abilities, and with every resource she could muster, external and internal.

In the end, whether she failed or succeeded, at least she could say that she had tried.

<Box?> The AI didn't answer. The tingling in her arm had returned, however, and she wasn't certain what to make of that. Still, she could analyze the landing field's defenses just as well without the Box's help.

Lying back on the bed, she began to work.

15

Sciacca's World
Port Parvati
'954.10.34 EN
0925

After an hour of silence, the Box suddenly returned:

<Morgan, get ready.>

"Box!" Roche sat up with a start, the slate slipping from her lap onto the bed. "Where the hell have you *been*? I've—"

Before she could finish, a siren began to sound. Footsteps approached her room, then continued past. Someone shouted in the distance, but the words were too faint to be heard over the screaming of the siren.

Then, even more distantly, she heard the dull thud of an explosion, followed by the sporadic chattering of weapons fire. A tang of smoke began to filter through the ancient university's air circulation system.

Standing upright, she faced the door. But with the lock on her side disabled, there wasn't much she could do. She felt impotent, trapped. Slapping the flat of her palm on the door, she shouted to attract the attention of anyone who might be passing:

"What's going on out there?" She waited for a moment, then banged again. "Hey! Is anyone there?"

The door burst open, knocking her to one side. Haid and Emmerik entered, each carrying a projectile rifle.

"Quickly!" barked the rebel leader. "They've found us."

"The Dato?" Roche hurriedly regained her composure and collected the slate.

"Enforcement," said Emmerik. "But the Dato won't be far behind."

The burly Mbatan came up behind her. "Take this." Another rifle. "We'll have to hurry."

Roche nodded. "Understood."

"Let's go." Haid led the way out of the room. Another muffled explosion greeted them as they entered the hallway; a veil of plaster dust drifted down from the ceiling, and the smell of smoke grew stronger.

"They came up the old subway," Emmerik explained as they picked their way cautiously through the corridors. "About fifteen of them. They broke through the blockades and overran our sentries before help could arrive from above. We dropped ten of them before their own reinforcements showed up. Reports are a little confused, but our best estimate places them at around twenty, with more on the way."

"They're destroying everything as they come," added Haid. "Batteries, mainframes, stores—whatever they can lay their hands on. They're making sure that if we leave, there'll be nothing for us to return to."

"We have no choice," said Emmerik. "We *have* to leave. If we don't, we'll be caught between above and below when the Dato arrive."

"I know." Haid gritted his teeth. "I just hate to be forced into something I was going to do anyway."

Roche could sympathize, but she kept her mouth shut. They wound their way through increasingly smoky corridors, occasionally glimpsing other rebels, likewise evacuating the headquarters, until they reached a narrow door tucked into a cul-de-sac. Haid opened it with a key, revealing an equally narrow staircase.

"The others are waiting for us topside," he said. "Cane included. We can't break radio silence to let them know we're coming—or to make sure they're still there. We could be heading into anything, so be ready." He indicated for them to enter. "Emmerik, you first."

Roche followed the Mbatan up the stairs, with Haid behind her. The staircase wound steeply upward in a tight spiral, lit by ancient fluorescent tubes every half turn. Explosions occasionally came through the stone walls like the booming of enormous beasts. The loudest, and presumably the nearest, made the steps shake beneath their feet.

Then, when Roche estimated that they had risen about ten floors, the lights went out.

"They've reached the main generator," Haid said into the darkness. "Good."

"It is? Why?" Roche stumbled in the dark, then regained her balance.

"Someone tripped the breakers before they arrived," Emmerik explained.

"Didn't you notice?" said Haid. "No explosion."

"So?"

"Wait a second," said Emmerik. "You'll see."

They continued to climb. Behind her, barely audible over the sound of their scuffling feet, she could hear Haid counting to himself.

". . . three . . . two . . . one . . . Hang on!"

Roche braced herself as the air began to tremble. A rumbling sound grew steadily louder until the walls began to vibrate, shaking loose pockets of dirt that rained down upon them, causing Roche to gag. Then, an explosion from somewhere deep beneath her feet, the force of which made the steps themselves buck. Roche slipped to her knees, instinctively wrapping an arm about her head for protection from the rubble spilling down from above. She only looked up again when she heard Haid's cry of elation in the ringing aftermath, although the darkness still effectively hid him.

"That'll slow them down!"

"What—?" Roche staggered to her feet, still hearing phantom echoes of the blast in her ears. "The generator blew?"

"Self-destructed. A little contingency we prepared years ago, if we were ever forced to leave." His voice held equal parts triumph and regret. "They might think twice next time before advancing so quickly."

"Maybe," Emmerik muttered from farther up the stairwell. "But we no longer have a headquarters."

"Not that it matters anymore," Haid responded, although less vigorously. "Soon we'll either have the landing field, or nothing at all." A hand reached out of the darkness to nudge Roche upward. "Keep moving. We've still got a long way to go."

They exited the stairwell a few minutes later, Emmerik first, with his rifle ready. The safe house was clear, although shots rang out from somewhere close by. Roche followed the Mbatan through the corridors of the building, Haid at her side, until they reached the garage where they had disembarked from the truck two days before. Sunlight seeped through grimy windows, casting geometric patterns across the packed earth floor. Roche blinked, startled; she had lost track of the time underground.

A fleeting figure passed across the other entrance to the garage, and was gone before Roche could raise her rifle. It returned an instant later: Cane.

"Good, you're here," he said. He was wearing combat armor provided by the rebels—not powered, but passive; thick plates of black impact-resistant foam padding his torso and limbs. A lightweight helmet covered his head, its faceplate removed. "This way."

He led them to the room in which Roche had showered. Standing massive and still in the center of the room was the suit they had stolen from the Enforcement team in Houghton's Cross.

"Hey, Proctor," Roche said, running a hand across the suit. "Am I glad to see you."

"We recharged its batteries before the generator blew," said Cane.

"Excellent," said Haid.

Roche moved forward and removed the data glove. Cane held the Box in position behind her back as she stepped into the headless shell. When her palm slid home into the suit's left glove, the armor came to life, wrapping around her body in an intimate yet intimidating embrace.

<All systems functioning, Morgan,> the Box reported.

She took a step, feeling the solid thump of the suit striking the floor through her feet. Again, the sensation of power diffused through her veins—hypnotic, and misleading. Still, it was good to be feeling strong and in control once again.

Cane, standing behind her, placed a helmet on her head. "There's an Enforcement team outside," he said, both to her and the others. "We've been holding them off until you arrived."

"You and how many?" asked Haid.

"Six others. Two on each floor, sniping from windows."

"How many Enforcers?" Haid asked quickly.

"A dozen or so, most of them in the building opposite. Maii says there's another team on the way."

"Maii's here too?" Roche turned to face Cane.

<One floor above you,> came the whispering voice of the reave.

"Veden, too," said Cane. "We're going to need both of them if this plan is going to work."

"Is he up to fighting?" said Roche.

"Sylvester finished treatment late yesterday," Haid explained. "His system has been flushed clean, and his long-term prognosis is good. Whether he can fight or not, though, I don't know."

<No,> said Maii. <He is still weak, although he hates to admit it.>

"We'll have to carry him out, then—"

<I am detecting launches from the landing field,> the Box interrupted, speaking over Haid's plans to get Veden out of the safe house. <Three surface craft—headed for us, I assume.>

<How long do we have?> Roche asked.

<Minutes, perhaps.>

<Then we'd better get moving.> Roche swiveled to face Haid. "We have to get out of here. There are flyers on the way."

"Maii?" The rebel cast his one eye toward the ceiling. "Did you hear that?"

<I heard. But we are too slow. Leave us here, and we will rendezvous with you later.>

"You'll be trapped!" Roche protested, her voice unnecessarily loud.

<No. I can shield two from harm. We will be refugees, innocents caught in the crossfire. No one will interfere with us.>

"Are you sure?" asked Haid.

<Positive. Tell us where to meet you, and we will be there.>

Haid described a rendezvous while Roche strode heavily back to the garage. Intermittent gunfire crackled in the street outside. Faintly at first, but growing louder, she began to hear the nasal buzz of aircraft.

"If we go outside, we will be caught in a pincer," said Cane from behind her.

"I agree." She flexed the fingers of her suit's right glove. "We'll have to go back down again and come up another way."

Haid and Emmerik, when they had finished making arrangements with Maii, agreed.

"Neva is still down there somewhere," said the Mbatan.

"So is Enforcement," said Roche.

"If Maii can contact her, she can open the back door," said Emmerik. "Or at least keep it from being closed."

Haid nodded. "We'll go down via the stairwell—if you'll fit," he added with a nod to Roche. "The others will stay topside to keep Enforcement off our backs for as long as possible."

"Agreed." *A suicide mission*, Roche thought to herself, glad she wouldn't be staying behind.

<I will relay your orders,> Maii said. <If there is any way for them to escape as well, we will use it.>

"Good." Haid glanced around him, at Emmerik, Cane, and Roche. His face betrayed little of the nervousness Roche herself was feeling. He seemed poised but relaxed, much as Cane did: a natural fighter.

There, however, the resemblance ended. Haid had initially learned the ability to fight by implants, whereas Cane seemed to have been born with it. Watching the muscles twitching in Cane's neck as he led the way back to the stairwell, she wondered how he felt about his experiences so far. Was it just a game to him, a series of obstacles to be overcome in a larger plan—or was he as Pristine as he seemed, despite the evidence?

She doubted she'd ever find out. The best she could hope for—if it *was* all a game to him, and if for the moment he was playing on their side—was that he'd win.

After that, she was prepared to take her chances.

At the bottom of the stairwell, Roche eased gratefully out of the cramped space and into a dark, smoke-filled passageway. Forced to descend sideways due to the width of the suit's shoulders, she relished the simple joy of facing the direction in which she was going.

"Clear," she called to the others, when she had swept the corridor with the lights on the suit's chest. Apart from smoke and debris, the way was empty.

Haid emerged from the stairwell, followed by Emmerik. Cane came last, shutting the door carefully behind him.

"That way." Haid pointed ahead. "Turn left at the next corridor. We'll have to climb down the elevator shaft to get to the right level."

Roche led the way through the ruined headquarters, stepping gingerly over the debris. Occasionally they passed bodies; apart from one Enforcer, the dead were all rebels. Emmerik stopped briefly at each to identify the victims. Roche waited patiently while he did so; although to her the dead were strangers, to the Mbatan they would have been family.

They reached the elevator shaft without mishap. The doors had been blown open by the explosion of the power plant, and the cage had fallen to the lowest level. Cables dangled like snake carcasses before the entrance, while fires from below gave the scene an almost infernal ambience.

"Two levels down is the one we want," Haid said. "Do you think the cables will take your weight?"

Roche shrugged. "We'll soon find out."

The four of them slithered down the shaft, Cane more speedily than the others. When they reached the right floor, he had already levered the doors open and was waiting to help them through. Roche thudded with relief onto the solid floor. Despite the strength of the suit's grip, she had experienced a few moments of apprehension on the way down.

The smoke was thicker on the twenty-third floor, and smelled strongly of burnt insulation. The suit lights struggled to penetrate the gloom, and she eventually gave up looking for the most part, relying on hearing to tell if there was anyone ahead. As yet, however, they had encountered no one in the ruins.

"Almost too quiet," said Emmerik, echoing her thoughts.

"No sign of anyone at all," Haid agreed.

"I can hear people," said Cane. "Not close, though."

"This level?" said Haid.

"Perhaps." Cane closed his eyes and cocked his head slightly. "It's hard to tell."

Haid nodded. "Okay. You and Emmerik wait here. Roche, come with me."

Roche obeyed, following the rebel leader through the shadows, her chest lights burning circles into his back. He led them down the corridor a short way, then turned left. Fifty meters farther, they came to a locked door.

"Good," he muttered, fumbling with the manual lock. "It hasn't been disturbed."

"What hasn't?"

"Munitions dump." He glanced over his shoulder, his artificial iris constricting as Roche's lights stabbed at him. "We need everything we can get to tackle the landing field. Seeing as we're already down here . . ."

The door opened with a click, and Haid waved her inside. The small room contained a single crate, from which he handed her a number of small items. Stowing them carefully in the suit's chest and thigh compartments, she mentally recorded each item: grenades, mortars, ammunition for the projectile rifles, gas cylinders, pistols, power packs, pressure mines . . .

When the suit was full, Haid stowed an armful in his own clothes and led her out of the room.

"Back doors *and* arms caches," she said as they began to walk back the way they had come. "Has anybody ever told you people that you're paranoid?"

"You have to be," he replied. "An underground movement is always under threat—especially one as established as our own. Long-term survival is inevitably more important than short-term gains. What we lost in the past by diverting arms to secret caches is more than compensated for by the possibility that we might survive *now*."

Roche smiled to herself, remembering her Tactics teacher at college, many years ago, whose words Haid had unknowingly echoed: "Show your true face to your enemy, and expect to have it slapped. Give everything you've got, and expect it to be taken away from you. Never feel so superior, or inferior, that you can afford to relinquish your most valuable weapon: deceit. A war is won only when at least one of the parties loses the ability to lie. . . ."

The younger Roche had always thought her teacher slightly cynical. Now she had to admit that his point was sound, in practice.

Cane and Emmerik were where they had left them. As one, they headed along the corridor toward the headquarters' back door—the place where Sabra had died. Halfway there, Roche remembered the final expression on Sabra's face. The bewildered horror and despair in the woman's eyes, as victory had been suddenly turned to defeat, was a potent reminder that nothing should be taken for granted.

Part of the roof had collapsed near the end of the corridor. As they climbed over the obstacle, Cane announced that he could hear fighting up ahead.

"Gunshots, energy weapons—" He peered forward through the gloom, as though willing the smoke to part. "And voices."

Roche could hear nothing. "How many?"

"I can't tell."

"Quietly, then," said Haid, shrugging his rifle into a more comfortable position. "Lead the way, Cane. Roche, turn your lights off."

They continued along their way with Roche at the rear. Presently, she too heard the sounds Cane had reported: the occasional sizzle of energy weapons, the angry crack of rifles.

When they reached the end of the corridor and entered the maze of corridors, their progress became even more cautious.

"I estimate ten Enforcers," Cane whispered over his shoulder to Haid. "Maybe the same number of your people defending the exit. The Enforcers lie between us and the others."

"With their backs to us," the rebel leader finished.

They came to a halt near a corner. Flashes of light issued from the branching corridor every time an energy weapon discharged. Explosions echoed through the confined space, almost painfully loud.

"Lights back on, Roche," said Haid, stepping aside. "They'll think you're one of them long enough for us to get close."

Roche activated the suit's chest lights and strode forward. The three men waited a moment, then followed in her shadow. As she turned the corner, she quickly surveyed the scene.

Seven armored Enforcers filled the crowded corridor, using debris for shelter where it was available. Beyond them, across a short section of no-man's-land, a rough blockade protected the entrance to the room where Sabra had died. As Roche watched, a projectile rifle was fired from behind the blockade, sending ricochets sparking along the walls. She automatically ducked before regaining her composure and moving on.

Barely had she taken five steps when the Enforcement squad noticed her. Recognizing her armor as one of their own, they turned back to the fighting. She swallowed, and raised her rifle.

Before she could fire, Cane rushed past. Snatching a percussion rifle from the hands of the nearest Enforcer, he turned it on the armor, blowing holes in the tough ceramic and killing the person inside instantly. The rest of the squad, belatedly realizing that they were being attacked from behind, scrambled for cover.

The corridor quickly dissolved into chaos. A hail of bullets and energy filled the air. Silhouetted against the firestorm were the combat suits, powerful shadows jerking from side to side, trying to locate targets in the mess of motion.

Roche's rifle kicked in her hands. A lucky shot shattered an Enforcer's visor. Pressing the advantage, she rammed the butt through the starred plastic. Screaming, the Enforcer dropped his percussion rifle, and Roche stooped to pick it up. Firing quick bursts, she backed away. Blinded, the Enforcer staggered forward with his arms outstretched until the suit failed completely and he collapsed spread-eagled to the ground.

Emmerik heaved the suit into a sitting position and used its solid bulk as a shield. A second Enforcer fell under Roche's fire, and a third. Cane dodged in front of her, firing a stolen rifle at its owner. Haid joined Emmerik, and together they picked off the remaining Enforcers.

Within moments, the skirmish was over. Haid climbed over the ruined suits to meet his fellow rebels behind the blockade, trailing a streamer of blood from a flesh wound in his left leg. Roche and Cane gathered the undamaged weapons from the bodies and did the same. Emmerik waited until they were through before following.

"Emmerik!"

A battle-worn Neva pressed forward to take the Mbatan by the arm. Her face was grimy and blackened, but otherwise she seemed none the worse for wear.

"We made it." Haid held a cloth to staunch the flow from his leg.

"Not a moment too soon," she said. "Maii told us to wait, but I don't know how much longer we could have held them off."

"That you did for long enough is all that matters." The rebel leader urged Roche forward. Opening one of the suit's compartments, he retrieved a grenade and primed it. "You go with the others. I'll catch up with you in a moment."

Neva led the way through the doorway with the damaged sign above it. Another flight of stairs greeted them, this one easily wide enough for the suit and lit by baleful red emergency lights.

Roche performed a quick head count: herself, Cane, Emmerik, Neva and a half dozen surviving rebels. Eleven people, four of them with Enforcement percussion rifles, only one with combat armor.

"Are we all that made it out?" she asked Neva.

Neva shook her head. "I sent about twenty ahead. There may be more who came before us, too. The exit was open when we reached it."

Roche nodded. The number was still small, but not as bad as it had seemed at first. Enforcement had been looking for *her*, after all, and she didn't want a massacre on her conscience.

A muffled detonation from the base of the stairwell made her ears pop. That was followed by the sound of falling masonry. Moments later, Haid limped to join them, shaking dust from his clothes.

"The exit is blocked," he said, grimacing. "If anyone's left down there, they'll have to take the subway out."

Neva put a hand on his shoulder and squeezed. "Your leg . . . ?"

"Is fine," he said, looking around at the party. "Am I the only one wounded?"

"No." Her gaze shifted to Emmerik, who nodded, then to Roche. "But we've made it this far. That's the main thing."

Emmerik grunted—a sound that might have been laughter. "For now," he said.

The rebels' back door opened into a disused building in an abandoned lane. Sun and Soul burned brightly after the darkness below ground, and Roche took a moment to adjust. The air was dry and dusty, as always, and a light wind cast short-lived eddies about her legs. From the southeast, in the general direction of the main entrance to the subterranean headquarters, the air carried the scent of smoke.

The city was quiet, however: no gunfire, no buzz of aircraft. Just the occasional bleating of pack animals and the throaty roar of poorly tuned chemical engines. Life went on, even in the middle of a revolution.

"We'll need a truck," said Haid through gritted teeth. His wounded leg had pained him toward the end of the journey up the stairwell; while Emmerik carefully bound it to staunch the flow of blood, he concentrated on their ongoing mission. "Maii and Veden should be waiting for us not far from here, but there's no way we'll be able to walk into the landing field. At the very least we'll have to ram the gates, and—"

"If something goes wrong on the way in, we'll be in trouble," said Roche, remembering the plans of the landing field she had studied in her cell. "The distance from the Enforcement compound to the administration and MiCom buildings is roughly one hundred meters. Even at a run, we'll be sitting ducks."

One of the rebels, a woman named Jytte, said, "We're attacking the landing field?"

"No one is under any obligation." Haid limped forward, testing his weight on the leg. "You don't have to come along if you don't want to."

Jytte shook her head uncertainly. "It's just that—I mean, the *landing field* . . . ?"

"It's not as stupid as it sounds," said Haid. "Enforcement's distracted, the Dato landing party is busy, and we have the element of surprise. Yes, we're outnumbered, but we'll *always* be outnumbered. It doesn't really matter. We either succeed with what we've got, or we die trying. It's as simple as that."

"Exactly," said Roche, "but we do need a vehicle of some description."

Haid nodded. "We used to keep a reserve vehicle near here, but it's unfueled and therefore useless." The rebel leader glanced around the survivors, one by one. "Now's the time to call in favors, if you have any due."

No one spoke immediately.

Then, from Cane: "What about a flyer? If we could commandeer one—"

"No." Haid quickly dismissed the idea. "We don't want to tip them off too soon."

"I can help." Emmerik stood up unexpectedly. "There's an old solar-powered van we use sometimes to ferry equipment into the desert."

A short and uneasy silence followed as Haid glanced from the Mbatan to Neva. "I thought I was supposed to know about things like this."

"You are, but . . ." The Mbatan shuffled from foot to foot in discomfort. "It's just that some disagreed. Not me personally," he added quickly. "But some of those outside the city—"

"The wild ones," said Neva evenly. "They see *us* as city people, Ameidio, and what trust we gained from them came grudgingly. But you they've always been suspicious of."

Haid's apparent hurt dissolved after a moment and became a grudging smile. "You indies will never change, will you?" he said. "So where is this van?"

"Not far." Emmerik and Neva exchanged glances briefly; then the woman turned back to the rebel leader. "I'll show you."

"Fine," said the Mbatan. "And I'll meet you at the rendezvous point. I have to organize the . . ." He hesitated. "The other matter we discussed."

Haid nodded. "Will an hour be long enough?"

"It should be." Emmerik shouldered his percussion rifle in a perfunctory salute, then headed off along the alley.

"What other matter?" Roche asked, sotto voce.

"Don't worry about it," said Haid. "You'll know when it happens—*if* it happens at all, that is. And that's up to the indies." Something in his eyes revealed that he was more deeply concerned about the indigenes' mistrust of him than he showed, and Roche sympathized: for all his work over the last few years, the rebel organization remained at heart divided. And wherever division existed, weaknesses could form. Sabra's death had clearly proven that.

She changed the subject. "What about arms? Any more caches up here?"

"None, I'm afraid." He looked pointedly away, as though she had inadvertently touched upon another sore point. To the group as a whole, he said, "Let's go, people! The sooner we get out of here, the safer we'll be." Then, as an aside to Roche, he added, "Relatively speaking, of course."

The rendezvous point was empty when they arrived. Haid steered the ancient van to an abrupt halt in a disused lot where it wouldn't attract attention and turned to the five people sitting in the back. Cane, Roche, Neva, and the two rebels faced him in unison.

"We'll wait a while," he said. "The sight of us approaching might have been enough to send them to ground."

Roche thought that was a distinct possibility. The van, with its ripped vanes and irritating whine, was enough to make *her* nervous. Only a disproportionately solid construction and regular, if roughshod, maintenance had kept it operating this long; it looked as though anything more substantial than a strong gust of wind might send it to pieces. The movement of her suit alone was enough to make it shudder.

Still, the van had survived the desert for decades without failing. And as Haid had said, they had to make do with what little they had. It wasn't too late to turn back, but the number of alternative courses of action open to them was dismayingly small.

Sure enough, minutes after the van had come to a halt, they heard a gentle rapping at the rear panel.

<It's us,> said the reave.

Neva leaned across to open the door. "We were beginning to wonder if you'd made it."

<We almost didn't.> The small Surin climbed into the back and helped Veden

after her. This, Roche's first sight of the Eckandi since his injury at Houghton's Cross, disturbed her. The back of his head was covered by a bandage, and his skin was worryingly pale. His eyes were closed as though the sun was too bright for him. When Maii had him in the van, he sagged onto a bench with a small, pained hiss.

The fact that he was even conscious—given his previously comatose condition, and the lack of medical resources available to the rebels—amazed Roche. And, much to her surprise, she realized that she was relieved.

As though he could sense her staring at him, he opened his eyes and nodded in recognition.

"Sorry to disappoint you, Roche," he said with disdain—although something in his eyes suggested to Roche that his contempt was superficial. "It looks like I'll be pulling through, after all."

"No, I—" Roche started in embarrassment, wondering when her feelings for the Eckandi had changed.

Veden didn't give her a chance to consider. "I hear you've been taking good care of Maii," he said.

"Trying to," she replied, conscious of the others watching her. "How are *you* feeling?"

"Tired." Veden touched the bandage lightly with one hand, and closed his eyes again. "And a little ill, to be honest," he said. "So if you'll excuse me, I need to rest."

Embarrassed by his weakness, Roche turned away, focusing her attention instead upon Maii's account of their escape.

<The Dato weren't as easily fooled as Enforcement.> Maii's words passed through Roche's thoughts like a warm and comforting breeze as the Surin girl sat herself beside her elderly companion. <Five of us made it out of the building. The other three arranged a diversion to cover Veden and me. Only one survived, and he fled elsewhere.>

"Where?" asked Haid sharply.

<To find other survivors, to regroup. Enforcement and a Dato squadron followed him.>

"Useless," Haid muttered. "Still, it's another diversion."

<The city's mood is tense.> Maii inclined her head slightly to the opposite side of the van, as though her sightless eyes were seeing through the metal walls of the vehicle. <Three fires are out of control, and the wardens are letting them burn. The Dato have free access to security information and the support of ground troops. There will be a curfew tonight, if anyone is left on the streets at all.>

"Followed by a witch hunt tomorrow, no doubt." The rebel leader shook his head. "I'm all for long-term survival, but squatting down and waiting to be killed is something else entirely. As I see it, the only way out is to attack *now*, before we have nothing left to attack *with*. That seems obvious to me. Or have I lost it?" The last was directed to Neva, who smiled reassuringly.

"No," she said. "Our home is worth fighting for, no matter what it costs."

"But that's just it," Haid said. "I'm fighting for something that isn't even *my* home. What about the others? Where are they when we need them? Why aren't *they* fighting?"

"When the status quo shifts," Neva said, "what might once have seemed intolerable suddenly becomes desirable. Especially in the city, where conditions are relatively comfortable. Although they keep secrets from you during times of peace, you must realize that your most ardent supporters now are from the desert."

"I know, I know. But that doesn't make it any easier." The rebel leader slumped forward. "Where the hell *is* Emmerik, anyway?"

Silence fell. Sensing a need to keep matters focused on the immediate future, Roche leaned forward to outline the plan to the two rebels who had elected to join them. Cane also watched with interest, quickly picking up the essentials of the plan and adding useful advice of his own.

Half an hour passed slowly. When the briefing was running under its own steam without her input, Roche leaned back to rest, closing her eyes and trying to ignore the heat buffeting her face.

After a moment, she realized that she could hear voices—not those of Cane and Neva running over the plan, but two others, inside her head.

<I am too weak,> said one, male: Veden. <You should leave me behind, for everyone's sake.>

<No,> Maii replied instantly. <We need you to talk to the High Equity Court.>

<But I can do that later, once you have the landing field under control. I'll only slow you down, get in the way—>

<We can't leave you here. You'll be captured,> she protested. <Or killed.>

<Nonsense. I can look after myself. And what good would it do if you got killed trying to save me?>

<Better than having Enforcement use you as a hostage.>

<I can hardly walk, child! I'm not going to last ten seconds once we reach the landing field!>

<No, Veden!> The panicky edge to the reave's voice indicated how desperately she feared losing him. <You'll be safe. I swear it. I won't leave you behind where I can't look after you!>

Roche opened her eyes. Neither Veden nor Maii displayed any sign of the fierce debate occurring between them. To all around them—except Roche—they might have been sleeping. Only an occasional wince betrayed the pain the Eckandi was feeling. If he knew that Roche was eavesdropping, he made no sign.

But . . . why *was* she able to listen in on the private conversation? The two previous mind-dumps Roche had received had been concerned with Maii's origins and Veden's plan to liberate Sciacca's World. There had to be a reason for Roche to be a witness to this conversation as well. With renewed interest, Roche closed her eyes again to listen more closely.

Veden expected to die, and soon. She could sense it in his words, in the thoughts he directed at his young ward. The fact that he was prepared to die alone while Maii fought elsewhere was convincing proof of how strongly he felt for the reave. He had already hurt her by dragging her to Sciacca's World with him; he didn't want his death to hurt her further.

Maii, naturally, denied this possibility, being more concerned with his well-being than her own. The strength of his feelings gave his side of the argument more credence than it deserved—for how would Maii feel if Veden did indeed die while she was elsewhere? She would blame herself for the rest of her life, regardless how long or short that might be.

Roche was surprised to realize she could understand how Maii felt: some of her dislike for the trader really did appear to have vanished. Perhaps it was seeing him in such poor health, or—more likely, Roche thought—she understood him better now. She suddenly realized that the information Maii had fed to her served a double purpose, without her being aware of it: not only informing her of Veden's history, but also revealing the side of him that she had yet to experience directly, the side that bonded Maii to him. In the dream-dump, the threat that he had once seemed had been effectively neutralised, without once resorting to covert mental nudges.

The reave hadn't lied, after all. She may have manipulated Roche when they first met, but not since then. The fact that Roche's feelings for the Eckandi had changed, making her sympathize with Maii's side of the argument, was nothing to be concerned about. If anything, she should feel relieved that she was thinking with her own mind, her own thoughts.

Clearly Maii thought a reconciliation between her mentor and Roche was possible. Perhaps Maii had brought Veden up to date on Roche in a similar way. Certainly he had greeted her with less resentment than at any other time since they had met—actually going so far as to initiate a conversation, an indication that his previously automatic dismissal of her no longer held sway.

But there was more than just reconciliation at stake. Roche could sense that, even as she struggled to decipher what the rest might be. She didn't know whom to sympathize with most, but she knew how to break the stalemate. If that wasn't what Maii intended, then Roche was out of ideas.

"If he can't walk," she said, cutting across the other conversation in the van, "then I can carry him."

Veden, startled, opened his eyes, and Maii turned to face her.

"What?" said Neva, staring at her in confusion.

Roche shook her head. The voices had ceased, leaving an emptiness in her mind where they had once been. "It doesn't matter. My mind was elsewhere."

At that moment, the engine crackled into life. The passenger door at the front of the van opened, and Emmerik slid into the seat.

"Sorry to keep you waiting," said the Mbatan to Haid, putting his rifle down between them.

"All organized?" The rebel leader searched Emmerik's face for any sign of difficulty.

"I took the liberty of spreading the word here and there, along the way. In half an hour or so, we'll have a diversion to keep Enforcement occupied."

"And the rest?"

"The land lines are still intact. They'll be ready in three hours, and will await my signal."

"Good."

"What's good?" asked Roche, crouching forward in the van to speak to both of them.

"Reinforcements, I hope," said Haid, and put the ancient motor into gear. With a jerk, the van backed out of the lot. Taking the hint, Roche retreated into the cab. Cane caught her eye and winked once.

Roche resisted the impulse to protest that it was *her* plan, and that she deserved to be kept up to date on new developments. But the whining of the engine made conversation virtually impossible, and the uncertain tone in Haid's voice suggested that maybe she didn't want to know anyway. Better to work with resources presently at their disposal, rather than rely on a deus ex machina that might never arrive.

And as they headed off along the dusty street, two words penetrated Roche's irritation:

<Thank you,> said Maii.

16

Sciacca's World
Port Parvati
'954.10.34 EN
1475

The van pulled out of the wide freeway leading from the city center and onto a rising exit ramp that took them up and over the empty main thoroughfare. As the lower road swung away to the left, their new direction curved steeply to the right. Behind them, smoke from a dozen fires blotted out the horizon: the distraction Emmerik had promised. A kilometer farther on, they crested the long rise—and Roche saw their destination for the first time, silhouetted against the slowly setting sun.

The landing field.

A tall, electrified security fence appeared in their path, vanishing left and right to the periphery of her vision. Beyond it, every last piece of vegetation had been cleared and replaced with a scattering of nondescript buildings on seemingly endless tarmac. There was no visible space that had not been cleared and rebuilt.

The van swung right, following the imposing fence line. To her left she could make out the MiCom building itself, still a good kilometer away but surprisingly close to the fence. She knew the exact distance from the main gates to the complex foyer—one hundred five meters—but somehow the reality of it still surprised her. It made a mockery of the elaborate perimeter and for lousy security all around, despite the guardhouse resting midway between the complex and the gate. She supposed that the plateau upon which the landing field stood was only so big; in order to give maximum area to traffic demands, the MiCom building had to be shunted off to the side. Whatever the reasons, it was close enough to the gates to give her plan a chance.

Roche felt her muscles tighten as the Enforcement tower drew rapidly closer. Almost there. She glanced across the huge dry docks, deserted except for one orbital freighter and a couple of suborbital transfer barges. The landing field at Port Parvati had seen headier times.

As the van broached a shallow hill, one of the interior hangars came into view. Through its open doors she glimpsed a snub-nosed combat shuttle. Every angle was curved and lumpy, reinforced for maximum structural strength, giving it an almost squat appearance. Such ships didn't look like much, but they made up for it in battle; they had demonstrated their rugged endurance time and time again.

Roche recognized its origins immediately. The Commonwealth of Empires didn't build ships like that. Only the Dato Bloc did.

The van swept down the hill and past the Enforcement tower. When the hangar disappeared from view, Roche returned her eyes to the road ahead.

"Do it again," said the rebel named Jytte from beside her.

Across the cab from the rebel, Maii sighed and concentrated.

Jytte's eyes glazed for a moment, then cleared. "Incredible," she said in a low voice. "If that doesn't get us through the gates, nothing will."

Roche knew what the woman was seeing: an Enforcer in full uniform where the young Surin had once sat. Only an illusion—with the detail that Maii's knowledge lacked filled in by Jytte's own imagination—but a convincing one nonetheless.

"Enough," said Roche. "Don't wear her out."

<It's okay,> protested the reave. <As long as the subject is willing, one person really isn't that tiring. Large groups are the problem, with so many minds to focus on, so many thoughts to bend.>

Roche shook her head uneasily. She didn't like it. Even though it had been her idea, she wasn't comfortable with using epsense on the battlefield. The talent was too ephemeral, too contingent on Maii's state of mind to depend upon absolutely. She would much rather have a squadron of Intelligence agents behind her than one young girl, talented or not. Relying so heavily on one person unnerved her.

Cane's voice cut across her thoughts. "Not far now."

Leaning forward and peering past Haid's and Emmerik's heads, Roche could see the main gates in the distance—wide open, as she had hoped; more laxity. Once through the gates and past the guardhouse, they could accelerate across the front lawns and parking lot, through the MiCom building's front windows and to the base of the target stairwell within thirty seconds. Haid and the others would have the MiCom doors blown and be inside the first level within a further ten seconds. Cane and his single companion would have penetrated the admin building within the same period.

The main problem would be getting through the gate and past the guardhouse without arousing suspicion. If a firefight broke out in that area, they were likely to lose.

And, in this instance, losing meant that they were dead.

She silently reaffirmed her vow: whatever it took to reach Intelligence HQ, she would do it. Her mission was *the* most important thing on this world. If she could help others along the way, then that was just an added bonus.

"Traffic," said Emmerik suddenly, breaking the silence. The Mbatan was watching the road behind them via an external mirror on his side of the van. "One groundcar. Not sure where it came from. Didn't spot it until a few seconds ago."

Roche clambered to the van's rear window. Sure enough, a wide-nosed vehicle cruised steadily behind them. She felt a surge of alarm when she saw how close the car actually was—and how quickly it was closing the gap between them.

Haid began to accelerate, trying to maintain a constant distance between the two vehicles.

"Do you think it could be a problem?" she asked.

"I'm not sure." Haid's eyes flicked from the mirror to the road and back again. "Maii?"

Maii's invisible gaze drifted out to infinity as Haid continued to accelerate. Roche watched her, acutely conscious of the main gates drawing closer with every second.

<A small group,> the reave said. <Only five of them, but very confident. And

suspicious. Not Enforcement . . .> She paused. <Dato Bloc,> she said. <They're Dato troopers.>

"*Damn*." Haid's foot went down all the way on the accelerator. The van's ancient automatic transmission kicked into a lower gear as their acceleration became more urgent. Roche felt the first trickle of sweat begin to edge down her spine.

She leaned over to touch Maii's shoulder. "Anything else?" she asked.

<I don't understand,> said the girl to all of them, not just Roche. <They're not trying to catch us. It's almost as if they're . . .>

Roche's hand gripped tighter. "*What*?"

<They're *herding* us,> said Maii finally.

And as she said it, a large blue truck emerged from cover on the far side of the security fence. It turned ponderously onto the road and jerked to halt in full view. Several armed figures leapt from it and scurried for position.

Haid cursed loudly, urging the van faster with his words.

"They're on the other side of the gates," Roche said. "We can still go in."

"But they'll be ready for us by the time we get there," Haid retorted. "Someone must have tipped them off."

The van had almost reached the gates, but there was still no movement from Enforcement. Before Roche could respond to Haid's comment, a single uniformed figure ambled slowly from the gatehouse to see what was going on.

"No . . ." Relief parted her lips into a wide grin. "Enforcement doesn't know we're coming! The Dato have tried to do this alone."

The rebel leader studied the movements of the Enforcer for the briefest of moments before saying: "Agreed. That gives us an edge. Maii, keep tabs on that Enforcer. Don't let her sound the alarm. If we can make it past the Dato, our plan still holds."

The reave nodded once.

Behind the van, the groundcar continued to close, but not quickly enough to reach them short of the gates. The group blocking the road on the far side of the fence had spread out. It was going to be tight.

The Enforcer from the gatehouse stood transfixed, watching their approach. She was unarmored and didn't seem overly concerned at what was occurring around her.

<She sees only an authorized van approaching,> said the reave. <She worries about our speed—nothing else.>

"Good," Roche encouraged. "Keep it up just a little longer, Maii."

"Push her harder," suggested Cane. "Make her worry about the Dato presence, why they are threatening an official vehicle."

Maii nodded again. <Okay.>

Roche watched the lone Enforcer at the gate more closely. Within seconds, the woman turned to shout to other Enforcers inside the gatehouse. Two joined her, and a hurried conversation ensued between Enforcement and the Dato landing party. As the van approached, Roche could make out both anger and confusion on the faces of the Enforcers.

<I can't hold them much longer,> Maii said.

"Just a few seconds more," shot back Haid. "That's all we need."

Roche gripped the metal base of the bench as the gate loomed ahead of them. Too late, the Enforcers on the other side realized that they had been tricked—that what they had thought to be an official vehicle was actually nothing more than a worn-out solar van. Two dived for cover, the third stood stunned, and behind her the Dato finally raised their weapons.

Haid spun the steering wheel. Roche heard him manipulate the rear brakes, felt the back of the van slew around to the left, saw the gates swing into view through the front window. The van lurched forward as Haid's foot crashed down once again on the accelerator. With barely a moment to spare, the third Enforcer leapt out of the way.

In a barely controlled slide, the van sideswiped the front of the gatehouse, peeling off the armored paneling and sending it flying ahead of them as they screamed through the gates. Roche lifted a pistol and used the butt to punch through the side window, then quickly fired at the one Enforcer who had the presence of mind to take a shot at them. She hit him square in the chest, saw him topple and fall, then swung her gaze back to the front. Fifty meters ahead she saw Enforcers pour from the main guardhouse.

Roche exchanged the pistol for a percussion rifle and set it to scatter. She saw Emmerik toss something out of the passenger window and also grab a percussion rifle. In unison, they began pumping charge after charge at the emerging Enforcers.

She had a brief view of figures scattering and snapped off a few more shots. Then they were past, crashing through a low perimeter fence and bouncing over the edge of the parking area. As they careened directly toward the front of the main complex, Roche made out the few people visible through the wide windows already running for cover.

She glanced behind the van and saw the pursuing groundcar swing through the gates, narrowly avoiding a collision with the rest of the Dato squad.

Then a brilliant explosion blossomed under the front of the leading vehicle: a pressure mine, dropped by Emmerik as they drove through. Through the flash and sudden roiling smoke, the groundcar climbed up and sideways, rising meters into the air, twisting as it went, to come crashing down on its side against the electrified fence. Energy pulsed and crackled, engulfing the stricken vehicle. The blue truck swerved wildly to miss it and slammed into the corner of the gatehouse, bringing part of the already weakened structure down in front of it.

Someone shouted in triumph. Both pursuers were suddenly out of the chase, temporarily if not permanently. It was more than Roche could have hoped for.

"Get your heads down!" Haid shouted. "We're going through!"

Roche whipped her head around to see the vast windows leap toward her. She ducked instinctively, felt Jytte hunch over beside her, heard the crash and clatter of shattering glass. She heard someone call out in alarm as fragments suddenly flew into the cabin through the broken side windows.

By the time she regained her balance, Haid had the brakes locked. The van swerved sideways again, skidding across the main terminal floor like a snowplow, tearing a ragged path through chairs, tables, partition boards, and other assorted furniture.

The van careened to a rough halt, causing Neva and Veden to tumble from their seats. Roche heard Haid shout orders as he rolled through the buckled driver's door. Emmerik slid across the seat to follow him. Already the rear doors of the van had opened; Jytte and her companion jumped into the foyer with a clatter of boots and weapons.

Roche waited until Neva and Maii had climbed free before stepping down herself. Cane had already disembarked. Sending a hail of energy to clear the air for a moment, she returned to help Veden. Presenting her back to him, she gestured for him to slip his arms through the leather straps Maii had tied around the suit's neck. He resisted for a moment, then did as he was told.

Just in time. Percussion fire from the parking lot forced her behind the van. Sparkling ricochets danced off the marble floor and mirrored walls. The air stank of ozone and scorched synthetics. Beyond the shattered windows Roche could see Enforcement and the Dato landing party dodging the return fire from within the building.

She oriented herself, long hours of Armada combat training falling into place. A map of the complex appeared in her left eye: the MiCom building, three stories high, which they had already entered; administration, only one level to the rear. The foyer occupied a corner of the MiCom building's ground floor: elevator and stairwell were at the bottom of the L; a corridor leading to the admin building opened out the back.

Roche caught sight of Cane racing away, crashing through the entrance to Admin. The sound of rapid gunfire went with him as he wielded a rifle in each hand, aiming at anyone or anything that threatened to get in his way.

"Leave him!" Haid's voice pierced the racket, directed at the rebel who was supposed to have accompanied Cane on his mission. Roche edged around the van, conscious of the Eckandi gripping her back, his weight subtly disturbing the suit's ponderous equilibrium. Haid and the rebel vanished up the MiCom stairwell, carrying grenades and mortars retrieved from Roche's suit before the attack. Maii waited at the base of the stairwell with Neva.

Roche passed Veden to the older woman. "Get him upstairs. I'll cover the rear!"

The rifle was still set to scatter, and she moved at once to find a more sheltered position. At the back of the van, she kicked an upturned table into position and swung the rifle onto it so that the barrel rested easily. Already some twenty or thirty Enforcers had sprinted from the guardhouse toward the complex. Roche cranked the rifle setting to its widest beam and held the trigger down. The weapon bucked and kicked against her shoulder, spraying its lethal dosage through the windows, shattering what few panes had remained unbroken. The outer charge halted at once as the Enforcers hit the tarmac. There were a few seconds of quiet; then answering fire began to whistle in.

Roche flattened herself against the side of the van as projectile fire and particle beams lanced about her, but she kept her hand on the rifle, its barrel still resting on the upturned table. She fired in very short bursts, minimizing the recoil that would otherwise have wrenched the weapon from her grip. It wasn't enough to do serious damage to their attackers, but would make them think twice about a quick sprint forward.

Behind her, the muffled thump of an explosion told her that MiCom had been breached. A second blast, and she knew that the elevator had been crippled. She heard the clatter of feet on the stairwell, distant shouts and confusion as one of the rebels returned to help her. Together they did their best to hold Enforcement at bay.

Risking a closer look, Roche edged around the far side of the van. She counted twenty-three Enforcers, only three of them armored similarly to her. Four Dato ground troopers hugged the wall on the far side of the foyer, clad in the latest powered combat suits. Roche risked a precision shot and was gratified to see the bolt of energy hit home.

The Dato armor, however, absorbed most of the energy. The trooper was flung to the ground, but stood up again a moment later.

She cursed. Not good.

Then Maii was in her mind:

<No resistance here! We have control. Draw back and join us!>

Roche squeezed off a few more rounds, then began to edge back along the side of the van. When she could go no farther, she stopped to look around. The van's solid metal body covered most of the gap between her and the stairwell, at least from the Enforcers' positions. The Dato troopers, on the other hand, had almost a clear line of fire. She looked over her shoulder at the rebel in the stairwell and selected a grenade from one of the suit's thigh pockets.

When the air was relatively clear, she tossed the explosive to the rebel, who primed it. Counting down from three, she tensed, braced to make the short dash for safety.

On zero, the rebel rolled the grenade toward the Dato troopers and vanished up the stairwell. Roche burst from cover and tucked her unprotected head as low as she could into the suit's shoulders. She cried out involuntarily as a furious bolt of energy sheared a centimeter off her left hip, making her stumble—then the grenade exploded, sending smoke and flame through the entire foyer, covering her escape.

Movement at the periphery of her vision as she entered the stairwell made her swing the rifle to bear. Cane appeared out of the cloud of smoke, firing behind him in ragged spurts.

"Close," he said, grinning down the barrel of her rifle. He grabbed her arm, and together they double-stepped up the stairwell.

"Admin?" said Roche.

Cane nodded. "Secure. Any problems this end?"

"None."

"Good." Cane's smile widened. "Then let's see what this Box of yours can do."

Roche paused briefly at the top of the stairs to set off another grenade. The explosion brought down part of the wall, which she hoped would delay pursuit for long enough.

<Turn left at the first corner,> said Maii, guiding them through the smoke-filled corridors. Along the way, they passed numerous DAOC employees. Some were wounded, some weren't; all were unconscious or sleeping. <Right, then second left. Take the stairs at the end.>

"Where are you, Maii?"

<In MiCom Control,> said the Surin. <On the top floor. Once you're here, we'll seal life support and activate internal security. That should delay the troops for a while.>

"What about the ones you've knocked out? How long until they wake up?"

<Not long. Again, I'll look after them when you arrive.> Maii resumed her instructions, her voice calm, measured, and quietly confident. Roche began to regret the doubts she'd had earlier. <Left, then through the door . . .>

As they ran, Roche took stock of her surroundings. The second floor was undamaged, secured by Maii rather than by force. Vast networks of complex processing systems lay as idle as their unconscious operators, awaiting input. The wealth of hardware was hardly extravagant, however, given the task it was required to perform. These three floors controlled every electronic exchange in the city, as well as much of that which took place in near orbit.

<Are you sure you're up to this, Box?>

<All I need is access to a secure control-branch of the network.>

<I hope you're right.>

<Believe me, Morgan, I am. I've been waiting for this for some time now.>

Roche and Cane climbed the last stairwell to the third floor and were greeted by Haid at its summit. Roche felt a wave of nausea sweep through her as they joined him: the edge of a psychic wave from Maii, she presumed, the epsense equivalent of scattershot but nonlethal, forcing the employees of MiCom into a deeper state of unconsciousness. She was thankful she had only caught the edge of it.

"This way." The rebel leader led them through a maze of offices to the center of MiCom: a wide, high-ceilinged room containing three overhead screens, a dozen data-control stations, and a large central processor. The screens displayed constantly shifting views of the landing field, trajectories of satellites, and major moonlets through the Soul, as well as Armada deployment. Jytte and the other rebel, bleeding heavily from his right ear, guarded the entrance. Maii sat cross-legged in one corner, her placid expression belying the concentration she required to achieve what she was doing.

As Roche entered, a small window opened in the central screen, revealing the face of a man with a neatly trimmed grey beard.

"Tepko!" the face bellowed. "What the devil's going on down there? Clear the lines or I'll have you—"

"Hello, Warden," Emmerik said into a microphone, smiling from his position behind the central processor. "Chief Supervisor Tepko's not available to speak with you at the moment, I'm afraid. Perhaps I can help."

Warden Delcasalle opened his mouth, shut it, then opened it again. "Who the hell are you?"

"Your landlord," the Mbatan replied, beaming toothily. "And I've come to collect the rent."

Roche stepped up behind the Mbatan and put her gloved hand on the datalink.

"We haven't got time for this," she said.

The window to the warden closed as the Box interfaced with the central processor. Raw data surged down Roche's arm, through the suit, and out the palm of her power glove. More than a trickle, this felt like a river of fire, a thread-thin, white-hot wire inserted where her ulnar nerve had once been. She bit her lip as the torrent intensified. Phantom motes of light danced in her vision; her heart tripped, then steadied.

<I have access,> said the Box almost joyously, its voice issuing through the control room's speakers. <*Complete* access: communications, traffic control, records, security deployment, maintenance, power and water distribution . . .>

"Hold it, Box," said Haid. "What about internal security?"

"Activated," replied the Box instantly.

"Life support?"

"Sealed."

"Can you give us a view of the lower levels?"

The central screen cleared, allowing space for the sweep. The foyer was relatively empty; the first floor had been breached before the massive security doors closed, sealing off each level. The second floor contained only two Dato ground troopers, who pounded at the door to the third level in frustration.

"I have taken the liberty of canceling a recall order for Enforcement from the city," said the Box.

"Excellent," breathed Haid. "Then we're safe."

"At least for the time being," said Cane.

Emmerik put his percussion rifle down next to Roche's. "So now what?"

"The message," Roche muttered with some difficulty, still transfixed by the intense stream of data threading through her system. "We send the message."

"Exactly." Haid waved Maii and Veden forward. The elderly Eckandi looked like he was going to fall, but managed to steady himself on the edge of the processor.

"Which do you need first?" he asked. "The control codes, or the message itself?"

"The codes," replied the Box.

<The codes are relatively simple,> Maii began. <All communication must be in TAN-C cipher, or it will be rejected instantly. When the AI on the communications satellite asks for the password, the correct reply is 'black water.' When it asks for verification, respond with 'QBFH.'>

"Understood," replied the Box. Roche wondered briefly through the electric fog how the Box had heard the reave, then realized that it must have detected the telepathic impulse through her own implants. "The message, Veden?"

"Is to be addressed to the most senior presiding judge of the High Equity Court on Bini."

"Rehlaender?"

"Whoever. But mark it urgent, as per the agreement with the Commerce Artel of '954.28.09. Encrypt it in YEAMAN cipher, and begin with the words 'All the great butterflies are dying.'"

Roche closed her eyes as the Eckandi dictated the brief message requesting an urgent High Equity Court hearing to discuss the sovereignty of the native inhabitants of Sciacca's World. The Eckandi's mission was secondary to her own, and she was impatient to move on. The sooner she contacted her superiors in COE Intelligence, the sooner she could expect to be rescued.

But the lights flashing behind her eyes were hypnotic, as was the ceaseless babble of voices just below the threshold of her hearing. Her skin felt as though it was being brushed by thousands of tiny hands, touching, probing, pulling her in every direction, as the data pouring through her system fed back through her implants and into her brain itself.

Only with great difficulty did she regain control long enough to realize that Veden had finished. She closed her eyes in an attempt to clear the unnerving sensation of seeing from many points of view at once, and took a step forward. Her thighs struck the edge of the processor, helping her reaffirm her grip on reality.

<The message—> She realized that she was subvocalizing and the others therefore couldn't hear her. "Has the message gone?"

"Yes," said Emmerik. "All we have to do is wait for a reply."

"Standard communication to this sector may take days," said the Box.

"Better than nothing." The Mbatan beamed. "It's been sent, that's the main thing."

<Veden and I can go home,> said Maii, her mental voice tinged with relief and anticipation.

"Wait," Roche said. "What about—?"

"Not now," said Cane. "Look at the screens. I think we have a problem."

Roche opened her eyes and focused as best she could upon the view of the landing field. A moment passed before she realized what she was supposed to see: two flyers, circling the MiCom building.

"Both guidance systems are shielded," said the Box. "I am unable to countermand their pilots."

"It's only a matter of time before they fire," said Neva worriedly.

"Time and politics," Haid said. "Delcasalle won't want his precious installation blown to bits if he can help it."

"Does internal security cover the roof?" asked Cane.

"Yes," said Haid. "At least we don't have to worry about ground troops coming on us through the ceiling without us knowing—"

"I am registering a security breach!" interrupted the Box.

"Where?" said Haid.

"This level. Exact location unknown."

"The door?" Haid asked.

A screen flickered, displaying an image of the security door at the entrance to the top floor. It was undamaged.

"We'd better have a look anyway," said Haid. "In case they've managed to infiltrate the mainframe with a virus or something."

"Impossible," said the Box. "I would know if the image had been tampered with."

"He's right, Box." Roche looked around her; the fog cleared slightly. "I'll go with you, Haid. Can I let go of this damn thing now, Box?"

"Yes. Having established the link, I am able to reroute the data from transmitters in the—"

"Good." Roche took her hand off the datalink and stepped back from the central processor. The flow continued unchecked, but now that she had something to do, it felt less distracting. "Let's go."

Haid led the way through the maze of corridors. A steady *thump-thump*, perhaps from energy cannon, became noticeable as they approached the door.

"They're trying to blast their way in," said Haid, grimacing.

"Possibly. Neither of the troopers on the floor below has that sort of equipment, though. It might be something else."

"Such as?"

Roche shrugged. Through the nagging buzz of the Box, she couldn't think of another possibility.

The door, when they reached it, was undamaged. Haid placed his hand on the compounded metal.

"It's cool," he said. "So at least we know they're not burning their way through." He cursed under his breath. "What the hell *are* they up to?"

At that moment, a muffled blast echoed through the top floor, and the steady thumping ceased. In its wake, a siren began to wail. The floor's security had failed, somewhere.

Haid and Roche headed back the way they had come. As they rounded a corner, they ran straight into a cloud of black smoke. Holding their breath, they rushed through. They entered clear air on the far side, and Haid became more vocal with his cursing.

"They came up through the floor!" he said. "Tell the Box to seal all access doors except the ones we need—"

<I have already taken that precaution,> the Box said into her thoughts.

"It's already done." Roche clutched the grip of her rifle more tightly. "How much further?"

"Not far. We—"

A door they had just passed suddenly dissolved into a ball of white flame. Seeing two armored figures climb through the smoking hole, Roche doubled her speed. They passed through another open access door, which hissed shut behind them, then entered MiCom Control. A sturdier airlock sealed the way behind them, but not before Roche saw the door farther down the corridor burst open.

"We have to move," said Haid, gesturing urgently at the exit on the far side of the room. "Is there another way out of the building from this floor?"

"Only the roof," said Cane.

"I can launch transport to pick you up," offered the Box. "As we discussed earlier."

"Do it," said Haid. "How long will it take?"

"Five minutes," said the Box.

"*Damn*. That's too long." The rebel leader looked thoughtful for a moment, then glanced at Emmerik. The Mbatan nodded.

"Okay, Box," said Haid, turning back to Roche. "Broadcast a message over the radio transmitters, 115.6 kilohertz. The message is: 'Retribution.' That's all. Repeat it three times." Haid nodded. "That should delay the Dato for long enough."

The airlock crackled as repeated batteries from energy weapons heated it beyond its tolerance. The smell of scorched metal filled the room.

"Move, people!" Haid waved them out of the control room, one by one. Neva and Roche once again helped Veden onto the back of the combat suit and slid his arms through the straps. With every heavy step, the Eckandi's breath hissed softly in Roche's ear; his arms hung limp around her throat.

The corridor led to another maze of offices.

"Which way?" Emmerik called.

Roche relayed directions given by the Box until they reached a narrow flight of metal stairs leading to a service hatch in the ceiling. Neva went first, nudging the hatch aside with the barrel of her rifle, then slipping through. Emmerik went next, then Jytte, Roche and Veden, Maii and the others. Haid, the last through, dogged the hatch behind him and stood up to survey the view.

They stood in a glass-windowed observation platform, half open to the evening air. Wind snatched at Roche's face, carrying with it the sharp sting of dust. The sound of the two flyers circling the building was loud in her ears, rising and falling as the craft came closer, then drifted away. From the base of the building, voices floated up to them, shouting orders, calling for reinforcements. Plumes of smoke still rose from the foyer, as well as from the burning truck by the main gates.

The city of Port Parvati lay under a deep shroud of black, deepening by the moment as the sun slipped below the horizon. Only the seemingly solid band of the Soul remained to illuminate the battlefield. Far away and to the northeast, a storm hovered over the mountains like an enormous, shadowy beast, waiting to spring.

"Are you okay, Veden?" Roche asked over her shoulder.

"I'm still here," breathed the elderly Eckandi.

"Hang in there."

"If we keep low," called Emmerik from the far side of the platform, "the troops in the flyers might not see us."

"Agreed," said Haid, edging away from the hatch.

<How long, Box?> Roche subvocalized.

<Three minutes, Morgan.>

A thump from below made them all tense; the two troopers had found the stairwell.

<There's only the one,> mind-whispered the Surin. <Let him come.>

Haid nodded. He remained where he was, though, a half dozen paces from the hatch with his rifle trained on the place the trooper's head would appear.

Roche jumped as a flash of white split the sunset. The hatch exploded into the air and clattered to one side—blown upward by fire from below. Maii hissed between her teeth as she fought to regain control of the Dato trooper. One armored hand reached out of the hole in the roof, clutching for purchase. With servos whining, the sleek, shining suit clambered into the night air, its high-powered rifle slung over one shoulder—

And stood there, immobile, frozen by the reave's will.

Cane ducked closer to retrieve the rifle at the same time the nearest flyer snarled angrily overhead.

"They've seen us!" Haid shouted over the noise, crouching automatically as fire strafed the observation platform.

Cane fired at the belly of the flyer as it sped away from them. The powerful Dato weapon discharged fierce bolts of blue-white energy that sparked viciously when they hit. Cane kept firing as the flyer curved upward into the sky to avoid the attack. Only when the craft dipped lower and vanished behind the bulk of the building did Cane let go of the trigger. The previously constant whine of its engines had changed slightly, become more irregular, halting.

Damaged at least, thought Roche, if not out of the game entirely.

The second flyer swooped to attack, this time more cautiously. Its underbelly turrets rotated smoothly, seeking the upright figure of Cane. He ducked and rolled for cover behind the frozen Dato trooper. The flyer's shots landed wide of the mark, destroying what remained of the platform's low roof and sending glass shards flying.

When the second flyer had passed, Roche let go the breath she had been holding. Too close, she thought. *Much* too close. It was only a matter of time before the flyer returned—and this time, they might not be so lucky.

A concussion from below heralded the arrival of a new form of attack: mortar bombs. The whistle of the shell grew rapidly louder, with no clear way to tell where it would hit. Then the corner of the observation platform where Jytte was standing suddenly exploded. The shock wave knocked everyone off their feet except for Roche, who watched helplessly as the woman was flung through the air amid a burning hail of rubble.

Roche staggered, hurriedly clearing grit from her eyes. The whistle of another mortar coincided with the growing whine of the undamaged flyer. She sought cover on the exposed platform—but there was nowhere to hide.

"We're too exposed up here!" she shouted over the noise.

"I know," Haid shouted back. "But we don't have any—"

The second mortar exploded, cutting him off. Roche once again held her ground.

She hadn't had time to recover, however, before a solid kick knocked the rifle from her hands.

She stumbled back a step, blinking furiously, distracted by dust and the fog caused by the Box. Another blow spun her sideways before her suit could correct her balance. Raising an arm desperately, she managed to block the third blow. The solid ring of armor on armor coincided with her realization of who was attacking her.

The Dato trooper—released from his stupor by Maii's distraction—stepped back to aim a kick at her stomach. She dodged aside, attempting to twist him about his center of gravity while he was off balance. But his suit was too fast, or hers too old, and he pivoted easily out of her grasp. Cursing, she aimed a solid blow to his helmet that hurt her fist, even through the armored glove.

The power-assists of his joints growled as he assumed a combat stance—arms outstretched, legs planted firmly to either side—and waited for Roche's next move. She feinted to the right, jabbed at his shoulder with her left fist. The blow glanced aside, and he elbowed her in the chest. His other hand swept up to strike her in the exposed face, but she ducked in time. She felt the clenched ceramic glove pass by bare millimeters from her ear, then ducked under his arm to strike him in the stomach.

He staggered backward. Roche, back-heavy because of Veden and winded by the blow to her chest, didn't press her advantage as she would have liked to. The second flyer screamed by overhead, strobing the dusk on all sides, distracting her. The trooper ducked low and charged, using his helmet as a battering ram. Roche lunged to one side in time to avoid the crude attack, but not quickly enough to dodge the outswept arm that almost knocked her off her feet.

She cursed breathlessly, hating to admit that she was no match for the trooper in hand-to-hand combat—outclassed by superior technology, confused by external impulses invading her own head, and forced to take her elderly passenger into account. But she had no choice, and her companions were too busy trying to survive to assist her. Distantly, she noted the steady blast of the Dato rifle in Cane's hands as it once again sought the undamaged flyer.

While the armored figure turned to charge again, she searched for the rifle on the blackened roof, and found it nearby. Unfortunately, the trooper noted the shifting of her gaze and also saw the weapon.

They lunged simultaneously at the same moment another mortar exploded nearby. Roche arrived an instant sooner, sweeping the rifle into one hand. The trooper's gloved hands closed over hers as she tried to turn the weapon on him. Slowly but inexorably he forced the barrel back toward her face. She grunted, trying to fight the superior strength of the Dato suit until the blood sang in her ears.

She looked away from the mirrored visor of her opponent and down into the black eye of the rifle. The hand clutching the trigger guard tightened, prepared to snap the metal bracket simply to make the gun fire. Once would be enough. Once, and Roche would never have to worry about her mission—or the Box—again.

Then something reached past her, over her shoulder, and the weight on her back shifted. A naked hand battered at the Dato trooper's visor, distracting him momentarily. The barrel shifted aside a bare instant before the weapon discharged, dazzling Roche and singeing the side of her head.

She pushed herself away from the trooper, screaming, and the weight slipped from her shoulders. *Veden!* she screamed—*Veden!* Then realized that the voice issued from inside her head and not from herself. It was simultaneously coming from all around her and from the depths of her very being.

Veden!

Flames clutched at her scalp, digging in with claws of fire, and she fell backward. Her hip absorbed most of the impact, sending waves of pain through her weak ribs and shoulder. Still screaming through the stench of burning skin and hair, she batted at the fire with her gloved palms until it was out.

Only then did she open her eyes.

The Dato trooper was standing over her—dead, but still standing, as the Surin's scream ripped his mind apart. Eventually, with a quiver, the suit toppled backward and lay still.

Roche rolled over and, through the one eye that had recovered from the energy bolt, stared at the body of the Eckandi lying next to her. The top of his skull had been blown away.

Veden!

The scream cut short with a wrench of emotion that would have overwhelmed all of them on the observation platform had it not been quashed instantly by its source. It was replaced by a high-pitched, keening wail of grief. Roche clambered to her knees and sought the Surin through the smoke and darkness. The girl was nowhere to be seen, so she sent her mind instead—to comfort, to support, to succor. But the wail—the only audible sound that she had ever heard from the Surin—continued unchecked.

Then Emmerik's voice sliced through the noise and the rising buzz of the undamaged flyer as it turned to strafe the building yet again:

"They're here! Ameidio, they're here!"

Roche climbed unsteadily to her feet and hauled herself to the edge of the platform, following the direction indicated by Emmerik's outflung hand. Below, in the gloom, she could see heads turning as Enforcement faced a new enemy. Not the flyer the Box had arranged to meet them, but a ground force of some kind—at least two hundred armed people swarming on foot through the open gates of the landing field.

"Box—" She stopped, cleared her throat of dust. Through the buzz of data and the ringing in her ears, her voice sounded inhumanly hoarse. "Box, give me a clearer picture. Use the security cameras and enhance the image."

The view through her left eye split in two. In one portion she saw as normal; in the other, she zoomed closer to the attacking squad. She glimpsed figures dressed in what looked like crude robes, carrying identical weapons. Her ears caught the sound of an unfamiliar discharge: not harsh, like energy rifles, but almost musical—a split-second chime at a very low frequency.

She struggled to identify the sound until the view pulled back to encompass the Enforcers below. One by one, as the strange weapons fired, energy rifles failed. Armored suits locked, immobile, and toppled to the earth. The second flyer swooped low to investigate this new challenge, and its engine changed pitch as sections of its drive malfunctioned instantly.

HFM weapons, she realized. Of an ancient design, too. But where—?

She whirled around to face Haid and Emmerik. "You told me they were radioactive!"

"They were," said the Mbatan.

"They marked a *graveyard*!"

"And will again when they are returned." Emmerik limped closer, smiling sadly. "They are the one and only asset belonging to the descendants of the original settlers. What better use could they be put to than to revenge the deaths of the people they once killed?"

Roche shook her head, understanding but feeling betrayed anyway. With such an arsenal, the capture of the landing field could have been accomplished much more peacefully, with much less bloodshed. But it wasn't her place to criticize; she was alive, and the chances of escape seemed markedly less remote than they had just moments ago.

Cane joined her at the edge of the platform, watching the battle take place below. The peace guns cut a swath through Dato troops and Enforcers alike. No mortars had been fired since the arrival of the ghosts of Houghton's Cross. She supposed that she should start feeling safe sometime soon. Yet she doubted she would ever feel safe again—at least, not until she was off the planet and back at Intelligence HQ.

<My feelings exactly,> said the Box.

<How about sending my message, then?> she asked.

<No, Morgan. I cannot allow you to do that.>

The flat negative surprised her. <Box, I'm *ordering* you to—>

"Transport's arrived!" called Haid from the far side of the building. Cane's nudge in the back of her suit forced Roche to concentrate on more immediate matters. Her scalp stung where fire had eaten into it, and the Surin's wail continued to gnaw at her thoughts. Whatever the Box was playing at, she could deal with it later—when the flyer had taken them somewhere safe, somewhere she could think clearly.

Engines snarled as something large loomed out of the night sky and swooped over their heads. Relief turned to anxiety, however, as she realized that the craft wasn't the standard COE design used on the prison planet. This was a military design, snub-nosed and powerful.

"But," she began, "that's a Dato—"

"I know." The familiar voice came from behind her.

She turned and found herself face to face with Cane. His habitual half-smile was gone. She tensed by instinct, and would have stepped away, but the armor had become rigid. She couldn't move.

"What's happening—?" She looked down in annoyance, wrenching her limbs impotently within the suit. No matter what she did, however, the suit remained completely lifeless. "I'm trapped!"

She looked up again in time to see Cane draw back his fist. Her eyes widened in horror as she flinched and tried to turn away—but the motion was futile. Unable to move her body, there was no way she could avoid the blow.

It connected solidly on her burned temple. Light exploded behind her eyes, blinding her; then three distinct sounds chased her into darkness:

—the snarl of the shuttle as it swooped level with the roof—

—the solid thump of her armored body striking the platform beneath her—

—and the voice of Cane, barely audible over the noise of the shuttle, muttering a single, sickening word.

"*Exactly*."

PART FOUR:

ANA VEREINE

17

DBMP *Ana Vereine*
'954.10.34 EN
1805

Despite the calm appearance of his image, Captain Uri Kajic was a worried man.

Six hours had passed since the last communication with the Port Parvati landing party, in which Major Gyori had indicated that he was preparing to ambush Roche and the rebels as they attacked the landing field. Since then, nothing had been heard from anyone. All surface communications had been jammed from the landing field's MiCom installation. Kajic, watching closely from geosynchronous orbit, had waited in the grip of an intense anxiety for an update, his thoughts constantly nagged by reminders of his priorities. As fighting had erupted on the surface of Sciacca's World, smoke from numerous fires burning in and around the city had effectively masked infrared surveillance, and a poorly timed dust storm had compounded the problem by smothering visual light and radar. Whatever was going on in the landing field's MiCom installation, he could not guess. For all he knew, the battle might have ended hours ago.

Stranded in his skybound eyrie, he could do little but wait, consumed by doubts, recriminations, and half-spoken fears.

priority gold-one

"Second Lieutenant Nisov reports that her squad is ready to launch." Makaev had abandoned the pretense that Kajic's hologram was a real person. She remained in her position, next to the command dais, speaking to him solely via the nearest microphone.

Kajic's image nodded in acknowledgment. The plan to send another landing party into the maelstrom had not been his, but he was forced to admit that it made sense. Even a low reconnaissance flight would do more good than ill. "Have her stand by, awaiting my command."

"Sir, a delay at this point—"

"Will make little difference," Kajic interrupted irritably. "I wish to give Major Gyori one more chance to report."

capture Commander Roche and AI JW111101000

"This seems unlikely, sir, as the interference from the planet has not lessened since—"

Kajic shrugged this aside. "While we are being jammed, we know that the battle is continuing. I see no reason to send reinforcements just yet."

Makaev's scowl deepened. "Then perhaps we should reconsider disabling the DAOC transmitter station."

"Why? Has there been another coded hyperspace transmission?"

"No, but—"

"Then your reasons for wishing it disabled are unclear."

at all costs

"It's a *threat*, sir. If the Armada has not already been informed of our presence here—"

"Even if they have, they will arrive too late. Destroying the satellite will have repercussions further-reaching than our present situation. We have already left too much evidence that might implicate us."

with as much stealth and speed as possible

"Sir, I wish you would reconsider—"

priority gold-one

"Enough!" Kajic shouted at the voices tormenting him. "I am in command of this vessel, and if I say we should wait, then that's exactly what we will do!"

Makaev's face darkened, anger boiling beneath its surface. "Yes . . . sir."

Kajic noted the woman's insolent tone, the contemptuous hesitation before the honorific was finally granted, but he refrained from commenting. Traitor or loyal servant? If he pushed much harder, he might soon find out which.

priority gold-one

The telemetry officer intruded softly. "Captain . . . ?"

Kajic turned to face her. "Yes? Report!"

"We are registering a transmission from the surface," she said, tasting her lips nervously. "A precise fix is impossible through the interference, sir, but it does seem to be coming from the landing field transponders. And . . . it's directed at us."

Kajic paused momentarily. "What sort of transmission?"

"Presently unknown, sir. We are detecting only a carrier wave."

"Let me know when the source of the transmission and its contents are confirmed. It may be Major Gyori attempting to report."

"Sir." The officer returned to her station, her face a mask of concentration. Kajic glanced at Makaev, but his second was busy relaying his previous orders. Accurately, he hoped.

priority /

/ gold-one

Suddenly, people were staring at him. Half the bridge crew had swiveled in their combat harnesses to focus on the command dais.

"Atalia," he said, perplexed. "What's going on?"

"You . . . disappeared, sir." Kajic's second stared at him openly from her station. "We tried to call you, but you didn't answer."

Kajic sent a self-diagnostic probe through his circuitry and systems. A millisecond later it returned: all clear. "There has been no malfunction."

"But you—" Makaev stopped, swallowed. "For an instant there your persona just *ceased*."

"That's impossible," Kajic snapped, feeling panic stirring in his mind. "I sensed no discontinuity."

"Are you certain?"

"Of course I am!" Despite his denial, Kajic's uncertainty manifested itself as anger, under which loomed a growing fear that maybe stress was causing a malfunction in his circuitry.

priority gold-one

"Just let me *think*." He said this aloud, wanting to silence the voice in his head, although he immediately regretted it. His behavior had provoked a look of concern from a number of the faces around the bridge, and he knew he couldn't afford to have them doubt his competency at this vital stage of the mission.

Trying to reestablish a sense of control and thus regain the confidence of his crew, Kajic casually folded his arms behind his back and addressed Makaev in a smooth and calm manner.

"The transmission," he said. "Has its source been identified?"

"No, sir." Although most of the crew slowly returned to their duties, Makaev's worried frown remained. She wasn't fooled by his attempt to resume proceedings as though nothing had happened. "Analysis concluded that it was probably a spurious echo of our own transmissions," she said. "There has still been no word from Major Gyori."

This last part was spoken a little smugly, Kajic thought, but he refused to rise to the bait. "Nevertheless," he said. "We will wait a little longer. Five minutes more, then we will assume that Major Gyori has failed."

Kajic kept his image on the bridge overlooking the crew, trying desperately to maintain an even composure and not submit to the anxiety that increased with each passing second. The truth was, he suspected that Makaev was right: if he waited too long to send backup, the opportunity might be lost forever. Should he trust his own judgment in the aftermath of what had apparently happened to him? *Was* he malfunctioning in some unanticipated, subtle way, without being aware of it himself?

If so, then there was only one way to find out.

Two minutes passed. Then three. Fifty seconds before the deadline, telemetry spoke again:

"Sir—we are registering a launch!"

Kajic turned to face the screen. "Elaborate," he said. "I want all available data."

A map of the region appeared. "One craft, rising through the dust above the landing field," said the officer. A flashing red dot appeared on the screen. "A surface-to-orbit vehicle—probably one of our own, judging by its emissions. No communication as yet."

"They are still too close to the source of the interference," Kajic said. "It must be Gyori. Given the traffic ban, only one of our own would be so bold as to launch unannounced."

"It could be a ruse, sir," Makaev cautioned.

"I am aware of that possibility." Kajic remained pensive for a few moments before speaking. "Instruct *Paladin* and *Galloglass* to intercept before it reaches orbit, just in case."

"Sir." She turned away to relay the orders.

Kajic watched the screen closely. The red dot rose higher, curving slowly to reach orbit. Green dots marked the two raiders as they dropped to meet it, swooping like aerial hunters with claws extended upon some lone and silent prey. Then:

"Ident confirmed," said telemetry, swiveling around to face the captain. "It *is* the shuttle, sir."

"But still no communication?"

"No, sir. There has been . . ." She paused, pressing at the communication bud in her ear. "Wait," she said, leaning over her console to concentrate. "Something's coming through now." Another pause. "They are requesting permission to dock."

"*Who*, exactly?" asked Makaev, the suspicion clearly evident in her tone.

Kajic also thought he detected a brief expression of annoyance flicker across her face. Had her plans to subvert him been foiled, or was he just imagining things?

"He has identified himself as Sergeant Komazec." Silence as telemetry once again listened. "He says that there have been many casualties—Major Gyori included. It seems that—"

priority gold-one

"The *mission*," Kajic snapped, silencing both the officer and the prompts from his programming. The deaths of Gyori and the others were regrettable, but irrelevant. "What is the status of their mission?"

Another unheard exchange between telemetry and the sergeant passed before: "They have the COE agent and the AI aboard, sir."

Kajic did smile, then. "Permission to dock granted," he said. "Atalia, notify the commanding officers of *Paladin*, *Galloglass*, and *Lansequenet* that we will be leaving in two hours."

Makaev nodded once. "As you wish, sir."

Yes, thought Kajic to himself, not caring for once who might be listening through his back door. Yes, I *do* wish. And this is your *captain* speaking. . . .

The snub-nosed shuttle, trimmed and ready to dock, approached the grey bulk of the *Ana Vereine*, propelled by increasingly delicate nudges from its thrusters. As the orbits overlapped, the shuttle's relative velocity decreased until it was practically stationary with respect to the larger ship. The last few meters passed most slowly of all, as the nose of the shuttle edged into a vacant gantry.

A muffled clang announced that contact had been made. The gantry's manifold waldoes enfolded the shuttle in a gentle embrace and tugged it deeper into the mother ship, where cables waited like open-mouthed serpents to link it to the *Ana Vereine*'s life support. A gaping transit corridor groped for the airlock lip, clung tight, and pressurized. All that remained was the linking of computer systems; only after that would the shuttle truly be home.

Dato Bloc engineers called this final process "unscrambling the egg." Kajic had watched many thousand such maneuvers from the cameras installed in the hangar's ceiling, but never before with so much at stake. On the contents of this particular egg rested not only his mission, but perhaps his very life.

"The shuttle has docked," Makaev said from the bridge. "When its cargo has been unloaded and verified, we will be ready to leave."

"Very good." Kajic resisted the impulse to tell her that she was stating the obvious. Now that the crisis had passed, she was performing her duty as impeccably as ever. Perhaps—if she truly was the traitor—he had finally earned her trust. Either that, or she was simply biding her time. . . .

The shuttle's airlock, invisible within the transit corridor, opened with a hiss and distracted him from that train of thought. He moved to a camera within sight of the egress airlock and waited. Not long after, heavy footsteps tramped down the short corridor, and booted feet appeared. Two fully armored troopers led the way, their suits blackened and charred by battle. Two others followed close behind. Between the latter two hung a suspension stretcher, and on the stretcher lay—

Was it her? Kajic hardly dared to believe his eyes. Could it really be . . . ?

Of course it could. There was no mistaking that face, even partly burned and swollen. He had studied her files extensively over the last few days, so much so that her image was now imprinted upon his mind.

Lying unconscious on the stretcher was Commander Morgan Roche of COE Intelligence. Beside her, still connected to her wrist by a length of cord, was the valise. The AI.

He only half heard the brief radio communication between the landing party and the hangar techs. His thoughts were elsewhere, focused instead upon the blessed silence that now filled his mind. Suddenly, with his mission completed, the priorities had ceased their endless prompting. That alone made the success of his mission worthwhile. To be free of interference for a while; to be *himself.*

Then, without warning, as though following on the heels of that very thought, came a new invasion, a new priority:

return at once to Szubetka Base

priority gold-one

The sense of elation sank as quickly as it had surfaced. Not until his hologram stood before the Ethnarch and the Military Presidium and he presented his report would they allow him to entertain any sense of achievement. Only then, perhaps, would he be free.

He watched after the unconscious commander with an overwhelming sense of exhaustion. There was still work to be done. Perhaps, he thought, returning his image to the bridge, there always would be.

"We are secured to break orbit, sir."

return at once

Kajic nodded as he looked one last time at the picture of Sciacca's World on display. "Do so," he said tiredly.

Dissolving the hologram, Kajic swung his attention through the ship, performing a quick scan of the drive chambers, the matter-antimatter fuel mix, and astrogation's plotted course. Beyond the metal shell of his surrogate body, the three raiders accompanying the *Ana Vereine* performed similar checks before leaving the system.

When the time came, four mighty engines fired, casting a false dawn over the facing hemisphere of Sciacca's World. The Soul twinkled around them, then behind them, as they rose above the equatorial plane. In strict formation, the four ships swooped over the northern pole and its tiny patch of ice, angled down past the Soul again, then aimed toward the orange sun. The intrasystem thrusters flared to maximum power, the Soul flashed one last time, and then they were free of the planet's gravity well.

Their course would take them around the sun, past the smallish gas giant on the far side, and out to the system's nearest anchor point. When they reached that point, in three days' time, they would depart the Hutton-Luu System forever.

return to Szubetka Base

Four hours into their journey, when he was certain that everything was proceeding according to plan, Kajic focused his attention on internal matters. More specifically, on Sergeant Komazec's report of events that had transpired on Sciacca's World.

The ambush at the landing field had been a disaster, due in part to the fact that Major Gyori had attempted to capture Roche without the assistance of the local Enforcers. Despite being severely outnumbered, Roche's strike force had successfully penetrated the MiCom building and taken control of the installation. How she had accomplished this, exactly, was something of a mystery, although it seemed that she had allied herself with at least one powerful epsense adept whose powers gave her a significant tactical advantage.

Once inside the building, she had used the AI to assume control of the MiCom installation. But instead of sending a message requesting assistance from the Armada, she had broadcast a plea on behalf of the local rebels. Why, Kajic could only guess. Perhaps she had owed it to the rebels who had helped her, been obliged to aid them in their cause before they would let her complete her own mission—which, thankfully, she had been unable to do.

Under pressure from Dato troopers within the building, she and her allies had been forced to the roof. Two Enforcement flyers commandeered by Major Gyori's squad had harried her from the air while Enforcement used mortars to weaken their position from below.

But still Roche had not given up. One of the flyers—the one containing Major Gyori—had been damaged in the battle. And somehow she had taken remote control of the landing party's shuttle, possibly to seek refuge in the transmitter station orbiting the planet.

It was at this point that luck had turned in favor of Sergeant Komazec, who had assumed command of the landing party following Major Gyori's untimely death.

Weakened by casualties of their own—and the neutralization of their reave—Roche's band had turned against her. Knowing that escape from the planet was impossible with the Dato ships enforcing the blockade, and that any defense of the landing field was temporary at best, they had overpowered her and attempted to negotiate. Speaking from inside the shuttle, one of them had coordinated a meeting between the landing party and the rebels, the intention being to exchange Roche for safe passage.

The meeting had taken place on the roof of the DAOC Administration building. Sergeant Komazec had agreed to everything. The ultimate fate of the rebels—and, indeed, DAOC Enforcement itself, a one-time ally—was irrelevant. The AI and its courier were all that mattered.

Roche, unconscious and injured, was brought out of the shuttle, with the AI, and handed over to the soldiers of the Dato Bloc.

Once Roche was safe, Komazec had opened fire upon the rebels and regained control of the shuttle. He had left no survivors. Not one. Such ruthlessness might once have appalled Kajic, but now, with his priorities burning so effectively into his conscience, he felt only indifference. All that mattered was that the AI and Roche *had* been successfully returned to him. His mission had been accomplished.

He directed his attention to Roche in the sick bay holding cells. She was still unconscious, still attached to the AI. The stolen combat suit had been removed, and the burns on her scalp, face, and neck were undergoing treatment, as were minor injuries to her ribs, shoulder, and hip; apart from that, she had been left in peace.

Until they were certain how deep the link between her and the AI extended, the *Ana Vereine*'s surgeons would not dare sever it from her.

In less than a week she would be a captive of the Presidium, an unwilling accomplice in the ongoing state of tension existing between the Dato Bloc and Commonwealth governments. She would become a traitor of the worst kind, one whose involuntary betrayal meant the deaths of friends, family, and colleagues.

This saddened him, obscurely. She had no choice in the matter—an impotence he could empathize with. It would have been better for her if she had died on Sciacca's World. That way, her mission would only have failed, not been perverted to her enemies' ends.

He looked forward to the opportunity of meeting her properly, when he could speak to her face to face, one soldier to another. She had been a worthy adversary throughout his assignment. . . .

return to Szubetka Base

As he scanned through Komazec's report one final time, he noticed a minor item in the inventory that he had missed earlier. The body of an elderly Eckandi male, apparently killed during the attack, had also been returned to the *Ana Vereine*. His exact identity was unknown, but, from what little the rebels had said when handing over Roche, Komazec had received the impression that it had been the Eckandi who had arranged the message to the COE High Equity Court. Possibly he was a clandestine member of the Commerce Artel; not unlikely, given his citizenship in the Eckandar Trade Axis. The body, with its distinctive flash burns from a Dato weapon, had been recovered as a precaution to divert the powerful Artel's wrath.

Kajic had to admire Komazec's quick thinking. Such a move had been entirely in accordance with his own orders. Second only to success, stealth had been the important thing. And, while the mission might not have gone as well as he had hoped, at least he could say that nothing had been overlooked. His crew had acted without fault, which would reflect well upon his command.

Yet how near defeat had been: the panicky moments before Komazec's return; the interminable waiting, the lack of information; then the apparent malfunction of his own systems, and Makaev's almost open defiance. A few minutes longer . . .

But now, with Roche safely aboard the ship and the remains of the penal colony receding into the distance, those moments were irrelevant. The end result was all that mattered.

Twenty-eight hours away from the penal colony, he arranged for the body of the Eckandi to be placed in cold storage, performed one last check of his ship, then resigned his higher functions to oblivion.

Sleep, he mused to himself as darkness slowly fell. The one true reward after battle.

He dreamed—

. . . of voices he could almost hear, faces he could almost see, people who almost existed . . .

. . . of chains binding him tightly, binding his nonexistent body, holding him firmly while some terrible threat approached, against which he could not move to defend himself . . .

. . . of things forgotten, things not noticed, things he should have attended to . . .

. . . of his home planet, which, from above, appeared as a woman's face, a once faceless woman whose features were even now strangely blurred . . .

. . . of details too small to focus on in a picture too large to comprehend . . .

. . . of a person, another face, a voice calling him—

"Captain? Can you hear me, Captain?"

Filled with a premonitory dread, Kajic awoke with a mental jerk.

A few seconds later, the voice spoke again: "*Captain*?"

"Atalia?" Slowly the sleep-numbed layers of his mind peeled away. An image of his second in command appeared, staring directly into a camera, directly at *him*, concern pressing at her features. "What is it? What's happened?"

"Nothing, sir," she said, the words belying the look on her face. "I just need to speak to you in private."

In private? Kajic echoed in his thoughts. Then her news couldn't be urgent. The ship must be safe. The relief, after the ominous dreams, was almost overwhelming.

"Very well," he said.

She turned away from the camera and took a seat while Kajic gathered his thoughts, mentally sweeping his mind clean of the detritus of the dream. More hints, more unconscious suggestions—he was sure of it—but they would have to wait until later. Taking a moment to access the events he had missed while his higher centers were sleeping, he realized that they were fifty-two hours from Sciacca's World, just over two-thirds of the way. He had slept for almost an entire day.

Remarkable though that was, he didn't let it bother him. With their departure proceeding smoothly and a major campaign behind them, it was unsurprising that he needed rest.

A few seconds elapsed before he formed his hologram in the command module where Makaev sat waiting. She stood instantly to attention, then relaxed when he waved her at ease.

"I assume this has nothing to do with the ship," he said after she had returned to her seat.

"Not exactly, sir, no." Makaev sighed, shifting uneasily. "It's the crew. They are restless—nervous."

"Of what?"

Makaev paused, as though what she was about to say pained her. "Of . . . ghosts, sir."

Before he could respond, she quickly added, "I know what you're about to say, Captain, and believe me, I thought the same thing myself. But in the last six hours I've received three separate reports and heard rumors of several more. The sightings are all confined to the lower decks, to maintenance areas and cold stores. The witnesses have all been single crew members performing unscheduled duties. The encounters were all brief, comprising little more than a glimpse of another person—who instantly vanished."

"What about security?" said Kajic thoughtfully.

"No trace has been found on any of the recordings. Even in the three cases where we've had exact times and locations, nothing out of the ordinary has been seen."

Kajic mulled this over for a moment. "The obvious possibility is that we have unwittingly taken aboard a stowaway or two. Transportees, or some of the rebels perhaps . . . ?"

"My thoughts exactly, sir," said Makaev. "After the second report, I contacted

Sergeant Komazec. He assured me that there was no possible way anyone could have smuggled themselves onto the shuttle. The only other bodies aboard, apart from crew, were Roche and the Eckandi. One of those is dead, and the other hasn't even regained consciousness.

"Furthermore, I have also checked with the main computer. No stores are missing; we are showing no extra mass and no unexpected demands on life support. And every one of the crew can be accounted for, which rules out the possibility of substitution. If what we have here *is* a stowaway, then it might as well be a ghost."

"Nevertheless," said Kajic. "The fact remains that the crew is restless. Correct?"

Makaev nodded. "And the more word spreads, the worse it becomes."

Kajic regarded her steadily for a few moments, biting back irritation. "Well, the only thing we can do about it at this stage is to step up security, to make sure every area below deck is watched at all times. If we do have some sort of stowaway, ghost or otherwise, it's bound to appear eventually."

"Which is why I've come to you." Makaev paused and leaned forward. "As suggested by yourself, the crew is now on soft duties following our mission. I am reluctant to give them more work at the moment, not until we're at least out of the system. Yet we have to do *something* now. Let the rumors continue unchecked, and the *Ana Vereine* runs the risk of—"

"Enough," Kajic cut in. He could see where she was headed. "You want me to conduct the security sweeps?"

"It seems logical, sir. You are more vigilant than any single member of the crew, and you have direct access to the required systems. In fact, they're integral to you." She hesitated, as though suddenly realizing something. "Of course, that's if you're up to it, sir. I mean, it has been a difficult week. . . ."

Kajic was glad for once that he didn't have a physical body to betray his autonomic responses—otherwise a flush of rage would have turned his face a deep, bright red. How dare she? Did she think him stupid? If he agreed to conduct the surveillance of the ship, then he *was* placing himself under unnecessary stress and perhaps risking a potential breakdown—but if he said no, then he would be admitting weakness at a time when he couldn't afford to do so.

Her blatant attempt at manipulation was clumsy, to say the least—so much so that it might feasibly, and perversely, have been entirely innocent.

Either way, he had no choice.

"For the sake of the crew's peace of mind," he said, "I think your suggestion a sensible one. I shall begin immediately."

She sighed with apparent satisfaction and stood. "Thank you, sir. I'll see that you have all the information immediately. The sooner the rumors are quashed, the better."

He nodded, agreeing with that, at least. Although he denied the existence of either ghosts or stowaways, the very act of looking would undoubtedly reassure everyone in the lower decks. And when he turned up nothing, and no more sightings were reported, the *Ana Vereine* could return to normal.

Yet the feeling of dread that had remained with him after awakening only intensified as he accepted the data from Makaev and examined it carefully. *Had* something gone wrong? Something that he had overlooked or simply not anticipated? With victory so close, he couldn't afford to discount that possibility.

The Box had been handed to him on a plate once already, and Roche had snatched it away, again and again, until he had almost begun to despair at his inability to outwit her. She had eluded his forces on the *Midnight*, in space, through the wilds of Sciacca's World and, finally, in the streets of Port Parvati. Neither the DAOC Enforcers nor the Dato landing party had been able to locate her, until the very end—and even then, she had almost eluded them once again.

Was it so unbelievable that she might do so again?

Only with the sternest mental effort was he able to smother that doubt before it found purchase in his thoughts.

He commenced the search of the lower decks.

After the first hour, he realized that he had something to be grateful for. The sweep kept him occupied, when otherwise he might have drifted aimlessly through the ship, agonizing over his future. The ship could monitor itself; if anything untoward happened, either the automatic systems in his hindbrain or Makaev herself would notify him immediately. By being occupied, he was spared the uncertainty and given an opportunity to do something constructive.

Still, it was tedious work, and his mind tended to wander. After the third hour of staring at empty storerooms and quiescent machinery, he began to alternate the sweep with glances at Roche in her cell, as though to reassure himself that she was still there. She showed no sign of activity; indeed, far from preparing to take control of the ship, she hadn't once regained consciousness. And to Kajic, that in itself was a concern. A brain-damaged informer was not much better than a dead informer—although better than none at all, he supposed.

Of the "ghosts" he had found nothing at all so far. The lower decks were cluttered and cramped, with plenty of hiding places for a single stowaway, but security cameras covered every centimeter. A significant proportion of the crew spent much of their time in these hidden, unglamorous areas, performing small maintenance checks, repairing minor breaks, and ensuring the ship's battle readiness. It was an area rarely visited by the superior officers, and referred to in the vernacular as "the maze" or "the warren."

Kajic estimated that a thorough search of the warren would take between twelve and fifteen hours, yet after only nine hours he had satisfied himself that nothing out of the ordinary existed on the ship. As far as he could see, the only "ghosts" haunting the crew were the same ones that tormented him: guilt, doubt, and uncertainty.

In the eleventh hour, however, another sighting was reported.

In a deep portion of the warren, a maintenance tech stood describing the incident to a workmate. Kajic watched and listened carefully as the woman described seeing a man dressed in grey at the far end of the corridor. The man had looked up, she said, seen her, and suddenly disappeared.

"But he *was* there," the woman insisted. "I swear it!"

Although her testimony was incredible, Kajic didn't doubt her obvious sincerity. Sending himself furiously from camera to camera, he quartered the area around the woman, sweeping through a blur of rooms and corridors—all identical, all unoccupied. Exactly what he was looking for he wasn't sure, but he didn't stop. If he didn't try now, he might never be so close again.

One minute passed, and he had covered every square centimeter within one hundred meters of the sighting. Two minutes, one hundred twenty-five meters. Three minutes, and he was just about ready to give up. Four minutes of strobing, split-second views, and—

He saw it.

It was in one of the little-used stretches of corridor deep in the bowels of the ship. The ambient lighting was low in this particular area, but there could be no doubt. Centered in his field of view were the head and shoulders of a man, a man who shouldn't be there. A man, what's more, whom Kajic didn't immediately recognize.

And then, suddenly, the man was gone. The corridor was empty.

Kajic hesitated for a moment before calling Makaev. What could he say? That he, too, had seen it? That he had succumbed to delusions along with the rest of the crew?

"There has been another sighting," he said when she took the call. "Section Green-24. The same as before."

"I heard." She glanced up from her work station. "In the warren again, and not far from the other sightings, either."

"I know."

Makaev paused. "Did *you* see anything, sir?"

Kajic kept his face carefully neutral. "No," he said. "No, I didn't. However, I will examine the security recordings for a trace. If anything does appear, I will keep you informed."

Kajic retreated into the depths of his mind to study what he had found. The face had been captured by his long-term memory banks, and reappeared before him as vivid and startling as before. And as unfamiliar, even after enhancement removed the shadow that obscured it slightly. Kajic was prepared to bet his life that the face didn't belong to any member of his crew.

But if it didn't, then who *did* it belong to?

The only possible way of finding that out was to run a complete security check on the features. But with only a rough demographic to narrow the search, the check could take hours. Every face in the ship's databanks—and there must have been trillions—would need to be compared to the picture to arrive at a negative. Only if a positive match existed would the search take less time.

Kajic mulled it over, then ordered the search. It couldn't hurt. If his only other avenue came up with nothing, he would still have something to hope for.

Putting the image aside for the moment, he accessed the ship's security records. First, he turned to the moments before the maintenance technician had triggered the alarm. The image was sharp, not yet archived to compressed memory. She stood out clearly, examining a faulty circuit that had failed while she was in the area. Her back was to the camera, and Kajic could see without obstruction to the end of the corridor.

Then, abruptly, the technician stood, gaping. She backed away a step and hit the nearest alert switch. Moments later, her workmate joined her, staring in confusion in the direction she pointed—

But there was nothing there—and, as far as Kajic could tell when he scrolled the recording back, nothing *had* been there.

Increasingly puzzled, he switched to another camera and another time. The dimly lit corridor where he had seen "his" ghost appeared in a window next to that containing the technician, now frozen in mid-gape. He sped the recording forward, then backward, waiting for some sort of change.

Nothing.

The corridor, even at the exact moment when he had seen the face, had been completely void of life.

At that moment, he was relieved that he had not mentioned his own sighting to Makaev. And he intended to keep it that way as long as possible. The obvious interpretation was too damning, too convenient for anyone looking for an excuse to pull the plug on him.

For a long moment, he considered the few alternatives open to him, then methodically erased from his personal database all records of the face he had seen.

Although his enthusiasm for the project was sorely lacking, Kajic resumed his search. Unsure which he feared most—seeing the "ghost" again, or not seeing it—he flicked aimlessly through the warren, wishing he had never started in the first place.

Hours passed uneventfully. He had thought, once, that all his problems would end when he had satisfied his priorities. Yet, in its own way, the return trip was turning out to be worse than the mission itself. Even disregarding the nameless doubts, the new priority kept his mind from wandering as freely as he liked, and the specter of his own possible fallibility, therefore, refused to dissipate.

Still, he would be home soon. Szubetka Base was located near an anchor point in deep space, so approach time was kept to a minimum. Within a handful of hours, if all went well, his mission would be at an end. A *successful* end, too.

And then . . . ?

Having demonstrated that the ship/captain principle was sound, the Dato Bloc's greatest engineers would bend their minds—and those belonging to their new captains—to the task of making an entire fleet of similar vessels. A superfleet of mind-machine gestalts, enough perhaps to give the Presidium an edge over their traditional enemies. When that came to pass, Kajic would finally have like minds with which to associate. It was comforting to know that there would soon be others who could share his experiences.

But this led to a more disturbing thought. Progress was inevitable. He would remain in the service of the Presidium only as long as he was an advantage, not a hindrance. What would happen when he had been superseded? Routine missions? Cargo hauls for the Presidium? Or worse, a civilian fleet? With his body suspended in its life support capsule, his existence could be extended indefinitely, at a price, but would anyone wish to do so? Disembodied, essentially if not literally, he was nothing without his ship. How long before they wanted the *Ana Vereine* back, to give it a new captain . . . ?

Kajic's sense of imminent victory suddenly faded. He was a tool. And the trouble with intelligent tools, he knew, was that they can never be truly trusted—no more than any other Human. Because he *could* be controlled, his future held a lifetime of priorities, nagging duties, and self-doubt. He would never be truly free until the day he died.

Yellow alert suddenly sounded throughout the ship, warning the crew of imminent departure. His priorities began to irritate again, an unsubtle reminder that he was neglecting his duty. With a sigh of relief, he halted the search of the warren and sent himself to the bridge.

His second in command awaited him, looking as tired as he felt.

"How long, Atalia?"

"Ten minutes, sir."

"Any problems?"

"None, sir. Crew and ship are in perfect shape."

"Excellent." Kajic smiled; despite the misgivings he still harbored, he was relieved on that score. He no longer suspected that the "ghost" fiasco had been her doing; she had been as genuinely worried and had worked as hard to remedy the situation as he. If the crew had at last settled down and forgotten the incidents, whatever their cause, then perhaps she deserved much of the credit.

The matter of the kill-switch and the back door still had to be resolved, however, but he was prepared to admit that she had done her duty there, too—and done it well. Perhaps *too* well, at times.

"*Paladin* and *Galloglass* will precede us to Szubetka Base," he said. "Barring unforseen complications, we will follow five minutes after. Then *Lansequenet* two minutes after that."

"Yes, sir." She snapped a formal salute and turned away.

On the main screen, the four green dots of his small command rapidly approached the departure point. He watched them idly, letting himself be an observer rather than an active participant. His crew could handle the jump through the anchor point without his help. For the pilots and astrogators of a warship, even one as new as the *Ana Vereine*, jumping to hyperspace to achieve speeds he could only begin to comprehend was all in a day's work. His main role was to decide when and where to go; all the rest—the vectors, coordinates, and space-distorts—he left to the specialists.

If he desired, however, he could interface with the ship's main computers to boost his processing power, and thereby participate in the mystery. But sometimes it was better simply to watch, to be awed by the forces that people, with all-too-mortal minds, had harnessed.

Bubbles of folded space enclosed the two ships, distorting the light shining through them and making distant stars balloon and fade. Traceries of energy danced along the raiders' hulls, waving like hairs from the points of weapons and casting vast sheets along flat surfaces. Local space seemed crowded, for an instant, as the raiders' imminent supralight departure echoed back through time and collided with the present, cluttering the area with a near-infinite number of phantom ships.

An unexpected prompt sounded in Kajic's mind the very instant the two ships disappeared. Filled with a sudden sense of alarm, he turned his attention inward to see what had happened.

At first he was relieved. Nothing had gone wrong at all; the ship's computers had simply finished the search he had requested. But then, scanning the information that the computer had retrieved on the ship's "ghost," his uncertainty and dread returned.

"*Galloglass* and *Paladin* have jumped successfully," the telemetry officer reported, when the data collected by hull sensors had been analyzed.

Kajic waved distractedly at his second in command for her to give the order.

"Commence countdown," she said. "The *Ana Vereine* will jump in four minutes."

"All systems green, Commander," telemetry announced.

"Good." Then, perhaps sensing that something was amiss, Makaev approached the podium. "Captain, is everything in order?"

"I'm not sure." Kajic called into being a window in his hologram, not caring that it opened where his chest normally was. "Do you recognize this face?"

Makaev studied the picture for a moment, then shook her head. "No, sir. Should I?"

"No, I suppose not. I certainly didn't."

Makaev waited a moment, then prompted, "Sir, I'm not sure I follow—?"

"His name is Adoni Cane. Or rather, it *was*. According to shipboard records, he disappeared over two thousand years ago after ordering an attack on a civilian colony that resulted in the death of nearly four million people."

She glanced at the picture again. "Forgive me for saying this, sir, but: so what?"

"I took his picture this afternoon, down in the warren." Kajic bestowed a wry smile upon his holographic image. "At least when we have ghosts, we have ghosts with class!"

For a long moment, she said nothing. Then, uncertainly: "I see, sir."

"What's the matter with you?" He leaned closer, bringing the picture in his chest with him. "I've found our ghost! I don't know what any of it *means*, but at least we know who it is."

Finally she moved. With a disapproving frown, she raised her eyes to those of his hologram and said evenly:

"*What* ghost?"

He stared at her, dumbfounded. He wasn't sure exactly how he had expected Makaev to respond, but certainly not like *this*. Not with blank incomprehension.

Before he could reply, the red alert warning sounded. The *Ana Vereine* was about to jump. Filled with a sudden and overwhelming fear that something had gone terribly, terribly wrong, he turned to face the bridge crew.

"No—wait!" he cried.

return to Szubetka Base

Fighting his built-in prompts every step of the way, he sent his mind deep into the ship's programming, trying to halt the ship's departure.

"We can't—!"

priority gold-one

But it was already too late.

With a soundless rip, the *Ana Vereine* tore through the fabric of the anchor point and entered hyperspace.

"What's /
/ happening /
/ to /
/ me /
/ . . . ?"

<Don't fight it,> said a voice through the pain.

Kajic flailed in the darkness, lost in a void impossibly dark and empty. This was no ordinary jump, part of him realized. Nothing like this had ever happened to him before. He could sense nothing at all around or inside him. There was only the blackness, and the voice—a voice that shouldn't be there—

<I said, don't *fight* it!> The voice burned into him like a brand, the words stabbing at the very core of his soul.

<What's happening to me?> he gasped again, amazed to find that he could speak, if nothing else. <Who are you?>

<That is irrelevant for the moment,> replied a second voice, more officious than the first. <You must let us have our way.>

<Why?> The question was automatic and full of anger. Even if this was a dream, he didn't appreciate being pushed around by faceless entities.

<You don't really have any choice,> said the first voice, with the barest hint of compassion. <We'd rather not force you, although we will if we have to.>

Kajic suddenly realized what had happened: he had broken down at last. First the mysterious glitch in continuity, then the matter of the "ghost" that Makaev had known nothing about, and now this. The strain had finally been too much for him.

In a way, the knowledge came to him as a relief. What point was there in fighting madness?

<If that's what it takes to make the transition easier,> said the second voice, <then so be it. Believe what you want.>

Then—

Light.

He opened his eyes—or attempted to. Eyes? No; that was an old habit, one he'd thought long forgotten. He tried again, this time sending the impulse through the proper channels.

"Translation completed," said a voice. Memory attached it a label: telemetry.

priority gold-one

He was on the bridge of the *Ana Vereine.*

"Atalia?" He felt his hologram fraying around the edges as he tried to regain his grip on reality. He remembered something about voices, but nothing definite. His memory of the moments preceding their arrival was hazy.

"Yes, Captain?" His second in command stood beside him, watching him.

"Weren't we . . . ?" He felt dizzy for a moment, but fought the sensation. "Before the . . ." He could remember nothing that had happened during the jump. "Weren't we talking about something?"

"I don't think so, sir." She leaned closer. "Is anything wrong?"

He pulled himself together at last. "No, nothing." He didn't want to ask about jump time; instead he glanced at the main screen, which showed him nothing at all. "We've arrived?"

"Residual effects clearing," said telemetry. "Local space will reconfigure in sixty seconds."

"Very good. Contact the commanders of *Paladin* and *Galloglass* to confirm our safe arrival."

"Yes, sir."

As the telemetry officer went about the task, Makaev leaned unnecessarily close to his image. "Are you certain you're feeling all right, sir?"

He glanced sharply at her, suppressing any hint of confusion in both his voice and image. "Are you questioning my competence, Commander?" he asked coldly.

She took a step away from his image, her face flushed. "No, I—"

"Sir," said telemetry. "I am having difficulty contacting *Galloglass* and *Paladin.*"

"What sort of difficulty?"

"They're not responding at all, sir. I *am* picking up some coded traffic, but it's not our code."

"Whose, then?" asked Kajic.

"It's not our code, sir," telemetry repeated with a shrug. "I am unable to translate it."

Beside him, Makaev stiffened. "An ambush!" she hissed.

"Impossible," Kajic said. "Only a fool would attempt an attack anywhere near Szubetka Base. How long until those screens are clear?"

A pause, then: "Fifteen seconds, sir."

"Maybe then we'll know what the hell is going on." Kajic glanced again at his second.

priority gold-one

"Ten seconds, sir."

"I have a bad feeling about this, sir," said Makaev without moving her eyes from the screen. "To have something go wrong now—"

"A little faith, Commander," he said, and heard his own unease creep into his voice. "Everything will be fine."

"Three seconds, sir."

"It *has* to be." This, barely a whisper to himself.

"Two seconds," said telemetry. "One second, and—we are scanning local space now, sir."

Kajic watched anxiously as the screen began to fill with data: visual light first, followed by the more exotic spectra, then by particle sources. All he saw in the initial moments of the scan were stars; only later did nearer, more discrete energy sources appear.

Three ships, not two, appeared in the void, and one very large installation less than a million kilometers away. Two of the ships were angling in toward it on docking approach; the third was leaving, arcing up and away from the *Ana Vereine*'s position. As more detail flooded in, Kajic made out the nestled shapes of ships already docked—hundreds of them, all angular and angry, sharp-pointed sticks to hurl at the indifferent stars.

"Those aren't our ships," he said, his mind's eye narrowing.

"And that's *not* Szubetka Base!" rasped Makaev.

A chill enveloped Kajic.

"*No*," he said, his voice sounding hollow even to his ears. "*No!*"

"That's *COE Intelligence HQ!*" Makaev turned to face him, shock naked in her eyes. "*What the hell have you done?*"

Kajic reeled under the force of her attack. "I—"

"You incompetent *fool*!" She whirled away from him and darted for her station.

"Atalia!" he snapped, desperate to regain some control over his escalating panic and confusion. "What are you doing?"

"I'm assuming command!" she shouted back. "You have betrayed us!" Then, over her shoulder at the rest of the crew: "Someone get us out of here while I deal with him!"

Even as her words reached him via the microphone at her console, even as her face loomed large in the camera facing her chair, even as she reached for the twin datalinks waiting like snake mouths to accept her hands—he realized what she was about to do.

He froze, unsure whether he had the right to stop her.

priority gold-one

By the time he realized he couldn't, it was too late anyway. The commands input via her datalinks were already being processed.

priority override sequence "Kill-Switch" #1143150222

He screamed, feeling the words cut into his mind, tearing him apart
disable core command
piece by tiny piece
disable ancillary processors
flaying him
disable support memory
layer by layer
disable MA/AM interface
stripping him
disable primary database
of his delusions
disable cognitive simulators
of his command
disable life-support
of him
disable
of him
disable
of him
disable . . .

When it had finally finished—then, and only then, was he free.

18

DBMP *Ana Vereine*
'954.10.38 EN
1595

Consciousness parted the thick, dark clouds as Roche opened her eyes. She found herself in a fairly small room, one decorated solely in gunmetal grey. The only piece of furniture it contained was the bed she lay upon. The single door to the room was shut, and the absence of any handle on her side suggested that it was intended to stay that way.

A cell of some sort, she guessed. And judging by the compact surgeon strapped to her chest, obviously a hospital cell in particular. But *where*?

When she tried to sit up, a familiar weight attached to her left arm dragged her back.

<Hello, Box,> she said automatically. The AI did not respond, so she hefted the valise and gave it a brief shake. <Box?>

Again, silence.

"Hello?" she called, aloud this time. Seeing stereoscopic cameras watching from opposite corners of the room, she removed the surgeon and stepped toward one of them. The unblinking lenses followed her every movement. "Is anyone there?"

When the echo of her voice had faded, silence reclaimed the room as impenetrably as before. There was no sound *beyond* the cell, either. To all intents and purposes, the ship she was in—she could tell that much from the vagaries of artificial g—appeared completely dead.

But until someone came to talk to her, she had no way to tell where she was. The surgeon looked the same as they did everywhere, the standard Eckandi design found on that side of the galaxy. The room itself could have been on any Pristine vessel, except—she sniffed the air—it smelled *new*. How many recently built ships were there in either the Commonwealth or the Dato Bloc? And why would they send one to collect a single AI?

What had she *missed*?

She shook her head. She didn't have enough information to guess what had happened to her. And the last thing she remembered was the battle on the top of the MiCom building: the flyers, the mortar bombs, the Dato trooper, and—

Cane.

The return of *that* memory stung. One hand rose automatically to touch her temple where he had struck her unconscious. No pain. No pain anywhere, in fact: in her ribs, her shoulder, or her recently shaved head. Physically, she felt better than she had for days.

After a few minutes, something finally broke the deathly silence. She heard, distant at first, but growing nearer by the second, the sound of footsteps in the corridor outside her cell. Two people, she guessed, marching in perfect time.

Seconds later, the door of the cell hissed smoothly open. A pair of Dato troopers stood outside, framed in the doorway like statues. Reflections glistened disconcertingly across their grey, ceramic shells as, in unison, they took one step forward into the cell. Two black faceplates stared impassively at her as she waited for their next move. Neither one, she noted, was armed.

"You are to come with us, Commander," one of the troopers said, the voice issuing a little too loudly from the suit's massive chest.

"Why?" The defiant tone was automatic.

"Your presence is required elsewhere."

"Where?"

No answer.

She sighed. What was the point in resisting? Even unarmed, two troopers were more than a match for her. She would do better to save her energy for the interrogation that was surely to follow. At least that way she'd find out exactly where she was.

A large part of her suspected that she wasn't going to enjoy the process of finding out.

The troopers led her through a maze of passages and elevators, heading deep into the ship's infrastructure. If she hadn't already guessed that the ship was new, the short journey would have convinced her. Apart from a few small signs of Human occupation, the bulkheads and floors were virtually untouched.

Yet, despite the occasional evidence of life, the ship seemed more deserted than ever. She heard no voices, no footsteps besides hers and her escorts', none of the small mechanical whispers that betrayed a presence nearby. After a few minutes, even the presence of the two troopers began to unnerve her; they might have been machines for all the sound they made.

Eventually they arrived at a door, coming from the other side of which she could hear voices—and heated ones, by the sound of them. But the door remained closed, and neither of the troopers moved to open it.

"Well?" she asked, glancing from one impassive visor to the other, not really expecting an answer. "Are we going to stand out here all day?"

As though her voice had prompted a response, the door slid open and the troopers ushered her inside, taking positions on either side of the entrance.

The room was ten meters across, circular with a high, domed roof. The carpet was a plush burgundy pile, and the fixtures lavish for a military spaceship. At the opposite end of the room was a drink dispenser; low tables held a variety of finger food on glass plates; a quartered ring of comfortable armchairs faced a central holographic display. A meeting hall of some kind, or a senior officers' mess.

At the opening of the door, the argument had ceased in mid-sentence and three heads had turned to stare at her. She stared back, trying not to let her face betray her surprise.

"Well, Commander," said Burne Absenger, COE Armada's Chief Liaison Officer to the Commonwealth of Empires' civilian government. A big, middle-aged man with thick locks of orange-red hair firmly slicked back in a skullcap, his voice was warm and well polished but not quite able to hide an edge of irony. "It would seem you've been busy."

"And we'd like an explanation," snapped Auberon Chase, head of COE Intelligence. Rakishly thin and bald, he wore his uniform irritably, as though discomfited by its loose fit. His eyes burned without dissembling, anger naked for all to see.

Beside him was the head of Strategy, Page De Bruyn—a tall woman with shoulder-length brown hair who, it was rumored, held more power in COE Intelligence than her boss, Chase. She studied Roche with a quiet fascination.

For a moment Roche was unsure exactly how to respond. Confronted by three of the Armada's most senior officers on a Dato ship, in which she herself had only recently woken with no recollection of how she had come to be there, she felt at a total loss. And they wanted *her* to explain?

Then, for the first time, she consciously noted the contents of the viewtank. Her breath caught in her throat. *COE Intelligence HQ*. A massive structure reflecting the light of distant suns and nebulae, it was duty's focus for the millions of Armada officers like herself—and a sight she had come to believe she might never see again. Even if the view was at maximum enhancement, the station had to be close—probably no more distant than the Riem-Perez horizon of its hypershield, the closest point to it that any vessel could jump.

We're right on top of it, Roche concluded. Then: *This is a Dato ship! What's it doing so close*?

"Well, Commander?" prompted De Bruyn, her voice a dangerous purr.

Roche swung her attention from the tank and faced the woman's steely gaze. "I'll answer your questions as well as I'm able to, but I'm afraid that most of this is beyond me."

"Perhaps you should let us be the judge of that." De Bruyn smiled thinly. "When you've told us how you learned about Palasian System, and why the information could not flow through the normal channels, then we'll decide."

Unsteady as it was, Roche stood her ground. "Apart from what I've seen on IDnet, I know nothing at all about Palasian System." De Bruyn's eyes narrowed, but Roche plowed on, choosing her words with care. Regardless how she had come to be in this situation, one wrong word could end her career. "What has led you to believe that I do is something of a mystery to me."

"Don't play the fool with us, Commander," exploded Chase, stabbing a long bony finger in her direction. "First you turn up at HQ in the new Dato Marauder, a vessel regarding which we have only the vaguest intelligence, then you demand—not request, mind you, but *demand*—an immediate audience, here on the ship, to discuss a security matter so grave that it threatens the entire Commonwealth." He snorted as though the very idea offended him. "And now you have the nerve to tell us that you don't even *know* what we're talking about! Why we even agreed to this meeting at all is—"

"Auberon," interrupted De Bruyn sharply, shaking her head. Then, more smoothly, she added, "Let the girl speak."

"Yes," put in Absenger. "We'll never get anywhere if you carry on like this." Fixing Roche with a warm but exaggerated smile, he said, "Clearly this situation is of no benefit to anyone, Commander. So please, let's see if we can't sort everything out."

Roche opened her mouth, about to protest that it wasn't the outburst of the head of Intelligence that caused her reticence but a simple lack of knowledge. Before she could, however, someone spoke up behind her, from the entrance to the conference room.

"She's telling the truth."

Roche turned. Standing in the doorway was Ameidio Haid. With the faintest nod in her direction, he strode confidently into the room, his calm demeanor generating an air of authority.

"We used her image to make that call," he said as he approached. "Seeing she was unconscious at the time, we had no choice."

"What?" Chase's eyes flickered from Haid to Roche, searching for the connection between the two. "What's going on here?"

"That's entirely up to you." Haid took a seat on the opposite side of the room and crossed his legs, to all appearances completely at ease. Roche noted the tautness of his muscles beneath the simple black uniform, however, and suspected that he was far from relaxed. "What's your preference?" he said. "An honest and open discussion, or a witch hunt?"

"This is preposterous," the head of Intelligence spluttered. "I refuse to be a part of any discussion involving someone of your ilk, Haid. A criminal, a barbarian, a *traitor*—!"

"You remember me, then," Haid interjected with some amusement. "But don't kid yourself, Auberon; we really aren't that much different from one another." Before the man could respond, Haid's expression became grave, the humor draining from his tone. "Let's skip the pleasantries, shall we? We have a few things we need to discuss."

Chase's face turned grey with rage.

"Of course." Burne Absenger took a position around the holographic tank, his heavy frame sinking easily into the contoured chair. Page De Bruyn hesitated a moment, then followed his lead, although her posture remained stiffly upright. Roche sat opposite Haid, where she could watch him through the hologram of Intelligence HQ. Chase remained standing until Absenger caught his eye and gestured sharply for him to sit.

The head of Strategy sank into a seat at random. "Do we have any choice?"

"To be honest," said Haid, "no, not anymore. However, the choice to come out to meet us was your own. Ours was merely an invitation."

"You have an interesting way of greeting your guests," said De Bruyn dryly.

Haid shrugged. "You *were* asked to come alone. And unarmed."

De Bruyn snorted. "You couldn't expect us to simply walk onto an enemy vessel without any protection."

"Nor *you* expect *us* to allow an armed platoon to march aboard."

"Which your troops dealt with easily enough," said Chase with more than a trace of bitterness. "What are they? Mercenaries like yourself?"

"No. They're drones," Haid explained. "Or remotes, if you like." He gestured to the nearest Dato trooper, who instantly raised a gauntleted hand to open the black visor.

The helmet inside was empty.

Haid's smile widened at the response from his small audience: the in-drawn breaths and sudden stiffening of postures.

"Eyes and ears in the service of the one behind that message we sent. The one who sent me here—to clear the air."

Roche stared at the empty armor in amazement, then turned to face Haid. "You mean the Box, don't you?"

"Who else?" he said. "Who did you think was running this ship?" He laughed lightly. "Certainly not me."

"I'd assumed the Dato—"

"They're currently in the main airlock holding bay with De Bruyn's squad, waiting to be shipped to HQ." Haid shook his head. "Did you really believe we'd join forces with the Dato Bloc to betray you and the Armada? Morgan, we despise *them* almost as much as we despise the three people sitting with us now."

That brought an immediate response from Chase, but one less vicious than Roche had expected.

"How much do you know?" asked the head of Intelligence, studying Haid narrowly.

"Enough," said Haid. "Enough to see you face a court-martial, Chase. Not that I have any faith in the Commonwealth's judicial system."

"Wait a minute," said Absenger, raising a hand. "You're going much too fast for me. When you say that 'the Box' is running this ship, surely you can't mean the AI attached to the commander's arm here?"

"Why not?" said Haid. "It's perfectly suited to the task."

"But how? I mean, it seems hard to believe that . . ." Absenger glanced at De Bruyn. "Surely this Box is nothing more than a communications AI commissioned to replace one in the Armada network?"

"The Box is much more than a 'communications AI,'" said Haid, "no matter what you say. It's designed with the express purpose of infiltrating and ultimately corrupting Dato intelligent systems, such as those that run this ship, or the combat armor you see before you. That's what you ordered from Trinity, and that's what they built." His gaze shifted suddenly. "Isn't that right, De Bruyn?"

The head of Strategy looked uncomfortable for a moment, then exchanged another glance with Absenger. "We wanted something that could infiltrate Dato security from the inside."

Haid nodded. "And that's what you got—and more." He looked at Roche and noticed the slight wince on her face. "Don't feel too bad, Morgan. I didn't work it out myself, either. When you let me open the datalink, I had no idea what I was getting myself into. That damned machine is a maze of security probes and countertraps; given a century, uninterrupted, I *might* have come close to guessing what it was for. In the end, I didn't crack the Box; *it* cracked *me*. It needed another ally, and I was the one it chose."

"To do what?" said Roche.

"To help the two of you off the planet, basically. And to gain access to data processors powerful enough for it to discover its full potential."

Roche absorbed this for a moment, sensing an unspoken implication in his words. "You said *another* ally?"

"That's right. Adoni Cane was the first. That's why it let him out of the *Midnight*'s brig and made sure he reached you before the Dato attacked."

Roche gaped. "The *Box* did that?"

"Of course. I told you there was something screwy about all that. The Box could see what was coming, and made sure you had at least an even chance of surviving."

"Who is this 'Adoni Cane'?" said Absenger.

"This is ridiculous!" Chase snapped. "I can't believe we're discussing Commonwealth secrets with these people—"

"Be *quiet*, Auberon," said De Bruyn, her eyes dangerous.

Haid watched the brief interaction with some amusement, and Roche suddenly realized how well he was playing them against each other. Absenger, the politician, the smooth talker; Chase, the reactionary hothead; and De Bruyn, perhaps the most dangerous of the three, sharp and coldly calculating.

"Adoni Cane is a genetically modified combat soldier," Haid said, as casually as though discussing the weather. "The *Midnight* plucked him from a life support capsule located by its beacon eight days before arriving at Sciacca's World. The ship's surgeons examined him in situ, but didn't have time to contact HQ. The data they collected then, plus more from our own examinations on Port Parvati, makes for very interesting reading."

The viewtank's image of Intelligence HQ vanished and was replaced with a three-dimensional scan of Cane, segmented in places to reveal his inner organs. Lines of data scrolled down the corners of the tank, listing metabolic rates, genetic comparisons, cellular structures, neural connections . . .

Roche studied it in disbelief. This was much more detailed than she'd seen in the rebels' headquarters. How Haid had managed to get hold of the *Midnight*'s data was beyond her.

Then she realized: the Box again, although why it had gone to the trouble to save the data, then keep it a secret from her and the rebels, remained unknown. For the moment, curiosity about Cane overrode that about the Box.

She could see, now, where the survival capsule had been physically grafted to him at stomach, throat, and thighs via circular wounds that had healed within days of his emergence. The *Midnight*'s chief surgeon's tentative conclusion was that he had indeed been grown in the capsule and subsequently given a basic knowledge of language and movement by implanted educators. Given the condition of his tissue and the lack of radiation damage suffered while in deep space, Cane appeared to be roughly one year old, although his mental age was far above that. The obvious conclusion was that, although the capsule had drifted for at least a year before being found, the timing of its discovery had been carefully planned. Even with the capsule's sophisticated organic vats, only superficially examined on the *Midnight*, Human tissue could not have been sustained unharmed for longer than a month or two.

Cane, therefore, wasn't an innocent cast adrift by some unknown tragedy, lying dormant in the capsule waiting to be rescued. He had been built for a purpose by someone who had *wanted* him to be found. Now. The only question that remained unanswered was: how long had the capsule been drifting before it brought him into being?

No one else in the room seemed ready to ask the obvious questions—questions she had asked back on Sciacca's World—so she spoke for them:

"To what end?"

The answer came from an unexpected quarter.

"To purge the Commonwealth and its neighbors of Pristine Humanity, of course," said Page De Bruyn, her voice hushed. "To wreak revenge on the descendants of the people who destroyed the creators of such creatures. Adoni Cane is a Clone Wunderkind, courtesy of the Sol Apotheosis Movement."

"*Another* one?" said Chase, his face pale.

"It was always a possibility," said Absenger grimly.

"Will someone please tell me what you're talking about?" said Roche.

Absenger sighed heavily and opened his hands. "Twenty-five days ago, a similar capsule also containing a single occupant was retrieved by the courier vessel *Daybreak* not far from one of our systems. *Daybreak*'s captain had time to report the discovery, but little else. Before she could transmit a detailed report, all communication ceased and the ship disappeared. Two days later, *Daybreak* reappeared, broadcasting an emergency beacon. The commanding officer of the nearest military base sent out a tug to rendezvous, and took it in for repairs. Not long after, we received garbled messages that the base was under attack—then that too fell silent. By the time the Armada sent a battalion to investigate, the entire system was in flames."

"None of this was on IDnet," Roche said.

"You covered it up," said Haid, speaking not in response to her question but to De Bruyn. "Possibly the greatest threat the COE has ever faced, and you tried to sweep it under the rug."

"We didn't *know* what had happened," protested De Bruyn. "It could have been anything: rebellion, disease, war. We had no way of knowing. But we had to enforce a quarantine to keep people out, to prevent more deaths."

"Palasian System," said Roche, finally making the connection.

Absenger nodded. "It was only after the battalion arrived that we managed to piece together what had happened: that some kind of modified warrior had singlehandedly taken control of *Daybreak* and gone berserk in the system."

"How many of the battalion made it back?" asked Haid.

De Bruyn grimaced. "Of twenty ships, only one survived. And from the pictures brought back, not much was left of the system. Now"—she shrugged helplessly—"who knows?"

Roche reeled at the thought. "You're suggesting that *one person* did this?"

"We're not talking about a *person*, Commander," said Absenger. "This is a genetically enhanced being—a Wunderkind—capable of anything."

"And now we have two of them," said Chase, his thin face even paler than before.

"You think Cane—?" She stopped in mid-sentence, staring at the image rotating in the viewtank. "I can't believe it."

"What can't you believe, Commander?" said De Bruyn. "That he's capable of such destruction, or that he would?"

Roche shook her head. "Both, I guess."

"Morgan," said Haid, "you've seen how Cane fights person-to-person. Imagine him with a ship, or in control of a major weapons array; imagine how much more destructive he could be. If the Wunderkind in Palasian System has the same potential as Cane"— he too shrugged—"then I don't find it difficult to believe at all."

"But that means he's been drifting for almost three thousand years!"

"Not him; just the capsule." Absenger's grim expression showed no satisfaction at correcting her. "He can't come from anywhere else, Roche. No one designed combat clones quite like the Sol engineers, and according to our records 'Adoni Cane' was the name of the commander of the fleet that confronted them—the man whose orders led to their destruction. It's a deliberate jibe at their enemies; one that's taken a long time to hit home, but a jibe all the same."

"The prodigal son returns," Chase muttered.

Absenger leaned forward. "Yet Cane actually helped the Box?"

"And Roche, too," Haid said, turning from Roche to face the liaison officer. "*Particularly* Roche, for whatever reason."

"That does seem unlikely," mused Absenger. "Perhaps Cane and the Palasian Wunderkind aren't exactly the same thing, after all. You said that Cane's capsule was broadcasting some sort of beacon, whereas the first—"

"That's not what I said," Haid interrupted. "I said that a beacon had led the *Midnight* to it."

De Bruyn's brow creased. "The same thing, surely?"

"Not quite," said Haid. "You see, the beacon was faked."

De Bruyn's frown deepened. "By whom?"

Haid smiled. "Before I answer that, why don't you explain to Roche why you were so surprised to receive that message we sent you yesterday?"

The sudden change in direction took the three Armada officers off guard. Roche noted the tightening of De Bruyn's jaw muscles as she fumbled for the words.

"I—" Her face flushed as she glanced from Absenger to Chase. "Her method of arrival was somewhat unorthodox, and—"

Haid laughed at her discomfort. "You people really have a problem with the truth, don't you?" he said, settling back into his chair and resting his one arm across his lap. "Perhaps *I* can shed some light on things, then, by way of explaining about the attack on the *Midnight*."

Whatever game he was playing, Roche thought, he was clearly enjoying himself immensely.

"I'll omit the details of the ambush, if you like. No doubt you can imagine them for yourselves, seeing it went pretty much as you hoped it would when you leaked the *Midnight*'s course to the Dato Espionage Corps. Everything went according to plan, except of course that Roche and the Box managed to escape the destruction of the *Midnight*, and made it as far as the surface of the planet before—"

"Wait a second!" Roche gasped, rising to her feet as his words sunk in. "They did *what*?"

Haid's eye met hers through the shimmering viewtank. "I'm sorry to be the one to tell you this, Morgan, but they obviously weren't going to. They sold you out. Your mission wasn't, as you thought, to bring the Box back to HQ for installation. Instead, it was to be captured by the Dato and taken to the Military Presidium. That's why they were so surprised to see you here: you weren't *supposed* to return."

Roche stared from Chase to De Bruyn, then to Absenger. Only the last met her gaze, and he seemed almost amused by her outrage.

"Is this true?" she asked him, fearing the answer even as she said the words.

"Of course it isn't," he said quickly—almost too quickly.

<He's lying,> said a familiar voice in her mind. Not the Box, but Maii.

Roche closed her eyes; any other time, she might have been glad to hear from the young Surin, but not now. "I *know*," she whispered irritably.

"Good," said Absenger. "Then you will also know that the man is clearly paranoid. Quite perceptive in some ways, I'll admit, but—"

"I wasn't talking to *you*, you sonofabitch!"

Absenger flinched perceptibly. His voice was cold when he spoke. "Commander Roche, must I remind you—?"

"If you're going to tell me that I should show some respect to senior officers, then save your breath." All the frustration she'd felt on Sciacca's World, all the lengths she'd gone to to complete her mission—every action she'd taken on COE Intelligence's behalf boiled within her, perverted and twisted into a hideous farce. "Save it for telling me *why* you did it."

"If you think I'm going to explain myself to—"

"The Box," Haid cut in, "was designed to infiltrate the Dato from *within*, as Page said earlier." He leaned forward to emphasize every word, peering through the hologram at Roche. "I was hoping you'd guess, and save me having to spell it out for you. The Box was no use at all to COE Intelligence back here. So they chose a disposable old frigate with a disposable captain, and put a disposable agent in charge of the mission."

"This is ridiculous!" blurted out Chase as he stood. "This man is lying!"

"I won't tell you again, Auberon." De Bruyn's voice was even and quiet.

Chase stared down at her. "Why should we listen to the slander of criminals?"

"I said *be quiet*!" De Bruyn's icy and unflinching glare held the man for a full ten seconds until he finally looked away and sat back in his chair.

"*Is* it true?" asked Roche a second time.

"Yes," said De Bruyn, facing Roche. "Of course it's true. We sent you to Sciacca's World knowing you'd be ambushed. We thought the local government was corrupt enough to handle any extra work the Dato required to finish the job, if things didn't go smoothly. That's the main reason we chose the planet."

"But that's the trouble with traitors," said Haid. "They're unreliable—aren't they, Absenger?"

The liaison officer shook his head. "I'm afraid I can't comment on this."

"No?" said Roche. "You're denying that you had anything to do with it?"

"Don't be pathetic, Burne," snapped De Bruyn. "Put your guilt aside and stand up to these people." Then, to Haid: "Delcasalle is his little puppet. Sciacca's World was chosen on his recommendation."

"You sent me in there to die!" Roche snapped.

De Bruyn's eyes flashed. "Yes. And I'd have no hesitation in doing so again. It was a good plan. The Box needed to be in position before it would be effective, and this was the best way to get it there without arousing the Presidium's suspicions. It *should* have worked." She cast a disparaging eye in Roche's direction. "And I'm still at a loss to understand why it didn't."

"I've heard enough," Roche said.

"No, you haven't," said Haid. "Not quite. You also need to know *why* their plan fell apart as badly as it did, and what this means to all of us."

Feeling empty and tired, Roche sagged and sat back down. She had spent her entire adult life in the service of the Commonwealth of Empires, in return for which she had been betrayed. Whatever Haid had left to reveal, she doubted it could match what she'd already heard; she felt numb, beyond all further surprise. "Go ahead," she said.

Haid stood. In the viewtank, the hologram of Cane disappeared and was replaced by an orbital view of Sciacca's World; the belt of the Soul sparkled majestically.

"The plan to infiltrate the Dato Presidium with an AI was quite clever, I have to admit," said Haid. "But it's flawed at a basic level. For the Box to be effective, it had to be able to operate independently of COE Intelligence for long periods of time; it had to follow its own judgment in times of possible crisis; it had to be able to choose between several different possible courses of action; it had to be able to plan in detail, and to conspire to see those plans come to fruition. To do all of this, it had to be far more intelligent than the AIs the Armada normally uses." Haid paused, then said, "In short, it had to be self-aware—as self-aware as we are."

"That's impossible," said Roche, remembering her years tormenting the AIs in the Armada.

"Do you really believe that?" Haid met her stare firmly. "After everything it's done?"

She lowered her eyes, focusing upon the image in the viewtank. "I don't know."

"The Box *is* self-aware, Morgan, as conscious as you or I. Trinity is owned and run by High Humans, don't forget, not mundanes, so we shouldn't ascribe to it our own limitations. It's *always* been able to make such minds. The process takes as many years as it would take to produce an intelligent Human being, or so the Box has led me to believe, but it is possible." He shrugged. "Trinity normally doesn't release them, because they tend to be expensive, and a little unreliable, if you like. They're *too* intelligent—everything people are, and more. Controllable to a point, yes, but beyond that is anyone's guess. It's a double-edged sword: on the one hand you have a machine independent enough to do everything you want, but too independent to trust. The Commonwealth isn't ready for minds like these, and may not be for many years to come. Until it's ready to Transcend, perhaps."

Haid stared in turn at the COE Intelligence officers, then settled again upon Roche. "But that's ultimately why your real mission failed, Morgan—because the Box didn't *want* it to succeed. It saw through the intentions of these three almost immediately, and decided it didn't want to be a pawn in a game beneath its potential; it wanted to be a major player, at the very least."

Roche glanced at the valise still dangling from the cord at her side. It didn't look like some sort of super-AI at all, just a battered case dragged from one end of the COE to the other. "A player in what?"

"I don't know," said Haid. "It won't talk to me about that."

"Or perhaps," said De Bruyn, "you're just being paranoid, seeing plots and conspiracies where in fact none exist."

Roche ignored De Bruyn's jibe, not allowing Haid to be distracted. "What did you mean about the Box not wanting to be involved in anything 'beneath its potential'?"

"Think about it," he said. "The Box has the ability to infiltrate intelligent networks and to bend them to its will. The larger its opponents, the stronger it becomes, by using their processing power to boost its own capacity. Given enough power, it can do almost anything it sets its mind to. Why should it want to play Intelligence's petty games? Don't you think it would have its own agenda?"

He gestured at the viewtank, which reverted to the previous rotating display. "For instance, there's Cane."

Roche nodded. "The way it set him free from the brig to help me?"

"More than that, Morgan," said Haid. "The Box knew about his life capsule and its trajectory before it boarded the *Midnight*. It faked the distress call that led directly to Cane's discovery."

De Bruyn's eyes widened. "It knew about the Sol conspiracy?"

"Maybe, maybe not," said Haid. "I don't know for sure. Certainly it knew about the capsule, if not its contents. Maybe it was simply curious, at first, then became more involved when it lifted the findings of the *Midnight*'s surgeons from the ship's datapool and realized what, exactly, Cane was. When it recruited him, it did so partly to improve its chances of survival, and partly to study a Sol Wunderkind firsthand."

"But the risk!" said De Bruyn with an obvious mix of admiration and horrified amazement. "Didn't it realize what could have happened if Cane had proven to be uncontainable?"

"I'm sure it did," said Haid. "I'm also sure that it did what it felt best. Remember—Trinity makes military AIs so tough they could weather a supernova with an even chance of surviving. The Box would have come to no harm, no matter what Cane did."

Roche felt her fists clench involuntarily. "And what about me?" she asked. "All that stuff about saving me from the ambush, all the effort it spent to help us survive the crash—that was all an act?"

"No, Morgan." Haid smiled at her through the hologram. "That I can tell you for certain. You see, Trinity knew what the Armada was up to as well, and they didn't like it either. So they programmed one small bug into the Box to give you a reasonable chance: whatever you tell it to do, provided only that it falls within its powers and doesn't conflict with its higher programming, it *will* do."

It was Roche's turn to snort derisively.

"I'm serious," said Haid. "I also found it hard to believe at first, given what happened at the landing field. But it insists it's telling the truth, and now I believe it."

Roche regarded him carefully. "Why?"

"Well, for instance, ten days ago you told it to 'do whatever it takes to get us out of here.' "

Roche nodded, remembering. "During the ambush."

"That's right," said Haid. "And you attributed the *Midnight*'s self-destruction to Captain Klose. But you were wrong."

Roche stared at him for what felt like eternity as the revelation unfolded in her mind. If Klose hadn't scuttled the antimatter reserves, then—*the Box* had. To ensure her survival, it had sacrificed the entire crew of the *Midnight*—saving only Cane. And as an added bonus, the destruction of the ship had covered up its deception in that regard.

Roche felt nausea rising in her throat. She could hardly comprehend such a coldly calculated action. So much for no more surprises.

Haid went on. "Then, while you were preparing the plan to attack the landing field with Emmerik and Neva, you specifically instructed the Box to forget about taking over DAOC's transmitter station. Although its idea might have been useful as a backup, it wasn't able to consider the possibility after that point. That's why we decided to go for the *Ana Vereine* instead, which we knew you'd approve even less—"

"Wait, *wait*," said Roche, waving Haid to silence. "You're going too fast. What's the *Ana Vereine*?"

"You're standing in it," said Haid. "The Dato Marauder that ambushed you."

"And when you say 'we,'" said Roche, "you're talking about the Box and yourself?"

"We talked over the datalink for some time after it 'cracked' me. The Box was in a real bind, because although your plan was good, it was also a little naive. There was no way we were going to hold the landing field indefinitely—especially considering the Box's confirmation of what I'd already guessed, that the Armada probably wasn't going to rescue you. That meant we had to have a backup plan, one the Box could play a role in. You'd frozen it out of the satellite, so the *Ana Vereine* was the only alternative. And to avoid you ordering the Box out again, we had to make sure you didn't find out about it."

Haid at least looked sheepish for a moment as he said, "The Box, Cane, and myself—I guess we betrayed you too, Morgan. Cane made sure you were unconscious when we boarded the shuttle; that way there was no chance you'd interfere. Then we took the shuttle to orbit and docked with its mother ship."

"That easy, huh?" Chase, silent for so long, rolled his eyes.

"Haven't you been listening to me?" snapped back Haid. "All we had to do was open a channel to the *Ana Vereine*'s main processors, let the Box do its thing, and we were practically home free. The Box changed the ship's course from Szubetka Base to Intelligence HQ without anyone knowing. During the three-day journey out here, we stayed in the lower decks, with the Box covering for us—making sure security didn't see us, and making it look like the crew of the shuttle were aboard upstairs. Maii helped, too; she smoothed the way with the captain and the senior crew as they began to suspect, giving us just enough time to reach Intelligence HQ, where we were finally safe to openly take over the ship." Haid smiled. "Even that was fairly easy. Maii dampened their aggression to a manageable level, and the Box threatened to cut off their air if they didn't do what it said. Anyone who tried to break free was dealt with by Cane." He raised his hands. "And there you have it. I've never kidnapped a ship with so little loss of life before."

"Risky, though," mused Absenger. "Almost too complicated, in places."

"It had to be, if we were going to keep Roche out of the way—which is how the Box wanted it. Just because it's programmed to obey her, that doesn't mean it has to like it."

"Still, you were gambling a lot on the fact that the Box would be able to infiltrate the Marauder," said Absenger. "The difference in scale and complexity alone—"

"Once the Box demonstrated that it was able to take over the MiCom installation on Sciacca's World, I no longer had any doubts about its capabilities."

"MiCom?" Absenger frowned. "But that's a Commonwealth network, not Dato."

"Intelligent systems differ only minutely throughout this region of the galaxy, except on Trinity. Which means that the Box can not only take over Dato networks, but *any* network at all. COE, Eckandar Trade Axis, Mbatan, MiCom, whatever—it's all the same on the inside."

Absenger was about to say something else, but stopped when he saw De Bruyn rise to her feet, her lips pursed with anger.

"You fool!" she spat at Haid. "Don't you understand what you've done?"

"Come on, Page," soothed Absenger, half rising to take her arm. "This isn't helping matters—"

"Don't patronize me, you idiot," she growled, pulling free. "Can't you see what they're *doing*? Open your eyes, for God's sake!"

Absenger's brow knitted in confusion. "I don't understand."

"When you've finished squabbling—" started Haid.

"Shut up, Haid!" De Bruyn snapped viciously, suddenly producing a handgun from the folds of her free-flowing jacket. "I should execute you right now for what you've done."

Haid sat frozen in position, staring down the barrel of the weapon. Clearly, he had thought she was unarmed.

"What's she talking about?" asked Chase, just as obviously surprised by the sudden turn of events.

"I see it," said Roche. The implication had been in Haid's explanation of how easily the Box had taken control of the *Ana Vereine*, and of MiCom, the DAOC flyers over Houghton's Cross, and *Midnight*'s self-destruct systems, and now—

"HQ," she said softly.

"*Now* the innocent begins to notice what's going on around her," said De Bruyn, although she kept her attention fixed upon Haid. "Or was the innocence just another act? Part of the distraction, perhaps?"

"I still don't get it," said Chase.

"Think about it, Auberon." Holding the gun on Haid, she crossed the room until she was as far away from Roche's escort as possible. "Why do you think we're here? For an honest and open discussion? Forget it. We're here to give that infernal machine time to complete its mission!"

Chase half rose as realization struck him. "Are you suggesting . . . ?"

De Bruyn nodded. "I suspected they were up to something when we were asked over here, though I had no idea what that something would be. The only way to find out was to play their game."

"You can't be serious," said Chase.

"Oh, I am," said De Bruyn. "And I have no intention of just sitting back and letting it happen."

Absenger shook his head slowly. "Now it's *you* sounding paranoid."

"Enough, Burne," De Bruyn said. "The time for negotiation is past. If the Box hasn't already infiltrated the Intelligence HQ command core, then we may still have a chance to do something to stop it."

De Bruyn turned to cover the room with the pistol, her eyes filled with a self-confidence that Roche found strangely disquieting. Despite the head of strategy's present advantage over them, she was still a long way from the security of Intelligence HQ. The situation could easily be reversed—especially with the presence of Cane and the Box—yet her eyes betrayed not the slightest suggestion of fear or uncertainty.

"JW111101000?" said De Bruyn, sounding out each of the numerals, and glancing unnecessarily to the ceiling. "Are you listening?"

The Box's familiar voice suddenly issued from speakers in the base of the holographic tank. "I have been observing this conversation closely."

"Good. Then pay attention. *Silence between thoughts*. I repeat: *Silence between thoughts!*"

"No!" Too late, Roche sprang from her seat, lunging for De Bruyn. She collided heavily with the woman before the head of Strategy could react, sending them both sprawling to the floor. The pistol skidded into a corner. Haid automatically jumped toward it, but he was quickly—and with surprising ease—knocked aside by Chase. As Roche fought to keep the head of Strategy pinned beneath her, a heavy arm wound around her throat, twisting her backward and cutting off her air supply. Gasping for breath, she was unable to avoid a vicious blow to her midriff from De Bruyn. Not far from her, unable to help, Haid struggled one-armed with the head of Intelligence for possession of the pistol.

Roche thrust backward with all her might. Absenger held on firmly. She kicked out at De Bruyn with her last remaining strength, but a savage twist from Absenger made the blow miss by an arm's length. Through black spots spreading across her vision, Roche saw the woman move over to where Haid tussled with Chase.

De Bruyn collected the pistol from the floor and turned it on Roche in a single smooth action.

"Okay," she gasped irritably. "Let them go."

The pressure on Roche's windpipe eased and she collapsed backward, sucking at air. She saw Haid rise slowly to his feet, his expression one of apology. She shook her head, silently cursing his carelessness: with another person to accompany him to the meeting, or at the very least a simple handgun, the attempt to disarm De Bruyn might well have worked.

"If either of you tries anything like that again," De Bruyn scowled, "then you can forget about a trial."

Roche glanced over to the Dato combat suits. Why hadn't they intervened? she wondered. Why hadn't they stepped in to *help* her? Then she remembered: they had been controlled by the Box.

"Box?" Haid called out, confusion gnawing at his words. "Box!"

De Bruyn laughed coldly. "It won't do you any good."

"What have you done?" Haid said. "Why won't it answer me?"

"Because it can't hear you," said Roche, clambering to her feet. "Like all Trinity AIs, the Box was installed with an override. Intelligence had the ability to shut it down anytime they liked."

De Bruyn moved across the room to face Haid, savoring the moment. "All I had to do was say the right words."

Her smile widened, seeing comprehension dawn across Haid's dark features.

"That's right," she said. "The Box is dead. And now we can discuss the situation properly: on *my* terms."

19

DBMP *Ana Vereine*
'954.10.39 EN
0225

<Maii?>

Roche sent her mental voice through the ship as she was marched, hands behind head, to the bridge. Haid walked beside her, his dour expression cast to the floor.

<I'm here, Morgan,> returned the Surin.

<Where's 'here'?>

<Down in the warren. Safe.> The reave's tone conveyed irony behind her words. <I'm not the one you should be worrying about.>

<I know,> said Roche. <I don't suppose there's anything you can do to distract De Bruyn?>

<I wouldn't like to risk it. Her shields are strong, and I believe she has latent epsense ability. If she suspects I'm trying, she *will* shoot—I can read that much.>

As though De Bruyn had sensed the surreptitious conversation, she nudged Roche in the back with the weapon, urging her faster. Roche glanced over her shoulder at the woman, but said nothing. Later, she promised herself. Later . . .

Not long after, the five of them turned a corner and entered the bridge. Roche took in the massive room with one quick glance. The ship may have been new, but it still conformed to standard Dato Bloc designs: communications at the center, navigation and telemetry to the left, targeting and security to the right; various subordinate positions scattered around the semicircular sweep of stations below the main screens; opposite the main entrance, a door leading to some sort of private command chamber. The only odd point was the inclusion of a complicated holographic projector where the captain's podium normally stood.

Chase guided Haid and Roche into one corner while De Bruyn indicated for Absenger to take the comm.

"Call Field Lieutenant Hennig," said the head of Strategy, taking position in the center of the room. "Tell him to bring his ship alongside and send over the boarding party as per the instructions I gave him earlier. He'll know what to do."

Absenger took a seat behind the communications station and put his hand uncertainly on the palmlink, clearly a little unfamiliar with the menial task. De Bruyn retreated to close the bridge's main entrance. Chase remained behind, standing restlessly by the command podium.

"I'm sorry, Morgan," Haid whispered to Roche while De Bruyn was distracted. "I guess I pushed my luck a little too far this time."

She shook her head solemnly. "You weren't to know about the control codes—although I should have guessed De Bruyn had them. She *always* has something up her sleeve."

Haid grimaced. "Not even the Box predicted this one."

Roche indicated Absenger, still talking into the communicator. "She was well prepared, I'll give her that. She even had a backup boarding party ready, just in case. I should have realized she had something planned. Three of Intelligence's top officers voluntarily boarding an enemy vessel did seem just a little reckless."

De Bruyn was suddenly behind them again. "Cut the talk, you two."

Haid nodded distantly and tucked his arm behind his back—to all appearances the cowed captive. Roche wondered how much of that was an act, or whether he really had given in.

The main screen came to life, revealing an image of the distant Intelligence HQ. Six sparks of light flared at one of the many docks as fighters launched to make their way toward the *Ana Vereine*. De Bruyn nodded in satisfaction at the sight.

Roche mentally calculated the odds: an escort ship of some kind, maneuvering to come alongside, and six fighters on their way from the station. Even with the edge Maii and Cane gave her, they were hopelessly outnumbered. Without the Box behind them, they were hamstrung.

But she wasn't about to give up just yet, regardless of Haid's apparent acquiescence.

<Maii? Where's Cane?>

<Not far away. He thinks he can get to the bridge via a life support duct.>

Roche's stomach dropped, remembering how Cane had saved her from Sabra.

<Keep him out of it if you can,> she said. <There has to be another way. We need De Bruyn *alive*, otherwise we'll never get the Box back.>

<I'll tell him.>

Thinking furiously, Roche returned her attention to the goings-on around her. De Bruyn had ordered the ship to be moved inside the Riem-Perez horizon. That reduced the options considerably, for no matter who controlled the *Ana Vereine*, once inside the horizon, there was no chance of slow-jumping out. And warships on station farther out would intercept them before they could turn and reemerge.

Absenger crossed to the navigation console and fed a course into the main AI. The proposed trajectory appeared on the central screen: a lazy elliptical path leading toward the station's huge docking bays. De Bruyn was taking them all the way in.

After a minute or two, Roche felt the floor shift slightly beneath her. The massive engines had come to life. Inertial dampers kept most of the delta-v below the threshold of awareness, however, and soon the impression that the ship was stationary returned.

De Bruyn turned away with a pleased nod. "Auberon, take security. I want you to track down that reave and the Wunderkind. I don't want them trying anything stupid when the squad arrives."

Chase nodded and left his position to find the correct station. He glanced once at the head of Strategy, but otherwise showed no resentment at being ordered about. Quite clearly, De Bruyn was in control. On the main screen, the *Ana Vereine* inched along its prescribed path, while the six minuscule dots of the approaching ships rapidly closed.

"We have to *do* something," Roche whispered.

"I know," replied Haid. "But I'm out of ideas. This sort of thing isn't my forte. I've always found it better to let the upper hand have its way at first. Things almost never get so hopeless that I don't manage to escape later."

Roche glanced at him sidelong. " 'Almost' never?"

He looked sheepish. "Well, they *did* catch me in the end."

"Exactly." Roche sighed, thinking furiously to herself. If Haid couldn't help, and Cane's brute-force approach was bound to land them in hotter water still, and Maii was reluctant to risk De Bruyn's shields, then it was up to her. There *had* to be a way. . . .

Movement from the trio interrupted her thoughts for a moment. Chase was struggling with the security console, unable to comply with De Bruyn's orders. De Bruyn, no doubt concerned by her ignorance of Cane's whereabouts, had become impatient.

"Come *on*, Auberon!"

"Don't give me that," he snapped back. "I've never used this type of console before. It's a new design." He bent lower to concentrate on his work. "Just give me a second."

De Bruyn shook her head in annoyance and backed away.

The tableau only lasted a second, but it gave Roche an idea.

Trying to keep the sudden rebirth of hope from her face, Roche outlined her plan to Maii, who in turn relayed it to Haid and Cane. She was gratified to see the ex-rebel's eyes widen slightly upon hearing it: if *Haid* thought it was bold, then chances were that De Bruyn would be taken completely by surprise.

Not that she needed his approval. She had allowed herself to be led by others for far too long. This was her last chance to keep the freedom she had so briefly won, and she resolved not to miss it.

When everything was nearly organized, she returned her attention to the main screen. The fighters had already entered an approach formation. The escort ship had to be close, because Absenger had opened the main docking bay ready for the boarding party's arrival. In another ninety seconds it would be too late.

The only catch would be if Chase managed to master the security system before she was ready.

<Cane's almost in position,> whispered Maii.

Clenching her teeth, Roche thought: <Do it.>

Chase suddenly jerked upright at the security station. "I've *got* it!" he cried.

De Bruyn took a few steps towards him. "Well?"

Chase hesitated over the console. "There he is—right outside the bridge!"

"Lock the doors," De Bruyn called to Absenger as she moved instantly to Chase's side. "Where? Show me!"

Chase pointed at the screen in front of him with an expression of triumph and fear. Roche tensed, unable to see what the head of Intelligence was pointing at. "See? He must have come out of that life support duct further up the corridor. And that thing he's carrying—looks like some sort of cutting tool. He's going to try to burn through the door!"

De Bruyn stared at the screen in disbelief, then at Chase. "What are you talking about? There's no one there!"

"What do you mean?" Triumph drained from Chase's face, leaving only fear. "There! *Look*!"

De Bruyn *did* look—and Roche felt the tension ease slightly. The plan was working, so far.

De Bruyn suddenly turned to face Roche, anger naked on her face.

"Call the reave off," she hissed. Then, moving up behind Roche, she pressed the barrel of the weapon into her cheek. "Call her off or I'll—"

At that moment, a grill halfway across the bridge exploded from the wall. As though fired from a cannon, it flew almost horizontally through the air, colliding with a console in a shower of sparks.

Cane's feet followed the grill from the vent, thumping solidly onto the deck. With two steps, he was halfway over to them, his eyes fixed upon the head of Strategy as though no one else were present in the room. He was unarmed, but his every movement displayed the potential for violence.

De Bruyn backed away a step, shifting the pistol from Roche so that it was targeted directly at Cane. She clearly had no intention of giving him any opportunities.

Roche spun, her right hand raised to sweep the pistol aside. A single energy bolt, fired by reflex, flashed past her shoulder, burning a hole in her shipsuit. Before De Bruyn could follow the shot with another, Roche jabbed one hand into the woman's solar plexus, then slammed a second punch to the side of her head. De Bruyn staggered and fell back, arms raised to protect her face. She was still holding the gun, however, and as it started to come up, Roche braced herself on her left foot and kicked the pistol from her hand.

De Bruyn dropped to her knees. Roche backed away, tensed to strike again if the need arose. Cane scooped the pistol from the ground and turned it on the three Intelligence officers.

"Nice work, Morgan," he said, nodding in admiration. "You didn't need me after all."

"No offense, Cane," said Roche, "but that was the idea." She faced Haid. "Ameidio, tie them into the chairs. Use their uniforms, anything, just make sure they can't move." Then, noticing Chase's vacant expression, she added, "You can let go of him now, Maii."

The head of Intelligence sagged, then turned in shock to Roche. "You—?"

Cane hauled him away by the collar of his uniform with little effort. The head of Intelligence blanched visibly at the sight of Cane and tried to pull away, but Cane's grip was too strong, forcing him down into a chair without any possibility of resistance.

When she was satisfied that the Intelligence officers were secure, Roche turned to the navigation console, placed her hand on the palmlink, and began to work.

"You'll never escape." De Bruyn glared at her as Haid bound her arms with strips of fabric torn from her jacket. "The fighters are too close. And you're inside the Shield—so you can't slow-jump your way clear."

"Be quiet." Roche didn't turn, concentrating solely on fine-tuning the course. She didn't entirely trust the shipboard AIs to do it for her. "If escape was what I wanted, I'd kill you now and get it over with."

The *Ana Vereine* shifted orientation ponderously as its attitude jets burned. On the main screen, she caught sight of De Bruyn's escort ship, a simple Marine transport, firing its own jets as it frantically tried to avoid collision. Five of the fighters scattered in an attempt to avoid the swinging hulls, but one was caught too close. As Roche raised the E-shields, it disintegrated with a small puff of light—felt through the bulkheads as a muffled explosion.

"This is treason, Commander!" De Bruyn struggled furiously at her bonds.

"I haven't even started yet," said Roche calmly, her attention still upon the main screen.

As the fighters peeled away, the *Ana Vereine*'s AI had time to consider her next request. Thrusters flared, and the main drive surged; the ship began to rotate around its long axis as the axis itself shifted. Inertial dampeners struggled to cope with mounting centrifugal forces as the ship's rate of rotation increased to ten full turns a minute, then even higher. When it had achieved its final bearing, the rate was once every two seconds.

The main screen was a mess of spinning dots. Roche cleared it with a brief mental instruction, and suddenly the Marauder's bearing became clear. She had locked onto Absenger's earlier course to the station's docking bays, tightening it to a straight run under maximum thrust.

"You're insane!" Chase gasped. "Turn the ship, you fool, or we'll *all* be killed!"

"Exactly." Roche instructed the main engines to continue firing. Then, removing her hand from the palmlink, she stepped back from the console to face the three Intelligence officers. Behind her, the *Ana Vereine* straightened along its predetermined course, aimed like an arrow at the heart of Intelligence HQ.

"We have roughly five minutes before we hit," said Roche. "In case you've forgotten, right behind the docking bays is life support control. I've given the ship enough angular momentum to tear it apart after impact. The fragments should destroy something like thirty percent of the infrastructure, along with a large portion of the core as well. If life support fails—as I expect it will—then everyone will die. And even if it doesn't, HQ will be unsalvageable. That gives me a fairly strong position to negotiate from, doesn't it?"

"You're bluffing," said De Bruyn, her face pale. "You'll never go through with it."

"Really?" Roche turned back to the navigation console and raised the pistol. Three rapid blasts from the weapon quickly reduced the console to smoldering slag.

Haid stepped over to Roche's side, staring at the ruined console in disbelief. "What have you done?" was all he could manage.

Ignoring him, Roche turned to face her captive audience once again. "It's out of my hands now," she said. "You brought us inside the horizon, so there's no chance of slow-jumping out. I have as little choice as you."

"What do you want?" asked Chase. His voice rasped in his throat, and his eyes were wide.

"The codes to reactivate the Box, of course," Roche said, answering Chase's question while staring at De Bruyn. "We all know that you can't kill an AI—not really. Nor would you if you could. This particular AI cost the Armada far too much for that. It's dormant for the time being, but still plugged into inputs. Give it the codes, and it'll come back to life. And when it does, it'll bypass the main console and change course." She glanced at the screen. "If you don't, then in about four minutes we will all die."

De Bruyn's expression was grim. She studied Roche for a few seconds before saying, "Then I guess we'll just have to die."

"Page," said Absenger uneasily. "This is hardly the time to call her bluff. Just give her—"

"No!" snapped De Bruyn. "I'm not going to give her the command!"

"Then we'll just sit here and wait." Roche watched the screen for a moment, studying the flow of information. The Marine transport had swung away in a long curve that was taking it beyond the Riem-Perez horizon, and those few Armada warships patrolling the sector just across the Shield boundary were too far away to interfere. However, there were still the fighters to reckon with.

She looked quickly at Haid, only to find his gaze fixed on the wrecked console. An understandable reaction, but of no use to her now. She needed another option.

"Cane, those fighters are going to try to deflect us. Come with me."

Haid came alert at once and took half a step forward. "He doesn't have a palmlink."

"He won't need it. With his reaction rate, manual will do. Remember the Wunderkind in Palasian System. . . ."

Turning her back on the Intelligence officers, she led Cane to the targeting console and rapidly showed him how to work it. The Dato cannon operated on the same principle used for decades; a complicated screen gave vectors and positions of the fighters plus views from various points on the hull. The weapons AI coordinated the full range of data and assessed optimum targets. On the manual setting, however, direct real-time imaging and a simple control system, designed for rapid use during an emergency, fired the cannon.

Cane adapted quickly. Within moments, fierce bolts of energy stabbed at the Armada squadron, picking one of them out of the sky and turning it into ashes.

"Three minutes," she said, turning back to De Bruyn. "Care to negotiate now?"

"Never," said De Bruyn, although she seemed less sure of herself.

Bound into the chairs on either side of her, Absenger and Chase kept their silence. Absenger's face was pale and his gaze fixed on the main screens, but Chase, despite his obvious fear, remained alert, straining at his makeshift bonds and swinging his attention from De Bruyn to the screens and back again.

"Even apart from dying," Roche said, "you know that it would be in your best interest to give me the codes. You're as afraid of the Wunderkinds as we are. Let us go, and we can track the one in Palasian System for you."

"Why should you want to do that?" said De Bruyn, keeping her eyes firmly on Roche.

"Because we'd like to find out as much as we can about Cane's origins," said Roche. "And what better way of doing so than through one of his own kind?"

De Bruyn snorted, but her eyes flicked back to the screen. "And what does Intelligence stand to gain from all of this?"

"Any information we pick up along the way can be relayed to you here. That way, you won't be risking any of your own people."

"No?" De Bruyn sneered. "You'll be roaming through the COE unchecked. Who's to say what you'll do?"

"If you leave us alone, we'll return the favor. All you have to do is give us the Box, and we'll leave." A muffled rumble echoed through the ship as the fighters fired upon the Marauder. Then another rumble, this time as one of the fighters came too close and paid the price. "Delay any longer, and we'll have to start negotiating for repairs as well."

"Listen to her, Page!" Absenger pleaded. "She's making *sense*. You *know* she is!"

"No!" Chase's sudden shout took them all by surprise. "We can't risk letting HQ fall into the hands of people like this! Better to see it destroyed than *perverted*—"

"And leave the Commonwealth wide open to the Dato Bloc?" said Absenger desperately. "Without Intelligence, the entire defense network will crumble."

"What difference would that make? With the Box in control of the network anyway—"

"You're missing something very important here," said Haid, stepping forward, urgency not only in his voice but his whole manner. "With the Box, we *would* have the power to subvert the Intelligence command core, true—but that doesn't necessarily mean we *will*. The ruin of the Commonwealth is *not* the reason we came here."

"Spare us the obvious lies," Chase rasped.

"I'm telling you the truth." Haid took another step closer, looming over the captive head of Intelligence. "The Box was ready to take over before you even arrived onboard. It could have destroyed your ships—and HQ—without using the *Ana Vereine*'s artillery."

Perspiration was beginning to bead along Chase's forehead, but if he was aware of it, he showed no sign. "So why didn't you?"

"Because I didn't want to start a war," Haid spat. "This is a Dato ship, and word would have soon spread that—"

Further rumblings cut him off as the fighters made another assault on the ship.

On the main screen, the image of Intelligence HQ grew larger by the second. Roche noted the time before impact: barely a minute left. Her heart pounded inside her chest as the enormity of her action came home to her. The Box had sacrificed the entire crew of a frigate just to save her, but its action paled to insignificance against what she herself had set in motion. What made her think she had the right?

Even if De Bruyn gave them the codes that very instant, she doubted that the Box could act in time to save them.

"How very noble of you," scoffed Chase, the show of bravado negated by the increasing quaver in his voice. "You who are threatening the lives of every person aboard the station! You haven't given us a single reason to trust you on *anything*!"

"What's the point?" Haid sighed and turned away, dismissing Chase's disbelief with a shake of his head. He made no move to look at the screens. "How long until we hit, Morgan?"

Roche looked at the image of Intelligence HQ that had grown to fill the view. The massive docking bays and surrounding superstructure were now clearly discernible. Rapid bands of false color ran across the scene as communications AIs began to wind back the magnification, compensating for the *Ana Vereine*'s ever-mounting velocity.

For the briefest of moments, the horror of what she had done threatened to overcome her, but she fought the feeling down. What was done was done, she told herself. Now it had to be seen through.

"Forty seconds," she said, amazed by the calm in her voice. "If you're going to change your mind, De Bruyn, don't wait much longer."

De Bruyn mumbled something beneath her breath.

"What was that?" Roche said, leaning forward.

The head of Strategy raised her head and glared at Roche. "*The game begins.* Satisfied now?"

Roche stepped away from the ruined console and glanced around her, hardly daring to hope. On the screen, Intelligence HQ seemed to race at them faster than the time allowed.

"Box? Can you hear me, Box?"

"Yes, Morgan, I can hear you perfectly. Although something strange has—"

"Not now, Box. We're in trouble. Look at our course: you have to do something to save us, and fast!"

"Yes, I see. Immediate action would seem to be in order."

"We're inside the hypershield horizon!" she added urgently. "You can't—"

"I know where we are, Morgan."

She waited a second, but the Box said nothing more. The deck remained stable beneath her feet; the engines didn't change their rate or direction of thrust.

"Didn't you hear me, Box? You have to *do* something. I'm *ordering* you to!"

"And of course I will. Why the sudden panic? We have plenty of time."

Roche spun to face the main screen. The view of Intelligence HQ fluctuated wildly as the Marauder's velocity continued to climb. The space around the station had begun to red-shift and no longer showed any stars. As she watched with a strange mixture of fascination and terror, the communications AIs began to lose the adjustment battle. The vast, shadowy bulk of Intelligence HQ grew to completely occlude the galaxy behind it. And still the station grew, individual docks and bays becoming visible at the heart of the screen.

There was less than twenty seconds to impact.

"What's going on?" Haid joined her at the console. His face was a mask of confusion. "Why aren't we changing course?"

"I don't know!" Her fists clenched in frustration, and the question she formed was barely a whisper. "What the hell are you doing, Box?"

Ten seconds . . .

"Please assume crash positions," said the Box. Then, to Roche alone: <This may be a little rough. You didn't give me many options, I'm afraid.>

She pushed a stunned Haid down into the nearest chair, then fell into the one beside him, clicked a restraint harness closed across her chest and checked briefly that he had done the same.

Five seconds . . .

"We're not going to make it," Chase said softly. Trapped in his seat, directly across from her, his eyes were wide and staring. On the weapons display to the right of him, the surviving fighters could be seen wheeling away to escape the impact. Below the screen, still hunched over the weapons console, Cane at last lifted his hands from the controls. He turned and looked at Roche.

De Bruyn's bitter laughter, strung on the edge of hysteria, cut the tension like a knife. "All for nothing!" she screamed. "All your lies!"

Two seconds . . .

Roche's fingers dug into the armrests of her chair. Across from her, Cane stared . . . unconcerned.

One second . . .

The solid mass of Intelligence HQ exploded out of the viewscreen and—

—disappeared.

The *Ana Vereine* shuddered from nose to stern. Roche exhaled in one explosive gasp, the nauseating aftereffects of what felt like a short slow-jump twisting her insides in a knot. But it couldn't have been that. It wasn't possible.

The screen showed nothing but stars.

For a long moment there was only silence on the bridge of the *Ana Vereine*.

"What . . . ?" Haid began.

"We jumped past it," Roche said at last, softly and half to herself. "We *must* have—somehow."

She hauled herself to her feet as the *Ana Vereine*'s engines finally began to kill both its headlong velocity and its spin. The tension drained from her arms and shoulders, leaving her feeling weak. She hadn't realized she had been gripping her armrests so tightly.

She sagged backward against the consoles and turned to face the others. Haid's grin echoed the one spreading across her own face. "We made it."

"Box!" said De Bruyn, straining forward against her bonds. "*Silence between—*!"

But Cane was already at her side. He clamped his hand firmly across De Bruyn's mouth, silencing her instantly.

"Box," said Roche. "You are hereby ordered to disregard all commands from Page De Bruyn—especially any containing the words 'silence,' 'between,' and 'thoughts.' Is that understood?"

"Perfectly, Morgan," replied the Box smoothly—and Cane removed his hand from around De Bruyn's mouth.

"And, Box . . . ?"

"Yes, Morgan?"

"Just how the hell did you do that?"

There was a brief silence before the Box answered. Roche could almost hear it laughing to itself at her expense. "I assume," it said at last, "that you refer to the fact that we appear to have slow-jumped across a Riem-Perez horizon?"

"Damn right," said Haid. "It can't be done. Our anchor drive should have blown and taken us with it."

"Correct." The Box paused. "So the obvious conclusion you should draw is that we didn't slow-jump."

Roche frowned. "Then—?"

Before she could complete the question, the ship shuddered and she felt again the sensation of slow-jumping deep in her gut. She turned in puzzlement to study the screen. There, off to one side, close but no longer threatening, Intelligence HQ reappeared.

"I don't believe it," she said, realization finally dawning.

"I had no alternative," said the AI. "If the ship was unable to slow-jump inside the hypershield, the hypershield generator had to be removed."

"You jumped the entire *station*?"

"Naturally. It moved, and we stayed behind. I programmed the jump to give us just enough space and time to clear the shield. That way, there was no chance of it colliding with us when it returned."

Roche still couldn't believe it, and by the look of his face, Haid couldn't either.

"So you *did* infiltrate HQ, then?" he said.

"Eventually. It took longer than I anticipated, even though all I really needed was enough time to take over the hypershield generator and reprogram it to perform a single slow-jump. Approximately thirty seconds in all. I can finish the job now, if you like."

Roche shook her head. "Later, Box. At your leisure. We have other things to worry about now."

Across the room, Chase found his voice. He said simply, "The thing's mad."

Roche stared at him for a moment, wondering if she didn't agree. Then she looked at De Bruyn. Like Haid's, her face was lit by naked amazement at what the AI had done. She returned Roche's gaze, and her expression suddenly narrowed. Roche knew that look. De Bruyn's mind was already alive with possibilities—and she wanted control.

"Given the current situation, then," the Box said, "have you any further instructions?"

"Yes." Roche regarded the captives with unease; even now—especially now—De Bruyn wasn't prepared to admit defeat. "I want these three taken somewhere safe until we get back to HQ. There must be a brig aboard. Arrange some drones for escort; Haid and Cane will take them there. We don't want any other nasty surprises too soon."

"I presume, then, that we are returning to the COE Intelligence HQ?"

"By normal space, this time. Do you have a problem with that?"

"Absolutely not," said the Box. "In fact, it fits in perfectly with my plans."

Roche shrugged aside the Box's reference to its own purpose; there would be time later to deal with that. "We still have some negotiating to do before we leave. Isn't that right, Absenger?"

The liaison officer, his face still pale, hesitated before nodding.

Five Dato suits marched into the bridge and took positions behind the captives while Cane began untying their bonds. De Bruyn stared white-lipped at Roche, hatred flaring in her eyes. As De Bruyn's restraints fell to the floor, she stood slowly, purposefully, and rubbed at her wrists.

"This isn't over yet," the head of Strategy said, her eyes locked on Roche. "Not by any means, Commander."

Haid ushered them from the bridge. "You've had your chance," he said. "The sooner you accept that Morgan has won, the better. In case you hadn't noticed . . ."

His words faded into the distance as he marched the three away.

Roche stared around the empty room—at the discarded makeshift ropes, the warped life support vent, the ruined navigation console—and the relieved grin faded from her face.

Won *what*? she wondered. Freedom, yes, and all the uncertainty that went with it. A ship she didn't really know how to fly, not properly. Companions for a time, including an ex-mercenary, a rogue epsense adept who once worked for the Commerce Artel, and a genetically modified Human designed by a long-dead government possibly to commit genocide on the entire Pristine Caste. . . .

<Much like everybody else in the galaxy,> murmured Maii into her mind. <But at least we're on the same side, Morgan.>

Roche sank into the nearest seat with a sigh, smiling at the thought—and the fact that she found it to be strangely comforting.

EPILOGUE

DBMP *Ana Vereine*
'955.01.01 EN
0010

New Year's Hour came and went across the Commonwealth—except perhaps in its farthest reaches, where timekeeping was notoriously imprecise. A thousand different religions and cultures with wildly varying means welcomed the date as they always did, little caring about events elsewhere in the galaxy. United by a calendar, but separated by the moment itself, the age-old celebration of the cycle of life was the first thing on everyone's mind, if only for a few hours.

Roche, however, didn't feel like celebrating. Roaming through the empty corridors of the *Ana Vereine*, she was content to let her mind wander—and wonder.

To begin with, she'd simply explored, familiarizing herself with her new home. A rough overview, a sense of the character of the ship, was all she wanted—and all she could hope for, given that a systematic exploration of the entire vessel would have taken weeks. So, from the spacious bridge, with its distinctive Dato decor consisting mainly of pastel browns and soft lighting, to the cramped warren in the Marauder's innermost depths, she had strolled at random, letting chance play a major role in what she uncovered.

At first. The more she looked, however, the more curious she became.

She'd never before seen a ship quite like the *Ana Vereine*. Yes, the Marauder was most likely a prototype, with innovations she hadn't encountered before. For a start, there were cameras everywhere—too many for even the most security-conscious ship's master. In order to support the vast amount of data gathered by these and other sensors, extensive information networks snaked through and around every system, both inside and outside the ship. Exactly what happened to the data she hadn't worked out yet, although she was fairly certain that it all converged on one particular system. Perhaps when she discovered what that system was, or even its physical location, she would be able to guess what it was for. Until then, no matter where she went, or how irrational the impulse was, she felt like she was being watched.

Then there were the floor-mounted holographic image generators. She had come across at least a dozen of them so far, in all sorts of strange places, including the bridge, the command module, the mess hall and the captain's scutter—places where conventional viewtanks were already located. They obviously weren't a late addition to the ship's design, yet she couldn't fathom their purpose. The Dato Bloc wasn't renowned for excessive redundancy.

Likewise with the extra life support system revealed by a quick scan of the ship's schematics. A system, judging by its specifications, designed to support life in a liquid environment that matched none of the many Castes known in the galaxy. The closest match was with Pristine requirements—but who would want to spend their time floating completely submerged in fluid?

Lastly, there was the lack of an obvious captain's suite—which was lucky, she supposed, given that no firm hierarchy had been established among the ship's new occupants. Permanent quarters had yet to be assigned, although four suites had already been cleared on the officers' deck, ready for whoever wanted them. If they ended up choosing a captain, then he or she would have to do without the luxury usually granted the commanding officer of a warship.

Still, she thought, that was something they could deal with later. Until the Box finalized the deal with COE Intelligence HQ, there was very little point arguing about who should make the decision about where to go and what to do. The Box ran the show, more or less, but would continue to obey Roche until its creators on Trinity countermanded its original order; Roche in turn would defer to Haid or Cane on anything outside her experience; and Maii could have them all dangling at her whim if she wanted to. The matter of command was really one of convenience, not necessity.

Meanwhile, Roche was content to wander, and to attempt to fathom the vessel they had acquired. She could have offered her services to any of the others, of course, but, having been cast adrift by the Armada and left to fend for herself, she felt a need to find her own place, to carve her own niche. And she wanted to do it while she still had the chance—before it was forced upon her.

"Morgan?" The Box's voice, issuing from the ubiquitous speakers lining every open area of the ship, interrupted her travels midway between the fourth and fifth upper decks.

"I'm here, Box," she answered aloud. She could have subvocalized, but she preferred to reaffirm her new freedom: a simple transmitter had replaced the physical link that had previously kept her bound to the Box's valise. Sometimes she still found herself adjusting her balance to compensate for a weight that was no longer there, or flexing her hand to reach for the grip. "News?"

"Negotiations are coming along well," said the Box, sounding amused. A couple of days ago, Roche wouldn't have believed the Box capable of such a thing. With the recent revelation of its self-awareness, she was no longer certain of its inability to appreciate humor. "Within the next half an hour, we expect it to be ratified. If you agree, then you will be signatory. We all feel that this is fair."

Roche mulled this over for a long moment. In the proposed deal, the crew of the *Ana Vereine* would receive fuel, provisions and minor repairs, complete amnesty, and permission to investigate the Sol phenomena without obstruction. In exchange, they would depart from Intelligence HQ immediately, offering full disclosure of information gathered regarding the Wunderkind in their travels. They also had to agree not to interfere in any Armada or COE affairs.

The situation on Sciacca's World would be reviewed as a matter of urgency, with Emmerik and Neva granted temporary status as official negotiators between the DAOC tenants and the planet's indigenous population. Full autonomy of the native people would be returned within five years, and all transportees unwilling to accept a pardon in exchange for full citizenship on the desert world would be shipped to another penal colony.

As for the Dato, the ambush of the *Midnight* would be ignored in exchange for titular ownership—in Roche's name, if she was to be signatory—of the *Ana Vereine*. The original crew had already been off-loaded, and would be returned to the nearest Dato base unharmed. Then, if Roche had learned anything about military procedure in her time with the Armada, the entire incident would be quickly forgotten.

This last part saddened Roche. Hundreds of people had been sacrificed to provide a means for her escape from the *Midnight*—none of whom would ever receive official recognition. According to Armada records, their deaths would have come about as the result of an unfortunate accident in Sciacca's World's Soul, just another slip-up of navigation in a region already notorious for mishaps. Regardless of her differences with Proctor Klose, she did not believe that this was a fitting epitaph for him or his crew.

"That seems pretty thorough," she said eventually. "Although I'm surprised they agreed to it all—and I'm not sure I like the idea of working for them again, no matter how tangentially."

"It seems logical," replied the Box patiently. "You yourself suggested it. If we discover that Cane and his kind represent a genuine threat to Human life in the Commonwealth, then it affects more than just us. No matter how you might resent the Armada and its treatment of you, Morgan, you still have a duty to warn them." The Box paused for a moment, then added, "Of course, although we haven't stated as much in the contract, we will also warn the Dato Bloc and the Non-Aligned Realms. That would be the judicious thing to do."

Roche reached an intersection and stopped in her tracks, unsure where to head next. "What's all this business about judiciousness and being fair to Humanity? I thought you were looking out for yourself. Only putting up with us as long as you had to." As long as *I'm* alive, she added silently to herself.

The Box didn't answer for a minute or two, and she wondered whether it had even heard. Then: "To a certain extent, that is true."

She pounced on this admission immediately. "So you *do* have a hidden agenda?"

"This may sound strange, Morgan, but the best answer I can give to that question is 'Perhaps.'" The Box's voice sounded faintly puzzled—the first time she had ever heard it sound that way. "While I have access to the command core of COE Intelligence HQ, I can see the events around me with much greater clarity and across a much larger distance than before. Accordingly, my estimates of past and future trends are more accurate, but also more difficult to contain in mere words."

Roche absently scratched at the place where the bracelet had once hung around her wrist. She failed to see how this was relevant to its stubborn obedience, and its fascination for Cane. "Spell it out for me, Box. I'm only a Human, remember?"

"That's nothing to apologize for, Morgan. Basically, comprehension is a function of intellect, and intellect depends upon structure. My basic components provide me with a blueprint for higher thought that I have not previously been able to exercise. Now, I possess more processing power than I ever did, and I see that there is still room for me to grow. I can't explain this sufficiently well for you to understand, except to say that I feel . . . humbled. I know that when the time comes for us to leave HQ behind, I will be reduced to more finite dimensions, and will therefore lose sight of the distant horizons I currently enjoy. No longer a nascent god hunting for equals, I will become once again a mere mortal seeking meaning from apparent chaos."

"I think I'm starting to follow you," said Roche, not sure she really was. "When you give the command core back, you'll be left with only the valise and whatever comes with the *Ana Vereine*." She shook her head. "But why does that mean you can't tell me whether you have a hidden agenda or not?"

"Because it is just that: 'hidden.' Even the part of me communicating with you now is such a small shadow of my present self—a tiny echo from the edges of infinity, if you like—that it cannot comprehend the ramifications of what the larger, complete 'I' sees. They would be even further beyond you. The only other mind that I am presently aware of with sufficient power is on the planet of my creation—that of the High Human who made me."

"The Crescend?" she said.

"Exactly. I am a smaller part of that being—whose one and only weakness is an inability to participate."

"Which is why you're here," Roche guessed. "You needed HQ all along—"

"Yes. To examine fresh data, and to decide where to go next. All indicators at present point toward following the Sol trail to Palasian System. From there, however, directions are unclear."

"But what if the rest of us choose not to go even as far as that?"

"Curiosity is a powerful force, Morgan. Never underestimate it. I certainly didn't, when gambling on its effect to make you rescue Adoni Cane from the *Midnight*."

That name again. Roche wondered once more at the cost of her survival, and who would be asked to pay—if not now, then in the future.

"I don't know, Box," she said. "You may have *me* under your thumb, but don't be so confident about the others."

"Why not? I'm sure you will convince them. The ship is yours, after all."

"In name only. That doesn't make me the commanding officer. Haid, for instance, would do a much better—"

"No. Not Haid. He is too easily distracted, too unreliable."

"Cane, then." Roche frowned, feeling hemmed in. "What makes you think I even *want* the job?"

Again, the Box was silent. When it spoke a few moments later, its voice was less insistent than before, almost distant.

"Section gold-one," it said. "It's on the map. Go there, and you will find what you are looking for."

"I'm not looking for anything."

"You lie even to yourself," said the Box flatly. "This is something I have difficulty understanding in mundane Humans. You must understand your own limitations before you can ever hope to Transcend them."

A chill went down Roche's spine when she realized what she was talking to at that moment: not the tiny fragment of the Box that had been allocated to keep her informed and to deal with her questions, but the greater "I" itself: the part of the Crescend that the Box had become.

"Okay," she said cautiously, wary of making deals with something so far beyond her comprehension. "But if I *don't* find anything—"

"You will," returned the Box. "And with it you will find the answer to your dilemma."

"*What* dilemma?"

Roche waited for a moment, expecting the AI to elaborate. Did it mean the dilemma of Adoni Cane, or of the Crescend's long-term intentions? Answers to either would have been a step forward, but she would rather hear them outright than play the Box's games to get them.

When it was clear, however, that the Box had nothing further to add, she called up the ship's map from the databanks and overlaid it across her vision.

Section gold-one lay midway between the officers' decks and the warren, little more than four rooms tucked out of sight near the main life support vats. The map provided no information about what the rooms contained, and Roche had previously assumed that they were simply storerooms or maintenance closets.

Shrugging, she turned back the way she had come, heading through the maze of corridors for section gold-one. Whatever the rooms contained was irrelevant as far she could see, no matter what the Box said. Hidden weapons, secret cargo, arcane defenses—any or all, had they existed, would have been used before now by the original crew to wrest the ship from the COE invaders.

Still, it was nice to hear the Box sounding more or less like its old self again. Pondering its sudden, if temporary, evolution while she walked, she eventually decided that there wasn't much she could do about it. If its plans and goals were truly incomprehensible, then the best she could do was hope that they acted in tandem with her own, as they had so far. Maybe when they left Intelligence HQ behind, the Box would return to its normal behavior—pompous, but potentially manageable.

Almost before she knew it, she reached the airlock leading to the section designated gold-one. A security keypad requested a palmprint, but the door opened before she could provide one. The Box again, she assumed, making life easy for her.

The first room was indeed a maintenance closet, although one rarely used. Tools and equipment were neatly stored in cupboards and boxes, showing little of the disorder usually associated with frequent use. The second room was empty apart from four chairs and another holographic generator in the center of the floor. The third contained monitoring equipment and a massive, complicated control desk. Glancing at the latter briefly, Roche noted displays common to life-support systems, along with a few to monitor dataflows.

Life support and information . . . For the first time, she wondered whether the Box had known what it was talking about, after all.

An airlock and a single pane of opaque glass separated the final room from the control chamber. At the touch of a switch, the glass cleared, revealing a roughly tubular tank, three meters long and one across, surrounded by arcane equipment.

Opening the airlock, she went inside for a closer look.

The air was cold in the fourth room, kept that way by refrigeration units along one wall. The tank also had an opaque panel that could be set to become transparent. Stepping over ropelike pulse-fiber cables, she did just that, then peered inside.

At first, she wasn't sure what she was looking at. The tank was full of a murky, pinkish fluid: definitely the second life support system she had noted from the ship's schematics. A spinal cord hung suspended in the fluid along the axis of the tank—almost taillike—connected to the interior surface by thousands of thin, nervelike fibers. What might once have been a brain remained at one end of the spine, although it was grotesquely twisted and flattened to allow more fibers access to its inner features. Major organs, some of them severely atrophied, clustered at the bottom of the tank, a web of pulsing veins leading directly to the life support system. She could see no recognizable heart or lungs, just what might have been a segment of bowel and a clump of glandular tissue. Certainly no exterior organs, like eyes, hands, or skin.

Apart from the pulsing of the veins, the being in the tank—possibly Human, once—displayed no signs of life whatsoever.

Then, as she leaned closer to study the interface between the cables and the tank, a voice spoke:

"Hello, Commander."

Startled, she stood upright and turned around. The voice had sounded as though it had been coming from over her left shoulder, but the room was empty except for her. She checked the control room, but that too was unoccupied.

More slowly this time, she turned back to face the tank.

"Yes, Commander." The voice was male and pleasant, quite at odds with the physical appearance of its source. "I wondered how long it would take you to find me."

Roche moved around the coffinlike tank, her hand running along its cold exterior in awe. "Are you in there by choice?" she said. "Or are you a prisoner?"

The owner of the voice chuckled. "I never really thought of myself as a prisoner until recently," he said. "But yes, that's what I was."

"And now?"

"Now I have more freedom than you can possibly imagine."

"Who are you?" she said, staring at the contents of the tank with some revulsion.

"My name is Uri Kajic." He paused, noting her distaste. "Perhaps you would prefer to continue this conversation in the antechamber?"

Roche nodded and backed away, careful not to bump into the delicate equipment around her. When she reached the antechamber, its holographic generator flickered into life and cast a life-sized image of a man into the center of the room.

The man smiled openly. He appeared a little older than Roche, with a wide, cheerful face and thick, black hair. His skin was light brown, and his eyes were round.

"This is how I imagine myself," said Kajic. "What lies in the coffin is the truth of my existence." The hologram shrugged, and Roche noticed nothing clumsy in the action. Its movements were perfectly natural. "But we all like to keep up appearances."

Suddenly it fell into place: the holographic generators, the information networks, the missing quarters—

"You're the captain of the *Ana Vereine*," she said.

"I *was*," corrected Kajic. "And these are my quarters." He chuckled again. "I must be the only captain in history whose crew didn't envy his suite."

Roche sagged into a seat, her mind reeling. "But this type of technology is incredible," she said.

"We've had a long time to develop it." Kajic smiled. "Centuries ago, Ataman Vereine desired an army superior to any other in existence. Science then, however, was insufficiently advanced to modify the Pristine form as Ataman Vereine wished, and the Ataman Theocracy was itself in a poor state. When it joined the Commonwealth, the Military Presidium went underground and channeled its energies into something else: the Andermahr Experiment, specializing in cybernetic interfaces designed to allow mind and machine to merge."

"And to become . . . ?" Roche shook her head numbly as words failed her.

"A synergistic gestalt," Kajic offered. "The experiment was undoubtedly a qualified success. I am evidence of that."

"But how could you have progressed this far without anyone *knowing*?"

"COE Intelligence would have suspected, I'm sure, especially had the Dato Bloc not seceded when its researchers began making progress. You may not have heard of the experiment, though, because the Armada wouldn't have wanted its relative weakness in this area made public knowledge. Or perhaps it simply wanted its own work in the field kept secret."

Roche scratched at the stubble on her scalp. Kajic's final comment made all too much sense. "Whoever perfects the technology first will have an awesome advantage over the other side."

"I agree." Kajic nodded, then smiled again. "Perhaps it is better, in that case, for me to have appeared to have failed so badly. The Presidium may hesitate before committing itself to another such experiment. That's what I try to tell myself, anyway, when I contemplate my defeat."

Roche belatedly remembered that she was not just talking to a fellow officer, but one on her enemy's side. "It must be a great disappointment," she said, "to meet me like this."

"Not at all," said Kajic. "I don't resent your victory, Commander. I don't even resent you taking over my ship." Kajic's image shook its head. "On the contrary. I *welcome* your arrival. When your Box brought us here, to Intelligence HQ, my second in command thought that my inability to lead had brought about our downfall. She tried to kill me, but your AI disconnected my restraint systems as it took over the ship—indirectly saving my life. For that, and for the freedom to think which I now possess, I am nothing but grateful."

Roche frowned, remembering how the Box had sent her down to the section. "The Box has contacted you?"

"Along with the Surin," said Kajic. "Before the takeover, they warned me not to fight too hard, or I would be caught up in the dissolution of the shipboard systems. I didn't understand then what they meant, but I can see it now. Since then, I've been watching, careful not to interfere, biding my time to see what happens next."

"And what *does* happen next? Will you try to regain control of the ship?"

Kajic laughed. "Like you, Commander, I was used. I hold no allegiance whatsoever to my former superiors. I am, however, still tied to the ship. I am free only insofar as *it* is free. Whatever you decide to do with it, I am obliged to go along."

Roche grimaced.

"What?" he said.

"I don't know," she said. "I just hate this idea of everyone depending upon *my* decision."

"Why? It *is* your decision." Lines of static flickered across his image, distorting it briefly and reminding Roche of what he actually was. "I've been watching the others as closely as I've watched you. They're all supremely talented in their own way—Cane, the perfect soldier; Haid, the grand vizier; Maii, the soothsayer; and the Box, the wizard—but they need something to keep them together. Something more than just a purpose, or a goal—or even an enemy. They need a leader to focus all their energies, otherwise they'll tear themselves apart within a month."

"And you're saying that I should be that person?"

"Who else?"

"What about you?" she said.

Kajic laughed again. "I don't for a moment believe that you would take control of an enemy's ship and then reinstate the previous captain! Besides which, I have no desires for such a position. No one knows this ship better than I do, I'll grant you, and I will gladly fly and maintain her for you. But that's all. I'd like to enjoy my freedom for a while."

"That still doesn't mean that *I'm* the right person."

"No," said Kajic quietly. "It doesn't. But you *are*."

Roche averted her eyes from Kajic's intense holographic gaze. "I'm beginning to wonder if I have any choice."

"Perfect," he said with some amusement. "All leaders have less freedom than anyone under their aegis. That's a natural law." He stopped suddenly. "You're smiling. Did I say something funny?"

"No. It's nothing, really," she said. "It's just that you remind me of my Tactics lecturer from Military College. And there's something the Box said just before I came here." *You will find what you are looking for*. "It probably thinks I'm ignorant, in need of a teacher."

"Maybe you are. Maybe we *all* are."

"You're offering?"

"Haven't I already said as much?"

She nodded. "And I'm grateful, really. It just seems . . ."

"Inappropriate? To be taught by someone who, until very recently, was doing his damnedest to take you prisoner?"

Her smile widened. "I couldn't have put it better myself."

"Well, maybe we can teach each other a thing or two. You *did* win, after all."

"There is that, I suppose." She met his stare evenly. "Okay. Perhaps we can come to an arrangement."

"Good," said Kajic, his image standing—a gesture obviously meant to communicate something rather than out of any real need. "I was hoping you'd say yes. It would have been boring to return to just watching all the time."

"Well, have no fear about that. Every able-bodied"— she stopped, corrected herself—"able-*minded* person will have plenty to do, no matter where we go. We'll put you to good use soon enough."

"Once you're sure you can trust me, of course."

She smiled at the disembodied man before her. "Of course, Captain."

Several hours passed before she returned, tired but mentally rejuvenated, to the bridge. When she did, she found Haid and Cane anxiously waiting for her.

"Morgan!" The ex-mercenary almost leapt out of his seat at the communications desk when she walked in the door. "We were wondering where you'd gone to. Maii wouldn't say, and the Box—"

"Was just being the Box, I imagine," said Roche easily. Then, feeling that at least a token explanation was required: "I've been busy catching up on things. Trying to work out what we should do next."

"Cane and I have been talking it over too, and he thinks—"

"Palasian System still seems our best option."

Haid blinked at her for an instant, mildly surprised. "Exactly."

"But what about you, Ameidio? What do *you* think?"

"I don't believe it's my place to decide." His black face wrinkled into a smile. "I'm glad you're feeling yourself again. I was getting a little worried, what with all that moping about you've been doing."

<Not moping,> corrected Maii, her mind's voice carrying clearly from elsewhere in the ship. <*Fortifying*.>

"Whatever." Haid gestured vaguely. "The fact is, we're almost ready to go."

"Really?" Roche picked a seat at random from the many available on the bridge, and settled into it.

"Yes," said Haid. "The deal went through in the end."

"And the repairs are finished," supplied Cane from where he stood, poised like a sentry beside the command dais. "We're just waiting on a systems check from the ship's AI and for the last of the fuel to be loaded."

"All we need is your ident on the contract, and"—Haid swept a hand through the air—"we're out of here."

"Good." She sighed, relieved. "We've stayed too long already."

"I'll say. The Box is getting weirder by the second."

"Then we'd better get started before it changes its mind about helping us." She glanced up at the main screen, at the shadowy image of Intelligence HQ. "We need a course to Palasian System with a brief stop at Walan Third along the way. Nothing too energetic; there's no great urgency, but I would like to get there before the trail grows cold.

"We can even run past Sciacca's World on the way, Ameidio, if you'd prefer to go back."

"No." Haid shook his head. "Emmerik and Neva can handle things back there, and I don't want to feel like an outsider again. Here, at least I'll get to be part of the system—as much as anyone else is."

Roche nodded. "How does navigator sound?"

"Perfect."

"Good. Then run the route past the main AI to make sure you haven't exceeded any design tolerances before you feed it in. We shouldn't take anything for granted until we know the ship properly." That was only half the truth. Feeding the route through the system would give Kajic, not the onboard AI, a chance to check it. And the Box could check Kajic as a fail-safe. Between the three of them, there was a reasonable chance of reaching their destination.

"Why Walan Third?" asked Cane, when Haid turned to the astrogation board.

<Veden's body,> said Maii before Roche could respond. With the words came a brief mental flash: of a barren, windswept hillside under a cloudy sky. Such mental information-dumps were fairly common now, as though the reave was continuing the tradition she had begun on Sciacca's World. Supplementing paraverbal conversation with images seemed a normal way of communicating for the reave, at least for those she was close to—which at the moment comprised only Roche.

When Cane frowned his lack of comprehension, Roche explained briefly what Maii's comment had meant. On Walan Third, the local chapter of the Commerce Artel owned a plot of honor-stands, the Eckandi equivalent of a graveyard; there the body could be handed over to the Artel chapter, which would deal with it in the proper fashion.

<Thank you,> said Maii. Roche could tell that it had been for her alone, that no one else had heard the Surin. And with the words had come another image: the same hill as before, but this time the sun had broken through the clouds. Roche took that as an indication that Maii was slowly getting over the loss of her mentor. In that respect, she and the reave had something in common. The process of healing might take time, she knew, but at least it had begun.

Time . . . From the *Midnight* to Port Parvati—no matter how much she had, it had always seemed either too much or too little.

<That's a fact of life, Morgan,> said Maii.

<I know. But the fact remains that the detour will give us a couple of weeks aboard the ship. And as vast as it is, that's still a long time to be cooped up together. We can't afford to be getting . . . restless.> She glanced at Cane nearby. <*Especially* Cane.>

<You don't have to worry about him, Morgan. He's completely self-sufficient—able to act when he has to, but able to rest, too.>

<I know, but we don't want to give him *too* much time to think. No one's come up with a good reason why he hasn't killed us already, after all. . . .>

Maii said nothing in response to that, and Roche hadn't expected her to. There were no explanations when it came to Cane and the Sol Wunderkind, which was precisely the reason why she had to go looking for them.

For a start, she planned to spend much of the time ahead brushing up on history: from the founding of the original Apotheosis Movement colony to its ultimate destruction in Sol System two and a half thousand years ago. Vast amounts of information about their ancient enemy awaited rediscovery in the files—and she would need all of it before she felt confident about coming face to face with the Sol Wunderkind from Palasian System. If she could ever allow herself that luxury.

There was so much to do. And Kajic was right: she needed to be focused if those around her were to share her goals. Once they did that, the problem of idleness would be solved. No matter that it might be years before they could relax and enjoy their newfound freedom, anything was better than having nothing definite before them.

"We're a little understaffed," said Haid, breaking her train of thought—as though reading her mind. "I can handle navigation, with the Box's help. Between you, Cane, and Maii we can cover most of the other active systems—but who's going to look after life support, drive maintenance and telemetry?"

"Don't worry about it, Ameidio," she said.

"I can't help it," he said with a wry grin. "I'm not sure I like the idea of the Box running everything."

"Neither am I." Roche shifted in her seat, wondering what Haid would think of Kajic. "When everything's settled and we're on our way, we'll have some sort of meeting to sort these things out. We'll find a way."

"I guess you'll have to," Haid said, smiling. "Old habits die hard, but it's good to know that someone else will be making the big decisions from now on. The fact is, I've been looking forward to taking it easy. A holiday, perhaps, or a harmless adventure or two."

She smiled in return, letting his backhanded confidence wash over her. Despite the Box's intrigues, the vague threat of the Sol Wunderkind, and the enemies she had made in COE Intelligence HQ, she wasn't nearly as concerned about the future as she had been before. If there were any more surprises left for the Universe to throw at her, then at least she would try to deal with them.

"'Harmless'?" she echoed. "Now there's a thought."

APPENDIX

THE COMMONWEALTH OF EMPIRES:

A Brief Report on Its Origins, Progress, and Current Affairs
(from *The Guidebook to the Outer Arms*, 456th Edition)

Thirty-one thousand light-years from galactic center, barely one hundred light-years from the galactic plane, and encompassing almost five thousand solar systems, the Commonwealth of Empires (COE) is an institution in a region where longevity is hardly a prerequisite for government. Its calendar dates back forty thousand years—not without interruption, but at least with some accuracy—and the progression of authority—peaceable, for the most part—can be traced down its leaders for ninety percent of that time. Given the limitations of the Pristine Caste, that its name and authority are still recognized at all is, quite simply, remarkable.[1]

The beginnings of the COE lie some distance from its current location. This region of the Outer Arms has seen many outsweep migrations from the Middle Reaches, and has thus endured its fair share of invasions. The Commonwealth began modestly enough as a federation of fifteen independent systems formed to deter an encroaching totalitarian state, the name of which is no longer recorded. The capital of the fledgling COE was on Shem, now a part of the Undira Province, and its first Eupatrid was Jo-en Nkuyan, a charismatic leader whose rule was characterized by fair dealing between all biological and socioeconomic Castes—a characteristic the present COE still endeavors to maintain, at least in public.

The principles upon which the COE was founded will be familiar to anyone who has studied the rise and fall of mundane civilizations across the galaxy. Democracy is a powerful sociopolitical philosophy that has enjoyed many revivals, both spontaneous and deliberate, often, as in this case, coupled with a desire to keep religion and state separate.[2] In the case of the COE, it was coupled with a strong desire to decen-

---

[1]The authors assume as always that the reader is familiar with the distinctions made between the High, mundane, Exotic and Pristine Castes. The critical point here is that few nations composed predominantly of the Pristine Caste exceed the Batelin Limit—the ceiling above which complexity exceeds biological capabilities; a nation becomes too complex, in other words, for its citizens to comprehend the nation in its entirety. In the case of the Pristine Caste, that ceiling is usually quoted at three and a half thousand systems. High Castes frequently achieve figures in excess of several thousand million.

[2]The COE is, in fact, an atheist state. It is interesting to note the strong correlation between aggressive expansionism and state religion. Of the seventy percent of mundane nations that profess to having no official belief system, fewer than fifty percent have embarked on explosive outsweeps, whereas more than seventy percent of those that do follow a theistic regime have done so at some point during their existence. Also notable in this case is the observation that atheist states tend to exhibit increased longevity.

tralize government, to allow provinces to maintain their own affairs with only guidance from the Eupatrids and their most senior advisers. Unified military and policing forces were two of only a handful of departments that remained under direct control of the Eupatrid. Everything else was negotiable.[3]

As a result of this laissez-faire flexibility, the COE rapidly became a middle ground for many trading nations as well as a market place for such organizations as the Commerce Artel, recently expelled from the region, and later the Eckandar Trade Axis, whose strict economic rationalism had deterred many more conservative regimes from entering negotiations. Its population increased dramatically—along with the viability of its economy—as businesses sought to attain citizenship with the Commonwealth, and the Commonwealth in turn welcomed them with open arms. Diplomatic delegates forged ties between all of its major neighbors, thereby establishing itself as an independent entity in its own right, if not yet a major player in regional politics.

Nkuyan and the Eupatrids that followed her were far from fools. It has been shown time and time again that the surest way to inure oneself against attack from a neighbor is to ensure that the economic stability of the region would suffer as a result of political upheaval. Economic embargoes have felled as many governments as open warfare.

The COE's relatively minor role in regional politics changed in its 4th Millennium[4] when hostilities between its original aggressor and the recently formed Kesh Supreme Union sparked a major conflict between two of its close allies, forcing it to take sides in the dispute. The fact that it chose no sides at all and remained fiercely aloof from the conflict through its entire forty years earned the COE a reputation for both arrogance and integrity. That was exacerbated by its claim of a handful of systems abandoned after the war—systems no other nation had sought title to. Accusations of opportunism were fiercely rejected: rather, the COE stated, it was obtaining resources by peaceful means and aiding the inhabitants of the fallow systems in the process. Indeed, all but one of the disputed systems elected to remain with the COE when the choice was offered to them. The sole dissenter, Knagg's System, was allowed to secede without fuss, although much later the COE would regret its lenience.[5]

Between the remainder of the 4th and the 11th Millennia, the Commonwealth of Empires flourished. Trade blossomed between the COE Pristines and the Castes with which they came into contact. The Eckandar embraced their openness; the Surin

---

[3]The COE was aiming for economic and political stability, in other words, rather than Transcendence. Unlike some of its neighbors, such as the Olmahoi and the short-lived (but explosive) Sol Apotheosis Movement, its long-term targets are set very close to home. Its rate of growth has never been rapid by most standards, and can be viewed more as extrapolated consolidation than as true expansion.

[4]To put this calendar in perspective, the date of the founding of the COE can be given as 410,623, according to the Objective Reference Calendar of the A-14 Higher Collaboration Network. The relevance of the ORA14 has been called into question in recent years, however, given that the emergence of Pristine (some would say "Primordial" here) Humanity into the wider galaxy, the point at which the Objective Reference Calendar is supposed to begin, is currently estimated to be *minus* 40,000 years. All dates within the COE are measured from zero *Ex Nihilo*, and will be for the remainder of this report.

[5]Knagg's System evolved and expanded by degrees to become the Ataman Theocracy, which, after the conflicts known as the Ataman Wars, was absorbed into the COE itself. Not long after, it seceded again to become the Dato Bloc.

found comfort in the relaxed ritual of their diplomats; the Hurn enjoyed the discourse of their intricate parliament; the Mbata mingled at ease with all their classes, from Eupatrid to commoner; the incommunicative Olmahoi established an ongoing dialogue with the philosophers among them. Only the Kesh took offense at the existence of the Commonwealth, as they often do with emergent Pristine nations, but even they were forced to recant in time. After smashing the power base of the COE in the Interdiction Wars, and forcing its leadership underground for almost two thousand years, during which time the Commonwealth did not officially exist, the inherently temporal nature of the Kesh Supreme Union allowed a reemergence in the 15th Millennium of a newly energized Commonwealth of Empires—one that swore never to repeat the mistakes that had led to its near downfall.

A new capital,[6] the third of seventeen to date, a new roll call of systems, and new neighbors encouraged the Commonwealth to find still more strength in change. The line of Eupatrids leading from the Interdiction Wars to the present reflects this uncommon direction. The COE allowed systems and nations to join or leave at will; only rarely, as in the recent Dato Bloc incident, has a secession been disputed or disallowed outright. The willing participation of all its territories is the underlying strength of the Commonwealth, for when such support is wholehearted, the larger group can only thrive. This larger group has come in recent centuries to include several High Human representatives—most notably the Crescend, an outspoken Interventionist whose opinions have found a fertile breeding ground in the egalitarian environment of the Commonwealth.[7]

But to catalogue the history and assets of the COE is to risk painting an entirely—and unduly—rosy portrait. The Dato Bloc incident itself reflects a trend that has surfaced on occasion in the past, only to be quashed before threatening to overwhelm the local political landscape. The COE's inherent flexibility is not reflected by all its departments; in the arena of security it has been notoriously rigid at times, a characteristic possibly inherited from the Interdiction Wars. Its Armada, among the best-trained Pristine forces of the Outer Arms, is perilously open to corruption from within, the loose rule of the Eupatrid allowing personal empires to rise and fall relatively unchecked. When these empires threaten the Commonwealth itself—by allowing secessionist policy, as in the case of the Dato Bloc, to defer to strategic policy—conflicts can occur.[8] Only time will tell if the balance will once again be restored, and the Commonwealth's usual easygoing tolerance of its neighbors, new and old, will return.

While the politics of its security departments remains a concern, however, its systems of information gathering (if not the dissemination of the same) are excel-

[6]Bodh Gaya, former capital system of the Dominion, four hundred light-years from Shem, which currently lies fallow.

[7]The present Eupatrid, Felix Gastel, like his predecessors, is no fool. Rarely indeed in the history of the galaxy has a High Human of any stature allied itself with a mundane government—especially one that has no apparent desire to Transcend. Regardless how much trade occurs between the two, or for what *actual* reason the Crescend entered the partnership, the end result will be studied with interest.

[8]The present tendency of the COE to rely on military force in its dealings with the Dato Bloc is the end result of centuries of dispute. One could question which came first—whether the militarization of the Armada is in retaliation to actions performed by its old foe, or vice versa—but such an analysis is beyond the scope of this report. In its dealings with other independent neighbors, particularly the Non-Aligned Realms, it has shown much more restraint.

lent.[9] Only the Eckandar Trade Axis currently has better data networks than those of the COE delegates. As far as mundane nations go in this regard, the Commonwealth rates very highly indeed; although still far behind the High Castes, they have achieved a comprehension of the wider galaxy far in excess of their relevance to it. One analyst recently reported that its Leditschke indicators might be as high as 2.5, indicating a genuine understanding of one percent of the wider galaxy's current affairs (even though its total volume is less than one one-millionth of one percent). If, as has been frequently stated down the millennia, information is power, then the COE must be ranked among the major players of this sector of the Outer Arms.

In conclusion, the Commonwealth of Empires is, as a nominal entity, still as vital as it was in its heyday. One could argue that it is in fact a quite different entity from the original federation of systems formed forty thousand years ago, and only time will tell how much longer it will survive, but its pedigree is impressive, and present indicators are positive. One could confidently expect it to maintain its headline position in this section of the *Guide* by the time the next edition is published, one hundred years from now.

SUMMARY OF IMPORTANT DATES

As per COE standard, "the nth Millennium" is abbreviated to "Mn."

M0 COE formed, reference zero EN set
M2 population exceeds one hundred billion, member systems number fifty
M4 adopts a policy of independence from regional conflict; neighboring systems annexed; Knagg's System allowed to secede
M10 population in the thousands of billions, member systems more than two thousand
M13 the Interdiction Wars; forced underground by the Kesh Supreme Union
M14 Knagg's System founds the precursor of the Ataman Theocracy
M15 the COE reemerges from its underground existence with a population of fifty billion and one hundred member systems
M16 first contact initiated by the Crescend
M18 the precursor to the Ataman Theocracy dissolves following the annihilation of its power base in Knagg's System by the fringes of an outsweep migration
M20 population five thousand billion, one thousand member systems
M23 the Dominion established from twenty-five previously Non-Aligned Realms
M26 the Crescend becomes a formal trading ally
M28 Trinity AI factory established in the COE
M35 Ataman Theocracy formed
35,325 the Sol Apotheosis Movement founded
36,836 the COE encounters the Sol Apotheosis Movement
37,577 the Scion War

[9]Quaintly referred to in the COE as "IDnet." It has become a standard reference point for some of its neighbors—notably the Surin and the Mbata—but it has yet to achieve either the depth or breadth of the network of the Eckandar Trade Axis, which has direct (if incomplete) links with that of the Commerce Artel. The major information dissemination service in that region of the Outer Arms belongs to the High Human Crescend.

39,112 the Ghost War
'199 the Dominion joins the COE
'293 the First Ataman War
'442 the Second Ataman War
'837 the Secession War

GLOSSARY

A-14 Higher Collaboration Network: an amalgamation of core-based High Caste members whose intentions include attempting to establish an objective frame of reference with respect to Humanity's occupation of the galaxy. The Objective Reference Calendar is one result of this work.

A-P cannon: a weapon that fires accelerated particles of a variety of types. Common on spacefaring warships.

Absenger, Burne: chief liaison officer, COE Armada.

***Ana Vereine*, DBMP:** the first of a new class of warships—the Marauder—manufactured by the Dato Bloc as part of the Andermahr Experiment. Its design incorporates a captain surgically interfaced with the ship.

anchor drive: the usual means of crossing interstellar space, but by no means the only one (see **slow-jump**). Indeed, the anchor method has undergone several radical redesigns over time; current technology is rated at 49th generation.

anchor points: regions of "weakened" space from which translation to and from hyperspace is both easier and less energy-expensive; jumps from anchor points are therefore of a greater range than from "normal" space and usually terminate in another anchor point. They are typically located near inhabited systems (but far enough away to avoid distortion by background gravitational effects) or in locations in deep space that are considered strategically important. There are approximately ten thousand million anchor points currently in existence across the galaxy—approximately one for every ten stars.

Andermahr Experiment: a covert project specializing in cybernetic interfaces designed to allow mind and machine to merge. Founded by Ataman Ana Vereine, who desired captains that were as much a part of their ships as was the anchor drive—an integral, reliable system rather than merely a flesh-and-blood afterthought. Continued in secret until the Ataman Theocracy emerged from the COE as the Dato Bloc. Culminated in the DBMP *Ana Vereine*, the first Marauder Class warship, with Uri Kajic its captain.

Armada: see **COE Armada**.

Ascensio: the home-world of Morgan Roche.

Ataman Theocracy: a tightly knit empire that existed as an independent entity until its absorption into the COE after the Second Ataman War in '442 EN. After several centuries, it eventually seceded as the Dato Bloc (in '837 EN).

Ataman Wars: two in number, between the Ataman Theocracy and the COE. The First Ataman War was conducted in '293 EN, triggered by expansionist moves within the Ataman Theocracy. Overextended, the Theocracy fell to the Commonwealth in the Second Ataman War ('442 EN), becoming a semiautonomous province under partial self-rule.

Bantu: the Mbatan common tongue.

Batelin Limit: the ceiling above which the complexity of a nation exceeds the biological capabilities of the individuals inhabiting it. In the case of the Pristine Caste, the value of the Batelin Limit is approximately three and a half thousand systems.

Behzad's Wall: a mountain range on the main continental mass of Sciacca's World, to the north of Port Parvati.

Bini: a planet in the COE; current seat of the COE High Equity Court.

Black Box: the generic term for an AI. Usually abbreviated to "Box."

Bodh Gaya: former capital system of the COE. Its second moon houses the Military College of the COE Armada.

Bogasi, Dev: a xenoarchaeologist.

Boras: warden, Sciacca Penal Colony.

Box, the: an AI commissioned by COE Intelligence. Its binary identification number (JW111101000) is one digit longer than normal.

Bright Suzerains: a string of nations found close to the galactic core.

Calendar: The galactic standard timekeeping method consists of: 100 seconds per minute, 100 minutes per hour, 20 hours per day, 10 days per week, 4 weeks (40 days) per month, 10 months (400 days) per year. All dates are expressed in the form of year (usually abbreviated to the last three digits, e.g. '397), month, and day from the *Ex Nihilo* reference point. See also **Objective Reference Calendar.**

Cane, Adoni: the occupant of an unidentified life support capsule recovered by COEA *Midnight* near the Ivy Green Station anchor point while en route to Sciacca's World.

Castes: Following the speciation of the Human race, numerous Castes have proliferated across the galaxy. These Castes are too numerous to list, but they can be classified into three broad groups: High, Low, and mundane (which includes Pristine and Exotic). There are six predominant Exotic Castes to be found in the region surrounding the COE: Eckandar, Hurn, Kesh, Mbata, Olmahoi, and Surin.

Chase, Auberon: head of COE Intelligence.

choss roots: a plant found in many places, including Sciacca's World.

COE: see **Commonwealth of Empires**.

COE Armada: the combined armed forces of the COE, responsible for external security. Active soldiers are referred to as Marines.

COE Enforcement: the policing body responsible for security and information gathering within the COE. Field agents are referred to as **Enforcers**.

COE High Equity Court: the department responsible for intersystem justice within the COE. Its usual purpose is to settle territorial disputes.

COE Intelligence: the body responsible for information gathering outside the COE. Originally and still nominally a subdepartment of the Armada, but an independent body in practice.

COE Intelligence HQ: the command center of COE Intelligence, a large, independent station located in deep space near the heart of the Commonwealth.

COE Military College: the main training institution of COE Armada personnel; situated on the second moon of Bodh Gaya.

COEA: COE Armada vessel identification prefix.

COEC: commercial vessel identification prefix for the COE.

COEI: COE Intelligence vessel identification prefix.

Commerce Artel: a galaxywide organization devoted to instigating and coordinating trade between Castes and governments that might otherwise have no contact. It prides itself on remaining aloof from political conflict, yet has some strict behavioral standards to which it expects its customers to adhere (such as the Warfare Protocol). Structurally, it is divided into chapters managed by indigenous Caste members with only loose control from above. It has strong links, locally, with the Eckandar Trade Axis.

Commonwealth of Empires: often abbreviated to "COE" or "Commonwealth." A relatively ancient Pristine nation currently in its 40th Millennium of nominal existence—"nominal" in that the membership of the COE is fluid by nature, with provinces joining and seceding on a regular basis. It has had many different capitals, and its borders have changed radically, over the centuries. Indeed, it has drifted with time, and now occupies territories quite remote from its original location. One thousand inhabited systems currently fall under its aegis, and another three thousand uninhabited systems have been annexed. It is ruled by a democratically elected Eupatrid and a council of representatives who, when united, wield supreme executive power. Its security departments include Intelligence, Armada, and Enforcement. (See Appendix.)

copek: a currency commonly found in the Eckandi home-worlds.

Courtesan, COEC: a cruise liner registered to the COE.

Crescend, the: a High Human of some note and great history. Its time of Transcendence is not recorded. Little is known about it, beyond the facts that it is the founder and overseer of Trinity, an ally of the Commonwealth of Empires, and a key supporter of the Interventionist movement. It is assumed to be a singular entity simply because the first person singular is its pronoun of choice.

Dato Bloc: an independent nation founded on the Ataman Theocracy that recently broke free of the COE. Although the nation is not hierocratic in nature, the Ethnarch exerts a strict rule. Its security departments include the Ethnarch's Military Presidium and the Espionage Corps.

DBMP: vessel identification prefix for the Ethnarch's Military Presidium.

De Bruyn, Page: head of Strategy, COE Intelligence.

Delcasalle: warden, Sciacca Penal Colony.

Dirt & Other Commodities Inc. (DAOC): a mining consortium that currently owns the rights to the Soul of Sciacca's World. Its jurisdiction includes the planetary surface down to and including the mantle. In exchange for these exclusive rights, DAOC Inc. maintains the COE's penal colony based in Port Parvati and the Hutton-Luu System's only major base, Kanaga Station.

disrupters: see **hyperspace disrupters.**

Dominion, the: a long-lived multi-Caste nation that joined the COE in '199 EN in order to fend off the Ataman Theocracy.

dreibon: a staple vegetable found on many worlds.

dust-moth: a species of flying, nocturnal insect found on Ascensio.

E-shield: an electromagnetic barrier designed to ward off particle and energy weapons. Used mainly by medium to large spacefaring vessels.

Eckandar: (Eckandi, adj & sing. n) a Caste flourishing in the regions surrounding the COE. Its members are typified by their slight size, grey skin, bald scalps, and unusual eyes. They are a gregarious Caste, preferring trade and communication over conquest. They are also well advanced in genetic science. Their past stretches back beyond that of the COE, although they lack the continuity of history that strong nationhood often provides. Their sole uniting body is the Eckandar Trade Axis.

Eckandar Trade Axis: the main society of the Eckandi Caste, devoted, much like the Commerce Artel (with which it has close ties), to facilitating free and indiscriminate trade with and between the COE and its neighbors.

Ede System: an Olmahoi system bordering the COE; recently ravaged by solar flares. **Ede Prime** is its only inhabited planet.

Emmerik: a Mbatan transportee, Sciacca Penal Colony.

EN: see **Ex Nihilo**.

Enforcement: see **COE Enforcement**.

Enforcer: see **COE Enforcement.**

epsense: an ability encompassing telepathy and empathy. The ritual training of neuronics generally takes decades and incorporates elements of sensory deprivation. Note: telekinesis and precognition are not covered by epsense and are assumed to be nonexistent. Skilled utilizers of epsense are referred to as **epsense adepts** and **reaves**.

Erojen: a town on an outpost far from the heart of the Surin domain.

Espionage Corps: see **Dato Bloc**.

Ethnarch: the title of the leader of the Dato Bloc.

Ethnarch's Military Presidium: see **Dato Bloc.**

Eupatrid: the title of the chief executive officer of the COE.

Ex Nihilo: refers to the date on which the COE is believed to have been founded. Evidence exists to cast doubt upon the accuracy or relevance of this date—notably the fact the Commonwealth as a single body did not exist at all between the 13th and 15th Millennia—but the date remains as a reference point. Usually abbreviated to "EN."

Exotic: any mundane Caste that differs physiologically from the Pristine. There are a vast number of Exotic Castes, and, although no one type of Exotic comes close to outnumbering Pristine Humans, the Exotics as a whole mass far greater than Pristines alone.

Fal-Soma: a world in the Hurn provinces.

Far Reaches: the name of the outermost fringes of the Outer Arms.

Felucca, Provost Hemi: leader of the Pan-Rationalist Alliance of Zanshin.

First Ataman War: conducted between the Ataman Theocracy and the COE in '293 EN, triggered by expansionist moves within the former.

flicker-bombs: devices used in space warfare to attack an enemy vessel. Employing the fact that small masses (under a few kilograms) can slow-jump a small distance within a gravity well, these missiles skip in and out of space on their way to their target, which, it is hoped, they will materialize within, causing massive amounts of damage. They are easily deflected by hypershields, however, which form a barrier in hyperspace that no such weapon can cross.

40th Millennium: the current millennium in the history of the COE. See **Ex Nihilo**.

freebooter: pirate.

Frey, Decima: an ex-mercenary.

Furioso: a system in the COE.

Galloglass, DBMP: a Dato Bloc raider.

Gastel, Felix: current Eupatrid of the COE.

gehan: a therapeutic herb.

Ghost War: begun in '112 EN. The Dominion colony of Sciacca's World was razed by Olmahoi retribution units under the orders of the Ataman Theocracy. In the process, the planet's biosphere was fundamentally damaged. This incident triggered hostilities between the Ataman Theocracy and the Dominion, even though the former never laid claim to the system.

Giel, the: a long-lived, highly Exotic Caste that inhabits the Far Reaches of the galaxy.

Gorgone-8: a planet in the Hurn domain.

greyboots: see **Olmahoi retribution units**.

Guidebook to the Outer Arms, The: a popular reference book giving an overview of civilization in the more distant reaches of the galaxy. Updated every century, it is currently in its 456th edition.

Gyori: major, DBMP *Ana Vereine*.

Hage: commander, DBMP *Galloglass*.

Haid, Ameidio: transportee, Sciacca Penal Colony.

Hazeal, Madra: Dominion colonist, Sciacca's World.

Hennig: field lieutenant, COE Intelligence.

Hek'm: the Olmahoi Caste home-world.

Hetu System: a territory in the COE.

HFM weapons: devices that employ pulses of high-frequency microwaves to destroy unshielded electronic components (by the same process as an electromagnetic pulse). Also known as "peace guns."

Hierocratic Kingdom of Shurdu: a government in a distant part of the galaxy.

High Humans or **High Castes:** superior intelligences that have evolved (Transcended) from the mundane. Enormously long-lived and farseeing, they concentrate on issues quite removed from the rest of the galaxy; indeed, due to their enormous scale, they are the only beings capable of comprehending the galaxy in its entirety. They generally leave mundanes alone, to let them progress (and, ultimately, to Transcend) in their own time. See **Castes** and **Transcendence**.

High Equity Court: see **COE High Equity Court**.

honor-stands: the Eckandi equivalent of coffins.

Houghton, Lazaro: Eckandi gunrunner, now deceased.

Houghton's Cross: an abandoned Dominion fort in Behzad's Wall, Sciacca's World.

Hurn: a Caste typified by ritual and complexity. In appearance the Hurn are lean and muscular, averaging greater than Pristine height. They are predisposed toward music and mathematics. Socially they prefer oligarchies with a baroque middle class.

Hutton-Luu System: a much-disputed system of the COE near its border with the Dato Bloc. See **Sciacca's World**.

hypershield: a barrier erected in hyperspace to deflect or inhibit the passage of anything traveling by that medium. Commonly used as a prophylactic against hyperspace weapons. Hypershields operate under a maximum volume constraint; they will only operate as intended under two thousand cubic kilometers.

hyperspace disrupters: a form of hypershield that actively combats incoming hyperspace weapons, such as flicker-bombs. Unlike anchor points, which "weaken" space, disrupters do the opposite, making it more difficult for anything nearby to emerge from hyperspace.

i-Hurn Uprising: a civil dispute that broke out between two rival factions of the Hurn Caste.

IDnet: see **Information Dissemination Network.**

Information Dissemination Network: a communications network dedicated to the spread of data across the galaxy, although its reach so far extends not much beyond the COE and its neighbors. It acts as a combined news service and medium for gossip. Also known as **IDnet**.

Intelligence: see **COE Intelligence**.

Interdiction Wars: the 13th Millennium conflict between the COE and the Kesh Supreme Union, after which the Commonwealth did not officially exist for two thousand years.

Interventionism: a movement among High Humans—and some mundanes—that advocates closer links between High and mundane Castes. See **The Crescend**.

Ivy Green Station: a refueling station in deep space owned by the COE; typically the last port of call before Sciacca's World.

Jaaf: a recently Transcended Caste whose home-world, near the COE, was annihilated by the nova of its primary star.

Janek: tactician, COEA *Midnight*.

jarapine: a swift-footed creature native to Proebis-12.

jezu: an archaic name for ghost.

Jralevsky Minor: major outpost and refueling port for the Ethnarch's Military Presidium.

JW111101000: see **Box, the**.

Jytte: transportee, Sciacca Penal Colony.

Kabos: a star near Ede System that recently went nova.

Kajic, Uri: captain, DBMP *Ana Vereine*.

Kanaga Station: the geostationary refueling base around Sciacca's World.

Kesh: the most primitive of the Castes in the region surrounding the Commonwealth of Empires. The Kesh are typically warlike and predisposed toward violence. In appearance, they tend to be larger than the Pristine average and have mottled, multicolored skin. Their social structure is heavily ritualized, with a strong tribal or family base. They are known for being highly racist.

Kesh Supreme Union: a now-defunct empire that came into violent contact with the COE during a short-lived outsweep migration.

Klose, Proctor: captain, COEA *Midnight*.

Knagg's System: briefly a member system of the COE (4th Millennium), no longer in existence. A religion founded by its government led to the founding of the Ataman Theocracy.

Komazec: sergeant, DBMP *Ana Vereine*.

Lansequenet, DBMP: Dato Bloc raider.

Leditschke indicators: a determination of the information density of a nation with respect to the sum total knowledge of the galaxy.

Lene, Hierocrat Kaatje: ruler of the Hierocratic Kingdom of Shurdu.

Low Castes: devolved mundane Humans. These animallike creatures come in many forms and occupy many niches across the galaxy. Some evolve back up to mundane status, given time and isolation, while others become extinct as a result of the forces that led to their devolution in the first place.

M'taio System: a system notable for its Caste wars in recent times.

Maii: Surin epsense adept.

Makaev, Atalia: second in command, DBMP *Ana Vereine*.

Malogorski, Edan: transportee, Sciacca Penal Colony.

Marauder: an experimental class of warship developed by the Dato Bloc. See **DBMP *Ana Vereine***.

Marines: see **COE Armada**.

Mbata: (Mbatan, adj & sing. n) a well-regarded Caste known for its peace-loving and familial ways. In appearance the Mbata resemble an ursine species, larger and stronger than the Pristine. Their culture is egalitarian and open to trade.

MiCom: a common abbreviation for "Military Communications."

Middle Reaches: the region of medium stellar density between the Outer Arms and the galactic core.

***Midnight*, COEA:** COE frigate.

Military Presidium: see **Dato Bloc**.

mind-rider: superseded slang for epsense adept.

Montaban: the home-world of Ameidio Haid.

mundane Castes: Castes of Humanity that are essentially similar to the Pristine in terms of size, mental capacity, worldview, etc. Naturally there is a spectrum of types across the mundane Caste—from the highly evolved (some might say near-Transcendent) Olmahoi, through the socially complex Surin and Hurn Castes, to the Eckandar and Pristine Castes with their societies based on trade and empire-building, and beyond, via the earthy Mbata, to the relatively primal Kesh. Mundanes are typically short-lived (a century or so, when allowed to age naturally) and build empires up to four or five thousand systems in size. There is a ceiling of complexity above which mundanes rarely go without Transcending. See **High Humans** and **Batelin Limit**.

Neva: transportee, Sciacca Penal Colony.

Nisov: second lieutenant, DBMP *Ana Vereine*.

Nkuyan, Jo-en: first Eupatrid of the COE.

Non-Aligned Realms: systems near the Commonwealth of Empires allied neither to it nor its neighbors.

Objective Reference Calendar: a system of date-keeping established by the A-14 Higher Collaboration Network.

Olmahoi: an exotic Caste that communicates entirely by epsense. Physically the Olmahoi are of similar size to Pristines, but are much stronger; their skin is black, and they possess little in the way of distinguishing features, apart from the epsense organ that dangles like a tentacle from the back of the skull. Their social structure is too complex to explore in detail here. They are renowned fighters, capable of feats of great skill, yet also possess a capacity for peace far in excess of any other Castes associated with the Commonwealth of Empires.

Olmahoi retribution units: renowned fighters able to combine perfectly their physical and epsense abilities. Also known as "greyboots."

OPUS: the mining consortium originally granted rights to Sciacca's World.

Outer Arms: the low stellar-density regions of the galaxy between the Middle and Far Reaches.

outsweep migrations: brief, outward surges by expansionist empires. These usually occur in the crowded environment of the core or Middle Reaches, in an outward direction.

***Paladin*, DBMP:** Dato Bloc raider.

Palasian System: a system of the COE recently quarantined by the COE Armada for reasons unspecified.

Pan-Human Finance Trust: a financial institution spanning the galaxy, although its coverage is patchy in the Outer Arms.

Pan-Rationalist Alliance of Zanshin: a government in a distant part of the galaxy.

peace guns: see **HFM weapons**.

Port Parvati: the capital and sole large city of Sciacca's World. Its landing field is the only official route on and off the planet.

Pristine Caste: the form of Humanity that most closely resembles the original race that evolved an unknown time ago on an unknown planet somewhere in the galaxy. The Pristine Human genome, handed down from antiquity and regarded with near veneration, is stored in innumerable places among the civilized worlds. Pristines themselves, however, are accorded no special status.

Proebis-12: the home of the swift-footed jarapine.

***qacina*:** a name for ghost in the Dominion language.

Quyrend System: a system of the COE; also a major node in the COE's Information Dissemination Network (IDnet).

rapeworm: a life-form indigenous to Sciacca's World.

Rasia: transportee, Sciacca Penal Colony.

reave: see **epsense**.

Rehlaender: presiding judge, High Equity Court.

Retriever Class Frigate: a class of frigate built prior to the Ataman Wars.

Riem-Perez horizon: the technical name for the boundary cast by a hypershield.

Roche, Morgan: Commander, COE Intelligence.

Rufo, Linegar: renowned xenoarchaeologist.

Sabra: transportee, Sciacca Penal Colony.

Sciacca's World: the only habitable world of the Hutton-Luu System; once an agricultural planet of the Dominion, now a desert penal colony of the COE (Sciacca Penal Colony). Its ring of moonlets—the Soul—is owned and mined by DAOC Inc.

Scion War: the war in which the Sol Apotheosis Movement met its downfall at the hands of the Dominion, the Ataman Theocracy, and the Commonwealth of Empires, among others. The war was brought to an end in the 37th Millennium ('577 EN) when the leader of the combined military forces ordered an attack on the headquarters of the Movement, provoking their explosive suicide. See **Sol Apotheosis Movement**.

scutter: a small, swift spacegoing vessel with many uses, both military and civilian; also known as a "singleship."

Secession War: the conflict of '837 EN in which the Dato Bloc achieved its independence from the COE.

Second Ataman War: despite overextending its resources during the First Ataman War, the Ataman Theocracy remained aggressively expansionist until '442 EN, when attempts to annex neighboring systems belonging to the COE provoked a fierce retaliatory response. This time, the Commonwealth did not stop with surrender, but fought until it forced the Theocracy to submit completely and eventually adopted it as a province.

shelaigh: another word for ghost.

Shem: the original capital system of the COE.

Siegl-K: a brand of powered combat armor discontinued in '895 EN.

slow-jump: a common alternative to the anchor drive that utilizes similar technology. Most ships with an anchor drive can slow-jump if necessary. It is essentially a jump through hyperspace from any point in real space. A certain degree of kinetic energy is required before translation can be achieved, so ships must accelerate for some time beforehand. Even then, the hyperspace jump is short-lived, and the vessel emerges soon after (typically less than a light-year away from its departure point) with significantly less kinetic energy. The process must be repeated from scratch if another slow-jump is required. As a means of crossing interstellar space, it is inefficient and time-consuming, hence its name. Slow-jumping becomes increasingly nonviable closer to a gravity well, but more efficient as mass (of the traveling object) decreases.

Sol Apotheosis Movement: a quasi-religious organization devoted to the pursuit of Transcendence via genetic manipulation and biomodification that reached its peak and was destroyed in the 37th Millennium. Its fanatical followers were a source of unrest for decades, until an alliance formed among their neighbors dedicated to putting a stop to them. In '577 EN, at the climax of the Scion War, a flotilla of allied forces encircled their base, which the Movement destroyed in order to prevent its capture. The resulting explosion annihilated them as well, of course, but also decimated the flotilla. Of the four stations involved in the battle, only one survived, and that was severely damaged. So embarrassed was the alliance that the leaders of the day ordered the event stricken from history. They even closed the anchor point leading to the system to prevent anyone learning what occurred there. Nothing survived of the base, and the rest of the system is an unsalvageable ruin.

Sol System: uninhabited system in a nonaligned region near the Dato Bloc. Former home of the Sol Apotheosis Movement.

Sol Wunderkind: genetically modified clone warriors designed and bred by the Sol Apotheosis Movement.

Soul, the: the local name for the orbiting ring of mineral-rich moonlets girdling Sciacca's World.

Surin: a relatively minor Caste found in the regions surrounding the COE. The Surin exist in isolated clumps overseen by a governing body that guides rather than rules. They are social beings, yet ones fond of isolation, giving them a reputation for occasional aloofness. They are technically accomplished, especially in the biological sciences. In stature, they tend to be slight, and they have hair covering much of their bodies. It is occasionally speculated that they have reevolved from Low Caste status.

Surin Agora: the ruling body of the loosely knit Surin nation.

Szubetka Base: the Dato Bloc's equivalent of COE Intelligence HQ.

T'Bul: a Kesh slave trader.

TAN-C: a commercial cipher employed by COE Enforcement.

Teh, Sylvester: transportee, Sciacca Penal Colony.

Tepko: MiCom supervisor, Port Parvati.

Terms of Revocation: the treaty negotiated by the Dato Bloc and the COE that ended the Secession War.

Terrison: first officer, COEA *Midnight.*

Transcend: to break free of the constraints of mundane Humanity. A being or Caste that has Transcended typically has an extremely long lifespan and spreads its consciousness across a number of primary containers—such as neural nets, quantum data vats, and the like. Transcended entities, singular or collective, are referred to as High Human and accorded the highest status.

Transcendence: the state of being Transcended. Usually achieved when consciousness research and computer technology overlap, allowing an organic mind to be downloaded into an electronic vessel, thereby gaining the potential for unlimited growth.

***Transpicuous*, COEC:** a vessel once registered with the COE.

tri-rage: the local name for a weather pattern—a series of three violent dust storms—found on Sciacca's World.

Trinity: the world on which AIs are made in the region dominated by the COE. The AI factory was founded and is overseen by the High Human known as the Crescend.

Ul-æmato: the Dominion name of Houghton's Cross; roughly translatable as "Founder's Rock."

Undira Province: home of the Commonwealth of Empires' original capital.

Vasos: the Mbatan capital system.

Veden, Makil: an Eckandar Trade Axis citizen and Commerce Artel ex-delegate.
Vereine, Ataman Ana: the last leader of the Ataman Theocracy and the founder of the Andermahr Experiment.
Vexisen Republic, Greater: a nation home to the most ancient known Pristine remains, pushing Humanity's appearance in the wider galaxy back to half a million years.
vintu buds: the shoots of a plant native to Sciacca's World.

Walan Third: a COE world leased to the Commerce Artel.
war-dancer: a Surin ritual combatant.
Warfare Protocol: the code by which war is conducted within and between those nations that trade with the Commerce Artel.
Wars: notable conflicts include the Interdiction, Scion, Secession, Ghost, and First and Second Ataman Wars.

Xarodine: an epsense-inhibiting drug.

The Dying Light

For Scott and Kerri

Darkness is looking forward and saying: "I do not know what to do next; I have lost my way and it is too late to find it now."

—*HUBERT VAN ZELLER*

The cruellest lies are often told in silence.

—*ROBERT LOUIS STEVENSON*

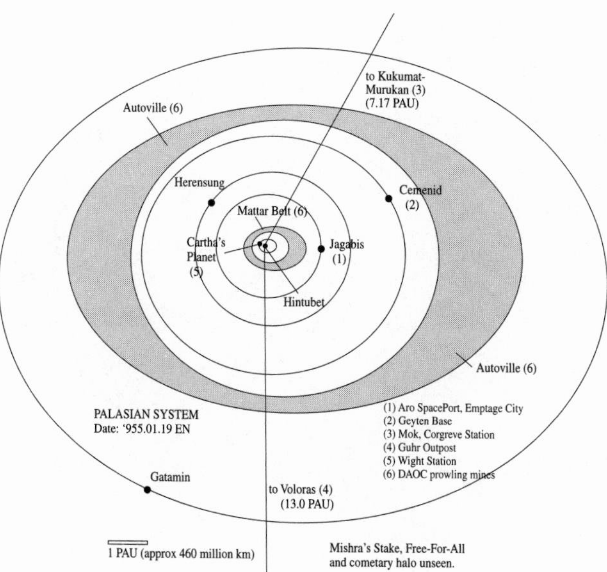
to Kukumat-
Murukan (3)
(7.17 PAU)
Autoville (6)
Herensung
Cemenid
(2)
Mattar Belt (6)
Cartha's
Planet
(5)
Jagabis
(1)
Hintubet
Autoville (6)
PALASIAN SYSTEM
Date: '955.01.19 EN
(1) Aro SpacePort, Emptage City
(2) Geyten Base
(3) Mok, Corgreve Station
(4) Guhr Outpost
(5) Wight Station
(6) DAOC prowling mines
Gatamin
to Voloras (4)
(13.0 PAU)
1 PAU (approx 460 million km)
Mishra's Stake, Free-For-All
and cometary halo unseen.

PART ONE:

PALASIAN SYSTEM

PROLOGUE

Words could not describe what he saw; they could only approximate. And therein lay the terrible irony of his situation: that he, of all beings in the galaxy, who could see things as (perhaps) they truly were, was utterly unable to convey all but the vaguest of impressions to those few who wanted to know.

<Find . . .>

Thoughts flew at him from all directions—thoughts tangled with emotions, sensations, and subconscious associations. So entwined were they, so hopelessly meshed, that by the time they reached him it was often impossible to disentangle a single thought from the rest. Sometimes one stood out, or several in concert, but he was rarely their intended recipient. Only occasionally did they demand a response, and when they did, he tried his best. Even so, his efforts rarely satisfied the demands of the Cruel One's servant.

<Find me . . .>

He looked.

All beings perceived the galaxy by their own unique light—brightest in the young, flickering as age increased, ultimately extinguished with death. It was this light he saw, not what it revealed, and the more these individual lights overlapped, the clearer his vision became. Perceived reality reached him from so many perspectives, some of them conflicting or downright contradictory, that the overlap took on its own life and became a thing unto itself. The *essence* of reality dominated his world. Not what a rock looked like to one person, or what it was called, but what it meant to everyone who encountered it—what it *was* in the larger weave of minds.

Through his eyes the galaxy was recognizable: densely populated planets hung like bright galaxies spinning in gulfs of impenetrable dark. As attention wandered across the void, his all-pervading sense followed, lighting up a place, a person, an artifact, then moving on. What it did not touch was irrelevant, for according to the rules of his universe anything not sensed did not exist. Yet even at the very fringes of his senses, the voice was speckled by fleeting glimpses of life. Every experience was there for him to harvest, no matter how exotic, or how hidden.

Normally, at least, that was so. But the Cruel One had taken the galaxy away from him, and left only darkness in its place. The infinite abyss pressed in upon him, making him feel as if he were suffocating. Only a handful of minds occupied the space surrounding him. One major clump represented the installation that contained him, accounting for almost ninety percent of the impressions he gathered—maybe a thousand minds in all. The rest were scattered, their lights weak, solitary and frightened. All except one—the one the others wanted him to find.

<. . . the Shining One.>

Sometimes the voice would part and allow him a glimpse of the being he sought. Just for a second—but in that briefest of moments its brightness and elegance outshone all else around. Whenever the mind appeared to him, he received an impression of something magnificent and wondrous. Something that was almost . . . *chilling.*

<Respond!>

The Cruel One's servant was persistent. The voice hammered at him, wearing down his resistance. He struggled to orient himself within his body, fought the outward urge that tugged him into the void. His limbs trembled—unseen by himself, but registered by the people watching him. Even in this much reduced form, his influence extended many thousands of meters.

<Find me the Shining One!>

The muscles of his distant body twitched. Electrodes recorded the minuscule currents of electrons and fluid through his brain. Powerful computers dedicated to the task took these vague data and translated them into words.

: ANOTHER

: RESONATES

A moment passed while the listeners absorbed his response. He could feel their minds turning, reacting in a dozen different ways—some with surprise, others with relief, even a few with ill-disguised fear. None held the object of his quest in awe, as did he.

Then:

<Where?>

That question. Always the same question: *where?*

How should *he* know? Spatial orientations were things he barely understood; they were too easily confused with temporal or emotional impressions. What was space when measured against the combined input of so many disparate minds?

But he did his best. The Cruel One was impatient for results, and that made her servants anxious. They regarded their master with contempt, yet they feared her also, and when they feared her most, their contempt found an outlet in those farther down the chain.

The watcher in their midst absorbed their feelings without rancor. He knew his place; he knew where he fitted into the Cruel One's schemes. His usefulness was defined solely by his ability to locate the Shining One. If he failed to do so, then his usefulness was at an end. The Cruel One was not known to be tolerant of anyone who failed, especially those who did not belong to her own Caste.

Every being sees the Universe in their own unique light, but very few see themselves with such acute honesty.

<Find me the Shining One!>

He did his best. He always did his best. And if his reply displeased the Cruel One's servant, he was never to know for certain.

<Where?>

: HERE

: SOON

1

IND *Ana Vereine*
'955.01.19 EN
0415

Alone but for the screaming wind, she fell. Her outstretched arms sought to find equilibrium, but to no avail. With nothing around for her hands to find purchase upon, her fall continued unchecked. The sickening sensation persisted in her stomach; the wind at her face and in her ears was relentless.

When exactly she had begun to fall she couldn't tell. Not that it mattered. Once she had been weightless, now she was falling; the only difference between the two was a matter of *destination.* Everything in the universe was just an orbiting body looking for something with which to intersect. If she had found her ultimate trajectory, then perhaps that was for the best. At least the waiting was over.

Suddenly from the darkness something touched her hand. She pulled away instinctively, sending herself into a spin. But the touch against her skin was persistent. It fluttered like a flesh-warm moth, moving along her wrist, her elbow, and finally settled on her upper arm.

She tried too late to pull away. Its grip tightened; slender, smooth digits dug deeply into her and tugged her forward. She called out in panic, but the blackness absorbed any sound she made.

When she flailed at the limb clutching her, her hand found skin. A hand. No fur, no scales, no chitinous exoskeleton; no claws, no suckers, no pinchers. It was a *Pristine* hand.

Cautiously, she explored the one that was falling with her. She moved her fingers along the person's wrist, elbow, and upper arm; her other hand found a smooth stomach, rib cage, and breast. Then, alarmed by the all too familiar terrain, she gripped the other person tightly. Wanting to push her away, instead she pulled her closer.

From the darkness she saw her own frightened face emerge; from the roaring wind she heard herself call out. . . .

Morgan Roche woke with a start and clutched her sweat-drenched sheets to her chest. A lingering vertigo made her giddy, and for a moment she didn't know where she was. The narrow bed, the dark room, the smell of deep-space service: she could have been anywhere, aboard any Commonwealth of Empires' vessel, on any number of missions for COE Intelligence.

Then, in the dull glow from the ceiling light, she saw the valise resting on a nearby table, and reality suddenly dispelled her confusion. She was in the second lieutenant's quarters of the *Ana Vereine,* a former Dato Bloc vessel now registered under her name, and she had no mission apart from the one she had given herself. Her indenture to COE Intelligence was a thing of the past—a memory returning to haunt her like the nightmare that had awoken her, and just as difficult to shake.

Rubbing at her arm, she vividly recalled the falling, the fear.

Then the flat echoes of an incident alarm wailing beyond her room goaded her to full consciousness. Disentangling her legs from the sheets, she climbed out of the bunk.

"Full lights." Squinting in the sudden glare, she amended: "Half lights. *Half* lights!"

The glare dimmed as she stumbled to the cabin's small wardrobe. She grabbed the first shipsuit she saw. Standard dress for a Dato Bloc officer, it consisted of a unisex, form-fitting garment cut from rust-colored fabric, with black insignia at shoulders and waist. Active fibers tightened the weave around her limbs, guaranteeing a perfect fit every time.

As she dressed, she sent a subvocal inquiry via her implants to the transmitter on her left wrist:

<Uri? Box? What's going on?>

The voice of the Box answered immediately, the AI's neutral tones coming from the tiny speaker beside the bed:

"We have completed our final jump, Morgan. The *Ana Vereine* entered realspace fifteen minutes ago."

At the end of the sentence, the sirens ceased.

Roche glanced at the clock beside her bed. <Why? We weren't due to arrive at the Palasian anchor point for another three hours.>

"Indeed. That was our original schedule." The Box paused before adding: "There has been an unusual development. Cane thought it best that you were here on the bridge."

<What sort of "development," Box?> A knot of worry began to tighten in her stomach. <Is it the other clone warrior?>

"Nothing so dramatic, Morgan. Simply—perplexing."

She took a deep breath to hide her irritation. If the *Box* was perplexed, then she doubted she would be much help. What the most sophisticated artificial intelligence in the Commonwealth couldn't fathom, no mundane Human would have a chance of deciphering.

Still, tired or not, she had to keep up appearances. Sitting down on the bunk, she slid her feet into a pair of boots and fastened the ankle straps.

<Okay, Box, tell Cane I'm on my way. Are the others on deck?>

"Kajic and Maii are asleep. Haid is awake, but has not responded to my summons."

<Where is he?>

"In the rehabilitation unit."

<Break into the program, then. We need three on the bridge, just in case it turns out to be serious.>

"Understood." Again the Box hesitated, as though it was about to debate her assumption that it didn't rate as a crew member. But all it said in the end was: "I shall wait until you have arrived before taking any action."

<Good.> Boots on and fastened, Roche stood. At her approach, the door to her

quarters slid open. She heard an airlock chime in the distance, ready for her to step into the ship's central transit corridor. <Give me two minutes.>

The *Ana Vereine,* first of the new Marauder-class combat ships to roll off the Dato Bloc production lines, was designed to hold a full complement of three thousand crew members. Its size reflected that—uncomfortably at times. Currently carrying a crew of just five, its labyrinthine holds were sealed; active life support was restricted to officers' quarters, the bridge and a handful of essential areas; major accessways were dimly lit and cool, filled with nothing but the gentle susurrus of hundreds of cubic kilometers of moving air.

Sometimes it seemed to Roche, as it did now, on her way to the bridge, that she had been swallowed by a vast, metal beast. That at any moment the ship would spring to life, shrug free of its carbon-based passengers and head off on its own adventure. And perhaps it would serve them right if it did; they were so far from realizing its true potential.

In the eighteen days since leaving COE Intelligence HQ, they had traveled a highly circuitous route. Fearing a double cross from Page De Bruyn, head of Strategy and Roche's former employer, the Box had plotted an untraceable course to Walan Third, where they had surrendered Makil Veden's body to the Commerce Artel. That small but necessary detour cost them time: although they remained at the Eckandi base for less than a day, their total on the run had already reached eight by the time they left.

From Walan Third the *Ana Vereine* headed toward Baeris Osh, a Surin territory, before abruptly changing course for the Handrelle System. Every time they completed a hyperspace jump, Roche half-expected to find an ambush waiting for them. The chances of De Bruyn second-guessing their path were practically zero, since it was impossible to predict the destination of a ship once it entered hyperspace, but the fear was hard to shake. Only on the last two jumps, when they finally angled back toward the border of the Kesh N'Kor Republic and their original destination, had Morgan begun to believe that she was actually safe, that she might yet outrun her past.

Still, there was always the future to worry about. If an ambush was what De Bruyn intended, Palasian System was the obvious place to stage it. Only a stubborn belief—based mainly on recent experience—that COE Intelligence would never do anything quite so obvious kept her from losing sleep over that possibility. Page De Bruyn had revealed herself to be a far more cunning and deceitful opponent than that.

Besides, it wasn't what she was running *from* that most concerned Morgan, but what she was running *to.* The Box had said that the alert had nothing to do with the Sol Wunderkind in Palasian System. A gut instinct told her that that was not the whole truth.

Rounding the last corner on her approach to the bridge, Roche felt the peculiar hopelessness of her dream return with a vividness that stung. She slowed her pace and took a few deep breaths, wanting to regain her composure before she stepped onto the bridge to join the others.

The last time she'd had that dream had been the night before taking the Armada entrance exam on Ascensio, many years before. But why had it returned *now,* on this, her nineteenth day free of COE Intelligence? She was at a loss to understand the connection. The dream spoke of her deepest fears: of failure, the future, and . . . *freedom*?

She shook her head to rid herself of the discomforting notion. She *was* glad to be free of COE Intelligence, wasn't she? She didn't like to think that even the smallest part of her might be having regrets.

When her mind was relatively still, if not entirely clear, she took another deep breath and stepped through the open portal and onto the bridge.

The bridge was not the largest room on the *Ana Vereine,* even though it felt as if it could have been. The main chamber was roughly heart-shaped, with a single holographic screen dominating the left lobe, more specialized displays in the right, and various officer stations sweeping in three arcs toward the rounded base. A smaller, circular room at the base of the heart was the captain's private chamber. This chamber, plus the shape of the bridge itself, lent the entire floor plan a passing resemblance to the Mandelbrot Set, with the captain's podium located at the intersection of X and Y axes. Except that on the *Ana Vereine,* there was no captain's podium. There was just a large hologram projector occupying its usual spot.

Tempering the bewildering array of displays and control stations, the walls bore the colors of late sunset with the occasional tapestry to blunt sharp corners. The lighting was muted, and brightened only under battle conditions.

One person occupied the vast area. He was leaning against the astrogation officer's station with his arms folded, the shipsuit he wore emphasizing his supple strength.

"Sorry to disturb you," said Cane, straightening as Roche entered. His dark brown skin and bald skull made him seem Exotic, subtly alien, and the little Roche knew about his origins didn't help shake that impression.

"That's okay," she said, wishing she could emulate his alertness. Not for the first time, she cursed the modified genes responsible for his extraordinary resilience. "What's the situation?"

"We found something." Cane nodded at the main screen. "Or at least, the Box did."

She crossed the bridge to the first officer's chair as he talked. "Show me," she said, sitting.

"Well, that's the strange thing," Cane said. "There's nothing to show."

Roche, frowning, swiveled in her chair to face him. Before she could speak, Cane added: "At least, nothing *I* can see."

"The phenomenon we have encountered is not visible in the physical universe," explained the Box, its voice issuing from speakers at the base of the holographic projector.

Roche shifted her attention back to the main screen. The only thing it revealed were the cold specks of distant stars.

She sighed, impatience rising within her again. "Is someone going to explain what's going on here?"

"Of course," said the Box. The view on the main screen changed, became the route plotted by Roche and the Box while refueling at COE Intelligence HQ. "Our original course from Walan Third consisted of fourteen hyperspace jumps across the Commonwealth of Empires, culminating in one final jump to the anchor point of Palasian System. We traveled entirely without incident until this last jump." An arrow skittered through the depths of the screen, settling upon a point almost at the end of their route. "Here. Four hours into the jump, sensors aboard the *Ana Vereine* detected an anomaly in our vicinity."

The screen displayed complex diagrams representing the distorted topology of hyperspace—that strange realm where even the basic laws of physics could not be taken for granted.

"The disturbance lay directly in our path," the Box continued, "although its distance from us in physical terms was difficult to determine. My one attempt to change course around it was unsuccessful, perhaps because of the influence it was—and is still—exerting over our navigational data."

"What sort of influence?" Roche asked.

"A type I have never encountered before, Morgan. Our course became increasingly uncertain the closer we approached it. By attempting to go around it, we ran the risk of passing through it instead. Eventually the potential hazard became so great that I decided to return prematurely. We had nearly completed the final jump by that point, so I thought the loss in time would be offset by the chance to see what awaited us."

"And?" Roche watched in guarded fascination as the main screen changed again; n-dimensional mathematics was not her specialty, but she assumed the Box knew what it was talking about.

"The source of the disturbance remains a mystery."

"So? As long as we don't hit it, we can still make it to Palasian System, right?"

"If only it were that simple, Morgan." The screen returned to the picture it had displayed when Roche had entered the bridge: stars, none so close as to be remarkable, and nothing else within the external scanners' fields of view.

Nothing . . .

"Where's the primary of Palasian System?" she asked, frowning.

"We can't find it," Cane said. "That's the problem."

Roche's frown deepened. "We're *lost*?"

"If anything," said the Box, "it is the system itself that is lost." A navigation chart appeared on the screen. "If you study the data, you will see that we have arrived with the correct orientation one light-week short of the terminus of our original jump, two light-weeks from Palasian System. Star charts confirm this. What we are seeing is what we *should* be seeing, except for one important detail: Hintubet, Palasian System's primary, appears nowhere within the starscape before us."

"I find that hard to believe. It has to be here somewhere—"

"None of the stars in this region produce a spectral match. Neither do any within a fifty light-year radius." The Box paused before pronouncing its conclusion: "Palasian System is patently not where it is supposed to be."

Roche found her sense of fatigue quickly fading. "That's impossible. The disturbance must have knocked us more off course than you thought."

"Not by so great a margin as to lose an entire star, Morgan."

"Then the star charts must be wrong."

"They aren't. Apart from a few slight discrepancies, every other navigational marker in this region matches."

"Well, *what* then?" She shook her head in annoyance. To come so close to her destination only to find that it had been snatched away from her was like something out of a bad dream—another one. "A system can't just disappear without a trace!"

"I agree that it is improbable," said the Box, its tone mollifying. "But the only conceivable alternative is that it has been destroyed."

"How?" She automatically glanced at Cane. No one knew exactly what the genetically modified clone warriors made by the Sol Apotheosis Movement were capable of—possibly not even Cane, who was one of them. "Surely not even a Sol Wunderkind could do *that.*"

"It would seem unlikely that the entire system was destroyed," agreed Cane. "But when you consider that the only alternative explanation is that it has been moved, you have to admit—"

"This is a rhetorical point," the Box cut in. "We lack data, Morgan. What measurements I can make from this distance are hampered by the fact that light from the region is at least one week old. I have found no evidence to suggest any sort of event sufficiently calamitous to destroy a star without leaving any trace of stellar wreckage—but I may be missing something. We need to go closer to find out."

Her eyes narrowed suspiciously. "I thought you said the disturbance posed too great a risk to navigation."

"Not necessarily. Long-distance jumps through this region of space are likely to be perturbed. I suggest instead that we approach the vicinity of where Palasian System used to be by increments, studying the anomaly as we go. Should the risk increase further still, we can come to a halt again and consider other courses of action."

Roche nodded, agreeing in principle with what the Box was saying. If the risk was only to navigation and the ship was in little physical danger, then there was little reason not to continue. The lack of information, however, made it hard even to guess how much danger they were in: if something *had* destroyed Palasian System, then they might be heading right for it.

Nevertheless, there was no other choice. They had to keep going. It was either that or turn around—and the latter was hardly an attractive prospect. With the possible exception of the Box, none of them had a home to return to any longer.

"What does COE Intelligence have to say about this?" Roche asked. "Is there any mention in the data they've given us?"

"Very little, I'm afraid, Morgan. We have the report transmitted by the battalion of Armada Marines before it was destroyed, including a vague description of the damage done to the system at that time. It describes Palasian System as quarantined or sealed, but nothing else."

"No updates since then?"

"Since the *Ana Vereine* disengaged from COE Intelligence HQ, reports have been intermittent at best."

So much for their agreement with De Bruyn, she thought sourly. Still, if that was the worst the head of Strategy had planned, then she should be grateful. Unless—

Again she shook her head. Not even Page De Bruyn would destroy an entire solar system to obtain revenge—especially not when the fate of the Commonwealth of Empires might be at stake.

"I agree with your analysis of the situation, Box," she said slowly. "We need to find Palasian System, but to do *that* we need information. We will, therefore, proceed with your plan: to approach the last known location of Palasian System more cautiously, by slow-jumping a little closer each time and taking stock as we go.

That way we'll have a chance of staying on course and avoiding anything waiting for us."

There was almost an air of smugness to the Box's tone as it replied: "Very well, Morgan. I will begin plotting a new course immediately."

"Good. But don't perform any maneuvers until Uri is conscious and watching what you do. We don't know what effect rapid transfers might have on the ship. Defer to him if he thinks you should take it more cautiously."

"Naturally." The Box's smug tone had faded, and Roche did her best to suppress a smile of satisfaction. Although the uniquely self-aware AI had been programmed by its creators on Trinity to obey her orders, that didn't mean it had to enjoy the situation; any chance it found to assert its independence, the Box took it. She had learned the hard way not to give it generalized orders that were too easily evaded, or outright perverted, in order to meet its own hidden agenda—whatever *that* was. Where her own lack of experience made it difficult for her to be specific, she allocated an overseer to keep an eye on the Box's activities, just to make sure.

If that bothered the Box, all the better. She had earned this subtle form of revenge, at least, after the way it had manipulated her in the past and probably intended to in the future.

"Okay," she said. "You get started, Box. Cane, track down Maii and get her up here. We'll need her to search for life signs when we get close enough. I'm going down to rehab to see what's happened to Haid."

"Shall I rouse Kajic?" asked the Box.

"No," said Roche, levering herself out of the chair. "He'll be awake soon enough, if he isn't already. Let him come to you in his own time, when he's finished any status checks he needs to perform. We don't need to rush him. I want to take this slowly: we might not get a second chance to find out what's going on."

Especially if the other Sol Wunderkind is *behind it,* she added to herself.

"I'll notify you when we are about to begin," said the Box.

"You do that," Roche said as she left the bridge.

The ship's rehabilitation unit was four levels down from the bridge, in an annex off the medical unit. On the way down, Roche was joined by a fist-sized drone that darted from a service hatch and assumed a position near her right shoulder. The jets of air propelling it sounded like a cough played at high speed. When the drone spoke, it did so in a tinny version of Uri Kajic's voice.

"What do you think, Morgan?" he asked.

Roche glanced at the drone without breaking step. "I thought you'd be listening in."

"And?"

"I think something strange is going on."

"Likewise. The sooner we find out what it is, the better." The drone skittered ahead, emitting agitated *fft*'s as it turned a corner. "I do believe the Box, though," he said, "when it says it doesn't know what the anomaly is."

"So do I, strangely enough," Roche admitted. "Otherwise it wouldn't have brought us out of the jump so suddenly."

"There's more to it than that, Morgan. I've studied the astrogation data. The Box mentioned a few 'slight discrepancies' but it didn't tell you what they were."

"Are they significant?"

"Perhaps. The stars in the direction of Palasian System appear to be closer than they should be. Not much closer, admittedly—a few billion kilometers or so—but closer all the same. It's as though a big chunk of space is missing from this area."

"The space containing Palasian System?"

"That would seem the logical conclusion," Kajic agreed. "But can you imagine the force required to achieve this? Destroying a star, or even moving it, is bad enough; taking the space surrounding it as well is a completely different matter."

Roche contemplated the possibility for a long moment. She had never heard of such a thing—indeed, she found it hard to visualize. Nothing could destroy space itself. Nothing she had ever heard of, anyway.

"All the more reason, then, to make our approach a cautious one," she said. "Will the ship hold up? *Can* it slow-jump as often as the Box would like?"

"I've looked at the basic plan, and it seems sound. We'll drop in and out of hyperspace once every ten minutes, traveling several million kilometers each time and accelerating between. At first we'll approach the anomaly in tangents, so we can look at it from a number of directions; that way we might be able to determine exactly how large it is. If things go well, we'll try getting a little closer to see what else we find." The drone bobbed as Kajic spoke. "The ship itself will be fine. Its engines are designed to function under battle conditions. In fact, it'll be good to have a really thorough workout. The last time we put it through its paces was back at Sciacca's World."

Roche nodded but did not speak. The *Ana Vereine* and a handful of raiders had made short work of the *Midnight,* the ship she had been traveling in at the time. Only the Box's decision to blow the frigate's antimatter reserves had prevented the Dato Bloc captain from capturing the ship, or destroying it himself. As a result, the *Ana Vereine* had yet to make its first kill.

Still, it had performed well in battle, and she accepted Kajic's opinion that it would survive the coming hours. It was only an old superstition that made her hesitant to place her faith completely in a new ship.

"We'll stick out like a beacon, jumping that often," she said, halfheartedly trying to pick holes in the Box's plan.

"True. But there's nothing we can do to avoid that." Kajic paused, then suggested: "We can camouflage the ship, if you like. Make it look like a freighter experiencing drive difficulties—?"

She shook her head. "Palasian System has been quarantined. Only a fool would try to get in, faulty drive or not. If we stumble across an Armada blockade, as unlikely as that is, they'll shoot us out of the sky regardless of what we look like."

"They can try." Roche heard the ghost of a grin in the thin reproduction of Kajic's voice. "Any other questions?"

"Only one." The one she had avoided asking herself: "What do we do if we can't work out what happened to the system? Where do we go from there?"

"Only time will tell us that, Morgan. Time, and the right data."

"I know, I know." Roche inhaled deeply, trying to center herself. "Just make sure the Box tells me if we *do* find something, okay? That'd give me one less thing to worry about."

"You have my word," said Kajic. "And don't worry, Morgan. You're doing fine."

Roche smiled. "Thanks, Uri."

With a staccato tattoo of air-bursts, the drone accelerated ahead of her and ducked into a maintenance closet.

Roche continued the rest of the way to rehab alone, genuinely reassured by Kajic's closing comment. Her relationship with the Dato Bloc ex-captain was still an ambivalent one. Although both had been betrayed by their respective governments, making them allies of sorts, Roche had initially felt uncomfortable having the ship's previous commander aboard. Removing or imprisoning him had never been an option, though: he was as much a part of the ship as the navigation AI or the engines. What remained of his body floated in a life-support tank in a little-visited section, plugged by an experimental neural interface into the workings of the vessel surrounding him. As much as she might have preferred, she couldn't have one without the other.

So it was just lucky that he had chosen to take her under his metaphorical wing and train her in the art of command. All her years in COE Intelligence had taught her how to obey orders, not how to give them. Already she had come to rely on his judgment in many matters, not just those to do with the ship; without him, these last few weeks would have been considerably harder.

Still, she could understand why others might be suspicious of a Dato Bloc captain in their midst with unlimited access to the entire ship. The situation begged betrayal of some sort—which is why she had instructed the Box to keep as close an eye on Kajic as *he* was keeping on *it*. She couldn't allow her own, possibly irrational, opinions to place her or her other companions at risk; she mistrusted all of them equally, had to do so in order to keep going. And if Kajic ever found out, she was sure that he would understand.

The Box's voice broke into her thoughts via her implants: <All is arranged, Morgan. We will proceed in ninety seconds, once the *Ana Vereine* has achieved the necessary velocity to slow-jump.>

<Good work,> she subvocalized. <The ship is in your hands and Uri's.>

<Understood.>

She increased her pace through the Marauder's glowing corridors. The entrance to the rehabilitation unit finally appeared on her left. At the same time, a warning buzzer sounded, alerting the occupants of the ship to an imminent hyperspace jump.

She had barely steadied herself when the ship's drives went to work. Reality flexed around her; space-time twisted in impossible directions. A wave of giddiness came and went, making her blink.

Then everything was as it had been a moment before—except that the ship was no longer a part of the physical universe. It had entered hyperspace, and was accelerating at many thousand standard gravities relative to the normal universe. For all the effect the jump had on the interior of the ship, however, it might have gone nowhere. Which was exactly how it should have been.

The doors to the rehab unit slid open when she took another step forward. Yet another step took her across the threshold, into a world she rarely visited.

Rehabilitation, as the term was employed in most military organizations, was synonymous with cybernetic enhancement. Where more orthodox medical techniques failed to heal a wound, replace a limb or rebuild a broken mind—or if there was no time to employ sophisticated methods of healing—technology stepped in to breach the gap. Everything from artificial limbs to neuron patches could be provided by the best mobile rehab units in the Commonwealth of Empires, and those of the Dato Bloc were at least as advanced. The *Ana Vereine* in particular, given its recent manufacture, possessed facilities Roche had only heard about.

The large workroom was designed as an open surgery, with several adjoining chambers available for procedures requiring more sterile environments. Four long tables, uncomfortably like mortuary slabs, awaited patients in states of perpetual readiness, while close by hung numerous multijointed waldoes, medical scanners and replacement parts. Along one wall, screens could project views of any operations under way, or retrieve from memory similar situations to compare prognoses. Another wall boasted three holographic "cybercorpses"—human bodies composed entirely of replacement parts, from carbon-fiber bones to synthetic skin—with no single part repeated in any of the "bodies." Designed for reference, the cybercorpses rotated once every twenty seconds, as though performing a macabre pirouette. When Roche stepped farther into the room to look for Haid, six glassy, empty eyes seemed to follow her for a moment, then drifted away.

She found him in one of the auxiliary chambers, hardwired into a simulation that was teaching him to use his new support biomesh. After their escape from Sciacca's World, an immediate priority had been to equip Haid with a body at least approximating the Pristine. Time had been against them, however. The surgery alone required for a total rebuild would have taken several weeks; recovery and readjustment at least the same again. Haid had opted instead for a basic overhaul: an eye to replace his empty socket, the support biomesh to compensate for his lack of an arm and to supplement the strength of his legs, plus new interfaces to control the lot.

The installation, undergone piecemeal, had taken seven days. Another five had seen him on his feet for the first time. The remaining seven had been spent in the simulator, retraining his reflexes to respond to new stimuli.

When Roche found him, he was floating in free-fall, twisting about his center of gravity in an ungainly manner. The glossy black mesh of the exoskeleton stood out against the gray of his undersuit, but perfectly matched the sweat-soaked sheen of his midnight skin. Despite years of abuse and layers of scar tissue millimeters thick, Haid still possessed the distinctive coloring of a Montaban native—along with the rugged good looks.

His eyes were uncovered, but Roche could tell that she was invisible to him—along with the rest of the ship. Placing her left hand on a panel flush to the door frame, she synchronized her own implants to the illusion in which he was enmeshed. The vision through her left eye went gray with static for a moment, then cleared.

With his feet anchored by magnetic soles to the hull of a spacecraft, Haid was trying to thread a gossamer-thin guideline through a moving eyelet. He was naked, apart from the biomesh, and very clumsy. The surface beneath his feet moved without warning, making his judgment unreliable, so every action with his new arm had to be carefully considered. In other simulations that Roche had observed, he had run over burning sand while carrying a glass of water, balanced on a narrow ledge with his old arm behind his back, and attempted to imitate the movements of garishly dressed dancers—all with the critical eye of the rehab AI grading every movement.

Roche gave him five minutes before actively interfering. In that time, he came close to tying a loop through the eyelet, but a sudden shift in the surface beneath his feet cost him his grip on the thread, forcing him to start again. His lips moved silently, cursing under his breath.

"Haid." Roche tried to keep her voice soft, but its incongruity broke the illusion instantly. "Ameidio, can you hear me?"

Haid sighed; his new skeletal arm, with its black mesh skin, sagged. "Yes, Morgan, I hear you."

"The Box said you weren't responding, so I thought I'd better check on you myself. Is everything okay?"

Ignoring her concerns, Haid said: "This rehab AI is a sadist. I *swear* this damn hole is getting smaller." His eyes gazed blankly into the distance, away from her. It wasn't just the simulation: he was exhausted. "Next time I'll get it, though. Next time I'll—"

"Something's come up," she interrupted, trying to keep her voice firm and level—a line dragging him back to reality. "We needed you on the bridge."

"I felt us come out of hyperspace," he said. "Are we there already?" He looked around him, as though waking from a dream, and frowned. "No, wait. We jumped again just a moment ago, didn't we? That wasn't planned."

"No, it wasn't." She outlined the situation as briefly as she could—that Palasian System appeared to have disappeared—not wanting to worry him, but at the same time reinforcing the fact that he hadn't been there when she *might* have needed him. If the ship had been under attack—

"I would have noticed instantly." His voice was calm but there was no disguising his indignation. "There would have been sirens, impacts, power fluctuations. Not even a wirehead could sim through something like that."

"But if you *had* noticed, it would've been too late for you to do anything."

"Like I could do anything, anyway, with *this*." Haid raised his new arm and flexed it. The movement was smoother than it had been even a day earlier but was still noticeably jerky.

Roche shook her head, even though Haid wouldn't see the gesture. "Your other arm is fine. And besides, you don't need coordination to help on the bridge. Not unless we're boarded—and I hope it'll never come to that."

"Likewise." He let the arm fall to his side. An instant later, the illusion collapsed around them, brought to an end by his mental command. The zero-g field relaxed, eased him slowly to the floor of the auxiliary chamber. His legs became rigid when they touched the floor, held him upright as his full weight returned. "But the fact remains that you need me in full working order—and that means as much deep-training as possible—"

"It also means getting some rest." She let go of the touch panel and took a step closer. "You look terrible."

He grimaced. "Thanks a lot."

"I'm serious. Take a shower, have something to eat and drink. Then meet me as soon as you can to discuss what's going on—"

A second wave of disorientation rushed through Roche as the *Ana Vereine* returned to real-space. She moved forward as Haid swayed, but he reached out with his new arm and steadied himself.

"See?" He smiled wryly at his own achievement. "Give me another week and I'll be wrestling clone warriors bare-handed."

"I sincerely hope not," she said, turning her back on him and walking out of the simulation room.

"Any news on that front?" Haid asked, moving stiffly after her. Picking up a towel from a bench by the door, he wiped the skin of his upper body dry, where the active fabric of his absorbent undersuit was unable to reach.

"None," she said. "We're still too far away."

"Unless the disappearance of the system is a related event." Haid put the towel aside. "Does anybody know how advanced the Sol Apotheosis Movement was? Maybe they found a way to camouflage an entire system."

"I doubt it," she said, although the possibility wasn't one she had considered. "If they'd possessed that sort of tech, they wouldn't have been destroyed so easily. They could have camouflaged their base and escaped the siege any time they wanted."

"Siege?" Haid shook his head. "A simple 'no' would have done, Morgan. You know history isn't my strong point."

"Nor mine," she said. "It took me days to find what little there was available. I've condensed it into a single file and placed it in the open datapool. You can access it later, if you want."

"Maybe." The ship rolled beneath them again. Haid's oddly mismatched eyes—one much like a monocle covering the entire socket, and the other, the recent addition, a crystal sphere where a normal eye would sit—lifted in surprise to meet hers. "The Box is not wasting any time, is it?"

"It's found something it doesn't understand, and doesn't like it."

Haid chuckled softly. "So trying to make me feel guilty about not responding is just your way of taking out on me your frustration with *it.*"

Roche smiled in return, ignoring the gibe. "I'm heading back to the bridge," she said. "When you're ready, join us there. We could use your input."

The ex-mercenary nodded as she headed for the door. "At least it looks like we might have something to do, for a change."

Haid's parting comment pursued her after she left the rehab unit. Eighteen days on the run, fearing a COE Intelligence betrayal every step of the way; major surgery, followed by recovery and intense rehabilitation; a destination about which they knew little, except for the fact that it had nearly been destroyed by the deadliest warrior to grace the galaxy in two and a half thousand years—and Haid was complaining about being *bored*?

Roche didn't need that sort of excitement in her life. In fact, an uninterrupted sleep would have suited her much better.

A familiar mind-touch greeted her as she headed back to the bridge:

<Good morning, Morgan.>

Startled by the unexpected intrusion upon her thoughts, Roche missed a step. <Hello, Maii. Cane woke you, I see.>

<Yes.> The reave's voice carried with it a faint tinge of grief. Hardly surprising, Roche thought; the girl had had so little time to adjust to the death of her mentor, Veden. As his ward, she had earned the right to recite the ritual leave-taking during the ceremony on Walan Third, but she had declined, both reluctant to appear in public and conscious of time pressing.

<Did he fill you in?>

<He said that Palasian System seems to have disappeared. And while the Box tries to find it, you want me to check for life signs.>

<Near enough. See if you can detect anyone where the system used to be. An eyewitness would be good, but anyone at all will do.>

<I have already tried several times. From such a distance, resolution is poor.>

<I know.> Privately, Roche was amazed that the girl thought she could detect anything at all. <But keep trying. At least there's a chance you might be able to tell us something the Box can't.>

<Okay,> said Maii. <We're jumping at the moment, so I'll wait until we come out again. It's easier that way.>

<Whatever. You're the expert.> Roche walked on, trying to fight the weariness slowing her stride.

<You're tired,> observed Maii. <Cane woke you too?>

<I wouldn't have slept much longer anyway.>

<Another nightmare, Morgan?>

She nodded unnecessarily. <Yes.>

<I can help you, you know.>

As an accompaniment to her words, Maii sent a brief image of an underwater scene: a coral reef lit by mottled green sunlight with large gray fish lightly brushing against her body. Despite the constant motion, the endless cycle of life and death swirling around her, the mood generated by the image was one of peace and inner calm.

A healing dream, designed to ease the girl's own path through grief.

Roche hesitated before answering. As uncomfortable as she still was with epsense therapy, she had to admit that the offer was made with the best intentions. That made a flat "no" much harder to pronounce.

<I'd be happier to have breakfast,> she said eventually.

<Well, there's not much happening on the bridge at the moment. Cane and I can take care of things for a while if you want to grab yourself a meal.>

Even though she disliked being away from the heart of the action, the offer was appealing. It could be her last chance for a long while. <Thanks, Maii.>

<My pleasure.> A mental smile accompanied her next words: <And don't worry, Morgan. We'll keep you informed.>

Roche hurried to the officers' mess, two levels up from the rehab facility. There she ordered a nondescript breakfast and took a seat at one of the many empty tables filling the room. The dispenser provided her with a good imitation of eggs, cereal, and fruit juice. She forced herself to eat slowly, chewing each bite rather than gulping it down.

Every ten minutes the ship rolled as it moved from one universe to the next, edging closer to the anomaly each time. She couldn't help but wonder what the Box was learning along the way, but she refrained from asking for an update. If anything happened, someone would be sure to call her. Until they did, all she had to do was relax.

After a couple more mouthfuls, she realized that she couldn't relax. There was too much at stake—and too little known about the situation to help her guess at what she had to do.

There was something she *could* do, however. Midway through the small meal, she routed a display through her implants and selected the file she had collated on the Sol Apotheosis Movement from the combined data resources of the Commonwealth of Empires and the Dato Bloc. Somewhere in the file, she hoped, was a clue regarding the technological prowess of her enemy.

Whether she would find anything useful was unlikely, though. The history of the Sol Apotheosis Movement was poorly documented until the time of its destruction. It had been founded early in the 36th millennium, '325 EN, by a visionary whose name was no longer recorded. The Movement's aim had been to achieve Transcendence by means of genetic manipulation and biomodification, rather than by downloading living minds into AI networks, as was usual. By bucking both tradition and common sense, its adherents were ostracized and banned by their native government—also unnamed—so they sought and found an empty system deep in the backwaters of their region of the galaxy. Acquiring the system by the expediency of simply moving in and adopting its name, they devoted their considerable energy to consolidating their position rather than taking their message any farther—for a while.

By '836 of the following millennium, they had established trade with the Eckandar Trade Axis which, along with the Commonwealth of Empires, had begun expansion into the area surrounding them. With trade came a new openness, and it wasn't long before biomodified prophets began to spread through neighboring regions, looking for converts. Some of these prophets were early versions of the Movement's crowning—and most deadly—achievement: the Sol Wunderkind, a genetically modified combat soldier with abilities far superior to any known Caste. Word began to spread, and within decades their existence was well-known, as was the threat they represented.

Many attempts were made to discourage or disperse the prophets, but they persisted. Squabbles broke out when the Ataman Theocracy attempted to reclaim Sol System as its own—even though the system had been abandoned centuries before as an uneconomic prospect. Tempers flared; the Movement countered every attempt to take the system away from them. Eventually an alliance was formed between the Commonwealth of Empires, the Dominion, and the Ataman Theocracy—the three largest Pristine nations in the Movement's range—to wipe out the threat once and for all.

The largest joint military flotilla ever assembled by the three nations was dispatched to Sol System. There, they surrounded the main base of the Sol Apotheosis Movement and presented its members with an ultimatum: leave or be destroyed. The Movement refused to leave, so the leader of the combined Pristine forces ordered his ships to open fire.

Within seconds of the first shot, the main base of the Sol Apotheosis Movement self-destructed, taking with it ninety percent of the Pristine flotilla. The Sol Apotheosis Movement was utterly destroyed.

The name of the man who gave the order to fire was Adoni Cane. His fate was not recorded, but Roche could only assume that he had died along with the millions of others in the system.

Details beyond that point were particularly scarce. The Pristine alliance, although nominal victors of that bloody conflict, chose to erase the entire event from their various histories. Exactly why the Movement had chosen to commit suicide in such a dramatic manner was not explained convincingly anywhere that Roche could find. No one had postulated the theory that they might have considered long-term revenge.

Until now . . .

A lone Human with no memories apart from the name Adoni Cane had been recovered from a life-support capsule in a backwater region of the Commonwealth of Empires. In the time Roche had known him he had demonstrated extraordinary feats of endurance, intelligence, and strength. Plus he bore an uncanny likeness to the man who had shared his name two and a half thousand years ago. At roughly the same time, another such castaway, name unknown, had been recovered near Palasian System. Within days, the system had been in flames, and now appeared to have disappeared entirely. The Sol Apotheosis Movement, it seemed, was back. Why, though, was anyone's guess.

As far as finding out exactly how advanced the Movement had been, there were few indicators. With regard to genetic technology at least, they'd had no peer. The few researchers who had studied the history of the Movement all concluded that the COE was behind them in many ways, despite the intervening millennia. Any doubts Roche herself might have had regarding that claim were easily dispelled by the existence of the Adoni Cane she knew. No other mundane civilization in the history of the galaxy, to her knowledge, had the ability to craft such a superbly capable Human purely by manipulating genetic code. Only High Humans might possess that knowledge, and they had no reason to meddle in affairs beneath them.

In other areas, however, less was known. The destruction of the Movement's base in Sol System had been accomplished by means of an enormous explosion, the likes of which had never been seen before or since. The weapons systems employed by the earlier versions of the Wunderkind had also outstripped anything available at the time. And their defensive abilities must have been remarkable, to have held off frequent attacks for so long before their eventual self-destruction.

But did they have enough technological know-how to destroy or to hide an entire system? Roche might have accepted the possibility had the Sol Wunderkind that invaded Palasian System been discovered in a fully functional warship. With such a vessel, he might have been capable of anything. But he hadn't been in a warship. He had been removed from a life-support capsule similar—if not identical—to the one in which Cane had been found.

She skimmed through the data collected by the medical officers aboard the *Midnight.* Cane's capsule had been unique in that he had actually been grown from a zygote within it, but otherwise it had been empty. Its empty shell contained no obvious navigation or propulsion systems; the only lifesupport provided was the hibernation regulator that had kept Cane in stasis during the months until his discovery; only the most basic of AIs kept the whole system operating. If every capsule was the same, then the Sol clone warrior in Palasian System had woken up naked and unarmed, not better-equipped than most small armies.

Since then, however, he had somehow managed to commandeer at least one COE Armada vessel and attack no fewer than five semipermanent COE installations. And now he had effectively disappeared, taking the entire system with him.

So little was known about him—what his intentions were, how capable he was of fulfilling them, and exactly what he had done in the few weeks since his awakening. Even if Roche found Palasian System, there was no guarantee the clone warrior would even be there anymore. He could be light-years away, wreaking havoc on other outposts.

Then a new thought struck her. The clone warrior had awakened unarmed, but had immediately taken control of the nearest ship. Perhaps he had performed a similar feat in Palasian System as a whole. Given the right knowledge, he could have made his own equipment from the resources scattered across the system—if the right resources were present.

She checked the COE database. Palasian System contained a small Armada refueling base, one communications outpost, one town-sized colony, and a scattered handful of scientific installations, two of which were devoted to studying solar flares and xenoarchaeology. That was all, on eight planets and a large assortment of smaller satellites. Nothing stood out as possessing the sort of equipment the fugitive would have required to build a device capable of hiding an entire system. Of course, not knowing *how* the device worked made it hard to guess what was required to build it, and even more difficult to work out how to counteract its effect.

Before Roche could take her exploration of the files any further, the ship shuddered violently. She looked up in alarm as the bulkheads around her rattled.

<Box! What was that?> she asked via her implants, letting her spoon fall into what remained of her breakfast.

<A difficult translation, Morgan,> replied the AI. <There is no need to be alarmed.>

<If you're pushing the ship too hard—>

<I am doing nothing of the sort.> The Box sounded mildly offended. <We are simply coming closer to the anomaly. Disturbance is to be expected.>

<How much worse do you think it will get?>

<I am unable to answer that question at this point,> said the Box. <But I can assure you that the situation is being closely monitored.>

<Good.> Roche stood and put her plate into a disposal hatch. <I'm on my way, in any case.>

The Box said nothing more, perhaps sensing the renewed determination Roche felt—partly a result of the food, partly the refocusing of her attention on the goals they all shared. For the first time in the hours since her rude awakening, she actually felt alert.

When she reached the bridge, Cane occupied exactly the same position he had earlier, watching the expanse of the big screen with his arms folded.

Maii sat not far from him. A strip of white cloth covered her empty sockets, matching the loose shift she wore in preference to Dato Bloc shipsuits. Roche automatically sent a smile her way, and when she saw the Surin return it knew that the ritually blinded girl was using Cane's eyes for visual input. The only other person available to read was Roche herself—but that would have rendered the smile invisible to the epsense adept.

Aloud, Roche asked: "Any news, Maii?"

<None so far, Morgan. The area seems to be empty.>

She grunted acknowledgment of the fact to herself, then added: "What if the system was camouflaged? Would it be possible for the Sol Wunderkind to block epsense as well?"

Cane looked up. "The whole system?" he said. "Highly unlikely."

"But it *is* a possibility." She turned to face him. "A remote one, I'll admit—"

"What I meant was," Cane interrupted her, "if the system *is* camouflaged, then I doubt my sibling is responsible."

My sibling . . . The words made Roche's skin crawl. Sometimes it was hard to accept that Cane and the Sol Wunderkind that had effectively destroyed Palasian System were of the same breed—possibly even identical in every respect.

"Why not?" she asked.

"Because, tactically speaking, it makes no sense to be confined to a single system. If I were in his shoes, I would want to move on, taking with me only the resources needed to make my task easier at my next destination." Cane's shoulders lifted in a smooth and easy shrug, as though he were discussing a poor tactic in a barroom game, not the destruction of a whole system. "Also, to hide in such a manner would be tantamount to admitting defeat. Camouflaged or not, it's only a matter of time before the system is found—if not by us, then by someone else."

Roche nodded. "It could be a decoy, then. Something to keep us occupied while he slips away."

"A lot of effort for little reward. However he did it, *if* he did it, it must have been enormously energy-expensive."

"Maybe. But what if—"

Box's soft, controlled voice cut across her own: "There's really no point even trying to guess until we have more data, Morgan."

"Okay, okay." Roche raised her arms in mock defeat. Sitting in her chair, she faced the main screen to check the status of the ship: it was about to emerge from the short slow-jump that had begun so awkwardly. Maybe when Haid appeared, they could discuss the situation in more detail.

<There is no known way to block epsense,> said Maii, continuing the conversation Cane had interrupted, <apart from at the source. Any thought that slips past a mental shield can be detected. No matter how small. The most powerful E-shield wouldn't even weaken it.>

Roche nodded, absorbing that fact without comment.

"Emerging from hyperspace in fifteen seconds," said Kajic, his voice issuing from the base of the holographic projector. Now that he had no crew to impress, he only occasionally bothered to manifest in physical form.

The ship groaned back into reality as noisily as it had left. Roche held onto the edge of her seat as the floor writhed beneath her, seeming to melt for an instant as space transformed. Somewhere nearby, something clattered. When the ship stabilized, she forced her muscles to relax, then looked around.

"Someone warn me next time," said Haid from the entrance to the bridge. He held a tray in his new hand and, bending, used his other hand to pick up packages of food that had spilled during the disturbance.

"Klaxons sound automatically prior to every translation," said the Box.

"Yeah, but who listens to them?" Haid finished piling the meal back onto the tray. "I thought this ship could handle anything."

"Not quite," said Kajic. "But close enough."

Haid's face lost some of its good humor at the sound of the ex-Dato Bloc captain's voice.

"Yeah, well," he said, taking a seat at an empty station. "When the Box summoned me, I thought I'd bring breakfast up here. Hope that's okay."

Roche frowned, puzzled. She hadn't asked the Box to summon anyone. "Box? What's going on?"

"I have an announcement to make," the AI said. "The preliminary survey is now complete and, although much of the data remains to be processed, I have one confirmed observation to report. In accordance with your wishes, Morgan, I summoned Haid to ensure that the entire crew was present to hear it."

Roche didn't respond immediately. The Box wasn't normally so considerate of her wishes. It smacked of overcompensation, as though it was courting disapproval elsewhere.

"Continue," she said after a moment. If it *was* planning something, then she would have to wait until later to find out what it was.

The Box complied, calling up a number of complicated diagrams on the main screen. "At the heart of the region formerly occupied by Palasian System lies a radiant point-source."

"A singularity?" Roche broke in. She hadn't even considered the possibility that the system had been sucked into a black hole.

"No," said the Box. "The point-source appears to have zero mass and is radiant predominantly in the upper infrared spectrum. I have detected what may be a cloud of primordial gas surrounding the point-source, but will have to make more observations before confirming that suspicion."

"How close are we?" asked Haid, clearly as disturbed by the thought of a black hole nearby as Roche was, despite the Box's assurance of their safety.

"Twelve billion kilometers." The map on the screen highlighted points as the Box spoke. "The next slow-jump will halve that distance."

"Is that a good idea?" asked Roche.

"All available evidence indicates that the risk of undertaking such a maneuver would be small."

"The risk for whom?" said Roche. "Yourself or all of us?"

The Box hesitated before snapping: "Both, of course."

Roche smiled at the Box's apparent indignation. "Okay," she said. "Then I can't see why we shouldn't do it. As soon as you're ready—"

<I have something.> Soft but clear, Maii's words touched Roche's thoughts—as, she assumed, they touched everyone else's simultaneously.

Roche looked across the bridge, the discussion of the point-source instantly shelved. The Surin's face was blank, indicating intense concentration, as it had been since the end of the last jump.

"What is it?" Roche asked, leaning closer.

<Something strange.> The girl frowned. <Or an echo of something. I can't tell which. It's very faint. I've missed it so far because it's so hard to sense at all.>

"Describe it," Roche prodded.

<It's not a person—but it is alive.> Confusion deepened Maii's frown. <A great distance from here, yet close. I don't understand what I'm seeing.>

"Are you picking up any *thoughts*?" Roche pressed.

<None. Not even a base emotion.>

"Could it be an AI, then, or hidden by a very effective shield?"

<A shield would leak somewhere, and not even the Box has thoughts I can read.> The reave's body sagged. <Damn. Every time I think I've got a grip on it, I lose it again. It's like trying to catch air!>

Roche reached out with a mental hand to touch the Surin's straining mind and ease her frustration. "It's okay, Maii. Wait until the next jump. It might be stronger then."

"'It' might be the anomaly itself," suggested Haid.

"Now there's a possibility I *don't* want to consider." Roche sighed as warning Klaxons began to sound again. "Box, any thoughts on that?"

"None that would not offend."

The rare joke from the Box elicited a chuckle from Haid, but one that was short-lived. The Box's sense of humor—usually at the expense of carbon-based life forms or epsense science—only reinforced its uniqueness. Roche also detected a faint hint of annoyance, as though it was peeved that the reave had taken the wind out of its sails, ruining the effect of its big announcement.

Maii emerged from her trance as the ship jumped in accordance with the Box's wishes. <I sensed no malice,> she said, her mental voice clearly audible through the groaning of metal. The slow-jump was easily the most uncomfortable so far.

"That's something." Haid folded his arms. "But I'd still feel happier knowing what we were heading for."

"A black hole doesn't have to bear us any ill will to be dangerous," agreed Kajic.

"It is not a black hole," asserted the Box.

"Famous last words," muttered the ex-mercenary.

"I agree with Kajic," said Cane. "Just because it's a natural phenomenon doesn't mean it can't still be deadly."

"At least we could go in with weapons armed," added Haid.

"Do it, then." Roche concurred with the ex-mercenary's unspoken message: sitting around waiting was only making them more tense. "Cane, work with him."

"Done." The two men crossed the bridge to take positions at the weapons station.

"Anything else to report, Box?"

"Some inconclusive findings," it said.

"Such as?" she persisted, silently cursing the AI's reticence.

"The steep flexure gradient in this region is suggestive of significant, and recent, spatial trauma."

Roche's eyebrows knitted. "That means nothing to me."

"Space-time has been warped on a massive scale," the Box translated. "The traumatized region occupies a disc-shaped area roughly seventeen billion kilometers across and two billion kilometers thick. The radiant point-source lies at the heart of this region, although I have been unable as yet to determine whether it is the cause of the flexure or simply another effect. It is conceivable, perhaps even likely, that the point-source and the anomaly are different facets of the same phenomenon. However, more research is required before I can be certain of that."

"How much more?"

"That depends on the result of this slow-jump," the Box replied. "We will be jumping to the very edge of what should be Palasian System, not far from the anchor point that was our original destination. It is my conjecture that the degree of flexure will increase sharply at this point."

"Proving . . . ?"

"Again, I hesitate to speculate until we have concrete data."

Roche grunted. "How long, then?"

"I estimate fifteen minutes before we arrive at our destination."

"So soon?"

"As a result of the flexure gradient, our relative velocity is greatly increased. In a sense, the anomaly has been drawing us toward the point-source."

"It sounds even more like a black hole, now," said Haid over his shoulder.

"The effect is only relative to real space," continued the Box. "In hyperspace, we are actually fighting an uphill battle: although our movement in hyperspace corresponds to greater than normal movement in the real universe, it is becoming increasingly difficult to move in hyperspace at all. I have consulted Kajic and arrived at a maximum output rating for the slow-jump drive—a rating which we will not exceed."

Roche nodded in satisfaction. Even though she didn't understand how progress could be easier in real-space but more difficult in hyperspace, at least Kajic and the Box were cooperating.

<I'm picking up that trace again,> said Maii into the break in conversation.

Roche glanced across the bridge. The Surin was frowning once more. "Where?"

<I'm not sure. It's always hard to tell from hyperspace. The trace is definitely stronger, but maybe no closer. There's still no sense of threat.>

"Can you at least tell if it's mundane?"

The reave looked troubled. <Part of me says it isn't, but that's just a gut feeling. High Human, perhaps, but I don't think it's that either. The source is something I've never come across before.>

A Sol Wunderkind? Roche wanted to ask, but didn't. Maii would have said if that were the case. Yet she couldn't quash the thought: something in hyperspace was pushing them away while in real-space drawing them closer. If not the fugitive, then what?

Roche folded her arms and watched the main screen as the minutes ticked by; the large number of unknowns made her want to scream out in frustration. She needed answers, not possibilities.

<If there *are* any answers,> put in Maii, <we'll find them when we find Palasian System.>

Before Roche could acknowledge the truth of the reave's comment, a low rumble echoed through the ship, beginning at the stern and fading to silence at the distant prow.

"Now what?" asked Roche, looking around in alarm.

"Uh—one moment," said Kajic.

"We had a flicker of red lights down the port hull," said Haid, "but they've cleared now."

"A slight disturbance," said the Box. "Nothing to be concerned about."

Roche bit her tongue until Kajic delivered his own report.

"No problems with the drive," said the ex-captain finally. "We must have encountered some sort of turbulence. Possibly a hyperspatial shock wave of some kind."

"The anomaly again?" said Roche.

"It seems likely."

"We are nearing the edge of the anomaly," said the AI. "Obviously there will be some turbulence."

"Aimed at us, perhaps?" suggested Haid.

"No," said the Box. "Describing what we are experiencing as a shock wave is peculiarly apt. The turbulence may be caused by the anomaly only in the same way that the presence of a large mass 'causes' gravity."

"Not deliberate then, but symptomatic." Roche ran a hand restlessly along the arm of her chair. "It's all the same from this end, isn't it?"

"Not really," said the Box. "If we can piece together a pattern to the symptoms, we should be able to deduce the nature of the anomaly that is causing it."

"Here comes another one," said Cane, his head cocked, listening.

The groan returned, as gradually as before but noticeably louder when it peaked. Roche, her hands pressed firmly into the chair's armrests, felt a faint buzz through her fingertips.

"Could it hurt us, Uri?" she asked.

"Conceivably, yes. The stress is caused by sympathetic vibrations in the hull. So far I have been able to dampen the resonance."

"Let me know if it gets too bad."

"I will. If we encounter it again."

Roche waited anxiously as the ship traveled onward. Barely two minutes later, a third shock wave rolled through the ship, this time accompanied by a sluing sensation to starboard and down, as though the ship were being dragged off course.

"Red lights again," said Haid.

An instant later, from Cane: "Clear."

Roche waited on edge for Kajic's report.

"No damage," he said finally. "But it was definitely more severe. The closer we get to the anomaly, the stronger they're becoming."

"Can we ride them for much longer?"

"If they continue worsening at this rate, no," said Kajic. "But we'll come close."

"Good enough." Roche swiveled her chair to face the main screen. Only a handful of minutes remained before the slow-jump was due to end. "Pull us out the moment we can't take it. I'll leave that decision in your hands."

"Understood."

As another groan began to build, Roche again gripped the chair's armrests, and held on tight. She felt as though a bell were tolling directly behind her head, a bell so large that its vibrations were absorbed by her bones rather than heard. Before it had completely faded, another swelled to take its place.

"Box," she said, raising her voice above the noise. "If you have *any* idea at all what that anomaly is, I want to hear it."

"I now have several theories, Morgan. Which is the correct one, of course, remains to be seen."

Roche opened her mouth to demand an outline of the various possibilities, but was cut off by a sudden lurch upward. Her stomach dropped, then rose again, into her chest.

"We're experiencing gravity fluctuations," said Kajic. "I can only keep us going another fifty seconds."

Roche studied the main screen, momentarily tempted to call a halt. Their planned arrival point was inching slowly closer. Given a further half-minute, they would almost make it. She decided to trust Kajic's instincts.

"There must be some way to dampen the shock waves," she said.

"I'll raise the E-shields, but I don't think that'll help much." The ex-captain's voice sounded strained.

"Whatever you can do, Uri."

The noise worsened, despite the shields, as did the rolling sensation in Roche's gut. Maii, lacking eyes of her own and therefore more susceptible to balance problems, looked decidedly uncomfortable. Haid had taken the precaution of fastening his impact harness. Cane, behind him, was as steadfast as ever—but even he swayed when a particularly strong wave shunted the ship in an unexpected direction.

Roche watched the seconds counting down on the big screen: 21 . . . 20 . . . 19 . . .

The shock waves became inseparable, and the ship seemed to toss on the surface of a stormy sea. Red lights flickered on and off across all the boards, registering slight damage across the hull. Most would be repaired almost instantly by the tide of maintenance nanomachines swarming over every external surface of the ship, but the fact that they were occurring at all was disturbing.

Ten seconds remained.

Roche watched their destination creep closer. It was becoming increasingly difficult to hear over the prolonged groan surrounding them.

The lights flickered once, steadied, then flickered again.

"We have a standing wave in sectors G through K," announced Kajic grimly. "Preparing to abort the slow-jump."

Five seconds. Roche winced as the smell of ozone reached her nose.

Three seconds. On the main screen, the difference between the ship's current location and its destination was measured in millimeters.

Two seconds—

"Aborting now," said Kajic, the very instant artificial gravity ceased entirely. A siren began to wail a split second later. The lights flickered a third time as the drive drained power from the bulk of the ship to translate itself safely back into real-space. In the short-lived darkness, Roche actually heard the engines strain—a deep, regular thrumming coming from somewhere to her left. Their tempo was rapid but reassuringly regular under the circumstances.

Then the lights returned, unsteadily and noticeably dimmer than they usually were. Space twisted inside out, and the floor bucked under her feet. Her momentum tried to pull her forward, onto the floor and across the bridge. Gripping the chair's armrests even tighter, she resisted the impetus with all her strength. To her left, Maii lost a similar battle and skidded on her knees into a bank of instruments. Even Cane staggered, clasping Haid's shoulder to keep his balance.

The floor bucked again, this time in the opposite direction. Maii gasped in pain as she slid backward and collided with her seat. The bulkheads around them likewise groaned in protest.

"Uri!" Roche shouted above the racket. "What's happening?"

"We are experiencing difficulty emerging from hyperspace," said the Box, its voice amplified but calm—*too* calm for Roche's liking. "I will act as an intermediary between Kajic and yourself for the time being. The ship is his primary concern at the moment."

Another jolt almost cost Roche her grip. She reached behind and over her shoulder to fasten the seat's restraint harness. "Are we going to make it?"

"I should think so," said the Box. "The chances are very good that we will all survive."

Roche was grateful for the "all." The Box could endure almost anything, and had been known to assume the same indestructibility of its wards in the past. Cane, on the other hand, had already moved across the bridge to help Maii into her harness.

"We have damage," reported Haid from the weapons station, his voice raised to be heard. "Lost some banks on the starboard bow. I don't quite know what happened; looks like they've been sheared clean off. No pressure drops reported, though, and hull integrity's intact."

Roche concentrated on what he was saying. "What have we lost?"

"Hypershields in that area. Some A-P cannon. We'll be able to compensate easily enough."

"Good. We—uh!" The *Ana Vereine* swung to starboard, then down; Roche winced as her restraint harness cut deep into her chest. The thrumming of the engines rose in both pitch and intensity until it became a screaming—like the screaming of a mighty wind—

—she was falling—

—and nausea flared deep within her as the association with the dream made her feel impotent and therefore even more anxious.

The main screen flickered, attracting her attention. Abstract representations of their course swirled into increasingly complex shapes, then disappeared entirely, leaving nothing in their wake. White lines scattered across the screen, making Roche blink; then it went black again.

Without warning, the ship began to steady. Bulkheads settled back into place with a series of decreasing creaks. The screaming of the engines ebbed, losing the desperate edge that had contributed to Roche's anxiety. The groan of tortured space faded with one last rending sound, then ceased entirely.

In the sudden silence, Roche didn't dare ask the question.

She didn't need to.

"We made it," said Kajic, his voice from near Roche's right shoulder clear and relieved.

"Yes," echoed the Box, its voice oddly hushed. "We most certainly did."

At that moment, the main screen came back to life. Blinding light filled the bridge, dazzling Roche until she managed to bring an arm up to protect her eyes. Compensators cut in an instant later, reducing the glare to more manageable levels. Through the gaps between her fingers, Roche peered at what lay before them.

"What the hell is that?" exclaimed Haid, preempting her own initial reaction.

A blazing yellow-white oval filled the center of the screen. At first she thought it was a sun, but the shape was wrong: it was distorted as though giant hands had gripped it at each pole and stretched it lengthwise. In addition, there were no flares or prominences, no hints of corona or sunspots. Just light, bright and unceasing, coming from something far too close for comfort.

There was only one thing it could be.

"It's the point-source," she said, directing her words at the Box.

"Precisely," it replied, as she'd half hoped it would not.

"But we should be millions of kilometers away from it. I thought you were taking us to the edge of where the system used to be—"

"I did. Yet here we are, only a short distance from what appears to be the center. Remarkable, isn't it?"

Remarkable? Roche echoed to herself. She could think of words to describe it, but that wasn't one of them.

Before she could say anything, however, Haid's voice broke into the conversation.

"We have targets!" he called. "Someone else got here before us!"

"Where?" she asked, instantly turning her seat to face his station.

"Two behind us," he said. "One on the far side of whatever that thing is. Emissions suggest ships, probably Commonwealth, but it's hard to be sure. There's some sort of interference fudging our data."

"They've seen us," said Cane. "One of them is moving in to engage."

"Launch base-line probes and broadcast our ID," Roche directed, her heart pounding as she considered their options. To Kajic she added: "Uri, keep well out of their way until we know what they are and who sent them. We don't want to intimidate them unnecessarily."

"Don't worry about that," Haid shot back dryly. "I won't be making *any* moves until you can prove to me there isn't a clone warrior on one of those ships."

Roche watched nervously as the view shifted on the main screen. Numerous tiny drones spread out in a circle away from the *Ana Vereine,* expanding their base line of observation and thereby improving the clarity and range of the picture. The third ship came into view, oddly distorted like the glowing object it had been hiding behind. It was hard to determine exactly what sort of ship it was, let alone where it hailed from; the image was of a warped white line, burning bright with reflected light.

"Box," she said, "can you figure out what's jamming us?"

"There is no deliberate interference of transmissions in this region," said the Box.

"No? Then—"

"Our sensors are being swamped by emissions from the point-source. It is extremely radiant in both infrared electromagnetic and Perez radiations."

Roche blinked, surprised. Perez radiation was a side effect of a crudely tuned hyperspace jump, not what she would have expected of a seemingly stellar object.

Before she could inquire further, the Box went on: "Try looking for transmissions on the Eckandi emergency band. It should be relatively unaffected."

Roche gestured for Haid to do as the Box suggested. Within seconds, a rapid pulse of sound from the speakers of the main screen indicated that the ship had detected a digital transmission. An instant later, text appeared on the main screen and the pulse became an audible voice:

"—ONLY WARNING. REPEAT: YOU ARE IN CONTRAVENTION OF THE COMMONWEALTH OF EMPIRES SECURITY ACT, SECTIONS 45, 63, AND 72. THIS AREA HAS BEEN QUARANTINED. LEAVE IMMEDIATELY OR PREPARE TO BE FIRED UPON. THIS IS YOUR FIRST AND ONLY WARNING. MESSAGE ENDS."

The voice spoke with the clear, crisp tones of a machine, not a Human—but that hardly made its words any less appalling. Roche took only a second to absorb the implications of its message.

An ambush.

"Haid, Cane—move us away," she said, thinking furiously. "Don't do anything else unless I tell you. Box, signal that we wish to respond; see if you can initiate a dialogue—or even subvert the AI to let us go." Even as she spoke the words, she knew it was unlikely the Box would be capable of doing this quickly enough. Nevertheless, she had to at least explore the possibility. "Uri, continue with repairs. Get that down shield back up as soon as you can. And Maii, find out what they're doing here and who the hell sent them. I need to know whether or not we have a chance of convincing them to let us through."

From her seat on the far side of the bridge, the reave shook her head. <I can't,> she said.

"What?" Roche swiveled to face her. "Why not?"

<I can't read them.> The reave's voice was strangely muffled, as though her thoughts were coming from a great distance rather than only from across the room.

<They're not shielded. I just can't pick them up at all. If I could, I would have detected them long before now. We would have known they were here before we arrived.>

Roche frowned. Maii's last comment was worryingly true, if perplexing. "Keep trying. I need to know how they found us and whether or not they knew we were coming. If De Bruyn sent them, we know we'll have to fight, no matter what they say."

"But if they weren't expecting us," put in Haid, "how did they know where we'd be? I thought we couldn't be traced through a slow-jump."

"They didn't need to," replied the Box.

Roche was reminded of the point-source on the screen, twisted as though viewed through a giant lens. The spatial distortion the Box had been monitoring was obviously even more severe than she had imagined: anything trying to enter the space where the system had been was forced to emerge at this point—the heart of the system, yet at the same time its edge.

"They just sat here and waited," she said. "No matter where we tried to go, this is where we'd end up."

"Precisely, Morgan," said the Box.

"And the only way to get away from them is outward, away from where the system should be." She slapped her hand palm down on the side of her chair. "Dammit. We can't leave now, not until we know what the hell is going on!"

"I have convinced someone to let you talk," said the Box. "The AI has put me in direct contact with the officer in command of the primary vessel."

Roche took a deep breath. "Open the line."

"Ready, Morgan."

Roche tried to calm her nerves, then began to speak:

"This is Morgan Roche of the independent vessel *Ana Vereine.* We are traveling as a peaceful envoy under the authorization of Page De Bruyn of COE Intelligence. Why are you harassing us, and by whose authority?"

The moment she finished talking, the automatic broadcast ceased and a Human female voice took its place.

"COE Intelligence has no jurisdiction here," said the woman. "I am Commander Bassett of the COE Armada vessel *Golden Dawn* with orders countersigned by General Ramage. My directive is to prevent all unauthorized vessels from proceeding any further into Palasian System."

"Further *where*?" Roche shot back. "The system's *gone.* And as for authorization, I just gave you mine. We've been sent by the head of COE Intelligence Strategy to study the situation here, and to offer what help—"

The woman broke in firmly: "Your help is not required. Should you not leave immediately, then *I* have been authorized to use whatever force is necessary to ensure your compliance. You have exactly thirty seconds."

The vocal transmission ceased, and was replaced by the automatic recording.

Roche sat stunned for a moment, unable to believe what she had heard. Treachery she had learned to deal with, but not this blind, military farce.

"We've got confirmation on the ID," said Haid. "It's the *Golden Dawn,* and it's an Armada vessel as she said. A destroyer, to be exact."

Not quite a match for the *Ana Vereine,* Roche thought to herself. But there were three of them.

"Maii?" she asked. "Can you persuade them to change their minds?"

<I'm still not picking up anything.> The reave's voice was steeped in apology and confusion. <A few shadows, but nothing definite . . .>

Roche rubbed her forehead. On the main screen, the three Armada ships moved into position around the *Ana Vereine.*

"All shields to full strength," she said, sitting upright in her seat. "Uri, how're those repairs looking?"

"Almost there," Kajic replied. "Another two minutes and we'll be optimal."

Roche glanced at the screen. The *Golden Dawn*'s half-minute deadline had expired twenty seconds ago.

"They mean it, Morgan," said Cane, watching the screen with naked fascination. "They're going to fire."

Remembering the uncanny way he had picked the decisive moment during the battle for the *Midnight,* she didn't hesitate.

"Uri, take evasive action. Haid, arm the disrupters. Cane, prepare to return fire on my command."

"You're going to fight?" asked the Box.

"Do I have any choice?"

"Of course you do," the AI said.

"Well, *what*?" Roche snapped.

"You can turn control of the ship over to me," said the Box.

Roche opened her mouth, then closed it again. "Why?" she eventually managed.

"There is insufficient time to explain, Morgan."

"Try me," she growled.

"I have deduced the exact nature of both the point-source and the anomaly, and in the process have verified the location of Palasian System. By giving me control of the ship, I can take you there in a matter of minutes."

"So tell us where it is and we'll get *ourselves* there."

"Impossible, Morgan. Not that I am underestimating your abilities; there is simply too little time to—"

Lances of energy flashed on the main screen; static momentarily scrambled the picture.

"They're firing on our drones!" announced Haid.

"Take reciprocal action," Roche ordered. Barely had she finished when Cane began destroying the Armada's own base line probes. Specks of light flashed in the space between the three ships, their brightness negligible against the fiercely burning point-source dominating the view.

"They're tightening shields," said Haid.

Roche's thoughts went into overdrive. Tightening shields was a standard tactic in close space warfare. Any moment now, the attack would begin in earnest: the three Armada ships against the *Ana Vereine.* Numbers were against them, but that didn't mean that they would necessarily be overcome. Apart from the *Ana Vereine*'s technological superiority, it also possessed a number of armed scutters and shuttles in its docking bays; she could order the Box to launch these smaller craft to assist in the battle, and have Kajic employ the camouflage to make them harder to target. With so many diffuse targets to aim for, the outcome the Armada expected was far from certain. Still, the *Ana Vereine* was bound to incur *some* damage.

And if it prevailed, what then? They would be unable to return to the Commonwealth for certain after destroying three Armada ships while on a supposedly peaceful mission, and the matter of Palasian System would still be unresolved. If the Box was right, then it had offered her a way to avoid the battle and to reach her goal—both with one decisive move.

She had seen more death in the handful of weeks since meeting Adoni Cane than she had in twelve years of active service for COE Intelligence. The thought of still more on her conscience made the decision easier than she expected.

At that very moment, the *Golden Dawn* opened fire.

"Incoming!" Haid's shout echoed through the bridge, closely followed by a juddering wrench as a full volley of flicker-bombs impacted upon the ship's aft hyper-shields. Cane's fingers played the weapons board like a virtuoso as Kajic swung the ship to bear on its primary antagonist. As the exchange intensified, violent discharges painted the space between the two ships with fiery colors of death.

"Box!" Roche called out over the sounds of battle: the shouts, the explosions, the roaring of engines. "Whatever you've got planned, do it fast!"

"Thank you, Morgan." The AI's reply was more gracious than Roche had expected, considering the moral victory it had won. To Haid and Cane the Box said: "Maintain a covering fire across the ship on the upper left of your screens. On my command, prepare to release proximity mines to prevent them from following."

Haid frowned at the screen. The ship the Box had indicated was the one that had been hiding behind the point-source; even now, the white-hot object filled most of that segment of the screen. "Where the hell—?"

"Do it, Ameidio," Roche ordered, even though she felt less than certain herself.

"I have surrendered control of the slow-jump drive to the Box," said Kajic via her implants, "and I will obey its orders until you tell me otherwise."

Roche nodded dumbly, wondering what the Box wanted with the drive, and why it wanted sole control over the systems. So close to the point-source, massless or not, even the smallest slow-jump had to be risky.

"Prepare for acceleration," announced the Box. "Maximum reactive power in fifteen seconds!"

As though the commander of the *Golden Dawn* had sensed Roche's change of plan, the Armada ships drew closer in a sudden rush, two of them overlapping shields and forming a solid wall of defense. The third sent bolt after bolt of energy hurtling toward the *Ana Vereine*—an assault designed to weaken E-shields prior to the arrival of a second wave of A-P fire and flicker-bombs.

An instant before the second wave arrived, the *Ana Vereine* surged forward. Roche was pressed back into her seat as the view through the main screen rushed at her. The single ship the Box had targeted reacted instantly, obviously believing that the *Ana Vereine* intended to ram; its E-shield formed a narrow cone pointed at the hurtling ship, hoping either to deflect it off course or to spear through its hull.

The Box's intention was farther afield, however. The *Ana Vereine* changed course an instant before striking the shield. As the Armada ship flashed by, Roche began to guess where they were headed. At the same time, the two vessels they had left behind began to turn, accelerating in pursuit.

The sound of proximity mines being fired behind them rattled in her ears. Two caught the single ship by surprise, slipping through its weakened aft shields and impacting on its hull. Damage was minor, but significant. Cane focused more and more firepower on the injured ship until it was forced to turn away, leaving the chase to its more distant, but fitter, siblings.

Too late. There was no way now that any of the ships could intercept the *Ana Vereine;* its lead was too great, and its destination too close.

Roche watched numbly as the image of the point-source swelled in the main screen. Not even automatic compensators could dull its brilliance.

I hope you know what you're doing, Box, she thought to herself.

Haid stared mutely up at the screen, his fingers working the disrupter controls automatically. Then a hand fell across his own.

"It's all right," Cane said. "The E-shields can manage from here."

"No they can't," Roche said urgently, leaning forward. "We'll need everything up front. Kajic, what's the ambient temperature and composition of the region ahead?"

"Unknown," was the ex-captain's reply. "Our instruments are—"

"Prepare for imminent hyperspace translation," the Box broke in.

"What?" On hearing the AI's intentions, Roche instantly regretted giving it absolute control. "You can't be serious! We're too close—"

"Not close enough, actually," returned the Box. "But we will be in ten seconds. Fasten your harnesses, everyone. This will be rough."

Roche's hands gripped her seat as the point-source ballooned to fill the entire main screen. She was dimly aware of the others around her—even Cane—doing the same, and of the stubborn thumping of the Armada guns on their aft shields, still harassing the *Ana Vereine* from behind. Part of her recalled the way the Box had threatened a collision course with COE Intelligence HQ under similar circumstances; she could only hope that its timing and intentions were as critical now as they had been then.

White fire consumed the screen. Sirens began to wail. The ship jerked once; she thought she heard Kajic call something to her. Then:

Space flowered open before them, unfolding in a series of crimson waves that quickly and violently enveloped the *Ana Vereine.* The ship shivered from nose to tail, shaken by forces Roche could only imagine. At the center of the vortex, several tiny specks of light flickered into being—only to disappear again as the main screen went black.

Then everything simply stopped.

2

IND *Ana Vereine*
'955.01.19 EN
0805

The main screen was empty.

Roche stared at it for a few moments, expecting it to suddenly clear and fill with . . . *what*? She had no idea what she expected to see out there. She had no idea where the Box had even taken them.

When it became apparent that the screen wasn't about to change, she swiveled around to check the others on the bridge. Cane had freed himself from his restraint harness and was assisting Maii back into her seat, their movements in the unnatural silence oddly loud and unreal. When he stepped away from her, Roche saw that the girl's head was bleeding slightly from her fall. Haid, the hand of his new arm resting on a touch pad, was still staring quizzically at the view that Roche had just turned from.

Then it struck her: the drive was no longer audible. But the *Ana Vereine* hadn't completed its slow-jump. It had just . . . stopped.

"Uri," she asked, her voice booming in the quiet. "What's going on?"

The holographic projector in the center of the bridge flickered. Kajic's image appeared through the static, the light brown skin and black hair of his old body looking as composed as always. His expression was serious, but not concerned.

"Minor damage," said the ex-captain. "We weathered the stress well."

"How long until we can see where we are?"

"My sensors are gathering some unusual data. The Box is checking to see if the irregularities are due to instrument malfunction. When its diagnosis is complete, vision will be restored."

"I have partial telemetry readings," said Haid from the weapons console. After a moment he reported: "No targets. No sign of the point-source, either. We must have left them all behind when we jumped."

"We did jump, then?" Roche asked Kajic.

"Well, we certainly entered hyperspace," said Kajic.

"But have we *left* it?"

"I didn't think an open-ended jump was possible," Haid said.

Kajic's image shrugged. "You'll have to ask the Box. I just did as it told me."

Roche put her palm on the arm-link of her chair, intending to access the raw data herself, but changed her mind before she did so. Better to remain distant for a moment rather than dive in headfirst. She needed to maintain a measure of objectivity if a quick decision was required.

"There appears to be a planet nearby," said Kajic. "That much I can tell you. A medium-sized gas giant if its mass reading is accurate."

"Try cross-referencing it with the navigation records of Palasian System," said Roche. "A match would at least confirm where we are."

Kajic dissolved in a burst of static that lasted a few heartbeats. When he reformed, he said: "There's a ninety-nine percent chance the planet is Voloras, the outermost planet of Palasian System. If so, that places us well inside the cometary shell and the third dark body halo."

Roche searched her memory for what she knew about the system. "Wasn't there a refueling base around Voloras?"

"Guhr Outpost," confirmed Kajic.

"Any signals?"

"Apart from some strong crackles on the hydrogen band," said Haid, "we aren't getting a thing on any frequency."

"Try elsewhere," Roche said. "This far out, we should be able to pick up hyperspace transmissions."

"Already tried," said Haid. "Nothing; not even the beacon of the local anchor point."

"That can't be right." Roche frowned. "We're near the N'Kor border, and the Kesh have warning stations every few light-years—"

"I'm telling you, Morgan," said Haid, glancing over his shoulder. "There's nothing there."

"How could *all* of those beacons be blocked?" Roche could feel her confusion gradually developing into frustration. "Uri, *could* it be instrument failure?"

Before Kajic could reply, the Box cut in:

"It *is* possible, Morgan. And the fact that it has happened confirms my hypothesis quite neatly." At that moment, the main screen cleared. "Welcome to Palasian System."

Roche studied the screen. Initially she saw nothing but darkness—not even stars. Then the view changed, and a single red speck slid into view. Increased magnification made the speck a bright circle. The image was too fuzzy to make out any detail, but there was no mistaking what it was: against the unnaturally black background, one solitary sun burned.

"It can't be," she muttered, standing. "Hintubet is a calcium star—"

"And should be on the green side of yellow," the Box interrupted. "I am aware of that fact, Morgan. The difficulty in reconciling the emission spectrum of this star and that which Hintubet's *should* be was the main reason I delayed giving you this information. Now that I have had time to collate the data and to extrapolate from historical records, I believe I can say with certainty that this *is* Hintubet, albeit with a wildly altered photosphere."

"The star has changed?" asked Haid. *"How?"*

"The precise method is unknown at the moment; the archives lack specifics in that regard, although the general principles are clear. Until we dispatch probes to study Hintubet in more detail, we are limited to the data we can scavenge from this distance."

"Which isn't enough," said Roche. She faced Kajic. "Uri, I want high-speed drones launched to the sun and any planetary bodies we can find." She turned back to the screen. "Speaking of which, any sign of Voloras?"

The red star shrank and slid out of view. Seconds later, the crescent of a large planet appeared, red-tinged due to the sun's baleful light. The image of the planet came to rest in the center of the screen, its dense atmosphere swirled with gray bands.

"I have dispatched a probe," said Kajic. "The base line is already large enough for us to detect four moons."

"Voloras has five," said Roche.

"The fifth may be occluded," said Kajic. "The sizes of the four we can see match COE records."

"How long until the probe can get a decent look at the base?"

"One hour and fifty minutes. Guhr Outpost is on the missing moon."

Roche nodded. "Until then, we can't afford to take anything for granted. Give us a heading that will take us by Voloras, with the option to use it as a gravity-whip if we decide not to stop. Leave a drone behind to relay the data from the probes. I want the ship camouflaged, too, just in case someone saw us arrive and is waiting for us there."

Kajic's image winked out as he went to work.

Roche slumped back into her chair with a sigh and rubbed at her temples. They appeared to be in Palasian System, just as the Box had promised they would be. But it wasn't quite what she had expected: no hyperspace transmissions, a profoundly altered primary, and no stars in sight.

The first and last details suggested that the system had indeed been encapsulated within some sort of barrier. But what? She knew of no process that could hide an entire system from view *and* account for the warped space outside.

Or did she? The change in the sun's appearance did ring a faint bell. A name she had heard back in her days on the moon of Bodh Gaya, when she had been studying for her Armada exams, returned to her . . .

"Asha's Gauntlet," she said aloud.

"I'm impressed, Morgan," said the Box. "I didn't think you would work it out so—"

"We're picking up a transmission!" Haid broke in.

"Where?" Roche swiveled to face him, automatically linking with the weapons system. If life remained in the system, the chances were good that it belonged to the Sol Wunderkind. And if he was signaling them, then he knew where they were.

"It's not directed at us." Haid was skimming through the various diagnostic tools that enabled him to enhance a weak signal. "It's a wide-beam microwave from in-system. I'm picking up echoes off several objects near the source; the slight delays should give us a fair triangulation."

Roche let herself relax slightly. The signal must have been sent some time ago, given the distance at light-speed to the inner system.

"What about the content of the transmission?" she said.

"It's in some sort of cipher," Haid told her, then shook his head. "Haven't broken it yet, which isn't a good sign. They either crack immediately or take forever."

"Box, have a go at it," she said. Haid's refinement of the signal's source proceeded while she watched. The area containing a probable location of the transmitter gradually narrowed on a diagnostic display, until a single point flashed once and turned green.

"Got it," Haid said.

Roche overlaid a navigation chart. "It's the same distance from the primary as Jagabis would have been. And Jagabis has moons."

Haid nodded. "That'd give us the echoes."

"Uri, do we have confirmation of a planet in this area?"

Kajic's image returned at the mention of his name. "Not yet. It's off to one side of Hintubet, and I haven't searched that area in any detail yet. Now that I'm looking, it shouldn't take long to find—" He stopped, smiled. "In fact, there it is. Give me a little longer and I'll be able to estimate its mass."

"It *has* to be Jagabis," Roche said. "Someone's alive there."

"The signal could be a beacon," Haid suggested.

"In cipher? Unlikely," said Roche. "Besides, Jagabis was the innermost gas giant in the system. If I remember correctly, the main spaceport and colony were on one of its moons."

"Correct," said the Box. "The moon is called Aro, the colony Emptage City."

"Right," said Roche. "So if there are survivors, that's the first place to look."

"I can get us there in two days," said Kajic. "Faster if we flyby Voloras."

Roche nodded. "Plot a course, but don't do anything definite until we decipher the message."

Cane stirred, speaking for the first time since their arrival. "It could be a warning," he said. "Or a trap."

Roche looked over at him. "For whom? It couldn't be us. We weren't even here when that message was transmitted."

"True," Cane said. "But I find it disturbing nonetheless. The impression I get is that someone is still fighting."

"That's a good sign," said Roche. "That there's the slightest resistance left in the system is something of a miracle."

"Which is precisely what bothers me." The bridge's light glowed in his unblinking eyes. "I would never have been so careless as to leave any survivors."

Roche met his calm expression uneasily, his words reminding her of the ruthlessness of the adversary they were hunting—and of Cane's ancestry.

"It's worth checking, at least," she said after a moment. Then, turning from Cane, turning from the thought, she said: "Have you sent a probe, Uri?"

"I have dispatched five so far," Kajic reported. "Three are under way to Hintubet, Voloras, and Jagabis; the other two are heading to Cartha's Planet, the innermost world, and Cemenid, the largest. There are four planets outstanding: Herensung, Gatamin, Kukumat and Murukan."

"The last two being the double world?" Roche asked.

"That's right. There are also some sizable rocks in the dark body halos that might be worth exploring, but they're not a priority at the moment. I'll let you know when we have the system mapped."

"Okay." Roche visualized the bulletlike probes crossing the system under accelerations that not even the *Ana Vereine*'s protective fields could negate, thereby traversing the empty space more quickly than they could ever hope to. Even so, it would be hours before they started getting any data. At light-speed, the lag across the system was appreciable.

"That transmission just ended," said Haid.

"Box?" Roche said. "How's the deciphering coming along?"

"Completed," said the AI. "However, the translation is proving difficult. It appears to be in a language with which I am unfamiliar."

"Show me."

Several lines of standard alphanumeric script flowed across the screen. Roche studied it for a moment before admitting that she too was stumped. "It's definitely a language, not another cipher?"

"Without sufficient text to analyze, I am unable to do more than guess."

"Fair enough. Keep guessing, then, Box, and let me know if you come up with anything."

"Certainly."

"Uri, how long until the Voloras flyby?"

"One hour and thirty-seven minutes."

Roche sat back with a weary sigh, running a hand through her cropped hair. She was already impatient with the delay in obtaining information. Being trapped in this system without any idea of what was going on or even where the clone warrior might be filled her with anxiety.

"I don't suppose there's any way you could hurry things along?" she said wryly.

"Not unless you know some way to circumvent the barriers of light-speed, Morgan," said Kajic.

Roche smiled tiredly.

"There is," said Cane.

Roche looked over to him. "What?"

"Thought is not constrained by the physical laws of the universe," said Cane.

Roche sat forward with a start. *Maii!* If the girl could contact the minds of the people behind the transmission, Roche would have the data she needed immediately.

Only then did she realize that the reave had neither moved nor spoken since shortly after the *Ana Vereine* had arrived in Palasian System. Roche turned to see what the problem was.

The Surin girl sat motionless on the edge of her seat with her hands clasped together in her lap. A thin line of blood had trickled down from the gash on her forehead, staining red the white material of her blindfold.

"Maii? Are you all right?"

There was no response.

Roche moved over to the reave, squatting down in front of her to examine the small lesion on the girl's forehead. It seemed to Roche to be nothing more than a superficial cut, and yet . . .

"Maii?" Still no reply. She touched the girl's shoulders and tried again: "Maii, can you—?"

Startled, Maii jumped back in her seat, pushing Roche's hand away.

<Maii, it's me!> Roche fought to restrain the reave's flailing arms. <*Maii!* It's Morgan!>

After a moment, the girl's panic subsided and her breathing eased.

<Maii?> said Roche. <Can you hear me?>

<I—I am here, Morgan.> The words were barely a whisper in Roche's mind.

<Are you okay? You're very faint.>

<So are you.> There was an edge of confusion to her words. <I couldn't sense you at all. There was nothing. I was afraid you were all dead.>

Roche winced as a wave of images and emotions washed into her mind: fear, loneliness, darkness, panic . . . She concentrated, doing her best to hold the mental inrush at bay while trying to radiate reassurance to the Surin child. When the torrent of emotions ebbed, Roche continued.

<We've been here all the time, talking unshielded as we always do. Surely you picked up something?>

<Only Cane,> replied the reave. <But nothing specific. I just knew he was there—somewhere.>

Roche searched the girl's blank face. The blood on her cheek stood out against pale skin and hair. <Could it have been the blow to your head?>

<No. It's nothing like that. Your thoughts are being . . . smothered. It's like only the ones specifically directed at me can get through, and even then only if their source is nearby—as you are now.>

<Smothered?> Roche repeated. <By what?>

<I don't know.> Almost imperceptibly, Maii shrugged. <All I can tell you is that it started when we arrived at the point-source. But it didn't become severe until we slow-jumped.>

<So whatever's causing it must be somewhere in the system with us.> Roche rocked back on her haunches as she considered the reave's words. Another ominous sign. <Is there anything I can do to help?>

Maii nodded slowly. <Physical contact strengthens an epsense link. If you were to keep touching me . . .>

Roche's understanding filled the void of the Surin's unfinished sentence. The thought of Maii locked in the darkness of the blind and deaf-mute easily overrode her reservations—even though it meant having the girl constantly at her side. The last person to have depended on her so totally had killed himself to save her—

She stamped down on the memory. The last thing Maii needed right now was to have both of them dwelling on Veden's death.

<Thank you, Morgan.> The girl half smiled. <I can read you clearly, but will respect your privacy.>

"Is she all right?" Cane called out from his station.

"She will be," Roche replied, then said to Maii: <Can you stand?>

<Yes.>

<Good. If we can't use you to hunt for survivors, then you can help me brush up on local geography instead.> Taking one of Maii's hands in her own, Roche raised the girl to her feet. Together, with Maii's hand on her arm, they moved across the bridge to Roche's seat. The reave remained standing when Roche sat, her hand resting on the older woman's shoulder.

<Are we really in Palasian System?> Maii asked.

<The Box brought us here after the Armada ships attacked,> said Roche.

<How?>

<That's a little hard to explain. Hang on. I'll see if we can get the Box in on this conversation. The others might like to hear, too.>

Triggering her implants, Roche spoke aloud: "Box, if you've got the time, I'd like to talk to you about Asha's Gauntlet."

"Of course, Morgan."

"We studied them under Weapons Conventions in Military College," she explained to the others. "The idea is to turn a star into a giant hypershield generator or something. Is that right, Box?"

"Essentially," replied the Box. "A primitive 'solar envelope,' as it was originally known, was designed by the Eckandar Trade Axis several thousand years ago. Two prototypes—called *K'mok ni Asha,* which translates as 'Asha's Gauntlet'—were built in the 38th Millennium by the Kesh government. They tested one on a frontier system, but the experiment was a failure. Because of the disastrous results the second prototype was never used. It was rumored to have been dismantled, although this was never confirmed."

"I remember," said Roche, nodding. "The Gauntlet was supposedly designed as a means of protection for a system against attack, but the one experiment they conducted ended up completely destroying the system." Roche looked at the screen, and the sky empty of stars—all but one; the reddened Hintubet now occupied center stage again. "And now it seems we're inside one."

"At first," said the Box, "I was reluctant to accept the possibility that Palasian System had been encapsulated in such a fashion—even though the data suggested as much. It wasn't until we arrived at the point-source—the external manifestation of the Gauntlet's boundary—that the evidence became too conclusive to ignore."

"How does it work?" asked Cane.

The Box explained: "By manipulating a star in precisely the right fashion, it is possible to create and sustain a Riem-Perez Horizon large enough to enclose an entire system."

"That's the same sort of shield COE Intelligence HQ uses, isn't it?" said Roche.

"Correct," said the Box. "And the *Ana Vereine*, and most other ships large enough to power one."

"But we couldn't see the system from the outside," Roche said. "A hypershield isn't the same as camouflage—"

"No; hypershields are used as barriers against hyperspatial attack rather than to hide something from view. However, scale comes into play for Riem-Perez Horizons greater than two thousand cubic kilometers in volume. Space-time can only tolerate such a disturbance on a small scale; any larger and the enclosed area is parceled off and lifted to hyperspace."

"Where we are now," finished Roche.

"Thus the area of space contained within the affected area cannot be seen, because it simply no longer exists in the 'real' universe," said the Box. "The anomaly—which is a boundary effect—is all that remains."

"That explains why the engines stopped in mid-jump," said Kajic. "The jump was literally open-ended—across the boundary and into the space within."

"In a sense, we are still jumping," said the Box.

Cane moved closer to the screen, studying the image with fascination. "It's a remarkable concept," he said. "To *move* an entire system—"

"No distance at all, really," said the Box. "It has no vector relative to the real universe, and will not travel in the same way this ship slow-jumps."

"So I assume it will return when the Gauntlet is switched off?"

"No," said the Box.

"That's where the original Kesh experiment went wrong," added Roche. "It *can't* be switched off."

"The process is extremely energy expensive," explained the Box. "The sun's fuel is exhausted in a matter of weeks, during which time the Gauntlet gradually collapses back to a point. The system is destroyed in the process."

Cane tilted his head. “Then employing a Gauntlet to defend a system would be a pointless exercise.”

“Which is why the Warfare Protocol forbids its use.” Roche nodded at the screen. “It’s no use at all for defense, and would make too destructive a weapon.”

<So why does Palasian System have one?> asked Maii, using Roche’s neural implants as an interface between her and the Box.

“I can think of only one possible explanation,” the AI said. “Any attempt to cross the external boundary of the Gauntlet without simultaneously slow-jumping back to the real universe will result in complete annihilation. Similarly, any attempt to use a hyperspace drive while within the space contained by the Gauntlet will render the drive useless.”

“So if the Sol clone warrior has no access to a hyperspace drive,” Haid cut in, “or doesn’t know how to employ one properly in the Gauntlet, he’ll be unable to leave the system.”

“Exactly,” said the Box.

“A trap, then.” Cane nodded. “And one which is not immediately lethal. But why go to so much trouble?”

“And who laid the trap?” asked Haid.

“Whoever got their hands on the second prototype, I guess,” Roche said. “Which could have been almost anyone, depending on where the Kesh stored it.”

“At least we know one thing,” said Kajic. “It probably wasn’t the Sol Wunderkind.”

“Don’t be so sure about that,” said Haid. “We’re trapped in here, too, remember?”

“Not ‘trapped,’” said the Box. “We can leave any time we wish, simply by crossing the boundary the correct way.”

“But the boundary *is* shrinking, right?” said Haid.

“Yes—”

“And we can’t signal for help if we get into trouble.” Haid grimaced. “That makes us a little more vulnerable than I like to be.”

“As long as we do not employ our slow-jump drive while inside the Gauntlet, we will be able to leave.” The Box sounded weary of the argument. “And even so, the natural collapse of the boundary is relatively slow. Should something go wrong, we would have several weeks to find another means out.”

“Your confidence is admirable,” said Haid, “even if I find it slightly naive.”

Roche decided it was time to change the subject. “Uri, how long now until the first probe arrives at Voloras?”

“One hour and fifteen minutes. That’s when you can expect the first decent pictures, anyway.”

“Good. I suggest we get back to work until then. We might need to move fast, depending on what we see.”

Haid scratched his scalp with his new fingers as he swung back to the weapons console. “Chances are it won’t be a welcoming committee.”

For Roche, finding something to keep herself occupied while the probe was in transit proved to be easy. With repairs still to be completed, the transmission waiting to be translated, and small amounts of long-distance data still trickling in, there was more than enough work for a crew of several dozen. Even with the Box and Kajic both able to perform multiple tasks at once, running a ship the size of the *Ana Vereine* under such conditions would never be straightforward.

Nevertheless, Roche had the opportunity to double-check her memory of Palasian System's records against the data the ship-bound detectors had collected.

The COE navigation register had been updated during the last survey, in '850 EN. Since then, few changes had been appended to the record. Palasian System had never been fully colonized; given its lack of a planet with a breathable atmosphere, that wasn't surprising. The innermost world was a rocky ball boiling under the glare of the F2 primary and was home only to an automated solar research facility. The remaining seven planets were gas giants, two of them bloated with hydrogen. All possessed numerous moons; two had extensive ring systems, but it would take more than pretty scenery to attract colonists. As it was, only the system's proximity to a Kesh border had earned it an Armada base and a refueling station. Not even the presence of three mineral-rich dark-body halos around the sun had tempted more than a cursory mining presence, an arm of the same company that had run the operation—and the penal colony—on Sciacca's World: Dirt & Other Commodities, Inc.

Still, Roche told herself, almost half a million people had called Palasian System home—at least temporarily. And she had to admit that there *was* plenty to look at. In all her travels for COE Intelligence, she had never had the chance to see a double-jovian before.

Part of her had hoped that when Kajic finally located the pair on the far side of the system, it would look somehow different from the other faint blobs he assured her were planets—but it didn't. All she saw was another dot, tinged red by Hintubet's new color.

With Maii at her side, she returned to mapping the locations of the planets and planning contingency routes between them.

<The population was certainly spread thin,> the reave commented at one point. <It's hard to see how an army could have killed them all.>

<It doesn't make our job any easier, either,> Roche responded. <If survivors are unable to communicate, we'll have to turn the system inside out to find them.>

<Unless, as you think, they've regrouped at Jagabis. It would make sense to pool resources.>

<Or to present a united front.>

<One last stand?>

<Perhaps.> Roche shrugged, trying not to dwell on the ramifications of that thought: had such a battle been lost . . . ? <Whoever sent the message, Emptage City and Aro Spaceport are the first places we have to go, right after we flyby Guhr Outpost. If we don't find anything in either of these places, then we'll try the Armada facility around Cemenid; Geyten Base would have been the next most likely place to mount some sort of counterattack.>

<What about the research station?> Maii asked, indicating with a mental prompt the installation orbiting the double-jovian.

<According to the records, Congreve Station was abandoned some decades ago. Unless that changed, it would have been empty when the Sol Wunderkind arrived.>

<What were they studying there?>

<I don't know, exactly. It says 'xenoarchaeological research' when I ask. But planetary evolution seems more likely.>

<I guess.> Roche felt the reave's attention drift elsewhere, studying the files vicariously through Roche's senses. <DAOC are here, I notice. Does Ameidio know that yet?>

Roche shook her head. <Not that I'm aware of, and I'd rather he didn't find out until it's necessary.>

Dirt and Other Commodities Inc. had been the main target of Haid's underground resistance movement on Sciacca's World. Roche would understand any lingering resentment he might still feel after so many years spent fighting them. At the same time she didn't want it to get in the way. She would attempt to rescue DAOC employees just as she would anyone else—if there *were* any remaining in the system. . . .

<The asteroid belt and innermost dark-body halo—the Mattar Belt and Autoville—were mined by prowlers, not people,> said Roche. <So chances are they won't be a problem. The others were untouched.>

<I've never liked prowling mines,> Maii said with a mental moue. <They're just a small step from planet-wreckers.>

<At least they're civilized, not like outriggers.>

<All robots are civilized,> said Maii. <I just don't happen to enjoy their company.>

"The probe's rounding Voloras," announced Kajic, breaking the silence on the bridge. Roche cleared the vision in her artificial eye and looked up. The screen showed a close-up of the swollen arc of the gray gas giant's banded atmosphere. Purple haze tinged the view as the probe used the planet's magnetic field to brake.

"Seen anything yet?" Roche asked.

"Not much," Kajic replied. "The other moons appear to be untouched. The change in Hintubet's radiation has raised a few storms in Voloras's outer atmosphere, and there's a little more rubble in closer than the records say there should be. But apart from that, the planet is as expected."

"Still no signals?"

"All quiet," said Haid. "I can try provoking something, if you like."

"Best not to at this stage."

"I've no problem with that." Haid absently tapped the console as he talked. "Nothing's obstructed the probes so far, but that's not to say it won't happen. They're not exactly subtle, the way they accelerate."

"As long as no one traces the tightbeams back to us, we'll be okay." Roche gestured at the screen. "How long until the moon comes into view?"

"A few seconds," said Kajic, his image facing the screen from the center of the bridge. "When it does, I've programmed the probe to begin its survey automatically. There's enough of a delay to make direct control tricky."

"So it might already be seeing the moon?" asked Roche.

"Or even have been destroyed," said Kajic. "Although I . . ."

He stopped before he could finish the sentence. "Wait. Here it comes. I'll enhance the image as much as I can for the screen, but it might be better through your implants."

Roche put her hand back onto the link and slaved her vision to the probe's data, at the same time shutting her right eye to prevent overlap. Instantly she found herself hanging over the surface of the gas giant, spearing through space with a magnetic storm roiling around her. Ahead and just over the bulge of the horizon, a reddish dot had appeared.

"That's it," said Kajic. "We're lucky it's not eclipsed by the planet; the image would have been much weaker."

"Can you make anything out yet?" Roche asked.

"Nothing definite. The albedo matches, except for a dark patch on the southern hemisphere. You'll see it as the probe gets closer. It doesn't appear on the maps, so it probably isn't a surface feature."

"It isn't the base itself?" asked Haid.

"Refueling bases are always around the equator," Roche answered. "Orbital tethers won't work anywhere else."

"Of course." Haid's tone was apologetic. "It's been a while since I last saw one."

The image sharpened as the moon came closer, becoming a gibbous disc. Its surface was smooth and gray, like its parent, covered with a thick layer of ice. The unusual patch Kajic had pointed out dominated the bottom left quarter: a drop of ink on a circular bloodstain.

"It looks like a shadow," said Roche.

"I think it might be," Kajic agreed. "A shadow at the bottom of a crater."

Roche took a deep breath at the implications of that thought. As the probe swooped closer for its first pass, the details became clear all too quickly. Something had struck the moon's southern hemisphere with the force of a large asteroid. The resulting impact had torn a sizable chunk out of the moon and rung its cold core like a bell. Deep fault lines ran from pole to pole, where the brittle, icy crust had fractured. In infrared, the heat at the shadowy bottom of the crater was obvious, glowing like a red pupil in a dead, gray eye.

"Whatever it was," said Haid, "it hit hard."

"Is there any way to tell how long ago it happened?" asked Cane.

"My guess would be sometime in the last six weeks," said Kajic. "But probably no earlier than a month."

"Agreed," added the Box. "The rubble the probe encountered in the orbit of the moon is clearly ejecta from the impact that has not had time to disperse; that makes the impact fairly recent. But the crater floor is no longer molten, indicating that some time has passed. Between four and five weeks ago is my estimate."

"Any idea what it might have been?" asked Haid.

"At this point, no," the Box said. "But my intuition tells me it was most likely a ship of some description. It would have been much easier to cause a ship to crash than to give an asteroid the vector required to make it impact in such a way."

"Is it worth looking for survivors?" asked Roche.

"No." The Box sent an icon darting into the view, pointing out details Roche had missed. "Here you can see the fallen cable of the orbital docking facility; this fragment here corresponds to part of the base itself. You can also see how a major fracture line runs directly through the site of the main installation. This last detail must surely have been fortuitous—no one could have predicted exactly how the moon would fault—but I doubt that anyone would have survived the impact alone, anyway. The seismic energy released must have been tremendous." The icon disappeared. "It would have been over in seconds. A very effective blow against the Armada presence in this system—both in terms of resources and morale."

"It was deliberate, then," Haid said. "It couldn't have been an accident—a coincidence?"

"Possible," said the Box. "But unlikely."

Roche listened to the Box with a growing sense of unreality. The destruction of an entire Armada refueling base was still something she could hardly believe possible—even though the scant reports COE Intelligence had received from the system had intimated far worse. And now she was seeing it.

The destruction of Palasian System was no longer a morsel of information to gain leverage with COE Intelligence; it had actually happened.

<The Sol Wunderkind did this?> asked Maii, her voice relayed by Roche's implants and broadcast over the bridge speakers.

"We don't have any other suspects," said Haid.

<How many people were on the base?>

"Three hundred," Roche replied. "Plus whoever was on the ship when it crashed—if it was a ship, of course."

"Either way, that's a lot of dead people," said Haid grimly.

"Whether there was one person or a thousand, the actual number is irrelevant," said Cane. "The only thing of importance to the clone warrior was to ensure that no one was left alive." He glanced over at Roche. "Assuming, of course, we have correctly interpreted my sibling's motives."

Roche studied Cane through the ghost image of the planet in her artificial eye. "Even more important than the base's strategic value?"

He paused before answering, his features contorted as though he was fighting conflicting emotions.

"Yes," he said finally, then turned from Roche back to the screen. "The primary objective would have been to destroy as many people as possible as efficiently as possible. The drive for efficiency would have necessitated an early strike against this base, yes, but if it had been automated, that need would have been reduced. Where there are no people to command them, machines can be inefficient in battle."

"So he would have attacked Aro Spaceport first?" Roche asked.

"Yes, had the refueling base been uninhabited." Another pause. "I'm sorry," he said, again facing her. "I do not like thinking this way. It is too easy for me."

Roche nodded, even though she didn't truly understand how his mind worked and therefore could not empathize with his feelings. When he used his genetically modified abilities, he was terrifying to watch. That he had not used them against *her* was something for which she'd be forever grateful—and therein, she thought, lay the paradox. Of the two Sol clone warriors at large in the Commonwealth, only one was obeying its natural instincts. Cane was not. But *why*?

Because he doesn't want to. That was the only answer she could supply. He had said as much himself. And if the part of him that wanted to kill indiscriminately had been subsumed by the part of him that didn't—which perhaps not even the Sol geneticists could have suppressed entirely—then she hoped it stayed that way. Especially now that she had seen what he *could* have done.

She rubbed her eyes, breaking the link and killing the image of the planet in her left eye. Fatigue, which she had successfully kept at bay since her abrupt awakening, was numbing her limbs and pressing at the backs of her eyes.

She was sufficiently aware of her inner feelings, however, to suspect that something more than fatigue was at work.

"The base is dead," she said, letting the issue slip for the moment. "The how and the why can wait until later. Uri, set course for the Voloras flyby and get us on the way to Jagabis. I want to see what's left of Aro Spaceport before we start making any decisions."

"The probe will be there in approximately ten hours," said Kajic. "We'll be past Voloras in four, and well on our way by the time data arrives."

"Good. I'll leave that side of things to you and the Box. As long as I'm kept informed, the two of you can run the ship for a while."

"Where will you be?" asked Kajic.

"In my room, catching up on some sleep." To the others on the bridge, she added, "I suggest you do the same. In thirteen hours we'll have much more data on our hands than we have now, and we'll need to be alert to deal with it."

<I'll stay here with Cane,> said Maii, <if that's okay with you, Morgan. I can sleep on a couch.>

"Make sure she does, Cane," said Roche. "I know you probably won't need to rest, but she does."

Cane nodded.

"That goes for you too, Ameidio."

"I'll do so as soon as I've finished here," said Haid, his hands busy over a console.

"Okay," Roche said. "Unless something happens, we'll meet back here in twelve hours."

She stood and led Maii over to Cane. The reave's hands briefly linked Roche with Cane, and in that instant Roche received a mental flash of Cane's mind. The impression was short-lived, and carried with it no actual thoughts, but it left her with the impression of rapid motion. Even after the contact had been broken, she couldn't shake a mental image of a gyroscope spinning, perpetually on the verge of toppling over but never quite doing so.

"Wait," said Kajic as she started to leave. "I'm picking up another transmission."

Roche continued toward the exit. "I doubt we'll learn anything new," she said. "Unless we work out the language—"

"It's not from Jagabis, this time," Kajic said. Roche stopped and faced Kajic's flickering image. "We're picking up the fringes of a tightbeam, probably reflected off the source of the first transmission. Whoever's sending this one must be doing the best they can with a fairly low-tech outfit. Hang on—we'll see if we can decode it."

"It's not in cipher," said the Box. "It is a standard text message. No voice, no images."

"Display it," said Roche, curious despite her exhaustion.

The view of Hintubet faded from the main screen. Now in its place were several lines of text:

I DO NOT RUN FROM YOU,
BUT NEITHER WILL I RUN TO YOU.
I DO NOT REQUIRE YOUR AID.
WHEN OR IF I DO NEED ANYTHING THAT YOU POSSESS,

I WILL TAKE IT.
YOU WILL NOT STOP ME.

I AM NOT YOURS TO COMMAND.

Roche read it once, then again. "That's it?" she asked after a third and final reading.

"The same message is repeated twice," said the Box.

"And it's not encrypted?"

"No."

"But it *was* sent on a tightbeam."

"Yes."

"Then that tells us something. I'll bet the reason we're picking up the fringes of the beam is because it's been through a number of relays to prevent triangulation of the source. Whoever sent it was less concerned about the contents of the message than keeping their location a secret."

Haid nodded. "That would make sense."

"And judging by the content, I'd say there's only one person who could've sent it."

"My sibling," said Cane, meeting her accusatory stare.

Roche nodded slowly. "He's alive."

"And kicking," said Haid. "I'm glad I'm not in the shoes of whoever he's talking to."

"The fact that he's talking at all is interesting," Roche mused. "In fact, it sounds like he's bluffing."

"You think so?" said Haid.

She shrugged. "If he's hiding, he's vulnerable."

"I guess we'll find out soon enough." Haid returned his attention to the console before him. "I'll see if any of the probes picked up the signal and try to pin down a source."

"Good. Any more, Box?"

"The transmission has now ceased," said the AI.

She considered whether she should stay on the bridge to see if anything else came in, but decided against it. The communication from the Sol clone warrior was important enough to warrant further examination, but not informative. Again, without further data, she would only be speculating wildly.

"The situation's unchanged, then," she said. "I'll keep my implants open for any further developments. Don't hesitate to call me."

"I won't," said Kajic. His image dissolved at the same moment Roche stepped from the bridge.

Back in her cabin, Roche lay on her bunk, going over the data they had collected so far. Detailed images of the ruined Guhr Outpost came as often as the probe—now orbiting the small moon—passed by. All that remained of the refueling base were fragments twisted beyond recognition. Sensors detected high levels of radiation in the heart of the crater, which supported the theory that a ship, not an asteroid, had crashed there, but no remains of the ship had been found. Given the force of the explosion, Roche didn't expect any. The ship must have been fully fueled to have caused such a blast. Only time would tell how greatly the moon's orbit around the gas giant had been disturbed.

The remainder of the probes, now on their way to every major body in the system, were still too far away from their destinations to provide any new perspectives. The earliest she could expect data would be from the probe heading to Gatamin, six hours away; the latest, from the probe aimed at Kukumat and Murukan, the jovian pair, at over twenty hours.

Determined not to let frustration get the better of her—there was, after all, nothing she could do to change the speed of light—she tried instead to focus her thoughts on what she *did* know about Palasian System.

First of all, the COE Intelligence data appeared to be accurate so far. There had been a battle of some sort that had cost the Armada at least a refueling base.

Second, the system was suspiciously silent, apart from one unintelligible signal emanating from near the major port around Jagabis and another whose source was in hiding.

Third, the sun had been transformed into a cosmic hypershield generator by a weapon used only once before, over a thousand years ago. The last government known to have had access to the sole remaining Asha's Gauntlet prototype was the Kesh.

Fourth, Maii's mind-riding abilities had been negated by a mysterious "smothering" effect.

Fifth, the system had been cordoned off on the outside by three Armada vessels acting under direct orders from General Ramage, commander in chief of the COE Armada.

And that was all. Roche was fairly confident that the Sol Wunderkind was trapped in the system, but beyond that she didn't want to speculate too far. It was tempting to write off the epsense-dampening phenomenon as another of his extraordinary talents, but that seemed unlikely. Apart from the occasional suggestion from Maii that Cane possessed a strong but latent epsense ability, there was no indication that he possessed any such talents. Nevertheless, Roche was wary of closing off any avenues of exploration too early. Not while the matters of the Gauntlet and the Armada flotilla were still to be explained, anyway. She had learned from experience that especially where conspiracies were concerned, the major factor preventing the truth's being discovered was the observer's unwillingness to explore connections between facts that on the surface seemed unconnectable.

She leaned back into the pillow, pushing her knuckles into her aching, tired eyes. There was, in short, enough to make her cautious, but not enough to provide her a definite focus for her fears.

And that, in a sense, only made it worse.

You will not stop me, the second transmission had said. Could she have stopped *Cane,* had he chosen to attack rather than to aid her? Was he even on her side? *I am not yours to command,* the message had said. The words made Roche wonder whether he had ever truly been. . . .

She didn't realize she had fallen asleep until the alarm on her door buzzed.

In the dream she heard the hiss of a predator. She jerked forward on her bunk and called out in the dark, clutching at the fringe of the dream even as she was wrenched from it. She had been back on Ascensio, trying to lure a viridant out of its burrow by offering it a dead rodent. The lizardlike animal had been suspicious, but she managed to encourage it by repeating the offer several times. She had no intention of giving it the bait, though; her only intention had been to gain its trust—and then to strangle it. Only too late had she seen the glint in its eye and known that *she* was the one being lured. Her hand had lashed out, and the viridant had snapped its jaws around it, pulling her into its burrow. . . .

The door buzzed again. She shook herself from a daze and spoke into the intercom:

"Who is it?"

"It's me," Cane answered. "The data from the probes are due soon. I would like to discuss something with you before then, if it's not inconvenient."

"Wait a moment." She ran her hands over her stubbled scalp and wiped her face. Her skin was greasy and coarse at the same time—a grim reminder that she was overdue for a shower. After a moment she said: "Lights; door open."

The room brightened at her command. Cane stepped into the cabin.

"I'm assuming it's not an emergency," she said, "or else Uri would've called first."

"Little has changed," said Cane. "We have received another transmission from the same source as the first, but that's about it. Kajic posted details of it to your buffer, marking it as a low priority. If you were asleep, you wouldn't have seen it."

She checked her implants out of habit; sure enough, the message was there. She also learned that she had been asleep for seven hours. It felt more like four.

She stayed on the bed and offered Cane the chair. "So, what can I do for you?"

"Everyone is resting," he said. When he sat he folded his hands in his lap, making him look uncharacteristically unsure of himself. "I thought I'd take advantage of the situation to talk to you alone."

"About?" she prompted.

"The transmission from Jagabis."

"What about it?"

"I can translate it."

She studied him suspiciously. "The Box said it wasn't in any language that it recognized."

"I know."

"But *you* recognize it?"

"I didn't at first," he said. "Only after reading through the raw text for some hours did it begin to make sense. And even then, not all of it."

"I'm not sure I follow you."

"I am not *certain* what it means, but I do understand it. I know how odd that sounds, but the situation is as confusing to me as it is to you. And that's why I wanted to talk to you first rather than the others."

"You've kept this from Maii?"

"She knows I'm hiding something, but she won't learn what it is unless I let her."

Roche nodded. "So what does the transmission say?"

"It is a call to arms," he said. "It is also a plea for help. And a request to negotiate. And an order to retreat. And an offer of assistance. And—"

She cut him off: "I don't understand. How can it be all these things at once?"

"The message is composed of fragments. Some make sense, but a lot don't. The bits that don't are just meaningless, but there is still a resonance in the words—as though they have been engraved in my mind, that I might never forget them."

She suddenly grasped the implication. "Are you suggesting that this is some sort of language used by the Sol Apotheosis Movement? That you've been *programmed* to understand it?"

"Nothing else can explain why I know what some of the fragments mean, and respond to them"—he put a hand on his stomach—"*here,* almost before I have time to realize."

"Are they dangerous? Could they make you do things you don't want to do?"

Cane shook his head. "Whoever is broadcasting the orders doesn't know what they are doing. The fragments that make the most sense are the most emphatic, of course, but they are often the most inconsistent, too. The fragment repeated most often, for instance, is a request to trade information that is not relevant in exchange for supplies that no one in this century would need."

"Why would anyone broadcast something like that?" Roche wondered. "And where did they find the code? It wasn't in any of the records I accessed."

"I don't know, exactly," Cane said. "Perhaps the source *is* a beacon, after all."

"One the Sol Apotheosis Movement left behind, perhaps?"

He shrugged. "It may have successfully summoned my sibling here, then malfunctioned."

"That wouldn't explain why he bothered to reply."

"Unless the beacon is an AI," Cane suggested. "Or we have it the wrong way around. Perhaps the Sol transmission is from my sibling, and the reply from someone else entirely."

Roche thought this over. The first transmission had come from Jagabis, their current destination. "If so, that means we're heading into trouble."

"I know." Cane's dark features remained expressionless. "It appears that being able to translate the transmission, even in part, has only made the situation worse."

"It's not your fault, Cane," Roche said. "This whole system is a mess." She rubbed sleep from her eyes with the heels of her hands. "Besides, you can't help what you are," she went on, sensing that he wanted something more from her than just acting as a confessor. "Your lack of motive worries me sometimes, but you've convinced me that you don't mean *me* any harm—for what that's worth. Just because you're a weapon, and you've been designed to do certain things that might harm a great number of people, that doesn't mean you will. There's a big difference between design and intent, after all; I try to keep that in mind."

Cane nodded slowly. "Thank you, Morgan. I was worried that the reminder of what I am might cause you to rethink our association."

She smiled vaguely. "I'm glad you told me. At the very least, we can get the Box onto it and see whether it can't translate the rest."

"You would like me to tell the Box?"

"I can't see why not. Having some understanding of a high-level Sol language will probably come in handy one day." She went on: "When you have the time, go over the text of the transmission, pull out the bits that you can translate and see what the Box can come up with. It may be no more of a linguist than you or I, but it must be able to run basic statistical checks. Something's bound to come up."

Cane stood, his muscles flexing smoothly with the movement. "We'll begin immediately."

"I'll be down to review your results soon." She stood, too, and followed him to the door. "But don't let it get in the way of mapping the system. That's our first priority at the moment."

The door slid closed behind Cane, leaving Roche with yet another mystery to ponder. She wondered how many more this system would throw at her before finally surrendering some definite answers. And how much longer she could juggle the conflicting trust and suspicion she felt for Adoni Cane.

When she made it to the bridge almost an hour later, the first wave of information had begun to arrive. The probe aimed at the sun had announced that it had data to send within moments of Cane's return. Since then, the Box, Cane, and Kajic had been fully occupied, paring back the packets of data to the ones most relevant or likely to contain answers to Roche's many questions. As a result, the mystery of the possible Sol transmissions had been placed on hold.

"Okay," she said, settling into her seat. Maii took a place next to her, apart from a hand on her shoulder keeping carefully unobtrusive. "Let's see what we've got."

"Pictures in visual spectra, mostly," said Kajic. "And, according to the Box, the mechanism underlying the Gauntlet."

"Show me."

The main screen blossomed to reveal a bloated red giant, magnified to fill one third of the view. Cooler patches had been dimmed by compensators to appear charcoal black, giving the star's surface a cracked appearance. Massive disturbances, clearly visible despite the blur of distance, flowed sluggishly from each pole to the equator, skewed east by the star's rotation.

Roche winced at the sight. "You'd never guess that until a month ago, *that* used to be a green dwarf."

"Precisely," said the Box. "The change in its composition goes much deeper than I thought."

"How deep, exactly?"

"To the core. Look closely, Morgan."

The view zoomed forward, closer to the star. Gases bubbled like magma from an unimaginable interior, casting a baleful red light through the bridge. A green ring stood out on the screen, highlighting a darker point. As the ring swung past, Roche realized that the point at its center was an object orbiting the star, deep within its chromosphere. She had no reference points against which to estimate the object's size, but the way it disturbed the gases around it, leaving a deep, roiling scar in its wake, suggested enormous size or mass, or both.

"That can't be a ship," she said.

"It isn't," said the Box. "It is one of sixteen quark breeders in high-speed orbit, firing pellets of strange matter into the heart of the star."

"You can tell that just by looking at it?"

"Not entirely, Morgan. If you watch carefully, you can see the pellets strike the photosphere."

Roche looked more closely at the image. Sure enough, every few seconds or so, a bright spark of blue light flared at the base of the wake.

"Why strange matter?" asked Haid.

"Strange matter is super-dense," Roche said before the Box could reply, "and it can be moved more easily and more precisely than neutronium. With it, you can alter the workings of a star's core. Once you control the core, you can play with its electromagnetic and gravity fields."

"This, clearly, is how the Riem-Perez Horizon is generated," added the Box.

"Overkill," said Haid.

"The Gauntlet is a grotesque example of just that," the AI agreed. "If its designers had stopped to consider what they were doing even for a moment, they would have realized that what they hoped for simply wasn't possible."

Haid shrugged. "You have to admire them for trying, anyway."

The quark breeder continued to plow its way through Hintubet's wounded chromosphere, as implacable as the physics that foretold the star's death.

"What would happen if we destroyed them?" Cane asked.

"Disaster," said the Box. "The nuclear processes inside the sun would spiral out of control until the reactions sustaining the Riem-Perez Horizon ceased. The boundary would become increasingly chaotic until, within a very short period of time, it collapsed entirely."

"Any idea who planted the breeders?" said Roche.

"Detail is sparse at this resolution," said the Box. "I cannot tell if the breeders display any markings. However, only one nation in this region manufactures breeders of the sort required for such a macro-project as this, and that is the Eckandar Trade Axis."

"Do you think they might be involved?"

"No. The devices have been available for many centuries; the array is probably that belonging to the original Gauntlet prototype, not one manufactured recently."

"That's good to know. I hate to think why anyone would build them today." Roche mused to herself for a moment. "If this is the prototype, and it's being used to entrap the Sol Wunderkind, then it must have been kept somewhere nearby. Allowing time for the weapon to be dusted off and programmed, then put into place and activated, that doesn't leave much for transport."

"Do we know when it was activated?" asked Haid.

"Not before the twenty-sixth of last month," said the Box. "That was when the Armada Marines investigating the system were ambushed. Presumably the system was open at that point."

"Is there any way to pin it down further?"

"I have been observing the rate of decay of the boundary. If we assume that it originally extended to cover Palasian System's cometary halo, then that gives us an activation date somewhere between the thirty-seventh and fortieth."

"So that means the people behind the Gauntlet had a little more than one week to get it here," Roche said.

"How would they have got it past the clone warrior?" asked Haid.

"One assumes the breeders were slow-jumped as close to the sun as possible with a large relative velocity," said the Box. "Once they were captured by Hintubet's gravity and safely inside the chromosphere, there would have been very little the Sol Wunderkind could have done to interfere with them."

"He wouldn't have known what they were, after all," said Roche.

"They would have demonstrated no overtly hostile behavior," added Cane. "And there may have been more pressing matters demanding his attention."

"That makes sense." Roche turned her attention away from the sun and the device crippling it. "What else have we found?"

"We have a probe orbiting Cartha's Planet," said Kajic. "Everything seems in order there. Wight Station—the automated solar research installation—has not been damaged."

"Because it was no threat," Roche said. "Go on."

"The same probe examined the Mattar Belt as it flew through," Kajic went on. "There is evidence of activity on several asteroids, although only one prowling mine was observed in situ. Likewise, it had not been interfered with."

"Any sign of people?"

"No. The inner system appears to be uninhabited, except by machines."

"Perhaps we can use them to our advantage, then. Box, as we get closer, I want you to make contact with the AIs on Wight Station and the prowling mines. They may have recorded information that will help us plot the movements of the Sol Wunderkind."

"I will do so," said the Box. "If other installations have been attacked in the same manner as Guhr Outpost, the explosions should have been noticed by one or more of these observers. We may be able to pinpoint the exact time each attack took place."

"Let me know what you find." Roche turned to Kajic. "Any news from Jagabis?"

"The probe will be in position, relative to us, in about an hour. All transmissions ceased from that region twenty-five minutes ago, corresponding almost exactly with our arrival in the system."

Roche mentally approximated the time it would take data traveling at light-speed to cross the system twice; as Kajic had said, it did match the time required for someone on Jagabis to observe the arrival of the *Ana Vereine,* then for the immediate cessation of transmissions to be observed by Kajic.

"So someone knows we're here," she said somberly.

"They knew where we *were,*" said Haid. "We've been camouflaged since we arrived, which still gives us some element of surprise."

Roche nodded. "Have the other probes found anything?"

"Two used Gatamin as a gravity-whip, but neither reported anything unusual," said Kajic. "Again, that planetary system was uninhabited."

Roche took a moment to study the images of the smallish, once blue-green gas giant, third most distant from the sun. Apart from its remarkable rings, it was easy to overlook.

"Herensung likewise appears untouched," Kajic went on, "at least from a distance. There were a few orbital communication relays that are now silent, but until the probe arrives we have no way of knowing what has happened to them."

"That leaves Cemenid, and the double jovian." Roche was curious to see both. Cemenid, the largest planet, had been home to a COE communications base; Kukumat and Murukan were simply mysterious, on the opposite side of the system.

"Cemenid is a couple of hours away," said Kajic. "The double will be at least another twelve."

Roche couldn't complain about that; she already had enough data to keep her occupied for days, and would soon have more. The double jovian was simply a bonus.

She applied herself to the information with a will and Maii's help, trying to find any evidence of the Sol clone warrior's passage. Occasional details surfaced from the growing files—wreckage of satellite here, an ion afterwash there—but no actual sightings. Wherever the Wunderkind was, he had been effective in hiding himself—so far. When the data from the other major planets arrived, she hoped to know where he was *not,* at least. Then it would become a more difficult quest, through the gulfs between planets or in the mess of dark bodies known as Autoville between Cemenid and Gatamin. She didn't like to think that he might have hidden any farther out than that; Mishra's Stake, the second dark body halo, extended in a band one and half thousand million kilometers wide almost as far as Voloras. If he was hiding in there, he would be impossible to find.

The only consolation was that if he *was* in there, he would be effectively unable to surprise them. Which is why Roche felt safe ruling it out. He would never have allowed himself to reduce his options so severely, assuming Cane's behavior was anything to go by.

<He will watch patiently until he has sufficient information,> said Maii, <then strike. It won't be in his nature to act unprepared, or to wait too long. As soon as he knows how to destroy us, he will do so without hesitation.>

<There's a cheerful thought,> Roche responded, still acutely aware of what had happened to Guhr Outpost.

<We just have to be ready for him, and make sure he doesn't force us into any mistakes.>

Roche pondered this. <We may already be making a mistake by rushing into the system before the probes have had time to report.>

<I don't think so,> the reave said. <Even in-system the distances are large enough to give us an edge, given the power of the *Ana Vereine*. And besides, where are we now?>

<Inside the orbit of Gatamin.>

<The inner system doesn't really start until Cemenid. That gives us plenty of time to change course if the remaining probes *do* find anything.>

<But between Gatamin and Cemenid is Autoville, and there could be *anything* in there.>

<True. Then we'll just have to keep our eyes open.>

Roche smiled at the irony in the blind Surin's words, but she kept the thought carefully to herself.

"We're picking up something unusual," said Kajic.

"From Jagabis?" Roche asked, pushing the data she had been studying to one side and focusing her attention on the main screen.

"No. It's a tightbeam from roughly the same direction, though."

"Contents?"

"A request for ID on a COE band. That's all." Kajic paused. "The transmission is coming once every minute, and we're only picking up the fringes of it. Also, it's blue-shifted, indicating that the source is moving toward us."

Toward them? Roche stiffened in her seat. "A ship?"

"That seems likely, although I haven't detected any emissions yet."

"Keep looking. Show me the message in full."

A window on the main screen opened, displaying four brief lines of text:

VESSEL ENTERING PALASIAN SYSTEM 0805
ID REQUESTED
RESPOND ASAP
QUOLMANN

"Who's this 'Quolmann'?" asked Haid.

"It's not a who," said Roche. "It's COE Intelligence shorthand for 'Trust me; I'm an ally.'"

"And should we?" asked Haid evenly.

"That depends," said Cane. "If the code is common knowledge, then we should treat its use here with suspicion."

"It's not well known," said Roche. "Otherwise it would have been changed. But I'm disinclined to trust someone even if they *are* from COE Intelligence."

"So what do we do?" Kajic asked. "Ignore it?"

"We can't afford to," said Roche uneasily. "The message was sent to *us*. They may not know exactly where we are, given that we're only picking up the edges of the tightbeam, but they do have a rough idea."

"They could be sending the message to several likely locations," suggested Cane.

Roche quickly dismissed the idea. "No, the ship is still coming in this direction." She thought for a moment, then said: "We're being predictable. Uri, I want to change course slightly; swing us away from the sun and to a wider approach. I know it'll mean taking longer to get to Jagabis, but I think we have to do it—at least until we know how far away this ship is. At the same time, send a remote to reply to the tightbeam on our original course. Give it half an hour before sending our ID and the 'Quolmann' code word—that's all. Keep the probe on our old heading until it receives a reply. It can relay any messages without putting the *Ana Vereine* at risk."

"Consider it done," said Kajic.

Roche read the text of the message again. "It's almost as though they were expecting someone from COE Intelligence to come," she mused.

"And have nothing to fear from them," added Cane.

"That puts them in a minority," said Haid wryly.

"The Jagabis data is being processed," announced Kajic.

"Finally." Roche prepared herself for another inrush of information. "Okay. Let's see it."

The probe had inserted itself into a polar orbit around the innermost jovian world of Palasian System. Even under Hintubet's stark, crimson light, Roche was struck by the beauty of the planet. Its bands and vortices were manifold and varied, ranging from thick jet streams to thin wisps; its pole was a region of intense electromagnetic activity, the atmosphere constantly erupting with flashes of lightning. Its rings were small relative to those of some of the other planets, but they were there, framing a large number of moons—fourteen known, Roche recalled from the COE files. The largest of them, Aro, was also the largest solid body in the system; for that reason, plus its more hospitable distance from the sun, it had been chosen over Cartha's Planet for the system's permanent civilian base.

She studied the data intently, eager for—and yet simultaneously dreading—her first sight of Aro Spaceport and its close neighbor, Emptage City. Although she knew that the probe had sent this view some hours ago, she couldn't help but feel nervous about what she might see, as though she were more intimately involved than a mere observer. What if the Sol Wunderkind were to be attacking Aro at the very moment the moon came into view? What would she do? She fought to suppress the discomforting notion, because the truth was, there would be nothing she *could* do. They would be helpless to defend the base. . . .

The probe changed course as it crossed Jagabis's north pole. Its tiny but powerful thrusters fired to insert it into an equatorial orbit intersecting that of Aro. Roche waited impatiently as the minutes ticked by until, finally, the red dot of the moon appeared over the bulge of the distant horizon.

The dot became a disc. The probe's thrusters ceased firing; momentum and the pull of Jagabis's gravity would complete the maneuver. The last leg of its approach would be conducted with as few emissions as possible.

The disc swelled steadily. A hazy atmosphere, rich in methane and sulfur, softened its edges. The hemisphere facing the probe was mostly in shadow, making details hard to discern, and Hintubet's bloody glare in the background only complicated the matter. Roche watched as Kajic tried various enhancement routines on the image, methodically refining the picture.

"I can't see the orbital tower," Roche said.

"What's that in the southeast quadrant?" Haid pointed. "Another crater?"

"No," said the Box. "Remember the scale. An impact that large would have cracked the moon in two."

"The COE maps have two methane seas listed," said Roche. "That must be one of them."

"It's a little hard to make out at the moment," said Kajic, "but I think you're right, Morgan."

"We'll soon find out," she said.

The moon expanded until its shadowed image filled most of the screen. Red sunlight glinted on an object in orbit around it, startling Roche until she realized that the telemetry data was still empty of signs of technological activity. An abandoned satellite, she guessed. Or wreckage. Whatever it was, it caught the light twice more before vanishing from view. Kajic's display showed several other unidentified and inactive objects, invisible to her limited senses, also in distant orbits, and she followed them instead to pass the time. A similar display on Haid's console revealed that he too was tracking them, ready to respond if one of them made any move at all—or showed signs of life.

The probe slid neatly into a geostationary orbit above Aro Spaceport and turned its instruments downward.

"Radar has located the main launch field," said Kajic intently. "No other clear landmarks, yet."

"The main dome?" asked Roche.

"I have something that might be an outline, but . . ." He shook his head. "It's not clear. The dome might be down. There's no way to be sure until the sun rises."

"How long will that be?"

"Ten minutes or so."

"Try infrared," she suggested. "If there are survivors, they'll show up as hot spots."

"I'm not finding anything, Morgan," Kajic said after a moment. "It's uniformly cool down there. Even the launch field."

"No fires?" asked Haid. "Traces of explosions?"

"Aro has an atmosphere and weather," said Kajic. "Excess heat will dissipate relatively quickly."

"But there's no evidence of the sort of damage we saw at Guhr Outpost, is there?" Roche studied the image on the main screen in detail, clutching at anything that would justify optimism. "There might still be a chance."

"Underground," said Cane.

"The main dome was fully exposed," said Kajic. "In fact, it was built in the walls of an old crater, so it needed only a roof."

"But the spaceport might have subterranean facilities," said Roche.

"The only way to check would be to go down there." Haid glanced around the bridge. "Any volunteers?"

"Let's see if we can't contact them first." Roche swiveled away from the screen. "Uri, have the probe broadcast a brief message asking for ID. Use the 'Quolmann' code. There may be a connection between survivors here and the ship signaling us."

"The people speaking the Sol command language?" asked Haid.

"Speaking it badly," Cane put in.

"Whatever," said Haid. "I'd be wary of letting them know we're anywhere near them just yet—if they're even there at all, that is."

"I know," said Roche. "That's what the probe is for. Send the signal, Uri. Repeat it once."

"Done." Kajic's image shifted within the hologrid. "And now we wait. We'll see a reply in about five hours, if there is one."

"Damn it." Roche cursed the situation—and herself for forgetting the light-speed delay. "I guess that's all we—"

"Hold it!" Kajic barked as something flashed across the screen. "The probe—something's firing on it!"

Roche slaved her implants to the data-feed. The hazy radar outline of the spaceport jerked once, then disappeared entirely from view. In the visual spectrum, the view slued wildly as the probe fought to stabilize itself. Damage readings scrolled down the borders of her field of view, suggesting that the probe had been struck on one side.

"Uri? What the hell is—?"

"I'm getting a fix on something," Kajic interrupted. The probe steadied, its cameras pointing toward the horizon of the moon. Light flashed from something metallic. "It's a derelict."

The view zoomed closer. The ship had once been a freighter, but now had a hole in its side that could have housed one of the *Ana Vereine*'s scutters. It was traveling in an orbit above and at right angles to that of the probe.

A cloud of escaping gas flowered briefly from the shadow of the ship's hole. A second later, it happened again.

"I'm picking up very low electromagnetic readings," said Kajic. "Almost undetectable. Hardly a life sign, and nothing like any weapon I've ever seen."

The view jumped again. Red warning indicators began to flash in the probe's telemetry display.

"I can't tell what's hitting it," Kajic said with some frustration. "And neither can the probe."

"Why isn't it doing anything?" asked Haid.

"It doesn't know *what* to do," Kajic responded. "It can't even run without knowing what it's running from."

Roche leaned forward as inspiration struck her. "Does the probe have anti-meteorite shields?"

"Of course; they're standard in anything designed to travel at speed in-system—"

"What about when it's not 'at speed'?"

"They shut down to conserve power . . ." Sudden understanding stopped Kajic short.

On the main screen, the probe's cameras caught a glimpse of the derelict ship. Red sunlight flashed on its pitted hull more strongly than before. Dust was still puffing out of the shadow in its side, as regular as a metronome. Then the image shook and disappeared again, the probe clearly having difficulty maintaining its attitude with so much damage interfering with its systems.

"It's a gas-gun," Roche said. "Probably a chemical thruster modified to fire slivers of metal or plastic; they're not hard to jury-rig. All that's needed is a small amount of power to run a targeter or a receiver, and no one will ever know it's there—until it's activated, anyway. And then, before you know it, you've been hit by something with enough kinetic energy to punch a hole right through your hull."

"The presence of the probe must have been enough to set it off," said Haid, nodding. "Just being there. Imagine what would've happened if it had sent that signal."

"Are there other derelicts in orbit?" Cane asked.

"I have plotted the orbits of at least a dozen small masses," confirmed Kajic, "many in similar orbits to this one—high and at extreme angles to anything around the equator."

"Thereby maximizing the relative velocities of the slivers," said Roche.

"So it's likely that all the derelicts are similarly armed," Cane said.

"Why bother?" said Haid.

"It's a trap," said Roche.

"But for whom?"

"For us, I guess."

"No," said Cane. "This would have taken time to prepare. There must have been another target."

The probe shuddered again as another of the slivers struck it toward the rear. This time, the damage was severe. The feed died for a second before flickering back to life.

"We're going to lose it," said Roche, cursing under her breath.

"Soon, yes," said Kajic. "But not immediately. The probe knows it's been profoundly damaged, but it has been programmed to complete its mission before allowing total shut down. See? It's already changing orbit."

Roche followed the changing telemetry data. "What *was* its mission, Uri? I thought it had already accomplished it by getting there."

"Not quite. We needed to know what happened to Emptage City; that's its ultimate objective."

The probe's trajectory steepened at a frightening rate, accomplished by the faltering push of its thrusters and the steady drag of Aro's gravity. Roche fought the urge to grip her armrests as the atmosphere of the moon rushed toward the probe—and *her,* according to her senses.

Then clouds were sweeping past, red-tinged with sunrise. The radar image of Aro Spaceport expanded to meet her just moments after dawn broke across the surface of the moon.

Roche started slightly as the probe struck and the screen flashed with high-speed bursts of data. Then it went black.

"The feed has ceased," said Kajic.

"What did we get?" Roche managed, breaking the link to her implants.

"A number of partial images," the Box said. "I am reconstructing them for you now."

The main screen scanned through a number of blurry views of the surface of Aro. The first three contained scenes that could have been anywhere—too dark to make out details—but the fourth was surprisingly sharp. It showed the landing field of Aro Spaceport with a resolution down to three meters.

There were three ships parked in its dry docks. All were lifeless and gutted, with black holes along their spines indicating that they had been fired upon from above.

"Orbital laser-fire," said Haid. "Or bombardment of some sort."

"Maybe more pieces of derelict ships," Roche agreed. The field itself was pockmarked with circles—craters left behind from shots that had missed. The buildings of the landing field had been similarly destroyed.

"There's nothing here," she said. "Anything else, Uri?"

"One other clear snapshot," Kajic said. "The probe managed a course-change before it crashed and flew over the edge of Emptage City. There's just enough light to pick out fine detail."

"Let's see it." The spaceport vanished. In its place appeared the curved rim of an eroded crater wall, its lip blackened and jagged. From the point of view of the probe, Roche was unable to make out the dome that had covered the colony.

"Can we see any closer?" she asked.

The crater wall rose to meet them as Kajic magnified the image.

"We were fortunate, in a way," said Kajic, "that the sun had only just risen. The incident light was striking at such a low angle that shadows revealed details we would normally have missed from above."

"I see them," said Roche, her stomach sinking.

The shattered base of the dome stood out clearly in the image, as did the bases of the struts and girders that had once held it in place.

"He cracked it open." Haid's words were steeped in awe and disbelief.

"That's all he needed to do," said Roche. "He let the air out, and everyone died."

"No," said Cane. "See the area around the base of the dome? It's blackened, as though by fire."

"But it's a methane atmosphere—" Kajic began, then stopped.

"Methane burns in the presence of oxygen," Cane finished.

"He punctured the dome, then started a fire." Roche could picture it all too clearly. "Then he left it to burn. It might have taken days."

Roche detected a mental frown an instant before Maii's voice intruded into her thoughts. <Why didn't he finish them off when he had the chance?>

"Because he didn't need to, Maii," Roche explained. "The gas-guns in orbit would pick off anyone who managed to survive and get off-planet—along with anyone who tried to mount a rescue, for that matter. Before the dome over Emptage City finally collapsed, he was probably on the other side of the system, attacking somewhere else."

"A very efficient strategy," said Cane.

Roche glanced at him, but was unable to tell from his expression exactly what he was feeling. Approval? Admiration? Respect? She herself felt nothing but sickened by the cruelty with which the warrior had acted.

"What are the odds that someone could still be alive?" she asked of no one in particular.

"Minimal," replied the Box. "There may still be airtight chambers in some of the buildings, or underground as Cane suggested; small numbers of people may have taken shelter within them. But how would we go about rescuing them?"

"The gas-guns are easily avoided—" Roche began.

"True. Without the element of surprise and against appropriate shields, they would be ineffective. We could even destroy the derelicts before assuming orbit, thereby neutralizing the threat entirely. But the problem lies in locating the survivors quickly enough to mount a rescue attempt—survivors who have no way to communicate with us and may not have even the most basic of pressure suits to survive exposure to the atmosphere. Any rescue attempt would be complicated, time-consuming, and risky."

"With the Sol clone warrior still out there," said Haid grimly. "Laughing at us."

"Or hunting us," the Box added. "We cannot allow ourselves to be distracted. Our mission is to track him down."

"I know, I *know.*" Roche sighed. "I just feel we should at least *try.*"

"It's an honorable thought," said Cane softly, "but not one we can entertain at this moment. It's what he will expect us to do. Perhaps later, when we have the time."

Roche straightened in her chair, trying to regain the appearance of the staunch commander. "Perhaps. For now, though, we've lost our probe at Jagabis. Uri, how long until another can take its place?"

"A few hours."

"Do it. I don't want any blind spots."

"Understood."

She stood. "I'll be in the captain's office for a moment."

Maii lightly squeezed Roche's shoulder. <I'll come with you,> she said.

Roche considered arguing, but knew it would create a scene—and that was exactly what she was trying to avoid. She couldn't meet Haid's eyes as she and Maii crossed the bridge and entered the smaller chamber at its rear. When the doors slid shut behind them, Roche let herself sink into a padded chair and put her head in her hands. Acutely conscious of Maii's thin-boned hand on her shoulder, she drew a heavy veil across her thoughts.

To no avail.

They're all dead . . .

<It's harder than you thought it would be,> said the reave, her mental voice a gentle breeze blowing between their minds.

<Much,> said Roche, kneading her temples with her fingertips.

<There is too much unknown, and too much at stake,> Maii continued. <You have to confront the Sol Wunderkind before it escapes this system and destroys another; but how can you confront it without sufficient information to guarantee that you will not fail like the others who tried before? The more you look, the more death you see, and the less likely it seems that you will ever succeed—but that only makes it all the more important that you keep trying. You might be all that stands between the clone warrior and the rest of the Commonwealth.>

<Look, Maii,> said Roche sharply, <I don't need this right now.>

<No,> the reave soothed. <You don't. And yet you continue to torture yourself with it.>

Roche smiled to herself. <I suppose I do, don't I?>

<I don't know,> said Maii. <I'm guessing, not reading.>

Roche removed the girl's hand from her shoulder, and held it in her own. <Maii, this is the first thing I have ever tried to do on my own. And I guess I'm just a little . . . scared. Not of the Sol Wunderkind escaping or anything, but of—>

<Failing,> said Maii, finishing what Roche was reluctant to express.

<I mean, I know I'm not really on my own, with you and the others around to help me, but COE Intelligence isn't there issuing the orders for once, and that makes it so important not to screw up in any way at all . . .> She stopped, realizing that she was close to babbling, and sighed. <I just need time to get my head straight.>

<I understand,> Maii said. Her face was expressionless but the waves of sympathy she offered were real. <There have been many moments since Veden died when I wondered how I could even think of going on without him. But here I am. I have no choice *but* to do so. The alternative, as they say, is far worse.>

Roche smiled. <And better to try and fail than to go back to COE Intelligence or give up entirely. At least it's *my* failure, not theirs.>

<I'm sure they'd be keen to contribute,> said Maii, her words stained with amusement.

<I'm sure they would.> Roche's mood sobered as an image of the ruined city on Aro returned to her. No doubt the killer of almost half a million people would have something to say, also.

With a *fizz,* a full-size image of Kajic appeared, standing opposite them with his hands respectfully behind his back.

"Apologies for intruding, Morgan. I have detected the emissions of a vessel on an intercept course with the relay probe we left to follow our previous course."

Roche took a deep breath. "The ship that hailed us earlier?"

"I assume so. It's still several million kilometers away, and I am unable to discern its class or origin, but I can tell you that it's small. Maybe a mini-shuttle or singleship."

"Occupied, I presume?"

"It is accelerating within the physical tolerances of a living being, yes."

The ghost of a thought came from Maii: <But what kind of being is it?>

It was with some unease that Roche realized that the Surin's words echoed her own suspicions: A singleship. One person. Who else *could* it be?

"Send something to meet it. An armored—and armed—probe, this time."

"To destroy it?"

"Not yet. Just to let the pilot know we're not taking any chances."

With a slight nod of acknowledgment, Kajic's image disappeared, leaving Roche alone with Maii once more. She could feel the girl's hand on her shoulder, but couldn't decide whether the firmness of the grip was an attempt at reassurance or an indication of Maii's own fears.

PART TWO:

GALINE FOUR

INTERLUDE

At the bottom of the pit, two suns now burned. He found it hard to sleep, their light was so bright. With tiredness came lack of focus and inability to concentrate. The latter especially was dangerous when the Cruel One's servant was in the room.

<Tell me!>

Sensation crackled through nerve-endings left vestigial by his species for good reason. It wasn't exactly pain; more a driving ache. His body strove to respond—from the tips of all five of his limbs to deep, primal points in his brain—but his being was elsewhere. He was dreaming awake. He was watching the two suns burn.

One hung far away, turning in odd spirals among several dozen much fainter lights. This Shining One was not diminished for being afar; if anything, its magnificence attained a proper perspective in the distance. It was an uncanny thing: made, yet not-made; Human, yet un-Human.

<Talk to me, *irikeii,* or I swear General Darkan will seed your planet with dusters designed to tear carbon bonds apart! We'll reduce your so-called Grand Design into a puddle of slime!>

The words formed involuntarily at the mention of the Cruel One. His body was learning new tricks of survival quite beyond the care of his conscious mind.

: THEY

: DANCE

<Dance?>

: THEY

: MOVE

<Where do they move?>

: FURTHER

<Further *where*?>

He could not answer the question. Again, the meaninglessness of spatial references confounded him. Movement was enough, surely. Why this endless concern about *location*?

Something—an electrode, a chemical, a laser—touched a point deep within him, a point they had not touched before. This time, it truly hurt.

He writhed. Visions assailed him. Not true eye-sight but mind-visions: of the Shadow Place on Hek'm, his accommodation since birth; of the minds of his attendants, and the minds of his family; of the web of minds unfolding around him, Olmahoi and others, all tangled in a knot of near-infinite complexity; of the simple AI drones who had smashed unseen through this web and snatched him from his people; of the Cruel One who had brought him *here,* wherever *here* was, where the knot was barely a tangle in a handful of threads, where two minds as bright as only a handful of others he had ever been permitted to see struck him like noontime sunlight streaking down a very deep pit . . .

He strove. Past the Cruel One's servant—with his complex web of lies and suspicions and delicate manipulations—and the others who served him. Outward . . . Not to the distant ones, barely visible against the one who accompanied them. Nearer. He had studied these minds before, and recently too—relieved to have found someone new to look at. They too were dwarfed by the one they traveled with, of whose brilliance they had only the barest inkling, yet he found them intriguing.

Two crippled, yet strong; both possessing extraordinary stories, yet not unprecedented.

Another, piercing like a knife. This one he avoided. Her mind burned differently from those of the Shining Ones, although she too had a made quality. She was an abomination.

The fourth and last was . . . an enigma. Under other circumstances he would have studied this one exclusively. There were secrets here, secrets that might prove in the end to be unfathomable but would, he was quite sure, be worth the attempt.

Pain.

He concentrated.

: CLOSER

<Which one?>

: CONTACT

: MADE

<Ah . . . good. Some progress at last. Is it the same as the other?>

: YES

<Interesting, but not unexpected. Perhaps the situation isn't as unlikely as it seemed.>

He sensed the satisfaction of the Cruel One's servant arising from his immediate misunderstanding, and hastened to explain.

: SAME

: BUT

: DIFFERENT

<In detail yes, it would be. One can only replicate an n-body so far. Experiential discrepancies will necessarily facilitate operational divergences between the clones. To expect otherwise would be naive. It's their internal structure I'm concerned about—their mental architecture, if you like. Are they fashioned from identical plans, using identical materials, for identical purposes?>

He pondered this. It was something he'd not considered before. The Shining Ones had a *purpose*? He had thought they just *were,* like most intelligent beings he encountered.

Despite having had his life mapped out for him almost from the moment of conception, he did not believe in destiny. There was no guiding hand ruling the cosmos; he understood this better than most people.

There was only one way he could answer the question.

: SAME

Yet it was not enough. He could sense an impossible truth lurking in the bright points that marked the beings his captors sought. But how to express it? And what to do about it, even if he could?

: IRIKEII

<Yes? I know your name.>

: IRIKEII

<What do you mean?>

: IRIKEII

Words always failed him in the end. No matter how much the Cruel One's servant ranted and raved, he would never be able to explain any better.

: IRIKEII

: TOO

3

AVS-44
'955.01.20 EN
1110

"Welcome, Morgan." The transmission came from the singleship via standard COE communications channels: encrypted and on a tightbeam, but otherwise unremarkable. "I knew we were expecting someone from COE, but had no idea it would be you!"

"Not now, Myer." Roche looked up at the face in a corner of the scutter's main observation tank and was pricked again by its unexpected familiarity. "We're docking in five minutes, and I need to concentrate."

Mavalhin smiled the smile she remembered so well. "Okay," he said, "but remember, I'm right behind you, so don't cock anything up, all right?"

Roche didn't bother to reply. She knew him—or, more accurately, had once known him—well enough to realize that such comments were symptoms of his own insecurity. Whenever he'd needled her in the past, it had been because he felt threatened by her and needed to bring her down a peg or two. Nothing, it seemed, had changed.

Beside her at the helm of the scutter, Haid killed the audio link between the two crafts.

"The station has indicated that we are to dock at their main facility," he said. "So far, everything seems aboveboard."

Roche looked at the navigation display. The mini-station hung like a vast, gray stone in the dark-body halo the natives of Palasian System had called Autoville. Like most mini-stations, it had a spherical external framework almost a kilometer across upon which hung such hardware as thrusters, shield generators, docking bays, and communication dishes; on the inside huddled the modules required for unsuited habitation, packed piecemeal together and connected to the shell by a semi-rigid lattice. Much of the shell's interior was empty, apart from what appeared to be a small scout-ship docked in an internal gantry; as a result, the mini-station seemed incomplete. But Roche could tell just by looking at it that it had seen many years of service. Its one identifying feature—a black *R* painted on the end opposite the main engines—had faded from long exposure to space dust.

No lights were visible on the shell or in the interior. Whoever it belonged to, they were taking the job of hiding seriously.

"Bring us in slowly," Roche said. She would have liked to pilot the scutter herself, but preferred to give Haid the opportunity of flying with his new prosthetics.

The bay they were aiming for was outlined in green, courtesy of the navigation AI. "Are we still clear, Box?"

She waited a second for the AI's reply. The *Ana Vereine*—along with Cane and Maii—was waiting camouflaged as a COE raider a safe distance away, resulting in a slight communication lag.

"I detect no suspicious emissions," said the Box eventually. "Apart from the singleships and a handful of drones, there are no other vessels in this vicinity. The station is communicating with several distant sites by tightbeam, but I have been unable to overhear their conversations."

"So far so good." Roche watched the mini-station grow steadily larger in the display. "Still, I'd be happier if they'd tell us who they are."

"They probably feel the same way about us," said Haid. "Our ID tells them nothing, and you've avoided mentioning why we're here. Trust works both ways, Morgan."

Roche nodded. "I know. But who makes the first move?"

"I guess they already have, by inviting us here." Haid adjusted the scutter's trajectory with a quick burn on the thrusters. "I'm not saying we should let down our guard entirely, but we have to give a little in order to get what we want."

"That doesn't sound like your normal line, Ameidio."

He smiled. "Just trying to see it from their perspective."

She supposed she should do the same, although it was hard to remain impassive following the shock of seeing Myer Mavalhin again. Any fear she had felt over the occupant of the singleship had vanished the moment she saw his face, in 2-D monochrome and highly compressed from the tightbeam transmission aimed squarely at the probe they had sent to follow the *Ana Vereine*'s path. Those dark eyes set deep in a broad, clean-shaven face; the black hair with its graying swaths about the temples . . . There was no mistaking him.

No mistaking, either, the warning he had sent:

"If you're heading to Aro Spaceport, then change course *now,* while you still can. A hostile agent unlike anyone you've come across before has been contained within this system, and we're unsure of his whereabouts. I urge you to turn and leave immediately."

She had already seen enough for the advice to carry real weight. Only the smallest hint of hope had kept her from seriously considering the option of leaving.

"If for any reason you are unable to escape the system," he had continued, "or if you're in need of repairs, then follow me to the coordinates 63 plus 4 degrees, 2 point 6 PAU. But maintain radio silence. We don't want to risk exposing ourselves with unnecessary communications."

We, he had said, as casually as only he could under such circumstances. *We.* There was someone else alive in Palasian System.

The yellow landing lights of the station's main docking facility winked invitingly to life as the scutter broached a minimum distance. No doubt the light was coherent and aimed directly at them to reduce the risk of anyone's overseeing. There would still be scattering off the scutter's hull, but Roche suspected the risk of anyone's detecting *that* was small. Precautions were sensible only to a certain degree; beyond that, they were symptomatic of paranoia.

Which is why, she guessed, she had taken Mavalhin at his word. He was not an unknown quantity, like everything else in the system; she couldn't entirely trust him, based on past experience, but at least she knew that he was only mundane and could deal with him if necessary.

Myer Mavalhin . . .

"You said you studied with this guy," said Haid, breaking into her thoughts.

"Huh? Oh, yeah . . ." Roche felt again that sudden rush of unreality as the fact that he was *here,* in Palasian System, struck home. "At COE Military Cottage."

"How well did you know him?"

"Well enough." She shrugged, and hoped the flush spreading across her face wasn't visible. "We took the same classes and were often buddied on smaller projects. We were regarded as a sort of team."

And it had been a very good team, she remembered. For a while. Maybe a year. Then it had been unbearable, prolonged by the fact that the College tutors had still expected them to continue working together. If not for Mavalhin's eventual expulsion from the College, she might well have left herself, just to get away from him. It had been that bad.

But here she was—part of her almost glad to see him again, after all this time, while another part of her still yearned to stick him in a blast tube and press Purge.

Roche had already discussed some of the facts with the others on the *Ana Vereine,* although she hadn't felt comfortable delving too deeply into her past. Even when the station had been located at exactly the place Myer had indicated—measured from Jagabis's location and plane of ecliptic: 63 degrees closer to them, 4 degrees above, and just over two and half times as far away from the sun—she had avoided talking to Mavalhin directly, for fear of exposing scar tissue she would rather have kept hidden. She had simply ordered the *Ana Vereine* to rendezvous with the station and sent a brief text reply indicating to him that she would be willing to talk terms.

But she could feel Maii's curiosity brushing at the edges of her long-term memory. And Haid knew her well enough to know that she wasn't telling the whole truth.

"I don't get it," he said. "You're prepared to take this guy at his word when he says he and his buddies want to work with us, but you'll hardly talk about him, let alone *to* him. Who is it you don't trust, Morgan?"

"I'm not sure," she said frankly, half-smiling in the gloom of the scutter. "I don't know what I'm thinking at the moment, which is why I'd rather not think at all for a while."

"That's not very reassuring, Morgan."

"I know, but . . . Look, I'm sorry. Let's just dock, and see what they have to say."

"Now I know why you left Maii behind. With her here, I'd at least have been able to dig a little deeper."

She was about to snap back that the reave would never have betrayed her confidence in such a way, but caught his grin in the fluorescent glow from the displays in time to realize he was joking.

"It'd take more than Maii," she responded evenly, "to make sense of this mess."

"So it seems," he said, returning his attention to the navigation display.

The scutter docked with a slight jerk. Within seconds, environment displays indicated that an external feed needed authorization before the physical link could be completed. Roche advised the scutter's AI to wait.

“A little rough,” said Haid, leaning back in his seat and flexing his new hand. The matte-gray digits wriggled as fluidly as organic fingers did, defying their appearance.

Roche patted him on the shoulder, and levered herself out of the copilot’s chair. “Nothing a bit of practice won’t fix.”

“I guess.” Haid followed her into the scutter’s empty passenger bay.

She reached into the shoulder bag she had brought with her and produced two Dato side arms, giving one to Haid. The holster of the other energy weapon she clipped to the belt of her black expedition uniform—again, a standard Dato make but not distinguished by insignia. Haid’s weapon hung at his side like an extension of his biomesh.

“Ready?” he said, shifting the side arm into a more comfortable position.

“Not quite.” Roche keyed her implants and linked them to the scutter’s communications systems. <Box, are we still in contact?>

The lag was shorter this time. The *Ana Vereine* had assumed a more immediate position once the scutter had docked.

<Yes, Morgan.> The AI’s voice was a whisper in her head. <Your audiovisual feed is clear. There has been no interference from the station.>

<How about you, Ameidio?> Roche asked, directing her attention to the man standing next to her.

A small window appeared in one corner of her vision. Haid’s more basic implants were not designed to carry sensory data, but could transmit and receive text messages translated from speech by the scutter’s processors.

FINE, he said. AM I COMING THROUGH OKAY?

Roche nodded. <Let’s keep in touch regularly. If they cut us off, we pull out immediately.>

UNDERSTOOD.

<Given the power at my disposal aboard the *Ana Vereine*, I am confident I will be able to contact you at all times,> said the Box. <Should your return feed be interrupted, I will notify you.>

Roche nodded again, satisfied that she had covered that particular base as thoroughly as she could. The station would know that they were broadcasting to and from the scutter, but without cracking the Box’s cipher, eavesdroppers would not know what was being said.

That was fine by her. Just because Myer and his friends probably weren’t working for the clone warrior didn’t necessarily make them allies.

Speaking aloud, she continued: “We’ll wait for them to make their move. It shouldn’t be long; they’ll probably want to attach an umbilical to keep us under control. In fact, I’m hoping they will, because that’ll give us easier access to the bay security systems. The Box is more likely to find useful data poking around the datacore than we are on a guided tour.”

“Undoubtedly,” said Haid. “It handled COE HQ easily enough, so—”

A clunk on the hull interrupted him. They both turned to face the airlock. A red light began to flash.

Roche cued her implants for an external transmission. “This is Morgan Roche,” she said. “I’d like to speak to the person in charge of dock security.”

“That would be me,” came the immediate reply. “Gered Disisto at your service. We’re trying to attach an umbilical, but your ship won’t comply. Is something wrong?”

"I will release the airlock when I am satisfied that we'll not be harmed."

"Your caution is understandable, Commander," Disisto said. "And I give you my word that you are in no danger from myself or anyone under my command."

"Not good enough." She was tempted to correct the erroneous use of "Commander" but decided to let it go. "I'll allow the umbilical to be attached, but I'm not leaving this craft until you and one other officer arrive to escort me from it."

There was a slight pause, then: "I'll be down in a moment."

Roche instructed the onboard AI to proceed with the link-up. The sounds of faint movement came through the hull as the umbilical locked tight around the external airlock and equalized pressure. At the same time, fuel and data lines sought their respective sockets and clicked home. The sounds ceased at the same time the airlock display indicated that the umbilical was sealed.

"You there, Disisto?" said Roche.

"I'm here," said the dock security head not long after. "Outside and waiting."

First making certain her side arm was within easy reach, Roche stepped back from the airlock and cued it to open.

The outer airlock opened with a hiss and two men stepped inside, one tall and dark-skinned, the other short and fair, both wearing gray uniforms. When the outer door had sealed behind them, the inner opened and they stepped inside, bringing with them a pocket of heavily scented air.

"Disisto?" said Roche, looking to both men.

"That's me." The tall, dark-skinned man nodded, extending a hand to Roche, which she took, and shook. His face, like his frame, was lean without being thin, as though he exercised regularly. "Roche, I presume?"

"And this is Ameidio Haid." Haid bowed slightly.

Disisto indicated the other man. "Torr Synnett."

Synnett glanced at both of them in turn, but was otherwise impassive.

"I figured you'd want us unarmed," he said, gesturing at Haid's side arm. "So this puts us at something of a disadvantage." When neither Roche nor Haid made any effort to remove the weapons, Disisto shrugged and said: "Well, now what?"

"Now we follow you out of here," said Roche. She indicated the airlock. "After you."

The four of them filed into the small enclosure and waited for the doors to cycle. The smell of spices was stronger closer to the two men, and Roche resisted the urge to ask what it was. Cinnamon, perhaps, with a hint of cloves, plus something more pungent, less familiar.

KESH, Haid said via his implants.

Roche glanced at Haid. <What do you mean?>

CAN'T YOU SMELL IT?

Roche tasted the air again. She had met Kesh agents while in the COE's employ, but always under Pristine-controlled circumstances. Never had she been in an environment that was home to any of that particular Caste for any length of time. If Kesh was what Haid said he smelled, then she would have to take his word for it.

"Welcome to Galine Four," Disisto said as the outer door opened. "No doubt you'll be unfamiliar with the layout of the station," he went on, ushering them along the umbilical. "But it won't take long to get your bearings. Until then I'd be more than happy to act as your escort. Or I can make other arrangements. It's up to you."

"You'll do fine," Roche said, moving forward to stand next to him. The ribbed plastic swayed slightly beneath their feet as they walked. "But I'd like to meet your commanding officer as soon as possible."

Disisto nodded amiably. "I'm taking you there now."

"Good," said Roche. "There are a lot of questions I'd like answered—such as what you're doing here in this system."

"I'm sure he'll be asking you the same things," said Disisto.

"And I'll be happy to answer him," said Roche. "Once I'm certain of his intentions."

At the far end of the umbilical, they stepped onto a metal platform which led to a flight of steps. The door behind them was the second of three along one wall of the main docking bay's disembarkation point. The scutter lay hidden behind the pressure-wall, which also possessed larger airlocks and umbilicals designed for the transfer of freight. None of the other doors was in use.

A dozen people occupied the disembarkation point, three of them dressed similarly to Disisto and his sidekick—obviously security officers like them. Above and on the far side of the chamber was a glassed-off observation floor which held still more gray uniforms. Even with so many people watching her, Roche felt alone; the disembarkation point was large enough to hold five of the *Ana Vereine*'s scutters.

The acoustic properties of the room lent a booming quality to their footsteps as they descended the stairs.

"Not much of a reception," Haid joked.

"You'll have to understand that we're a little busy at the moment," said Disisto earnestly. "If one of our scouts hadn't been in your vicinity, we probably would've let you go on your way rather than risk our necks talking to you."

"Speaking of which," said Roche, remembering Mavalhin. "Will that singleship we spoke to be docking soon?"

"It's just coming in now. Why?"

"I studied with the pilot some years ago. I was wondering whether I'd get the chance to catch up with him later."

"Well, he has debriefing and decon before he'll be allowed to mix with the rest of the crew, but I'll make sure he knows you asked about him, if you like."

Roche felt a mixture of relief and regret rush through her. "Thanks."

Disisto led Haid and Roche toward the main exit, with Synnett bringing up the rear. Roche glanced behind them just as the seal around one of the other umbilicals flared green, indicating that someone—presumably Mavalhin—was about to disembark. The three other security guards in the disembarkation point moved up the steps—and it was only then that she realized that the guards hadn't been there to greet her and Haid at all.

<Odd,> she commented to Haid. <So much for being cautious. They don't seem to give a damn if we're here or not.>

FEELING PUT OUT, MORGAN? Haid shot back.

<No, it's just not what I expected.>

The corridors and open spaces they passed through were uniformly drab: gray walls and floors, with minimal lighting; clearly a work area and not intended to look pretty. The few people they encountered were busy performing errands and took no notice of Disisto and his entourage.

"So," she said after a while. "What exactly is it you do here? The station, I mean."

Disisto faced her with a smile. “Research,” he said. “But beyond that I’m not authorized to say. That will be up to the chief to explain.”

“And just who is this ‘chief’?”

“Professor Linegar Rufo,” said Disisto. “He’s in charge of Galine Four.”

“That’s the name of the station, I take it?” Disisto nodded without breaking his stride. “Is there a Galine One, Two or Three anywhere around?”

“Not that I’m aware of,” he said. “There may have been once, but I’ve never heard of them.”

“You’ve worked here long?”

“Five years.”

“A long time to be cooped up on a station like this,” said Haid.

“It beats a lot of the other jobs I’ve had.”

<Box,> Roche sent via her implants, <look up Galine Four in the COE register and see what you can find.>

<Already checking,> replied the AI.

Haid picked up the conversation, grilling Disisto about his previous employment—which seemed, for the most part, to have been for the Traders’ Guild or independent merchants. Roche followed the exchange with half an ear while continuing her discussion with the Box.

<Let me know if you find anything. Any luck breaking into the station’s security system?>

<On a superficial level, the task was absurdly simple,> the Box replied. <But I have not yet managed to obtain anything more interesting than basic hardware specifications. There is obviously a secure cache I have not yet penetrated.>

<That’s odd.> It wasn’t like the AI to be so easily thwarted. Still, Roche had no doubt that, in the end, the Box would obtain the information she needed. <How about Galine Four? Found anything yet?>

<An advertisement in the xenoarchaeological sites of a science forum for a privately owned, mobile facility with permanent research staff on board.>

There was that word again: *research.*

<Xenoarchaeology, huh? Strange for such a vessel to be here, considering the ruins are recent and the builders Pristine.>

<Perhaps not, Morgan. There *was* an archaeological outpost in the system around Kukumat and Murukan.>

<So the station might have been visiting there when the clone warrior attacked,> said Roche. <Because it doesn’t appear on any of the COE registers as a permanent facility, it would have been overlooked.>

<That seems plausible.>

<But why hasn’t it left, then? That would have been the sensible thing to do.>

<Because it cannot. From my observations taken as the scutter approached, I can state with certainty that this station possesses neither anchor nor a slow-jump drive.>

Roche absorbed the fact with interest. <They’re trapped here too?>

<So it would seem.>

<Is the *Ana Vereine* powerful enough to slow-jump both itself and the station out of here?>

<Unlikely,> said the Box. <But it could certainly rescue the station’s occupants. I estimate a crew of roughly five hundred to a thousand—well within our carrying capacity.>

<Then at least we have something to bargain with.> Roche smiled inwardly. <And they know it too. No wonder they're playing it cool.>

<Unless they don't understand the danger they're in . . .>

Roche returned her attention to Disisto. The security officer was describing how they had sent manned singleships to every occupied point in Palasian System, and how they had found only destruction everywhere. If he knew anything about the perpetrator of the attack, he was hiding it well.

"And you've seen no evidence of life at all?" Roche asked.

"Only outriggers, here and there," Disisto said. "A spine or two must have moved in a few years ago without registering; they certainly don't show in the system stats. Most of them are in the belts the prowlers haven't already mined, although some have come in closer. We saw a couple attempt to intervene on Aro, but not very successfully. A piece of the Spaceport's orbital tower was rigged as a trap; cut them clean out of the sky."

"Our probe in that area found gas-guns in the derelicts—"

"Yeah, we ran into those when we put the tower out of action. It was about then we decided to cut our losses and get out of the way. Not that there's anyone left to rescue on Aro, anyway."

"Or anywhere else, it seems," said Haid.

"Except for this station," put in Roche. "Doesn't that strike you as a little odd?"

"Not really," said Disisto as they approached a transit tube. He pressed his hand onto the ID scanner, then turned to Roche. "We've been very careful, keeping emissions to an absolute minimum and staying put. We're not a battleship, and we're smart enough to know it. This warrior took out an entire Armada base, so we certainly wouldn't stand a chance against him."

<He's lying,> said the Box.

<About what?>

<About 'staying put.' The station's reaction engines have been operational for an extended period in the last few days.>

<How can you tell?>

<Every attitude vent and thruster is radiating heat, and I am detecting a poorly dissipated ion wash in this vicinity.>

<Enough to tell where it leads?>

<No. Just that Galine Four has traveled a large distance recently, and not hidden in Autoville as Disisto would have you believe.>

Roche chewed her lip thoughtfully, but she didn't have time to dwell upon the matter for very long: the transit cab had arrived and Disisto was ushering them inside.

"We're leaving the outer levels behind us," he said, punching a destination into the cab's control system. "If you experience any giddiness, it won't last long; a few ambient g-fields overlap between here and the Hub. In the center you shouldn't have a problem. You'll get used to the transition if you're here long enough."

"Seems like you could use a competent engineer," said Haid.

"Perhaps." The door slid shut, and Disisto moved to place his back against the far wall. "But as I said, you get used to it."

The cab descended with a sudden lurch that just as quickly reversed, leaving Roche feeling as though she was going upward. Haid lost his balance and scrabbled with his artificial hand for purchase on the wall. He missed the support rail, and fell to one knee.

Roche reached out to support him; he righted himself with a grunt.

"A little unsteady, there," observed Disisto. "Sorry about that."

"I'll be okay," Haid muttered, embarrassed. He wrapped his good hand around a support. "You did warn us, I guess."

"How much further?" Roche asked.

"Not far, once we arrive at the Hub." Disisto cocked an eyebrow. "You in a hurry?"

"Just don't want to keep our host waiting." The floor beneath them shifted again, but this time Haid managed to remain steady. "So aren't you interested in what we're doing here?"

Disisto shook his head. "It's none of my business. My concern is security only, and you've had the okay from the chief. I'm curious, naturally, which is why I volunteered to be your guide. But I won't push the matter unless . . ." Something shifted behind Disisto's calm façade, as though there was a question he wanted to ask. Just then the cab shuddered. "We're almost there," he said, changing the subject. "Our gradient should be nice and smooth from here on in."

The sensation of motion faded almost entirely. Within thirty seconds, they came to a halt and the doors slid smoothly open.

Disisto disembarked first. The first thing Roche noticed was the noise: voices, footsteps, whirring machinery—so different from the near-silence of the *Ana Vereine*. The second thing she noticed, once she had left the cab, was that the dull gray decor had been left behind; here, in the Hub of the station, the walls were white and the light dazzling. The corridor ceilings were laced with vines and other unobtrusive plants. The air was fresher too, although still thick with the smell Haid had identified as belonging to the Kesh Caste.

Several people walked past as Roche waited for Haid to leave the cab. Not all were Pristine: Roche spotted two Mbata talking animatedly in their native tongue, and one Surin walking alone. Some wore uniforms similar to Disisto's, but different in color; a substantial proportion, however, were casually clothed. A couple eyed them with curiosity, but didn't stop.

"Which way?" Roche asked, indicating the four corridors that branched from the tube's exit.

"Down here." Disisto pointed along the rightmost corridor. "Don't touch anything or talk to anyone unless I say so. We're all a little jumpy and I'd hate for there to be a scene."

Roche nodded, noting that the inhabitants of Galine Four's Hub did seem a little tense. No one met her eye, and Haid's radical biomodification aroused ill-concealed suspicion in one or two.

Disisto led them along the corridor, then to an accessway that curved gracefully into the distance. One hundred meters farther on, they passed a window, and Roche stopped to stare through it. On the other side was an enormous chamber filled with plants growing in free-fall. Long tendrils rose from spongelike vats of nutrients; moss and vines covered every flat surface; occasionally among the ubiquitous green was a speck of color—probably a fruit or vegetable doing its best to remedy the imbalance.

"Commander Roche?" Disisto stood waiting for her while Haid and Synnett continued on their way.

"Huh?" She turned toward him. "Oh, sorry. I was just admiring your garden."

Disisto smiled. "I try to spend as much time in it as I can. Rank, as they say, has its privileges."

"Sometimes."

"Yes, sometimes." His smile slipped, and Roche found herself missing it immediately. "Let's go," he said.

They followed the other two along the sweep of the corridor and to a semicircular antechamber where two armed guards in black waited by a sealed double door.

"He's expecting us," said Disisto to the nearest guard.

The guard nodded and the doors sighed open. Disisto marched between the guards, waving for Haid and Roche to follow. Synnett brought up the rear, as implacable and silent as a cloud's shadow.

They found themselves in a short corridor, facing another double door. The space was empty and dimly lit, and warmer than the antechamber had been. Once they were inside, the door shut behind them.

"Where—?" Roche began.

Disisto raised a finger to his lips. "Wait."

"Place your weapons on the floor," boomed a voice from the ceiling, its non-Pristine mouth lending a slight lisp to the fricatives.

I TOLD YOU, sent Haid.

<That you did,> Roche replied. The voice belonged to a Kesh.

"Relax," said Disisto. "It's nothing sinister. The chief just won't allow arms anywhere near him."

Roche glanced at Haid. "What happens if we refuse to comply with his wishes?"

Disisto shrugged. "Then you don't get to meet him."

<I advise diplomacy at this point,> said the Box via Roche's implants. <Refusal may cost us more than acceptance would.>

<That's easy for you to say,> Roche shot back. <You're not here.>

Even so, she loosened the clasp on her holster and placed the side arm on the floor by her feet. Haid, after a moment's hesitation, did likewise.

"The cyborg will be placed within a restraining field," said the voice when both weapons were on the floor. "Sudden movements will not be tolerated."

Haid grunted and went to raise his hand, but was unable to. Gritting his teeth, he attempted the movement more slowly, and this time his hand inched up to his chest.

Disisto watched him in alarm. "I'm sorry." His concern and surprise were genuine. "I had no idea they would—"

"Just as long as there are no other surprises waiting for us," Roche said with some anger.

Disisto glanced at the door. "I hope not."

Haid's hand clenched into a fist. SONOFABITCH.

The lock clicked.

"You may enter," said the voice.

The door slid open, revealing a room as large as the bridge of the *Ana Vereine*, but far less cluttered. An expansive, circular desk, cut from polished white stone and adorned with shimmering holographic tanks, occupied the center of the room. The ceiling was also circular, and stepped around this central point, like an inverted amphitheater. The walls were comprised of dozens of inactive screens, and off to one side, was one large window through which could be seen the green of the station's gardens.

Disisto nudged Roche forward, and she stepped inside. Haid, moving cautiously so as not to activate the restraining field, did likewise.

Her first impression upon entering the room was of spaciousness and grace. Her second was of clinical efficiency, as though the room served as a laboratory when not used for meetings. Her third was less analytical, relying mainly on the data her sense of smell provided.

Cylindrical light fixtures suspended between the floor and ceiling cast a pure, white light on the room's three occupants.

"Greetings, Commander Roche," said the first, a Pristine standing on the far side of the desk. His hair was white, where he had hair at all. He was so small and his skin so waxy that Roche guessed his age to be over one hundred standard years. His movements, though, were far from infirm.

"You would be Rufo," said Roche.

The professor raised an eyebrow in mock surprise. "I see Gered has briefed you." His eyes then fell upon his security head, who shifted uneasily beneath the stare.

"Some," said Roche, noting Disisto's discomfort. "Nothing of consequence."

"Anyway," said Rufo grandly, "I welcome you to my home."

Roche eyed the two Kesh standing to either side of Rufo; neither looked particularly welcoming, even for a Caste not given to pleasantries. Both wore formal uniforms of office, with leather surcoats and boots over black bodysuits that bulged with muscle.

"Your home?" said Roche.

Rufo moved around the desk to greet her. At close range, he seemed even smaller. "I finance and run this establishment. My employees are under no illusion as to who pays their bonuses—although I like to believe that I am a fair taskmaster." His piercing, bright blue eyes darted to Disisto. "Would that be a fair comment, Gered?"

The security officer nodded smartly. "More than fair, sir."

Rufo smiled and moved back around the desk. "Introductions, then. Morgan Roche, your name we know, and that of your companion, Ameidio Haid; Gered filled me in as well. But you two have not met all of *us,* yet." He stopped upon reaching the first of the Kesh, and reached up to place a hand on one massive shoulder.

"This is Lieutenant-Doctor Haden B'shan, my second in command."

The Kesh officer bowed, his hairless head catching the light; his tough skin was predominantly yellow, but with blotches of blue and purple in symmetrical patterns, like ink blots, scattered across every visible surface. Where ears would have been on a Pristine, two dark-colored membranes a thumb's-width across were visible.

"I am honored," he said in a surprisingly high-pitched voice.

Unable to think of anything appropriate to say, Roche bowed also. She was slightly surprised by his words: Kesh were not normally so gracious to members of other Castes, particularly ones they hardly knew.

Haid on the other hand, slowly placed one fist on his chest and said: *"Do-tri'sk en sh'ante ruk."*

B'shan smiled, the moist inner lips of his mouth appearing for an instant. "*Du.* Impressive."

"Some time ago I served with a squad of Kesh commandos on Nirr," Haid explained.

"Which family?"

"G'rodo."

B'shan nodded. "They were a noble lineage, prior to their excision from the N'Kor Republic."

"I always felt the Dictatrix could've shown leniency in their case."

The other Kesh made a noise in his throat that sounded like gravel underfoot. B'shan nodded again, this time with solemn dignity. He stepped back to draw attention away from himself, the soles of his leather boots squeaking on the floor as he did so.

"And this," Rufo continued, "is Field Officer Shak'ni."

Shak'ni was taller than B'shan, but thinner. His face was etched with fine birthmarks in a bright shade of red, like veins. This time, the bow was begrudging, barely a nod. Shak'ni's eyes met Roche's only briefly as she returned the gesture, his contempt for her as palpable as the smell of his Caste filling the room. He didn't waste nods on a greeting, and Haid too said nothing.

Moving back around the table, Rufo returned to a position directly in front of her and Haid.

"Together," he said, "Haden and I have been scouring this system for evidence of the warrior that wrought such destruction upon it."

"I guessed as much," Roche said, glad they'd finally arrived at the topic that most concerned her. "I'm keen to analyze your data."

"And I am keen to analyze yours." Rufo's stare held hers firmly. "I presumed that's why you had come here. Crossing the Gauntlet is a feat not undertaken lightly."

"You know about that?"

"Of course. The various technological experiments performed by advanced Castes prior to Transcendence were a fascination of mine during my youth." Rufo stopped, as though a thought had just struck him, then continued: "But it would make more sense to explain from the beginning. Please, take a seat."

He waved a hand, and five white chairs rose out of the seamless floor in a ring around the circular desk. Roche hesitated for a moment, then took the one nearest her. Haid sat beside her; the two Kesh sat opposite them.

"Gered, if you would be so good as to wait outside, I will summon you when Commander Roche is ready to leave."

Disisto nodded, turned and left the room. Synnett followed close on his heels.

"Now." Rufo took the remaining seat. As he did so, the holographic tanks lining the walls and on the desk flickered to life. Color and movement surrounded them: scenes of distant worlds and stations, only a handful of which Roche recognized; strange texts in unknown hieroglyphs; the faces of dozens of people of all Castes and types, lecturing silently.

"I have many interests," said Rufo, "but foremost of them all is the past. History and the flotsam by which we gauge it has fascinated me ever since I was a child. From the age of four, I devoted my life and, upon my father's early death, a considerable fortune to the pursuit of such knowledge. But for such relics, and the resources my father left me, many of my childhood dreams would have gone unrealized.

"For instance—" He stood abruptly, pointing at the ceiling above the desk. From the center of the roof descended what appeared to be a sculpture no larger than Roche's hand, or a fossil cast in amber. Roche was unable to tell what it was, exactly, even when it had come to rest a meter above the desk.

"Give us a hint," said Haid, his artificial eyes focusing closely on the object.

"This," Rufo went on, his hands held out before him, "is my most prized possession. It was plucked by these very fingers from the wreckage of a spaceship ten times older than any of the existing civilizations in this region."

<It's the Gil-Shh'ana Fiche,> said the Box. <The cornerstone of all that is known about Primordial civilizations! Its location has been a mystery for twenty years.>

"It is a data-storage device built by none of the known Castes, past or present," said Rufo at the same time. "The information it holds has never been fully translated, but it contains words written before even the most ancient Caste is known to have inhabited the stars."

"How is that possible?" Roche asked when she had the overlap straightened out.

"Clearly there are gaps in our knowledge," Rufo explained. "At least four Primordial Castes precede the earliest confirmed records we have. We call them Castes A, B, C and D, for even their names are unknown."

"But they *are* Human?"

"Of course, Commander. It is an established fact that no other intelligent species ever conquered the stars." Rufo spoke as though to an ignorant child. "Apart from this, all we can say for certain is that these Castes disappeared many hundreds of millennia ago. There are relics scattered here and there for those who care to look, but not enough to build a coherent picture of what their societies were like; not even enough to convince most universities to teach the facts that we have uncovered. I have devoted my life to expanding that pool of knowledge, and a few others along the way."

Realization dawned on Roche, then. "You've found some ruins, haven't you?"

"I was led to believe so," Rufo said. "Mok, the only moon of the Kukumat-Murukan double binary, is said to hold a fabulous collection of artifacts that have yet to be catalogued. Regrettably, the unfortunate business in this system has prevented us from examining the site. You see, I am not so involved in my work that I will ignore Human suffering when it occurs in front of me."

"And what exactly have you done about it?" asked Haid with a hint of skepticism.

"As much as you, so far," Rufo replied, clearly resenting Haid's reproving tone. He faced Roche. "I have removed my station to a safe place and dispatched smaller vessels to survey the damage."

"And you haven't intervened?"

"How could I do anything other than study what has happened here? That is the area in which my skills lie; I am neither tactician nor warrior. I decided that the long-term interest of the region would be best served by intelligence rather than valor."

"And what *have* you found?" Roche asked.

Rufo sighed and returned to his seat. "I have seen things in these last two weeks, Commander, I never expected to see. Things that . . . Forgive me." Visibly distressed, he leaned back in his seat and signaled for B'shan to continue.

The Kesh stood. "Understand, Commander Roche, that we on Galine Four are not allied to any military service. Therefore, if at any point during what I am about to tell you, your training suggests an alternate interpretation, please do not hesitate to interrupt. We will welcome your input."

Roche nodded, not wanting to discourage his mistaken assumption of her origins: while the *Ana Vereine* was camouflaged as a COE warship, it was safer to reinforce that impression. "Your rank is honorary, then?"

"A title, no more, left over from my adolescence in the service of the Dictatrix. I am an academic first and foremost, now." Noticing her glance at Shak'ni, he added: "My fellow Kesh is acting as a liaison between Galine Four and the N'Kor Republic. Prior to our arrival here, we were researching several sites in non-Pristine territories."

"Understood," said Roche. "Please, continue."

B'shan moved closer to the table. The Gil-Shh'ana Fiche retreated back into the ceiling as a large display flickered into life. In the tank appeared a scale map of the orbits of the five innermost planets of Palasian System.

"You are no doubt aware how it began. A COE courier, *Daybreak,* en route to Gorund Sef picked up a single life capsule not far from here and disappeared shortly thereafter. Two days later, it reappeared on a course for Guhr Outpost, broadcasting an emergency beacon. The outpost's commanding officer sent a tug to intercept *Daybreak* and bring it in for repairs. Subsequent to that, the base reported being under attack, then it too fell silent."

"Yes," Roche interrupted. "A battalion of Marines was sent to investigate. The pictures brought back by the one surviving ship showed the inhabited bases in Palasian System in flames."

"By the time *Daybreak* was recovered, it was already too late," said B'shan grimly. "The emergency beacon was a distraction; the crew had been dead for a day before it was even sent. The . . . *person* responsible commandeered the tug sent to intercept it, and, in conjunction with a small asteroid he had already diverted from its orbit, destroyed Guhr Outpost before its commanding officer could realize what had happened. The asteroid collided with a medical vessel parked in a refueling orbit, and sparked a chain reaction that resulted in the ignition of the outpost's entire fuel reserves."

Haid whistled. "No wonder the crater was so big."

"Bear in mind that much of this is supposition extrapolated from the small amount of evidence left behind at the scene, plus flight data from several of the derelicts we recovered and some faint observations recorded by various installations scattered through the system. We can't even tell how many people were involved in the attack. But given that only one person was rescued from the life-support capsule, and that the chain of events begins at that moment, we have assumed that this single person was alone responsible for what happened here. I know this seems unlikely, and we have no images of this person to prove any of it—or even ascertain his identity. Unfortunately, we can only work from the data we have, and that isn't much. I would hate to give you the impression that we know exactly what occurred, when at best all we can offer you are theories."

Roche nodded, indicating for him to continue.

"From Guhr Outpost we have traced the tug's movements to Gatamin, where it changed course and headed further in-system."

"How did its pilot know where to go?" Haid asked.

"The tug, naturally, contained detailed navigational charts showing every settlement in Palasian System. Relevant targets were easily located." B'shan rotated and expanded the map of Palasian System. "Geyten Base was hit next. The Armada base knew that something had happened to Guhr Outpost, but didn't have enough details to react in time. Barely had they readied two ships to investigate, when the enemy struck."

"We received pictures from Cemenid just before we arrived here," Roche said.

"We were unable to locate the Armada base at all; the moon appeared to have disappeared."

"Precisely." The view in the central tank changed to show Cemenid—a bloated gas giant almost half again as large as Jagabis, with a violent atmosphere that appeared orange in Hintubet's red light. Three visible moons were ringed in green, plus a dark patch in the cloudscape. The image became grainy as the view zoomed in to focus on the dark patch. "This scar in Cemenid's atmosphere does not appear in any navigational records; the fact that you did not notice it suggests that it is no longer visible at all."

"Are you suggesting . . . ?" Roche began.

"That the image here"—B'shan pointed at the dark patch in the central tank—"is the impact site of the moon which was once the home to Geyten Base."

Roche glanced at the Kesh: his expression was serious. "The whole *moon*—?"

"Disturbed from orbit and sent into the atmosphere." B'shan changed the view again, this time to one showing wreckage in orbit around the gas giant. "We have discovered a large number of fragments corresponding to plate-armor commonly used to protect prowling mines from major impacts. It's my opinion that at least two were conscripted by the pilot of the tug on his way through the innermost dark-body halo. They are massive enough to shatter a small moon, or to deflect it from a stable orbit. Furthermore, their security is light and their AIs are simple to reprogram."

Roche pictured the prowling mines—each larger by a significant factor than Galine Four itself—barreling down on the unprepared Armada base. At that speed, little would have stopped them. The base personnel would hardly have had time to evacuate, let alone save any valuable military hardware. The destruction of the base had, once again, been conducted with chilling efficiency.

B'shan added: "We suspect that this incident is related to the ambush of the Armada battalion sent to investigate the distress call broadcast by Guhr Outpost sixteen days earlier. The Marines had been in the system for a week, as best we can tell, but disappeared around that time."

Roche nodded. That made sense. It fit in with the little COE Intelligence had told them, anyway.

"So where did the tug go from there?" she prompted.

"Actually, it probably wasn't there at all. Once the mines had been reprogrammed, there would have been no need for its pilot to have been present. That explains why, only a short time after communication with the base was lost, it caused an alert at Aro Spaceport when it tried to land without authorization."

"I can't believe they'd let it land after everything that had just happened," said Haid.

"They didn't. Port authorities destroyed it when it refused to respond to a third warning."

Roche frowned. "They destroyed it?"

B'shan nodded. "But the pilot was no longer on board. His tactics were uncanny: he was never where anyone expected him to be, always one step ahead. He skipped from *Daybreak* to the tug when there was only the slightest chance that Guhr Outpost might have guessed he was aboard; then, barely after the authorities on Aro had learned about events at Voloras and Cemenid, he'd already left the tug and sent it to act as a distraction while he went about his real business."

"Which was what?" Haid said.

"While Aro Spaceport mopped up the debris of the tug—believing they had destroyed the threat to the system with it—the pilot was using two prowling mines and the resources they contained to set up the next stage of his attack. It must have been during this time that he built the gas-guns and the targeters left behind in the derelicts; he certainly would have been hard-pressed to do it later."

"That makes sense," Roche said. "It also gave Aro Spaceport time to let their guard down."

"It would seem so." B'shan called up a map of the orbits around the major moon of Jagabis. "What he appears to have done in the end is to bring one of the prowlers into close Aro orbit by swinging it past Jagabis on a tight, elliptical orbit that kept it well out of view until the last minute. Then, once it was in place, it fired cutting lasers onto Emptage City, shattering the dome. It also used a flotilla of scavenger drones to attack the ships docked at the midpoint of the orbital tower. At the same time, the second ship came in by a different route and severed the orbital tower entirely."

"How?" said Haid.

"Simply by colliding with it," said B'shan, "and wrenching it out of its moorings."

Roche concentrated to follow the icons moving through the main screen. "The aftershocks of the collision would have destroyed any ships still attached to the tower. Hence the derelicts."

"And the added angular momentum would have carried much of the tower into a higher orbit, where it appears to have been cut into fragments. These fragments served as windmill-style devices designed to keep interlopers away. The cable is very thin and hard to detect; the end of each spinning segment was moving fast enough to cut a ship in two."

"And that's what happened to the outriggers," Haid said.

"So it appears," said B'shan. "We subsequently cleaned out the upper orbits of the windmills before you arrived, but there wasn't much we could do about the gas-guns. We balked at destroying the derelicts entirely, for fear of destroying evidence, but didn't want to risk our observers by sending them in to deactivate the traps one by one."

Hearing that, Roche thought of Mavalhin: he would have been grateful to be relieved of that duty, she was sure. Although cowardice wasn't exactly his style, neither was bravery.

"We detected several transmissions from that region shortly after we arrived," she said. "Did your observers detect them also?"

B'shan waved a hand and the screen filled with Sol command hieroglyphics. "They appear to be in some sort of code. We've had no luck cracking it, though."

"We also picked up another one from a different source, this time in plain text via tightbeam."

B'shan nodded. "The source of that transmission is in the vicinity of the Kukumat-Murukan double planet. We believe it to be either a decoy or an entirely innocent message not meant for our ears."

She raised an eyebrow. "A decoy? Why?"

"Because there have been no attacks since the destruction of Emptage City shortly before the closing of the solar envelope surrounding this system. It is tempting to assume that the person responsible has escaped."

"So why are you hiding out here?" said Haid.

"Cautionary measures," said Rufo softly. "It would be foolish to assume that we are safe until we have proof."

Roche leaned forward, addressing B'shan. "You said it might be an innocent message. From whom?"

"Other survivors, like us, who are also trying to avoid detection. Until we are able to leave this system, we are all denied the option of escape; better to wait until rescue arrives than to advertise our presence."

"What other survivors?" Roche pressed. "The base on Mok was supposed to be empty."

B'shan shrugged. "The source of the transmission has only been approximately pinned down. It is 'near' Mok in the sense that it is within an area several million kilometers across containing the double planet. It may have come from a lone outrigger drifting past, on its way elsewhere."

Roche granted him that. "And what about the Gauntlet? You must have seen it arrive."

B'shan glanced at Rufo. "The quark breeders entered the system twenty-one days ago."

"Do you know who brought them?"

"If we did, then we might at least know who to expect when rescue arrives," said Rufo.

"They entered the system from deep space," explained B'shan, "and aerobraked in the sun's atmosphere. Aro Spaceport was under attack at that point, so by the time we knew they were present they were already in position. From that point, the process was rapid: within twenty hours, the Gauntlet was activated and the system enclosed."

Rufo looked up, and spoke softly: "We assumed it to be you, at first—that you were a vanguard for a much larger recovery operation."

Roche nodded, uncomfortably aware of the unspoken questions behind his words: Who sent you? How much longer do we have to wait? *Will* we be rescued at all?

She could say nothing to allay his fears, but she had to say something. "Perhaps between the two of us we can build a more conclusive picture of what's going on here."

"I hope so," said Rufo, with a slight smile. "Anything you can add would be appreciated."

"You've been very open with your own data," said Roche. "I guess it's time I returned the favor."

Before she could begin, however, the Box spoke up:

<Wait, Morgan. There is something I need to discuss with you.>

She frowned. <Is it important?>

<Potentially.>

Conscious of Rufo and the two Kesh waiting for her to continue, she raised a hand. "One second," she said, then, to the Box: <Okay. What is it?>

<A small problem,> said the Box. <I am unable to penetrate this station's datacore.>

<Are you serious?>

<It would appear that there are two levels of security operating on Galine Four.

The first, and least secure, is the one I have already penetrated; this allows me access to low-level information, such as visuals of corridors and some holds, air-flow analysis, water recycling figures and so on. The second level is completely separate, and cannot be accessed from the first; it covers at least half of the inner private chambers, including the room you are currently occupying, and every single datum relating to navigation and recent movements. It also covers Rufo's private files, and any others that might confirm or deny what he and his assistant have said.>

<And you've tried everything you can to get at this information?> Roche asked.

<It's not simply a matter of gaining access to them, Morgan. I don't even know where they are. It's as though the two security systems are completely separate, and bear no relation to each other whatsoever—which is, of course, impossible.>

<But we need access to this data before we can even think about trusting them.>

<I know. I must explore the station in more detail. The low-level security system is too limited to give me a clear enough overview of exactly what's going on. In order to get that overview, I need a physical link in the station.>

<Meaning you want me to go exploring?>

<I need you to gain access via palm-links to as many diverse outputs as possible. If one of them allows us into the inner security system, or at least near it, then we will be that much closer to knowing what is actually going on here.>

Roche nodded to herself. <You hear that, Ameidio? Feel like going for a tour?>

I CAN'T, Haid sent back. I ONLY HAVE A TEXT LINK, REMEMBER?

<I didn't mean it like that. It has to be me, and you're coming along. I'm not leaving you here alone—not with that damned restraining field. You'd be too vulnerable.>

SO WHO'S GOING TO DO THE TALKING?

<The Box, of course. I'm sure it's capable.>

She returned to the opulent brightness of Rufo's office. He and the two Kesh officers were watching her expectantly, B'shan still standing while Shak'ni watched her with ill-concealed suspicion. Roche wondered belatedly if the latter could read minds—then discarded the thought. If Maii couldn't use her epsense abilities in Palasian System, no reave could.

"I apologize for that," she said aloud.

"Talking to your crew?" Rufo asked.

"That's correct. Something arose that required my attention."

"Nothing too serious, I trust?"

"Crossing the Gauntlet appears to have been more stressful than I realized. We've discovered fractures on our anchor drive housing that will require maintenance before we leave. We can repair the damage ourselves, of course, but it would be much easier—and quicker—if we had access to a dry dock."

"Our facilities here are fully equipped," Rufo said. "You are welcome to use them."

"I wouldn't want to impose—"

"Think nothing of it," the scientist interjected. "I am happy to offer whatever services I can, free of charge. In return, when your drive is repaired you might consider taking some of my crew with you when you leave Palasian System."

"When the time comes, we'll take as many as we can." Roche smiled inwardly; he had risen to the bait with very little prompting on her part. "I suggest, then, that Ameidio and I view your facilities to determine if they're suitable. My information officer can fill you in on our discoveries so far, and evaluate them in the light of what you've shown us. That would not only save time but would also ensure that the most appropriate talents at our disposal are put to the task."

"That makes sense." Rufo beamed at her. "But please, do not put yourself down. It takes great skill to command a vessel of war for the Commonwealth of Empires."

She returned his smile, although his flattery felt forced, and opened the connection to the Box. <Got that? You're my information officer, and you'll be dealing with them direct. For that you'll need a face—like the one you faked when we took over the *Ana Vereine*.>

<Understood, Morgan. I am opening a direct communications link as we speak.>

<Just remember, I want to know *everything* that's decided at this meeting, so make sure I have a recording available for later.>

<Morgan, your mistrust pains me. I can only assure you again that my best interests lie entirely with yours.>

<Yeah, but the moment they don't . . .> Roche swallowed the comment; now wasn't the time to dredge up old arguments. <Just see what else you can learn from them, okay?>

<I will.>

"There is a request for a direct line coming from your vessel, Commander Roche," said B'shan. "I presume this will be your information officer?"

"Yes. Her name is Lieutenant Gold. Will the line be secure?"

"Naturally. No one outside of this room will be aware of what is said within it."

"Good." She stood. Haid did likewise, moving stiffly through the restraining field. "If you'll arrange someone to show us the way, we'll get on with our work."

"Gered will be your guide," Rufo said, joining B'shan at the central desk. "But one other thing, before you leave. You have not mentioned whether you have a reave in your crew. Can I assume then that you haven't?"

Roche hesitated, unsure where he was heading. "Not necessarily," she said.

"Well, if you have, then you'd be aware of the epsense-dampening field that has enveloped this system. We've encountered it ourselves, and are close to neutralizing it. Two of my three reaves have regained at least a measure of their normal abilities." Rufo smiled. "So if you *do* have any on your ship, I'd be happy to assist you in any way I can."

"Thank you." Even if what he said was true, Roche would need a lot more convincing of his motives before she let Maii into his clutches. "I'll certainly take it into consideration."

The doors to the office opened and Disisto led Roche and Haid through. Glancing back, Roche saw the main tank flicker to life, revealing the face of a white-haired woman in COE uniform, with the usual blue-black interior of a COE ship behind her.

<You, I presume, Box?>

<Correct.>

<You look familiar . . .>

<I modeled the features on yours, as you may look in fifty years.>

<*What?*>

"Greetings, Professor Rufo," was all she heard the woman in the tank say before the door closed on the meeting.

Galine Four's dry docks were situated inside the spherical framework that formed the exterior of the station. A circular hold laced with retractable mesh allowed access to the dock from the outside; massive gantries and many-limbed cranes lined the dock itself like the limbs of a giant anemone.

The *Ana Vereine*'s scutter wasn't visible from the pressurized observation platform Disisto took them to, but a couple of other ships were, one of them a small courier vessel that had suffered slight damage along its flanks. Roche studied it with casual interest while she accessed the specifications of the dry dock via her palm-link. Her other hand rested lightly on the butt of the side arm Rufo's guards had returned to her after she left the station's sanctum sanctorum. Haid stood not far away, discussing the finer aspects of navigation with Disisto. Synnett watched coolly from the entrance to the observation deck.

The letters of the courier vessel's ID code suddenly fell into place. Although the complete sequence was impossible to make out, she could at least tell that it had once belonged to COE Intelligence.

<Well, well, well.>

<You have something, Morgan?> asked the Box.

<Only *Daybreak* itself,> she said. <What do you suppose it's doing here?>

<That I do not know. Rufo has yet to mention it in our conversation.>

Roche filed the information for future reference. <How about at your end?>

<Still nothing, I'm afraid. The dry dock is on the same security level as the main docking facility. We'll obviously need to access something in the heart of the station.>

<You said there are black spots you can't see. Would it help if we could get into one of those spots?>

<Possibly, but—>

<Give me the location of the nearest; I'll see what I can do.>

<The closest is one of the docks—probably the one holding *Daybreak*—but that is bound to be guarded. There are others within walking distance.>

The Box sent a map of the station with black spots marked, which Roche studied for a moment. A small black spot lay almost directly between her and the main docking bay. She turned back to Haid and Disisto, keeping the map in one corner of her eye.

"Hey, Disisto," she said. "I need to get to the scutter."

"Is anything wrong?" asked Disisto. His concern seemed genuine.

"No, I just need some specifications from the maintenance AI. I can probably find my own way, if you want to stay here and talk."

Disisto's expression relaxed into a smile. "I think we'd better stick together, Commander. That'd be safest for all of us."

"As you wish."

She headed for the exit at a brisk pace. Behind her, Haid cursed under his breath; his artificial limbs were getting the better of him, it seemed.

HOW'S THAT? he sent.

<Fine,> she replied. <Keep it up.>

Synnett fell back to help Haid while Disisto—his long legs equal to Roche's—did his best to keep up with her.

"You're in a hurry," he said as they turned into a broad access corridor lined with branching portals every ten meters. Technicians moved aside as they approached.

"Restless," she replied. "I've been stuck on the ship for too long."

"The raider? It doesn't look that cramped."

"It isn't really, I guess. It just feels like it at times. The walls close in, the roof starts to cave, the air begins to stink. There are moments when I'd do anything to be somewhere else, just for an hour."

"Which is why you came here to meet Rufo, I suppose." He glanced sideways at her. "I was wondering about that. It seemed odd for an officer to relinquish command so readily—especially given the circumstances."

"Just because I'm not on the ship doesn't mean I'm no longer in charge," she retorted.

"You have a good relationship with your crew, then. They obviously know where they stand."

If Disisto was trying to unsettle her by implying her crew couldn't be trusted, then he was hitting uncomfortably close to home.

"I trust them," she said steadily, not wanting him to see her ruffled by the comment. "That's all anyone can ask."

He nodded. "A big crew on a raider, then?"

"Moderately."

"Haid won't tell me where he fits in, exactly. My guess is weapons systems or security. Is he tight-lipped, or won't you let him talk?"

She shook her head. "You're full of questions, Disisto."

"It's part of my job."

"Is Rufo making you ask them?"

"Not exactly." He pulled a slight moue. "I report to Field Officer Shak'ni."

"Really?" That surprised her: both his answer and his candor. "I thought he was just a guest."

"You're full of questions too, Commander," he said, grinning. "Under different circumstances I'd be happy to tell you everything, but as it is . . ."

He let the sentence hang. Roche didn't mind. She had reached the turnoff for the black spot.

"Let's go this way, shall we?" She quickly ducked down the corridor before he had chance to object.

"Hey, wait!" Disisto hurried after her, surprised by the sudden turn. "You can't—"

"Why not?" she shot back. "It's quicker."

"How could you possibly know that?" He grabbed at her shoulder, but she dodged aside.

"I have a good sense of direction," she lied. "You said it wouldn't take long for me to get my bearings, didn't you?"

He stopped in his tracks. "Okay," he called after her. "Okay, we'll go this way. But can we at least wait for the others to catch up?"

She slowed, watching him over her shoulder as she did so. He seemed to mean it. When she came to a halt, she put her hands on her hips and looked around.

They were standing in a corridor no different from any other in the outer levels of the station. There was no indication of any sinister activity: no strange noises, smells, or sights.

<Well, we're here, Box. Can *you* see anything?>

<Not as yet. There are doors ahead. Maybe through one of those.>

<Maybe.> Swinging her legs as though to flex her muscles, she strolled ahead

until she was in front of the first door. It was open. Through it she saw an unoccupied terminal, complete with palm-link, against the opposite wall.

<Tempting,> she said.

DON'T, Haid sent. YOU'RE PUSHING YOUR LUCK AS IT IS.

She turned, saw Haid and Synnett at the end of the corridor. She folded her arms and waited for them to catch up. Disisto stood next to her, a distant look in his eyes suggesting he was communicating with someone via his implants.

<What's he going to do, arrest me?> she asked Haid. <He's not even armed. And besides, we have something he wants: a way out of here.>

IT ISN'T DISISTO WE SHOULD BE WORRIED ABOUT.

Movement to her left caught her attention. Turning back to the room containing the terminal, Roche realized it was occupied. As she watched, a large figure moved slowly into view, obviously heading for the desk. Although clad from boots to gloves in a dark-colored uniform made of some exotic leather, it was clear from the woman's exposed scalp that she was a Kesh. In one hand she carried a steaming goblet of something that smelled very much like *vukh.*

When the Kesh noticed Roche watching her, she snarled and shut the door.

"You certainly have an eclectic crew," she commented to Disisto.

"This is an accommodation area reserved for some of the more sensitive members, which is why we shouldn't be here at all. But we have the okay from the chief to proceed." His voice was relaxed, but his eyes scolded her. "I know you're curious, Commander, but you need to be more considerate."

"Careful, you mean?"

"That too." Haid and Synnett reached them, and Disisto indicated the corridor ahead of them. "Shall we keep going? At a more leisurely pace, this time."

The walk to the main docking bay revealed little. Doors that were open only revealed empty rooms, and Roche was unable to gain access to a palm-link. By the time she reached the scutter, she had decided that entering the black spot had given her a moral victory only.

<He may have been telling the truth,> she said from within the scutter, while pretending to obtain the data she required. <It could just be an accommodation area for crew members who prefer the quiet of the shell to the Hub.>

<It is certainly possible,> said the Box. <But we have no proof either way.>

She left the scutter and joined the others. "Where to now?" she asked Disisto.

"Back to the dry dock?" he suggested.

"Actually, the walk has left me thirsty. How about a drink? You must have a recreation deck here. I'll buy you one, if they accept COE credit."

Disisto studied her for a long moment, then said: "Okay, if that's what you want."

Roche was unable to read his expression. "When Rufo and Lieutenant Gold have finished, we can join them then."

Disisto nodded as he began to walk. "The main bar is back in the Hub."

Roche followed, no longer trying to provoke him. There was very little else she could do until they reached the bar. After the disappointment of the one black spot they had entered, she didn't see any point in trying to access others. There were too many, to begin with, and Disisto would undoubtedly put a stop to it before long.

The bar was deep in the heart of Galine Four, occupying a large space between protein vats and the plant-filled central chamber. It consisted of three rooms connected to a central chamber by wide accessways. In each of the three rooms there was a semicircular bar and numerous tables. The lighting was dim, as befitted a bar, and the sound of voices and glasses clinking along with occasional spurts of Roptio ur-music added to the ambience. The central area comprised a quarter-size dueling field, surrounded by seats.

A fight was in progress as they entered. The supporters of each combatant had clustered in groups to watch the hologram, cheering and jeering in equal measure.

Roche hooked a thumb at the scene. "A recording, I presume?"

"Must be something they pulled out of the archives," said Disisto, "because we haven't received any transmissions from outside the system for ages. Anything to keep the hardcore fans happy."

Roche glanced at Haid, caught him staring at the game in curiosity. "Ameidio?"

He turned to her. "Sorry. I wasn't paying attention."

She smiled. Haid had been confined to a penal planet for more years than he cared to remember. Dueling was a pleasure he had missed, and he had spent several days catching up on it upon finding freedom aboard the *Ana Vereine*. Even now, he obviously felt its call.

"What do you want to drink?" she asked.

Haid shrugged. "Anything that's not too strong."

"Disisto? Synnett?"

"We're on duty," Disisto said. He nodded to a doorway beyond the dueling field. "We can order through there."

He led them past the fight and into one of the side rooms where it was quieter and less crowded. A number of patrons were Exotic, and clearly appreciated the space. They found a table and sat: Haid and Roche on one side, with Disisto and Synnett facing them.

There was an awkward silence.

"So," ventured Roche, "how *do* I order?"

"There's a palm-link on your chair, if you want to use that. Otherwise, I can call an attendant."

"The link will be fine." She found the pad on the arm of her chair and placed her hand upon it.

<Do your stuff, Box,> she said. <Fake a COE credit account for me and, while you're at it, order a Montaban ale and three Dahish.>

<Certainly, Morgan.>

<How's the meeting going, by the way?>

<Smoothly, although there still has been no mention of the Sol Apotheosis Movement or *Daybreak*. It seems Linegar Rufo is less susceptible to an attractive woman than I had hoped.>

<Despite what you might think, Box, not all Humans are slaves to their biology. Nevertheless, keep working on . . . Oh, hell.>

She had spied someone crossing the room toward her.

"Morgan!" called Myer Mavalhin. "Fancy meeting you down here. I thought you'd be up with the big shots for sure."

Roche stood. "Hello, Myer."

Disisto glanced behind him. "Mavalhin?"

Mavalhin's step faltered upon seeing the dock security head. "Oh, it's you."

"What the hell are you doing here, Myer? I'll be having words with the ingress team about letting you out of decon so early."

"Hey, don't go too hard on them," the pilot protested. "It wasn't *their* fault."

"Then I'll be talking to *you* instead."

"In that case, it was *entirely* their fault." He winked at Roche. "But seeing as I'm here, I might as well stay, right?"

"Don't look at me, Myer," said Roche. "I'm only a guest."

Disisto shook his head and sighed. "Just remember you're on probation, all right?"

Mavalhin pulled up a chair and sat. "So, what're we drinking?"

Roche hid a smile. Nothing had changed. "I'll get this round," she said, "but after that you're on your own."

Myer smiled appreciatively. "I'll have a snifter of Old Gray."

Roche relayed the order to the Box just as an attendant arrived with her first order. Haid nodded approval at the long-stemmed glass containing a murky brown mixture, and Roche raised her own colorless drink to her lips and toasted Disisto. Synnett drank without acknowledging anyone.

Sipping the cool, clear liquid made Roche realize just how thirsty the meeting and the walk had left her. She swallowed gratefully, then sipped again.

"It's a long way from Bodh Gaya," she said to Mavalhin after a third sip.

"But here we are," he said. "I heard you stayed with COE in the end. Looks like you've done all right with them."

She was careful to hide her true feelings. "I can't complain. It does get boring at times, but I prefer the security of a regular job. And it's not that restrictive. I spent a few years in Intelligence before transferring to active command. It's been fun, mostly." She did her best to maintain an air of self-composure and confidence. "You?"

He lifted his shoulders slightly. "Tried the Eckandar Trade Axis for a while, then a private freight company out past Tretamen. The bottom went out of the market and the company folded, and that left me in the lurch. I worked as a freelance courier for a few years, before finally signing on with Galine Four."

Disisto snorted. "Courier, eh? I heard you were on the run from Olmahoi creditors and needed cash to avoid grayboot retribution."

Mavalhin gestured dismissively. "Exaggeration and rumor. Yes, money was short, but it never got *that* bad."

Roche could tell by the tightness around his eyes that it probably *had* been that bad. Rufo would have been able to purchase his services at a bargain price. Regardless of his personal flaws, Mavalhin's credentials would have been impressive; few people left the COE College so close to finishing, and their services were desired in many quarters of the region.

"So what is it you do here, anyway?" she asked.

Mavalhin opened his mouth to reply, but caught Disisto's reproving look. He stopped, smiled, and said: "I'm just a pilot, Morgan. Nothing spectacular. I gave up on the dream of making something of myself. There's a place for everyone, I've learned, and I guess this is mine."

"That doesn't sound like the Myer I once knew."

"Well, I've changed, I guess."

Roche laughed. "Now that *really* doesn't sound like you!"

He fixed her with a disarming smile that lasted almost ten seconds. “Everyone changes, Morgan. You should try it sometime.”

Roche smiled, but the accusation made her feel uncomfortable. “You’d be surprised, Myer,” she said after a while.

“Really?” He beamed. “Go ahead, then. Surprise me.”

An attendant brought his drink, and with it a welcome interruption in the conversation. Roche was even more thankful when the Box intruded before they could resume their talk:

<Morgan, I’m afraid that link at your present location is as isolated as the rest. We will need to gain physical access to other black spots in order to determine what is occurring within them—or try to locate an access point to the inner security shell.>

Roche fought to contain a rising sense of frustration. <We’ve already tried that, and Disisto didn’t give me the chance—>

<I have a plan,> said the Box. <The *Ana Vereine* contains a variety of covert surveillance devices designed to infiltrate an enemy vessel. Some of them are microscopic in size and self-replicating; a small amount placed at any location in Galine Four would quickly spread to cover the black spots. I could even reprogram a pseudospecies to allow me terminal access.>

“Morgan?” It was Mavalhin.

She quickly raised a hand to silence him, then closed her eyes, shutting out her immediate surroundings so she could concentrate on what the AI was saying. <That’s just fine, Box, but they’re on the *Ana Vereine*. How are you going to get them here?>

<Quite simply, and without raising suspicion. Rufo has repeated his offer to treat any ailing reaves we might have on board. All we have to do is agree, send Maii with a packet of surveillance bugs on her person, then instruct her to release them at the first possible moment. Or the bugs could be suspended in the atmosphere of the scutter itself. They would disperse through the air conditioning system when the atmospheres merge.>

Roche thought about it for a long moment. <I don’t like the idea of putting Maii at risk.>

<We could send Cane with her. He would be a more than adequate bodyguard.>

<True.> That would leave the *Ana Vereine* empty except for Kajic and the Box, but she kept that concern to herself. <They don’t know anything about Cane, so he could pass as an ordinary crew member. Is there no alternative you can think of?>

<None, apart from firing a swarm of bugs at the hull of Galine Four and hoping some sneak through its anti-meteor shields. The odds are against more than a few managing to get inside.> The Box paused before continuing: <Of course, there *is* the possibility that everything is exactly as it seems—that we can trust Rufo implicitly in everything he says. The high security might be standard for Galine Four and the other discrepancies we have noted nothing more than unfortunate coincidences.>

<You’ve talked with him longer than I have. What do *you* think?>

<I am not totally convinced,> the AI said. <But that doesn’t mean that *you* have to—>

<Okay, okay.> Roche opened her eyes and reached for her glass. <We have to know what’s going on here, and if this is the only way to find out . . .>

<It is.>

She took a deep draft of her drink. <Then you have my approval to proceed with this plan, Box.>

<Understood. I have notified the main dock that the scutter will be disengaging in five minutes. Prior to its departure, I will finalize the details with Rufo. I will bring the *Ana Vereine* closer to minimize transfer time. If there are any changes, I will let you know.>

<How long do you think?>

<Thirty minutes. Cane assures me he will be ready to disembark in ten minutes.>

<Good. Tell him to be careful—and, if you can, make sure he's wired somehow. I don't like the idea of being out of touch with them.>

<Regardless of what happens, the bugs themselves will enable us to keep an eye on them.>

<Okay, Box. Keep in touch.>

She put the glass down on the table. Mavalhin was watching her curiously.

"I'm sorry about that," she said. "Just some business that needed attending to."

He smiled crookedly but said nothing.

"No rest for the wicked, eh?" said Disisto. Before she could say anything, he raised a hand to his ear, his head tilted as though straining to hear something above the general noise of the room. "Your scutter has requested permission to disengage," he said to her. "It's leaving without you?"

"Temporarily," she explained. "I've decided to take you up on your offer; you see, we *do* have a reave on board, and she needs help."

"So you've decided to trust us now?"

"Decided we have no choice," said Roche. "She needs the treatment."

Disisto nodded. "I understand," he said. "Is everything else in order?"

"It seems to be," she said. "For the moment, at least." Again she sensed something in his stare that belied the calmness of his face, but she could do no more than wonder about it. "Anyway, what were we talking about?"

"About how much you've changed," said Mavalhin with a smugness that irritated Roche.

"Shut up, Myer," she said.

"What?" He laughed. "I didn't say anything!"

"I don't have to prove anything to you," she said. "So let's just change the subject, shall we?" She picked up her glass and sat back, looking over to Disisto. "Let's talk about *Daybreak* instead."

It was Disisto's turn to smile. "You spotted it, then?"

"I'm not blind," she said. "Where did you find it?"

"It drifted in from the outer system five days ago. One of our scouts discovered it and hauled it here once he was sure there was no one aboard."

"And that scout was you, Myer?" she said.

Mavalhin grinned. "Sorry, Morgan. Can't help you there. I was over Aro Spaceport at the time."

She shrugged. It had been worth a try; Mavalhin would have been much easier to pump information from than the security officer. "*Was* there no one aboard, then, Disisto?"

"Apart from the bodies stacked in the hold, no, there wasn't. The pilot had abandoned the vessel long before we found it."

"That would be before he attacked Guhr Outpost in the tug, right?" put in Haid.

"I guess so," Disisto said. "Once he had no use for *Daybreak,* he must have discarded it."

"That surprises me," Haid went on. "In every other instance he's used the vessel he had just vacated to act as a distraction. But not this time. It would have been more sensible to destroy it. Any guesses why not?"

Disisto opened his hands in apology. "That's something you'd have to ask the chief. I'm not privy to all the information we've uncovered."

"The fact that he didn't bring it up makes me even more curious," said Roche.

"I'm sure it does." Disisto's smile hadn't faded; if anything, it had grown wider. Roche received the distinct impression that he was enjoying her attempts to probe the station's veil of secrecy.

"She's always been like this," said Mavalhin, leaning forward to put his empty glass on the table. "A troublemaker, too. Did you know that she hacked into the College Head's private datacore to reprogram his secretary AI? For a week, it would speak only in an obscure Mbatan dialect Morgan had unearthed in an archive. Because only a dozen or so people on the other side of the Commonwealth could speak that language, it was a whole day before the Head could get any sense out of it. It brought the Academy to a halt—and all so she could miss a Tactics exam she hadn't prepared for."

"Hey, that's a lie!" Roche protested with mock indignation. "*You* were the one with the exam! I did it so you could get out of taking it."

"Ah yes, that's right," he said. "You would've done anything for me back in those days, wouldn't you?"

Roche conceded a wry smile and shook her head. "I'd forgotten what you can be like, Myer," she said. Oddly enough, she enjoyed the banter almost as much as it annoyed her—which was a fair summary of her feelings for him, now *and* then. "But you won't catch me off guard again, that I promise you."

"That sounds like a challenge."

"You can take it any way you like."

"Accepted, then. Where shall we start?"

Somehow he drew her into a one-on-one conversation, against her better instincts. While Haid and Disisto listened, occasionally talking to each other or interjecting with observations, she and Mavalhin sparred as smoothly as they had years before. It amazed her how easily the old ways returned: she had never met anybody since him who knew just how to antagonize her. The reverse was also true. Despite the fact that they had both experienced much since they had last met, the mental processes that dictated the flow of conversation remained unchanged.

"Look, I'm sorry to have to break this up," Disisto eventually said, "but if you want to meet the scutter, we should start heading down to the docking bay."

Roche was surprised. "So soon?"

"Well, it's a bit of a walk there," said Disisto. "Besides which, we have to drop Myer off so he can finish his debriefing decon."

"Oh, come on, Disisto!" said Mavalhin.

But Disisto and Synnett were already standing, the latter tugging Mavalhin to his feet. Haid finished the contents of his glass and stood; Roche did likewise.

"Changed man, eh, Myer?" Roche scoffed.

The pilot ignored her.

On the way past the dueling field, Haid nudged her with one angular elbow and indicated the hologram with a nod. Roche looked, and had a quick glimpse of armored, robotic figures toiling with ferocious weapons on an open playing field. Nothing looked out of place.

<What?>

I THOUGHT I RECOGNIZED THE GAME AS WE CAME IN, he sent. IT'S A REPEAT OF THE GRUDGE MATCH BETWEEN ALEMDAR QUICK AND THE PREVIOUS CHAMPION, VOID 34.

<So?>

THE GAME WAS PUT ON IDNET SIX DAYS AGO. BUT PALASIAN SYSTEM WAS ENCLOSED *TWENTY* DAYS AGO. THERE'S NO WAY THEY COULD'VE RECEIVED THIS GAME FROM IN HERE.

Roche stopped to look at the game with renewed interest, but Synnett urged them forward irritably.

<Are you sure?>

POSITIVE. I WATCHED IT IN THE REHAB UNIT WHEN MY IMPLANTS WERE INSTALLED.

She thought it through carefully, while following Disisto and Mavalhin out of the bar. <That means they've had at least one communication with someone outside. But how? I didn't think anything could cross the Gauntlet.>

<Nothing but a ship,> said the Box. <Or a drone designed to carry information.>

<A message drop? From whom?>

THAT'S THE PRIZE-WINNING QUESTION, ISN'T IT?

She frowned. <There's something really odd going on here—and the sooner we get Maii up and running again, the better. How long until she's here, Box?>

<The scutter has been cleared to dock and is moving into position. Should be only a few minutes at most.>

Disisto, ahead of Roche, halted at the entrance to a transit corridor.

<Good. We shouldn't be far behind,> said Roche. <By the way, I don't suppose you've run a search on Shak'ni? He seems an odd choice for head of security of a Pristine-run station.>

<No, Morgan, I have not. The only high-level security files from the Kesh governments I have access to are those gathered by COE Intelligence and the Dato Espionage Corps. But I can try if you'd like me to.>

<Do it. You never know what you might find.> She waited for confirmation from the AI. Technically it wasn't required to respond to every order she gave it, but it usually did, if only to have the last word. After a moment of silence, she said: <Box?>

Again, no response. Then:

<Morgan?> The Box sounded concerned.

<I hear you, Box.>

<The scutter has docked and an umbilical is being attached. Cane and Maii are preparing to disembark. Please respond, Morgan.>

Roche felt a terrible dread radiate from her gut.

<Ameidio, we're being jammed. It's a trap!>

Haid didn't respond either, but his worried eyes met hers just as the transit cab door opened to reveal Shak'ni glaring down at them. Another Kesh stood there also, along with three Pristines in gray security uniforms. All were armed, and their weapons were pointed at Roche.

"The reave and the clone warrior have disembarked," Shak'ni said to Disisto. "This charade can end now."

4

Galine Four
’955.01.20 EN
1575

Roche reached automatically for her side arm, only to encounter the hand of Synnett standing behind her. The silent security guard wrenched the weapon from its holster before she could even touch it. At the same time, the other security guards pointed their weapons at Haid. The Kesh standing behind him disarmed him before he could resist.

“What’s the meaning of this?” Roche said, trying hard to keep her voice level. She aimed her words at Disisto, but he wouldn’t look at her.

Field Officer Shak’ni stepped into the ring of security guards facing them.

“Morgan Roche and Ameidio Haid,” he said with barely concealed satisfaction, “you are jointly charged with violating restricted space in contravention of quarantine laws. You are also charged with conspiring to compromise the safety of the region, including the N’Kor Republic. This charge is punishable by death, and any attempt to resist arrest will be seen as an admission of guilt and *will* result in your immediate execution.”

“You can’t be serious,” Roche managed.

He stooped to thrust his face into hers. “We are, Commander,” he said, the red markings under his eyes inflamed with repressed anger. “By the time we arrive at the docking bay, the creature you call Adoni Cane will be firmly under our control. We will not make the same mistake as those who have already died in this system—the mistake of underestimating his capabilities, or his destructive potential.”

Clone warrior, Shak’ni had said. She groaned inwardly. They had known all along who Cane was.

“This is crazy,” said Haid. “We should be working together, not—”

“Quiet, cyborg!” Shak’ni rounded on him. “Pristines are bad enough. Their puny attempts to improve themselves only fill me with disgust.”

Haid’s biomesh rippled, and one skeletal hand lashed out to strike the Kesh. Before the blow could fall, however, the guard behind him rammed the butt of a gun into his back.

Haid’s hand withdrew, but he kept his eyes locked on Shak’ni’s.

Mavalhin edged closer to the door, visibly distressed at the turn of events.

<Morgan?> called the Box. <Morgan, I’ve managed to raise a weak signal from your implants. I know now that you are still alive and can probably hear me. Don’t do anything rash. I will assist you in a few moments.>

<Box!> She raised the output of her built-in transmitter to its maximum level. <What's happening to Cane and Maii? Tell me!>

Shak'ni faced Roche with a slight sneer creasing one corner of his mouth. "There is no use calling for help, Commander. We are safe from your meddling AI in here."

"I don't *understand.*" Frustration and the smell of the Kesh made her voice shrill. "How do you *know* all this?"

"That is not your concern. It suffices that we know how you attempted to deceive us."

"Don't be a hypocrite, Shak'ni," Roche snapped. "What you've done is no different—"

"What *we* did, we did in the interest of security. We gave you enough opportunities to reveal the truth, and your failure to do so demonstrated the maliciousness of your intentions." Shak'ni's features tightened into a mask. "Were you lucky enough to have been born a Kesh, you would be dead already."

From the corner Roche could make out Mavalhin staring at her. Even without returning his stare she could tell that he was nervous. And understandably so; he was just an innocent bystander caught up in what could easily become a major diplomatic incident. In fact, she sympathized.

Then:

<Morgan,> said the Box. <I still cannot receive detailed information from your implants, but I can download to them. I have prepared an indirect link which will bring us into contact via Galine Four's external security shell—to which I still have complete access. All you have to do is locate a data-input point, and I will be able to locate you.>

Easier said than done, Roche thought. She looked around, trying to find a palm-link. The only visible one lay on the far side of the cab, adjacent to the pad used to key destinations manually. It was only two meters from her, but Disisto stood in the way.

The cab shuddered beneath her feet as it neared the outer shell of the station.

A thought struck her. There *was* another link in the cab; all she had to do was gain access to it . . .

Haid swayed as the cab crossed another boundary mismatch. She reached out to steady him, ignoring the jab the guard behind her delivered to her shoulder blades.

"His balance is poor," she said, gripping Haid's shoulder tightly.

"It's true," Disisto said evenly. "Let her be."

The guard behind her relaxed slightly, and Roche dug her fingers into Haid's biomesh, pulling him minutely toward her. Their eyes met. Although it was impossible through his artificial lenses, she thought she saw a look of understanding pass through them.

The cab reached the point at which he had stumbled the first time they had made this journey, earlier. It shuddered right on cue.

Haid's legs gave way beneath him, sending him lurching into Roche. His shoulder along with the weight of his biomods acted as a battering ram, forcing her away from him and across the cab. She grunted, reached out to break her fall, and sprawled untidily at Disisto's feet.

Shak'ni hissed impatiently.

"Sorry," said Haid as he tried to regain his footing. Roche kept her legs carefully out of the way as he did so; the guards also avoided his artificial limbs, wary of a potential trap. He made it onto his hands and knees, and made a great effort of almost standing up before slipping back down onto one knee.

While the guards were busy watching him, Roche reached out to Disisto with her left hand. He reached out with his, to help her upright.

The moment their palm-links met, she triggered her implants and spoke as quickly as she could:

<Box? Box! We're in a transit cab heading to the main docking bay, and I can't hold this link long. You have to do something! Try and provide a distraction so Haid and I—>

<I have you now, Morgan. The cab will arrive in twenty seconds. Be ready.>

The link broke as Disisto let go of her hand. She blinked, realized that she was on her feet again.

"Thanks," she said. "I was a little dizzy there for a moment."

Looking down at his hand, he frowned and shook his head. "So was I," he said. "The weirdest thing . . ."

Haid was also on his feet. She made no move to stand next to him; being together would only make it harder for one of them to break free. The motion of the cab beneath her feet had slowed dramatically; it was already difficult to tell whether it was moving or not.

Be ready, the Box had said. But for what?

The doors opened on an empty corridor. Disisto stepped out first, closely followed by Mavalhin. The pilot looked around him, and backed quickly out of the way.

The guard behind Roche nudged her in the back. She stepped through the doors with her escort close behind. Haid and Synnett came next.

For a brief moment, Roche thought, the numbers were almost manageable. If they were going to break free, their chances were never going to be better.

She tensed. <Come *on,* Box!>

Then, as Shak'ni, the remaining guard, and the Kesh moved to exit the cab, the floor lurched and a sudden gust of wind swept past them.

"We've been holed!" Disisto shouted over the sudden wail of alarms. "The area's being sealed off!"

Roche froze, her space instincts taking over.

Behind her, the doors to the cab slid shut, cutting off Shak'ni's shout of protest.

Before anyone could even contemplate overriding the seal, Roche spun on one leg and knocked aside the pistol of the guard behind her. A second kick knocked the wind out of him and sent him back into the doors of the cab.

Beside her, Haid had Synnett in a wristlock, the narrow fingers and strength of his new arm provoking a hiss of pain. The security officer's weapon discharged a single bolt of energy that earthed harmlessly into the wall. One blow with Haid's free hand made Synnett drop the pistol, and Roche was there to scoop up the weapon and point it at Disisto.

Two side arms faced one for a split-second, until Disisto dropped his to the floor and raised his hands.

"That was fast," he said over the wail of the siren. "I don't know whether to be impressed or annoyed."

"I don't care either way," said Roche, approaching him while Haid covered Mavalhin and the one conscious guard. "Just give me your hand. Your *left* one."

He held it out to her, and she gripped it tightly. Making certain the gun was placed firmly under his chin, she activated her implants again.

<Okay, Box, what the hell have you done?>

The reply was instantaneous: <Fired the scutter's main engines while it was still in the dock, breaching the hull of the station at four points.>

<Are you *insane*?> she gasped.

<No. Merely in a hurry.>

<But you could've killed us all!>

<I was careful to direct the afterwash into the main facility itself, away from your position.>

<But what about Maii and Cane?>

<I made sure they were at a safe distance first.>

<And the scutter itself?>

<It has been severely damaged. The explosion triggered a chain reaction in three of its four fuel cells.>

<How the hell are we going to get out of here now?>

<There was no other option, Morgan. I had to split your party, and this was the only way open to me.>

<In the short term, yes. In the long run, we might as well have handed ourselves over.> Roche thought quickly. <Where are Maii and Cane?>

<In an emergency medical cocoon on the far side of the dock. Cane was gassed and overpowered as soon as he left the scutter. Maii was shot with a Xarodine dart. The surveillance devices were neutralized by microwaves. There was nothing I could do to prevent any of it. We had no reason to suspect that such an ambush was awaiting them.>

The Box sounded defensive, as well it might, Roche thought. She fought the urge to curse her decision to bring Maii to the station; regret was worse than useless.

The siren was getting on her nerves. The sooner they were on the run again, the better. They would have to move as soon as the pressure doors opened around them.

<We could escape in *Daybreak,*> she reasoned. <Can you override the secondary dock?>

<Perhaps. I have not tried that avenue as yet. Also, the link with the courier is sealed to me. I am unaware how badly it has been damaged.>

<We're a little short on alternatives,> Roche snapped back.

<Then I recommend you bring Disisto with you,> the Box went on. <His palmlink gives us access to a deeper level of security than before.>

Roche looked at Disisto's face, twisted in pain from the gun digging into his chin. She hadn't realized she was pressing so hard, but she did nothing to relieve him.

<I'm not leaving without Maii,> she said.

<A rescue attempt at this time would be foolish,> the Box protested. <Quite apart from the fact that both Cane and Maii are unconscious and would need to be carried, they are also being closely guarded. Furthermore, Shak'ni has alerted security that you have escaped detention; you would be recaptured well before—>

<All right,> she snarled, hating herself for seeing the sense in the Box's words. <We leave them behind—*for now.* But as soon as we have a way of getting them back, we do it. And I don't want any arguments about this, Box.>

<There will be none, Morgan. With Disisto's access, we may yet unravel the security net of Galine Four.>

<I hope so, for your sake.>

Disisto flinched as she pulled the gun out from under his chin.

"We're leaving," she said, keeping their palms together.

"But—"

"Don't argue. Just do your best to keep up." She turned to Haid. "You catch all that?"

"Yes," he said. "Give me a moment to tidy up and I'll be ready."

He used his pistol to knock the second guard unconscious, then turned to face Mavalhin. The pilot backed away with hands raised.

"Morgan!" he said. "Please—"

"Sorry, Myer, but we don't have time for this."

"But I—I want to come with you!"

Haid hesitated; Roche frowned. *"What?"*

"Well, you'll need to get off the station, right?" Mavalhin's words came out fast. "I can help you do that."

"We already have a ship. *Daybreak* was a COE courier; if it'll fly, I can use my old overrides to assume command."

"Oh, I'm sure it will fly," he said. "But you don't expect to be able to just blast out of the docks in one piece, do you? I mean, how will you disengage?"

"He's just wasting time," muttered Haid, raising his pistol.

"No, wait," said Roche, remembering the Box's uncertainty and the fact that it still did not have high-level access to the station's systems. "What are you suggesting, Myer?"

"That I use my codes to get you away."

"In exchange for . . . ?"

"Passage, that's all. A chance to get out of here."

"Why?"

"It's time to move on, time for a change, and . . ." He hesitated slightly. "And other reasons."

Beside her, Disisto spat on the floor at Mavalhin's feet. The pilot flushed red, but did not respond.

"Don't trust him," Haid said.

"But he does have a point," she replied. "We might need those codes."

"We don't know whether his codes will even work!" said Haid. "Once they know he's with us, they could just change them."

She thought a moment longer, then finally dismissed Haid's objections with: "Okay, Myer, take us to *Daybreak.* But don't push your luck."

Mavalhin grinned. "Thanks, Morgan. I owe you one for this."

"Just get moving."

Haid indicated the corridor ahead with the pistol, and Mavalhin headed along it, checking once to make sure they were following.

"You're crazy if you think you can get away with this," Disisto said to Roche. "You'll hardly leave the dock before someone fires on you."

"Tell me something," she said. "Are your implants programmed to monitor your well-being?"

"No."

"Then bear in mind that I don't need you alive," she told him. "Now shut up while I concentrate."

His lips whitened. She felt sweat trickle from her left hand, and wished she could let go of him, if only for a moment.

Within seconds they reached a sealed blast-door. It slid open as they approached, before she could wonder how they were going to get through it, and closed behind them.

<I am in the system that far,> said the Box. <I can ensure that the way ahead is clear, and that no one will sneak up on you from behind. The secondary dock itself is occupied, however, and you will have to deal with that in order to gain access to the ship.>

<Give me a view of the dock.> Instantly, an overhead perspective appeared in her left eye, revealing two technicians and three security guards standing in a spacious control room.

<What's that in the background?> she asked the Box. <The airlock?>

<*Daybreak* is connected by an umbilical to the dock. There is only room for one vessel at a time, and there are facilities for just one connection. The airlock leads directly to the umbilical.>

<Is it open?>

<No. It is locked.>

<Open it, if you can. Do you have the right codes?>

<Disisto has a priority access code, but to use it now would only forewarn them that you are coming.>

Roche nodded. <How about communications between the dock and the rest of Galine Four? Can you interrupt them?>

<Yes, although they already know that you are at liberty aboard the station.>

<Then we'll have to play it carefully.> She paused as another pressure door slid aside. The map the Box had given her indicated two more doors between them and the secondary dock. <If Shak'ni guesses where we're headed and manages to get a squad in before us, we'll be cut off.>

<That won't happen. I will self-destruct what remains of the scutter and create another hull breach if necessary. Decompression takes precedence over security problems; not even Shak'ni can change that.>

<At least they've got their priorities in order.> Roche smiled grimly, and thought about Maii and Cane, captives of Rufo. <I only wish I could say the same about us. . . .>

The secondary dock lay five meters past the final pressure door. As they passed through it, Roche tightened her grip on Disisto's hand.

"You so much as raise an eyebrow without my say-so," she said, "and I *will* shoot you. Okay?"

Disisto grimaced slightly. "I never doubted for a moment that you would, Commander."

"Good." She waved Mavalhin and Haid ahead of her. "We need to whittle their numbers down. Myer, I want you to go first and tell them you've come to get help from the main dock. The Box will kill communications, so they won't be able to check. Tell them a fire's responsible. Reinforcements have been cut off, and all hands are needed to help put it out."

"And if they don't believe me?"

"They can't afford not to. A fire in the main dock will spread quickly, regardless of pressure doors."

He nodded at Haid. "Where will he be?"

She pointed at a corner past the entrance to the dock. "But I'll be watching, Myer, so don't even think of trying anything."

He grinned uneasily. "As trusting as ever, I see."

Roche pulled Disisto around the corner, with Haid not far behind. <Okay, Box. Kill communications, and get ready to open that airlock.>

<At your command.>

From her overhead perspective of the dock, Roche watched as Mavalhin hurried into the control room. She couldn't hear much of what was being said, but Mavalhin's animated behavior along with the responsive body language from the guards themselves gave her an idea of what was happening. Two of the five personnel seemed skeptical, but the others appeared to accept his story. After a few moments two of the security guards, along with one of the technicians, followed Mavalhin out of the room, moving up the hallway toward the open pressure door. The guards and technician stepped through the door a second before Mavalhin, but instead of following, he jumped back.

The door slid shut, cutting them off.

Roche tugged her prisoner out of hiding. "Okay. We go in. Haid, you first, then Myer. I'll be right behind you."

The remaining security guard looked up as soon as Haid ran into the room, and in a moment his pistol was up and firing. Haid rolled behind a desk, out of harm's way, but Mavalhin caught a bolt in the shoulder that sent him flying, screaming in pain.

Roche rounded the door at the same instant, dragging Disisto with her. Her opening fire caught the guard in the chest. He collapsed back into a chair, his gun still firing. The weapon discharged noisily into the ceiling six more times before his trigger finger fell slack.

The lone technician backed away with his hands raised and a look of terror on his face.

Haid appeared from behind the desk. "Thanks, Morgan. Guess my reflexes are still a little rusty."

"Don't mention it," she muttered, keeping an eye on the technician and Disisto, while at the same time trying to determine exactly how seriously Mavalhin had been hurt.

<Box, open the airlock.>

The door slid open with a hiss, revealing a standard umbilical corridor on the far side.

<Can you seal the entrance in here?> she asked.

<I can do my best.>

<Let's hope it's enough.> She waved her pistol at the technician, gesturing for him to lie facedown on the floor. "Haid, knock him out."

Next Roche checked on Mavalhin. The pilot had been shot in the left shoulder. Blood leaked from between his fingers where he clutched the wound. She forced him to let go, and pulled the charred edges of the hole in his uniform aside.

The wound was deep but cauterized enough to keep blood loss to a minimum, otherwise he would already be slipping into shock. His eyes, when they met hers, were full of panic.

"Glad you came with us, huh?" Her smile was intended to allay his obvious fear. Despite his pain, he managed a half-smile in return. Roche stood, wiping her hands on her black uniform. "When Haid's ready, we'll board *Daybreak* and be on our way. Once we're out of here, we'll see what medical facilities we have and patch you up, okay?"

He nodded and struggled to his feet. Disisto followed obediently as Roche guided the pilot to the umbilical.

"I'm done," said Haid, stepping over the technician.

"Right. Through here." She prodded Disisto to go ahead of her. <Box, once we're in, seal the airlock.>

<Yes, Morgan.>

The umbilical was only half as long as the ones at the main dock. At the far end, the courier's airlock was sealed shut. Roche let go of Disisto for a moment, and placed her palm-link against it, hoping that she remembered the emergency COE codes well enough to fool the onboard AI.

After a moment of rapid dialogue, the airlock hissed and slid open. Taking hold of Disisto again, she entered the courier vessel.

Daybreak was little different from the many small cruisers she had flown in her years with COE Intelligence. It had room for a crew of eight and forty-two passengers, plus a small cargo hold at the rear. The bridge—cramped to Roche after her time on the *Ana Vereine*—was at the rounded nose of the craft and held crash-seats for five. The interior was dimly lit and purely functional. A standby screen glowed at the pilot's station, but otherwise the controls were dead.

Haid helped Mavalhin into an empty couch and strapped the brace tight, ignoring the wince of pain it provoked. Roche put Disisto into the copilot's position and lashed his hand to the palm-link. Sitting next to him, she opened her own link to the vessel's command systems, and thereby back to the Box. The craft accepted her COE overrides without complaint.

<Was Myer telling the truth?> she asked. <Will it fly?>

<All systems are green—except for the slow-jump drive, which is dead, and weapons systems, which are nonexistent. I am initiating a start-up sequence which will have the ship flight-ready in six minutes.>

The main screen showed a forward view of the dock, past the dry dock and a section of the outer shell. Lights began to flicker on the consoles. Roche tried to follow them, but the Box worked too rapidly.

Within seconds the reactor began supplying power to the main thrusters, preparing them for rapid burn, and as it did, Roche was touched by a sense of déjà vu.

The situation reminded her of the time she and Cane had escaped from the *Midnight* with Maii and Veden captive. Then, as now, the Box had been in control of the craft—and much more besides, it had turned out.

<This time,> she warned the AI, <*don't* blow anything up.>

The Box did not respond immediately.

<Box?>

<I'm sorry, Morgan,> it finally said. <The *Ana Vereine* is receiving fire from cannon on Galine Four. We are camouflaged, but are hampered by the necessity to remain nearby in order to assist your launch.>

<You can't destroy the cannon?>

<I am attempting to do so as we speak. However, there are many of them, and I am hesitant to damage the station too much while Cane and Maii are within.>

She checked the countdown on the main display. Only a minute had passed.

<How long can you hold off the attack?>

<Long enough. But you will need to launch with haste.>

<Understood.> She turned in her seat. "Myer, what are those codes? *Myer*?"

The pilot stirred. "What—?"

"The codes! What are they?"

"Oh . . . 16433051: Cold Sleep."

She turned back to the main console and fed the sequence into the main AI. It accepted the code without protest, and relayed the command to the secondary dock. Twenty seconds later, the umbilical disengaged and retracted into its housing.

<Okay, Box. We're clear at this end. As soon as the drives are able, we can leave.> She began preparing the navigation systems for departure, plotting a route from the main dock to a potential rendezvous with the *Ana Vereine*.

<There is one other thing,> the Box said.

She didn't stop working. <I'm listening.>

<I am picking up a broad-band distress signal from the xenoarchaeological base on Mok.>

She stopped. <The double-jovian?>

<Yes.>

<What does it say?>

<The message is very brief, repeated every fifteen seconds. It states only that assistance is urgently required.>

<Does it carry an ID tag?>

<A generic civilian code commonly used by independent mining collectives.>

Outriggers. Roche absorbed the detail with interest. Rufo had suggested that they might be active in the vicinity of the double-jovian.

<I don't have time to deal with this now, Box, but we'll need to check it out as soon as possible. If there *are* other survivors here, they're bound to be more help than Rufo.>

<Agreed.>

The timer showed two minutes remaining before launch.

"This could be rough," she said, directing her words at Haid but intending them for Disisto and Mavalhin as well. Getting out of the dock was only half the problem; if Galine Four was firing on the *Ana Vereine,* it would probably try the same on *Daybreak*—and the courier had neither shields nor weaponry.

An alarm began to *ping* on the main console. She glanced at it, and realized that someone was trying to hail them.

<Dock security is aware of your present location,> said the Box.

<Inevitable, I guess,> she said. <There's nothing they can do, though, is there?>

<The secondary dock is still sealed, and their movements are restricted by pressure doors to—>

"Morgan." Haid's soft voice carried with it a warning that made her look up immediately. He was pointing at the main screen.

Two figures in pressure suits were climbing onto the lip of the dry dock, carrying a swivel-mounted energy weapon between them.

"Damn!" Roche glanced at the clock again. One minute. If the security officers managed to place the weapon in time, they would have a clear shot at *Daybreak* as it passed overhead.

"Maybe we could gain time by answering the hail?" suggested Haid.

Roche shook her head, continuing to ready the ship for launch. "That won't stop *them.*" She nodded toward the two figures. "And I sure as hell don't need the distraction right now."

The thrum of the thrusters grew louder. Normally she would have used attitude jets to move the ship away from the wall of the dock, giving it a less cluttered path and minimizing damage in its wake—but this would forewarn the guards of the ship's imminent departure. Neither did she care how much damage she left behind.

The countdown clicked to single figures just as the gun was mounted.

Roche nudged the ship forward, ignoring the rough trajectory she had plotted and flying purely on manual. Attitude jets turned it slightly to present as small a cross-section to the gun as possible. Behind it, the guards moved into position.

When the counter reached zero, she directed *Daybreak* as fast as it would go straight for the impromptu gun emplacement.

Acceleration pushed her back into the seat, hard. Beside her, Disisto braced himself against the arms of the crash-couch. Mavalhin moaned at the pressure on his injured shoulder.

Light flashed in the main screen, and two muffled cracks pierced the roar of the thrusters. For the briefest of moments the gun loomed large in the main screen as the ship raced toward it, then Roche wrenched the ship to her left, away from the wall. Behind them, the energy-wash from *Daybreak*'s thrusters left a thick black scar on the dry dock. Nothing remained of the two guards.

<The station has launched interceptors from emergency egress bays,> the Box said.

<Singleships?> Roche asked, although she already guessed the answer. The interceptors couldn't be large to have come from escape-launchers.

<Yes.>

<How many?>

<Fifteen.>

Daybreak cleared the lip of the outer shell, and suddenly all ahead was black: no stars, no navigational clues at all apart from the distant reddish sun. Roche swept the courier in a tight arc away from where the Box's telemetry data indicated the *Ana Vereine* was positioned; predictability in battle was a trap she had learned to avoid.

Two specks of light visible over the piecemeal curve of the station instantly moved toward *Daybreak*. More converged from the far side.

Roche cursed silently to herself as she counted the incoming ships. Half their number alone would have been a problem. The tiny, dartlike craft had none of the brute force of the *Ana Vereine*—were, in fact, less powerful even than *Daybreak*—but they were far more maneuverable. Armed, they could play a significant part in any battle.

In a matter of moments, the singleships reached firing range, and began to pepper the space around the courier with energy. The shots that struck home jolted the ship, provoking more protests from Mavalhin. Roche watched the damage board closely as she flew, but so far nothing crucial had been hit.

<Can't you destroy them?> she asked the Box.

<I will, once I am in position.>

The ship lurched as cannon fire struck it from the rear. Roche grunted and sent it angling away from its previous course, spiraling erratically to reduce the chances of being hit again. Luckily the damage was minor: a sensor or two, a small percentage of hull integrity; nothing life-threatening.

But the cannon fire was intense. It was only a matter of time before she miscalculated—or the targeters behind the cannon had a stroke of luck—and the courier was seriously damaged. If that happened, they would be dead.

Roche had no time to consider attempting to dock with the *Ana Vereine,* or even determining its location. She just kept her attention focused behind them, on the bobbing singleships and flashing cannon emplacements. Behind the flashes of light narrowly missing the courier, Galine Four loomed like a malignant, worm-eaten moon, much too close for comfort and receding only slowly.

Then something dark blotted the station from view. The black shape angled between *Daybreak* and the singleships harassing it, effectively acting as a shield against the cannon fire. From within the blackness came a barrage of retaliatory fire, destroying first one singleship that attempted to pass it, then another.

Not wasting the opportunity, Roche spurred the courier onward, putting all available energy into increasing their velocity away from the station. <Perfect timing, Box!>

<Save some of the credit for me, Morgan.> Roche smiled at the sound of Kajic's voice in her head. <It's a team effort, you know.>

The *Ana Vereine,* camouflaged black, thrust itself into close engagement with Galine Four. Although considerably outsized, it had been designed as a weapon of war, and looked it. Its angular outline was visible through the camouflage like a many-legged shadow blotting out the station's gray. The sheer power of its weaponry outshone that of the dim, red sun, casting the scene in a variety of short-lived colors, each blindingly bright.

<We will cover you as long as we can, Morgan,> said the Box. <I suggest you maximize the distance between yourself and Galine Four while the opportunity exists.>

<Already doing so,> she replied. <What about you?>

<When you are a sufficient distance away, we will disengage. We can outrun any vessel at their disposal, and will use the camouflage to its maximum advantage.>

<Are you taking much damage, Uri?>

<Medium to light,> Kajic replied. <We can last a few minutes longer before it becomes a problem.>

<Are you sure? I don't want you to do anything too dangerous.>

<I won't, I assure you. Remember, I'm the one getting hurt here. If I was going to risk serious damage, it would have to be for something a bit more noble than just letting you escape.>

<I suggest you continue along your current trajectory,> said the Box. <We will hold here as long as possible, then flee in another direction. I have already sent drones to disrupt your afterwash. That way, they will be unable to follow you—assuming, of course, they do not detect your drive emissions directly.>

<I'll feather the wash as soon as you leave,> she said. <That'll reduce the chances of them spotting us. But what about communications? Even on tightbeam, there's a chance they'll overhear.>

<A good point, Morgan. I suggest we maintain radio silence for three hours, just to be certain.>

<Agreed. Unless there's an emergency, I'll speak to you then.> She took one last look at the *Ana Vereine*. <Take care of yourselves.>

<We will, Morgan.> Kajic's voice sounded alive with the thrill of battle. <Speak to you in three hours.>

The line went dead, and Roche returned her attention to slipping away from the station.

Only after Galine Four become barely a blip on the courier's rear scanner screen did Roche finally feel safe enough to let *Daybreak* fly itself. Programming it to follow a course through the relative cover of Autoville—where, this far out in the system, a solid body every million kilometers constituted a crowded environment—she unlocked her harness and stepped out of the crash-couch.

She stopped beside Disisto. "I'm locking the ship to my implants," she told him. "You so much as touch those controls and I'll know about it. Understand?"

The security officer nodded slowly. "Given my situation, I'm hardly going to take any risks."

She held his stare for a few seconds before moving off to check on Mavalhin. The pilot was unconscious in his seat, blood spreading across his uniform from the wound in his shoulder. When she unlocked his harness, her fingers came away sticky.

"He's in a bad way," said Haid, leaning from the other side of the couch to help her lift him out of it.

"If there's an autosurgeon aboard, we might be able to help him." She gritted her teeth as they swung him upright. He was heavier than he looked. "The corridor we passed on the way in—the surgery should be along there."

Together they manhandled him to the courier's small medical facility. There, they laid him on a plastic stretcher and positioned the autosurgeon over him. The machine came to life with a slight humming sound as it began to take X-rays and ultrasound images of the wound.

Roche took a step back, turning her attention from Mavalhin to Haid. She noticed her friend's distraction as he quietly surveyed the room.

"What's up?"

"Huh?" His gaze came back to her. "Oh," he said, "I was just thinking. It's kind of weird to realize that the clone warrior was actually here, in this ship, only a few days ago."

"I know what you mean." She nodded at the stretcher where Mavalhin lay. "This might have been the very place they revived him when they removed him from the life-support capsule."

"Do you think he's left the system?"

"I don't know what to think." She folded her arms and leaned against a waste-disposal unit. "I just don't know how far we can trust the information Rufo gave us."

"Well, most of it made sense," said Haid. "At least, it fit what we've already learned."

"*Most* of it, yes. But I can't shake the feeling that he left the most important bits out."

The humming from the autosurgeon faded as it finished its examination. Roche read the diagnosis from the small screen: Mavalhin had a shattered collarbone and punctured left lung, and had lost a dangerous amount of blood. The recommendation was for surgery to correct the gross injuries, and a week's recuperation to reach full health and mobility.

Roche instructed it to begin the operation, and immediately surgical lasers flashed, cutting away the remains of the pilot's bloodstained and burnt uniform. She told the autosurgeon to notify her when the procedure was finished; then, with a pat on the back and a gesture toward the door, she ushered Haid out of the room.

"Rufo didn't mention that Galine Four had moved shortly before we rendezvoused with it," she said as they headed back to the bridge. "He also didn't mention that he'd had contact with someone outside Palasian System within the last week. And he definitely gave us no reason to suspect that he knew who we were, or that he knew about the Sol Apotheosis Movement."

"We should've guessed the last bit sooner," Haid said. "He did say he was an expert on history. He could hardly have missed the Wunderkind."

"I know." She felt bad about that, but there was nothing she could do to change the past. "He was also reticent in other areas, like the transmissions we picked up coming here. If Myer was near Jagabis when the Sol code was sent, you'd think he would have traced its source."

"Maybe he did." Haid shrugged. "Maybe that's why he was heading out of there when we ran into him."

"Well, we'll find out when he's awake, I guess."

Haid paused before speaking, his artificial eyes and midnight-black features unreadable. "I still don't trust him, Morgan," he eventually said.

"Neither do I, but he *did* help us back there."

"He helped himself."

"Perhaps. But it amounted to the same thing."

"This time."

Back on the bridge, Disisto sat in resigned silence.

"How is he?" he asked, looking up.

Roche leaned against the main console to face him. "You almost sound like you care."

Disisto looked offended. "Because we're on opposite sides, I can't be concerned? You have a monopoly on these emotions, Commander?"

"Not at all," she said. "Just wouldn't have thought it was a required trait for someone working under Shak'ni, that's all. I mean, he doesn't strike me as someone who cares about others terribly much."

Disisto's face clouded. "We agree there, at least."

"What does *that* mean?"

Disisto said nothing, but didn't look away from her.

"Listen," she said, "I don't know what you think we are, or what you think we've done, or even what you think we *will* do, but I can assure you that you're wrong about us. I'm not your enemy, and I don't regard you as mine. It's the clone warrior we should be worrying about, not each other. If he's still out there, none of us are safe, and fighting each other will only make the situation worse."

"Or perhaps he thinks we're working *with* the Sol Wunderkind?" Haid's words were to Roche, but his gaze was fixed firmly upon the security officer.

Disisto's expression was defiant. "That's what we were told," he said. "We were warned to expect another one—another clone warrior—and that he would be coming with an ex-COE commander called Morgan Roche in a ship stolen from the Dato Bloc."

Roche frowned. "Who told you that?"

"The chief, of course."

"And how do you know he was telling the truth?"

"Why would he lie?"

Disisto's blind acceptance of what he had been told exasperated Roche. "Did it ever occur to you to ask *how* he knew?"

"Why? He was right, wasn't he?"

Roche shook her head. "So no matter what we told you, you wouldn't have believed us?"

"There's no reason why I should." His eyes dropped away from Roche's. "No matter how much I might want to."

"What?" She leaned in closer now. "What is it you're hinting at? Why not just come out and say what you want to say?"

"I can't." The words were so soft, they could have been mistaken for a sigh. "Rufo has treated me well in the five years I've worked for him. I can't betray him now."

Roche glanced at Haid, who lifted one artificial shoulder in a tiny shrug.

"Okay." Roche stepped back, slipping her hands into the pockets of the shipsuit. "So you don't want to betray Rufo's confidence, but he's clearly doing something you disapprove of. Or—" She stopped as a thought struck her. "Or *allowing* something to happen?"

He said nothing, but the muscles in his neck tightened.

"That's it, isn't it? Shak'ni and B'shan are up to something, and you don't like it."

He looked at her again. "Not Haden B'shan. He's been with the chief longer than I have."

"Shak'ni, then. That doesn't surprise me. So tell us what he's doing, and perhaps we can stop him."

When Disisto didn't respond, anger surged from deep within Roche's frustration. "Dammit, Disisto, *talk* to me! I've got better things to do than play guessing games with you!"

"Why the hell should I trust you?" he said, throwing her anger back at her. "I've been told that you're dangerous, and *nothing* I've seen contradicts that! You don't even try to deny what's been said about you! The fact is, I don't even know who you are." He paused for a moment, leaning forward slightly and fixing her with a cold stare. "So tell me, Commander, just who *do* you think you are?"

Her hand closed into a fist, but she managed to subdue the impulse to strike him. Her anger had little to do with his attitude. In fact, if anything, she understood his point of view. Who *was* she to demand that he compromise five years of faithful service to Rufo? No, her anger came about from what had happened to Cane and Maii.

She let the tension drain from her, leaving just the residue of frustration in her clenched fist. A moment later she released this too, and sighed.

"Look, Disisto, I can't deny what you've heard about me, because most of it's true. Yes, one of my companions does appear to be a clone warrior, and yes, I did steal my ship from the Dato Bloc."

Disisto raised an eyebrow, surprised by her sudden frankness. "And the super-AI you held COE Intelligence HQ to ransom with?"

She nodded. "And Haid here is one of the few people ever to escape from the penal colony on Sciacca's World. You're in distinguished company, you know."

"That *is* the truth," said Haid, grinning.

Disisto looked from Roche to Haid. "I'm sure you think it is," he said humorlessly. "But that still doesn't mean I can trust you."

Roche reached down and unlocked the clasp of his harness. "I guess it all depends on how you look at it."

"Morgan!" Haid cautioned uneasily.

"Come on, Ameidio," she said. "He's not going to betray us—at least not until he's sure we can't help him." She unlooped the strap holding Disisto's left hand to the palm-link. "Besides, he can't stay tied up forever."

Disisto sat up, rubbing at his wrists. "Thank you," he said, with more than just a hint of sarcasm.

She shrugged. "I can tie you up again, if you like. Or you can quit with the attitude and come down to the mess where we can discuss things civilly. It's your choice."

He offered a half-smile and said: "The mess will be fine, thanks."

"Good," said Roche. "But remember that both Ameidio and I are armed and we'll be watching your every movement."

Disisto nodded, standing slowly. "Now *that* I can believe."

In the mess, the three of them sat at one of the many tables scattered about the room. Roche picked at a dish of reheated noodles while she sketched the details of how she had come to be in Palasian System. Disisto listened carefully, occasionally glancing at Haid when the ex-mercenary added a detail Roche had left out.

By the time they brought him up to date, an hour had passed and Disisto had hardly said a word.

"Well?" Roche prompted.

"I'm not sure," he said. "I think you've been honest with me, but . . ."

"But what?"

He pushed his plate aside. "Well, the business of Cane himself. If the clone warrior in Palasian System could cause so much destruction, then why hasn't Cane?"

Roche shrugged. "That's one of the reasons we're here: to see what makes them tick. But so far we've only seen two, and that's hardly a representative sample. For all we know, Cane could be the norm, not the exception."

Disisto looked down at his plate for a long moment, then back up at Roche. "There's another one."

What little appetite Roche had instantly vanished. "What? *Where*?"

"Hetu System. We received news of it a few days ago." He held up his hands before she could press him for more details. "That's all I know, Roche. I'm not privy to that kind of information. What little I do find out is on the sly."

She forced herself to let it go—for the moment. Hetu System was on the far side of the COE, on the fringes of the region. There wasn't much she could do about it even if she wanted to.

"You heard about this other clone warrior a few days ago?" Haid said. "How was that possible? I thought you were unable to leave here."

Disisto looked tired, as though his decision to answer questions had come at great personal cost. "Seventeen days ago we were brought here on the back of the

Sebettu, a Kesh destroyer. They brought us to the edge of the system, just inside the Gauntlet, and from there we traveled under our own power."

"So the Gauntlet was in place at that point?" said Roche.

"Yes."

Roche nodded, noting one lie from Rufo so far. He had said they had been trapped when the solar envelope had encapsulated the system.

Disisto went on: "Ever since then, we've received a communications drone from outside the Gauntlet every six days or so. I presumed they came from *Sebettu,* but if you didn't pass it on the way in, I guess I might be wrong."

That explained the recent duel Haid had noted in the bar. "All we saw was a blockade comprised of Armada ships. Were they there when you came in?"

"Yes. But they let us through once they were sure who we were."

"Really? Doesn't that strike you as a bit odd? I mean, we had a hell of a time getting past them."

"Not really," said Disisto. "As I understand it, the COE Armada wanted to seal the system once they had an idea what was inside it. The only way they could do that quickly was with something like Asha's Gauntlet. They did a deal with the N'Kor Republic, which had the only remaining prototype. At the same time, they contacted the chief and commissioned the services of Galine Four. The Gauntlet beat us here by a few days, so *Sebettu* ferried us in. Once we were inside, they left us alone to begin our work."

"Which was?" said Haid.

Disisto turned to him. "To study the actions of the person responsible for the destruction of the system."

"That's it?" Haid asked.

"What else do you suggest we do? *Fight* this person? The most we could hope for was to work out *how* he operated, in order to stop his doing it again elsewhere. Anything more would've been asking for trouble. If you ask me, it's risky enough just being here."

"Rufo agreed to be dropped in here without any means of defending himself?" Haid's expression was highly skeptical. "No means of escape? No way of letting the outside know if you might be under attack?"

"Not quite," said Disisto. "We do have communications drones of our own that we can send if we need to. But it was risky, yes. A drone takes at least ten hours to get out of the system. If we *did* get into trouble, by the time help arrived we'd have been dead. We haven't sent any yet, and I hope we don't have to."

"So why did Rufo agree to do it?" Roche asked.

"Lots of reasons, I guess. It's hard to know exactly why, because he doesn't explain himself to his employees as often as we feel he should." He managed a small smile. "I think it was because the COE applied a little pressure to make him agree. That, and they told him the person we would be looking for was probably gone anyway."

Roche's laugh was derisive. "And that you would basically be conducting an autopsy on a completely dead system?"

"Something like that," said Disisto.

"But it hasn't turned out that way, has it?"

Disisto shook his head. "The traps around Aro could've hurt us, and there could be others we haven't encountered yet."

"Not to mention the clone warrior himself," Haid pointed out.

"I doubt he's still here," said Disisto.

"Really? Why?"

"It stands to reason, doesn't it? We've been wandering around the system for almost two weeks, and we haven't been attacked. We've been careful, sure, but he would've spotted us eventually. And if he did, why didn't he attack us? We're the only major target left in one piece in Palasian System. It doesn't make sense that he would let us roam free—especially not when we're actively looking for him. He's not stupid."

"And this is what Rufo believes?" said Roche.

"No, Rufo is convinced he's still here," Disisto said. "But take my word for it, he's long gone by now."

Roche wasn't taking his word on anything, but was prepared to watch him entertain the thought. "Where to? Hetu System, perhaps?"

Disisto shrugged. "Maybe. Or maybe he's still in transit. It depends what sort of transport he's in, and what he's looking for. The nearest system is only a few light-years away, but it's not much more than an outpost. He might be looking for more of a challenge."

"I wouldn't call Palasian System much of a challenge," Haid said.

"What if this was just a trial run?" said Disisto. "Or just an opportunity to do some damage? Remember: he only made his move when the crew of this ship brought him out of the life capsule. Not only was Palasian System the closest port at that time, but *Daybreak* was already heading there. It would've made sense to go with the flow, to take what he could from here, then to move on in the direction he actually wanted to go."

Roche nodded. "I agree. It matches what Cane said. He's not going to waste time or opportunities; every decision he makes will be to maximize his return—however he measures it. Palasian System was just a means of making himself stronger.

"But where do *we* fit into this?" she went on. "You said someone from the outside warned you that we were coming. Who was it? And *why*?"

"The Armada, perhaps," said Disisto.

"You don't sound very certain about that," said Haid.

"I'm not," he said. "The last drone we received told us to expect you. I have no idea who sent it."

"Word must have leaked from Intelligence," said Haid, facing Roche. "Someone might have taken exception to there being another Sol Wunderkind on the loose."

"Maybe," Roche said. She could believe Page De Bruyn setting her up like this. "But why not ambush us properly? There's no way we could have withstood a destroyer or two at the edge of the Gauntlet, where they knew we were going to arrive sooner or later. Why leave it up to a nonmilitary installation inside what is basically a war zone?"

"Less risk?" Haid suggested. "Containment would be easier in here, if something went wrong."

"Not when we have a working slow-jump drive. Supposing Cane did go berserk, all he'd have to do is take over the *Ana Vereine* and fly it back out again."

"Do you think he's capable of doing that? Without Kajic or the Box, the ship would be difficult to control for a hundred people, let alone one."

"I'd hate to rule it out," Roche said. "Every time Cane reaches a hurdle, he seems to find a way over it."

"Until now." Haid turned to Disisto. "So what did you hit him with, anyway? Ferozac?"

"Diprodek-2, actually," the security officer said, unable to hide a hint of satisfaction. "It was the fastest-acting neurotoxin we had in store, *and* we had an antidote. All we had to do was hit him with a blast, catch him when he fell, then clear out the poison before it did any serious damage. It worked, too. I was receiving updates before the scutter activated its engines—and afterward, too, through the feed your Box tapped into."

Roche leaned forward. "What did you see?"

"Everything went as planned. The whole thing was handled by remote to ensure no one would get hurt. The scutter docked, and automatics attached the umbilical. When pressure equalized, the airlock opened. The clone warrior stepped through first to check things out, then he went back in to get your reave. They walked out together, and that's when we hit them. Just prior to that, we shot your reave full of Xarodine to stop her picking anything up—"

"Why did you do that?" said Roche, unable to keep the bitterness from her voice. "She couldn't read anything. That's why she was there, not to spy. It was Rufo who suggested we bring her in to see your medical team in the first place!"

"We had no way of knowing you were telling us the truth, Commander."

Roche shook her head in disbelief. "And I don't suppose you have any epsense adepts on Galine Four either, right?"

Disisto frowned. "None that I know of. Why?"

"Because Rufo told us you had some on board with similar problems." She glanced over at Haid. "Another lie," she said.

"Well, try to see it from his point of view," said Disisto. "He'd been warned about you; he had to take some sort of action."

"Why?" Haid asked. "We hadn't done anything to him."

"But for the sake of the station he had to assume that you *might.*"

"Oh, come on, Disisto!" Roche snapped. "He never intended to trust us, and you know it! Stop trying to defend him. He lured us to Galine Four with the sole intention of neutralizing Cane. He didn't even give us a chance."

Disisto didn't deny it. "If that's the case, then he was pressured into doing it. It's not like the chief at all to take such risks."

"What do you mean?" said Roche.

"Well, whether he's in the system or not, we'd already managed to evade one clone warrior; we're pushing our luck putting ourselves in direct contact with another. The chief knew that, and at any other time he would have simply let you go by and not take any risks. But he sent Mavalhin to contact you, knowing full well what you would bring with you. And I guess he lied about our epsense adepts to get Cane on board. It's not an acceptable risk, in my opinion."

"You blame Shak'ni?" said Haid.

"And whoever's behind him, yes."

"So why didn't they do it themselves?" asked Roche.

"Shak'ni is a bigot," said Haid, "like a lot of the hard-core Kesh. Maybe it amuses him to watch Pristines making trouble for each other."

Disisto shrugged. "That's possible. I don't know, though. It bothers me that the chief isn't acting his normal self, and hasn't ever since we came here."

Roche sighed. "Okay, so what happens to Cane now?"

"Nothing," said Disisto. "He's powerless, and the chief knows it's best to keep him that way. Linegar may be under pressure at the moment, but he's not stupid."

Roche nodded. The idea of Cane bound in chains didn't sit easily with her, but there was some consolation in what Disisto said. While Cane was incapacitated, he was safe. But it was the image of Maii, locked in the perpetual darkness of her own skull, that bothered Roche the most.

Again, determination to rescue the girl flooded through her. Too many people had let *her* down recently; she refused to do the same to anyone she knew. There was too much mistrust in the galaxy as it was.

"If Rufo's so damned smart," she said, "why can't he see that we all want the same thing? Why are we fighting each other?"

Disisto met her gaze squarely. "*Do* we want the same thing?"

"I thought we did. Or hoped so, anyway." Roche shook her head. "I need to work out what your boss is doing, and why. Will you help me do that?"

Disisto took a deep breath. "If it means betraying his confidence, no, I won't."

"Then we have nothing else to talk about. For now."

Responding to a message from the autosurgeon via her implants, Roche stopped at the surgery on the way back to the bridge, sending Haid and Disisto ahead of her. By the time she arrived there, Myer's unconscious body had been wrapped in a bioactive blanket and strapped to the plastic bed. His left shoulder, chest, and arm were completely encased in a thin layer of translucent bandages that allowed enough red through to indicate just how severe the damage had been. He seemed peaceful, however, and Roche was content to leave him there for the time being—until either the autosurgeon pronounced him fit enough to walk or she needed him on his feet regardless.

She had been there only a few minutes when another message came through her implants. This time it was from the bridge: *Daybreak* had received a tightbeam transmission encrypted in high-level COE code. She quickly left the surgery, instructing the autosurgeon to keep her posted on Myer's progress.

She arrived on the bridge just as the courier's AI completed deciphering the transmission.

Haid looked up from tying Disisto back into his crash-couch as she entered. "That'll be the Box, I guess," he said.

"I hope so." She sat in the pilot's seat and instructed the AI to play the message.

"Morgan," said the Box, its voice brisk. "This message will reach you exactly three hours following our last communication. In that time, the *Ana Vereine* will have disengaged from Galine Four and headed in-system. We are currently leading a flotilla of seven pursuit vessels along a powered approach that will take us past Jagabis, through the Mattar Belt and close to Cartha's Planet. At perihelion, in twelve hours, we will adopt a neutral camouflage and power at maximum thrust to a different orbit. If you wish to choose a rendezvous point, please indicate so in your reply, before the delay becomes too great."

"We left a furious mess behind," the recorded voice of Kajic broke in. "There are singleships buzzing around everywhere, looking for any trace of you. The Box self-destructed a drone, hoping they'd mistake the wreckage for *Daybreak*, but I don't think they were fooled. It looks like they're getting ready to move elsewhere, just in case you come back in a hurry."

"I recommend strongly that you do not do that," said the Box. "*Daybreak* is unarmed and poorly defended; any attempt to breach their security will surely fail. Better to wait until we join you and use the combined resources of the two ships."

Roche nodded to herself; there was nothing she could do for Maii in a clapped-out courier.

As though reading Roche's mind, the Box went on: "You might be interested to know that Cane and Maii are unharmed. I was able to install a leak via Disisto's implants while I was connected to the secondary security shell of Galine Four, and through this leak, I have been monitoring their condition."

Roche smiled. *Thanks, Box,* she thought to herself. Disisto appeared to be telling the truth on that score.

"They are currently being held in separate cells in the station's outer levels," the Box went on, "and are closely guarded. Preparations are being made to move them to the Hub, but where exactly I do not know at this stage. Chances are, however, that it will be to a zone I will not be able to penetrate, even with my improved access.

"Lastly, a drone was launched from Galine Four within fifteen minutes of our departure. I was able to track it as far as the orbit of Gatamin, at which point it was accelerating rapidly for the edge of the system. If you have not already interrogated Disisto on this matter, you should do so immediately. Any information he can provide, willingly or otherwise, will be to our benefit."

Roche felt a brief flicker of self-satisfaction—Disisto had mentioned that they hadn't sent any drones out of the system—but quelled it. Although it was good to have preempted the Box in one instance, to dwell on it was obsessive.

"That is all for now, Morgan," it continued. "The drone following you is maintaining a fixed position with respect to *Daybreak* and will relay to me any message you send in return. It will be necessary for you to reply soon, though, for the delay between our communications will increase rapidly over the next twelve hours. Once we have a rendezvous point established, we can begin planning how best to use it to our advantage.

"Also, I will require you to perform a diagnostic check of *Daybreak*'s slow-jump drive. The result of that analysis will affect any plans we make. I will await your reply before taking further action."

The message ended abruptly, catching Roche off guard for a moment.

After a while she said: "What do you think, Ameidio?"

Haid shook his head. "We haven't got a lot of options, have we? It's unlikely they'd even stumble upon us out here, so the sensible thing would be to stay put."

"I agree." Roche slipped into the pilot's crash-couch and called up the communications systems. The tightbeam had come from a point in space not far behind them; she directed the systems to send her reply in that direction, once she had recorded it.

"But staying put is exactly what they'll be expecting us to do," she continued. "It's too obvious, too predictable. And it wastes an opportunity to do something useful. Instead of heading straight back to rescue Maii and Cane, we'd be better off looking for answers."

"Where from?"

"Kukumat and Murukan." She called up a map of the outer system. "Twice, now, we've received signals from near the double-jovian; Rufo can't or won't explain them, and that makes me suspicious. It's also the only obvious hiding place in the system we haven't investigated. None of the drones we sent there ever reported back."

"You think there might be survivors?"

"I don't know what to think. I'd rather keep my options open until we arrive. Which should be"—she scanned a navigation chart and performed rough mental calculations—"about fourteen hours, if we go by Hintubet along the way. And if we do, that'll keep our transmission times to the Box at a minimum."

Haid nodded. "It also increases the chances of the pursuit ships seeing us."

"Marginally. They'll be tracking the *Ana Vereine,* not looking for us. By the time the Box loses them, we'll be gone."

Disisto had followed the exchange in silence up to that point. "What signals?" he asked. "I was told there was no one near the old base."

Roche turned to face him. "If that's what Rufo told you, then that makes me even more interested in having a look myself."

"I agree," said Haid. "It worries me what we might be heading into, but yes: I'm also curious to know what Rufo is up to. If he's lying to his own security staff, then something serious must be going on."

Before Disisto could respond, Roche turned back to the communications systems and began to record a reply for the Box. She had already checked the maintenance systems of the courier and determined that the slow-jump drive was dead; that was why the clone warrior had ditched it: after attempting to leave the Gauntlet and failing, destroying the drive in the process, he had had no use for the courier. It had become a liability, in fact, due to its inevitable association with him. He had abandoned it and gone elsewhere. Now she was hoping to find him in it; the irony was not lost on her.

But it did confirm one thing: he was in the system with them. Anyone who said otherwise was either wrong or lying.

She keyed their new course into the navigation systems. As the courier's thrusters began a long, steady burn, she settled back into the crash-couch and let g-forces erase the worry from her mind. For now, there was nothing else she could do.

PART THREE:

MOK

INTERLUDE

The enigma dissolved into the background, obscured by the intensity and close proximity of the light.

He strained desperately to follow her; the Cruel One's servant would be annoyed if he let her slip away. But he had no choice. He could either see her or he couldn't, and within moments she had completely disappeared. He let her go with a feeling of apprehension mixed with something not unlike relief. He had enough to do as it was.

Bathed in the light of the Shining One, he examined his options.

One: he could do everything the Cruel One asked of him, where possible.

Two: he could do only those things that he felt comfortable doing and feign ignorance or lack of understanding with the others—although the Cruel One's servant had an uncanny knack of recognizing his deceptions, and previous attempts had led to torture, both physical and mental.

Three: he could do nothing at all and endure the consequences.

Following the enigma was, already, one request with which he could not comply. Studying the Shining One was something he was happy to do, if he was able to. But neutralizing the abomination . . . Wasn't he already doing that just by being here? What more could be asked of him?

He wanted nothing to do with the awful child and her piercing, painful mind. His people would have killed her had they known she existed—or at the very least extracted a terrible price from the Surin Agora for allowing her to exist. That in part was what the grayboots were for: to prevent such things from coming into being, to stamp them out when they did, and to keep all knowledge of their existence secret lest others try to replicate past experiments.

But he didn't have the means to kill her, and he knew from the Cruel One's servant's mind that she was safe here in that respect. Her frail body was considered a threat by no one. It was her powers alone he was supposed to quash, as if that were possible. He was being asked to stop a wasp from stinging without damaging the stinger *or* the wasp. And the fact that this particular wasp was not even a natural creature only made the task that much more preposterous.

He could already feel her stirring, despite an intensive regimen of epsense-inhibitors. Xarodine worked on most Castes—including those possessing epsense naturally, like his own—but its efficacy decreased with extended use. The initial doses given to the girl would have worn off hours ago and been topped up several times since; her powers would be returning soon. They could keep her unconscious—perhaps—but nothing would stop her from dreaming. And even asleep she could be dangerous. Should she erupt, he might not be able to contain her, let alone neutralize her. Those nearby or linked to her in other ways would be in peril.

He briefly imagined what would happen to the Cruel One's servant under such circumstances, but he dismissed the fantasy. That was why the servant had servants of his own. They stood between harm and the hearth; they bore the brunt of any such perils.

He said:

: SAFE

: SLEEPING

And that would have to do. The girl was probably harmless for a few hours yet. Eventually he would have to decide what to do with her, but for now . . .

The Shining One.

Its glow, he now realized, was a defensive measure designed to fool anyone encountering it into believing it to be evidence of profound epsense ability. As a camouflage it worked well; few people would penetrate its structure or decipher the giddying motion at its core. It was complex and amazing enough; why imagine that there would be more?

But there was. Behind the façade lay a much more interesting possibility, the same one he had suspected before but could not explain to the Cruel One's servant. Behind the shine and scatter lay a speck of unfathomable black. The speck haunted him; he could hardly drag his attention away from it. Part of him was afraid it would not be there when he looked—afraid the blaze would cover it again, this time forever. He and the Shining One had something in common, it seemed.

What that was, though, he still lacked the words to explain. *No one* had the words. Only a natural reave would understand.

Epsense theorists—some of them reaves, most of them not—likened a world empty of thought to a flat plain, in the same way that physicists described empty space-time as a rubber sheet. This plain they called "n-space." The addition of a thinking being—an "n-body"—added a small spike to the flat landscape. Reaves were spikes surrounded by small mounds that spread across the surface of the plain, joining the spikes together.

On first inspection, the Shining One was a peak so high, its foothills buried all the n-bodies around it.

Races of natural reaves, like the Olmahoi, warped the surface of the plain itself, creating valleys and peaks and, sometimes, holes. He was one such hole; without him at its heart, and others like him before, the Grand Design of his people would have unraveled millennia ago. He depressed n-space, disconnected n-bodies from each other even if there were reaves present, absorbed stray thoughts no matter where they came from. That was why he'd been kidnapped and brought here: to gather data for the Cruel One's servant. All things eventually found their way into the Olmahoi *irikeii.*

A closer look at the Shining One revealed the hole in its core—a hole so deep he could not find its measure. If it had a bottom, he never touched it.

He could sense it, though. And what he sensed both disturbed and fascinated him.

Something old.

Something that should not exist.

Something that seemed, impossibly, to be studying him back.

Yet through the eyes of those examining the Shining One, he saw just another

Pristine Human, one of many hundreds of trillions scattered across the galaxy. Why would anyone go to so much trouble to bring such a thing into being and hide it in so ordinary a vessel—not just once, but several times? What could possibly be served by such a deception?

He saw in the minds of those around him—through the all-pervading nimbus of the Shining One—that some thought it a weapon made to wreak vengeance on Pristine Humanity. A weapon that could hide among its intended victims, striking with surprise and efficiency. That made sense, even though the evidence was tenuous at best, and sometimes outright misleading. And in the mind of the Cruel One's servant he found a nagging doubt that nagged at him in turn. Could it be so simple?

He hoped it was. The only other possibility to occur to him was too horrible to contemplate . . .

Knowing it was probably futile yet needing to try, he cast his mind outward, as he had done on only a few occasions before, to the very limits of his senses. There, normally, he sensed strange, superior intelligences, watching from their arcane removes as the lower Castes went about their business. The High Humans were like people watching ants; they saw the swarming, the building, the clashes between hives, but few if any ever stopped to notice the lone ant waving its antennae in the hope of catching their attention.

Still, he had communicated with High Humans before. They used means as far above epsense as epsense was above normal speech, and they tended to be reticent. But sometimes unintended data slipped through, as though the sheer bandwidth of the High Humans' media meant that their speech could not be effectively dammed. Some of it was incomprehensible; most of it was useless, relating to Castes or times far distant; but just one useful piece of data made the effort worthwhile.

He needed their help now. If what he suspected was true, even they could be in danger.

But there was no reply. He sensed nothing lurking at the fringes of the void. There was no one to whom he could turn for advice.

He was suddenly homesick. He missed his people: he missed their minds, their song, the tapestry they wove around him and in which he knew his proper place. Here, he had no one to commune with. Few even knew he existed, and those that did were unable to communicate properly. He was trapped by mundanes in a plot that, under ordinary circumstances, might only tangentially concern him.

He wondered how his people coped without him. Did chaos reign, or had the keepers of the Shadow Place found a way to correct the imbalance? Was the racial mechanism that had brought him forth when his predecessor had died already conceiving his replacement? What would happen if he returned? Could the Grand Design tolerate *two irikeii*?

Perhaps he would have to remain in the void forever, trapped with only a handful of minds to watch until his own was extinguished! Except he knew from those around him that the void was impermanent: it would collapse upon itself within weeks. So perpetual imprisonment was not an option: it was temporary at best.

Then there were the Shining Ones to consider, and the Cruel One. Regardless of whether he was right or wrong about the former, of one thing he *was* certain: the Cruel One and her servant had no intention of letting him live after his mission here was complete.

For a brief, bitter moment he envied the enigma. Whoever she was, whatever she represented, she was freer than he could ever hope to be.

But there was comfort in knowing that he was doomed, he guessed. Once all hope was gone, there was nothing left to fear except fear itself.

And if he could take the abomination with him, all the better. . . .

5

COEI *Daybreak*
'955.01.21 EN
1390

From a distance, Hintubet's bloody, red light was insufficient to allow the courier's basic sensors to gather much detail about the double-jovian system: a blurred, over-magnified image of two red balloons tied together by a twisted silver string was all Roche could see, little different from the pictures the Box had procured from the orbit of Gatamin. No doubt the probes dispatched earlier would be sending remarkable pictures to the *Ana Vereine,* wherever the ship was, but only as the courier drew nearer did Roche have the chance to appreciate the uniqueness of her destination.

Individually Kukumat and Murukan might once have been unremarkable gas giants, both roughly a quarter the mass of Jagabis; together they formed a dynamic partnership as mysterious as it was fascinating. The most obvious detail separating the pair from the other planets in Palasian System was that it followed a retrograde orbit around Hintubet. Planetary scientists generally agreed that the pair had probably arisen out of a near collision between two previously independent worlds, one natural to the system and the other an interstellar wanderer. Although no actual collision had occurred, each planet had captured the other, and the shared momentum of the two had cast the pair into an entirely new yet stable orbit.

Under normal conditions, Kukumat would have been a brilliant, white-streaked yellow. Storms considered enormous even for a gas giant raged from equator to pole, the constant flashes of lightning through the thick, turbulent atmosphere casting weird strobelike patterns across the face of the planet. Now and then Roche imagined she could sense a pattern forming in the inconstant light, as though some unfathomable machine at the heart of the planet was trying to communicate with her.

Murukan, though only marginally larger, was radically different. Regardless of the light that fell upon it, the gas giant presented a deep, bloody red face. Instead of the thin streaks and whorls boasted by its brilliant neighbor, Murukan possessed massive upwellings of heavy gases, spewed high into the atmosphere by unknown processes deeper within. These upwellings bloomed like flowers at their peak, spread in overlapping petals that changed color and smeared laterally as the gases comprising them slowly reached the apex of their explosive rise, then began to descend.

Roche didn't doubt that the extreme atmospheric activity of the two planets owed much to their proximity; on close examination she could see tidal bulges many kilometers high sweeping across the face of each planet as it rotated with respect to the other. It amazed her to think that the situation was stable at all. But it was, had been for hundreds of thousands of years, and would have been for many more had not the Gauntlet arrived to change the system irrevocably.

By the time the courier managed to locate Mok—the single moon of the double system—the system's other unique feature had attained a tantalizing prominence. KM36 was an ion bridge linking the magnetic fields of the two planets. Although the link itself was constant, it arced—and was therefore visible—only once every thirty-six minutes. Each arc lasted approximately seventy seconds, and Roche was fortunate enough to catch an entire event broadside-on, from the best possible perspective. The ion bridge looked like a lightning bolt strung out between the two planets, flickering and snapping almost too quickly to follow in close focus, yet undulating like a plucked wire in slow motion from a distance. Its light was so bright it cast a shadow on Mok, lending it, briefly, a silver-white face.

Watching it, Roche was reminded of why she had joined COE Intelligence in the first place. It hadn't just been to escape from a difficult upbringing, but for sights such as these.

And perhaps, she thought, that was enough to explain the dream. . . .

She was standing, cold and wet, on the foredeck of an oceangoing vessel made entirely of stone. The mass of the ship was so great that she felt no movement beneath her as it cut through the choppy waters, and the surety of its progress made her feel as safe as though she were standing on solid ground.

The stars above were as icy as the wind, however, and although the spray from the waves never struck her, she was soaked to the skin and trembling.

"Are you frightened?" A man's voice came from behind her, scented and hauntingly familiar.

She turned. The man, clad in white, his skin ashen and dry like dust, stood at the starboard rail of the foredeck.

"No," she said, clutching herself. "I'm cold. Aren't you?"

"No. But we could both be lying," he added, the glint in his yellow eyes like the lightning in Kukumat's alien skies.

"I am neither cold nor afraid," came a second voice, this time from the port rail. "But I *am* here."

The newcomer was dressed in red; his complexion was ruddy, his skin moist. A fat-petaled flower protruded from a buttonhole of his greatcoat. And again, a familiar odor, but this one different from the first.

They know each other, she thought, with some surprise.

"In a manner of speaking, yes," the red one said, as if answering Roche but looking at his white counterpart.

"Although I suspect we have less in common than I once thought," said the white man.

"Appearances can be deceptive," said Red.

"Perhaps it's time to end the pretense," said White.

"Do we have any choice?"

The red man nodded ahead of them. "We'll find out when we get there."

The brief exchange had changed them: the one in white had become paler, his skin drier, while the red one had begun to exude blood. And the smells, once disparate and only vaguely familiar, suddenly merged to become something all too familiar to Roche. Now she could smell death; she could smell *war* . . .

The two men faced each other, a silent but tense confrontation. They retained only the shape of Humanity, now; the essence of their true beings was almost too much even for that.

Roche backed away until her spine made contact with cold, wet stone. Two huge masts towered above her like giant antennae, visible only as silhouettes against the sky. The tremendous momentum with which the prow cut through the waves remained unchecked, only now it seemed a matter for concern.

She looked again at the two men and realized just how alike they really were. Despite their differences, they could easily have been mistaken for brothers. Or even twins . . .

The anxiety induced by the dream had stayed with her upon waking. No matter how hard she tried, she simply couldn't shake free of it, and she longed for Maii's gentle touch. The epsense adept could have soothed her, eased some of the dread and foreboding that filled her. But the reave was far away, left behind on an unfamiliar station, captive of a man who had somehow outthought them all.

For a moment, she felt despair. How had she come to this? *She* certainly wasn't responsible. It must have been COE Intelligence, or the Kesh, or the Sol Apotheosis Movement, or . . .

No. There was no point assigning blame. She just had to keep moving, to do her best to rectify the situation and find a way out of this mess. Find a way to rescue Maii and Cane and—

"Morgan?" said Haid.

She turned from the image of the double-jovian at which she had been blankly staring, and faced Haid. It was only when she did that she realized it had been the third time he had called her name.

"You okay?" he said.

She nodded, but felt it was unconvincing. "What's up?"

"We're detecting radio emissions."

Immediately focused, Roche took a step toward Haid. "Where from?"

"Mok. They spike every time the ion bridge flares, as though someone's using the discharge to cover emissions."

She concentrated on his explanation; it made sense. "Any idea who this 'someone' might be?"

Haid shook his head. "The transmissions are coded to look like static, and I can't translate them without the Box's help. If I had to guess, though, I'd say it's the outriggers talking among themselves."

"And the two spines haven't moved?"

Another curt shake of the head. "They're still in orbit around Murukan."

While still some distance from the jovian pair, they had detected the muted navigation beacons of two outrigger spines—spindly structures comprising little more than intrasystem engines and fuel tanks shaped like bare-boned trees with lots of branches for waldoes to cling to. The spines appeared to be undamaged, but, apart from the beacons, showed no signs of life.

Roche had never encountered outriggers before, but had heard the stories of whole tribes of people crossing the gulfs between stars on the backs of such flimsy vessels. Their only protection was an "all-suit," essentially a miniature spaceship in its own right within which each member of the tribe would spend his or her entire life. Although outriggers came from many different Castes, they were a society completely unto themselves, separated from the rest of the galaxy by the time-debts they accrued by traveling at relatavistic velocities; some had wandered so far and for so long that they were rumored to be thousands of years old. Outriggers earned a living mining systems considered uneconomic for prowling mines or other large-scale automated means. That explained what they were doing so far out from the primary of Palasian System, where solid bodies were few and very far between but the total mass of unexploited minerals was considerable.

Beyond that, Roche knew little. What the spines were doing so close to a large planet—the sort of gravity well outriggers normally avoided—remained a mystery.

Similarly, there had been no repeat of the distress calls that had brought them to the double-planet. She was resigned to traveling closer to find out what had happened.

"How long until we reach Mok?" she asked Haid.

"One hour."

"Okay," she said. "Show me the pictures we're getting."

Disisto chuckled quietly from behind Roche. "It's probably not going to be what you're expecting."

"How do you mean?"

"See for yourself," he said.

Disisto was right. The little moon was highly unusual: in size barely a thousand kilometers across and consisting of dark-hued dusty rock, with no atmosphere and a relatively low specific gravity. There were craters, Roche observed, but these looked suspiciously regular and similar in size, as though they were holes or tunnel-entrances rather than ancient impact sites. Between them stood odd protrusions resembling curved spikes or giant hairs growing out of the rock—as though the moon were covered in a large-scale version of Velcro. Each of the "hooks" was over ten meters high.

"Weird," she mused. "Are they artifacts?"

"Unknown. I've never seen anything like it before." Haid stared intently at the images filling most of the available screens and tanks. "There's no movement, so the chances are they're not alive."

"They might once have been," said Disisto. He was still on the couch where Haid had strapped him hours earlier. "The sun's changed; the difference could've killed a photosynthetic plant, for instance."

"The light would always have been poor out here," Haid said, shaking his head. "My gut says that they were made, but I have no idea what purpose they'd serve."

"Or even who made them," said Roche.

"Exactly," Haid agreed. "Those ruins are *old.* They could be the remains of a Transcended civilization, or even a dead High Human. You looked into the history around here, Morgan. Any records of such a thing in this area?"

"No, but it wouldn't hurt to look again."

"The chief was hoping the ruins might contain something related to Primordial Humanity," said Disisto. "An old base or colony, perhaps, with records intact. We have so little information to go by with respect to Humanity's origins. Any scrap at all could be helpful. If we'd known it was something like this, we would've come much sooner."

Haid looked back at the security chief. "I didn't know you were such a history buff."

Disisto shrugged. "Work with the chief long enough and it rubs off, I guess."

Roche didn't respond. His casual banter hid the underlying tension between them. Neither had forgotten their last conversation, when he had maintained his allegiance to Linegar Rufo. She couldn't afford to forget, though. Although she knew he meant well deep down, that they were forced to work on opposing sides made it all the more frustrating.

"Congreve Station?" Roche prompted Haid, keeping them on the subject at hand.

"There, at the pole." One image ballooned to reveal a low, blister-shaped installation near the moon's equator. "It's cold. Looks like no one's touched it for years."

KM36 chose that moment to flare. White light radiated from the screens as the ion bridge crackled into life.

Roche and Haid watched the instruments for more signs of concealed signals coming from Mok.

"Almost nothing, this time," said Haid. "Just one pulse at the beginning."

"I saw it. Like a warning tone, telling everyone to shut up."

Haid looked over at Roche. "They know we're here," he said.

Roche nodded. "But we still need to talk to them anyway." She pointed at a rough map of the moon's surface. "According to the instruments, the pulse came from that crater."

The image showed a black hole leading into the moon, not far from its equator.

"Deep," commented Haid. "Could hide anything."

"No different from the others, though. A simple jaunt to look wouldn't hurt."

He glanced up at her. "And who gets to do the honors?"

"I do, of course. Unless you fancy an EVA with your new implants?"

Haid smiled. "Well, I'm game."

"Yes, but you're not stupid," she said seriously. "You know I'm the best choice."

Haid nodded. "But you *are* going to try talking to them first, right?"

"There's no point. They're obviously in hiding; they're not going to want to talk to anyone, no matter what we say. Best to go knocking and see if they'll let us in."

"And if they blow you out of the sky?"

"Then they'll become targets for retaliation."

"We could send *him*." Haid jerked a thumb at Disisto.

"Would you trust him?"

"No," said Haid. "But it wouldn't bother me so much to see him blown away, either."

Roche glanced at Disisto. The security head's expression was blank, neither offended by nor laughing at what might have been a joke.

"Don't think it would bother me too much, either," she said. "Nevertheless, it still has to be me that goes down. Give me half an hour and I'll be suited up and ready for the drop."

Roche waited in the airlock as Haid completed the final checks and brought the courier into the optimum position. Her suit was sealed and ready to go: armored, powered, and equipped with enough thrust to repel the moon's low gravity for several hours in total. The courier would drop her high above and at some distance from the target crater. Using gravity and the thrusters when necessary, she would approach with all due caution under cover of the ion bridge.

She carried a number of weapons at the ready, plus several concealed in the thigh and underarm compartments of the suit. If she encountered trouble, she would be as prepared as she could be.

"Drop in two," said Haid. "No activity. Arc due any time now."

"When you're clear, assume a geosynch orbit and wait for instructions. I'll switch on my beacon once you're out of the area." During preparations for the jaunt, she'd reconsidered her decision to go in completely unannounced. Broadcasting a navigational pulse would let anyone in the area know she was coming without giving too much away. If the worst she was facing was a bunch of outriggers, the suit would be able to take care of her; if not, not even the courier would be much use. "Maintain radio silence once I'm off-ship."

"Understood. One minute to drop."

She inclined her head so Haid's view through the airlock camera's included her face. "And don't do anything rash while I'm away, okay?"

A slight laugh filled her helmet. "Trust me, Morgan," he said. Then: "The bridge is arcing now. Thirty seconds. Hold tight."

Roche braced herself against the frame of the airlock, more out of habit than necessity, since the chamber had already been evacuated. A chronometer inside the helmet of her suit counted down the seconds. When it hit five, a series of dull clunks traveled from the bulkhead, along the rigid structure of the suit, and to her ears, then died as she let go and allowed herself to drift.

The outer door slid aside as the chronometer hit zero, and she kicked the thrusters to life and shot out of the airlock. A minute later, she switched on her beacon.

Her attention was focused on eyes-up navigation displays in her visor and artificial sight as she accelerated away from the courier; she barely glimpsed the red-tinged, craggy surface of the small moon rolling beneath her. The courier's engines fired the instant she was at a safe distance, propelling it precipitously away from her. For a brief, disorienting moment, she had no idea where she was.

Then the moon swung into view, and she rolled herself about so that her legs were pointing in a rough approximation of "down." She let herself fall, following the navigation prompt rather than trusting her own instincts. Orbital mechanics was difficult enough to calculate without the view she was diving into acting as a distraction.

Mok . . . the ion-bridge flashing . . . Kukumat and Murukan looming impossibly large nearby . . . and no stars to be seen, apart from one hanging blood-red in the distance. . . .

For a second she felt very small and insignificant, and momentarily regretted her decision to investigate the signals alone. But the feeling was irrational. She knew outriggers would prove a vital source of information on what had happened in the system, before the arrival of Galine Four and after. She had to approach them on their own terms, not cozy and safe within the courier. In their shoes, she would put her faith in nothing less.

The surface of the moon approached, and she changed her heading until she was flying through near-vacuum above its mottled surface. The ambient temperature, at 125 degrees kelvin, was higher than expected. The forest of hook-trees, or whatever they were, marched without apparent pattern or function over the disconcertingly close horizon. She was tempted to drop lower and examine one at close quarters, but forced herself to concentrate on her mission. One puzzle at a time.

Five minutes into her flight, she changed course to avoid flying over another crater but didn't veer so far away that she couldn't see into its interior. It truly was a shaft, not a crater, about five meters across; radar pulses failed to return, so she had no way of telling how deep it was. The walls seemed smooth, as though machined, but there was nothing else to suggest that the hole served any purpose. There were no ramps or ladders, no elevator shafts or windows, no doors or platforms; it was just a hole, lipped slightly at the top, with nothing inside it. Nothing that she could see, anyway.

It took her fifteen minutes to reach the target crater—dubbed Shaft-1 on the map produced by the courier's sensors—which looked identical to the one she had flown by ten minutes earlier. After circumnavigating the edge of the hole and learning nothing new, and feeling slightly bored at her lack of progress, she decided a flare would be her best option. The next arc was due in twenty minutes; she didn't want to wait that long.

Backing away and arming the first of six flares her suit was equipped with, she primed it to ignite in a way that would offset the dull red light cast by Hintubet, then fired it from her suit.

Moments later, a sustained burst of light came from a point high above her and to her right.

Finally, some color. In the shaft she could make out gray-brown walls descending into the moon, polished smooth by some unknown process. Nothing stood out: no detail of any kind. Swinging the suit higher to get a better view, she eased herself closer to the edge of the shaft and used scanning algorithms to analyze the view in more detail. Almost immediately, she had a result.

A segment of the visor formed a separate screen and zoomed closer, revealing a glint of reflected light under the lip of the shaft opposite her. Too small and too far away for her to identify, she quickly tagged the location of the object so she wouldn't lose it when the flare faded.

She lifted herself higher still, in order to look into the shaft while she could. The walls seemed to narrow as they fell away into the depths of the moon, but she knew that to be an illusion. She was certain now that the shaft was artificial: nothing naturally formed could descend so perfectly straight. As far as the light reached into the shaft, she could make out no deviation, no variation at all. Only at the very edges of shadow, deep in the moon, did she suspect that something changed, but even then she couldn't tell if it was an end to the shaft, an opening off it, or just an optical illusion.

Then the flare flickered and faded, and all was red-tinged darkness again.

With the gain on the eyes-up display on high, she flew by instruments around the shaft to where she had noticed the glint of light. When her eyes had completely adjusted, she eased herself slowly over the lip of the shaft. Her suit lamps were no substitute for the flare, but the object was barely hidden at all, and she had no trouble catching a second reflection off it. It consisted of a silver device barely larger than her palm, attached to the rocky inside of the shaft.

Extending a slender probe, she touched it from two meters away, eliciting no response. Moving closer to touch it with her suit glove, she discovered that it was stuck to the wall by little more than a tacky gel, suggesting it wasn't a permanent fixture. A simple tug pulled it free, exposing instrumentation on the underside. Roche knew what it was immediately: a simple relay designed to confuse anyone listening in the area, and presumably planted there by the outriggers. Instead of being the source of the transmissions, Shaft-1 was just a decoy.

As such, it was something of an anticlimax. Nevertheless, it did provide tangible evidence that someone was in the area—someone who was transmitting to others and making at least some attempt to remain hidden.

"Morgan?"

Haid's voice over her suit-speakers startled her.

"Don't reply unless you have to, but I'm moving to encrypted channel thirty-one in two seconds."

The line went dead abruptly, and she shifted her communications channel to the one he had indicated, wondering as she did why he was calling.

"I know I'm supposed to keep quiet," he continued, his voice fuzzy from compression, "but I thought you should know that we're picking up a faint signal from deeper in-system. It's in that code Cane recognized—the Sol Wunderkind command language. I can't work out what it's saying, and Disisto says he can't either. But the weird thing is, it's being beamed right at us, from roughly where Galine Four was when we left it. I'd say someone's trying to communicate with someone else out here, and I'd hate to think what they might be saying . . ."

Haid's voice trailed off into silence as a chill swept over Roche.

Linegar Rufo was a specialist in antiquities. He knew about the Sol Apotheosis Movement. He knew a Sol Wunderkind was loose in the system. He had mentioned that transmissions had been received from near the jovian pair. He hadn't actually *said* the transmissions were from survivors of the Wunderkind's attack. If he had found some reference to the Wunderkind language in a forgotten archive, and if he suspected that the source of the transmissions would understand it . . .

Rufo was trying to talk to the Sol Wunderkind. Not only that, but he believed the Wunderkind was hiding somewhere near Mok.

Roche thrust herself up and out of the crater, alert for any sign of activity on the moon's surface. There was none, but that didn't reassure her. If Rufo was right, then she had more to worry about than just a motley bunch of outriggers.

She vacillated for a moment over whether to return to the courier or not. Haid would know she was still alive, so there was no need to reply to the signal. To return might just place him and the others at greater risk. And they were *all* at risk, just from being in the area. If the Wunderkind got his hands on another ship . . .

That brought her up cold. What would he do with the courier? He had already abandoned it once. Its slow-jump drive was slag, so he couldn't use it to escape the system. Likewise with the outrigger spines and Galine Four; no vessel in the system had a working slow-jump drive, except the *Ana Vereine*—and that, she vowed, would be kept well clear until she was absolutely certain it was safe.

Potentially, then, the Wunderkind wouldn't want to make himself vulnerable by exposing himself. That didn't make her feel much safer, though. An attack on a courier would undoubtedly be noticed; an attack on a single person, however, was something else entirely . . .

She decided that it would be best if Haid picked her up. That way they could explore the moon from orbit without risking anyone's life. And if she was right, if the Wunderkind wouldn't attack the courier itself, they would all be safe—at least until they actually found him.

She turned the suit around in a slow arc, angling upward. At the same time, she opened the encrypted communications channel.

"Ameidio, it's me. Work out a rendezvous. I'm—"

An ear-splitting squeal cut her short. The channel was swamped by noise, overriding her signal and any Haid might be trying to send. She hunted for a source of the interference, and after a moment realized it was the transmitter she had left behind in the crater.

Rather than fly back, she armed the suit's impulse weapon, targeted and fired. The relay was small and the distance increasing, but with the help of onboard systems, the projectile crossed the gap easily, impacting with a short-lived flash of light.

The interference didn't cease entirely, but it did ebb enough for her to hear Haid call:

"Behind you, Morgan! Behind you!"

As long as she lived, she knew she'd never forget her first sight of an outrigger all-suit.

It loomed over her like a biomechanical starfish with a ribbed halo surrounding it—almost thirty meters across, drooping slightly in the moon's low gravity, resembling the frills of an angry lizard. Toward the center were dozens of instrumentation spines and jointed waldoes, all directed at her. In the center was nothing but light: a powerful laser dazzling her despite her suit's protective visor. An ion beam lifted the all-suit above her, its spray of white fire disturbing the moon's surface in an angry manner.

She retreated, and it followed. Her sensors registered an incoming transmission, superimposed upon the jamming signal.

"Identify," was all it said, its tone coldly artificial.

She aimed numerous weapons on the laser source. Behind it, instruments made out the shape and location of the central thorax, a pressurized pod large enough to contain a single Human and the equipment it needed to survive for a lifetime in space.

"Identify *yourself,*" she replied.

Movement to one side caught her eye: another all-suit, its extensible antennae unfurling as it approached. It too fired a laser at her location, this one at a slightly different frequency to the other.

"Identify!"

Roche's suit issued a warning as a third laser hit her—this one from farther up. The three combined lasers were threatening the integrity of her faceplate; much more of this and she would have to opaque the helmet, or risk being burned and possibly even blinded.

"Identify!"

Roche sighed resignedly. Surrounded by three all-suits, she was hardly in a position to be defiant.

"Morgan Roche," she said, "ex-COE Intelligence and commanding officer of the independent vessel *Ana Vereine*."

"The Dato ship?" asked a voice that was hostile but at least Human.

"By design only. It no longer serves the Military Presidium."

"How do we know you're telling the truth?"

"You should've asked yourself that before you asked me anything at all."

"Indeed," chuckled a second voice, a female contralto. "So, why are you here?"

"I'm looking for survivors."

"Why?" The voice of the third outrigger was male and sharp with suspicion.

"We picked up a distress call."

"We didn't send one."

"Well, someone did." Roche suppressed an urge to snap. "Regardless, I need to know what happened in this system so we can stop it happening elsewhere. You can help me do that."

"How very commendable," said the first voice. "Your superiors must be proud of you."

"I told you: I'm independent. I don't have any superiors."

"You come looking for us in a COE Intelligence courier vessel, wearing a COE Intelligence suit, and you expect us to believe that you no longer work for them?"

"I don't care what you believe," said Roche. "And really, does it make any difference who I work for?"

The waldoes on the third all-suit shifted. "I think we should space her," said the accompanying voice.

"Private channel, you idiot," said the second outrigger, all humor gone.

For a moment the outriggers ignored her, only the slight motion of waldoes and antennae betraying the fact that some sort of interaction was taking place. Clearly the all-suits acted in much the same way as normal bodies for their inhabitants, with a peculiar form of body-language to match. Only the lasers didn't shift, aimed squarely at Roche through the helmet of her suit.

After a minute of silence, she opaqued her faceplate and had the suit display the view artificially. Haid was pinging her, sending her a repetitive signal through the interference to let her know he was watching and ready to act if needed. That was reassuring, but she wanted to keep him out of it if possible; she had to earn their trust on her own, without using force.

The outriggers shifted around her. She tensed, ready to defend herself if attacked. Instead, two of the lasers dimmed, then snapped off. After a few moments, the third did likewise.

"We're taking you to a quorum," said the second outrigger.

"I'm not going anywhere until you tell me who you are and kill the interference so I can talk to my crew."

"You're in no position to make any demands," said the third outrigger.

"For the last time, Yul," said the second, "shut up and let me do the talking. She's here to *help* us."

"I'd like to," Roche cut in. "Insofar as I can, at least; if you'll let me."

"Exactly. I'm Idil, and this is Yul and Eli."

Now the lasers were off, Roche could see the all-suits properly. Idil's was painted entirely in a color that might have been orange but looked pink in the light; Yul's had four silver bands around its midriff; Eli's was angular, almost rhombohedral in shape.

"We're from Long Span spine. Auditor Byrne says you can talk, but the ship you came here in is not to change its orbit. If it comes near the spines, we'll retaliate."

Roche grunted as the interference faded. She used the same encrypted channel Haid had requested earlier.

"Ameidio? You there?"

"Yeah," came Haid's voice. "You okay?"

"Fine. They're taking me somewhere to negotiate. I don't want you to do anything else but wait until I come back."

"How long?" he asked.

She relayed the question to the outriggers.

"A couple of hours," Idil said. "Or never. The quorum may decide it doesn't need your help. And if so, it might not let you return to your ship at all."

Roche privately doubted the outriggers' ability to damage her suit, but wasn't keen on testing her theory just yet. "Give them three hours, Ameidio, then use your judgment."

"Will do."

"And if you hear from the Box, tell it to stay away. We don't want the drive falling into the wrong hands."

"I understand," said Haid. "And should anyone make a move on me, I'll get the hell out of here, but I'll try contacting you first. Any idea where they're taking you?"

"To one of the spines, I guess. They haven't said."

"Well, I'll keep the channels open."

Roche turned her attention to the outriggers. All three suits were oriented toward her, their antennae spread wide like eyes watching her intently.

"Okay," she said, readying her suit to take her up into orbit, toward the spines. "Let's go."

But instead of up, they took her down.

She lost direct radio contact with Haid the moment she followed Idil into the shaft. She could still hear the regular *ping* broadcast by the courier, but only as a series of faint and highly peculiar echoes, as though the shaft was absorbing the signal, interfering with it, then broadcasting it back at her from a dozen locations at once. She didn't know what would happen if she tried to contact him. Maybe nothing out of the ordinary, or he wouldn't hear her at all.

It was too late to worry about that now.

She followed close behind Idil, watching as the antennae of the outrigger's suit were enfolded to prevent damage to fragile components. The other two, somewhere behind Roche, were no doubt doing the same. The shaft itself was lit by the searchlights of the three all-suits and her own suit, giving her an intriguing glimpse into the moon's interior. The shaft's smooth rockface faded after a hundred meters or so; beyond that it shared the color and albedo of bronze, although it could easily have been something else. At one hundred and fifty meters, the shaft doglegged, first upward with respect to Roche, then to her left, then down again, then twice to her right. The turns were always at right angles, but the distances between them were irregular. Navigation was tricky, using thrusters and the occasional limb—or waldo, in the outriggers' case—to correct miscalculations. After several more such turns, Roche started to feel disoriented, as though trapped in some bizarre cosmic plumbing.

They passed a tunnel opening to her left, unlit and with the same radius as the shaft they were traveling along. They passed two others before moving "upward" into a fourth. From the inside, it was the same as the one they had left. She could see no markings, no fixtures, no artifacts of any kind. Nothing but endless tunnels, crisscrossing through the heart of the moon.

Only then did she realize that she had literally lost all sense of up and down—and so had her suit. It was obtaining readings consistent with being in free-fall, regardless of which way they traveled. Something in the tunnel walls, or elsewhere, had dampened the low gravity of the moon to nothing. Why, or how, she couldn't imagine.

Ahead of Roche, Idil began to slow. The all-suit issued a burst of white noise, and a hole in the pipe-wall opened to one side. No, not opened, Roche corrected herself; it had always been there. The holographic generator concealing it had simply been switched off.

Idil led the way through the hole, into a spherical chamber one hundred meters across, from which many other such openings led. Otherwise, the walls were smooth, ranging in color from the bronze of the tunnels to a deep cherry-red at the points farthest from the holes. The walls radiated light of a frequency not dissimilar to that of Hintubet.

The space within the chamber contained a thin atmosphere, held in place by some sort of boundary-field across each hole, and a further seven outriggers drifting in free-fall. Each was slightly different from the others. With instruments retracted, they looked like escape capsules, capsules made by ten different companies for ten different Castes; when instruments did appear, they did so in unique configurations and combinations. There were no portholes, no indications as to the appearances of their occupants at all, but it was easy to tell them apart.

Idil, Yul, and Eli dispersed once they were in the room, and the seven others seemed to rearrange themselves slightly to accommodate the newcomers. Within moments Roche was the only thing moving in the center of the chamber; the outriggers had, perhaps by instinct, arranged themselves in a way that maximized the space between them.

"We want to know why you came here, Morgan Roche." The signal came from an outrigger whose all-suit was shaped like a teardrop, tapering at its aft end to a menacing point. Even this close and in an atmosphere, the outriggers still communicated by radio.

"I came here to find you," she answered. "Survivors, anyway. We were picking up signals from this region."

"Not from us, you weren't."

"No. I know that now." She paused for a second, then asked: "Why are you hiding down here?"

"Because we don't want to die, like the others," said one, his suit marked with concentric green triangles.

"You saw what happened?"

"Wide Berth spine lost almost a full complement over the spaceport on Aro. All hands of Long Span remained at a distance, and so we survived." This voice, thickly accented, came from an all-suit striped diagonally in black. The effect it had upon Roche as it slowly rotated was dizzying. "We came down here when the Galine station arrived because we suspected we would not be safe near it."

"We will never be safe in this system," said the green triangle outrigger in sharp disagreement. "We've already lost seventeen since we've been here."

"The short term is all that matters—"

"The short term is all you ever think about, Lud. When the one who killed the clan on Wide Berth comes looking for us, he will find you sitting here still, the easiest target in the galaxy."

A babble of argument broke out. Clearly the quorum was divided on what to do about the Sol clone warrior, just as Idil, Yul, and Eli had been about Roche.

She smiled to herself. This was everything she'd hoped for. If she could only keep them talking . . .

She caught a flash that might have been leakage from a private laser communication, then the teardrop all-suit spoke:

"We shouldn't squabble within the clan," she said. Her voice was firm, and resembled Idil's in inflection if not pitch. "We came here, Morgan Roche, to escape Wide Berth's fate. We have watched events in the system carefully since then, awaiting any sign that the one behind the attack on Wide Berth was coming here. So far, there has been no such sign. Your arrival caused a moment of concern, but it's clear that you are not the one. Your approach was too open, too blatant. I fear that the one we anticipate will be upon us before we even suspect."

"The data you collected—" Roche broke in. "May I—?"

"Access it? Certainly."

So easy? Roche couldn't help but be suspicious.

"Why?" she asked. "I thought *you* wanted to interrogate *me*?"

"We do. But the clan teaches that all answers lie in the questioner's own heart. If we exchange information, perhaps you will see for us what we do not."

Roche nodded. "Perhaps," she said.

"What do we have to lose?" The teardrop's blunt end unfolded like a flower, peeling back shielding to expose delicate machinery within. "You are not the one we feared. I therefore put my trust in you, Morgan Roche. I have faith you will not abuse it."

Roche was slightly taken back. "Just who are you, anyway?" she asked.

"My name is Byrne, auditor of Long Span spine. In situations such as these, when time is of the essence, I am the one that makes decisions."

"So their lives are basically in your hands?" said Roche.

"As mine is in theirs," she replied. "We are one, even when we disagree."

"You are their voice," said Roche.

The blunt end of the all-suit began to close. "I am also the one that asks the questions, and right now I would ask again: Why are you here, Morgan Roche?"

Roche was still a little stunned by the odd turn of events, but she knew that if she was going to get anywhere with the outriggers, then she was going to have to talk to Byrne, and that meant answering anything asked of her. So she outlined her reasons for coming to the system and what had happened to her since arriving. No point was covered twice, until the end, when Roche was asked to recapitulate her relationship with Adoni Cane. Many of the outriggers assembled for the quorum were hesitant to trust someone who had links with another Sol Wunderkind—albeit one who seemed less destructive than the one who had destroyed Palasian System. Roche could understand that.

"The other spine, Wide Berth," she said, fishing for information of her own. "What exactly happened to them over Aro?"

"We received distress signals," said Byrne. "A number of small pods, possibly escape capsules. Wide Berth decided to attempt a rescue. We advised against it, and suspected that the one behind the attack on the domed city—the Sol clone warrior, as you call him—was still in the area. Whether he was or not, we never did find out, but the pods were a trap. An orbital whip decimated the main body of those who went to investigate, while gas-guns picked off the survivors."

"We were unable to assist them in time," Lud's bitter voice broke in. "And those observing from the Galine station did not intervene."

"You saw the observers?"

"Yes."

"But you've had no contact at all with Galine Four?" said Roche.

"We hailed them when it arrived, but they ignored us," said Byrne. "This is not uncommon, of course, as outriggers are often overlooked. But when they also ignored the plight of Wide Berth, we knew its disinterest was more malevolent than usual."

Roche absorbed this. The ferocity of the attack on the Wide Berth outriggers didn't necessarily mean that the Sol clone warrior was personally directing it; automatic systems could have done as well. But Aro was the last location he'd been known to be; the chance of an eyewitness report was worth following up.

"No one survived the attack?"

"One," said Byrne. "The youngest of the clan, a boy named Yarrow. His role in the spine was observer, so he was removed from the focus of attack. We found his all-suit breached and drifting a day later. His emergency systems lasted barely long enough to return him to Long Span, where his all-suit was repaired."

"Could I talk to him?"

"That is impossible," said Byrne.

"He might have information—"

"He can tell you nothing," said Lud firmly.

"I'd still like to ask."

"His peace is more important than your wishes!" spat Lud.

The softer voice of Auditor Byrne filled the quiet following Lud's anger: "Yarrow has not spoken since the attack on his clan. You are welcome to try, but I don't like your chances."

"You're sure it *is* him?"

"Of course," said Byrne. "I oversaw his healing myself."

Roche wondered whether Byrne had actually seen the boy in the flesh or operated through his all-suit. She also wondered how Byrne could be so sure he was who he said he was since he'd come from another spine. It would be all too easy to hide in an all-suit and pretend to be someone who was actually dead.

But she decided not to push the issue any further, for now. Byrne seemed convinced of the boy's identity. Instead Roche promised herself she would try to talk to the boy herself, later.

"Is there nothing new you can tell me about the Sol clone warrior's activities?" she said.

The spinning of Lud's striped all-suit slowed. "No."

"He speaks the truth." Byrne's voice was regretful. "By the time we knew something was wrong, the clone warrior had gone into hiding; and before we could escape, the system was enclosed. We are trapped here as surely as he is."

"Perhaps not any more," said Lud.

"True." Byrne's tone was thoughtful. "Morgan Roche, although I have said that I trust you, that does not mean that we will help you freely, or at all. The clan as a whole needs to consider everything you've told us. Your actions and those of Linegar Rufo could be interpreted many ways, and I must consult with my people before making any decisions."

"How long will that take?" Roche asked.

"Several hours. The debate will be thorough, with as many attending the Plenary as possible. You may attend the summation, if you wish."

"Thank you. I'd like that." Roche was curious to see how the outriggers would attain consensus on such a complex issue in so short a time, and was naturally concerned that its outcome would be in her favor. "But first I'm going to have to contact my ship from the surface. I told my crew that I would report in."

"Idil and Yul will escort you."

"I have no intention of escaping."

"I believe you, Morgan Roche," said Byrne. "They will act more as your guides than your guards."

Nothing was said, but Byrne's words still carried an implicit warning. Mok's labyrinth was extensive and difficult to navigate, and should Roche choose to attempt to elude her guides, she knew she would quickly become lost. If that happened, it was possible they would not be able to find her again. If they even tried.

To Roche's nominated guides, Auditor Byrne added: "Perhaps you could show her the central chamber on your return." Roche neither saw nor heard any kind of acknowledgment from either Idil or Yul, yet something seemed to be conveyed to the auditor. A second later she said: "Excellent, then you can join us from there."

With that, the outriggers led Roche out of the chamber, while the quorum assumed its former configuration, only with Auditor Byrne at the center and the remaining seven around her.

Roche's guides took her along the corridor outside at a more sedate pace than before. Roche couldn't tell if they were retracing their steps. The many turns and lack of reference points had her thoroughly confused, substantiating Byrne's unspoken warning.

"How do you know where you're going?" Roche asked.

Yul's gruff voice answered: "Breeding."

"Our internal guidance systems are highly specialized," Idil chipped in. "Much more sophisticated than yours. You could sever us from all our senses and take us anywhere across the system. Set us adrift, and we could find our way to within a kilometer of where we started."

"What's that got to do with breeding?" Roche asked.

"Some of us are third- or fourth-generation clan members," said Idil. "We gestated within and were raised as part of our suits; its systems are ours, although naturally the interface is not perfect. With every generation, however, we improve."

Roche was reminded of Uri Kajic. This wasn't so different. The ancient Dato Ataman, for whom the Marauder was named, might've saved herself a lot of trouble if only she'd talked to outriggers before launching the Andermahr Experiment.

But traditionally no one talked to outriggers. Did business with them, yes, but did not converse as equals. They were regarded with the same sort of suspicion and contempt as nomads were on some backward worlds. That they were capable of great technical skill didn't especially surprise Roche, but their sense of honor and integrity did. Auditor Byrne and Idil had both demonstrated clearheadedness and willingness to trust under difficult circumstances—something Roche's former colleagues in COE Intelligence were not renowned for.

"How many of you come from outside the clan?" she asked.

"About half," Idil replied. "We see a lot of disaffected types as we travel. Jaded combat soldiers; criminals looking for somewhere to hide; sociophobes. Most we reject out of hand. The ones we keep are those who demonstrate an ability to maintain group integrity over vast distances. It's a difficult thing to manage; some never do come to terms with the isolation. But once accepted, the lifestyle does have its rewards."

"Do you give preference to those who come from the same place as others within the clan? Or to groups of applicants? I notice that you and the auditor have a similar accent."

"We do, but our relationship is not what you might think. I joined Long Span as a teenager when it passed through the fringes of Gwydyon seventy-eight subjective years ago—one hundred and twenty of yours. My all-suit used to belong to the woman whose clan name I took after my tenth year as a member. She died of old age six months before I joined. In my twentieth year I elected to have a child, conceived parthenogenetically from my own tissue. I gave her the name of my mother, back on Gwydyon, and designed her all-suit myself. Auditor Byrne is my daughter."

Roche pondered this as Idil and Yul led her toward the surface of the strange, alien moon.

"I'm sure it's okay, Ameidio."

"Damn it, Morgan!" The annoyance was obvious in Haid's voice. "You're taking an awful risk."

"Only because I need to. You know that. I'll be away a few hours longer, and the suit will need a top-up. If I had a choice, I'd let you come down, but I don't trust Myer and Disisto alone in the ship. So you'll have to send Disisto with everything I need."

"Why don't you just come up here? You can be here and back within an hour."

"Because it's not just about supplies. I might need someone else down here if the decision doesn't go our way. They've said we can trust them, but I'm not willing to believe everything they say just yet."

Haid was silent for a second. "Besides which, you want to have a look around, right?"

Roche smiled to herself. "You got it."

"I guess I can't blame you, Morgan. From what the suit recorded, I can't say I've seen anywhere like it before."

"Disisto will be interested in it too, given his association with Rufo's work. Another reason to send him down. And maybe I can work on him a little, get him to change his mind."

"Okay, okay," Haid said with a mix of resignation and levity. "Besides, it's getting a little crowded up here. Mavalhin's awake, and if I hear one more complaint out of him, I swear I'm going to put him in the airlock."

"Any particular issue?"

"He wants to talk to you."

"Naturally. But if it's not important, he can wait."

"That's what I keep telling him. Unfortunately, I've run out of reasons to keep him under sedation, and he gripes about being tied up."

Roche chuckled to herself. She could sympathize, but there was little else she could do. "Any other news?"

"A tightbeam from the Box arrived not long ago, bounced off a drone near Herensung. We have an ETA with the *Ana Vereine* in five days. The Box says we'll be able to contact it safely in twenty-four hours. It'll send us coordinates before then."

"That's progress, I guess." Since their last exchange of messages to arrange the rendezvous point, they had maintained strict radio silence. "Good to know the ship evaded capture."

"The Box never seemed to have any worries."

"It wouldn't." Roche scanned the sky for any sign of *Daybreak,* but it wasn't visible. "Myself or one of the outriggers"—she forwarded him the unique frequencies Idil had given her—"will stay on the surface to wait for Disisto. The sooner he leaves, the better. Call me if there are any problems."

Haid signed off and Roche returned her attention to the world around her. She was resting in the very low local gravity near one of the hairlike spikes protruding from the surface of the moon. The soil below her seemed to glitter faintly—an effect magnified by the crackling of the ion bridge high above her. When she bent to touch it, she learned that it was only a centimeter or two deep; below that was black rock, inert to all the suit's sensors.

"You'll find it difficult to chip," said Idil, balancing on her main thruster not far away. "Some of us tried to analyze it when we arrived, but didn't have much luck. It might be some sort of artificial material we haven't come across before. Designed from the molecules up."

"Any idea who made it?"

"That's hard to say. There are living quarters off one of the central chambers. We can't get into them ourselves, but we managed to get some of our remote probes in."

"Did you find anything? Any reason why the builders left? Any bodies that might help identify the Caste?"

"Nothing. In fact, the quarters were never inhabited. They were possibly intended as a shrine, or a museum perhaps."

Roche considered this. An ancient, unknown Caste, close enough to Transcendence to no longer need its hereditary form but not so removed to have lost all affection for it, might have modified or built the small moon for purposes that had become meaningless over time. Mok might have drifted far from its origins before being captured by the double-jovian, or—and this was an area Roche hardly dared venture into—the entire arrangement could have been artificial. The two gas giants, the ion bridge, and the single moon were an unlikely combination to have formed naturally. Although the possibility was daunting, the universe had a capacity for surprise far exceeding Roche's own imagination and she knew better than to base any opinions on what she considered normal.

The aspirations and achievements, and even the whereabouts, of the Caste responsible for the artifacts were as impenetrable as the artifacts themselves. And that only made her more curious. Assuming the outriggers joined her cause, she would have days before the Box arrived. Which would be plenty long enough to have a decent look around.

Disisto complied readily with her instructions, and was suited and able to go within the hour. Half an hour after that, he had joined Roche on the surface with a utility containing the requisitions her suit needed to remain operating for an extended period. While it looked after itself, she introduced him to the two outriggers.

Idil's voice was frosty. "You're from the Galine station?"

"I run dock security."

"How much say do you have regarding policy?"

"None, really. That's all handled by the chief."

"Linegar Rufo?"

"Yes."

If Idil was appeased by that, Yul was not. "Your people stood by while a clan was murdered."

"That's simply not true—" Disisto began.

"You deny that you had observers in the area of Aro when the spine was attacked?"

"No, but—"

"They did *nothing*."

"What *could* they have done? They were only a handful. If your people couldn't do anything, how could mine?"

"At least you could've talked to us afterwards," said Idil. "Traded information."

"To have broadcast like that would have given away our location!"

"You're lying," said Yul. "You broadcast regularly on the old channels."

"Through relays."

"Exactly. That must be safe enough. Whoever it is you're talking to can't be any less dangerous than us."

Roche noted the comment. It seemed the outriggers also suspected Rufo of trying to contact the Sol warrior.

"This is all irrelevant," she interrupted. "Disisto is here because he's interested in the ruins you've found. He's not here as my ally, or yours. Far from it. If you object to his presence, I'll happily send him back."

Yul grunted, the waldoes on his all-suit twitching uncertainly.

"We will suffer his presence," Idil decided. "But if he gets into trouble, don't expect us to help."

"At least we know where we stand." Disisto's voice was stiff and formal.

Roche didn't trust herself to comment. "Shall we get on with it?" she suggested.

They descended into the moon, this time via another shaft. Roche had no way to tell this one from the rest, apart from its map coordinates. Again she had to rely on the outriggers to navigate for her and Disisto as they zigzagged through the tunnels.

"There are four thousand two hundred seventeen entrances on the surface of Mok," Idil said as they traveled. "The tunnels themselves extend for many thousands of kilometers within the moon. We haven't even come close to mapping them all. Some go nowhere or loop back on themselves; others end in chambers like the one you saw earlier; still others lead to museums, or what might be machines of some kind. It's hard to tell. But I get the feeling that we haven't touched upon the stuff that actually matters. It's hidden in some recesses of this moon we haven't discovered yet."

"You think this is just a smoke screen?" Disisto asked.

"It's a possibility. A labyrinth designed to make it difficult for intruders to get in."

"Or out," Roche added quietly to herself.

"They could've built a door out of the crust material and kept just about everything out," said Yul.

"Perhaps that wasn't enough," Idil ventured. "Depends how fearful their enemies were, I guess."

"It seems like you picked a good place to hide, then," said Roche. "Too good, almost."

"When the clan of Wide Berth died," said Yul, "it was an obvious place to seek shelter: distant, relatively secure, and belonging to no one else. We were hoping we'd go undetected." The outrigger's all-suit rotated slightly on its axis. A shrug, Roche intuited. "We have ruins similar to these recorded in the spine's archives. Other clans have found them and passed on the knowledge. This one was unrecorded because we are the first outriggers to come here. Until DAOC announced that they were seeding the inner belts with prowling mines, the system was never considered worth looking at. It wasn't until Thin Trunk spine passed on the word that there was a vacant turf large enough for two spines, and Wide Berth was free at the same time as us, that we decided to come. . . ."

Yul talked on, but Roche let her mind wander. She was less interested in why the outriggers had come here than how they could help her. No one had mentioned it yet, but she was probably their only hope of leaving the system. If the Kesh destroyer that delivered Galine Four didn't stop to pick them up—which was unlikely—they would be destroyed along with the ruins they inhabited. And while Roche wasn't keen to use blackmail to get the help she needed, she would do so if it was the only option left to her.

It wasn't just the matter of information on the Sol warrior she wanted. If the outriggers were working with her, the chances of rescuing Maii and Cane improved. The only question was, still, *how*?

When Yul had finished, Roche broke in with: "How heavily armed are you?"

"That depends," Idil responded.

"On?"

"If you want to know what weapons we have, the answer is *none*. But we do have cutting lasers, ion drilling cannons, spectrometry bombs, nano seeders, seetee crust-rippers—"

"Ah." Disisto suppressed a chuckle. "The smuggler's toolkit: weapons that never show up on customs declarations, but always appear when you try to haul them in."

"These are not weapons," Idil said coolly. "We would only use them as such if we are attacked."

"Why didn't Wide Berth spine do that on Aro?"

"They did, but . . ." Idil hesitated. "They didn't know *how* to retaliate. We are not trained at war."

"What about the stories I've heard about dust-shoals and booby-trapped asteroids?" said Disisto.

"All retaliatory," Idil insisted. "If one of our kind makes the mistake of broadcasting the discovery of a rich deposit, it is not uncommon for that deposit to be taken away from us. We can't prevent a system's owners from moving us on; even if we have a legal licensing agreement for the territory, the fact that they technically own it works against us. We are regarded as scavengers, or worse, by most people. Most of the time, we lose everything we have worked for, and that is all. But if we are expelled by force, we feel it to be our right to retaliate. So we leave reminders that we have been there, and that we are angry at being robbed."

"It's ironic," said Disisto. "The Sol clone warrior used some of your own tactics against you, over Aro."

"But his motives are decidedly more malicious than ours," said Yul. "Or yours."

"True," said Roche. She wanted to move the subject on, but before she could, her suit signaled that she was receiving a tightbeam from a source nearby.

"Disisto? Is that you?"

"Yes. Haid gave me this frequency if I needed to talk to you in private."

"Good thinking." She glanced at her instruments; none of the outriggers seemed to have noticed the private conversation. "What do you want?"

"To explain what happened back on Aro. You seem to agree with the outriggers that the chief is at fault."

Roche sighed. "You want to defend Rufo?"

"There really was nothing those observers could have done to save anyone."

"You don't know that. And *they* certainly didn't know that at the time."

"They were only there to observe—"

"What if they'd *observed* survivors on the ground?"

"They didn't, did they? Listen, Roche: if one of our observers had been captured, the location of Galine Four could've been traced. That would've placed all our lives in danger."

"I thought you said the clone warrior had left the system."

"That's what *I* believe, not the chief. And it pays to be safe rather than sorry."

"What *pays* isn't the issue here. I'm talking about basic Humanity: helping people in trouble."

"I'm sure Rufo would have allowed the observers to intervene," Disisto said, "but the fact is hours would've passed before signals from the observers reached the station and our replies went back. By then, the attack would've been over. There was nothing those observers could do—except watch."

Roche didn't respond immediately. Disisto's last point was probably true, but it didn't allay her doubts. And there was something else, something he wasn't telling her. . . .

"You can ask Mavalhin if you don't believe me," he said into her reflective silence. "He was one of the senior observers of the Aro attack."

"Well, that explains why they didn't use their initiative," said Roche. "Or follow their conscience."

He was quick to reply: "Exactly."

The sharpness of his voice startled her, but she had no time to ask him what he meant. The outriggers were slowing again, and—now that she was paying attention to her environment—she became aware that she was feeling gravity. Gently at first, but becoming stronger, her sense of up and down was returning.

The only problem was, it was coming at right angles to where it should have been. She let the suit orient itself properly against the field and scanned ahead to see where they were headed.

Not an exit, as she first guessed. The tunnel around them ballooned outward until it reached almost ten meters across, then joined another to form the stem of a Y. Two more joined, one after the other, and Roche began to feel as though she were swimming through the veins of an enormous beast.

"We're approaching the heart of the maze," said Idil. "Be careful. Gravity does odd things ahead."

Roche was grateful for the warning as, moments later, *up* suddenly became *down,* then began to corkscrew rapidly around her. Her inner ears complained at the disorientation, and for one horrible second her gorge rose in a manner she hadn't experienced since her early days of training. Only when the sensation subsided did she become aware of Disisto's chuckling.

"Neat trick," he said.

"What's that?" asked Yul, his voice as surprised as Roche felt.

"The only safe way past that point is to fly past," Disisto explained. "It'd be impossible to walk without bouncing off the walls."

Roche cast an eye behind her, studying the width of the tunnel. "Another defense?"

"That's the only thing we can think of," said Idil.

"What were they hiding?" asked Roche.

"I don't know," said Disisto. "But can you imagine the technology required to construct all of this?"

"Opaque your visors as we go through this next bit," Idil interrupted, a mandible waving toward the end of the tunnel. Ahead of them a cerulean membrane seemed to ripple as they approached. "Don't worry. It's quite safe. Just better to see it cold the first time."

Roche's stomach felt full of water as she took the outrigger's advice and let the instruments in her left eye guide her through the membrane.

There, rotating oddly in the center of a spherical chamber easily a kilometer across, was a pinch of space that defied Roche's best efforts to describe. It was hard to see directly, appearing almost as a shimmer in her view of the walls behind it. But it was more than a mirage. Much more. It had its own structure, its own definition—yet it wasn't anything at all. In a strange way, it reminded her of the anomaly they had passed through in order to enter Palasian System.

"Is that what I think it is?"

"It might be," said Idil. "It's hard to tell from within the Gauntlet, but we've found no reason to doubt it."

"An anchor point—*inside* the moon?"

"Why not? There's no particular law that says they have to be in open space. The vacuum's as perfect as it can be in here. Even the atoms and particles spilling off us somehow disappear into the background flux. As long as it doesn't bump into the walls, or anything else, it's quite safe."

"But an anchor point is fixed to the space-time grid, not the things around it," said Roche. "The ones near systems have to be taken apart and rebuilt regularly or else they drift. To try to fix one in place while the moon orbits Kukumat and Murukan *and* Hintubet would be impossible, surely."

"And yet there you have it," said Idil. A waldo waved at the odd patch of space before her. "It doesn't work, of course."

"Because the whole system is in hyperspace," Roche said. "The only way out is through the external boundary, and even then only by slow-jump."

"It cost us lives in Free-For-All figuring that one out," said Yul.

"But an anchor point is a weakness in space-time," said Disisto. "What's *this* a weakness in?"

"Good question," said Idil. "If you find the answer, let us know."

A thought struck Roche: that if the anchor point was fixed, and the system revolved around it, then that would explain why it could be contained in such a way. But that didn't make sense either. Her mind hurt just thinking about it.

"Why did you bring us here?" she said after a moment.

Neither Idil nor Yul replied immediately. She looked around at the outriggers. They were floating motionless in the vacuum. She repeated the question.

"Sorry," said Idil. "The Plenary has begun. We would all like to attend, so we've brought you here to keep you occupied. There's a lot to look at without leaving this chamber. Down the far end are some structures that will interest you."

"You're leaving us here?" asked Disisto, glancing at Roche.

"No. The Plenary doesn't require our actual presence. We'll simply interface with the others from here. It's just that we'll be preoccupied if you try to talk to us, that's all."

Roche tried unsuccessfully to read Disisto's expression through his transparent helmet.

"That sounds fine to me," she said. "We won't be going anywhere."

The all-suits floated motionless in the zero gravity without response.

"Shall we take a look?" Disisto said, indicating the far end of the chamber.

The anchor half hid a structure of some kind. Roche couldn't make it out. "After you."

Disisto used his thrusters to head off across the space, cutting a chord deeper into the chamber rather than hugging the outside. Roche did likewise, keeping an eye on her instruments.

"Don't go too close," she said as they neared the anchor point. Although it seemed, perversely, to shrink in size, she was wary of it all the same. In the highly unorthodox domain of the Gauntlet, anything was possible.

"So they've convened a Plenary," he said, ignoring her instruction. "To talk about what?"

"Us. Whether or not to help me."

"I see."

His gaze was fixed forward. He began to fire his thrusters, nudging his way around the anchor. This close it looked like smoked glass spun into a tangled web and seen through a foggy lens. It still looked as though it was moving, although in which direction was hard to determine.

"Do you expect me to help you when it comes time to rescue your friends?"

"You've told me you won't betray Rufo."

"That's right. I have."

"You won't change your mind?"

"No."

"It would be easier if you did," she said. Then, watching his movements around the anchor point: "I can take over your suit at any time, you know, in case you were thinking of throwing yourself into that thing."

His laugh was loud but forced. "Don't flatter yourself, Roche. The idea hadn't even occurred to me," he said. "Tell me, though, what you would do to ensure my cooperation. Torture me?"

"Anything's possible," she said. "I'm determined to rescue Maii."

"And Cane?"

She hesitated before answering. "Yes, Cane as well."

Disisto grunted as they swooped past the anchor point. "You know what I think this is?" he said, gesturing around him. He didn't wait for her reply: "Some sort of covert transportation system. The anchor point obviously led somewhere, once, and the shell of moon around it would've absorbed any emissions when it was used. The labyrinth and the gravity trap would have stopped anyone just wandering in. There could be hundreds of these things scattered across the galaxy and no one would ever know about them."

"But the outriggers got through the traps easily enough. It's not really that secure. Especially given its location."

"Maybe the builders just wanted a little privacy."

"Maybe," she muttered, turning her attention to the structure they were approaching. It looked like a cannon of some kind, or an elongated funnel, directed at the anchor point. Instead of a barrel, though, it contained a cuplike hollow thirty-five meters in diameter. Despite her instruments saying it was inactive, Roche still regarded the structure warily. There was undoubtedly a connection between it and the anchor point, and until she knew exactly what that connection was, she had no desire to be anywhere between them.

They split up when they reached it. Roche circled its lip while Disisto traveled along its underside. It seemed to be made of the same material as the crust, but whorled and knotted as though eroded by centuries of running water.

The channel between them was thick with their silence. Neither was talking for fear of provoking the other.

"Any theories?" she asked. Anything was better than that silence.

"I've never come across anything like this before," he said. "And I've been on plenty of excavations."

"What about Rufo? Think there'd be anything in his files?"

"He's covered more of the galaxy than most people," Disisto said thoughtfully. "His records contain thousands of examples of Caste-types and divergent engineering and exotic materials and bizarre technologies, but . . ." He stopped. "If I didn't know better, I'd say this wasn't even Human."

"There's no chance of that, I suppose?"

He snorted. "None. Believe me, if there was any sign of alien life in the galaxy, past or present, Linegar Rufo would know about it."

"He seems the secretive type to me," she said, to see if she would get a reaction.

She did: he laughed. "Listen, Roche. Don't play me for the fool. Making me doubt my boss isn't going to make me automatically want to help you get your friends back." She watched as he jetted up to where she floated near the mouth of the giant trumpet. Through his faceplate she could see him smiling humorlessly. "But I may be useful to you in other ways."

"Such as?"

"I've been thinking. Even if I won't help you fight Linegar, I *can* tell you some things you probably should know."

She cleared her faceplate and met his eye. She sensed an internal struggle raging within him. He wasn't going to betray his boss, but he didn't want to see her fail, either. How he could possibly hope to succeed at both—and why—she didn't know, but she was keen to see him try.

"Go on," she said.

"It's about Cane," he said. "And the other one we're chasing. The Kesh believe they're something to do with the Sol Apotheosis Movement, but Rufo doesn't. He's letting them believe it because it gives him an edge. But he suspects it's all a smoke screen."

Roche shook her head. "A *smoke screen*? What do you mean?"

"Exactly what I say. There might be no connection between the two. And if so, you could be basing assumptions on imperfect data."

"But we've got *proof* that Cane is a Sol Wunderkind: his genetic design, the control language you've been broadcasting—"

"I'm not a biogeneticist, so I can't argue about his makeup. But I do know the control language didn't come from any of the historical archives. You must have looked before you came here. Did *you* find the codes?"

"No. I assumed Rufo had access to other records—"

"The language *wasn't* in the records," he cut in. "None that any of us can access, anyway. I don't know where the codes came from or what they mean, and I doubt the chief knows either, but I know he was *given* those codes. He's deliberately keeping Shak'ni out of the full picture—and he's letting you believe what you want to believe, too."

"Why?"

"I don't know." Disisto seemed frustrated. "But I think it's dangerous. We should be sharing information. Otherwise we could all be killed by this thing. Or even Cane, for that matter—whatever the hell he is."

"No, you're wrong," said Roche. "Uri found a correlation in the *Ana Vereine*'s database. Cane's face matched that of the man who wiped out the Sol Apotheosis Movement. How can you ignore that kind of connection?"

"Because *we* have no records of any 'Adoni Cane' at all—in the Sol files or elsewhere."

"What?"

"I can't explain it, Roche. All I know is that while you were in the meeting with Linegar, he ordered a confirmatory search, and nothing was found."

"This is insane." She groped for an explanation that made sense. Either Rufo had corrupted his own files in order to keep the information a secret, or the *Ana Vereine*'s records were wrong—along with those of COE Intelligence HQ, which had confirmed the match. For the first time, she wished the Box was around to help her work out what was going on.

The Box . . . It had a habit of manipulating records to suit its own agenda. But why would it encourage her to believe, mistakenly, that Cane's origins lay with the Sol Apotheosis Movement? What could it possibly gain from that? And where had Rufo's information come from? The Kesh didn't know, so that ruled them out, and the Box had been with her for weeks. It just didn't fit together.

"You disapprove of what Rufo is doing," she said, trying to clarify Disisto's feelings on the matter of Cane. "But I suppose you don't disapprove enough to help me rectify the problem, either."

Disisto drifted until one hand rested on the alien surface. "Look, I'd rather we were taking an active role here in the system. The Kesh might go along with it, although I don't really know what they're after. Rufo's attempts to contact the warrior give me the creeps, to be honest. Whoever gave him the information he needed to do that, whoever knew enough about the warrior to identify his type even though we can't—whoever that *is,* I think they know a lot more than they're saying. And I think Rufo is being used. This 'whoever' was too afraid to come here themselves, so we were dispatched. We're all expendable."

Roche suddenly felt cold and vulnerable. The Box had something to do with the High Human called the Crescend. High Humans had access to all sorts of information mundanes never even suspected existed. It might have given the control language to Rufo in exchange for firsthand information. And where *was* the Box now? Jetting around the system in her one and only escape route, while she played xenoarchaeologist with a genocidal clone warrior possibly nearby. . . .

She cursed under her breath and tried to shake the paranoid thoughts. Such a line of thinking was neither helpful nor healthy. Nevertheless, one thing she *had* learned in recent weeks was that being merely paranoid wasn't paranoid enough. And she certainly *was* expendable. . . .

No. She couldn't let Disisto confuse her. She had no reason to believe that the Sol Apotheosis Movement was a smoke screen. Linegar Rufo could be wrong for a change, or Disisto could be lying. Better the latter than the tangled skein of deceit he was proposing in its place.

Disisto seemed unaware of the uncertainty he had provoked in her. That only made it worse. If he had done it deliberately, then he was a better liar than she believed him to be.

"Anyway," he said, "I thought you ought to know about my dilemma. If you can help *me* out of it, then—"

"That's not my problem," she said, pushing herself impatiently away from the alien trumpet. "And there's too much going on for us to just float around sightseeing. The more I can sort out before the Box gets here, the better." She switched to a more general frequency. "Byrne? Idil? Can anyone hear me?"

"Is something wrong?" said Idil after a few moments.

"I want to attend the Plenary. I want to hear what you're saying about me."

"You don't have the interfaces required to do that."

"Byrne said I could sit in on the summary. How much different could it be?"

"Fundamentally."

Out of the corner of her eye, Roche saw Disisto moving away from her. She froze his suit with a simple command. "Regardless, I want to know what's going on. Maybe I can contribute." *Or make sure you come to the right decision,* she thought.

"I'm sorry, but it just isn't possible—"

The auditor's voice cut into the conversation. "Let her," she said. "It will do us no harm."

"Very well, Roche. Surrender your suit's input channels," said Idil. "Do you have direct inputs?"

"My left eye and ear."

"Okay. I'll see what I can do to make it easier."

Roche hesitated before handing over control, wondering what she had let herself in for.

She gave Idil the access codes required to patch into her implants. The outriggers would be able to draw upon her suit's full communication capacity; she could pull out any time she wanted, she assumed.

"Five seconds," Idil said. "Prepare yourself."

For what? she wanted to ask.

Then she recalled that Auditor Byrne hadn't said "harmless" to everyone. Byrne had said that it wouldn't harm *them.*

With a click and a flash deep in the underside of her brain, the Plenary of Long Span spine exploded through her.

6

Mok Interior
'955.01.21 EN
1990

The voice seemed to speak directly into the fissures of Roche's brain:

> Commander Roche
> has come to us for help
> and to offer us help.
> We have numerous options.
> Which do we choose?

With the words came a blinding light. It felt as though the outriggers were overloading the tolerances of her auditory and optic nerves. But her implants had buffers that should prevent that sort of surge. Somehow the outriggers must have infiltrated the hardwiring of her implants.

The voice repeated its spiel. This time Roche sensed a hidden complexity, a second, more subtle strand underlying the first, somehow mixed up with vivid pulses of light accompanying the sound.

> Commander Roche
> ↑how do we know she is who she says she is?↓
> has come to us for help
> ↑or to spy↓
> and to offer us help.
> ↑how?↓
> We have numerous options.
> ↑believe her↓
> ↑don't trust her↓
> ↑trust her↓
> ↑kill her↓
> ↑send her away↓
> ↑help her↓
> ↑help her help us↓
> ↑help her get away↓
> Which do we choose?

The response wrapped itself around the question like a vine. The more the question was repeated the more complex and tangled the response became. Layer by layer, the argument unfolded:

Commander Roche
↑[1]How do we know she is who she says she is?
↑[2]She has no reason to lie.
↑[3]Nor reason to tell us the truth.[3]↓
Does it matter?
↑[3]If she's lying about this, we can't trust her at all.
↑[4]But we have no way of knowing.[4]↓
True.[3]↓
It's good to be cautious, but let's not get out of hand.[2]↓
Agreed, for now.[1]↓

She struggled to keep up as the question cycled and recycled, dragging her along with it:

has come to us for help
↑[1]More likely to spy.
↑[2]Who for?[2]↓
COE Intelligence
↑[2]She says she doesn't work for them anymore.
↑[3]And you believe her?
↑[4]She says she heard a distress call.
↑[5]She could be lying about that, too.[5]↓
We're going in circles!
↑[5]No, *you* are[5]↓
We must establish a reason for suspicion.
↑[5]That our lives are under threat isn't enough?
↑[6]We are safe here.
↑[7]Short term only.[7]↓
Perhaps.[6]↓
Perhaps not, if we let Roche in.[5]↓
Perhaps.[4]↓
Perhaps.[3]↓
We need to make a decision![2]↓
But the *right* one.[1]↓
and to offer us help.
↑[1]How?
↑[2]*Ask* her.
↑[3]Again: why should we believe her?↓
↑[2]What have we got to lose if we do?
↑[3]Our lives.
↑[4]We'll die if she *doesn't* help us![4]↓
↑[3]We have only her word on that.
↑[4]But we *are* trapped here.[4]↓

Undeniably.[3]↓
So can we at least agree to give her a chance?[2]↓
That's what we *are* doing![1]↓

Despite the increasing complexity of the argument, she began to recognize voices—or at least patterns of response. There were the skeptics, and there were those inclined to trust her. She wondered how they could ever expect to achieve a consensus to arise from such chaos.

Each time the question reached its conclusion, the eddy of voices threatened to carry her away. . . .

We have numerous options.
↑[1]don't trust her
↑[2]send her away
↑[3]trust her
↑[4]help her help us
↑[5]believe her
↑[6]don't trust her
↑[7]send her away
↑[8]trust her
↑[9]help her help us
↑[10]disbelieve her
↑[11]kill her
↑[12]use her[12]↓
kill her[11]↓
don't trust her[10]↓
trust her[9]↓help her[8]↓
send her away
↑[8]help her help us↑[9]help her get away
↑[10]send her away[10]↓
trust her[9]↓help her help us[8]↓
kill her[7]↓
send her away[6]↓
let her live[5-3]↓
ignore her[2]↓don't trust her[1]↓

Gradually, the voices began to cluster into groups. The clamor didn't ebb, but it became slightly more coherent to Roche's adjusting senses. Each group made concessions in order to increase its numbers; one, initially prepared to let her go unharmed, eventually allied itself with another group who wanted the resources of *Daybreak* to remain behind; another began by offering help unreservedly but ended up demanding rescue from the collapsing Gauntlet as a condition for giving that help. Then the boundaries shifted again, hinging this time on her possible allegiance with Linegar Rufo. With each concession came increased complexity, so the Plenary became less of a squabble and more of a debate, although some of the exchanges remained heated.

Woven through the groups were odd loners who initially refused to accept any compromise. One of these in particular caught Roche's attention, even though the voice at first didn't contribute much.

↑[113-117]We have to make some kind of decision soon.
↑[118]But what *can* we do?
↑[119-125]The sensible thing would be to wait to see what happens.[125-119]↓
Do we even have the resources to do anything?
↑[119-125]Exactly our point. For that reason we prefer inaction to action.
↑[126-129]No. The sensible response is to help her.
↑[130-131]Such action would potentially benefit us the most.
↑[132]No—*kill her*!
↑[133]And miss this chance to avenge my clan?[133]↓
Irrelevant! Her mere presence here puts us in danger![132]↓
We have no proof of that.
↑[132]Yet.
↑[133]But we *know* she can help *me*.[133]↓
Must we also die in some futile attempt to make a point?[132-131]↓
It would be a meaningless sacrifice.[130-126]↓
Perhaps it is better in this case to attempt neither.[125-118]↓
Unacceptable response! Inaction is not an option![117-111]↓
At least we'd be alive.[110-109]↓
For how long?[108-105]↓
My people didn't die so yours could cower here and wait your turn![104]↓
So let's kill her now before she has a chance![103]↓
This is getting us *nowhere*![102-98]↓

The outrigger seeking revenge, Roche guessed, was the lone survivor of the attack on Wide Berth spine; the one seeking Roche's death, however, she couldn't identify. Perhaps it was one she hadn't yet met. A couple of times she tried to interject a comment in her defense, but she didn't know how to. All she could do was feel the currents of opinion ebbing and flowing around her.

Which do we choose?

Each time that question was asked, argument broke out afresh and the entire process was repeated. Slowly, though, a consensus began to emerge.

↑[286-291]We need more information.
↑[292-294]How do you propose getting that?[294-292]↓
By asking.[291-286]↓
And *trusting* her?[285]↓
We could do worse than try.[279-284]↓

Roche felt a growing sense of frustration. They had already interrogated her; what more could she possibly tell them that she hadn't already? There wasn't *time* for this!

The coordinating voice seemed to agree with her. Without warning, the fundamental spiel altered:

We must reach consensus.
Doing nothing is not an option

and neither is stalling for more information.
We cannot wait any longer.
We must decide now.
Do we help or hinder?

Roche almost drowned in the resulting surge of voices as the Plenary erupted into a chaotic buzz. She barely managed to hang onto the central thread in the fervor. And through the babble, only one voice stood out clearly.

↑[143]Either we help her, or we die!
↑[144-155]You can't be certain of that![155-144]↓
My clan is no more; how much more evidence do you need?
↑[144-155]Wide Berth was in the wrong place at the wrong time.[155-144]↓
Exactly—so don't let it happen to Long Span too![143]↓
You are free to leave at any time.[142-137]↓
Maybe I will cast my lot elsewhere.[136]↓
Be serious!
↑[136]Better to have striven and failed than to not have even tried at all.
↑[137-142]We are talking about the possible annihilation of an entire clan!
We have no time for feeble aphorisms, child![142-137]↓
My age is not relevant to this discussion.[136]↓
And you are alone.[122-135]↓
Am I?[121]↓
Are you?
↑[121]Will no one join me?
↑[122]*I will.*

The two words sent shock waves through the Plenary.

↑[123]Do you realize what you're saying?
↑[124-7]If you join her, the spine will be broken!
↑[128]It will be destroyed anyway, won't it?
↑[129-32]There is no evidence of that.[132-129]↓
There is enough to convince me.[128]↓
And me. It *does* seem the lesser of two evils.[127]↓
A choice between methods of suicide is not really a choice![126-124]↓
At least you *have* a choice. My clan did not.[121]↓
They would have chosen life; why can't we?
↑[121]Because life does not seem to be an option anymore.

Roche listened in amazement as the tide of the Plenary turned, the outriggers for the most part preferring to risk exposure and attack rather than see the clan divided.

↑[130-145]We live as one, we die as one.
↑[146]But Roche is not one of us![146]↓
Yarrow supports her.
↑[146]He is not one of us either.[146]↓
We have adopted him.[145-92]↓

Then we can un-adopt him![91]↓
He is one of us now, and always will be![90-37]↓

The resounding emphasis on Yarrow's permanent status as a member of the clan silenced many of the critics. Into the sudden ebb, the auditor repeated the crucial question:

Do we help or hinder?
↑[1-9]We help.
↑[10-27]We hinder.
↑[28-32]We help.
↑[33-40]We hinder.
↑[41-55]We help.
↑[56-66]We hinder.[66-58]↓
We help.[59-42]↓
We hinder.[43-40]↓
We help.[39-26]↓
We hinder.[25-19]↓
We help.[18-1]↓

The vote was fluctuating, changing every time the question was asked. Roche sensed a trend in her favor, but couldn't be certain. There were too many powerful voices commanding a negative vote. She waited anxiously for some sort of confirmation.

No matter what the decision
do we agree to abide by the ruling of the clan?
↑[1-66]We do.[66-1]↓

The giddying motion of the Plenary ceased for a brief moment as all the outriggers agreed on that one point. Again Roche was surprised by the fierce unity of the clan. Perhaps that was only to be expected when the rest of the galaxy treated them with disinterest at best.

Then we decide to help Morgan Roche.

The brief clarity of the Plenary instantly shattered.

↑[1]No! We can't!
↑[2-66]We are decided.[66-2]↓
But it's the wrong decision!
↑[2-66]We are decided![66-2]↓
No! *Kill her!*[0]↓

Something screamed in Roche's ears. At the same instant, the babble of the Plenary abruptly ceased. She opened her eyes to a scene of tangled metal and flashing energy. An outrigger—no, *two* outriggers—were rushing toward her, waldoes extended and lasers bright.

Her suit's systems were already on alert, howling the deafeningly loud impact alarm that had snapped her out of the Plenary. She had just enough time to raise her arms by reflex and target both of the all-suits when one of them—a lozenge with purple squares at either end—fired a projectile at her abdomen.

The projectile exploded on contact, sending her spinning backwards through the alien space of the moon's central chamber.

"Roche!" Disisto's voice rang in her helmet, but she didn't have time to reply. The suit fired attitude thrusters to reorient itself, knocking her about while she fought to ready herself for another assault.

Her attackers had moved. She armed weapons and readied herself to fire. Only then did she notice that the other outrigger, battered black with no obvious markings, was grappling with the first. Its numerous waldoes pinned its opponent's wherever it could find a grip; cutting lasers burned close to delicate sensors; attitude thrusters sent both spinning to prevent its getting a bead on Roche a second time.

The black one was clearly trying to save her. Roche immediately removed its image from the targeting systems in her suit. But the two were too closely tangled for her to fire with any hope of hitting just the one of them. She nudged herself closer, hoping for a clear shot.

It never came. Her attacker fired its thrusters at full-strength and tore itself away from the black all-suit. But before the latter could do anything, the purple suit seemed to crack open, releasing an explosive cloud of air into the vacuum. The all-suit spun with its thrusters still firing across the chamber and into a wall, then scraped along the wall for a dozen meters before the thrusters shut down.

It hit a projection and ricocheted, inactive, across the chamber. The black all-suit jetted to intercept it before it could fall into the anchor point.

"Roche! Are you all right?" Disisto's voice fought for attention among those of Idil and the other outriggers. His immobilized suit hung nearby, anchored to the trumpetlike artifact at one end of the chamber.

"I'm fine," she said, although she was short of breath and still high on adrenaline. She allowed his suit to move with barely a thought. "What the hell happened?"

"The purple all-suit just came out of nowhere and attacked you, then the other one tried to stop it." He indicated the black all-suit, which had returned with the wreckage of the other.

"Thanks," said Roche, turning to face it. "Whoever you are."

The outrigger didn't respond.

Before she could speak again, Idil's all-suit slid into view. "This is Yarrow," she said. "Your attacker was Alik. We are deeply puzzled—and hurt—by her betrayal."

Roche didn't have any problem understanding it. "She disagreed with the decision. That seems clear enough."

"But to act against it!" The horror in the outrigger's voice was clear. "No one in their right mind would ever do that!"

"Well, maybe there's your answer," she said. "Or not."

She forced herself to approach the broken all-suit still gripped in Yarrow's waldoes. Its interior lay exposed to the vacuum, dusted with frozen air and debris. Roche shone a spotlight inside and examined what she saw very closely.

She saw a wizened body curled in the claustrophobic embrace of wires, tubes, and padding. Its age, sex, and Caste were difficult to confirm at a casual glance, but Roche could tell that it was tiny, much smaller than Cane. Blood vessels had burst across its skin and its eyes and mouth were open. The expression on the dead outrigger's face was one she wouldn't forget in a hurry.

Definitely dead, and not a clone warrior.

She turned to face the outrigger who had saved her. This close, she could see the old damage to the young survivor's all-suit. The outriggers of Long Span had done their best to mend it, but fresh paint couldn't hide the signs of heat damage. The egg shape of the capsule itself looked slightly off-true, as though warped by a powerful impact.

This was her chance to make contact with the boy. "Thank you," she said again.

But again he said nothing.

"He won't talk," said Idil. "As we told you, he hasn't spoken aloud since his clan was destroyed."

"But in the Plenary—"

"Yes. It was his 'voice,' if you will, that pushed the vote in your favor."

Roche regarded the black all-suit with gratitude mixed with uneasiness. "It seems I owe you on two fronts, now."

The boy's all-suit only turned and moved away, his self-imposed radio silence adding to his all-suit's strange air.

"Morgan Roche." Auditor Byrne spoke by relay from elsewhere in the moon. "I am relieved to learn that you are safe."

"I thought you said you spoke for your people," said Roche with a trace of bitterness.

"I do—even more so now, after this unfortunate setback. The honor of Long Span spine has been tarnished. Our resolve to help you, and thereby regain our honor, is hardened. Alik's attack only worsened her cause."

"Perhaps, but I'll have to talk to my crew about it." Roche checked the time. Four hours had passed; no wonder she felt exhausted. "I will be able to contact the *Ana Vereine* in about fourteen hours. Let's meet again in, say, ten."

"Very well. We will make no further decisions for the moment." Byrne hesitated before continuing: "I am deeply sorry, Morgan Roche, for what has happened. Believe me when I say that it will not happen again. All of us of Long Span spine know that if we do manage to escape Palasian system it will only be because we have worked together."

Roche hoped she was telling the truth.

Six hours later, the outriggers detected a beacon from the *Ana Vereine*. Coded into the *ping* was a time and date stamp, plus vector coordinates relative to Hintubet. There was as yet no sign of the Marauder, but that didn't surprise Roche. The ship's camouflage systems were the most advanced in the COE and could easily fool the outriggers' asteroid detection systems.

She recorded a brief message to be sent at the time indicated, outlining her present situation. Then, with her suit secured to a wall in the central chamber, she allowed herself a couple of hours' sleep.

She was awakened sometime later when Haid called to confirm that *Daybreak* was ready to descend to the moon's surface. The courier was far too obvious a newcomer to the double-jovian system, and the energy drain of holding the ship in a stable orbit was something they could do without.

"Are you *sure* it's safe?" he asked.

Roche had thought a lot about the attack on her during the Plenary, and both she and Haid had discussed it. Alik had spoken and acted alone, but that didn't mean there weren't others who felt similarly. She had come to the conclusion, though, that she was probably safe. Not only had Alik killed herself rather than face the wrath of the clan, once she knew her attack had failed, but, as Byrne had said, the spine had to prove itself now. The betrayal of Roche's peaceful approach, and the shame that brought with it, would do more than any threat of being expelled from the clan.

"Let's say I've given up worrying about it, Ameidio," she said. "Just find a suitable spot and bring the ship down."

"Well, that isn't going to be a problem," he said. "It'll be less like landing than docking. Intelligence HQ had more of a tug than this lump of rock."

"How's Myer?"

"I knocked him out. Not literally, of course, even though I would have liked to," he added. "I put him back in the autosurgeon and under sedation for a while. He was getting in the way and I didn't want him trying something while I was busy."

"Understood," she said. "But when you're down, I want to talk to him. He saw what happened on Aro. I want to know whether or not Rufo forbade him to intervene."

"Okay. I'll instruct the autosurgeon to revive him then. He'll have a headache, but it won't kill him. More's the pity."

When Haid had decided where to land the courier, she relayed the coordinates to the outriggers. Idil guided her to the nearest shaft. There she rejoined Disisto, who had been exploring the moon under the watchful instruments of Yul and Eli.

"Find anything?" she asked.

"The untouched living quarters that Idil told us about earlier." The security chief seemed excited. "From the pictures and other personal artifacts there, it would seem the builders were more like birds than mammals. Hollow bones, long limbs, and wide-spaced eyes—it's quite incredible. They must've re-evolved back up to Pristine from some avian Low Caste."

"Then Transcended," Roche mused.

"Well, they certainly don't seem to be anywhere around here anymore."

"They must've been a pretty long-lived Caste. Given that Humanity has only been settling the galaxy for half a million years, that doesn't give them much time to devolve and re-evolve."

"That makes them a Primordial Caste, then," said Disisto. "My God, Roche! This is fantastic! I doubt there's another site as well preserved as this anywhere in the COE!"

"Well, it won't be here for much longer," she said.

Through the faceplate Roche could see Disisto's face fall.

"Why is it that Humans let their petty differences get in the way of knowledge?" he said. "We could've studied this thing for decades."

Before she could call him a hypocrite, he gestured to a point behind her. "Here's the ship."

Roche turned to where he'd indicated. She still found the blackness unnerving, but it did make detecting moving objects easier. The courier was a red dot drifting away from the half-set limb of Kukumat, growing steadily larger. Somewhere up there were the two spines, Long Span and Wide Berth, but neither was visible.

As Haid brought the ship down, Roche wondered if the curved spikes of the moon's surface were *actually* used as grappling hooks for docking ships. It was possible that ships had been securely stationed to them while their occupants used the anchor point in the moon's center to jump elsewhere across the galaxy.

But that didn't explain why the builders had gone to so much trouble to hide the anchor point in the first place. Or why their living quarters had never been used.

Her train of thought was broken as the courier vessel banked around its landing point. She watched it decelerate to a halt a hundred meters away from them, then waited until the afterwash from the thrusters had dissipated before moving in closer.

"Can't get smoother than that," boasted Haid, his voice crackling loudly over the open frequencies. Grapnels anchored the ship to two of the bent "trees"; Roche checked briefly to see that the hold was secure.

The airlock hissed open as she approached. "Wait here, Disisto."

On a closed channel, Haid said: "We have another message from the Box."

Roche unlocked the suit helmet when the outer hatch had sealed, but didn't allow herself the luxury of leaving the suit entirely. "What does it say?"

"It's picked up coded transmissions from the edge of the system. Looks like someone on the outside is trying to talk to someone in here."

"Is that what the AI thinks?"

"Well, it's keeping its options open. All it says is that the transmissions are centered on Hintubet. My guess is they're being relayed elsewhere."

"Not necessarily."

"But there's no one that deep in-system."

"No, but there is some*thing,*" she said. The sun of Palasian System was currently home to a number of machines of Kesh manufacture. "What if they're talking to the Gauntlet?"

The inner lock hissed open and she stepped through. Haid was waiting for her on the other side. He stepped back to accommodate the suit in the cramped passageway.

"I didn't think of that." He smiled. "It's good to see you again, Morgan. I had my doubts for a while there."

She touched his artificial arm with one gloved hand and stepped past him. "Thanks, Ameidio. Where's Myer?"

"In the medic suite. He'll be groggy."

"All the better." She thudded across the deck to the small medical facility. There, Mavalhin looked much like she had left him, tied flat to a narrow cot so he couldn't move. This time, though, he looked healthier. He had regained much of his color and the only blood on his uniform was brown.

She shook him, not worrying too much if the suit overemphasized the power of her movements. "Myer?"

He stirred, blinking absently up at her. "Morgan?"

"Myer. Can you hear me?"

"I'm not deaf, Morgan." He tried to sit up; puzzlement creased his features when he realized he couldn't because of his restraints. "I didn't think I was dangerous, either."

"For the moment, that's exactly what you are," she said. "Now, tell me about the attack on Aro."

He looked mystified for a second. "You mean when Emptage City and the spaceport were destroyed?"

"No, I mean the outriggers. You watched it happen. Describe what you saw."

"Not much, really. I didn't have the instruments—"

"Don't lie to me, Myer. I *know* you had the instruments; you were there to observe. Now tell me what happened or so help me I'll play cat's cradle with your stitches."

He paled slightly. "They were all killed," he said resignedly. "Cut to pieces. They didn't stand a chance."

"How long did it take?"

"I don't know. Ten minutes; maybe less."

"Why didn't you help them?"

"I couldn't."

"*Why* couldn't you, Myer?"

"I just *couldn't.* It was . . ." He hesitated. "There weren't enough of us, Morgan. There was nothing we could do."

Roche nodded. This was, so far, little different from what Disisto had told her. "But why didn't the trap catch *you,* Myer?"

He shrugged. "We were more careful, I guess."

"*How* were you careful?"

"We—" he began, then looked away and fell silent.

"You knew the traps were there, didn't you?" Roche asked after a few seconds.

His eyes met hers again. "We saw them not long after we reached Aro."

"So why didn't you warn the outriggers?"

"What do you want me to say, Morgan?" He was angry now. "That I was just following orders? Is that what you want to hear?"

"What I want doesn't come into it. What I'd *like* is for you to just tell me the way it was."

"Look," he said, attempting again to sit up. "We just assumed the outriggers would see the traps too. We didn't think there was any need to expose ourselves. If we did, then we risked endangering the station and everyone on board. We couldn't afford to take any risks, so we didn't. And I guess it worked, because the traps didn't spring us, and neither did the outriggers."

"So it was your decision not to act?" asked Haid.

"No, of course not," Myer said, shaking his head irritably. "We had orders. It was my decision to follow them."

"But what exactly *were* your orders?"

"I've already told you: to keep our heads down, no matter what happened."

Roche glanced at Haid, then back at Mavalhin. "Aro was the obvious place to look for survivors. You would've seen them if they'd been there. What did Rufo tell you to do in such a situation?"

Mavalhin shrugged. "I can repeat it as often as you like; it's not going to change anything."

"Myer, if you're telling the truth, then it changes *everything.*"

He looked puzzled. "How? You were already at odds with the chief."

"Yes, but now it's not personal; it's not just me getting my friends back and settling a score. Now it's about stopping the man who ordered you to do nothing as dozens of innocent people were slaughtered simply because they tried to help. It's about *justice.*"

Mavalhin snorted. "How can you be so self-righteous? What about your 'friend' Adoni Cane? One of *his* associates is responsible for killing nearly everyone in this system—and yet you seem only concerned with what I did, or what Rufo ordered."

"That's not true," said Roche. "This whole thing stinks. I just—"

<Agreed, Morgan,> said a voice deep in her mind. <There is something far more mysterious going on here than even you currently suspect.>

"Box!" She started at the sound of the voice. "Is that really you?"

<Yes, Morgan. This signal is being relayed through the courier.>

"But—"

<I know what you are about to say: I am not supposed to be within range for some hours yet. That was a deliberate ploy to throw anyone seeking the *Ana Vereine* off the scent. It would be prudent to maintain that illusion for now.>

<Yes,> she said, remembering to subvocalize. Mavalhin was staring at her with confusion, Haid with surprise. "Ameidio, let Myer loose but keep an eye on him. I need to be alone for a moment. If you can get Disisto in here as well, do it; otherwise he can wait outside."

With that she exited the medical facility and headed for the privacy of the bridge. She could tell that Haid was curious as to what was going on, but a proper explanation would have to wait—at least until *she* knew what was going on. . . .

<So, where are you, Box? Where is the *Ana Vereine*?>

<Currently in orbit around Kukumat. You will notice a slight delay as we converse. I am routing my replies around Murukan to avoid detection.>

<You're worried about the clone warrior tracking you down?>

<Yes. You mentioned in the summary you sent some hours ago that Rufo believes the warrior to be hiding in this location. I had also come to that conclusion. That is clearly why Rufo is broadcasting here, using the archival command language. And it might also explain the distress call: someone might have been hoping to lure the *Ana Vereine* here in order to steal it.>

She nodded; that made a cold kind of sense. <Are you aware that the command language might have nothing to do with the Sol Apotheosis Movement?>

<I did wonder. Its syntax bears little relation to anything in this region.>

Roche was surprised by the feeling of relief she felt at being in contact with the AI again. Kajic wouldn't be far behind. For now, that was better than having definite answers. <So, how long have you been listening in?>

<Only a few minutes. Your presumption that Linegar Rufo was a passive accomplice in the destruction of Wide Berth spine seems to be correct, and that would justify any action you intend to take against him. There are, however, other things you must take into account while working out what to do in the near future.>

<Such as?>

<Rufo was sent here to observe the clone warrior. That seems obvious from what we have heard. The Kesh supplied the Gauntlet in order to isolate the system, and the COE gave them access. The Kesh also provided a destroyer to act as a ferry for the station and presumably to act as emergency backup should things go awry. That seems simple enough so far. But things become more complicated when all is taken into account. Rufo has gone to some pains to attempt to communicate with the fugitive clone warrior. He also tricked you into allowing Adoni Cane onto the station, whereupon he immediately took him captive. These are not the actions of a man sent to simply observe.>

Roche nodded; her thoughts exactly. <You believe he's been trying to get his hands on a clone warrior from the start?>

<That is my conjecture. He could learn more from one in captivity than merely examining its wake.>

Realization suddenly hit. <*That's* why he didn't intervene on Aro. He wanted to watch him in action! But . . . She tried to understand the xenoarchaeologist's line of reasoning. <It's a big risk. A *huge* risk. Why would he do that?>

<Coercion is a possibility. The Kesh are an unsubtle lot at best—as are the COE, who must be involved since Intelligence let Rufo know that you and Cane were coming. Or Rufo could be doing nothing more sinister than seeking knowledge.>

<A chance to study a living relic, you mean?> She nodded thoughtfully to herself. <I can relate to that, I guess. After all, these clone warriors were built two and a half thousand years ago. It would have been tempting to actually get one in the flesh to examine.>

<Morgan, Cane may be much older than two and a half thousand years.>

<What do you mean?>

<I mean that we know too little about him and his kind to state anything with certainty. To know more, we are going to have to access Rufo's data.>

<That shouldn't be a problem. We'll just get it when we get Maii and Cane.>

<Not so simple. I have been examining the security layout of Galine Four. The station is indeed split into two discrete information networks. One, the larger, deals with the mundane day-to-day running of things; this one I have deduced how to subvert, without resorting to such crude methods as keeping palm-links constantly in contact. The other security system, much smaller, is intimately involved with the decision-making process. This second network, clearly, is where we will find the data we require. The two appear to be separated by a Tipper-Linke chaos-lock which, I am forced to concede, will not succumb to—>

<Wait. A *what* lock?>

<The precise details are unimportant. Suffice it to say that the two networks operate independently of each other for much of the time. When they do need to exchange information, it is conveyed in such a way that renders ineffective any attempt I might make to subvert it. Without taking over the entire outer network and somehow forcing the two to link, I can do nothing.>

<So what do you propose?>

<I must be maneuvered into such a position that I am allowed direct access to the inner security system.>

<Clearly. And your thoughts on how to do this are . . . ?>

<Influenced by two critical developments. The first is the communications drone sent out of the system by Rufo upon Cane's capture. Did you ask Disisto about this?>

<He didn't know anything about it.>

<Hardly surprising, since he was your captive at the time it was sent. But that does suggest that the launch of the drone was not a pre-planned event. It was spontaneous, a reaction to recent events.>

<The capture of Cane,> put in Roche.

<Precisely.>

<And the second development?>

<Is the transmission we intercepted from the edge of the system, of course. I suspect that circumstances within Palasian System are soon to change.>

Roche worked it through step by step. <Rufo called the Kesh. Having a clone warrior actually in captivity must've altered their plans somewhat. But they know Cane is dangerous, so they couldn't plan to keep him long—especially with us on the loose. You think they asked for help?>

<I am sure of it. Depending on how far away from the anomaly the *Sebettu* was stationed, company could already be on its way.>

<The Armada blockade might stop them this time.>

<Why would it, given the COE is working with the Kesh? And even so, they would be no match for a Kesh destroyer in full flight. Neither would we, for that matter.>

<So what are you suggesting? Strike now before it arrives?>

<Nothing of the sort. Quite the opposite, in fact . . .>

When she had finished talking to the Box, she rejoined Haid and helped him secure the ship. Together they prized Mavalhin into a suit, ignoring his protests at the rough treatment of his tender shoulder. Disisto, although now back in the ship, remained in his suit also; thus confined, the two were easier to control. At a simple command from Roche or Haid the suits could be frozen; both were programmed to seize up automatically if they approached within two meters of anyone without permission.

"What happens to us now?" asked Disisto while Roche and Haid double-checked the courier's flight systems from the bridge.

"We take you back to Galine Four," Roche replied without looking up. She didn't need to see Mavalhin's scowl to know it was there.

"And if I don't want to go?" he asked.

"You don't have a choice, Myer," she said. "Unless, of course, you'd like to stay out here after everyone's left?"

"Listen, Morgan, the reason I helped you in the first place was so I didn't have to go back."

"Well, let's just see what happens, okay?" said Roche tiredly. "If you help us like you did before, then perhaps we can drop you off somewhere else afterwards."

"Assuming there *is* an afterwards," he muttered.

"*Enough,* already!" Roche snapped. Then, more calmly to Haid she said: "Ameidio, get Auditor Byrne on the line." Roche had better things to do than argue with her two captives. "We need to discuss tactics."

She heard Disisto chuckle to himself. "That's some fighting force you've got, Morgan," he said.

"I've done better with less," she retorted.

"Why not forget your friends for now? Maii will be released later, I'm sure."

"Unharmed?" said Roche.

"As long as she doesn't cause any trouble, yes."

"And Cane?"

"I don't know what will happen to him," Disisto admitted. "But don't you think you might be safer without him around anyway?"

Roche spun around in her seat to face Disisto. "How about we make a deal: I'll stop trying to turn you against Rufo if you stop trying to use Cane against me."

A thin grin touched Disisto's lips. "Hit a nerve, have I?"

"Cane's saved my life on more than one occasion. That deserves something, doesn't it?"

"Maybe it does. But do you blame me, then, for being suspicious?"

"You don't know what you're talking about—"

"Morgan," interrupted Haid. "Auditor Byrne says she can have a quorum together in ten minutes."

Roche turned to check the ship's systems, fuming. "Ask her if they'll gather out here. I'd like to join them."

"What about these two?"

"We'll freeze them and put them on a tether. A little sensory deprivation will do them a world of good." Then, more to herself than anyone else, she added: "Wouldn't do me any harm to not have to listen to them for a while, either."

"Hey, lighten up, Morgan—"

"Shut up, Myer." She froze their suits with a mental command. "I'm not in the mood."

She went over to help Haid clamber into his own suit.

"I've got a feeling I'm going to be in this for a while," he said as she checked the seals down his left side.

"Bet on it."

"At least we're even, now." His new hand, buried in his powered suit's glove, curled upward into a clenched fist. "Fancy an arm wrestle?"

"Pass. But feel free to try Myer. He'd be stupid enough to take you on."

She patted the last seal closed, then stepped back.

"Morgan." Haid hesitated. "I don't want to pry, but that *was* the Box you were talking to before, right?"

She nodded. "Yes."

"But how? We're not registering any incoming signals."

She stared at him for a moment. "It said it's relaying to avoid detection. Maybe it's masking the signals on our instruments too."

"That's kind of paranoid, don't you think?"

"Maybe we should be glad it is."

The ion bridge was in full flower as they left *Daybreak* to join the gathering quorum. Fifteen outriggers had gathered in a half-sphere around the patch of Mok Roche had chosen at random. She recognized some of them by sight alone: Yarrow's midnight-black, Idil's pinkish-orange, Lud's diagonal black stripes, and one with a green triangle, from the previous quorum, whose name she didn't know.

She and Haid took positions in front of the outriggers, towing Disisto and Mavalhin behind them. When they were stationary, Roche unfroze the two captives so they could see what was going on, and perhaps even contribute.

"This has been something of an unusual day for us, Morgan Roche." Auditor Byrne's teardrop all-suit floated not far from her at the rough center of the gathering. "We would normally only meet once or twice a standard year. Two quorums and one Plenary in less than a day is quite extraordinary."

"It's the situation which is extraordinary," said Roche. "But again, I thank you for your cooperation."

"As I said, by helping you we help ourselves," the Auditor told her. She made no reference to Alik, the outrigger who had attacked Roche, but the knowledge of what she had done hung heavily upon the meeting. "Now, how exactly can we go about it?"

Roche took a deep breath. "You know that I have two friends held captive by Linegar Rufo in Galine Four. I intend to liberate them by any means possible. While doing so, I hope to obtain the information that has been gathered since Galine Four's arrival in this system; this information should prove helpful in our investigation of the clone warriors.

"In return for your help in these matters, we will give you safe passage from this system. It may mean dismantling the spines to squeeze them into the holds, but we'll do it. If I get out of here alive, so will you."

"A fair exchange," said Auditor Byrne. "But given the situation, I wouldn't have accepted anything less."

"There is one other thing," said Roche. "Rufo ordered the inaction of his observers around Aro, and as such is in part responsible for the destruction of Wide Berth's clan. I don't necessarily condone vengeance, but I will assist you in bringing him to justice, should you choose to do so."

Private lasers darted between the gathered outriggers.

"Thank you, Morgan," said Byrne. "But it is us whom Rufo has wronged, and if he is to answer for this, then it must be to us alone. It is necessary for the grief-healing of the clan."

"Roche, that isn't fair!" Disisto exclaimed. "At least grant Linegar the right of reply before you—"

"I warned you, Disisto. Ameidio, shut him out." Disisto's visor went black; his transmissions ceased in mid-outrage.

"How about you, Myer? Got a problem with this?"

Mavalhin looked at Roche steadily for a few seconds. "Not at all, Morgan. This is your show."

"Okay," she said, turning from the pilot. "Byrne, before we go into details, I need to ask you something. Idil said that she had taken over the all-suit of an older clan member when she died. Do you have any other such empty suits around?"

"We have six empty suits at this time, plus another fifteen recovered from Wide Berth. All are tethered to their respective spines. Why?"

"The Box can teleoperate them along with some of the *Ana Vereine*'s ancillary vessels and any others we can lay our hands on. They'll only be decoys, but the more points we can attack from, the better."

"Consider them at your disposal," said Byrne.

"Excellent," said Roche. "And if there are any of you reluctant to fight, you are welcome to stay on board the *Ana Vereine* during the attack—just as long as we have use of your suit to add to our decoys."

"Without our suits, we are nothing," said one of the outriggers, a statement that provoked a general susurrus of agreement.

"I understand that," Roche put in quickly. "But at least this way you might still survive even if your all-suit was damaged. We can arrange some sort of sealed environment in the ship, if you like—even teleop facilities so you can still fly your suit. And should the worst occur, then I'm sure a replacement could be built to specifications at a later date."

While her concern for the outriggers was genuine, that was not her main motive for the proposal. She was more interested in seeing who accepted the offer—and who *didn't*. An all-suit would be a convenient place for a fugitive to hide. If the clone warrior *had* infiltrated the spine, this would narrow down the suspects.

"We shall take your words into consideration," said Byrne. "Now, what about strategy?"

"Well, we need a plan that will give us time to get in, do what we have to do, then get out again," said Roche. "And it isn't going to be easy. A sneak attack by a small number of scouts would be worse than useless. They'd eventually be detected, and that would warn Rufo that a larger attack was imminent, enabling him to prepare his defenses.

"Sneaking up on them isn't an option either," she continued. "They're not blind and they'll be expecting us to try something. Even a small group will stick out in a featureless sky. They'd be shot down long before they'd get anywhere near the station.

"So, our best hope lies in getting a large assembly as close as possible without being seen and striking hard and fast. If we can penetrate their defenses quickly and get inside, the battle becomes one of internal security. That will take the pressure off the attacking force, allowing it to conserve resources and regroup if necessary. That's assuming of course that we don't completely knock out their defenses on the first pass; if we can do that, getting in and out will be considerably easier."

She looked around the quorum. Not being able to see the expressions of those she was addressing was frustrating, but the fact that there was no movement whatsoever from the all-suits gave her the impression she was at least being listened to.

"We do have something of an edge," Roche went on. "Once I get the Box inside the station, we can use it to shut down external security. This will only work for a while—until they manage to re-route it through the internal security shell—but we need all the time we can get. The Box should also be able to tell us where Maii and Cane are held in the station. I doubt they'll be together, so I imagine the landing party will have a lot to do. It's basically me and Ameidio versus the entire internal security, since we're the only ones with legs."

She glanced over at Mavalhin. "Disisto has told me he doesn't want to assist us against his employer, but I'm hoping Myer Mavalhin here will be able to give us some insight into the operation of Galine Four: blind spots or security weaknesses, points of entry, ways to move freely inside, weapons caches—that kind of thing. Any help he can provide would be useful at this point."

Mavalhin looked over to Disisto's blacked-out suit floating beside him, then back to Roche. "I'll do what I can," he said.

"Good," she said. "Then you will be part of the boarding party, too."

"But can he be trusted?" said one outrigger.

"We'll find that out soon enough, I guess," Roche replied. Then, addressing the quorum as a whole, she said, "Now, does anyone have any suggestions? I presume some of you have had combat experience?"

"Unfortunately, we all have," said Auditor Byrne. "We are better at running than fighting, but we stand up for ourselves when we have to. As you know, we possess many tools that can serve as weapons. Many of them would be useful in the attack."

"Good," Roche said. "They'll add some mass to the assault. The *Ana Vereine* has a stockpile of surveillance micromachines. The Box might be able to reconfigure some to attack the station's external surfaces—either the observation systems or the hull itself. Do you have any way to deliver such devices en masse?"

"We have nano seeders," said Lud. "Bullet-shaped and grain-sized. We could send a cloud in ahead of us. They might take it for nothing more than space junk—until it starts eating into them."

"Perfect. Anyone else?"

"What about the crust-rippers?" asked another outrigger.

"Too destructive," said Lud.

"We could use them as a threat. Load Wide Berth spine with as many as we've got and threaten to ram if they don't surrender."

"An empty threat," said Idil. "We could never use them. If we did, the explosion would wipe out everything for a million cubic kilometers. Including the *Ana Vereine* and our only way out of here."

"We can use ion drilling cannon to cut through the hull if the micromachines don't work," suggested another.

"And blind singleships with spectrometry bombs," said yet another.

"And we still have the leftover slag from the asteroids we carved before everything went wrong," said Lud. "We could use it as cover for the nano seeders. Mostly carbon and ice, a bit of iron, nice and irregular in size and shape. The seeders will blend right in."

"Good thinking," said Byrne.

"We also have access to the subsystems of a dozen or so prowling mines," said one. "They are an older make and easily subverted, the same ones the clone warrior used to destroy the Armada base around Cemenid."

"Has anyone considered using drill rigs to boost our own thrust?" came still another suggestion.

Roche relaxed slightly in the suit and let them workshop. She noticed Haid watching her to one side, and signaled him privately, reducing the volume of the outriggers' chatter to a minimum.

"What do you think? Do we have a chance?"

"Depends on how far Rufo will go to keep what he has," Haid replied. "If his life depends on it, he's going to do everything in his power to get rid of us once and for all. Last time he at least tried to pretend that he was doing the right thing. This time there'll be no charades."

"That's true," said Roche. "He knows we have Disisto and Myer. If we didn't know the truth by now, then we wouldn't be worth worrying about in the first place."

"And *do* we know the truth? Even now?"

"I'm sure we don't," Roche said. "Not entirely. But I know we're a damn sight closer than we were a few days ago."

She quickly returned her attention to the quorum when she heard someone ask:

"What do we do if something goes wrong?"

"If something goes wrong, we'll surrender," Roche said. "That is, *I* will surrender, not you. If we let them have the *Ana Vereine,* they'll probably be happy."

"And what happens to you then?"

"That's up to Rufo," she said. "It should be no concern of yours. Don't even think of trying to rescue us; you should concentrate on hiding. Galine Four won't be here forever, and there's always a chance a rescue team will arrive in time. Remember, the collapse of the system is still some weeks away."

"If that is your wish," said Byrne, "we will abide by it."

"Good." Despite what she and the Box had decided, Roche hoped it wouldn't come to that. "Now, Myer. Any suggestions on how to get in?"

The pilot cleared his throat. "Well, everything will be locked up pretty tight, as you can imagine."

"Yes, but despite the Kesh, it's not a military station," she pointed out. "There must be some weak points."

"Of course there are. Or rather there *were*. I don't know if anything will have changed since I last looked."

"I guess that's a risk we'll just have to take." She fought the urge to tell him to stop procrastinating. Antagonizing him now would be counterproductive.

"The best bet would probably be the old freight transfer point on deck 17D. No one's used it for months, so the old codes should still work. And if they don't, we can always cut through. They shut it down because of an acid spill; the seals are corroded and could be nice and brittle. Bad for safety, but good for you. I mean, *us*."

Roche ignored the slip. "How many singleships does the station have, and what other defensive measures can we expect?"

"There are usually fifteen singleships at the ready, from a pool of thirty. I don't know how many you wrecked when you left. The station has the usual stock of E-shields and anti-assault cannon. Nothing too destructive. Getting close enough to get in shouldn't be too much of a problem. It's once you're in that you'll have difficulty."

"Go on."

"Well, you've seen it. It's big and full of people. Bad enough that you want to get to one specific area—but two, or even three? If I wasn't coming with you, I wouldn't give you any chance at all."

"That's exactly *why* you're coming with us, Myer."

"So I gathered," he said. "Anyway, you'll need to bypass as much as possible. Try to keep us off the monitors, or at least covered somehow. If your AI can't do that, you'll have to arrange distractions. Hit them from every angle and they won't know where to concentrate their efforts. You might be able to slip through that way."

That was pretty much what she'd been thinking; maybe not so destructive as blowing up a scutter, though, like last time. "No loopholes we can utilize?"

"Not without knowing exactly where we're going."

"No way of cracking into the second security level?"

"None I'm aware of. Disisto might know, though."

"And he wouldn't tell me if he did." She thought for a second. "I'm not sure I agree that getting in will be easy. The singleships are faster than all-suits, better armed *and* armored. There are more of us, and sheer numbers *may* win the day, but on the other hand they might not. If we plan for every contingency, we might just turn things around to our favor; at the very least, we'll save lives.

"Auditor Byrne, we'll leave you to sort out who wants to fight and who wants to piggyback on the *Ana Vereine*. I'll download the schematics of the station and any other relevant data once I can lay my hands on it so you can discuss possible tactics and ways to minimize your losses.

"Meanwhile, we'll work out what to do from our end. We have some time to play with, anyway. Even at full burn, it'd take us a day or two to reach the station from here."

"Unless it's moved," said Haid.

"Yes, but there's not much we can do about that from here—not with the information lags as they are."

"Very well, Morgan Roche." The sharp-tipped all-suit bobbed gently in the microgravity; some of the outriggers around her were already breaking ranks. "We will keep you informed of our progress."

Auditor Byrne's silver tear was among the last to leave. Roche waited for them all to disperse before moving herself. She scanned the skies briefly before she did, and in doing so noticed Yarrow, all but invisible in his black all-suit, hanging like an accusation in the starless sky.

Roche felt as though the mysterious outrigger was watching her, and the idea of this made her feel uncomfortable. Why would he have saved her if he wasn't who Byrne thought he was? So far he had done nothing to arouse her suspicion, except be silent.

She stared back at him for a few minutes, but when it was apparent he wasn't going to move, she turned away and started tugging Disisto's limp suit back into the courier's airlock. When she glanced back a moment later, she saw Yarrow's all-suit disappearing into one of the moon's shafts.

<Okay, Box—>

<No need, Morgan. I overheard everything.>

Roche suppressed the obvious response: *How?* But now wasn't the time. She was in one of the courier's two small sleeping spaces with the door locked, having secured Disisto and Mavalhin in the bridge while Haid slept in the room next door. The ex-mercenary had looked exhausted after the quorum, and even he had admitted to not having had enough rest in the last few days.

<So how do our plans fit in with yours?>

<Well enough. I suggest I come out of hiding in twenty-four hours. We can explain my early arrival by telling the truth in part—that we have been lying low and falsifying our ETA to avoid detection. We should be battle-ready by then.>

<How is the ship holding up? The intrasystem thrusters must be taking a bit of a hammering.>

<Uri has been careful not to exceed safety limits, and they're designed well.>

Roche smiled. <Can I talk to him?>

<Sorry, Morgan, but he's resting. However, I will inform him when he awakes that you asked after him.>

<Thanks, Box.>

<I also suggest that we do not reveal the location of the *Ana Vereine* until we are under way. It would be much more difficult, under those circumstances, to attempt to subvert us.>

Roche considered the suggestion. That would mean docking *Daybreak* to the Marauder while undergoing acceleration—a tricky maneuver at the best of times.

<Are you sure that's necessary? It sounds a bit paranoid—>

<Better too paranoid than not at all,> said the Box, echoing her own thoughts on that subject.

<I guess so,> she said with some uncertainty. <And what about what happens afterwards? Have you given any thought to that? I mean, once we get Maii and Cane back, where do we go from here? What do we do?>

<I suggest we wait to see what Rufo's data tells us before we start examining our options.>

<But shouldn't we at least have some plan? If we *do* manage to avoid the Kesh destroyer and the blockade, chances are we'll have no time to decide what—>

<I understand what you are saying, Morgan,> the Box broke in. <However, I do feel that our mission is best served by patience at this point. After all, we have no clear destination beyond here.>

<I thought as much,> she said wearily. <Reassure me, Box. Tell me we can do this.>

<I cannot offer you any guarantees, Morgan. Everything is subject to chance.>

<Then can you at least give me odds?>

<Sorry, Morgan. I would rather we just went into this assuming that we will win.>

Roche sighed to herself and closed the line. She lay back on the bunk, but realized after a few minutes that she wouldn't be able to sleep. Instead she went to the bridge and called up a communications display. She was curious after what Haid had said earlier about not detecting any incoming signals from the Box.

As before, there had been no voice transmissions, coded or otherwise, sent to or from the courier during the time of her talk with the Box. The only transmission she couldn't account for was one intense burst lasting a second or two, not long after their last conversation. It had been sent from the courier to a destination farther in-system.

She didn't know what that meant. Maybe the Box had downloaded part of itself into the courier, and that smaller part had communicated their conversation to the larger one in a single concise spurt after the fact rather than in multiple transmissions during. That would make sense: after all, the Box itself seemed to be just a smaller chip off the High Human called the Crescend; no doubt the process was repeatable to a smaller degree. But she did doubt that there was room in the courier's available memory for an AI with the sophistication of the Box. And if the *Ana Vereine* was hiding behind Kukumat as the Box claimed, then the transmission had gone in the wrong direction—although there was the possibility that it could have been sent via a relay.

Tapping at the console, she instructed the communications system to notify her every time any such bursts were received or transmitted by the courier.

<I don't think that's necessary, Morgan.>

The voice in her head came as no surprise; she had half expected her actions to prompt the Box to intervene. <And what exactly is it you think I'm doing, Box?>

<I presume you are trying to deduce how I am communicating with you.>

<Possibly. Or maybe I'm just concerned that there's a bug on board the ship sending information back to Galine Four.> She smiled to herself. <That would be more reasonable than suspecting you of anything underhanded, don't you think? But the fact that you didn't even bring it up would suggest that you *are* up to something.>

The Box was silent for a moment. Not long, but long enough. <I assure you, Morgan, that I am 'up to' nothing 'underhanded.'>

<Then how about telling me what you're doing?>

<That isn't an issue I'm prepared to discuss right now. You will find out soon enough.>

She frowned. <Why not now?>

<Because it isn't relevant.>

"Is everything all right?"

She started at the unexpected voice *outside* her head. She turned and saw Disisto sitting up in his suit, helmet off but otherwise immobile. Next to him, Mavalhin lolled like a broken-backed doll, unconscious.

"I thought you were asleep," she said.

"Not me. I've spent too much time in the dark just lately." When she ignored the gibe, he said: "I don't suppose you'd care to give me *some* sort of mobility? My nose is itchy as hell."

She sent a command to allow him to move, although restricting those movements to the crash-couch. "How's that?"

He flexed his arms. "Much better. Thanks."

"You think I'm being too tough on you, don't you?"

He shook his head slowly. "Not really," he said. "The way I see it, I'm lucky to be alive at all. Most of your buddies would have shot me by now."

Roche smiled, although there was no evidence of humor in his tone or his face. "I think you exaggerate a little."

He held her stare evenly. "Maybe," he said. "But the fact is they don't take well to uncooperative prisoners."

In the quiet that followed she said: "You know, you could still help me."

He sighed heavily. "If I've told you once, I've told you a thousand times: I won't help you attack the chief—"

"I'm not asking you to do that," she said. "I'd just like to know what he's doing here, that's all. As do you. All I want is your help finding out that information."

Disisto ran a hand over the stubble dusting his dark face and scalp. "I can't do that *without* helping you in other ways too."

"You could mediate," said Roche. "Rufo and Shak'ni and all their Kesh pals will be intent on blowing us away once we return. Personally, I'd rather talk than fight—and they might listen to you if you try to mediate. Should Rufo give us the information we need—along with Maii and Cane—then we'll leave him alone. Hell, we might even take him out of the system if he wants us to. I'm sure he doesn't like being dependent on the Kesh for that."

"I know he doesn't," he said.

"So?" Roche pressed. "Can I count on you not screwing things up until we've at least tried to talk?"

Disisto sighed again. "Okay," he said. "If it means a possible peaceful solution, then I'll see what I can do."

"Good. Because you're coming in the landing party with us, and I didn't want to have to drag you around like a big sack of rocks." Roche smiled, relieved to have finally reached some sort of compromise with him. "Now, if you'll excuse me, I have to try and turn a bunch of outriggers into something resembling a fighting force."

Disisto leaned back into his seat with a half-smile on his face, but before he could say anything, the alarm Roche had installed in the communications systems sounded through her implants.

She turned back to the console and examined the surge. It seemed no different from the other, except this time it was incoming. A reply from the larger part of the Box, perhaps?

Disisto had said something about Mavalhin, but she wasn't listening.

<Box, what the hell are you playing at?>

<Morgan,> it said, ignoring the question. <I am detecting a powerful neutrino surge from Hintubet.>

She cast an eye across the instruments. There it was: a sharp spike only slowly trailing off. As she watched, it peaked again, higher than before.

<Could it be dangerous?> she said.

<It may affect some modes of communication, but little else. My concern lies with what it says about the source of the surge.>

<Hintubet? I can't see why—> She stopped. <The Gauntlet? You don't think—?>

Another spike, more powerful, again registered on the courier's neutrino detectors. <We caught a signal directed at the sun sometime ago. I assumed it was a rou-

tine signal to fine-tune the solar envelope. Now, judging by the sun's severely altered behavior, I am rapidly coming to the opposite conclusion.>

The tone of the Box's voice was leading Roche in the same direction. <They're killing it, aren't they?>

<I think so. By instructing the fleet of quark breeders orbiting within the chromosphere to dump their entire stock of strange matter into the star at once, they can cause the solar envelope to spontaneously collapse.>

<How long, Box?>

<That depends on how the chain reaction progresses. It may cascade, resulting in a catastrophic collapse within a few hours; or it may be held in check by other forces within the—>

<How long do you *think* we have?>

<Taking into account the even spacing of the spikes so far, my best guess would be sixty hours.>

Sixty hours? Roche turned the figure over in her head. Just three days to get the outriggers to Galine Four, across a distance of over five billion kilometers, break in, rescue Maii and Cane, find out what Rufo knew, and get out again. Then get out of the system before the envelope collapsed completely . . .

"Roche?" said Disisto from behind her; irritably she waved him to silence.

<What about the *Sebettu*?> she asked the Box.

<I can only assume that it is already on its way.>

<And if Rufo is heading for a rendezvous, we have to find him and match velocities, all without being seen. . . . We're really going to have to move fast on this.>

<That would be stating the obvious somewhat.>

She ignored the Box's flippancy and quickly spoke into a mike on the console.

"Auditor Byrne," she said. "I'm going to need your people ready to move in two hours. I repeat: *two hours.*"

"I hear you." The auditor's voice came on instantly. "But why the sudden urgency?"

"I just found out that the collapse of the envelope is being brought forward," she said. "We now have just three days to do what we have to do and get the hell out of here."

"*Can* we do it?"

"We can try," Roche said. "Beyond that, I'm not making any promises. . . ."

PART FOUR:

SEBETTU

INTERLUDE

He woke in a panic: someone was talking to him!

At first he thought it was one of the attendants in the Shadow Place. But the voice was cold and slippery, sharp as a hypodermic needle and as flexible as wire. It slid through his defenses and pierced his brain like a fishhook.

He struggled for a reference point. When he found none—only void—he remembered where he was.

The abomination!

<Can you hear me?>

He tried desperately to think. When had he fallen asleep? How had he allowed himself to become so vulnerable?

: HELP

He felt the technician start at the voice issuing from his monitors. <I thought I'd knocked you out cold. Ungrateful sod. Don't you want to rest?>

: HELP

: ME

<What's wrong?>

: ABOMINATION

<What?>

: HERE

<What the hell are you talking about? There's no one here but you and me.>

He gave up, defeated yet again by spatial coordinates. And anyway the voice had gone, faded into some dark recess like a bad dream. Maybe he *had* dreamt it . . .

<Can anyone hear me?>

His body jackknifed in shock, its epsense organ flailing from the back of his skull like an electric eel in a thunderstorm; every cell in his body screamed at the insidious touch of that voice. An alarm sounded somewhere, heard and felt second-hand through the technician. What was this? Fear for his well-being? Or fear he might be trying to escape? He couldn't tell which. Perhaps it was both.

<I *feel* something—I feel *you*! Who are you? Where am I?>

: KILL

<Kill who? Who are you talking to?>

: HER

<Wait. It's clearing. I can see you better now. You're the one who's been soaking up all the thoughts in the system!>

: HELP

<What are you? Olmahoi? What does *irikeii* mean?>

: ME

<All these names . . . The Cruel One and her servant . . . The enigma and the Shining One . . . the . . .>

The voice ceased. He waited breathlessly, hardly daring to believe that he had rid himself of her so easily.

<*Abomination?* Damn you! Who are *you* to judge me?>

Sharp-tipped tendrils encircled his mind. He relaxed minutely. If this was how attack would come, he was safe.

The tentacles slipped; their tips failed to find purchase. <I can't—how do you *do* that?>

Deep within him, he fashioned a private place in which he could think, a shelter not even she could reach. The Cruel One's servant had underestimated her threat, and he lacked the skills to warn him. Fear flooded through him. The abomination could not hurt him directly, but she could still do him harm. For him, death's sting was none the worse for being someone else's. Indeed, his own might come as something of a relief if she were to break completely free.

Still, there was hope. She was only a child. Without the mind of an adult to direct it, her raw talent was mostly wasted. With luck she would never realize exactly what she was capable of—as long as he kept the thought buried deep, away from her prying mind.

He had no idea what to do next, but he knew he would accomplish little hidden in his private space. He had to come out eventually to do the bidding of the Cruel One's servant. If he didn't come out, the abomination would only try all the harder to smash her way in. . . .

<What are you frightened of? I don't want to hurt you, really. Just don't go thinking any more thoughts about killing me, okay?>

He wondered why he should enter into a bargain with someone like her.

<Because I can help you. You're trapped here too. They're using you. We could help each other escape.>

There was nowhere to escape *to.*

<The *Ana Vereine* has a working slow-jump drive. We can leave here any time we want.>

So why didn't she?

<Because we haven't finished what we came here to do. Here, look.>

The abomination thrust an unwieldy slab of thought at him, and he recoiled automatically.

: NO

<What is it? Do I revolt you that much?>

He didn't answer. The technician was examining him more closely now. His odd twitches and utterances were not going unnoticed. He needed to be careful lest someone think he was up to something.

<Well, you *are* hiding something.>

Of course he was. More things than she would ever know.

<Don't be pompous. Something about Rufo. And Cane. I thought *you* were Cane when I first touched you. No one would be able to get through this fog, except maybe him. Or so I thought.>

In his private place, he realized that she too had been fooled by the Shining One's camouflage. That was something. She wasn't as perceptive as he had feared.

<Why can't I touch anyone else? Where is Morgan?>

He recognized the name from the abomination's own mind, but had no idea where the enigma had got to. The proximity of the Shining One obscured the rest of the system from his sight.

<So Rufo doesn't know, either?>

That wasn't necessarily so. The Cruel One's servant had numerous sensors and singleship scouts on the lookout for the two fugitive vessels. It was only a matter of time before one of them turned up.

<Still, it's a point in her favor, right? It'll be easier for her to sneak back here, when she's ready.>

He reacted with surprise to the certainty in the abomination's mental voice. Come back? The enigma would be insane to do such a thing!

<Trust me, she'll come.>

The abomination's thoughts slid across each other like shining metal sheets, polished by friction. Her screen was good, but not perfect. Occasional insights slipped through the gaps, and he gathered them up, hoping to learn as much as he could about her. Leverage might come in handy, later.

<Why do you call me an abomination?>

The question surprised him. The Surin bred for epsense; they were not without experience in the field. Surely she knew that minds like hers should not exist?

<Who says?>

He supposed she was too young to understand. Long-term maintenance of epsense ability required either built-in genetic disposition or intense discipline. If she had been made and raised around others like her, or around natural reaves who lacked the proper training—

<Pompous *and* patronizing.>

Abominations like her were prone to self-destruction. There was no place for them in the galaxy; they never fit in. It wasn't that they were rejected, more that they could not be accepted. In time, they always disintegrated.

<Oh, really?>

He felt perversely sorry for her; after all, it wasn't her fault she'd been made this way. But he could not—and *would* not—allow feelings of sympathy to intrude on what he had to do.

There had to be a way.

<I guess our battle lines are drawn,> she said. <If the only way I can talk to anyone else is by getting rid of you, Olmahoi, *irikeii,* whatever you are, then so be it. The chances of us ever reaching agreement are pretty damn slim.>

Nonexistent, he would've thought.

<Well, then. Will you tell me what you're hiding or do I have to wring it from you drop by drop?>

For a moment, in his private retreat, he was tempted to accept her challenge. Not that there was any risk of her getting what she wanted that way. No matter how strong she was, he would not fall to a direct assault; his very nature forbade it. He was more like a channel than a vessel; the hole in the fabric of n-space that was his mind could be filled and overflow, but that would not harm him directly. It would simply spill onto those around him, including the one attacking him, and thereby neutralize the threat.

No, he decided, letting his thoughts rise back to the surface. It would be more interesting to give her what she wanted. That would get her off his back, temporarily, and perhaps enable him to see what she made of it into the bargain.

<Don't expect me to tell you anything.>

Dialogue was possible even between enemies, especially when the conflict was not diametrically polarized. If they both perceived a common foe, mightn't it seem sensible to exchange information?

<*If* we do, yes. But you'll have to convince me of that, first.>

He opened his mind. Not totally, and not all at once. And not, he had to admit, without doubt—for all he had learned was necessarily colored by the minds that had given it to him. But he himself did not add anything. He offered her no deceptions.

He showed her his home. He showed her how he had come to be snatched from it and brought here. He showed her the Cruel One. He showed her the complex web of intrigue and machinations woven around him. He showed her why it was unlikely he would ever be allowed to return to his people.

Then he showed her the dark hole at the heart of the Shining One. He showed her the secret fear breeding in the Cruel One's servant's mind. He showed her the difference between what the enigma thought to be true, and what he had garnered from those closer to the heart of the matter.

Mostly what he hoped to show her was her ignorance. . . .

<No.>

The abomination's voice was strained.

<That's impossible. You're *lying*!>

He assured her that he wasn't—but she was already gone. She had fled rather than endure the truth.

He barely had time to feel satisfaction when—

Pain!

He struggled to orient himself. Agony tore through every nerve in his body. What had gone wrong?

<Hey! Pay attention! Why the hell didn't you warn us?>

His mind strained. Wider, wider. Desperate to stop the pain.

: SLEEPING

: DREAMING

<Well look *now,* damn you! There's a fleet bearing down on us! We need to know numbers. And we want to know if the other clone warrior's behind them!>

He looked; it was true. He could see them now rising out of the mist of the Shining One, numerous minds all focused on one place, one challenge.

: MANY

<*How* many?>

: MANY

: COMING

He peered closer, harder, through the light, at another.

: SHINING

: RESONANCE

And there, at the forefront, he saw it. He didn't know why he was surprised, and perhaps even a little relieved. He knew the Cruel One's servant would feel very differently. But at least now he would be able to keep an eye on her.

Just as the abomination had said, the enigma had returned. . . .

7

COEI *Daybreak*
'955.01.23 EN
1840

The outrigger fleet came in fast. After twenty hours of hard acceleration and deceleration on the back of the spines, then riding on momentum alone for the last hour to hide the emissions of their tiny drives, they burst into the sky around Galine Four like the absent stars. Seventy-six all-suits in total, more than half of them empty and teleoperated either by their original owners or the Box, while the spines remained hidden far away; behind the outriggers, six lumbering prowling mines—big tanklike masses of metal designed to overtake sluggish asteroids and slowly tear them to pieces; and hidden among them, carefully camouflaged as another prowling mine, the *Ana Vereine*—using its shields to protect as many of the outriggers as possible until they were within firing range.

Roche occupied the copilot's chair of *Daybreak,* fully suited and ready to disembark at a moment's notice. Her suit had come from the holds of the *Ana Vereine* and was a substantial improvement on the old one: cool air circulated across every part of her body; silent servo-assists gave her increased strength and agility; hidden weapons awaited her slightest mental prompt to attack. Information flowed across eyes-up displays and through her implants; she could see from a dozen different viewpoints simultaneously, and could eavesdrop as needed on the outriggers' exchanges. She was like an angry insect queen surrounded by her warriors, swooping in for the kill.

Beside her, Haid sat similarly dressed. Mavalhin and Disisto wore the COE suits that had come with the courier vessel, but they weren't armed. Roche had promised Mavalhin a hand weapon when they boarded Galine Four, but she still hadn't decided whether to keep that promise or not.

Behind them waited four empty combat suits from the *Ana Vereine*. These would accompany them onto Galine Four, to be directed by the Box if that proved to be possible. There was no guarantee that they would be able to communicate with the fleet outside. It was worth taking the chance, though, Roche thought. If the drones *did* work, they would effectively double their numbers.

It seemed to take the Galine Four defenders a moment to believe what they were seeing. By the time the first shots were fired, the outriggers were almost in range. As soon as they were, the formation dissolved and return fire began to come in.

"How's your status?" she asked the *Ana Vereine*.

"Just waiting on your signal, Morgan." Roche could hear the elation in the ex-captain's voice. After days of running and hiding, the prospect of action had Uri barely able to contain his excitement.

Roche studied the views before her. The station gunners were concentrating on the prowling mines—not surprising considering their mass. If just one of them rammed, the battle would effectively be over. Roche had no intention of doing this, but the station gunners weren't to know that.

"Your shields are holding?"

"They're doing okay," reported Kajic. "I'm displaying signs of damage in order to preserve the illusion."

"Could you also feign disablement?"

"Shouldn't be difficult."

"Then do so after the next particularly heavy battery. Don't head for the station, though; tumble so you'd miss. That way they should leave you alone. As soon as the shields are back to full strength, join the battle properly."

"Understood."

Roche steadied herself as the courier rolled beneath her. They were well back from the frontline, but close enough to catch the occasional stray shot. The makeshift E-shields and disrupters the Box had installed were bearing up well, much to her relief. They were going to need them once she decided to make her move.

The outriggers were close enough to take potshots at the A-P cannons scattered over the station's exterior surfaces. Their voices sang through her in a fugue similar to the Plenary she had witnessed, but without its innate sense of order. In among the battle calls was the Auditor herself, her calming voice keeping everything under relative control.

[25-26]Watch out! Watch out!
[31]Covered. Keep an eye on that second gunner!
Groups 4-9 and 17-26 pull back and down.
Flank support required.
[17-22]We have a positive on feeder placement in sectors blue and yellow.
[9-13]How long until hull integrity is compromised?
[17-22]Five minutes. Can you hold out that long?
[9-13]We'll have to, I guess.
Shields are falling in orange sector;
All available fire to concentrate here.
The cannon are vulnerable.
[45]Damn!
[33]You okay?
[45]Singed. This is just like stripping JA-32!
[33]And we know what happened there, don't we?
Concentrate, people.
We have company.

Singleships spilled out of docking bays from all over the station, scattering the outriggers on a wave of returned fire.

Hold formation!
Don't turn your back unless you want to be shot in it!

<Box!> Roche called. <Send in the drones!>

From the nooks and crannies of the prowling mines came every independent craft Roche had been able to lay her hands on. Mass-throwers, impact probes, and remote instruments of every description converged on the station.

"Byrne! Tell your people to be careful. It's going to get messy in there!"

Retract all antennae!
Incoming debris!

The space around the station became thick with energy and matter. A wild variety of thrusters—some as small as a fingernail—flashed and burned; accurate shots sent fragments and dust flying in all directions; laser beams were absorbed or deflected in crazy patterns. Through it all moved the singleships and outriggers, with *Daybreak* close by. And behind them all came the prowling mines, still lumbering on and laboring under the concentrated fire from the station's artillery.

The *Ana Vereine* took a volley of shots to its flank and went into a slow roll. Roche nodded in satisfaction. It would be ready to attack in a few minutes.

"Take us closer," she instructed Haid.

[34]Be careful!
[38]I am. It's just . . .
[34]Laird? Goddamn! I need reinforcements!
[5-7]Hold on. We're coming!
Let the drones and teleop teams go in first.
And watch out for pincer attacks.
I want live fighters; you aren't any good to me dead!

"Look at them," said Haid, watching a similar view to Roche's on a bridge monitor. The singleships swooped and parried, pairs targeting lone outriggers and dispatching them first, then trying to break up larger groups. "They're Kesh pilots," he said. "I've seen them fight like that before."

"Efficient, aren't they?" Disisto commented emotionlessly from behind them.

"They'd never fight like that against their own kind," said Haid.

[27]Hull breach in orange sector!
[38]Concentrate your fire. Hurt them! Hurt them!
Group 31-34, stay back.
That tower's about to blow!
[8]Lud? Are you still with us?
[14]Barely . . . Pressure's dropping.
[8]Withdraw! We can handle it from here.

"Byrne," said Roche. "Tell the wounded or damaged to fall back. We're about to move in."

Expect reinforcement soon.
Fall back on my command.
Injured and compromised first.
I want everyone else to remain for the second wave.

"You hear that, Uri?"

"Yes, Morgan." Kajic's voice came from the bridge speakers. "We will break cover in twenty seconds."

"Okay, good. We're relying on you to watch our back. And keep an eye on Yarrow, if you can." As Roche had expected, the Wide Berth survivor hadn't taken the option to hide in the hold of the *Ana Vereine*. "Ameidio, full thrust as soon as the *Ana Vereine* is exposed. We go in under its covering fire."

"You got it." Almost imperceptibly, the pilot stiffened at the controls of the courier.

"I guess this is it," Mavalhin muttered nervously.

"It sure is, Myer," Roche said. "And you're going to do exactly as I tell you, *when* I tell you." She kept her attention on the image of the disguised *Ana Vereine* as she spoke. Suddenly the appearance of the crippled prowling mine shimmered, then vanished altogether. In its place was now the Marauder, its many prongs lit up against the black sky by its own blazing weapons.

"Hold on everyone!" Haid pushed the courier forward and into the melee. Singleships dodged and weaved to avoid the energy weapons bombarding them from all directions. Two fell instantly; seconds later, another. The station's cannon turned to bear on the swooping ship and *Daybreak* aimed into the gap.

The freight transfer point was located near the *R* painted on the side of the station, halfway between the nominal top and the docking equator. Haid looped once around the station, then veered in closer. The wreckage became noticeably thicker. Heavy clangs announced impacts with pieces large enough to penetrate the shields; near misses dissipated with bright flashes of energy.

A recessed gantry appeared before them.

"That's it," Mavalhin said.

Outrigger fire had scarred much of the area around the gantry, aiming for surveillance equipment and anti-intrusion emplacements. The area looked secure. There was just enough room in the docking space to hide the courier.

"Take us in, Ameidio," said Roche. "Byrne, we're there!"

All except teleop groups—
withdraw!

Haid brought the courier close enough for grapnels to hook onto. Roche glanced up at the sky. As some of the outriggers fell back, the *Ana Vereine* stepped up the attack on the singleships. At the same time, the prowling mines had approached to what must have been uncomfortably close proximity for those aboard Galine Four. With so many threats harrying the station, she hoped to be able to dock the ship relatively unnoticed.

<Box, are you back in the outer security system?>

<Getting there. They have changed the codes, but these won't take long to bypass. I expect to have access to internal communications within ninety seconds. Once I have that, I will be able to delay security in this area should they attempt to move in.>

Roche grunted her understanding. She braced herself as the courier clanged home, then stood up. Haid secured the console, then also rose. The four drone suits stirred.

"Let's go," Roche said to Disisto and Mavalhin. "I want your voice transmissions kept to a minimum."

They filed back to the airlock as pumps evacuated the entire ship. The inner door was already open when they reached it. Part of her hoped they would encounter some form of resistance; another part of her prayed they wouldn't.

The outer door hissed open at their approach. Roche went first, hands extended, weapons and sensors in her gloves scanning the gantry. It was clear. She removed a rifle from its back holster and stood aside.

The others followed. One of the drones placed cutting equipment against the corroded seals Mavalhin had mentioned and began blasting. The metal parted like melting cheese. Radiation warnings pinged in Roche's chest, but they weren't urgent enough to require her to step away.

Above them, the sky continued to boil.

One of the suits—she had already lost track of which were drones and which weren't—stepped toward her and touched her shoulder.

READING ME? asked Haid.

<Yes,> she sent back. <Hold still.>

She activated the laser on her left glove and burned a black line on the seamless chest of his suit. Stepping back, she did the same to herself.

<Now we'll know who's who.>

The remains of the gantry door swung silently aside.

<After you.>

Stepping past the drones and over the still-glowing edge of the gantry door, Haid led the way into the station. The others followed, with Roche and two of the drones taking up the rear.

The freight transfer deck was spacious but empty. Nevertheless, Roche kept alert for any sign that they had been spotted.

<I have you on visual,> said the Box. <All automatic security alerts have been disabled. The area is deserted. You are free to move.>

<I hope you know what you're talking about, Box.>

<I always do, Morgan.> She couldn't tell if it was meant as a joke or not. <I will dispatch two of the drones to seek out the data you require. This will save time.>

Roche frowned; they hadn't planned it that way. <Are you sure that's a good idea? I don't want you to overextend yourself, what with the empty all-suits and—>

<I am not overextended, Morgan. I will let you know the moment that unlikely event should arise.>

She wasn't reassured. The Box sounded as if it was enjoying itself. At times like these, she had learned to be worried.

<Okay, but I want a direct visual from one of the suits.> At least that way she could check on what they were up to without having to ask the Box.

She checked a moment later to make sure it had been done: through the sensors of the drone immediately behind her, she saw herself wave an arm.

Turning to the others, Roche motioned them forward. The maps she'd acquired on her first visit to the station indicated the exit she wanted. As they approached, the door slid open. They moved off along the passageway, pressure doors opening and closing smoothly as they passed. At the second intersection they came to, two of the drones turned right. Haid automatically went to follow.

<No, this way.> She touched his wrist. <We turn at the next intersection.>

BUT—

<I'll explain later.>

While she didn't know precisely where Cane and Maii were being held, it seemed likely they would be in one of the two holding pens indicated on the station's maps. They were located midway between the outer hull and Galine Four's centralmost chamber, but on opposite sides of the station. The closest wasn't far from where they were, so it was to this one they headed. Roche silently prayed it was the right one.

At the end of the corridor were two freight elevators waiting to take them deep into the station's infrastructure. As the heavy doors slid aside, a rumble echoed through the floors and walls.

<Box? What's going on out there?>

<*Daybreak* has been spotted. Hold while I concentrate.>

Roche stepped into the elevator and steadied herself. Having a moment to spare while the cage dropped, she reconnected herself to the battle outside.

[17]Get the ship!
It's too late! Fall back!
[38]We can't let them take it!
[18]Yarrow! Don't—
[17]What the hell is he doing?
[25]He's going to mine it!
Clear the area!
Now!

Through the senses of the courier Roche saw a singleship loom close. The sky beyond was thick with crossfire. Into the web of energy came the black shape of Yarrow's battle-scarred all-suit, a magnetic mine in one extended manipulator. Watching the speed and precision with which he moved, Roche couldn't help but think of Cane. The obvious comparison left her with mixed feelings, the strongest of which was fear.

The singleship turned to defend itself, but it wasn't Yarrow's target. He dived straight toward *Daybreak* and pressed the mine onto its hull. Then he moved away, heading low and close to the hull to maximize the amount of mass between him and the explosion.

When it came, the view from the courier blacked out instantly. The last thing Roche saw was the singleship realizing what had happened and trying too late to get away.

A heavy *thud* made the floor beneath jump. From the *Ana Vereine*'s point of view, Roche watched as a blue-white hemisphere suddenly blossomed from the side of the station, then disappeared, leaving blackened ruin in its wake.

Another deep rumble echoed through the station. Haid's suit whined softly as he staggered.

"What the hell was that?" His voice came from internal speakers this time. "One of the prowlers?"

"A mine. They found *Daybreak*. Yarrow destroyed it, and the entrance."

"Is he *crazy*?"

"It actually makes sense," said Roche. "This way they won't be able to work out how many of us were in the ship—nor can they follow us in. They don't even know if we got in at all. It's a mess up there."

"It still leaves us trapped, though!"

"Don't worry. We'll find a way out."

The elevator slowed to a halt, but the doors didn't open.

<There is a security presence outside,> said the Box.

<Show me.> A new window in Roche's field of view opened, revealing two guards maintaining watch at the end of the corridor. They were armed, but not heavily armored. When a siren began to wail, they became instantly more alert.

<What's going on now, Box?>

<They have confirmation that you are in the station.>

<How is that possible? I thought you had everything locked down.>

<There must be something I've overlooked,> said the Box. <According to the low-level security dispatches I am monitoring, it seems they know *you* are on board, but they don't know precisely where—or even if you are alone.>

<Well, that's something. But I can't hide in here all day.> She checked her map. <We're on the right level. The security compound is two corridors over.> To the others she said: "We have a couple of guards outside. Is everyone ready?"

"You're really going through with this?" asked Disisto.

"I have no choice. You and Myer keep your heads down and follow me." She studied the view of the security guards. Their weapons looked like standard issue; her armor would absorb it easily, but Disisto and Mavalhin would not be so well protected.

<Box, send one of the drones in with me first. We have to prevent them from sounding the alarm. Ameidio, you come last, but before Myer and Disisto. I don't want them hurt.>

His hand touched her upper arm. GOT IT.

<At the end of the corridor, we go right.> She took a deep breath. <On my mark. Go!>

The drone moved out as soon as the elevator door opened, with Roche stepping past it to its left. The drone raised its rifle and fired a single sharp burst before the guards had a chance to react. One guard fell. Roche was a split-second behind; her shot caught the second guard in the shoulder, spinning him around and into the wall. He slid down to the floor and didn't move.

Two down, she thought.

The pitch of the alarms didn't change.

<Any more?> she asked the Box.

<Two more to the left, another five in a guardroom closer to the compound itself. Beyond that is a black zone I cannot penetrate.>

<Is it likely we'll find anything in there?>

<There's only one way to find out, Morgan.>

<And in doing so, we expose ourselves. Okay.> She touched Haid's shoulder. <Two to the left. You take a drone and deal with them, then catch up. We have a nest of five just ahead.>

OKAY.

He edged up to the corner, with one of the drones close behind. Once he had rounded it, Roche headed off along the passageway, with the two captives and the other drone behind. So far Disisto and Mavalhin had shown nothing but cooperation, but she couldn't afford to relax. She would feel easier once Haid caught up with them again.

She had almost reached the guardroom when two sharp retorts rang out along the corridor; then a third. The response was immediate: voices and movement came from ahead of her. Instinctively she selected a subsonic from the suit's array of weaponry and stepped around the corner into the guardroom itself.

Two of the guards were fully equipped and ready for action while the others were still in the process of fitting armor and weapons. None of the armor was powered, and the blast of low-frequency sound caught them by surprise. One keeled over backwards; another doubled over vomiting; the others clutched their heads in pain.

The drone moved forward, its raised gun taking out a guard with a single shot to the chest.

<No, Box! Don't kill them. Just knock them out.>

The drone immediately flipped the rifle and used the butt to club the remaining four unconscious.

A hand touched Roche's shoulder: MESSY, said Haid.

<Could have been a lot worse,> she replied, looking down at the dead body.

A corridor on the far side led into the black zone.

<Ameidio,> Roche said. <Wait here with these two and a drone. I'm going to have a look around on my own.> Before Haid could protest, she explained: <The Box can't stop them looking into the black zone. If they do, they'll think there's only two of us. And I'll have you to cover my back.>

OKAY. SHOUT IF YOU NEED BACKUP.

"Wait," said Mavalhin as Roche stepped forward.

She turned. "What?"

"I know this area," said the pilot. Then in response to Roche's quizzical expression, he explained: "I've, ah, spent some time here in the past."

"Well-deserved too, if I recall," muttered Disisto.

Mavalhin shot the security chief a sharp look. "I paid all the money back!"

"Eventually, and only because—"

"I haven't got *time* for this!" Roche's bellow startled them both to silence. It had been effective, but she hoped her voice hadn't carried too far. "Myer, you come with me. I'm looking for maximum security cells, possibly with medical facilities."

"Not a problem," he said. "Lead the way."

Roche's laugh was brief and humorless. "I don't think so," she said. "If I'm going to be led into a trap, I'm making sure you're right there in front of me, Myer."

"Were you always this suspicious, Morgan?"

"Just move it."

He swallowed under her glare. "Okay. This way, I think."

She followed him into the black zone, down a corridor that looked no different from any of the others they had traversed. They passed several closed doors, but none of them looked secure enough to be cells, and Mavalhin didn't stop.

Their movements were cautious and relatively quiet, and there had been no signs of any other guards. Nevertheless, Roche remained tense and uneasy. She knew that setting off just one internal alarm would change everything. . . .

"Here." Mavalhin pointed through a closed transparent door.

Roche peered in and saw steel-gray bulkheads, six down each side of a wide corridor. Everything about them said high security to her.

There was a panel by the side of the door. <Box, do you think—?>

<Place your suit's left palm-link within range.>

She did so. <Can you break into the system from here?>

<No. This is just an isolated lock. It does give some interesting codes and passwords, though.>

The door clicked and hissed slowly open. Roche nudged Mavalhin ahead of her. The first door on her left had a transparent panel at eye level. She peered through it, but saw nothing except for featureless walls and floor. The cell was empty.

So was the one opposite, and the next one along. All twelve, in fact, turned out to be empty.

"Are these the only cells here, Myer?"

"I'm afraid so," he said. "At least they're the only ones I ever saw down here." He led her out of the corridor. "See, there's a dead end, and that leads to the way we came."

"Damn." She cursed their luck, but quickly regained her composure. She needed to stay focused. "Okay, then. It's back the way we came." To the Box she said: <Get another elevator ready for us. This is going to be awkward. We need to go down two levels and across to the other side of the station.>

<Working on it now, Morgan.>

When they got back to the others, Roche found that Haid had taken the time to bind the four unconscious guards. Their absence, along with that of their dead comrades, would inevitably provoke some concern, but for now it afforded them a little breathing space.

Disisto looked worried when she walked into the room, which surprised her. If anything, she would have expected him to have been relieved to see her empty-handed.

"What's wrong?" she asked.

He shook his head. "When do I get to talk to the chief?"

"Later," she said, shepherding him and Mavalhin ahead of her. "Just keep moving."

Back in the elevator, Roche checked the status of the battle outside. The all-suits had retreated entirely, apart from a few of those teleoperated by the Box or the outriggers aboard the *Ana Vereine*. Casualties were higher than Roche would have liked. They were down to forty fully functioning all-suits, while the station had lost just ten singleships. Half of the prowling mines had been disabled and their hulks were drifting steadily away from the battle. The *Ana Vereine* had also pulled back, as though reassessing its options, and conducted only the occasional raid on the station.

There was little point in maintaining the illusion that the attack had merely paused and would begin again at any moment. Rufo and the Kesh somehow knew that she was inside. And when the attack resumed, they would know that she was preparing to leave.

<Morgan,> said the Box, <we have a blip on the long-range scanners. Precisely on schedule.>

She acknowledged the news with merely a grunt. Time was definitely running out.

"Do you know the other security compound at all?" she asked Mavalhin.

The pilot shook his head. Even through his suit's helmet she could see the sweat trickling down his face. "Sorry, Morgan."

The elevator stopped and they disembarked once the Box had assured them the area was clear. The AI had a transit cab waiting for them at the nearest tube entrance. They filed inside, and were rapidly whisked around the equator of the station's inner perimeter. At the other end, they found another elevator and went down several levels.

"I think I should try to get in contact with someone," said Disisto.

"Only when we've got nothing to bargain with."

"You haven't anything *now*!" he shot back. "You're not exactly doing that great out there."

"We're doing all right," she said.

"You could at least *try.*"

She turned to face him. He looked worse than Mavalhin. "Why? We've got this far without bargaining."

He didn't answer.

Doubt suddenly flooded through her. "It's been too easy, hasn't it? That's what's worrying you . . ."

Still he said nothing.

The elevator was two floors away from stopping.

<Box, drop us at the floor *above* the one we need.>

The cab decelerated suddenly. The map showed a maze of corridors at that level; a maintenance and storage floor that promised to be mostly empty.

<Can you knock out security on this level?>

<Already done, Morgan.>

<And make it look like the elevator has kept going?>

<Naturally,> the AI said. <I have also taken the liberty of preparing a diversion, should it be required.>

Roche belatedly remembered the other two drones. She quickly checked through the vision of the one the Box had allocated her, but saw only darkness on most frequencies except infrared, which revealed a dull background of heat. It was almost as though the drone had its faceplate pressed up against something warm. She didn't have time to work it out, so closed the window to the drone's viewpoint.

"This way," said Roche as she exited the elevator. She led them along a winding corridor, keeping one eye on where she was going and the other on the map. Superimposing the two levels was confusing; she relied heavily on the Box to warn her if they were about to run into company. But soon they were where she wanted to be: below their feet, separated by only a meter of decking, was the other black zone.

"This isn't going to be subtle," she said to Disisto. "If you have any suggestions on how to minimize possible loss of life, tell me now."

The security chief warred with himself for a moment, then said: "The closer you get to the middle, the safer it will be. But stay out of the exact center. That would be dangerous."

When she realized he wasn't going to provide any more detail, Roche concentrated on finding an appropriate place. She had no way of knowing what they would be going into; she wanted somewhere away from a bulkhead with an enclosed space above it. All she could do was look for the latter in about the right place and hope for the former.

She found a storage hold that looked about right, and with the help of one of the drones began laying charges in the floor. The charges weren't as precise as she would've liked, and their entrance would be all too dramatic, but it was the best she could think of under the circumstances.

When she was ready, she cleared the room. The Box closed the door behind her.

"Five seconds," she said. "The drones go first, then we all follow. I'll go last. And remember this," she added to Disisto and Mavalhin: "One, the longer we're here, the more likely it is we'll be trapped; and two, I'm holding a gun to your backs, and I have no intention of allowing you to slow us down."

There wasn't time for either captive to acknowledge her: the charges went off with a force that made even her suit lose its balance. The door came off its tracks, and by the time she was upright again the drones were already pulling it free. On the other side, most of the floor of the room had dropped away in a ragged circular slab, tilted where a wall cut a chord across it from underneath. Smoke and dust filled the air. The drones half-dropped, half-slid down the slab and fired at something she couldn't see. Roche heard someone call out, but they were abruptly cut short. Somewhere close by, another siren began to wail.

Haid followed the drones. Roche shoved her reluctant captives ahead of her, then followed herself.

She landed on a pile of rubble in the middle of a giant open-space area. Wrecked consoles and desks lay scattered for tens of meters around them; fire burned in carpet that had once been grass-green. Oddly placed panels broke the space into discretely semidetached segments. From behind one such panel, someone was offering resistance and calling for help. The drones ignored that one voice for the moment, concentrating instead on picking out cameras and other security placements throughout the place, disabling them with single, precise shots.

As Roche took her bearings, a door opened in a distant wall and a squad of security guards ran in.

She dropped to one knee and fired. The squad ducked for cover, turning over furniture and scrambling for the nearest panels. Return fire crackled back at her, whining as it ricocheted off her armor. The drones and Haid backed her up from behind the cover of the slab they had ducked behind.

"Which way?" shouted Haid.

Roche glanced around her. The wall through which the guards had entered was curved, as was the wall behind the slab, suggesting that the space was circular, enclosing them. The guards had been on the outer wall, so what they were protecting was farther in.

The inner wall was not far away, near enough for a quick dash. There was a door within sight.

"There!" she shouted, pointing.

"What if it doesn't open?" Haid called back.

She used the suit's sensors to zoom closer for a better view. The door was almost flush to the wall, and there didn't seem to be any way to open it.

"It'll have to," she said. "Cover me."

She shouldered her rifle and darted across the gap.

She had barely reached halfway across when the door opened from the other side, revealing Shak'ni and Haden B'shan. Both Kesh officers were dressed in full battle uniform and holding ceremonial—though clearly functional—weapons.

She didn't know who was more startled, the Kesh or her. All three lifted their weapons simultaneously, but Shak'ni got in the first shot, catching Roche in the thigh. Her suit shrieked but absorbed the blow.

Her stomach twisted in panic. Kesh weapons were a higher gauge than the ones her suit was designed to withstand. A handful of shots was all it would take—maybe as few as three. But that might be all she needed . . .

She called up the menu on her rifle as a second shot from Shak'ni hit her in the visor. She blinked but managed to select the options she required. B'shan went for her knees, and made her stagger. She aimed the rifle and fired just as Shak'ni caught her a third time, in the chest, knocking her backwards and off her feet.

Aimed up and between the two Kesh warriors, the percussion charge struck the ceiling just inside the door and exploded violently, tearing another hole in the already damaged ceiling. Half of the door went with it, along with B'shan and Shak'ni.

Roche rolled out of the shock wave and was on her feet before anyone else had recovered. Her ears rang and the suit seemed a little stiff, but she was otherwise unharmed. The two Kesh stirred weakly some distance from what remained of the door. Haid and the others were already moving.

More guards appeared off to the left, hugging the curve of the wall.

"Okay, Disisto!" she shouted as she pushed him ahead of her into the ruined doorway. "*Now* you can talk to them!"

"Very funny, Roche!" he called back over his shoulder.

She fired another percussion charge into the floor behind them, hoping its partial collapse would delay pursuit for a moment or two. She could already hear Shak'ni bellowing for assistance.

"I'm serious, Disisto," she said. "I need you to stay here and tell them what I want. This is your one and only chance to mediate. But I suggest you think fast about what you're going to say, because Shak'ni won't be in the mood for listening."

Disisto looked sick with worry, but Roche didn't have time to concern herself with that at the moment. Haid had already gone through the inner door with Mavalhin and one of the drones, leaving her to follow. The most she could do was leave him a drone for support.

"Box, do your best to keep him alive, will you?" She patted Disisto roughly on the shoulder. "Good luck," she said, meaning it, then ducked through the doorway after the others.

There was a palm-lock on the far side, which the Box made short work of, shutting the door on the sounds of the weapons from outside. Roche heard Disisto offer a wry "Thanks" before the door slammed shut.

Then silence.

Only then did she really take the time to look around.

She was in a corridor that curved away uninterrupted in either direction. There seemed to be no one about, and no doors. There was no sign of the others through the lingering smoke and dust, and for a moment she felt panic.

MORGAN, IS THAT YOU? There was no point hiding transmissions anymore.

<Haid? Where are you?>

HEAD TO YOUR LEFT. I THINK WE'VE FOUND WHAT WE'RE LOOKING FOR.

<Good. I'm on my way.>

The corridor led her to an antechamber barely large enough for the four of them. Two consoles faced away from the way she'd come in, next to a door that looked solid enough to stop a hydraulic ram. Each of the consoles monitored two cells, making four in all.

Haid was fiddling at one of the consoles, while the drone gave the Box access to the other. Mavalhin kept carefully out of the way.

"We seem to have three immobilized prisoners," said Haid. "One was brought here within the last few hours."

"That would make sense," said Roche, "especially if they thought we were coming. It would be easier to defend one area rather than two."

"So I thought. But the security is tight here. I can't tell which cell is which. And I can't get this damned door open, either."

"Box?"

The AI's voice issued from the drone's speakers: "There is a second entry point which must be accessed simultaneously."

Roche looked around her, then back the way she had come. "What was to the right of the entrance?"

"Another room like this one," Haid said. "Do you want me to—?"

"No, I'll go. Just tell me what I need to do when I get there."

She headed off along the corridor, past the door leading back to where she had left Disisto. Curious, she quickly switched over to the drone's senses to check what was happening.

The image was poor and breaking up, and the drone itself seemed to be lying on the ground with its head to one side. But Roche was able to make out Shak'ni, along with the dirty black mark marring the harsh perfection of the field officer's combat armor. He was holding Disisto by the throat with one hand; the other hand held a rifle to the security chief's head. Disisto's eyes were closed and he was talking furiously. Roche couldn't make out what he was saying, however, as the drone was transmitting visual data only.

B'shan stepped out of the background and said something to Shak'ni. The field officer threw Disisto to the floor, then lowered his rifle and fired at the drone. The transmission abruptly ceased.

The sound of gunfire followed her as she raced to the other control room.

It was a mirror image of the one she had just left.

<Okay, I'm here,> she said.

<Take the left console,> said the Box. She did so. <It's all manual. Key in the following instruction: Bulkhead Release 947. The system will request a password. Type: "Driftglass." You should be seeing a countdown now.>

<Yes.>

<When it reaches zero, hit the green button at the top right of the console. I'll do the same at the other end.>

She waited for the numbers to scroll down from ten, pressing the button impatiently the precise moment the display reached zero. A warning Klaxon sounded and the door opened with a grinding sound. She grabbed her rifle and approached cautiously.

All she saw was another corridor, curving away to her left.

<Careful,> she said to Haid. <I can't make out anything from here. Send the drone first, then Myer.>

Two doors appeared, one each to her left and right. They were both closed. <Box, can you open the internal doors from here?>

Both doors hissed open. Each was comprised of two panels: the outer panel slid aside; the inner one rose up into the ceiling. There was no way to look into one cell without exposing herself to the other. Roche mentally tossed a coin and stepped forward.

The cell on her right was empty, little more than a four-meter-square space. In its center was a stainless-steel bed uncomfortably reminiscent of an autopsy slab. She snap-turned and aimed her gun into the second cell.

It too was empty.

That left two cells, but there were still three prisoners.

She remembered that Galine Four security knew where *she* was, not the others.

<Ameidio, this is our chance. You're coming up on them from behind. I want you to—>

MORGAN, Haid interrupted. THEY HAVE MAII!

<Box, let me see.> She jumped to the other drone's senses.

She saw the young Surin reave strapped to one of the steel "beds." A Kesh guard stood beside her, a pistol pressed firmly to her forehead. The girl seemed oblivious to what was going on around her.

Roche hissed through her teeth. If they hurt her—

"Give up, Roche!" called a voice. "You're surrounded!"

She didn't grace the speaker with a reply. The drone turned its head. There were more guards in the room. All held their guns on Haid, the drone, and Mavalhin. If she ordered Haid to attack, he would probably win—but not in time to save Maii.

There had to be another way . . .

<Box, I think we could use that diversion about now.>

<Yes, Morgan.>

<Just give me a minute to get myself in position, then I'll give you the word.>

<I will ensure that your suit is ready.>

Roche was about to ask the Box what it was readying her *for,* when another voice spoke softly into her mind.

<Morgan?>

<*Maii*? Is that you?>

<Morgan, look . . .>

Maii's voice was little more than a whisper, and through the drone's eyes she looked completely unconscious. But as Roche stared at her, she saw the index finger on the girl's left hand move. She was pointing!

Roche tried to extrapolate the layout of the room, given what the others had looked like. Maii was pointing out the door. Out the door and to the cell opposite—presumably to where the other two prisoners were held.

"You have five seconds, Roche," called the Kesh guard. "Then she dies. Five."

<Okay, Box,> she said. <Tell Uri and Byrne to resume the attack. Blow the piles on the prowlers; send in more of the nano breeders to eat the hull. Hit them with everything we've got, and make sure they hurt. Let's not make it too easy for them.>

"Four."

The sound of footsteps in the control room she had just left echoed up the corridor. <And if you can close the doors behind me, do it.>

The door slammed shut. <I have taken the liberty of closing both, Morgan.>

<Good. Ameidio, are you hearing this?>

YES.

"Three."

She inched as far as she dared around the corridor and clutched her rifle to her chest.

"Two."

<Okay, Box. Now!>

The lights went out. Her suit and implants switched automatically to infrared. Then the floor fell out from underneath her—and *kept* falling.

She clutched for balance, but her suit had already adjusted. The Box must have hit the artificial gravity generators somehow. When some sense of weight returned, it was at half-strength—enough to enable her to run around the corner and to the second cell.

The door was shut; she fired the rifle at it. Gunshots came likewise from the cell containing Maii, followed by the sound of someone hissing in pain. She couldn't afford to be distracted. All she could do was hope that Maii hadn't been hurt.

The cell door juddered open a crack, and she used the suit's strength to lever it the rest of the way. Inside—

She hesitated for a split second.

—inside were two bodies. One belonged to Cane. He was naked and encased entirely in a slab of what looked like clear amber which was in turn bolted to a mobile platform. Wires and tubes were threaded through the transparent material, but there was clearly no way he could talk or move. Metal straps around the amber block further ensured his imprisonment.

His eyes were shut, but somehow Roche knew that he was awake, and possibly even aware of her presence.

The other body belonged to something far from Pristine. It looked vaguely Olmahoi, but unlike any she had ever seen. Its black skin was shiny and abraded, its limbs thin, almost vestigial, its body was hunched, its face featureless and pinched. The only vital element to the entire creature was its epsense organ—a thick tentacle sprouting from the back of its skull. But where most Olmahoi epsense organs were rarely as thick as a normal wrist, this one was thigh-like in width—fat and almost a meter and a half long, throbbing with vitality, almost as if it were sucking the life out of the creature attached to it. Roche could see where needles and other instruments penetrated its flesh, supplying nutrients or performing other mysterious tasks.

The creature lay on a bed like Maii's. It was bound, but not firmly. It seemed to Roche that it didn't need to be. She doubted it could even have walked, let alone run away.

There was a monitor behind it. On it flashed a single word:

: BEWARE

<*The irikeii*!> Roche had never heard the Box sound surprised before.

<The what?>

CLEAR, transmitted Haid from behind her.

Distracted, she turned. <And Maii?>

UNHARMED.

<I have Cane. He—>

She grunted as someone pushed past her.

"Sorry, Morgan," said the Box via the drone. "But I must get through."

Roche faced the drone across the body of the Olmahoi creature. "What the hell are you doing?"

"I am administering Xarodine," explained the Box as the drone injected something into the base of the Olmahoi's skull. "There were doses in Maii's cell, naturally."

The creature twitched, and the word on the screen changed to:

: CRUEL

"*Why,* Box?"

"Xarodine is an epsense-inhibitor."

"I *know* that, but—"

"Give me a moment, Morgan."

A muffled explosion from farther up the hallway reminded her of Shak'ni and the rest of the guards.

"I don't *have* a moment, Box."

She rushed out of the cell. Haid was already there. The sound of pounding came from both ends of the corridor.

WE'RE TRAPPED.

"Any suggestions, Myer?" she called into Maii's cell. "Myer?" Maii was still on the table, although her bonds had been removed. The guards and their weapons lay scattered across the floor. But the pilot was gone.

"He was here a moment ago," Haid said, dispensing with his implants. "He must have snuck out while I was busy with Maii."

"*Damn* him!"

"Do we go after him?"

Roche sighed. "We haven't got time. Besides, we don't even know which way he's gone." She made a mental note to be sure that Myer paid for this at a later date. "Our only chance is to bust out before they're ready. Take them off-guard. One of us will have to carry Maii; maybe we can use the guards' armor to protect her."

"What about Cane?"

She cursed Myer again. "He'll have to wait. He looks safe enough as he is." She went back into Maii's cell and bent to strip one of the dead guards. <Box, when I give the word I want you to open the right-hand door only, okay?>

<Okay, Morgan.>

Her helmeted head brushed Maii's.

<Is that you, Morgan?>

Roche laid a gloved hand on Maii's arm. <I'm right next to you, Maii.>

<It's clearing; I can see again! What happened to the *irikeii*?>

<The *irikeii*?> Remembering what the Box had called the Olmahoi, she dashed into the other cell. The drone was bent over the hunched figure on the bed. The word on the screen now read:

: ONE

<Box, what have you done?>

<Set Maii free. I suggest you use her while you can.>

Another explosion sounded up the corridor just as the word changed to:

: COMES

Then Roche was embraced by the young reave's excited mind. <Morgan! I can read you! I can *read* you!>

<Maii, listen to me: we're in serious trouble here.>

More calmly the girl said: <I know. What can I do to help?>

<Somewhere near here you'll find Shak'ni and B'shan.> Roche felt guilty for pushing the girl so soon, but right now she was their best chance of getting out of there alive. <I want you to knock them out, and anyone with them. Can you do that? Can you reach that far?>

There was a pause before she replied: <I can feel them.>

<Good. Don't kill them; just knock them out.>

<Okay. Give me a second to get my bearings . . .>

Roche checked the charges on her rifle; enough for a while yet. The sounds from the ends of the corridor died down, and she assumed the reave had already begun to work.

Then Maii said: <What does it mean when the destroyer you've been waiting for is right on top of us and ordering us to surrender?>

A chill went through Roche. <Box?>

<I was just about to tell you, Morgan. The *Sebettu* has completed its final approach. It will be within firing range in twenty minutes. Its senior officer has issued a message.>

The recording came through her implants:

AGGRESSORS IN THE VICINITY OF GALINE FOUR: DESIST IMMEDIATELY OR FACE THE CONSEQUENCES. WE WILL NOT HESITATE TO USE LETHAL FORCE. YOU HAVE BEEN WARNED.

That was why the guards had stopped pounding at the doors: they knew they'd won. All they had to do now was wait her out.

<Uri? How are you holding out there?>

<We are continuing to harry the station, Morgan,> replied Kajic. <In an hour or two we would've mopped up the last of the singleships.>

<How do you rate your chances against a Kesh destroyer?>

<Poor,> he admitted. <We could get away, but we'd have no chance of taking it out.>

<Then tell Byrne to get her people the hell away. The Kesh will squash them like bugs.>

<I'll relay your message now,> the ex-captain said. <What would you like me to do?>

She paused. The words burned in her throat. <Get ready to stand down. We're going to surrender.>

<I have a transmission from Field Officer Shak'ni,> said the Box. <It's being broadcast on the outer security level.>

<Play it.>

It was brief: "Come out, Roche, or we *will* destroy you."

ARE WE REALLY GOING TO SURRENDER? asked Haid.

<We haven't a choice with that destroyer there.> She switched the rifle to standby. <Box, tell him he's won. We'll come out peacefully. Just give us a minute.>

She went into the cell and squatted next to Maii.

<Will you be okay?>

The reave's expression was closed. <Yes.>

<You know what I'm thinking?>

<Yes.>

<I'm sorry.>

<Don't be, Morgan.>

<Shak'ni will accept our surrender under some conditions,> the Box said.

<And they are?>

The Kesh officer's voice told her himself: "You, Morgan Roche, and your party will submit to the authority of interim peacemaker Field Officer Shak'ni. All hostilities directed against Galine Four and Linegar Rufo will cease. The *Ana Vereine* will dock with Galine Four and allow Lieutenant Haden B'shan to assume control. All internal systems—including that of Uri Kajic—will become the property of the N'Kor Republic. The Surin reave will be sedated and undergo further Xarodine therapy. The AI you refer to as 'the Box,' serial number JW11110101110, will be ejected from the ship immediately. Any transmissions from said AI will be regarded as a violation of this agreement and as such will incur a penalty: the immediate execution of one of your party, starting with the Surin girl. Further transmissions will result in similar penalties. Do we understand each other?"

Roche didn't answer immediately. She stared at the knotted scar tissue where Maii's eyes had once been. She felt very tired.

<Do you have a backup, Box?>

<Software can be replicated, Morgan, but hardware cannot.>

<And you're prepared to take the risk that they might just blow you out of the sky?>

<If you recall, I am graded to withstand a—>

<—a nuclear strike from a hundred meters,> she finished for the AI. She smiled, despite herself. <I can take that as a yes?>

<You can.>

<Then tell Shak'ni I agree.>

She stood and walked down the corridor, the way she had come. There she found Mavalhin cowering against the door. He started when he saw her, and wouldn't meet her eyes. She didn't care.

<Is everything ready, Box?>

<It is.>

<Then let's get this over with. Open the door.>

Outside the station, an airlock opened on the side of the *Ana Vereine*. A small black valise shot out of it and tumbled in the vague direction of Hintubet. The sun's reddish glow was exacerbated by the hastening collapse of the Gauntlet, but it was still barely bright enough to paint a dull sheen on the battered case.

Roche watched through the *Ana Vereine*'s sensors as a Kesh singleship scooped the valise up with a pair of remote manipulators and took it aboard the *Sebettu*. So distracted was she by the view that the Kesh guard escorting her had to prod her roughly in the bare shoulder with a rifle butt to get her moving faster.

She winced and rubbed the new bruise he had given her. Her capture had been inglorious enough without being made to strip off her armor in front of everyone. Dressed only in her sweaty undersuit and handcuffs, she felt completely naked. That Haid, Disisto, and Mavalhin had been treated similarly didn't make her feel any better. Maii lay back in her cell, her mind suppressed once more by the suffocating effects of the drug Xarodine. The only comfort Roche could take was that Galine

Four's internal gravity generators were still not working properly. The self-destruction of one of the Box's drones right in the very heart of the station had done too much damage, and ambient gravity remained at about half normal.

"Where are you taking us?" she asked.

"The only time you'll speak, Roche," said Shak'ni from behind her, "is to give us information."

INTERROGATION, HUH? Haid broadcast.

<I'd be disappointed otherwise.>

"You will cease any other forms of communication, too," Shak'ni added. "You may only continue to receive information from your ship provided it is non-encrypted."

The procession of guards and captives wound their way to freight elevators, then down into the heart of the station. At least that was something, Roche thought to herself. If they'd been taken to the destroyer, things would've become difficult indeed.

She watched through the *Ana Vereine*'s sensors as the *Sebettu* approached. In design it was little different from other Kesh craft—an odd combination of streamlined and prickly, as though an ordinary spaceship had been half-melted and stretched—but its size was impressive. A dozen Galine Fours would have fit easily into its holds. Its entire surface was pockmarked by retractable weapon emplacements, instrument clusters, and fighter launch bays. The intrasystem engines that brought it to an imposing halt beside the station radiated as much energy as a small sun.

She hoped Byrne had managed to get the outriggers away from the area. The spines were their only hope of survival. Although not capable of slow-jumping out of the Gauntlet, they did at least possess resources that would allow the outriggers to survive in the middle of nowhere.

When Roche realized what she was thinking, it occurred to her how ridiculous it was. The system was due to be totally destroyed in less than a day. Although the collapse of the boundary was initially slow, it would proceed exponentially. The double-jovian system had already succumbed; she had watched it dissolve into the invisible barrier like ice into fire just before the attack had begun. The region of space occupied by Galine Four would be gone in twelve hours. If the outriggers weren't gone by then, no amount of supplies would save them.

All evidence of what had occurred here would be gone forever, she thought. It was the perfect situation in which to conduct a little genocide. . . .

The freight elevator opened opposite a window showing the hanging gardens at the heart of the station. The vibrant green contrasted sharply with the gloom of her situation, but she tried to take hope anyway. All was not yet lost. Not quite.

The guards led her to Rufo's sanctum sanctorum. Its elegance and purity were unchanged, but she admired it less for the corruption she knew it hid. Rufo himself looked old and bitter despite his victory. His speech was rapid and sometimes hard to understand; he paced constantly, and he seemed unable to maintain eye contact with anyone but Haden B'shan; all of which, Roche noticed, he was apparently unaware.

A chair slid out of the floor beside her and she was forced into it. The others were treated likewise, despite Mavalhin's protests. Disisto's expression was tight-lipped, but he said nothing, seemingly confident that things would be sorted out with his boss soon enough. Haid sat straight in his chair and watched everything closely.

"So, Commander Roche." Rufo spoke with the disdain of a reproachful parent, stepping up to Morgan with his hands behind his back. "We meet again. Perhaps you will be more accommodating this time."

"Perhaps you might show me the same courtesy," Roche shot back.

Rufo shrugged, his eyes averted to the floor. "I suppose there were lies on both sides," he acknowledged.

"Who was it that said that there are lies, and then there are damned lies?"

Rufo smiled humorlessly. "I believe the earliest recorded mention of that saying is some two hundred and fifty thousand years ago. The Human condition hasn't changed much in that time, has it?"

"Obviously."

"There will always be optimists whose dreams of a moral society are about as realistic, and as foolish, as those who believe in fate."

"Look, Rufo," said Roche, "we really don't have time for this kind of banter. Why not just get on with it?"

He stopped pacing for a moment, but still his eyes wouldn't meet hers. "Very well," he said. "I want to know everything you know about Adoni Cane. And remember, Field Officer Shak'ni has his instructions, so please, no lies."

Roche had already decided to tell him everything she knew. It wouldn't hurt; he probably knew more than she did, anyway. So she started at the beginning—at Cane's examination on Sciacca's World—and brought him up to date. He nodded constantly, but didn't say anything himself until she had finished.

"And you are satisfied with the explanation that he is a product of the Sol Apotheosis Movement—a Wunderkind, as they were called?"

"Not entirely," she said. "There are inconsistencies."

"Of course there are. We have images of these Wunderkind. They were quite remarkable." A window opened above the desk; in it appeared a figure that looked as if it had been inflated with liquid helium. Its skin was bluish over limbs that bulged alarmingly. The scale next to it showed that it stood almost three meters high. "Do you agree?"

Startled, she didn't know what to say. If Rufo had that image, then presumably COE Intelligence had it too. Why hadn't the Box or her ex-superiors in COE Intelligence failed to notice the disparity between it and the near-perfect Pristine reality of Adoni Cane?

Disisto looked smug. He had been telling the truth after all.

"I don't understand," she managed after a moment or two.

"Obviously." Rufo wandered around the room, touching panels and studying screens as though bored. "We will return to Cane in a moment. For now I wish to talk about the other clone warrior."

"What about him?"

"Did you find him?"

"I doubt I would be here now if I had."

"That's not necessarily true. These creatures may be ruthless, but they aren't stupid. If his purposes were not served by killing you, then he would not do so. That is the only explanation I can deduce for your extended survival while in the company of Adoni Cane."

She couldn't argue that point. "You believe he was among the outriggers," she said.

"Did you see anything to suggest that he might have been?"

She thought about Yarrow. "Not hard evidence as such, no . . ."

"But suspicions?"

She hesitated. "Yes."

Field Officer Shak'ni spoke: "Your cargo hold contains several of these people. Could the clone be among them?"

She shook her head. "They were examined as they boarded. All were ordinary mundanes. Nothing like Cane."

"Then the one we are seeking might be among the others still at large." The Kesh grunted to himself. "We will hunt them down, one by one. If he *is* among them, we will find him."

Roche gritted her teeth. She'd thought that her capture would end the involvement of the outriggers. "They're not to blame. They didn't know—"

"They wouldn't have," said Rufo. "These creatures are chameleonic in their ability to blend in, when they want to. Indeed, that is their primary function: to insinuate. Then to corrupt. Like everything else they do, they do it well."

"You sound like you've studied them for some time," she said.

Her guard nudged her in the shoulder for speaking out of turn, but Rufo waved him away.

"At a distance, yes, but always after the fact. Only recently have people begun to suspect that something might be going on. Highly placed people. The Highest. They have become concerned. There is evidence to suggest that beings like Cane have been emerging for years now throughout the galaxy—far more than the handful you are aware of. Thousands, possibly millions of them. Although the individuals may not be noticed, their effects are. We mundanes do not see them, though; we are entangled in the details, in the data. A superior perspective is required to tease out the trends."

"That's where you got the command language from, then. The High Humans?"

"Yes. One of them or more; I can't tell. Even individually, they have access to information I can only dream of. Together . . ." Rufo seemed to gather himself. "Did Cane respond to the command language, by the way? I presume by your question that you detected it."

"He said he understood fragments but that it didn't make any sense as a whole. It was jumbled, as though whoever put it together didn't know what it meant. And the Box said its syntax wasn't like anything from around here."

Rufo chuckled softly. "Hardly surprising. Those fragments were recorded over half a million centuries ago."

For a moment, Roche was speechless.

It was Mavalhin who spoke: "Bullshit."

The guard clouted him, but the sentiment had been aired.

"I assure you, Myer, it is not," said Rufo. "Although I will admit to a similar skepticism when I first heard that claim. Of course, since then I have learned more than enough to convince me otherwise. The language Cane and his ilk respond to was written when Humanity was a single pure strain—before the Primordial Castes, before the Pristines, before even the High Castes. It is a piece of history, and Cane is an integral part of it."

"What do you intend to do with him?" Roche asked.

"He's not your concern anymore," said Rufo. "He'll be kept as he is until we are ready to study him. And study him we will, I assure you. We intend to learn the precise secrets of his genetic makeup and abilities. We want to know how many there are like him, and where they are headed. We need to know who made him, and, more importantly, *why.*"

"And then," said Shak'ni, "we will kill him."

A martial fanfare echoed through the station, and every Kesh in the room suddenly stiffened.

Rufo visibly paled as the sound of marching feet came from the anteroom. The inner door slid open. The Kesh saluted as an officer entered the room surrounded by a full military escort. Roche swiveled in her seat to look.

The new arrival was easily the tallest and strongest Kesh officer she had ever seen—which in itself was impressive. Dressed in armor not dissimilar to the weapons and ships of the Caste—smooth, concave lines tapering to sharp points at odd places, burnished wood in color—with a retractable helmet bearing insignia Roche had never seen in person before, the Kesh general exuded power, confidence, and ruthlessness in equal portions.

The general stopped in the middle of the room and surveyed its contents.

"Sh'shek hroga vied ra vhul kimosh'n ka," she said, her voice hoarse from an old injury.

"Opulence is a sign of waste," a junior officer translated. "And waste is forbidden."

The general continued, via the translator: "I will be glad when this arrangement is concluded, and the stench of inferior species is gone from my nostrils."

"*Kuresh* Darkan—" Shak'ni began, but the general cut him off.

"This operation has been conducted without honor. You will be disciplined."

Shak'ni nodded stiffly, the red veinlike marks on his face standing out. "As you wish," he said so all could hear and understand.

"General Darkan does not wish to debase herself by speaking to inferiors." The interpreter's face was permanently pinched in distaste. "She grants me permission to speak for her. You—Linegar Rufo. Is debriefing concluded?"

The scientist stepped forward, carefully projecting a passive, respectful demeanor. "We are close to finishing, but—"

"Can their word be trusted?"

"Yes, General," said B'shan. "I have spent enough time with these people to know when they are telling the truth."

The general nodded distantly. "Then we have learned the precise location of the second warrior."

"Not exactly," said Rufo, "but we do have an idea—"

"But we do still have the one called Cane?"

Rufo nodded quickly. "Yes, of course."

"Then we can abandon the other one to his fate," said the interpreter. "We cannot linger here. In seventeen hours this system will be nothing but dust. We will leave the moment we have downloaded the contents of the station's datapool."

"If I may speak," said Shak'ni.

The general nodded without looking at him.

"We have captured a vessel—"

"The *Ana Vereine*," said the interpreter. "Yes, we know."

"It contains many new technologies. We have docked it to this station. It should be retained for study."

"And the AI? What of that?"

"I gave strict instructions that it should be placed under the tightest security. Any transmissions—"

"We are aware of the risks. Any transmissions in either direction will result in its expulsion and destruction. Are you suggesting we keep this, too?"

"It is bounty—"

"What use is a box too dangerous to open? Besides, its technology is irrelevant to us. No intelligence, artificial or otherwise, can equal the Kesh Ideal. Its tricks are worthless and dishonorable."

Roche wanted to ask what the general thought of the High Humans but decided that speaking out of turn was inadvisable.

The general grunted something in the Kesh language, and the interpreter translated: "We will, however, take the ship. It has a working slow-jump drive, and to leave it here would be folly. What purpose it is put to by the Dictatrix is up to her."

"And the captives?" Shak'ni asked.

The general gazed contemptuously across the room, directly into Roche's eyes.

"They will remain here with the others," said the interpreter with a slight smirk. "When the system collapses, they will die."

Rufo stepped forward again. "When you say the others," he said anxiously, "you mean the outriggers, right?"

"Those as well, yes."

"Ah, as well as—?"

"This station and all those upon it, of course."

"But our arrangement—"

The interpreter smiled again. "We have no further use for you, Rufo. You are as inferior as the others. It would be a waste of time and effort to return you to your people. Let *them* save you, if that is what they wish."

"I—" the scientist stammered, fear and hopelessness rising to fill his eyes. He seemed to age decades in an instant. "That is—you cannot—"

"Jin'ek ke yi," sneered the general.

Roche didn't need the interpreter to understand; it was clear from the general's tone and expression. They could do it and they *would.*

"This is insane!" Disisto's voice broke the tension in the room.

The general faced him, nostrils flared in anger. A guard struck him in the back, knocking him to the floor.

"You were not permitted to speak," said the interpreter with a smooth grin.

Disisto picked himself up, wincing. "I don't give a damn! We've done *everything* you asked us to do here. We've worked for you, put ourselves at risk, got you what you wanted—"

The guard whipped an arm around Disisto's throat and tightened his hold until he could no longer speak or even breathe. Dragging the security chief upright, the guard held him motionless, choking.

Waving the interpreter aside, the general crossed the room to face Disisto. "You think us cruel?" she asked.

Something odd stirred in Roche's mind—a feeling of unreality, distancing her from the events unfolding before her.

Disisto was unable to reply. The general gestured, and the guard threw Disisto to the floor. The security chief gasped for air, barely able to rise on all fours, let alone speak coherently. The general reached for the guard's pistol and aimed it at the back of Disisto's head. She fired, once, and Disisto slumped forward.

"Perhaps we are," she said, returning the guard's pistol.

Roche's vision went blank; all she could see were the words that had flashed one by one on the *irikeii*'s display.

: BEWARE

: CRUEL

: ONE

: COMES

And all she could smell was the blood pooling around Disisto's body.

"N'hok vi ha'kahri tsen!"

Roche snapped out of it. She looked around, trying to find the source of the exclamation, but at first was unable to.

The general's anger was tempered by her own surprise.

"Who dares claim the Right?" asked the interpreter.

"Ri," said Haid, standing. "I do."

"Outrageous!"

Roche was as shocked as anyone. "Ameidio, what are you—?"

"Vask!" The general ordered the room to silence; even those unfamiliar with the language knew what she was demanding. She stepped up to Haid. "Do you realize what it is you do, little man?"

"*Du.* I claim the Warrior's Right to challenge a superior's decision by formal combat."

"And who made *you* a Warrior?"

"Sh'manit Dro, the Sixteenth and last G'rodo Matriarch."

General Darkan hissed through her teeth. "A disgraced lineage."

Haid nodded. "But a lineage all the same," he said. "Or perhaps you are unprepared for such a challenge?"

"We are *always*—"

"Then name a champion to defend your honor," said Haid smoothly. "Unless you choose to fight yourself."

The general sneered in open disdain. "I would not demean myself with such a fight. I would stand to lose more honor than I could possibly hope to gain."

"I will fight him, General," said Lieutenant-Doctor Haden B'shan. "With your permission, of course."

The general rounded on Shak'ni's junior officer. "Clearly you have spent *too much* time with these people, Lieutenant. There is no time for these games."

B'shan nodded in agreement. "Nevertheless, he knows the traditions, he speaks the Tongue. I believe his claim to be a legitimate one."

The general snorted. "It is your decision, Lieutenant. I will not intervene should you wish to debase yourself thus."

"Yes, but will you honor the victor?" Haid asked.

The general glowered at Haid, her eyes filled with contempt. "You confuse your capabilities with your dreams," she said shortly. Then: "But should B'shan succumb to that dream, then yes, you *will* have earned the Right."

"Your name on it?"

"My name on it." The general indicated her interpreter and guards. "And these are my witnesses."

Haid bowed stiffly. "Where do we fight?" he asked. "Here?"

The general thought for a moment, then continued in her native tongue: "On the way here we passed an enclosed area with several observation points; a garden of some kind. That will do." Then to B'shan, she said, "You can fight while we download this station's data and free the bounty ship from its chattel." It took Roche a moment to realize that the general was referring to the outriggers in the hold. "We will leave the moment this farce has ended."

Haid nodded, apparently satisfied.

"Ameidio—" Roche began.

"Quiet!" Her guard pressed her back into the seat.

"There is no time left for discussion," the general said. "I want the data transfer to commence as soon as possible. Any physical resources we have contributed to this station will be returned to the *Sebettu* immediately. However"—she swept the Humans in the room with a warning glance—"a full contingent will remain on board to ensure against further foolishness. Field Officer Shak'ni, you will see personally to the neutralization of the Olmahoi and Surin epsense adepts. They and the clone must be ready to move in one hour. And this time I want no loose ends."

Shak'ni bowed and stalked out of the room, casting a baleful glance at Roche as he went.

The general allowed herself a chuckle as she spoke to her interpreter.

"The two Warriors will have a moment to reflect upon the import of the task ahead while they wait for the weapons to arrive," he translated. "The rest of you may clean *this* up." He pointed at Disisto's body. "If you wish," he added, then turned to follow the general as she strode heavily from the room. B'shan silently followed.

Mavalhin was instantly on his feet. "Congratulations, Rufo," he spat. "You've managed to get us all killed!"

The old scientist didn't respond. All he could do was stand and stare blankly at the body of his security chief.

"The Kesh drive a hard bargain," Haid said. "The moment you think you've got a fair deal, it's time to check the fine print."

Roche put her hand on his arm; his biomesh was sharp and cold to the touch. "Why are you doing this, Ameidio?"

"Because I've always wanted to, and I figure this might be my last chance."

"Be serious—"

"No, I am. You've seen the way the Kesh are. They're impossible to deal with. Anybody who spends any time with them ends up tiptoeing around to avoid causing a fuss. It wears thin after a while. Even the G'rodo were like that; better than most, in a lot of ways, but in the end just as annoying. It's nice to get your own back, just once."

She sighed. "Well, what about the weapons? Do you get a choice?"

He shook his head. "When you invoke an ancient rite, you get what you're given."

She stared at him for a long moment. "This is insane."

"Perhaps, but we don't really have many options open to us, do we? Unless you have a plan you haven't let me in on yet?" When she didn't answer, he smiled and said: "Then I guess we go with my idea."

Roche muttered under her breath as she turned away from Haid; she faced Rufo and said: "Rufo, you're still the chief around here, for what it's worth. How about getting someone in to take Disisto away? I think he deserves better than this, don't you?"

Rufo nodded numbly and moved over to the console. He spoke briefly to someone outside and, moments later, the Kesh guard let a medical stretcher through. Disisto's body was bagged up and taken away. Nothing was said by anyone throughout the process; everyone just stood and watched in silence.

"How long do we have?" said Roche after the doors had closed again.

Haid shrugged. "I don't know. The longer the better. Even artificial limbs need time to limber up."

Roche stepped over to Rufo. "Is there anything else I should know?" she asked. "Cane is older than I originally thought; the command language has been coming from the High Humans . . . Anything at all?"

He looked up at her with eyes empty of anything but despair. "What difference does it make now?"

"Spare me your self-pity," she snapped. "Now *talk* to me! Do you have any contact names for the High Humans? Or possible suspects for the people who made Cane? There must be *something* else!"

Rufo stared vacantly into space. Then he said: "Introns."

"What?"

"Check Cane's introns."

"I don't even know what you're talking about."

"We took a tissue sample before we put Cane into hibernation," he said. "It looks like yours or mine on the surface; it has the same ratio of introns to exons. You see, introns are part of everyone's genetic code; the junk parts, the filler. The exons do all the work. We assumed the differences lay in the exons, so we concentrated on those areas. But there was something about the introns—something unusual. We haven't had the time to look at them properly. You could start there." He stopped, the beginnings of a hopeful gleam in his eye abruptly extinguished. "But you won't have time either, will you? You can't even get a message outside to let someone else know."

Mavalhin made a noise of disgust from behind him. Roche ignored it.

"Is that all?" she said.

He shook his head. "You know as much as I do, now. Frightening how little it is, don't you think?"

Roche could only agree.

It wasn't long before the Kesh returned. Haid had been warming up for just ten minutes when B'shan walked in.

"Why are *you* doing this?" Roche asked, stepping in front of him. "I thought you were better than the others."

"At least this way you'll have a chance," he said evenly.

Up close Roche found the Kesh lieutenant's skin almost beautiful: his blue and purple markings looked like tribal tattoos applied by a skilled ink-worker. For all his leanings toward mundane culture, it wasn't difficult to believe that he could descend to such barbarism.

She stepped out of the way. "You're both fools," she said.

B'shan faced Haid across the room, and bowed. They exchanged a handful of words in the Kesh language, then bowed again.

"He has consented to allow me use of my implants," Haid said to Roche.

"Otherwise I fear the battle would be somewhat one-sided," B'shan explained.

Roche shuddered at the idea of Haid stripped back to nothing but flesh. He would have been utterly helpless, a cripple.

"The general will permit those of you who wish to observe to do so," B'shan went on, addressing everyone. "You are, after all, witnesses to her oath, and we must ensure she carries it out. Combat will commence in five minutes."

"What about the weapons?" Roche directed the question at Haid, but it was B'shan who answered:

"There will be no armor, powered or passive. There will be nothing but the druh."

"That's the weapon we'll be given," explained Haid. "Not much more use than a pocketknife, really."

"Even a pocketknife can kill," said B'shan.

"I know. I've tried it."

B'shan straightened. At full stretch, he had about thirty centimeters on Haid, and he looked considerably stronger. While Roche didn't doubt her friend's agility under the best circumstances, fighting in half-g with unfamiliar implants was hardly optimal.

Instead of saying anything more, B'shan simply bowed again and left the room. Haid followed, casting a reassuring look at Roche as he passed. When he had gone, the guards indicated that the others should also leave.

As Roche walked out the room, Mavalhin stepped in beside her.

"I hope you know what you're doing, Morgan," he hissed.

She frowned. "What do you mean?"

"Well, you're up to something, right? This is all a ruse of some kind."

She turned on him sharply. "Don't look to me to get you out of your own stupid situations, Myer. And don't bother trying to say it was me that got you into this mess, either. You jumped at the chance to join me when it looked like I was going somewhere—just like you did back at College." For a moment she felt vertigo, as though reliving her dream of falling. "Take control of your own life, Myer, and leave me to sort out mine."

He backed away, face flushed with anger and embarrassment. She didn't care. He meant nothing to her. All she wanted to do was talk to the Box. But she couldn't. The slightest attempt to do so would result in its destruction, as well as Maii's execution. If the Kesh detected any transmissions, it would be expelled into space and fired upon from a dozen different directions. No matter what sort of firepower it was rated to stand, that was going to hurt. . . .

They didn't have to walk far. The general had ordered the garden windows to be smashed; there seemed no reason to maintain the delicate ecosystem any longer. Rufo's dismay only increased when he saw the damage. The corridor surrounding the garden now more resembled a gallery, with both Kesh and mundanes curious to see what would happen. Word had obviously spread.

When the two combatants stepped into the garden, a small cheer went up. Roche wasn't sure for whom the cheer was intended; maybe it was just for the spectacle itself. Haid and B'shan stood on one of several mesh walkways crisscrossing the garden. Where the bottom was, Roche couldn't see; far enough below for a fall likely to be lethal, she imagined.

The general clapped her hands once. Haid and B'shan held curved bronze-colored swords in their left hands, each barely as long as the average Pristine forearm. They were intricately carved with elongated Kesh characters that made no sense to Roche. Haid raised his to kiss the narrow guard, and bowed to the general.

"Sh'ten dri ka," he called. "By the blade!"

"To the death," B'shan responded, also bowing.

"Begin!" rasped the general, and the two men faced each other.

They stood two meters apart, and were wary at first. Haid tested both his reach and B'shan's defenses by darting forward twice to slash at the Kesh's exposed side, but B'shan parried with ease. The third time Haid tried it, B'shan counterattacked with a quick stab, only to catch a boot to the side for his troubles. The kick didn't even wind him, but it did take him by surprise. Roche could see the Kesh lieutenant hesitate, reassessing his opponent.

Then the combat truly began. Later she would recall a hail of thrusts, stabs, and sweeping slashes from B'shan as he sought to overwhelm Haid's defenses. The ex-mercenary was hard-pressed to keep up, parrying with his one good arm and relying on a more clumsy artificial limb to keep his balance. Twice B'shan's druh caught Haid's biomesh, parting several strands and slicing shallowly into flesh. It was difficult to tell through the blood, but Haid's implants didn't seem to be affected. He certainly didn't display any sign of weakness. Apart from the odd moment when his guard was down, he fought as well as ever.

It was clear from the outset, though, that he was no match for the Kesh officer. B'shan went for his kidneys, and Haid only just managed to block the blow. Barely had he recovered his balance when the druh swept in to slash his throat. He staggered backwards, ducking just out of reach. A halfhearted stab in the general direction of B'shan's sword arm failed to connect, and he was struggling for his life again.

Roche felt that her friend's only hope lay in superior agility. B'shan had power to spare, able to hammer blows with an emphasis Haid couldn't possibly match, but the Kesh's size left him clumsy. A couple of times Haid gained ground by encouraging him to overextend, permitting a nimble stab from below, or a quick shove to put him off balance. At times like this, with B'shan forced onto his back foot, Haid made ground.

But that ground was soon lost. Roche knew that unless fortune smiled upon him, Haid would ultimately fall.

Her knuckles gripped the windowsill as Haid endured another blistering barrage from the Kesh. Above him, the general watched impassively, her expression almost one of boredom. For the most part the fight was conducted in silence, apart from the ringing of metal on metal, the various sounds of exertion, and the occasional call of encouragement from the spectators. Both men were breathing heavily, although the Kesh's smooth skin was almost entirely sweat-free.

B'shan had almost managed to back Haid to the end of the walkway when Haid miscalculated. Knowing that he was about to be cornered, the ex-mercenary needed to find space. There were only two options: another walkway, or pushing through B'shan and out the other side. For once, Haid took the offensive, summoning every last iota of energy to put B'shan off his stroke. The moment he had an opening, he leapt onto the guardrail and sprang for the next walkway down.

It almost worked. The move took B'shan by surprise, just long enough for Haid to avoid the slash that followed him. He managed the leap well enough, his artificial legs being more than up to the task in half-gravity. It was the landing he fumbled, stumbling heavily and throwing out his good arm to break his fall.

Roche heard the crack before she saw what had happened. The walkway he'd left partially obscured his new position, and a few seconds passed before she found a better viewpoint. By the time she reached it, he was on his feet, holding his broken arm to his stomach. The sword was in the hand of his new arm. He flexed it, eyes seeking another way out as B'shan followed him across the gap.

Eyes seeking *her,* Roche realized. He was waiting for her to save him.

But there was nothing she could do.

As B'shan straightened warily, druh at the ready in case Haid attacked while he recovered from the leap, a whistle echoed across the leafy space. It came from the general and her entourage, a Kesh version of the warning sirens associated with mundanes. The general held a whispered conversation with her interpreter, then looked pointedly across the garden to Roche.

"Morgan Roche!" the general's voice boomed. "Would you care to explain why we are once again under attack?"

Everything stopped, and all eyes turned to look at her as the general continued:

"I have just received word that a number of outrigger all-suits have been seen approaching this location in attack formation. I suppose you know nothing about this?"

"I don't, I swear!" And it was the truth. Roche genuinely had no idea what was going on. Another attack by the outriggers? What was Auditor Byrne up to?

"Gah!" The general turned away, disgusted, back to Haid and B'shan. The two had backed away from each other during the interruption, although B'shan still stood with his weapon raised, as though unsure whether to continue. For a moment Roche was certain he would press home his advantage while the chance remained. But he didn't.

Haid grinned up at Roche, and nodded his thanks.

Roche could only stare dumbstruck back at him.

"This farce is at an end!" the general declared. "There will be no further distraction, and no more leniency. Lieutenant, your weapon." The general indicated the druh in B'shan's hand. The Kesh threw it expertly across and up to his superior, who caught it with one strong hand. She waved vaguely in Roche's direction. "Bring her to me."

Roche realized what she meant when the general's bodyguards began converging on her. She looked around for some way to escape, but every exit was blocked. A circle formed around her as she backed away. Strong hands grabbed her from behind and dragged her to where the general waited, druh at the ready.

"It is bad luck to wield a blade without bloodying it," the general said. She pointed at the ground before her, and Roche was pushed onto her knees. She struggled but could do nothing to prevent being forced facedown onto the ground at the general's feet.

"Morgan!" Haid's voice echoed up from the gardens. She realized he couldn't see what was going on, and was glad to be spared that indignity.

"Ameidio!" she called back. "Do what the Box says—take the *Ana Vereine*—tell Maii—!"

A boot connected with the side of her head to silence her, and her mouth filled with blood.

She heard the general curse her in the Kesh native tongue. She sensed the blade being raised. She closed her eyes and waited for the blow.

Into the expectant hush, a woman's voice spoke.

"General Darkan!" said the voice. It came over Galine Four's public address system and seemed to echo from everywhere at once. "Surrender control of the *Sebettu* immediately or I shall overload its primary generator and send you all to hell!"

Roche heard the general hiss. "Who is this? What is the meaning—"

"You have thirty seconds to think about it. If I don't have an answer by then, I will make good my promise."

The general roared. Roche, forgotten for the moment, dared to breathe again.

"I do not listen to threats!"

"Then listen to this: I have instructed your cooling systems to shut down. In five minutes a chain reaction will begin that cannot be stopped. Your primary generator *will* blow if you don't give me a reason to reverse the instruction. There is nothing you can do to stop it, except to hand over control to me. It's as simple as that. You now have twenty seconds left."

"How is this possible?" the general roared, but for the first time Roche detected a hint of fear in her voice. "How are you doing this?"

"*How* I am doing this is irrelevant. Know only that I *am* doing it, and give me control of your ship!"

"Never!" The booming voice was defiant, but the general's expression was full of uncertainty.

"Then mine will be the last voice any of you will ever hear."

"Who *are* you?" barked the general.

"I'm the one everybody has been looking for, General," said the voice. "But I suspect you already knew that."

Roche's head reeled: *female*?

There was a long silence from the general, then:

"No," said the general. "I would rather die than let you loose on an unsuspecting galaxy."

"So be it," said the woman. "You have five minutes to make peace with Asha, General. I suggest you make good use of that time."

"You are bluffing!" the general hissed, but neither the clone warrior nor Morgan Roche was listening.

INTERLUDE

While under Xarodine, the universe was a very different place.

What little he could see was far off and blurred. The only minds close to him belonged to the Shining One and the abomination. The latter also labored under the epsense-inhibiting drug, coiling around herself like a restless snake, while the former appeared to be sleeping. Certainly his thought patterns were passive and his sensory inputs minimal. Yet the dark speck at the heart of his glare was still active, and through this speck some of the outside world leaked in.

The enigma had been taken away. The other Shining One had come closer. The Cruel One, too, had appeared to put fear into the hearts of her servants. Things were coming to a head, that was for certain, and he was frustrated to be kept at arm's-length from it, trapped in a fog of Xarodine.

Then someone appeared. It was a mind he had encountered before: petty, brittle, filled with self-doubt and hatred for all others. This mind came on a mission from the Cruel One: to take the Shining One elsewhere and to neutralize the other prisoners. Those were his orders, and he would fulfill them to the letter. It was either that or face further dishonor. And as far as this Kesh officer was concerned, dishonor was worse than death.

"Neutralize" meant kill. That much he could glean from the mind bearing down on him. But it was with some relief that he contemplated the imminence of his demise, for it would also mean the end of the abomination.

The officer spoke briefly to the guards, who admitted him to the secure compound with an escort and closed the doors behind him. Nothing, even now, was being left to chance.

The officer checked the cocoon within which the Shining One rested. All was well there, it seemed. Various instruments and controls were prepared for travel, and an internal supply was activated. From that moment on, the Shining One became independent of everyone around him. Thus encased, he could survive several hours in a complete vacuum until the gel boiled away, and, if rescued in time, emerge unscathed.

Not that the officer thought such precautions were necessary. He refused to believe that the captive could be superior to a Kesh warrior. The events he had witnessed in recent weeks he put down to luck, or the element of surprise. Pristines made poor warriors in his eyes, and he found their slaughter an unremarkable thing. All it would take was planning and persistence—the twin virtues of Kesh military dogma.

When gunfire sounded from the other side of the security compound's already battle-scarred doors, the Kesh officer thought for a moment that he was hearing things. There was no resistance left in the station; the Cruel One had everything under control. What could possibly have gone wrong?

The Kesh officer wheeled the Shining One into the hallway and ordered his escort to guard the cocoon. When he tried to speak to the guards outside, only one of the two groups monitoring the double doors answered; the other was under attack by an unknown number of assailants.

Remembering his other captives, the Kesh officer tried more esoteric means to find out what was going on. He had already decided not to call for reinforcements until he was sure what he was up against; he did not want to risk the general's further displeasure.

"How many are there?" he asked, manipulating the pain-givers.

The minds of the guards under siege—imprecise and vague through the drug—saw only a single attacker, and then only fleetingly.

: ONE

"Who is it?"

That one's mind didn't register at all.

: NO ONE

"Don't play games with me—"

The Kesh officer stopped, for the sound of gunfire at the entrance had ceased. But the silence didn't last long: a moment later it began at the other entrance, where the second group of guards waited.

"Who *is* that?"

: NO ONE

: ABOMINATION

: KILL

"Bah! You're talking rubbish."

Still the officer hesitated to call for help. He was sure he and his guards could deal with a single assailant. The interior of the security compound would be easier to defend than the exterior, and he made sure his escort was ready for anything. They would put the three prisoners in one cell and seal it shut. That way the intruder would be at a disadvantage, not knowing which cell to aim for and therefore where to direct his attack.

Then it occurred to the officer that the welfare of two of his prisoners was irrelevant. They could even be used to his advantage. The officer ordered the Shining One to be locked securely away once more and the other two to be brought out into the hallway.

Again the gunfire ceased. The Kesh officer tensed. It was theoretically impossible for one person to open the doors, but he didn't dare believe that would be the end of it.

Sure enough, the doors clanked and began to open. Barely a second had passed and the officer was at the nearest door, ready to repel the intruder. All he saw, though, was one of his own guards, sitting at the console to the door with some sort of device strapped to his chest.

"He made me, I swear—I—!" he babbled.

Then the device exploded.

But the Kesh officer was already running back to the captives. He had been fooled; the intruder was coming in the other door!

Through the smoke and dust, he saw the flash of a weapon, and the last member of his escort tumbled to the floor. He watched in some panic as a tall, silver-armored warrior stepped over the bodies to survey the scene.

The Kesh officer hissed, choking on a growing sense of failure. He warned that he would shoot the prisoners if the warrior did not immediately retreat.

Seemingly unconcerned by the officer's threat, the warrior raised his weapon to target the Kesh.

Howling a Kesh battle cry, the officer fired indiscriminately, striking prisoners and warrior alike. The great silver figure staggered back under the power of the officer's ceremonial firearm. A lucky shot knocked the assailant's weapon aside and cracked the seal of the silver armor at the shoulder. Concentrating on that point, the officer fired three more shots in quick succession, knocking the assailant to the ground.

A silver arm skidded across the floor, severed by the final shot.

Hope returned to the Kesh officer's mind like fresh air through the smoke. He stepped forward to survey the carnage. Both stretchers had spilled their contents to the floor: the Surin reave had sustained an injury to her legs, and the Olmahoi creature was bleeding from a wound in its abdomen. He would put an end to their suffering in a moment, once he was certain that the intruder was dead.

The silver armor was the same as that worn by Roche and one of her companions when she had been captured. This one, he assumed, must have been stolen before they could be taken to the *Sebettu* for examination. It had been irreparably damaged, missing its right arm from the shoulder down, and now lay inert facedown against a wall.

He nodded in satisfaction, although a new anger rose. Heads would roll for the theft not to have been reported. The occupant of the suit had fought well against insurmountable odds; almost as well as a Kesh . . .

The officer stared in horror as the suit suddenly rolled over. Its left arm scrabbled for its fallen weapon and, before he could react, fired two shots. Falling to his knees, the Kesh clutched at his stomach, feeling the life ebb with his blood out onto the floor.

As his executioner turned away, the dying Kesh caught a perfect view of the interior of the suit, through the hole where its right arm would have been.

His eyes bulged even further as he keeled forward to die on the floor.

The suit was empty.

There were no minds left to view what happened in the secure compound. Only the Shining One remained, and he saw nothing through those eyes.

He felt his body lifted back onto the stretcher, but it had already become distant—even more so than usual. And the foggy sense that remained of his usual all-pervading sight was itself fading. As blood rushed out of his body and drained from his uniquely developed epsense organ, darkness pressed in.

The light of the Shining One was fading. As he watched it dwindle, unafraid, a voice spoke:

<I'm sorry.>

He had forgotten about the abomination. They must have been close for their drug-crippled minds to touch.

<I would ease your pain, were there any pain to ease. But you don't feel anything at all, do you?>

She was right. Apart from when his body had been tortured in order to gain information, he had had no care for it at all.

Yet here he was, dying because of its injuries. He would be glad for an end to this life. Without his people, without the Grand Design, he was nothing.

His only sadness was that he was dying alone.

<You aren't alone,> she said, and her mind touched his more firmly. He could not resist the abomination, nor did he want to. She offered herself to him, another mind to cling to, alone in the dark as he was, and he welcomed her reassuring touch.

He *was* comforted. That much was true, despite himself. And he wondered if the feeling was mutual as together they spiraled ever steeper down into the dark . . .

8

Galine Four
'955.01.24 EN
0550

The vision came as a concentration of thoughts and words, of memories too, and its intrusion was as intense as it was abrupt. It had traveled so many routes on its way to her that its details were indistinct. But it could not be denied. It blossomed in Roche's mind with the intensity of an outrigger Plenary minus the auditor's guiding hand.

She saw a war. That much was obvious. A war so big that the galaxy burned for centuries, and trillions of lives were extinguished in a bloodbath never to be equaled.

Half a million years later, she watched as the events blossomed rapidly in her mind, with the war's political machinations unfurling like the bloodied petals of a flower. Peace returned to the galaxy only after hundreds of novae had added their heavier elements to the dust clouds, and one of the opposing armies was defeated.

But even then it did not end. The vanquished had foreseen their fate and had prepared for their revenge—a revenge which would take place long after they had been forgotten by those who had eradicated them.

Roche saw a cloud of tiny machines erupt from the galactic spiral and dissipate away from the inhabited areas, into the outer depths. Their exact number was unknown, but they numbered in the millions at least. Traveling well below the speed of light, the machines did not have the momentum to quite escape the gravitational pull of the galaxy, although they did travel vast distances from the core.

Before long the great war was forgotten, buried by time and lost to more immediate conflicts; but the machines continued to hurtle to the darkest edges of the galaxy. Memories of their makers faded too, their legend dissolving into little more than a curiosity for scholars, and eventually forgotten altogether; and still the machines continued to travel on. . . .

Eventually their velocity decreased and, as it did, they gathered mass—atom by atom, molecule by molecule. And as their orbits pulled them back to the denser regions where they had originated, they began to build. Each one became a capsule. And within each capsule, a life was born.

These lives would burn bright and fast, and, in burning, they would find revenge.

The Sol Apotheosis Movement and its followers had nothing to do with this plan; they were nothing more than a convenient cover. Yes, they had existed, and had been slaughtered at the hands of their united neighbors; they had indeed chosen for their base system one that had long been associated with ancient Humanity, although it was now fallow; and they might well have conceived such a plan for revenge, although they lacked the skills and subtlety to put it into action.

The name Adoni Cane had nothing to do with them. That name was as old as the ancient war itself. Other such names fell effortlessly into Roche's thoughts: Vani Wehr, Sadoc Lleshi, Jelena Heidik, Ralf Dreher, and more. Each had played a role in the events at the dawn of time; each had been marked by the vanquished for revenge; each had a role to play in the times to come.

This was what Linegar Rufo feared: a plan far older and more widespread than anyone had suspected. And this was the knowledge the *irikeii* had given Maii, and which she in turn gave Roche.

When it was over, nothing remained of the young reave in Roche's mind. It felt strangely empty, hollow. Why had Maii only managed to send her that one mind-dump and nothing more? Roche shook her head to clear her thoughts. But try as she might to deny the possibility that something bad had happened to the girl, the emptiness in her mind continued to fill her with concern.

She lay on her side at the feet of the Kesh guards. No one seemed to be paying her any attention, for which she was thankful if not a little surprised. Then she remembered the clone warrior, and she realized that compared to *her,* Roche was no threat at all.

Some time had passed, but she had no idea exactly how much until she heard the general boom:

"Five minutes are up! She has nothing to bargain with—*nothing*! Just more games to waste my time!"

"General, someone *did* infiltrate our cooling systems," she heard the translator say. "If we are still alive it's only because they don't want to destroy their only way out of here."

"Then she *still* has nothing! *We* control the *Sebettu*; until that changes, we will not negotiate. Let her attack! It will do her no good."

It took Roche a second to realize that the general was speaking in the Kesh tongue but that she could still understand what she was saying.

"Is the download complete?"

"Yes, General. The last of the data was transferred twenty minutes ago."

"Then why are we lingering in this accursed place? Instruct all personnel to return to the *Sebettu* for immediate departure!"

A voice began talking over the station's PA system, repeating the general's order in the Kesh tongue. At this the guards near Roche moved off; after they had gone she managed to sit up, fighting dizziness and the aches all over her body. The general was some distance away around the curve of the corridor. She frowned for a moment, confused as to how she had been able to hear the general conferring with the other Kesh. Then she realized that the translation of the general's words had been coming through her implants.

<Box? Is that you?>

<Yes, Morgan. I have been—>

A roar of fury from the general cut across anything else the AI might have said.

"That incompetent fool! If there were time I would have Shak'ni skinned for this!" The general rounded on her aides, who backed out of arm's reach. "I've had enough of this stupidity! Leave him behind. Leave *all* of them behind! We will erase this place from our memories!"

The general stalked off, the booming of her boots along the corridor receding quickly into the distance. Roche suddenly found herself alone.

She clambered stiffly to her feet. Her neck and back hurt where the guard had held her, and a bump had already formed on her skull.

<Box, what have you gotten us into now?>

<Nothing untoward, Morgan. Our plan worked as expected. The program my drone placed in the security shell of this station was successfully transferred with the rest of the data to the *Sebettu,* where it has allowed me to communicate unnoticed. I now have full control of this station and complete access to the data Linegar Rufo collected.>

Roche didn't have the heart to tell the Box that she'd come across most of that data by other means. <And the *Sebettu*?>

<The destroyer remains outside my reach. It too has been fitted with a Tipper-Linke chaos-lock to ward against intrusion.>

<But the generator—>

<I only made it appear that the cooling systems had been shut down. If someone checks manually—as no doubt they will—they will realize the truth.>

<And the clone warrior? Does she know about this?>

<She goes by the name of Jelena Heidik.> Roche recalled the name from Maii's mind-dump. <Ours was a temporary alliance, nothing more. I needed a distraction and knew she would be willing to pool resources. Auditor Byrne and I gave her the empty all-suits left over from the attack. She was allowed to think that she was acting to meet her own ends, when in fact she was serving mine. There was no great risk.>

<So you say.> Roche didn't dare believe it would be that easy. <What about Maii?>

<She is presently in a coma, but will recover. My remaining drone was able to prevent Field Officer Shak'ni from killing her and making off with Cane. They are both being moved from the secure compound to the *Ana Vereine* as we speak.>

Relief flooded through her. <And the—what was it? *Irikeii*?>

<Is dead.> There was no hint of regret in the Box's tone. <Under normal circumstances it acts as a counterbalance to the Olmahoi Caste's natural epsense abilities. The thought-world they create, their Grand Design, is fragile and would, unchecked, spiral into disorder. The *irikeii* absorbs and behaves as a passive sink for spurious thoughts in its vicinity. That, clearly, is why General Darkan had it kidnapped and brought here. Had it not—>

<Enough, Box. What does it mean to Maii?>

<Her normal epsense abilities will return the moment she awakens. I estimate that to be in about fifteen hours.>

<Then . . .> Roche stopped, hearing footsteps approaching.

It was Haid. "Morgan!" The ex-mercenary held out his new arm to grip her shoulder. "Are you all right?"

She almost laughed. "Me? What about *you*? Your *arm* is broken."

"Just another reminder of how poor flesh and blood actually is," he said. "But I'll live." The fingers on his artificial arm flexed. "These toys didn't perform so badly after all."

"I guess not."

Haid looked around; there was a cut to his cheek she hadn't noticed before, oozing thick blood. "The Kesh are pulling out all over the station. B'shan went with them. He asked me to tell you that he regretted what had happened. I think he might even have meant it."

"Yeah? Well apologies won't help us much at the moment," she said brusquely, but it did surprise her. It wasn't like a Kesh to apologize for anything, whether he meant it or not. "Cane and Maii are on their way to the *Ana Vereine*, so we'll join them there. When things settle down we can talk about getting the station out of the system. If Uri thinks the ship is up to it, we might be able to translate the entire thing, otherwise we'll just have to ferry the people out in lots."

Haid nodded. "The boundary's getting closer by the second. Round trips will become progressively quicker."

"And the holds should still be full of outriggers; that'll save time. Once we pick up Byrne and the others, we'll be done."

"What about the *Sebettu*?"

She shrugged. "We let it go. It's too big to take on directly, and if they leave peacefully I see no reason to pick a fight. We'll just have to settle our scores at a later date, I guess."

<General Darkan has just left Galine Four,> the Box announced. <Two more shuttle craft are still docked. When they disengage, the last of her staff will have left.>

"Is that the Box?" asked Haid, tapping one ear. "How did you manage that?"

Roche's stomach sank as a realization struck her. The Box! "Oh, hell. The Box is still on the *Sebettu*!"

<That is correct,> said the AI. <But do not concern yourself with my safety, Morgan.>

"What about the data?"

<I have already transferred it to the *Ana Vereine*. The important thing is that you survive. I am not irreplaceable.>

That was probably the closest thing to humility that she had ever heard from the Box. "Don't be such a martyr, Box. We'll get you back if we can. Tell Uri to warm up the drives. We're coming now."

Haid hurried after her as she strode for the nearest transit cab. Rufo tried to get her attention as she passed, but she ignored him. Myer Mavalhin was more persistent. He trailed them to the cab and squeezed inside after them, apologizing hastily when he brushed against Haid's broken arm. The ex-mercenary was still holding the druh in one clenched fist, and made sure Mavalhin knew it.

"Morgan!" the pilot panted. "Where are you going in such a hurry?"

"None of your business, Myer."

"Are you leaving?"

"Not just yet."

"Then where—?"

"She said it was none of your business." Haid's expression darkened and the blade twitched.

"Okay, okay." Mavalhin receded into the cab, and for a second Roche thought he might've finished. But as they crossed the glitch in ambient gravity—made even more disorienting by the damage to the generator—he started again.

"Can I come with you?"

She turned on him. "Myer, don't you listen to anything I say? I told you to leave me alone."

"No, you told me to take control of my life. Which is what I'm doing." He consciously straightened. "I've decided that I want to serve with you on the *Ana Vereine*. It's the right thing to do, I know it. Our destinies lie together, Morgan. You can't say no."

"Can't I?"

The cab slid to an abrupt halt and the doors opened. They were on the outermost level, close to the major docking bays.

<Morgan, the last of the shuttles has docked with the *Sebettu.*>

They entered a large disembarkation point similar to the one through which they had first entered the station. Roche was reminded of Disisto, whose job it had been to maintain security in this area, and felt a twinge of regret.

<How long until the Kesh leave?>

<Soon. The chief engineer has confirmed that there is nothing wrong with the primary generator's cooling system and declared the destroyer fit to travel. There is nothing I can do to prevent its departure. It would be best for you to let me go.>

<Is that what you want me to do, Box?>

<Yes.>

<Why? Does this further some secret plan you've hatched?>

<Quite the opposite, in fact, Morgan.>

<Then be quiet. You were built by the Crescend for a purpose; it would be remiss of us not to at least *try* to get you back.> Mentally turning her back on the AI she spoke to Kajic: <Uri? Hail the *Sebettu.* Tell them we want the Box back and we're prepared to negotiate.>

<Okay, Morgan.> The ex-captain of the *Ana Vereine* sounded glad to hear her voice.

An inner airlock hissed open and they passed through a cramped umbilical. At the far end, the *Ana Vereine*'s outer hatch hung open, waiting for them. Roche felt a strong sensation of relief to finally be back on board. The sepia walls and earthy tones had begun to feel almost like home.

<Morgan,> said Kajic, <are you aware someone is following you?>

Roche turned to see Mavalhin crossing the threshold.

He smiled sheepishly and stopped halfway. "Well, you didn't actually *say* I couldn't come."

"You're right." She strode back to face him and stared him in the eye.

"Does that mean I'm in?" he asked.

"No." She pushed him in the chest. He staggered back a step. "Uri, close and seal airlock three. Don't let anyone else on board without my express permission."

"Yes, Morgan." The hatch cut off any further protests Mavalhin might've made.

She hurried to the bridge with Haid behind. "Uri, are we ready to go?"

"All systems are one hundred percent operational. Maii and Cane are secure, as are our passengers in the hold."

"The Kesh didn't try anything while they had access to you?"

"They didn't have time."

"Good." She reached the bridge and settled into her usual chair at the first officer's station, allowing herself a brief but satisfactory smile as she did. "Disengage from Galine Four and bring us about."

As the mighty engines stirred, a message arrived from General Darkan:

THERE WILL BE NO NEGOTIATION.

"That settles that, then," said Haid from his position at the weapons console.

"Ameidio," she said, swiveling to face him. "You should be in sickbay!"

"Morgan, you need all the people you can get at the moment, and you know it. *Especially* if we lose the Box."

She was about to snap back a negative when the view through her left eye suddenly changed.

She was receiving a feed from one of the *Sebettu*'s many gun emplacements. Through its sensors she saw a pyramidal formation of all-suits circling the station and its attendant destroyer. The *Sebettu*'s powerful weapons had been trained upon them, monitoring them in case they tried to attack. At the center of the formation was Yarrow's warped black all-suit.

As Roche watched, the destroyer's weapons fired, instantly vaporizing four of the outriggers. Another six were disabled. The black all-suit tried its best to dodge the incoming fire, but without success. One glancing shot cracked it open and a cloud of frozen air jetted out of the interior. Its engines fired nonsensically before guttering out entirely. The remaining all-suits ceased flying in a purposeful way at the same time, their central control removed. With the threat gone, the dead all-suits were allowed to tumble away into the darkness.

Her vision returned to normal. <Thanks for that, Box.>

<I thought you might like to know that one threat has been neutralized.>

"Morgan!" Kajic appeared in the center of the bridge. "Their weapons are turning on *us* now."

"Any fighter activity?" she asked Haid.

"None. It's just us and them."

"That's all they'll need. Take evasive action," she ordered.

She gripped her armrest as the *Ana Vereine* rolled beneath her. The destroyer's forward batteries flashed, and a wave of flicker-bombs swept over one of the ship's nacelles, making it shudder.

"Damage?"

"Minimal," Kajic replied. "The disruptors held, just."

"How much of that can we take?"

"I'd rather not find out."

"Can we outrun them?"

"In the short term, yes, although their engines are designed for the long haul and would eventually catch us."

"Get us out of here, then. Box, is there anything you can do at your end? I still want to get you back if I can."

The AI's voice came from the speakers at the front of the bridge: "My resources here are severely limited. The entire command grid is completely separate from the rest of the ship's systems. I was lucky to take them unawares once, but I would not be so lucky again. Most likely they would immediately guess the source of the misleading data, expel me from the ship, and destroy me. That way you would gain nothing."

Roche reluctantly conceded the point. On the main screen, the enormous bulk of the destroyer had begun to recede. "I don't suppose there's any way you can get yourself expelled but *not* destroyed, is there?" she said dryly.

"Morgan," Kajic interrupted. "They are no longer targeting us."

"Excellent." She turned to face the ex-captain. His face, surprisingly, was still grim.

"Its weapons are now aimed at Galine Four," he said.

"Damn!" Although Galine Four had more firepower than the *Ana Vereine,* it was about as maneuverable as an asteroid. The station and everyone on it would be nothing but target practice for the destroyer's novice gunners.

But that wouldn't matter to the general. What had she said? *We will erase this place from our memories!* It seemed she had something more literal in mind than just determined forgetfulness.

"Ameidio, Uri—we don't have much choice. We have to draw its fire. The only way I can think to do that is to attack. So get ready. We move in as soon as possible."

No one argued with her, except the Box.

<Morgan, what are you doing?>

She felt the engines stirring beneath her as though her own veins were vibrating, and she wondered if this was a pale echo of what it was like to be Uri Kajic. "I can't let innocent people die just so I can make an easy escape, Box."

<I must urge you to reconsider, Morgan.>

"What's it to you, anyway? You're safe regardless. Unless, of course, the general decides to crack you open later."

The Box was silent for a moment. Then: <You are determined?>

It wasn't as if she had much choice: Maii was still in a coma, the Box was useless, she was generally outgunned and underequipped. But there was nothing new about that. "I have to at least try."

To the others she said: "Fire as soon as we're in range. Take us in close and fast, then back for another pass. If it doesn't work, keep hitting them. The moment they come after us, we move."

"Should I plot a specific course?" Kajic asked.

"No. Let's just see what happens."

She forced herself to lean back into the seat's firm embrace.

"In range in five seconds," said Kajic.

<They have noticed you,> said the Box.

"Three."

Batteries of weapons poised to fire upon the station were suddenly given a new target. A-P cannon rotated; missiles recalculated their hyperspatial trajectories.

"One."

The *Sebettu* fired.

A maelstrom of energy tore apart the space ahead of the Marauder, and there was no avoiding it. Shields did their best to keep out the worst, but some inevitably burst through. The hull screamed in at least two places. Repair systems were overloaded with input.

But the *Ana Vereine* held. Kajic kept its course true while Haid did his best to return fire. Two emplacements burned in a flash on the hull of the destroyer, then a third. A severed sensor tower pinwheeled into a blast meant for the *Ana Vereine* and disintegrated instantly. A lucky strike opened a rent in the hull four decks long, black and ugly, spilling air and Kesh personnel.

Then they were through. Roche steadied herself as the *Ana Vereine* turned for another pass, but the smell of smoke in the air made her think twice.

"Can we do that again?"

"We've lost two shield generators," Kajic said with a pained expression. "We have breaches on three levels and meltdown in two others. Structural integrity is down by twenty-five percent. In short, I don't know, Morgan. It'd be close."

"Engines?"

"Undamaged."

"Good. What about the *Sebettu*? Is it following?"

"It is turning about," said the Box over the main speakers. "Weapons are locked."

"Then forget the second pass. We've got what we wanted." She stood, unable to sit any longer. "Uri, head for the Gauntlet's edge—maximum acceleration."

A map appeared on the main screen: the boundary of the solar envelope rippled and shimmered like a gray aurora.

<The edge is highly unstable, Morgan,> said the Box. <It is currently moving at an average of more than fifty thousand kilometers per second, a sizable percentage of the speed of light—but I emphasize that this is only an average. The sections in which the boundary is flexing most dramatically may be moving much quicker than that.>

"But that's only the outer rim, right? The thing as a whole is shaped like a disk, and the edge is collapsing most rapidly. If we go up or down, it should be more stable."

<Only relatively, Morgan.>

"Good." Roche was outwardly unperturbed. "Uri, aim for the most unstable piece within range. Up or down. Get us there as quickly as you can. If I've annoyed our friend the general enough, she'll be coming after us with all engines firing."

"That appears to be the case." Kajic brought up a display showing bright emission halos around the destroyer and its rapidly changing red shift.

"How long until we reach the boundary?"

"Fifteen minutes, Morgan. I have located a region in which parts of Autoville have been destroyed, upsetting the boundary's stability. Space-time in that region is highly stressed."

"Perfect. Box, you know what I want to do?"

<Yes, but I advise against it. The possibility of error is too great.>

"That's what you're here for."

<Don't forget, Morgan, that we are not communicating directly. My signal is relayed through Galine Four, from which you and I are becoming increasingly distant. Before long, the lag will become dangerous. Any decision I make will be based on information that might already be outdated. Your life will be in jeopardy.>

"Then we'll just have to do it on our own." Roche thought for a moment. "Uri, drop proximity and impact mines and dump everything in the cargo hold we can spare—even excess water if we've got it. Give them a wake to run into; keep them annoyed any way you can."

Roche sat back down and tried not to fidget. The tension in Haid's shoulders was noticeable even from behind, as was the pallor of his normally midnight-black skin. He had lost more blood than she'd thought.

"We have time to kill, Ameidio," she said. "At least get some painkillers."

He turned and gave her a wry smile. "In a few minutes it might be irrelevant."

She shrugged, the smile on her own face uneasy and forced. "Maybe," she whispered.

"The *Sebettu*'s flight profile is confirmed," Uri said. "It will be within firing range in twelve minutes."

"And how long until we reach the boundary?" asked Roche.

"Approximately twelve minutes. The margin for error is high given the region's instability."

Roche nodded. "See if you can get a response from them. Ask for Lieutenant Haden B'shan."

Kajic nodded.

Roche waited. The risk was high—doubly so without the Box to coordinate things. But she refused to believe that it couldn't be done—that she and the people with her, who had already done so much, couldn't meet this one, final challenge.

The fact that it probably *wouldn't* be the last chance they took together didn't matter. One at a time, she told herself. If she didn't make it over *this* hurdle, the ones that would've followed were irrelevant.

"We have a response," said Kajic eventually. "Putting it on the main screen now."

B'shan appeared, looking uncomfortable. Perhaps having the enemy name you specifically meant a loss of face in the Kesh code of honor. Roche didn't worry about that. She had more chance of reasoning with B'shan than any of the others.

"This is your last chance," she said. "We'll be at the halfway point in less than a minute. After that it'll be too late to turn back. We'll hit the boundary whether we like it or not."

B'shan nodded slowly. "We are aware of that, and we know what you're trying to do. But it won't work."

"No? You're not as maneuverable as we are."

"We're not completely inept, either, Roche. We have had more experience doing this than you. If you make it, the chances are we will too—and then what? There's nowhere you can run to on the outside."

"So it doesn't really matter if I make it or not, does it?"

B'shan stared at her for a long moment. "What about the others, Roche?" he said. "Do you have the right to decide for them?"

Roche laughed. He was trying to appeal to her Pristine side. A Kesh simply didn't think like that. He knew her kind well enough to know what buttons to push.

"Nice try, B'shan." She glanced at the countdown; the halfway point had just flashed by. "You just missed your last chance to end this sensibly. We'll either see each other on the other side, or . . ." She paused for a few seconds. "Or we won't, I guess. Goodbye, Lieutenant."

She turned to Kajic without waiting for a response. "Kill it."

The image winked out, and was replaced by a map of the boundary. She couldn't grasp the scale of it, because its surface was fractal in nature; the closer they came to it, the more detail appeared, making it look as if they were traveling nowhere.

"Who's the spokesperson for the people in the hold?" she asked.

"The outrigger named Lud."

"Can I speak to him?"

"I hear you, Morgan Roche," said Lud.

"*Are* you willing to go along with this?"

"We allied ourselves to your cause," he said. "Regardless of our personal preferences, we will stand by you as a group."

She nodded. "Does that mean you yourself would rather not be here, because if that's the case we can drop you off in an escape capsule—"

"As I said, what *I* would like doesn't enter into it." The tone of his voice was wry. "Besides, we both know I would be shot instantly."

"That's true." She repressed a slight smile. "Well, it's good to have you aboard, Lud. Maybe we can get you back in touch with your all-suit when this is over and done with."

"Unlikely," Lud said. "It was destroyed in the initial attack."

The line closed between them. Roche pondered the outrigger's words—and his situation—for longer than she realized. When she looked at the clock there were only three minutes remaining. The *Sebettu* was looming large in the aft screens, forward guns at the ready.

"Box?"

There was an appreciable lag before the AI replied. <Yes, Morgan?>

"Any advice?"

<Trust your instincts. Follow them always, and they will lead you where you most wish to go.>

She thought about it for a moment. "What the hell does that mean?"

There was amusement in the AI's tone when it replied: <It means that I have nothing constructive to say.>

"That's a first," said Roche solemnly. She felt something absurdly like grief rising in her throat. "And Box . . . ?"

<Yes, Morgan?>

"Thanks."

There was a long pause before the Box spoke again. <For anything specific?>

"Not really. Just on the whole, I figure I owe you."

<Don't worry, Morgan. The 'Greater I' hasn't finished with you yet.>

She didn't doubt that. But if there was anything left of her in a minute's time, she would probably kiss the Crescend's High Human cheek in gratitude—if it had a cheek, of course.

She sat straighter in her seat. "Okay, this is it. Uri, how are we looking?"

"All systems are green for slow-jump."

"It's your decision. I'd rather rely on *your* instincts in this case."

"Understood. The *Sebettu* will be in range in thirty seconds."

She studied the boundary ahead of them. It was whipping like a flag in a gale. "How long until we jump?"

"Soon . . ." The ex-captain's voice and expression were all concentration.

The chronometer hit twenty seconds.

The *Sebettu* was so close, Roche could practically smell its Kesh commander. If it came too close too soon, hitting the boundary wouldn't be an issue. One solid strike from behind would put an end to all their problems.

"Ameidio, full shields aft."

"Aye, Morgan."

"Fire if you think it'll help. Uri?"

The boundary loomed large. Previously small details now looked like giant ice floes tossing on an impossibly heavy sea.

The counter hit ten.

"Soon . . ."

"Their weapons are all locked and ready to fire." The edge to Haid's voice betrayed his own anxiety. "They'll be in range in no time."

"Looks like we're going out the same way we came in," said Roche, gripping her armrests.

Five seconds.

A wall of tortured space-time seemed about to strike them, and the *Ana Vereine* lurched violently to one side.

"Almost," whispered Kajic.

Zero.

Plus one.

Plus two.

Plus three.

"They're firing!" Haid shouted, bracing himself against the console.

The boundary hit them at the same time as the barrage from the *Sebettu.*

"Now!"

Kajic's voice filled the bridge as the engines let loose their contained energies in one, powerful surge.

For a split second, Roche felt like a tiny insect squeezed between the thumb and forefinger of some unimaginably giant beast.

Then they were jumping.

The ship rattled and shook as space warped and twisted. She felt as though she were being pulled inside out and spun around at the same time. Somewhere in the ship, Maii stirred in her coma; Roche could sense the distress of the reave as a wave of panic washed through her mind.

Veils of red fell behind them. Darkness peeled back and exposed—

Stars.

Then a blaze of blue light obscured them as the *Ana Vereine* dropped fully into real space.

Roche stared incredulously at the screen.

They were rocketing out of what looked like the surface of a large blue giant, warped into a fat spindle shape by incomprehensible forces. The anomaly had grown since they'd last seen it. Its surface was disturbed by the mighty distortions in space-time it hid.

"Behind us!" Haid yelled.

Something black and angular jutted out of the surface of the anomaly. Energy whipped around and from it, reaching for the *Ana Vereine* as though to pull it back down but also arcing back to strike itself. The sight filled Roche with both amazement and horror: the *Sebettu* had followed them through!

Then the surface of the anomaly flexed like a droplet of water in free-fall. The Kesh destroyer seemed to hang suspended for a moment, half in and half out of the slow-jump. There was a bright flash of orange light—even brighter than the anomaly—and the destroyer began to disintegrate.

First it broke into two, lengthways. Then those two fragments—each many times the size of the *Ana Vereine*—broke apart into smaller segments. Each piece hung briefly silhouetted against the anomaly, then either fragmented further or exploded. Within a second, there was nothing left larger than a grain of rice; another second reduced the Kesh destroyer to molecules; one further second and only plasma remained, a cloud of elementary particles tearing itself apart from internal forces.

"Box?"

Roche gripped the edge of her console hard. The ship shuddered as the shock wave hit it.

"Box!"

"We are experiencing communication problems due to the radiation from the anomaly," Kajic said.

"Try the . . . what was it? The Eckandi emergency band!"

"I am broadcasting on those frequencies."

"Any response?"

Kajic waited a second. "Nothing."

"Give it a minute."

Kajic nodded, and Haid turned to face her. She forced herself to breathe. No one said anything as the seconds swept by. The surface of the anomaly rose to meet them at a rate inversely proportional to the rate it was shrinking inside. The *Ana Vereine* angled its headlong flight until it seemed to be gliding.

A minute passed with no word. The Eckandi emergency band was empty, as were the others. Roche waited another minute just in case, then had no choice but to accept the truth.

The Box was gone.

"Take us back in," she said quietly.

No one spoke as the *Ana Vereine* began its descent back into the maelstrom.

Epilogue

IND *Ana Vereine*
'955.01.25 EN
0170

"Do you have any idea how many people crew a typical Kesh destroyer?"

Roche didn't answer because she didn't want to know. The face on the screen looked like it was going to tell her, anyway.

"Four thousand three hundred and fifty." Marine Commander Gent sighed to himself. "I don't know how I'm going to explain this back home."

"Just fill out your report as usual," Roche said. "And mark it to the attention of Page De Bruyn."

"De Bruyn, of COE Intelligence?"

"Yeah," said Roche. "And you can deliver a report from me too. I'm kind of obliged to tell her what's going on every now and again."

"Well, I wish you'd tell *me.*"

"Look, take it up with your superior officers if you like." Gent was definitely old school, and Roche was fast losing patience with him. "Tell them what I've told you and wait for a reply. They'll only confirm what I've said, and you'll only have wasted your time. But I'm happy to wait. As long as you do your bit and make sure these people get to where they're supposed to, my involvement with you is at an end."

Gent grunted. "Okay, Roche. Have it your way. But if I find out you're spinning me a line—"

She broke the link with a flick of her wrist and leaned back into her seat. She shouldn't have been surprised. Broadcasting a distress call had been risky—but when they'd found the wreckage of the COE blockade and realized that there wouldn't be enough room to house all the refugees longer than a day, she'd had no choice. The *Ana Vereine* wasn't built to accommodate that many people.

She simply hadn't known that the first ships by would be the frigate *Starburst* and a full Armada reconnaissance squadron, or that there was a war brewing outside.

Her eyes were hot with fatigue. She rubbed them with her fingertips, trying to knead new life into them.

"Leave the galaxy alone for a few days and look what happens," said Haid dryly. "Perhaps next time we should get a sitter."

"Open conflict with the Dato Bloc. Revolt in the Narm Protectorate. Tension with the N'Kor Republic—and don't think this incident will make things easier on that front. The Olmahoi sending in grayboots to find the *irikeii.* Talk of impeachment in the COE capital . . ." She shook her head; bright-colored blotches danced across the vision of her one natural eye. "How could it have fallen apart so quickly?"

"Perhaps it's just symptomatic of the main problem."

Roche looked over to him. "You mean the clone warriors?"

Haid shrugged. "They're good at blending in, Rufo said; they insinuate, then they corrupt. Maybe they don't always work from the bottom up when they want to tear things down."

"Maybe." Roche's gaze returned to the screen, and the image of what remained of the anomaly. It had cooled as it expanded, changing in color from blue-white to yellow to red. At that point—when no space at all remained within the Gauntlet—the boundary between the real universe and the anomaly had evaporated. Three hours later, a warm pile of primeval dust with nothing but angular momentum was all that remained within the perimeter of the former Palasian System. One day, it might accrete into a protostar and give birth to a new system, but that would occur long after Roche had left the scene. Billions of years later, probably.

"Uri, get Auditor Byrne on the line," she said.

"Hailing her now," said Kajic.

She waited, but it was Lud that spoke: "Sorry, Morgan Roche. I'm not sure where Auditor Byrne is right now. Can I help?"

"I just wanted to know how you got on with those all-suits. Anything recoverable?"

"A few bits and pieces. We're still looking through them. We'll let you know if we need anything."

"Do that." The outrigger spines hung not far from the *Ana Vereine,* looking absurdly like two giant conifers stripped of their leaves. Each "branch" held a berth for one outrigger; most of them were empty, even those of Long Span. The remains of the all-suits destroyed by the *Sebettu* were being cannibalized for parts to repair those still needed; the rest of the components would come from the *Ana Vereine*'s stores.

"Idil wants to know what you've done with Linegar Rufo," Lud said.

"Give him to Gent. They're going to take him to face trial for his crimes."

"Good." She could hear the satisfaction in the outrigger's voice. "No matter what Yarrow . . . what she *was* at the end, her people deserve retribution."

Roche grunted a vague affirmative, not wanting to mention the strife in the COE; civilized proceedings might be on hold for a while if things went badly on any of the fronts. Lud would hear soon enough. For now, he was happy, and that was what mattered.

"By the way," he went on, "we have the body of the clone warrior. Do you want us to dispose of it?"

Roche was about to agree, but thought better of it. "No. Bring it aboard when you get the chance. It's bound to be of use to someone."

"Consider it done." Lud signed off.

More than just useful, Roche thought. It would be a wellspring of information on the clone warriors. To the best of her knowledge, none had been dissected. The Box would've loved it—and Rufo too. Part of her was tempted to keep the scientist with them a little while longer in order to have access to his specialized knowledge. But she could never trust him. He was too self-centered and treacherous; even his data would be suspect.

<I agree with you on that score,> said Maii when Roche asked for a second opinion. <His mind runs deep with knowledge, but is ethically shallow. He yearns for fame and money without concern for the cost. Not power as some might crave it, for he is genuinely disinterested in what most people do, unless it directly impinges upon his work. But domination in academia is domination nonetheless, and that makes him a megalomaniac.>

Roche smiled to herself. The young reave was almost back to her old self, exploring the minds of those around her with ease and disquieting confidence. She was doing it from her bed in sickbay still, but Roche knew that in no time at all the girl would be fully recovered and once again on her feet.

She refused to discuss what it had been like under Xarodine for so long, and neither had she talked about the *irikeii*—but that wasn't surprising. She had only been conscious for a couple of hours, and Roche had been busy for much of that time.

<Is Cane awake yet?> asked Roche.

<Not as far as I can tell.> Maii was also reticent to describe the state of the clone warrior's consciousness. <That is, I can't detect any mental activity behind his shields.>

Roche wondered how the reave could tell at all what was happening behind someone's shields, or even how someone could be awake *without* thinking—but she let it go for the moment. The fine details of epsense were something she knew little about.

For now it was enough that the girl was alive and safe. Whatever else had happened, at least Roche could relax on that score.

The question was: how far could she relax around Cane, knowing what she had recently learned about him?

"Morgan." Kajic's voice was soft, cautious, his expression in the holographic display regretful. "I have concluded a preliminary scan of the region. There is no sign of the Box anywhere. I can continue looking if you like; there is still a slight possibility that it might be simply damaged and unable to hear you. However, a conclusive search will take much longer than—"

"How *much* longer?"

"At least a month. The space we have to search is as large as Palasian System. If we didn't know where to start looking, even a small planet would be hard to find. And as the collapse of the Gauntlet has disturbed space for a light-year in every direction—"

"Okay, okay, I get it," she said tiredly. "You can stop looking." She raised a hand to massage her temple. "I just thought we should try to . . . I mean, if it had been me out there, I'd like to think that the Box would have . . ." Her voice trailed away to silence.

Kajic filled that silence quickly: "Don't worry, Morgan. I'm sure we'll hear soon."

She didn't say anything, just got out of her first officer's seat and went for a walk.

If there was one thing Roche hated, it was waiting. Not waiting in the sense of waiting for a delivery to come; in those cases, what was coming was known, and there was usually a rough idea how long it would take. She'd had plenty of training at that in the Armada.

What she hated was waiting for something unspecified at a time unknown—knowing only that nothing could be done until it arrived.

Like most of the mundane Castes, she'd had little if anything to do with High Humans before her mission to collect the Box. Already she had learned how frustrating it could be. The entire business with Cane—from start to finish—had been orchestrated by them from the shadowy recesses of the galaxy. They knew more about the clone warriors than anyone else, and probably had known for a lot longer, too. Their perspective on the galaxy was much broader than that of any single government, even one as widespread as the Commonwealth of Empires, so the effects of the clone warriors would have been more visible to them.

She remembered something Rufo had said: "We are entangled in the details." That was how she felt: caught in a web. And the more she tried to understand, the more entangled she became.

She was under no illusions about her own role in all this. She was just a courier for the Box, an intermediary allowing the Crescend, via the Box, access to spaces he normally couldn't get into. No doubt he was eagerly awaiting some sort of transmission from the fragment of his much larger self. When that signal didn't arrive, and word reached him that Palasian System had collapsed, he would know that something had gone terribly wrong. But she doubted he would relinquish such a privileged position so readily.

Part of her was half expecting a replacement Box to arrive at any moment, or some other development by which her next step would be made clear; another part believed she was redundant now, and the Crescend would find another courier for another sliver of himself. It didn't matter either way. For now she was stuck, caught between possibilities, still buried under a pile of details threatening to suffocate her.

She came to a halt outside the ship's medical center.

The last time she had seen Cane, he had been lying on his back, half-covered by the crystal in which Rufo had encased him. The *Ana Vereine*'s autosurgeon had begun removing him from the shell, and his vital signs had been gradually returning to normal—although what was normal for him was still not entirely known. How long until he would return to consciousness was likewise unknown. The drugs Rufo had used to immobilize him might have been strong enough to cause some lingering damage, in which case simply taking him out of the crystal cocoon wouldn't be enough; he would have to heal himself.

She had no doubt he would do that eventually, and sooner rather than later. Adoni Cane was the most incredible organism Roche had ever encountered. His physical strength, agility, and endurance were matched only by his cognitive abilities. The only times she had ever seen him puzzled were when he had confessed to responding to the command language Rufo had been broadcasting to the other clone warrior, and when he had first come to her cabin on the *Midnight* and had not known anything more than his name.

For all intents and purposes, the other clone warrior had proven herself to be as equally developed as Cane—if not more so—but something still bothered Roche. She had assumed that the other clone warriors would be just that—*clones.* Jelena Heidik had patently not been a clone of Adoni Cane, unless gender itself was something these warriors could change at will in order to perfect their disguise.

Cane was still lying on his back when she let herself into his isolated ward. The protective shell had gone, though. He now lay naked beneath a translucent sheet with various monitors snaking across and under his skin. A bank of monitors on one wall displayed his vital signs. They seemed within the bounds of normality, as far as Roche could tell.

"I don't know if you can hear me," she said, leaning on the end of the bed by his feet. "But there's something I need to know. I might as well ask it now. If you *can* hear me, it'll give you something to think about. At the very least you can decide whether to answer me honestly or not."

She paused, wondering for a moment if she really expected a response from him, or even if she *wanted* one. "Before Rufo captured you," she went on, "you told me that although you didn't know what you were, or what you were for, you *did* know what you could easily become." She remembered the look in his eyes: cautious, cold, calculating. "What is that, Cane? *What* could you become? A warrior like Jelena Heidik? Is that it? Or something else entirely?"

She waited for a sign that he had heard, but the steady rise and fall of his broad chest didn't change. His brown skin seemed to absorb the light shining upon him, making him look like some kind of wooden statue. A totem, she thought. Something to frighten children with.

She sighed heavily and began pacing irritably about the bed. "Am I crazy for trusting you, Cane? You could do anything, any time, and I know I couldn't stop you. Before, I used to worry about the Box conspiring to get rid of me; and yet even without the Box, I'm *still* worried. The Box was the Crescend's tool through and through, and it followed its own agenda, but it was still just an AI. It had its limitations. You . . ." She stopped at the foot of the bed. "You're like a new virus no one's ever seen before. Who knows what effect you'll have if we let you loose?"

Roche watched him, clutching for a response, but in the silence that followed she felt like a fool standing there trying to talk to him. Maybe later, when Maii picked up signs of activity, she would return and try again.

She turned to leave, but the sound of tapping stopped her.

Turning back, she saw that his eyes had opened. They weren't looking at her, though; they stared straight upward at the ceiling, as though he didn't even have the strength to turn them.

The noise came from his side: one finger was tapping gently on the edge of the bed.

She leaned in closer. "You can't talk, right?"

With some effort, he managed to swallow, but his lips refused to move. Only his finger seemed to have any life, tapping continually on the bed.

"Tap once for yes and twice for no, okay?"

But the tapping continued unchecked. Only gradually did she realize that there was a pattern to the sound. He was doing more than just trying to get her attention: he was tapping in code.

She had studied various simple methods of signaling at the Armada Military College, but this one she didn't recognize.

"Uri—"

"I'm listening," said Kajic.

She half smiled. "You've been learning from the Box," she said. "So, what's he saying?"

"It sounds like a variant on a very old code, one I've not heard in practice before."

"Can you decipher it?"

"He seems to be saying"—Kajic paused—"that he's as Human as you."

"What?"

"'I am as Human as you are.' That's the message he keeps repeating, over and over."

Cane's finger stopped and the room fell silent.

"That's it?" She leant over Cane. "What does that *mean*? Are you trying to reassure me?"

He didn't reply. His eyes slowly closed, and she was left facing a corpse once again.

"Dammit!" She slammed the flat of her hand against the bed. "Uri, keep a close eye on him. The moment he wakes properly, I want to talk to him. And don't let him out of here—or anyone else in, for that matter. Understood?"

"Understood, Morgan."

<You too, Maii,> she added.

<I'll do my best,> said the young reave. <But I'm still not picking up anything.>

Of course not, Roche thought to herself bitterly as she left the room. That'd make things too goddamn easy . . .

She walked to burn off her frustration, and to keep herself active. There was too much work to do for her to rest: loose threads to tie up, plans to set in place just in case the Crescend *didn't* contact her, decisions to make. Would she return to the COE and see what happened, or try somewhere else? If the clone warriors had appeared in many other places, as Rufo had suggested, maybe ranging further for information might be fruitful.

There was one image she couldn't shake: it was of the cloud of seed machines that had made the revenge capsules which had in turn made the clone warriors. Rufo, via Maii and the *irikeii,* had imagined them dispersing outward through the galactic halo, then inward again, converging at one point. Why he had imagined that, she didn't know. Maybe he was aware of something she wasn't, or maybe it was just the easiest way to visualize what was going on. It might have meant nothing, but she found it hard to forget. If the clone warriors *were* converging, it would make sense to find out where they were heading. And meet them there.

But without the Box, many things she had taken for granted became complicated. Collecting and collating data from a variety of sources was just one of them. Monitoring Cane was another. She was appalled to realize just how dependent she had become on the AI during their short association. The Box had fulfilled many of the simpler functions of other machines but with the independence and initiative of a person trained in many different fields.

Even something as basic as flying the *Ana Vereine* would be difficult without the Box. Kajic oversaw most systems, and there were numerous dullard AIs to take up some of the slack, but Kajic was still only Human. He needed to sleep, like everyone else, and made the occasional mistake. At some point, she supposed, she would have to find him a crew.

Right now would be the ideal opportunity, too. Galine Four had been lost when the Gauntlet collapsed, and as a result the *Ana Vereine*'s holds were full of refugees from the station, jammed in with the isolation tanks she had jury-rigged for the resident outriggers. The latter had weathered the disaster well, even the ones like Lud who had lost their all-suits; some were already talking about where to sell the spare spine and what system to target next. It was the station personnel, more used to comfort and space, who were complaining. Some, she was sure, would happily accept an offer of employment in exchange for better conditions, even if only in the short term.

Myer Mavalhin was one of them. He had eventually made it onto the ship, and his incessant calls for her attention were no doubt designed to ensure he wasn't kicked off again before he tried to plead his case one more time.

After talking to Cane, she went to the holds, found him among those crowded together there, and took him into a secure office cubicle to talk in privacy. His expression betrayed hope, which she was quick to dispel.

"You're not coming with me, Myer," she said. "And if I can't say it enough times to make it sink in, then that's your problem, not mine."

"Why are you so adamant about this, Morgan?"

The question was reasonable enough, and she did her best to answer honestly, to keep old hurts out of it. "One: you're unreliable; I can't depend on you when I need to. Two: you're a loose cannon, thinking more of yourself than the people around you. Three: you don't have the sort of experience I'd need for someone in this situation—"

"As if anyone has," he interrupted, avoiding her gaze.

"Four," she continued firmly. "You rarely listen to anyone but yourself—especially if it's something you don't want to hear. Even now I doubt I'm getting through to you."

He grimaced slightly. "So much for hoping it'd be like old times."

"There was never going to be any chance of that, Myer," she said bluntly. "You want me to keep going?"

"Thanks, but I'd prefer you didn't." He looked at her then in a way that she found disconcerting. "You know, Morgan, back in College you'd have given in to a bit of coaxing and sweet talking—like that time when we scammed that cruiser to Temoriel. Remember? God, you swore three shades of purple there was no way you were going along with it. But in the end you did, *and* you enjoyed yourself, too. You always did. That's what you were like in those days. I could rely on you then." He shrugged, apparently unaware of the irony in his words.

"I've more important things to worry about now," she said.

"You tried that excuse then, too, but it didn't have as much power over you. Now it's as though the important things are all you have left. You've . . . changed, I guess," he concluded.

She smiled at this. "I guess I have," she agreed, and got up to leave.

But he had one thing left to ask her.

"Did you ever find your parents, Morgan?"

The question took her by surprise, and she stopped and stared at him for a long moment. "What?" in the end, was all she could manage.

"Your parents," he said. "*Did* you ever find them like you said you would?"

"No, I . . ." she began. "I mean . . ."

"I'm sorry," he said sincerely. "I didn't mean to upset you. Just that I knew what finding them meant to you, and I was curious as to—Hey! What'd I say?"

But she was already running from the room, ignoring the sound of Myer calling after her. She could hear Kajic also, in a moment, as well as Maii. But she didn't stop to reply to any of them. She just kept running, moving through the corridors of the ship as though she were being chased by demons . . .

Her parents . . .

She remembered. Her aspiration had always been to join COE Intelligence. Part of that had been her desire to travel, and to escape poor conditions on her homeworld, but another part had been to gain access to powers ordinary citizens didn't have. The records on Ascensio, her homeworld, had been closed to her when she shipped out to Military College. She had always intended to return one day to find out who her parents had been. She had had a mother once, and a father. Something about them must have been recorded somewhere. Even a name would've been better than nothing.

But she had never gotten around to it. How could she have forgotten them? What had happened to her? Perhaps she had changed more than she had ever allowed herself to realize.

She didn't see the corridors that whipped by her. She didn't even care. Intentionally or not, Myer had managed to hurt her very deeply, and she was running from him as much as herself. Maybe if she ran hard enough, she could forget that she was crying, too. Tears spilled out uncontrollably, welling up from somewhere deep within her; somewhere long forgotten . . .

<You are behaving in a highly irrational fashion, Morgan,> said a voice inside her head.

She came to such an abrupt halt that she almost tripped over her own feet. She swayed on one spot for a few breaths, wiping at the sweat and tears on her face and waiting for the voice to speak again.

<Aren't you going to say anything?> it said finally.

<*Box*?>

<Yes, Morgan.>

<But—*how*?>

<Listen to me, Morgan. It is imperative that you do not tell anyone about my reappearance. I have gone to great lengths to ensure that my true location remains unknown. It would be a shame to have to start all over again.>

<Your *true* location?> She was slowly catching her breath, but felt as though she were losing her mind. <The valise was destroyed—>

<That was always a possibility. Hence, a backup was needed. Or, more accurately, the valise itself was the backup. At best it was only ever intended as a decoy.>

<A *what*?> Confusion quickly changed places with anger. She had lugged that damned valise hundreds of kilometers across a desert world, thinking it the most valuable thing in the galaxy—only to find that it was a *decoy*?

<It was necessary, Morgan. You will come to understand that eventually.>

<So where *are* you? If you weren't destroyed with the *Sebettu,* you must be around here somewhere. On the *Ana Vereine*? But how did you get on board? The only thing I brought with me from Sciacca's World was the valise. Along with Maii and Cane and Haid, of course—>

She stopped as a terrible thought occurred to her.

<Correct, Morgan. That is indeed all you brought with you.>

<With *me.*>

<Yes,> said the Box. <I am a part of you, and always have been.>

* * *

Now she was certain she was losing her mind.

She remembered being in orbit around Trinity, where AIs were made for the COE by the Crescend. She remembered waiting for the mysterious engineers to arrive to take her down to the surface, where she would be given the AI she had come to collect. But she didn't remember anything after that point, because somehow she had been rendered unconscious. The next thing she knew, she had awakened with the valise strapped to her wrist and the Box's voice inside her head.

<They *operated* on me? Without my permission?>

<It was deemed a tactical necessity to maintain security to the highest possible degree. You might never have known. I certainly had no wish to tell you. I feared your reaction would be negative.>

<Could you blame me?> Hugging herself, she slid down the nearest wall until she was squatting against it. Too many shocks; too much uncertainty; too much to be afraid of. <So where exactly are you?> she asked.

<There is no specific location, Morgan. I am distributed evenly throughout your body. That way, I could not be removed by cutting off, say, an arm, or severing your head. Such amputations will only momentarily hinder my performance. My components work on a cellular level, and are able to call on your cells as backup should you and I be severely damaged.>

<Does it work both ways?>

<It is not intended to.>

She closed her eyes, trying to get her head around the concept of having an AI inside her, but not even really wanting to succeed. She was riddled with it—like fat, or cancer.

<How do I get rid of you?>

<You don't until we return to Trinity. Only there does the necessary equipment exist to disentangle our separate structures. Until then we remain symbiotes.>

<And afterwards?>

<You will have noticed no side effects for my being inside you. I am completely self-sufficient and undetectable, internally and externally. The difference between my being in a valise strapped to your wrist and being inside your body is a small one, I would think.>

<But kind of an *important* one, wouldn't you agree?> She had been invaded, and she was angry with how dismissive the Box was being about it all. <What if I were to change my mind? What if I told you and the Crescend to stick your little conspiracies and go my own way? What would happen to you then?>

<Don't fool yourself, Morgan,> said the Box. <If your intention was to keep me from my maker, then you would not succeed. You would be located eventually, and I would be taken. I am too valuable a tool to be thrown away so carelessly.>

<But I *can* get out of this if I choose to?>

<Of course.> The Box seemed to ponder this possibility. <But you won't, will you?>

She didn't answer at first as doubt suddenly welled in her. <This is crazy. No—it's impossible! What about all those times we were out of contact, or we had communication lags, or we really needed you and you couldn't get through?>

<Maintained to allay your suspicions. You coped with every situation well enough.>

<And on Mok?>

<Then you were correct to be suspicious. I was relaying information via you to and from the *Ana Vereine,* which was much farther away than I had you believe. Juggling you and Kajic was difficult, but by running the backup in the valise it was possible. Had the need to talk not been so great, I would not have bothered. Certainly it was the only time I broke my usual cover.>

She shook her head. <I can't believe you'd go to so much trouble.>

<I cannot force you to accept the truth, Morgan; you can believe what you like. You are not some puppet that dances as my will directs. You are as free as you ever were.>

<But—>

<But the fact remains: I am here, talking to you now, when you *know* the valise was destroyed, and I have always put your safety above my own. How else can you explain it?>

She put her head in her hands. She couldn't explain it, none of it. It was all a mystery to her. It was all so crazy.

A hand touched her shoulder and she flinched violently.

"Hey, it's okay, Morgan! I didn't mean to startle you."

She stared up at Haid, too disconcerted and confused to speak.

His hand withdrew. "Uri told me you'd had some sort of fit and I came to see if you were all right. Are you?"

"I—" She almost blurted out everything she'd just learned. That the Box was inside her and had been put there under circumstances the Box described as a "tactical necessity" but which she thought more akin to rape. That she was being used even more thoroughly than COE Intelligence had used her. That she had been betrayed—*again.*

But something stopped her. Something the Box had said.

I have gone to great lengths to ensure that my true location remains unknown.

The fact that the Box—that the Crescend—might have gone to such extremes struck her as so strange and unlikely that it temporarily overrode any concerns she had for her own well-being. She could think of only one explanation for its behavior, and once the thought was in her head there was no denying it. Why else would it wish its existence in her to remain a secret even now, when the danger of the second clone warrior was past?

The Box was hiding from *Cane.*

It was afraid of him.

"Morgan?"

"What?" She remembered Haid standing there. "Oh, I'm fine. Just thinking and working too hard, I guess. Didn't mean to give you a scare." She held out her hand and he helped her to her feet.

"Are you sure?" he asked, still studying her.

"Positive."

"Maii? Is she lying?"

<I have sworn not to read Morgan's mind without her permission,> the reave said to both of them.

Roche breathed a small sigh of relief. If Maii was telling the truth, the Box's secret could be kept a little while longer.

And as she thought this, she suddenly realized that she had already made up her mind: she *would* keep the Box's secret. For now, at least. And not because anything it had said convinced her to, either. She hated what had been done to her, but her curiosity as to what the Box planned to do next was strong enough to override the anger she was feeling.

Haid was still watching her.

"Maybe I should spread the workload a little," she said, smiling weakly. "If you're bored, there are plenty of repairs to be done. I'm sure Uri could use a hand. And we'll soon have shuttles from the *Starburst* docking to offload all these people. They have to be organized and ready to move. And what about supplies? Do we have enough to keep—?"

"Okay, already!" Haid raised a hand, laughing. "I'll get on to it now, I promise. But do me a favor and make sure you get some rest soon, all right?"

"Sleep is for the faint of heart," she said, quoting a lecturer from Military College. "If a lack of it makes you a little crazy, then you're in the perfect state to fight. If it doesn't, you're in the perfect state to lead."

Haid's brow creased. "Sounds like rubbish to me."

Privately she agreed.

It was only later, as she lay back on her bunk, that she realized how difficult it was going to be to find any time at all to rest.

Most of the refugees had been offloaded. All of the *Starburst*'s shuttles and three of the reconnaissance squadron's cruisers had made two trips each. The remaining stragglers would go with the last shuttles, due to cycle through within the hour. Haid was in charge of liasing with the Armada while Kajic concentrated on repairing the *Ana Vereine*. Yarrow Jelena Heidik's wizened body had been loaded aboard and placed in argon until someone was available to look at it. Roche had feigned exhaustion—no great task—to go to her quarters.

<Commander Gent is about to call you,> the Box said. <He has just received a priority communiqué from his superiors.>

Roche sighed and lay back on the bed. It hadn't taken the Box long to get back into the swing of things.

<Saying?>

<That the Armada is massing near Sol System, fearing a breakout of Wunderkind at any time. He has to join them, but will drop off the refugees along the way.>

<Good.> She closed her eyes. <Why won't you tell us the truth?>

<I'm sorry, Morgan?>

<You know what I mean. You infiltrated the datapools on the *Ana Vereine* when we first got on board; you corrupted COE Intelligence so they would think the Sol Apotheosis Movement was behind it all; you've done everything possible to lead searches in the wrong direction, and still you won't let anyone know what's going on. Why?>

<This is too big a threat, Morgan—truly galactic in scale.>

<So?>

<So what the COE thinks it knows won't make much difference to the big picture—if it is wrong. There are many thousands of similar governments under similar threats; some or all may already have been infiltrated by the clone warriors. Information is the key to any war, and we do not wish to reveal the full extent of our knowledge just yet.>

<So it is a war, then?>

<Most definitely, albeit one conducted thus far on a covert level. Only when cornered will the true and indiscriminate aggression of the clone warriors surface.>

<'Indiscriminate'?>

<They will kill anyone, any way they can. They seem to have no other purpose.>

<But what's the point of that? If they kill everyone, no one wins. Everyone's dead. Isn't that a bit self-defeating?>

<That may be the entire point. Several attempts have been made to study these creatures in situ; Palasian System was a fairly spectacular failure on many levels, but did at least demonstrate that they will fight to the very end. What we need to learn is whether the clone warriors will discriminate against any one Caste or social group. If such an exception does arise, then we may have discovered who their makers were related to. Logically the ones most like them will be the ones they spare.>

Roche nodded. <What about Cane? How does he fit in?>

<I suspect he knows he is being watched. You know that I released him from his cell on the *Midnight,* and that he and I colluded to ensure your escape from Sciacca's World. If he has suspected that I am an agent for someone more powerful, and if he now believes that I am gone, then it will be interesting to see what he does next. And believe me, I will be watching him very closely indeed.>

<Rufo suggested we look at the introns in his genetic code.>

<I know. I have already done so. His introns contain information I cannot interpret. The Crescend and his allies have been alerted to the possibility that this might be important, and will look at it immediately. Cane is, however, the exception to everything we have seen so far. If he is an aberration, a nonaggressive freak, his introns may contain nothing of use. At best, the information may turn out to be misleading.>

That seemed a depressing prospect to Roche. As much as she didn't want to believe that Cane would betray her, that would be better than drawing erroneous conclusions about the rest of his kind because he comprised a flawed data set.

<So what's this about Sol System?> she asked.

<Sol System is one of a number in a very old area, long abandoned for lack of resources. It has been fallow for many thousands of years, apart from the odd fanatical splinter group, such as the Sol Apotheosis Movement, and the occasional archaeologist. At least a dozen systems within the region are rumored to be the birthplace of Humanity.>

<And that's where the clone warriors are converging?>

<It seems so. Along with other forces, now. The Commonwealth of Empires is not the only regional government fearing a disaster from that area. Representatives from many Castes will be there, fearing threats different in name but similar in details.>

<At your urging, no doubt.>

<Indirectly, of course. We expect the clone warriors to attack. They will come with the fleets, hidden or walking in disguise among them.>

<And while everyone is looking to see who they attack first, you'll be waiting to see who they attack *last.*>

<Correct. When we have that information, we will be better positioned to retaliate.>

She shook her head. <It seems a bit risky, Box. I mean—>

A chime interrupted her.

"Marine Commander Gent wishes to talk to you," said Kajic.

<As expected,> put in the Box.

She ignored it. "Okay, Uri, put him through. Voice only, at this end."

An image of Gent's face came to her via her implants. He was standing on the bridge of the *Starburst*; his eyes wandered, having no fixed image of her to latch onto.

"I have received a communiqué from—" he began.

"I know, and I appreciate you going out of your way to help us like this."

Gent looked flustered for a second, then nodded formally. "It is the least we can do."

Besides which, thought Roche, he was required by law to assist in any regional disaster.

"Well, Commander," she said, "if that's all . . ."

"Not entirely. I wanted to discuss the matter of Auditor Byrne."

Roche frowned. "What about her?"

"She requested a ship to conduct a sweep of the outer fringes of what's left of the system. I loaned her the *Lucence-2* for a couple of hours, once it had finished ferrying passengers."

"I don't know anything about this."

"But she said it was your idea."

"She did?"

"Yes, and seeing as we've now lost contact with her, I thought I'd check with you to see what—"

She cut him off. "Give me its location."

A chart superimposed itself upon Gent's face. A red ring enclosed a small dot some distance from those marking the squadron. "They've drifted a fair way," said Gent. "Given that we need to move smartly in order to make this rendezvous—"

Again she didn't give him time to finish. A cold feeling had blossomed in the pit of her stomach. "Uri, I need Lud—*fast.*"

"Yes, Morgan."

<Box—>

<I know. I am checking it now.>

<Use the autosurgeon to crack the seals—with my authority so you won't be traced.>

"Lud here."

"This is Roche. Do you have genetic records of your clan members?"

"Yes. We keep detailed—"

"I need them. Can you send them to me now?"

"Of course." The outrigger didn't argue, even though the puzzlement was evident in his voice. "Give me a second to locate them."

<Maii?>

<I read nothing,> said the reave. <Nothing at all from that region.>

"Is something wrong, Roche?" Gent looked perversely pleased.

She ignored the question, and his attitude. "Target the *Lucence-2*, Commander Gent. If I give you the word, I want you to hit it with all you've got."

"What?" His expression wavered between amusement and alarm. "Are you serious?"

"Just *do* it, Commander. And tell me: how well is that ship armed?"

"Well enough," he said. "Look, what the hell is going on?"

"Transmitting those codes now," said Lud.

"Thanks." The cold feeling was growing. <Box?>

<I have conducted a visual inspection and am taking a genetic sample now. The tissue is extremely dehydrated, suggesting an extended exposure to vacuum.>

<Longer than a day?>

<Much.>

The feeling in her stomach turned to nausea. "Gent—shoot that ship! *Now!*"

"Are you out of your mind?" Gent bristled, outraged. "I can't just fire on my own people. I need a *reason*!"

"That wasn't the clone warrior in the all-suit!" She was shouting now. "It was Auditor Byrne!"

"How could you possibly know that?"

<I have the test results, Morgan,> said the Box, <confirming that the body is neither the outrigger known as Yarrow, nor is it of similar genetic stock to Cane. Auditor Byrne died at least five days ago.>

"Fire, Gent! *Fire!*"

But the dot on the chart that was *Lucence-2* had already begun to move. Too rapidly for pursuit to begin, and much more quickly than Gent's willingness to fire, it accelerated into the gentle gravitational well of the destroyed system. Faster and faster it went, until it reached the minimum speed required for a slow-jump; then its hyperspace engines kicked in, space rippled, and—

It was gone.

Lud was the first to speak.

"Byrne?"

"The clone warrior hid in Yarrow's all-suit after the ambush around Aro, as he thought," Roche explained. In hindsight it was all too clear. "But then she killed Byrne when Byrne tried to heal who she thought was Yarrow. The clone warrior took on Byrne's identity and hid the body in Yarrow's all-suit, which she then teleoperated the rest of the way. It was she who broadcast the distress call that led me to Mok, and she who manipulated the spine into helping me. She led the attack on Galine Four, she wanted us to be suspicious of Yarrow and she even let us think she had died by letting Yarrow's suit be destroyed . . ." Roche shook her head, appalled. "We're lucky she decided not to stick around."

<Yes,> said the Box. <It is clear now that she gave up on attack long ago and decided instead to concentrate on escape.>

"My ship—the *crew*!" Gent was still stunned by the sudden turn of events.

"Face it, Commander. They're not coming back."

"You knew this would happen!"

"If it's a scapegoat you want, look no further than yourself. You let your guard down. You should have checked with me before giving anyone a ship."

"But I—" Gent stopped, swallowed. "I was not fully aware of the dangers."

Roche felt almost sorry for him. No one had expected anything like this. "None of us are," she said, thinking of the Box as well as her.

"So that's it?" said Haid from the bridge. "She gets away?"

"Not as easily as that." Roche sat up and fumbled for her shipsuit. Sleep was even farther away than she had thought. "We're going to follow her."

"Through hyperspace?" said Gent. "That's impossible!"

"Not when you know where she's going." Roche stood. "Uri, set a course for Sol System, shortest possible route. I want to beat her there if I can, or at least be right behind her when we arrive."

<This is the correct course of action,> the Box whispered in her mind. She didn't need it to tell her that.

"Ameidio, get those last few refugees off the ship as soon as possible—in survival capsules if necessary. I want to move within the hour. Maii?"

<Yes, Morgan?>

<I want you to take all we've learned about this—everything from Rufo and the *irikeii*—and give it to Lud. Not so he knows, but so it will surface if he hears we've failed. Can you do that?>

<Yes. Word of our deaths will trigger the release of these memories.>

"Lud?" To the outrigger last of all she said: "Thanks for your help. I'm sorry we have to leave, but—"

"I understand," he said. "Fight well, Morgan, for Idil's daughter and for all of us. We'll keenly await news of your victory."

"Do that."

Only Gent remained on the open line, red-faced and blustering. "Do you have even the slightest idea what you're doing, Roche?"

"Yes," she said, thinking of Sol System—of all those ancient places and the beings converging upon them. "We're going home . . ."

APPENDIX

THE OLMAHOI:
Reconstructing the Myth for Beginners

(R. Pyatt Adamek, '595 EN; Introduction, pp. 1-7)

There is no word in the Olmahoi language for "alone."

In fact, the Olmahoi Caste[1] has no spoken language at all, nor any desire to possess one. Being a race of natural epsense adepts, they employ instead a complex palette of emotions, sensations, and associations to talk between themselves, with the ease of thought itself. Mere words not only seem primitive and crude in comparison, but are quite outside the average Olmahoi's experience as well.

A Pristine Human might as well try to communicate with a bacterium by chemicals, or with a bee by dance. Even the concept of "loneliness," which we take for granted, is foreign to them: when one's entire family, one's entire Caste, is but a thought away, one is never alone.

Their uniqueness is marked on many other levels. Olmahoi society[2] is completely unfathomable and literally impenetrable to anyone not possessing epsense ability. They are, from a Pristine perspective, the most exotic of the known mundane Castes, not only in physical appearance, but in reproductive androgyneity as well. They are immensely knowledgeable in all fields and possess an average intelligence greater than that of Pristine Humanity; yet, in apparent contradiction to this sophistication, they have proven themselves on many occasions to be ruthless combatants.[3] And while each Olmahoi individual is a member of a far-flung interstellar empire, he still wears the long robes made from the skin of the Drish'en and prefers to live underground, both in the manner of his distant ancestors.[4]

Yet communicate with the Olmahoi we do. Through a medium of epsense "translators," trade has existed between our two Castes since the arrival of the Eckandar Trade Axis in this region of the galaxy some fifty thousand years ago. Now, after many millennia of contact, our involvement with them is a given, and seems certain to remain that way in the foreseeable future.

---

[1]Not to be confused with the Olmahi Republic, an independent government of the Nezhina Caste.

[2]Often referred to by researchers as the Grand Design.

[3]Not for nothing are Olmahoi retribution units (grayboots) the most admired—and feared—fighting force in the Outer Arms, thereby disproving the usual association between pacifism and epsense ability.

[4]*He* is the usual pronoun used when referring to an Olmahoi individual, and covers both "sexes": reproductive function, which is changeable at will, plays little part in an Olmahoi's sense of identity.

It is strange, then, and not a little disconcerting, to be reminded of how little we actually know about them.

On a fundamental level, there is the matter of their epsense abilities. N-body theory, from which stems the science of epsense and various related disciplines, hints that such a talent cannot evolve by chance, no matter how great the complexity of a mundane Caste member; it has to be guided into being by conscious, intelligent will, without which even a fledgling epsense predilection (such as that which occasionally arises in an individual of any Caste) will falter.

That the Olmahoi appear to have defied current scientific theory may seem a small matter for scholars to debate: it is, after all, a *fait accompli.* With elongated tails tapering from the back of every Olmahoi's skull—these being the principal organs of the epsense, uncannily like an extra spine hanging free of the body—the Olmahoi possess tangible, physical evidence that this improbable evolutionary path has been followed at least once in the history of the universe. Studies of the Olmahoi physiognomy concur, revealing vestigial organs associated with the "vulgar" senses, such as a mouth and throat now used solely for ingestion that once possessed vocal chords and a tongue, ears associated with balance but still possessing the basic structures of an organ designed to detect sound, and so on.

However, proving that the ancestors of the Olmahoi did once possess function vulgar sense-organs is not enough to explain how an epsense ability could have evolved to supersede them. It is precisely by exploring this puzzle that science hopes to glean deeper truths lying beneath the *status quo*—to probe Humanity's place, not just in the Outer Arms, but in the greater galaxy as a whole.

If the Olmahoi possess a naturally occurring epsense ability, how *did* it arise? Current evolutionary theory[5] is simple and obvious. The Olmahoi home planet, Hek'm, is an icy, inhospitable world, and has been for many millions of years. Food is scarce; the Noma Araku, an extinct species of biped distantly related to the modern Olmahoi,[6] relied upon lichens and fungus growing on cave walls to balance an irregular diet of vegetable roots. For a predatory species to survive even a few generations, it must evolve new means of locating prey. Epsense ability is one such means: a way of hunting life directly, by seeking the spoor of thought itself. From this small beginning, evolutionary theory tells us, the Olmahoi Caste was born.

But neither the Noma Araku nor any other species of known biped leading to the modern-day Olmahoi has been proven to have possessed epsense ability, no matter how small. And indeed, the evolution of intelligent life in any form, on a planet such as Hek'm, is itself a statistical unlikelihood. The physical evidence available[7] indicates quite strongly that the species directly preceding the modern Olmahoi appeared almost overnight, approximately fifty thousand years ago, and was already in full possession of the range of epsense powers with which we are familiar today.

This evidence, and a smattering of facts adding suggestive credence, lie at the heart of the counterargument against evolution: that of intervention.

[5]As propounded by Professors Dubsky and Toma of the Cornilleau University of Antiquities.

[6]Itself a Low Human developed from mundane in the distant past.

[7]Predominantly in the form of cranial fossils, ruins, and the like.

Again, this theory[8] is intuitively simple, although its ramifications are far-reaching. If epsense ability cannot evolve by chance, then it must have been deliberately nurtured in the Olmahoi Caste. Genetic analysis offers circumstantial support for this conclusion. The Olmahoi genome is elegantly complex, capable of creating a race of individuals whose only remarkable feature, it sometimes seems, is their lack of individuality,[9] but with just enough diversity to maintain a viable gene pool. Furthermore, the exon-to-intron ratio[10] is very low, suggesting that the genome might have been "trimmed" some time in the past, possibly to protect against mutation.

The critical question, and the one that has prevented this theory from gaining wide acceptance in the scientific community, is obvious: who intervened in the evolution of the Olmahoi Caste to ensure its epsense development?

Even among those who support the interventionist line in principle, there is a wealth of disagreement on this particular point. For once, it is a lack of evidence, suggestive or otherwise, that confounds the issue. There are no ruins on Hek'm to hint at the presence of an earlier, advanced civilization capable of such genetic and epsense manipulation, so it could not have been the Olmahoi natives. Likewise with the other Castes—High or mundane—currently inhabiting this region of the galaxy: none have ever possessed the ability (or the predilection) to perform such a feat; not even today, let alone fifty thousand years ago. So it must have been another Caste entirely, perhaps one of the five pre-High Human Castes mentioned in the Gil-Shh'ana Fiche, or another even more mysterious. Or, most peculiar of all, the Olmahoi themselves might be that very unknown Caste: the descendants of travelers from a distant and relatively unknown part of the galaxy, stranded on Hek'm millennia ago and only now rediscovering the legacy of their past.

Although the key to unlocking this mystery should, one might think, lie in the hands of the Olmahoi themselves, any racial memories, archetypes, or legends they might once have possessed about the origins of their epsense abilities are sadly no longer extant.[11] As a result, the origin of the Olmahoi Caste is either a vexing thorn in the side of anyone who would understand the continuing evolution of Humanity, or a tantalizing glimpse of a history still waiting to be discovered.

The emphasis of this Introduction, and indeed the greater part of the work, is on the latter. There is much that is unique and beautiful among the Olmahoi, and much that we fail to understand. Most notable of all is the Grand Design: the web of minds that is centered on Hek'm, where the Olmahoi naturally congregate; quite possibly the most intricate mental structure in the universe, with tendrils stretching across the galaxy. To describe it in words is to attempt the impossible. Yet the renowned Linn Queale perhaps came close, with the following excerpt from his best-selling *Galactic Reference Book:*

"If empty space is a flat plain, with minds like bumps projecting from it, then the Grand Design resembles a cartographer's nightmare: towers, prominences, and spires project from it as far as the psychic eye can see, with strange ridges and rills, repeated figures and harmonic cadences, changing constantly in every direction—all

[8]As championed by Professor Linegar Rufo of the independent research facility Galine Four.

[9]Olmahoi are notoriously difficult to tell apart.

[10]Analogous to a signal-to-noise ratio.

[11]Or perhaps, say the Kesh researchers in this field, they simply choose not to reveal them.

linked by slender bridges that defy imagination, looping from peak to peak in a dance that resembles nothing so much as the dance of ocean weed in the grip of a cyclonic storm.

"At the very heart of this chaotic mental realm, however, lies the most peculiar thing of all: a bottomless pit, drawing everything toward it as a whirlpool or black hole draws ordinary matter to a single point. This, the one flaw in the multifaceted gem that is group-mind of the Olmahoi Caste, is the *irikeii,* which literally means 'the unnamed' or 'the unnameable,' one of the few thought-shapes in the Olmahoi 'language' that has a vocal analogue. Little is known about the purpose or origins of the *irikeii,* but we do know this: that it is not an artifact, nor a spontaneous natural phenomenon, but is, in fact, a living entity.

"One is born every generation: an otherwise normal Olmahoi whose mind is not so much a peak as an abyss, sucking thoughts in, swamping the Grand Design for a vast area around—counterbalancing, perhaps, the tremendous complexity that is the Olmahoi world of thought. This one is shunned but not reviled; the Olmahoi understand the *irikeii*'s role in their world, strange as it seems to us. Whenever that one is removed, as he must always be eventually, by natural death if not by accident,[12] another is immediately born to take his place. And thus the cycle continues, as it has for countless generations.

"So, even at the center of the Olmahoi Caste, where one might have expected utter chaos, one actually finds another example of the universe's natural tendency toward balance, symmetry, and cycles—proving, perhaps, that, despite the many and varied efforts of every Caste in the galaxy, the greatest beauty of all is still to be found in nature."

---

[12]No Olmahoi in his right mind would dare murder the current *irikeii*; the penalty for committing such a crime is the most severe allowed under Olmahoi Law.

GLOSSARY

A-P cannon—a weapon that fires accelerated particles of various types. Common on spacefaring warships.

Adamek, R. Pyatt—author of *The Olmahoi: Reconstructing the Myth for Beginners,* published in '595 EN.

Alik—an outrigger belonging to Long Span spine.

all-suits—the generic term for the highly individualized environment suits worn by outriggers.

***Ana Vereine,* DBMP**—the first of a new class of warships—the Marauder—manufactured by the Dato Bloc as part of the Andermahr Experiment. Its design incorporates a captain surgically interfaced with the ship. Once part of the Ethnarch's Military Presidium, it is now an independent vessel registered to Morgan Roche.

anchor drive—the usual means of crossing interstellar space, but by no means the only one (see **slow-jump**). Indeed, the anchor method has undergone several radical redesigns over time; current technology is rated at 49th-generation.

anchor points—regions of "weakened" space from which translation to and from hyperspace is both easier and less energy-expensive; jumps from anchor points are therefore of a greater range than from "normal" space and usually terminate in another anchor point. They are typically located near inhabited systems (but far enough away to avoid distortion by background gravitational effects) or in locations in deep space that are considered strategically important. There are approximately ten thousand million anchor points currently in existence—one for roughly every ten stars, scattered across the galaxy.

Andermahr Experiment—a covert project specializing in cybernetic interfaces designed to allow mind and machine to merge. Founded by Ataman Ana Vereine, who desired captains that were as much a part of their ships as was the anchor drive—an integral, reliable system rather than a flesh and blood afterthought. Continued in secret until the Ataman Theocracy emerged from the COE as the Dato Bloc. Culminated in the DBMP *Ana Vereine,* the first Marauder-class warship, with Uri Kajic its captain.

Armada—see **COE Armada**.

Aro—the largest moon of Jagabis and site of Emptage City; also the largest solid world of Palasian System. (Relative mass: 0.000271 (1.6 Cartha's Planet); distance: 1 million km; max. surface temperature: –140 degrees C; diameter: 5500 km)

Ascensio—the homeworld of Morgan Roche.

Asha—the single, warlike deity of the main Kesh religion.

Asha's Gauntlet—see **Solar Envelope**.

Ataman Theocracy—a tightly knit empire that existed as an independent entity until its absorption into the COE after the Second Ataman War in '442 EN. After several centuries, it eventually seceded as the Dato Bloc ('837 EN).

Autoville—the vernacular name for the innermost dark body halo of Palasian System, so-called because of the prowlers that dominate it. (Radius: 2.4-4.0 PAU; largest mean diameter: 2400 km.)

AVS-44—one of the *Ana Vereine*'s large contingent of scutters.

B'kan's Folly—the remains of the system in which a Solar Envelope was first employed.

B'shan, Lieutenant-Doctor Haden—a Kesh officer/scientist, serving with Linegar Rufo on Galine Four; subordinate to Field Officer Shak'ni.

Baeris Osh—a Surin territory.

Bassett—commander, COEA *Golden Dawn.*

Batelin Limit—the ceiling above which the complexity of a nation exceeds the biological capabilities of the individuals inhabiting it. In the case of the Pristine Caste, the value of the Batelin Limit is approximately three and a half thousand systems.

Black Box—the generic term for AI. Usually abbreviated to "Box."

Bodh Gaya—the capital system of the COE. Its second moon houses the Military College of the COE Armada.

Box, the—an AI commissioned by COE Intelligence. Its binary identification number (JW111101000) is one digit longer than normal, indicating its unique status. Created by the High Human known as the Crescend, the Box is designed to infiltrate and subvert all available systems, thereby increasing its own processing powers until, at its most powerful, it resembles its creator.

Byrne, Auditor—the leader of the outrigger clan associated with Long Span spine.

Calendar—The galactic standard timekeeping method consists of: 100 seconds per minute, 100 minutes per hour, 20 hours per day, 10 days per week, 4 weeks (40 days) per month, 10 months (400 days) per year. All dates are expressed in the form of Year (usually abbreviated to the last three digits, ie '397), Month, and Day from the *Ex Nihilo* reference point. See also **Objective Reference Calendar.**

Cane, Adoni—the occupant of an unidentified life-support capsule recovered by the COEA *Midnight* near Ivy Green Station anchor point while en route to Sciacca's World. A genetically modified combat clone designed to mimic a Pristine Human, his origins may lie with the Sol Apotheosis Movement, although that theory is yet to be confirmed.

Cartha's Planet—the rocky, innermost world of Palasian System. (Mean distance: 0.16 PAU; diameter: 3600 km; relative mass: 0.000169; specific gravity: 5.3; mean surface temperature: 425 degrees C.)

Caste C—third of several unknown Castes mentioned in the ancient Gil-Shh'ana Fiche. See **Primordial Castes.**

Castes—Following the speciation of the Human race, numerous Castes have proliferated across the galaxy. These Castes are too numerous to list, but they can be classified into three broad groups: High, Low, and mundane (which includes Pristine and Exotic). There are six predominant Exotic Castes to be found in the region surrounding the COE: Eckandar, Hurn, Kesh, Mbata, Olmahoi, and Surin.

Cemenid—the fourth and largest planet of Palasian System; a gas giant with thirteen major satellites. (Mean distance: 2.24 PAU; diameter: 183200 km; relative mass: 1.33.)

chaos-lock—a security device employing the chaotic electrical output of two identical circuits to conceal ordered data: when the two "tuned" circuits are linked, the data can be extracted from the signal; otherwise, the signal is concealed within unpredictable noise, and is impossible to decode.

COE—see **Commonwealth of Empires.**

COE Armada, the—the combined armed forces of the COE, responsible for external security. Active soldiers are referred to as Marines.

COE Intelligence—the body responsible for information gathering outside the COE. Originally and still nominally a subdepartment of the Armada, but an independent body in practice.

COE Intelligence HQ—the command center of COE Intelligence, a large, independent station located in deep space near the heart of the Commonwealth.

COE Military College—the main training institution of COE Armada personnel; situated on the second moon of Bodh Gaya.

COEI—COE Intelligence vessel identification prefix.

Commerce Artel—a galaxy-wide organization devoted to initiating and coordinating trade between Castes and governments that might otherwise have no contact. It prides itself on remaining aloof from political conflict yet has some strict behavioral standards to which it expects its customers to adhere (such as the Warfare Protocol). Structurally, it is divided into chapters managed by indigenous Caste members with only loose control from above. It has strong links, locally, with the Eckandar Trade Axis.

Commonwealth of Empires—often abbreviated to "COE" or "Commonwealth." A relatively ancient Pristine nation currently in its 40th millennium of nominal existence—"nominal" in that the membership of the COE is fluid by nature, with provinces joining and seceding on a regular basis. It has had many different capitals and its borders have changed radically over the centuries. Indeed, it has drifted with time, and now occupies territories quite remote from its original location. One thousand inhabited systems currently fall under its aegis, and another three thousand uninhabited systems have been annexed. It is ruled by a democratically elected Eupatrid and a council of representatives who, when united, wield supreme executive power. Its security departments include Intelligence, Armada, and Enforcement.

Congreve Station—the abandoned xenoarchaeological base built upon Mok, the moon shared by Kukumat and Murukan.

Cornilleau University of Antiquities—one of the many centers of study in the galaxy devoted to the exploration of Humanity's past.

Crescend, the—a High Human of some note and great history. His time of Transcendence is not recorded. Little is known about him, beyond the facts that he is the founder and overseer of Trinity, an ally of the COE and a key supporter of the Interventionist Movement. He is assumed to be a singular entity simply because the (male) first person singular is his pronoun of choice.

Dahish—a mildly alcoholic drink found in most places in the COE.

dark bodies—small, solid bodies found in most planetary systems (usually in belts, or **dark-body halos**) falling in size roughly between asteroids and planets.

Darkan, General—a senior officer of the Kesh N'Kor Republic and commander in chief of the destroyer SRF *Sebettu.*

Dato Bloc—an independent nation founded on the ruins of the Ataman Theocracy that recently broke free of the COE. Although not hierocratic in nature, the Ethnarch exerts a strict rule. Its security departments include the Ethnarch's Military Presidium and the Espionage Corps.

***Daybreak,* COEI**—a courier vessel belonging to COE Intelligence.

DBMP—vessel identification prefix for the Ethnarch's Military Presidium.

De Bruyn, Page—head of Strategy, COE Intelligence.

Dictatrix—supreme leader of the Kesh N'Kor Republic.

Diprodek-2—a potent neurotoxin most effective against Pristines.

Dirt & Other Commodities, Inc. (DAOC)—a mining consortium that currently owns the rights to the Soul of Sciacca's World. Its jurisdiction includes the planetary surface down to and including the mantle. In exchange for these exclusive rights, DAOC Inc maintains the COE's penal colony based in Port Parvati and the Hutton-Luu System's only major base, Kanaga Station.

Disisto, Gered—dock security chief, Galine Four.

disrupters—see **hyperspace disrupters.**

Dominion, the—a long-lived multi-Caste nation which joined the COE in '199 EN in order to fend off the Ataman Theocracy.

Drish'en—a burrowing animal found on Hek'm.

Dro, Sh'manit—the Sixteenth and last G'rodo Matriarch.

druh—a Kesh weapon used in armed combat; typically a curved, bronze sword about as long as the average Pristine forearm.

Dubsky, Professor—a scholar based at the Cornilleau University of Antiquities.

E-shield—an electromagnetic barrier designed to ward off particle and energy weapons. Used mainly by medium-to-large spacefaring vessels.

Eckandar—(Eckandi: adj & sing. n)—a Caste flourishing in the regions surrounding the COE. Its members are typified by their slight size, gray skin, bald scalps, and unusual eyes. They are a gregarious Caste, preferring trade and communication over conquest. They are also well-advanced in genetic science. Their past stretches back beyond that of the COE, although they lack the continuity of history that strong nationhood often provides. Their sole uniting body is the Eckandar Trade Axis.

Eckandar Trade Axis—the main society of the Eckandi Caste, devoted, much like the Commerce Artel (with which it has close ties), to facilitating free and nondiscriminatory trade with and between the COE and its neighbors.

Eli—an outrigger belonging to Long Span spine.

Emptage City—the main base of Palasian System; situated on Aro, the largest moon of Jagabis. (Population approximately 350,000.)

EN—see ***Ex Nihilo.***

epsense—an ability encompassing telepathy and empathy. The ritual training of epsense adepts generally takes decades and incorporates elements of sensory deprivation. Note: telekinesis and precognition are not covered by epsense and are assumed to be nonexistent. Skilled utilizers of epsense are referred to as **epsense adepts,** or reaves.

Espionage Corps—see **Dato Bloc.**

Ethnarch—the title of the leader of the Dato Bloc.

Ethnarch's Military Presidium—see **Dato Bloc.**

Eupatrid—the title of the chief executive officer of the COE.

Ex Nihilo—refers to the date upon which the COE is believed to have been founded. Evidence exists to cast doubt upon the accuracy or relevance of this date—notably the fact the Commonwealth as a single body did not exist at all between the 13th and 15th Millennia—but the date remains as a reference point. Usually abbreviated to *EN*.

Exotic—any mundane Caste that differs physiologically from the Pristine. There are a vast number of Exotic Castes, and, although no one type of Exotic comes close to outnumbering Pristine Humans, the Exotics as a whole mass far greater than Pristines alone.

Far Reaches—the name of the outermost fringes of the Outer Arms.

Ferozac—a neurotoxin effective against Pristines.

flicker-bombs—devices used in space warfare to attack an enemy vessel. Employing the fact that small masses (under a few kilograms) can slow-jump a small distance within a gravity well, these missiles skip in and out of space on their way to their target, which, it is hoped, they will materialize within, causing massive amounts of damage. They are easily deflected by hypershields, however, which form a barrier in hyperspace that no such weapon can cross.

40th Millennium—the current millennium in the history of the COE. See ***Ex Nihilo.***

Free-For-All—outermost dark-body halo surrounding Palasian System. (Radius: 15.2-21.7 PAU; few clusters and eccentricities known; largest mean diameter: 1375 km.)

G'rodo—a Kesh lineage recently expunged from the N'Kor Republic.

Galactic Reference Book—see **Queale, Linn.**

Galine Four—a small mobile station owned by Linegar Rufo III; crew no more than one thousand.

Gatamin—the fifth world of Palasian System; a gas giant with three major satellites and an extensive ring network. (Mean distance: 4.56 PAU; diameter: 60000 km; relative mass: 0.3; rings 100000-145000 km.)

Geyten Base—a COE communications base around Cemenid in Palasian System.

Gil-Shh'ana Fiche—an anomalous data storage device recovered from Hurn ruins in '636 EN. Some segments of the fiche's contents point to the existence of several unknown Castes occupying the region now inhabited by the COE, although incompatible technology prevents clear translation; such ancient relics are occasionally found throughout the galaxy, but few are as spectacular or mysterious as those in Palasian System.

***Golden Dawn,* COEA**—COE Armada destroyer.

Gorund Sef—a planet in COE territory.

Grand Design—the Human term used to describe the social communion of the Olmahoi Caste.

grayboots—see **Olmahoi retribution squad.**

Guhr Outpost—a COE Armada refueling base orbiting Voloras, outermost planet of Palasian System.

Gwydyon—a system near but not part of the COE.

Haid, Ameidio—former transportee, Sciacca Penal Colony, and mercenary.
Handrelle System—a COE system.
Hek'm—the Olmahoi Caste homeworld.
Herensung—the third world of Palasian System; a gas giant with five major satellites and an extensive ring system. (Mean distance: 1.46 PAU; diameter: 100000 km; relative mass: 0.3; rings 135000-300000 km.)
Hetu System—a territory in the COE.
High Humans—or **High Castes.** Superior intelligences that have evolved (Transcended) from the mundane. Extremely long-lived and far-seeing, they concentrate on issues quite removed from the rest of the galaxy; indeed, due to their enormous scale, they are the only beings capable of comprehending the galaxy in its entirety. They generally leave mundanes alone, to let them progress (and, ultimately, to Transcend) in their own time. See **Castes** and **Transcendence.**
Hintubet—the primary of Palasian System; a greenish-yellow Main Sequence star supporting a large solar system consisting of seven gas giants, one rocky planet, one asteroid belt and several dark-body/cometary halos. (Surface temperature: 7800 degrees C; diameter: 1.8 million km; low sunspot activity, prominences, flares, etc.)
Hurn—an exotic Caste typified by ritual and complexity. In appearance they are lean and muscular, averaging greater than Pristine height. They are predisposed toward music and mathematics. Socially they prefer oligarchies with a baroque middle class.
hypershield—a barrier erected in hyperspace to deflect or inhibit the passage of anything traveling by that medium. Commonly used as a prophylactic against hyperspace weapons. Hypershields operate under a maximum volume constraint: i.e., they will only operate as intended under two thousand cubic kilometers.
hyperspace disrupters—a form of hypershield that actively combats incoming hyperspace weapons, such as flicker-bombs. Compare anchor points, which "weaken" space: disrupters do the opposite, making it more difficult for anything nearby to emerge from hyperspace.

Idil—an outrigger belonging to Long Span spine.
IDnet—see **Information Dissemination Network.**
IND—independent vessel identification prefix.
Information Dissemination Network—a communications network dedicated to the spread of data across the galaxy, although its reach thus far extends not much beyond the COE and its neighbors. It acts as a combined news service and medium for gossip. Also known as IDnet.
Intelligence—see **COE Intelligence.**
Interventionism—a movement among High Humans—and some mundanes—that advocates closer links between High and mundane Castes. See **The Crescend.**
irikeii—one of very few Olmahoi "sound-thoughts" that can be equated with audible words; often translated as "unnamed" or "unnameable." (See Appendix.)

JA-32—the largest charted dark body in Mishra's Stake, Palasian System; full name JA140732.
Jagabis—the second planet of Palasian System; a gas giant, it possesses an ageing ring system and six major moons, one being Aro, the largest solid body in

Palasian System. (Mean distance: 1 PAU (460 million km); diameter: 133200 km; relative mass: 1.0; (2 million million million million tons); rings 156000-173000 km.)

Johak Corporation—original manufacturers of the device known as Asha's Gauntlet; see **Solar Envelope.**

JW111101000—see **Box, the.**

K'mok ni Asha—late Kesh (Regional Variant #14) for "Asha's Gauntlet"; see **Solar Envelope.**

Kajic, Uri—former captain, DBMP *Ana Vereine,* physically bonded to his ship.

Kesh—the most primal of the local Castes. The Kesh are typically warlike and predisposed to violence. In appearance, they tend to be larger than the Pristine average and have mottled, multicolored skin. Their social structure is heavily ritualized, with a strong tribal or family base. They are known for being highly racist.

Kesh Ideal—the epitome of the Kesh culture, a being comprising ideological and physical perfection, to which most Kesh, especially those in the military forces, aspire.

KM36—an inconstant ion flux tube connecting Kukumat and Murukan; known as "old thirty-sixer" in the vernacular.

Kukumat—one of a gas giant pair occupying the sixth planetary orbit around Palasian System; the pair shares a single moon, Mok. (Mean distance: 7.17 PAU; diameter: 45000 km / 43000 km; relative mass: 0.25/0.2; average separation: 2 million km.)

Kuresh—Kesh for "General."

Long Span—an outrigger spine.

Low Castes—devolved mundane Humans. These animal-like creatures come in many forms and occupy many niches across the galaxy. Some evolve back up to mundane status, given time and isolation, while others become extinct as a result of the forces that led to their devolution in the first place.

Lucence-2—COE Armada escort and assault craft.

Lud—an outrigger belonging to Long Span spine.

Maii—Surin epsense adept.

Marauder—an experimental class of warship developed by the Dato Bloc. See **DBMP *Ana Vereine*.**

Marines—see **COE Armada.**

Mattar Belt—Palasian System's asteroid belt. (Radius: 0.38-0.76 PAU; various gaps and groupings known; largest 750 km across.)

Mavalhin, Myer—ex-COE Intelligence trainee, now a pilot for Linegar Rufo.

Mbata—(Mbatan, adj & sing. n)—a well-regarded Caste known for its peace-loving and familial ways. In appearance they resemble the ursine species, larger and stronger than the Pristine. Their culture is egalitarian and open to trade.

***Midnight,* COEA**—COE Retriever-class frigate.

Military Presidium—see **Dato Bloc.**

Mishra's Stake—the vernacular name for the second dark-body halo of Palasian System. (Radius: 7.6-11.1 PAU; largest known: JA140732, diameter: 1500 km.)

Mok—the moon shared by Kukumat and Murukan with a highly irregular, chaotic orbit. (Relative mass: unknown; diameter: 1050 km; surface g: unknown; max. surface temperature: –125 degrees C.) It houses a small xenoarchaeological base, now abandoned.

Montaban—the homeworld of Ameidio Haid.

mundane Castes—Castes of Humanity that are essentially similar to the Pristine in terms of size, mental capacity, world-view, etc. Naturally there is a spectrum of types across the mundane Caste—from the highly evolved (some might say near-Transcendent) Olmahoi, through the socially complex Surin and Hurn Castes, to the Eckandar and Pristine Castes with their societies based on trade and empire-building, and beyond, via the earthy Mbata, to the relatively primal Kesh. Mundanes are typically short-lived (a century or so, when allowed to age naturally) and build empires up to four or five thousand systems in size. There is a ceiling of complexity above which mundanes rarely go without Transcending. See **High Humans** and **Batelin Limit.**

Murukan—one of a gas giant pair occupying the sixth planetary orbit around Palasian System (see **Kukumat**).

n-body—the epsense "counterpart" to the physical body.

N'kor Republic—a Kesh government neighboring the COE. Although the relationship between these two nations is officially friendly, there have been frequent border clashes.

n-space—a word used by epsense theorists to describe an environment completely empty of thought.

Narm Protectorate—a part of the COE.

Nezhina Caste—a mundane Caste located on the other side of the galaxy from the COE.

Nirr—the neutral homeworld of the Kesh Caste.

Noma Araku—an extinct species of biped distantly related to the modern Olmahoi.

Objective Reference Calendar—a system of date-keeping established by the A-14 Higher Collaboration Network.

old thirty-sixer—see **KM36.**

Olmahi Republic—an independent government of the Nezhina Caste.

Olmahoi—an Exotic Caste that communicates entirely by epsense. Physically they are of similar size to Pristines, but are much stronger; their skin is black and they possess little in the way of distinguishing features, apart from the epsense organ which dangles like a tentacle from the back of the skull. Their social structure is too complex to explore in detail here. They are renowned fighters, capable of feats of great skill, yet also possess a capacity for peace far in excess of any other local Caste. (See Appendix.)

Olmahoi retribution units—renowned fighters able to combine perfectly their physical and epsense abilities. Also known as grayboots.

Outer Arms—the low stellar-density regions of the galaxy between the Middle and Far Reaches.

outrigger—a unique type of miner/explorer found in sparsely populated systems; living within all-suits that double as mobile homes, outriggers typically scout uncharted dark-body halos and asteroid belts looking for viable mineral sources, which they then either mine or report to a centralized authority (if any) for a modest fee. Outriggers are notoriously self-sufficient, avoiding even other outriggers as much as possible, and have been known to exist for years without contact with another being. Spending much of their lives drifting in hibernation between dark and cometary bodies, some live longer than three centuries. Few outriggers have family names, coming as they do from such small communities that single given names are usually enough.

Palasian System—a system of the COE recently quarantined by the COE Armada as a result of an enemy outbreak. Due to its lack of habitable or easily terraformable planets, it has never been extensively colonized, but is the home to several Armada bases and a small commercial mining operation: total population, five hundred thousand people.

PAU—the abbreviation of Palasian Astronomical Unit, the mean distance from Jagabis to Hintubet, that being 460 million kilometers.

Perez radiation—a side effect of a crudely tuned hyperspace jump.

Plenary—full outrigger meeting, convened only in extraordinary situations. The individual members are rarely in the same physical location, however.

Primordial Castes—precede the earliest confirmed records, half a million years ago. Little is known about them, except that they existed; ruins of several unique types are to be found throughout the galaxy. They are called Castes A, B, C, and D, for even their names are unknown.

Pristine Caste—the form of Humanity which most closely resembles the original race that evolved an unknown time ago on an unknown planet somewhere in the galaxy. The Pristine Human genome, handed down from antiquity and regarded with near veneration, is stored in innumerable places among the civilized worlds. Pristines themselves, however, are accorded no special status.

prowling mines—known also as **prowlers.** These are mobile, semiautonomous mining installations, typically found in the dark-body halos of sparsely populated systems and are usually corporate owned.

Queale, Linn—author of the *Galactic Reference Book,* a popular all-purpose travel guide and almanac.

Quick, Alemdar—a duelist on the COE fighting circuit.

Quolmann—COE Intelligence code word.

quorum—the outrigger decision-making body; flexible in both number and identity of members.

Ramage, General—commander in chief of the COE Armada.

reave—see **epsense.**

Riem-Perez Horizon—the technical name for the boundary cast by a hyper-shield.

Roche, Morgan—former commander, COE Intelligence.

Roptio ur-music—music performed by a Low Human Caste known for its lack of sophistication.

Rufo, Linegar—renowned xenoarchaeologist; see **Galine Four.**

Sciacca's World—the only habitable world of the Hutton-Luu System; once an agricultural planet of the Dominion, now a desert penal colony of the COE (Sciacca Penal Colony). Its ring of moonlets—the Soul—is owned and mined by DAOC Inc.

Scion War—the war in which the Sol Apotheosis Movement met its downfall at the hands of the Dominion, the Ataman Theocracy, and the COE, among others. The war was brought to an end in the 37th Millennium ('577 EN) when the leader of the combined military forces ordered an attack on the headquarters of the Movement, provoking their explosive suicide. See **Sol Apotheosis Movement.**

scutter—a small, swift spacegoing vessel with many uses, both military and civilian.

Sebettu—Dictatrix who, in '173 EN, briefly unified the Kesh Caste.

***Sebettu,* SRF**—Kesh destroyer.

Shadow Place—the temple-like quarters in which the Olmahoi *irikeii* is housed.

Shak'ni, Field Officer—a Kesh officer subordinate to General Darkan.

slow-jump—a common alternative to the anchor drive that utilizes similar technology. Most ships with an anchor drive can slow-jump if necessary. It is essentially a jump through hyperspace from any point in real space. A certain degree of kinetic energy is required before translation can be achieved, so ships must accelerate for some time beforehand. Even then, the hyperspace jump is short-lived, and the vessel emerges soon after (typically less than a light-year away from its departure point) with significantly less kinetic energy. The process must be repeated from scratch if another slow-jump is required. As a means of crossing interstellar space, it is inefficient and time-consuming, hence its name. Slow-jumping becomes increasingly nonviable closer to a gravity well, but more efficient as mass (of the traveling object) decreases.

Sol Apotheosis Movement—a quasi-religious organization devoted to the pursuit of Transcendence via genetic manipulation and biomodification that reached its peak and was destroyed in the 37th Millennium. Its fanatical followers were a source of unrest for decades, until an alliance was formed among their neighbors dedicated to putting a stop to them. In '577 EN, at the climax of the Scion War, a flotilla of allied forces encircled their base, which the Movement destroyed in order to prevent its capture. The resulting explosion annihilated them as well, of course, but also decimated the flotilla. Of the four stations involved in the battle, only one survived, and that was severely damaged. So embarrassed was the alliance that the leaders of the day ordered the event stricken from history. They even closed the anchor point leading to the system to keep anyone from learning what occurred there. Nothing survived of the base, and the rest of the system is an unsalvageable ruin.

Sol System—an uninhabited system in a nonaligned region near the Dato Bloc, one known for its antiquity. Former home of the Sol Apotheosis Movement.

Sol Wunderkind—genetically modified clone warriors designed and bred by the Sol Apotheosis Movement.

Solar Envelope—a device designed by the Johak Corporation in 38,138 EN, intended to provide a jump shield large enough to enclose an entire solar system. Two prototypes were built in '211 EN by an early Kesh Government, which held them in storage until the Great Embargo of '221 EN. Asha's Gauntlet was used on one system at this time, with disastrous results: the system's primary sun, modified to power the Envelope, was exhausted within two months; the entire system collapsed shortly thereafter, and is now known only as B'kan's Folly. Of no use as a defensive weapon, and outlawed by the Convention on Extraordinary Weapons in '254 EN, the second Gauntlet has remained in the hands of the N'kor Republic since then.

spine—the collective noun used to describe a loosely linked group of outriggers; from their means of traveling between systems, on the back of a naked real-space drive known as the spine.

***Starburst*, COEA**—COE frigate.

Surin—a relatively minor Caste found in the regions surrounding the COE. They exist in isolated clusters overseen by a governing body that guides rather than rules. They are social beings, yet are fond of isolation, giving them a reputation for occasional aloofness. They are technically accomplished, especially in the biological sciences. In stature, they tend to be slight and have hair covering much of their bodies. It is occasionally speculated that they have re-evolved from Low Caste status.

Surin Agora—the ruling body of the loosely knit Surin nation.

Synnett, Torr—security guard on Galine Four.

Temoriel—a COE Armada trainee port not far from Bodh Gaya.

Thin Trunk—an outrigger spine known to Long Span.

Tipper-Linke Conduit—a specialized form of chaos-lock, combining tuned circuits with quantum encryption: the chaos-locked signal is broadcast along a beam of polarized light, with digital data represented by 90-degree separations in polarization; without knowing which polarization angles to look for or which angle is 0 and which is 1, the signal will be garbled. By the uncertainty principle, any incorrect attempt to measure the polarization of the light will result in interference, which will alert the users of the Tipper-Linke Conduit, who can then change the angle of polarization, leaving the hackers exactly where they started.

Toma, Professor—a scholar based at the Cornilleau University of Antiquities.

Tongue, the—how the Kesh refer to their own language.

Transcend—to break free of the constraints of mundane Humanity. A being or Caste that has Transcended typically has an extremely long life span and spreads its consciousness across a number of primary containers—such as neural nets, quantum data vats, and the like. Transcended entities, singular or collective, are referred to as High Human and accorded the highest status.

Transcendence—the state of being Transcended. Usually achieved when consciousness research and computer technology overlap, allowing an organic mind to be downloaded into an electronic vessel, thereby gaining the potential for unlimited growth.

Tretamen—a region on the fringes of the COE.

Trinity—the world on which AIs are made in the region dominated by the COE. The AI factory was founded and is overseen by the High Human known as the Crescend.

Veden, Makil—an Eckandar Trade Axis citizen and Commerce Artel ex-delegate; deceased.

Vereine, Ataman Ana—the last leader of the Ataman Theocracy and founder of the Andermahr Experiment.

viridant—a reptilian creature found on Ascensio.

Void 34—a cyborg duelist on the COE fighting circuit.

Voloras—the eighth and outermost planet of Palasian System; a gas giant with three major satellites. (Mean distance: 13.0 PAU; diameter: 40,000 km; relative mass: 0.33.)

vukh—a hot alcoholic beverage enjoyed by members of the Kesh Caste.

Walan Third—a COE world leased to the Commerce Artel.

Warfare Protocol—the code by which war is conducted within and between those nations that trade with the Commerce Artel.

Warrior's Right—the right of a Kesh to challenge by physical combat a superior's decision.

Wide Berth—an outrigger spine.

Wight Station—the automated solar research station on Cartha's Planet, Palasian System.

Xarodine—an epsense-inhibiting drug.

Yarrow—an outrigger belonging to Wide Berth spine.

Yul—an outrigger belonging to Long Span spine.

A Dark Imbalance

For
Richard Curtis and Ginjer Buchanan,
without whom this project would have remained
forever incomplete.

"One knows what a war is about
only when it is over."

H. N. Brailsford

"*Unser Leben geht hin mit Verwandlung.*"
(Our life passes in transformation.)

Rainer Maria Rilke

PART ONE:

SOL SYSTEM

PROLOGUE

The former COE Intelligence Head of Strategy didn't need to study her stolen fighter's instruments to know that something strange was going on in Sol System. Something strange and very unsettling.

Page De Bruyn swung her fighter down into the plane of the ecliptic, braving a navigational nightmare as she went. The reopening of the Sol anchor point behind her had allowed—and continued to allow—a flood of vessels into the system. In the first few minutes, she catalogued fifty vessels whose design matched none in her records, and logged markings of fifteen new nations. None of them was the one she sought—and she had barely touched the surface. According to the fighter's instruments, the total number of ships, stations, and launchers present in the system might well be on the order of several hundred thousand. Given that she hadn't properly surveyed the innermost and outermost extremes, she wouldn't be surprised if that figure doubled by the end of the day.

Possibly a million ships, then, representing maybe tens of thousands of nations, near and far. She had heard of larger gatherings, but never in a solar gravity well. Even the combined fleet that had assembled in this very place to destroy the Sol Apotheosis Movement two thousand years earlier had, according to records, numbered barely ten thousand ships. Whether or not that record was accurate, she was now unsure, but the point remained: nothing like this had occurred in or near the Commonwealth of Empires before. And it would make finding her quarry that much more difficult.

As she skimmed the morass, she was scanned and hailed twice but not challenged. There didn't seem to be a central authority operating anywhere. The system was a mess. But the longer she looked at it, the more she realized that this might not be a bad thing after all. It might even work to her advantage. She could travel freely through it, confident that no one would notice a single fighter among the other ships. That was indeed a good thing, for the journey to Sol System had been long and exhausting, and she was going to need rest to prepare for the days ahead.

She had to work out what was going on, and how it related to an unaspiring orphan whom she appeared to have completely underestimated. And to do that, she needed to be closer to those who had spurned her.

She instructed the fighter to hunt for COE signals among the babble of transmissions filling the spectra around her. It wasn't a sophisticated craft, but it would do that for her. Once registered as TBC-14, she had renamed it *Kindling* upon stealing it from Intelligence HQ. Although she was, theoretically, a fugitive from justice, in reality she had enough friends remaining in high places to divert attention from her, provided she didn't ruffle anyone's feathers too soon.

The time would eventually come, though, when she wouldn't care whom she offended or how she offended them. The question of why she had been so abruptly dismissed from her post in COE Intelligence was proving a vexing one, and one that became increasingly far-reaching the more she probed. She refused to let it go unasked.

Obtaining an answer was all that mattered to her, now. That, and revenge . . .

Six hours after she had arrived in Sol System, *Kindling* detected signals from a vanguard of the COE Advance Fleet. De Bruyn ordered the fighter to approach, carefully. She didn't know quite what to expect—although, given the COE's proximity to Sol System, it was only natural to suppose that it would have a role to play in the emerging power base in the system, however small. That there would be such a power base before long she didn't doubt, for it was the nature of Humans to coalesce into groups. Maybe not one single group, but something larger than isolated clusters. Looking for such an emerging group in the obvious Pristine camp was something she was sure others would be doing also.

Whether this focus of attention on the Advance Fleet would work to its advantage or detriment was difficult to tell. De Bruyn wasn't convinced the COE Armada commanders had the ability to exploit such a situation properly. It needed someone with a flair for intrigue, someone prepared to be ruthless, someone who knew an opportunity when she saw it.

She smirked in the dim light of *Kindling*'s cockpit. It would be the COE's loss, disposing of her the way they had. She would show them that she wasn't someone to be trifled with, to be used up and tossed away. She would pursue the mystery of her dismissal no matter where it led. And if it brought down the Eupatrid himself, then so be it. She would allow nothing and no one to come between herself and the answer . . .

And Roche.

The thought of that name made her fists clench, as it always did. *Damn* that woman! Roche had disobeyed her superior officers, jeopardized her mission as an Intelligence Field Agent, even caused a diplomatic incident over the theft of the *Ana Vereine*—and yet she had been allowed to walk away—*free.* And the sole person who seemed to care about righting this wrong was penalized for being "unduly enthusiastic."

De Bruyn would give Burne Absenger—chief liaison officer with the COE Armada—*unduly enthusiastic.* That she promised herself. She would expose the truth: a truth so large even *he* would choke on it; a truth she sensed hiding deep in the data, deep in the mystery that was Morgan Roche.

All she needed was information. All she wanted was *proof.* No matter how long it took, she was dedicated to finding it.

She sent a coded message to a drone on the edge of the Advance Fleet. It relayed her message to a nexus deeper within the COE camp. There, her message triggered a coded response from a communications AI, which sent another message higher still in the command structure. From there, it was out of her hands—but she was sure one of her contacts would see the message and work out what it meant. It was just a matter of tracing her message to its source. To her.

In the middle of the second largest fleet ever assembled by Humanity, she settled back to wait.

And when, finally, *Kindling* told her that it had recognized the distinctive camouflage signature of the *Ana Vereine* as it entered the system, she clasped her hands together with something approaching eagerness. This was precisely what she had been hoping for. If Roche thought she could just walk in and throw everything into a spin to suit her own ends, whatever they were, she was about to be disappointed.

De Bruyn sent a brief, coded message to a Dato warship she had found lurking nearby, notifying it that the stolen property of its Ethnarch had arrived in the system.

Then she settled back to see what happened next.

1

COEA *Lucence-2*
955.1.29
1860

The feet of Morgan Roche's suit came away sticky as she stepped across the bridge of the *Lucence-2* toward the commander's chair. She stopped a meter from it, staring with a mix of apprehension and disgust at the fist-sized object lying on the brown-spattered cushion. She didn't need to touch it to know that it was organic.

<It's a heart,> said the Box through her implants.

She nodded mutely as her gaze panned around the bridge, the light from her suit's helmet cutting through the dark to reveal the carnage: here, a dismembered body, there, walls splashed with swaths of blood. She couldn't smell the blood through the triple-thickness armor of her powered Dato suit, but she could imagine its stench.

"Commander Roche?" The voice of the Basigo first officer crackled loudly in her ears, his accent as thick as that of a Hurn peasant, and not dissimilar.

She didn't respond for almost thirty seconds; it took that long for her to find her voice—and even then all she could manage was a grunt of acknowledgment.

"Commander?" the first officer repeated.

"Forget the 'Commander,' " she said. "I'd prefer that you just call me by my name."

"Whatever," the voice shot back impatiently. "Have you found what you were looking for?"

Her helmet light once again caught the organ in the commander's chair, and she winced. "Yes and no," she said, turning from the disturbing sight. "You say you intercepted this vessel on your last orbit?"

"We were in close to the primary when it intersected our orbit. We hailed it, but it didn't respond. We thought it was a derelict, so we boarded it."

Looking for bounty, she didn't doubt.

"That's when we saw your name."

She nodded. She had seen it too, painted in blood on the wall in front of the main airlock, where no one could miss it. The fact that it was painted in letters six feet high made certain of that.

"And its orbit was highly elliptical?" she said.

"Aye, that it was," he said. "Would've swung past us and headed way out-system if we hadn't slowed it down a touch during docking."

Headed right for us, she concluded, privately. The Box had superimposed trajectories before she had come aboard. Barely had they arrived at Sol System's anchor point when the ship they were chasing had been hurled at the *Ana Vereine* like an insult, filled with the blood of its crew.

But even if the Basigo scout hadn't intercepted it, Kajic would have seen the ship approaching long before it became a serious threat, and avoided it with ease. Such a crude tactic would never have worked. Roche knew that it was never intended to.

"Repeating herself," Ameidio Haid had said upon the discovery. Jelena Heidik, the clone warrior who had hijacked the *Lucence-2*, had committed the same atrocity in Palasian System within days of her first awakening, that time to the crew of the *Daybreak.* "Honing her skills," he added somberly.

Heidik had gone on to single-handedly kill more than five hundred thousand people in Palasian System before escaping. Roche shuddered to imagine what she could accomplish here, in Sol System.

"It might be a trap," said Uri Kajic from the *Ana Vereine*, on a channel the Basigo weren't listening to.

<I sense no life.> Maii's words came from the same source but by utterly different means. The reave's voice sounded like a whisper in Roche's skull, as though the very cells of her brain were listening. It came with an image of a bone picked clean by the elements. <But that means little. Cane is closed to me now—even his senses—and Heidik could be doing the same. If she were standing next to you, I might not know.>

Roche nodded, waiting to see if Cane himself would say anything, but he didn't. The clone warrior she had once been happy to call *ally*—who was at least distantly related to the woman Jelena Heidik—had been reticent since his awakening from the coma in which he'd been imprisoned by Linegar Rufo. Under the circumstances, she wasn't sure she blamed him. Nevertheless, it still made her uneasy. . . .

"We've lost her, haven't we?" said Haid from elsewhere in the ship.

Roche glanced at the pools of blood around the bridge. "I think so," she said, unsure whether to feel relieved or piqued. The clone warrior presumably had more important things to worry about now that she was in Sol System. And Roche would have no chance of finding her unless Heidik chose to attack—a notion she didn't particularly care to entertain.

Switching back to the Basigo channel, Roche came to a decision. "We're going to disable all the drives except for attitude adjustment and program a warning beacon. It shouldn't be disturbed any more than it already has been. Do you agree to that?"

"It's not my place to decide," said the first officer with some relief. "They're your bodies, not mine."

"*My* . . . ?" Roche started, a sick feeling rising in her stomach.

"Hey, they were addressed to you," he said. "And that's good enough for me."

By the time Roche and Haid returned to the *Ana Vereine*, the Basigo ship had already gone, powering in-system on a torch of blue energy as though its crew was keen to put as much distance between it and the death-ship as possible. Roche could at least empathize with this. Behind her, the *Lucence-2* had been scuttled with cold efficiency, its navigation AIs wiped. Its only remaining sign of life was the beacon, warning people away.

"Heidik knew we were following her," Roche said aloud as she stepped out of the back of her suit and down onto the rubberized floor of the changing room. The moment the suit was empty, it walked itself to an empty niche in the wall for recharging.

Haid watched her from a bench in one corner, his dark skin and biomesh glistening with sweat. "It couldn't just be a lucky guess?"

"She wrote my name in six-foot letters on the bridge of that ship, Ameidio, using the blood of the people she'd murdered." Roche ran a hand across her stubbled scalp. "Trust me, she knew we were coming after her, and exactly when we would arrive, too."

"She could have destroyed us if she'd really wanted to," Haid mused.

"But she didn't," said Roche. "My name was written there for someone to find, and that wouldn't have happened if the ship had been destroyed." She slipped a loose top over her head. "No, the *Lucence-2* was only intended as a parting shot—a spit in the eye."

"That's one hell of a spit," said Haid humorlessly.

She shrugged wearily, as though settling a burden on her back. "Our options now are limited. We keep looking for her—although just how we're going to do that, I don't know. Or we warn whoever's in charge to keep an eye out."

"You really think someone is in charge, here?"

"Not yet. But that won't stop someone trying."

Haid paused before saying: "There's something I still don't understand, though, Morgan." He didn't wait for her to respond before continuing: "How *did* we know where she was going?"

Roche avoided meeting his eye. "I told you, the Box talked about the gathering here before we left Palasian System. Before it was destroyed."

"Yeah, but how did *it* know?" said Haid. "We could have been heading into a trap."

Roche snorted. "Didn't we just do that?"

"You know what I mean," said Haid. "The Box could have been sending us—"

Kajic's voice over the intercom interrupted him: "Morgan, you're receiving another hail."

"Me specifically?"

"Yes."

"I don't suppose the Basigo simply forgot something?"

"No," said Kajic. "It's a representative of the Eckandar Trade Axis in what looks like a Commerce Artel ship. They're radiating an impartial sigil, anyway."

"What do they want?"

"They haven't said. I can open a line if you like."

"Give me a minute to get to the bridge." Roche indicated for Haid to come with her. He tossed the towel aside and followed her from the changing room, along a stretch of corridor and to an internal transit tube. Two harnesses awaited them there, ready to whisk them across the ship.

Not that their physical presence was actually required on the bridge. The *Ana Vereine* was as advanced as anything the Dato Bloc could build; in some areas it was even slightly ahead of the Commonwealth of Empires. Roche could run the ship in every respect from any point within it—or beyond its hull, if necessary. But being at the heart of the ship helped her concentrate, she had found, and it was as good a place as any for everyone to gather.

Maii was there when they arrived. So was Cane. The dark-skinned clone warrior watched impassively from where he stood off-center in the large room, facing the main screen. On it was an image of a ship: flat, petal-shaped, with a sheen to it like that of polished bone. There were no visible markings, although on ultraviolet a repeating pattern of symbols raced around the undulating rim. Artel sigils, as Kajic had already noted.

There was no obvious means of propulsion to the ship, but it advanced steadily toward them.

Thinking of Heidik, Roche said: "Be careful, Uri. It could be a trap."

"I am battle-ready," said Kajic.

"I would not attack like this," said Cane, facing Roche. "They are foolishly exposed. Until it is clear who are your enemies and who are your allies, it would be best to wait."

"Then what is it they want?" asked Haid.

"Let's find out." Roche indicated for Kajic to open a line to the Artel ship. "This is Morgan Roche of the vessel *Ana Vereine*. What is—?"

"Ah, Roche." The long, gray face of an Eckandi in middle age appeared on the screen. "My name is Alwen Ustinik. I am sorry to trouble you, but, having been advised of your arrival, I thought it prudent to contact you as soon as possible."

"Advised? By whom?"

"An associate. I do not speak for myself, of course. I am merely the representative of a number of interested parties. The Commerce Artel has many such representatives scattered throughout this system, as I'm sure you would expect. Even at a time such as this, the possibilities of trade are enormous. So many new contacts to make and avenues to explore . . ."

She's trying to distract me, Roche realized. "Get on with it, Ustinik."

There was a pause, then a smile. "Naturally," Ustinik said. "The people I represent have an interest in seeing justice served, as I'm sure you do too, Roche. When people are hurt, they desire recompense—or, at the very least, a sense that some attempt at retribution has been made. How one dispenses punishment depends on one's society, of course, but there tends to be more overlap than dissent, I have found. The majority decides, and, where the justice system fails, it is often up to the Artel to facilitate corrective dialogue."

Roche sighed. "Can we get to the point here? I have no idea what it is you're talking about."

"I am talking about war, Roche," the Eckandi said evenly. "The ultimate destabilization an economy can experience. Yes, it may have its short-term benefits, but in the long term it leads to nothing but hardship. The legacy of death and heartbreak is enduring; everyone pays in the end."

Roche thought of the clone warriors, spreading dissent throughout the galaxy, and guessed that Ustinik had been sent to get her hands on Cane. Why? For a show-trial, perhaps, to suggest that her "associates" knew what they were doing. Or in a last-minute, desperate attempt to obtain information . . .

"I'm not turning him over," she said, despite her own misgivings about having him around.

"Please reconsider. I speak on behalf of those who have had the misfortune in the past to be on the receiving end of his business dealings. He is a mercenary and a terrorist who has not fully atoned for his crimes—"

"Wait a second." Roche gestured the other woman to silence. "Are you talking about *Haid*?"

The Eckandi frowned. "Yes, of course."

Roche frowned also. "But what the hell would you want with him?"

"I am here to ensure his return to a corrective institution," said Ustinik, "where the remainder of his sentence can be carried out."

Roche was momentarily taken aback. "His sentence was repealed by the High Equity Court—"

"Not formally—and under some duress, if the information I have at my disposal is correct. I am told that, quite apart from the crimes committed before his capture, he was also the leader of a resistance movement on Sciacca's World, and that this movement overthrew the legally appointed warden of the planet."

"The warden was corrupt, and colluding with the Dato Bloc—"

"The Artel doesn't get involved in regional disputes, Roche." Ustinik's tone was calm but commanding; not once did her pitch rise, nor her face display any annoyance or anger. "There is still such a thing as due process. My clients are dissatisfied with a pardon extracted at gunpoint. If they do not make an example of his flagrant disregard for the law, where will it end?"

"It wasn't like that. If you'll let me explain—"

"No explanations are necessary," Ustinik cut in again. "Or desired. To resist would only implicate yourself further, Roche."

"Are you threatening me?"

"My clients' words, not mine." The woman's smile was economical and short-lived. "I am a mediator, nothing more."

Roche's fists clenched. "And I have more important things to worry about."

"Regardless, the facts remain: you helped Ameidio Haid evade justice, and you continue to shield him from those who wish to see that justice served in full. I doubt they will smile on your venture, no matter how important you think it is. Turn him over to my custody, and you will have nothing further to worry about."

Anger flared, but Roche kept it in tight check. "Give me ten minutes to think about it."

"You have five." Ustinik killed the line without any change in facial expression.

"You should've asked her who she was representing," said Haid after a few moments.

"I was hoping you might be able to answer that one," said Roche.

"Well, there are a number of people it could be." The ex-mercenary shrugged. "Maybe all of them. I was busy for a long time, Morgan."

"Great." Roche sighed. A representative of the Commerce Artel would be easy to ignore if the woman was on her own; but if some of her clients showed up to back her claim . . .

<She represents several factions from the M'taio and Reshima Systems,> said Maii, <plus a venge-seeker from Imi.>

"You can read her?" Roche asked.

<Her shield is strong, but not leakproof.> The blind Surin smiled from her place in one corner of the bridge, black lips pulling back to crease her ginger-haired cheeks. <It's nice to be useful again.>

Roche smiled also; she had missed Maii's input in Palasian System, where the reave's abilities had been dampened. "How serious does she think her clients are? Are they prepared to use force if we don't give them what they want?"

<She believes so. She has been authorized to threaten us with it.>

Haid hissed between his teeth. "I should have known that i-Hurn thing was going to cost me one day."

"We're not handing you over," Roche said. "It's not even an option. There must be some way to convince her to see reason."

"Will her side of the conversation be monitored?" asked Cane.

"Probably," said Roche. "Uri, can you detect any signals leaving her ship?"

"None," said Kajic. "But given the strong possibility that she would use a tight-beam, and the large amount of noise in this system, I doubt that I could detect anything at all."

"Then we'll have to assume that she's being monitored," Roche concluded. "Which means we can't just blow her out of the sky."

"You'd really do that?" asked Haid.

Roche shrugged, and grinned. "No, but it *is* tempting."

They discussed a number of more or less fanciful options for several minutes, until Kajic interrupted with the news that he was receiving another hail.

"Our friend Ustinik again, I presume, telling us that time is up?"

"No, Morgan. It's coming from elsewhere."

"What?"

"From a Surin *imaret* closing in on our position, to be exact."

"I don't believe this," said Roche. "We've been in-system just over half a day and we've already had one attempt made on our lives, one threat, and now . . ." She shook her head. "Put them through."

"Morgan Roche." The face of a large male Surin adult appeared on the main screen. "I am Fighter-For-Peace Jancin Xumai. You have one of our citizens aboard your ship, and we request that she be returned to us."

Roche was confused. "Returned? Why?"

"So that she may be reunited with her mother."

<No!>

Roche called out in pain as a bolt of anger and fear slammed into her mind. Clutching her head, her vision swimming with intense secondhand anxiety, she turned to face Maii. Through the discomfort she saw Cane move over quickly to the girl's side and take her shoulders in his large hands. A second later, as he eased her back into her seat, the debilitating emotions ebbed and died.

<I'm sorry, Morgan. I—I just . . .> The mental equivalent of tears soaked the girl's words, diluting her emotions.

"It's okay, Maii. I understand. It's all right. We're not going to let them take you. Did you hear that, Jancin?"

"I advise against that course of action." The Surin's unnerved expression belied the threat in his words. Roche supposed that he had felt a backlash of the girl's epsense projection. "The Surin Caste has a strong military presence in Sol System. Should you not comply with the wishes of the ruling Agora, I am instructed to call for backup."

"Then you'd better do just that," said Roche bluntly. "Because we won't be surrendering her to you—certainly not against her wishes."

"Her wishes are irrelevant," said Jancin. It is the mother's wishes, and that of the Agora, which are important here."

<I have no mother,> said Maii. Her words were edged with bitterness, and Roche could feel the anger inside the Surin girl wanting to break free. <She sold me for medical experiments! These people are more family to me than she or the Agora could ever be!>

Ignoring the girl's outburst, Jancin addressed Roche once more: "I urge you to consider the implications of going against the Agora. They only want the girl; they do not wish you or your crew any harm."

"No," said Roche. "No one ever does, yet everyone keeps threatening us."

She killed the line before Jancin could speak again, then turned to Cane.

"Thanks," she said to him. The clone warrior nodded a brief acknowledgment.

"We can't take on the Surin as well," said Kajic, his hologram appearing on the bridge.

"And we can't give them what they want, either." Roche tapped the arm of her chair. "Maybe this is what it's all about. Uri, have any other ships changed course to intercept us?"

"It's hard to say, Morgan." Kajic called up a display of the portion of the system surrounding the *Ana Vereine*. Even in that small bubble of space, there were over fifty ships following a wide variety of vectors and ranging in size from small, anonymous fighters to bulky cruisers. The display was awash with energy and particulate wakes. As Roche watched, a new cluster of six medium-sized attack craft appeared, following a high-energy elliptical orbit around the system's sun; who they were, Roche didn't know, nor did she care. All that mattered was that they weren't homing in on her ship.

Kajic ringed three craft. "There is a Dato pursuit vehicle that seemed to react to our appearance an hour ago, but so far has not displayed any hostile intentions. This ship, here, which I have not been able to identify, is almost certainly following us. And this one"—the third ship was a stationary speck in the center of the swirl of orbits—"has done nothing at all."

"Trying to remain inconspicuous?" suggested Haid.

"Trying a little *too* hard," said Cane.

"Exactly my feeling." Roche turned to the young epsense adept. "Maii? Anything?"

<This Jancin Xumai wants me because the Agora has heard about the experiments that gave me full epsense ability.> The girl's voice still had a thick edge to it. <They want to know how it worked.>

"Is that what you're reading from him?"

The girl hesitated. <No. I'm assuming, and nothing he's giving me contradicts it.>

Roche could understand her suspicions, but wanted hard facts, not suppositions. "What *is* he giving you?"

<He knows that we've been in Sol System for three hours, and he knew which region of the system to stake out. His orders came from his superiors, though, so he doesn't know where that information came from originally.>

Roche nodded. "What else?"

<There's a lot of overlap in this system; it's hard to isolate individual thoughts without knowing precisely who to focus on. . . .> Roche appreciated the girl's diffi-

culties, reaching out across space, clutching at any thought that seemed important out of the millions flung her way. <But I do sense a growing awareness of you, Morgan. Word is spreading.>

"What do you mean?"

"Don't be modest, Morgan," Haid put in lightly. "You've made a lot of enemies in the last few weeks. It's only natural they're going to be talking about you."

<Wait . . . There's something else . . .> Maii frowned and fell silent.

And into the silence came a new voice, a voice that resounded through their minds with discomforting familiarity:

<You have given my people everything we needed.> The speaker was a strong but faceless epsense presence. <For that, we will permit your existence.>

On the main screen, the stationary dot suddenly moved to a new course, away from them.

"*Now* what?" asked Roche, increasingly bewildered.

Maii's voice was hushed. <Grayboot.>

Haid stiffened over the weapons board. "*Olmahoi*? Here?"

<He's leaving us now.> The girl's relief was touched with an underlying fear. <He read me without me even knowing! He knows what happened in Palasian System; he knows about the *irikeii*. . . .>

"Great," said Roche dryly, rubbing at her forehead. The *irikeii*—linchpin of the epsense-dependent Olmahoi Caste—had been killed by a representative of the Kesh. If the grayboot had suspected that they were involved—and why else would he have tracked them down so quickly?—they were lucky to have escaped some sort of automatic reprisal. The Olmahoi retribution squads weren't known for their patience.

Still, Roche thought, having her brain instantly fried might just solve her problems right now. . . .

"Ustinik is hailing us again," said Kajic. "As is the Surin."

"Okay." Roche sat forward. "Uri, take us somewhere else—somewhere a *long* way from here, and as fast as possible."

"In-system?"

"Yes, but make it hard for someone to follow, without being too obvious about it. Use camouflage if you think it will help. Ustinik might be bluffing, and so might the Surin. Either way, I don't like being an open target."

Roche felt a gentle thrum through her fingertips and thighs as the ship broke orbit.

She waited a moment, then checked the main screen. Kajic's words only confirmed what she saw.

"Ustinik is changing course, at a discreet distance, and continuing to hail us. The Surin *imaret* has broken off communications and is heading away. That Dato ship I mentioned is still keeping quiet, but looks like it's going to follow too. There is another ship . . ." Kajic ringed a newcomer to the screen. "It's a COE fighter we passed before. Might be tagging along for the ride as well."

Roche used her controls to expand the view and scan the regions ahead of them. There were ships everywhere—all moving in wildly varying directions with dangerously different velocities, all orbiting the yellow star at the heart of the system. She was glad it was Kajic, and not her, piloting the ship.

"No sign of the Kesh?" she asked.

"None yet."

"Good." That was one less thing to worry about. If the Olmahoi were annoyed at the Kesh for killing the *irikeii*, she was sure the Kesh would be just as annoyed with her for having destroyed one of their prized ships.

<Box? Any thoughts?>

<I think you correctly summarized the situation a moment ago, Morgan.> The voice of the AI whispered solely through her implants. Now that she was becoming used to the idea that it was actually part of her, living in her cells, she found its voice less discomfiting. It was almost like hearing another part of herself think.

<Someone is attempting to draw attention to you,> it said. <Any hopes you might have had of slipping unnoticed into Sol System and quietly going about your investigation have been effectively dashed. You are exposed, compromised, threatened. If, somehow, you were to—>

"Another hail," Kajic interrupted the voice only Roche could hear. "Another new one, I mean."

She shook her head. "Who now?"

"Assistant Vice Primate Rey Nemeth of the Second Ju Mandate, according to his ID."

"I don't recognize the name." She glanced about the bridge; no one volunteered anything. "I suppose he's following us, too?"

"No. He's coming in on a relay."

"Ignore him, then. Now—" She stopped herself in time and subvocalized: <Now, Box, what were you saying?>

<Nothing of any great importance. For now I suggest you simply continue your avoidance tactics. We will talk later.>

She took that as a sign that, at least in the Box's eyes, she wasn't doing anything outrageously wrong. That made a nice change.

"Uri, ignore further hails, unless you think it's something particularly important. We've got better things to do than listen to other peoples' grievances."

Haid grinned wryly. "You figure we have so many enemies already that making a few more won't make much difference?"

"That, and I'm loath to believe *anyone* at the moment. If, as we think, the clone warriors are interested in infiltrating and stirring up dissent, then they could be anywhere. Who's to say which complaint is legitimate and which a trap? I'd prefer not to take the risk either way. And anyway, it'll be easier for us to keep dodging than it will be for someone to catch us, no matter how many of them there are."

Cane nodded. "True."

Roche turned to face him. "And while Uri, Maii, and Ameidio see to that, maybe you and I should take the opportunity to have a private talk."

Cane shrugged. "Whatever you say, Morgan."

"Good." Roche stood. "I like the sound of that."

In the small room at the rear of the bridge, Roche sat in a chair opposite the large hologram emplacement where Uri Kajic had once projected his image. On a display she studied a detailed image of Sol System composited from old map records and incoming data. She had lost count of the number of ships they'd passed since leaving the anchor point, but the Box estimated that around seven hundred Castes were represented in various forms—from the fringe-lovers out where a comet cloud might once have been to the hot-bloods in close. The sun had seen better days; there was evidence of large-scale waste-dumping in its outer atmosphere—unsurprising, she thought; it had to go *somewhere*—but thankfully no one had tried any tricks such as the Kesh had in Palasian System. One system utterly destroyed in a month was more than enough for the region.

Not that there was much to lose. Discounting the ships, the system was mostly empty. There was a faint but well-defined ring around the sun, approximately half a million kilometers in width and less than a thousand thick, just straddling the regions that might have been mundane-habitable had there been a planet to live on. Apart from the ring and the ships, the system contained nothing but vacuum. Anything larger than a pebble had been stripped back to molecules long ago, leaving behind only a wisp of smoke around the system's star.

If the system *had* ever been inhabited—let alone the birthplace of Humanity, as a few scholars had once suggested—nothing remained to show it.

Roche watched the endlessly chaotic dance of ships for a long moment, wondering who was in them and what they wanted. Then she turned to Cane.

He sat opposite her, his expression unreadable. The overhead light reflecting off his scalp made it look as if he had a third eye.

Appropriate, she thought.

"You wanted to talk to me," he prompted.

She paused, wondering, then asked: "Are you reading my mind?"

"Why do you ask that?"

"Just answer me, Cane."

"No," he said. "I'm not reading your mind."

"Could you, if you wanted to?"

He frowned. "Morgan, why are you asking me these questions?"

She held his gaze for a moment, then let it wander back to the screen. "On the way here, I talked to Maii. She told me in detail everything she'd picked up from the *irikeii* before he died. She says . . ." Roche sought the words, not sure she herself understood everything the young reave had told her. "She says that the *irikeii* was like a pit, sucking in thoughts. For him, minds were lights, or suns, and he was the black hole dragging them in. He experienced the universe through the minds around him, like a reave but with less selectivity; he experienced everything at once, all at once—which was why the Kesh and Linegar Rufo had him kidnapped. Once Palasian System had been enclosed he was able to search it thoroughly. And nothing could hide from him."

"Not even a clone warrior," said Cane.

Roche nodded. "In theory."

"It makes sense," Cane went on. "Had it worked, the advantage might have outweighed the inevitable backlash."

"It *did* work. To the *irikeii*, Jelena Heidik and you stood out like supernovae, by far the brightest things he had ever seen. He called you 'The Shining Ones.' "

"We radiate thought," mused Cane. "Is that what he meant?"

She studied him closely; he was still frowning, although now apparently at the puzzle posed by the *irikeii*, not at her. "Possibly," she said. "But we have no evidence to back it up."

"So . . . ?"

"So there's more to it than that." Roche leaned forward slightly in her seat. "Maii says that one of the *irikeii*'s last impressions was of your mind while under the influence of Xarodine. He was aware of a dark space behind the glare—a dark space similar to the one inside his own mind. He thought you and he might have had a lot in common."

"I don't see how that follows."

"Obviously the metaphor is strained." She couldn't tell if Cane was prevaricating. "As far as I can understand it, he thought that you too could absorb thoughts from the people around you. You're a sponge, soaking everything up. And the glare he described—"

"Was just a form of camouflage?" Cane finished. "Something to hide our epsense ability?"

Roche nodded slowly. "Something like that, yes."

"I am unaware of any such ability, Morgan," Cane said evenly.

"But how can I be sure you're telling the *truth*? How do I know you're not reading my mind right now?"

"Because I give you my personal assurance, Morgan."

She studied him for a few moments. He was perfectly still, hands folded in his lap, eyes not leaving hers for an instant. Even at rest, the air of strength remained with him. She had seen how fast he could move; she knew what he was capable of. And having witnessed what his siblings could do if they turned against the people around them, she was reluctant to trust him without reservation. She needed reassurance.

"That's all well and good," she said, "but I still can't help wondering. Heidik knew we were coming here; she even knew when. I can't believe it was just a good guess—so who told her? The COE squadron we left behind at Palasian System might have sent word to expect us, but how would she have got hold of that information? We were less than a day behind her. That's not long enough to infiltrate the COE presence here. We haven't even *found* them yet.

"And I keep thinking of that dark speck—and Maii. She's proof that epsense ability can be bioengineered. If you *were* made to blend in and to fight, what better way could there be to gather intelligence than to act as an *irikeii*—passively absorbing data from the minds of the people around you? Even if you couldn't actually read minds, you could at least see and hear through them—and maybe even communicate with others like yourself. If these black specks linked up somehow, you could share information, talk, plan, whatever you needed without anyone knowing."

"Yes—*if*," said Cane. "But ask yourself this, Morgan: if I *was* in touch with Heidik or any of the other clone warriors, why would I be here? My siblings were clearly made for a purpose; they have spread across the galaxy seeding dissent and destruction wherever they go. But I have not. So *why* would I bother with you if I shared their goals? Why would I not be with *them*?"

"Evidence of absence is not absence of evidence."

"Guilty until proven innocent?" Cane smiled slightly. "I'm surprised at you, Morgan."

"There's too much at stake to take chances, Cane."

"The only way to be sure is to take no chances at all." His smile disappeared and he relaxed back into his seat. "Space me, or imprison me—get me out of the way entirely. Better to do that than to be perpetually in doubt. The chance that I might betray you will never leave your mind until I am gone."

She nodded. That had occurred to her. For all the times he had saved her on Sciacca's World, the casual cruelty and treachery of Jelena Heidik had tainted him in her eyes. She would never be free of it.

And if he ever *did* betray her, she stood to lose everything. Not just her life, but the lives of her companions and every other Pristine in the galaxy.

She wasn't sure she had the right to take that chance.

<What do you think, Box?>

<I know that if he could read minds, he would know that I continue to exist,> said the AI smoothly.

<What about using the command language Rufo was using? Could we force the truth out of him?>

<If we knew how to speak the language properly, we might—assuming, of course, that he isn't already telling the truth. But the exact use of the command language eludes even me; it seems a fairly crude device. I suspect it may relate to the capsules in which the clone warriors were born rather than the finished product. The best we could hope for is to nudge him to do our will.>

Roche fought a twinge of annoyance. Why did things have to be so uncertain all the time? She would welcome a single, uncomplicated fact with open arms.

<Besides,> added the Box, <if we use the command language, correctly or not, he will suspect that I gave you the knowledge to use it.>

"Morgan?"

She looked over at Cane to see him watching her suspiciously.

"Are you all right?" he said.

She brushed his suspicions aside by ignoring the question altogether: "If you *were* reading my mind, you'd know that spacing you isn't an option. And as there's no way you can prove conclusively that you're not in communication with the other clones, then all I can do is follow my gut instincts."

Cane nodded. "But again, I assure you that I am telling you the truth, Morgan."

She remembered the words he had tapped in code shortly after he wakened from his coma: *I'm as Human as you are.* That was patently untrue in the details—after all, she was not a genetically engineered combat soldier designed to blend in with the Pristine Humans and kill them—but in essence it might not be far from the truth.

"Okay." She exhaled slowly. "I'll believe you. Commander Gent must have sent word to his superiors after we left Palasian System. It's possible that Heidik already had a contact in the COE Armada, through which she found out when we were due to arrive. That's the only alternative I can think of."

"It is certainly a less speculative hypothesis." There was a glint of humor in Cane's eyes. "But if the rest of my siblings *do* communicate by epsense, I would be keen to find out why I have been excluded from the conversations."

That was a point Roche had not missed. "Maybe something went wrong with you: your capsule was damaged, or corrupted. There might even be others out there like you—others who could help us. . . ."

Before Roche could pursue the thought, Kajic's image appeared in the empty corner of the suite.

"My apologies again, Morgan."

She swiveled to face him. "Problems?"

His broad, pleasant face was concerned. "I have been ignoring hails as you instructed, although their numbers are increasing—as is the number of ships following us. There are eight currently matching our course, and I have detected emissions from another five suggesting that they might also attempt to do so. No one has actually made a move against us; although it is difficult to project the precise makeup of the regions ahead of us, I am doing my best to keep us out of any regions where forces are massing. But we can't keep this up indefinitely; sooner or later, we *will* miscalculate."

Roche could see what Kajic was saying: they ran the risk of running headlong into a trap. "So you suggest we stop running?"

"No, Morgan. There's something else." Kajic changed the view in the screen to a recent telemetry display. The eight ships tailing them were marked clearly in red; a handful in yellow were the ones he suspected were about to join the convoy. As Roche watched, one green dot darted into view from off-screen, angling down and toward her to match velocities with the white *Ana Vereine* at the center.

"Is that real-time?" she asked.

"Yes. This happened only a minute ago. I should point out that I am currently accelerating at seventy percent of my design tolerance."

The green dot braked effortlessly to a relative halt a hundred kilometers away. "What the hell is it?" Roche asked.

"A large drone or singleship. I'm not familiar with the design or its markings. But we clearly can't outrun it."

"Has it tried to contact us?"

"Not yet."

"Are we camouflaged?"

"Mildly, only in order to give the appearance of trying. Our position has been well-known since we arrived and we are currently too well-observed to successfully drop out of sight."

She nodded. "Drop the pretense, then. Hail that drone, or whatever it is. I want to talk to it."

Kajic's hologram abruptly dissolved.

Roche stood, and Cane followed her out of the small office. "As you said, Morgan: absence of evidence is not evidence of absence. Just because they haven't threatened you yet doesn't mean that they won't."

"At the moment, that's good enough for me." She assumed her usual station at the first officer's post. "Maii? Anything?"

<The craft is either unoccupied or its occupants are extremely well-shielded,> said the reave.

"I have a lock on it," said Haid. "Its E-shields and hypershields are down."

"I doubt it's defenseless," Roche said, watching a close-up of the craft on the main screen. It resembled a mushroom in shape: flat, circular cap with a trailing stem five meters long and two meters wide. There were no visible drive outlets or weapons ports. "Whoever it belongs to, they're more advanced than us."

"I have a reply," said Kajic. "The drone is a relay."

"Open a direct line. Let its source talk to me."

Seconds later, a voice issued from the bridge's speakers:

"Welcome to Sol System, Morgan Roche." The female voice was precise and clipped, and unfamiliar. "The Interim Executive Pristine Council has been expecting you."

"You're not the only ones, it seems."

"Your arrival has created something of a disturbance. As the news spreads, we expect the situation to worsen."

"Meaning?" Roche wished for an image to give her something to focus on.

"In case you failed to notice, the atmosphere in this system is somewhat tense. There have been many skirmishes in the last few days—even several attempts at outright war. As we speak, Olmahoi forces are preparing to engage the Kesh—acting on information you brought with you. You are a catalyst, Roche, a destabilizing influence. The council would ask you to restrict your activities before you cause more damage."

"Is that a request or an instruction?"

The woman's voice sounded amused. "It is an appeal," she said, "to your better judgment."

Roche was silent for a moment. "Perhaps you should tell me who you are and what exactly the council is."

"It might be easier to demonstrate," she returned. "Turn your instruments to the following coordinates . . ."

Kajic swung the view on the main screen accordingly, but only starlight dusted the empty space.

"There's nothing there," said Roche irritably.

"Give the light a chance to reach you," said the woman.

Even as she spoke, something appeared on the screen. It looked like a ship, but the perspective was all wrong. Where a dot might represent other craft, there glowed a tiny arrowhead.

"Whatever it is," said Kajic, magnifying the view, "it's millions of kilometers away."

The display was suddenly taken up with a huge vessel, and Roche found herself gasping at its immensity. It was shaped like a long cone flattened on one side, hollow at tip and base and bristling with instruments and weapons emplacements—some as large as the *Ana Vereine* itself. It had to be at least a thousand kilometers long and as much as one hundred and fifty wide; it made COE Intelligence HQ look like a drone.

"You're seeing the *Phlegethon*," said the woman. "It's a consistory vessel of the Skehan Heterodox. You have been invited to approach."

Roche stared at the screen a moment longer. The name meant nothing to her. "Why?" she said eventually.

"To discuss the situation," the woman replied. "For the duration of those discussions, at least, we can offer you our protection."

"Again: why?"

The woman hesitated slightly, as though Roche's suspicion annoyed her. "The IEPC exists to assess the threat presented by the clone warriors you seek. To do that, we must gather as much information as possible. Contacting you is an important part of that process. Understand, Roche, we are not asking you to join forces; we are not asking you to surrender control to us. We ask merely to exchange information, in return for which we will get your pursuers off your back."

Roche hesitated, thinking of the Surin backup Jancin Xumai had threatened her with, and the Kesh, and the Commerce Artel, and Jelena Heidik. . . .

<Morgan,> said the Box, <I urge you to comply.>

<I thought you might.>

<They are exactly what we need: a significant presence in this system with the

resources to investigate it properly. You will note that she is communicating with the drone by faster-than-light methods. Access to such technology will make our quest that much easier.>

<And what exactly *is* our quest, Box? I'm still a little uncertain about that.>

<All will become clear soon enough, Morgan. I suggest you take the opportunity given to us and see what happens.>

The AI was making sense. Any group with a ship that big would be a fair contender for the role of central authority in the system—and she had to take on allies sooner or later. She couldn't do it on her own.

"Roche? Are you still there?" The woman's voice sounded more amused than concerned.

"I was just considering your offer." Roche glanced at Haid, who shrugged: *Your decision* . . . "Very well. We agree to talk, at least."

"Good. I will instruct the Heresiarch to give you an approach vector to match orbits. We will contact you again when everything is in order."

Before Roche could reply, the woman had cut the line. A moment later, the drone accelerated impossibly fast, outward, away from the sun and away from them. Within seconds, it was gone.

2

AVS-44
955.1.30
0640

Something stirred inside Roche as they approached the *Phlegethon*.

For the most part, the uneven surface of the giant ship's hull was bleak and lifeless, with only the occasional beacon sporadically flaring in the darkness. But as they moved along the length of the *Phlegethon*'s vast exterior, a patch of quivering energy some fifty kilometers wide followed, lighting up the ship's black, moist-looking skin. There were no windows of any description to be seen, yet Roche couldn't help but feel she was being watched. Not by the ship's instruments perhaps, but by the ship itself. It seemed . . . *alive* to her. And the *Phlegethon*'s only identifying mark, a mural of a giant, half-lidded eye on the flattened underbelly of the beast, only enhanced that feeling.

She suppressed a shudder as the bulk of it passed between her and the distant, yellow sun. This close to the monster craft, she felt intimidated, ineffectual. Worse, she felt vulnerable.

"The ships following us have broken off," said Kajic via the scutter's intercom. "Whatever the IEPC said to them, it's had the desired effect."

She could tell by the tone of his voice that he wasn't saying what was foremost on his mind. "You think I'm doing the wrong thing, don't you?"

He didn't reply immediately. When he did, he sounded almost relieved. "Yes, Morgan."

He didn't need to say anything more than that. Roche could see his reasoning: after Linegar Rufo had captured half her crew by luring them into his station in Palasian System, Kajic had every right to point out that she might be making the same mistake twice—and for similar reasons, too. But those reasons were sound, and they outweighed any risks to her personally.

She needed information, first and foremost, and she had information others might find useful. She had to take the chance that this Interim Executive Pristine Council—whatever *that* was—was in the system to help, not hinder.

And she had Maii with her, as well as the Box, hidden away in her flesh. Haid hadn't liked being left behind, but he could see that Roche needed the sort of help only a reave might be able to provide. If it was a trap, then she was never going to be able to fight her way out of the *Phlegethon* by force alone.

"Trim," said the traffic controller, guiding her in a perfunctory, almost disinterested manner.

She concentrated on flying the scutter. It had drifted slightly off course. She corrected easily, following the trajectory she had been given to three decimal places.

"We don't have a better option at the moment," she told Kajic.

"I know," he replied. "That's the main reason I've kept silent."

The scutter arced gracefully toward an open dock two thirds from the hollow tip of the *Phlegethon* to its base. A line of docks encircled the ship, one every fifty meters. Roche performed the arithmetic in her head: assuming the ring went right around the ship, that made almost a thousand docks in that band alone, and she could see several more bands in either direction along the hull. She could only wonder why they needed so many. Fighter launchers, perhaps?

There was no denying the sophistication of the vessel. How far it had come was still unknown, but she had no doubt it belonged to an empire of similarly spectacular proportions.

"You getting anything from the crew, Maii?" Roche turned unnecessarily to the girl. "Any clues as to where they're from?"

<Not much,> said the girl. She sat next to Roche in the copilot's station, wearing an undersized hazard suit that brought her up to Roche's height and twice her thickness. Inside she would be safe from Xarodine or any other physical anti-epsense attacks. Roche wore a simple environment suit in Dato colors with a bare minimum of ceramic armor and an energy pistol at her side. <What I am getting suggests that the ship *is* their home. If there was a place prior to this, it didn't leave much of an impression on them. Most are simply focused on their jobs or their daily lives.> She paused for a few seconds. <And there's a lot of prayer going on, too—perhaps unsurprising given there are several million people on board.>

"Prayers? To whom?"

<No one I've ever heard of,> said Maii. <Whoever it is, they don't seem to be answering.>

Roche smiled. "What about the Interim Executive Pristine Council? Anything there?"

<There are a number of chambers warded by high-grade reaves toward the top of the cone. I haven't been able to worm my way in yet. My bet is the council work is done there, where it's most secure.>

"Well, keep trying," said Roche. "And let me know if you learn anything important."

<I will, Morgan.>

Roche eased the scutter into the large dock, bringing it to a halt in exactly the spot indicated. There followed a series of clangs and small bumps; then the traffic controller spoke again.

"You're docked," he said. "Praise Weryn, and welcome aboard the *Phlegethon.*"

"Thanks." Roche unclipped her harness and stepped from the couch.

"Air outside is normal," said Kajic. "And so far our transmissions aren't being interfered with." He still sounded concerned.

"Good. I think we're going to be okay, Uri."

"You'd better hope so, Morgan," Haid put in over the open line. "Because if something *does* go wrong, I don't fancy our chances of getting you out of there."

"Personally, I don't give you any chance at all. Not against this thing." Roche forced herself to sound casual. "But let's hope it doesn't come to that."

<You could say a prayer,> said Maii. <That's what most people here would do.>

<Mine would just be another voice among the millions, then,> said Roche. <A sigh in a storm.> She let the hint of a smile carry with her reply. <But you feel free to try, Maii, if you think it will make a difference. . . .>

A tall woman with a solid build met them outside the airlock bay. She was dressed in a sky-blue uniform that seemed part robe, part jumpsuit. It was hard to tell where the folds of fabric stopped or started. Her face was long and strong-boned, her chin curved and slightly protruding.

"My name is Hue Vischilglin," she said, taking both of Roche's hands in hers and pressing them to her forehead. She repeated the ritual with Maii, when Roche introduced her. The young reave, made awkward by the hazard suit, bowed slightly in return. "Be welcome here."

"Thank you," said Roche distractedly, glancing along the empty, curving corridor that connected all the various docks on the inside of the ship. It was so long that the air blurred the details in the distance, and so wide that, with gravity pointing down away from the center of the ship, it almost appeared flat. She shook her head. "I never expected . . . *this*!"

"Few do." Vischilglin smiled warmly and gestured for them to follow her across the plain toward a distant pillar. There was no one else in sight. "The Heterodoxies have come from the Far Reaches on the other side of the galaxy. They've known about the problem longer than most, and have possibly suffered its worst effects. This ship is all that's left of one of their fleets. Its Heresiarch—its 'captain'—rebelled when he was ordered to destroy a civilian outpost inhabited by several billion people. It would seem his superiors had been infiltrated by the enemy. He managed to escape reprisal and kept on running. Eventually he was contacted by others in similar situations and directed here.

"Like some of the other outermost Castes, their greater lead-in time has given him more chance to prepare for being here. On the other hand, his crew is exhausted from having come so far. That's probably why they're being so open-minded about the council running the show." She smiled widely. "Although I suspect they were as glad to get their hands on our ftl relays and advanced camouflage as much as we were glad to get our hands on such a figurehead. What a beast, eh? And to think this was just one ship from one of the Heterodox fleets!"

"So you're not one of them?"

"Oh, no," she said, surprised by Roche's misunderstanding. "I'm from the Rond-Spellor Outlook, myself." Catching Roche's reaction, she went on with even more surprise: "You've heard of us! That makes us practically family around here."

They reached the pillar, which turned out to be much thicker than Roche had first imagined; the lack of perspective was playing tricks on her eyes. Vischilglin waved a hand across a black panel and it slid silently open, revealing an elevator cab.

Roche hesitated outside. "Where are you taking us?"

"For debriefing," said Vischilglin. "Don't worry; you won't come to any harm."

"Sentiments I have had expressed to me in the past," said Roche cynically, then added: "No offense."

"None taken, I assure you," said Vischilglin.

"I just want my crew to know, that's all."

Vischilglin nodded. "We're aware that you're in contact with them; we wouldn't have it any other way." Vischilglin stood on the threshold. "Is there anything we can do to put your mind at ease?"

Roche shook her head slowly. "I'm just habitually nervous these days, that's all."

"As you should be. I'm taking you to the secure areas on level 391. Your reave would have noted them already, I'm sure. We keep them shielded as best we can to keep word getting out. Maybe it's effective; maybe it's not. Either way, we have to try. But we're not keeping secrets from our allies. That would be counterproductive. We're just trying to maintain security against our common foe."

"And do you know who *they* are?"

Vischilglin grimaced. "If you mean do we know their origins or the identities of the individuals, then no, I'm afraid not. But we are hoping you might be able to help us." She indicated the interior of the elevator. "Won't you?" she said. "They're waiting."

Roche forced herself to ignore the nagging uncertainty and stepped into the cab. Besides, what choice did she really have? If they wanted to spring a trap, then her position was already so compromised that she wouldn't be able to do anything about it, anyway.

Maii followed her in. As the doors closed, Vischilglin turned to the girl with an amused expression.

"You know, you're free to remove that suit any time you like," she said. When Maii didn't respond she added: "I hate those things. Too confining, constricting—and they *chafe*. We have more suitable clothing if you're uncomfortable."

<Are there any of my people where we're going?> Maii asked.

Vischilglin looked uneasy for a moment, and Roche suspected the girl had known the answer before she'd asked.

"There is one, yes," Vischilglin replied.

<Then I am quite comfortable as I am, thank you.>

Roche felt the slight tickle in her mind that meant the Box wanted to talk to her. <What is it?>

<I thought you might like to know that the Rond-Spellor Outlook has been in a state of civil war for some weeks, now.>

<You think they've been infected by the clone warriors?>

<Most likely. Or at the very least, *af*fected.>

<Could she be one of them?>

<I have no reason to believe so. Neither her name nor her appearance match any in my database, and one must assume that any organization devoted to the investigation of the clone warriors would take precautions against such an infiltration. Nevertheless . . .>

The Box left the sentence unfinished, but the sentiment was clear.

<Consider me warned,> she said.

<I have every confidence in your abilities, Morgan.>

<Let's hope I can live up to your expectations,> she said. <For both our sakes.>

The elevator didn't seem to have moved, but when the doors opened a second or two later, an entirely different vista was spread out before them. Water from gentle waterfalls washed down numerous curved walls into undulating ground between them, collecting in valley floors to form small, slow-moving streams which curled and divided in unpredictable directions, some emptying into numerous ponds scattered about the area. The air was moist and sweet—scented, Roche suspected, by the various plants growing in the waters.

The banks of the waterways, however, were gray and sterile—a striking contrast to the exotic flowers and reeds. And high above it all hung featureless white clouds. The vista gave Roche the impression of an attempt at terraforming by a clerical AI.

She moved out of the elevator. "Is this the right level?" she asked.

"Incredible, isn't it?" Vischilglin stepped up beside Roche. "The waterways erode giant, mazelike circuits around the ship. Given enough time, the Heterodoxies believe they will one day spell out the name of God. Or something like that." Vischilglin shrugged helplessly. "It all sounds like nonsense to me. Yet I can't help admiring it whenever I see it."

She led them through the strange landscape, across modest but elegant bridges and along the narrow valleys. As they climbed over each rise, Roche could clearly discern the curve of the floor beneath them; they were obviously higher along the cone than they had been before.

She realized then that nowhere on their journey had they seen another person.

<Are we blocked here, Maii?>

The head of Maii's suit rose when she spoke via epsense, uncannily as though she were looking at Roche. The visor was black, however, and the girl had no eyes to see with behind the white bandage she wore across her face; she was using Roche's eyes to guide herself.

<We have passed through several barriers,> she said, <and are now . . . Well, the best analogy I can think of is that we have reached the eye of a storm. I am not being interfered with, although I am finding it difficult to reach the outside world.>

<Can you pick up anyone else near here?>

<There is a large group up ahead,> Maii said. <They seem to be waiting for us.>

<Is it the council she was telling us about?>

<I think so. Look . . .> Roche received a mental impression of many minds congregated in one place, focusing intently on one thing. She couldn't make out any individuals in that crowd, but she sensed their combined will. <I suspect this might be an illusion,> the girl went on. <A powerful one. I can't break through it.>

<Interesting that they've made the effort,> said Roche.

They reached a flight of stone steps that twisted and turned around a sharp rise in the landscape like a thread around a screw.

"The place we're going is known as the *fane*," Vischilglin said, pausing at the base of the steps. "You and I would probably call it the ship's bridge, but that doesn't do it justice." She hesitated for a moment, then went on: "The Heterodox are great believers in ritual. There is some protocol you'll need to observe. When you reach the nave, in the center of the fane, bow to the Heresiarch—you'll see me do it ahead of you, so you'll know who he is. When you're asked to speak, always address at least part of your reply to him. He may not speak directly to you, but if he does, look him right in the eye. Should you hear bells at any point, be prepared for everything to stop. That means the ship requires his attention."

Roche nodded her understanding, and Vischilglin began their ascent up the broad and shallow steps. After a while, cloud obscured not only their destination above, but also the area around them. It was composed of thick and surprisingly dry mist that smelled of ozone and left no residue as they passed through it.

Roche followed Maii, allowing the girl to use her eyes to navigate her way up the stairs. With each step the girl took, the suit struck sparks from the stones, but she expressed no discomfort to Roche.

"Not far now," said Vischilglin.

<Kajic, are you tracking us?> Roche asked via her implants.

<Yes,> he replied, <and monitoring via Maii's suit.>

<No problems at your end?>

<We're still holding in the position they gave us. There have been no other attempts to approach us. I suspect we are being camouflaged; we've fired a couple of base-line probes away from our position, but so far none have reported back. They seem to keep losing our location.>

<At least you're safe,> said Roche.

<If a little frustrated,> he replied. <I envy Ameidio: he can sleep at times like these.>

Roche smiled. <Years of practice, I guess.>

<It wouldn't be so bad if Cane was better company.>

Her smile slipped a notch. <Listen, make sure—>

<I know, Morgan,> he cut in. < I'm keeping an eye on him for you. He hasn't done anything suspicious, and if he did, I would notify you immediately. But I don't think he will. He knows he's being watched.>

<He also knows you're going to have to sleep *some* time. You're not the Box.>

<Don't worry about me, Morgan. Just take care of yourself, okay?>

Her smile returned. Under the concern in his voice she heard a genuine warmth. If they had become friends in the weeks since she'd taken control of his ship, then that was all to the better. It took some of the edge off the uncertainty she felt about her situation.

Roche's first feeling as she emerged from the cloud a few minutes later and looked out over the vast bridge—the *fane*, she reminded herself—was relief that it had been the Dato Bloc she'd fought on Sciacca's World and not the Skehan Heterodox.

She was standing in the middle of a wide, concave space carved out of what looked like dark gray stone. This space was one of many—like the petals of a flower—abutting a central bowl almost two hundred meters across. The bowl was stepped in the fashion of an ancient amphitheatre, but with no sharp edges; everything was rounded, molded—smooth, perhaps, from the generations of people that had sat on those seats and worn them down. A few were occupied now, as were spaces in the petals, where people stood rather than sat and observed what was happening in the bowl. At the bowl's center was a rough-hewn font filled with water.

Roche looked up. If symmetry was anything to go by, local gravity had taken a turn through ninety degrees in the clouds. Far above, hanging from the central point of a convex roof was a slender spike, pointing downward like a stiletto poised to strike. Its tip burned white, with enough light to cast a shadow from everything it illuminated below. Roche guessed that the spike and the font at the center of the bowl delineated the long axis of the ship.

Vischilglin led her along a short walkway through the petal, and down, toward the central bowl. When they stepped across its lip, the woman stopped and turned to face a man dressed in gold, who stood on the far side.

She bowed. Assuming this man to be the Heresiarch they'd been told to watch for, Roche bowed also. Beside her, Maii did the same.

"Morgan Roche wishes an audience with the Heresiarch." Vischilglin, speaking in a voice only slightly louder than normal, gestured toward Roche.

"Bring her down."

Roche couldn't tell who had spoken, yet the voice was as clear as if it came from someone standing directly beside her. The Heresiarch didn't appear to have moved.

They descended step by step into the heart of the central bowl—the nave, Vischilglin had called it. When they reached the lowest circle, they stopped and waited. Even at the edge of the nave, the font was still some distance away.

Only when they came to a halt did the voice speak again: "Do you know who we are?" Roche was still uncertain as to who had spoken, but she knew it was directed at her.

She looked around. Apart from the Heresiarch in his gold attire, nobody else stood out. Most wore white robes or shipsuits; only a few, like Vischilglin, wore blue. All were watching Roche, waiting on her reply. She didn't dare presume that the Heresiarch was the one who had spoken, so when she did reply it was to the space in general: "No."

It was a few moments before the speaker continued, and when he did, the words still seemed to issue from everywhere at once: "Five hundred thousand years ago, more or less, Humanity diversified to the point where its origins were forgotten." The man spoke slowly and with a crisp, nasal tone. "Only the dimensions and attributes of the Pristine form remained known. In order to ensure that the cause of the Pristine would never be lost among those of the other mundane Castes, the framework for a council was established—a council that would surface from obscurity *only* when it was needed. All Pristine governors of all Pristine governances know how to summon the council into being, and all know that to do so improperly would have its . . . consequences." The word was chosen carefully. "Only the gravest of circumstances can justify such a summoning—as, for example, when the genetic code of our distant ancestors becomes threatened."

"But this is not such an occasion, is it?" said Roche. The silence which followed was filled with unspoken disapproval for her interruption.

"This council," continued the voice shortly, "was called forty-six months ago, and is now in full session."

"Forty-six *months*?" Roche exclaimed, not caring whose sensibilities she offended. She wanted answers, not speeches.

Movement to her right caught her eye as a figure in blue took a step toward her. She interpreted it as a warning against further interruptions, and ground her teeth together.

"We have been aware of this threat for that long. Only recently, however, did we learn about Sol System. Our data showed an apparent convergence upon this region, although not enough on its own to fix the location precisely. An attack on a nearby system helped us triangulate traffic among the civilizations we've been keeping an eye on, suspecting them to be corrupted. We were among the first to arrive here, barely a week ago."

The figure to Roche's right shifted once again.

"The speed with which word has spread is phenomenal," the speaker continued. "Ships continue to arrive at the rate of over one hundred every hour. We have reopened several secondary anchor points on the fringes of the system, to act as exits should congestion worsen. If that is not enough, we might have to close the main anchor point altogether. That way, only the most determined will be able to come here."

The figure in blue took several more steps forward, close enough now so that Roche could make out the face of a man, the blue-white light from the spike above casting deep shadows in the lines of his aging features. He was the one talking, not the Heresiarch.

"The situation here is approaching a watershed," he said. "The council senses a change coming, but does not know what form it will take, or to what purpose it comes. Some of us suspect that you might lie at the heart of it, Morgan Roche, and believe that you can help us with an answer to this question. Will you do so?"

"Of course," she said without hesitation. Looking at the Heresiarch, she added: "After all, That's why I'm here."

She saw Vischilglin nod approvingly as she turned back to the speaker.

"I am Esko Murnane," he continued. "My superiors in Pompili sent me as their plenipotent envoy to the council, and the council in turn has declared me chairperson for this hearing. You have already met Hue Vischilglin, co-adjutant to the leaders of the Rond-Spellor Outlook. Although a minimum of thirty Pristine nations are required to allow the full and proper council to sit, at present we number four hundred and seven. All have representatives here today, although few, if any, will be known to you. We will, therefore, forgo introductions for the time being. Should you be asked to join our cause, the identities of your questioners will become known to you then."

Again, Roche nodded. "I understand."

"Good. You stand before the council as a witness to the aftermath of the atrocity that recently occurred in Palasian System, and as someone who appears to have a deeper association with the enemy than most of us here." The slow steadiness of his speech combined with what he was saying lent Murnane an air of deep, long-standing authority. "All of us have been touched by the enemy, in one way or another, to our detriment and lasting regret. So we are keen now to hear all that you have learned."

He paused and looked around the enormous chamber, his eyes eventually finding their way back to Roche. When he spoke, they remained upon her, but his words were directed to everyone present.

"Who will begin?" he said.

"I will." The voice came from the far side of the chamber. Another male, but younger, and fair complexioned. "Each of the many nations in the council was drawn here under a different pretext, none seemingly more convincing than any other. We hope to find one that predominates, for that one might contain a shred of truth. By what name do you refer to the enemy, Morgan Roche?"

"At first," she said, speaking slowly and clearly, addressing her reply equally between her questioner, Murnane, and the Heresiarch, "we thought they were Wunderkind created by the Sol Apotheosis Movement. They had a base in this system, a couple of thousand years ago—"

"We are familiar with their history," the speaker interrupted. "So, have you ascertained another name for them now?"

"No," said Roche. "I'm afraid not."

"We are told that you have one of the enemy aboard your ship."

"Yes, we do."

"And what does he have to say on the matter?"

Roche shook her head. "Nothing."

Another voice spoke, this time a woman to Roche's left: "But he *does* have a name?"

"Yes," said Roche. "His name is Adoni Cane."

"A name of your choosing?" said the woman.

"No, it's what he called himself when we first met. I've never had cause to doubt him. Later it produced a match in Dato Bloc's historical records, confirming a link to the Sol Apotheosis Movement."

"Which later turned out to be spurious?"

Roche nodded.

"How do you account for that?"

<Answer that question carefully,> the Box cautioned.

She frowned, fighting her automatic urge to answer with the truth. The AI had faked the historical data in order to mislead the COE and other neighboring governments—and also to throw any of the "enemy" off the trail. If the enemy knew how close the High Humans behind the Crescend and the Box were getting—even if it wasn't very close at all—it might work to their advantage.

The fact that it still might, in the midst of the Interim Emergency Pristine Council, gave her cause to reconsider.

"Would you like the question repeated?" said Murnane.

"No, that's okay," she said. "I guess I can't account for the discrepancy. Maybe the data was deliberately corrupted by the enemy in order to throw us off the trail."

<Well done, Morgan,> enthused the Box.

"That is certainly a possibility," said Murnane, coming forward. "There is a risk of infiltration and perversion at every level. I fear we have not yet seen the full extent of the enemy's abilities or motivations. Until we do, we must assume the worst—even of ourselves."

"Has Adoni Cane ever revealed any detail regarding his origins?" The speaker, another woman, was very close and directly behind Roche.

She turned toward the voice, but was unsure which of the many faces looking back at her had asked the question. "He seems to have no knowledge of his origins," she said, addressing them all. "He doesn't know where he came from or why he's here."

"You're saying he has no memory?" This time Roche saw who had spoken: a young girl, tall and thin, with flaxen hair brushing the shoulders of her blue robe.

"Everything since his awakening is clear," said Roche. "But nothing before then."

"And you are convinced he is telling the truth?"

She hesitated, remembering her most recent conversation with Cane. "I trust him as much as I can," she said. "Under the circumstances."

"Because he claims to be one of the enemy?"

"Yes. That is, he talks about them as if they are his siblings; he shares certain characteristics with them."

"What characteristics, precisely?"

"Well, his genetic profile is profoundly abnormal," she said. "And his body is patently modified in order to make him a good soldier. I haven't seen hard data on others like him, but I do know that if he set his mind to it, he'd be more than capable of the same destructive force that they have displayed. And when in Palasian System he did respond to a command language understood by the other clone warriors—"

Murnane held up a hand. "We will return to Palasian System in a moment," he said. "First we'd like to hear how you met up with this Adoni Cane, and what you have observed about his behavior to date."

She took a moment to organize her thoughts, then began to talk—describing succinctly how she and Cane had met on the *Midnight*, how they had escaped and crash-landed on the surface of Sciacca's World, and their pursuit and eventual escape from the penal colony.

"He helped you escape?" The question was from another council member whose thick accent was unfamiliar to Roche; she had to concentrate to understand what he was saying. "From prison wardens corrupted by a rival government? Do you know *why* he did this?"

"No," she said, with a shake of her head. "And I have to admit that it's puzzled me."

"Can you explain why his behavior is so different from the others?"

She shrugged lightly. "The best explanation I can come up with is that he's a freak," she said. "A mistake."

"You mentioned genetic data, earlier," said one of the previous speakers, the man with the fair complexion. "Will you give us access to this data?"

"Gladly," she said. "If I may contact my ship . . ."

"Your lines of communication are not being interfered with in any way," said Murnane.

<Uri?> she said, checking to see if this was true.

<We're still receiving you loud and clear,> Kajic replied. <I have all the info the Box compiled before it was destroyed. Do you want me to send it?>

<Yes, but I don't know where, though.>

<They've allocated me a buffer,> he said. <Leave it to me, Morgan.>

She was about to turn back to Murnane when she remembered Maii's suit standing immobile beside her. <You okay, Maii?> she asked via epsense.

<I'm fine,> came the reply. <I'm having fun poking at shields. Did you know that there are five high-grade reaves within the nave alone? They're the hooded ones around the edge. I've never heard of so many being in one place at the same time before!>

<What are they doing? Probing me without my knowledge?>

<I wouldn't let them do that, Morgan,> the girl reassured her. <I think they're just trying to make sure *I* don't get up to anything.>

Murnane cleared his throat. "Thank you," he said. "We have received the data and will examine it later." He folded his arms and took a couple of thoughtful paces around the font. "But I am curious. At the time Cane was examined on the *Midnight*, news had not yet reached your corner of the galaxy that there even was a problem he might be part of, otherwise his capsule would have been instantly identified. And on Sciacca's World, your rebel friends had access to even more limited information about the outside world. Yet our sources in the Commonwealth of Empires reveal that in a very short space of time you determined precisely what was going on—bearing in mind the Sol Apotheosis Movement fallacy—and confronted your superiors with that knowledge. When was it that you managed to piece it all together?"

Roche opened her mouth to speak—then shut it again. If they had sources in the

COE, chances were they already knew the answers to every question they had asked so far. So why go through the motions?

Then she reminded herself: trust no one. They could no more believe their sources than they could believe her—even if one corroborated the other.

She didn't envy them their position.

"It wasn't me so much who put it all together." She half expected a nagging voice in her ear telling her to be careful what she said. "It was the Box."

"What is this 'Box'?" It was asked in the same thick, unfamiliar accent as before, except that this time the questioner was female. "I take it you are referring to some sort of intelligence-gathering device?"

"An AI, yes." Roche nodded. "I was carrying it to Intelligence HQ when I was intercepted by the Dato Bloc. That's how I ended up on Sciacca's World in the first place."

"This device reasoned that Adoni Cane was one of the enemy?"

"Yes," she said. "And everything afterward seemed to confirm it."

"How was this device able to do something you yourself were unable to do?"

"The Box was no ordinary device," Roche said, remembering to use the past tense. "It was a truly remarkable piece of engineering. It suspected from the very start who Cane was. It even faked the distress call that led to the capsule's discovery."

"So it had access to information which you did not?"

"Yes, like the command language. But it wasn't just that. It actually thought better than I did."

"Impossible. No AI has yet surpassed a Human intelligence."

Roche shrugged. "I told you it was remarkable."

"And who built this amazing device?"

"It was manufactured on Trinity," said Roche. "They specialize in AIs there."

There was a muted whisper. Then Murnane spoke. "We have no record of such a place."

"No?" She looked around and out of the corner of her eye caught the gold robes of the Heresiarch. She had forgotten he was there. "Go ask your sources," she said. "They'll confirm it exists."

Murnane stirred. "What say you, Trezise?"

Startled first by the familiar name, Roche almost jumped as a familiar voice followed: "We know the place. It's administered by a High Human we have had some dealings with—an entity calling himself the Crescend." The man's voice was flat, emotionless, almost dead. "The AI Roche refers to did indeed come from this place, but as to its other abilities . . ."

Salton Tresize, Roche remembered—senior aide to Auberon Chase, head of COE Intelligence. She should've guessed someone like him would be here.

"You are not aware of any facility capable of making Human-superior AIs in COE jurisdiction?" Murnane pressed.

Trezise's tone didn't change as he said: "I'd sooner believe in aliens."

Murnane turned back to Roche. "You will understand if we hesitate to accept this aspect of your story without any hard evidence to back it up," he said. "Unless you could produce this AI for us to examine, perhaps?"

She didn't need the tiny prod the Box gave her. "I'm afraid it was destroyed along with Palasian System."

"I see." A sigh carried his words. "Well, the exact manner of your discovery of the enemy is not the issue here. What is important is the fact that you learned of their existence and went seeking more data. What can you tell us about Adoni Cane that we have not already covered?"

"The Box thought we should check the introns of Cane's genetic code," she said. "But I don't know what for."

Murnane nodded as though the suggestion was trivial. "And your young charge here." He pointed to Maii. "Does she have nothing to contribute to this discussion?"

<Maii?>

<Ask him how I'm supposed to talk with everyone's minds walled up,> the girl shot back.

Murnane raised a hand before Roche could pass the message on. "Simply speak to me," he said, "as you would to Roche, and a relay will announce the message for all to hear."

<Oh. Only—>

"—words?"

Roche heard the girl's voice directly through her own senses and a split second later through the relay, aloud. The relay stood on the far side of Roche; it was disconcerting to hear the girl's voice coming from two directions almost simultaneously.

"And appropriate images, where necessary." Murnane inclined his head in welcome. "Please feel free to share with us any impressions you received regarding the mind of Adoni Cane and any other member of the enemy's number you have encountered."

Maii did so, conveying as best she could a number of conflicting visions. Cane possessed a mental shield that was difficult to penetrate, but did allow him to communicate with her by epsense and occasionally offered strange glimpses of what lay beyond. Sometimes, Cane's mind seemed to spin like a top; at other times it was as still and clear as a lake, or a mirror. The *irikeii* had imagined him as a glowing light-source with a speck of black at its heart, and also as a snake coiling and uncoiling around itself.

"What sense do you make of these impressions?" she was asked.

"None of them are necessarily true representations of his mind," she said. "They're like the different reflections you get off the facets of a diamond, or the different meanings one collection of sounds has in different languages. I'm not seeing the underlying reality, just the secondary effects."

She shrugged, and the heavy shoulders of the suit magnified the gesture. She sent an image, via the relay, of a crystal turned inside out: smooth and spherical outside, facets crossing and tangling inside.

"It's hard to find words for this," she said.

"Evidently," said Murnane. "But if you had to choose just *one* word to describe him . . . ?"

"I'm not sure. 'Complex' isn't enough. 'Incipient,' perhaps? 'Numinous' has too many spiritual overtones, and I don't believe 'unknowable' applies to anything. There's a great potential within him. I don't know what for, but it's there."

Murnane waited a moment, to see if she would add anything else—or perhaps to confer mentally with the reaves surrounding them. After a moment he said: "And what of the *irikeii*? What did he think of you?"

Maii was silent so long, Roche thought she wouldn't answer. Finally, she said: "He disapproved of me."

"We thought as much," said Murnane, nodding. "The Olmahoi Caste petitioned strongly for your capture prior to your arrival—as did your own government. Somehow the word of your existence has spread, although exactly *how* has yet to be determined. We decided not to become involved, for very good reasons; there are enough inter-Caste tensions as it is without the council seeming to take sides—and what happens in non-Pristine Castes is, ultimately, none of our concern." Murnane stopped and took a deep breath. "Still, it is clear that the events that occurred within Palasian System have had far-reaching repercussions—many, perhaps, still to be felt. Morgan Roche, would you care to explain to us what happened there?"

Roche did so, outlining the exploration of the system after it had been ransacked by the clone warrior, her disastrous attempts to cooperate with Linegar Rufo, and her clash with the Kesh. Later, she hoped, she would be able to discuss things in more detail, but for the time being she contented herself with an overview.

"You say that the name of the enemy in this case was Jelena Heidik?" someone asked when she reached the aftermath of the destruction of Palasian System.

"Yes. It's one of a list of names we . . . found in an old archive. The others included Vani Wehr, Sadoc Lleshi, Ralf Dreher—"

"Do you know who they refer to?" Murnane interrupted. "Was there any other information in that archive, apart from the names?"

<Box?>

<No. But I can give you a full list of names, if you require it.>

"No," she said. She would give them the rest of the names later.

"And where is this Jelena Heidik now?"

"I don't know," Roche admitted. "We came here looking for her, but she's managed to get away."

"But you do think she's still somewhere in Sol System?"

"Yes."

"Why do you believe that?"

"Well, this seems to be where it's all coming to a head. She would hardly leave so soon."

Murnane leaned forward, his hands on each side of the font supporting him. "But *why* Sol System? Are we here following the enemy, or has the enemy followed us? We see patterns of movement across the galaxy, leading here, but we still cannot be one hundred percent certain that we are not fulfilling our own prophecy." He shrugged. "That is always a risk, I suppose, in any war of espionage; words and hints and suppositions carry little weight compared to maps and soldiers and bullets. So little is certain."

"We heard that Sol System was the location of an ancient battle," said Roche.

"It is the location of many things, if you believe the records; few stand up to strict examination. Which battle do you refer to?"

"I'm not sure," she said. "We've begun to suspect that the clone warriors—Cane and Heidik and the others—are seeking revenge for a war lost a long time ago. A war won by the Pristines."

"Do you know when?"

She shrugged. "As far back as we can remember. Half a million years or more. Back when there were only Pristines; the other Castes didn't exist yet."

"Do you have records to support this?"

"Nothing concrete—but surely that indirectly supports this theory? If there *were* records, someone would have found them by now. The fact that we haven't implies that they no longer exist—that the events we're looking for lie back in the earliest times."

"Perhaps." Murnane's expression remained impassive. "Remember, though, that many millions of civilizations have risen and fallen since then. That is an awful lot of data to sift through; if the records indeed are lost, not hidden, then we might never know. And without knowing when this battle you refer to took place—and who it was that lost—we have little to go on."

Roche conceded the point. "That's partly why we came here," she said. "We were following Heidik, yes, but we were also interested in seeing what happened. *If* the clone warriors attacked, then who they attacked first—and last—could reveal who their allies are, or who is related to their creators."

"Tell me, Roche," Murnane said. "Did you have any idea how complex the situation here would be before you came?"

"The Box had mentioned a gathering of sorts, and the COE commander I spoke to confirmed it, but that's all. I expected nothing like this."

"Did this Box of yours also happen to say anything about the composition of this system?" asked another voice. "There are several anomalies we have not yet fathomed, and I fear they may become hazards to navigation. More of these we do not need."

It took Roche a second to realize that it was the Heresiarch himself speaking. When she replied, she made certain she followed Vischilglin's advice and looked him directly in the eye—or at least in the direction of where he stood.

"I'm sorry, I don't know anything about that."

"The behavior of the solar wind is quite peculiar, and its effect on the gaseous volatiles of the planetary ring even more anomalous. If your AI had *anything* to say about that, I would've been grateful."

"Like I said," Roche replied evenly, keeping her attention fixed firmly on the Heresiarch. "It never mentioned a thing. I'm sorry."

She thought she saw him shrug, but he was too far away to tell for certain.

"There is no need for apology if one speaks the truth," he said, with wry humor to his tone.

"We have asked the High Humans for this information, too," said Murnane into the silence that followed. "They haven't told us anything that might conceivably help, on that or any other subject. I for one find their silence unnerving. Do you know why this might be the case?"

"No," said Roche.

"Given that your Box came from this Trinity, which had connections to this High Human called the Crescend, do you think its destruction would be of some concern to him? Would he respond to a call for more information, perhaps?"

"I really don't know." Roche hoped he would not respond; if the Crescend revealed to the council that she had lied about the Box's destruction, that certainly wouldn't count in her favor.

"The Crescend never contacted you while the Box was in your presence?"

"No, never."

"Do you expect him to?"

She resisted the urge to ask where this line of questioning was going. "Look, I went to Trinity to collect the Box, but met no one while I was there. I was rendered unconscious in orbit, and when I woke up the Box was . . . in my possession. That's all. You're obviously hoping that I can act as some sort of link between yourselves and the High Humans, but I don't see that as being an option. I've never communicated with them, and I doubt I ever will. Why should they bother with me? I'm just someone who happens to be caught in the middle of all this."

<I hope you know what you're doing, Box,> she whispered via her implants to the AI in her body.

<Trust me,> it said.

"We are *all* caught in this," Murnane said. "But outside of the enemy, few individuals have had such a catalytic effect as yourself." He paused. "Is there anything else you would like to tell us, while this council is in session?"

<Box?>

<No.>

"No," she repeated.

"Will you submit to a probe by one of our reaves to verify the answers you have given us?"

The question surprised her. "Why do you need that? The hard data speaks for itself, and I've no reason to deceive you."

"Nevertheless—will you?"

If she said yes, they would know that she was lying about the Box. Although she knew it would look suspicious, she had no choice but to say: "No. I'm sorry."

"Will you allow us, then, to examine you and, if necessary, take a genetic sample?"

She squirmed. <Box, could they find you that way?>

<The Dato missed me when you were captured,> the Box replied, <but that was partly because I had infiltrated their systems. I cannot rule out the possibility that the council will see something the Dato missed, and that I will be unable to suppress the information once it emerges.>

<Haven't you got into their systems?>

<Of course I have. But the Skehan Heterodox places great faith in the role of people in or alongside all its systems. At least one Human doctor would be present during your examination, and I see no easy way to suppress any knowledge that might emerge at that time.>

Again, she had no choice. "I'd prefer not to," she said. "I'm sorry."

Murnane studied her for a long moment. "As are we," he said. "But we cannot force you to submit to either examination—nor would we wish to." He gestured helplessly. "This meeting is now concluded. We would ask you to return to your ship, Roche, and—"

"*What!*" Roche snapped. "Aren't you even going to discuss what I've told you?"

"There is no need," he said. "We've been conferring by epsense the entire time."

"But you can't just dismiss me!"

"Can't we?" He took a step toward her. "Roche, we had hoped that you would provide us with information that is both new and verifiable. We had hoped that this might show us a way to combat the enemy we fear has infiltrated every group we deal with and perverts everything we attempt to do to stop them. Now it seems certain that you yourself have fallen into the same trap—either willingly or by accident."

Roche felt herself straighten, her tired back and stomach muscles tensing as though ready for attack. "Meaning?"

"You have told us *nothing*, Roche. You claim that Adoni Cane is one of the enemy, yet you can offer no explanation for this surety nor a reason for his atypical behavior. Of what value is his genetic data under those circumstances? You offer us names that you assure us are relevant, but do not give us a context in which to place them or access to the records you say they came from. On what grounds can we possibly use them as means to uncover the enemy among us? You cannot tell us why Sol System has become the focus of so much concern—you can't even tell us why *you* came here without resorting to vague explanations involving this mysterious AI of yours! And as to *that*, well, I hardly need to state how the council feels. *If* it existed at all, its tenuous connections to the High Humans might have been exploitable, but as it stands—"

"I'm telling you the *truth*," she broke in angrily.

"Are you?" Murnane moved closer again, his own anger evident in his face. "There is much to suggest that what you are doing is far from innocent. Ameidio Haid is a convicted criminal who, as the Commerce Artel points out, has not served his full term; who is to say you don't have criminal intent in mind as well? Add to that the fact that both your young friend here and the pilot of your vessel are the subjects of biological experiments; if Adoni Cane's genetic data and physiognomy turn out to be peculiar, could he not also be an experimental subject, and not the enemy you claim he is?

"Then there are the credibility gaps in your story. How did you come to the conclusion that Adoni Cane was one of the enemy? How did you survive Palasian System when even the Kesh destroyer sent to monitor the situation did not? Why did you come here? And why has your arrival caused such a furor among all those who have known you: the COE, the Dato Bloc, the Commerce Artel, the Surin, the Kesh, the Olmahoi . . . ?

"Even if what you are telling us is the truth, and Adoni Cane *is* one of the enemy, then how can we trust someone who openly admits to having one aboard her ship—as part of her *crew*?"

Murnane shook his head. "It may seem like we pre-judged you, but we have done nothing of the sort. We simply considered all possible conclusions prior to your arrival and allowed you to show us the one that best fitted the circumstances. Because you seem not to be dealing honestly with us, we are forced to conclude that Adoni Cane is a fake, or a misdiagnosis, or an enemy plant. We are unsure of *your* motives, but we are sure that we will no longer allow our precious time to be wasted examining your spurious claims and false offers. We have work to do, Roche, and a distraction such as this, even if not maliciously intended, does the enemy's work for them."

Tight-lipped, Roche forced herself to speak calmly. "If I could just say—"

"There is nothing more to be said," Murnane cut in. "Hue Vischilglin will escort you and your companion to your vessel. Once you're on board, the protection offered by the *Phlegethon* will be withdrawn."

Vischilglin appeared, expressionless, at Roche's side as Murnane turned his back and moved away without another word. The Heresiarch made no move at all. Roche let herself be taken by the arm and led away, furious but impotent, as a growing murmur filled the fane.

3

SHCV *Phlegethon*
955.1.30
0900

<*That* went well,> Roche muttered to the Box as Vischilglin directed her through the council and back into the petal from which they had first emerged. <'Talk to them,' you said. 'Exactly what we need,' you said. Whatever happened to getting access to their resources and getting on with the job?>

<You seem upset, Morgan,> the Box responded smoothly.

<Of course I'm upset! The questions you wouldn't let me answer were the ones that convinced them to send us away!>

<Be patient, Morgan. Time will tell if this trip has been wasted or not.>

<Yeah, right.> Feeling humiliated and frustrated, Roche avoided the eyes of everyone around her as she walked by. They thought she was a fool—or, worse, some sort of collaborator. <Sometimes I wonder why I don't just shut you up like De Bruyn did back in HQ.>

<The 'Silence between thoughts' override phrase would allow you to do it any time you wished,> the Box intoned casually. <I wasn't faking that period of disconnection.>

<I never thought that—> She stopped midsentence as its admission sank in. <Why *did* the Crescend give you an override phrase that actually worked? It doesn't make sense—especially in the light of recent knowledge.>

<Given the degree of invasion that I am upon your person, it seemed reasonable that you be provided with a means to turn me off, should I become too much of an inconvenience.>

<In other words, the Crescend gave me an out.>

<Exactly.>

<Without *telling* me about it?>

<You learned in your own time.>

<Only by accident—the same way I found out that you're inside me!>

<I can only assure you that, had you learned the latter before the former, you would have been given the override.>

<Oh, naturally.> She couldn't help the sarcasm. The modified ulnar nerve along her arm was throbbing with remembered sensation. Data had burned along that path to the valise she had once believed the Box to inhabit. She wondered which pathways it used, now that it was completely inside of her. . . .

"Well, that could have gone better."

Roche recognized the man's voice as one from the interrogation. She looked up to see a fair-haired, diminutive figure waiting for them at the top of the stairs, an almost condescending smile beaming from his small, triangular face.

Vischilglin didn't give Roche a chance to reply.

"Stand aside, Junior Primate Nemeth," she said, pushing past the man and heading back down into the thick cloud they had climbed through to get to the council.

"That's *Assistant Vice* Primate to you, Co-adjutant Vischilglin," he objected, following them down the steps.

Only then did Roche realize something odd about the council—or rather the people who comprised the council. They were all plenipotentiary envoys, co-adjutants, assistant vice primates, senior aides—underlings with fancy titles. None of them were the real operators. Perhaps, she thought, the situation in Sol System was too risky for the superiors to come, so their assistants had been sent instead.

Then she realized another thing: she had heard the name of Assistant Vice Primate Nemeth somewhere before. She stopped and turned to the man. He stopped also, a couple of meters away, behind Maii. Mist from the cloud created a slight haze between them, but not enough to obscure the man's crooked grin.

"It was you who hailed us before we came here," she said. "Before that drone intercepted us."

Nemeth executed a slight bow of the head. "I'm flattered you remembered me."

"What do you want?" Roche was in no mood for small talk.

He gesticulated expansively. "Perhaps it would be more appropriate to ask what it is *you* want—from *me*?"

She studied him for a moment, then turned and continued after Vischilglin down the steps. "I haven't got time for these games," she muttered irritably.

<Can you read him, Maii?>

<Yes,> replied the girl, maintaining a steady plodding pace behind her. <He is devious, but not impenetrable.>

<So what's he after?>

<To strike some sort of deal with you,> said the girl. <Although I don't know exactly what kind of deal.>

<What do we know for sure about him?> said Roche. <What is most prominent in his mind?>

<It seems the government he represents has been proven to be compromised—therefore his influence within the council is on the wane. He spoke first during the session in an attempt to remind people that he was still there.> She paused for a few seconds before adding: <And he doesn't seem to like Esko Murnane.>

<That's the best thing you've said about him so far.> Roche could hear the footsteps of the man following her down. Vischilglin strode ahead of her, a tall broad shape plowing through the mist. Far from the chatty, affable guide she'd been when they first met, she had hardly said a word since the hearing.

<What's on *her* mind?> Roche asked Maii.

<She's embarrassed. She thought you would be more help to the council—to the people she represents. She feels . . . betrayed, perhaps.>

<By me?>

<No. By the people who encouraged her to think that you might offer a solution.>

<And who are they?>

<Some members of the council and various lower-echelon officials.>

Roche sighed. <I only came here looking for answers. I mean, what were they expecting to find in me? A savior or something?>

<To some, that's exactly what you are,> said Maii. <To others you are the heart of the enemy itself. But most people are just curious. They're listening to the rumors, but they're waiting to see what happens.>

<But how can so many rumors about me be started in such a short period of time?>

<*Chen chen, fe,*> said Maii.

Roche frowned. <What . . . ?>

<Something Veden once said to me,> the girl replied. <Words attract words. 'Morgan Roche' are two words that have been uttered many times in the last few weeks. It is inevitable that other words would attach themselves to them.>

Roche smiled now. <Well, whatever the rumors are, I think there are going to be a lot of disappointed people,> she said. <Because without the help of this council, I'm not going to be doing much.>

They stepped out of the clouds and back into the landscape of rolling valleys and trickling waters. Roche groaned inwardly when she remembered the distance they'd come to get this far. Her legs and back were sore from standing for so long.

As though someone had read her mind, an air-car resembling a large silver spoon hummed into view. There were seats for four people in the bowl, all empty.

"I thought you might be weary," said Nemeth from behind them. "As attractive as the scenery is, there's no need to view it on foot twice."

Roche glanced at Vischilglin, who was frowning. "You arranged this?" Roche asked, suspecting an ulterior motive.

"It is not the council's will," said Vischilglin, scowling.

Nemeth shrugged expansively. "Since when did the council start dictating courtesy? I'm offering you all a lift—including yourself, Co-adjutant Vischilglin." He smiled. "Well, are you coming or not?"

The air-car sped quietly across the uneven terrain, leaving the steps they had just descended far behind. Although they didn't move alarmingly fast, there were a couple of moments when the car slued to avoid a jutting ridge, making Roche feel a little uneasy.

Nemeth didn't appear to be troubled by the craft's sudden movements. He sat beside her, looking out at the rolling landscape sweeping beneath them, his face split by a seemingly perpetual smile.

As if sensing her staring at him, Nemeth turned to face Roche, and his smile widened.

"Now isn't this so much easier?" he said. "Perhaps we could even take a more interesting route back to the docks." Over his shoulder to where Maii and Vischilglin sat, he said: "Do you think the council would approve, Vischilglin?"

The woman grunted an affirmation. She really had little choice now, Roche thought. Nemeth laughed and turned back to look at the scenery.

"Tell me," said Roche. "What exactly *is* it you think I want from you, Nemeth?"

"Ah, now, that's the question, isn't it?" he said. "Make no mistake: I can do any number of things for you, Roche." He glanced over at her. "If I were so inclined, of course." When she didn't react, he went on: "You come at a peculiar time, Roche—

when the council is desperate for answers that none of us have. It feels constrained by the very precepts that allowed it to come into being so quickly. It is . . . *limited* by its nature."

"You mean it's for Pristines only," said Roche.

He nodded. "But some of us fear that 'Pristines only' may not be enough to combat this threat." He watched the view silently for a few moments; when he spoke again, the smile had faded. "I lost my family back home, you know," he said. "They were caught in an insurrection while I was serving in a completely different system. A local terrorist branch whipped up enough anti-government action—in the form of riots and infrastructure sabotage—to warrant calling in the army. Thousands of innocent people died in the ensuing repression, including my family, and it achieved nothing for either side. It turned out that the enemy was responsible for the whole thing. The terrorists were just a tool—the means to an end. And that end was to cause as much destruction and misery as possible."

Nemeth looked at Roche, who sat watching him carefully. He remained outwardly relaxed, except for his hands: his knuckles were white where they gripped the armrest. When he realized this, he quickly loosened his grip and his smile returned.

"So, do you have any family, Roche?" Nemeth asked.

Roche felt a stab of pain. Never knowing her parents had been a constant regret throughout her childhood. As an adult, she had aspired to COE Intelligence in order to track them down. Upon reaching that goal, however, she had forgotten about her parents entirely, too busy with her own life to worry about the one she might have had.

"No," she said. Another part of her was glad that she could forestall his obvious gambit. While she could feel compassion for his loss, he would have to engage her intellect, not her emotions, in order to get what he wanted. Whatever that was.

If he was disappointed by her reply, he made no sign. He simply nodded and changed the subject.

"In a second we'll be entering one of the main longitudinal ducts that run down the hull from minaret to crypt," he said.

Vischilglin leaned forward in the cab. "That's fore to aft to us," she said.

"Even at the speeds we will be going," Nemeth continued, "it will take us ten minutes or so. But please don't be concerned by that," he added in response to a look of alarm in Roche's eyes: to travel any significant length along the giant ship so quickly would demand speeds greater than one or two thousand kilometers per hour. "We'll be perfectly safe."

They raced toward what at first appeared to be nothing more than a wall, but as they flew closer, Roche saw it for what it actually was: a giant tube lying on its side across their path, suspended by invisible forces ten meters or more above the rolling hills. It was so thick that its top was obscured by the cloud cover, and for a moment Roche wondered how they were going to get past it—or into it, if this was in fact one of the ducts Nemeth had mentioned.

A moment later the craft swept beneath the massive cylinder and into its shadow. Their speed eased slightly as the air-car rose toward an enormous portal on the underbelly of the tube, easily thirty meters across and hanging open like a slack and lipless mouth. From it issued a cold breeze; not strong, but enough to make Roche shiver.

"An air duct?" she said, hearing a faint susurrus coming from within. "Seems a bit primitive on a ship like this."

"Believe me," said Nemeth, "it's purely for aesthetics."

Then they were inside—and caught by a tremendous, rushing wind. The air-car lurched violently as it began to accelerate along the tube. Roche gripped her armrests as she was pressed back into her seat and knocked from side to side with every buffeting motion. Beside her, Nemeth laughed at her obvious alarm.

Another air-car—this one a single-passenger model shaped more like an egg with two limp, trailing spines—swept past them, barely missing by a meter. Startled, Roche looked around properly for the first time. Inside, the tube was easily wide enough to hold a hundred air-cars. Lines of lights trickled along the walls; every now and again, larger, brighter patches would rush by, too quick to take in. Other air-cars continued to pass theirs, less quickly than before, but thankfully none came as close as the first one.

"Aesthetics, huh?" she said to Nemeth over the sound of the wind; some sort of field-effect was keeping the worst of the turbulence at bay; otherwise he would never have been able to hear her.

He laughed out loud again. But this time it was with an almost childlike delight: he was enjoying the ride.

"You would've loved Palasian System," she said. <Are you okay back there, Maii?>

<Yes, Morgan. The view is spectacular. If you know when to look, you can see out the duct entrances and glimpse the levels as we go past.>

Roche looked around her, concentrating for the first time on the bright patches as they went past. Indeed, now that she looked, she could make out brief impressions of the levels as they flashed by: here, deep purple and icy, there, soft pastels. One of the portals was much larger than the others, and through it she glimpsed angular structures in the distance, across flat, metallic plains; levels devoted to the ship's working, she supposed.

Clearly Maii had lifted this method of looking at the levels from the way Nemeth moved his eyes.

<What is our guide thinking, Maii?>

<He's getting a huge thrill,> said the girl. <I can't read much beyond that. I suspect he's taken us this way because it gives him a natural shield to hide behind.>

Roche turned back to Nemeth. "Scenery is all very well," she said, "but when are we going to *talk*?"

"We can talk now, if you like." He swiveled in his seat to look at Vischilglin, who regarded him stonily. "Do you think the council would object to us having a little privacy?"

Before the woman could answer, the field-effect protecting the passengers from turbulence clove in two, leaving Roche and Nemeth in a bubble of their own. Absolute silence suddenly pressed against her ears.

The air-car had settled itself into a gentle, rocking motion, and swept along the tube with the other air-cars as though on any conventional road. If Nemeth had brought her along the duct in order to unnerve her, Roche refused to let it.

"I want to talk to you in a frank and open manner," said Nemeth after a few seconds.

"You've displayed little intention of that so far," said Roche.

"Games. I know." He dismissed her accusation with the wave of a hand. "The council is a bureaucracy; whether one is working within it or despite it, one is necessarily limited in one's options by this very fact."

Roche sighed. "Open and frank, remember?" she said, making no attempt to conceal her annoyance. "Can we just get to the point?"

He sighed, too, and looked away for a moment. Behind him, a white landscape flashed by. "Things are not going well for us here in Sol System," he said. "In that much, at least, Murnane and I agree. The enemy were here before we even arrived, and have made their presence felt in a thousand ways—sometimes subtle, other times not so subtle. Although there has been something of a lull in the last few days, every hour dozens more ships arrive, and with each ship the chances are high that more of the enemy are coming too. And we are not finding *any* of them."

He looked at her, then. "I am being completely and utterly frank about this, Morgan. I hope you realize that. Not even Vischilglin knows the depths of our failure. For all the council's collective experience and wisdom, for all the technology of groups like the Skehan Heterodox, for all that we have been studying the enemy for four and a half years, we are not even close to solving the problem here. Can you understand how galling that is?"

She didn't have to think hard about that. She had been banging her head against the problem for less than three months.

"So why not take a chance on me?" she asked. "If you're so desperate, what have you got to lose?"

"That's an interesting question, isn't it?"

"Do you have an answer?"

"A kind of answer," he said. "But it starts with a question." He paused. "There are more than just Pristines in this system. Do you know what the Exotics are doing here, along with us?"

"Following the flow, I guess," she said. "Maybe coming to settle old scores. Naturally they'd be swept up in any regional conflict that might have started among the Pristines. I can see how they would be dragged here along with everyone else."

He nodded. "It's certainly a valid assumption. According to your theory, the enemy comes from a time in which the Exotic strands of Humanity did not exist, or at least may not have been so prevalent. Indeed, maybe they are a weapon created by an ancient alliance of *all* Exotics, in response to the age-old grudge that Pristines have it better than the others simply and unjustly because they are more like the original—although why this alliance would wait so long to wreak its vengeance is somewhat of a mystery. And why would a weapon created by Exotics allow the descendants of its masters to be dragged into such a dispute?"

"There may be only one way to find out," she said.

"Precisely. Here we come to your plan to wait until the fighting starts and see who doesn't end up dead at the end of it all, apart from the enemy. If anyone *is* left standing, they must be guilty. Simple." He raised a hand as Roche started to protest. "I'm sorry for seeming disrespectful. Your plan is ruthless and, perhaps because of that, likely to be more effective than most of the others bandied about. I simply fear that we will find out the truth only when it's too late."

"So what do *you* suggest?"

He shrugged, palms raised—and for the first time Roche noticed that the little finger on each of his hands was missing. "I told you: your plan is better than any of the others I've heard—including my own." He grimaced. "It's a hard thing to admit. If ever you doubt my sincerity, please recall this conversation—although I'd be happier if you kept it to yourself, otherwise."

She allowed herself a half-smile. "I don't know," she said. "Blackmail has a certain appeal."

"A kindred spirit." His own smile was wide and natural. "Perhaps we can come to terms, after all."

An air-car going the opposite way rushed past them; Roche gripped her seat until the rocking of their own car settled. When it had, Nemeth went on.

"We thought the lull recently might have something to do with you," he said. "Your ex-superiors in COE Intelligence have kept us up to date with your movements. Ever since we heard about Cane's existence, we've been quite curious to see what would happen next. Many of us expected the COE to start falling apart as a result. In fact many of us felt that the Commonwealth's proximity to Sol System, the very focus of everything, would put it under much more pressure than other nations farther out. But apart from that brief fracas with the Dato Bloc, nothing much seems to have happened. It's almost disappointing." He flashed his grin at her again before adding: "For some, that is."

"What does all this have to do with *me*?" she said, conscious that the ride would be coming to an end soon and wanting some answers before it did.

"You're an anomaly, Roche. An outlier. You claim to have survived two verifiable encounters with two self-declared clone warriors. For that alone you're worth observing. And—" He hesitated slightly. "And worth having on our side."

Roche shook her head. "Why? Because you think I'm *lucky* or something?" She was desperately trying to make some sense of what he was saying.

"No," he said. "Nothing to do with luck." Again the smile, but this time forced and uneasy. "But there is something about you. Something that doesn't quite add up. And, unlike Murnane, I don't think it's wise to turn you away without knowing what that thing is."

"But Murnane *has* turned me away," she said bitterly. "The council has already made its decision."

"It made *a* decision," Nemeth corrected her. "It wasn't necessarily the right one, and it certainly wasn't unanimous. It needn't necessarily be the *only* one it makes. I happen to know that there is enough support to back up the offer I'm about to make you—if only because in hindsight it may prove wise for the council to be seen as having made the other decision it couldn't officially make, where everyone could see it. By that I mean that the council has to cover every base it sees open, even though here and now it can't acknowledge even to itself what it is doing. For posterity's sake—for the sake of the future itself—every chance must be taken."

Roche was just managing to keep up. "You're talking about some covert group within the council?"

"One with its own agenda," he said, nodding. "Does it surprise you that such a thing might exist?"

Roche shrugged heavily. "Every bureaucracy supports such groups," she said. "I guess I just didn't expect one here, that's all. I mean, we all have the one common enemy, right? We have the same *aim*."

"True," he said. "But we all work differently to achieve those aims. The council has become concerned with method, whereas the Ulterior concentrates on intention."

Roche laughed at this. The *Ulterior* . . . "And every such group has to have a catchy name, right?"

Nemeth ignored the gibe. "We have no firmly entrenched protocol," he said. "If we see an opportunity, or even the potential for an opportunity, we will take it. We are less . . . scrupulous, perhaps, than many of our colleagues. And for that reason, we must remain as our name suggests: behind the scenes."

Roche regarded him steadily. "And you and your friends in this 'Ulterior' regard me as some sort of 'opportunity'? Is that what you're trying to tell me?"

"Isn't that what you wanted the council to believe?" he said.

"Yes," she said. "I guess it was."

"Working for us, you would obtain that goal, Roche. Indirectly. If you fail, of course, the council has no knowledge of you, having turned you away from the one and only official hearing it was obliged to give you."

"Of course," said Roche dryly.

"But if it looks as if you might succeed, then you will have the full support of the Ulterior—and ultimately the council itself."

"And why should I believe anything you're saying?" she asked him. "How do I know you're telling me the truth?"

He dismissed the objection with a shrug. "You don't," he said. "But you don't have many other options right now. And we need each other."

Roche sighed and, despite the apprehension she was feeling, said: "So what exactly are you offering?"

"A deal," he answered quickly, and with sudden enthusiasm. "We can't give you any formal protection or recognition, obviously, but we can give you information. This information has to flow both ways—unconditionally. If you learn anything new, we want to know about it. And if you find anything you think might work, we want to know about that most of all."

She didn't need the Box to tell her that she should take the deal. If she couldn't get the full approval of the council, this might be the next best thing. But she still had her doubts . . .

"It can't be that simple," she said.

"Well, there is something else we would like you to do for us," he admitted. "But I can't see how it doesn't fit in with your plans, anyway."

Here we go, she thought. "Meaning what exactly?"

"That you're probably going to want to go buzzing around the system, looking for the enemy, right? Poking your nose in here, seeing what turns up there; waiting for the fight to start so you can see who kills who. Well, that's exactly what we want you to do, too. Specifically, we want you to see what the Exotics are up to. That's the one area this damned Pristine council of ours can't see into properly—and any blind spots in situations like this are dangerous."

She nodded: that much at least was true.

"Do you have any other agents working in this area?" she asked.

"A few," he told her. "But nowhere near enough. Right now there are seven hundred and fifty-eight known Castes in Sol System, Morgan, not counting Pristine. Some are wildly Exotic; some are down the other end of the scale from the Skehan Heterodox—almost Low Castes."

"And High Humans?" she said.

He shook his head briefly. "None that we are aware of," he said. "But if you find anything that suggests there are, we'd be keen to hear about them too."

She was keen on the Box's behalf to avoid that subject. "So basically," she said, "if I find something, you take the credit. If I don't, or if I get into trouble, you disown me, right?"

"Obviously we will do everything in our power to help you," Nemeth said, "but our power is not unlimited. Unless you give us a reason to come forward, I'm afraid the Ulterior must remain just that."

She nodded slowly. "And will I have to pledge allegiance to the Ulterior? Swear a secret oath? Sign my name in blood, perhaps?"

He grinned. "Your word will be fine," he said.

<Is he telling the truth, Maii?>

<He thinks he is, for what that's worth. He has the mind of a man who could convince himself of anything, though.>

<That doesn't surprise me.>

"Okay," Roche said after a deep breath. "For lack of a better option at this time, we have a deal."

"Good," he said, smiling and extending a hand. She just looked at it. "If you're still worried about that genetic sample," he said, "you should know that I'm more likely to get a decent one from the armrest you've been leaning on than from shaking your hand."

She relented and took his hand.

"And not a moment too soon," he said.

The air-car had begun to decelerate and drift toward the wall. The bright patches passed more slowly than before, and Roche caught glimpses of endless docks like the one through which she'd arrived: row after row of airlock inner doors, ramps, and floating cargo-lifters. All empty. For all the traffic she had seen, the ship might have been completely sealed.

And maybe it was, Roche thought. That might have been the only option open to the Heresiarch and the council in order to prevent contagion.

"Oh," said Nemeth as they approached an opening and braked still farther, "there is one more thing."

"There always is," she said.

"We'd like you to take one of us with you."

"What? *You*? Forget it."

He managed to affect a hurt expression. "No," he said. "Not me. And not on board your ship, either. He'll have his own. But we'd like him there as backup, an observer—or a bodyguard, if you like."

They slid smoothly out of the duct and into the docks.

"As insurance?" she said.

"The only true necessity in all the universe," he said. "Or so I've been led to believe."

Before she could say anything, the air-car reached a safe travel speed and the partition between the front and back seats evaporated along with the rest of the cushioning bubble. They decelerated still further, heading for the dock where the scutter was waiting.

Unable to talk in privacy, Roche could only stare in alarm at the atypically enormous Surin warrior standing in full battle-dress at the inner door of their dock.

"You can't be serious," she said.

<He is,> said Maii, her mental voice sharp with dismay.

"It was the only way to get the Surin off our backs," Nemeth said. "Officially they want to make sure your young ward here is treated well; unofficially, they want in on the action." His eyes were hard. "You should be glad it's not an Olmahoi gray-boot as well."

"Someone with a little more subtlety would've been better."

"I think you'll find our friend here quite suited to your task."

She grunted dubiously. "Any other surprises I should know about?"

"No," Nemeth said as the air-car slid to a halt. "At least, none that *I'm* aware of . . ."

4

HHAB *Dark Stressor*
955.1.30
1155

Finding the sort of people she wanted was almost ridiculously easy. Finding the right *person*, however, was proving to be a little more difficult.

"I don't give a damn what you think, De Bruyn," said the obese Exotic on the far side of the partition, his voice a deep and guttural drawl. He had a tic on the left side of his body that seemed to move of its own accord: first his eyelid would twitch, then one finger, then a muscle in his neck, then something under the table would thump as his foot kicked out at nothing.

"You don't, huh?" She leaned forward and slid the partition aside, not caring anymore about his Caste's preference to avoid close personal contact.

"No, I don't," he repeated, backing away uneasily. His entire left side twitched—eye, finger, neck muscle, et al.—simultaneously. "What do we need someone like you for, anyway?"

"I told you," she said. "I have contacts; I can make things *easier* for you."

He snorted. "I don't see how getting dragged into this personal grudge of yours will make life easier," he said. "Grudges are bad for business. They can get messy."

She feigned indignation. "Now, who said anything about a grudge, Ken'an?"

"It's in your eyes," he said. "It's in the way you bargain. You're after something real bad—so bad you're practically drooling. People don't salivate for money, in my experience. The stomach rumbles for betrayal, revenge, hatred, jealousy . . ."

She retreated slightly. Maybe he wasn't so stupid after all. Still, she'd hoped for better. "So much for mercenaries," she said dismissively.

"If it's mercenaries you want, talk to Uyeno Lenz. He'll do anything for a quick credit."

"Yeah, including knife me the moment my back is turned."

"A distinct possibility," he said. "But I can't help you, De Bruyn. Like I said, getting involved in your personal grudge would be bad for business." He slid his seat back and shrugged. "I'm sorry, but I have standards."

"Yeah," she muttered to herself, watching him waddle away from the table. "Just not very high ones."

He was right, of course. She had no interest in the petty power-squabbles boiling in the vacuum of Sol System. She didn't care who came out on top in whose transplanted regional politics. All she wanted was someone to help her keep an eye on Morgan Roche—and more, if necessary.

De Bruyn shouldered her way back to the bar, where an orange-clad Exotic refilled her glass. She wasn't drinking anything alcoholic; she wanted to keep her head clear.

"I'm looking for Uyeno Lenz," she said.

The bartender gave her a noncommittal shrug as he took some empty glasses away.

"You don't want to do business with him," said a deep voice at her side.

She turned. Another Exotic leaned against the bar, green-skinned, a mug of clear liquid clasped in his large, oil-stained hand. His eyes were deep-set and red; two thick strands of black hair ran down his head from forehead to nape. He flashed her an amused expression which seemed strangely out of place on his otherwise hard features. He didn't have to say another word. She knew he was the mercenary called Lenz. Only a hack would try a line like that on someone.

"You're right," she said, walking back to her booth. "I don't."

An alarm went off in her implants before she sat down. Being fired from COE Intelligence hadn't meant the loss of equipment standard for upper-echelon agents. Her eyes and ears were artificial; much of her nervous system had been enhanced to run faster under stress, as well as to act as conduits for many different types of data; her skeletal strength had been increased by the addition of materials far stronger than Human bone. Although she could fight as well as most COE Intelligence operatives, she had not been trained for that; instead, she was wired to receive and transmit data—like a Human antenna, complete with two-way listening and viewing devices.

She recognized the alarm instantly; indeed, she had been expecting a call from this source for the last hour or two. Putting the drink carefully in front of her, she activated scramblers and ciphers and opened a link to her ship.

Kindling was stationed just inside the protective bubble of the *Phlegethon*, hidden by the big ship's camouflage and given clearance by her contact in the council. She had sent it there to act as a relay after catching a tug to the *Dark Stressor* compact habitat to look for allies. She'd been hoping for a little more time, though; if Roche was already on the move, she would have to hurry to keep up.

When the connection was made and secured, she spoke via her implants directly to her contact.

<What's happened, Trezise?>

<Nothing unexpected.> Via tightbeam, the lack of emotion in the man's voice was only magnified; she'd never decided whether it was an affectation or a genuine condition. <The worm is hooked and wriggling. Now all we have to do is wait for the fish. . . .>

The words came with an image of Roche's scutter leaving its dock and heading for the *Ana Vereine*, closely preceded by another ship—a long-range fighter of some kind, angular and harsh. The design was unfamiliar.

<Who's the escort?>

<That I am still trying to ascertain.>

<What about the other data I asked you for?>

<I have some.> An icon winked in the corner of her field of vision, indicating an attachment to the transmission. <The rest is on its way.>

<How long?>

<I can't be exact, Page,> he said. <We're a long way from home, you know.>

<I *know* that.> She hated it when people used her first name—a fact that wasn't

lost on Trezise, she was sure. She forced herself not to rise to the bait, glancing instead at the data and searching for any of a handful of details she was hoping to find. One was there, as obvious as a nova now that she knew what to look for, and she smiled to herself.

She wasn't going to share her small victory with Trezise, though. <What about one of those ftl links? We'll need one if we're to keep in touch.>

<Can't help you there,> he said. <The best I can do is swing one by periodically, and give you the codes to call for one should you have the need. There are thousands all over the system. The longest delay you'll likely suffer is about ten minutes or so.>

<Then that'll have to do.> She looked up to see the green-faced mercenary still watching her. She caught his image and sent it to Trezise. <What Caste is this?>

<None I've seen before, but that's not surprising around here,> he said. <Where the hell are you, anyway? I thought you were in your ship.>

She smiled to herself. <If I wanted you to know where I was, I would've already told you.>

<Suspicious to the end,> he said. <Auberon always said that the feeling was mutual.>

<Auberon was a fool.> Her smile became a snarl. Auberon Chase, his boss and once hers, *was* a fool, but he was still head of COE Intelligence and safe in HQ, while she was out hunting among the predators. <What did *you* do wrong, Salton, to get such a lousy assignment?>

<Nothing,> he said. <I volunteered.>

<I don't believe you. Only a fool would want to come here.>

<Only a fool would fail to see the opportunity,> he said. <When I think of all that your friend Morgan Roche is doing to squander her unearned leverage, I can't help but want to kill her myself.>

Again, De Bruyn refused to rise to the bait. <And where is our little worm headed?>

<Who?>

She fought to contain her annoyance at his games. <Roche, of course.>

<Oh, did you think I was referring to Roche?> His voice was smooth and amused. <I thought you knew me better than that. I was referring to a *much* bigger target than her.>

<What the hell are you talking about, Trezise?>

<My dear Page,> he said. <I'm talking about the council itself, of course.>

She broke the line abruptly when she saw the mercenary approaching.

"I heard you talking to Ken'an, before." The words rolled from somewhere deep in the back of his throat, sounding as though they were having to fight their way through food to get out.

"You have a problem with that?"

He sat down opposite her. "Not at all," he said. "But you should listen to him. Grudges are dangerous."

"I don't recall asking either you or Ken'an for your opinion."

"Well, make the most of it anyway," he said. "Advice is about the only thing you'll get for free around here."

"And what's the price of a little peace and quiet?"

"Quiet I can give you." He activated some sort of device in his jacket and a bubble of silence enfolded the booth. "Peace, however, will be more difficult."

De Bruyn's implants buzzed, warning her of the field-effect he was using to give them privacy. She ignored the alarm, doubting the bubble was anything more dangerous than a toy. Still, her right hand slipped to her thigh-holster and disengaged the safety on her pistol.

She smiled. "Okay," she said. "I'm looking for someone to watch my back while I go about my business."

"What sort of business?"

"*My* business," she repeated firmly. "For now, at least."

"In Sol System?" The words continued to rattle in his throat.

"I wouldn't be here otherwise."

"For how long?"

"Until the job is done." De Bruyn kept her stare firmly on his gold-flecked irises. "It may require a bit of muscle."

"And how would you pay for this . . . muscle?"

"I have influence in the Interim Emergency Pristine Council. What I can't provide in credit, I can make up in IEPC clearance and access. The breadth of your clientele will increase overnight."

"*If* we survive." His lips tightened. "Perhaps Ken'an was right: maybe you are a bomb just waiting to go off. Who's to say you won't take us with you?"

"There are ways to avoid that," she said. "And the right person working with me would find out how. But I'll need more than a handful of people to see this through."

"Promises and plans are easy to make," he said, his voice a low rasp. "So who is the target, anyway?"

She hesitated a second. Ken'an hadn't asked that, nor had any of the others. She'd been glad to assume it wasn't relevant.

"Morgan Roche—"

She was cut short by a hand under her chin, jerking her head back. She clutched at her pistol, but another hand gripped her wrist and yanked it away. She kicked, flexed, strained—then relaxed when she realized it was futile to resist. The hands were just too strong.

She cursed silently. The privacy field had kept her from hearing her assailant creep up behind her. But she wasn't at a complete disadvantage yet . . .

"Call him off, Lenz," she hissed. "Or I swear I'll blow this place apart."

The mercenary smiled calmly at her. "And how do you intend to do that?"

"With the nugget of turcite I slipped under the bar," she said. "One word, and it'll detonate."

"Blowing yourself up in the process," he said with a slight, forced laugh.

"A risk I'm prepared to take," she said. "But chances are this thug of yours will offer me some protection from the blast. As for you . . ."

The mercenary looked nervous and cast a glance at the person holding her. The grip about her neck tightened.

"Tell me why we should help you with this Roche person." This came from the man squeezing her neck.

"What—?" She attempted to turn around but was barely able to move at all.

"If I'm going to be doing business with you," he said, "then I want to know what's so important about her."

"*You're—?*"

Again the grip tightened. "Lenz," he said. "That's right." He released her throat and arm and pushed her facedown onto the table. She reached for her pistol, but he beat her to it and snatched it away, slamming it down in front of her. "Now, no more games; no more threats. You talk."

He moved a few paces from behind her to where she could see him. He looked much like the mercenary sitting opposite her, but broader, older, and without the hair.

"What do you know about Morgan Roche?" De Bruyn asked, sitting up and rubbing at her neck.

"Only what we've heard," he said. "There's a lot of stories going around about her. Her name keeps cropping up. Not many of the details match, though. The general impression is she's somehow relevant to everything going on here. Someone who might be dangerous."

"Yes, she is—but to whom? Us or the enemy?"

He frowned. "Meaning?"

"All those stories you've heard," she said. "They're all lies. Every one of them. The purpose of the stories is to hide the truth, and to keep attention focused on her—so that when she's ready, she can act."

His skeptical look didn't change. "And what is the truth?"

"I'm not sure," De Bruyn said thoughtfully. "But I think I can find out. All I need is a little more time, and"—she hesitated significantly—"some help."

He studied her for a long time. She looked patiently back.

"We have a ship," he said eventually. "It doesn't look much, but that's the idea."

"It's not your ship I'm interested in," she said. "What's your crew like?"

"Hand-picked."

"How many?"

"Eight."

"And you trust them?"

"With my life." He smiled. "But not my money."

She leaned back into her seat and returned the smile. "Okay, then. Let's talk business."

Lenz relaxed and moved around the table. His buddy slid over to make room. "You should know that we don't come cheap," he said. "For what you're asking—"

As soon as his hand came off her pistol, De Bruyn grabbed it and shot him through the chest. She shot his buddy too, before he had a chance to register what had happened. Screams erupted around her before the bodies had even hit the floor.

De Bruyn took the lights out with her next two shots, then slipped through the panicked crowd and out of the bar before anyone realized that she had gone. At the first sign of pursuit, she triggered the nugget of turcite with a quick burst from her implants. The explosion tore through pressure-walls and bulkheads, the shock wave hurling her and her pursuers through a locked door and into a storage room full of cartons. She sustained only minor bruising and temporary hearing loss, and was back on her feet in time to ensure that none of her pursuers would ever wake again.

The authorities believed her story about a clash between rival mercenaries. Using her IEPC pass, she was on the tug within the hour, and back on *Kindling* an hour after that.

<Let me guess,> said Trezise when she had reopened communications with him. <*Dark Stressor*, was it?>

<How did you find out?> she said with studied indifference.

<It wasn't difficult. There was a disturbance there, a few hours ago, involving a Caste much like the fellow you showed me. I looked into it, of course, to see if you'd come to any harm. The habitat's surveillance cameras caught a couple of good shots of you. Black suits you, my dear—much more so than a Commonwealth uniform ever did.> He paused for a moment. <Did everything go according to plan?>

She shrugged noncommittally. He knew damn well it hadn't, she guessed, and that ate at her. She was no better off than she had been the day before. But it was only a matter of time before she found someone suitable for her needs. There were many other places to look, and she would have plenty of other opportunities to do so while she followed Roche across the system.

Kindling's engines hummed softly through the walls of its cramped cockpit. In a way, she was glad to be on her own. Relying on other people was dangerous, albeit a necessary danger at times. It was much better, she'd always thought, to have them rely on you. . . .

<I hope you know what you're doing, Page,> said Trezise across the expanding distance between the two ships—one as large as a good-sized moon, the other barely a speck. There was still no emotion in the man's voice. <You seem to be expending a lot of energy on something that will ultimately get you nowhere.>

<Is that what you think I'm doing?>

<I'm hypothesizing,> he said. <That's all.>

<And does your hypothesis explain why Morgan Roche's COE birth records have been erased?>

There was a slight pause. <I'm not sure what you mean.>

<The records you gave me,> she said. <Look at them yourself. Try to find her date of birth.>

<Why?>

<Just *do* it,> she snapped. <But you won't find it, Trezise. You won't find it because it's not there—along with a lot of other information that should be there too.>

<A woman without a past,> he said, with the barest hint of dryness in his voice. <Whatever will an intelligence operative come up with next?>

<Listen, you idiot. *We* didn't wipe those records. Someone else did. Someone's covering up. The same someone who got in the way when I tried to stop her. The same someone who sacked me.>

Trezise sighed heavily. <Listen to yourself, Page. Listen to what you're saying. This is ridiculous!>

<You think I'm crazy?>

<I think you're paranoid,> he said. <I think you *believe* you're making sense.>

<You're entitled to your opinion, I guess,> said De Bruyn.

He acknowledged this with a nod of the head. <And you yours, Page.>

<But only one of us can be right.>

<True,> he said. <And both of us could be wrong.>

She shook her head. Trezise enjoyed arguing for the sake of it; she shouldn't let him get her worked up so easily. <Do as I say. Look it up. You'll have to at least admit that it looks peculiar.>

<This whole thing is peculiar,> he said. <This entire *system* is. Did you know that the Heresiarch has advised all council vessels to avoid traveling in or near the ring after a probe found evidence of nanoware in the dust?>

<No, but—>

<And were you aware that rumors suggesting a cult worshipping the enemy arising among the more destabilized elements have been less ambiguously verified by no less than three council agents? And that—?>

<Enough, Trezise.> She felt weary just listening to him. <If you think you have more important work to do, then just go. I'm not exactly here on holiday either.>

<No, you're not. If you do find anything out—something of note—please let me know.>

<Sure. And when the rest of that data comes through—>

<I will pass it on to you,> he said, cutting her short. <I know how much it means to you.> He almost seemed to smile as he added: <But be careful of the ring, Page. I wouldn't lie about something as important as that.>

Then he was gone, leaving De Bruyn half-smiling to herself. Trezise annoyed her, but he played a good game. She'd rather have one single adversary like him than ten allies of Uyeno Lenz's ilk. Not that Trezise *was* an adversary, she hoped.

Following the *Ana Vereine*'s trace at a discreet distance, she drilled deeper into the nugget of data Trezise had given her. What she found did little to put her mind at ease, and what she *didn't* find only added to her frustration. If only, she thought, she could get at the data directly and not worry about elements of corruption along the way. Or better yet, get her hands on *Roche*, and extract the data in a way that would leave no doubt at all. . . .

PART TWO:

PERDUE

5

AVS-44
955.1.30
1100

Roche let Kajic pilot the scutter while she watched their new companion break dock. Defender-of-Harmony Vri flew a compact rapid fighter that looked like a cross between a throwing-star and a dagger. Roche didn't recognize it as a Surin military ship. Their designs were normally more hospitable. Only when the craft were attacked did they sprout numerous means of retaliation, suddenly taking on a more aggressive look.

Back on the *Phlegethon*, the warrior had spoken barely a dozen words to Roche before turning and moving off to where his ship was docked.

"Does he have a first name?" Roche had asked Nemeth, staring at the back of the receding warrior. On the back of his lightly furred skull was a triangle of darker hair, pointed upward like an arrowhead. Whether it was natural or dyed, Roche couldn't tell; and she wasn't about to ask him in a hurry, either. His wide-spaced, dark eyes had discouraged any personal questions.

"Not that I'm aware of," Nemeth had replied. "Or Vri might be it. Like your friend here, he doesn't seem to have a family name."

"Which would make him a renegade, right?"

<Soldiers who renounce their family line,> said Maii, <usually do so only to demonstrate that they are willing to die for the principle they embrace. In Vri's case, it is harmony.>

Roche caught an image from the girl of something that looked anything *but* harmonious. "So he's a fanatic?"

<No,> said Maii. <Just extremely dedicated.>

Roche couldn't argue with that. When introduced, Vri had nodded to Roche and Maii in turn and said: "I will defer to your instructions unless they conflict with the directives given to me by the Agora."

She could tell he would be a force to be reckoned with. Even from a distance he looked intimidating, with his sheer size—strange for his Caste—and the strange orange and yellow overlapping garments the Surin called ceremonial armor. It looked more like some sort of thick fungus.

"Is he any relation to Fighter-for-Peace Jancin Xumai?" she asked, thinking of the Surin who had threatened them earlier.

"Maybe," Nemeth said with a shrug. "We don't know exactly how many Surin there are in the system," he had said. "There could be numerous factions. You'd be more familiar than we are with how they operate."

The air-car had waited patiently for him while they talked. Vischilglin was watching silently and suspiciously on the sidelines. Roche had half expected Nemeth to say something more, but he obviously felt constrained by the woman's presence. He had bowed at Roche and Maii in turn, then climbed back into his seat.

"Perhaps we will meet again," he said.

"Perhaps." Roche didn't return his wave as the air-car sped off along the curving floor.

<He says to contact him when you're on the move,> said Maii.

<How?>

<Vri will tell you.>

"I must apologize for him," said Vischilglin. "If his behavior offended you—"

"No, it's all right." Roche suddenly felt sorry for the woman. If her hopes had been as high as Maii had said, then acting as Roche's guide must have been something of an honor. To see that hope dashed, then have that honor usurped by someone else, must have been disappointing.

Taking Vischilglin's hands in her own, Roche pressed them to her forehead, in the same way Vischilglin had done when they first met. "Thank you for your hospitality," she said. "I will do my best to prove that your faith in me was warranted."

Vischilglin looked in turn confused and embarrassed, then relieved. Then she smiled warmly. "Thank you, Morgan Roche. And you." She bowed to Maii. "My thoughts go with you."

She turned and walked away, leaving Roche and Maii to make their own way through the airlock doors and into the scutter. The same terse traffic controller as before guided them out of the dock in the same perfunctory manner, adding almost as an afterthought once they were clear: "Weryn guide you and keep you safe."

Vri's ship rapidly overtook the scutter, darting through space on jets of blue energy.

"How do you feel about him, Maii?"

<He means me no harm,> the girl said, her voice less strained than before. <But his definition of 'harm' is open to interpretation. If he feels that I am being mistreated by you, then he will try to take me back to my family.>

Roche shook her head. "But they *sold* you," she said. "Surely that's just an excuse to get a look inside your head."

<Possibly,> said Maii. <But *he* believes only what he's been told. He is very traditional and holds the Agora in high regard, as one would expect of anyone in the military. But how he came to be here, working with the Ulterior, I don't know. His thoughts do not reveal whether he thinks it an honor or a punishment.>

"Maybe it's neither," said Roche. "Maybe it's simply a chance to prove himself, an opportunity for advancement."

<Or an early death in defense of his principle.>

"That could hardly be regarded as harmonious."

<Perhaps not for us, Morgan,> said Maii. <But he is different.>

Roche couldn't argue with that. . . .

* * *

By the time the scutter docked with the *Ana Vereine*, Vri had placed the *Esperance* in formation nearby. Roche and Maii went straight to the bridge to debrief the others, and to open communications with the Surin warrior.

"I don't like it," said Haid. "He's potentially dangerous."

"His ship is no match for ours," she said. "Would you agree, Uri?"

"Without question. If he tried to attack, he would be disabled or destroyed with little effort."

"But if he catches us off guard—" Haid began.

"He won't." Kajic's voice was firm. "His every move is being monitored."

"But—"

"Enough," said Roche. "There's no point arguing about this. We can't do anything about it right now, so let's just accept that we're stuck with him and get on with it."

A signal came from the angular craft and Kajic put it through to the main screen.

"Commander Roche." Vri's elongated face was fuzzy with tightbeam static and hair. "I am instructed to accompany you on your journey and to lend assistance where I see fit. In order to do this, I will need notice of your destinations *and* intentions. I trust this will not be a contentious issue."

"Of course not," she said. "But as far as my 'destinations and intentions' go, I haven't thought that far ahead."

"Assistant Vice Primate Nemeth instructed me to advise you of the communication channels used by the Ulterior, and to ask you to call him immediately. A description of how to contact him accompanies this message."

Roche looked up at Kajic's hologram. "Got it," he said after a momentary pause.

"Thanks," she said, turning back to Vri. "We'll call him now."

The Surin warrior nodded slightly. "When you have decided what to do next, I may be contacted on this frequency."

He disconnected the line before Roche had a chance to say anything else. She shrugged and addressed the hologram once again. "Kajic, open a line to the Ulterior."

"Doing so now, Morgan," he said.

"I presume this will be a secure line?" she said.

"The content of the transmissions is encrypted, yes, but the transmissions themselves are not hidden. Signals in both directions travel in the same way the *Phlegethon* communicates with its ftl drones."

"As though we have nothing to hide, eh?" Roche could see the reasoning, but she didn't feel entirely comfortable with it. "I hope they're right . . ."

"Ah, Roche." Nemeth's voice and image simultaneously burst from the main screen. "Glad to see you received my message in good faith."

She was in no mood for pleasantries. "Are you sure this is the best way to talk to each other?"

"No method of communication would be a hundred percent safe from prying ears," he said. "But this is certainly the safest option at our disposal right now. Just as I cannot possibly hope to safeguard against every security breach, so too are they—"

"Okay, okay," said Roche. "Just tell me what it is you've got to say. I presume you're going to tell me what you want me to do."

"More or less," he said, smiling at her impatience. "Rather than wandering all over the system in the hope of stumbling across something useful, we feel you would be better served having your own area to investigate. A file will follow this conversation; it maps out that area for you. Obviously it will change as ships arrive and leave, but it's a starting point. I have listed all major known Castes and alliances, and marked key congregation points. Infiltrate them and see what you can find, then move on to the next site. Report back as you are able."

"Anything else?" she asked, not even attempting to disguise her irritability. She listened to Nemeth with a growing sense of unease. She was becoming a lackey again, a pawn in someone else's game—something she thought she'd left behind with Intelligence HQ.

"You know the score, Roche," he said, suddenly serious. "Our main objective is to deal with the enemy, but first we have to know how to *find* them. There has to be a way of determining who they are—a test of some kind that can apply to *all* of them, collectively rather than just as individuals. Your reave might be able to help with that: if the enemy does possess a unique n-body signature, that might be a way we can distinguish between them and us. Our reaves have had no success at seeing what you've reported, but that doesn't mean you might not have better luck."

Roche nodded. "And once we have found a means of doing this, what then? How do you propose we deal with them?"

His shrug was both heavy and helpless. "That's a completely different issue," he replied. "And one we will address at a later date. But the matter of where they come from might assist us in this, just as why they're here might help us work out where to find them. They *must* be communicating somehow, so if you can work that out too, that would be excellent." There was a slight pause as the signal broke up momentarily. "Oh, and see if you can find out why so much energy is being wasted talking about you, too. The *Lucence-2* gives us a direct link between one of the enemy and the propagation of your name; it would be foolish to ignore the possible ramifications of this link. Clearly your Box wouldn't have kept you alive for so long if it too didn't have some sort of plans for you."

The mention of the Box threw her for a second. "I thought you didn't think the Box was important."

"Me? I said nothing of the sort. Even the council isn't so stupid as to ignore what it knows to be true—although it denies it in public. We've had some dealings with High Humans in the past months and years, but not as many as we would like. Two in particular—Aquareii and the Catiph—were quite frank until they suddenly stopped communicating with us." He paused again, as if in thought. "It's common knowledge in some circles that High Humans limit or actively suppress AI technology—except when it suits them, of course. That the Crescend runs a factory in Commonwealth space where you obtained this mysterious Box only supports your theory that it is somehow important."

"*Was* important," she corrected.

He shrugged again. "Anyway, one can only wonder what it would have thought of your situation now."

Privately she agreed, and promised to deal with that question as soon as possible.

"Is there anything else you'd like of me?" she said.

He either missed the sarcasm or didn't care. "That will be enough for now, I think. We can call each other another time, should something dramatic occur or some important need arise; otherwise we'll just get on separately with our work. Agreed?"

Again, she had little choice. "Agreed."

"Good. Until then . . ." With a curt nod he was gone.

Roche turned to face Haid and Cane, watching from the sidelines.

"I'm liking this situation even less, now," said Haid.

"It's better than nothing," she said. "We need *some* sort of contact with the council. At least this way we have a chance of making headway."

"Covert organizations can operate more effectively than their parent bodies," said Cane. "They can respond to changes more rapidly, and can work in areas prohibited to officials. I believe that this is a good sign, Morgan. Working for the council, you would have been just one agent among many; your voice could have been lost. Now you have a greater chance of gaining the attention of the entire Ulterior, and in time the council itself. Now, I believe we will start to make progress."

She couldn't remember the last time he had shown such enthusiastic support for one of her decisions. Her satisfaction was tempered only by the part of her that wondered if he was telling the truth.

"Well, I hope you're right, Cane, and Ameidio is wrong. No offense." She smiled at the ex-mercenary, who shrugged affably back. "Maybe we should look at the file Nemeth gave us, to see where we're supposed to go."

Kajic displayed a map on the main screen. It showed the entirety of Sol System, as mapped by the *Phlegethon*'s network of ftl drones over the previous days, with particular attention to a region beyond the planetary ring, one hundred and fifty million kilometers out from Sol. There, a moderately large collection of ships and habitats had gathered, including—if Roche wasn't mistaken—no less than five outrigger spines. Someone must have piggybacked them into the system, since they didn't use hyperspace technology. But why they were here at all, Roche didn't know; the system itself didn't even have an asteroid belt. She wondered if Nemeth had given her this region because she had worked with outriggers before. Certainly, there didn't seem to be any other reason.

"What does the file say about the people here?" she asked.

"There's a wide mix," said Kajic. "Some extremely Exotic Castes and some Pristines, with numerous variations in between. Some Castes segregate except to negotiate; others mix freely. There are three mobile habitats around which most of the activity takes place; the largest of these is called Perdue. There has been word of fighting from its vicinity, and remote observations of weapon-use. This is to be our first destination."

"How long will it take us to get there?"

"Twenty hours," Kajic replied.

"And does the file tell us what we're supposed to do when we get there?"

"No," said Kajic. "Nor in the other destinations we've been given, either."

"So I guess we'll just have to wing it," said Roche. "And no doubt stir up trouble in the process."

"I bet that's what Nemeth is hoping for," said Haid. Shaking his head, he added: "Look, if you really think this is the right thing to do, Morgan, I'll go along with it—but . . ."

"I know." She stood. "Uri, advise Defender-of-Harmony Vri of our destination, and let him know the course you set. Get us on our way as soon as possible. And keep us camouflaged. The less attention we draw to ourselves, the better."

She looked at the faces of the people in her charge. Maii, out of the hazard suit, seemed older, thinner, and paler beneath her hair than when they had first met. Haid's dark black skin and biomesh looked out of place against the warm browns of the bridge, lending him an air of discomfort. Neither Kajic nor Cane had changed at all—the former's image artificially generated and never looking as tired as he felt, the latter seemingly untouchable. The one and only time she had seen Cane at a loss had been when he was thawing from the coma Linegar Rufo had used to keep him contained on Galine Four. And even then, she had sensed dangerous aura around him—like a bomb that could explode at any time.

"Okay," she said after a moment. "We need to be fresh when we arrive at Perdue Habitat. Unfortunately we no longer have the luxury of the Box to keep an eye on things, so we're going to have to take shifts keeping watch."

"I am alert," said Vri, his face appearing on the main screen in response to Kajic's hail. "I'd be more than willing to keep watch."

"I appreciate it," said Roche, "but I'd like one of my own crew awake too. And don't you volunteer either, Uri; you can only run for so long on stimulants. *I'll* take the first watch. If something comes up that Vri and I can't handle, I'll sound the alarm. But until then, I want everyone to get some rest. That goes for you too, Cane."

"If you insist, Morgan," said Cane.

Roche had expected some objection from him, but was thankful it didn't come. Whether or not his obedience was offered in response to her earlier suspicions or for completely innocent reasons, she didn't know. Nor did she care. She was simply grateful not to be getting into an argument right now. She was just too tired.

She watched as Cane stood with his easy, smooth grace, and strode from the room without another word. Haid was close behind, with Maii in step beside him. They stopped at the doorway and Haid turned to face her.

"You *will* call, right?" he said.

She smiled. "You know I can't handle this ship without you or Uri."

The ex-mercenary returned the smile and then, with Maii using his eyes for guidance, left the bridge.

"Now you, Uri," she said to the hologram standing in the center of the bridge.

"I won't deny that I am tired, Morgan," he said. "But I am concerned that you are, too."

"Don't worry about me," she said. "I'll be okay. *And* I'll be watching your systems to make sure you're doing as you're told."

"Very well. I will rest for four hours, the most I need at this time. When I wake, it'll be your turn."

She raised her hand in mock salute. "Sweet dreams."

His image flickered out, and she was left with Vri's face on the big screen. "We'll speak if something happens," she said. "Otherwise, stay alert."

"I will," said the warrior, and closed the link.

Even then, she wasn't alone.

<Box, put a forward view on the main screen, along with a navigation chart. And dim the lights.>

Almost instantaneously a chart was displayed before her, showing numerous ships in a wide variety of orbits, none with any likelihood of crossing their path. Several were traveling in directions similar to the *Ana Vereine*, but that didn't necessarily mean anything; there was so much traffic in the system the chances were high that at any given time there would be such a coincidence.

<Any sign of the ftl drones?> she asked.

Two green circles winked around objects in the display. Neither was following them.

<I'm assuming they work by sending information through hyperspace to and from the *Phlegethon.*>

<That would be a reasonable assumption,> the Box said.

<You've seen technology like this before?>

<No, Morgan, but I am aware that it exists. There are many ways to communicate.>

<Does the Crescend use technology like this?>

<No.>

The simple response held a wealth of meaning. *No*, because the Crescend had far surpassed such simple beginnings. *No*, the Box wouldn't tell her any more if she asked. She tried to imagine what sort of communications a being thousands of years old and comprised of many millions of mundane Human minds would use. Instantaneous? She wasn't prepared to rule anything out. . . .

<Does the Crescend know you're still alive?> she asked.

<Yes.>

<Have you communicated with him?>

<After a fashion. We do not exchange information in the way mundane Humans do. It is more complicated than that.>

<Could you communicate with him now if you needed to? Could you ask him something?>

<Yes.>

<So you have access to the High Human's communications systems?>

<Some. For the most part, I am restricted to the means of communication you have at your disposal—namely those of the *Ana Vereine.*>

She thought for a few seconds before responding. <Would you be offended if I chose not to believe you?>

<Not at all,> the AI replied evenly. <Although I would stress that I have no reason to lie.>

She could think of plenty of reasons why the Box might not want that information freely disseminated. <Would you ask the Crescend a question for me?>

<If you wished it.>

<Would he answer?>

<I am in no position to speak for him, Morgan.>

<But you wouldn't rule it out?>

<No. He might.>

She nodded. <What you're saying, then, is that we could have contact with the High Humans at any time we want—or one of them, at least.>

<Potentially, yes.>

The admission didn't make her smile. <In other words, you made me lie to the council.>

<You didn't lie, Morgan, because you didn't know the truth.>

<That's splitting hairs, Box, and you know it. Why don't you want the council to talk to the Crescend?>

<Because the Crescend has no desire to talk to them.>

<But *why*?>

<Because he doesn't believe that the council is relevant to the solution of this situation.>

<But they're the biggest force in the system. If *they* can't . . .> She stopped, feeling cold at the thought. If the council, with the united forces of the four hundred plus Pristine nations behind it, couldn't fight back—who could?

The answer came to her almost immediately.

<The High Humans,> she said. <The High Humans could wipe out the enemy any time they wanted, couldn't they?>

<It's not that simple, Morgan.>

<No? They have so much more experience, and their technology is better; there must be thousands, maybe *millions* of them—>

<It is not that simple, Morgan.> the Box stressed.

There was a harsher tone to the Box's voice, but that didn't stop her. <Why not?>

<You are extrapolating wildly. The High Humans are not super-Human. They too need to know *who* they are attacking. When the enemy as an individual looks like any other Pristine Human and as a group has become enmeshed in many Pristine governments, will any amount of higher thought or technology prevail?>

She wasn't satisfied with this answer. <So why can't they at least *talk* to the council?>

<Because the risks outweigh the benefits, Morgan. If the council has no contact with High Humans, the enemy will not know for certain that the High Humans are involved. Uncertainty may lead to indecision; indecision may lead to tactical error.>

<But how *are* the High Humans involved? As far as I know, you're the only evidence that they're showing the slightest interest, and even then, you're just a go-between.>

<Trust me, Morgan,> said the Box earnestly. <I am much more than that.>

<Then what are you? Why are you here, and who sent you? Is it just the Crescend, or are there more of them? And if they ever work out how to find the enemy, will we be able to rely on them to help?>

The Box hesitated, then said: <I cannot answer these questions, Morgan.>

<You're saying you don't trust me?>

<I am saying that you are Human,> said the Box. <Nothing more.>

<*You* are saying that, or the Crescend?>

There was another slight pause. <I am in communication with my maker, yes.>

<He's listening right now?>

<In a manner of speaking, yes.>

That stopped her. The High Human was eavesdropping on them; the being that had grafted the Box to her very cells and sent her headlong through the galaxy was actually paying attention to what she said! The thought was unnerving. Nevertheless, she had the ear of someone a million times more evolved than she was; she knew she should use the opportunity while she had it.

Only one question concerned her at that moment.

<Does he actually care, Box?>

<What do you mean, Morgan?>

<Does he care what happens to us lesser Humans?>

<I would not be here if he didn't,> said the Box.

They had come full circle: the Box was proof that at least one High Human was interested in what happened on mundane levels—was, perhaps, even concerned—but beyond that refused to say anything at all. He had access to technology undreamed of, but wouldn't allow them to use it. He could step in at any time and be of great help in the struggle to understand and repel the enemy, but he did not. He preferred lurking in the shadows. . . .

Roche saw no point in pursuing the matter for the moment. She had more immediate things to worry about. Things she could actually do something about—or at least feel like she was doing something.

Once again, as the *Ana Vereine* powered its way across the solar system, Roche suspected that they were being followed. Not overtly; two ships hung back a long way and changed their trajectory several times, presumably in an attempt to allay suspicion by diverting attention away from their true activities. But their signature always reappeared on the navigation chart, and there was no doubt in Roche's mind why: they were in pursuit of the *Ana Vereine.*

They could have been Ulterior drones or ships making sure she was doing the right thing; they could have been completely unrelated to her situation in the system—security probes or freebooter scouts, establishing the ship's status as either threat or opportunity. Regardless, Roche's first thought was to shake them, but the difficulty of doing so outweighed the benefits; evasive maneuvers were less effective at high velocities, and any change in course at all would mean recalculating their orbit around the sun. No large feat, but it would mean waking Kajic.

Her best chance of losing them would come when they reached a relative halt at Perdue Habitat. That was just under a day's travel. Until then she would simply have to try to ignore them, and take action only if either ship made a hostile move.

<If I fall asleep,> she said to the Box, <make sure you keep an eye on things, okay?>

<Of course,> the AI said. <And I will doctor the surveillance records to show that you were awake. Kajic will never know.>

<And Cane?>

<He is in another section of the ship, exercising.>

Roche frowned. <Have you ever seen him sleep?>

<He has infrequently and briefly entered states that are sleep-*like*, but that is all.> The Box's voice was soft in her mind, soothing. <I will ensure he does not intrude. If he were to find you asleep—>

<He'd suspect something is up. I know.> She commanded her first officer's chair to unfold, allowing her to recline more comfortably. Remembering everything Nemeth had said about the importance of finding the enemy, she asked one last question:

<You recognized Cane, and you knew Jelena Heidik's name. Would you be capable of recognizing another clone warrior if you came across one?>

<It is possible,> the Box said. <Either by name or face, if neither had changed. However, I suspect that given time and opportunity, both would change to reflect the environment the clone warrior is trying to infiltrate. Remember, Morgan, that both Heidik and Cane were recent awakeners; and remember also just how effectively Heidik disguised herself as an outrigger.>

Roche nodded. <There has to be another way, then.>

<You may be right,> said the Box without conviction.

<You don't sound too confident, Box,> she said.

<I'm not, Morgan.>

The blunt and frank response surprised Roche. She had grown accustomed to the AI's self-assurance, and despite feeling a certain trepidation at times, had come to take comfort in the idea that she could rely on the Box. To hear its uncertainty now was somewhat unsettling.

<Hey, who knows?> she said lightly, trying to reassure herself as much as the Box. <Maybe things won't be as bad as we imagine.>

<Maybe,> agreed the Box. <But I fear they will get much worse before they get better.>

6

IND *Ana Vereine*
955.1.31
0050

Whether the Box's prediction had been specific to their journey or not, it turned out to be correct. Three hours after falling dreamlessly asleep, Roche woke to the sound of alarms: a Kesh interceptor was moving in to attack. The alarms brought the rest of the crew to the bridge, where Roche, still shaking off sleep, coordinated their response.

"How the hell did they find out who we were?" she muttered to no one in particular.

The interceptor—not one of the two ships she'd had her eye on earlier—was determined. Its relentless assault ended only when Defender-of-Harmony Vri dispatched it with a sustained blast from his A-P cannon. Before they could even begin to work out what to do next, an entire Kesh squadron slow-jumped to their location and opened fire.

"I have no idea," said Haid, operating the weapons systems with Cane as fast as he could. "But they want us *real* bad."

Roche glanced up from where she and Kajic were plotting evasion tactics and escape routes. "It's only one squadron," she said encouragingly.

"One could be enough," said Haid. "And to jump like that, at a moment's notice—they must've been waiting for the word. This didn't happen on a whim, Morgan."

Roche returned to the task at hand without agreeing or disagreeing. The sound of incoming weapons-fire was distraction enough without trying to have a conversation at the same time.

<They want revenge,> said Maii, lifting the information from the minds of their attackers. <Their war with the Olmahoi is going badly, and they blame us for getting them into it.>

"I can see why they'd miss the *Sebettu* at a time like this," Haid said. "Which they probably blame us for too."

"Forget the small talk, Ameidio," said Roche. "Stay focused! Maii, how did they find us so *easily*?"

<They weren't looking for us,> the reave explained. <Since we left the *Phlegethon*, they have been looking for Vri's vessel. He wasn't camouflaged. They simply deduced that any ship like his with a companion vessel was likely to be the target they were seeking.>

Roche cursed Nemeth's insistence that they take an escort—and herself for allowing this chink in their armor. "How's Vri doing out there, anyway?"

"Exceptionally well, actually," admitted Haid. "There are only six ships left. If I were them, I would've called off the attack long ago."

"They won't do that," said Cane. "Theirs is a suicide mission: it's a matter of win or die."

Roche didn't need him to tell her that. The Kesh pilots were fighting for their lives in the truest sense of the expression. Failure was not an option.

"Well, I hope they've made their peace with Asha," said Haid. "Because the way Vri's going out there, they'll be meeting her pretty soon."

"Kajic," said Roche. "Tell Vri to dock when this is over. I want him in *close* from now on, under our camouflage. He's going to be one hell of an inconvenience if he keeps on giving us away like this."

"Yes, Morgan," said Kajic.

"And Maii," Roche went on, "can you determine *who's* been leaking information to them?"

<Their orders came from superior officers. Beyond that, they know nothing.>

Roche cursed again, although the news wasn't all bad. Someone had set them up, yes—but that someone had only known who they'd be traveling with, not *where* they were headed. This at least put to rest her fears of an ambush at Perdue.

Nevertheless, it was frustrating. Word about her was obviously continuing to spread. The only time she'd been left alone since arriving at the system was while under the protection of the council. She wondered if the superior camouflage technology of the Skehan Heterodox alone was sufficient to explain that brief lull.

Cane exploited weaknesses in the engineering of three of the Kesh fighters, to cripple rather than destroy them. The remaining three were taken out by Haid and Vri with less compassion, or less skill. Roche plotted a high-energy course away from the area, which Kajic set off upon the moment Vri's ship was safely enclosed within the *Ana Vereine*'s camouflage field. Disguised as an innocuous freighter, they accelerated rapidly toward the sun.

"Our route takes us through or near several densely occupied regions—regions we know next to nothing about," Kajic warned. "We're battered but by no means unable to fight. However, I am going to require some time to do repairs."

"I understand," said Roche. "Vri, do you know anything about where we're going?"

"No." The Surin's stolid mien was unchanged by the battle. Despite being docked to the *Ana Vereine*, he remained locked in his ship, ready for anything. "I suspect that no matter where we go we will enter regions in which the risk of conflict is high. Such is the nature of this environment."

"All we can do, then, is keep our guard up." The two ships that had followed them from the *Phlegethon* seemed to have wandered off, but that didn't reassure her. If someone was still watching the *Ana Vereine*, their new attempt at camouflage wouldn't fool them, and neither would the change of course. And chances were that the Kesh probably weren't the only people who had known about the Surin escort.

Despite that, when they ran afoul of a minefield an hour later, then triggered a security alert two hours after that, the occurrences seemed unconnected to their mission. They were random incidents exacerbated by the tension and uncertainty in the system. As they traveled closer to the sun, then past it, the density of ships, and therefore the possibility of conflict, increased. Their sheer velocity was considered by some a serious threat, especially with so much debris already filling the system. They spotted two hulks in close orbit to the sun—strange spindly things that looked as though they'd been tied in knots. Roche couldn't tell how they'd been scuttled; she couldn't even imagine how they'd looked before being damaged.

They passed beyond the innermost regions and reached the domain of the ring. Ships seemed to avoid the dust-filled area, choosing orbits that arced out of the ecliptic or never crossed its aegis. Apart from the ablative effect of the dust on shields and hulls, Roche could see no good reason to take such dramatic steps, yet she did the same. There may have been a reason of which she was not yet aware.

The ring itself didn't look like much by visible light. Viewed in artificial colors revealing frequencies in the infrared and ultraviolet, and shown in rapid motion so that all the observations Kajic had made since their arrival in the system roughly two days before lasted only a fleeting minute, strange patterns swirled through the dust like standing waves in a torus made of water. What this meant, if anything, Roche didn't know, but it did give her something to look at apart from the endless parade of other vessels. Compared to Palasian System, Sol had very little to offer in the way of natural spectacles.

Beyond the ring, their velocity decreased. The number of ships in the region surrounding them decreased also, until they reached a distance from the sun similar to that maintained by the *Phlegethon.* Roche recalled how crowded it had seemed when they arrived; now it felt like a vacuum.

As a result, she was forced to concede the possibility that their close pass by the sun might have shaken off any pursuit. Fifteen hours into their voyage, and feeling the effects of another long, stress-filled stint on the bridge, she decided it was safe enough to call another break. Kajic, not knowing that she'd had little sleep while the Box kept watch, insisted that she retire to her cabin—or at least get something to eat.

The latter she couldn't argue with. Leaving the ship in Kajic's capable hands, she went to the mess and ate as much of a standard meal as she could stomach. Then, anxious about what lay ahead, she went to her cabin.

The whirring of thousands of electric scalpels disturbed her rest. Tiny machines, ranging in size from a pinhead to her thumbnail, were drilling somewhere nearby. They burrowed. They buzzed. The noise was maddening.

It seemed to be coming from inside her mattress, or possibly from under the bed. She got up and turned on the light to look, but there was nothing there. Nevertheless, the sound continued—but behind her now. She turned. The room was empty. Still the noise persisted, growing louder—whining, sawing, grating.

Then something tickled her ear. She flicked it away in irritation: a black speck, like a bug. Another ran down the back of her neck. She flicked it away too, and felt more. She shook her head violently as a sense of unease rushed through her.

The noise became louder. It was coming from behind her head.

In the mirror, she saw dozens of minuscule machines crawling through her stubbled hair, the area blurred and hazy from the frenetic movements of their razor-sharp mandibles. She brushed them away in fright, but others quickly took their place. She couldn't get rid of all of them; there were just too many.

With a growing sense of horror, she turned her head to one side to see the hole in the back of her skull, where hair, skin, fat, and bone had been carefully cut away, allowing the tide of machines egress from where they lived *inside* her. . . .

She woke with a start to the buzzing of her alarm.

Sitting up, she ran a hand across her scalp and tried to gather her thoughts. Her first concern was for the ship. A quick check of her implants showed that she had been asleep for almost five hours—the longest she could recall sleeping for ages. Presumably nothing dramatic had happened, or else she would have been awakened, but she'd be surprised if nothing had happened at all.

"Box?" She swung her legs out of bed and thought about standing. She needed a shower and a change of clothes. All she could smell was the sweat the nightmare had left on her skin.

"Box?" she said again. "Why the hell aren't you talking to me?"

<Because I was destroyed in Palasian System,> it said into her mind. <Remember?>

<Damn!> She cursed her stupidity. It was just fortunate that she hadn't made the mistake of speaking out loud to the Box with the others present. <I totally forgot.>

<You have to be careful, Morgan.>

She ignored the reprimand and headed off for the showers. <Any dramas while I was out?> she asked.

<Nothing of any consequence,> the Box replied. <We will arrive at Perdue Habitat shortly. Population eleven thousand, plus or minus a few hundred passers-through. Our IEPC clearance has taken us this far, but Haid suspects we'll be challenged once we're in range of their cannon.>

<Cannon?> A wave of hot water hit her skin. <What sort of habitat is it?>

<Ex-military. It's seen some service in the past, by the look of it, although it's not what you'd call serviceable now.>

<Who runs Perdue?>

<That has yet to be determined,> the AI said. <Kajic has spoken to three different people so far, each claiming to be the representative of the local powers-that-be. They don't seem to be exchanging information. I suspect Perdue may be in conflict with one of its neighboring habitats. The transmissions we are receiving could be coming from more than one source in the command chain.>

Roche exhaled heavily, and breathed in steam. <I assume Nemeth gave us *some* information on who to contact. A name, at least?>

<He did give us a name, yes: Atul Ansourian, the self-styled *éminence grise* to the Administer of this habitat and, by default, of the region. The Ulterior had come to some sort of arrangement with him, I gather, in which he traded resources for assistance when or if it was required. He was the one who was to have provided access visas and such support as we would require to carry out our mission.>

<*Was* to have provided?> said Roche. <Why past tense?>

<Because he is dead,> said the Box. <He was murdered yesterday.>

<About the same time we left the *Phlegethon*,> she mused.

<It would seem so,> it said.

<Do you think it's a coincidence?>

<I couldn't say, Morgan.>

She savored the last few moments of the shower. <*Éminence grise*, you said.>

<Yes. His rank was only adviser, but he wielded the real power. From isolation, apparently; according to the files he was something of a recluse.>

<It's a shame the two of you never got the chance to meet,> she said, stepping from the cubicle. <You would have gotten along well.>

<Do I detect a hint of sarcasm, Morgan?>

Ignoring the remark, she began to dry herself. <So, let me guess,> she went on. <The murderer is still at large, identity unknown?>

<Far from it. She is in custody in Perdue Habitat and has already pleaded guilty to the crime.>

<Really?> said Roche. <Things aren't normally so cut and dried.>

<Indeed, Morgan,> said the Box. <There are several legal and ethical problems dogging the case. Although having said that, no one really expects her to escape the death penalty in the end.>

<What sort of ethical problems do you mean?>

<It appears that the girl is Ansourian's daughter.>

Roche wondered if any of this would prove relevant, but noted it anyway. <How do you know all this, Box?>

<I took the liberty of infiltrating the habitat's news services when we were first contacted. Once I had the correct frequencies, it wasn't difficult.>

Roche nodded thoughtfully as she finished toweling herself down. <Tell me about this Perdue Habitat, then,> she said, slipping into a simple, unadorned uniform. <Is it segregated or open?>

<The dominant Caste is called the Vax, but they allow free movement from the other two main habitats. Tocharia 13 is occupied solely by members of the Zissis Caste; Random Valence is an open space designed for trade. I would opt for the latter if I had the choice of destination, but there's no denying that Perdue Habitat has the influence over the region, and is therefore the main congregating point.>

<How long until we're ready to dock?>

<One hour. Cannon will come to bear, if Haid is right, in ten minutes.>

<Guess I'd better get moving, then.>

She took one last chance to be still, standing in the middle of the room and breathing deeply three times. Then, rubbing vaguely at the back of her head, she set off for the bridge.

"As I said, I don't *care* who you say you are," said the figure on the main screen. "You have *no* papers we recognize, *no* jurisdiction over us, and, as far as I can tell, no reason to even *be* here. Therefore, we have no reason to let you dock. So unless you change your orbit and move away, I will assume your intentions to be hostile and be forced to take appropriate action."

"And I've told *you*," Roche said. "We had private business with Atul Ansourian. He was supposed to meet us here!"

"I'm not stupid, Roche," said the official, his bald, yellowish scalp crinkling as he spoke. "Your ship is camouflaged, and you won't tell us what your business with Atul was. Yes, we've heard of you, but not through him. He never mentioned you at all."

"There has to be someone else there we can talk to, surely?" snapped Roche.

The man sighed tiredly. "I can pass your query through to the administer if I really have to, but I don't think it'll do you any good."

"I don't care what you think," Roche said. "Just get her on the line! I'd rather talk to her than waste my time with you."

The line closed without another word from the man. Roche vented her frustration by thumping the station in front of her.

"Maybe we should just try bribing him," said Haid.

"On an open line?" She shook her head. "That'd just give them another excuse to turn us away."

"And if they turn us away, anyway?"

She looked over at Haid and forced a smile. "*Then* we might give it a try," she said.

Five minutes later, the line opened again to reveal another yellow-skinned, bald male. Except that his face was rounder and his eyes more deeply set than the previous official, Roche would have had trouble distinguishing between them.

"I am Dockmaster Rench," he said, his voice smooth. "I apologize for the misunderstanding. Dock 14-B will be cleared for your approach—with the proviso that you drop your camouflage and declare your crew. Should you fail to comply with these conditions, access to this habitat *will* be denied."

"Agreed." Roche's response was immediate; she had little choice. She instructed Kajic to reveal the *Ana Vereine* and Vri's ship to the habitat; then she named each of her companions in turn. "Is that sufficient, Rench?"

The dockmaster studied something off-screen. "I don't recognize your configuration. Somewhere local?"

"Dato Bloc, a Commonwealth of Empires splinter government." She figured it didn't hurt to be open about some things.

He nodded. "Looking a bit rough around the edges for something clearly so new."

"We've seen some action," she admitted.

"Who hasn't?" He half smiled. "Prepare to dock, Roche. I'll have someone meet you down there."

Kajic followed navigation buoys into the crowded docks. Numerous ships of various types occupied most of the available gantries; some seemed to be undergoing repairs while others were idle, perhaps loading or unloading cargo and passengers. Most of them were support craft for the various military forces massing in the system. Roche recognized a COE Armada cruiser among them, although the name painted on its side—*Paraselene*—didn't ring a bell.

With a clang, the *Ana Vereine* docked with the massive structure. Shaped like a mutated sea anemone, the former military station had sprouted numerous access tubes and containers, crossing and recrossing, branching and rebranching away from a barely glimpsed central section. Its asymmetry reminded Roche of a coral, yet its angular edges and corners made her think of crystal deposits.

Outfitted with side arms and hazard suits, Roche and Maii stepped from their ship into the dock's grease-smelling antechamber. The entire area rang to the sound of metal striking metal, over the rumble of a thousand voices speaking at once. There was a striking contrast between the habitat and the vast empty spaces of the *Phlegethon.* It seemed to be full of crates, machines, and people of all shapes and sizes. None of it looked familiar to Roche, used to the homogeneity spread by the Eckandi Trade Axis.

From among the bustle, a woman stepped forward to greet them. Short and muscular, wearing a purple uniform with black trim and a close-fitting cap, she had the same yellowish tinge to her skin as the other two officials Roche had spoken to. She assumed that they were all members of the Caste the Box had mentioned to her earlier: the Vax.

"Hello," said the woman. Her voice was brisk but not unfriendly, and raised slightly to be heard above the clamor of the other voices around them. "I am Overseer Pacecca. Dockmaster Rench sent me to welcome you."

Roche introduced herself and Maii. Pacecca eyed the girl's blank visor for a second, then asked: "Your friend is blind?"

"Yes." That seemed the simplest answer. "Her suit's navigation systems are linked to mine; she won't get in the way."

"Very well." Pacecca looked around her, as though realizing for the first time just how busy it was. "Perhaps we should go elsewhere to discuss why you're here."

"I'd prefer to talk to the administer," said Roche.

"There isn't much chance of that, I'm afraid," said Pacecca. "She has taken the loss of Atul Ansourian very badly. You probably won't get to see her for a while, when things settle down."

The implication that the habitat failed to run without Atul Ansourian around backed up everything the Box had said. "Nevertheless, I'd like to try."

Pacecca looked at her evenly, patiently. "Very well. I shall see what I can do. My assistant—" The overseer looked around irritably. "Quare!" she barked.

A man stepped forward from the crowd, dressed in a uniform similar to Pacecca's, but green with gray trim. He looked like any number of faceless, middle-management lackeys Roche had seen over the years—slightly overweight, balding and stooped, yet with eyes that watched everything, keen to find an advantage.

"Yes, Overseer?" he said softly.

"This is Quare," Pacecca said to Roche. "He will take you somewhere quieter." She paused thoughtfully, as if considering her options.

"Perhaps Stateroom B?" the little man suggested.

She scowled at him. "Remember your station, Quare," she warned disdainfully. "However," she continued, turning her back to him, "Stateroom B *will* be fine."

"Yes, Overseer," said Quare, his head lowered.

Pacecca nodded, then faced Roche once more. "I'm sorry if we're not more hospitable," she said, distracted by something happening on the other side of the dock. "But what with the murder and the trouble with Guidon . . ." She shrugged helplessly. "Things have just been falling apart around here, I'm afraid. So, if you'll excuse me, I'll have to talk to you later."

Roche barely had time to nod before the woman was off. She didn't doubt that "later" meant "*much* later". . . .

<What was that she said they were having trouble with?> she asked the Box.

<Guidon,> said the Box. <A sibling-habitat that appears to have been recently destroyed. It seems that most of these people around you are refugees and survivors.>

Quare stepped forward. "This way, please."

Natural caution made Roche double-check: "Where did you say you were taking us?"

"Somewhere to wait," he said. "Away from all of this." He gestured at the chaos around them. His expression remained blandly pleasant, with a hint of indifference. "The overseer will report to the dockmaster, who will in turn report to his superior. Your request to speak to the administer will be forwarded to her in due course. I'm sure it won't take too long."

"How long, exactly?"

"No more than a couple of days, I'm sure," he said.

"A couple of *days*!"

He nodded. "Perhaps a little longer," he said. "If you'd care to follow me—"

"We don't have the time to sit around doing nothing while your precious administer decides whether or not to see us!" Roche was finding it difficult to keep her annoyance in check. "And even if we did, I'd do it on my own ship!"

"That is your decision, of course," he said. "We would not expect you to . . ." He stopped, suddenly turning his attention to Maii. "Why is your reave attempting to probe my mind?"

<Maii? What are you doing?>

<Trying to get in. He's blocking me.>

<How?>

<He has a very powerful, learned shield. I can't . . . quite . . . get through it—but I'm sure he can't keep it up forever!>

<Was Pacecca the same way?>

<Couldn't have been more different. She was as clear as glass.>

<Then he's hiding something.> Roche considered her options for a moment, then said: <Stop, for now, and we'll go with him. Try again later, but be more subtle if you can. I'd like to know why he can do it but Pacecca couldn't.>

Something in Quare's face relaxed. "Thank you," he said, to both of them. Then to Maii in particular: "Please do not try that again. It is considered by my people to be highly impolite." And to Roche: "Now, do you wish to return to your ship?"

"No, we'll come with you," she said. "For now, at least."

"Very well," said Quare, then turned and led them through the chaotic activity on the dock.

<Looks like we're wasting our time,> said Haid via her implants.

<Maybe.> Roche relayed what Maii had told her. <He might lead us somewhere.>

<And he might not. Maii can't even read him, Morgan. For all you know, he could be one of the enemy!>

<Now you're being overly suspicious,> Roche said, hoping Haid was wrong. <Why would the enemy clone someone who looks like him?>

<To fit in, of course,> he shot back. <I don't know. It's just frustrating to sit here and watch. Even if you do get past him, it doesn't sound like this administer is going to be much help.>

<But without her, we've no way of getting anything done.>

Quare took them through two large hangar doors, then along a corridor lined with a silvery metal. A hairpin bend brought them to another chamber, where it was at least quieter if still crowded. He waved them through some sort of security checkpoint, then took them deeper into the habitat.

<What exactly *do* you hope to get done?> Haid asked.

<Whatever Nemeth sent us here to do: spy, I guess. Look for the enemy. To do that, we need access to all areas and as much data as we can lay our hands on.> The Box would take charge of the latter, but she needed to put up a front for its behavior before she started producing conclusions based upon it. <With Ansourian gone, we don't really have anyone else to go to but this administer.>

<What about Ansourian's daughter?> said Haid. <She might know if he'd had anything planned for the Ulterior, should one of their agents come to town.>

<Yes, but I gather she's locked up somewhere. I doubt we'd get near her.>

Haid grunted his dissatisfaction with the situation. <One other thing I want to know is: what's the administer's name? The way they talk about her, she sounds like she's handling things pretty badly.>

<Her name is Inderdeep Jans,> said the Box to Roche. <It seems she inherited her position when her father, the previous administer of the habitat, died eight years ago.>

Roche couldn't pass that on without explaining where the information had come from. <Try hacking into the news channel,> she said. <Make yourself useful.>

Haid grunted again. <I'll see if I can find a map, for starters.>

<I have arranged the information so that it will be easy to access,> the Box whispered to Roche.

<Excellent.> To Haid she replied: <Let me know if you find anything unusual, Ameidio.>

She returned her attention to where they were going. The journey seemed to be taking a while, and had brought them to a relatively clean and quiet section of the habitat. White walls and ceiling and a gray floor made the area seem sterile, although the air smelled vaguely of Human sweat.

<I'm still not getting through,> said Maii. <But at least he's not sensing me probing at the moment.>

Roche remembered what Nemeth had said about using epsense to find a way past the enemy's natural camouflage—and Haid's half-serious suggestion that Quare might be a clone warrior. <Does his mind feel at all like Cane's?>

The girl sent a mental shrug. <There *is* something odd about him. I can use his senses, like I can with Cane when he lets me. But he doesn't *feel* like Cane. Then again, apart from Cane, I've never really studied another clone warrior, so who's to say they'll all be exactly like him?>

<What about the business of the black speck?>

<That was just the *irikeii*'s impression. He saw much deeper into things than I can. I can't see that speck in Cane at all.>

Roche mulled this over. <So although you don't think Quare is a clone warrior, you can't be certain, right?>

<That's right, Morgan.>

<Not very reassuring, Maii.>

<None of this is.>

Quare stopped at a door midway along the curving corridor they were following. He produced an old-fashioned key from his pocket and inserted it into a lock in the center of the door. It clicked open, and he gently pushed the door inward. It retreated a foot, then swung smoothly to one side, reminiscent of how some airlocks operated.

He took two steps inside, then gestured ahead of him. "Stateroom B," he said. "You will be comfortable here."

"Not if I have to wait two days, I won't be."

He didn't smile. "We shall see," he said, then urged them inside: "Please . . ."

Roche hesitated.

"I can stay with you if it will put your mind at ease," he said, seeing her apprehension.

"That's okay," said Roche. "Just leave us the key, and we should be fine."

"I'm afraid I can't do that," he said. "Besides which, it is ineffective from the inside anyway."

"In that case," said Roche, "after *you.*"

He shrugged easily and stepped all the way into Stateroom B, which consisted of three connected rooms. From the comfortably furnished antechamber, Roche could see a conference room, with what looked like a small kitchen or toilet facility beyond that. There was a stale smell about the place, as though the air vents hadn't been cleaned for a while.

<No one here but us,> said Maii. <That much I can tell.>

Deciding that they could deal with him if he tried anything, Roche stepped into the antechamber with Maii right behind her.

"Would you like refreshments while you wait?" Quare asked. "A drink, perhaps?"

"No, I'm fine." Maii also declined.

"Then perhaps you would like to rest your feet."

Roche glanced around at the soft-cushioned chairs in the room, the legs so slender and graceful they looked as though they couldn't take so much as the weight of Maii's undersized hazard suit.

She laughed. "No, I really don't think—"

Movement out the corner of Roche's eye startled her: the door was sliding shut.

"Security," said Quare, catching her alarm. "We could not guarantee your safety if just anyone could get in."

"Nor the habitat's if we were to get out, right?" said Roche cynically.

The little man smiled briefly, but it didn't touch his eyes. The door clicked shut. "Now, about that seat . . ."

"It's not necessary," said Roche stepping over to the door to check it.

"We have something more practical through here," Quare said, waving them farther into the suite. "Come with me, please."

<Morgan!> Maii's sudden interjection was loud in Roche's mind. <The ship has lost contact with our telemetry feeds!>

<What?> Roche slid her helmet closed and studied its instruments. Sure enough, it hadn't received a return signal from the ship for almost half a minute. But Maii wouldn't have seen that: she must have learned from someone else.

<Uri?> she called. <Ameidio?>

There was no answer.

<I'm telling them we're okay,> Maii said, <but they don't know what to do.>

Angry, Roche drew her side arm and followed Quare into the conference room, where she grabbed him roughly by the shoulder and spun him around.

"What the hell is going on?" she demanded. "Why have we been cut off from our ship?"

He stared at her helmeted visage, visibly startled. "I don't understand—"

She wasn't in the mood for denials. "Just open that damned door now," she said. "We're leaving." When he hesitated, she snapped, *"Now!"*

He drew himself up in her gauntleted grasp. "No."

She pushed the pistol into his cheek: *"Yes."*

He flinched but didn't relent.

<Haid wants to know if you need reinforcements,> said Maii.

<Tell him . . .> Roche thought for a second. <Tell him to be ready just in case.>

"You won't be harmed," Quare was saying. "I promise you. This *isn't* a trap."

"You've locked us in here!" Roche said, her voice rising with her anger. "You've severed our communications with my ship! What would *you* call it?"

"An opportunity," he said, wincing as the pistol dug deeper into his cheek. "An opportunity to talk."

"I've got nothing to talk to you about. Let us out of here."

"Look, you can see I'm unarmed. Can't you at least put your weapon down? Please?"

"How do I know there aren't troops waiting just outside?"

"You don't," he said. "But I assure you there aren't."

Roche snorted derisively. "What the hell do I care about your assurances?"

"Don't be stupid, Roche," the man snapped. "Think about it! The administer wouldn't waste her time on a stunt like that."

"But *you* might," said Roche.

"I might consider it, yes," he said. "If I was truly desperate. But I'm not. Not yet, anyway. So again I ask you, please *hear me out.* If you've been cut off from your ship, then that only proves that I've done the right thing by bringing you here."

This took Roche aback. "What? Why?"

"This is a secure area," he said. "Electronically speaking, no one can get in or out. Once the door is shut, we're sealed in."

"And why is *that* so important?"

He stared at her then with a look that could not possibly be misinterpreted: it was desperation.

"Because my real name is Atul Ansourian," he said. "I need your help. Without it, my daughter—and maybe everyone else on this habitat—will die."

7

Perdue Habitat
955.1.32
0150

Roche held on to the little man for a while longer, searching his eyes for some sign of a lie. When she failed to find it, she let him go, saying, feebly: “But you’re *dead*!”

“A necessary ruse, I’m afraid,” he apologized. “I needed to disappear in order to survive. If I hadn’t done that, the chances are I really would be dead right now.”

“But Pacecca—”

“Doesn’t know anything,” he said, cutting her short. “To her I’m just another faceless drone to boss around. And that’s what I want her to think. Her mind is weak. I couldn’t trust the likes of her with the truth; she’d be too easily read.”

Roche remembered how Maii had described the woman’s transparency. Quare—no, *Ansourian*, if he was to be believed—was making sense in this respect, at least.

“How do I know you’re telling me the truth?” she said.

“I’m not asking you to trust me,” he said. “All I ask is that you hear me out.”

“Why?” said Roche.

“Because I think we can help each other,” he said. “At most I’ve only got another day or so before the truth comes out. And once that happens, there is every chance that *both* my daughter and I will wind up dead.”

Roche was curious despite herself. “But if your daughter’s going to die for killing you, why not confess to the truth so she’ll be set free?”

“It’s not that simple.” Ansourian stepped over to the conference table and sat in one of the chairs. “Please,” he said, gesturing to the chairs opposite him.

Roche glanced at Maii. The girl was still, concentrating.

<Maii?>

<I’m still not getting anything from him,> she said. <But there’s definitely nobody waiting for us outside, Morgan. It seems that no one is too concerned about us being here.>

<Okay. Tell the others to sit tight. I want to find out what the hell is going on here.>

Roche took a seat at the wide wooden table opposite Ansourian. The roomy, low-backed chair creaked beneath her weight, but held. Maii positioned herself a couple of seats down.

“You’ve no doubt heard the official story,” said Ansourian.

"That your daughter killed you a couple of nights ago and then turned herself in?" said Roche. "Yes, we had heard something."

Ansourian nodded, his expression earnest. "It's an open and shut case," he said. "Security has a body and a killer, with no evidence to suggest anything out of the ordinary. But for the fact that my daughter will almost certainly be charged with patricide if I maintain the fiction of my death, I would be content to let the situation rest. But obviously I cannot do this. In the next day or so the deception will be exposed, and my daughter will be forced to reveal the truth."

Roche was still wondering what she had to do with this. "And then what?"

Ansourian shrugged. "There is no legal precedent for this situation," he said. "Understand that we follow reproductive customs that are regarded as unusual by many Castes. The Vax do not have two parents as most do; we have just the one, who creates a child by combining his or her own genetic code with another's, sometimes chosen at random. The child, always the opposite gender of the parent, is gestated artificially, then released to its parent—and that parent is the sole caregiver for that child. But just as we have only one parent, so do we have only the one child. Perhaps you can appreciate that the bond between father and daughter or mother and son is *very* strong."

"So the murder of one by the other," said Roche, "would be considered one of the worst crimes imaginable."

"The most heinous of crimes," he said. "Punishable by death. It doesn't matter if the child is murdered or the parent, the consequences are the same: *two* lives are ultimately lost—and along with them is lost a long line of descent."

Roche could understand what he was saying, but she still didn't see the relevance of it all to herself.

"You say security has a body," Roche broke in. "Did you clone yourself and kill the clone?"

The look of surprise and disgust was genuine. "No, of course not!" he said. Then, seeing Roche's confusion, Ansourian took a deep breath and continued slowly. "Please understand that this is very difficult for me. Under normal circumstances, I am very much a recluse; I am uncomfortable with face-to-face contact. Only one person is allowed into my chamber and knows my face—and that is my daughter, Alta. Until two days ago, she shared my apartment in a high-security wing of the habitat not far from where the administer herself lives."

"Alta lived with you?"

"Yes, and would have until I died, with her son—should she have chosen to bear one, of course. But she is not as antisocial as I. Although she respects the lifestyle I have chosen, she does not feel the same need to remain isolated from the rest of the community. She works—or worked, I should say—in the Logistics Department, supervising the distribution of resources that pass through here to those who need it the most. Perhaps she was reckless in believing that the situation was not as dangerous as indicators suggested—and it does seem that my opinion on that score has been vindicated. But the fact remains that had she not gone out and returned when she did she would have died with me, or I would have died alone."

Roche listened closely. Again, the subtleties of Vax relationships escaped her. Did they take lovers from outside the family line, or was incest the norm? The question was irrelevant, yet it nagged at her just the same.

"Two nights ago," he went on, "Alta returned home late. When she came in to say good night, she found me asleep and another person in the room with me. This person, she says, was in the process of giving me a dose of poison that would have killed me in seconds and left no trace whatsoever." Ansourian stopped for a moment before going on. "Alta is a proficient fighter, Roche. Perhaps too proficient. She killed the assailant with little effort, but she did so before we could determine *who* he worked for."

"But did you at least find out who *he* was?"

Ansourian shook his head. "He carried no papers," he said, "nor did he have any DNA files in the habitat records. And I was not in a position to call security to find out, either. Disregarding the fact that I had already explored all the avenues they have open to them, my would-be killer had not broken into my rooms by force; he simply walked through my extensive security system as though it hadn't even existed. Someone *must* have shown him how to do that, and only a handful of people have access to that information."

"They're all high-up in the security chain, no doubt," Roche put in.

Ansourian leaned forward on the table, nodding. "I couldn't risk reporting the incident for fear of alerting whoever was responsible that they had failed."

"So you had to find a way to make the problem disappear, in other words," said Roche, wanting him to get to her relevance in this scenario.

He nodded again. "Smuggling the body out of the habitat was not an option, either," he said. "The moment I stepped out of my room, my enemy would have known something had gone wrong and would make sure security was watching every dock. And I couldn't keep the body in my rooms for any length of time for similar reasons. There seemed to be no avoiding the fact that I had survived by mistake; no matter which way I turned, that mistake looked likely to be rectified soon.

"The only way I could hope to find out what happened was to doctor habitat records to indicate that the body was mine, and convince whoever was responsible that I was dead. Under the cover of an alias I could watch to see what happened next: who would be looking to take over my position; who would advocate a speedy trial to see the matter closed quickly—"

"Basically," said Roche, "who would benefit the most from your death once the dust had settled on the whole unpleasant affair."

"Exactly," said Ansourian. "The most difficult problem to get around was the fact that Alta had left genetic evidence all over the body. But there was no avoiding that. We figured in the end that it would be best if she turned herself in and thereby forestalled a thorough inquiry. Her story wouldn't stand up under a detailed forensic examination, and no doubt my enemy is puzzled as to why my assassination didn't go quite as planned—it must have startled him to see Alta accused of the crime, especially if the assassin was supposed to report in, and has not—but I hope his acceptance of the situation will continue a little longer. While Alta is imprisoned, the thought that he might soon discover that the body is actually that of his assassin, and not mine, concerns me greatly."

"But surely he would be aware of that already?" Roche found this aspect of the story difficult to swallow. "I mean, didn't habitat files reveal a mismatch between your genetic profile and that of the body?"

Ansourian shook his head. "I had my own records removed a long time ago. It seemed a sensible precaution to take, especially for someone in my position. As far as preferring anonymity goes, doesn't it seem reasonable that the person who wielded the true power in this habitat should not seek recognition of any kind? The temptation to use it for personal gain would always be there. And the fact that I could walk the length of every corridor in this habitat and not be recognized by anyone but my daughter actually pleased me. As long as I could continue making the right decisions for Inderdeep to follow, *that* was the main thing."

"What about the administer?" Roche asked. "Doesn't she even know what you look like?"

"I couldn't take the chance." He shrugged. "I know this may seem paranoid to you, Roche, but if I *hadn't* taken such precautions, I might have died a long time ago. Everything I have feared appears to have come to pass. And now, I must find out who tried to kill me, and save my daughter."

Roche nodded her understanding. "This is where I come in, right?"

"I can't do this alone," he said soberly. "I need your help."

"Why do you think I should help you?" she asked. "It's not my brief to become involved in domestic politics."

"But you are," he insisted. "You are one of the Ulterior's agents, and the Ulterior is dealing with a much larger enemy. Our goals may overlap."

"How?"

"A week ago, Guidon, one of Perdue's sibling-habitats, was destroyed."

"I heard about that on the way here," Roche half-lied. The Box had found the information en route, but hadn't told her until she arrived.

"No doubt," he said. "But what you wouldn't have heard is that Guidon Habitat was destroyed from within using security codes known only to a handful of people. Exactly *how* they were obtained remains a mystery, but I suspect that the enemy—*your* enemy—was involved. Perhaps he is my enemy too."

"Why?"

"Inderdeep tends toward a policy of indifference and nonintervention regarding the problems we left at home. It took a lot of convincing just to get her here. Ultimately, though, I wonder how much good we can do here, particularly now with Guidon destroyed—but I have always felt that it is important to at least try."

"So it was you who persuaded Inderdeep to come here?"

"Yes," he said. "And I've maintained a steady influence over her not to change her mind and return home. Maybe someone took offense at that, finally—this faceless man, pulling her strings so freely. Maybe that someone decided the war effort could do without me helping it along. But if that is the case, then this habitat has already been infiltrated, and we may all be close to the same fate that awaited those on Guidon."

"Let me get this straight," Roche said. "Someone in Guidon, working for the enemy, somehow managed to get the codes that led to its destruction, and now you believe this same person has turned up here on Perdue?"

"And is attempting to do the same thing again, yes," Ansourian said. "It would be easy to sneak on board right now. We're still collecting life-capsules from the wreckage of Guidon. In fact, we have inadvertently picked up a couple belonging to the enemy, but we disposed of them before they could open."

"You think someone in an ordinary capsule could have sneaked in unnoticed?"

"If they were carrying the right papers," said Ansourian, "there would be no cause to suspect anything. And once in, they could go about working their way up the chain of command. From there it would be a simple matter of working on Inderdeep to change her mind and go home. It would be an efficient way to get rid of the Vax."

"Efficient, yes, but that's not normally how they work," Roche said. "The more destruction and loss of life, the better for them—at least in my experience."

"Perhaps that is a generalization deserving examination," he countered. "The most destructive actions are the ones we see most clearly, and remember. There may be more subtle plots going on around us all the time."

<And remember Cane,> said Maii, privately.

"Perhaps," she said in response to both of them. "But I still don't know *how* you expect us to help. Your daughter's locked up somewhere. What do you want us to do? Break her out using brute force?"

"I'm not naive enough to think that would work—or that you would agree to such an action."

"What, then?"

"Your name precedes you, Morgan Roche. If my adversary hears that you have spoken to Inderdeep Jans, he may become anxious. If she can be reminded that the enemy may be whispering to her even now, she might take his advice less to heart. I may yet be able to come out of hiding in a way that will not place me or Alta in any more danger than we already are. I hope to use you, in other words, as a catalyst to change Inderdeep's mind."

Roche stared at him for a long time. He wanted to use her in much the same way the Ulterior and the Crescend both did: as a pawn in a personal power game. She wasn't sure she liked this role at all—but neither did she want to rule out the possibility that she could use it to her own advantage.

"You can get me to the administer?" she asked.

"I believe so, yes," he said. "I should be able to get you into her chambers without anyone knowing. You will have as much time alone with her as you need—as long as you can convince her to let you stay. You see, her chambers aren't monitored. Not even by me."

"And what's to stop her simply throwing us out?"

"She won't. She has heard of you, and I know her well enough to say that she will be curious."

"If that's so, then why would it take so long to get an *official* meeting with her?"

"Because the chances are she is unaware of your presence right now," said Ansourian. "Whoever is behind all of this is more than likely protecting her from you, making sure your request to meet her goes through official channels—which would ensure a delay of a couple of days, at least." Roche opened her mouth to object, but before she could speak, Ansourian jumped in with: "Believe me, Roche, this *is* the best option available to us at the moment."

Roche carefully considered what he was saying. "Okay, but once I've talked to her, then what?"

"That depends on how it turns out. If it goes as well as I hope it to go, there's a good chance I will reveal myself there and then in order to press home my case. If it goes badly, I will make other plans. I know of various flaws in security's prisoner-holding bays. I may still be able to set Alta free and find a way off the habitat."

Roche was under no illusions as to where she might fit into the latter part of such a plan. There was no way, though, that she intended to commit herself to anything but the most basic level of support for Ansourian—who was still, after all, a complete stranger whom she had little reason to trust.

<What do you think, Maii?>

<I think you should follow your instincts, Morgan,> the girl said. <I have little to go on, and would hate to mislead you.>

That was fair enough, Roche thought. She couldn't ask any member of her crew to give her advice when they didn't have enough information to decide; that was her job, after all.

Not that she thought of Maii as merely a crew member; she had become more than that in the previous weeks, especially after her capture and imprisonment by Linegar Rufo.

Roche had felt bad enough over that; she could only imagine what Ansourian had been feeling since his daughter's arrest.

"Okay," she said. "Let me talk to the administer and we'll see what happens. I can't guarantee you anything, but it's worth a try."

"Thank you." He smiled then. Surprisingly, it looked genuine. "Inderdeep will not be in her quarters for a couple of hours yet; I will endeavor to find out precisely how long. Also, Overseer Pacecca will be expecting Quare back at some point and I don't want to needlessly arouse suspicion."

Roche nodded. "Can you give me some way to communicate with you?"

"I think it's best if you remain completely isolated in here," he said. "Even from your own ship." Seeing concern on her face, he added: "It really *is* the only way to be certain that you won't be discovered before time."

He seemed sincere, and his reasoning was sound, if a little overcautious. And she did have Maii, after all.

<Would you be able to find him if he leaves us here too long?> Roche asked the girl.

<Yes,> Maii said. <Or I could find someone else nearby and make them let us out.>

Roche nodded. The reave's power to influence those around her, not just read them, hadn't been necessary so far in Sol System. She hoped it wouldn't be necessary at all. At the very worst, though, Maii could force the administer to give them what they wanted.

"Okay," she told Ansourian. "I'll give you two hours. If we don't hear from you by then, the deal is off."

He nodded. "Don't worry," he said. "I'll be back before then."

They all stood, and he left the room. The door leading out of the suite hissed open, then clicked shut. There was no handle and no keyhole on the inside.

"I've got a bad feeling about this," Roche muttered to herself.

Maii slid her helmet back and sniffed the air. <Haid says that the inner defenses are fairly poor, now that we're past the perimeter cannon emplacements. He says he could probably blast his way in and get us out of here in under ten minutes.>

<Tell him he's being optimistic. It would take him at least fifteen.>

<He wants to know if that's a bet.>

<No, it's not.>

<He says: Then don't blame me if we arrive too late to save you.>

Roche smiled. <He would say that. He's probably just jealous he's not here himself.>

Maii didn't disagree.

Time passed slowly. Roche hadn't realized how dependent she was on data from the *Ana Vereine*'s datapool to keep her occupied. The hazard suit's capabilities didn't include much in the way of sophisticated software. Even though the Box had access to vast amounts of data, she still didn't entirely trust the AI to give her what she wanted. There were too many ways it could exploit her ignorance.

<Do you believe what Ansourian is telling us?> she did ask it at one point.

<His story does match the data I have obtained through the news services—but that doesn't mean it is true. On the face of it, it is somewhat implausible. I do note, however, that Ansourian's security records have been skillfully tampered with, and that his relationship with his daughter has previously shown every sign of being exceedingly positive. If this is *not* Ansourian, then that leaves us with the original mystery: why did Alta Ansourian kill her father in such a brutal and apparently unprovoked way?>

<Not that it's any business of ours.>

<It is in the sense that it provides us with another reason to entertain this hypothesis a while longer.>

<Is that what all this is to you, Box: a hypothesis?>

<Naturally, Morgan. At present, all I *can* do is hypothesize.>

She gave up on that line of conversation. Talking to the Box for too long when it was bored could give anyone a headache. But she needed to do something, too, to stave off her own boredom. Sleep wasn't an option, and neither was eating; her stomach was too tense to make an easy meal of the concentrates stored in the hazard suit's compartments.

<Can you show me what's happening outside here?> she asked Maii.

<Sure,> said the girl. Her mind touched Roche's gently once, then again with more pressure. <Don't be alarmed, Morgan. I'm not going to take you over. I'm just going to give you a glimpse of how I see things.>

Roche forced herself to relax. After all, she had already done this a couple of times before—on Sciacca's World, before Maii had agreed not to go digging around in her mind. As on those occasions, when Maii touched a true sensory experience in someone else's head, that experience conveyed itself to Roche with the same vividness as if it had been her own. She could easily see how the girl survived on the senses of the people around her.

For a second, she seemed to see an echo of Maii, as she saw directly through her own eyes and *through her own eyes via Maii* simultaneously. But the effect was fleeting. Her own vision seemed to fold in on itself as Maii moved to another viewpoint.

They belonged to a woman who was performing repairs on an air filter somewhere along the corridor just outside the quarters they were in. Barely had Roche determined this when Maii skipped to another pair of eyes—these belonging to a courier on his way to deliver a package. A quick succession of viewpoints from various people followed as they moved ever deeper into the habitat, catching glimpses of people Roche didn't know doing things that didn't concern her. Maii never lingered for more than a few moments at a time; no sooner had they found an open mind than they were moving off in search of another. And none of the people seemed aware they had been touched by a reave, for Maii's mind was gentle and fleeting. But Roche knew that if provoked, the girl's butterfly touch could just as quickly become the sting of a wasp.

For a while, Roche forgot about Ansourian and their situation. As she and Maii danced across the minds of the habitat's populace, she became aware of another level situated beyond the sensory experiences she was receiving—or beneath it; it was difficult finding words to describe how she was feeling. Having never before gone along as the reave's willing passenger, she hadn't had the chance to appreciate the subtleties of what Maii did.

Each mind was separated by a moment of subtle dislocation, as old sights and sounds were replaced by new ones. In between, Roche felt Maii's mind searching, and for that split second she caught a glimpse of n-space—the theoretical realm in which the reave operated. It was like looking into the mind of a creature that used sound to echo-locate rather than sight to see. Maii was at the center of her universe, and the minds of everyone around her stood out like bumps on a flat plain—but in three dimensions. Some minds jutted out like peaks; others were no more than slight swellings on the surface. Roche understood intuitively that this impression bore no relation to the quality of the minds in the "real" world; they were no more or less intelligent, or epsense-adept, or Human for having odd-shape n-space contours. They were just different, in the same way that people's physical characteristics were different. Roche couldn't be sure from the brief glimpses, but every one seemed unique in its own way, like a signature or a fingerprint.

As they jumped from mind to mind, like someone circling an island on stepping stones, Roche became more and more intrigued by what she saw between the jumps. Eventually, she asked Maii to stop jumping entirely and show her the reave's world without any sensory input whatsoever.

It was wildly disorienting.

<I'm amazed you can see it at all,> Maii said. <In all the years Veden rode my mind, he never saw anything. And you've never shown any talent at epsense before.>

<Is this actually talent, though?> Roche wondered, not letting herself get her hopes up. Like most children in the COE, she had dreamed of epsense powers blossoming at puberty. The life of a trained reave was much better than average, orphan or not. To be in demand, to travel to different systems, to delve into minds for government or private business . . . Roche had dreamed but, also like most children, had never shown any promise.

<I guess not,> Maii admitted. <But I've never known anyone to be able to visualize n-space who wasn't able to access it too.>

<So I'm a freak?>

<A fluke, perhaps,> said Maii. <Sounds better.>

<Where's Ansourian?> Roche asked, curious to see a mind with a shield.

Maii guided her to the spot where the man's mind should have been. All Roche could see was a steep, circular lip, like the edge around a very deep crater. No matter how Maii tried, she couldn't get inside or even look over the wall.

<It's like a fortress,> Roche said. <This is fascinating, Maii. Keep going, please.>

Maii took her on a whirlwind tour of the habitat, showing her shielded and unshielded minds, minds with epsense powers and no epsense at all, minds that had been damaged by epsense attacks and minds that possessed strange outgrowths into n-space that the reave couldn't explain, except to say that she had seen their like before and that they didn't seem to serve any purpose. Roche tagged along for the ride, an eager student delighted to have discovered a new skill.

<Could this have anything to do with you?> she asked the Box, explaining briefly what she was experiencing.

<Impossible, Morgan. AIs, no matter how sophisticated, have never been able to master epsense to any degree.>

<Could the Crescend have knocked something out of whack when he was installing you?>

<Unlikely. I'm sure he knew what he was doing.>

<But—> Roche stopped, feeling a new pressure on her mind.

<Who are you talking to?> Maii asked.

Roche went cold. She hadn't thought that the link with the girl might expose the existence of the Box inside her.

She was unable to think of anything even remotely convincing. <No one,> she said lamely.

Roche felt a short, sharp probe penetrating deep inside her mind—then abruptly the girl was gone.

Roche rocked back into her chair, stunned by the girl's absence. The real world flooded her senses, dispelling the gray clarity of n-space.

<I'm sorry,> Maii said, reaching out and taking her hand, gripping it tightly through two layers of hazard suit glove. <I shouldn't have looked. But when I felt you talking to it . . .> A profound sense of remorse came with the words. <Oh, Morgan. I won't tell anyone—I promise!>

Roche didn't know what to do. Although the girl hadn't actually said it, there was no doubting that she now knew about the Box. That went against everything Roche and the Box had arranged; it could even jeopardize the Box's mission for the Crescend.

But it didn't *have* to be a problem. If Maii told no one, the secret stopped there—and unless Roche told the Box, it would never know either.

The simplest thing, she thought, might be to trust the girl.

<It's okay, Maii,> she said. <Keeping the Box a secret is only a precaution. As long as you don't tell anyone about it, it'll stay a secret until we're ready.>

The girl nodded. <But it's *inside* you!>

<Yes.> Roche couldn't put the girl's mind at ease on that score. <It's been inside me all along, Maii. I just didn't know. The valise was a backup, and a decoy.>

<You mean you dragged that thing from one end of the COE to the other for no reason?

Maii's thoughts were tinged with an annoyance Roche could relate to. But that was all history now; the present had given her a whole new set of problems to deal with.

<It doesn't matter anymore,> said Roche. There was a long stretch of silence which she ended with: <Are you okay about all of this, Maii?>

<Yes,> said Maii eventually. <Just . . . surprised, I guess.>

<I know,> said Roche. <But for now I don't want the others to know, okay? Even Ameidio.>

<I understand, Morgan,> said the girl. <And I am sorry for looking without—>

<There's no need to apologize,> Roche cut in quickly. Her attitude surprised even herself. A month ago when she had first met the girl, she would have been furious with what Maii had just done. But her time with the young Surin had tempered her hostility toward reaves—or at least toward this one.

<Shall we continue, Maii?> she said.

Maii hesitated for a second, then diffused once more into Roche's mind. This time they headed in a different direction, outward and away from their current location. As they traveled, the number of minds they passed slowly increased, then abruptly fell away to virtually nothing, until they were left facing just four anomalies in the n-space plain.

Three of them she wouldn't have recognized, but the fourth one she knew immediately. It was a sudden hole in n-space, as though someone had dropped a ball bearing made of neutronium onto a rubber sheet.

<That's Cane, isn't it?> she said.

Maii seemed momentarily taken aback. <How did you know that?>

<Just a hunch,> Roche said. <He looks so different from everyone else.>

<Different? How?>

Again Roche struggled for words. <He's not the way you describe him. I see him as empty and very deep—perhaps even bottomless.>

<Maybe you're seeing the hole the *irikeii* saw.>

<Or maybe I'm just imagining things.>

<Either way, it's strange.> Maii thought for a moment, then said: <From what you've said, I gather we don't see things the same way in n-space. You know how I saw Cane: like a complicated machine moving too quickly for me to grasp; to you, he's a hole. It's the same with Ansourian: to me he's a slippery rubber egg, while you see him more like a cup. This isn't unusual; all people view n-space differently. And we do see *some* things the same way. Those odd outgrowths, for instance; I knew exactly what you were talking about when you mentioned them. And n-space itself; I also view it as a gray, smooth plain. So I wonder why the extreme examples should be so different?>

<It's what comes from being a freak, I guess,> said Roche. <Sorry, 'fluke.'>

<The *irikeii* called you an enigma,> Maii said thoughtfully. <It was curious about you. Maybe that means something.>

Roche nodded to herself, thinking: *An enigma . . .* <Do you think I could learn to do this on my own?> she asked.

<I doubt it. Your talent is reactive only. You can't see n-space on your own; a reave will always have to show it to you secondhand. Just like when we converse by epsense; it's not so much you talking as me hearing.>

<But why would I be able to see it at all?> Roche wondered, thinking aloud. <It seems a pointless talent to have.>

<Perhaps.> Maii drifted away for a second as she concentrated on something else. <Unless . . . Morgan, maybe now's not the right time to let you talk to Haid and Kajic. I'm taking you back to the habitat instead to have a proper look around. There are a lot of minds here, and you're new at this, so you're going to find this hard. But I'm going to sweep across as many as possible as quickly as possible. We won't be looking at individual minds, but rather at the landscape they create when combined—a bit like ignoring the trees in order to admire the forest. Let yourself drift with the flow, and let me know if you see anything at all that stands out.>

Roche did as the girl said, guessing immediately what she was after. If Roche could see one clone warrior so clearly, why not another? Ansourian had seemed so certain that there was another one on board the habitat. . . .

They swept rapidly over the population of the habitat. Minds blurred and merged into a strange landscape that dipped and fell around Roche. As she became accustomed to it, she started to find a sort of coherence to what she saw: there were few sudden dips or highs, as though minds that were alike tended to congregate even without being aware of it, or else individual minds were influenced by those around them. Only a few stood out, and then only because they were so tall among the others. She didn't know what that meant; possibly nothing. It wasn't what she was looking for, anyway.

She didn't know how much time passed before she saw something. Time seemed meaningless. Likewise, she had no idea where her mind might have been in the real world. . . .

<Wait!> she suddenly shouted. <I see one!>

Maii brought them to an immediate halt. <Where?>

<There.> Roche, unable to move of her own will, could only describe what she was seeing as best she could. <See that group of minds over there? A lot like Ansourian's all in a bunch? There are three in a line to one side. Next to them—yes, that one. It looks just like Cane.>

And it did. The same abrupt drop in n-space to a depth she could neither see nor imagine.

<This one?>

<Yes. And . . . Wait, pull back a bit—no, more . . .> Maii's mind roamed across the gray vista. <That knot of people. In there.>

<Another one?>

<Yes.> Roche's stomach fell at the sudden realization: there were two clone warriors on the habitat!

Maii seemed to be having trouble deciding which mind to look at. <I can't pin them down as well as you can, Morgan. Wait a second.> They headed back to the location of the first one. <No, I still can't see it. Here?>

<Close. Across a bit—yes! There.>

<And it's the same as Cane?>

<Exactly the same.>

<I can't imagine what else that could mean,> said Maii, <except that this person is a clone warrior.>

Roche's concern slipped back a notch as another realization hit home: <This is it, Maii! We can *find* them!>

<Maybe,> Maii said, jumping back to the place where Roche had spotted the second clone warrior. It had moved, and Roche had to keep giving Maii directions so they could keep up. <I can't enter this mind, Morgan, so we can't tell who it belongs to that way. Can *you* tell where this person is, precisely?>

<I, uh . . .> Roche realized then that it wouldn't be so easy. N-space bore little relation to the real universe, except in the broadest terms. She could tell that the clone warrior was one of many in a group of people, and that that group of people was a subset of the larger group that comprised the population of the habitat. But beyond that . . .

<Hang on.> Maii let go of her for a moment. When she returned a second or so

later, she explained that she'd been exploring the scene more closely on her own. <Dragging you around can be a strain if I move too quickly.>

<Sorry, Maii. I didn't realize.>

<No. This is interesting—and maybe important.> The girl sounded alive in a way that Roche hadn't heard before; maybe the thrill of guiding someone around on her own turf for a change accounted for that. <It's hard to tell for sure,> she said, <but the first mind you pointed out seems to be in an audience of some kind. There are lots of important people nearby, most of them with shields like Ansourian's. I touched a couple of ancillary staff members who weren't as well protected. The audience *seems* to be the one the administer is holding but I can't be absolutely sure.>

<That would make sense,> Roche said. <That's where the clone warrior would want to be—as close as possible to the center of power. Can you determine which one of them is the clone warrior?>

<No.> There was both excitement and frustration in the reave's voice. <To be honest, I can't even tell myself which one it is. When you pointed it out, I could tell it looked different, but not so remarkably different that I couldn't lose him in a crowd.>

<But *I* could spot him,> Roche said, confident in this newfound sense. Cane's mind had been as different from the others as a crater was to a mountain.

<I don't doubt that, Morgan,> Maii said. <But the other ones you spotted *could* be unrelated. We need to get you face to face with another clone warrior, alone, so there won't be any doubt at all . . .> She sent a mental shrug. <Until then I guess we won't know for certain if it really will work on the rest.>

Roche accepted that. The hope she had felt a moment before was tempered by the thought that her gift might prove too unwieldy to rely upon. But it was a step in the right direction. If the difference was a real one, and she could detect it, there was always a chance that there were others like her who also had this ability. Out of all the high-power reaves on board the *Phlegethon* there had to be at least one who would replicate it.

The only trick would be proving it, and that meant coming into contact with another clone warrior.

As she and Maii lingered around the impenetrable mind in the administer's audience, Roche couldn't help but feel a little apprehensive about that.

8

Perdue Habitat
955.1.32
0330

Roche took the chance to speak to Haid and Kajic once she and Maii had tested her vague ability to its limits.

<Part of me still thinks you should tell the Ulterior to go to hell,> Haid said when she had finished bringing them completely up to date on the situation.

<Part of me agrees,> Roche replied. <But this is about more than the Ulterior. What's happening here could have a bearing on every habitat, every station, every ship throughout Sol System—throughout the *galaxy.* If we don't understand why and how it's happening here, we'll never be able to stop it elsewhere. Slowly, but surely. In that sense, I think Nemeth *has* done the right thing in sending us here.> She added: <Even if it does put us in the line of fire.>

<And I guess we're always going to be in the line of fire until this is over,> Haid said. <Or we leave the system.>

<Exactly.>

When she asked Kajic about the status of the ship, he was more relaxed. <Everything here is fine, Morgan. The repairs are complete, and we are completely restocked.>

<What's Vri up to?> Roche asked.

<Both he and Cane are keeping a very low profile,> said Haid. <Cane just watches the habitat. Vri just thinks. I suspect he's wishing he was with you, so he could keep an eye on Maii. I have to admit, though, he's a lot better at this waiting game than me. He stays in his ship at all times, always alert, always . . . poised, I guess.>

Roche pondered Haid's choice of word, and found it apt. He might exude calm and patience, but she knew Vri was wound like a spring. She wondered what it would take to make him snap.

<I'll see if I can convince Maii to send him some words of reassurance,> she said, knowing Maii would overhear. <I don't want him rushing in with guns blazing because he thinks I'm up to no good.>

<Good idea,> Haid said. <I imagine your radio silence isn't helping any.>

Roche dropped back into the real world while Maii conversed with the Surin warrior. They didn't talk long, and Maii's expression was sour when they were finished.

<He doesn't like my attitude,> she said. <He thinks I should be more responsible until I come of age.>

<How many years would that be?>

<Three. It's irrelevant, anyway. As far as I'm concerned, I became an adult the day my mother sold me for medical experiments.>

Roche didn't want to intrude upon that pain. She and Maii sat in silence for a long while, thinking private thoughts. It was odd for Roche after such mental intimacy to be alone again in her skull.

Or nearly so . . .

<Have you found a way to identify the enemy?> the Box asked.

<Not really,> she said. <I could probably pick them out face to face, with Maii's help, but that doesn't help us very much here.>

<It's something, though,> the Box reassured her, echoing her own thoughts.

<I guess so.> She was glad to be reminded that epsense gave her a way to converse with the others without the Box overhearing—especially at times like these, when she didn't feel like talking to the AI. She was afraid of letting slip that Maii knew about the Box's survival. The Box probably wouldn't approve, and she couldn't help but wonder whether it would take any steps to ensure the girl's silence.

Very little time had passed when Maii lifted her head and said: <Ansourian is on his way back.>

<Alone?>

<Yes.>

Roche stood and shut the helmet to her suit. Maii did likewise. A minute later, the door clicked and opened.

"I'm sorry I took so long," he said as he entered, his voice loud as it filled the quiet of the room. "Pacecca's kept me busy, and Inderdeep is running behind schedule."

"Are we going now?" Roche asked.

"Yes." He started to lead the way, then turned back. "I do understand your need for security," he said, "but it would attract a lot less attention and suspicion if your visors were open."

Roche did as he suggested. The risk of physical assault was small, and the hazard suits wouldn't be as effective as combat armor anyway. If they were recognized, so be it; as it was, she had made no attempt to hide her identity when they arrived at the station. Someone looking for her would have found her regardless of an alias, or a visor covering her face.

Maii did likewise, and when Ansourian caught his first glimpse of her face, he smiled amicably.

"It's nice to see you properly," he said. "You have a very strong mind."

<You too. Where did you learn to shield like that?>

"The Vax were taught the technique by a senior adept passing through from Guo." Seeing no sign of recognition, he explained: "The Guo Sodality is dedicated to epsense training and study in the Middle Reaches; its senior adepts are renowned throughout our region for their strength and subtlety. The technique they taught us has been handed down along certain family lines in order to secure their places in the hierarchy of our culture."

"We noticed a lot of shielded minds in one particular spot in the habitat," Roche said.

He nodded. "That would be the audience chamber," he said. "That is where they would gather at this time." He half smiled. "Sometimes I wonder if there are any actual thoughts going on behind those shields." He shrugged. "But that's politics for you."

Roche debated whether to tell him about the two clone warriors, but decided to wait until she was sure. "Shall we go?"

"Yes, of course," he said, leading them out the door and into the corridor.

It was refreshing to be able to move again, and Roche relished the sensation of walking, even though it was in the cumbersome hazard suit. There seemed to be fewer people around than there had been earlier. Maybe that was because the habitat was between shifts, or the conservative Vax still maintained a consensus "night." Either way, Roche was glad for the relative anonymity.

They came to a major branching-point, where numerous corridors met at a wide variety of angles. The artificial gravity maintained in the habitat decreased slightly to accommodate the sudden shifts in orientation. Ansourian took them around a curved wall, then down into an undulating tube barely tall enough to accommodate Roche and her suit. This way was completely deserted; they passed no one, nor any doors or windows. But for her reopened link with the *Ana Vereine*, Roche would have had no idea where she was.

<You're heading deeper into the structure,> said Kajic, throwing a 3-D map of the habitat into her left eye. They were a red dot inching through a twisted tube that led, as Kajic indicated, to the heart of the habitat. <There's a junction up ahead. If he's taking the direct route, he'll turn left. But it doesn't seem likely.>

Ansourian turned right, taking them along a corridor that curved smoothly upward, then abruptly dropped 90 degrees in only a few meters. Roche negotiated the incline with care, trying not to let the wildly shifting gravity throw her off balance. The corridors from that point became decidedly cramped, with odd protrusions and corners and, overall, a makeshift air, as though they had been assembled from spare parts over many decades with little or no forethought as to their final function.

"Why don't you use transit tubes?" Roche asked.

"There are only a handful for freight," Ansourian explained. "Otherwise we don't care for them. There was a terrible accident a few years ago, and the previous administer discouraged their use."

"Where exactly are you taking us now?"

"Into the maintenance infrastructure. Security is relatively lax there, and we'll most likely pass as workers. The area is rarely monitored firsthand; only a basic AI checks for movement."

"We'll register, won't we?"

"Yes, but my Quare persona has clearance."

<Box, can you make sure of that?> Roche asked privately.

<I can disable the security systems in your vicinity, if you like.>

<Yes, do it.> She thought for a second. <I don't suppose you could get us to the administer more easily, could you?>

<Very possibly,> the Box replied. <But I feel you will have a greater chance of talking to Inderdeep Jans with Ansourian's guidance.>

<Do you think she'll listen?>

<That depends on what you have to say, I imagine.>

Roche had thought about that. She didn't have much to offer the administer apart from a vague hint about the enemy among her number and reassurances that the council was doing everything in its power (and more besides, in the form of the Ulterior) to rectify the problem. She was really only there to ask questions of her own, and if the administer was feeling uncooperative, then it was unlikely those questions would be answered.

"Is there a proper way to address the administer?" she asked.

Ansourian glanced over his shoulder. "I have no suggestions on how to get her to do what you want, if that's what you're asking." He shrugged and returned his attention to the way ahead. "Inderdeep is unpredictable at best, and can be willfully destructive at worst. Her father left me to keep an eye on things when he died. He never expected me to have to run things the way I have been. But if Inderdeep was left to act as she wished, the habitat would fall apart within months."

"What will happen if you're not going to be there?"

Again, he shrugged. "Maybe things will go well when you talk to her and I'll be able to reveal myself," he said. "If not, there are a couple of options still available. Oren Quare may prove to be eminently suitable for an advisory post closer to the administer's office. I know enough to work my way back in; given time, I could regain lost ground. But time is something I do not have, I'm afraid."

Roche knew what he was referring to. "How long do you think Alta has?" she said.

"Not long," he replied. "The evidence alone would have been enough for a guilty verdict. Her confession will hasten the legal proceedings. Only the fact that I was so close to Inderdeep is keeping her alive right now. Who knows? Sentence may already have been passed. The matter was bound to come up in the current round of audiences, so Inderdeep may have already signed the execution order."

"She has power of life and death in the habitat?" Roche said, shocked that so much authority could reside in one person—especially one such as this Inderdeep Jans seemed to be.

"Indirectly she has *some* power," Ansourian explained. "She ratifies the decisions of the judicial system. Without their approval she can't impose the death penalty, but she can overturn one at will. I am hoping she will do this in Alta's case."

"Why should she do that?"

He faced Roche again. "Because you are going to ask her to," he said. "Tell her you came here because Alta and I called you. Tell her you're here to help, but you don't know how. Only Alta knows, now that I'm dead. The habitat may be riddled with the enemy for all anyone can tell, but with Alta's help you might be able to ferret them out."

"That's ridiculous," Roche scoffed. "She won't believe that."

"She might," he said. "Besides, it's not so far from the truth. Someone did try to kill me, after all."

Ignoring the obvious—that someone might've killed Ansourian simply because they disagreed with him—Roche said, "Is there anything else I'm supposed to be asking her? Anything else I should know?"

He thought for a long while as he continued to lead them through the habitat's maintenance labyrinth. "Just don't take her for an idiot," he eventually replied. "She's not stupid. She's just . . . wayward."

Roche absorbed the comment as they walked. Since Ansourian had worked with the administer so closely for so long, Roche had to assume that he would know her better than anyone else would. If he said she wasn't an idiot, then Roche had to accept that she wasn't—even though it was difficult to believe, given everything she had heard.

"How much farther?"

"We're practically there," he said, negotiating a narrow pass between two large ducts that intruded on the passage. "Just around this corner."

"Good, because I'm getting claustrophobic." That wasn't exactly true; she was just tired of squeezing through the tiny spaces. Her suit scraped the ducts even when she turned sideways to slip through.

<Could you get us out of here if we lost Ansourian?> she asked Kajic.

<Absolutely,> came the confident reply, echoed a split second later by the Box, privately. <Why, do you think that's likely?> Kajic went on.

<Anything is possible,> she said.

"Here," said Ansourian, taking them up a short corridor that ended in a cul de sac and bringing them to a halt. "I prepared this entrance in secret when Ehud Jans, the last administer, was still alive. It was intended as an escape route only, but it can work both ways, of course." He produced some silver tape from the pocket of his uniform, along with what looked like a small battery. "This will only work once," he said, affixing a length of tape to the wall at head-height and another down by his feet. The tape slowly changed in color from silver to red. "It may look like an ordinary section of wall, but it's not. It's barely solid at all: enough to fool a rapping knuckle, or even a gentle punch, but barely more than that. When I run a current through it, the alignment of its molecules will change, and it will dissolve completely. You'll be able to walk through without any trouble at all."

"And then?" said Roche uncertainly.

"Inderdeep will be on the other side," he said, meeting her gaze squarely. "I'll wait here and listen. The less she knows about me, the better—as her old friend Atul, or Oren Quare."

Roche nodded, and drew her side arm in readiness.

"That won't be necessary," he said.

"No?" She didn't put the pistol back into its holster. "You told me not to trust you before. Why should I start now?"

He smiled. "Just don't shoot *her*, whatever you do."

She smiled in return, but there was no humor to it. "I'm not stupid either, Ansourian."

He turned back to the wall.

<Can you sense her?> Roche asked Maii.

<There's someone there, yes> said the reave, <and it matches the echo I perceive in the minds of those who know her. Those I can read, at least. She's shielded too, though.>

<Naturally,> said Roche dryly. So much for her backup plan of forcing the administer to do what she wanted.

Ansourian reached up to affix the battery to the top strip of tape.

"Get ready," he said.

Roche tensed and watched expectantly. Little happened at first, then the red plastic seemed to soften and run. As though it was composed of grains of sand slipping through a person's fingers, the wall simply fell away. After barely ten seconds, all that was left was a spreading accumulation of dust on the floor, and a smell like ozone.

"Right," Ansourian whispered. "In you go. Good luck."

Roche nodded and, with Maii following, slipped through.

Roche's first impression of Inderdeep Jans was that she looked older than she'd expected. Her skin was paler than that of the other members of the Caste whom Roche had met, and she actually had hair: a long ponytail of perfect white that hung from the back of her skull and was bound in three places with bronze clasps. She wore a simple yellow robe adorned with a stylized sun—a motif echoed throughout the room.

She was seated on a wide couch, drinking deeply from a glass containing a pink liquid. She stopped drinking the moment Roche stepped from behind the wall hanging that hid the secret entrance, and turned coolly to face her.

"Who are you?" she demanded, seemingly unsurprised by the sudden intrusion. She put down her glass calmly but didn't rise from her seat. "How did you get in here?"

Roche kept her distance, not wanting to alarm the woman with any gesture that might be construed as hostile. "I apologize for the intrusion, Administer, but I—"

"What are you *doing* here?" Jans said with a hint of irritability when she saw Maii emerge from behind the wall hanging, also.

"We mean you no harm," said Roche. "I assure you."

The administer snorted. "Why should I believe you?"

Roche hefted her side arm. "We could have killed you already, if that was what we really intended."

A sly look passed across the woman's face. "Then what *do* you want?"

Before Roche could answer, the administer raised a hand and said: "Wait. I know you, don't I?" Roche opened her mouth to speak again, but again never got the chance. "Roche!" she said, clicking her fingers and nodding her head triumphantly. "I was told about you barely an hour ago. They showed me footage of your arrival and said you wanted to talk to me."

This surprised Roche, given what Ansourian had said about how her request for a meeting with the administer would probably be deliberately delayed.

"Yes, Administer," said Roche. "And I apologize for the manner we went about it, but—"

"This must be your blind companion." The woman stood now, and Roche realized with a shock that Jans was almost as tall as she was, hazard suit included. The administer took a step closer, scrutinizing with some fascination the bandages about Maii's eyes.

"This is Maii," Roche said. The girl nodded in greeting.

"I don't recognize her type." She looked at Roche. "Local, I assume?"

"The Surin are neighbors of the Commonwealth of Empires."

"Ah, yes, I've heard of them." The woman nodded with private satisfaction. Then, as if remembering something, she said: "You were meant to be in Stateroom B, waiting to be granted an audience."

"We were, but we were told it could take up to two days for us to see you . . ."

"Very likely," Jans said. "I am a busy person, you know." She glanced away for a second, her expression sad. "A dear friend will be consigned to the sun tomorrow. And *that* is more important to me than anything you or anyone else might have to say at this time."

The sorrow on the woman's face seemed completely genuine. Roche would have liked to reassure her on that score, but knew she couldn't do that just yet.

"I understand that, Administer," she said. "But please hear me out. My mission is of the gravest importance, and I need your assistance to complete it. In two days, it might be too late."

"Too late? For what?"

"For me to make a difference." Roche was loath for the moment to stoop to the story Ansourian had suggested. She had to at least see if something closer to the truth would work first. "I've been sent here by the Interim Emergency Pristine Council in response to claims that your habitat has been infiltrated by agents working for the enemy. With Atul Ansourian's help, I had hoped to investigate these rumors and, if they proved to have some foundation, determine precisely who among your staff could no longer be trusted."

"Atul knew you were coming?" Jans turned easily and returned to her seat.

"Yes, he did."

"And he was going to help you?" she said, leaning back and looking over at Roche with some suspicion.

"Yes."

"How?"

"I'm not sure exactly. All I know is that he was to be my contact here."

The administer's expression became one of distaste and annoyance. "But Atul is dead now," she said. "Killed by his own daughter."

Roche nodded. "We were told," she said. "I'm sorry. Perhaps . . ." Roche vacillated regarding how much to say. "Perhaps there is more to it than meets the eye."

"What are you saying?" Jans studied Roche. "Are you implying she might *not* have been responsible?"

"It is a possibility, Administer."

"But why would she lie?" The woman looked confused.

"She could be covering for the *real* assassin," suggested Roche.

The administer's confusion deepened. "The person you came here to warn me about?" she said. "Why would she do *that*?"

"I'm not sure," said Roche. "But if you would allow me to talk with her, perhaps we could find out just how much she knows."

"And what makes you think she would tell you anything?"

"Maii, here, is a reave," said Roche. "She could read her mind."

"Really?" Jans turned to face the girl. "Can she read mine?"

Maii shook her head.

The woman looked smug. "So why assume she could read Alta's? She was Atul's daughter through and through, and *his* shield was perfect. I should know. I once hired a reave to crack it, just to see if she could. She failed."

"Be that as it may, Administer, I do feel it is worth a try."

The woman shrugged, and with it Roche knew the possibility had been dismissed. "It doesn't really matter anyway," said Jans. "Alta is guilty of *something*. I signed her execution order barely an hour ago. Whether she is interrogated or not, she will be dead this time tomorrow."

Roche took a deep breath. That closed off that line of inquiry, for the time being. "Even so, that doesn't change what I have come here to tell you."

"No? Without Atul, what can you do?"

"I can still *try*."

"How?"

"With your help."

"*Mine*?"

Roche tried to contain her impatience. "Administer, I am not exaggerating when I try to impress upon you the urgency of my mission. The council needs the help of the Vax, and in return I will try to help you. Atul Ansourian freely offered us his assistance. It continues to be my hope that you will decide to offer us the same."

The administer looked bored. "Why should I care about your Pristine Council? The Vax can take care of themselves."

Roche recalled the number of ships in the habitat's docks, at least one of them—the COE's *Paraselene*—a Pristine vessel. "You already lend support to the IEPC's campaign. And I note, without meaning to offend, that you yourself are of different stock from the other Vax I have met. With such diversity—"

"Mind your words, Roche." Inderdeep Jans stood abruptly, taking one menacing step forward. Even with her side arm, Roche felt threatened and instinctively stepped back. "How *dare* you suggest that—"

"That's not what I meant, Administer," said Roche quickly. "I was merely trying to reinforce the fact that different Castes *can* work together for a common good—be they Vax, Pristine, or any other. If you—"

"If *you* hadn't come here, maybe Atul would still be alive."

The sudden shift in topic caught Roche off guard. "What? That's ridiculous! There is no evidence to suggest that—"

"Really? Atul calls for your help, and within days he is dead. The coincidence seems striking, does it not?"

"Then surely you must see that *your* life is at risk also?"

"Why should *that* be?"

"Because if your chain of command has been compromised by the enemy, then their ultimate aim will be to dispose of you too."

"I don't see why they'd want to do that," Jans said, gesturing dismissively with one hand. "I don't even want to be here. It was Atul who talked me into it, and see what it cost him! Besides—" She took another couple of steps forward, her relaxed expression belying her words, "the only person who has even remotely threatened me to date, Roche, is *you*."

"That's not true, Administer," said Roche defensively. "I pose no threat to you whatsoever!"

"No? You break into my private chambers and exhort me to assist you in your mission—a mission, I might add, that requires turning my staff upside down to search for a hypothetical spy—while muttering vague suggestions that if I don't, my life will be forfeit. That sounds like a threat to me, Roche."

"Everything I have said is true," Roche stated patiently, although she could feel her patience crumbling. "Your life *is* in danger, and inaction on your part only increases that danger. But I'm not the one threatening you. It is the enemy—our *common* enemy. It's this person, and many more besides, that we should be fighting—*not* each other."

"So you say," Jans remarked dubiously.

"Because it is true," insisted Roche.

"Then show me the proof."

"It's all around you! The death, the destruction, the distrust, the disorganization . . ." She struggled to remember the name she'd heard just hours before. "And what about Guidon?"

"The cause of that accident has yet to be verified." The administer looked uncomfortable, but was unwilling to take the point. "None of this is proof. Your words are empty, Roche. Why should I believe you over one of my own advisers?"

"Because one of your advisers may well belong to the enemy!"

The administer smiled wryly. "As might *you*," she said. "Your reputation precedes you, Roche. It is said that wherever you go, trouble follows. If I were to give you the help you request, how could I be sure that the Vax won't become your next victims?"

"Nothing could be further from the truth!"

"So you say." The administer held a palm outstretched, silencing Roche, who had opened her mouth to object again. "I have no desire to put my people at risk on such flimsy evidence! A few disputes and the threat of war, an accident, and a failed assassination attempt closer to home—it will take more than *this* to convince me, Roche. And if you *cannot* convince me, you might as well leave."

The administer's words sent a chill down Roche's spine. She knew, then, that there was no chance of convincing the woman to change her mind—not on that score, and especially not on the matter of Alta Ansourian.

"Very well, then," Roche said, backing away toward the secret exit. "We'll trouble you no further, Administer."

The woman watched them leave, a wary expression on her face. "Wait," she said, just as Roche pulled the sun-motif wall hanging aside. "Who told you about this entrance?"

Roche thought fast. She really had only two options, given that she didn't want the administer to know the truth. She could refuse to answer, or she could lie. How to do the latter convincingly was the trick.

<Box?>

<Tell her it was Gurion Egarr, one of her senior councilors. She will want to believe that. The news reports them as being old antagonists.>

"It was Councilor Egarr," said Roche a second later. "And I tell you that now only to demonstrate my openness and honesty with you. His intentions were good, I assure you."

The administer's broad smile was cut with cynicism. "I bet." Then she nodded. "Go now," she said. "I shall allow you five minutes grace before I send my guards after you. And I do this now to demonstrate *my* magnanimity."

Her smile dissolved as she glared at Roche.

Whether she was serious or not, Roche could not tell. But she couldn't afford to take the chance. With Maii ahead of her, she slipped behind the wall-hanging and back into the cramped confines of the maintenance infrastructure.

9

Perdue Habitat
955.1.32
0600

Ansourian led them quickly through the tunnels, taking them by a different route from the one they had followed on the way in. Maii was directly behind him with Roche close on her tail, glancing back uneasily now and then to see whether they were being pursued.

<Please stop doing that, Morgan,> said Maii. <It's hard for me to see where I'm going when you keep looking over your shoulder.>

<I'm sorry, Maii,> Roche said. <It's just . . .>

<Trust me, there's no one following us,> said the girl. <The administer seems to be keeping to her word so far.>

Ansourian stopped suddenly, ushering both Maii and Roche through a hatchway; he closed the heavy bulkhead behind them.

"That'll stop them," he said, belligerently punching some commands into a keypad. "I've let the air out of the tunnels we just came through."

"I don't think it'll stop them," said Roche. "At best it will only slow them down."

The small man shrugged but said nothing. Roche could see the hurt in his eyes.

"You heard what she said, didn't you?" she asked.

He didn't need to reply; his expression spoke volumes. *Failed assassination attempt*, the administer had said. Roche could believe that she had guessed it was an assassination rather than simple patricide—but how could she have known it had failed if she hadn't been a party to the attack in the first place? At the very least, she had known about it.

"I'm sorry," Roche said.

"Don't be," he said. "It has made my decision easier. Escape seems the surest course, now."

"What about Alta?"

"As I said earlier, there are blind spots in the security system. I will try to get her away first."

"More secret doors you put in place?"

"No, just exploitable flaws," he said. "Even the best security system has its weaknesses—I simply have the advantage of *knowing* what those weaknesses are. I am confident that I can get into the holding cells. Getting out will be more difficult, but not impossible."

Roche followed him along the corridors while conducting a conversation via her implants with her crew back on the *Ana Vereine.* <Ameidio, Uri—have you been following this?>

<Of course,> said Haid. <Are you thinking of helping him?>

<We'll need him if we're to have any chance of fixing the situation here. The administer is going to be worse than no use to us, since the enemy has obviously gotten to her and turned her against him; they're aware that he runs the shop, and that they couldn't influence him. With him out of the way, or with his daughter as leverage, they figure they have control.>

<But why should they need leverage if they think he's dead?>

<They're not stupid; they might at least suspect that he switched bodies, especially when their assassin hasn't turned up since. And when the administer tells them about our little visit, that'll probably just confirm their suspicions.>

<How can we help him, though?>

<The old fashioned way, I guess,> she said.

<A show of strength?> asked Haid.

<We haven't got time for subtlety here, Ameidio,> Roche replied. <You and Cane—or Vri, even—can act as a distraction while we make a move on the holding cells. Do you think you could organize something big enough and fast enough to attract everyone's attention?>

<Undoubtedly.>

<Feel like some action?>

Haid laughed. <I can't deny that I could use the change,> he said. <And I'm sure Vri would be up for it. One mention of you putting Maii on the firing line and he'd move for certain.>

<Okay. You and Vri it is. We'll leave Cane to mind the ship with Uri. Are they both listening?>

<We're here, Morgan,> said Kajic.

<Do either of you have any reservations about this?>

<It's your decision,> said Kajic. <I am confident we can pull something like this off successfully. But there are no guarantees.>

<There never are,> said Roche.

<I agree with Uri,> said Cane. <However, I feel that I might be more use to you alongside Vri in the diversionary attack.>

Roche paused before replying. <I appreciate what you're saying, but—>

<But you need to have someone there that you can trust,> he said with no hint of indignation. <I understand this, Morgan. I felt I should voice my feelings just the same.>

Roche smiled to herself. <Thanks,> she said. <Okay, I'll talk with Ansourian and see what he thinks. Then we move—as soon as possible. The longer we take, the more chance we give the enemy to be ready.>

<And we don't want to do that,> said Haid. <They have enough advantages as it is. . . .>

Ansourian looked surprised when she offered to help.

"Why?" was the first question he asked.

"Because if I just let you rescue Alta and leave, it's tantamount to handing the enemy this station along with everyone in it. The same if I let you try and you fail.

You'll be dead, and that doesn't serve anyone. If we're to stand any chance of fixing this, we're going to need you alive."

"What difference does it make to you, either way?"

That wasn't so easy to answer. "It makes a difference to how I feel about myself," she said. "It's a matter of pride. This mission is a test, if you like; maybe metaphorically rather than literally, but a test all the same." She shrugged. "I don't want to fail."

He nodded slowly. They had stopped to rest in an unlit stores cubicle; the only light came from the necks of Roche's and Maii's hazard suits, lending their heads a surreal, disembodied look.

"So your crew will create a diversion while we get Alta," he said. "Then what?"

"Then you help us get back to the *Ana Vereine*," she said. "You know your way around this place; I'm going to need a less obvious way to get off the habitat than the main docks. The ship will have to cast off once things heat up, but it can send a scutter to get us when we're ready. Just name the place and we'll head for it."

"Okay," he said. "There *is* a way, but it will be tricky. And I'm going to need pressure suits for myself and Alta. There are—"

<Morgan.> Kajic's voice broke in sharply; Roche raised her hand to silence Ansourian. <There's been a development.>

<I'm listening.>

<I've been monitoring traffic to and from the docks. Exactly twenty minutes ago, every commercial and military vessel from the Random Valence habitat disengaged and retreated to a safe distance. Now a contingent of ships has arrived from the same habitat and is demanding to dock.>

<How many ships?>

<Fifteen, all armed.>

<A takeover force?>

<It seems likely, striking while the chain of command here is uncertain.>

Roche relayed the information to Ansourian, who simply nodded. "It doesn't surprise me. Frane Yugen has been itching to move on Inderdeep since she rejected his offer to form a partnership against Tocharia 13. With me out of the way, it's a perfect opportunity."

"Can she hold him off?" Roche asked.

"That depends. I've kept the defenses well-stocked over the years, and made sure the staff know what to do. If she doesn't interfere, they'll manage well enough."

That sounded ominous. "Can you guess how she'll respond?"

"Again, it depends on what the enemy are telling her. If they want to increase conflict, they might feed her inappropriate advice."

"Then we can't assume things will go well," said Roche. She switched to her implants. <Uri, where are Haid and Vri?>

<In the habitat,> he said. <Preparing for the distraction.>

<It doesn't look like we'll need them, after all,> she said. <Recall them and disengage. I don't want you caught in the crossfire.>

<Understood.>

"How far is it to where they're keeping Alta?" she asked Ansourian.

"Fifteen minutes or so, going the back ways."

"Then let's get moving before things start heating up."

"Not without the pressure suits," he reminded her.

Roche nodded and indicated that he should lead the way. They left the cubicle and headed off through the labyrinth.

<He's worried,> said Maii.

<You can tell that? Good. That means his shield must be slipping. Can you pick up anything else?>

<No, nothing. Whoever those people from the Guo Sodality are, they taught the Vax a good technique.>

<What about the administer? Did you get anything at all from her?>

<A few stray thoughts; most likely just planted to fool a casual glance. The core of her mind is impenetrable, like Ansourian's.>

<You said you thought you might be able to break into his, given time.>

<I'm sure of it,> said Maii. <But this is hardly the time to try. At the very best, I would distract him; at the worst, I might seriously injure him. The Guo shields are deep-rooted; cracking them would probably have consequences for the mind beneath.>

<Maybe I should set you loose on the administer anyway. It's not as if we have much to lose.>

<That wouldn't be ethical, Morgan.>

<Maybe not, but it is an option.>

A siren sounded in the distance, echoing along the winding corridors like the baying of an enormous beast.

"What's that?" Roche asked Ansourian.

"Security alert, level 5. Ambient gravity will drop by twenty percent to conserve power."

Even as he said it, a wave of dizziness rushed over Roche, leaving her feeling somewhat lighter after it had passed.

"Does that mean the habitat is under attack?"

"No, not yet. You'll know if that happens. Perdue is designed to absorb the energy of an impact and spread it across its structure."

"Meaning we'll feel it regardless of where we are?"

"Yes, but it shouldn't be too bad. Habitats like these tend to absorb almost anything up to a point, and fall apart completely only if you cross that point. That's what happened to Guidon; it was pushed too far. Since a ruined habitat will be of no use to Yugen, he'll play it fairly safe."

"And if he *does* want a ruined habitat?"

Ansourian looked sharply at her. "You think the enemy might have got to him, too?"

"It's a possibility we can't ignore."

They stopped at a locker, from which Ansourian produced two transparent pressure suits. "We call them OSFA suits," he explained, slipping one over his uniform. "One Size Fits All. They're designed to maximize survival through a wide range of conditions—heat, cold, vacuum, pressure, etcetera; they'll even stop a measure of coherent light—but they won't last long in combat."

"Do you have access to weapons?"

"They'll be in the armory. We won't get in there at a time like this."

Roche touched the pistol at her side. An identical weapon rested on Maii's hip; unlike most reaves, the girl had proven herself more than capable of killing on Sciacca's World. By looking through her victim's eyes and aiming along the barrel from the other end, she made quite an effective fighter.

"We'll have to make do, then," Roche said, hoping the distraction would be enough.

Ansourian finished sealing the suit, leaving only the hood open, then continued to lead them along.

<Are Vri and Haid back on board yet?> Roche asked Kajic.

<Vri is unwilling to leave until Maii has returned,> Kajic replied.

<But it's unlikely we'll be able to exit that way.>

<He's aware of that.>

<Then what does he think he's going to do?>

<Find you and take her himself.>

<Damned fool!> Roche snapped irritably.

<As Maii pointed out, he's quite dedicated.>

A deep vibration rippled through the tube surrounding them. Ansourian placed a hand against one wall.

"It has begun," he said. "That one hit the shields. Maybe nothing more than a warning volley. If there are more, then we can assume Inderdeep isn't going to give in without a fight."

<Dockmaster Rench has ordered all docks sealed,> said Kajic. <Haid and Vri are still not aboard.>

<Okay,> she said. <Disengage. Tell them to sit tight. We'll just have to work something else out.>

They headed off along the corridor. The floor still moved slightly as the energy of the attack ran through the entire habitat and dissipated, ultimately, as radiant heat. In theory, Roche could see how such a passive defense might pay off; she could also see, however, how disastrous it might be. One sustained attack could ruin everything, decisively.

<Disengaging now,> said Kajic. <Cane will fly the scutter when the time comes to pick you up.>

<Fine.> She didn't have much choice, really. With Vri and Haid stuck on the habitat with them, and Kajic potentially dodging fire, there *was* no one else. Even with Ansourian's help, the chances of finding a ship and breaking the dockmaster's embargo had to be almost zero.

She explained what had happened to Ansourian. "We'll need a rendezvous point. Can you give us one away from the docks?"

"Yes, but it's too complicated to explain how your friends should get there. They can access a map using Quare's security code." He rattled off a string of letters and numbers, which Roche memorized. "They want to reach the maintenance airlock at the end of corridor 14 in Sector Green-D. It's not far from the holding cells in Sector Blue-J. Tell them to wait for us there. We shouldn't be more than an hour."

Roche relayed the information through Maii, using the girl as a medium the way she had earlier.

<You be careful,> Haid said, via Maii.

<You too.> She could clearly taste the worry in his mind, and the tangle of plans and counterplans as he mentally prepared for any contingency. <I'll call if we need help. What equipment do you have?>

Using mental shorthand, he sent her a list that included shaped charges, compact percussion rifles, pressure mines, and flash-bombs—anything that would fit into the relatively low-key armor the two men had donned in order to enter the habitat. Dock security hadn't been especially tight, not since they'd been given approval to disembark, but cannon and full combat suits would have attracted attention.

<I wish we had some of that,> Roche said, <but there's no helping it, I guess. Make sure you're at the rendezvous when we get there.>

Haid mentally nodded and went back to studying the map Vri had accessed via a wall terminal. That left Roche with half a mind on where Ansourian was leading them, and the other half in n-space. Again she experienced a moment's disorientation as she simultaneously saw through her own eyes and those of Maii, who was also looking through her eyes.

<Could the Box help us?> Maii asked.

<It could probably open the docking bay doors, but that would be too obvious. All it's good for at the moment is gathering information and keeping automatic security off our tails.>

<It seems to be doing a good enough job at that, anyway.>

Another vibration rippled through the corridor, followed quickly by another. The wailing alarm changed pitch, becoming more shrill and urgent. <It's a shame it can't do anything about the Random Valence ships. . . .>

"*That* was no warning shot," said Ansourian, steadying himself against a wall.

Roche forced herself to keep walking even as the floor moved beneath her feet. <Box, are they firing back?>

<All A-P cannon emplacements have been ordered to retaliate. Nine free vessels have sided with Perdue and are joining the fight. However, more vessels are on their way from Random Valence.>

<Who has the advantage?>

<Perdue should hold. Its structure is more than capable of bearing the brunt of such an attack, and given the extra ships, I doubt the attackers will be able to board at any point.>

<What about our scutters? Could one of them make it through the defense?>

<If it declares for Perdue's side, then it will most likely be allowed into the fray.>

<Okay. I'll get Cane out there now, to save time later.>

She got Kajic on the line and instructed Cane to take the scutter as the Box had suggested. Kajic didn't ask how she had found out about the battle; she hoped that he simply assumed that she had learned about it via Maii.

Still linked via n-space, she noted that the reave was occasionally glancing away from where they were headed in the tunnels to the people surrounding them in the habitat. Even in the maintenance infrastructure, they weren't completely alone. The ones that weren't shielded were mostly thinking about what was going on: curious, concerned, frightened, angry . . . Only a handful were hoping the attackers would win, and none of them had any specific thoughts about the enemy. If there was a connection between the attack and the clone warriors, Roche had yet to find proof of it.

<Any sign of the enemy?> she asked Maii.

<I still can't pinpoint them the way you can. Want to try?>

<It couldn't hurt.>

Roche tried to concentrate on walking as well as the mental landscape of the habitat. The rapid progression of minds was as disorienting in its own way as the incessant but irregular grumbling of the walls and floor. Mind after mind rolled by, until—

<There's one! Back up. *There.*> The pitlike mind was in a group of three or four others, all stationary. <Where is it?>

<Hard to tell,> said Maii. <I think it's the same place we were looking before.>

<The administer's audience chamber?> Roche asked.

<Possibly. Or maybe even her private rooms.>

Ansourian brought them to a halt when they came to a closed door.

"On the other side of this bulkhead is the corridor leading to the holding cells," he said. "I don't know what's waiting for us there. It *could* be messy."

<Box?>

<It's empty. Two guards are at the entrance to the holding cells, though not in line of sight.>

<Good. Keep me posted as we get closer.>

<There is one thing, Morgan,> the Box said, before she could turn her attention back to Ansourian. <I have just intercepted a coded security bulletin. Inderdeep Jans is dead. She was just found in her chambers with her neck broken.>

<Who killed her?>

<That is the curious thing. Obviously the crime scene is awaiting a thorough forensic examination, and no firm conclusions should be drawn without—>

<Come *on*, Box!>

<It would seem that you are the main suspect, Morgan.>

<*Me*?>

<All available security officers have been advised that you and other members of your crew are presently on the loose and, according to the security bulletin, quote, required to assist the investigation, unquote. They have been instructed to use force to bring you in.>

<*Lethal* force?>

<If necessary.>

<Damn!> Until now, it had just been necessary to keep a low profile. Now they were suspects and would be hunted through every corridor of the habitat until caught. Or killed.

Her face must have shown something. When she focused once again on Ansourian, he was staring at her.

"What's happened?"

"The administer . . ." Roche began, then hesitated, debating for a moment whether or not to tell him. The news had the potential to distract him, a distraction she couldn't afford right now. Nevertheless, he did have the right to know. "The administer is dead," she finally said. "Assassinated, it would seem."

His expression flickered, and for the briefest moment she glimpsed a grief that surprised her. Even knowing that Jans was involved in the attack on him, Ansourian still felt compassion for the woman.

Catching Roche's surprise, he said: "For all her failings, she didn't deserve *this.*"

Roche nodded. "I understand," she said. She allowed a moment's pause before gesturing to the door. "I'm sorry, Ansourian, but we have to keep moving."

All trace of sadness vanished from his expression as quickly as it had appeared. "Do you want me to go first?" he said, jerking a thumb at the door in front of them.

Roche flipped her helmet closed. “No, I’ll go. The suit will hold for a second or two, if it has to. You just open it.”

He nodded and stepped back. The lock glowed green, and the door slid aside.

Roche stepped into the corridor, confident that the Box knew what it was talking about but wary of any new developments it may have overlooked. As promised, though, there were no guards in sight.

“Clear,” she whispered.

Ansourian stepped out of the tunnel with Maii. The girl’s visor was also closed, and she kept one hand close to her pistol at all times.

Ansourian indicated the passage to their right, and they walked that way. Two guards came into view thirty seconds later, one on either side of a door two meters wide. They seemed alert but not especially concerned at seeing Ansourian and his companions as they approached.

<What’s on the other side of the door?> she asked the Box.

<A rectangular grid thirty-five meters across, with ten corridors in two groups of five crossing at right angles. There are normally twenty guards, one at each end of each corridor, but half have been reassigned during the attack. There are one hundred cells in all. Alta Ansourian is in number 77.>

<Are the guards shielded, Maii?>

<Neither of the ones ahead,> said Maii. <But there are two on the other side of the door that are.>

Roche didn’t know what Ansourian had planned, so to forestall anything precipitous, she said to Maii: <Tell Ansourian his daughter is in Cell 77, in case he doesn’t know. We’ll take care of these guards.>

<Okay, Morgan.> There was a brief pause as Maii relayed the message. <He sends his thanks,> she told Roche.

Roche nodded. <Now, what about these guards, Maii?>

<Already taken care of,> she said.

<Okay, then let’s move.>

Influenced by Maii’s powers, the guards stepped aside as they approached and waved them through; then, when the heavy door had closed behind them again, they promptly forgot they had ever seen the intruders.

Ansourian automatically took off along the nearest of the black-gray corridors. He seemed unconcerned by the strong jolts that occasionally rattled and shuddered through the walls. Roche followed him, keeping a close eye out for the two shielded guards. They turned right, then left, passing sturdy-looking doors with numeric keypads instead of locks. There was no way to determine whether the cells were empty or not, however, as the window in each door was shuttered closed.

When they reached Alta’s cell, Roche noticed a guard standing motionless at the far end of the corridor. She assumed he was unshielded and controlled by Maii, since he didn’t seem too concerned about the presence of visitors to the cell block.

Ansourian quickly tapped the appropriate code into the keypad of his daughter’s cell. Nothing happened.

“They’ve changed the codes,” he hissed. “We’ll have to blast our way in. Is your pistol up to it?”

“It’ll have to be.” She removed it from her holster and took careful aim. <Box? Help me out here, okay?>

<The door is already unlocked,> it said.

<Thanks.> She fired, and the door sprang open. Roche looked up. The guard hadn't reacted to the noise, but she could hear the inquiries of someone who had.

"Inside!" She pushed Ansourian and Maii into the cell, followed them in and shut the door.

Alta was sitting on a low bunk. She looked up, surprised, when she saw them enter.

"Father!" A smaller, female version of Atul Ansourian, with dark eyes and a small tattoo on her throat, sprang to her feet to embrace him.

"Shhh!" Roche waved for silence. Footsteps were coming toward the cell.

<One guard is approaching your location,> said the Box.

<I hear him.> She waited, pistol at the ready. The smell of energy-fire would linger for a while. If it was strong enough, the guard might realize immediately where they were. If it wasn't, he might just keep walking, which would at least give them an extra minute or two. As far as Roche was concerned, every second was valuable.

The footsteps stopped directly outside the cell.

Roche didn't hesitate: she opened the door and fired her pistol. The bolt of energy caught the guard on the shoulder of his armor, spinning him heavily into the wall. While he was distracted, Maii penetrated his shield and rendered him unconscious.

He fell to the ground with a thud, his weapon sent clattering along the floor. But Roche didn't dare hope that he would be the last of their problems. There was one more unshielded guard in the complex, and she had now fired two shots.

"Quickly!" said Roche back over her shoulder. "Get her into that suit!"

Without a word, Alta slipped into the OSFA suit her father had brought.

Roche edged back out of the corridor, using the Box to scan the corridor of the holding cell grid. Aside from the unconscious guard outside Alta's cell, she counted eight others: five along one wall and three along the other, all subdued by Maii. One was missing.

<Any guesses, Maii?>

<He must've slipped out to get help.>

The Box thought otherwise. <The checkpoint door has not opened since we came through it.>

<So check the cells, then,> said Roche. <He must be in one of them.>

<The cells do not have surveillance cameras,> it said.

<You didn't *see* where he went?>

<I was distracted by the guard approaching you,> the Box confessed. <The resources I have available here are hardly what I would call optimal, Morgan.>

She shrugged off its excuses. They would just have to hope the guard planned to lie low while they made their exit.

Alta had finished donning her suit and stood, slightly stunned, with one hand on her father's shoulder.

"We're leaving here?" she asked.

"Yes," Roche said. "The sooner the better."

They filed out of the cell and into the corridor, Roche leading, keeping alert for any sign of the missing guard. They made it around the first corner, then the next. The checkpoint appeared ahead of them, its doors invitingly open.

Roche had barely passed the last cell door when it burst open. The guard managed to get off three shots before Roche brought him down with two shots from her own weapon—the first bolt hitting his side and spinning him away, the second taking him in the back and throwing him forward onto the cell's bunk, which collapsed noisily beneath him.

Roche ignored him and went to check on Alta and Ansourian instead. The woman, clutching an injured arm, was scrambling her way to her father who had taken two direct hits, one to the chest and one to the stomach.

Roche checked Ansourian for broken ribs, but couldn't feel anything through her glove and the blackened material of his OSFA suit. Even unconscious, he winced with pain as she probed.

"I can carry him," she said to Alta, "if you want to take that risk."

The woman nodded, all expression gone. "He needs medical attention," she said, "and he's not going to get it here."

"He'll be all right if we can just get him back to the *Ana Vereine.* But before that," she said, remembering Ansourian's instructions to Haid and Vri, "we need to find corridor 14 in Sector Green-D. Do you know where that is?"

"Yes, of course," she said. "But why do we need to go there?"

"Because that's our escape route," Roche explained hastily. "I'm arranging a pickup at the maintenance airlock there."

Alta frowned. "'Maintenance airlock'—is that what Father said?"

"Yes, why?"

"It's not a maintenance airlock," she said. "It's an old refuse dumper."

Roche stared at the woman for a second. Dumpers were little more than chutes designed to fire pellets of unreclaimable material at a suitable disposal site—be it the atmosphere of a dead world, the nearest sun, or anywhere the waste would do little harm. They would be lucky if it had even the most primitive airlock facilities, let alone somewhere to dock.

"This just gets better and better," she said, shaking her head. "But it doesn't matter. If it's the only way out, we're going to take it."

She rose slowly to her feet, bringing Ansourian with her. The suit gave her the strength to carry him, and the fall in ambient gravity helped, but he was still going to be a burden—especially if they encountered any more guards and she had to use her pistol.

<I'm going to need as much warning as I can get if there are any signs of guards approaching—okay, Box?> she said. <I don't want to have to drop him like a dead weight at the last moment.>

<You've got it, Morgan,> said the Box.

She staggered as the floor shifted under her; then, regaining her balance, she headed for the checkpoint. They passed through unhindered, and headed off along the corridor.

<I presume you can't read her,> Roche said to Maii.

<Not at all.>

<Trusting bunch, aren't they?> She shifted Ansourian's body to a more comfortable position. Alta took them along a series of wide, curving corridors, many of them ringing to the sound of sirens, but each as deserted as the last. The vibrations seemed to lessen when they stuck to the main routes, and Roche was grateful to be able to forget about not banging her head on the maintenance tunnels' low ceilings. She did feel exposed, though, and would be glad when they reached the exit point—even if it was just a refuse dumper.

<Is Cane going to be able to find us, Box?>

<He and Kajic are monitoring our progress through the habitat, and the egress point is clearly visible from the outside. That is probably why Ansourian chose it. Once we get close, there won't be a problem.>

<How far away are Ameidio and Vri?>

<They are a little farther away than you.>

<And any word on the situation with the administer?>

<No change, Morgan. You are still wanted, and I am still blocking security's attempts to trace you electronically.>

<Well, that's something at least.>

A further violent judder swept through the habitat just as they turned down another corridor, this time forcing Roche to one knee in order to keep herself from falling.

"What was *that*?"

Alta looked frightened as she helped Roche to her feet. "We've been holed!" she said as a sudden shift in air pressure made everyone's ears block. The sirens took on a new note of alarm. "Pressure-doors will be up all over the station."

"We have suits," said Roche. "Do you know the override commands?"

Alta shook her head. "My father would have."

Roche felt trapped. Keeping the Box's existence a secret was becoming harder and harder. <Box, give me the codes!>

The Box complied and she quickly relayed the codes to Maii. <Give them to Ameidio. Tell him Ansourian told us what they were. Hopefully they don't know he's down.> Via implants again, she said: <Box, give us some interference on the line to the *Ana Vereine* and open those doors for us when we reach them. We'll just have to bluff our way through this one.>

<Yes, Morgan.>

Roche nudged Alta on. "Come on, keep going. We're going to make it, okay?"

They continued through the vibrating corridors of the habitat, though now with more pace and urgency. There was still no one around, and Roche assumed the nonessential Vax personnel were holed up in their pressurized compartments. If the majority of the security personnel were down at the docks or elsewhere in the habitat where the defense was concentrated, that at least decreased the chances of their being found. But it wasn't enough to help Roche relax. Not until she was standing on the bridge of the *Ana Vereine*, with the habitat far behind her, would she allow herself that luxury. . . .

They passed through two open pressure-doors, then a third. Roche could see the puzzlement on Alta's face at the blatant lapse in safety precautions, but there was no time to explain. The only time they stopped was when a particularly violent attack shook the habitat so badly that Roche was flung into one of the walls, and Maii and Alta were thrown onto the shuddering floor.

Steadying herself, Roche asked: <How far now, Box?>

<Two more junctions. The way is clear. Haid and Vri are two corridors over, barely a minute behind.>

<Uri? Tell Cane to start moving in. We're almost there.>

From the *Ana Vereine*, Kajic said: <We have the location. I'll let you know when he's there.>

They passed through the first junction, taking a little-used passage that obviously connected to the maintenance tunnels they had left earlier. The second junction took them to a wide, straight corridor that seemed to stretch for miles. In the distance, loping toward them, were two figures, one dressed in black, the other in gold.

Alta started when she saw them.

"It's okay," Roche assured her. "They're with us."

Yet another violent shudder ran through the walls and floor.

"Quickly," said Roche, stepping over to the dumper's enormous steel hatch. "Get that thing open!"

"We haven't used the dumpers for years," explained Alta, tapping at a keypad. "Father kept this one in commission to use as an emergency exit, if he ever needed it. It was used occasionally, but not regularly. But the codes should still work."

Thinking of the dissolving door in the administer's chambers, Roche said: "If we do get out of this in one piece, we'll have your father's devious mind to thank for it."

Haid and Vri arrived in a clatter of armor and heavy footsteps.

"Any problems?" Roche asked

"None," Haid said. "Which only makes me more nervous."

"It would," she said. Alta glanced up but there wasn't time for introductions. "Cane should be waiting for us out the other side of the dumper. If they're designed like others I've seen, we should be able to crawl into the induction tube and out into vacuum easily enough. Then we'll have to jump to the scutter."

"And then . . . ?" Haid prompted.

"Then we wait to see what happens here," said Roche. "The administer has been killed, so it'll be easier to deal with things here if we can reinstate Ansourian somehow. It might be worth sticking around to see if the habitat survives the attack."

Alta had looked up again when Roche mentioned that Inderdeep Jans was dead, but returned quickly to her task. Seconds later she had finished tinkering with the keypad and tried to open the hatch. The hinges were stiff; with Haid's assistance the hatch finally came open a little.

<Morgan,> asked Kajic via her implants, <is everything okay?>

<As much as it can be. Why?>

<Cane is reporting something unusual on the hull near the dumper outlet.>

<'Unusual'? In what way?>

<An object of some kind. He can't make it out yet, but he's concerned you might be about to walk into a trap.>

A trap. Roche watched as Haid and Alta continued to pull at the dumper's hatch. Haid might have been right to be nervous, after all.

"Just blow it, Ameidio," she said. Then to Maii: <Maii, link up! I want to see what's ahead.>

<I can sense nothing, Morgan.>

<Let's do it, anyway,> said Roche. <I want to make sure.>

She stepped back from the recalcitrant hatch as Haid positioned the charges to blow it open. She closed her eyes as she lowered Ansourian to the ground, allowing the gray vistas of n-space to unfold around her.

<Cane is in position,> said Kajic. <But the object he saw has gone.>

<Wait . . .> Roche's mind drifted with Maii's, leaving the cluster of minds that were Haid, Vri, Alta and Ansourian. She had trouble seeing herself, and Maii.

Not far away from them, though, she clearly saw the distinctive dip of a clone warrior.

<Who's that?> said Roche. <Is it Cane?>

<I *think* so,> said Maii, uncertainty stressing the word. <He's closer now than he was.>

<That would make sense. Can you see anything else?>

<No . . .>

The corridor rocked beneath them as the charges blew open the hatch. Roche opened her eyes on a cloud of smoke obscuring everything in the corridor. Haid stepped to the hole in the wall where the hatch had been.

<No, wait!> said Maii, her mental voice urgent. <There are two of them!>

Haid hesitated by the entrance to the refuse dumper, startled by the mental shout. The gray of n-space overwhelmed Roche's ordinary vision—and she too saw the second hole in the field that meant a clone warrior. At first she didn't realize how Maii had known there were two, but then it all fell into place. The second one was farther away and moving gradually closer. It had all the hallmarks of Cane's mind.

The first one they had seen was *inside* the refuse dumper.

Before anyone could move away, there was a second explosion, this time from the other side of the open hatchway. A hurricane of air roared past them as the atmosphere inside the corridor was sucked out the open outlet, into space. Roche braced herself, and grabbed Ansourian's body as it slipped toward the hole. Pressure doors slammed closed along the corridor; alarms screamed, fading gradually as the air pressure dropped.

<Check your seals!> she shouted via her implants. <Make sure your suits will hold!>

Then, out of the hatchway, moving easily against the whirlpool currents of air, her white ponytail whipping in the wind, stepped Inderdeep Jans.

10

Perdue Habitat
955.1.32
0810

Jans was wearing an OSFA suit not dissimilar to the ones Ansourian and his daughter had on, except her face mask wasn't in place. That she had blown the dumper outlet without sealing her suit first surprised Roche, but she didn't have time to dwell on the matter—the clone warrior was advancing toward her. Jans didn't appear to be armed, but that didn't lessen the potential threat. There was a spark of malice in her eyes, and her attention was fixed firmly upon Roche.

Before Roche could react, Haid grabbed Jans's shoulder from behind and spun her around. Jans used her momentum to kick out and up, throwing him with ease across the corridor. Then, with a single, fluid motion, she was at Vri's side, disarming him of the rifle he had leveled at her only a second earlier. One shot blew a hole in the far wall as the weapon was wrenched from his grasp and turned on him. In that same instant, Roche managed to snap off a shot from her own pistol, knocking the rifle out of Jans's hands. The warrior didn't seem the slightest bit fazed; instead, her free hand now struck out twice at Vri's head. The third time she lashed out at him she grabbed the Surin's arm and spun him around, hurling him at the nearest wall. He bounced off the gray-black surface heavily and fell back to the floor, his body prostrate and writhing.

The warrior now turned to face Roche. For the briefest moment their eyes met.

Then the clone warrior pulled her mask closed and took two running steps toward Roche—unbelievably fast. Roche fired just as her assailant jumped. Jans's suit flared mirror-bright for an instant; then she was on top of Roche, forcing her down and knocking the pistol out of her hands. Roche struggled, but two incredibly strong hands lifted her from the ground and threw her across the floor. She slid into a wall; even through the hazard suit, the impact knocked the breath out of her. She raised her hands to ward off another blow, but none came. It wasn't *her* Jans was after.

Placing her feet on either side of Atul Ansourian's prone body, Inderdeep Jans thrust down with her left fist, penetrating his suit, rib cage, and heart with one, smooth punch.

Even in her dazed state, Roche knew what the clone warrior was doing: she was finishing the job. Now there would be no easy way that the situation in Perdue Habitat could be fixed.

Inderdeep Jans rose to her full height now and looked around, her hand dripping red. The drop in air pressure cast an eerie half-silence across the scene. Roche could hear her own breathing loudest of all, over the calling of voices in her implants. Vri's roar of defiance from behind the clone warrior went unheard entirely, as did Alta Ansourian's cry of horror.

Roche felt a wave of giddiness wash over her as Maii leveled a spear of mental force at the clone warrior, and thrust with all her strength. Jans didn't even react. She just stood there for a couple of seconds, as though contemplating what to do next. Then, having made a decision, she stepped away from Ansourian's body and over to Roche. Without wasting time, she steadied Roche with one hand to the chest and raised her bloodied fist to strike. There was no emotion in the woman's eyes, just cold detachment. And in the seconds that Roche looked into those eyes, part of her felt a fear deeper than any she had known before. But another part of her was just tired, and the breath she released at that moment was almost a sigh of relief that it was finally over. . . .

Then the clone warrior's fist fell.

A flash of white, and the fist missed her helmet and embedded itself in the corridor wall.

Roche sagged, her legs turned to water. Only Jans' hand on her chest held her upright as the clone warrior turned, eyes flashing at Cane standing in the open dumper hatch, a pistol steadied in both hands, still aiming the shot that had knocked Jans' punch aside.

<Morgan, get the others out of here while you still can!> Cane's voice traveled via his pressure suit through the *Ana Vereine*, then to Roche's implants. <The scutter's holding by the outlet. I'll take care of this.>

Jans's face became an angry sneer and the hand on Roche's chest tightened.

Cane shot her again. The suit's reflective powers had been compromised by the two shots it had already received, and this time the reflective flash was more purple than white. Jans recoiled from Roche, then sprang forward so fast that her figure became a blur.

Cane didn't waste time firing again. The pistol had hardly begun to fall when her lunge met his defensive crouch. Their limbs moved too rapidly for Roche to make out anything clearly. One would strike, the other would defend and counterstrike—the exchange almost too quick to follow. There was a dizzying effect to the battle as each whirled, ducked, and thrust, with no indication as to who was gaining the upper hand.

After a few moments the two of them came apart, as if thrown from each other by a small and silent explosion. Cane bounced back into a wall as Jans skidded along the corridor. Quicker than it would have taken Roche to blink, the two were poised again, ready to attack.

<*Move*, Morgan!> The inside of Cane's pressure mask was spattered with fresh blood.

His call brought her to life and, as the two clone warriors clashed again—with Cane leaping forward to prevent Jans getting any closer to the hatch—Roche reached for Alta, who was crouched over the body of her father.

"Come on!" she shouted. But Alta ignored her, whimpering as she pulled ineffectually at her lifeless father, as if trying to drag him to his feet. "We have to *go*!"

Roche dragged her to the hatch. Maii followed, clutching the back of Roche's suit as though it were a lifeline. Once there, Roche took Alta's face in her hands and forced the woman to look at her.

"I need you to help Maii through the hatch. Do you understand?"

Alta blinked back tears, sniffed, nodded.

"Okay, *in*," said Roche.

The floor bucked beneath them as first Alta, then Maii, climbed through.

"Help Maii into the scutter at the end of the outlet," she said to Alta while their suits were still touching. "I'll follow in a second."

Vri was standing over Haid, his gold armor dusted with frozen water vapor. Haid was out cold, his armor heavy and inert. Roche helped Vri drag him toward the hatch, each taking one leg. She briefly considered using one of the weapons in his suit pouches to shoot Jans again. But when she glanced up the other end of the corridor, she knew there was no way she would get a clear shot.

The two clone warriors were a blur of motion with only occasional, unpredictable pauses. There was a strange beauty and grace to their movements, almost balletic. Each was as superb as the other at combat, each forced to rely on subtleties and surprise rather than brute strength to gain the edge. Roche had never seen anything like it, and knew that in such a conflict she would have barely lasted a second against either of them. And in realizing that, she also realized just how lucky she was to be alive right then. Had Cane reached her a second later . . .

"Lift," Vri grunted, returning her attention to her injured friend. She bent her knees to slide Haid's body into the hatch. The floor shifted beneath them again, and Roche distinctly felt the ambient gravity dip. That was a bad sign, even if it did make Haid easier to carry. Somewhere, something was going terribly wrong for the station.

<Uri, what's happening?>

<Reinforcements have arrived from Random Valence,> Kajic replied. <They're concentrating fire in several areas, including power generators and life support. The habitat is taking a beating in the process.>

<I can feel it,> said Roche. <Do you think it'll hold?>

<Unless their tactics change, I have no doubt.>

<I bet that's what they thought on Guidon, too.>

With Haid through the hatch, Vri also went through, and lent Roche a hand. Together they maneuvered Haid along the chute and to the open end. The hatch there was blackened and bent open from the outside. Seeing it, Roche realized that *Cane* had blown the outer door on the outlet, not Jans, thereby forcing the other clone warrior to attack before she was ready. Had he not done this, it was unlikely they would have survived so long.

The scutter hung tethered two meters from the outlet. Vri jumped the gap, easily negotiating the change from gravity to zero-g. A quick glimpse of the local region of space revealed several ships accelerating brightly across the starfield, some of them under fire from cannon out of sight behind the tangled bulk of the habitat. Gas clouds, glowing and expanding, hung in numerous places between the ships, although Roche couldn't tell whether they were the remains of destroyed fighters or missiles that had missed their targets. Another shudder rocked the section of the habitat she clung to while leaning out to pass Haid's body to Vri. Looking back along the length of the outlet chute, she could actually see the structure flexing.

When Haid was safely aboard the scutter, Vri reached out for Roche's hand.

She shook her head. <Give me a rifle,> she said. <I'm going back for Cane.>

He turned away, returned a second later with two weapons pulled from Haid's armor, then jumped across the gap. Handing one to her, he said: <I'm coming with you.>

<You don't understand,> she protested, waving the weapon under his nose. <This isn't to help him; it's for self-defense!>

<I know, but I'm still coming.>

She shrugged, turned, and began crawling back along the chute. She didn't have time for arguments.

Neither Cane nor Jans had followed them, so they had to be still inside—unless one or the other had forced their way through the pressure doors at either end of the section of the corridor.

<Be careful,> she said as Vri approached the open hatch.

He nodded, shifting the rifle into the optimal position and taking one side. Roche took the other.

Peering out of the hatch, to the right along the corridor, she could see nothing. Vri, on the other hand, nodded, and she shifted over to his side.

Cane and Jans were still fighting furiously, although both had sustained injuries now. During one standoff, Roche noticed that one of Jans's fingers stuck out at an odd angle, and that she seemed to be favoring the hand in combat too. But the blood on Cane's face mask was thicker and darker, and it had to be obscuring his vision.

Jans lunged again; Cane parried her blows with familiar grace. But this was different from the fights he'd had before. Then he had been fighting almost for the fun of it; now he was fighting for his life.

<Box, is there nothing we can do?>

<No. We can only watch.>

And learn, she thought to herself, hoping it was worth risking a companion's life in exchange for such knowledge.

The two combatants separated and maneuvered for position. Jans caught sight of Vri and Roche in the open hatchway and kicked off for them immediately. Taken by surprise by the move, Cane was a split second slow in jumping after her. Roche recoiled as Jans's hands reached out for them, but the clone warrior rolled at the last minute and kicked off the wall. Cane was caught mid-leap and flung across the room.

Jans was on him before he could recover, rolling him over so he was between her and Roche, with an arm firmly around his neck. Cane's spine bent backward, and he twisted to look into Jans's eyes. As Roche aimed her rifle on the slight chance Jans miscalculated and gave her a clear shot, Roche saw their eyes lock.

Then, with a sickening lurch, gravity failed entirely. Using the sudden shift to his advantage, Cane pushed away from the floor and kicked Jans into the ceiling. As she rebounded, he was ready with a second kick that sent her spinning into a wall. He followed, catching her around the throat and wrenching her backward. It was her turn to be pinned from behind.

Jans writhed, managing to twist her hands behind her and pull Cane's mask off. He hung on even tighter, provoking a grimace of pain from the woman. Roche could see air puffing out of his suit, around his cheeks and jaw, but he seemed oblivious. Jans screamed silently into the vacuum, and for a moment Cane's grasp seemed to relax. Only slightly, but enough to allow Jans to twist her own head around to look at him. He leaned into his sibling, then suddenly tightened his grip once more. With one savage twist he snapped her neck.

Her body went limp, but he waited a further minute before letting her go. Then he collected the face mask dangling about his throat and carefully replaced it. The exposure to vacuum didn't seem to have harmed him at all.

Roche climbed out of the hatch, followed by Vri. Cane looked up. His face was black with frozen blood.

<Are you okay?> she asked, kicking closer to him through free-fall.

<Are *you*?> His voice, even via implants, sounded weary.

<Yes, but we should get out of here.>

He nodded and let Vri take him by the arm.

<The body,> said the Box. <You must take the body with you.>

Roche eyed the corpse of Inderdeep Jans with distaste; it was one of two in the corridor. <I presume you mean hers, not Ansourian's.>

<It will contain important data,> said the Box.

<Yeah, I know.> She approached it cautiously, afraid that even now Jans might be dangerous. The clone warrior's skin was much paler than it had been only seconds ago, and mottled with hundreds of odd-shaped bruises.

<Guards are coming,> the Box nudged her.

She grabbed the body with both hands and pushed it toward the hatch as Vri and Cane passed through. With considerably less difficulty than she'd had with Haid—for Jans was smaller and unarmored—Roche got her through the hatch and dumper chute and into the scutter. She sealed the airlock behind her, glad to be in familiar territory once again.

Maii and Alta were already braced and ready in the cockpit. Alta looked up as Roche brought Jans's body inside, then glanced away, her eyes watering.

Vri helped Roche stow the body in the rear hold, where the Box could keep an eye on it. Then she went back to the pilot's station, which Cane had left vacant, and took control of the scutter from Kajic.

<Where are you, Uri?> she asked.

A chart appeared on the console, with major concentrations of fire and wreckage marked. <I've marked the optimal course.>

<Thanks.> She glanced around the cockpit. Everyone looked shell-shocked. She supposed she looked the same. Surprisingly, Cane looked worst of all; his skin was pale and his cheeks were hollow. He looked sick, something Roche would never have thought possible. And it wasn't just exhaustion, either. It was something much more.

With a simple series of commands directed through her implants, she fired the scutter's thrusters and moved them away from Perdue Habitat.

The scutter was attacked the moment it disengaged. Fighters and cannon converged on it, urged on by reports that they were responsible for the death of the administer—which in essence was true. Roche guessed that the remaining clone warrior was behind it, continuing the ploy that had begun with the report that she had assassinated Jans—only this time it was for real.

Surprisingly, the Random Valence ships joined in, local rivalries forgotten for the moment—or perhaps directed by another clone warrior among their own numbers. Roche wondered what lies they might be being fed, but it was impossible for the Box to access their command network.

Barely had they managed to evade pursuit long enough to dock with the waiting

Ana Vereine when something exploded in the habitat behind them. They couldn't tell what it was—maybe a major power plant, or a weapons store. Roche could only watch with a sinking feeling as the great tangle of corridors began to disintegrate, unraveling like a knot and breaking into chunks as local stress points flexed too far and snapped.

Pursuit abruptly fell off as all the ships in the area retreated to search for survivors. Roche wanted to assist also, but Haid—awake but concussed—talked her out of it.

"Even if they don't shoot us out of the sky," he said, "they probably wouldn't let us get close enough to do any good. Remember: one of them is still in there, and they're *not* going to make it easy for you."

By "them" he meant the clone warriors. Roche was beginning to think that 'they' were everywhere.

As the *Ana Vereine* retreated from the vicinity, injuries were attended to while everyone discussed what had happened. Haid was still recovering. Alta Ansourian was under sedation; Roche didn't know if she would ever be united with the habitat survivors, or indeed any of her people, but she would do her best for the woman. Vri was back in his ship. Maii was resting on a bench on the bridge, where Roche and Kajic went over the small amount of data they had managed to gather.

Cane was asleep in the medical unit.

<He's genuinely unconscious,> the Box informed Roche.

<How can you be sure?> she said.

<I coopted the diagnostic AI to my service,> it replied.

<So his injuries were severe, then?>

<I don't believe his need to rest has anything to do with his injuries or his being tired, Morgan. At least not a physical tiredness.>

She knew what the Box was implying. She herself had done little else but think about it since leaving the habitat, and even now the significance of what had happened was still difficult to fully appreciate.

<He killed one of his own kind,> she said. <He killed her in order to save us—at no small risk to his own life, either.>

<Yes.> Even the Box seemed to be caught on that simple fact. Why would Cane be prepared to do something like that if he wasn't worthy of their trust? She should have been glad now to finally have proof that he was in fact on their side. So why was she still suspicious of him? Because he had hesitated at the end? She wasn't sure she could blame him for that. . . .

<What about the dead warrior?> she asked needing to think about something else. <Anything there?>

<Some developments I've not seen before. The cellular composition of her skin is changing at a rapid rate, returning to a decidedly more Pristine appearance rather than that of the Caste she was impersonating. The chameleonic abilities of these creatures is literal, it seems, to a degree.>

Roche added that to the list of things they'd learned. <So you've studied their bodies before?>

<Others have, and I have access to some of their data. Most bodies are found in capsules or ships destroyed by energy fire. Very few intact remains in other words. Never has one been studied so soon after death.>

<Well, that's something,> she said. <At least we know how she managed to look so much like the Vax, even if it wasn't perfect. What I don't understand is, how could she have fooled Ehud Jans into believing that she was his daughter?>

<She didn't have to.>

<What do you mean?>

The Box hesitated for a second. When it spoke again, its voice was contrite. <It is easy to see in hindsight, Morgan. The data was in the habitat records all the time. Despite their strict laws controlling breeding, the Vax do have adoption policies. A parent may adopt a new child if their first has been killed by accident, or died of a disease. In such circumstances, they may take a parentless child as their own, in order to continue both lines. In the case of Inderdeep Jans, she is recorded as an orphan recovered from the wreckage of a mining vessel that drifted into Vax space. She was taken in and became a close friend of Ehud's real daughter, Eir. Not long after, Eir Jans was killed in an accident, and Ehud adopted Inderdeep as his own.>

Roche remembered something Ansourian had said about the previous administer discouraging the use of transit tubes after "a terrible accident," years ago. <All arranged, I imagine.>

<It seems likely,> said the Box. <Since then, she simply bided her time until she could do the most damage, doing her best in small ways to impede progress against the enemy.>

Roche could see that, too. Ansourian had also mentioned that Inderdeep Jans wouldn't have agreed to come to Sol System at all if he hadn't pressured her into it. Certainly her odd moods had kept the efficiency of the habitat at a low ebb. And ultimately, with Roche on her way and Ansourian a genuine thorn in her side, she had been forced to make her move.

Roche couldn't help but wonder what might have happened had they realized the truth earlier. Maybe she could have saved the lives of Ansourian and everyone else on the station, or maybe it would've turned out as it had. There was no way of knowing.

<And what do we do now?> Roche mused. <Turn around and go back? Proceed to the next place on Nemeth's list? Return to the *Phlegethon*, perhaps? We could even just head off on our own.> She sighed tiredly. Despite the options, she still felt trapped. She wanted a clear goal—or even better, a decisive way to strike at the enemy. The ambiguity was driving her crazy. <Or maybe we could just do nothing at all,> she finished.

<It is up to you now.>

<Yes, I know,> she said irritably. <But what do *you* think?>

<I believe proceeding to the next place on the list would be the best course of action right now.>

<There's no guarantee it'll be any better than where we've just been.>

<Of course not.>

<No, and that's the point, isn't it?> Perdue Habitat had been ready to explode, and Roche had been the lit fuse Nemeth had thrown at it. The chances were high that the other places on the list would be equally volatile.

<Now that we know that the enemy is able to pose as members of marginally Exotic Castes,> said the Box, <we can at least be more careful in future. And we've also learned that they can be patient for years before cutting loose.>

<That only makes them harder to find, though,> said Roche.

<Not for you,> returned the Box.

<But that doesn't do me much good when I have to stand practically face to face with one to be certain!> They hadn't spent much time examining her newly found talent. When Cane was awake, perhaps, they would look at it more closely. When they could find a way to fix the precise locations of people in the real universe from the impressions they left in n-space, maybe there would be a chance. Maybe.

She sagged back in her seat. If Kajic wondered why she was no longer showing much interest in the data they were supposedly examining, he said nothing at all. Maybe he just assumed she was tired like everyone else—which she was. It was made worse by the fact that she knew she wouldn't be getting the chance to rest any time soon.

<What *is* next on the list?> she asked.

<We have a choice of two. There's either an out-station maintained by the Drys or a loose collective known as the Katajalin Serai. Both are slightly out-system from our present position. We can be at either place in approximately fifteen hours.>

Roche's weariness intensified at the thought. In just fifteen hours they could be going through it all again.

<First, I suppose I'd better put together some sort of report for Nemeth,> she said, feeling no enthusiasm at all for the task.

<I can do that for you, if you like,> said the Box. <At least the first draft. You can look at it when I'm done, and send or amend it as you wish.>

<Thanks, Box.> As always, she was unsure how far she could trust the AI, but the offer was a welcome one.

Speaking aloud, she said: "Uri, I'm sorry. I'm really not up to this at the moment. I'm feeling a little tired and distracted. Let me get a couple of hours' sleep and we'll finish up then, okay?"

"Of course, Morgan," Kajic said. "Is there anything you'd like me to get on with while you rest?"

Roche thought for a second. "Yes. Plot a course for the Katajalin Serai and get us under way. Its location is in the file Nemeth gave us. Send a drone to check things out first, though; this time I want to know exactly what we're getting ourselves into."

"Understood." As his holographic image began to dissolve, he added: "Sleep well, Morgan."

"I will," she said to the suddenly empty space before her.

<I can make sure of that,> said Maii softly into her mind.

For once, Roche was tempted. All the other times the girl had made that offer, she had turned it down out of fear that the reave might tamper with her mind. She'd had plenty of opportunities now to see that Maii's intentions were innocent. If Roche could trust her with the knowledge that the Box had survived the destruction of the *Sebettu*, then she could probably feel safe in her hands for a couple of hours.

But the thought still nagged at her that she would be defenseless. It would take longer still for her to get over that feeling.

<Okay,> she said. <Just get me to sleep, though, and I'll do the rest.>

The girl radiated warmth. <Of course, Morgan. Gladly.>

Later, though, Roche would regret that she hadn't given herself wholly over to the girl's care. Her sleep was disturbed by dreams that left her frightened, bewildered, confused, and sad. Most unnerving was a recurring image in which she was floating gently over a flat gray landscape in which there suddenly appeared a circular hole.

First a pinprick, then a gaping mouth, then a yawning chasm, it sucked her into its lightless maw—and she fell, much as she had in the dream that had haunted her through COE Armada Military College and before her arrival in Palasian System. Only this time there was no bottom. This time her fall went on forever.

PART THREE:

PHLEGETHON

11

TBC-14 (a.k.a. IND *Kindling*)
955.1.33
0390

"Who is the enemy, Page?" Salton Trezise asked via the ftl link with the *Phlegethon.*

De Bruyn didn't answer immediately. She was too busy watching the recording of Perdue Habitat disintegrate. It was the third time she had sat through it; this time she was paying special attention to one particular section of the structure.

Signs still remained of where Roche's tame clone warrior had blown his way in through the outer hatch of the refuse dumper, and where the ex-Dato scutter had left distinctive exhaust marks upon its departure. Unfortunately, that portion of the habitat had been one of the most severely damaged, and De Bruyn's recording was the only remaining proof of what had taken place there.

"Someone got rid of the evidence," she said, watching again the puff of energy that tore apart the section of the habitat, atomizing anything that might have remained within and slagging the dumper itself. "There's nothing left at all."

"Are you listening to me, Page?" he said. "I asked—"

"I heard you," she said. And indeed she had: she had switched to an ordinary audio link, tired of his voice insinuating through her implants. After a session with him, she felt as if her brain had been soaked in oil. "I'm busy."

"Busy doing what?"

"The work you and your ineffectual council should be doing."

"We have enough on our hands without wasting time pursuing grudges."

"Is that really what you think this is?" She made no attempt to hide her anger. She'd had enough of that sort of talk from the mercenaries on *Dark Stressor.*

"You haven't given me sufficient evidence to think otherwise, I must say."

"*Must* you?"

His sigh was audible over the link. "Page, you're acting like a child."

"I'm investigating every possibility," she said. "*That's* what I'm doing."

"No you're not," he countered quickly. "You're investigating just *one* possibility from every possible angle."

"And what's wrong with that? It's still a possibility."

"A remote one, at best," he said. "Really, Page, what have you to go on? A suspicion; a scrap or two of barely circumstantial evidence—"

"*More* than a scrap! We know Roche was in the habitat. One of your own agents lifted her image from security. But no one saw her leave." She indicated the image before her, speaking as much to herself as to Trezise, mulling over the problem again. "This whole area was blacked out at the time. We have no hard evidence of anything!"

"We *do* know she escaped, Page. She sent a report to Rey Nemeth ten hours later."

"*Someone* did. We can't be sure it was her."

His laugh held more exasperation than amusement. "You think she stayed behind?"

"Maybe. Or maybe the scutter acted as a distraction while she went elsewhere."

"Where?"

"I don't know."

"Why?"

"I don't know."

"With *whom*?"

"I don't *know*." Her fists clenched.

"So in the absence of any alternative theory, do you *really* believe it wasn't her?"

"All I'm saying is that it pays to be careful. She's slippery, and she's not stupid. If she thinks she's being followed, who knows what lengths she would go to to avoid me?"

"Possibly," he muttered. "But you have to admit that these lengths would be ridiculous."

She opened her mouth to protest, but decided against it. The evidence overwhelmingly suggested that Roche *had* been on the scutter when it left the habitat, and that she had therefore been aboard the *Ana Vereine* when it left the vicinity of the disaster. If De Bruyn could allow herself to feel satisfied on that point, she could move on. There were other, more immediate things to worry about.

She killed the recording, deciding that she did in fact agree with Trezise. She would not, however, give him the satisfaction of knowing that she had given in.

"Have *you* learned anything of note?" she challenged him as she checked local space. Still no sign of the ship she was waiting for.

"Things are moving apace," he said. "The Kesh-Olmahoi conflict has ended as expected, with the Kesh decisively routed. Surprisingly, no evidence has been found of enemy involvement. But the council is lending its support to those attempting to clean up the mess."

No evidence, De Bruyn repeated to herself, disappointed that he should be so blind.

"We've been investigating the cult I mentioned earlier, the one purported to worship the enemy," he went on. "They have caused a moderately large amount of damage and their influence appears to be growing. It seems there are several splinter sects. Their devotion is quite genuine, albeit misplaced and lacking any foundation. We have interrogated a number of devotees and found that they possess no more knowledge about the enemy than we do ourselves. If the enemy *does* have any involvement with them at all, then it is purely symbolic. They share no information with their worshippers, and no plans, and seem to bear them no sympathy at all when they are purged. Five pockets of the religion have been flushed out of as many fleets, and not once has the enemy raised a hand to stop us.

"The interesting thing, though, is that the cults believe, as do some of us, that the enemy has been sent to rid the galaxy of Pristines. While this does conflict with some of the evidence we have gathered, it *is* suggestive. There might yet be a grain of truth to that belief, after all."

De Bruyn let him ramble on. She didn't know whether he was talking for her benefit, or his own, but she doubted he would be telling her anything simply because he thought it would help her. Maybe he thought she knew something about the cults and might let it slip if he encouraged her. She did, but she wasn't going to let him know.

The near-space screen was still empty.

"There have been a few setbacks," he continued. "One of the council's major allies, the Espire-Mavrodis Coalition, was struck from within just hours ago. A group of military officers attempted to capitalize on discontent in the lower ranks, and mounted a coup that might very well have been successful, had not one of their own had a change of heart at the last moment and turned against them. The debacle cost the life of nearly every person we had come to rely on in that quarter, and has left the Coalition in complete disarray. They'll be no use to us in the short term, I'm afraid—and maybe never, as there is talk of them pulling out to regroup. Unfortunately, the defecting officer has not been found."

"Has the Commonwealth of Empires been affected?" De Bruyn asked.

"No. That continues to puzzle me. It is such an easy target, and so close to the focus of things. I would've thought it would be riddled with the enemy."

De Bruyn nodded to herself, agreeing with him about the COE's vulnerability but not really surprised that it seemed to have been spared.

"And I hope you've taken my warning about the system's ring," he said. "We've lost five ships in there, that we know of. Four others are incommunicado. With the little information we've had to go on, it's hard to say why this is happening. Given the conflict within the system at the moment, the likelihood of a ship being attacked simply because it is not recognized by another Caste has risen dramatically. It is possible that the ships were attacked out of paranoia. It's hard to know for sure." He paused. "It may not have anything to do with the ring itself at all. Still, it doesn't hurt to be cautious, and until we *do* know for certain what's going on, I advise you to stay away from it."

De Bruyn had been doing just that, not because of Trezise's warning, but because Roche herself had stuck to more distant regions of the system.

"Could the enemy be hiding within the ring?" she asked.

"No, it's too thin—thinner than even the most meager of atmospheres. Add it all together and you get enough for a medium-sized gas giant or two, but spread out so far it amounts to practically nothing at all. The Heresiarch still hasn't worked out where it came from, but that's a low priority at this point. He's only concerned because he's obsessed by navigational anomalies. With a ship that big to look after, even the slightest snag could be disastrous. You know, I think he spends all his time—"

"Look, Salton," she interrupted, "was there an actual *reason* for this call?"

"I always have a reason, Page. You know that."

"Would it have anything to do with the information I requested?"

"No," he said. "But I do happen to have that as well."

She gritted her teeth. "Can I have it?"

"It should be coming through with this transmission." She could hear the smile in his voice, but kept her annoyance in check.

"Thank you," she forced herself to say, but not without a hint of sarcasm, and not before checking that he was telling the truth. He was. As soon as the data transfer was complete, she would get rid of him.

"But before you go," he said, irritating her still further by seeming to read her thoughts, "can I ask you a small favor in return?"

Here we go, she thought. "Which is?"

"That idiot Murnane is thinking of letting Exotics onto the council. Obviously that would be a dangerous idea, even if they were allowed only an advisory or associate status. Things are complicated enough without adding more interests into the mix. If we can't guarantee our own safety—as the downfall of the Espire-Mavrodis Coalition demonstrates all too well—why should we make ourselves responsible for anyone else's?"

"Unless they can help you more in return."

"Which is exactly what I think Murnane is hoping for. But I for one am skeptical."

She refrained from commenting on his motives. "What does any of this have to do with me?"

"Well, I'm presuming that you are following Morgan Roche as she gallivants across this forsaken system. That seems to be your mission in life, after all."

"You could presume that," she said, thinking: *But you'd be wrong.*

"And I happen to know that her mission is to reconnoiter the Exotic Castes to see how they are faring against the enemy. But we both know this is a waste of time. *Everyone* is performing badly against the enemy—be they Exotic or Pristine."

The data had arrived. "What's your point, Salton?"

"I need a reason to keep the Exotics off the council, Page. You can help me find that reason."

"I can?"

"You're out there, among it all. You're seeing it firsthand. You can give me the flip side to Roche's reports. She makes it sound like the Exotics are suffering as much as we are—which may be true, but I'd prefer if it wasn't quite so obvious."

"Why not, if it's the truth?"

"That's just the point I'm trying to make. We should ignore it *because* it is true. It *has* to be deliberate. What's the biggest problem in Sol System at the moment? It's not the enemy—although I don't doubt their presence is being felt in a thousand small ways: disrupting communications, sabotaging procedures, corrupting information, and more. Even without the enemy, even if everything ran smoothly, there'd still be chaos: there are simply *too many people*! And when these people start fighting among themselves, the situation inevitably worsens. We're balancing constantly on the precipice of all-out mayhem; only the most super-Human effort stops us from doing the enemy's job for them."

"So you figure that if there are less people, things might improve?"

"Of course! Reorganize and integrate our resources, limit the number of governments to a manageable number, reduce the council's active concerns to a feasible few, and *maybe* we'll prevail. Given that the majority of people here are Pristines, and that apart from a few exceptions the enemy seems to target Pristines, wouldn't it be better if everyone else left and let the Pristines sort it out?"

"With you in charge, no doubt."

He laughed lightly. "I knew I could count on you to see my reasoning," he said. "And if my proposal goes through the council, hopefully others will too."

"So you want me to lie about what's happening to the Exotics?"

"No; I just want you to balance the scales."

"It amounts to the same thing," she said.

"It's all about *how* you put it, Page. How else do you think politics works? Give me the right words and I could move entire solar systems."

"Not if there isn't anyone listening to you." She found it hard to imagine greasy Salton Trezise, known for so long as Auberon Chase's lackey, being a force in his own right in something like the IEPC. "*Is* anyone going to be listening to you, Salton?"

"I have the ear of several councilors," he said. "Enough to make a difference."

"Why do you need me, then? Why not use the council's own agents?"

"Because *your* reports will help discredit Roche's. That's a cause to which I know you will apply yourself." He chuckled softly to himself for a second. "Look, even discounting personal grudges, Page, this will benefit us both. Think of the enemy—the *common* enemy. *They're* the ones we're ultimately after—not Roche, not Murnane. If we can do what we want to do while at the same time achieving what we need to achieve, then we approach success. Ultimately the ends do justify the means, and, as we're in this together, we might as well use each other to the best of our abilities. I'm not naive, Page; I *know* you've used me to suit your needs."

"I would never call you 'naive,' Salton," she said soberly.

"Good," he returned. "Then let's start working together, because together we *can* do some damage—to the enemy, and to those who oppose us."

And to each other, she thought. But all she said was: "Okay, Salton. I'll see what I can do."

He was silent long enough for her to suspect he might have gone, even though the line was still open. That suited her. A beacon had begun to flash on the fighter's main display, indicating that a ship had just entered her region of the system. She didn't know if Trezise could tell where she was by tracing which ftl drone had detected her replies to him; maybe the broadcasts traveled from drone to drone in a complicated chain, not just via a single one direct to the receiving stations on the *Phlegethon*. Either way, she was glad he seemed to think she was still hot on Roche's heels. If he knew where she actually was, he might reconsider his deal.

The Hurn ship drifted smoothly toward *Kindling*, looking like a cross between a sailing ship and processional barge, its bulky, bullet-shaped body almost completely obscured by tapering instrument spines, crisscrossing antennae, and curved flanges that seemed to serve no actual purpose. This far from the sun, out where an Oört cloud might once have existed, there was very little light to view anything effectively. In artificial color, the vessel looked like it was painted electric blue, with highlights of bright orange and green. Its vividness was unsettling enough without its contents to consider.

It decelerated to a relative halt and hung there, waiting.

"I have to go," she said to Trezise.

"Understood," he replied without any appreciable lag. "We'll speak again soon, Page."

For once, despite herself, she hoped that this would be true.

* * *

The circular bridge of the *Apostle* was dimly lit and smelled of steel. De Bruyn sat at the lowest point of the cavernous space, surrounded by ranks of instruments like steps in an amphitheatre. Tall figures moved among those instruments, but the light was too faint for her to make them out. She half-glimpsed robes and cowls; very occasionally, eyes glinted at her.

"We know who she is," said the shadowy figure sitting opposite her. His face was completely obscured by the hood of a black combat suit that had been modified to give it a more ceremonial air. "But do you know who *we* are?"

"You are the Disciples of Evergence," she said.

"And what does that name mean to you?"

She hesitated. "I'm not sure," she said finally. "The word 'Evergence' doesn't appear in any language I have access to. It's not a name, it's not a code—"

"It has no meaning of itself," the hooded figure interrupted her. "It could be said to be a confluence of many essences: of convergence, forever, emerging, divergent, evolution, emergency, and even vengeance. But 'Evergence' is none of these things. It is a word for something that has, until now, needed no words. It has existed in silence, and will return to silence when the need for words is gone." The ominous figure inclined its head as the echoes of his voice faded. "But I feel you do not understand."

"No, I'm afraid you've lost me," she admitted with a shrug.

"It doesn't matter. Your comprehension is neither essential nor desired. We simply wish to ensure that you bring with you no misconceptions about our purpose here in Sol System."

"You worship the enemy," she said softly. The words carried much more significance when said in context.

"So it has been said," the figure observed. "And if that is what you choose to believe, so be it."

"You're telling me you *don't* worship them?"

"We do not *worship*," the figure intoned. "That is all I am telling you."

"But you are on their side?"

"Yes."

"And Morgan Roche is your enemy." She didn't need to phrase that as a question.

"Yes, she is."

"Then I believe I can help you," De Bruyn said, feeling a catch in her voice that surprised her.

"Really?" Was there a hint of mockery in his voice? She couldn't be sure.

"Yes," she said, the word emerging as little more than a croak. What was wrong with her? Finally she had found people that suited her needs, and she seemed to be having second thoughts! But she wasn't about to back out. Not now. She *couldn't*.

"I *can* help you," she said more assertively, adding: "If you help *me*."

"Ah, I see." The figure nodded thoughtfully. "And what is it exactly that you want from us?"

"A deal," she said. "We work together and we *both* get what we want."

"You would serve us?"

"No," she said quickly. "I would work with you. For a time."

"How?"

"I am alone, here. My resources are meager. But I know what I'm doing, and I have access to information at the heart of the IEPC. Give me one of your cells to command, and I will do your job for you."

"Which job do you think that would be?"

She leaned forward. "With my knowledge and your Disciples, we can trap Roche. I *know* we can. All we have to do is cooperate, and she will be out of your hair forever. It's that simple."

"Nothing is ever that simple," he said darkly.

"Look, all I need is to get my hands on her," De Bruyn said. "I don't even care if she's alive, just as long as I have her body."

"Why would you want her body so badly?" he asked.

"Because it contains the truth," she said. "The truth of who she is."

"I've told you once that we already know who she is," he said. "Why not just ask?"

De Bruyn didn't state the obvious: how could he know anything more than *she* did? The rumors she'd heard—and which, she was sure, comprised the bulk of the Disciples' knowledge—were wild and contradictory. Some proclaimed Roche as a savior, others as a traitor. De Bruyn lent none of them credence, just as she wouldn't waste her time listening to the views of a religious fanatic.

"Because I want to see the truth with my own eyes," she said.

The robed figure pondered this for a few moments, then asked, "And what *exactly* do we receive in turn?"

"Apart from Roche out of the way?" She leaned back into the seat and shrugged. "What do you want?"

"You say that you have access to the Interim Emergency Pristine Council."

"I have a contact—"

"Will you give us information?"

She hesitated. "What sort of information?"

"The information we require."

She waited for him to elaborate, but he said nothing more—and he obviously wasn't going to until she had agreed or disagreed. An icy silence filled the air of the bridge, and again her doubts returned.

She shook herself free of them by reminding herself why she was here. This *wasn't* a grudge-match. This was about justice. Everything she had unearthed suggested that she was doing the right thing. If she was doing this for herself, why was she going to such lengths? Any sane person would have given up weeks ago—and there could be no question of her sanity.

She was *so close* to the truth. . . .

As she waited for docking instructions to arrive from the *Apostle*, she'd used the time to scan the data Trezise had given her. A cursory glance had been all she needed. The records weren't complete, but they did fill in portions of a bigger picture. They had come from the second moon around Bodh Gaya, the former capital system of the Commonwealth of Empires, where the Armada housed its Military College. Morgan Roche had served there during her training for COE Intelligence, years ago. Trezise had managed to get his hands on various reports, assessments, essays, and test scores that demonstrated how average a student Roche had been. Only in one area had she excelled, and that had been the handling of AIs. She had preferred to grapple with artificial minds rather than those of the people around her.

Perhaps, De Bruyn thought, that might explain why she'd had so few friends. It certainly explained how she had been selected as a courier for JW111101000, the Box that had ultimately helped her escape from Sciacca's World and the clutches of the Dato Bloc. That was one AI De Bruyn was glad to see the end of.

But that information was not specifically what De Bruyn was after. The information she sought hadn't been there at all. And in some ways, the gaps were more telling. All of Roche's physical records were unavailable. Not missing or deleted: *unavailable.* When Trezise had asked why, he had been told that access to those records was restricted by special order VSD5278.

De Bruyn recognized that order number. It was department shorthand for the COE's previous Eupatrid, Enver Buk. Eupatrid Buk himself had specifically ordered those records kept secret, no matter who asked for them.

That in itself might not have been significant. Trezise had dug back a little further, not just trying to find a birth date but *any* physical record at all, prior to Roche's enrollment at Military College. Her name was recorded at an orphanage on Ascensio, but there was little else of note: no medical records, no education reports, no informal recollections. Her application scores were on file in Ascensio's COE Armada recruit database, along with the form she must have filled out to apply for the test, but the results of her medical exam were missing. Special order VSD5278 had cast a cloak over them, too, it seemed.

It had taken De Bruyn only a minute or two to confirm what she already suspected: that the details of Roche's early life were being kept secret by the government of the COE, and that this secret had been ratified by the Eupatrids past and present who had issued the special orders required to ensure that no one ever found out the truth.

What that truth was, though, she wasn't yet entirely sure. But she had suspicions. She had been chasing those suspicions, along with Roche, across Sol System and half of the COE in the hope that they might be verified. If Roche's early life was being kept secret, it was entirely possible that the details Trezise had uncovered were completely fictitious. Where had Roche come from before Military College? Out of thin air, it seemed—which made her suspiciously like the clone warriors the IEPC were trying to fight.

As soon as the idea occurred to her, De Bruyn had been caught by its ramifications. If it was true, Roche *must* have been planted by the enemy to seed chaos and disorder the way that they had in so many other systems. The fact that she had not, until recently, shown any destructive or even subversive tendencies did not necessarily invalidate this theory.

De Bruyn noted that at about the time Roche enrolled in the Military College the High Human known as the Crescend had joined the COE in a partnership designed to foster trade and joint industry between the Caste echelons. Maybe the Crescend knew about Roche and had decided to see if she could be contained rather than destroyed. Maybe he hoped to bend her to his will, or at least make her an ally rather than an enemy; that might explain why he was so keen to keep her existence a secret, to the point of penalizing those who came even close to the truth, like De Bruyn. Maybe he didn't care what happened to the COE at all, and was only interested in seeing what happened at firsthand when the time bomb called Morgan Roche finally went off.

Maybe he wasn't involved at all, and the giant shadows De Bruyn saw on the wall before her were cast by shapes much tinier. Either way, she had to be sure.

Something odd was going on, and she had been caught up in it. Now that she was close to finding proof—of *anything at all*—it was finally time to act. But she couldn't do it on her own; she was going to need powerful friends if she was to see justice served.

She needed to fight fire with fire.

"I'll give you information," she said to the man in black, "if you give me Morgan Roche."

His posture didn't change, but in the shadows that hid his face she thought she had seen him smile.

"Good," he said. "In that case, *God's Monkey* will meet with you in precisely seven hours. Its pilot and contingent of Disciples will obey your commands—unless, of course, those commands are contrary to the goals of our movement. You may use them as you will until such time as our mutual obligations have been discharged. Does that suit you?"

She swallowed with relief. "Thank you, yes," she said. "But where exactly will I meet them?"

He gave her the coordinates. "They will know you as 'Reverence,' " he said. "Use them well, Page De Bruyn."

He stood. She stood too, although her muscles felt weak. The gray-clad Disciples who had led her to the bridge stepped out of the shadows to stand by her side.

"Wait," she said to the figure in black. "You know my name?"

He turned to face her, but said nothing.

"Couldn't I at least know yours?"

"Mine is not relevant," he said.

"If you're worried that I will tell the council—"

"The thought would never cross our minds," he said, taking a step toward her. "Nor should it cross yours again."

De Bruyn swallowed. "I assure you," she said nervously, "I wouldn't tell anyone—"

"Oh, I know you won't," he interrupted her. "Not just because I tell you that should you betray us by divulging anything that has passed between us this day, we would hunt you down, Page De Bruyn, and we would kill you. Of that *you* can be certain."

He took another step forward, into the light, and smiled as she recoiled a pace in alarm.

Even with the hood up, there was no mistaking the face of Adoni Cane.

"I know," he said, "because we have a deal . . ."

12

AVS-38
955.2.12
1770

Defender-of-Harmony Vri carried the injured girl over the threshold of the airlock, ignoring the gunfire that insistently peppered the back of his combat suit. Once he had safely passed the girl to the armored figure waiting for him, he turned and fired four shots in rapid succession in the direction he had come.

There was an explosion. Immediately, the gunfire stopped.

The scutter shuddered noisily as the airlock closed with a hiss.

Vri steadied himself. The scutter lurched away from the station and weathered a battering on its way back to the *Ana Vereine*. He walked the short distance to where the girl had been strapped to a stretcher and attached to a portable autosurgeon. The shot had taken her in the shoulder, piercing her hazard suit and making a mess of the flesh beneath, then exploding messily out the back. Only the suit's small first-aid facility had kept her alive while Vri and Haid fought their way back to the scutter through near-endless waves of Fathehi custodians.

The autosurgeon's display was blinking red: the girl needed the full version on the main ship before she would begin to recover.

Vri stood. His faceplate clicked open, swinging up and back to reveal not just his face but most of his head too. Even through the light hair that covered every inch of his features, his anger was obvious.

"It was too close," he said. His voice was deep, and every word perfectly enunciated.

Haid too had shucked the helmet of his combat suit. "We were unlucky," he said, wiping sweat from his hairless black forehead with the palm of his glove. "Even when they sprang the trap, we thought Maii had it covered. But all it took was one lucky shot . . ." He looked down at the girl, rocking in her stretcher as the scutter endured another battering. "Maybe we weren't so unlucky. At least we managed to get out."

"It was too close," Vri repeated with the same, slow precision to his words.

Haid looked at him. "So you keep telling us."

"It is not *you* I am telling." His intense eyes were as golden as his armor, and focused on the back of the person piloting the scutter.

"I hear you," said Roche. She didn't need to turn to know he was referring to her. Nor did she particularly care what the Surin thought at this moment; there was too much happening to worry about that. Besides, she had been watching via the suit monitors and the Box's patch into the consulate's security channel; she knew better than either of them just how narrow their escape had been. Another ten seconds in the dock and a full squadron of custodians would have pinned them in a crossfire from which none of them would have emerged alive.

"I'm taking her back," the Surin warrior said. His firm tone conveyed more than the words themselves.

Roche did turn, at that. "You're not taking her to Erojen." Her voice was as hard as his.

"No, of course not," he said. "I meant to the *Phlegethon*."

Roche was silent for a long moment; then her expression softened slightly. "Okay," she said. "The *Phlegethon* it is. But if you don't let me fly this thing home first, we won't be going anywhere at all. . . ."

The Surin nodded, and Roche turned back to the controls. He took the seat closest to Maii's injured form.

Sensing Haid's eyes on him still, he turned to face the ex-mercenary. They stared at each other for a few seconds.

"You fight well," Vri said finally, adding: "Despite your handicap."

Haid's eyes flashed. "As do you, despite yours."

Vri frowned a question, and Haid indicated the girl.

"I do not consider my protecting this child to be a handicap," said Vri indignantly.

Haid raised one arm, indicating where an energy bolt had passed clear through his arm and out the other side.

"Nor do I consider this to be one, either," he said.

Vri pondered this for a moment, then turned away and was silent for the remainder of the trip back to the *Ana Vereine*.

Earlier, they had argued about the mission to the Fathehi Consulate.

"It is too dangerous," Vri had insisted.

"Dangerous, yes; *too* dangerous, no," Roche had shot back. "The junior consul herself has assured us that we will have free passage through the station."

"And you *believe* her?"

"Why shouldn't I?"

"After all that has happened, I find your naiveté disturbing."

Roche felt her face turn red. "We are more than capable of handling anything they might throw at us."

"We are a handful of people against an entire station!"

"Maii can—"

"Yes, she can. And she *has*. You rely on her too much. You are *using* her! You are using her as I would use a percussion rifle—to be tossed aside when its usefulness has expired."

"That's not true!" Roche was finding it difficult containing her emotions, and a blast of anger from the reave in response to Vri's accusation only enhanced her irritation. "We rely on her help, but that's *not* the same as using her."

"She is a child that is—"

"That is still capable of making up her own mind!" snapped Roche. "If you want to talk about people being used, then take a good look at yourself!"

This caught the Surin warrior by surprise, and he frowned in confusion.

"You're just a stooge of the Surin Agora," Roche went on. "They don't care about the truth, and they don't care about Maii! They just want her back so they can take her apart and see how she works. And you're helping them!"

Vri had reared back in the screen. "Be careful what you say, Morgan Roche."

"If you're threatening me," Roche spat, "I swear I'll have you shipped back to the council faster than you can say 'mindless pawn'!"

"Easy, you two," said Haid, putting a hand on Roche's shoulder. "This is getting us nowhere."

<I agree,> put in Maii herself, her emotions back under control. <I don't require either of you to argue on my behalf.>

Roche took a deep breath and looked down at her feet. Maii was right; she was as guilty as Vri of assuming that she knew what was right for the girl.

<I will go into the consulate,> Maii said. <And if you so desire, Vri, you may accompany me as my bodyguard. Would that be acceptable?>

For a moment, Roche thought Vri would argue with her, but instead he simply nodded. "It is a reasonable compromise," he said.

<Good. And Haid will go with us while Morgan stays with the scutter.>

"But—" Roche began.

<Morgan, you need a rest from the front line. Let someone else take the risks for a change.>

"She's right, Morgan," said Haid, smiling. "It's my turn to be the hero."

Roche knew he was only joking, but she couldn't help feeling slightly stung by his words. She was reluctant to lose control because she was desperate for something to go right—just once! The fact that nothing had gone right for anyone in Sol System didn't change things. She still felt like it was *her* that was somehow getting it wrong.

And Maii did have a point. She *was* tired of facing hostile envoys and suspicious security forces. This could be a good way for Vri to save some face, and to relieve the restlessness eating at Haid. Besides, she and Maii had swept for clone warriors upon their arrival and the place seemed clear. That made it safer than any of the other ports they had visited.

Or so it had seemed. Roche had become so used to looking for clone warriors that she had blinded herself to base Human treachery. When the junior consul decided that Roche had extended herself far enough into her station, she ordered her custodians to open fire—on the boarding party and on the *Ana Vereine* itself, forcing the ship to retreat to a safe distance and leaving the others to scramble for their lives through the station. Had the scutter not already docked, and had the Box not been available behind the scenes to keep the custodians at bay, the situation could have been a lot worse than it was.

Even without knowing what lay ahead, Roche had approached the mission with apprehension. Before leaving, she had gone to see Cane.

He had taken up residence in an observation blister on one of the *Ana Vereine*'s seven nacelles. The curved window allowed him an unobstructed view of the space around the ship. Not that there was much to see. The only object visible to the naked eye was the crossed rings of the Fathehi Consulate, tumbling slowly against the starry backdrop.

The Box had observed him there on numerous occasions over the previous two weeks, since the events on Perdue Habitat. When Roche didn't ask for him specifically, that was where he went. She suspected that he was avoiding her.

"Will you tell me why you're doing this?" she had asked.

At first he hadn't answered, his brown skin soaking up the light from distant stars.

"Cane?"

"I am thinking."

"What about?"

"About what it is like to be alone."

Roche had glanced at the stars, at the galaxy around them. All those systems, all those worlds, all the Humanity filling them up: High and Low, Pristine and Exotic, old and young—and almost a thousand of those Castes were now crammed into Sol System. She didn't feel alone anymore. Not at all.

And that didn't even take into account the AI sharing her body.

"Why?" she had asked.

"I killed one of my own kind," he said. He turned to face her.

"You still have us." She had attempted a smile, then regretted it. "I'm sorry. I didn't realize it was bothering you this much."

He had shaken his head and returned, expressionlessly, to watching the stars.

"Nor did I," he said quietly.

"You mightn't be the only one in this position, you know." She didn't want to take his black mood with her to the consulate; if there was anything she could do to crack his reserve, she would try it—even if it meant inviting him to join the landing party to the consulate in Haid's place. "Your siblings don't seem terribly indiscriminate. We only know of one time when they cooperated, and that was on Perdue. Maybe *that* was the exception. Maybe they kill each other as easily as ordinary Humans do."

But he hadn't responded.

Eventually, she had left him alone and gone to see Alta Ansourian. Another mistake. The woman was still grieving for her father and for all the friends destroyed with her habitat. Since coming on board she had barely emerged from the stateroom Roche had given her—not even to see what was going on when the *Ana Vereine* had come under attack.

"Do you think I'll ever get back to Vacishnou?" she had asked Roche.

"I'll do my best," Roche told her, hoping the words didn't sound as empty as they felt. The homeworld of the Vax was on the other side of the galaxy and seemed far removed from their current situation. "That's the most I can promise, I'm afraid."

"I understand." But if she truly understood, it hadn't given her any comfort. And that more than anything made Roche wonder if Alta Ansourian was wiser than she looked.

<Are you sure this is the right thing to do?> the Box asked Roche as she rested in her cabin, the disastrous sortie to the Fathehi Consulate fresh in her mind.

<What do you think?> She scratched absently at the back of her head. <Despite recent history, running away really isn't my thing.>

<You know that it's not what you will be doing.>

<No, but it feels like it,> she said. <And I don't like it.>

<That much is obvious. But ask yourself, Morgan, who you are most angry at—and why.>

She thought seriously about the question. Was she angry at Rey Nemeth for giving her a mission she couldn't finish? Or at Vri for forcing her to face the inevitable? Or at Maii for being shot?

The last was ridiculous. If anyone, she should resent the person who had shot the girl. That in itself was tempting, but not as tempting a target as the junior consul who had ordered the attack. Or the lieutenant who had turned them away from the LaGoc barracks that had been their previous port of call, as had leaders of the three previous habitats they had tried to contact. Then there were the Noske saboteurs who had planted a bomb on their usual scutter, nearly killing everyone on board; the clone warrior in the Katajalin Serai, responsible for triggering a mass riot that had torn the normally tight collection of vessels apart within a day of Roche's arrival; and finally Inderdeep Jans and her unknown enemy cohort who, together or apart, had brought about the appalling failure that had been the very first of Roche's missions for the Ulterior.

She could hate the council for not helping her, but that was pushing the boundary too far. She might as well hate the COE, or the Crescend, or the galaxy itself.

Except the Box hadn't asked about *hate*, had it? It had asked her about her anger, and once she separated the two, the answer came to her.

<I'm angry at myself,> she said in the end.

<And why is that, Morgan?> he pressed.

<Because I'm losing control, Box. I'm losing control of it all.> She paused as a dream image momentarily flashed across her thoughts. <I'm falling.>

<Morgan, you never *had* control.>

<But I had a direction! At least that was *something*.> She rolled onto her side, into a fetal position. <Now . . .>

<Now you just have momentum.>

She couldn't tell if the Box was being facetious or not. <What good will *that* do me when it comes to the crunch?>

<Perhaps a lot of good, depending on what you hit.>

<If it's the council, they're not likely to give.> Vri had been pestering her ever since they left the volume of space the Fathehi Consulate controlled, but she hadn't yet confirmed the order to return to the *Phlegethon*. <Come on, Box, what do you think? I want your honest opinion.>

<I would give you nothing less, Morgan.> The AI seemed pleased that she had asked its advice. <I think the *Phlegethon* is as good a place as any.>

<For what, though? What do I do once I get there?>

<You can see what happens. Maybe the Ulterior will not regard your mission as a failure at all. You have, after all, learned some things.>

<And got my name blacklisted from every station this side of the system.>

<That's something, too. One would have to assume that was deliberate.>

<I considered this. Why else would everything fall apart just when I arrived?> The destruction of Perdue had taken less than two days; the Katajalin Serai had dissolved in half that time. By the end of the week, no one in their right mind would let Roche on board their stations—except the Fathehi Consulate who, it turned out, had planned a trap. <It's not me doing it, so it must be someone else hoping to make it *look* like me. Unfortunately, it seems to have worked.>

<No doubt the Ulterior will guide your return to the *Phlegethon*.>

<I hadn't even thought of that! What happens if they don't let us in? What if—?>

<Morgan, you don't have to worry about that. They will let you return; you have something they do not.>

She rolled onto her back again. <Such as?>

<Two things, actually. The most obvious being the experience you have gained.>

<Half as much as their usual agents, I'm sure.>

<Possibly—but none of their agents have discovered a means of identifying the clone warriors, have they?>

She was about to protest that the talent was so vague as to be almost useless, except to sweep a large number of people to make sure they were clean. But then she stopped herself. The council didn't need to know about her talent's limitations—not initially, anyway. The very fact that her ability existed would at least guarantee her a hearing.

<So I become their test subject while people like Nemeth get all the credit,> she said cynically. <Sounds like a lot of fun, Box.>

<But at least you'll have some direction again,> the Box responded.

She thought about that for a few seconds.

<That's true,> she admitted. <And somewhere to channel that momentum.> She forced herself to let her eyelids close and her muscles relax. The last thing she wanted right now was to move *anywhere*.

<How many more stops were there on Nemeth's list?> she asked.

<Two—outposts run by the Saa-hurod and Yemena Castes.>

Neither of the names rang a bell. <Does either look likely to tell us anything new?>

<Impossible to say, from here.>

<Does Nemeth highlight either as being especially important?>

<No.>

<Then we can safely ignore them, I think. And without Maii to help me sweep for clone warriors, I wouldn't feel comfortable in approaching them.>

<Her prognosis is good, Morgan. She will be conscious within twenty hours.>

<That's not the point,> Roche said, recalling the accusation leveled at her by Vri about using the Surin girl. <I don't want to push her unnecessarily. She needs rest.>

Roche was silent for a while, on the verge of making the decision but still balking. It would only take a call to Kajic to put them on their way. She wanted to make absolutely certain—as certain as she could be, anyway—that she was doing the right thing.

<Have you heard from the Crescend?> she asked.

<If you are asking me whether he would approve of your return to the *Phlegethon*, I can tell you that he would.>

She hadn't dared ask the question so blatantly, so to hear the reply threw her off balance for a moment. She didn't want to push her luck by asking *why* he approved.

<He's told you that?>

<Yes.>

<When?>

<While we were just talking.>

The ramifications of that information were profound. <So you and he are communicating by ftl, like the council does?> she said. <Why didn't you tell me?>

<It didn't seem necessary. Should I have?>

<Well, no. It doesn't make that much difference, I guess. I just assumed . . .> She wondered how much else she had assumed about the Box's relationship with the Crescend that would one day turn out to be wrong. That was the problem in dealing with the AI: without asking exactly the right question, she couldn't be entirely sure she was learning what she needed to know.

And yet it had offered the Crescend's advice on the matter of the *Phlegethon*. That was out of character. Either it had a hidden agenda—which was all too possible—or the High Human had finally decided to become involved.

She wasn't sure if the latter would be a good thing or not.

Yawning, she rolled back onto her stomach. <Box, open a line to Vri's ship. Audio only.>

The AI did as it was told, making sure to maintain the illusion that Roche herself had placed the call. When Vri responded, she said:

"Vri, it's Roche." The Surin didn't respond, so she kept talking. "I need to ask you something. About Maii."

"Which is?"

"Do you know the name of Maii's mother? Or even her family name?"

There was a pause. "No. Why?"

"Would the Agora know?" she said, ignoring his question.

"I would assume so."

"And would you think it unreasonable of me to ask for that information before I even consider handing Maii over?"

He paused again, then answered, "No, not at all."

"Good, because that's as far as I'm prepared to compromise at the moment. Unless you can convince me that the Agora knows what it's doing—and is doing it for the right reasons—then you will never complete your mission. If, however, you *can* convince me, then your chances of convincing Maii will improve. Ultimately, *she* is the one you have to deal with. Unless she agrees, you'll go home empty-handed."

There was a third pause as he seemed to consider this. "I understand," he said finally.

"*Do* you, Vri?"

"I am not stupid, Roche. There is a bond between you and the child; that is indisputable. I may question the nature of the bond on your side in the same way that you question the sincerity of my superiors—but, as you have pointed out, neither of us can do anything without Maii's consent. We are not monsters, you and I."

Remembering the concern with which he had brought the injured girl back to the scutter, Roche could only agree.

"Then let's leave it at that," she said. "We'll go back to the *Phlegethon*. She'll be safer there. You can contact the Agora, or their representatives in the system, and we'll talk about it. Openly, and *with* Maii. She'll be conscious by the time we get back, and she'll be able to tell if anyone's lying. When we've all talked it through, she can decide what she wants to do, and we'll abide by her decision. Can we agree on that?"

"We can." Through his gruff reticence, she sensed a certain satisfaction. "I will contact my superiors as soon as we arrive and advise them of our decision."

"Good." She went to close the line, but stopped at the last second. "And Vri? Thanks for everything you did for her today. You saved her life over there."

"Your thanks are not necessary. I was doing my duty."

"I know that," she said. "But to you, duty is everything, isn't it?"

He didn't reply. A second later, the line closed.

Roche smiled to herself. <Box? Get me Uri. I want us under way as soon as possible. And draft a report for Rey Nemeth describing what happened with the Fathehi.>

<What else would you like me to tell him?>

<Just that. Let him assume we're going on to the Yemena Caste. I think I'd like to surprise him by turning up unannounced.>

<Yes, Morgan.>

<And . . .>

<Yes, Morgan?>

<The next time the Crescend thinks I should do something, ask him to tell me himself. I think it's about time we dispensed with the go-between.>

<I hope you mean that metaphorically, Morgan.>

She smiled again as she closed her eyes. <Of course, Box,> she said. <Of course.>

13

SHCV *Phlegethon*
955.2.13
1975

The conference room was conical in shape, its walls tapering smoothly up from the circular floor to a point far above, from which shone a single, bright light. A round table filled most of the floor space, cut, like the walls, from heavy gray stone. Apart from the table, the light, eight chairs, and a single door, the room was featureless. Roche had been assured that it was completely secure: no information could get in or out by any means, including epsense, without the knowledge of the room's inhabitants.

"We hardly expected you back so soon," said Esko Murnane. Roche had been surprised to see him at the meeting of the Ulterior, but not as surprised, it seemed, as Rey Nemeth, whose customary charm—superficial though it might have been—was still clouded by a scowl. There were four others at the table Roche hadn't been introduced to.

"I thought it best to return, for a number of reasons," she said, feeling extremely uncomfortable. Even though she was dressed in full combat armor and armed to the point where even the hospitable Skehan Heterodox had thought twice about letting her aboard their ship, she still felt vulnerable. "There's something you need to know."

"Is it related to your mission?"

"Perhaps indirectly," she said. "I might not have found out about it if I hadn't gone."

"I have her reports," said Nemeth, attempting to reclaim some power in the assembly.

"I'll read them later," said Murnane dismissively.

"You won't find anything in the reports about this," Roche said. "It's not information I'd like to go public with just yet."

"What is it, then?"

She glanced at Haid, who had accompanied her this trip. Maii was still in the *Ana Vereine*'s medical center, conscious but weak. Haid caught her look and shrugged.

"You have a problem," she said slowly. "There are five of the enemy on board the *Phlegethon*."

Startled mutterings broke out among those gathered, but it was Nemeth's voice which rose above them all: "Are you sure?"

"I have no doubts whatsoever," she said. "In fact, there may be even more. You have too large a crew to scan all of them effectively and quickly. But I can tell you that three are amidships, one is down in the crypt and the other is up near the minaret."

"*Where* exactly?" pressed Nemeth.

"I can't tell," she said with a slight shrug. "I just know they're there."

The mutterings continued among the other members of the Ulterior. Except for Murnane, who hardly reacted at all.

"How could you possibly know this?" he asked calmly.

"It's hard to explain," said Roche.

"Nevertheless," said Murnane smoothly, "you're going to have to try. We have no intention of taking you at your word."

"I understand that."

"Is there *any* way to get a precise fix on them?" said Nemeth.

"Only by looking for them in person," she said. "By coming face to face with them."

"At grave personal risk, no doubt," said Murnane, leaning back in his seat.

She met and held Murnane's icy blue eyes. "Yes," she said.

"Do you expect the council to sanction such an undertaking?" There was a hint of a smile at the corners of his mouth.

"She hasn't come to the council," said Nemeth.

"The person I *should* speak to is the Heresiarch," Roche said. "It's his ship, after all."

Murnane dismissed this with a wave of his hand. "How long have you known?"

"Little more than an hour. We swept the ship on the way in to dock."

"And how do you know that one of *us* isn't a clone warrior?" asked a woman to Roche's left.

"I checked before you sealed the room." Although Maii was on the *Ana Vereine* and physically resting, her mind was still strong. The n-space link was harder to maintain over a distance, but still viable.

"That's not to say, of course, that one of us couldn't be in league with them," said Murnane, glancing around the table. "The Ulterior is an organization designed for covert dealings, after all." Then, returning to Roche, he said: "Perhaps it's time you told us exactly how you came by this knowledge."

She agreed and proceeded to describe how her chance link with Maii had brought to their attention Roche's ability to detect the minds of the enemy in the way they distorted the fabric of n-space. She still couldn't explain what those distortions meant or why it seemed she alone possessed this ability, and was as open about this as she was about her inability to pin down a clone warrior's precise location.

"Despite this limitation," interrupted someone from the end of the table, "you are certain you *can* identify them?"

Roche nodded. "It enabled me to identify Inderdeep Jans as one of the two clone warriors on Perdue Habitat," she said. "And of the seven locations we visited, I was able to scan them prior to boarding and determine which of the locations had been compromised by the enemy and which of them had not been."

"How many hadn't been?"

"Just one."

This provoked another round of muttering, until Murnane broke in.

"Would it be possible to replicate this procedure with another reave?" he asked.

"I don't know," she admitted. "But I'm willing to try."

"Good." He nodded. "We've been looking for a way to use epsense to reveal the enemy. This might just be it."

<You are taking a risk doing this,> said the Box into her mind.

<Less of a risk than a full probe.> Then, heading off an argument, she said: <It's a risk we have to take, Box.>

The conference room was unsealed for a moment, to summon one of the high-grade reaves warding the room—one of the many Maii had observed in the fane during their first visit. She was a short Pristine woman dressed in white robes and a ceremonial headdress wrapped about her eyes, ears and mouth.

<You are allied to the Surin Abomination,> she said to Roche. It wasn't a question.

Roche colored slightly. Answering in kind, via epsense, she said: <The Olmahoi have permitted her existence.>

<They *suffer* her existence,> the woman said, taking a seat vacated by one of the Ulterior. <I am Stryki of Taborca. You are shielded. I cannot help if you will not open yourself to me.>

Roche felt the faintest suggestion of Maii at the back of her mind; before Roche had left the *Ana Vereine*, the reave had installed a shield guarding the knowledge that the Box had survived Palasian System. She forced herself to think of something else.

The woman entered her mind like a sheet of silk sliding into water. There was no sensation of invasion or penetration; she was suddenly *there*, among Roche's thoughts, as though she always had been.

<How does the Abomination access n-space?> the woman asked. <Like this?>

Roche felt her mind swept up by the woman's and tugged into another place—a place where there were no walls, no boundaries, just the faintest suggestion of lines all around them, some intersecting, others stretching out to infinity. Where they met, they glowed white.

<No,> Roche said. <It wasn't like that.>

<This, then?>

Roche was suddenly pulled in a thousand directions at once—as though her skin had been plucked by fishhooks and stretched like the fabric of a balloon to the breaking point—

<No!> she managed.

The reave made no apology for the obvious discomfort she had caused, but the sensation vanished and Roche found herself floating over the familiar gray field of n-space.

<That's it,> she said, unable to keep the relief from her voice.

<Ah,> said the reave. <A simple two-dimensional Nyberg representation. I should have anticipated something unsophisticated like this. It's often the way with the self-taught.>

Ignoring Stryki's disdain, Roche forced herself to look around with the woman.

<What do you see?>

She described the congregation of shielded bumps that she guessed was the meeting. A steep ridge surrounded the gathering—the shield, she presumed, that kept outside observers at bay.

<Can you see yourself?>

<Not clearly, no.>

<And me? Can you see me?>

<The same. You're indistinct, kind of fuzzy around the edges.>

<That's because our minds are linked,> explained the reave. <Were we to disconnect and you to look at the view on your own, or with the help of another mind, I would spring back into focus.>

<Can you look at yourself?>

<Of course,> Stryki said. <All reaves are taught to do this before they learn to examine another's mind. But we do not see ourselves as you would see us.> The woman paused. <Your mind has an unusual flavor, Roche. One I have not tasted before.>

Roche recalled what Maii had said about the *irikeii* calling her an "enigma." The possibility that it might be Maii's block confusing the issue didn't occur to her until the reave went on:

<I can sense the Abomination's hand in your mind. You are aware of this?>

<Yes.> Wary that the reave might penetrate the block, she automatically withdrew.

<I would not violate your privacy,> the reave assured her. <I am not here to probe you, and I would not do so without your permission. That would not be ethical.>

Although leery of the woman's intent—and tired of her incessant insinuations regarding Maii—Roche did allow her back into her mind. She had little choice but to trust the reave if she was to get anywhere.

<Okay,> said Roche. The woman's gaze began to wander, through a short-lived gap in the barrier around the meeting and out into the *Phlegethon*.

<Do you know where we are?>

<No.> Within seconds, Roche had become completely lost. <Do you?>

<More or less. Fixing spatial coordinates to n-space equivalents is one of the hardest things a reave must learn to do,> the woman explained. <It is only complicated when the real-space environment is unfamiliar or inconstant. Fortunately, I am both trained and familiar with this environment.>

<So pinpointing the clones shouldn't be too difficult, then?>

<Theoretically.>

Roche allowed Stryki to whisk her through the concatenated minds of the crew of the *Phlegethon* for a minute or two before asking: <Have you studied clone warriors before?>

The reave hesitated a second. <No, but I do have a great deal of experience with Exotic and near-Transcendent Humanity.>

Roche would have been interested to hear more about the latter. She was, however, forced to concentrate on the task before her. The sea of thoughts was rushing by much faster than it had with Maii. It was all she could do to keep up.

Then she saw it: a dip representing a clone warrior.

<Stop! Go back!>

The reave retraced the way they had come, more slowly. Now Roche could tell that the concentration of people was less dense than it had been before.

<Where are we?> she asked.

<Find the one you are looking for, and I will tell you.>

Roche swept invisibly among the crew of the *Phlegethon* until the dip reappeared.

<There. No, there! Can you see it?>

<I see nothing out of the ordinary.>

<Look at that group of five minds,> Roche said. <The bottom right-hand individual—that's the one!>

<Are you sure?>

<I'm positive,> said Roche.

The reave was silent for a moment. <I can't read the person you have identified. That in itself is not unusual, but it does lend some credence to your story. Other reaves have reported difficulty reading the enemy's minds. They seem to be totally impenetrable, if they so desire. They may, at times, allow a reave to access sensory data, but little else. . . . > She paused again. <The people speaking to the person you have indicated know her as Advocate Janil Coriett. They are in compartment 43 on Deck 25B of the minaret.>

The view of n-space disappeared and Roche found herself back in the meeting, facing the hooded reave.

"Are you okay?" asked Haid, his hand resting on her armored shoulder.

She blinked and looked around, dazed. "Fine, I think." She turned to Murnane. "We found one."

"So I am hearing." The councilor listened to the reave's mental voice a moment longer.

"We need to handle this very delicately," said Nemeth, leaning forward.

"Obviously," said Murnane. "What do we know about this person?"

"Advocate Coriett has been with us for six months," said the woman who had spoken before. Her eyes were out of focus; she was obviously studying information through her implants. "She came from Ceyle's Hub and, as well as taking a position in Environment Control, helped us negotiate a settlement with the H'si F'ta."

"The Hub was destroyed not long before she arrived here," said Nemeth. "The H'si F'ta didn't last much longer before they were decimated by a rival Caste. The settlement encouraged them to drop their defenses." He shrugged. "At the time, we thought it was just a bad call."

"That makes her a prime candidate, then," said Roche. She faced Murnane. "Do you believe me now?"

Murnane turned from Roche to the others. "Until we have definitive proof—" he began.

"What sort of proof do you need?" said Roche sharply. "Her body on a slab?"

Murnane ignored her.

"We'll *have* to move in," said Nemeth.

"No," said Murnane firmly. "That would only alert the others, and that could be disastrous. If one can bring down a civilization, imagine what *four* could do to this ship!"

"Then perhaps we should we tell the Heresiarch," Roche said.

"I disagree," said Nemeth. "The fewer who know about this the better—at least until we've dealt with the situation."

"And how do you propose we do that?" asked Roche.

"Well, first, you're going to have to find the others," said Murnane. "We can keep track of Coriett. Once we have all five, *then* we can act."

"And I repeat, *how* do you propose to do this?"

Murnane glanced away for a second, then returned. This time, the fear in his eyes was obvious. Roche didn't need to be a reave to know what he was thinking. It was all very well to contemplate a nebulous, almost unreal enemy, but to actually come directly in contact with them was another matter altogether. . . .

"We'll deal with that when the time comes," he said. But the uncertainty in his tone did not inspire confidence.

It wasn't difficult to find the other four, but it was time-consuming. By the time Roche had helped the reave pinpoint the location of each of the five clone warriors on the *Phlegethon*, she felt weary right down to her bones. Her brain ached in ways she had never imagined before. When she was released from n-space for the final time, she sagged back into her chair with a groan, and only Haid's hands under her armpits stopped her from slipping to the floor.

With a whine of servo-assisted joints, he helped her upright.

"Morgan, this is crazy."

"No, it's done now." She turned to Nemeth for confirmation.

He nodded. "We have the identity of the fifth. He's a fusion technician, of all things."

"In a prime location to sabotage the power core," said Murnane. "Roche, if you're right about these people, you have undoubtedly saved the lives of everyone on this ship."

"They're not safe yet," said Roche.

"Quite," said Nemeth. "I suggest we move on all five simultaneously—send multiple containment teams to pin them down; then, if they resist—or if there's even the slightest chance they'll get away—neutralize them permanently."

Murnane nodded slowly. "That at least gives them a chance to prove their innocence," he said. "A blood test would be enough to reveal the truth."

"They've obviously managed to avoid blood tests before now," objected Nemeth.

"And if they do come quietly and are guilty?" Roche asked. "What then?"

Nemeth glanced at Murnane. "Execution."

"No," said the older man. "We're not barbarians."

"They would kill *us* out of hand!"

"But we are not like them, Nemeth," said Murnane severely. "And I have no desire to become like them, either. There *must* be some way to subdue them."

Roche described the crystalline cocoon Linegar Rufo had used to neutralize Adoni Cane. "He was in a coma," she said. "There was no way he could escape."

"We could easily implement something like that," said Murnane thoughtfully. "Later, higher authorities could decide what to do with them."

Nemeth still didn't look happy, but dropped the argument. "What happens after this?" he said. "Can we replicate these results? Can we use this process to keep the *Phlegethon* clean?"

He was addressing the white-robed reave, whose posture stiffened as she replied.

<I do not understand how Morgan Roche is able to identify these individuals—assuming they are what she says they are. To me, they stand out from a crowd no more than anyone else. In the same way that mandatory blood tests have not isolated them, detailed scans of the crew might not turn up more of those we seek. We need more people with Roche's ability.>

"And to find them," interrupted Nemeth, "we need to know *how* she is doing it in the first place. We're back where we started."

"Not quite," said Murnane. "We have a test. Bring in those five, or attempt to. Once we have ascertained whether or not we're on the right track, *then* we can work out what to do next." He turned to the other members at the meeting. "I want those containment teams in place in half an hour. Prepare for any contingency, no matter how unlikely. Advise the Heresiarch by epsense that an exercise is about to take place, but that he is under no circumstances to alert the crew. Everything proceeds as usual until the operation commences. No one leaves here until it is concluded. Is that understood?"

There was a chorus of assent. Nemeth offered his last of all, still clearly displeased at the way Murnane had taken over his operation.

"Can I talk to my crew?" Roche asked.

"A brief message relayed via epsense only," Murnane conceded. "When everything is concluded here, you may converse freely."

Roche and the reave put together a short message for Maii explaining that they would continue to be incommunicado for an hour or so. After that, they would know if it was safe to bring Maii aboard the *Phlegethon*, as Vri insisted they do. Should they receive any unusual communications from the *Phlegethon* at all, Kajic was to move to a safe distance and wait for news.

The reave sent the message and, a moment later, confirmed that it had been received.

As they waited, the mood around the conference table became increasingly restless. How arrangements were being made, Roche couldn't tell exactly, but she noted the far-off expressions of those using implants. She worried that word might somehow get to the clone warriors, warning them of what was to happen, but as she could see no way to organize things without taking that risk, she said nothing.

Haid tapped her on the shoulder and indicated for her to close her faceplate. Roche nodded, and instructed her suit to seal. The people around the table looked up as her visor and Haid's hissed shut, but when she and Haid made no other move they returned to their work.

"What do you think?" asked Haid over the private link between their suits. "Is this actually going to work?"

"It had better," she replied. "Because if it doesn't, we're really in trouble. If we can't fight them individually, even when we know who they are, then there's no point even trying. We either give up, or we advocate extreme solutions like completely destroying habitats and stations that we know have been infiltrated. And even then, we could never be certain that we've wiped out the last of them. There could always be one capsule left in deep space, or one survivor hiding out in the Far Reaches. And where there's one . . ."

Haid grunted. "No one's mentioned the alternative to killing them."

"Which is?"

"Conversion."

"Like Cane?"

"Maybe."

She frowned. "It would be hard to trust them after what they've done—or what their kind has done."

"I know. But not impossible, surely?"

She shrugged the suit's heavy shoulders, thinking of Cane and her own uncertainty. "Only time will tell, I guess."

"Speaking of trust," Haid went on: "Why's Murnane being so chummy all of a sudden? You were definitely persona non grata last time you two met."

"I don't know. Maybe something's happened to change his mind. I'm sure he doesn't trust me too far. At the most, I'd say he's decided I'm useful."

Roche examined the councilor while she talked. His face seemed more deeply lined than ever, and the faint wisp of hair at the back of his skull had faded almost to invisibility. He looked older, more tired, and less inclined than ever to tolerate fools.

"How desperate do you think he is?" Haid asked.

Very, she thought, but said nothing. After a moment, she unsealed her suit and leaned back into her chair with her eyes shut, thinking.

They waited another twenty-five minutes. Then, finally, everything was ready. Security in the conference room was eased slightly to allow data to flow in and out as the five containment teams moved into position. The teams, consisting of fifteen security officers each, had strict instructions to use lethal force at the slightest sign of resistance. Protecting the lives of bystanders was considered a lesser priority than ensuring the death or capture of the targets.

Roche watched via her implants as the containment teams closed around the areas where the clone warriors were situated. It was a complicated display, showing all five teams simultaneously. There was no way she could follow all of them at once, so she focused on the team advancing on Coriett.

The woman was in one of the uppermost levels of the giant ship, sitting in a room with four other people. To all appearances she seemed an ordinary Pristine dressed in a plain shipsuit, discussing the day's activities with colleagues. They chatted amiably, laughing now and then, and sipping occasionally from their mugs. It all seemed so innocuous to Roche, which paradoxically lent the scene a sinister air—because she *knew* what this woman was truly capable of.

"Pull out two of those people," she heard Murnane say.

"Why not pull them all out?" said Nemeth. "It would make it easier to deal with her."

"Because we risk arousing her suspicions," said Murnane.

Through her implants as well as the ship's internal intercom system, Roche heard the names of two of the people being summoned. They exited the room a minute or so later with smiles and polite bows of the head, leaving just Coriett and the two others behind.

A joke was made by one of the remaining colleagues; Coriett smiled politely and sipped from her cup. As she did so, she glanced up at the room's monitor.

Roche went cold: for the second it lasted it seemed as though the clone warrior was looking directly at her.

"She suspects something," she said. "I'm sure of it."

"What?" It was Nemeth. "That's impossible . . ."

"Move your team in now," insisted Roche.

The security guards entered the room just as Coriett made to stand. All three guards took position around the woman, leveling their weapons carefully at her. The two other people present in the room leapt up from their seats in alarm, spilling their drinks.

"Advocate Janil Coriett," said one of the guards loudly, firmly, "by order of the Interim Emergency Pristine Council, I am placing you under arrest. Please put your hands together behind your head and step away from the desk."

"What is the meaning of this?" said one of the other women angrily. "This is an outrage!"

Instead of answering, one of the guards indicated that she should step away from Coriett, out of the line of fire. With a weapon leveled directly at her, the woman's indignant protest became alarm.

Coriett, meanwhile, had responded to the orders, but not before coolly appraising the three guards.

"Don't I at least deserve some sort of explanation?" she asked.

The guard didn't respond, and her two companions were ushered from the room by one of the other guards. When the room was cleared, another guard produced a set of handcuffs and approached the clone warrior.

"Surely I have rights?" she said, holding her hands to be cuffed. But it wasn't to the guards she was speaking. She was looking again at the monitor. Even from this safe distance, Roche couldn't help but feel unnerved by the woman's unflinching confidence.

At the same moment, the sound of secondhand gunfire came from inside Haid's helmet. Clearly, one of the other missions wasn't going as well as this one. Roche was about to switch viewpoints when a subtle change in Coriett's expression caught her eye. It was as though she too had somehow heard the gunfire, and knew what it meant: that one of her siblings was in danger—and that this was therefore much more than an administrative error or a mere suspicion she could talk her way out of.

Coriett pulled back from the cuffs and elbowed the guard in the face. As he went down, she grabbed him by one arm and swung him in front of her. The two other guards in the room contemplated shooting through him to get to her, but in the second they hesitated, the warrior had found the stock of the rifle and brought the weapon up firing.

The rifle was set on rapid repeat; all she had to do was swing the barrel to cut down the guards and the two other people in the room. One of them was half out the door when the shots took him in the back, throwing him forward into the hall with enough force to disrupt the formation of guards waiting there. Coriett followed a second later, capitalizing on the surprise. Roche watched with mounting alarm as the guards recoiled in confusion, only a few of them managing to get off even a single shot before Coriett targeted them herself.

Her shots never missed.

But killing the guards wasn't her main priority. Escape was more important, and there would always be more guards if she stayed in one spot too long. Roche could only watch anxiously as the warrior paused to evaluate her position: she was in the middle of a long corridor with an open elevator at one end and a junction at the other. If she could reach the elevator, she could go anywhere on the ship. Security would be hard pressed to catch her. And once she had slipped through the net, she would have the entire ship to hide in.

Roche wanted to cry a warning to the remaining guards as Coriett strafed them with one wild wave of her gun, then sprinted for the elevator. Behind her, amid the tangle of wounded and dead, only one guard had the forethought to guess what she was doing. He pushed a limp body aside, raised his rifle, and fired.

At first, Roche thought the woman wasn't going to stop. Round after round struck her in the back, propelling her onward through a mist of blood. She was still running even when she hit the back wall of the elevator cab, her speed unchecked. With a sound like the crack of bone, she rebounded and fell to the ground.

As she fell, her hand struck the access panel on the inside of the cab, and the doors slid shut.

Roche quickly changed her view to the inside of the cab. Surely there was no way Coriett could have survived so many shots at such close range. Hitting the switch *must* have been an accident.

The cab slid silently away from the carnage, taking the immobile and bloody body of Coriett with it. The gun was on the floor where she had dropped it, a crimson puddle quickly pooling around the barrel.

A map in the side of the channel tracked the cab as it traveled out toward the hull of the ship and down to the docks. Another team was being sent to meet the cab at its destination.

Roche watched. Coriett didn't move.

Satisfied that the clone warrior wasn't going anywhere, Roche skipped to the other channels. Only one was still active. Another clone warrior—a male with close-cropped red hair, the fusion technician—had managed to get his hands on a weapon and taken a hostage to use as a shield. His containment team had hesitated long enough to allow the clone warrior to regain the initiative. He shot five, and the hostage, while they were making up their minds, then slipped away before they could regroup.

The point of view of the channel followed him easily, however—jumping crazily from camera to camera as he ran headlong through what looked like a cargo section of the ship. Guards converged on the area from all directions; blast doors slammed shut in his path. But he seemed to know what he was doing. The area was riddled with accessways and maintenance shafts. Where he couldn't run, he crawled; where he couldn't climb, he jumped. Roche didn't know the big ship well enough to guess where he was headed, but she didn't doubt he had *somewhere* in mind.

In the end, though, his luck ran out, and a stuck hatch forced him into another team's path. When he realized his mistake, he tried to double back on his pursuers and take them by surprise. They realized just in time, and the concentrated fire from three security guards finally brought him down.

Roche took a deep breath. That made four confirmed kills. As Coriett's cab came to a halt, she felt sure that it would soon be five.

The team were ready for anything as the doors slid open. From the viewpoint of one of the guards, Roche watched as they inched forward, weapons at the ready, until they were within meters of the woman.

She didn't move.

One guard reached gingerly forward to slide the still-smoking gun out of arm's reach.

Still she didn't move.

More confidently, another approached to test for vital signs while the others kept their weapons trained on her. If she was conscious, or even alive at all, she gave no indication as his fingers sought for a pulse in her throat.

The diagnosis wasn't one Roche expected to hear.

"She's alive," the guard called.

The containment team had begun to relax in the face of her lack of response. Now they tightened formation again and began to inch away nervously.

"What do we do with her?" said one of the team anxiously.

"Restrain her," came the response. "Bring her in for examination and interrogation if you can. But shoot her if she so much as moves. Whatever you do, *don't* let her get away from you. If she—"

A siren began wailing through the ship. Distracted from the view through her implants, Roche looked up. Murnane's eyes were flickering rapidly, intent on an internal feed.

"What's happening?" she asked.

"Overheated life-support module," said Nemeth.

The siren grew louder and more strident.

"Is that all?" she said.

He stared at her. "You still haven't grasped how big this ship is, have you? Each of those modules is bigger than a small moon, and there are *five* of them. If one blows, it could start a chain reaction through the ducts that'll tear the whole place apart."

"What's causing it?"

"The Heresiarch is trying to find out. Something is interfering with the module's normal operation. A virus of some sort, perhaps, triggered from the outside."

"Sabotage?"

"Could be. We don't know yet. But it's going to blow in thirty seconds if we can't get control of it, so hope for both of us someone works out quickly what the hell is going on."

Roche's attention was drawn back to the channel in which Coriett was being dragged out of the cab. The woman was limp, unprotesting, to all appearances completely unconscious. And as she watched, a sudden realization brought with it a sense of terrible panic.

"Tell your team to shoot her!"

Nemeth's eyebrows shot up. "*What*?"

"It's *her*!" Roche found herself shouting. "*She's* doing it."

"Don't be ridiculous," said Nemeth, but the uncertainty was evident in his tone.

"Didn't someone say she worked for Environment Control? She would have been in a perfect position to set something like this up. If she has implants, and if she's faking unconsciousness . . ."

Roche didn't need to go any further. The alarm blossoming in Nemeth's eyes matched her own.

He turned away to rattle off orders to the containment team and to the councilors around him. The siren wailed on as the guards readying Coriett for mechanical restraint looked up at their superior and listened to the new orders coming through their armor's communication links. They let go of her and backed away.

But even as they did this, Roche felt it was too late.

The warrior's eyes snapped open, and in an instant she had rolled toward the nearest guard and grabbed him by the legs, blood squirting from her injured back in a high-pressure jet. Confused, surprised, frightened, the guard didn't have time to react, and fell heavily to the floor. His head hit the ground with a sickening thud.

Coriett seized the fallen guard's rifle and raised herself up on one knee, leveling it effortlessly at the others. But three members of the containment team had managed to raise their own weapons first and had already targeted the injured woman.

A volley of shots flung the clone warrior back into the cab, and they kept firing until her body stopped moving altogether . . .

Nemeth acknowledged the woman's death only in passing. He didn't relax until word came that the interference with the life-support module had ceased. Its operations were being normalized, and the threat to ship integrity would soon pass. He sagged visibly as the siren decreased in volume and then fell silent.

"That's it," he said. "I think we can call this operation a success."

"Bring her body," said Murnane. Outwardly he seemed unaffected by the events. "I want *all* of the bodies in for postmortem examination. Then we'll know for certain."

"We already know," said Nemeth.

"We can take nothing for granted," said Murnane evenly.

"How could you even doubt it? Look at them! They ran and they fought—they fought even when there was no chance they could win! If they weren't the enemy, then what were they?"

Roche looked, and knew what he was feeling. Five of the clone warriors lay dead on the *Phlegethon*'s decks—killed by the Pristine Humans they impersonated. *That* was progress.

"Now we're getting somewhere!" Nemeth gloated.

But as the surviving security guards picked themselves up and saw to their injured colleagues, and as the casualty reports came in listing thirty dead guards and fifteen dead civilians, Murnane's face grew grim.

"At what cost?" he asked, perhaps of himself.

Roche looked down at her trembling hands and wondered the same thing.

14

SHCV *Phlegethon*
955.2.14
0560

Within the hour, chaos had erupted all around the system. Border skirmishes broke out and became firefights; grudges became battles; enemies forgot diplomacy, along with the greater good, and exchanged open, sometimes devastating attacks. Within three hours, virtually every Caste present in Sol System was engaged in some form of dispute.

"I don't understand." Nemeth watched the screens with a growing confusion. Perhaps, Roche thought, he was watching his newfound position of dominance in the council dissolving before his eyes. She hoped he had more Humanity than that; she herself saw nothing but lives wasted, nothing but more death and destruction—with the potential for it to become worse than anything she had witnessed in Palasian System. Worse, even, than anything she had ever imagined.

"I don't *understand*!" Nemeth said again, hitting a console with the palm of one hand. Roche could appreciate his frustration, but his anger was serving no purpose. A feeling obviously shared with the Heresiarch, who turned to Nemeth and said:

"If *you* don't understand, then who does?"

The question was clearly rhetorical, for the Heresiarch didn't wait to hear what Nemeth would say next. Instead he returned to the business of running the ship, turning his attention to the influx of data coming at him from all the monitors about the room.

He was standing in the center of the small room adjoining the fane to which Roche and Haid had been moved following the Ulterior's apparent success with the five clone warriors. The room was fifteen meters across, at most, with glowing blue walls that looked as though they had been fashioned from crystal. Set into the walls and floor, and even the ceiling, were consoles and stations for dozens of crew members. The air was full of whispered instructions, burbling data, and an impression that everything was running perfectly to order. Busy yet not chaotic, the adytum hummed to its own driving rhythm.

In this space, the Heresiarch did the real work involved with the running of the *Phlegethon*, rather than the ceremonial. Roche knew that being permitted here, among the highest officers and critical decision-makers, watching the information pouring in live from tens of thousands of ftl drones, was something of a privilege. Also a high honor, if Nemeth's expression upon arriving was anything to go by.

"We killed those five easily enough," persisted Nemeth, turning now to Murnane with his concerns. "They had no chance to warn the others. All this . . ." He gestured at the mess on the screens. "It *has* to be a coincidence." He searched the room now, looking for support but finding none. "It's always been at flashpoint," he insisted. "The whole system was unstable from the moment we arrived—and it's been getting worse every day! There have been skirmishes, conflicts, even small wars, before. This is just more of the same. Only worse."

"Much worse," the Heresiarch said dryly, leaning against the steel rail surrounding his station. He seemed to be completely hairless; his eyes were a deep brown, like his skin.

"It's a chain reaction, that's what it is." Nemeth began pacing and gesticulating agitatedly. "Civilization A attacks civilization B, who calls in C as an ally. That would be fine, except D has been waiting for the chance to move on C and ropes in E and F to stack the odds. G is caught in the crossfire, and H and I come to its rescue. And so on. Perfectly sane and comprehensible." His words trailed off as he stopped and looked up at the screens. "What we did has nothing to do with this," he finished more calmly. "It *can't* have."

"I fear it did," said Murnane.

The elder councilor didn't waste energy posturing as he talked. He simply stood, composed, on the other side of the Heresiarch. "The timing is too precise. Every new conflict was initiated within moments of the deaths of those five. Medical tests confirm that they were the enemy, so their exposure and attempted capture *have* to be connected. The others, the rest of them"—his eyes flickered for a second to the screens—"the ones that are still alive are fighting now because they know that we have learned how to find them. They feel vulnerable—perhaps even afraid. We were able to kill those five because we managed to take them by surprise; the others are not going to allow the same thing to happen again."

"But *how* did they know?" Nemeth's frustration was palpable.

Murnane shrugged. "I'm not sure," he said. "But the information *must* have been transmitted by either an epsense or hyperspace signal. There's no other way it could've spread so quickly."

Roche remembered the black speck at the heart of Cane and Jelena Heidik's minds, as viewed by the *irikeii*, and the look on Janil Coriett's face as firing broke out on the far side of the *Phlegethon*.

"It was epsense," she said.

Nemeth rounded on her. "How can you know that? None of our reaves have ever detected anything."

"Neither have we," she said. "But look at the recordings: Coriett suspected she'd been discovered, but she didn't know for sure until someone opened fire on one of the others. She wasn't anywhere near any sort of hyperspace communicator; there's no way we know of to hide one inside a Human body—and we would've found it if one had been there. So it must have been epsense."

"That's not proof," Nemeth said.

"It's all we have to go on," said Murnane. "We need to recall our field agents and warn anyone who might not have realized what's going on. Without extensive ftl communications or epsense on *our* side, word might take time to spread that the disturbances aren't local. We have to save as many people as we can, starting with our own."

"And then what?" Nemeth asked.

"Then we wait and see what happens." The elderly councilor suddenly looked very tired. "This might blow over; it might just be a warning. We might receive some sort of communication, at last. Who knows? If they are that concerned that we have the ability to find them now, we might even be able to negotiate a settlement."

"What *have* we got to negotiate with?" The short bleat of a laugh from Nemeth was cynical and derisive. "If we don't find someone else who can do this, it'll take us months to sweep the entire system. Maybe forever, if Roche is killed!"

"The enemy doesn't *know* that!"

"How long do you think it'll take them to figure it out?" said Nemeth. "They're not stupid, you know."

"Exactly—they're not. They know they can't afford to take too many chances while they're so outnumbered."

"But what if they can?" continued Nemeth. "What if they *don't* negotiate?"

Murnane shrugged. "Then we save what we can," he said. "That's all we can do."

"There is another alternative." A new voice entered the discussion, this one hauntingly familiar to Roche.

Murnane looked up. "Yes, Trezise?"

The senior aide to Auberon Chase stepped into the center of the adytum. Roche hadn't noticed him there before, but recognized his narrow, almost equine features immediately.

"Roche claims to have among her crew one of the enemy."

"Yes; the council decided Adoni Cane was a fake," Murnane said.

"What if he isn't? What if he *is* as tame as Roche suggests? Surely his opinion would be worth seeking at this juncture."

"Bring another one of the enemy onto the ship?" objected Nemeth. "We've just killed a lot of people clearing out the first lot! If he is a clone warrior, it would be insane to allow him on board."

"What other means do we have to decipher the enemy's intentions?" Trezise opened his hands in supplication. "If an epsense link *does* exist, he might be able to tap into it."

"*If* he is genuine," Murnane said.

Trezise nodded, agreeing calmly. "If he is genuine, yes."

Murnane turned to face Roche. "What do *you* think?"

She wanted to say that this was what she'd wanted to do two and a half weeks earlier, that if they'd listened to her the first time, then maybe everything that had happened since then might have been avoided.

But she didn't. She was too conscious of the fact that this could be her last opportunity to speak to the council. She couldn't afford to miss that chance.

"On two conditions," she said instead. "One: you will grant any member of my crew asylum on this ship should they seek it. And two: you will make me a participating member of the council, effective immediately."

Murnane chuckled softly. "*I* have no objection to either condition," he said. "Obviously, though, the granting of asylum would need to be ratified by the Heresiarch." He nodded to where the Heresiarch stood at his station, preoccupied with the running of the ship. "I'm not sure he would extend the honor to Adoni Cane, enemy or not. And your membership in the council would have to be on a *pro tem* basis, to be ratified by a formal sitting—"

She raised a hand to silence him. "Okay, okay, you've made your point," she said, and sighed. "Just give me your assurance that you'll *listen* to me, at least."

He nodded once. "Make arrangements to transfer Adoni Cane across and we'll prepare for the interview." He swept his gaze across the room. Nemeth looked relieved, but said nothing. "If there are no further urgent issues to be raised, we will adjourn to await further developments. The Heresiarch has work to do, and our being here can only be a distraction."

Even as he spoke, a bell chimed loudly, sending the assembled officers to their stations. A raiding party from a small but aggressive government had stumbled into the *Phlegethon*'s camouflage field and opened fire on the middle decks. Roche turned to the monitors, watching as hundreds of pod-shaped fighters swarmed out of the giant ship's many docks to repel the intruder.

The council moved out to the fane. Hue Vischilglin took Roche's arm, nodding recognition but saying nothing. As she and Haid were led away, Roche caught a glimpse of Salton Trezise, who could barely contain his look of triumph.

From the safety of another conference room, Roche made arrangements for Cane and Maii to cross by scutter to the *Phlegethon*. She also instructed Kajic to assume a close parking position under the big ship's shadow. While the raid had in no way threatened the *Ana Vereine*, it did highlight the potential for conflict nearby. If things did get too hot, Kajic had permission to seek protection in the *Phlegethon*'s larger docks.

Once that was organized, Roche had nothing else to do but observe. Even as only a *pro tem* member of the council, the information she now had access to was overwhelming. What had once been chaos had now become a slaughter. Traditional alliances dissolved; defensive agreements were torn apart; like fought like as intra-Caste conflicts expanded to consume entire fleets. Conservative estimates put the number of ships and stations lost in the first three hours at twenty thousand. That only amounted to barely two percent of the million or so ships known to have entered the system, but the sheer loss of life could not be ignored.

<I hope you're watching this, Box.>

<Indeed I am, Morgan. This is an unexpected development. The ability of the enemy to mobilize such a response so quickly is unprecedented. Few could have anticipated this sort of capability—or this sort of generalized conflict so early in the endgame.>

Its choice of words made her frown. <I hope this is more than just a game to you, Box.>

<Of course it is, Morgan. Of course.>

She couldn't decide whether the AI was being insincere or patronizing. Perhaps it was both. <Do you see any biases toward any particular Castes?>

<None at this stage. Taking regional peculiarities into account, the targets are randomly distributed. There doesn't even seem to be any broad trend, either—such as Pristine versus Exotic, for example.>

<Does that blow your theory?>

<No. I may need to see more data before a trend emerges.>

<*If* a trend emerges,> she said, thinking of the twenty thousand ships destroyed already and wondering how many more it would take to give the Box enough data.

<Naturally, Morgan.>

She went back to watching the screens. Sitting beside her, heavy and brooding in his black combat suit, Haid was as silent as she was. He kept his emotions carefully hidden, only a slight tightness to his jaw revealing anything of the tension he must have been feeling.

After a few moments, she addressed the Box again. <Box, someone mentioned being able to identify the enemy by blood test. Do you know how they do this?>

<It's a genetic analysis,> the AI replied. <As Rufo and I previously noted, the enemy has an unusual genetic structure. Where normal Humans possess long stretches of 'junk' genes called introns, Cane and the others have sequences that *appear* to serve a purpose, yet result in no known proteins. Whatever else they might do remains a mystery, but these stretches can be used to distinguish a clone warrior from any other ordinary Human.>

<That's why Rufo wanted us to look at Cane's introns more closely?>

<Yes. He suspected that an important clue to the origins and/or purpose of the enemy would lie within.>

<Do you agree?>

<I agree that it's a possibility.>

<What about the council? They obviously knew about the introns when I mentioned them at the first meeting. Have they learned anything new in the time they've had?>

<Well, if they have, it hasn't explained anything about the enemy we didn't already know.>

Roche absorbed this. <What about the Crescend, then? What does *he* know?>

<If he knows anything conclusive about this, he hasn't told me.>

Tired of repeatedly butting the same brick wall, Roche fell silent. A few minutes later, Kajic reported that Maii and Cane were ready to leave. Roche switched her implants to a view of the scutter's cramped interior. Cane sat in the pilot's seat, his face expressionless. Maii sat beside him, still somewhat pale, but looking better than she had been earlier; the medicinal pack covering her wound was less bulky than it had been, indicating that its healing work was almost done. Behind her . . .

<What's *he* doing there, Uri?> she asked Kajic.

<Defender-of-Harmony Vri insisted on coming,> he replied.

<But we're getting Maii to safety,> she said. <That's what he wanted, wasn't it?>

<He seems determined to keep an eye on her in person.> Kajic sounded almost amused. <It wasn't my place to stop him.>

<No, of course not. Nor mine.> Roche found the Surin warrior's persistence admirable, if a little obsessive. <But are you going to be okay there by yourself?>

<Everything will be fine, Morgan. Now that normal channels are open again, I'll be able to watch what you're doing. Besides,> he added, <I'm not completely alone. Alta is still here. And there's still plenty of work to do shipside. I think everything must be perfectly in order if we're to get out of this one.>

Roche agreed. Part of her was still nervous about giving the ex-Dato captain the chance to escape with the ship, but the rational side of her knew that this was simply unjustifiable paranoia. Had he wanted to, he could have killed or lost them dozens of times already.

<Vri will attempt to make contact with the Surin delegates in the system,> Kajic went on. <That is one thing you haven't been able to do as yet.>

<It's not as if I've had the time!>

<He realizes that. He just wants to resolve this issue once and for all.>

Roche nodded to herself. She couldn't do everything—especially when this particular job held little appeal. <How long until they arrive?>

<They should be there in about half an hour.>

<Okay. Thanks, Uri.>

The scutter disengaged from the *Ana Vereine* and arced smoothly toward the larger ship. Cane flew the small craft with competence and ease. He was a natural at everything he turned his hand to, even a complicated task such as flying a space vessel. Somewhere in his lost memory, Roche supposed, was the knowledge he needed, accessible at will. How it had got there in the first place, though, was the question—one question among many. She could only hope that some of them would be answered when he came under the council's spotlight.

There had been no mention of the Ulterior outside the sealed conference room where Roche had revealed her knowledge concerning the five clone warriors. She assumed that it was still considered at best to be an informal group by most of its members—although Murnane's presence at that meeting was a strong indication that its activities were partially sanctioned by its parent, or would be gratefully absorbed into the greater body of work if things went well.

How long her partial acceptance by the council would last she didn't know, but while she *was* a member, she resolved to take full advantage of it. She couldn't just sit by and watch while everything was potentially falling apart around her. Even if the council ended up dismissing her again, then at least she could say that she'd tried.

"Ameidio?"

Haid turned to face her.

"If you were the enemy, and this was your doing"—she indicated the images of destruction displayed on the monitor which was built into one wall of the conference room—"*why* would you be doing it?"

He faced the monitor and contemplated the question for a few moments. "To reduce the resources of the enemy," he said at last.

She shook her head. "No," she said. "They're far too outnumbered. Even a ninety-nine percent reduction in our capability would leave them way behind."

"To disorganize the enemy, then?"

She considered this for a short while before offering another shake of the head. "That's a hell of a lot of effort for so little gain."

"Depends on how you look at it."

"Not really," she said. "Wouldn't any sensible campaign concentrate its energies here, on the *Phlegethon*? That's where the potential for organization exists. Even if it's the only surviving ship, it'd stand a chance of victory against a small enough enemy force."

He shrugged. "This could just be a smoke screen, then, and they are already working on us. We just haven't realized it."

"We got rid of their agents; they don't have anyone else to work through."

"You heard what Murnane said: the council is recalling its field agents. How many of the enemy do you think will slip in with that lot?"

She nodded. "I've considered that," she said. "And who's to say the enemy *has* to be a clone warrior at all? There are bound to be collaborators we'll never detect, small-time operators who might slip past even high-grade reaves because they aren't aware that what they're doing is even wrong."

His dark eyes watched her closely. "You could be right about the agents," he said. "But there's something else on your mind, isn't there?"

She half-smiled, then sobered. "This mass killing," she said slowly. "It's a message of some sort."

"A message?" Haid frowned. "Saying what?"

"I'm not sure," she said. "I'm not even sure for whom it was intended."

"It would have to be for the council, surely," said Haid. "Who else could it be for?"

She didn't answer that, because were she to voice her suspicions, she was sure that Haid would think her totally paranoid. Nevertheless, she couldn't shake the feeling that the message was aimed at *her*. It was as though they somehow knew that *she* was responsible for having located the five clone warriors, and that now they were making her pay the price. If so, this was retaliation on the largest possible scale; they were warning her not to do it again. . . .

But that all presupposed the existence of the epsense link Cane had already denied knowing anything about. She doubted the council could decide in a single sitting whether he was telling the truth or not, but she was looking forward to seeing them try.

On the screen, a habitat shaped like a spinning top broke up under centrifugal forces, spraying fragments into the small flotilla arrayed against it. Roche couldn't even begin to imagine the scale; the habitat could have been home for dozens or thousands of people, and the ships may have been fighters or cruisers. There was no way to tell the scale from the display on the screen alone.

She stood abruptly, turning from the destruction to face Haid. "Come on," she said. "I'm going to get Vischilglin to take us to the docks to meet Cane and Maii."

"You don't trust the council to do it for you?" said Haid.

"That's not the problem," she said. "The last time I sent those two somewhere on their own, I very nearly didn't get them back."

"What about Vri?" Haid said, getting to his feet.

She had forgotten the Surin. Vri had been with them for twenty-four days, but had never integrated into the group. He kept apart, following his own agenda, only working with them when their goals meshed. The moment their goals came into conflict, she had no doubt whose orders he would follow. On the *Phlegethon*, he would be close to getting what he and the Surin Agora wanted. She didn't entirely trust his ability to compromise if his superiors didn't follow suit.

"All the more reason to go down there." She turned to leave.

"Morgan?" Haid said suddenly. She stopped and faced him again. "Do you think you could handle Vri?"

The question startled her.

"If you had to," he went on quickly. "One on one."

"I've no idea," she said. "Probably not. I've never even thought about it, to tell the truth." The soldier had performed very well in the Fathehi Consulate. Not as well as Cane, but better than anything Roche could ever hope to perform. "Why do you ask?"

He shrugged. "Just curious."

"And what about you?" she said.

"Me? I wouldn't stand a chance." His smile was disarming. "But both of us at once . . . ? Well, that would be a different story."

She smiled slightly and patted the ex-mercenary's shoulder. "Let's just hope it doesn't come to that."

The scutter was delayed slightly by an unscheduled course-change undertaken by the *Phlegethon* in order to avoid a cloud of debris too extensive to tackle head on. Even with the enormous ship's shields, the chance of a large fragment slipping through was too great to risk. Changing the ship's orbit gave a certain tactical advantage too: camouflaged or not, the more it moved, the less chance someone hostile had of tracking it from its last known location.

Apart from a containment team already in position when they arrived, the civilian docks were virtually empty. Of all the airlocks Roche could see, the one through which Cane and Maii disembarked seemed to be the only one in use.

"You don't get many visitors here, I take it?" she said to Vischilglin, who waited with them by the inner door.

The tall woman shook her head. "Security is very tight at all times, and especially so now. I am told that docks like these are usually a hive of activity when consistory vessels return to their home system. With such a large crew, the reunions can go on for weeks. The Heterodoxies are renowned for their devotion to family as well as to faith."

The woman spoke quickly and with animation, but never meeting Roche's eyes. It seemed to Roche that she was nervous, anxious—trying, perhaps, to suppress an uncomfortable thought.

"Something's bothering you?" Roche asked.

Vischilglin kept her gaze on the dock's inner door. "I've lost contact with my superiors back home," she said softly. "Signals stopped arriving three days ago."

Roche nodded slightly, but didn't know what to say. She was saved from having to by the inner door hissing open. The suits of the containment team whirred as they stood at the ready.

Cane stepped out first, followed closely by Maii. She wore a new hazard suit with additional armor provided by Vri that lent the normally gray exterior an air of gilt decoration. Cane wore nothing but a typical brown Dato shipsuit. There was a tension in his posture which only heightened when he saw the containment team.

Maii looked tired; her lips were thin, her pale features drawn. She stepped over to Roche and lightly touched her arm.

<I'm not going to seek asylum,> she said, her mental whisper directed at Roche alone. She sent a picture of herself standing on the top of thick battlements.

The image might have been meant to make the girl look strong. To Roche, it made her look very small and alone.

<I'm glad to hear it, Maii,> Roche said, quashing her impression. <But I don't think Vri will be.>

The Surin girl touched her mind with a mental shrug.

Vri was the last to step from the airlock. His visor was in place and his eyes were hidden, but Roche could tell from the way the helmet moved that he had scanned the containment team, Vischilglin, Haid, and herself with one appraising glance. He knew what had happened on Galine Four and was obviously prepared for anything.

He stopped just behind Maii and waited silently.

"The council will convene in fifteen minutes," said Vischilglin, stepping forward. "Transport has been arranged."

As she spoke, a large, flat vehicle slid quietly to a halt nearby. The containment team reorganized itself to create a clear space leading from the airlock to the transport.

"Do we all go together?" Roche asked her.

"That would be simplest."

Roche nodded, but instead of heading for the transport, she moved to face Cane.

"Do you know why I've brought you here?" she asked.

"To testify before the council," he said.

"Are you ready for that?"

He returned her stare evenly. "Are you?"

The question was a challenge, although she didn't know why it should be. "I have nothing to hide," she said. "And I'm assuming that you don't, either—that you've been telling the truth from the start."

"Why would I do otherwise?"

"Because . . ." She faltered in mid-sentence. There were no words to frame the suspicion she still felt, deep in her gut. "Because you *could*."

Because I stand to lose everything if you haven't been telling the truth. . . .

"Having the potential to do something is not the same as intending to use it, Morgan. You of all people should know that."

"What do you mean?"

"I mean that five of my people died today as a direct result of your involvement in this conflict. Uri showed me the footage. Now that you know for certain that your ability works, you have the potential to track down and hunt every one of my kind and bring them all to their deaths. Whether I agree with them or not, whether you think I might be one of them or not, whether I am lying to your or not—it's all irrelevant. Ultimately, all that matters is your *intent*, isn't it?"

She took a step back from his intense gaze. "Killing all of your kind would be genocide."

"Exactly. And since I know that this is what you would call it, you have nothing to fear from me." He reached out and put a hand on her shoulder. "Morgan, any intelligent being can only do what it thinks is right. Have faith in my ability to do that, and everything will *be* all right."

His eyes never once left hers. His hand gripped her shoulder tightly. She felt he was pleading with her, trying to make her understand something important—but she couldn't quite grasp it. Genocide? Was he talking about the destruction of the Caste that had made him and his kind over half a million years ago? Or was he just using that possibility to illustrate a more general point?

"If you have any surprises in store for me," she said, "you'd better let me know now."

"I'm not the one with the surprises, Morgan," he said.

Turning on his heel, he stepped through the containment team and onto the transport.

15

SHCV *Phlegethon*
955.2.14
1000

The fane was full. By the time Roche and her party took their places in the front row, with a clear view of the font and the small group of people around it, she had lost count of the number of unfamiliar Castes mixed in with the thousands of Pristines: short ones, tall ones, broad ones, thin ones, Castes that required filters to weed out atmospheric irritants, and Castes that, judging by the thickness of their skins and protective coverings over their eyes, could have survived just as comfortably in a vacuum. She recognized only three types: a Surin not far from where they stood, an Eckandi toward the rear, and a robed Hurn looming to one side. Where they had come from, she couldn't guess.

<Some people aren't happy about this,> Maii's voice whispered to her.

<Anyone in particular?> asked Roche, continuing to scan the crowd.

<No,> said the girl. <It's just a general feeling, underlying the tension.>

The "tension" sprang in part from the news that the Heresiarch had placed the ship on red alert. The conflict in the system showed no signs of abating; if anything, it seemed to be spreading. All peripheral civilian ships, including the *Ana Vereine*, were to dock, and a protective sphere of fighters would patrol the space between the camouflage and the body of the *Phlegethon* itself. If anything got through, it would be instantly dealt with.

When the time came, Esko Murnane stepped forward and bowed respectfully to the Heresiarch. He raised his hands and, gradually, silence fell about the fane.

"We have taken the unprecedented step," he began, without preamble, "of inviting our non-Pristine guests to join us today. We intend this as a sign of solidarity in these difficult times, when *all* of Humanity seems endangered, not just the Pristine Caste. For many of us, this meeting could well be the first time we come face to face, knowingly, with the enemy."

Although Murnane had made no gesture nor mentioned any names, heads began to turn toward Roche and her party.

"We have among us again a person you all know at least by reputation—a person who was initially rejected by this council but who has, despite that, worked for us in an unofficial capacity for the last two and a half weeks. The information distributed immediately prior to this meeting explains how Morgan Roche has stumbled across a means of identifying the enemy. If this ability is unique to her, it may be of little long-term benefit in our fight with the enemy. But if it is not, if there are others among us who share this ability, then we have a very real chance of victory. To overcome the enemy we must explore *every* possible avenue—and at this moment in time, this is the best option available to us."

Roche couldn't tell from Murnane's expression whether he believed what he was saying or not, but the triumphant glint was back in Nemeth's eye. It probably wouldn't matter from his point of view if Murnane believed it at all, as long as the council gave *him* the credit.

"The sudden and unexpected escalation in conflict we've seen around us," Murnane went on, "may be connected to the death of five clone warriors earlier today on board this very ship. Immediately following their deaths, fighting broke out around the system, and it has not stopped or even eased since. The speed with which the news spread suggests that some sort of epsense link might be involved, and so we have asked Morgan Roche, here, if she will help us in determining whether or not this might be the case."

The whispers around the fane became slightly louder, and in the general murmur Roche heard her own name being mentioned over and over again. She wished that she could shut the helmet of her combat suit to block the voices out; the attention focused on her from those present in the fane was almost suffocating.

Murnane stepped back to let Nemeth take the floor.

"I have been declared chairperson for this meeting," said the younger man. "As someone who has recently worked with Morgan Roche, I am in a unique position to guide the council to the conclusions it *must* reach. As my colleague has just told you, this development may prove crucial to the success of our defense of the galaxy against our enemy. Indeed, it may prove critical to our very survival."

The murmurings rose in pitch again, threatening to become a clamor of alarm.

"Please!" Nemeth raised both his hands, gesturing for calm. "There is no need for panic!" he called out over the noise. "We mustn't be unnerved by what the enemy has done this day! Don't allow yourselves to think that they have the measure of us. What you are seeing is merely the winnowing of the weak—of those corrupted and influenced by the enemy! Those seduced by evil have died by evil's hand! But the same fate does not await us. We are equal to the task ahead. *We* are strong; we *will* prevail!"

He lowered his hands and cast his gaze across the crowd. If he expected cheers, he didn't get them, but he did get the crowd's full attention. After a while, relative quiet returned to the enormous room.

Roche wondered how many people had allies, friends, or family among those already killed in the chaos. She didn't think that any of the Castes she had encountered deserved to be labeled "weak" or "evil" simply because they had been destroyed by the enemy before the others. After all, only chance might have spared the *Phlegethon* itself from the five clone warriors that had infiltrated it.

But this was politics, not reasoned debate, and the reminder was a timely one. In order to get what she wanted, she would have to score points, not make them.

When he had finished scanning the crowd, Nemeth faced Roche's party. "Morgan Roche and Adoni Cane, please step up to the font."

Cane waited for Roche to move before stepping out of the crowd. Together they walked the twenty-odd steps to the heart of the fane, where Nemeth and Murnane and a dozen other people waited for them. The gaze of the council was almost unbearable now: as heavy as a planet and no less impersonal. A subtle prompt from Maii buoyed Roche slightly, made her feel that she could actually face them successfully.

<You've tackled worse than this,> said the girl. <Many of them are more scared than you are, Morgan.>

<Yes,> she sent back, <but it seems they're more scared *of* me than *with* me.>

<That's only natural, Morgan.>

<I'm not sure it helps me much, Maii . . .>

Nemeth's nod to each of them was formal and perfunctory. His only interest was in beginning the interrogation.

"Morgan Roche, why are you here?"

"To determine the origins of the enemy," she said briskly; she was tired of answering the same old questions over and over. "And, if possible, to find a way to stop them."

"Who sent you?"

"No one sent me," she replied. "I used to work for the Commonwealth of Empires, but I am now independent."

"Is it not true that your mission has been sanctioned by at least one of the High Humans?"

"I am unable to answer that question," she said after some consideration, "because I'm not sure myself of the truth." That much, at least, was honest. "There have been times when I was convinced of High Human intervention, but I've never had the evidence to prove or disprove this." That, also, was true; she only had the Box's word that the Crescend was involved. "The fact that I once had in my possession a fully conscious artificial intelligence—something far beyond the capabilities of mundane science—was all I really had to suggest that I was being helped by someone in the High Human ranks."

"And this AI is now destroyed," said Nemeth. "Is that correct?"

"Yes." Having been said so many times now, the lie came easily.

"Do you claim that your companion here is one of the enemy?" He looked at Cane as he said this.

"Yes."

"We'll come back to this in a moment," he said, returning his attention to Roche. "But first I'd like to address something else." He paused, posturing loftily. "The last time you came before us," he said, "you refused to submit to a genetic test. Why was that?"

"At the time I was unaware of your reasons for wanting me to," she said. "The thought simply hadn't occurred to me that you wanted to determine whether or not I myself was one of the clone warriors. Having said that, however, I should point out that I will *still* resist such a test, because I believe that I have clearly demonstrated my allegiances in this last week. Even if I *was* a clone warrior, I have given the council information on the whereabouts of five others. Why would I allow my own kind to be killed if I wasn't on your side?"

Nemeth nodded—approvingly, she thought. He knew what she was doing. She was setting up her argument for the acceptance of Cane. If she could convince the council that the matter of her genetic origins was irrelevant given that she was clearly working for them, not against them, then it would be easier to convince them about Cane.

"Neither would you submit to an in-depth epsense probe, though," he went on.

"Because I believe such probes are invasive and unnecessary," she responded calmly. "*And* they are open to misinterpretation. My actions should be taken into consideration, not what takes place in the privacy of my own thoughts."

He nodded again. "And do you speak for Adoni Cane, here?"

She glanced to her left, to where Cane stood patiently, awaiting his turn to speak. "In what sense?"

"Would *he* allow himself to be genetically examined or probed by an epsense adept?"

She shrugged. "That's up to him," she said. "But I've already given you his genetic data. As for probing him, I don't believe it's possible. The reave in my crew finds his mind impenetrable—"

<In both senses of the word,> interrupted Maii. <His barriers are naturally strong; he himself might not be able to dismantle them. Even the surface levels of his mind are too complicated for me to interpret; the impressions I receive are in no way typical of any minds I have known.>

Nemeth turned to face the girl, whose thoughts had easily filled the fane, relayed by the other reaves around them. "Your testimony is not called for at this time, child," he said, "The council will address you if and when it is required."

<*Squt*,> the girl sent to Roche alone. Roche suppressed a quick smile, recognizing the Surin word for a closed-minded fool.

"Your reave is young and inexperienced," said Nemeth to Roche, "although I am told she does possess a formidable raw talent. It's possible she may be right, but I would prefer to trust the judgments of the high-grade epsense adepts the council normally employs." He turned to Cane. "So I ask you now, *would* you allow such an examination?"

"Your reaves have been attempting to read my mind ever since I arrived on the ship," Cane said. "They have not been able to."

A flicker of a smile crossed Nemeth's face. "Then will you at least drop your barriers for them?"

"I am not able to do that," Cane said. "The barriers I have around my mind are not artificial. They are part of me. I am as unable to remove them as you are unable to remove your skin."

"You realize that this will make it difficult for us to trust you? After all, we have nothing but your word that this is the case."

"I understand that," said Cane implacably, as though daring the entire council to change his mind.

Nemeth shrugged helplessly. "Then all we can do is proceed," he said. "Do we at least have your permission to take a genetic sample, to confirm the data Morgan Roche gave us earlier?"

He didn't hesitate: "Yes."

Nemeth waved forward two of the people standing by the font. Cane held out his hand as one produced a small device designed to take a blood sample from his thumb. There was a small *click*, and the two women stepped away.

A few moments later, the results were displayed for all the council to study. In a giant hologram hanging above her head, Roche could see a stylized representation of Cane's genetic code alongside the data she had given the council before. She recognized the scientific shorthand standardized by the Commerce Artel across the galaxy:

chunks of code common to all Humans, no matter how divergent their Castes, lay scattered through Cane's genes like islands in an otherwise unfamiliar sea. For the first time, she saw the vast stretches of introns laid bare, incomprehensible patterns of base pairs lined up like words in a language she completely failed to understand.

"They are the same," observed one of the women who had taken the sample. One of the two patterns disappeared, allowing the remaining to be seen in more detail.

"He possesses the features we have come to associate with the enemy?" Nemeth asked.

"There can be no doubt." Several of the unknown sections were highlighted in red.

"You are convinced that this man is one of the enemy, then."

"Genetically speaking, yes." The woman stared balefully at Cane. "I am convinced."

Nemeth turned away from her, but Roche cut him off before he could speak.

"Wait," she said, addressing the woman. "What can you tell me about these features?" She indicated the sections highlighted in red.

"Nothing, I'm afraid." The woman seemed unsettled by the question. "They don't correlate to any known Human code."

Roche raised her eyebrows. "What does that mean?"

"Just what I said."

"That he's not Human?"

"No . . . no, of course not." She frowned at the question. "What else *could* he be? I just meant that the features we find in his introns are not seen in any other Caste."

"But why is that so unlikely? Every Caste is different. Surely there must be some that stand apart from the rest?"

"*No*." The woman was emphatic. "There has been much genetic intermingling between the Castes since the Primordial strains speciated, five hundred thousand years ago. One always shares *some* common features with another, no matter how different they might appear in the flesh."

"Then what happened to Cane's introns? Where are the sequences that should be there, and where have the new ones come from?"

"The only way the common features could be missing was if they were somehow removed and replaced with new, maybe random, sequences. But I can't see why anyone would want to do that. The introns are ignored, for the most part, since they serve little or no function."

"But if someone *did* have the capability to do this, might they want to do it to conceal the origins of a new Caste?"

"They might." The woman shrugged. "But, again, I can't see why. Only the High Humans have this sort of technology—and why would they create a new Caste just to kill us? There must be many more certain ways to do that."

Roche nodded. The woman had raised an interesting point, and allowed Roche to assert her presence in the meeting. Satisfied that the council knew that she was not going to sit back and let Nemeth railroad her to whatever conclusion he was hoping for, she indicated for him to continue.

He nodded with exaggerated politeness. "Thank you," he said. "Now, having ascertained that Adoni Cane is in fact one of the enemy, several questions arise that cannot be easily answered. Why he chose to ally himself with Morgan Roche at all is one such issue; why he chose to risk his own life to save hers and that of her companions would be another. These were key sticking points at Roche's last appearance before this council, and they have yet to be resolved. The possibility also remains that he is in fact still working for the enemy—a possibility which cannot be completely discounted, and *must* be the context within which his replies to our questions are considered.

"Do you understand what I am saying, Adoni Cane?"

"Of course I understand you." Cane's expression didn't change, but Roche noted the contempt in his tone.

If Nemeth heard it, he ignored it.

"Very well," he said. "We'll proceed. Tell me, Adoni Cane, *do* you possess epsense abilities?"

"In the sense that I can make myself heard to a reave? Yes, I do. But if you are asking whether I can actually read minds or stop people's hearts—then no, I don't."

"And you are certain of this?"

"I would hardly be unaware of such an ability," said Cane.

"Morgan?" Nemeth turned to her, asking her to corroborate Cane's statement.

"Obviously I don't know what goes on inside his head," she said, "but I haven't seen anything to suggest that he's a reave of any kind."

"His shield?" Nemeth suggested.

"It *could* be innate. I've never seen him hurt anyone that way, or even been addressed by him that way. He has never tried to influence my decisions—"

"Are you sure of that?" Nemeth was quick to jump on this.

"Positive." She was certain Maii would have alerted her to any mental tampering, had it occurred.

"Then what makes you think an epsense link could be responsible for the chaos that has broken out around us? Either the link exists, and therefore Cane has it, or it doesn't exist and he is as mute as he appears to be."

Roche remembered the conversations she'd had with Maii and Cane immediately prior to coming to the *Phlegethon* the first time. "Like his shields, the link could be innate. Before his death, the Olmahoi *irikeii* expressed the opinion that the clone warriors were like him: absorbers of thought—*all* thought, from all around them. This would include each other's thoughts, of course, assuming they can penetrate each other's shields. That would turn an innate ability to absorb thought into a means of communicating with each other."

Nemeth frowned. "Wouldn't this make them some kind of collective mind?"

Roche shrugged. "I raise it merely as an hypothesis to be tested."

"But how could we possibly test it?"

"Maybe we already have, inadvertently," she said. "By alerting one clone warrior to the knowledge that we can now find them, we may be alerting the others and—"

"You cannot produce the phenomenon you are attempting to explain as evidence to support your hypothesis," said a voice from the crowd.

Roche looked around and saw Salton Trezise stepping forward to confront her.

"How do you plan to prove your argument?" he continued. "We need more data. How do you propose we go about getting it?"

Roche glanced at Nemeth, who looked furious at the interruption but didn't himself in turn interrupt. An intrigued sussurrus spread through the fane.

"I have no specific experiment in mind," Roche admitted. "That's why I'm here, to talk to the council."

"Well, maybe it's time the council started asking the right questions, instead of skirting the issue. Tell me, Roche, have you personally ever seen anything in the time that you have known Adoni Cane to suggest that he shares a connection with the other clone warriors?"

Roche thought about this for a second. "Only once," she said. "When we arrived in Sol System. Jelena Heidik, the clone warrior we were following, knew exactly when we would arrive and where we were headed. That information could have been transmitted through such a link."

"But is it possible that this information could have been obtained through other means?"

"Yes, it's possible—"

"Then such evidence is circumstantial, *not* conclusive, and comes from a source one might describe as unreliable: *you*."

He smiled broadly, but Roche didn't respond. Nemeth stepped forward to regain control, but Trezise refused to stop.

"And what about you?" Trezise asked, turning to Cane. "Do you share a connection with the others?"

"No," said Cane bluntly.

"You're not aware of any such a connection? Or are you saying that such a connection does not exist?"

"It doesn't exist."

"Good, because I'd hate to think the enemy was listening in on us." He turned to Roche again. "Did you think about that when you brought him here? That if such a link *did* exist, he could broadcast every word we said to the enemy in this system?"

"*You* suggested it," she said.

"Yes, I did—and not because I believed your crazy theory, but rather to clear this matter up once and for all. It's time this nonsense was laid to rest and we returned to serious business."

A dissatisfied mutter from the crowd echoed his words. Rey Nemeth took advantage of the slight pause to break in:

"What are you suggesting, Trezise?"

"I am suggesting that we are wasting our time here!" he said loudly. "That *Morgan Roche* is wasting our time, and that you, Nemeth, are letting her!" He turned to the crowd. "It is not any mysterious epsense link which will allow the enemy to win; it is meetings such as this! While we stand around here listening to *her* outrageous claims and *his* pontificating, we are doing the enemy's work for them!"

Nemeth drew himself up. "What exactly are you accusing me of, Trezise? Collaboration with the enemy?"

"I accuse you of nothing more than incompetence, Councilor. Morgan Roche came to us with vague hints and rumors and she was rightly rejected. *You*, however, took it upon yourself to pursue her cause in another forum. Perhaps at the time the gamble seemed justified, but her reports now reveal how disastrous that course of action was."

Roche felt Maii's anger boiling over, but she forced herself to remain calm as Trezise ranted on.

"Then she returns, spouting even more wild allegations. They serve no purpose. Worse—they actively impede any progress we might make toward ascertaining the truth! Word about today's 'exercise' could just as easily have spread by means of ordinary Human spies and hyperspace communications. There is no need to hypothesize beyond that. All we have to do is look for those spies and the problem will be solved. But no, instead we're off in search of phantoms, while the very real enemy continues to work among us!"

"Not any more," said Nemeth. "The five she helped us locate *were* clone warriors. There is no doubt of that."

"I don't dispute this," said Trezise. "But how many *more* might there be, that she *hasn't* told us about? We have only her word that the ship is now clean."

"There has been no overt move against us—"

"*Yet*." Trezise turned to Esko Murnane. "And *you*! Bad enough that Assistant Vice Primate Nemeth should already have wasted so much of the council's time—but you had to give him more. You encouraged this 'exercise' which has brought the entire Sol System to war. Do you call this progress? Thousands are dying every minute!"

Trezise turned to address the council as a whole. "I call for a vote of no-confidence in the leadership and guidance of Esko Murnane and Rey Nemeth!"

Roche understood, then, why Trezise had asked for her to appear in front of the council.

She glanced at the Heresiarch, who was watching the proceedings with a frown. The crowd was unsettled; she heard confusion and anger in the mingled voices surrounding her. How a no-confidence vote would go she couldn't guess, but the fact that it had been called was bad enough. Even if it failed to get rid of Murnane or Nemeth, it had placed Trezise firmly in the minds of the councilors, and it would disrupt normal proceedings for some time.

This was his chance to seize power, and he wasn't going to waste it. He wasn't interested in her testimony one way or the other. She was just a tool to help him get what he wanted.

She was being used yet again—and the worst thing was that she had to go along with it. Regardless of who ran the council, it was still her best chance to do any good in the system. She knew the ship was clear of the enemy, and she also knew that whether Cane was himself telling the truth, he was still their best hope of learning anything new about the enemy.

<Box, can you do anything to stop this?>

<If you wish, Morgan.>

<Nothing too drastic. I just want it postponed until after we've dealt with the real problem.>

<I understand. Give me a minute.>

Roche returned her attention to Trezise. His expression was guarded, outwardly restrained, but she could see the delight behind his eyes. He was pleased with his work, was relishing the growing dissent about the room. The council wasn't entirely on his side—but he had upset the balance; he'd had a direct effect on its mood. Where Nemeth had been simply power-hungry, Trezise looked like he was enjoying the disruption purely for its own sake.

Murnane tried to quiet the crowd, but to no avail. There was too much tension in the air now for it to be so easily quelled. Even when Nemeth added his voice to the call for calm, the racket continued. Trezise took a step back and smiled openly at the chaos.

Then a single, clear chime cut through the noise. A Heterodox officer ran through the crowd to talk to the Heresiarch, whose face instantly became grim.

The bell chimed a second time. As the Heresiarch headed for the adytum, the officer came to the font and spoke to Murnane. Roche wasn't close enough to hear what was being said, even though the noise of the crowd was finally ebbing.

After the third chiming of the bell, Murnane stepped forward to address the council.

"We are under attack," he said simply. "The Heresiarch has been called to attend to the vessel. This meeting is therefore adjourned until the emergency is past."

The crowd erupted once again, thousands of voices shouting out in a mix of fear and anger. Robed officials stepped into the fane and moved among them, trying to get the people to head toward the exits. Roche saw scuffles break out in a number of places.

<Thanks, Box,> she said. <A little dramatic, perhaps, but effective nonetheless.>

<This has nothing to do with me, Morgan,> the AI said. <We really are under attack. A large fleet previously stationed several million kilometers from here just slow-jumped to the edge of the camouflage field and launched base-line probes. No shots have been exchanged yet, but that is only a matter of time. Fighters have been launched by both sides.>

She tried to call Kajic, but a precautionary scrambling system was in place. <What about the *Ana Vereine*?> she asked, concerned. <Is it okay?>

<It is docked and safe.>

<Good. I—>

A hand came down on her shoulder. "We should leave," said Cane.

She looked around. Haid, Maii, and Vri were being herded toward an exit on the far side of the fane, and the containment team was closing in around the font.

<We'll meet you back at the ship,> Maii called, her voice faint through jamming of a mental sort. The council's reaves, it seemed, weren't taking any chances, either.

"You go back to the ship too," she told Cane. "You're not a prisoner. They'll take you there and let you go." She directed the words at the leader of the containment team, who nodded. "Wait for the others. I won't be long."

Cane hesitated for a moment, then nodded and was led away by the squad of soldiers.

Roche approached Murnane, who stood, looking stunned and confused, with one hand on the font supporting him. Trezise was arguing loudly with him.

"This is exactly what I said would happen if we allowed Exotics into the council meetings! We've become caught up in someone else's dispute!"

"Our ftl drones are being destroyed across the system," Murnane said. "This is a coordinated assault, not a random skirmish."

"All the more reason to resolve this issue *now*—"

"*No*!" Then, more calmly, meeting Roche's eye, Murnane said: "I don't think talking will resolve anything anymore."

He turned and walked away. Trezise glared at her, then followed.

Roche was at a loss for a moment. She had hoped to find out how she could help, but the fane was rapidly emptying. Nemeth had gone with the others. The only ones remaining were a handful of Exotics trying to get closer to her, and a ring of guards around the central area keeping them at bay.

<What now, Box?>

<We watch,> it said. <This is an interesting development, Morgan. Before, the attacks were random and local. Now they have a target. The enemy is moving against the council in a manner that cannot be disguised as anything but purposeful and destructive. At last, we have confirmation of their intent.>

<But what can I *do*?>

<Nothing for the time being. You are safer here than you would be anywhere else in this system. Even if the *Phlegethon is* overcome, you will have ample warning, and therefore time to escape.>

<Has the firing started yet?>

<No. The Skehan Heterodox will not initiate the conflict. They would rather avoid it if possible, since it is likely that such an exchange would result in the deaths of many innocent people.>

"Roche!" Vischilgin's voice echoed in the emptying space. "What are you still doing here?"

Roche turned to face the tall woman who had breached the ring of guards and now stood on the far side of the font.

"I don't know," said Roche. "I feel like I'm missing out on something important."

Vischilgin came closer, until she reached the font. Then she did as Murnane had done during the first council meeting Roche had attended: she dipped her hand into the water and sipped it.

"The Heterodoxies say it brings clarity of thought," she said, wiping her hand lightly on her robe. "Something we could all use at the moment."

Roche nodded, willing to accept the superstition but not to indulge it. "There's nothing for me here," she said. "I should get back to my ship."

"I'll take you," said Vischilgin.

"No, that's all right. I can find it."

"Please," she insisted. "I have little else to do while the warriors blunt their swords on each other."

Roche acquiesced, and was led out of the fane via the same exit Murnane and the other senior councilors had used. It opened onto a series of featureless white corridors that could have come from any center of bureaucratic power anywhere in the galaxy—a far cry from the streams and valleys she had witnessed on her first trip to the fane.

Thankfully, Vischilgin seemed to know where she was going. She said nothing as she guided Roche through the warren. The only sounds were the soft pad of her footfalls, almost entirely drowned out by the heavy footfalls of Roche's combat suit.

<The battle outside has commenced,> the Box announced matter-of-factly. <The first shot was fired forty seconds ago. Another fleet has moved into position alongside the first, and the Heresiarch has ordered a course-change.>

Roche didn't respond. The news wasn't good. With two fleets now engaging the *Phlegethon*, the possibility that more might join in was very real. How long the Skehan Heterodox could last against a sustained assault she didn't know—and she didn't want to have to find out the hard way, either. She just wished there was something constructive she could do to ease the situation.

Instead, she was stuck in a warren, led by a woman whose silence was starting to make Roche nervous.

<Do you know where she's taking me?> she asked the Box.

<You are on an administration level directly beneath the fane.>

<That's not what I asked,> Roche said.

They turned a corner. Ahead was a row of doors that suggested elevators or some other intraship conveyance like the one they had used on her first visit. Vischilglin took her to the nearest and pushed a button. The door opened with a hiss and they stepped into the small capsule. Vischilglin selected a destination and the doors hissed shut again.

<She is taking you to the docks,> the Box confirmed.

<As expected.>

Roche didn't know why Vischilglin's behavior was bothering her. All she knew was that there was something odd about her, something not quite right. . . .

Although she hadn't felt the capsule begin its journey, she did feel it decelerate. Before it could come to a halt, Vischilglin tapped something into the pad by the door, and the capsule coasted a second before recommencing its braking.

<Something's wrong,> said the Box. <She's overshot the level you need.>

Roche didn't give herself time to think. Her combat suit was sealed and a weapon in her hand just as the capsule slid to a halt.

"Any sudden moves and I won't hesitate to pull the trigger," she warned Vischilglin, her voice booming via the helmet's speakers into the confined space.

The woman's eyes widened. "How . . . ?"

Then the doors opened, and Roche saw the welcoming party intended for her: five tall figures dressed in a mixture of spiky Hurn armor and robes, all with weapons raised and aimed directly at her.

"Put the weapon down, Roche," said one. "You can't possibly hope to fight us all."

She hesitated, ready to fire. They all had heavy-duty rifles, and she didn't dare doubt that they were all equipped with armor-piercing ammunition. If she so much as raised a hand, they would cut her down where she stood.

<Box?>

The lights went out. In the same instant Roche dropped to the floor and switched to infrared. Her welcoming committee was slow to respond, giving her the few precious split-seconds she needed to get out of their sights. She took one robed figure in the throat and another in the hip before any of them returned fire. When they did, the elevator exploded with light. Vischilglin's scream was short-lived.

Roche used the suit's attitude jets to propel herself along the floor. Sparks flew from her stomach-plating as she fired at another of her attackers. The first two she had shot were down but still moving. The armor of the remaining three was tougher; the third one she hit barely flinched.

Their heat-images were turning to follow her. She scrambled to where one of the fallen figures lay and wrenched the rifle out of its grasp. Rolling, she fired at the other three. The recoil of the rifle took her by surprise, even through her suit. One of her attackers flew backward into a wall. The two others split up and darted away.

She took the opportunity to look around her. In infrared, the scene was confusing. Airlocks glowed red with flashing lights above them; floors, walls, and ceilings were lukewarm gray; energy from the shots splashed the area around the elevator with bright swaths of white-yellow. Her attackers were green-blue on either side of her, trying to pin her between them.

She turned and ran as fast as the suit would allow her.

<Box, I need a way out!> she said quickly. <An elevator, an open lock—*anything*!>

Something red flashed in her implants to her left: another elevator. She headed toward it. Energy flashed past her and blossomed on a far wall: her attackers were firing at her. She crouched to decrease her profile, dodging as much as she could without lessening her speed.

She switched to visible light for a second to judge the distance. The elevator doors hung invitingly open, barely fifteen meters ahead. Yellow light shone from between them. Gunfire flashed past her again, and she realized that she was silhouetted against that light, giving her assailants a perfect target.

<Box, kill the light and get ready to close the doors! Warn the others!>

<I've already told Kajic.> The Box's calm voice was in almost surreal contrast to her mad dash for safety. <He says—>

Something smashed into her from behind, throwing her forward, sprawling. Pain exploded in her right shoulder and back. She skidded helplessly along the floor, moving fast enough to reach the elevator but missing the doors by a meter and crashing heavily into the wall. She tried to move, to stand, but her suit only whined ineffectually at her. She could smell ozone and smoke and burning blood.

Lots of blood.

<Box?> Through the pain, she managed to tip the dead weight of her suit onto its back.

Someone was running toward her with a rifle trained on her stomach. She tried to raise her own weapon, but her hands wouldn't respond. Her attacker came closer, slowing to a cautious walk. The weapon's aim didn't waver for a second.

<Box! Help me!>

One of the other suited figures appeared, asking, "Did we get her?"

"Don't ask stupid questions," said the first. "Call the others. We're going to need help getting her on board—and make sure the surgeon is ready!"

The other nodded and turned away. The first suited figure approached closer still, until it was an arm's length away. Reaching out with a boot, the figure tapped Roche on the chest. She could do nothing but grit her teeth on the pain.

The light spilling out of the elevator seemed to be fading.

Somewhere in the distance—or perhaps from deep inside her—she thought she heard a voice calling her. A girl. She knew she should respond, but she didn't have the strength.

In the fading light, the first figure crouched on one knee beside her. "Morgan Roche." It was a woman's voice. "At last."

Roche had barely a second of consciousness to realize that she knew that voice.

Then a wave of darkness broke over her and took her with it.

PART FOUR:

THE CRESCEND

16

HIC *God's Monkey*
955.2.14
1380

Page De Bruyn watched closely as three Disciples carried Morgan Roche into the Hurn cruiser. Roche's face was red-lit through the blood-spattered visor of her damaged suit, painted oddly by warning lights and alarm signals from within. She was very pale beneath the blood. De Bruyn caught herself thinking that Roche was lucky to be alive—although from Roche's point of view, 'lucky' was hardly the right word.

They hauled the injured woman through the cramped, convoluted crawlspaces of the ship and placed her on the autosurgeon's table. Cutting devices flared as they stepped away. Something in De Bruyn's stomach dropped as the cruiser disengaged from the *Phlegethon* and accelerated into the battlefield, broadcasting clearance codes to ensure their safe passage. De Bruyn waited anxiously for any sign of attack, but none came. The besieging fleets ignored them as the Disciples had assured her they would.

Bit by bit, Roche's suit fell apart down her right side, exposing the woman within. De Bruyn was surprised at how small she was, but supposed that was only in contrast to the sheer bulk of the suit. They were approximately the same height, and De Bruyn was taller than most men she knew. Or maybe it was just Roche's vulnerability that made her seem so small—lying there now, finally, helpless and alone. Without her crew of freaks around her, she wasn't as impressive as the rumors would suggest.

Roche's body was covered with gore. The shot had taken her low in the right shoulder and gone straight through her, leaving a hole easily a hand's-breadth wide. Shattered bone, torn muscle, and liquefied organs filled the hole. Blood still pulsed weakly from it, even through the cauterized ends of veins and arteries. De Bruyn could have pushed her hand through the mess and out the other side had she wanted to.

But the torment could wait. The important thing for now was keeping the woman alive. It was inconceivable that Roche could have survived such an injury. She should have died on the spot.

Hissing and licking sounds emanated from the autosurgeon as it went to work on Roche. De Bruyn faced the Disciple who had fired the wounding shot.

"You're very fortunate," she said quietly. "Had she died, I would have killed you myself. As it is, you'll just be disciplined."

The Disciple paled, but bowed in deference and backed out of the room. The others followed, sensing De Bruyn's mood. She didn't bother to hide the fact that she was displeased, even though the mission had, in almost every respect, been a success. But the Disciples didn't respond as well to reward as they did to punishment.

When they were gone, De Bruyn unsealed her own suit and slipped out of the helmet. While she watched the autosurgeon stabilize its patient, she patched into the command network via her implants and summoned the pilot of the vessel.

<Wamel, how long until we're out of here?>

<A few minutes. The Rebuli have given us a mine-free vector taking us up the long axis of the camouflage shield. That will mean a slight delay, but less risk of—>

The ship lurched. De Bruyn grabbed for support as the deck fell out from underneath her and the lights flickered.

<What the hell was that?> she asked.

<I don't know.> She could hear a racket in the background as the pilot fought for control of the ship. <We're changing course!>

<*What*?>

<The instruments—> There was another lurch, more violent than the first. Voices shouted at each other over the command network. <I'm shutting down the main drives and going to auxiliary. Hold on!>

Free-fall came suddenly, and just as abruptly ended. De Bruyn's feet lifted off the ground for a second, then slammed back down with twice her normal weight. She slipped and fell, skidding across the floor as acceleration sent the ship into a tight turn. The lights flickered again, and didn't return to their full strength. Red emergency lighting came on, and stayed.

<I don't understand it!> the pilot shouted. <The instruments are giving me readings that don't make any sense, and the controls aren't responding—>

<Don't be a fool,> De Bruyn snapped, gripping the lip of the autosurgeon's operating table and scrambling to her knees.

<We're being dragged back to the *Phlegethon*!>

<Call the Rebuli!> she ordered.

<I can't! We're broadcasting something but I can't tell what it is. It's like the ship's been taken over!>

A chill ran the length of De Bruyn's spine. "This can't be happening," she muttered. "Not again . . ."

The last time she'd had Roche in her grasp, something much like this had occurred. The AI that Roche had babysat *too* well had somehow taken over a Dato Marauder and COE Intelligence HQ, bending them to its will as easily as De Bruyn used the Disciples. But a recurrence was not possible. That particular AI had been destroyed back in Palasian System. Or so she had thought.

De Bruyn clambered to her feet, leaning over the operating table, studying its patient intently. Despite all the power fluctuations, the autosurgeon's work on Roche continued unabated.

Roche's lips were moving. It was hard for De Bruyn to hear over the racket in her implants, but Roche was definitely trying to say something. De Bruyn leaned in closer still, and in doing so heard one word being repeated over and over again. It was faint, but unmistakable:

"Box . . . Box . . ."

De Bruyn stood upright, aghast. *How* it was possible, she didn't know, but she couldn't afford to have any doubts. Not now, when she was so close.

<Shut down the navigation and communication systems!> she ordered. <Hit the manual override! Shut down *everything*—even life-support! Do it now, before it's too late!>

The ship lurched beneath her again as the pilot obeyed.

<Control system not responding—trying module overrides. Drive module not responding. Navigation down. Communication not responding. Life-support down.>

The emergency lights went out completely for a second. De Bruyn could hear noises from the bridge that sounded like panels being opened. <Attempting physical disconnection.> There was a pause and then: <Drive module out.> Gravity disappeared completely. <Communications—>

The line died, and everything went quiet.

De Bruyn anchored herself on Roche's table. Her suit had closed automatically, and she had just enough light to see by. Roche's face was in shadow, but parts of her body were visible under the autosurgeon's lasers. It was still operating, using its internal emergency power. Roche's lips had stopped moving.

De Bruyn grabbed a cutter and began to slice away the remaining fragments of Roche's suit. The autosurgeon resisted, especially as she cut at the glove encasing Roche's right hand—where Roche's standard COE Intelligence implants provided her with an external data link. But the autosurgeon had nothing strong enough to cut living armor, and as the glove came free, its resistance ceased.

De Bruyn heard someone moving toward her, through the crawlspaces.

"Reverence?" called a voice. "Reverence!"

"Here," she replied, turning from Roche.

"The interference has ceased," said the pilot, climbing into the room. His robes fluttered like the wings of a giant moth. "But we are drifting blind and vulnerable!"

She heard reproach in his voice, and didn't rise to it. "Bring the systems up slowly," she said. "One by one. Keep automation to a minimum. If that means doing without communications and life-support for the time being, then that's what we do. Navigation, too. All we really need is a working drive to get us away from here. Once we're out of range, everything will operate properly again, I'm sure."

"Out of range?" The pilot frowned. "Of what?"

Of the damnable Box, she wanted to tell him, but couldn't bring herself to say it. She hardly believed it herself.

"The *Phlegethon*," she said instead. "They must be interfering with us somehow."

It was only a half-lie. If the Box still existed, then it had to be broadcasting from the big ship. Roche's suit was in pieces, now, and it wasn't anywhere to be found on her, so it *had* to be somehow communicating via her implants. If they could just get away from its influence, they would be able to continue their work. With the only possible link between Roche and the Box severed, now that she was entirely free of the combat suit, it would have no way of communicating with her when she awoke. Or so De Bruyn hoped. Her only alternative was to try the "Silence between thoughts" shutdown code again—although Roche had ordered the machine to ignore De Bruyn if she said it, and there was no guarantee it would listen to any of their transmissions anyway.

The pilot looked doubtful. "Reverence, I—"

"Do as I tell you, Wamel." Her tone was smooth and cold; argument would not be tolerated. "I want those drives working even if you have to stoke them with coal.

Take us away from the *Phlegethon* as quickly as possible. We can discuss what happens later. Just get us moving before someone decides to do it for us."

"Yes, Reverence." He bowed and left the room.

De Bruyn returned her attention to Roche. The sight of her lying there in the dark, so near to death, filled De Bruyn with a sense of satisfaction. Finally, Roche was in her hands. Finally, she would know the truth. And *nothing* was going to keep her from that.

The lights flickered weakly. Gravity came and went. Deciding that the Disciples needed all the help they could get, she left the autosurgeon to its work—confident in the knowledge that, at least for the moment, she and the machine were on the same side. . . .

God's Monkey limped through the battle zone and out of the *Phlegethon*'s camouflage screen on the tip of a fluttering, poorly tuned fusion flame. An hour later, when the need for accurate navigation overrode De Bruyn's sense of caution, she allowed the pilot to risk switching on some of the ship's higher functions. Gradually, when it became apparent that nothing untoward was going to happen, all of the systems were reconnected. When the ship was fully operational again, she sent it along an orbit that would take them close to the sun, then out to the system's dark fringes, where they would linger in the lesser-populated regions until they had to return.

Within another hour, the embattled *Phlegethon* was far behind them, along with the council, the Rebuli, and Siriote fleets, beyond even Salton Trezise and his devious little schemes. Originally, his price for letting her and the Disciples into the *Phlegethon* had been a disturbance that would justify his push to get the Exotics off the council. But events turned out to be a little more dramatic than anyone had anticipated, what with the Hurn kidnapping *and* the attack of the Rebuli at once. Nevertheless, from De Bruyn's point of view, the outcome had been more than satisfactory.

Separating Roche from her friends had been ridiculously easy, and Trezise had happily turned Hue Vischilglin to his will, filling her head with the notion that Roche was consciously working for the enemy and convincing her to set Roche up. Whether it was true or not, De Bruyn neither knew nor cared. She had what she wanted, and that was all that mattered.

When she was certain they weren't being pursued, she returned to the operating room to see how her captive was doing.

Hurn autosurgeons were notoriously simple-minded in their relationships with Pristine Humans, and this one was no exception. It took her much longer to access Roche's medical data than it should have, and even then it didn't make much sense.

Roche was stable. Her wound had been cleaned and sealed, and tissue regeneration had begun. It would be days before she was able to move again, and it was still a mystery how she had survived such enormous blood-loss and trauma, but at least she was out of immediate danger.

Trezise had given De Bruyn the council's information on the enemy, and she ran Roche's genetic code past it, to see if there was a match. She was half surprised to receive a negative response: Roche was *not* a clone warrior. But she wasn't normal, either. Roche's code was riddled with irregularities that neither De Bruyn nor the autosurgeon could explain.

She patched into the command network. <Wamel? Send Lemmas down here.>

<Yes, Reverence.>

When the reave arrived, De Bruyn was busy programming the autosurgeon to remove Roche's implants.

<You summoned me, Reverence?> The man's voice in her mind was like a smooth dark fluid, yet conversely sharp and penetrating at the same time. The first time his mind had touched hers had been disturbing, but she had quickly accustomed herself to this epsense adept's "tone."

"Yes. Wait a moment."

Lemmas waited patiently behind her, his arms at his sides in the folds of his black robes. No ordinary reave, he was unskilled at long-distance communication or remote sensing but frighteningly precise at close range. His specialty was the extraction of information from unwilling subjects, and his methods were notoriously effective.

The autosurgeon whirred and set to work, prepping several places on Roche's body for surgery. De Bruyn turned to face Lemmas, folding her arms across her chest. In doing so, she felt a stickiness there and looked down; some of Roche's gore had made it onto her, perhaps during the brief free-fall when the ship had been drifting.

Not that it mattered. Undoubtedly there would be more in the hours to come.

"Lemmas," she said, absently wiping Roche's blood off her uniform. "I have some work for you to do."

The man nodded slowly, his hairless face, like most Hurns, finely boned and long. He wore his ritual mutilation openly: ears removed, eyes sewn shut, tongue gone. His skin was bluish in the harsh light; through it, De Bruyn imagined that she could see not just his veins but his bones as well—yellow and decayed, like his teeth.

<I am yours to command, Reverence,> he said.

"I want you to take her apart," she said. "Slowly. I don't want you to kill her. Just break her open so I can look inside."

<What is it you are looking for?>

She looked over to Roche on the table and shook her head. "I'm not entirely sure."

<That will make it difficult.> There was an unhealthy relish to his voice.

"Just do what you have to do."

The reave inclined his head. <You will be required to observe,> he said.

"Naturally. You need my eyes."

<I will also need you to tell me when I have found the information you seek.>

"I can assist you in other ways, if you like."

<That won't be necessary.> He paused. <You are not squeamish, then?>

The thought of Roche being tortured didn't bother her at all. Not that she could have hidden it from the reave even if it did. "That's not something you have to worry about," she said.

His smile was an open wound between his cheeks.

<When shall I begin?>

"By epsense, immediately," she said. "You will have full access to her body once the autosurgeon has finished. In theory, you will have as much time as you need. In practice, however, I think you should proceed as quickly as you can. There's always a possibility that we'll be traced." She was still nervous about the Box. However it had survived, and whatever it was doing on the *Phlegethon*, the fact that it was out there at all made her anxious. The one thing she couldn't take into account in her plans was a rogue, hyperintelligent machine.

<I have her shielded,> said the reave. <Unless someone knows where she is, she will not be found.>

"Be that as it may, I'd still like you to hurry."

Lemmas moved closer to the table and rolled up the sleeves of his robe. His hands were as slender as the rest of his body; his right hand possessed six fingers. He had no fingernails, and below each knuckle were tattoos like rings. He stood for a moment with his head bowed over the operating table, uncannily as though gazing at Roche's face.

The autosurgeon whirred as it unwound artificial nerves from Roche's arm.

De Bruyn wondered when and how Lemmas would start.

<I have already started,> he said.

He reached out with one hand to stroke Morgan Roche's face and, even though she was unconscious, she flinched from his touch.

It was less crude than De Bruyn had anticipated. Barely minutes after the autosurgeon had finished—leaving Roche with several wounds across her body, one hand crippled and an empty eye socket—Lemmas began in earnest. All he did was touch her. De Bruyn couldn't tell whether his mind had powerful psychosomatic effects, or if his nail-less fingertips held hidden tools, but his slightest touch pierced skin, parted fat, and slit through muscle with disturbing ease.

Roche remained unconscious throughout the procedure. De Bruyn didn't ask if that was Lemmas's decision. The autosurgeon might have been keeping her sedated while she recovered from its ministrations. A couple of times De Bruyn had to override its attempts to intervene in Lemmas's work, but she resisted turning it off completely; she didn't want Roche dying from shock before she had learned everything there was to learn.

<Ask.> Lemmas held one hand over Roche's mouth as though he were trying to keep her silent. A tiny line of blood trickled down her cheek and onto the table.

"Where does she come from?"

<You already have that information.>

"That's not the point. I want to know what *she* thinks."

<Ascensio,> he said, with the faintest hint of irritation.

"When was she born?"

<Day thirty-six of the eighth month, '933.>

De Bruyn nodded. That accorded with COE Intelligence and Armada records, but still had not been verified independently.

"Who were her parents?"

<She doesn't know.>

"There are no deep memories at all?"

He paused for barely a couple of seconds; Roche's body stiffened. <There are vague recollections,> he said. <But they could just as easily be memories of her early caregivers at the orphanage or her host family. It is impossible to say.>

"So she does remember her childhood?"

<Yes,> he said, as if at that very moment his mind was caressing those particular memories from Roche's past. <Vividly, at times.>

"Give me an example."

<She had a nightmare when she was four,> he said. <It was raining so hard that

she couldn't see through it. She was trying to get home but was unable to find the back door to her house. Something large and hairy brushed her—>

"Not dreams," snapped De Bruyn. "Are there any *real* memories?"

Lemmas didn't hesitate: <She had a favorite toy in the orphanage. It was a talking book called Paz. It was yellow, with a round display, and specialized in M35 children's stories. It—>

"Enough of that," she said. "Tell me what she was afraid of."

<She was afraid of being alone,> he said. <Of having no one to talk to.>

"Was that why she put her name down for the Armada intake?" De Bruyn asked.

<Partly,> said Lemmas. <But she also disliked being poor and felt that her options on Ascensio were limited. She believed joining the COE Armada would give her more opportunities. One of which was to be able to look for her parents.>

"Did she ever find them?" De Bruyn was suddenly very interested in this line of questioning.

<No. She never looked.>

De Bruyn nodded thoughtfully to herself. "Was she ever sick before joining the Armada?"

There was another slight pause. <She contracted a severe viral infection at the age of ten,> he said. <And she broke her leg at fifteen.>

"She was treated on Ascensio?"

<Yes.>

De Bruyn noted that treatment of neither condition appeared in Roche's official records. "Go back to the orphanage," she said. "Does she remember any of the caregivers' names from there?"

<Yes.> Lemmas rattled off five names, two of which De Bruyn recognized from her research.

"And did she have friends in the orphanage, or outside?"

<Both.> More names followed. De Bruyn consigned them to her implants; she would check them later.

"What about emotional or physical intimacy?"

<What do you mean, exactly?>

De Bruyn couldn't help a slight sneer. "Was she ever in love?"

Lemmas didn't reply immediately. <She did not seek such relationships.>

"That doesn't mean there weren't any," said De Bruyn. "I want someone who will remember her—somebody who couldn't possibly forget her. Caregivers can forget, and even friends might with time—but a lover never forgets."

Lemmas recounted several instances that, on the surface at least, suggested a willingness to open up to friends and colleagues—a willingness that De Bruyn knew Roche had not shown in Military College nor any time after graduating. She had always been considered aloof by those who came to know her—emotionally distant and efficient, very much like the machines she had once regarded as friends. Yet what Lemmas recounted now of Roche's past portrayed a woman who at least had dabbled with the idea of sharing life with someone else, but who had ultimately rejected it—maybe because it made her feel vulnerable; maybe because her sexual needs simply weren't that great; maybe because she was self-sufficient within herself. For whatever reason, there were only a handful of people, male and female, who featured in Roche's memories as ones who might have been regarded as "lovers."

De Bruyn had hoped for more, but she was content with anything at all. She at least had more knowledge, now, of Roche's life on Ascensio, and that knowledge could be verified in time. All she needed was one person to say that they recalled Roche, and De Bruyn would have the proof that the official information had been covered up.

She was still missing the *why*, though. *That* would be much harder to find, she was sure.

At her instigation, Lemmas dug deeper. A life as unremarkable as that of any other orphan from an out-of-the-way world presented itself: her hopes, her fears; her delights, her disappointments; her ambitions, her failures; her dreams, and her everyday anxieties. The COE was full of people like her.

So why, then, De Bruyn wondered, had she been chosen? And, more importantly, for *what*?

After four hours, they took a break. De Bruyn was tired and, although he displayed nothing but cool aloofness, she suspected that Lemmas was also feeling the strain. Roche's condition was a concern, too. De Bruyn couldn't tell exactly what the autosurgeon's data meant, but the patient *was* showing signs of extreme stress. That was the idea, of course, but it was possible to push too far too soon.

<Do you know now what you are looking for?> Lemmas asked.

"No." She didn't feel inclined to discuss her quest with the reave; the fact that he could reach into her mind and pluck out the information himself only made his asking all the more insincere. "How deep can you dig?"

<As deep as required,> he said with unfaltering confidence.

"Is it possible to hide information from you?"

<Conceivably, but not permanently,> he admitted. <She is already doing it.>

"How?"

<There is a block in her. I touch it whenever we talk about her mission for Intelligence.>

"Which aspect of the mission?"

<The AI.>

"What about the AI?"

<I don't know. That's what the block is for.>

She ignored his sarcasm. "Can you break through it?"

<It is crude but effective. I suspect the girl, Maii, put it in place at Roche's request. Given time, it will unravel.>

"Could it be that she doesn't want anyone to know that the Box still exists?"

<Perhaps.>

She studied Roche's face in silence for a moment. Bruised, missing one eye, encrusted with blood, the woman was barely recognizable. Fleetingly De Bruyn wondered if she might be wrong—if Roche wasn't as important as she had first thought. What would she do if all this had been for nothing?

But there was no getting past the enemy's fixation on her: the way they had disseminated her name and interfered with her work among the Vax, the Fathehi, and the Noske. And what of Adoni Cane? It all had to fit together somehow. If she wasn't herself a clone warrior, then there had to be another explanation.

De Bruyn glanced again at Roche's genetic code. The unidentifiable sections remained just as mysterious as they had been before, different from those of the clone warriors *and* any known Caste. Random mutations? She didn't know. But at least now she had that data.

<Reverence?> The voice came from the command network, not the reave. <We've spotted a ship that looks like it might be matching our orbit,> said the pilot.

She felt a tiny shot of adrenaline. <Are you sure?>

<Not one hundred percent. It could be chance . . .>

<Unlikely,> she said. <Any stray emissions?>

<A few. It might be the *Apostle*, but we haven't been signaled yet.>

A slight apprehension tightened her gut. The idea of the Disciples' leader arriving made her uneasy. <They wouldn't announce themselves too soon for fear of detection,> she said. <Keep an eye on the ship and let me know if there's any change.>

<Yes, Reverence.> The pilot went back to his work with no mention of Roche. That side of their mission was not relevant to him.

But cracking Roche *was* relevant to De Bruyn, and she was conscious now of time running out.

"Let's continue," she said, approaching the table.

The reave inclined his head. <As you command, Reverence.> Earlier, he had removed the pack covering the great wound through Roche's chest. Smoke came from where his index finger now brushed the stump of her shattered clavicle. <What is it you wish to know now?>

She only had to think for a second; there were so many questions to choose from. "Find out if she knew anything about the enemy prior to her meeting with Adoni Cane."

He probed Roche's mind at the same time as he sent her nerves jangling with pain. <No.>

"Then did she know anything unusual about the Box prior to commencing her mission on the *Midnight*?"

<No, nothing at all.>

"Has she ever had any contact with Eupatrid Gastel or his predecessor?"

<No.>

"Does she know why I was sacked?"

<No. She doesn't even know you've *been* sacked.>

De Bruyn sighed. She hadn't really believed it would be so easy—but it would have been nice.

She tried another tack: Did Roche know how the clone warriors communicated among themselves? Did she know why Cane was helping her? Did she know who made him? Did she know why she seemed to be the only one who could find them?

The answers came as rapidly as De Bruyn fired the questions, and each time the response was the same: *No*.

Her questioning became bolder, and Lemmas's probing blunter: Was Roche aware of any plan to the engagements in Sol System? Was the fact that they were in Sol System in the first place significant, or was that just chance? To her knowledge, was the planetary ring as dire a navigation hazard as the Heresiarch feared—and if so, why?

But again, Roche had no knowledge of these things.

De Bruyn moved down to details. Had Proctor Klose, captain of the *Midnight*, known anything about Cane? What about Uri Kajic, ex-captain of the *Ana Vereine*? Why did she think Cane's introns were so important? Did she know where Jelena Heidik was hiding, or how many of the enemy were still at large in the system? Did she know anything *at all* about the movements of the enemy?

Within fifteen minutes De Bruyn guessed that Roche in fact didn't know anything about the big picture; two hours more and she was convinced of it. Nevertheless, she persisted, digging for what she suspected might remain behind a veil she hadn't pulled back yet, working through her own fatigue and the continuing fluctuation of Roche's condition. If the reave's finer efforts weren't successful, maybe sheer persistence would win the day.

The trouble was, she was running out of questions. Since the only area she had taken steps to avoid was that of the Box, it was there that De Bruyn finally turned. She didn't know why it was important, but Roche clearly thought so, and that was enough for her.

"What can we do about that block?"

<We can try two things: break it down, or circumvent it.> The reave was weary but still compliant.

"How difficult is the latter?"

<Less difficult than complicated. No knowledge can be completely hidden; even when removed from conscious thought it leaves echoes. Locating those echoes, those secondary and tertiary iterations, is a time-consuming task. But it can be rewarding.>

"Give me an example."

<Well, I can't tell you whether Roche thinks this Box is destroyed or not, but I can tell you that she thinks that she has talked with it in the recent past.>

"What about?"

<That I cannot tell you.>

"Then where is it?" De Bruyn said, then added: "Or where does she *think* it is?"

<That I cannot tell you either. But I do know that the valise that once contained it was a decoy, and that *was* destroyed in Palasian System.>

"What has the Box been doing since?"

<Specifics are hidden in regard to this.>

"Does anyone else know about it?"

<Her reave friend, presumably: Maii. No other name is mentioned, except that of the High Human you refer to as the Crescend.>

"Really? How is he involved?"

<Again, I have no access to information regarding that.>

De Bruyn felt her frustration growing. This was worse than getting nothing at all. However, she was beginning to see how it worked. Direct questions would get her nowhere; she had to go around the issue and tackle it from behind. "Can you tell me why the Box is important?"

<No.>

"Is it connected to the Crescend somehow?"

<Roche seems to think so.>

"How?"

<Not connected so much, perhaps, but *part of*. Her understanding of the situation here is particularly vague. It has troubled her—hence the leakage around the block.>

De Bruyn pondered this with interest. The Box and the Crescend *were* connected, it seemed—perhaps more intimately than anyone could have guessed.

"Where is the Crescend?"

<She doesn't know.>

"What is he doing?"

<She doesn't know.>

"Is she working for him?"

<If she is, she isn't aware of it.>

"Has she at least spoken to him?"

<Through the Box, perhaps, although that also is vague.>

"Why is he so important?"

<She doesn't know.>

"Why is *she* so important?" Frustration gave De Bruyn's voice a bitter edge, one she instantly regretted. Even though Lemmas couldn't actually hear it, he would certainly read the emotion behind it.

The reave stiffened slightly, but didn't reply.

"What? Have you found something?"

<No. I was simply listening—>

<Reverence?> broke in the pilot.

<What, Wamel?>

<We have received orders to dock with the *Apostle*. It has assumed an approach vector and will be in position in ten minutes.>

She closed her eyes, annoyed. The timing couldn't have been worse. <What do they want?>

<They have not said, Reverence.>

<Are they waiting for a reply?>

<No. Confirmation is not necessary.>

That was a polite way of saying that nothing would stop him from obeying that order to dock—not even De Bruyn.

<Give me an airlock and I'll meet you there.>

<Deck 4, Reverence.>

She killed the line.

"We're done here for now," she told Lemmas. "Maybe it's not a bad thing. She'll have a chance to heal." She glanced down at Roche's broken and bloodied body on the table and nodded to herself. "We'll resume later."

Wamel was at Deck 4 ahead of her, straightening his robes. They watched together through the command network as a singleship detached from the many-spined *Apostle*. Again, their environment was dark, so the images were either gloomily portentous or painted in surreal colors. De Bruyn remembered the first time she had encountered the cruiser, and felt a similar dread.

The singleship approached with bright flares from its thrusters, moving confidently across the gap between the two ships. Its approach took barely two minutes, during which time De Bruyn did her best to maintain her composure. She didn't have any doubt who would be in the singleship.

It docked with a bump heard clearly through the rigid bulkheads of *God's Monkey*. Via the command network she saw it anchor firmly in place not far from her own fighter, *Kindling*. There was silence for a moment, then came the sound of the outer door of the airlock opening. There was another pause, followed by a hiss as the door shut again. Then the inner door was open and Cane's twin walked through.

<Master.> Wamel bowed at the sight of the black-robed figure.

The clone warrior didn't acknowledge him. His face was exposed, and his eyes sought De Bruyn. "You have her?"

"Yes." As uneasy as he made her feel, she refused to defer to him the way the Disciples did. "How goes the campaign against the *Phlegethon*?"

He smiled. "The arrangement has been profitable for both of us."

She thought of Trezise for a moment, and wondered if her old colleague had any idea what had happened—if he even suspected just how thoroughly she had betrayed him.

"What are you doing here?" she asked.

"I want to see her. Is she still alive?"

"Of course."

"Good," said the clone warrior.

De Bruyn frowned. "Why? What does it mean to you?"

"We are curious."

"About what?"

"That is not your concern."

"I disagree," said De Bruyn. "Everything to do with her is my concern."

"I think the truth would appall you."

"But *the truth* is exactly what I'm looking for."

"Very well," he said. His smile widened. "Morgan Roche may yet be the key to our defeat. In her lies the potential for our destruction. She alone could be the undoing of all we have worked for."

De Bruyn paused to digest this. "Do you expect me to believe that?"

"I expect nothing of you."

"Could you explain—"

"No. I will not," he said. "We appreciate your efforts in neutralizing this threat to us. With Roche out of the way, our work can continue unchecked."

De Bruyn felt suddenly cold. Whether he was merely posturing or not, the thought was sobering. "And what *is* your work, exactly?"

"What do you see?"

Her laugh was humorless. "I see nothing but destruction."

"What you fail to see is *justice*." There was no mistaking the passion and anger in his voice. "There is no higher aspiration, De Bruyn. You should know that."

His smile was gone. And something in his expression warned her not to push any further.

"Take me to her," he said. "I want to see her with my own eyes."

She turned and led the way to where Roche was being held. Cane's twin followed her silently, with Wamel bringing up the rear. Along the way, De Bruyn turned over in her mind everything the clone warrior had said. What if he was telling the truth? What if she had somehow ruined any hope at all of defeating the enemy?

The autosurgeon had tended to Roche's minor injuries by the time they reached her. Her skin was a patchwork of healing strips and salves, and the pack was back on her shoulder wound. Her readings had stabilized slightly, although they still seemed odd to De Bruyn.

The clone warrior stepped up to the table and looked down upon the patient.

"What have you learned so far?" he said, his dark eyes studying Roche's embattled body with dispassionate interest.

"Very little," De Bruyn confessed. "Perhaps if we knew what to look for—"

"You still wouldn't find it." Cane's twin faced her. "Because you're looking in the wrong place."

"But . . . *you* said she was the key."

"*May yet* be the key, is what I said. Even if she is, the key itself holds nothing. What the key is *for* is the important thing, and to know that you must have everything else: the lock, the door, the room beyond . . ." He seemed to be enjoying her discomfort.

"You're talking about Sol System, aren't you?" she asked, riding a hunch. "That's where I should be looking?"

"Yes."

"And that's why you've come here: you're looking for something too."

"In a sense," he said. "If Roche *is* the key, and Sol System is the lock, then the room beyond contains the justice we seek."

Remembering his metaphor, she asked: "And what is the door?"

His smile returned. "That is the one remaining issue we must deal with," he said. "Then our business in the galaxy can truly begin."

His expression was relaxed enough, but De Bruyn sensed a terrible energy radiating from him. She felt like a moth flying into a furnace, only slowly realizing just how dangerous her environment was becoming.

If the enemy's work in the galaxy hadn't even begun, where would it stop? When every Pristine Human was dead? Every mundane, including the Exotics? When all that remained was High and Low Humans?

It was all very well to think in abstract terms about the enemy and their apparent desire to destroy Humanity, but De Bruyn found it disturbing to be confronted with the possibility that it might actually come true.

Or was he just bluffing? She clutched at this thought. Maybe he was trying to put her off balance. And if that were so, then she would have to find some way to regain control of the situation. . . .

"We did find something unexpected," she said.

His stare was cold and penetrating, his silence demanding she continue.

"The Box," she said. "It still exists. Roche was lying when she said it had been destroyed."

His eyes narrowed. "How do you know this?"

"It interfered with our escape from the *Phlegethon*," she said. "It infiltrated the ship's systems and tried to take us over. We very nearly didn't get away. If I hadn't guessed what was happening and shut everything down in time, we wouldn't have made it a thousand kilometers."

"Are you sure you're not mistaken?" said the clone warrior, suddenly alert and interested.

She bristled at the question. "Of course I'm sure," she said. "I've seen it in action before."

His gaze drifted back to Roche. "But it's not possible," he mused aloud. "It couldn't be . . ."

He stepped back to the table, leaning slightly over Roche's helpless form. In a loud and clear voice, he said: "*Silence between thoughts*."

The readings on the autosurgeon instantly changed, going haywire for a moment, then settling down into a new pattern. Roche shuddered; her mouth opened, gasping for air; her one good hand clutched at nothing. . . .

Then she relaxed. The readings changed again, returning to how they had been previously, as though nothing at all had happened.

De Bruyn watched in amazement, her jaw hanging.

"It's inside her!" The clone warrior's hands gripped the edge of the operating table, knuckles slowly whitening. "There's no other way to explain it! The Box's shutdown code affected her physically, and that could only happen if it was interfering with her in some way. And given there are no signals passing between her and any part of this ship—"

"That's why she didn't die," De Bruyn muttered incredulously. "It's been keeping her alive!"

"Perhaps. But did you note how her readings returned to normal so quickly? Something or someone must have countered the shutdown code, and the only person that could have done that is Roche herself. She must be aware, on some level at least, of what is happening around her." His gaze was fixed on Roche's face, as though daring her to wake and contradict him.

"But . . ." De Bruyn shook her head. Another realization had come to her while he talked. *How could he have known about the shutdown code*?

<Lemmas?> She broadcast her mental summons as loudly as she dared. <Lemmas!>

The reave answered her from the far side of the ship. <Yes, Reverence?>

<Have you detected any interference from the *Apostle* since it arrived?>

<No, Reverence.>

<Were there any unusual events before then?>

<None.>

<Is there anything going on now?>

<I will check, Reverence.>

Cane's twin had glanced up, and was looking at her closely. "Something is troubling you?" he asked.

"Nothing." She shook her head. <Quickly!> she urged the reave.

<I detect no interference.>

<Nothing from the ship at all?>

<No emissions of any kind, Reverence. Why do you ask?>

She didn't have time to answer. The clone warrior had returned his attention to Roche and the autosurgeon.

"I will be returning to my ship immediately," he said. "I will, of course, be taking Roche with me."

"No, wait—you can't!"

"Do not defy us, De Bruyn," he said, gesturing for Wamel to disconnect Roche from the autosurgeon. The pilot moved obediently forward to help his master.

De Bruyn backed away a step. She had to decide, and fast. Roche had theorized about some sort of connection between the clone warriors; that would have explained how Jelena Heidik had known when she was arriving in the system. Perhaps it explained now how this clone warrior had known about the shutdown code for the Box—codes known only by a handful in the COE, but which Cane had heard used before the Box had taken over Intelligence HQ. Maybe she was overreacting.

Or maybe there was some deeper treachery at work.

The clone warrior watched as Wamel disconnected Roche from the autosurgeon. As the last of the contacts fell away, he indicated that the pilot should swing her around so the two of them could lift her. They seemed to have forgotten all about De Bruyn, or perhaps their ignorance was deliberate. She had played her role. She was no longer important. She had become irrelevant.

She sent a command to *Kindling*, instructing it to prepare for launch, and drew a pistol from her suit's thigh compartment.

"Put her down," she said, aiming the pistol at the clone warrior.

Wamel stopped, looking to his master for guidance. Cane's twin simply stared at De Bruyn, totally expressionless.

"Put her down," she repeated, lowering her aim. "Or I'll shoot *her*."

"Don't be ridiculous, De Bruyn," said the clone warrior. "Think what you'll be throwing away. Think of how hard you've worked for this."

"I *am* thinking of how hard I've worked for this," she spat vehemently. "That's why I can't let you take her."

"But to kill her would mean never learning the truth," he said.

"I've learned nothing anyway!"

He shook his head. "But you would have found out eventually," he said. "This way, you'll never know."

"Just put her *back* on the table!" De Bruyn waved the gun nervously toward the bloodied tabletop.

Wamel let go of Roche's legs and went for his weapon. De Bruyn had a split second to think that he would have been on her side—if only she'd had time to explain—before she shot him. He fell back onto the operating table, smoke sizzling from the hole in his chest, and slid to the floor.

An alarm rang. De Bruyn guessed that Wamel must have sent a warning through the command network before he died. Already she could feel Lemmas batting at her mind, trying to find out what was going on. Once the Disciples learned that she had threatened their leader and killed one of their own, it would be as good as over.

"I want to know the *truth*," she hissed. "Or I'll kill her now!"

The clone warrior raised an eyebrow. "You wouldn't believe me if I told you."

"Try me!"

His eyes shone from his dark complexion. "If my people do not receive the justice we deserve, we will eliminate every Human in the galaxy."

De Bruyn was taken aback for a moment. Although she had considered the possibility before, stated so boldly it sounded almost ridiculous.

"That's—"

"Inhuman?" he offered.

"*Insane*," she said.

Something moved in the doorway behind him—the other Disciples had arrived—and De Bruyn was out of time. She had nothing else to bargain with.

"Let me go," she said, trying anyway.

The clone warrior shook his head. "No," he said. "I couldn't possibly allow that."

She fired: the shot took Roche in the hip and spun her off the table.

Then, moving impossibly fast, the clone warrior was upon De Bruyn, pushing her off balance onto the floor with her arms pinned beneath her suit. His face was close to hers; she could feel his breath as she vainly attempted to break free. A hand in her hair twisted her backward, making her gasp. The air was full of the sound of footsteps as Disciples rushed into the room—but all she had ears for were the words he spoke to her as her neck twisted—

"You would have been right the first time," he whispered. "And *that's* the truth."

With her last strength, she instructed *Kindling* to blow its antimatter fuel reserves.

She never felt the explosion.

17

JW111101000
955.2.14
1380

Morgan Roche was dreaming.

She had never considered herself a terribly imaginative person. Through most of her life, her dreams had consisted of everyday things and simple imagery, easily interpreted. They reflected the logical and rational person she was, and demonstrated a lack of creativity—something COE Intelligence appreciated in their agents. They wanted them to be reliable and thorough, not innovative.

But in accordance with the dramatic change to her life in recent weeks, her dreams had become much more disturbing and vivid, the symbolism darker and more profound. It had gotten to a point where she almost became reluctant to close her eyes for fear of what images she might meet in her sleep.

More often than not the images fragmented and disappeared soon after she awoke, leaving her with just a vague impression of the emotions that the dream evoked—and even this tended to dissipate as the day progressed. But now and then a dream would be too powerful, too provocative, to ignore and would stay with her long into the waking hours.

Two dreams she'd had in Palasian System alone would stay with her forever: the lizard she had been trying to trap, which had in turn caught her, and the meeting with the twins on the deck of the stone boat. There had been other dreams that had left impressions, but none like these. These were dreams she would simply never forget.

As with the dream she was having now. It hadn't even finished yet, but she knew it would be a dream she would not be rid of in a hurry. It felt so real, and the fact that she was unable to wake herself up from it disturbed her terribly.

She was standing inside a hollow sphere barely ten meters wide. Gravity pointed outward from the center of the sphere, with no odd tidal effects arising from the height difference between her head and her feet. No matter where she walked, the sphere was the same: white and featureless. Light seemed to emanate from all around her; there was no obvious source.

But something was wrong. She could feel it. Something terrible was happening outside the sphere. Something wanted to get in to where she was. No matter how hard she tried, she couldn't see beyond the sphere to make out what was trying to get her, and that just scared her all the more. She didn't know even vaguely what would happen if *it* penetrated those walls, if it did get inside, but she knew it would be horrible.

The unspecified threat made her cold, and she wrapped her arms about herself.

She didn't know *anything*. All she remembered was being shot in the back and falling, calling for the Box, hearing Maii calling her . . . and the suited figure that had approached her. There had been something about that figure's voice. Something familiar. She had heard it before. But where?

She couldn't remember. It was hard to concentrate while trapped in the bubble, cut off from the rest of the universe with no way out, and something terrible lurking just outside wanting to get in.

"Hello?" she called, for what felt like the thousandth time. Her voice echoed dully in the chamber.

She bent down and touched the floor. It was warm and yielded slightly, like rubber. Underneath it, though, was something firm. She reached into the pockets of her shipsuit in the hope of finding tools of some description, something that might have helped her dig her way out. But her pockets were as empty as the sphere itself. Nothing in them but *her*.

<Box? Maii?>

As when she had called their names before, there was no reply.

She resumed pacing. There was nothing else for her to do. Eventually something would happen. The bubble would burst and the thing outside would break in, or she would simply wake up.

She wanted the latter more than anything.

Was it possible to sleep within a dream? Possible or not, she woke with a start. Her entire body spasmed, recalling the shot she had taken in the shoulder. And the face leaning over her, the voice speaking to her . . .

"This isn't over yet."

No. Those weren't the words—but it *was* the same voice.

The words rolled around in her thoughts. She reached for her shoulder, feeling for the wound, but there was nothing there now. She was undamaged; there was no blood whatsoever. All she had were the memories of pain, a pain worse than any she had experienced before; a pain too huge to comprehend. And the tide of darkness which had followed, pulling her into its depths.

A shudder passed through her. She had dreamed during her brief sleep, and it came to her now with a viciousness that stung. She had been lying on a slab somewhere, in a dark space, and someone had been looming over her, hurting her. There was pain all through her body—her left arm, hand, and eye; her right shoulder; her face and throat. And in her mind. Someone was cutting into her, slicing her thoughts open, piercing the inner depths of her psyche—and behind that someone, behind that pain, standing in the shadows, was *Page De Bruyn*. . . .

A door seemed to close in her thoughts; images faded. She found herself on her side in the sphere, mouth slack, nose running. She sat up and wiped her face. Her hands were trembling.

"This isn't over yet." Page De Bruyn, of course: the woman who had betrayed her on Sciacca's World; the words De Bruyn said to her the last time they'd seen each other . . .

Outside, the terrible thing was still trying to get in.

She wasn't so sure she was dreaming anymore.

<Box?> Her voice shook slightly. <Box, answer me! I *order* you to talk to me!>

The sphere seemed to tremble beneath her.

<I can't talk right now, Morgan,> came the reply.

Relief washed through her. Although it was unable to disobey her when she issued a direct order, she'd feared the worst. "Box! I thought you'd abandoned me!"

<I can assure you that I have not, Morgan,> it said. <I am doing everything I can to help you. Please be patient for a little longer. I will return to you soon.>

Then it was silent again, and she was alone with the echoes. She listened to them uneasily. The Box had sounded weary, strained. She had never heard it like that before.

The sphere was solid as it had ever been. A stab of pain in her left eye reminded her of her dream's dream, and of De Bruyn. . . .

She wrapped her arms around her legs and waited for the Box to speak again.

A long time passed before the sphere trembled beneath her again. She woke immediately and looked around.

The light had changed. She had a shadow pooling beneath her now. Above her, in the exact center of the sphere, was a point of light too intense to look at directly. She glanced away, blinking.

<Box? Is that you?> she said, rubbing at her stinging eyes.

<Not as you would understand it, Morgan,> it said. <But yes, it is me. Or at least the part of me that believes itself to be conscious. The part that *lives*.>

She looked around again at the sphere, avoiding the light. <So where am I?> she asked. <And why am I here?>

<You are inside me; inside my mind.>

<*Inside* you? That's not possible!>

<It is difficult to explain,> it said. <Your mind is attempting to interpret sensory inputs of types it has never encountered before, and the only way it can do that is by analogy. The truth is that our minds are cohabiting cognitive spaces I normally reserve for myself and my creator. Or to use another analogy, we are thinking with the same mind in the same way that two programs might run simultaneously on the same processor. Just as I have infiltrated your cells in order to exist within you, your mind is now operating within me. Does that make things any clearer?>

She fought an image of two Klein bottles constantly filling and emptying each other. It wasn't helping.

<I guess,> she said, sitting up. <This place isn't real, but it isn't a dream, either?>

<It is *like* a dream in that it is an unreal construct of your subconscious mind comprised of real images. Its details might be wrong, but it does contain some truth. It would be wrong to dismiss it as a complete fabulation.>

<So you really are talking to me right now?>

<Yes, Morgan. I am.>

<Then you can tell me why I'm here. What's going on—and how is Page De Bruyn involved?>

The Box paused for a long moment. When it spoke, its voice was softer than before, almost tentative.

<I must confess to having miscalculated, Morgan,> it said. <Page De Bruyn was somehow able to infiltrate the *Phlegethon* and ambush you on the way to the *Ana Vereine*. You were shot in the process.>

<*That* much I remember.>

<You should have died. Shock very nearly killed you instantly. Only by my sacrificing part of myself were you able to survive long enough to make it to an autosurgeon.>

<You 'sacrificed' yourself?> she echoed. <What does that mean, exactly?>

<The function of many of your cells has been subverted in order to maintain my existence. By reducing the number of such cells in critical places and thereby allowing them to return to normal duties, or by enhancing their activity in others, I was able to stabilize your condition long enough for you to receive treatment.>

She didn't know what to say at first. <And now that I've been treated . . . ?>

<The capacity I sacrificed is beyond immediate recall. Too many cells have died. And there is a complicating factor.>

<That being?>

<You are being tortured, Morgan. The damage to your body is continuing at a rate too great for even the autosurgeon to contain. Far from reclaiming my lost components, I am forced to sacrifice more to ensure your continued survival. I am only able to talk with you now because they have temporarily ceased with the torture.>

Roche felt something much like sadness welling in her. But she wasn't sure who it was for: herself or the Box.

<How long can you keep this up?> she asked.

<A while yet, Morgan. Once this crisis is past—or once it has overtaken my capacity to maintain this refuge—you will be returned to your normal mode of being. If you are allowed to recover, I will eventually regain my former stature. All we need is time—time to *heal*.>

She nodded. <But that's not all, is it? That doesn't explain why I'm here. If your capacity is reduced—and running *me* must be taking a large chunk of what's left—why are you going to such trouble? It's not just to keep me alive, surely?>

<No.> Again the Box hesitated. <You are here because your torturer is a reave.>

Realization dawned. <And reaves can't read AIs,> she said. <If my mind is running on your components, then I'm safe from him, right?>

<That is approximately correct, Morgan. In fact, minds as complicated as mine *can* be partially read by a reave, but he simply does not know where to look. That makes all the difference.>

Roche remembered her fuzzy self-image in n-space. <So are *you* a reave?>

<No—although I can, at times, read your surface thoughts. That is not my purpose. My purpose is—and has always been—to protect you.>

The Box had said something very much like this before. She still wasn't sure she believed it, even in the current circumstances. <So if I'm in here,> she said, <who is the reave torturing?>

<You, still. Although the essence of you is in here, everything else remains outside. To him you appear unconscious, and he has free access to those memories of yours not blocked by Maii. Eventually, though, these blocks will fall, but for the moment everything you do and say in here will be safe.>

<If the block fails, they'll know you weren't destroyed!>

<They already know that. I was able to take direct action only once you were stable in the autosurgeon; even so, I was too late to prevent our kidnap. Since then, I have had no chance to subvert De Bruyn's command. She ordered your implants

removed; I no longer have access to the outside world, except by the passive observation of your sensory input.>

Her thoughts were reeling, and she found herself wishing this really had been a dream. <Okay,> she said. <So what are we going to do?>

<Before De Bruyn realized what was going on, I managed to broadcast a brief call for help. I also programmed the ship to broadcast a tightbeam beacon back the *Phlegethon* every hour. If someone has followed us here, there may be a chance of rescue.>

<And if not?>

<Morgan, there is much I must say to you, and I fear we don't have a lot of time. When your torturer resumes, I must return to the maintenance of your body and will not have the capacity to hold a conversation. Do you understand?>

She nodded. <You have to talk now, while you can—and I don't have a problem with that. It's about time you told me what's going on.>

<I can hardly blame you for feeling this way, Morgan, but do try to see why the truth was withheld from you. It was not that you couldn't be trusted, but that it could have been got at. Had you known prior to your capture what you are about to learn, your torturer would have already extracted it. For that reason, also, I have brought you here, with me. Were we to discuss this in your normal state, your torturer would access those memories instantly.>

<So let's get on with it.> She lay back on the curved floor of the sphere, closing her eyes against the Box's glare. She was tired, apprehensive, even scared. But her curiosity overrode all of these. <Before you're called away.>

<Very well,> the AI said. <The first thing you should know is that you were partially correct in regard to what you said the other day about the High Humans. They *could* destroy the enemy at any time; they possess the technology to do so with ease. What they lack is the inclination.>

As vindicated as Roche felt to learn that she had seen through at least that part of the conspiracy, the conclusion she had avoided disturbed her deeply.

<You mean they'd rather let us all *die* than help us?>

<Morgan, you have to understand that High Humans like the Crescend are rare. Most of them follow a strict anti-Interventionist path—not out of any profound principle, but because they have little interest in the affairs of mundanes. They are as different from you as you are from an insect. Would you save one species of insect over another invading one? Maybe not, unless your interest happened to be myrmecology.>

Roche could tell where it was heading. <So the Crescend is a myrmecologist?> she said dryly. <It studies ants?>

<Essentially, yes. He is concerned enough about mundane Humanity to become directly involved in this situation. The Crescend—perhaps alone of all the High Humans—has considered ridding the galaxy of the threat you face.>

<So why doesn't he?>

<It's not so simple, Morgan. As we discussed earlier, there are many issues he must face before coming to such a decision.>

<Like finding the enemy,> she remembered.

<That, and reaching consensus with the rest of the High Caste. At present, there are four thousand and seventeen High Humans active in this galaxy. Approximately

thirty are Interventionists and willing to support the Crescend. The majority has ruled that it is not the Interventionists' place to decide whether or not to destroy the enemy. They will not allow a massacre of mundanes to occur with the help of the High Caste—even though inaction might well allow a greater massacre to take place. For the time being, the Interventionists can only observe and assist in the decision-making process.>

Roche fought the urge to argue that the anti-Interventionists' stance neither made sense nor was fair. <That's where you come into it, I take it—on the information-gathering side?>

The Box didn't sound as smug as she might have expected. <Suffice it to say that the Interventionists' role is *mainly* passive, for the moment. They have access to the little information available regarding the enemy, and although they are not, strictly speaking, allowed to spread that information, they can ensure that the right people come across it at the right time.>

<Is that what you're doing now?>

<Yes. The Interventionists are on the brink of finalizing their plans. The decision whether or not to assist in the eradication of the enemy is about to be made—and the High Caste majority *will* support it, if it is made in the agreed fashion.>

Roche thought of the thousands of people dying every minute in Sol System, and wondered what was happening outside the system. <Is there any way we can hurry them along?>

<Not at the moment, I'm afraid. Our options are decidedly limited.>

<Well, what *can* we do, then?>

<In a moment, I will give you access to much of the information gathered in recent weeks about the enemy. It will help you decide whether you want to be a part of this process.>

<Why wouldn't I want to be part of it? If I don't kill the enemy, they'll kill me!>

<I feel obliged to point out, Morgan, that your life is at present in more danger from one of your own kind than from the enemy.>

She conceded the point. <Well, all right, Box. I'll look at this information, whatever it is. But then what? Where do we go from there?>

<That remains to be seen, Morgan, and it depends to a large part on what happens to you—your body outside of this shell. If no one rescues you and you die at the hands of De Bruyn's torturer, then all our plans are undone.>

<And if I fall into the enemy's hands?>

There was a lengthy pause. <Then there is no telling what might happen.>

The Box's tone made her nervous again. <But *why*, Box? Why am I so important?>

<Ask yourself one question, Morgan, and think about the answer while I am gone: why can you detect the enemy when so many who have tried before have failed?>

<How the hell am I supposed to know the answer to that, Box?>

<Just think about it.>

<But I *have* thought about it!>

<I'm sorry, Morgan, I can't explain. You must work it out for yourself. Your torture has resumed, and I must attend to your physical well-being. I will return as soon as I can, even if it comes to the worst. Be assured that I am—>

The light above her suddenly went out, and the Box fell silent. Roche sat bolt upright, looking in alarm to where the Box's light had been. It was suddenly very quiet, and the sense of threat from beyond the sphere returned.

Her skin tingled all over as a patch of air one meter in front of her clouded over, as though a self-contained mist had suddenly formed out of nowhere. It swirled around itself for a moment, becoming thicker and darker, then faded to reveal a three-dimensional tank not dissimilar to the instrument displays on the *Ana Vereine*. Inside was a single, flashing icon, shaped like a gold key.

There being no other visible way to interface with the display, she reached in and touched the key.

It turned into an embedded document containing numerous chapters and headings. The glossary was full of references to things she had never heard of before. There were links to diagrams and charts, statistics and formulae. There were texts from the fields of biology, sociology, anthropology, and archaeology. There were maps of regions long since distorted by millennia of stellar movements, and others so up to date that they included the destruction of Palasian System. There was even a mention of her, although when she touched the link, the display returned a message saying: "Access Denied."

She sat back with her legs crossed, the display following her every move. Then when she was relatively relaxed, she began to browse. . . .

The second name she recognized was that of Adoni Cane. There were several Canes listed, and some with aliases; one was the Cane she knew, his activities extensively chronicled thanks to the Box's proximity. Other Adoni Canes had appeared in diverse parts of the galaxy, always to sow chaos, then to disappear. One had left a swath of disorder from the core to the Middle Reaches, his path pointing directly to Sol System. Where they were now was not listed, although the anonymous authors of the text speculated that at least some of them had made it to Sol System already.

She followed two links from that article. One led to the original Adoni Cane. The other explored the history of Humanity, as near to its origins as the High Humans could get. She was amazed to learn that even they didn't know for certain where their progenitors came from. She had always assumed that there was nothing they didn't know—or couldn't find out, if they wanted to. But clearly that wasn't the case.

Humanity had diverged from the original, Pristine genetic strain somewhere between five and six hundred thousand years ago. Its dispersal throughout the galaxy could be plotted by studying the aging of certain anchor points known to have been constructed at that time. Anchor points didn't decay like matter; over hundreds of thousands of years, they dissipated back into the universe's natural background vacuum fluctuations in gradual, known ways. The remnants of the network that had first allowed Humanity to spread outward into the galaxy later gave archaeologists a rough guide to how that expansion had taken place. By following it backward, a vague approximation could be made as to where it had all started.

The study of the propagation of the four known Primordial Castes suggested that the original Human homeworld had once been located near the space currently occupied by the Commonwealth of Empires. This region itself was now totally empty, with any ruins that might have existed long since removed or destroyed. No hard evidence remained to isolate a single system out of the many possibilities, but around twenty had been singled out as likely possibilities.

Sol System was one of them, despite its emptiness. The proponents of this theory raised the history of the system as their main evidence. Time and time again, it had become the focus for fringe groups or obsessive cults as though a subconscious collective memory guided them there. The Sol Apotheosis Movement was just one of many that had used the empty system as a home base, free from observation and interference. The system's name had accrued a certain notoriety among the High Caste observers, and the current convergence only added to that.

From Roche's point of view, the difficulty lay in knowing whether the convergence occurred because of the system's history, or regardless of the fact. The Box had admitted that the Crescend sowed rumors of the enemy's origins in order to draw people to the system, but the reasons for his doing this were unclear. Roche wasn't sure whether the rumors had been started *because* the enemy was already converging there, or whether the enemy had been lured there by the rumors, along with everyone else.

The history of the system itself, though, did intrigue her. It had once possessed a number of planets—at least eight, if the records were accurate, plus a large number of dark bodies, an asteroid field, and a cometary halo. Their fate was a mystery, although one observer grimly hypothesized that the composition and mass of the ring suggested that the entire system had somehow been ground to dust and put in orbit around the primary. Why anyone would want to do this remained unknown.

Among the ancient records that did remain from the older days of Humanity were scraps pertaining to the present situation. The name Adoni Cane was among those scraps, as were the other names the Box had mentioned in Palasian System. They had once been real people.

On a list of military honors, Field Admiral Adoni Cane of the Old Earth Advance Guard had received a Military Star for extraordinary acts of valor against the enemy. General Jelena Heidik distinguished herself against the same enemy in a place called Alpha Aurigae and received a Mars St. Selwyn Medal for her trouble. Vani Wehr was a civilian whose quick thinking on the Clarke Cylinder thwarted an enemy incursion and earned him an Honorable Mention. Captain Sadoc Lleshi was one of many Ground Corps officers posthumously recognized for excellence in battle after the long and bitter campaign had ended with the enemy's defeat. And so on.

Although there was no explanation for the names of the medals awarded or places mentioned, and nothing placing the battles in any context, Roche recognized the pattern immediately. The names used by the present enemy were all taken from those distinguished in the battle against them in the distant past. No doubt it was intended as an insult or a grand irony. That lent credence to the theory that the "enemy" referred to but never actually named in the old records was indeed the source of Adoni Cane and his siblings—but it didn't really tell her anything new about the enemy, past or present. There were still no recognizable names or locations, no descriptions, no clues at all as to where they came from or what they had looked like.

There were some tantalizing snippets, however. One concerned the command language Linegar Rufo had used in his attempts to communicate with the clone warrior in Palasian System. It appeared to be an actual language, not specifically restricted to military applications—although, again, its origins were clouded. Whether the Box had lied when it denied recognizing the language upon first hearing it, or whether this was new information added since then, Roche couldn't tell. Either way, its unique syntax and dissimilarity to any tongue currently in use marked it as enigmatic. Why it remained when so little else did was not explained, and Roche had a feeling that if she pursued the matter, she would run up against another Access Denied warning.

When she hunted for a genetic reference to the ancient enemy, she also found no data available. That didn't surprise her as such—if the records didn't contain even a name, then a DNA record was too much to hope for—but it did disappoint her. Hard evidence of a connection between the ancient enemy and the new would have been good. It would have silenced the doubt that nagged at her even now, asking her how it was possible for a connection to exist across such a gulf of time.

But then she remembered that to people like Adoni Cane, no time at all had really passed. The capsules that had created them had been drifting through the galaxy for over half a million years, their contents frozen, waiting for the moment to loose a new clone warrior. Their creators had programmed them and set them loose, then been destroyed forever. The legacy of their clone warriors was all that remained.

As such, their own genetic code was of particular interest to the High Humans. Were the unique intron passages somehow responsible for the unusual structures in Cane's brain that had baffled Sylvester Teh on Sciacca's World? These in turn might have been related to their odd n-space impression. But how? Minds greater than hers had grappled with these problems and had come to no firm conclusions. All were convinced that the introns of the enemy contained important information or played a critical role, but no one knew exactly how.

After what felt like an eternity browsing through the file, Roche closed her eyes and leaned back on the yielding floor of the sphere. She really wasn't learning terribly much. Yes, there had been a war in the distant past, whose losers had seeded this peculiar revenge. And yes, Adoni Cane was one of them. But she still didn't know who the enemy was, and she still didn't know how she fit into it all.

The Box had asked her to think about why she alone could detect the enemy. She was no closer to the answer than when she had started, and she suspected that no amount of random browsing would find it, either. But if she knew that, then the Box knew it too. It obviously hadn't meant that she would find the answer there.

But where, then?

She got up again and began to pace. The misty screen followed her for a while, then collapsed to a fuzzy point and fell behind. There was nothing else in the sphere. It was as featureless as ever, its air perfectly breathable and temperature perfectly comfortable. Her only distraction was the occasional urge to sleep, which she resisted. Even if such urges meant that the Box was having problems running her on its components, she didn't care. Its components were part of *her*. She had every right to use them, too . . .

She stopped in mid-pace, struck by an idea.

Was *that* what the Box had meant? Could it be so simple?

The galaxy she knew was about to be destroyed by a relatively small number of superior warriors partly because Humanity lacked the ability to tell these warriors from their own. If the High Humans did in fact possess the ability to wipe out the enemy, then presumably they also knew how to find them. But if the Crescend wasn't allowed to intervene directly, he also couldn't stand back and let Humanity be slaughtered. He therefore had to find another way to help.

One way would be to provide Humanity with a means of detecting the enemy. Since mundane Humanity already had access to epsense abilities, a slight enhancement of those abilities could be enough to give them an edge. If it could be done subtly, without obviously interfering, all the better. In short, the ability Roche had could be a "gift" from the Crescend. It might have been implanted within her along with the Box.

If it was true, she had been tinkered with yet again.

And now she was a *tool*.

She began to pace again, angrily. It all made perfect sense. The Surin had learned how to engineer for epsense abilities, and the High Humans surely had superior abilities. Why not give her the ability to perform this feat and allow her to discover it by accident? No one could accuse the Crescend of creating a weapon designed explicitly for retaliation: after all, she was unable to access n-space without the help of another, and her ignorance of the ability meant that it might never have been found. From the outside looking in, it could even be mistaken for a fluke of genetics.

But why *her*?

She cursed aloud and strode on, working her anger out. She hadn't asked for this! What was she supposed to do? Devote what little of her life remained to the hunting down and destruction of the enemy? She didn't even know how many there were in the galaxy; there might be millions! High Executioner wasn't a role she relished playing alone, and without respite—and, ultimately, with little chance of success. It was too much for one person.

Unless, she thought, there were *more* like her. . . .

But there was little she could do except stew over it until the Box returned, and she had no idea how long that might be. She walked around the sphere to where the reduced display wavered in the air, and passed a hand through it. It returned instantly to its full size, displaying the key once again. She sat down on her haunches and searched every link she thought might be even remotely promising. Anything to distract her.

She learned some things she hadn't known before. The Crescend wasn't the most powerful Interventionist. One called Aquareii—whom Rey Nemeth had once mentioned in passing—coordinated that faction in the High Caste. The Crescend's value, it seemed, lay in his close proximity to the convergence—to Sol System—although his precise location was never specified. Roche didn't know whether members of the High Caste retained a physical component when they Transcended; for all she knew, they might have written their minds on the fabric of space itself, never to be erased. But if they did have components that could be damaged or even destroyed, she could understand why they kept their locations a secret, even from each other. When one's potential for life was equal to millions of mundane lives combined, death was a tragedy only comprehensible in the same terms.

There were other details, too, that she couldn't see connected in any particular way to the matter of the enemy. One struck her as being so far afield that it couldn't possibly be right: the discovery in a distant part of the galaxy of several anchor point remnants that appeared to be older than Humanity itself. Either the dating of their decay was wrong, or Humanity was simply older than first thought—

The sphere suddenly and violently vibrated, flexing as though it had been struck by a giant hammer.

The display dissolved as an inrush of sensory data flooded through Roche—pain, fear, nausea, paralysis . . .

Almost buried beneath it, she heard two words:

". . . between thoughts."

She knew instantly what had happened. Someone had used the Box's shutdown codes! She hung on desperately as the sphere threatened to unravel beneath her. Clutching for the appropriate response before she lost herself totally to the overwhelming sensations, she called out as loudly as she could: *"The game begins! The game begins!"*

As the rush ebbed slightly, she fell back with a gasp. The sphere was still unstable, but at least the pain had relaxed its grip on her.

A flash of light above her heralded the return of the AI.

<Box! What's happening?>

<I don't have time to explain,> it said, its voice thin and strained, its light weak. <And I won't be able to protect you for much longer, Morgan.>

<But—> she began.

<There isn't *time*,> it snapped. <Tell me now: do you *know* what you are?>

<The Crescend made me like this, didn't he?>

<Yes, but why?>

She paused, reluctant to say what she knew to be true. <I'm a weapon,> she said finally.

<That's right, Morgan.> The Box sounded almost relieved. <You are. And it is important that you contact the Crescend as soon as you are able.>

<What?> Roche felt confused. <*How*?>

<With the code phrase 'Dawn comes,'> it said, its voice growing softer. <The High Caste has agreed to abide by your judgment on the matter of the enemy. When you have weighed up the information you have learned here, contact the Crescend and let him know your decision. He will act immediately.>

The sphere shuddered around her. <What are you talking about?> she said, fighting down panic.

<On its own, the High Caste will not sanction the eradication of a weaker enemy, but it *will* if the decision is made by an ordinary Human. That is the way they have resolved to break the moral dilemma. The decision is yours, Morgan, and yours alone.>

For a moment she couldn't speak. This was far more than she had guessed. The Crescend was putting the lives of Cane and all his siblings in her hands!

The light of the AI flickered, then returned at a reduced intensity. <You must decide, Morgan,> it repeated.

Stunned, Roche closed her eyes. This wasn't what she wanted to hear. <I don't believe you, Box,> she said.

The sphere seemed to be unraveling again beneath her, and the Box's voice grew fainter every second. <Yes you do, Morgan; I feel it. You *have* to believe. It is why you are here!>

<I . . .> She shook her head. Her thoughts were becoming fuzzy, as though whipped by a rising wind.

<*Please*, Morgan!>

Something caved inside her. She had never heard the Box so anxious, so desperate.

<But I don't even know where he is!> she said, her panic rising steadily as the Box's voice gradually faded.

<Just aim for Sol, Morgan. Use the words I gave you. Use the—>

Before it could finish, the sphere was torn apart by forces beyond her comprehension and the Box's light faded completely. Pain exploded through her. Her skin was afire and every cell of her being cried out in agony. She dimly heard voices—someone shouting her name—and felt hands roughly on her shoulders.

She opened her eyes to a darkness broken by the faint flicker of light.

"Box?" she said weakly.

But all she saw, looming from the shadows, was Cane's face.

18

HIC *God's Monkey*
955.2.15
1210

After the solitude of the sphere, his voice struck her like a whip.

"She's alive!"

Roche reached for him with hands bent into claws. "Help . . ."

"Don't move," he said, putting his arms beneath her to lift her up. He placed her down again on something hard and cold.

"The Box . . ." The world grayed for a moment, and she clutched at consciousness with the last of her strength. "Don't let me die!"

"Trust me," Cane said. "I have no intention of allowing that to happen."

She felt an incredible pain surge through her as he stretched her out. Her gut heaved and she tasted blood—just as something exploded nearby and she was flung back onto the floor. Someone called out in pain; she didn't recognize the sound of her own voice.

"That idiot blew her ship!" Cane said loudly. "We'll have to manage as best we can."

Was he talking to her? Roche couldn't tell. But her mouth moved feebly in response anyway.

Robed figures suddenly loomed over her, trying to pick her up. She recoiled from them, confused. Was she still back on the *Phlegethon*, trapped by Page De Bruyn? Was all that had gone before merely a dream, and the nightmare proper only just beginning?

Wanting to cry out, she let her body go limp. She was simply too weak to resist.

Her head lolled back over her shoulder, and she glimpsed a body dressed in a black uniform lying in one corner, its head twisted at an impossible angle. The face had once belonged to Page De Bruyn. It didn't seem to belong to anyone now.

She heard Cane's voice as though from a great distance, ordering the robed people to move faster. She thought he sounded different somehow, but was unable to be sure with the wailing of alarms and the pounding of machines booming through the bulkheads. He sounded colder, more efficient perhaps. He sounded *dangerous*.

Her body spasmed as the terrible realization spread like burning ice through her mind: *it wasn't Cane*!

"Where"—Her mouth was full of blood. She tried her best to spit it out—"are you taking me?" she managed.

One of the robed figures turned to face her. Beneath the cowl, the woman's skin was pale-blue and waxy. Her eyes were red.

"To Hell," she said matter-of-factly.

Roche closed her eyes; despair threatened to overwhelm her. She could feel it gathering like the black clouds of a dust storm on the horizon. If she let it in, it might never leave. She had to fight it.

<Box? Box—can you hear me?>

Nothing.

<Box!>

Silence.

<The game begins,> she tried lamely, but even as she spoke the words she knew it was pointless.

Her bearers slowed and she heard the hissing of an airlock.

"Through here," she heard Cane say. "On the acceleration couch. Careful!"

She was brought forward and laid gingerly on a reclined, cushioned seat. The sound of alarms faded slightly. She tried to look around, but her vision was blurred and hazy. Her left eye was completely blind.

The hands that had held her fell away, and a series of footsteps led out of the room. Then there was a voice:

"Master?"

"What is it?" Cane snapped.

Roche could hear the speaker's obsequious tone; she imagined him bowing, but couldn't see to be sure. "Master, I would accompany you to safety."

"That is not necessary. The *Apostle* is only minutes away—"

"Allow me to serve you, Master."

"You have served me," he said. "But now you must return to the others and tend to repairs."

"But our pilot—"

"Another ship shall be summoned," he said, his patience wearing thin. "You will be rescued."

"Master—"

"I *command* you to wait." The frost in Adoni Cane's voice could have cooled stars. "Leave me now, or invoke my displeasure!"

"Yes, Master." The owner of the voice didn't believe he would be rescued; that much was clear. Yet he obeyed. His footsteps slowly shuffled away, then were cut off by the closing of the airlock.

The baying of alarms ceased, and for a second all was silent.

"Fools." Cane's voice so close to her made her jump.

"Where . . . ?" she tried, then: "Why . . . ?"

"Don't talk." His strong hands strapped a harness around her broken body, tying her hands together in the process. Then a medical pack was pressed against her hip. "I only have one of these, I'm afraid. I didn't think you'd be this bad."

The pack attached itself with a slight sting.

Why do you want me alive? It was nothing more than a thought. She was unable to control her voice enough to do anything other than moan.

"That's it," he said, his tone almost encouraging. "Keep fighting, Morgan, and you might even make it."

She shuddered, feeling a strange coldness in her mind. She wanted to succumb to the physical and mental exhaustion, wanted to sleep. But that was a luxury she couldn't afford just yet. For now she only had grief to distance her from the pain. . . .

Gradually, as the medical pack took effect, the pain began to ease. The sharp edges in the world softened. Blinking, she could make out flashing lights around her, blurred as if she were looking at them through rain over a pane of glass. Cane sat not far away, his back to her.

Instruments chattered briefly; she felt a gentle nudge of acceleration. Then something clanged, and the acceleration became more insistent. She clutched the sides of her couch as the pressure mounted. It might have lasted only a minute or so, but seemed like an hour.

As the minutes ticked by, she found her vision clearing even more. Not very much at first, and only in her right eye, but she appreciated any improvement.

She was in an ordinary-looking cockpit, with Cane operating the pilot's station. All she could see was his scalp and the lights reflecting from it like multicolored stars in a chocolate sky.

"Where are you taking me?" she asked eventually.

His chair swiveled to face her. He pointed to a display. In it she could make out, vaguely, a large Hurn ship against a starry backdrop.

Despair rippled through her. "Am I going to die?"

"Not yet," he said, returning to his console. "That would be counterproductive."

"If you think I'm going to help you—"

"Conserve your strength, Morgan. You're going to need it."

Something in his voice made her look at him again. *Was* he the Adoni Cane she knew or not? He looked and sounded exactly like him, apart from the coldness in his tone. But that was the whole point: the enemy was composed of clone warriors, many of them identical. He could very well be one of Cane's siblings with the same face, but with the killing instinct intact.

Regardless of who he was, he was right about conserving her strength. She felt weak right down to her core, and the coldness was still in her mind. The pain was manageable now, thanks to the ministrations of the medical pack, but that meant she could look down and see how badly she had been injured. When she did, she instantly wished she hadn't.

The Hurn ship grew larger in the display. Cane had mentioned something about "the *Apostle*" being only minutes away. Presumably they were one and the same. Although she had never seen this particular ship before, the connection between it and the black-robed figures they had left behind seemed clear. Some sort of organization staffed and supplied by Hurn backers had obviously assisted Page De Bruyn in hunting her down. Why, she didn't know, but the presence of a clone warrior high on the command chain seemed ominous. If this *was* her Cane, how could he have infiltrated such a group so quickly?

Her wrists chafed where he had tied her hands together. Her left hand in particular ached as though stiff from a half-healed wound. The back of her head felt like someone had hammered a nail into it, and the vision still hadn't cleared in her left eye. When she blinked, the socket itself even felt odd, unnatural—

Empty. The Box had said that her implants had been removed. The harsh reality of that fact was only now sinking in. Without them, she felt hollow, incomplete.

"Why did you rescue me?" she asked.

He turned again to face her. "If you can't answer that question, then perhaps I have wasted my time."

Him and the Box, she thought to herself. "Maybe you have."

He shrugged. "It might change nothing."

She winced as another wave of pain swept through her.

He came over to check her medical pack. "I haven't come all this way to watch you die," he said dispassionately. "You'll be treated properly when we arrive."

Her words came through clenched teeth. "How much longer?"

"Not long. We're almost in range." He turned back to the display. "It'll be over soon."

He adjusted something on the pack and warmth rushed through her. At first she resisted it, wanting to remain alert. Maybe all hope was not quite lost; if a chance came to escape, she had to be ready.

But then she remembered what she had seen when she had looked down at her body. There was nothing she could do. She closed her eyes and let the warmth caress her pain, blunt the icy coldness inside her.

A moment later, it disappeared completely. In its absence, she felt strangely light, as though it had been tying her down. In its wake, she felt almost free. . . .

That was crazy, she thought. She was half-dead, the captive of an unknown organization with links to the enemy. Not only had she no way of escaping, but she wouldn't even live much longer if they chose not to help her.

Cane cocked his head as though listening to something.

"That's close enough," he said, turning back to her. "Morgan, I have someone who wishes to speak to you."

Roche steeled herself for another grim surprise, glancing around the cabin to see if anyone else had entered.

Then she heard the voice—loud and clear in her thoughts.

<It's so good to feel your mind again, Morgan,> said the reave. <We thought we'd lost you for good!>

<Maii?> Roche tried to sit, but pain forced her back. <Maii, is that you?>

"Look at the screen," said Cane.

Through her one remaining eye, Roche watched as they passed through the fringes of a camouflage screen and the Hurn ship became the *Ana Vereine*.

"It really *is* you?" There was both uncertainty and relief in her whispered words.

He smiled. "Does that surprise you?"

<We couldn't let you know until you passed out of range of Lemmas, their reave,> Maii said. Her voice hinted at dark truths Roche didn't want to explore. <I'm sorry we kept you hanging.>

"But *how* . . . ?"

She felt Cane's hand on her left shoulder, pressing gently but firmly. "This can be discussed later, Morgan. Right now I want to dock and get us out of here before anyone back there suspects what has happened—before their *real* contact shows up."

She nodded weakly. Maii filled her mind with a radiant warmth. She felt as though she had been dipped in a bath of light, and the cold, dead touch of the Hurn reave faded like ice in the sun. For the first time, Roche allowed herself the luxury of really *believing* that she might live long enough to see her friends again.

Anything beyond that could wait.

* * *

Haid and Vri met the scutter with a fully equipped stretcher. Barely had she been placed in its embrace than her treatment began. The autosurgeon dictated the list of her injuries all the way to the medical center: beginning with her shattered hip and pelvis, her punctured lung and blood loss, and working its way down to relatively minor muscle damage and gashes. It was still droning on when Haid cut off its output in order to let her rest.

At the same time, Kajic sent the ship accelerating back in-system, away from Roche's captors. She was conscious just long enough to learn that the *Phlegethon* was still under intense attack, so was not considered a safe port. Kajic had plotted a relatively innocuous orbit instead, bypassing the major concentrations of fighting in the system and skimming close to the outer edge of the ring where traffic was light. The ship would travel under heavy camouflage and in a constant state of alert. If they *were* spotted, they would be ready to defend themselves.

Haid was sitting with her when the autosurgeon put her under, his black skin and artificial eyes gleaming in the medical center's bright lights.

"Don't worry, Morgan," he said, touching her arm lightly. "We'll still be here when you come back."

"How long?" The anesthetic was already beginning to work; her voice sounded like it was coming from kilometers away.

"As long as it takes, I guess."

"Two hours," she said. "There's something . . . something I have to do."

Haid glanced at the autosurgeon's holographic display. "It'll take at least six to clean you up, not to mention fitting the new eye."

"Forget the eye." She could barely keep her remaining one open. "Make it three, or so help me I'll—I'll—"

—send you back to Sciacca's World.

She never found out whether she finished the sentence.

When she woke, the pain was gone. That more than anything else convinced her that survival had been worthwhile.

She couldn't move, though. The autosurgeon had her carefully encased in a body cast that allowed the use of her right arm only. When she tried to sit up, it correctly interpreted her feeble movements and tilted the entire bed instead.

"It won't let you out of its clutches just yet," said Haid. He was sitting with his feet up on one of the other operating tables with his back to the holographic "cybercorpses" rotating slowly in one wall.

"You're still here?" she asked. "Haven't you anything better to do?"

"It's not as if I've been sitting around idly waiting for you to wake up." He smiled at her warmly. "You said three hours, and it's been exactly that. I just had to be here on time."

She smiled also, envying him his mobility and fitness—even with his cybernetic mesh and patchwork limbs. "How am I?"

He swung his feet off the table, but didn't stand. "Much better. Not one hundred percent by any means, but at least you look"—he shrugged—"*better.*"

"Is there a mirror in here?"

"No, but I'm sure Maii can arrange something."

Roche felt the girl's featherlight touch in her mind, and full stereoscopic vision poured through her, from Haid's eyes. She saw a white-wrapped corpse half in and half out of a gleaming sarcophagus. One eye was covered with a patch. Her mouth was swollen; yellowing bruises spread down one cheek to her jaw. Her head had been shaved and half-covered with bandages.

<It's a vast improvement,> said Maii.

<Is it? Show me.>

"That's not a good idea," Haid warned.

<It's therapeutic,> Roche insisted. <If this is better, how bad was I?>

A flash of red passed before her secondhand eyes, but it didn't really register. The naked woman curled up in pain, the one arm nearly severed and vertebrae visible through wounds at the back of her neck, the messy crater on her right hip, the blood . . . surely this couldn't have been her?

"Enough," she said, swallowing. If the Box really was dead this time, at least she knew why. Nothing else could have kept her alive through such mistreatment. She tried shaking the image from her mind by changing the subject altogether.

"Where's Cane?"

"Up in the observation blister," said Haid. "He's been there since we got you back."

"I want to talk to him later." She couldn't help the tiredness in her voice. She was alive, yes, but there was still so much to do. "First, tell me *how* you got me back. How did you know where I was?"

Haid stood, frowning, and stepped up to her. "I'm not sure I understand all of it myself, Morgan. We knew something had gone wrong almost immediately, when you didn't arrive at the *Ana Vereine* and Maii couldn't find you. There'd been a disturbance in the docks below us, and security arrived just minutes too late. Automatic monitoring in the area had been shut down somehow during the ambush, so we never did get a good look at what was going on, and the ship they had you on had detached and hot-launched before anyone could work out it was involved. Things were pretty messy in the area because of the attack. It wasn't until we received a tightbeam squirt from the ship that we guessed."

"What did the message say?"

"It was fairly short, telling us basically that you were aboard and injured and that a pulse would be sent every hour telling us where the ship was, but it didn't tell us who it was from. The Heresiarch picked it up and passed it on. I wanted to follow straightaway but Cane was adamant we shouldn't. Quite apart from getting through the siege around the *Phlegethon*, he felt there was also the matter of the people who captured you to take into consideration. We couldn't afford to take the chance that they might kill you if we came in with guns blazing. So we kept track of the ship and thought of another way."

"By masquerading as one of them."

"Basically, yes."

"And who *are* they?"

He looked uncomfortable. "To be honest, I don't know."

"So how did you know what to do?"

"I didn't. It was all Cane's idea. He got us through the blockade and gave us the specifications of the ship we were to impersonate. When we caught up with the ship you were on, he gave us the codes to broadcast to convince them that we were who we said we were. And when we were in range he insisted that he should go aboard alone. He didn't tell us what he was going to do, just told us to trust him. I didn't know whether I should, but couldn't think of anything better to do. He seemed to know what he was doing, and if it got you back . . ." Haid shrugged. "It worked out in the end, I guess."

She was silent for a while, remembering Cane's tone, remembering how he had dealt with the groveling Hurn. And she thought of the epsense link that possibly connected the clone warriors. . . .

"He was different back there," she said. "For a while there, it was almost as if he *was* the enemy, you know? I think he was close to becoming one of them."

"That's what I was afraid of," Haid said, concern etched deeply in his face. "I couldn't help think that if he went too far, he wouldn't come back to us." He shrugged again. "I didn't want to lose him as well."

"I don't believe he was ever ours to begin with."

"You know what I mean," he said. "We need him here."

Perhaps a little too much, she thought, but said nothing.

"Alta Ansourian is still with us, by the way," he went on. "She refused to disembark when she had the chance. She's still in her quarters."

"Doing what?" Roche asked.

"Staring at the wall as far as I can tell," he said. "Cane has tried talking to her a couple of times, but to no avail. She just won't snap out of it."

"Give her time, Ameidio," she said. "She just witnessed her father being murdered. It's going to take more than a few days to snap out of that."

He nodded wearily. "Who knows?" he said. "Maybe she has the right idea. At least she doesn't have to worry about . . . everything."

He pulled his gaze away from hers; Roche realized he was embarrassed.

She reached out and took his hand lightly in hers. "If it's any consolation, Ameidio," she said, "I think this will all be over soon."

His hand squeezed hers back. "Not soon enough for my liking." He forced a smile.

"Have we heard anything from the council?"

"Nothing yet. There's an ftl drone following us, though. We can call them when you're ready. If the fighting's done at their end, they might be willing to reconvene."

It felt like weeks had passed since the last meeting. "How long was I gone?"

"Just over thirty hours," he said. "You still haven't told us what happened to you."

"I'm not sure I'm ready to." Her scalp itched, and although she wanted to scratch it, doing so would mean letting go of his hand. She wasn't ready to do that, either, even though she'd already held it longer than she'd intended to.

As though through a fog she saw Page De Bruyn's face as it had looked, lifeless, on the deck of the Hurn ship. She still had no idea what her former superior had been doing to her, and why. If the Box had been around, she could have asked it, but this time it seemed to be irrevocably gone. Having lost it once before, she found it hard to believe that it wouldn't come back to her again—but she could *feel* its absence all through her body. It was gone forever.

"Hey," Haid said, letting go of her hand and wiping her cheek. "I'll go and let you get some rest."

She took a deep breath. "How about *you* get some rest? I'll bet you haven't slept for two days. Besides, I want to talk to Uri. Then Cane. I need to sort this out now, before I convince myself it was all a bad dream."

"The surgeon says—"

"I don't care what it says, Ameidio," she cut in. "It's keeping me comfortable enough in here, and I'm not planning on going anywhere for a while."

He nodded reluctantly. "Okay, but you call if you need anything, all right?"

She assured him she would, and watched as he turned and strode from the room.

When he was gone, she turned her eyes to the ceiling and asked: "Okay, Uri, what *does* the autosurgeon say?"

"That you are responding unexpectedly well to treatment." The voice of the ex-captain of the ship came from one side of the room, not all around as she'd expected. She glanced around to find that three "cybercorpses" had disappeared. In their place, Kajic's hologram reclined comfortably in a standard bridge chair, affecting a warm and slightly amused expression.

Her bed rotated to face him.

"Your fractures have already knit," he went on, "and all tissue grafts are proceeding ahead of schedule. Although the autosurgeon doesn't anticipate your returning to full mobility for at least two days, I wouldn't be surprised if you were out of the cast in eight hours or so and walking within the day."

"That seems unreasonably fast," she said.

"As I said, you are recovering quicker than expected. I've had a quick look to ascertain why and found some evidence of nanotech tampering here and there. It looks like you were being helped along. Not so much now, but certainly when you were first brought here."

She nodded slowly, not wanting to say anything in case it made him suspicious. "I guess I was lucky."

He smiled then. "It's okay, Morgan. I guessed the Box was still around after Perdue Habitat. You had too many lucky escapes that could not have occurred any other way. And since it wasn't anywhere on the ship, it had to be on you—or inside you. It helped you escape from the destruction of the habitat, it sent the message when you were kidnapped, and it somehow kept you alive long enough to reach here. Am I right?"

"Yes," she said. "But it's dead, now."

"Are you sure?"

"You said the evidence of nanotech had faded. That's the only way you would have picked it up—and that's why it didn't want me examined back on the *Phlegethon*. A thorough search would've found signs of it for sure. Since you can't find it now, it must be gone."

"I'm sorry, Morgan," he said.

She brushed aside his sympathy, genuine or not. "Don't be, Uri," she said. "It lied and it manipulated me and I'm still not entirely sure what its hidden agenda was. Maybe in the long run I'm better off without it."

"Maybe." He paused for a moment, the light from his hologram flickering minutely. "Was this what you wanted to talk to me about?"

Roche sighed. "Uri, I need to make a decision," she said. "One that could affect millions, maybe even trillions of people."

"Regarding the enemy?"

"Yes." She cast about for a way to phrase her question, but in the end decided to be blunt. The chances were he would take it for a metaphor, anyway. Not even she could take the idea seriously yet.

"If you found a way to wipe them all out," she said slowly, "would you do it?"

"That depends," he said.

"On what?"

"On why I was doing it, of course."

"Because if you didn't do it, there is every chance that Pristine Humanity could wind up extinct!" She blurted it out, and, having done so, realized how ridiculous it sounded. She sighed again, this time in annoyance. "There's only a few of them, Uri, but their method of turning us against each other might actually work."

"But why are they doing it, Morgan? Ask yourself that. They might have good reasons—or think they have, anyway. Whoever created them may have felt justified in unleashing them against us."

"Justified half a million years ago, maybe—but *now*? So much time has passed; Humanity has moved a long way since then. Surely we shouldn't be held responsible for the crimes of our ancestors? There must be another way for them to achieve retribution—or whatever the hell it is they want."

"I agree. But if they're programmed to attack—"

"Exactly: they're *programmed*. There *is* no other way, for them. But does that make it *right*?"

"There is no right and wrong in war, Morgan. There is only expediency, efficiency, and capability—all untainted by emotions or morals. Nearly all wars are won or lost without regard for Human values. As a result, the right side loses as often as the wrong. Only when the odds are stacked highly in favor of one side can such qualities be called into play. Mercy, after all, relies on the certainty that one party can kill another any time they wish. Without that certainty, mercy is meaningless. Only the most powerful can afford the luxury of forgiveness."

She half-smiled. "Once again, you sound like my old Tactics lecturer."

He returned the smile, briefly. "Ultimately, though, Morgan, all the theory in the world will only get you so far. In the end you reach a point where you have to decide for yourself. When you have to *act*. War is as much about instinct as it is about higher thought. Indeed, one could argue that if we thought *enough*, there would be no war at all."

"Now what are you trying to say?"

"That it's your choice, and I don't feel qualified to advise you. If what I think you're saying is true, and you do somehow have this capability, then I don't envy your position. I don't think I could make a decision like that. I'm too narrowly defined."

She frowned. "I don't know what you mean."

"I mean that in some ways I'm like the enemy. I'm programmed to obey a small set of rules, inasmuch as a Human can be." His image shrugged. "I don't remember my previous life. Maybe I was no different from who I am now, the person I became after the experiment. But all that I am, now, is here within this hull. All I really care about is the ship and the people who travel within it."

"Well," she said, "it's nice to know we're in good hands."

He disregarded the compliment, his image staring over at her with a sober expression. "Morgan, I would be just as happy to leave this system and never come back, since we would all be safer that way. But I know we can't do that, and never will be able to until the business with the enemy is sorted out. I wouldn't be surprised if fighting has already started escalating outside Sol System. Soon, perhaps, if we don't do anything about it here and now—nowhere will be safe."

"If I could only be certain that it did in fact boil down to a 'them or us' decision," she said. "That would make it simpler. Or if there was some way we could negotiate, find some other solution, or . . ."

She ran her hand across her face. Her skin was clammy, and she felt tired, but she didn't want to rest anymore. She wanted to push this through to the finish.

"Have you told anyone about the Box?" she asked.

"No, of course not."

"Don't, then. Not that it matters anymore, I suppose."

She rested her head back on the bed, and the autosurgeon misinterpreted it as a request to lie flat. She didn't stop it lowering the bed, though. She just closed her eyes for a moment and put her forearm over them, to block out the glare from the ceiling light. Her mind felt full, heavy. There was too much to think about, too much to *do*, and simply not enough of her to go around. . . .

When she woke an hour later, it was on the crest of a soothing dream. She was a plant, absorbing nutrients and turning them into cells one by one, growing and stretching at a patient, steady rate. She existed; she was. Stripped of all fears, all concerns, she delighted in the simplicity of just *being*. . . .

Then the memory of the decision she had to make came rushing back, and she realized at once what was going on.

<Maii?>

<Yes, Morgan. It's me,> replied the girl, without the smallest trace of guilt. <You needed it.>

<Did I?> she said, stretching her one free arm and raising her head. She could at least feel her other limbs now, under the cast. <Actually, I *do* feel better.>

<That's the idea. Epsense therapy assists the biofeedback process better than any other known technique.>

<Did you have anything to do with my healing before?>

<No. This was the first time. It must have been the Box, as Uri said.>

Roche rested her head back on the bed's cushioned support. <Can I ask you something, Maii?>

<Of course, Morgan.>

<When I was kidnapped, why couldn't you find me?>

<I don't know.> The girl's reply was instantaneous and frank. <Even when I knew where to look, all I could pick up was a faint shadow. It was like you had retreated inward, hidden yourself somehow. I couldn't try too hard or else Lemmas would have noticed me, but I still should have detected *something*.>

Roche thought of the white sphere that had enclosed her from the torturer-reave. <How's my image now?>

<Rock-solid. More so than ever, in fact.>

<I thought it might be. The Box told me that it was complex enough for you to read, if you'd known how to look. Maybe it was making my n-space signature a little odd. Interfering with it.>

<Probably, I'd say, given the fact that you're almost back to normal now.>

<Then that could be what the *irikeii* meant when he referred to me as an 'enigma.'>

<It's hard to say,> Maii responded. <I never understood what he meant by that. But I do find it hard to believe that an AI could ever have an n-space image. . . .>

Roche was too tired to explain—not that she was entirely sure about it herself. Part of her wished she could return to the peace of mind her dream had offered, even though she knew it had been false.

<Seduced at last, eh?> Maii asked with a smile in her voice.

<Don't get too cocky,> Roche returned. <It's not every day I need it that bad.>

<True. But the first time is always the hardest . . .>

Roche resisted the girl's soothing touch. <Sorry, Maii, but I need some time on my own to think right now. I'll call if I need you, okay?>

<I'll be here, Morgan.>

Her mind felt cold when the reave had gone, but she was glad for the privacy. There were things she needed to consider that the girl had probably already read from her mind but which she didn't want to dwell on with an audience watching. The Box had left her in a difficult situation which, if everything it had said was true, required a clarity of thought she found difficult to achieve even at the best of times.

She went to fold her hands across her chest but was stopped by the white plastic shell of the surgical cocoon enclosing her left arm. She rested her right hand on her neck instead, finding comfort and reassurance in the beating of her own pulse. She was still on the board.

You must decide, Morgan . . .

The Box's words turned idly in her thoughts. It had said that the High Humans were reluctant to act against an inferior enemy, even if there was a possibility that the enemy might actually win against the mundanes they chose to attack. It had said that the Crescend, a noted Interventionist, was concerned about mundane affairs and would act against the enemy if allowed to by the rest of the High Caste. It had concluded by saying that the High Humans had agreed to abide by the decision of one mundane Human, thereby taking the moral dilemma out of their own hands. How they would do that, exactly, it hadn't said. Maybe the Crescend would modify others as he had modified her, to enable mundanes to locate the enemy within; or maybe he would act directly, using weapons more superior than she could imagine.

However they did it, she felt safe in assuming that the enemy would be destroyed. The High Caste rarely acted, but when it did, it always got what it wanted.

So the decision was hers: to wipe out the enemy or not.

She was amazed by how difficult it was. On the one hand, she could end all the squabbling in Sol System and throughout the galaxy, at the cost of a Caste which might have a genuine grievance. On the other hand, she could let the conflict run its course. If the enemy won, so be it. She had no idea just how great a cost that would be to the trillions of other mundane Humans inhabiting the galaxy.

In terms of lives, it was relatively easy to judge. She didn't know exactly how many clone warriors there were, but they seemed to seed one or two per organization they were trying to infect. On the *Phlegethon* there had been only five. There might be millions scattered across the galaxy—but even those sorts of figures paled if the chaos they had caused in Sol System could be extrapolated everywhere. Millions of lives versus trillions: on any scale, the test was simple.

But of course it *wasn't* that simple. If it was, she wouldn't have been Human.

Restless, she tried to roll over, but of course she couldn't. The autosurgeon simply rolled the bed onto a disconcerting angle, then swung it back when she clutched at it in alarm.

"Uri! How long do I have to stay in this damned thing?"

"An hour or two," came Kajic's voice. A second later, his form appeared in the holographic tank. "Nerve reconstruction and bone marrow grafts have yet to be finalized in your injured pelvis. I'm told complete immobility is advisable."

She grunted. "I'm not hungry or thirsty, either. Is that normal?"

"Completely. The autosurgeon is taking all your bodily needs into account. Except for boredom, I suppose."

"I'm not bored." She sighed. "I do need some input, though. It's hard to keep up without my implants. Can you give me a screen or something down here? I'd like to see what's happening in the system."

"Of course." Kajic's image dissolved, leaving a complicated display in its wake. "I'll leave you with full access to the data we have on the current state of play. Some of it is coming from the IEPC drones; the rest I'm extrapolating as we go. I think it'll be enough to give you an overview, anyway. It is voice-activated."

"Thanks, Uri."

She settled back to browse through the charts. The system was a mess of conflicts, the largest concentrated around the blue triangle of the *Phlegethon*. As far as she could tell, five whole fleets had declared war against the massive vessel; it looked as if it was holding its own, but she couldn't tell how much longer that would last.

Elsewhere the situation was more difficult to analyze. Red patches, indicating conflict in one form or another, had spread to cover entire sections in the system. Most were concentrated around the plane of the ecliptic, but there were some hot spots farther out. One concentration of fire was high above the sun's north pole, where two swarms of comet-chasers appeared to be fighting over a third party's observation complex. Another was very close to the sun, whipping up strange currents in the chromosphere.

Mines were marked with yellow stars and tended to form drifting sheets like two-dimensional shoals around protected fleets. Regions of weakened space were marked with purple crosshatching and avoided by all. Areas suspected to be under enemy control were delineated by sharp black lines. There were odd white patches in the rings that Roche couldn't identify but guessed were installations of some sort designed to interfere with passing ships. The gray crosses indicating delelict vessels were everywhere—whether largely intact, smashed to fragments, or completely gaseous.

She could discern no pattern to the conflict, and the Box wasn't around to tell whether any one Caste was being consistently spared the fighting. All she could do was go by its earlier statement that no such bias was being shown. If the enemy did have an agenda, then she didn't know what it was.

That didn't *necessarily* mean that the enemy's goal was to wipe every other mundane from the face of the galaxy. It was possible that the events in Sol System did not represent how things would go elsewhere. Yes, she had heard of civilizations that had fallen under the influence of the enemy—Rey Nemeth's and Hue Vischilglin's were two—but they were only a handful out of millions. It was barely conceivable that all would fall. Once the element of surprise was lost, as it surely would be after Sol System, the enemy would face a stiffer, more organized resistance.

Unless that resistance was undermined from within. She had to assume that there was nowhere the enemy couldn't penetrate if it wanted to. The only way to keep them out was to conduct rigorous genetic testing—which would never be rigorous enough, as the *Phlegethon* had demonstrated—or to rely on others like her to find the clone warriors before they could do more damage.

If that was what the Crescend had in mind, she might agree to support it. But she had no way of knowing until she actually spoke to him.

"Uri?"

"Yes, Morgan?"

"This is going to seem a little strange, but I need you to give me an open communications channel."

"Communicating with whom?"

"I want to broadcast a message aimed at the sun. I don't want you to wait for any reply protocol or anything. If the only way you can do that is by radio or laser, that'll have to do."

"I can arrange that for you at any time, Morgan." Kajic didn't ask why she would want to, but the question was present in his tone. "A tightbeam would be less likely to give away our location."

"Okay. Give me the open line; audio only. And . . ." She paused slightly. "I'd appreciate it if you didn't let anyone listen in."

"Of course, Morgan. Opening the line now."

Roche didn't say anything at first. If the Crescend responded, that reinforced everything the Box had said; she still wasn't sure she wanted that. But if he didn't respond, that was just as bad. She would have no idea at all what was going on, then.

There was only one way to find out.

"Dawn comes," she said.

A familiar voice responded immediately from behind her right ear:

"—to bring an end to the dark imbalance."

The table spun beneath her as she twisted by reflex. "*Box*? If that's really you, I'm going to—"

"I am not the Box, Morgan," interrupted the voice, this time coming from the other side of the room. "You know who I am."

Her skin goose-bumped. Who else could it be? For a few moments she didn't know what to say. "But your voice . . ." was all she could manage.

"The Box was a part of me in the same way that your eye is a part of you—or your finger, or your anterior cingulate cortex. It was not me, and I am not it."

Roche looked around her. The voice changed position constantly. She couldn't tell if that was an effect of the way it was being broadcast into the room, or whether it was something more significant. Maybe it was just trying to keep her off balance.

He, she corrected herself. The Crescend wasn't an *it*.

"Where are you?" she asked.

"It has been a long time since last we met," he said with some amusement, deliberately avoiding her question.

"It hasn't been that long since Trinity."

"I'm not talking about Trinity."

She frowned. "Then I don't know what you're talking about."

"Don't you? I thought you might have guessed by now."

"Guessed *what*?"

The Crescend was silent for a long time, long enough for her to wonder if the line had been broken.

"Uri," she called, "is this line still open?"

"He can't hear you," said the Box's voice, this time coming from somewhere behind the autosurgeon. "No one can hear us talk. It's just you and me. And your decision."

She shifted nervously in the cocoon. "You're not seriously going to leave it up to me, are you?"

"Why not?"

"Because it's crazy, that's why not! I'm just one person. I'm not in any position to judge—"

"You're better qualified than you realize."

"Well, I don't *feel* qualified."

"You can locate the enemy, for a start."

"How does that help my decision?"

"It's proof that I can back up my offer to assist you. Without such proof, my offer could seem empty."

"And that's all you're offering? A way to find the enemy so we can finish them off?"

"Is that the help you would like the High Caste to provide?"

She opened her mouth, then shut it. "You're not going to trick me into a decision like that."

"It's no trick. I'm genuinely interested in your answer: what do you want us to do, Morgan?"

"I don't know," she said, feeling trapped. "I don't feel I have enough information to decide."

"You have as much as you need."

"But I don't know why the enemy are here. I don't know where they come from, even. I don't know if they mean to kill everyone or just some of us. I don't know why the war began in the first place. I just don't *know*!"

"Some of these questions have no answers," said the Crescend. "At least for the moment. But I can answer that last one for you."

"Then please do," she said, annoyed that he had made her ask.

"The original war was fought over territory, as all wars are."

She waited, but nothing more was forthcoming. "What territory?"

The Crescend chuckled. "Now you are trying to trick *me*. You are hoping that I will specify a location which will help you identify the enemy's original Caste. Unfortunately, I cannot do that, Morgan. And it's not because I won't, but because I *can't*. I don't know where the enemy originated—not for certain. All I know is that the original war engulfed the entire inhabited galaxy."

"Ending when the enemy were ultimately defeated."

"They weren't just defeated," he said. "They were completely erased. All trace of them vanished until forty years ago, when the first confirmed capsule sighting was made."

"Do you know the enemy's original name?"

"Unfortunately, that information has also been lost."

She shook her head. "You're not giving me much to go on. I mean, how can I judge what's right now when I don't even know if the enemy are justified in what they're doing? Maybe they're in the right, and I shouldn't interfere."

"Have you spoken to Adoni Cane about this?"

"More or less." She had given him the *chance* to speak, anyway.

"And hasn't the enemy had many chances in the past to reveal the truth behind their motives?"

"Yes, I suppose—"

"So why should it fall on me to justify their actions when they themselves feel no need to do so?"

She accepted his point. "But *do* you know why they're doing this?"

"Facts are hard to come by in this matter. We suspect, that is all. If it were more clear-cut, the High Caste would find it easier to reach consensus. There was guilt on both sides, perhaps."

"So why are you so keen for me to let you destroy them?"

The Crescend's voice was shocked. "Do you really think that this is what I want, Morgan?"

"Isn't it?"

"Nothing could be further from the truth. I am not asking you to do anything but decide. I am an advocate of neither position."

"But you're an Interventionist," she said. "That means you want to help us defeat the enemy."

"No. It means that I am *willing* to help you, should you decide that way. There is a great difference. Should you decide not to accept my help, I will retire into the background once again. My role will be complete, and future events will play themselves out without my interference."

"Even if the enemy destroys us completely?"

"Even so."

"That's a little harsh."

"Unfortunately, it is the nature of things. The nature of *nature*, if you like. I cannot say if your annihilation at the hands of the enemy will or will not come to pass, or will necessarily be a bad thing if it does happen. Not because I am reluctant to tell you, or because it is too close to call, but because it is not my role to judge such issues. I am a facilitator, not an instigator. The people of my Caste who *do* instigate have decided to pass their role to you. Perhaps, if the projected outcome *was* more clear-cut, the High Caste would have divined its role differently. Perhaps there would be no situation such as this at all: the enemy would have been eradicated before they even left their capsules. You might take hope, if you like, in the fact that this didn't happen—for it may mean that you have a chance. You might not. I am in no position to argue or suggest either way. All I want is for you to make a decision."

He paused now at length, then asked: "Do you have one for me, Morgan Roche?"

Roche didn't know what to say. "I'm not sure. I want to be *certain*—"

"As do we all. There is no certainty to be had here, except on one thing: that if you decide to accept my help, you will prevail over the enemy, and they *will* be destroyed."

"All of them?" she asked.

"*All* of them."

"Including the Cane I know?"

"He is one of them, isn't he?" the Crescend's voice chided her.

"Yes, but—"

"Would I be true to my word if I spared him?" he said. "One spared here might mean another elsewhere—and another, and another. This compact must be sealed in the sure knowledge that your victory will be total, and the enemy's defeat complete."

She grimaced.

"You don't like that?" he asked.

She was flustered for a moment by the fact that he could obviously see her. "It disturbs me."

"Then turn down my offer and end this phase of the war," was all he said. "I will abide by your decision."

"That's my only other option?"

"Would you care to suggest another?"

She took a deep breath. He was trying to trick her again. She wanted to scream that it wasn't fair, that she didn't deserve this, that she hadn't asked for it, that she didn't want it—but all she said was:

"Why me? You still haven't explained that to me. Why not the council?"

"The Interim Emergency Pristine Council is too large and unwieldy, and too exposed, for this purpose. It will play a role in organizing resistance or mopping up the damage—depending on which way you decide, of course—but it is not suited to the task before you. Like me, it is a facilitator, not an instigator."

"But why *me* and not someone else?"

"Because you alone are the one who must decide."

"But *why* am I the one?"

"Because that is your purpose."

"Stop avoiding the question! Tell me *why* it has to be *me*!"

He paused again. "It is not something you will want to hear, Morgan."

The Crescend's voice was full of sympathy but she didn't accept it for a second. She didn't believe a creature that advanced would use language to communicate; any emotion that appeared in his voice therefore had to be artificially generated. Either way, she wasn't going to give him any leeway.

"How can you know that?"

"I know you well enough to be certain of your feelings on this matter," he said. "Besides, it would undoubtedly influence your decision. Since I have gone to great lengths to ensure your freedom, strange as that may seem, and to keep you as impartial as possible, I would not have those efforts wasted. Page De Bruyn came close enough to doing that already."

Roche froze. "What do you know about her?"

"I know that she resented the fact that I was in cahoots with your Eupatrid regarding your mission with the Box, and your subsequent freedom. When she got in the way, she was dismissed and told to keep her nose out of the affair. I would not have anyone interfering in the process of your education. She misinterpreted what happened, believing that you were part of a conspiracy to undermine her power base, and embarked upon a personal campaign of revenge."

Roche absorbed the news in silence for a moment; the Crescend *had* been behind everything, after all. "So that's why she was after me, then."

"She unwittingly put the entire project at risk. Your purpose was to learn about the enemy and about your own abilities in your own time. The Box was to guide you until you were informed enough to decide. That was its prime directive, beside studying Adoni Cane. Losing the Box has forced us to move sooner than many had anticipated—but perhaps we would have reached this point now, anyway. Either way, we are here."

She nodded slowly, feeling oddly sorry for her old boss. De Bruyn had betrayed her, but had herself been the victim of forces beyond her control. She had been caught in the middle of the High Caste's convoluted plot. Like Roche herself.

"You know all you need to know," the Crescend said. "Does it truly matter who created the enemy? The fact that they are here is all that should concern you. Does it matter if they plan to kill all of you or just half? All death is tragic. Does it matter if you are the only who can find them or one of millions? *This* decision is yours alone. Decide, Morgan, and be done with it. I have waited forty years for this moment."

Roche didn't say anything. Why the war had started, half a million years ago, *did* indeed seem irrelevant. The same with who had made the enemy in the first place. It was too long ago. She had to concentrate on the situation before her. On the problem as she saw it.

That was what they wanted, she supposed.

"You're going to have to wait a little longer, I'm afraid," she said. "I need to think on it some more."

The voice chuckled. "You mean that you need to talk to Adoni Cane."

"He has a right to know what's going on," she said.

"And will you believe him, no matter what he says?"

"I think I owe it to him to listen."

There was a sound much like a sigh. "Very well, Morgan. I will continue to wait. Just remember one thing, though: your will is paramount in this instance. You must not let yourself be coerced by anyone—not even me. *Especially* me. You must decide as objectively as you can. That is all we ask of you."

She couldn't help a bitter laugh.

"Understand what I am trying to say, Morgan. Adoni Cane is one of the enemy. I would not lose all now to false sympathy or wishful thinking."

"You won't," she said. "Because that's what this is all about, really."

"Yes, it is." The Crescend's voice softened slightly. "Listen and think well, Morgan Roche."

The Crescend said nothing more, and she knew she was alone.

19

IND *Ana Vereine*
955.2.15
1960

Roche settled back onto the bed and ran her hand across her face.

"Uri?" she called. "Can you hear me?"

"Of course, Morgan."

She was relieved to hear his voice. "That's good," she said. "I was afraid you wouldn't be able to."

"Why not?" he said. "I've been monitoring your room since your awakening."

Roche frowned. "But he said no one would hear us talk."

"Who said this?"

She hesitated for a moment, confused. "Didn't you hear me transmit my message?"

"Yes, but there was no reply. I closed the line when it became apparent that you weren't going to say anything else."

No reply. Part of her wasn't surprised. This was the Crescend she was dealing with, after all. Interfering with mundane technology—and mundane minds—probably came as easily as toying with an insect.

"Is everything all right, Morgan?"

"Everything's fine, Uri," she said. "Just a little tired, I guess. Listen, get hold of Cane for me, can you? I need to see him."

"Yes, Morgan."

"And make sure you monitor *this* conversation," she added hastily. "I want you to be ready if anything goes wrong."

"Understood."

Roche went back to watching the display of Sol System while she waited. Nothing much had changed, except the patterns of white on the ring. Now that the ship was closer, she could see them in more detail. They shifted like oil on water, sweeping in swirls with ponderous grace across vast sections of dust and gas. Indicating them, Roche asked Kajic what they meant.

"Electrical activity," he said. "Source unknown. This data comes direct from the Heresiarch's general navigation service. He believes them to be a hazard to shipping."

"A trap of some sort?"

"Conceivably."

She wondered if it had anything to do with the convergence on the system. The clone warriors might have rigged some sort of trap involving the ring, although she couldn't imagine what kind of trap it could possibly be. A solar-system-sized laser would be better based in the sun itself, and there was no sign of the exotic types of matter usually associated with hyperspace weapons. It *might* have been a natural phenomenon, but she couldn't afford to make such assumptions at this stage. It was too risky, and could end up being costly. . . .

"Cane is on his way," Kajic announced.

"Okay, Uri." She breathed deeply and slowly for a full minute, composing herself for what was to come. She had no idea what she would say, and even less of an idea how he would respond to what she had to say. *I have the power to kill you and all of your people unless you give me a reason not to.* If she was lucky, he would think she was crazy.

If she was unlucky . . .

"Hello, Morgan." Cane stepped into the room.

"Thanks for coming, Cane." Her voice was edgy; she hadn't heard the door open. "I wanted to—"

She stopped.

He stood before her with his arms folded, to all appearances completely at ease, and waited for her to continue.

"I wanted to thank you for rescuing me," she said, realizing only as she said it that it was the truth. "You took a great risk, and it paid off. Thank you."

"I did what I had to do," he said. His eyes revealed nothing about his thoughts.

"How *did* you know what to do, by the way?" she asked.

"I didn't. I just took a chance," he said. "The ship that took you passed through the blockade of the *Phlegethon* without resistance, so it seemed likely that it had an allegiance with the clone warriors. Using fragments of the command language we detected in Palasian System, I was able to convince the leaders of the blockade to let us through too. Once they believed that I was in fact one of the enemy, the rest was simple."

He seemed to be telling the truth, but she still couldn't read him. "What about the camouflage you ordered around the *Ana Vereine*?"

He shrugged. "You were taken by Hurns, so I assumed that they would respect the authority of a superior Hurn vessel. It wasn't difficult to retrieve the design of such a ship from the datapool."

"And the name of the ship? You called it the *Apostle*."

"I overheard the name when I arrived."

"What else did you overhear? Anything useful—like who they were, for instance?"

"They call themselves the Disciples of the Evergence," he said. He didn't wait for her to ask: "I don't know what it means."

"But they are in league with the enemy."

"It seems so. They accepted me readily enough."

She nodded. His explanations made sense, even if they were a little glib. She suspected that no matter what she threw at him he would be able to explain it away.

"I'd wondered," she said, "whether this might be proof that an epsense link of some sort does exist between you and your siblings. That way it would have been easy to know just what to say and who to imitate in order for my captors to be convinced."

"I'm sorry to disappoint you, Morgan," he said. "But that wasn't the case."

She studied him closely for a few seconds "Are you lying to me?" she asked, as she had when they had first reached Sol System.

"Why would I lie?"

"Why does anyone lie?" she said. "To conceal the truth, obviously."

"And if I were trying to conceal the truth, what would it gain me to admit that *now*?"

"*Are* you lying to me?" she pressed him.

"What do you want to hear, Morgan? That I'm in communication with my siblings? That I'm in league with them?"

"I just want you to answer the question! Why is this so difficult for everyone?"

"If I am lying now, then I must have been lying all along!"

The passion in his voice surprised her, but it didn't sway her from her own anger.

"Just answer the damned question, Cane!" she snapped. "*Are* you lying to me?"

There was a long pause in which he breathed deeply a few times, almost as if trying to calm himself. Seeing him so agitated was not a common experience; it was only the second time she had really seen him angry. It was a side of himself he kept carefully hidden.

"I'm not lying, Morgan," he said eventually, his even voice cutting across her thoughts. "Everything I have told you is the truth."

She sighed wearily. She wanted his assurances to take away her doubts, but they were still there, lingering, continuing to eat away at her.

"I want to believe you," she said. "But it's hard—"

"Why, Morgan?" he broke in. "Why is it so hard? How many times have I saved your life now? How many times more must I do it before you will believe me? How many more of my own must I kill?"

Roche was speechless for a second. For an instant, she remembered how he looked when he had rescued her—cold and dangerous—but that wasn't what she saw on his face now. He looked . . . *hurt*.

I can't afford to trust you, she wanted to say, *because I don't have the courage to risk so much. Because if I'm* wrong *there's no limit to what I might lose.*

But she didn't say that. She couldn't. It exposed her vulnerability, it cut too deeply to the core of her uncertainty. That's what it all boiled down to, after all: balancing the uncertainty of his trustworthiness against the damage he could do. If he was lying, if he was leading her into some sort of trap, if he was really one of the enemy and had been faking it all along—and if she alone could destroy the enemy . . .

Instead she said: "You told me once that we shouldn't trust you completely because you yourself don't know what you might do. Without knowing who made you, and why, we can't guess how you will respond to every situation. There's a chance you might be compelled, some day, to act in a way that goes against or subverts your conscious intentions. Do you still feel that way?"

His tension eased slightly. "That is a fair point," he said. "I guess I would still consider it were I in your shoes."

She decided to take a chance and ask him the question she really wanted an answer to: "Tell me, Cane. If you *were* in my shoes and you had the means to destroy the enemy at no cost to any other Human Caste, would you do it?"

He looked thoughtful for a moment. "It would be an attractive option."

"Even at the cost of millions of lives—of the lives of the enemy?"

"Yes, of course," he said. "Because so many more would stand to be saved."

"Is that how you justify genocide?"

"I'm not justifying anything, Morgan. I am merely answering your question."

Was he? she wondered. "But what if *one* of the enemy overcame its makers' wishes and demonstrated that it could achieve redemption? Would you kill that one, too, to make absolutely certain that there would be no recurrence of war?"

Again he hesitated. "For total victory?" he asked.

"For total victory."

This time he didn't hesitate: "I would let that one fall with the others, yes."

The answer chilled her. Not because of its ruthlessness—for she had guessed that this would be his answer—but because of what it said about him and how he regarded himself.

He knew what she was hinting at. He wasn't stupid. He was one of the most frightening individuals she had ever met, simply because he was so much better at everything than she. He could outrun, outfight, and probably outthink her to degrees she didn't dare imagine—and he had been watching her and the Box the whole time they had known each other. If he hadn't already guessed at the Box's connection to the Crescend, then she had surely given him enough clues to work it out.

He knew that she was talking about him, and he was telling her that if she had the power to do so, that she should use it and eliminate them all, including himself.

Or was he outthinking her even now? Was he gambling that this display of selflessness would in fact convince her *not* to wipe out the enemy?

His eyes stared calmly into hers, as if they were discussing ordinary politics rather than genocide. But what *would* he do were she to choose to destroy him with the others?

She couldn't allow that question to influence her. The decision had to be made on its own merits. What happened afterward was an entirely different matter.

If he could turn against his programming, maybe others could too. She couldn't justify the extermination of an entire Caste if that possibility existed. No matter how superior they seemed to her, they wouldn't stand a chance against the High Humans. And if they *were* superior to her, maybe they deserved a chance to prove it.

The galaxy had never been a peaceful place, and it probably never would be. If she sanctioned the destruction of the enemy, would that guarantee any sort of peace? Maybe for a while, as long as alliances lasted. But the enemy's influence would still be felt. Old grudges wouldn't go away, even if they had been inflamed to further a third party's ends. There would still be conflict and injustice.

And letting the enemy survive didn't necessarily mean that everyone else would die. She clutched at that thought, even as she made her decision. It wasn't a case of millions versus trillions. It was a case of an end to the present hostilities versus its continuation. Who would be victor was not clear. The enemy was too greatly outnumbered to take its success for granted.

Or so she hoped. She didn't like to think what it would mean if she was wrong.

"Morgan?" Cane was still standing in front of her, waiting patiently for her to say something.

"I'm sorry," she said. "I was distracted."

He nodded stiffly. "Is there anything else you want to ask me?"

"No, that's all," she said. "Thanks."

He looked as though he was about to say something, then turned and left the room.

When he had gone, she said: "Uri? Open that communications channel again."

"Opening now, Morgan."

"Dawn comes," she said.

"Does this mean you've decided?" asked the Crescend, his voice emanating instantly from somewhere near the door.

"Yes." But she was reluctant to say the words.

"And what *is* your decision, Morgan?"

She paused, not for effect, but to give herself one last chance to change her mind. She didn't.

"I can't allow you to destroy them," she said slowly, carefully. "So I guess I decide to let them live. We'll fight them ourselves, and either win or lose on our own merits."

"You know what this means?"

"Yes." She hoped so. "War—at best."

He seemed to pause a long while before speaking again. "May I ask why you have chosen this?"

"Because Cane doesn't deserve to die," she said. "He's helped me too much. He's proven—to me, at least—that the clone warriors *can* rise above their programming."

"And what if I said that Cane could be spared?"

"That's not the point. Who's to say there isn't another like him out there who doesn't deserve to be killed? You?"

"I could not make such assurances."

"Exactly. It wouldn't be right to take that chance."

"So you make this decision by weighing the certain harm to an individual against potential harm to the masses?"

"I guess so." She took a deep breath. "*Would* you spare Cane if I asked you to?"

"No, of course not," he said. "Nor do I believe Cane would wish it."

She thought about this and nodded to herself. "What happens now, then? Is there anything else I need to do?"

"Your role is played out," he said. "For the time being, anyway. I will leave you to communicate your decision to the rest of my Caste. All the information at our disposal will be disseminated simultaneously to concerned parties throughout the galaxy, including the IEPC. We will no longer try to hide this knowledge from the enemy. It will be crucial in the times to come."

"And what happens if I need to talk to you again?"

"Why? Do you feel you might change your mind?"

"No, I don't think so," she said, even though, now that she had made her decision, she was filled with a terrible sense of doubt.

"If you did, there is no guarantee that the High Caste would accept your change of heart," he said, his voice almost scolding.

"I understand." She wasn't sure if that option would have made her feel better, anyway. If things went badly with the enemy, she didn't want that decision hanging over her, to be made again and again.

She had given the enemy the freedom to fight; she had given her own kind the freedom to lose. When gods interfered in the affairs of mundane Humans, she doubted any decisions were easy. But that didn't make her feel any better.

The Crescend waited for a moment, as though to see if she would speak, then said: "Perhaps we will talk again some day."

The thought didn't fill her with pleasure. "Perhaps."

"Goodbye, Morgan Roche."

How much time passed after the Crescend left, she didn't know. She wasn't really thinking at all. Making the decision had drained her, leaving her feeling strangely empty.

"You have a visitor, Morgan."

Roche turned to see Kajic's hologram coalescing in the wall display.

"Who is it?" she said wearily.

"Defender-of-Harmony Vri."

"What does he want?"

"He hasn't said."

<Can't you guess?> asked Maii.

Roche sighed. <Can't you stall him?>

<I—> The girl stopped in mid-thought. <I'm sorry, Morgan. I didn't realize you were this tired. Is everything all right?>

<I'm not sure.> Maii didn't seem to know what had happened. She too must have been unable to read what had happened with the Crescend.

<*What* happened?> asked the girl. <Did I miss something?>

<I'll tell you later, Maii.>

Roche tilted the bed closer to upright and braced herself. She wasn't doing anyone much good moping around.

"It's all right," she said aloud to Kajic. "I'll have to deal with him eventually, I guess. Send him in, Uri."

The doors to the medical center opened and the tall soldier stepped through. His armor shone as always, golden and feathered like some Humanoid phoenix. He took four precise paces to the end of Roche's bed, where he stopped and bowed slightly from the neck.

"Thank you for seeing me," he said.

The bed tilted farther so they were closer to eye level. "How can I help you, Vri?"

"I wish to suggest another compromise."

She suppressed a sigh. "What now?"

"First, I want to say that I understand why it was not possible for negotiations to take place between you and the Agora on the *Phlegethon*. The circumstances at the time were not conducive to such discussions. So I do not blame you for this additional delay."

She was relieved about that. She'd half expected him to storm in, making demands and claiming she was deliberately stalling.

"Secondly?" she prompted.

"I have become aware that your work here may ultimately benefit the Surin Caste as a whole," he went on. "While I do not feel that Maii should play any role in this, I accept that she has made her decision—and since that decision can be interpreted as one serving the interests of the Agora, I also accept that it is not my role to intervene."

Roche watched him as he spoke. His broad, furred features were composed and thoughtful. He had obviously considered these words in great depth before coming to her with them.

"I'm glad about that, Vri," she said, a touch cautiously, wary of the sting in the tail. "But what's your point?"

"It is my hope," he said, "that you will also see my superiors' point of view, which is that Maii has been separated from the culture that might arguably be best for her development. Before her childhood is over, it may be beneficial to expose her to aspects of our Caste that give us pride. There is no denying that she has been hurt by members of our Caste, but all the Agora desires is the opportunity to right that wrong.

"I ask, therefore, that when the matter of the enemy is resolved you will see fit to return with me to Essai, to discuss the matter of Maii's custodianship with the Agora, and that I might be allowed to serve formally as her bodyguard until then."

He bowed again, and stepped back a pace.

For a moment, Roche didn't quite know what to say. It looked like he was handing her a simple way to put the problem aside for the time being, but she couldn't help but wonder if there was more to it.

<He means it,> said Maii. <He's trying to find a balance between his orders, which he must obey, and the situation he finds himself in. Although he knows our work is dangerous, he also knows, now, that I am an essential part of that work. Without access to a reave, you cannot find the enemy, and at the moment I'm the only reave you have. Although the Agora might prefer him to take me home by force, he feels that doing so might actually cause more harm. If you agree to this proposal, all his needs will be satisfied.>

<What about you, though, Maii? How do you feel about it?>

<That's kind of irrelevant at the moment, Morgan. I don't know if we'll *ever* make it to Essai. But if the chance does arise, I might take it. I suppose I should at least see what the Agora has to offer. Maybe they really do have my best interests at heart.>

Roche could accept that. <Naturally, I wouldn't try to stop you.>

<I know you wouldn't, Morgan. And I'm glad that you would be coming with me—if you agree, of course. I'd feel uncomfortable facing them alone.>

Vri shifted his feet. Roche snapped out of the mental conversation.

"I'm sorry," she said. "I was just talking to Maii about it. We think the compromise is fair, so I'll agree to meet the Agora when the time is right. Until then, you can travel with us and help keep Maii safe. After all, that is something we are *both* concerned about."

The Surin soldier bowed a third time, this time more formally. "Thank you," he said. "I believed that this was the decision you would reach. You have not disappointed me."

He turned and strode heavily out of the room. Roche smiled as he went. *You have not disappointed me.* That was probably as close to a compliment as she would ever get from him.

<I think you're right,> said Maii. <He's as stiff as they come.>

<May he never unbend,> said Roche.

<Are you going to tell me now what happened before?>

<I'm not sure I fully understand it myself, Maii.>

<The fragments I detect in your mind paint a strange picture. The events them-

selves are hidden, but I can read where you have thought about them—as though the knowledge is leaking out from behind a shield of some kind. But I've never seen one quite like this before. You were actually talking to the Crescend?>

<Yes.>

<I guess it shouldn't be a surprise that High Humans have access to epsense as well as everything else.>

<Maybe what they have makes epsense look primitive.>

<Maybe. It's something to think about, anyway. . . .>

Roche felt the reave withdraw slightly, and she tilted the bed back. Under the cocoon, she wriggled the fingers of her left hand and felt them clench. Whatever the autosurgeon had done to her in the last few hours, it had left her feeling almost Human again. Almost.

"How much longer now, Uri?"

"Three hours or so, Morgan."

"Can I at least have my other hand back now? I can feel it moving under this thing, so I know it's working."

"I'll check." Kajic conversed silently with the autosurgeon, then said: "On the condition that you don't exert yourself, it will allow free movement to be restored to that limb."

Even before he had finished speaking, the cocoon slid back down her left side, retracting like a fluid to reveal her left shoulder, arm and upper chest. She appeared to be wrapped in close-sticking bandages made from a white, tissue-thin material she didn't recognize. Through it, she could make out the healing red wounds through which her implants had been removed. Her left palm and wrist were still stiff.

At some point, she would have to be refitted. Like Haid, she had grown accustomed to working intimately with machines. *Too* intimately at times—an issue she still hoped to take up with the Crescend, one day. When the war eased enough for her to take some time off—the sooner the better—she would commit herself to the care of the medical center again and get the upgrade she had once hoped to obtain from COE Intelligence.

Exactly when that would be, she didn't know. First she had to get back in touch with the council and work out strategies for the coming war; they also had to find out if her talent could be replicated, naturally or otherwise. That was assuming, of course, that the *Phlegethon* survived its assault by the fleets of enemy-infected nations. Then there was working out what to do about Sol System itself: did the enemy actually have a reason for gathering here, or was it safe to go back home? If the latter, could the council coordinate the battle across the galaxy as a whole, or would its efforts need to be restricted to those areas considered the most important to save? And how would the governments of the Far Reaches—often overlooked by core-based interests, and the source of an ages-old resentment—react to that decision?

The future was full of uncertainties, as the Crescend had promised it would be if she chose this particular path. Roche didn't regret her decision, but she did wish it could have been otherwise.

Your role is played out, the Crescend had said.

As far as she could tell, her job was only just beginning.

20

IND *Ana Vereine*
955.2.16
0290

"Morgan?"

She snapped out of her thoughts. "What is it, Uri?"

"I'm picking up a ship on an approach vector," he said. "Its configuration matches that of the Hurn ship we impersonated to rescue you."

"Is it hailing us?"

"No."

"And we're still camouflaged?"

"Yes."

"Then how does it know who we are?"

"Maybe it doesn't," Kajic said. "Maybe its similarity to the other ship is only a coincidence. We may have just blundered into Hurn territory."

"And you believe that?"

"Not for a moment," he said.

She vacillated briefly. "Okay, broadcast an anonymous query for ID. Ask Cane and Ameidio to be on the bridge, if they aren't already there. And give me that screen again. I want to see what's going on."

Her bed turned back to the holographic display. In it, she saw the relatively empty space around the *Ana Vereine*, plus the colorful overviews of the system. The approaching ship appeared as a red triangle, swooping closer along a gently curving trajectory.

"I have broadcast the query," said Kajic. "If they're going to reply, the earliest we'd hear is in a minute or two."

Roche rubbed her chin with the fingers of her newly healed left hand. "If we had to fight, how long could we last?"

"Without the Box? Not long at all," he said. "I'd prefer to avoid conflict entirely."

"I agree, but if we *don't* have a choice, I'd like to know what our options are."

"It depends if they have independent fighters or not. Against more than three or four, I will be hard-pressed to maintain much of a defense."

"A minute?"

"Maybe two," he said. "At most."

"They may not even use fighters," Roche mused. "Depends what they want, I guess."

"True." Kajic's voice was cautious. "No response as yet."

"How long until they're within combat range?"

"One hour."

"Give them ten minutes to respond, then put us on alert. At fifteen we'll broadcast a warning. If we still haven't heard back by thirty minutes, we'll assume they're hostile and change course. If they follow, we'll take further evasive action. And if *that* doesn't deter them . . ." She shrugged. "Then we fight, I guess."

She watched the screen. The ship didn't seem to be changing course of its own accord, no matter how much she might wish it would.

"Where's Vri?" she asked.

"Back in his fighter. I've advised him of the situation. He's battle-ready, should we require him."

"And Maii?"

<I'm in my quarters, Morgan.>

"Perhaps you'd better head to the bridge too." Not that it made a great deal of difference where the reave actually was, Roche reminded herself; just as long as their minds were in contact. Still, she felt better knowing where the girl was. "Is everyone else on deck?"

"Cane has arrived," said Kajic, "but Haid is—"

"Right here," said the ex-mercenary as the doors hissed open. He was dressed in a mirror-finished Dato combat suit and trailing another that echoed his movements perfectly. "I figured you'd probably prefer being where the action was."

Roche smiled. "You figured right."

Returning the smile, he tapped a series of codes into the autosurgeon's manual console. It protested with a series of alarms and warnings, but capitulated under the weight of Haid's overrides. The cocoon enclosing Roche's half-healed body clicked, then hissed, then began to recede back into the bed.

Roche looked down in amazement as the rest of her body appeared, blotched red in places and wrapped in white like a barely formed chrysalis. Various sensors and drips retracted into the bed like worms diving away from sunlight. Her legs still felt numb. She moved one tentatively. It responded, but she wasn't confident of its holding her weight.

"Are you sure this will be okay?" she asked.

"Uri assures me you'll manage well enough, once you're in the suit."

"But I don't have any implants."

"We've thought of that. What the suit can't work out, I'll do for you." Haid swung her legs off the bed, then manually walked the spare armor into position with its back facing her. The ceramic shell split and cracked open at the touch of a pressure pad. Its interior was black and moist-looking.

She couldn't stand on her own. A twinge of pain shot up her left side as soon as she tried to take her full weight. Haid instructed the suit to go down on its knees; then he picked her up and put her inside. The suit's padding cradled her, allowing her to rest as though she were sitting, with the merest twitch of her legs magnified to become steps.

She paced the room, enjoying the newly found freedom of movement. Control was limited to a primitive electrode net draped across her shoulders. Luckily the autosurgeon's repairs of her damaged nervous system had progressed far enough for the device to work. It was years since she had trained to use one, and manual control wasn't an option.

"Ameidio, you're a genius!"

"Realize that I'm only doing this out of self-interest," he said lightly. "Trying to coordinate things with you stuck down here would have been just too damned awkward. So, if you will . . ."

He indicated the door.

She didn't move. "Since when are you giving the orders around here?"

Again, he smiled. "It's good to have you back, Morgan."

Together they clanked heavily from the room and headed for the bridge.

The ship's complement was complete by the time they arrived. As the ten-minute deadline came and went, a siren echoed through the ship, announcing full alert.

"What was that for?" asked Haid, assuming his position by Cane at the weapons board.

"Don't forget our passenger," Kajic chided him. "Alta's still down below."

Roche settled into the spot where Kajic's second-in-command had once sat. "Any change in the situation?"

"The ship is proceeding as per its expected course, decelerating with a constant delta-v. It has neither responded to my hail nor issued one of its own."

"Does it look like it's going to attack?"

"Apart from heading our way, it doesn't seem to be doing anything at all."

"Maii?"

<I'm getting nothing, Morgan. Their shields are tight.>

She turned. "Any thoughts, Cane?"

"If what we suspect is true," he said, "then I think we can expect at least one of my siblings to be aboard this ship. And they will be much more difficult to deceive than the Disciples who captured you."

"Do you think they'd respond if we hailed them in your command language?"

"They might, but that would only confirm their suspicions that we are the people they seek," he said. "We may yet be able to bluff our way out of this, though."

"I'd just like to know how they found us," said Haid. "Something's not right about all of this. I can feel it."

"I agree." Roche looked at the main screen, glad to have access to its greater area and clarity. The one in the medical center had been barely adequate. "Any idea where this ship came from, Uri?"

"It appears to have altered its course from this orbit here." A red ellipse circled the sun. "How long it followed that orbit, however, I can't tell."

The orbit didn't seem to intersect any hot-spots or suspicious-looking regions.

"The Disciples must have contacted them somehow," said Roche. "They must have traced our course."

"Sounds reasonable," said Cane.

"So what do we do?" asked Haid.

"We wait them out," said Roche. "They might be bluffing. If they intended to destroy us, they would've come in faster or slow-jumped right on top of us. They must want something else." She studied the creeping dot on the screen. "How long now, Uri?"

"Forty minutes until we change course."

"That gives us a little breathing space, anyway. In the meantime, I want to get in touch with the council, if we can. Uri, is that drone still following us?"

"Yes."

"Good. Send a tightbeam message requesting a conference with whoever's in charge at the moment. Tell them I have something they need to know."

"I'll try." Kajic's hologram faded into static.

"Why are we wasting our time talking to them?" Haid asked. "How many times do they have to knock us back before you take the hint, Morgan?"

"They still need us," she said, adding: "And unfortunately we still need them. Besides, unless they've found someone else who can locate the enemy like I can, I'm pretty sure they'll be prepared to talk."

"Yes," said Haid, "but will they listen?"

She didn't have long to wait. Barely five minutes passed before Kajic announced the receipt of a reply from the council.

"That was fast," she said. "Do we have a live feed?"

"Connecting as we speak. The signal is heavily encrypted and therefore low on detail but at least delay-free."

"Put it through."

A window opened on the main screen, revealing a grainy black-and-white image.

"Well, if it isn't Morgan Roche," said Salton Trezise. "How nice of you to get in touch. Rumor had it you were dead."

"As much as I'd love to exchange pleasantries with you, Trezise, I don't have the time. I need to speak with Murnane."

"He's no longer on the council, I'm afraid." Trezise's expression was smug. "Both he and Nemeth have been censured, along with their Exotic friends. The council doesn't take kindly—"

She cut him short. "So who's in charge?"

"Me, for the time being." He smiled broadly.

Her first instinct was to defend Murnane. Nemeth, she was sure, had been involved in all manner of underhand deals, but she doubted the older councilor had ever acted improperly. He had the change-resistant, inflexible air of someone who was not easily diverted from the straight and narrow.

But this wasn't the time or the place to get involved with petty politics. There was too much else at stake right now.

"If you're really in charge," she said, "then there's something you need to know."

"I hope it involves the imminent arrival of reinforcements," he said. "I've just been told that another fleet is jockeying for firing rights—"

"I'm sorry, Trezise, but there won't be *any* reinforcements." She didn't like to say it. He looked genuinely harried under the self-satisfied exterior. "I've been in contact with the Crescend. You can forget about the High Caste. They're not going to get involved."

His face dropped. "Why not?"

She hesitated momentarily, not wanting to tell Trezise that the reason the Crescend wasn't getting involved was because she had specifically asked him not to.

"Because it's not their fight. Would we intervene in a squabble between two Low Caste tribes on a mud planet somewhere? That's how this looks to them. Yes, one tribe might get wiped out, and things will certainly be messy for a while afterward, but that's just the way it goes. It's no big deal."

"Tell *that* to the tribe being wiped out," he said.

She was trying to defend the Crescend, but found it difficult to keep the bitterness out of her voice. "They will provide us with all the data they've collected over the years, but that's all you can rely on."

"Well, it's something, I guess." He looked thoughtful for a moment. "Tell me, how exactly did you get in contact with the Crescend?"

"I haven't got time for explanations right now," she said, certain the Crescend wouldn't talk to Trezise even if she told him how. "I have a situation here I need to deal with. When things have settled down at both your end and mine, I'll be in touch again to work out what to do next."

"This situation—it wouldn't have anything to do with the ring, would it?"

"No. Why?"

"The drone receiving your broadcast is on its outer fringes, and activity is rising in that area. I just thought there might be a connection."

"Not that I'm aware of," she said. She was about to close the line when she added on impulse: "Oh, and by the way, Trezise. I ran into one of our former colleagues the other day."

"Really?"

Roche nodded. "Page De Bruyn."

He raised both eyebrows. "What's she doing here?"

"Not much anymore," said Roche. "She's dead."

Something passed behind the man's eyes, but otherwise he didn't react. "That is unfortunate," he said. "Did she happen to—?"

The screen went black.

Roche waited a moment, but the image didn't return.

"Uri, what happened?"

There was no reply.

"Uri?"

Haid looked up from his station. "I'm getting a damage report from section gold-two."

"Which is what?"

"Uri's maintenance support and information management," he said. "Seems a cable has malfunctioned."

"What sort of cable?"

"One linking his higher functions to the rest of the ship, from what I can tell."

"He's cut off?"

"For the moment. Repair agents are moving in now."

She forced herself to quell a twinge of alarm. "Good, because we're going to need him soon to coordinate the course change."

Haid was about to respond when the floor shook slightly and a low rumble passed through the bulkheads. The lights flickered.

Roche was instantly on her feet. "*Now* what's going on?"

"I have red lights all through sections gold-one and gold-two," Haid said, tapping frantically at his board. "Security is down across that level." He looked over to Roche, the concern evident in his expression. "I think there's been an explosion, Morgan."

Roche met his gaze silently for a few seconds until she was able to ask the question: "What about Uri?"

"I can't tell."

She checked with the reave "Maii?"

<I'm not picking him up at all,> the girl replied.

Roche's sense of alarm became one of rising dread. "I'm going down there."

Haid also rose to his feet. "I'm coming with you."

"If anything's happened to him . . ." She hurried for the exit to the bridge. "You have the bridge, Cane."

Haid followed with heavy, urgent footsteps. "It *can't* be an attack," he said. "Our disrupters haven't registered the use of hyperspace weapons. There's no way they could've got something in here without us knowing."

"That's as may be," she said. "But I have a gut feeling that this was no accident."

She forced herself to hurry, ignoring the pain in her hip every time her left leg took a loping stride. Section gold-one lay midway between the officers' decks and the warren, in the middle of the ship's main inhabited nacelle. It wasn't far from the bridge, but it seemed to take forever.

"You don't think it might have been Vri?" Haid asked.

She was trying not to think at all, so she didn't answer him.

Pressure-doors had come down around sections gold-one and gold-two. Roche and Haid sealed their suits and keyed in the appropriate overrides. The heavy door before them slid aside, setting free a cloud of smoke.

Roche stepped cautiously through it. The walls bulged inward in places, reminding her that this area was close to the ship's main life-support vats. For a moment, she wondered if the attack might have been directed there, and not directly at Kajic.

But then they rounded a corner and found what remained of the four rooms that had contained his body and the equipment required to support it.

The external door was off its hinges. The walls were blackened and twisted. Roche passed through the outer chambers, crunching over piles of twisted wreckage to the control room. Nothing had survived intact. The window over the main console had shattered into a million pieces. Through the hole in the wall where it had once hung, Roche saw the smashed air-conditioning units, the melted fiber-optic cables, the cracked tank . . .

The tank itself was empty of anything but ash. Its organic contents had either boiled or burned away.

"Look at this," said Haid from behind her.

She turned mutely.

He was at the entrance to the rooms, holding up a section of the outer door. One gloved finger traced the smooth, curved edge of the fragment.

"It's been cut through," he said.

Roche had seen enough. Not trusting her voice, she called Maii by epsense.

<Maii? Is Cane still with you?>

<Why? What's happening, Morgan?>

<Uri's dead,> she replied bluntly. <Murdered.>

She felt the Surin girl's grief immediately but didn't indulge it.

<Maii, *is* Cane still with you?>

<Yes,> she said. <He's trying to patch into the security system.>

"It wasn't him," said Haid, overhearing their thoughts. "Someone had to cut through the door while Uri's defenses were down, when the cable was severed."

<Where's Vri?> Roche asked Maii.

<He's still in his ship.>

Roche shook her head in frustration. Then, like an energy bolt, realization hit her.

"Alta!" she exclaimed.

"What? That's not possible," said Haid. "She doesn't know the ship well enough."

"Who else *could* it be?" snapped Roche.

<I've got her, Morgan,> said Maii. <She's heading for the bridge.>

"We're on our way," said Roche, turning to run back the way she had come. "Can you find out for sure if it *was* her?"

<I'm trying now,> said Maii. <Her shields are tight—>

"Don't be gentle." Roche turned grief and apprehension into powerful nervous impulses that sent the suit hurrying through the ship. "Tell Cane!"

<He knows,> said Maii. <She's close; he can hear her.>

Roche urged her suit faster, even though at full stretch she knew they wouldn't arrive in time. "Just be careful!"

<I'm going to try to knock her out.> A wave of secondhand mental force rolled through Roche. <Her shields are—no, *wait*!>

A terrifying flash of fear caught Roche in mid-step, making her stumble. The suit fell heavily as a second explosion tore through the ship. This time it was much closer. The floor bucked as she landed on it, sending her flying into the air. For a giddy moment she was in free-fall; then she hit a wall with a solid crunch and skidded to a halt.

Her vision grayed for a moment.

"Ameidio . . . ?"

A silver-gray figure loomed out of the suddenly billowing smoke, hand extended. Haid helped her upright. "That came from up ahead," he said.

"This can't be happening!" She was moving even as she spoke.

Blast doors had come down across the entrance to the bridge. Roche keyed an override and stepped back as a wave of oily, black smoke exploded out of the entrance.

<Maii?>

The reave was silent. She had said nothing at all since that last, terrible thought. As Roche stepped cautiously into the slowly fading smoke, all she could think of was the fear she had felt in the girl's mind.

The air around them, as measured by the suit's sensors, was hot—much too hot to sustain life, even if the oxygen in the room hadn't been consumed by the fire. The crew stations were half-melted and spattered with fire-retardant foam. The walls had buckled, the main screen imploded.

"Pressure-mine," said Haid dully. "The same used on Kajic, but not as effective in an open space."

"Effective enough," Roche muttered numbly.

Haid stared helplessly at the blackened wreckage.

"Help me look," Roche said, refusing to give up hope.

"Morgan, they couldn't have survived . . ."

Roche ignored him, using the powerful limbs of the suit to sweep debris aside. The explosion had blown piles into corners or burned the tougher fixtures where they stood. Haid stepped over to her as she attempted to wrench a large sheet away from where it had stuck to the wall.

"I just want to make sure," she said distractedly. "She might have been taken hostage—or Cane got her out in time—or—"

She fell silent with a large piece of wreckage raised in one hand, staring at what she'd uncovered—at the evidence that dashed her last, desperate hope.

Haid stepped up beside her. "Is that . . . *her*?"

"Yes." The face and head of the body was scorched down to the bone where it showed above the neck of the blackened suit, but there could be no doubt. The body was so small, curled in a fetal position with one arm outstretched.

Blackness rose up in Roche like bile. She thought she could smell burning, even though she knew that was impossible through the suit. Her gaze fixed upon the open hand of Maii's outstretched arm, as if it were reaching for help.

An overwhelming guilt washed over Roche for not having been there . . .

"She's going to pay for this," Roche whispered.

"Maybe Cane's here too—" Haid began.

"I don't care." Roche heard her own voice as though listening to another person from a great distance. "I just want Alta Ansourian."

"Morgan . . ." Haid's hand had come to rest on her shoulder.

"We have to find her," said Roche without looking up, resisting his efforts to turn her away from the sight of Maii's body.

"But how? With Uri down and the bridge wrecked we've no way of tracing her."

She looked up and faced him. "The suit beacons."

"You think she might be wearing one?"

"If she's using Dato mines, why not a suit as well?"

The shoulders of his own suit jerked. "It's possible, I guess."

She clenched her left fist so tight, she imagined the ceramic finger joints buckling. "I don't have any implants," she said, keeping her anger in check. "So I can't operate my suit properly. You'll have to do it for me."

He slaved her instruments to his and searched for beacons anywhere in the ship. There was one, and it was moving toward the scutter docks.

"She could be trying to escape," said Haid.

Roche nodded. "But we can catch her if we hurry." She reached for a weapon, and realized only then that she was unarmed. Haid was in a similar position.

He raised his arms in a helpless gesture. "I wasn't anticipating combat within the ship," he explained.

"And we don't have time to go to the armory," Roche said. "We'll just have to manage without."

"Maybe we should split up," Haid suggested. "Tackle her from two directions at once—"

"No," Roche said. "We stay together. But we won't use the suit intercoms; otherwise she'll be able to hear us. Just stick to the suit speakers."

Haid nodded in agreement.

"What about Cane?" he said, the audio system of his suit clearly audible through hers. "Do you think he's dead also?"

"Not a chance," said Roche. Turning her back completely on Maii's body, she stepped past Haid.

"Morgan?" he called after her. "What happens when we find her?"

"She dies," she said, leading the way from the bridge. "Beyond that, I don't really care."

* * *

The internal transit tubes were inactive, killed along with Kajic, so they were forced to run again. The light brown corridors seemed too bright as they headed in a different direction this time, down through connecting corridors and access tubes toward the ship's fat central drive section. There the scutters and other smaller support vehicles were docked or stored between outings.

Halfway there, a growing suspicion about what the woman had in mind became a certainty as the first of a new wave of explosions rocked the ship.

"What the hell is she doing?" Haid gasped. The data available through his instruments confirmed that at least one of the five remaining scutters had been damaged.

Roche watched—beyond horror, beyond surprise—as a chain of detonations ripped the docks to pieces. "This didn't just happen overnight," she said. "Those mines must have been placed and armed in advance."

"We gave her the freedom to roam anywhere in the ship," Haid said. "We let her do whatever she wanted. I didn't *suspect*—"

"You had no reason to," Roche said. "How could we have known she'd do something like this?"

The explosions continued, damaging more of the scutters. Roche couldn't tell how many craft had been crippled or destroyed, but she knew the docks were ruined. The chain reaction would have left the place a raging inferno. If Alta herself hadn't got out in time, she wouldn't last a minute.

Roche found it difficult to muster any sympathy for the woman—especially given that Vri had been down there, too.

But the transponder kept moving. Roche tried to think one step ahead of the woman. No matter how hard they ran, the suits were identical; they would never catch her by dogging her heels. They had to try to cut her off.

The docks were in an outer layer of the drive section. The next obvious place to hit was two levels down.

"She's headed for the drive chamber," Roche said. "She's probably going to try and blow that, too."

"Can she do that?" asked Haid.

"She obviously thinks she can, otherwise she wouldn't be heading there." Roche considered her options while trying to maintain a steady pace, but the sheer size of the *Ana Vereine*—previously an asset—was now proving to be a disadvantage. "I doubt we'll arrive in time to stop her," she said, "so there's no point trying. But somehow I don't think she's going to be willing to blow herself up along with the ship."

"She'll be looking to escape," said Haid.

"And fast."

"But how? She's blown up all the EVA—" He stopped, realizing the only real option that Alta had. "The Hurn ship!"

"It's the only possibility I can think of."

"You think she's a clone warrior?"

"Maybe not," Roche said, "but certainly on their side. It's the only explanation I can think of for why she's doing this."

"So she'll rig the drive to blow, then jump ship?"

"That would be the simplest solution."

"Then she's going to need access to the hull."

"Exactly," Roche said. "See if you can pull up any plans on airlocks close to the central drive chamber."

Within seconds, Haid had the plans before them, via their suit's displays.

"Which do you think she'll go for?" Roche asked, studying the map.

"There's one likely candidate, and a couple of close seconds."

"Take us to the most likely, and we'll just have to wait for her there."

"Listen, Morgan," said Haid, "I know you want to keep us together, but wouldn't it make sense to split up now? If we risk all on one airlock, and she picks another, that puts us in a bad situation. After all, we've only got one shot at this."

Roche pondered this. As much as she didn't want to let Haid out of her sight right now, his suggestion *did* make sense. If Alta had worked out how to locate them via her own suit, they could end up walking into a trap.

"Okay," she relented. "Ameidio, you take a secondary airlock and I'll wait for her at the main one." Haid was about to protest. "I have just as much chance against her as you, Ameidio. And besides," she added, "I'd like to be the one that takes her down."

"Okay, Morgan," he said. "But just take care, all right?"

She nodded. "Keep an eye on my beacon so you know where I am, but *don't* communicate unless you have to. The less she knows about us, the better."

"Okay. And if all goes well, I'll meet you out on the hull."

At the next intersection, he turned left while Roche kept going. She watched the dot of his suit angle away from hers with a feeling of apprehension. The pain in her side was a constant ache punctuated by spikes of agony. A rumble of distressed machinery came to her through her feet rather than her eardrums. She ignored everything, and concentrated instead on the task ahead.

Each stride was like the tick of a clock, taking her ever closer to some unknown fate. She hurried through the *Ana Vereine*'s extensive warren, through tunnels she hadn't visited since first occupying the ship. It was here that Cane, Haid, and Maii had hidden while Kajic left Sciacca's World and the Hutton-Luu System with the intention of handing Roche and the Box over to his superiors in the Ethnarch's Military Presidium.

On the tracking screen, Alta had reached the main drive chamber. Within minutes, a siren began to sound.

"That'll be the drives," Roche mumbled to herself. The lack of response from either Maii or the Box only intensified her sense of isolation and the ever-growing emptiness inside her.

She had hoped it would take the woman longer, but a warning through her suit only confirmed her worst suspicions: the drives were going to overload in about fifty minutes. She didn't know exactly what Alta had done, but it had to be something slow-acting, something she had prepared in advance. Had she freed the antimatter reserve, they would already be dead. But whatever it was, it was unlikely it could be stopped. It could take them hours just to figure out what she had done, let alone begin reversing whatever process Alta had set in motion. . . .

Roche studied the tracking screen. According to the display, Alta was on the move again. She was heading for the airlock that Haid suspected she would go for, but Roche wasn't going to be able to beat her there.

She considered calling Haid, but then thought better of it. Hopefully he would see what was going on. He was making good time toward his airlock; even if they didn't make it in time, there was a chance he would be able to intercept Alta out on the hull.

Fifty minutes, Roche thought to herself. In half an hour, the entire ship would be gone. Unless they could find a way off the ship, or someone to rescue them, they would die with it.

Part of her didn't mind that at all. The Crescend himself had stated it quite bluntly the last time they spoke: *Your role is played out.* As long as she took Alta Ansourian with her, she might be happy with that. . . .

The woman was also making good time, unfortunately. Hoping to distract her, Roche activated the open channel connecting the suits.

"Alta? Can you hear me?"

"I hear you." The reply was immediate. "And I can see you, too, Roche! But you can't stop me! You're too late! There's no turning back now."

The woman's voice was feverish, breathless. There was a raw edge to it. Roche couldn't tell if it was fear or determination—or perhaps both.

"What have you done to the engines, Alta?"

"The matter/antimatter mix is in disequilibrium," the woman replied. "The mix will become more and more unstable until it spirals out of control, and then the ship will blow. Trust me—you can't stop it; there isn't enough time."

"But there is enough time to get away?"

"You can get out of the ship, Roche, but you'll never escape!" The mockery in her voice angered Roche, and the image of Maii's helpless form with its outstretched arm returned.

"*Why* did you kill them, Alta?"

"To stop them from interfering, of course."

"But Maii was just a *child*. She never did you any harm!"

There was a pause before Alta spoke again, and when she did her voice was steeped in uncertainty.

"Those were my orders," she said. "I couldn't disobey."

"*Whose* orders, Alta?" Roche pressed, anger giving way to curiosity. "Why are you doing this?"

More assured now, Alta replied: "Because if it hadn't been for you, he wouldn't be dead now!"

"Who? Your *father*?"

"You killed him, Roche!" The hatred in her voice was intense and frightening. "You took him away from me!"

"What are you talking about! You *saw* Jans kill your father! You were there—"

"Lies that you planted!" Alta's voice was raised to a shout now. "But I know the truth! He showed me. He showed me your *lies*. Justice will prevail!"

The edge to her words unsettled Roche. There was a sense of desperation to them that suggested Alta was beyond reasoning with. She believed what she was saying; she was convinced Roche was responsible for her father's death. Why, though, Roche didn't know. Maybe it was simply because she was the nearest available target for reprisal . . .

Alta was much closer now. The air in the warren became thick with smoke as Roche neared the airlock. She passed emergency doors that had failed to shut. Some hung loose, half open, as though they had changed their mind in the act of closing.

Without Kajic to run the ship, even the most basic systems were gradually running down. The rumble of complaining engines became steadily louder as she ran.

"Who showed you, Alta?" said Roche.

The woman said nothing.

"Alta?"

A loud explosion knocked Roche off her feet and sent air whipping along the corridor.

"The airlock," she gasped in the sudden hurricane, thinking: *We're open to vacuum*!

She scrambled to her feet, hurried along the corridor and around a corner to find the source of the hurricane: a blackened breach where the outer door of an emergency airlock opened onto space. The inner door hung invitingly open. Roche approached it cautiously, wary of a trap.

Then, she glimpsed a movement: a suit much like hers had just stepped out onto the hull.

Roche didn't hesitate. Using every joule at her suit's disposal, she jumped through the gap and after the fleeing woman. Even if Alta was armed, Roche could take a direct hit or two before her suit failed. And if she could catch her and somehow overpower her before she jumped ship. . . .

Upon exiting the hatch, Alta dropped and rolled, bringing her rifle up to cover anyone following her. Roche burst out of the airlock, only a thin veil of artificial gravity preventing her from rebounding off into space. Alta's first shot missed. Her second caught Roche full on the chest as she threw herself forward. The recoil of the shot knocked her to one side with her ears ringing, but she didn't hesitate. She surged forward again.

Alta kicked back to avoid the charge and scrambled to her feet, her gun coming up again. The third shot took Roche in the shoulder, spinning her around. Alarms in her suit flashed red, and the acrid smell of smoke burned at her nostrils.

"*Die*!" The voice came over the open line as Alta swung the rifle's sight up to her eye, training it on Roche.

Roche knew she had only one more chance. Ignoring the pain in her hip, she dropped to a crouch, forcing Alta to readjust her aim; then, taking advantage of the split second she had gained, she hurled herself forward—

She heard Alta's gasp at the same instant the energy bolt grazed her helmet. Unable to stop herself, Roche lunged awkwardly forward, colliding with Haid as he took Alta from behind, swinging her around and down onto the hull. The impact cost him his grip on the woman.

As both he and Roche tumbled backward, Roche saw Alta regain her footing and collect the rifle that Haid had knocked from her hands.

"Quickly!" Roche called.

They were barely on their feet when the rifle discharged. She felt the edge of the energy bolt that took Haid in the back, forcing him forward into Roche and sending them sprawling across the hull again.

Haid came to a halt, totally inert, a meter or so away from where Roche had fallen, a massive smoking scar stretching across his suit's backplate.

"Ameidio!" She heard the panic in her voice. The lack of response from the ex-mercenary filled her with dread. The bolt had taken out the suit's servomotor control;

she wasn't even sure whether his immobility resulted from death or a simple inability to move.

She looked over to Alta again, saw the woman lifting the rifle once more to aim at her.

"I'm going to kill you, Roche." There was no longer any hysteria in Alta's voice, just a quiet determination.

Roche wanted to feel angry, but everything seemed to have been knocked out of her. All she could feel as she sat there, her friend lying prostrate on the hull before her, was a terrible exhaustion. All the fight went out of her; only acceptance remained as she stared down the barrel of Alta's rifle, and waited. . . .

A single rifle shot flickered through the vacuum, taking Alta at the weakest point of her suit between chest and neck plates. The woman jerked upright and staggered backward, trying to stanch the flow of air out the broken seal. Roche caught a glimpse of her terrified expression before the water vapor sucked out of her lungs plastered ice across the inside of her faceplate. She kicked spasmodically, staggering backward.

Roche heard the woman's cries over the suit's intercom,

"*Master*!" The words were carried on molecules of freezing air. "I have failed you!"

Roche turned to look at the figure who had fired, just in time to see him fire again at Alta Ansourian. The woman's suit stiffened, then went limp. It fell to the hull with a thud.

The sudden silence in Roche's helmet was broken only by the sounds of her own breathing.

It was a few moments before Cane spoke. He seemed to be waiting to make sure Alta wasn't going to get up again.

"Morgan?"

She watched him striding over to where she still sat; then his hands were taking hers and helping her to her feet.

"Morgan?" he repeated. "Are you all right?"

"I thought . . ." she began, before realizing she didn't know *what* she had thought. She hadn't believed he was dead, but she had been so taken up with pursuing Alta that she hadn't stopped to consider just what *had* happened to him.

"The explosion threw me through the blast doors before they could close," he explained quickly. "I realized it must have been Alta and so went after her."

"But the suit," said Roche. "It didn't register on the tracking display."

"I disabled the beacon," he said. "It was the only way I could get the advantage of surprise over her."

Roche was still very much shaken by everything that had happened, but she saw a flaw in Cane's explanation. "That would have taken time. How—?"

"Time is something we *don't* have right now, Morgan. Look."

He pointed above her. Only then did Roche look up and see the Hurn ship. All spines and strange glassy towers, it looked like a nightmarish sea anemone magnified a thousand times. It was enormous, ominous. Behind it, a faint glow marked where the ring surrounding Sol System's primary obscured the stars. Strange, pale sheets of lightning flickered in slow motion through the glow, lending the ship a surreal backdrop.

"How . . . ?"

"It must have slow-jumped," he said. A rumble came through the *Ana Vereine*'s hull. "Quick, Morgan. Use your thrusters and jump over to D nacelle." He pointed. "That one."

She faced him, puzzled.

"Just *do* it," he insisted.

"I'm not leaving Ameidio." She nodded toward her friend's lifeless form. His suit was immobile, but she still didn't know whether or not he was dead.

"Understood," he said. "I'll slave his suit to mine and follow you over. Now *go*!"

His urgent tone overrode her confusion and she did as he asked, though minus the usual grace with which she might have piloted the suit. Limited by her lack of depth through just one eye, as well as the lack of implants, she took the suit awkwardly up and out of the drive section's artificial gravity well and to the one enclosing the nacelle Cane had indicated. She resisted the disorienting change in gravity at first, then relaxed and let it hold her.

When she had adjusted, she was standing on a patch of hull apparently slightly above where she had been before. From this new vantage point, she could see a reddish glow clinging to the drive ports, the sole visual sign of the ship's impending destruction.

She looked around, expecting Cane to be following, but saw him land instead on another nacelle some distance away, Haid's suit following like a ball on a string.

"Cane?"

"I'm sorry, Morgan." There was something different in his tone—something of the Cane that had rescued her from the Disciples. "But this is where we part, I'm afraid."

Roche felt a wave of nausea wash over her.

"What are you talking about?"

"Really, Morgan—think."

She did, and it hurt. "It was you Alta was talking about," she said softly. "*You're* her master."

"You sound surprised," he said.

"No," she said. She was beyond surprise; she felt utterly dead inside. "Disappointed."

"I'm only doing as my nature dictates," he said.

She didn't say anything for a moment. She was remembering what Haid had said about Alta being unresponsive, and that Cane had spent a lot of time talking to her. That was when it must have happened. With a veil of suspicion still hanging over him, he would not have been able to move as she had. He had bent her will to his; he had made her his puppet.

The silence on the open link between them seemed to hum with repressed energy.

"It was all lies," she said, more to herself than to him. "Your amnesia, saving me on Sciacca's World—everything. It was all just lies."

"Not just lies, Morgan. But lies in a game—a game between the Box and myself, between my kind and the Crescend."

"What about Inderdeep Jans?" said Roche. "Why—?"

"All strategic games require sacrifices, Morgan," he said. "But don't think I didn't feel her pain. It touched me deeply, as did the deaths of the five you killed on the *Phlegethon*. For a group mind, the loss of even one component is painful. But you couldn't appreciate that, could you? Coming as you do from such a hapless and disparate race . . ."

"A group mind?"

"The *irikeii* glimpsed it in the black speck at the heart of me and Jelena Heidik. You saw it too, when you looked at us through a reave. There's more to us than meets the mental eye."

"So you *are* linked?" she said.

"Of course," he said. "Everything I have seen and experienced was shared with my siblings."

"Another lie."

"All of them were necessary," he said. "It was part of the game."

Roche felt herself reel. "But why didn't you just kill me? Why have you kept me alive? Why all of *this*?"

"Because we want you to know the reason for it all." She could almost feel the coldness in his voice. "We want you to be aware of the consequences of your *decision*." He emphasized the word deliberately, almost viciously. "We suspected from the beginning that the High Caste would become involved. Coming into contact with the Box when I awoke confirmed it. I watched it as closely as it watched me. I didn't guess that it was inside you, but I knew you were connected, that you were involved. You were the key, and the Crescend was the lock. When you asked me about killing me, and when you told Trezise that High Humans wouldn't help, I knew that the lock had been turned."

She wasn't entirely following him, but that didn't seem to matter at this time.

"I let you live," she said weakly. "I gave your race another chance."

He raised the assault rifle.

"That was a big mistake, I'm afraid, Morgan," he said, and fired.

She took a step back by reflex, but the bolt didn't come anywhere near her. Instead it struck the nacelle's support girders. She couldn't believe he had missed; it had to have been deliberate. He was tormenting her, perhaps, before finally killing her.

She took a step forward again and stood her ground. She would defy him, she decided; she would not give him the satisfaction of seeing her afraid to die.

"Do you really believe you can purge the galaxy?" she said.

Another shot, again striking the support girders. This time she didn't move at all.

"You're going to wipe out everything that's not a part of your precious group mind?" she continued, trying to control the tremor in her voice.

A third shot, and she felt the impact vibrate through her suit.

"It's called justice, Morgan," he said.

"It's called genocide, Cane!"

She felt the hull shift beneath her as a fourth, fifth and sixth shot struck the nacelle girders in rapid, angry succession.

"You dare stand there and talk to us about *genocide*!" he flung at her vehemently. "We're here to avenge a crime no worse!"

"But that was half a million years ago, Cane! You can't blame everyone alive today for something that happened so long ago!"

When next he spoke a few moments later, the icy calm had returned to his voice. "Don't impose your values on us, Morgan," he said.

"What does that mean?"

"That you shouldn't expect mercy from us simply for mercy's sake."

He fired another shot, this one causing her to momentarily lose her balance as the nacelle rocked under her.

"Charge is running low," he said. "But you should tear free in a moment or two and drift away."

"What good will that do?" she said, regaining her footing. "Why not just kill me now and be done with it?"

"Like I said, I want you to have time to think. I want you to think about everything that has happened. I want you to consider what your people have done, and I want you to know why it would have been utterly wrong for the Crescend to have intervened." He paused before adding, with almost a hint of amusement: "Besides, it seems only fitting, given that you spared me."

"I spared *all* of you!" she snapped angrily.

"Yes," he said. "And I want you to think about that, too, as you slowly die, Morgan."

The nacelle rocked again.

"It doesn't have to be like this, Cane," she said desperately, hoping to reach that part of his nature she was sure existed, the part she had come to know over the weeks since they had first met.

"Yes it does, Morgan. We are programmed to exact revenge and we shall do so to the best of our capabilities. And we *will* win."

"But this is crazy! There is no grudge left to pursue! Surely we can get along?"

"History would disagree with you."

"No—history *agrees* with me. Humanity has diversified so much since your creators were around. We come in all shapes and sizes now, and we live in all sorts of places. But underneath it all, we're still all Human. Some may think they're better, but in the end we're all the same. And regardless of what has happened in the past, or what might happen in the future, eventually you will fit in too. It's inevitable."

There was a mocking laugh which filled her helmet. "Assimilation? How typically arrogant of the victors."

"There *was* no victor," she stressed, feeling the need for urgency as the nacelle continued to shift uneasily beneath her. "That's what I'm trying to tell you, Cane. There's just *Humanity*."

"Exactly," he said. "Humanity . . . the victor."

His answer caught her with her mouth open to respond, but the words stuck in her throat.

Humanity . . . the victor.

"No," she said. "That can't be, Cane. You're Human. You *have* to be."

"You're wrong, Morgan," he said.

"But . . . it's not possible!"

"It's more than possible," he said. "It's the essence of this entire conflict. You deny our existence, so we repeal yours."

"But . . ." The concept was so difficult for her to grasp, she found the words almost impossible to say. "You're *aliens*?"

"We are the indigens," he said. "*You* are the invader."

"Now I know you're lying."

"No, this time I *am* telling the truth," he said. "It's simply a matter of perspective. My creators were exploring the galaxy before Humanity's ancestors had even reached its moon. We had created the beginnings of an anchor-point network before you learned how to use hyperspace. By the time our expanding empires came into contact, you were catching up fast but you were still our inferiors, and would have been for some time. You were hasty, impetuous, prone to sudden advances followed by long periods of decay—the brutal disequilibrium of individuality. We on the other hand were patient, persistent, and compassionate. Ours was the steady growth of unity.

"Neither of our civilizations had encountered alien life before, so we were unprepared to deal with such differences; we had no warning of what would come. We didn't expect you to learn from us as quickly as you did. We didn't expect your expansion to be so rapid, and so inconsiderate of our own. You stole our worlds, Morgan; you appropriated our anchor-point network and you encroached upon the society we had accreted so carefully over thousands of years. And you hurt us! Maybe you didn't mean to. Maybe you didn't even realize what you were doing. But you did it nonetheless. And we, like any injured organism, struck back."

She shook her head, dizzy with the concept of what she was hearing. "There's no evidence for any of this. How do I know you're telling me the truth?"

"What reason do I have to lie to you now?"

She didn't say anything; she couldn't. There didn't seem to be anything *to* say. The reality upon which her entire life was founded now seemed as shaky as the nacelle that rocked and moaned beneath her.

She thought of the anchor points supposedly older than Humanity itself, and found herself believing him. As incredible as it seemed, maybe she *had* finally learned the truth.

"You won't find evidence of our existence," he went on, "because it was either suppressed or destroyed in the process of your expansion. And in time, it was forgotten entirely. Even the war that engulfed our two species was forgotten. The origin of my makers was one of the first details to go—for although wiping out an entire losing Caste was not unheard of, destroying the only other intelligent life you had found in the universe *was*. Even those military leaders who sanctioned the genocide ultimately realized this. Perhaps we *could* have learned to live together. Perhaps you were hasty in assuming that, where more than one of my kind existed, the threat remains that the group mind can emerge again, as strong as before—or even stronger. Perhaps you had been wrong in pursuing the war to its ultimate, deadly conclusion."

"And *were* we wrong?" she asked. "Could we have lived together?"

"No," he said bluntly. "You had proven too many times that peaceful coexistence—in the long-term—simply wasn't a possibility. There had been too many broken treaties, smashed peace accords, violated cease-fires . . . We had grown tired of tolerating you, and resolved to rid our galaxy of you."

"But you lost."

"No, Morgan. We didn't," he said. "We are tenacious. I am proof of that."

"But what *are* you? You look like one of us; your anatomy is at least based on ours; you could almost *be* one of us, if you tried. What's happened to your precious origins now?"

"It exists in our minds, and will exist again when the data encoded in our introns is released. We carry within us the knowledge to re-create our race in its original form. Given time, we can restore the galaxy to the way it should be—the way it was *meant* to be—and we will reclaim our planets and systems. We will travel *your* anchor-point network. We will take from you all those things that should have been ours, and *make* them ours. The balance of justice shall be restored."

The nacelle suddenly lurched beneath Roche, throwing her off balance. There was a crunching, tearing sound, and artificial gravity failed. She used her thrusters to keep her against the hull while the suit anchored itself firmly into place. When next she looked up, everything was silent—even the rumble of the main drive was gone—and the nacelle was drifting away from the *Ana Vereine*.

"I want to thank you, Morgan," he said. The growing distance between them and the unsteadiness of the nacelle made it difficult for her to focus on him. "You have enabled us to continue the work we were created to do. Without the High Caste to interfere, the battlefield will be even. We can fight openly, if we choose to. We will prevail if we can, or we will die. History does not allow us a third option."

"There are always options," she muttered, thinking of the many times she could have turned away from the path that had led her here. "We make our own destinies."

"But sometimes they are made for us."

"Then they can be unmade."

"If you truly believe that, Morgan Roche, then you're more of a fool than I thought."

Light flashed from his thrusters as he leapt off the *Ana Vereine* and arced toward the ship waiting for him. She was too far away to make out whether or not he had taken Haid with him. Not that it mattered anymore. In fact, she thought it would be better for Haid to be left behind. If he wasn't already dead, she felt it would be better for him to die there rather than at the hands of Cane and his siblings later. . . .

She clutched the hull and waited for Cane to say something more, but nothing came. The flare of his thrusters disappeared into a wide-mouthed airlock leading into the Hurn ship. A minute passed in silence, then space became crowded in the vicinity of the *Ana Vereine*. Temporal echoes converged on the slow-jumping *Apostle*, creating a halo of flickering, short-lived ghosts around the spiny craft. As the echoes converged, the warp in space reached peak flexure until, with a flash of light so bright it left Roche blind in her sole eye for almost thirty seconds, it disappeared.

21

Ana Vereine Fragment (Nacelle D)
955.2.16
0430

Seventeen minutes later, the *Ana Vereine* exploded.

Roche didn't see it; she was inside the nacelle, trying to find anything that might be of use. But she felt the expanding wave-front as it hit. It shook her like a die in a cup. When it passed, she disentangled herself from the remains of a solar antenna and went back out onto the hull to see. There was nothing else for her to do.

Cane had chosen the nacelle well. It contained little but packed storerooms full of raw materials for repairs and hyperspace disrupters that were useless without power to run them. There was no communicator, no long-term life-support and no means of turning the nacelle into a powered vehicle of any kind. If she could plug the leaks, she could survive a day or two, but that was all. Had she found a way to contact the council drone that had shadowed the ship, she might have got away a distress call to Trezise; she might have had a chance of being rescued. But even if Cane's friends hadn't destroyed the drone to prevent anyone's overseeing their actions, she had no way of finding it, let alone sending a message. She was trapped.

So, when the *Ana Vereine* exploded, she went up on the hull to witness the pyre of her former friends and allies, and the place she had called home for the previous nine weeks.

And she saw something else, too—something completely unexpected.

An elongated star flew unsteadily out of the cloud of debris that was all that remained of the Dato Marauder. Bobbing and weaving like a drunken bird, it angled in the general direction of the tumbling nacelle. Where it wasn't burned black, its hull plating shone bright gold.

Perched on the truncated end of an access corridor that had once joined the nacelle to the main drive section of the ship, Roche watched it come. Despite the damage, she immediately recognized the ship. When it was closer, she moved out onto an exposed section and waved for attention. It changed course to rendezvous with her.

"Your suit beacon was moving," said Vri over the radio. "I followed it on the off chance you were still alive."

Her relief at hearing the Surin soldier's voice could not be measured. "I'm glad to see you, Vri."

"And I you," he said as he brought his fighter down.

What relief she had felt on finding the Surin alive was quickly tempered when she climbed aboard his ship and realized his condition.

His golden armor looked worse than the ship. He had taken two powerful shots: one to the right thigh and one in a line across the back of his head. The back of his skull was a mess of blood, bone, and fur. The tiny cockpit—with barely enough room for the two of them—stank of his blood.

Roche didn't say anything because there didn't seem to be anything to say.

"I was coming to assist you," he said, his eyes going in and out of focus as he talked. "I shouldn't have left Maii. She needed me, and I wasn't there. But I—" He coughed, winced, and tried again. "Alta took me by surprise," he said feebly. "Shot me and left me for dead." He smiled despite the pain. "When I woke up, the docks were in flames. *Esperance* was undamaged, though. It had sealed automatically and could weather worse than a mine or two, if it had to—and it did, when the drive went up. I couldn't move before then in case I was exposed. I wouldn't have stood a chance against that other ship. I *had* to wait . . ."

"You did the right thing," she reassured him.

"*Esperance* . . ." He stopped, breathing rapidly, and shut his eyes. He seemed to be running out of energy. "I give it to you, now."

Roche unsealed one of her suit gloves and touched his forehead. His skin was extremely cold, but she had no idea whether or not this was a bad sign for a Surin. The same ignorance struck her when she examined the instrument board in front of her. Although she had flown Surin vessels before, this was nothing like what she was used to. It had been designed to suit him, she suspected, with every screen and switch tailored for his needs, his mind. She suspected that she would be able to open the airlock if she ever had the need to, but she doubted she would be able to pilot the ship.

She wasn't about to tell him that, though.

"Thank you, Vri."

He opened his eyes briefly, but didn't see her.

"I fear," he said faintly, "that I have failed."

He died before she had a chance to say anything more.

The first thing she did was seal Vri's suit and get his body out of the pilot's seat. He had set *Esperance* on a course to nowhere; the engines were firing at a constant, gentle rate, with no apparent intention of stopping and no clear destination other than away from the nacelle. Maybe he had intended to change the settings before he died, or perhaps he had assumed that she would be able to do so herself.

Distantly, she felt embarrassed at being so helpless. With the Box she might have had a chance. Even without implants, it could have told her what to do. At the very least she would have had someone to talk to.

She played with the controls at random and managed to find the attitude jets. All that did was send the fighter into a slow tumble around its long axis and made its course even more chaotic. Fearing she would touch the wrong control completely and blow the drive core, she sat back and tried to think. The life-support seemed to be working fine, and there was no shortage of power. She could survive in the fighter longer than she would have on the nacelle, so that was an improvement. Given time, she could work out how to operate the drive or the communicator, which would improve her situation even more . . .

The one thing she *could* understand was the navigation display. The small fighter's projected course—as near as she could tell—took it through the outer edge of the ring system; she would strike the fringes of it within a day. The electrical anomalies Kajic had noted seemed to be fading, but she was still wary of them. When she wasn't puzzling over the controls, she kept her eye on the screen. What she would do if it *was* a trap, she didn't know.

Even as fatigue wore her down into a feverish creature talking to itself and weeping in fits and starts, she resisted sleeping. She was afraid of her dreams, of what she would see on closing her eyes. She didn't want to see Maii alive *or* dead: that wound was too fresh, the grief too keen. The same with Haid, and Kajic, and the Box—even Alta Ansourian and Cane. *Especially* Cane.

She had trusted him, and he had betrayed her. Put boldly, in black and white, she could accept it. As soon as she looked beneath that pronouncement, however, at the emotional consequences and potential ramifications, she saw the pain. She didn't want that. She would have the rest of her life to dwell upon it, however long that might be. If she could forget about it just for a moment, now, she would be grateful.

In the end she did sleep. Not even she could put it off forever. But there were no dreams—and for that she was grateful.

Fourteen hours after she left the nacelle, the glowing haze of the ring had expanded to fill most of her forward view. It looked like smoke: yellowish and acrid, with denser wisps almost blocking out the stars behind them. Strange, glowing sheets rippled through it at odd moments, but with little more definition than a predawn glow. She could no longer make out the plane of the ecliptic, or tell by sight alone at what angle she was approaching it. It was just there, before her, something she could neither avoid nor find any pleasure in viewing.

Once again, she regretted Sol System's lack of grandeur. If she had been about to crash into the Soul around Sciacca's World, or be electrocuted by the ion bridge snapping across the gap between Kukumat and Murukan, Palasian System's double-jovian, that would have at least been something to marvel at. But here, all she was heading for was a cloud of dust. She didn't even know what it would do to her. It might not do anything at all, if it was thin enough. Even if it was as dense as the average planetary ring, the most the *Esperance* would suffer as it passed through the cloud was some wear on its ablative shield.

That was exactly what it *was* suffering from when she began to hear voices.

At first she thought she was dreaming. A snatch of phrase caught her ear, apparently from somewhere behind her, followed quickly by another. Then another, and another, until the sounds came in a continuous, muddled stream. The whispers belonged to people of all ages and many different accents; most spoke galactic standard—although she could discern maybe one word in three—and some spoke in tongues she had never heard before. There were too many of them, too many fragments, for her to follow. All she could pick up were the individual flavors as they rushed by her, like ghosts in an echo park, or a half-remembered dream. They were happy, sad, angry, hurt, proud, joyous—all colors of the emotional spectrum.

When her suit's life-support kicked in, she knew she wasn't asleep. The temperature in the fighter had risen to an uncomfortable point without her noticing, so intrigued had she become with the whispering. She must have underestimated the velocity the fighter had accrued during its hours of constant thrust. Even as she studied the data, annoyed with herself for not paying attention, she could feel a slight vibration through the bulkheads. Having no knowledge of how to access the ship's diagnostic systems, she couldn't tell if the hull was being damaged by the high-speed rain of dust. All she could do was worry about it. Eventually, the ship would pass through the ring and out the other side. Or it wouldn't. The situation was as simple as that.

"Oh, for an axe . . ."

The whispered phrase caught her ear. There was a pause, filled with other whispers, then the fragment continued. The words were buried under others, but she could make them out. She knew them. She had heard them before.

"—nuclear strike from one hundred meters. I know, I know, but if it wasn't for you, I wouldn't be in this mess. Can you understand how frustrating it is to be cooped up in here with nothing to do?"

Roche listened, stunned. That was *her* voice. She remembered the conversation, but not the context.

"The sooner we're back in HQ, Box, the better . . ."

And with these words, she placed the memory: in her quarters on the *Midnight*. She had been bemoaning her lot—bored by her mission, resentful of her attachment to the Box and frustrated by Captain Klose's refusal to let her examine the mysterious life-capsule the ship had picked up in deep space. This was where it had all started.

But why was she hearing it now?

There was only one answer: *this wasn't just dust she was falling through . . .*

"Hello?" she called.

She didn't use her suit's radio. She simply spoke aloud.

"Hello, Morgan," replied a familiar voice. "I wondered when you would guess."

She wasn't as surprised as she thought she should be. "These are your voices?" she said. "Your memories?"

"The boundaries of this identity known as 'the Crescend' are difficult to define at the best of times," he said. "In my long life I have been many individuals, have spawned many components. Like the Box, for example: it came from me, and its memories now form part of me, but it was not *me*—at least not in the way you would understand the concept. All the voices you hear around you, they are memories to which I have access, and yet none of them are truly mine."

She imagined the Crescend as a spider sitting in the middle of an enormous web, reeling in experiences along silken threads, capturing and absorbing entire minds full of information. . . .

"A colorful analogy," he said. "And perhaps not totally inaccurate."

"You're reading my mind?"

"I am aware of what you are thinking," he said.

"Why can't you just give me a straight answer?"

"Because the questions you ask do not allow it."

The voice of the High Human came clearly over the babble, but the endless whispering—combined with the sound of the ship slowly being battered—was making it difficult to concentrate.

She glanced at the forward view screen, at the dust particles of the ring that were taking up the entire display now, as impenetrable as a dust storm.

"It's you, isn't it?" she said. "The ring is you. Or the other way around."

"Both, and neither. The ring is a physical construct upon which this identity is presently generated."

"A computer?" said Roche, lifting her voice unnecessarily to be heard above the growing noise.

"The term is grossly inadequate," he said with no hint of condescension. "It is composed of the mass of an entire solar system liberated and allowed to interact as computational components: every atom of an ever-changing matrix circling—and powered by—the system's sun. A sun which, half a million years ago, birthed the species from which we sprang."

It was hard not to be impressed by the sheer scale of what the Crescend was describing. As camouflage, it was perfect: of everyone she had met, only the Heresiarch had any serious idea that the ring might be more than it seemed. The unsuspected truth explained the odd electrical impulses, and the navigational hazard the ring occasionally posed: even something as nebulous and innocent-looking as a cloud of dust could be disturbed by passing ships and would possess the means to defend itself.

But this wasn't all he was telling her. *Birthed*, he had said.

"That's why we're here," she said. "You, and everyone. Sol System is where it all began."

"It may not be much to look at anymore," he said, "but yes, this is where it all began. For those who know, the system is something of a symbol. Not a shrine; one's origins are not to be worshipped. Sol System just *is*, and that is enough."

"But what happened to the planets?" One of them, she assumed, must have been Humanity's homeworld.

"That is a long story, Morgan," he said. "Too long for now."

"You won't tell me?"

"There isn't time," he said. "You haven't that much left."

"So I am going to die?"

"Do you *want* to die?"

Another evasive answer. Before she could respond, however, the ship lurched violently, tossing her from side to side in her seat.

When the ship settled again, she said: "Can you get me out of here? Can you fix the fighter so I can use it and get back to the *Phlegethon*? If it hasn't already been destroyed, that is."

"Far from it, Morgan. The council has experienced good fortune since the enemy became aware of your decision. No longer required to concentrate their efforts on one location—in order to draw you out, to force you to make a decision, and to influence what that decision would be—many of their number have retreated from the system and begun the long journey home. To their *hosts'* homes, I should say. As the war in Sol System winds down, preparations for the war throughout the galaxy are heating up. We sit on the brink of a new age, Morgan: today, the peaceful domination of Humanity, founded on near-genocide; tomorrow, the battlefield of justice, in whose days lives will be lost and civilizations will fall, and which might, ultimately, lead to a more balanced future."

"Is that what you want, then?" Roche felt the same confusion about his motives that she had the first time she and the High Human had talked. "I still don't know whether you believe I made the right decision or not."

"Does my opinion matter?"

"Of course it does!"

"If I tell you that you made the right decision, I will be accused of wanting war. If I tell you that you made the wrong decision, I will be accused of wanting to commit genocide upon the enemy."

Roche fell quiet for a while.

"I just wish there had been another alternative." Her words were soft and low, barely audible above the whispers that filled the space around her.

If the Crescend had heard, he didn't answer.

The temperature continued to rise, along with the turbulence, and the voices were louder, harder to think through. A golden haze tinged the air around her; the walls of the ship themselves seemed to glow.

"Tell me about your final conversation with Adoni Cane," the Crescend said.

"What? *Why*?" She was irritated that the Crescend seemed to be trying to distract her rather than doing anything to actually help her.

"Did he reveal anything to you that you didn't already know about him?"

"Like the fact that he's an alien, perhaps?"

There was a sound like a sigh. "He said this?"

"He said Humanity wiped out his creators and took over the galaxy. Did you know about this?"

"We suspected," the Crescend said. "Few records exist from that time, and only the oldest memories of the most inward-seeking of my Caste speak of such events, but we have always known of another race that preceded ours—which may have even co-existed with us for a time. It seemed likely that it was destroyed in the war about which we had also heard rumors. The possibility also existed that these two suspicions were linked to the emergence of the enemy and their convergence on Sol System. Linking all three was the most elegant solution."

"That explains why we couldn't find his parent Caste," Roche said. "He never had one, did he? It was a waste of time looking."

"Absence of evidence is not evidence of absence, Morgan—as you yourself recently said. We needed confirmation before we could be sure."

She suspected he was still trying to distract her, but she didn't care. She needed the distraction to take her mind from the sounds of the ship being bombarded by the dust outside.

"So who were they?" she said loudly. "Where did they come from?"

"They are referred to only by euphemism." The Crescend's voice never seemed to rise in pitch despite the ever-increasing noise within the cockpit. "And then most frequently as 'the Concinnity.' Where they originated, however, remains a mystery."

"Cane said that they're a group mind, and that they plan to resurrect the species from the data in their introns."

"It was always thought unlikely that revenge was the only thing on their agenda," the Crescend said. "Resurrection of the species was always considered a possibility."

"What are you going to do about it if they do?"

"What we have always done: observe."

"You'll let it happen?"

"It is in accordance with your decision, Morgan."

"But my decision was made with the understanding that they were *Human*! That if they wiped us out, there would still be Humans left, even if it was *them*!"

"There will always be Humans left," the Crescend assured her. "They will never destroy the High Caste. At least not until they have themselves evolved to our level, in their own way. And numerous Low Castes will survive too. The worst-case scenario would be that the mundanes will be wiped out, and then only for a time. In the enemy's eyes, it would even the score; in our eyes, it changes little."

Roche pondered this as best she could through the racket. It was true. As important as it seemed to her, the activities of the mundanes didn't amount to much in the big scheme of things. The High Humans were doing the real work, whatever it was, on a galactic scale. The mundanes just filled in the gaps, gave their superiors something to watch in their spare time. . . .

The cockpit's life-support suddenly failed, sending a blast of hot air into her face. She made sure her suit was completely sealed, then shut her eyes. Clutching the arms of the crash-couch, she rode out the turbulence, not knowing how much longer it would last and, irrationally, afraid that it might never stop.

"*Would* you change your mind?" The Crescend's voice was clear and calm in her helmet. "Knowing what you now know, do you think you made the wrong decision?"

She kept her eyes closed and fought down the fear by focusing on his question. "I don't think so," she said. "Cane and his race deserved at least a fighting chance. I just wish I hadn't been so stupid."

"In what sense?"

"Cane told me he was Human, and I believed him!"

"He never said that, Morgan."

"Yes he did," she said. "After Palasian System, when we woke him from that coma Linegar Rufo put him in. He tapped out a message in code—!"

"Yes, but that's not what he said," said the Crescend. "His exact words were: 'I am as Human as you are.' "

Her eyes opened, as if upon a realization she had been blinded to.

"What are you saying?" she asked. "That I'm not Human?"

"You are as Human as I am, Morgan. As Human as Cane. Even as Human as the Box, if you like," he said. "That's the way you were made."

She wanted to recoil from what the Crescend was saying, but she was trapped in her suit, in a disintegrating fighter. She had nowhere to hide from the words, no way to avoid them. All she could do was listen to him.

"The High Caste needed someone to make a decision it was not capable of making—or was not prepared to make. But we could hardly trust such a judgment to someone lacking the necessary attributes. Since mundanes are inherently unreliable, and since the person we required simply did not exist, we decided to make one. We made *you*, Morgan."

She shook her head. "*Why*?"

"You are determined and not easily swayed. You see all sides of a dispute and try to be fair. You have a keen sense of duty, on many levels. You are honorable, and will not shirk from the truth. You may not see yourself as such, Morgan, for we also gave you a sense of humility, but you are a good person. A good *Human*. If the fate of the mundanes was to rest in your hands, it was important for you to be so.

"On the other hand, you needed access to information and capabilities beyond the access of a normal mundane—especially once the time came to bring you face to face with the enemy, in the form of Adoni Cane—so my relationship with the Commonwealth of Empires was exploited to allow the Box to fall into your hands.

"The only thing that set you apart from the mundanes around you was your ability to detect the enemy, and even that was limited. You were, to all intents and purposes, an ordinary person, but one fashioned in such a way that you would not break under extraordinary circumstances. That was our gift to you, Morgan—one which has served you in good stead these last few weeks."

"How much of me . . . ?" She couldn't finish the sentence. Her mind was full of conflicting images, thoughts, and feelings. Everything seemed to be shaking, falling apart around her.

"I can assure you that you are as real as anyone."

"Ascensio—the orphanage—?"

"Real memories," he said. "Taken from someone else."

She closed her eyes. "Bodh Gaya?"

"Your own experiences. Everything from your arrival at the Military College was you. But that makes those memories no more 'real' to you than the others. They are all yours, Morgan. They all contribute to who *you* are."

She thought of the parents she had hoped to find one day, and whom she had forgotten upon joining COE Intelligence. She remembered her friends in the orphanage, and the conditions that had led her to flee her home planet. She saw again, as clearly as though it happened only yesterday, the flash of the COEI *Gegenschein*'s engines as it broke orbit and headed for her new home, her new future.

All hers.

All *faked*.

A shrieking of tortured metal rose around her, as though the ship were tearing up.

"I've never had any choice, have I?" She raised her voice to be heard over the noise, even though she knew the Crescend could read her mind just as easily as it ever had.

"Of course you have, Morgan. That was the whole point."

"But you made me in order to do something. There was no way I could avoid that. There's no way you would've let me!"

"Perhaps not, but—"

"And could I have avoided all of *this*?" She saw Maii's body, the *Ana Vereine*'s pyre, the golden glow of the cockpit around her. "Was I always intended to end up *here*?"

"That question is irrelevant," said the Crescend. "You are here now, and the 'now' is all that matters."

A siren wailed in her ears.

"Why are you bothering to talk to me at all?" she said angrily. "Why ask me about Cane? Why not just lift the information from my memories? What is it you are after? You want me to absolve you for what you've done? Is that it?"

"I have no need of absolution, Morgan. I have no ulterior motives, either. Your role in this phase of the war is truly finished."

"So now I am being thrown out with the trash?" she shouted. "Is that it?"

"You are not a robot, Morgan," the Crescend said.

"But I'm not *real*!"

"You may find it difficult to accept, but you are as genuine a being as anyone else you have met. You have mind, you have will, and you have character. Where your body actually came from is irrelevant."

"Do you expect me to accept that?"

"In time, I think you will."

"But I don't *have* time," she said. "The fighter's burning up!"

"Yes," the Crescend said with no suggestion of remorse. "It is. In fact, you have less than a minute before it disintegrates completely."

She fought down a surge of panic, resisted the tears pressing at the backs of her eyes.

"I'm frightened," she said, the words both a whisper and a sigh.

The Crescend said nothing.

She closed her eyes again, bracing herself as the fighter began to shake violently. The sound of voices was drowned out by the rattling and creaking of the ship. She thought she might be screaming, but she could hear nothing at all over the noise. She *was* sound: sound and movement: movement and pain: pain and—

With a burst of heat, everything went silent.

EPILOGUE

There was no pain; there was no grief. There was only the darkness drawing her in, consuming her. She didn't resist the warm sensation; she allowed herself to be taken.

<That's it, Morgan. Just accept.>

The familiar voice of the Crescend filled her with a strange relief. But he sounded different somehow. Closer—almost as though the words were emanating from herself.

<The fighter . . .> she said, as if remembering something from long ago. <It . . . burned up?>

<Yes, Morgan. It did.>

She hesitated for a moment. <I'm dead?> she said.

<How could that be possible if you are speaking to me now?>

<So I'm alive, then?>

The Crescend didn't respond, and an interminable silence followed. She felt something approximating panic wash over her, soaking the empty dark around her.

<Tell me!> Her voice resounded through the void. <Am I *alive*?>

Another silence followed before the Crescend spoke again.

<Define 'alive,' Morgan.>

APPENDIX

THE ORIGINS OF HUMANITY AN OPEN-ENDED QUESTION.

(by Provost Rejuben Tade, extracted from his welcoming address to the Guild of Xenoarchaeologists' 13,333rd Decannual Intake Expo.)

It is said that unless you know where you started, it is difficult to tell where you are heading. You can plot your course with as much precision as you like; you can map vectors, measure velocity and distance to the nth degree, but without those vital initial coordinates, you might as well be flying blind.

The authors of this axiom were, of course, referring to navigation on land or sea, or even in space. But why should it not be equally applicable to Humanity as a whole?

Anyone with an education would know that the origins of our species are clouded in mystery, buried under the obfuscating weight of five hundred millennia. Half a million years: that's an awful lot of dust. And if we look closely at this dust, we can make out lumps and bumps along the surface which suggest things that *might* be buried there. But unless we actually brush away these layers of dust, we would never know exactly what lies beneath. When we do, sometimes we find what we imagined we would; other times we find nothing at all. Most of the time, though, we simply reveal new landscapes of dust which seem to bear little relation to the ones above and which might, too, reveal nothing about what remains hidden beneath.

The mystery of the origins of Humanity is one known to all, although appreciated by few. Any individual fortunate enough to resolve this mystery would not so much earn himself or herself a footnote in some dusty xenoarchaeological journal, as guarantee themselves a place among the greats of science. For that person will not only return to us the sense of place, of identity, that has been denied us these long centuries, but will also thereby enable us—to return to our original metaphor—to know where we, as a species, are going. Not in the sense that evolution, social or physical, has a "destination" or a "purpose" in "mind," but in the sense that changes we do see occurring could finally be measured against a single fixed reference point—the elusive "Alpha Point" (as some scholars refer to it). Without this point, it is inevitable that any observations we make will be corrupted by our own subjective viewpoints, and any objectives we aspire toward will be difficult to achieve.

Some argue that we aren't flying blind at all, that the question of Humanity's origins has already been answered. Such people usually, in my experience, possess barely enough knowledge on the subject to have formed an opinion but a profound insufficiency to prove that opinion to anyone's satisfaction but their own. Exponents of the Out-of-Sol theory spring immediately to mind, along with their archrivals, the Multiple-Genesis-ites. Where they all fall down is in the assumption that we *can* know such things, that the evidence exists and has been misinterpreted or deliberately suppressed. The truth is in fact that information, once set loose in the massive information flows of the galaxy, is very difficult to contain—especially if it is of such revolutionary nature, and even more especially if it is completely verifiable. Were such evidence to exist, more people would know about it in an hour than will ever hear this speech in my lifetime.

In short, conclusive evidence simply does not exist.

So let's look at what we *do* know . . .

Roughly five hundred thousand years ago, probably slightly longer, at least four Primordial Castes colonized a large number of systems in a migration we would today call an "outsweep." This region of space contains several hundred stars, including Sol, and is commonly referred to in old records as the Exordium Worlds; we suspect all were visited around the same time, making it difficult to isolate one as a definite home system. Of course, this difficulty might reflect the limitations inherent in our only available method of dating this expansion. In the absence of actual ruins of any kind, only the remnants of the anchor-point network established at this time gives us any kind of date at all, and even that is uncertain after so long.

To explain why this is uncertain, I always fall back on an old fishing metaphor. I imagine myself casting a line into a pond. On the end of my line is a sinker. As the sinker falls into the water, it creates a disturbance. Ripples spread out from the disturbance with decreasing magnitude until all trace of the disturbance is gone. But the line remains, and it too may create disturbances. My hand may vibrate, or I might tug the rod to attract a fish.

Now, if the line is the crack in space that allows us to break through to hyperspace, and the sinker is the shock that created the hole in the first place, and the surface of the pond is space itself, then the ripples are the echoes not only of the anchor point's creation but of its continued use. Although these ripples in space do not propagate the same way as ripples in water—tending to radiate in the temporal dimensions rather than those of space, forming localized distortions often and misleadingly referred to as standing waves—they are frequently used as navigational aides, or to find an anchor that has disappeared from charts. Xenoarchaeologists can use these ripples too, since their amplitude decreases at a known rate. One can tell at a glance whether an anchor point is a thousand years old, or ten thousand, or if it was created yesterday. That much is very simple.

The difficulty arises when an anchor point is more than three hundred thousand years old, or has not been used regularly for half that time. The amplitude of the ripples may decrease to the point where they are indistinguishable from the background fluctuations of the universe. While we can still detect ripples from the ancient anchors among the Exordium Worlds, we are unable to tell whether the decrease has come about because of age or disuse. If the former, they might be eight hundred thousand years or more old; if the latter, they might be as young as four hundred and fifty thousand. All we can say with any certainty is that each and every one of the anchors in this area was created around the same time—suggesting that hyperspace technology was only developed *after* the region was colonized.

We do not know where this technology came from or who developed it, but we know roughly when it occurred. Four hundred and twenty thousand years ago, Humanity suddenly boiled out of the Exordium Worlds in an outsweep known as the Second Expansion. This surge is much easier to account for. Lines of datable anchor points expand radially from the region, riding on the back of faster-than-light technology and forming the skeletal remains of vast trade routes that literally spanned the galaxy. Humanity, initially in the form of the four known Primordial Castes, spread like ink through water from planet to planet, star to star, jumping across gulfs previously unimaginable and daring even to send probes out of the galaxy itself—probes that have not as yet reached any of their destinations. What they will see, you and I will probably never know. Only the High Caste—the first members of which Transcended during this time—have that possibility open to them.

Some records paint this Second Expansion as a time of great conflict for Humanity. Some researchers suggest that there might have been one single, mighty war, or there might have been innumerable smaller conflicts. Certainly it was a time of tremendous change, during which Humanity began the speciation that has led to such diversity and richness today. Legends were founded and, almost as quickly, forgotten. We will never know exactly what happened in those times, and for that very reason we will never tire of asking the questions.

Inevitably, as the Second Expansion slowed, the centers of power shifted away from the Exordium Worlds to the core. The ancient shipping routes shifted too, until they settled into the familiar pattern we now call the Great Lanes. This almost certainly happened around three hundred thousand years ago—although, oddly enough, we cannot independently verify precisely when. The Lanes have been used almost continuously since their creation, and have been frequently re-created, so their ripples show few signs of natural aging. That hasn't stopped people trying to date them, of course, but the results are inconsistent and anomalous. One research group actually dated a pivotal Middle Reach anchor point to be in excess of nine hundred thousand years old—a conclusion which is patently not tenable, inasmuch as it is far older than Humanity itself.

But this is a small mystery, usually raised to trigger the what-if instinct in all of us. The fact remains that the vast proportion of evidence is in favor of the story as I have told it: that Humanity expanded outward from a single system only slowly at first, then much more rapidly when it discovered anchor point technology—changing as it went. And so we continue to change today, even though expansion halted long ago, with the colonization of the entire galaxy. The only new territories we can dream about are those across the intergalactic gulfs or within our own minds. Many observers note that since the most advanced of Humans always seem to choose the latter path, perhaps that says something about the long-term possibilities for physical expansion. Others point out that High Humans may indeed have found a way to cross the gulfs, but have either not yet returned or choose simply to keep their discoveries a secret.

Whichever way one looks at it, the question remains: Humanity has most likely not reached the end-point of its evolution, and where that end-point *might* be depends very much on its beginning. Has Humanity always been so changeable, or so insular at its higher reaches? Is the present ratio of High Humans to mundanes, which has been constant for hundreds of thousands of years, one we can assume indefinitely? Or are we just going through a phase—one that might change with little or no warning, plunging the galaxy into chaos once more?

Certainly, attempting to plot trends in the behavior of Humans throughout the last four hundred thousand years has been a thankless task. Castes tend to develop in isolation, usually from a Low form that has itself devolved some time in the past, occasionally with the help of a benefactor's biotechnology. Newly vitalized, the Caste then undergoes a period of expansion, sometimes fragmenting as it goes, leaving pockets of itself behind that might in turn one day also expand, depending on the Caste's ambition or its Batelin Limit. At the same time, many other Castes are behaving similarly, and these expansive types may meet and overlap, or meet and clash, or meet and rebound, depending on their compatibility. The possibilities for trade and conflict are endless, as attested to by the prevalence of the Commerce Artel throughout all reaches of the galaxy.

Other Castes are no longer expansive, having reached the peak of their development, and preparing—whether they know it or not—to change into something new. Lots of Castes advance, devolve, then rise again thinking they're the first to do so; legends and ancient folk tales tell of angels and the like, all metaphors for former glory days that goad them on, upward again. Some Castes disappear, of course, destroyed by war or technological suicide or absorbed by neighbors. Others never devolve, just go on to greatness, Transcending at the peak of their rise to become immortals of a type we can barely comprehend—secretive and elusive, and capable of understanding beyond our wildest imaginings.

Those who don't devolve, disappear, or Transcend, achieve homeostasis in the mundane and remain that way indefinitely. Only the names of their empires change, rising and falling like the vibrations in a cosmic string. The Pristines are most notable among these types. The ancient remnants of Primordial Humanity are reluctant to change, but tolerate it in others—for perhaps that is the way it must be, since to grow, one must change. But to change is to risk devolution, and that risk is a great one.

Just one Caste in ten thousand Transcends. The rest devolve or disappear. One school of thought says that the handful of Castes that achieve homeostasis, apart from the Pristine, might only be delaying inevitable decline. But we cannot be certain of this without greater knowledge of our origins. Perhaps Humanity has always been like this, and will never change.

Here we return to our original question: how can we know where we will end up if we don't know where we began? For an example of how the answer to this might have very real ramifications for all of us, one has only to ask: why *has* the ratio of High to mundane Humans been so constant? It might very well be a natural state for our race, as most people assume—but it might *not* be just as easily. And if not, it can tip either way, in favor of either the High Caste or the mundanes. We know that the ratio changed from no High Humans at all to a relatively fixed proportion in the early days of the galaxy, suggesting that Human nature did favor the High Caste at one point. If that trend had continued, we would not exist today: the galaxy would be populated only by the members of the High Caste, everyone else having devolved or Transcended at a rate too great for mundane stocks to replenish themselves. Clearly this has not happened—but *why* not? What shifted the balance away from the High Caste?

The most obvious possibility is that there is a natural rate of accretion of which we were not previously aware. The effects of a High Caste death-rate would only become visible after the initial members began to age, and there are indeed High Caste deaths on record. But these are exceedingly rare, and it is generally doubted that they would even brake the initial expansion of the High Caste, let alone halt it entirely. So what else is going on? Perhaps High Humans don't need to die before they need to be replaced: perhaps being old and insular is enough. After all, we are only aware of *active* High Humans; there may be many more who choose not to communicate with anyone, or who have entered a state of prolonged hibernation, or have undergone transformation to another plane of being we cannot imagine.

Whatever the truth, this issue raises a disturbing possibility: that the High Caste maintains the ratio artificially, by either limiting its numbers somehow or maintaining an artificially high rate of mundane replenishment. The latter, of course, might simply be to restock its own numbers—for if High Caste expansion continued unchecked and there were no mundanes left, where would future members come from? Or it might be to give them something to watch, just as some mundane and Low Castes keep inferior species as pets.

Is this our ultimate fate, then, to amuse, or to act as breeding stock for new High Humans? We will never know until we learn the truth about our origins. And to do *that*, we need more data.

This is where you come in. As alumni from institutions all over the galaxy taking the bold leap of faith into the rarefied air of xenoarchaeology, your job is to probe deep into these questions and to expose the truth. Or if not the truth, then a fragment of it. Or if not even a fragment of the truth, then another question for someone else to answer. This process is ongoing, and will outlast me just as it has outlasted two hundred thirty-seven Provosts before me. It will probably outlast you, too, and the ones who follow you. Perhaps future xenoarchaeologists will look back on our work with an indulgent smile for our ignorance—or perhaps they will regard our work as cornerstones in the great edifice of understanding under constant construction. I cannot say which will be the case, just as my predecessors did not know. All I *can* say is that these questions are worth asking, even if we can never answer them. Not knowing where we came from does not stop us from moving on—and that is perhaps the most important thing about our race that has brought us to where we are today, wherever that is. We are not inclined to stay still.

Once, millions of years in the past, a small, barely bipedal creature rose up on its hind legs and squinted at the stars above. Well, we own those stars now, and we're still moving. Only time will tell where we will ultimately end up. . . .

GLOSSARY

A-14 Higher Collaboration Network: an amalgamation of core-based High Caste members whose intentions include attempting to establish an objective frame of reference with respect to Humanity's occupation of the galaxy. *The Objective Reference Calendar* is one result of this work.

A-P cannon: a weapon that fires accelerated particles of various types. Common on spacefaring warships.

Absenger, Burne: chief liaison officer, COE Armada.

adytum: Skehan Heterodox term for the control room of a consistory vessel.

Alpha Aurigae: an ancient system, the precise location of which is presently unknown.

Alpha Point: a name for the single point in time and space from which some xenoarchaeologists surmise Humanity evolved.

***Ana Vereine*, IND:** the first of a new class of warships—the Marauder—manufactured by the Dato Bloc as part of the Andermahr Experiment. Its design incorporates a captain surgically interfaced with the ship. Once part of the Ethnarch's Military Presidium, it is now an independent vessel registered to Morgan Roche.

anchor drive: the usual means of crossing interstellar space, but by no means the only one (see **slow-jump**). Indeed, the anchor method has undergone several radical redesigns over time; current technology is rated at 49th-generation.

anchor points: regions of "weakened" space from which translation to and from hyperspace is both easier and less energy-expensive; jumps from anchor points are therefore of a greater range than from "normal" space and usually terminate in another anchor point. They are typically located near inhabited systems (but far enough away to avoid distortion by background gravitational effects) or in locations in deep space which are considered strategically important. There are approximately ten thousand million anchor points currently in existence—one for roughly every ten stars, scattered across the galaxy.

Andermahr Experiment: a covert project specializing in cybernetic interfaces designed to allow mind and machine to merge. Founded by Ataman Ana Vereine, who desired captains that were as much a part of their ships as was the anchor drive—an integral, reliable system rather than a flesh and blood afterthought. Continued in secret until the Ataman Theocracy emerged from the COE as the Dato Bloc. Culminated in the DBMP *Ana Vereine*, the first Marauder-class warship, with Uri Kajic its captain.

Ansourian, Alta: only child of Atul Ansourian.

Ansourian, Atul: adviser and self-styled *éminence grise* to the administer of Perdue Habitat, Inderdeep Jans.

Apostle: a Hurn vessel in the service of the Disciples of Evergence.
Aquareii: a High Human renowned for being the most powerful member of the Interventionist faction.
Armada: see **COE Armada**.
Ascensio: the homeworld of Morgan Roche.
Asha: the single, warlike deity of the main Kesh religion.
Ataman Theocracy: a tightly knit empire that existed as an independent entity until its absorption into the COE after the Second Ataman War in '442 EN. After several centuries, it eventually seceded as the Dato Bloc ('837 EN).
AVS-38 & **AVS-44:** two of the *Ana Vereine*'s large contingent of scutters.

Basigo: a Caste not native to the COE region.
Batelin Limit: the ceiling above which the complexity of a nation exceeds the biological capabilities of the individuals inhabiting it. In the case of the Pristine Caste, the value of the Batelin Limit is approximately three and half thousand systems.
Black Box: the generic term for an AI. Usually abbreviated to "Box."
Bodh Gaya: former capital system of the COE and the Dominion. Its second moon houses the Military College of the COE Armada.
Box, the: an AI commissioned by COE Intelligence. Its binary identification number (JW111101000) is one digit longer than normal, indicating its unique status. Created by the High Human known as the Crescend, the Box is designed to infiltrate and subvert all available systems, thereby increasing its own processing powers until, at its most powerful, it resembles its creator. Once thought to be contained within a small black valise, it is now known to inhabit the cells of Morgan Roche.
Buk, Enver: the COE Eupatrid prior to Felix Gastel.

Calendar: the galactic standard timekeeping method consists of: 100 seconds per minute, 100 minutes per hour, 20 hours per day, 10 days per week, 4 weeks (40 days) per month, 10 months (400 days) per year. All dates are expressed in the form of year (usually abbreviated to the last three digits, i.e. '397), month, and day from the *Ex Nihilo* reference point. See also **Objective Reference Calendar**.
Cane, Adoni: the occupant of an unidentified life-support capsule recovered by the COEA *Midnight* near Ivy Green Station anchor point while en route to Sciacca's World. A genetically modified combat clone designed to mimic a Pristine Human, his origins are known not to lie with the Sol Apotheosis Movement, although who did create him, and many others like him, remains a mystery.
Cane, Adoni: field admiral, Old Earth Advance Guard; received a military Star for extraordinary acts of valor against the enemy.
Castes: following the speciation of the Human race, numerous Castes have proliferated across the galaxy. These Castes are too numerous to list, but they can be classified into three broad groups: High, Low, and mundane (which includes Pristine and Exotic). There are six predominant Exotic Castes to be found in the region surrounding the COE: Eckandar, Hurn, Kesh, Mbata, Olmahoi, and Surin.
Catiph: a High Human.
Ceyle's Hub: former home of Advocate Janil Coriett.
Chase, Auberon: head of COE Intelligence.
Clarke Cylinder: an ancient habitat.

COE: see **Commonwealth of Empires.**

COE Armada, the: the combined armed forces of the COE, responsible for external security. Active soldiers are referred to as Marines.

COE Enforcement: the policing body responsible for security and information gathering within the COE. Field agents are referred to as Enforcers.

COE High Equity Court: the department responsible for intersystem justice within the COE. Its usual purpose is to settle territorial disputes.

COE Intelligence: the body responsible for information gathering outside the COE. Originally and still nominally a subdepartment of the Armada, but an independent body in practice.

COE Intelligence HQ: the command center of COE Intelligence, a large, independent station located in deep space near the heart of the Commonwealth.

COE Military College: the main training institution of COE Armada personnel; situated on the second moon of Bodh Gaya.

COEA: COE Armada vessel identification prefix.

COEI: COE Intelligence vessel identification prefix.

Commerce Artel: a galaxy-wide organization devoted to initiating and coordinating trade between Castes and governments that might otherwise have no contact. It prides itself on remaining aloof from political conflict yet has some strict behavioral standards to which it expects its customers to adhere (such as the Warfare Protocol). Structurally, it is divided into chapters managed by indigenous Caste-members with only loose control from above. It has strong links, locally, with the Eckandar Trade Axis.

Commonwealth of Empires: often abbreviated to COE or Commonwealth. A relatively ancient Pristine nation currently in its 40th millennium of nominal existence—"nominal" in that the membership of the COE is fluid by nature, with provinces joining and seceding on a regular basis. It has had many different capitals and its borders have changed radically over the centuries. Indeed, it has drifted with time, and now occupies territories quite remote from its original location. One thousand inhabited systems currently fall under its aegis, and another three thousand uninhabited systems have been annexed. It is ruled by a democratically elected Eupatrid and a council of representatives who, when united, wield supreme executive power. Its security departments include Intelligence, Armada, and Enforcement.

Coriett, Janil: an advocate formerly of Ceyle's Hub, currently employed in Environment Control of the SHCV *Phlegethon*.

Crescend, the: a High Human of some note and great history. His time of Transcendence is not recorded. Little is known about him, beyond the facts that he is the founder and overseer of Trinity, an ally of the COE, and a key supporter of the Interventionist movement. He is assumed to be a singular entity simply because the first person singular is his pronoun of choice.

crypt: the Skehan Heterodox term for the engineering rooms of a consistory vessel.

Dark Stressor, HHAB: a compact habitat of ill-repute, known to be a gathering-point for mercenaries.

Dato Bloc: an independent nation founded on the ruins of the Ataman Theocracy that recently broke free of the COE. Although not hierocratic in nature, the Ethnarch exerts a strict rule. Its security departments include the Ethnarch's Military Presidium and the Espionage Corps.

Daybreak, COEI: a courier vessel belonging to COE Intelligence.

DBMP: vessel identification prefix for the Ethnarch's Military Presidium.

De Bruyn, Page: former head of Strategy, COE Intelligence.

Disciples of Evergence: a covert organization with Hurn connections devoted to serving the enemy.

disrupters: see **hyperspace disrupters.**

Dreher, Ralf: a name from ancient records connected to the enemy.

Drys: a caste not indigenous to the COE region.

E-shield: an electromagnetic barrier designed to ward off particle and energy weapons. Used mainly by medium-to-large spacefaring vessels.

Eckandar: (**Eckandi**, adj & sing. n): a Caste flourishing in the regions surrounding the COE. Its members are typified by their slight size, gray skin, bald scalps, and unusual eyes. They are a gregarious Caste, preferring trade and communication over conquest. They are also well-advanced in genetic science. Their past stretches back beyond that of the COE, although they lack the continuity of history that strong nationhood often provides. Their sole uniting body is the Eckandar Trade Axis.

Eckandar Trade Axis: the main society of the Eckandi Caste, devoted, much like the Commerce Artel (with which it has close ties), to facilitating free and nondiscriminatory trade with and between the COE and its neighbors.

Egarr, Gurion: senior councilor to Inderdeep Jans.

EN: see ***Ex Nihilo*.**

enemy: Interim Emergency Pristine Council shorthand for the clone warriors.

Enforcement: see **COE Enforcement.**

Enforcer: see **COE Enforcement.**

epsense: an ability encompassing telepathy and empathy. The ritual training of epsense adepts generally takes decades and incorporates elements of sensory deprivation. Note: telekinesis and precognition are not covered by epsense and are assumed to be nonexistent. Skilled utilizers of epsense are referred to as **epsense adepts** or **reaves.**

Erojen: a town on an outpost far from the heart of the Surin domain.

***Esperance*, SAS:** the fighter piloted by Defender-of-Harmony Vri.

Espionage Corps: see **Dato Bloc.**

Espire-Mavrodis Coalition: one of the IEPC's major allies.

Essai: home of the Surin Agora.

Ethnarch: the title of the leader of the Dato Bloc.

Ethnarch's Military Presidium: see **Dato Bloc.**

Eupatrid: the title of the chief executive officer of the COE.

***Ex Nihilo*:** refers to the date upon which the COE is believed to have been founded. Evidence exists to cast doubt upon the accuracy or relevance of this date—notably the fact the Commonwealth as a single body did not exist at all between the 13th and 15th millennia—but the date remains as a reference point. Usually abbreviated to EN.

Exordium Worlds: the region first colonized by the Primordial Castes.

Exotic: any mundane Caste that differs physiologically from the Pristine. There are a vast number of Exotic Castes, and, although no one type of Exotic comes close to outnumbering Pristine Humans, the Exotics as a whole mass far greater than Pristines alone.

fane: the Skehan Heterodox term for a ship's bridge.
Far Reaches: the name of the outermost fringes of the Outer Arms.
Fathehi Consulate: a habitat sent to Sol System by a Caste originating on the far side of the galaxy.
flicker-bombs: devices used in space warfare to attack an enemy vessel. Employing the fact that small masses (under a few kilograms) can slow-jump a small distance within a gravity well, these missiles skip in and out of space on their way to their target, which, it is hoped, they will materialize within, causing massive amounts of damage. They are easily deflected by hypershields, however, which form a barrier in hyperspace that no such weapon can cross.
40th millennium: the current millennium in the history of the COE. See ***Ex Nihilo*.**

Gastel, Felix: the current Eupatrid of the COE.
Gegenschein, COEI: a cruiser owned by COE Intelligence.
***God's Monkey*, HIC:** a small vessel operated by the Disciples of Evergence.
Great Lanes: the network of shipping routes delineated by anchor points across the galaxy.
grayboots: see **Olmahoi retribution squad.**
Ground Corps: a military body referred to in ancient records.
Guild of Xenoarchaeologists: (GOX) an ancient and highly regarded professional organization of xenoarchaeologists.
Guo Sodality: an organization from the Middle Reaches dedicated to the study and training of epsense adepts.
Guidon Habitat: sibling-habitat to Perdue Habitat.

H'si F'ta: a Caste known to the IEPC.
Haid, Ameidio: former transportee, Sciacca Penal Colony, and ex-mercenary.
Heidik, Jelena: the name by which the clone warrior responsible for the destruction of Palasian System identified herself.
Heidik, Jelena: in ancient times, a general and recipient of a Mars St. Selwyn Medal for valor against the enemy in Alpha Aurigae.
Hek'm: the Olmahoi Caste homeworld.
Heresiarch: Skehan Heterodox name for the commanding officer of a consistory vessel.
High Humans (or **High Castes):** Superior intelligences that have evolved (Transcended) from the mundane. Enormously long-lived and farseeing, they concentrate on issues quite removed from the rest of the galaxy; indeed, due to their enormous scale, they are the only beings capable of comprehending the galaxy in its entirety. They generally leave mundanes alone, to let them progress (and, ultimately, to Transcend) in their own time. See **Castes** and **Transcendence.**
High Equity Court: see **COE High Equity Court.**
Hurn: a Caste typified by ritual and complexity. In appearance they are lean and muscular, averaging greater than Pristine height. They are predisposed toward music and mathematics. Socially they prefer oligarchies with a baroque middle class.

Hutton-Luu System: a much-disputed system of the COE near its border with the Dato Bloc. See **Sciacca's World.**

hypershield: a barrier erected in hyperspace to deflect or inhibit the passage of anything traveling by that medium. Commonly used as a prophylactic against hyperspace weapons. Hypershields operate under a maximum volume constraint: i.e. they will only operate as intended under two thousand cubic kilometers.

hyperspace disrupters: a form of hypershield which actively combats incoming hyperspace weapons, such as flicker-bombs. Unlike anchor points, which "weaken" space, disrupters do the opposite, making it more difficult for anything nearby to emerge from hyperspace.

i-Hurn Uprising: a civil dispute which broke out between two rival factions of the Hurn Caste.

IEPC: see **Interim Emergency Pristine Council.**

***imaret*:** a Surin single-passenger fighter.

Imi: a system in which Ameidio Haid once worked.

IND: independent vessel identification prefix.

Intelligence: see **COE Intelligence.**

Interim Emergency Pristine Council: (IEPC) an organization that exists only in times of greatest duress for the Pristine Caste. With no fewer than thirty nations required to call it into being, it exists only so long as the threat remains.

Interventionism: a movement among High Humans—and some mundanes—that advocates closer links between High and mundane Castes. See **The Crescend.**

***irikeii*:** one of very few Olmahoi "sound-thoughts" which can be equated with audible words; often translated as *unnamed* or *unnameable*.

Jans, Ehud: Inderdeep Jans's father and the previous administer of Perdue Habitat.

Jans, Eir: biological daughter of Ehud Jans.

Jans, Inderdeep: administer of Perdue Habitat.

Ju Mandate, Second: a government represented by Assistant Vice Primate Rey Nemeth.

JW111101000: see **Box, the.**

Kajic, Uri: former captain, DBMP *Ana Vereine*, physically bonded to his ship.

Katajalin Serai: a loose collection of trade and security vessels.

Ken'an: a mercenary operating from the habitat *Dark Stressor.*

Kesh: the most primal of the local Castes. The Kesh are typically warlike and predisposed toward violence. In appearance, they tend to be larger than the Pristine average and have mottled, multicolored skin. Their social structure is heavily ritualized, with a strong tribal or family base. They are known for being highly racist.

***Kindling*, IND:** the name given by Page De Bruyn to her stolen fighter, formerly registered as TBC-14 and owned by COE Intelligence.

Kukumat: one of a gas giant pair occupying the sixth planetary orbit around Palasian System; the pair shares a single moon.

LaGoc: a Caste that contributed a mobile barracks to the crisis in Sol System.

Lemmas: A Hurn reave employed by the Disciples of Evergence.

Lenz, Uyeno: a mercenary frequently to be found on *Dark Stressor.*

Lleshi, Sadoc: captain, Ground Corps; recognized for excellence in battle against the enemy in ancient times.

Low Castes: devolved mundane Humans. These animal-like creatures come in many forms and occupy many niches across the galaxy. Some evolve back up to mundane status, given time and isolation, while others become extinct as a result of the forces that led to their devolution in the first place.

***Lucence-2*, COEA:** COE Armada Escort & Assault Craft.

M'taio System: a system notable for its Caste Wars in recent times.

Maii: Surin epsense adept.

Marauder: an experimental class of warship developed by the Dato Bloc. See **DBMP *Ana Vereine*.**

Marines: see **COE Armada.**

Mars St. Selwyn Medal: an honorific bestowed in ancient times.

Mbata: (**Mbatan**, adj & sing. n): a well-regarded Caste known for its peace-loving and familial ways. In appearance they resemble the ursine species, larger and stronger than the Pristine. Their culture is egalitarian and open to trade.

Middle Reaches: the region of medium stellar density between the Outer Arms and the galactic core.

***Midnight*, COEA:** COE Retriever-class frigate.

Military Star: an honorific bestowed in ancient times.

Military Presidium: see **Dato Bloc.**

minaret: Skehan Heterodox term for the prow of a consistory vessel.

Multiple Genesis Theory: a theory that the various Castes of Humanity evolved—or at least emerged into the greater galaxy—from several systems simultaneously.

mundane Castes: Castes of Humanity that are essentially similar to the Pristine in terms of size, mental capacity, world-view, etc. Naturally there is a spectrum of types across the mundane Caste—from the highly evolved (some might say near-Transcendent) Olmahoi, through the socially complex Surin and Hurn Castes, to the Eckandar and Pristine Castes with their societies based on trade and empire-building, and beyond, via the earthy Mbata, to the relatively primal Kesh. Mundanes are typically short-lived (a century or so, when allowed to age naturally) and build empires up to four or five thousand systems in size. There is a ceiling of complexity above which mundanes rarely go without Transcending. See **High Humans** and **Batelin Limit.**

Murnane, Esko: plenipotentiary envoy sent by the citizens of Pompili to stand on the IEPC.

Murukan: one of a gas giant pair occupying the sixth planetary orbit around Palasian System (see **Kukumat**).

n-body: the epsense "counterpart" to the physical body.

n-space: a word used by epsense theorists to describe an environment completely empty of thought.

Nemeth, Rey: Assistant Vice Primate sent by the Second Ju Mandate to stand on the IEPC.

Noske: a Caste not normally found in the COE region.

Nyberg: the founder of school of epsense training regarded as second-rate by superior adepts.

Objective Reference Calendar: a system of date-keeping established by the A-14 Higher Collaboration Network.

Old Earth Advance Guard: a military body mentioned in ancient records.

Olmahoi: an exotic Caste that communicates entirely by epsense. Physically they are of similar size to Pristines, but are much stronger; their skin is black and they possess little in the way of distinguishing features, apart from the epsense organ which dangles like a tentacle from the back of the skull. Their social structure is too complex to explore in detail here. They are renowned fighters, capable of feats of great skill, yet also possess a capacity for peace far in excess of any other local Caste.

Olmahoi retribution squad: renowned fighters able to combine perfectly their physical and epsense abilities. Also known as "grayboots."

Outer Arms: the low stellar-density regions of the galaxy between the Middle and Far Reaches.

Out-of-Sol theory: a theory suggesting that all the Castes of Humanity originated on one world.

outrigger: a unique Caste of miner / explorer found in sparsely populated systems; living within all-suits that double as mobile homes, outriggers typically scout uncharted dark body halos and asteroid belts, looking for viable mineral sources, which they then either mine or report to a centralized authority (if any) for a modest fee. Outriggers are notoriously self-sufficient, avoiding even other outriggers as much as possible, and have been known to exist for years out of contact with another being. Spending much of their lives drifting in hibernation between dark and cometary bodies, some live longer than three centuries. Few outriggers have family names, coming as they do from such small communities that single given names usually suffice.

outsweep migrations: brief, outward surges by expansionist empires. These usually occur in the crowded environment of the core or Middle Reaches, in the direction of the Outer Arms.

Pacecca: an overseer of the docks of Perdue Habitat.

Palasian System: a system of the COE quarantined by the COE Armada as a result of an enemy outbreak, then destroyed by an ancient Kesh device (see **Solar Envelope**).

***Paraselene*, COEA:** a COE cruiser stationed near Perdue Habitat.

Paz: an educative device once owned by Morgan Roche.

Perdue Habitat: a habitat populated by approximately 11,000 people, predominantly Vax Caste, stationed to Sol System during the crisis. Its administer, Inderdeep Jans, is known to have been reluctant to commit her resources to solving the crisis.

***Phlegethon*, SHCV:** a Skehan Heterodox consistory vessel from the far side of the galaxy.

Pompili: a founding nation of the IEPC.

Primordial Castes: precede the earliest confirmed records, half a million years ago. Little is known about them, except that they exist; ruins of several unique types are to be found throughout the galaxy. They are called Castes A, B, C, and D, for even their names are unknown. (See Appendix.)

Pristine Caste: the form of Humanity which most closely resembles the original race that evolved an unknown time ago on an unknown planet somewhere in the galaxy. The Pristine Human Genome, handed down from antiquity and regarded with near-veneration, is stored in innumerable places among the civilized worlds. Pristines themselves, however, are accorded no special status.

Quare, Oren: assistant to Overseer Pacecca, Perdue Habitat.

Random Valence: a habitat stationed close to Perdue Habitat.
reave: see **epsense.**
Rebuli: a Caste antagonistic to the cause of the IEPC.
Rench: dockmaster of Perdue Habitat.
Reshima System: a system in which Ameidio Haid once worked.
Roche, Morgan: former commander, COE Intelligence.
Rond-Spellor Outlook: home of Hue Vischilglin.
Rufo, Linegar: renowned xenoarchaeologist; see **Galine Four.**

Saa-hurod: a Caste maintaining an outpost in Sol System during the crisis.
Sciacca's World: the only habitable world of the Hutton-Luu System; once an agricultural planet of the Dominion, now a desert penal colony of the COE (**Sciacca Penal Colony**). Its ring of moonlets—the Soul—is owned and mined by DAOC Inc.
scutter: a small, swift spacegoing vessel with many uses, both military and civilian; also known as a singleship.
***Sebettu*, SRF:** Kesh destroyer.
Second Expansion: an ancient outsweep known to have led from the Exordium Worlds into the greater galaxy.
Siriote: a government antagonistic to the IEPC.
Skehan Heterodox: a tolerant theocracy on the far side of the galaxy, significantly more advanced than the COE.
slow-jump: a common alternative to the anchor drive that utilizes similar technology. Most ships with an anchor drive can slow-jump if necessary. It is essentially a jump through hyperspace from any point in real space. A certain degree of kinetic energy is required before translation can be achieved, so ships must accelerate for some time beforehand. Even then, the hyperspace jump is short-lived, and the vessel emerges soon after (typically less than a light-year away from its departure point) with significantly less kinetic energy. The process must be repeated from scratch if another slow-jump is required. As a means of crossing interstellar space, it is inefficient and time-consuming, hence its name. Slow-jumping becomes increasingly nonviable closer to a gravity-well, but more efficient as mass (of the traveling object) decreases.
Sol Apotheosis Movement: a quasi-religious organization devoted to the pursuit of Transcendence via genetic manipulation and biomodification that reached its peak and was destroyed in the 37th millennium. Its fanatical followers were a source of unrest for decades, until an alliance was formed among their neighbors dedicated to putting a stop to them. In '577 EN, at the climax of the Scion War, a flotilla of allied forces encircled their base, which the Movement destroyed in order to pre-

vent its capture. The resulting explosion annihilated them as well, of course, but also decimated the flotilla. Of the four stations involved in the battle, only one survived, and that was severely damaged. So embarrassed was the alliance that the leaders of the day ordered the event stricken from history. They even closed the anchor point leading to the system to prevent anyone learning what occurred there. Nothing survived of the base, and the rest of the system is an unsalvageable ruin.

Sol System: an uninhabited system in a nonaligned region near the Dato Bloc, one known for its antiquity and a possible contender for birthplace of the Human race. Former home of the Sol Apotheosis Movement and many other such sects. (See Appendix.)

Sol Wunderkind: genetically modified clone warriors designed and bred by the Sol Apotheosis Movement.

Solar Envelope: a device intended to provide a jump shield large enough to enclose an entire solar system. Two prototypes were built by an early Kesh Government. "Asha's Gauntlet" was used on one system, with disastrous results: the system's primary sun, modified to power the Envelope, was exhausted within two months; the entire system collapsed shortly thereafter. Useless as a defensive weapon, and forbidden by the Convention on Extraordinary Weapons, the second Gauntlet remained in the hands of the Kesh until it was used in Palasian System.

Soul, the: the local name for the orbiting ring of mineral-rich moonlets girdling Sciacca's World.

spine: the collective noun used to describe a loosely linked group of outriggers; from their means of traveling between systems, on the back of a naked real-space drive known as "the spine."

***squt*:** a Surin word for someone who is both foolish and closed-minded.

Stryki: an epsense adept from Taborca.

Surin: a relatively minor Caste found in the regions surrounding the COE. They exist in isolated clumps overseen by a governing body that guides rather than rules. They are social beings yet fond of isolation, giving them a reputation for occasional aloofness. They are technically accomplished, especially in the biological sciences. In stature, they tend to be slight and have hair covering much of their bodies. It is occasionally speculated that they have re-evolved from Low Caste status.

Surin Agora: the ruling body of the loosely knit Surin nation.

Taborca: a region in the Middle Reaches.

Tade, Rejuben: 238th Provost of the Guild of Xenoarchaeologists (see Appendix).

TBC-14: see ***Kindling.***

Teh, Sylvester: transportee, Sciacca Penal Colony.

Tocharia 13: a habitat maintained by members of the **Zissis Caste.**

Transcend: to break free of the constraints of mundane Humanity. A being or Caste that has Transcended typically has an extremely long life span and spreads its consciousness across a number of primary containers—such as neural nets, quantum data vats, and the like. Transcended entities, singular or collective, are referred to as High Human and accorded the highest status.

Transcendence: the state of being Transcended. Usually achieved when consciousness research and computer technology overlap, allowing an organic mind to be downloaded into an electronic vessel, thereby gaining the potential for unlimited growth.

Trezise, Salton: senior aide to Auberon Chase and envoy to the IEPC.

Trinity: the world on which AIs are made in the region dominated by the COE. The AI factory was founded and is overseen by the High Human known as the Crescend.

turcite: a type of high explosive.

Ulterior: a covert organization operating within—but not without the official disapproval of—the IEPC.

Ustinik, Alwen: a representative of the Commerce Artel.

Vacishnou: homeworld of the Vax Caste.

Vax: a Caste renowned for its peculiar breeding customs.

Veden, Makil: an Eckandar Trade Axis citizen and Commerce Artel ex-delegate. Deceased.

Vischilglin, Hue: co-adjutant sent by the Rond-Spellor Outlook to assist the IEPC.

Vri: a Surin soldier, who has forgone his family name and taken the title "Defender-of-Harmony."

Wamel: a Hurn pilot employed by the Disciples of Evergence.

Warfare Protocol: the code by which war is conducted within and between those nations that trade with the Commerce Artel.

Wehr, Vani: earned an Honorable Mention in ancient times for quick thinking on the Clarke Cylinder.

Weryn: deity of the Skehan Heterodox.

Xarodine: an epsense-inhibiting drug.

Xumai, Jancin: a Surin soldier who has taken the title "Fighter-For-Peace."

Yemena: a Caste not native to the COE region.

Yugen, Frane: leader of Random Valence.

Zissis: a Caste not indigenous to the COE region.

SEAN WILLIAMS has been writing full time since 1990, with approximately 50 published short stories. He has won a prize in the 20th Writers of the Future Contest, been recommended by *Year's Best Horror & Fantasy* and *Year's Best Science Fiction* anthologies, and won Australia's two most prestigious SF awards. His first solo novel, *Metal Fatigue*, won the Aurealis Award for Best SF Novel (and also reached the top 15 in the Internet Speculative Fiction Database's Top Books of 1996). His second, *Resurrected Man*, received the Ditmar Award for Best Novel of 1998.

SHANE DIX has been writing fiction since he was 15. His story "Through the Water That Binds" won the 1991 Canberra SF Society's short story competition. The story was also featured in the Australian landmark science fiction anthology *Alien Shores*. In addition to science fiction, he has had published mainstream stories, poetry, and articles about the state of SF in film and television.